DRACULA AND OTHER STORIES

By

Bram Stoker

Cover Photograph: Majo's Photos

ISBN: 978-1-78139-378-9

Contents

DRACULA

THE JEWEL OF SEVEN STARS

THE MAN

THE LADY OF THE SHROUD

BOOK I: THE WILL OF ROGER MELTON

BOOK II: VISSARION

BOOK III: THE COMING OF THE LADY

BOOK IV: UNDER THE FLAGSTAFF

BOOK V: A RITUAL AT MIDNIGHT

BOOK VI: THE PURSUIT IN THE FOREST

BOOK VII: THE EMPIRE OF THE AIR

BOOK VIII: THE FLASHING OF THE HANDJAR

BOOK IX: BALKA

THE LAIR OF THE WHITE WORM

DRACULA'S GUEST

THE DUALITISTS

DRACULA

A Mystery Story

How these papers have been placed in sequence will be made manifest in the reading of them. All needless matters have been eliminated, so that a history almost at variance with the possibilities of latter-day belief may stand forth as simple fact. There is throughout no statement of past things wherein memory may err, for all the records chosen are exactly contemporary, given from the standpoints and within the range of knowledge of those who made them.

CHAPTER 1

JONATHAN HARKER'S JOURNAL (Kept in shorthand)

3 May. Bistritz.--Left Munich at 8:35 P.M., on 1st May, arriving at Vienna early next morning; should have arrived at 6:46, but train was an hour late. Buda-Pesth seems a wonderful place, from the glimpse which I got of it from the train and the little I could walk through the streets. I feared to go very far from the station, as we had arrived late and would start as near the correct time as possible.

The impression I had was that we were leaving the West and entering the East; the most western of splendid bridges over the Danube, which is here of noble width and depth, took us among the traditions of Turkish rule.

We left in pretty good time, and came after nightfall to Klausenburgh. Here I stopped for the night at the Hotel Royale. I had for dinner, or rather supper, a chicken done up some way with red pepper, which was very good but thirsty. (Mem. get recipe for Mina.) I asked the waiter, and he said it was called "paprika hendl," and that, as it was a national dish, I should be able to get it anywhere along the Carpathians.

I found my smattering of German very useful here, indeed, I don't know how I should be able to get on without it.

Having had some time at my disposal when in London, I had visited the British Museum, and made search among the books and maps in the library regarding Transylvania; it had struck me that some foreknowledge of the country could hardly fail to have some importance in dealing with a nobleman of that country.

I find that the district he named is in the extreme east of the country, just on the borders of three states, Transylvania, Moldavia, and Bukovina, in the midst of the Carpathian mountains; one of the wildest and least known portions of Europe.

I was not able to light on any map or work giving the exact locality of the Castle Dracula, as there are no maps of this country as yet to compare with our own Ordnance Survey Maps; but I found that Bistritz, the post town named by Count Dracula, is a fairly well-known place. I shall enter here some of my notes, as they may refresh my memory when I talk over my travels with Mina.

In the population of Transylvania there are four distinct nationalities: Saxons in the South, and mixed with them the Wallachs, who are the descendants of the Dacians; Magyars in the West, and Szekelys in the East and North. I am going among the latter, who claim to be descended from Attila and the Huns. This may be so, for when the Magyars conquered the country in the eleventh century they found the Huns settled in it.

I read that every known superstition in the world is gathered into the horseshoe of the Carpathians, as if it were the centre of some sort of imaginative whirlpool; if so my stay may be very interesting. (Mem., I must ask the Count all about them.)

I did not sleep well, though my bed was comfortable enough, for I had all sorts of queer dreams. There was a dog howling all night under my window, which may have had something to do with it; or it may have been the paprika, for I had to drink up all the water in my carafe, and was still thirsty. Towards morning I slept and was wakened by the continuous knocking at my door, so I guess I must have been sleeping soundly then.

I had for breakfast more paprika, and a sort of porridge of maize flour which they said was "mamaliga", and egg-plant stuffed with forcemeat, a very excellent dish, which they call "impletata". (Mem., get recipe for this also.)

I had to hurry breakfast, for the train started a little before eight, or rather it ought to have done so, for after rushing to the station at 7:30 I had to sit in the carriage for more than an hour before we began to move.

It seems to me that the further east you go the more unpunctual are the trains. What ought they to be in China?

All day long we seemed to dawdle through a country which was full of beauty of every kind. Sometimes we saw little towns or castles on the top of steep hills such as we see in old missals; sometimes we ran by rivers and streams which seemed from the wide stony margin on each side of them to be subject to great floods. It takes a lot of water, and running strong, to sweep the outside edge of a river clear.

At every station there were groups of people, sometimes crowds, and in all sorts of attire. Some of them were just like the peasants at home or those I saw coming through France and Germany, with short jackets, and round hats, and home-made trousers; but others were very picturesque.

The women looked pretty, except when you got near them, but they were very clumsy about the waist. They had all full white sleeves of some kind or other, and most of them had big belts with a lot of strips of something fluttering from them like the dresses in a ballet, but of course there were petticoats under them.

The strangest figures we saw were the Slovaks, who were more barbarian than the rest, with their big cow-boy hats, great baggy dirty-white trousers, white linen shirts, and enormous heavy leather belts, nearly a foot wide, all studded over with brass nails. They wore high boots, with their trousers tucked into them, and had long black hair and heavy black moustaches. They are very picturesque, but do not look prepossessing. On the stage they would be set down at once as some old Oriental band of brigands. They are, however, I am told, very harmless and rather wanting in natural self-assertion.

It was on the dark side of twilight when we got to Bistritz, which is a very interesting old place. Being practically on the frontier--for the Borgo Pass leads from it into Bukovina--it has had a very stormy existence, and it certainly shows marks of it. Fifty years ago a series of great fires took place, which made terrible havoc on five separate occasions. At the very beginning of the seventeenth century it underwent a siege of three weeks and lost 13,000 people, the casualties of war proper being assisted by famine and disease.

CHAPTER 1

Count Dracula had directed me to go to the Golden Krone Hotel, which I found, to my great delight, to be thoroughly old-fashioned, for of course I wanted to see all I could of the ways of the country.

I was evidently expected, for when I got near the door I faced a cheery-looking elderly woman in the usual peasant dress--white undergarment with a long double apron, front, and back, of coloured stuff fitting almost too tight for modesty. When I came close she bowed and said, "The Herr Englishman?"

"Yes," I said, "Jonathan Harker."

She smiled, and gave some message to an elderly man in white shirtsleeves, who had followed her to the door.

He went, but immediately returned with a letter:

"My friend.--Welcome to the Carpathians. I am anxiously expecting you. Sleep well tonight. At three tomorrow the diligence will start for Bukovina; a place on it is kept for you. At the Borgo Pass my carriage will await you and will bring you to me. I trust that your journey from London has been a happy one, and that you will enjoy your stay in my beautiful land.--Your friend, Dracula."

4 May--I found that my landlord had got a letter from the Count, directing him to secure the best place on the coach for me; but on making inquiries as to details he seemed somewhat reticent, and pretended that he could not understand my German.

This could not be true, because up to then he had understood it perfectly; at least, he answered my questions exactly as if he did.

He and his wife, the old lady who had received me, looked at each other in a frightened sort of way. He mumbled out that the money had been sent in a letter, and that was all he knew. When I asked him if he knew Count Dracula, and could tell me anything of his castle, both he and his wife crossed themselves, and, saying that they knew nothing at all, simply refused to speak further. It was so near the time of starting that I had no time to ask anyone else, for it was all very mysterious and not by any means comforting.

Just before I was leaving, the old lady came up to my room and said in a hysterical way: "Must you go? Oh! Young Herr, must you go?" She was in such an excited state that she seemed to have lost her grip of what German she knew, and mixed it all up with some other language which I did not know at all. I was just able to follow her by asking many questions. When I told her that I must go at once, and that I was engaged on important business, she asked again:

"Do you know what day it is?" I answered that it was the fourth of May. She shook her head as she said again:

"Oh, yes! I know that! I know that, but do you know what day it is?"

On my saying that I did not understand, she went on:

"It is the eve of St. George's Day. Do you not know that tonight, when the clock strikes midnight, all the evil things in the world will have full sway? Do you know where you are going, and what you are going to?" She was in such evident distress that I tried to comfort her, but without effect. Finally, she went down on her knees and implored me not to go; at least to wait a day or two before starting.

It was all very ridiculous but I did not feel comfortable. However, there was business to be done, and I could allow nothing to interfere with it.

I tried to raise her up, and said, as gravely as I could, that I thanked her, but my duty was imperative, and that I must go.

She then rose and dried her eyes, and taking a crucifix from her neck offered it to me.

I did not know what to do, for, as an English Churchman, I have been taught to regard such things as in some measure idolatrous, and yet it seemed so ungracious to refuse an old lady meaning so well and in such a state of mind.

She saw, I suppose, the doubt in my face, for she put the rosary round my neck and said, "For your mother's sake," and went out of the room.

I am writing up this part of the diary whilst I am waiting for the coach, which is, of course, late; and the crucifix is still round my neck.

Whether it is the old lady's fear, or the many ghostly traditions of this place, or the crucifix itself, I do not know, but I am not feeling nearly as easy in my mind as usual.

If this book should ever reach Mina before I do, let it bring my goodbye. Here comes the coach!

5 May. The Castle.--The gray of the morning has passed, and the sun is high over the distant horizon, which seems jagged, whether with trees or hills I know not, for it is so far off that big things and little are mixed.

I am not sleepy, and, as I am not to be called till I awake, naturally I write till sleep comes.

There are many odd things to put down, and, lest who reads them may fancy that I dined too well before I left Bistritz, let me put down my dinner exactly.

I dined on what they called "robber steak"--bits of bacon, onion, and beef, seasoned with red pepper, and strung on sticks, and roasted over the fire, in the simple style of the London cat's meat!

The wine was Golden Mediasch, which produces a queer sting on the tongue, which is, however, not disagreeable.

I had only a couple of glasses of this, and nothing else.

When I got on the coach, the driver had not taken his seat, and I saw him talking to the landlady.

They were evidently talking of me, for every now and then they looked at me, and some of the people who were sitting on the bench outside the door--came and listened, and then looked at me, most of them pityingly. I could hear a lot of words often repeated, queer words, for there were many nationalities in the crowd, so I quietly got my polyglot dictionary from my bag and looked them out.

I must say they were not cheering to me, for amongst them were "Ordog"--Satan, "Pokol"--hell, "stregoica"--witch, "vrolok" and "vlkoslak"--both mean the same thing, one being Slovak and the other Servian for something that is either werewolf or vampire. (Mem., I must ask the Count about these superstitions.)

When we started, the crowd round the inn door, which had by this time swelled to a considerable size, all made the sign of the cross and pointed two fingers towards me.

With some difficulty, I got a fellow passenger to tell me what they meant. He would not answer at first, but on learning that I was English, he explained that it was a charm or guard against the evil eye.

This was not very pleasant for me, just starting for an unknown place to meet an unknown man. But everyone seemed so kind-hearted, and so sorrowful, and so sympathetic that I could not but be touched.

CHAPTER 1

I shall never forget the last glimpse which I had of the inn yard and its crowd of picturesque figures, all crossing themselves, as they stood round the wide archway, with its background of rich foliage of oleander and orange trees in green tubs clustered in the centre of the yard.

Then our driver, whose wide linen drawers covered the whole front of the box-seat,--"gotza" they call them--cracked his big whip over his four small horses, which ran abreast, and we set off on our journey.

I soon lost sight and recollection of ghostly fears in the beauty of the scene as we drove along, although had I known the language, or rather languages, which my fellow-passengers were speaking, I might not have been able to throw them off so easily. Before us lay a green sloping land full of forests and woods, with here and there steep hills, crowned with clumps of trees or with farmhouses, the blank gable end to the road. There was everywhere a bewildering mass of fruit blossom--apple, plum, pear, cherry. And as we drove by I could see the green grass under the trees spangled with the fallen petals. In and out amongst these green hills of what they call here the "Mittel Land" ran the road, losing itself as it swept round the grassy curve, or was shut out by the straggling ends of pine woods, which here and there ran down the hillsides like tongues of flame. The road was rugged, but still we seemed to fly over it with a feverish haste. I could not understand then what the haste meant, but the driver was evidently bent on losing no time in reaching Borgo Prund. I was told that this road is in summertime excellent, but that it had not yet been put in order after the winter snows. In this respect it is different from the general run of roads in the Carpathians, for it is an old tradition that they are not to be kept in too good order. Of old the Hospadars would not repair them, lest the Turk should think that they were preparing to bring in foreign troops, and so hasten the war which was always really at loading point.

Beyond the green swelling hills of the Mittel Land rose mighty slopes of forest up to the lofty steeps of the Carpathians themselves. Right and left of us they towered, with the afternoon sun falling full upon them and bringing out all the glorious colours of this beautiful range, deep blue and purple in the shadows of the peaks, green and brown where grass and rock mingled, and an endless perspective of jagged rock and pointed crags, till these were themselves lost in the distance, where the snowy peaks rose grandly. Here and there seemed mighty rifts in the mountains, through which, as the sun began to sink, we saw now and again the white gleam of falling water. One of my companions touched my arm as we swept round the base of a hill and opened up the lofty, snow-covered peak of a mountain, which seemed, as we wound on our serpentine way, to be right before us.

"Look! Isten szek!"--"God's seat!"--and he crossed himself reverently.

As we wound on our endless way, and the sun sank lower and lower behind us, the shadows of the evening began to creep round us. This was emphasized by the fact that the snowy mountain-top still held the sunset, and seemed to glow out with a delicate cool pink. Here and there we passed Cszeks and Slovaks, all in picturesque attire, but I noticed that goitre was painfully prevalent. By the roadside were many crosses, and as we swept by, my companions all crossed themselves. Here and there was a peasant man or woman kneeling before a shrine, who did not even turn round as we approached, but seemed in the self-surrender of devotion to have neither eyes nor ears for the outer world. There were many things new to me. For instance, hay-ricks in the trees, and here and there very beautiful masses of weeping birch, their white stems shining like silver through the delicate green of the leaves.

Now and again we passed a leiter-wagon--the ordinary peasants's cart--with its long, snakelike vertebra, calculated to suit the inequalities of the road. On this were sure to be seated quite a group of homecoming peasants, the Cszeks with their white, and the Slovaks with their coloured sheepskins, the latter carrying lance-fashion their long staves, with axe at end. As the evening fell it began to get very cold, and the growing twilight seemed to merge into one dark mistiness the gloom of the trees, oak, beech, and pine, though in the valleys which ran deep between the spurs of the hills, as we ascended through the Pass, the dark firs stood out here and there against the background of late-lying snow. Sometimes, as the road was cut through the pine woods that seemed in the darkness to be closing down upon us, great masses of greyness which here and there bestrewed the trees, produced a peculiarly weird and solemn effect, which carried on the thoughts and grim fancies engendered earlier in the evening, when the falling sunset threw into strange relief the ghost-like clouds which amongst the Carpathians seem to wind ceaselessly through the valleys. Sometimes the hills were so steep that, despite our driver's haste, the horses could only go slowly. I wished to get down and walk up them, as we do at home, but the driver would not hear of it. "No, no," he said. "You must not walk here. The dogs are too fierce." And then he added, with what he evidently meant for grim pleasantry--for he looked round to catch the approving smile of the rest--"And you may have enough of such matters before you go to sleep." The only stop he would make was a moment's pause to light his lamps.

When it grew dark there seemed to be some excitement amongst the passengers, and they kept speaking to him, one after the other, as though urging him to further speed. He lashed the horses unmercifully with his long whip, and with wild cries of encouragement urged them on to further exertions. Then through the darkness I could see a sort of patch of grey light ahead of us, as though there were a cleft in the hills. The excitement of the passengers grew greater. The crazy coach rocked on its great leather springs, and swayed like a boat tossed on a stormy sea. I had to hold on. The road grew more level, and we appeared to fly along. Then the mountains seemed to come nearer to us on each side and to frown down upon us. We were entering on the Borgo Pass. One by one several of the passengers offered me gifts, which they pressed upon me with an earnestness which would take no denial. These were certainly of an odd and varied kind, but each was given in simple good faith, with a kindly word, and a blessing, and that same strange mixture of fear-meaning movements which I had seen outside the hotel at Bistritz--the sign of the cross and the guard against the evil eye. Then, as we flew along, the driver leaned forward, and on each side the passengers, craning over the edge of the coach, peered eagerly into the darkness. It was evident that something very exciting was either happening or expected, but though I asked each passenger, no one would give me the slightest explanation. This state of excitement kept on for some little time. And at last we saw before us the Pass opening out on the eastern side. There were dark, rolling clouds overhead, and in the air the heavy, oppressive sense of thunder. It seemed as though the mountain range had separated two atmospheres, and that now we had got into the thunderous one. I was now myself looking out for the conveyance which was to take me to the Count. Each moment I expected to see the glare of lamps through the blackness, but all was dark. The only light was the flickering rays of our own lamps, in which the steam from our hard-driven horses rose in a white cloud. We could see now the sandy road lying white before us, but there was on it no sign of a vehicle. The passengers drew back with a sigh of gladness, which seemed to mock my own disappointment. I was already thinking what I had best do, when the driver, looking at his watch, said to the others something which I could hardly hear, it was spoken so quietly and in so low a tone, I thought it was "An hour less than the time." Then turning to me, he spoke in German worse than my own.

"There is no carriage here. The Herr is not expected after all. He will now come on to Bukovina, and return tomorrow or the next day, better the next day." Whilst he was speaking the horses began to neigh and snort and plunge wildly, so that the driver had to hold them up. Then, amongst a chorus of screams from the peasants and a universal crossing of themselves, a caleche, with four horses, drove up behind us, overtook us, and drew up beside the coach. I could see from the flash of our lamps as the rays fell on them, that the horses were coal-black and splendid animals. They were driven by a tall man, with a long brown beard and a great black hat, which seemed to hide his face from us. I could only see the gleam of a pair of very bright eyes, which seemed red in the lamplight, as he turned to us.

He said to the driver, "You are early tonight, my friend."

The man stammered in reply, "The English Herr was in a hurry."

To which the stranger replied, "That is why, I suppose, you wished him to go on to Bukovina. You cannot deceive me, my friend. I know too much, and my horses are swift."

As he spoke he smiled, and the lamplight fell on a hard-looking mouth, with very red lips and sharp-looking teeth, as white as ivory. One of my companions whispered to another the line from Burger's "Lenore".

"Denn die Todten reiten Schnell." ("For the dead travel fast.")

The strange driver evidently heard the words, for he looked up with a gleaming smile. The passenger turned his face away, at the same time putting out his two fingers and crossing himself. "Give me the Herr's luggage," said the driver, and with exceeding alacrity my bags were handed out and put in the caleche. Then I descended from the side of the coach, as the caleche was close alongside, the driver helping me with a hand which caught my arm in a grip of steel. His strength must have been prodigious.

Without a word he shook his reins, the horses turned, and we swept into the darkness of the pass. As I looked back I saw the steam from the horses of the coach by the light of the lamps, and projected against it the figures of my late companions crossing themselves. Then the driver cracked his whip and called to his horses, and off they swept on their way to Bukovina. As they sank into the darkness I felt a strange chill, and a lonely feeling come over me. But a cloak was thrown over my shoulders, and a rug across my knees, and the driver said in excellent German--"The night is chill, mein Herr, and my master the Count bade me take all care of you. There is a flask of slivovitz (the plum brandy of the country) underneath the seat, if you should require it."

I did not take any, but it was a comfort to know it was there all the same. I felt a little strangely, and not a little frightened. I think had there been any alternative I should have taken it, instead of prosecuting that unknown night journey. The carriage went at a hard pace straight along, then we made a complete turn and went along another straight road. It seemed to me that we were simply going over and over the same ground again, and so I took note of some salient point, and found that this was so. I would have liked to have asked the driver what this all meant, but I really feared to do so, for I thought that, placed as I was, any protest would have had no effect in case there had been an intention to delay.

By-and-by, however, as I was curious to know how time was passing, I struck a match, and by its flame looked at my watch. It was within a few minutes of midnight. This gave me a sort of shock, for I suppose the general superstition about midnight was increased by my recent experiences. I waited with a sick feeling of suspense.

Then a dog began to howl somewhere in a farmhouse far down the road, a long, agonized wailing, as if from fear. The sound was taken up by another dog, and then another and another, till, borne on the wind which now sighed softly through the Pass, a wild howling began, which seemed to come from all over the country, as far as the imagination could grasp it through the gloom of the night.

At the first howl the horses began to strain and rear, but the driver spoke to them soothingly, and they quieted down, but shivered and sweated as though after a runaway from sudden fright. Then, far off in the distance, from the mountains on each side of us began a louder and a sharper howling, that of wolves, which affected both the horses and myself in the same way. For I was minded to jump from the caleche and run, whilst they reared again and plunged madly, so that the driver had to use all his great strength to keep them from bolting. In a few minutes, however, my own ears got accustomed to the sound, and the horses so far became quiet that the driver was able to descend and to stand before them.

He petted and soothed them, and whispered something in their ears, as I have heard of horse-tamers doing, and with extraordinary effect, for under his caresses they became quite manageable again, though they still trembled. The driver again took his seat, and shaking his reins, started off at a great pace. This time, after going to the far side of the Pass, he suddenly turned down a narrow roadway which ran sharply to the right.

Soon we were hemmed in with trees, which in places arched right over the roadway till we passed as through a tunnel. And again great frowning rocks guarded us boldly on either side. Though we were in shelter, we could hear the rising wind, for it moaned and whistled through the rocks, and the branches of the trees crashed together as we swept along. It grew colder and colder still, and fine, powdery snow began to fall, so that soon we and all around us were covered with a white blanket. The keen wind still carried the howling of the dogs, though this grew fainter as we went on our way. The baying of the wolves sounded nearer and nearer, as though they were closing round on us from every side. I grew dreadfully afraid, and the horses shared my fear. The driver, however, was not in the least disturbed. He kept turning his head to left and right, but I could not see anything through the darkness.

Suddenly, away on our left I saw a faint flickering blue flame. The driver saw it at the same moment. He at once checked the horses, and, jumping to the ground, disappeared into the darkness. I did not know what to do, the less as the howling of the wolves grew closer. But while I wondered, the driver suddenly appeared again, and without a word took his seat, and we resumed our journey. I think I must have fallen asleep and kept dreaming of the incident, for it seemed to be repeated endlessly, and now looking back, it is like a sort of awful nightmare. Once the flame appeared so near the road, that even in the darkness around us I could watch the driver's motions. He went rapidly to where the blue flame arose, it must have been very faint, for it did not seem to illumine the place around it at all, and gathering a few stones, formed them into some device.

Once there appeared a strange optical effect. When he stood between me and the flame he did not obstruct it, for I could see its ghostly flicker all the same. This startled me, but as the effect was only momentary, I took it that my eyes deceived me straining through the darkness. Then for a time there were no blue flames, and we sped onwards through the gloom, with the howling of the wolves around us, as though they were following in a moving circle.

At last there came a time when the driver went further afield than he had yet gone, and during his absence, the horses began to tremble worse than ever and to snort and scream with fright. I could not see any cause for it, for the howling of the wolves had ceased altogether. But just then the moon, sailing through the black clouds, appeared behind the jagged crest of a beetling, pine-clad rock, and by its light I saw around us a ring of wolves, with white teeth and lolling red tongues, with long, sinewy limbs and shaggy hair. They were a hundred times more terrible in the grim silence which held them than even when they howled. For myself, I felt a sort of paralysis of fear. It is only when a man feels himself face to face with such horrors that he can understand their true import.

All at once the wolves began to howl as though the moonlight had had some peculiar effect on them. The horses jumped about and reared, and looked helplessly round with eyes that rolled in a way painful to see. But the living ring of terror encompassed them on every side, and they had perforce to remain within it. I called to the coachman to come, for it seemed to me that our only chance was to try to break out through the ring and to aid his approach, I shouted and beat the side of the caleche, hoping by the noise to scare the wolves from the side, so as to give him a chance of reaching the trap. How he came there, I know not, but I heard his voice raised in a tone of imperious command, and looking towards the sound, saw him stand in the roadway. As he swept his long arms, as though brushing aside some impalpable obstacle, the wolves fell back and back further still. Just then a heavy cloud passed across the face of the moon, so that we were again in darkness.

When I could see again the driver was climbing into the caleche, and the wolves disappeared. This was all so strange and uncanny that a dreadful fear came upon me, and I was afraid to speak or move. The time seemed interminable as we swept on our way, now in almost complete darkness, for the rolling clouds obscured the moon.

We kept on ascending, with occasional periods of quick descent, but in the main always ascending. Suddenly, I became conscious of the fact that the driver was in the act of pulling up the horses in the courtyard of a vast ruined castle, from whose tall black windows came no ray of light, and whose broken battlements showed a jagged line against the sky.

CHAPTER 2

JONATHAN HARKER'S JOURNAL Continued

5 May.--I must have been asleep, for certainly if I had been fully awake I must have noticed the approach of such a remarkable place. In the gloom the courtyard looked of considerable size, and as several dark ways led from it under great round arches, it perhaps seemed bigger than it really is. I have not yet been able to see it by daylight.

When the caleche stopped, the driver jumped down and held out his hand to assist me to alight. Again I could not but notice his prodigious strength. His hand actually seemed like a steel vice that could have crushed mine if he had chosen. Then he took my traps, and placed them on the ground beside me as I stood close to a great door, old and studded with large iron nails, and set in a projecting doorway of massive stone. I could see even in the dim light that the stone was massively carved, but that the carving had been much worn by time and weather. As I stood, the driver jumped again into his seat and shook the reins. The horses started forward, and trap and all disappeared down one of the dark openings.

I stood in silence where I was, for I did not know what to do. Of bell or knocker there was no sign. Through these frowning walls and dark window openings it was not likely that my voice could penetrate. The time I waited seemed endless, and I felt doubts and fears crowding upon me. What sort of place had I come to, and among what kind of people? What sort of grim adventure was it on which I had embarked? Was this a customary incident in the life of a solicitor's clerk sent out to explain the purchase of a London estate to a foreigner? Solicitor's clerk! Mina would not like that. Solicitor, for just before leaving London I got word that my examination was successful, and I am now a full-blown solicitor! I began to rub my eyes and pinch myself to see if I were awake. It all seemed like a horrible nightmare to me, and I expected that I should suddenly awake, and find myself at home, with the dawn struggling in through the windows, as I had now and again felt in the morning after a day of overwork. But my flesh answered the pinching test, and my eyes were not to be deceived. I was indeed awake and among the Carpathians. All I could do now was to be patient, and to wait the coming of morning.

Just as I had come to this conclusion I heard a heavy step approaching behind the great door, and saw through the chinks the gleam of a coming light. Then there was the sound of rattling chains and the clanking of massive bolts drawn back. A key was turned with the loud grating noise of long disuse, and the great door swung back.

Within, stood a tall old man, clean shaven save for a long white moustache, and clad in black from head to foot, without a single speck of colour about him anywhere. He held in his hand an antique silver lamp, in which the flame burned without a chimney or globe of any kind, throwing long quivering shadows as it flickered in the draught of the open door. The old man motioned me in with his right hand with a courtly gesture, saying in excellent English, but with a strange intonation.

"Welcome to my house! Enter freely and of your own free will!" He made no motion of stepping to meet me, but stood like a statue, as though his gesture of welcome had fixed him into stone. The instant, however, that I had stepped over the threshold, he moved impulsively forward, and holding out his hand grasped mine with a strength which made me wince, an effect which was not lessened by the fact that it seemed cold as ice, more like the hand of a dead than a living man. Again he said,

"Welcome to my house! Enter freely. Go safely, and leave something of the happiness you bring!" The strength of the handshake was so much akin to that which I had noticed in the driver, whose face I had not seen, that for a moment I doubted if it were not the same person to whom I was speaking. So to make sure, I said interrogatively, "Count Dracula?"

He bowed in a courtly way as he replied, "I am Dracula, and I bid you welcome, Mr. Harker, to my house. Come in, the night air is chill, and you must need to eat and rest." As he was speaking, he put the lamp on a bracket on the wall, and stepping out, took my luggage. He had carried it in before I could forestall him. I protested, but he insisted.

"Nay, sir, you are my guest. It is late, and my people are not available. Let me see to your comfort myself." He insisted on carrying my traps along the passage, and then up a great winding stair, and along another great passage, on whose stone floor our steps rang heavily. At the end of this he threw open a heavy door, and I rejoiced to see within a well-lit room in which a table was spread for supper, and on whose mighty hearth a great fire of logs, freshly replenished, flamed and flared.

The Count halted, putting down my bags, closed the door, and crossing the room, opened another door, which led into a small octagonal room lit by a single lamp, and seemingly without a window of any sort. Passing through this, he opened another door, and motioned me to enter. It was a welcome sight. For here was a great bedroom well lighted and warmed with another log fire, also added to but lately, for the top logs were fresh, which sent a hollow roar up the wide chimney. The Count himself left my luggage inside and withdrew, saying, before he closed the door.

"You will need, after your journey, to refresh yourself by making your toilet. I trust you will find all you wish. When you are ready, come into the other room, where you will find your supper prepared."

The light and warmth and the Count's courteous welcome seemed to have dissipated all my doubts and fears. Having then reached my normal state, I discovered that I was half famished with hunger. So making a hasty toilet, I went into the other room.

I found supper already laid out. My host, who stood on one side of the great fireplace, leaning against the stonework, made a graceful wave of his hand to the table, and said,

"I pray you, be seated and sup how you please. You will I trust, excuse me that I do not join you, but I have dined already, and I do not sup."

I handed to him the sealed letter which Mr. Hawkins had entrusted to me. He opened it and read it gravely. Then, with a charming smile, he handed it to me to read. One passage of it, at least, gave me a thrill of pleasure.

"I must regret that an attack of gout, from which malady I am a constant sufferer, forbids absolutely any travelling on my part for some time to come. But I am happy to say I can send a sufficient substitute, one in whom I have every possible confidence. He is a young man, full of energy and talent in his own way, and of a very faithful disposition. He is discreet and silent, and has grown into manhood in my service. He shall be ready to attend on you when you will during his stay, and shall take your instructions in all matters."

The count himself came forward and took off the cover of a dish, and I fell to at once on an excellent roast chicken. This, with some cheese and a salad and a bottle of old tokay, of which I had two glasses, was my supper. During the time I was eating it the Count asked me many questions as to my journey, and I told him by degrees all I had experienced.

By this time I had finished my supper, and by my host's desire had drawn up a chair by the fire and begun to smoke a cigar which he offered me, at the same time excusing himself that he did not smoke. I had now an opportunity of observing him, and found him of a very marked physiognomy.

His face was a strong, a very strong, aquiline, with high bridge of the thin nose and peculiarly arched nostrils, with lofty domed forehead, and hair growing scantily round the temples but profusely elsewhere. His eyebrows were very massive, almost meeting over the nose, and with bushy hair that seemed to curl in its own profusion. The mouth, so far as I could see it under the heavy moustache, was fixed and rather cruel-looking, with peculiarly sharp white teeth. These protruded over the lips, whose remarkable ruddiness showed astonishing vitality in a man of his years. For the rest, his ears were pale, and at the tops extremely pointed. The chin was broad and strong, and the cheeks firm though thin. The general effect was one of extraordinary pallor.

Hitherto I had noticed the backs of his hands as they lay on his knees in the firelight, and they had seemed rather white and fine. But seeing them now close to me, I could not but notice that they were rather coarse, broad, with squat fingers. Strange to say, there were hairs in the centre of the palm. The nails were long and fine, and cut to a sharp point. As the Count leaned over me and his hands touched me, I could not repress a shudder. It may have been that his breath was rank, but a horrible feeling of nausea came over me, which, do what I would, I could not conceal.

The Count, evidently noticing it, drew back. And with a grim sort of smile, which showed more than he had yet done his protruberant teeth, sat himself down again on his own side of the fireplace. We were both silent for a while, and as I looked towards the window I saw the first dim streak of the coming dawn. There seemed a strange stillness over everything. But as I listened, I heard as if from down below in the valley the howling of many wolves. The Count's eyes gleamed, and he said.

"Listen to them, the children of the night. What music they make!" Seeing, I suppose, some expression in my face strange to him, he added, "Ah, sir, you dwellers in the city cannot enter into the feelings of the hunter." Then he rose and said.

CHAPTER 2

"But you must be tired. Your bedroom is all ready, and tomorrow you shall sleep as late as you will. I have to be away till the afternoon, so sleep well and dream well!" With a courteous bow, he opened for me himself the door to the octagonal room, and I entered my bedroom.

I am all in a sea of wonders. I doubt. I fear. I think strange things, which I dare not confess to my own soul. God keep me, if only for the sake of those dear to me!

7 May.--It is again early morning, but I have rested and enjoyed the last twenty-four hours. I slept till late in the day, and awoke of my own accord. When I had dressed myself I went into the room where we had supped, and found a cold breakfast laid out, with coffee kept hot by the pot being placed on the hearth. There was a card on the table, on which was written--"I have to be absent for a while. Do not wait for me. D." I set to and enjoyed a hearty meal. When I had done, I looked for a bell, so that I might let the servants know I had finished, but I could not find one. There are certainly odd deficiencies in the house, considering the extraordinary evidences of wealth which are round me. The table service is of gold, and so beautifully wrought that it must be of immense value. The curtains and upholstery of the chairs and sofas and the hangings of my bed are of the costliest and most beautiful fabrics, and must have been of fabulous value when they were made, for they are centuries old, though in excellent order. I saw something like them in Hampton Court, but they were worn and frayed and moth-eaten. But still in none of the rooms is there a mirror. There is not even a toilet glass on my table, and I had to get the little shaving glass from my bag before I could either shave or brush my hair. I have not yet seen a servant anywhere, or heard a sound near the castle except the howling of wolves. Some time after I had finished my meal, I do not know whether to call it breakfast or dinner, for it was between five and six o'clock when I had it, I looked about for something to read, for I did not like to go about the castle until I had asked the Count's permission. There was absolutely nothing in the room, book, newspaper, or even writing materials, so I opened another door in the room and found a sort of library. The door opposite mine I tried, but found locked.

In the library I found, to my great delight, a vast number of English books, whole shelves full of them, and bound volumes of magazines and newspapers. A table in the centre was littered with English magazines and newspapers, though none of them were of very recent date. The books were of the most varied kind, history, geography, politics, political economy, botany, geology, law, all relating to England and English life and customs and manners. There were even such books of reference as the London Directory, the "Red" and "Blue" books, Whitaker's Almanac, the Army and Navy Lists, and it somehow gladdened my heart to see it, the Law List.

Whilst I was looking at the books, the door opened, and the Count entered. He saluted me in a hearty way, and hoped that I had had a good night's rest. Then he went on.

"I am glad you found your way in here, for I am sure there is much that will interest you. These companions," and he laid his hand on some of the books, "have been good friends to me, and for some years past, ever since I had the idea of going to London, have given me many, many hours of pleasure. Through them I have come to know your great England, and to know her is to love her. I long to go through the crowded streets of your mighty London, to be in the midst of the whirl and rush of humanity, to share its life, its change, its death, and all that makes it what it is. But alas! As yet I only know your tongue through books. To you, my friend, I look that I know it to speak."

"But, Count," I said, "You know and speak English thoroughly!" He bowed gravely.

"I thank you, my friend, for your all too-flattering estimate, but yet I fear that I am but a little way on the road I would travel. True, I know the grammar and the words, but yet I know not how to speak them."

"Indeed," I said, "You speak excellently."

"Not so," he answered. "Well, I know that, did I move and speak in your London, none there are who would not know me for a stranger. That is not enough for me. Here I am noble. I am a Boyar. The common people know me, and I am master. But a stranger in a strange land, he is no one. Men know him not, and to know not is to care not for. I am content if I am like the rest, so that no man stops if he sees me, or pauses in his speaking if he hears my words, 'Ha, ha! A stranger!' I have been so long master that I would be master still, or at least that none other should be master of me. You come to me not alone as agent of my friend Peter Hawkins, of Exeter, to tell me all about my new estate in London. You shall, I trust, rest here with me a while, so that by our talking I may learn the English intonation. And I would that you tell me when I make error, even of the smallest, in my speaking. I am sorry that I had to be away so long today, but you will, I know forgive one who has so many important affairs in hand."

Of course I said all I could about being willing, and asked if I might come into that room when I chose. He answered, "Yes, certainly," and added.

"You may go anywhere you wish in the castle, except where the doors are locked, where of course you will not wish to go. There is reason that all things are as they are, and did you see with my eyes and know with my knowledge, you would perhaps better understand." I said I was sure of this, and then he went on.

"We are in Transylvania, and Transylvania is not England. Our ways are not your ways, and there shall be to you many strange things. Nay, from what you have told me of your experiences already, you know something of what strange things there may be."

This led to much conversation, and as it was evident that he wanted to talk, if only for talking's sake, I asked him many questions regarding things that had already happened to me or come within my notice. Sometimes he sheered off the subject, or turned the conversation by pretending not to understand, but generally he answered all I asked most frankly. Then as time went on, and I had got somewhat bolder, I asked him of some of the strange things of the preceding night, as for instance, why the coachman went to the places where he had seen the blue flames. He then explained to me that it was commonly believed that on a certain night of the year, last night, in fact, when all evil spirits are supposed to have unchecked sway, a blue flame is seen over any place where treasure has been concealed.

"That treasure has been hidden," he went on, "in the region through which you came last night, there can be but little doubt. For it was the ground fought over for centuries by the Wallachian, the Saxon, and the Turk. Why, there is hardly a foot of soil in all this region that has not been enriched by the blood of men, patriots or invaders. In the old days there were stirring times, when the Austrian and the Hungarian came up in hordes, and the patriots went out to meet them, men and women, the aged and the children too, and waited their coming on the rocks above the passes, that they might sweep destruction on them with their artificial avalanches. When the invader was triumphant he found but little, for whatever there was had been sheltered in the friendly soil."

"But how," said I, "can it have remained so long undiscovered, when there is a sure index to it if men will but take the trouble to look?" The Count smiled, and as his lips ran back over his gums, the long, sharp, canine teeth showed out strangely. He answered:

"Because your peasant is at heart a coward and a fool! Those flames only appear on one night, and on that night no man of this land will, if he can help it, stir without his doors. And, dear sir, even if he did he would not know what to do. Why, even the peasant that you tell me of who marked the place of the flame would not know where to look in daylight even for his own work. Even you would not, I dare be sworn, be able to find these places again?"

"There you are right," I said. "I know no more than the dead where even to look for them." Then we drifted into other matters.

"Come," he said at last, "tell me of London and of the house which you have procured for me." With an apology for my remissness, I went into my own room to get the papers from my bag. Whilst I was placing them in order I heard a rattling of china and silver in the next room, and as I passed through, noticed that the table had been cleared and the lamp lit, for it was by this time deep into the dark. The lamps were also lit in the study or library, and I found the Count lying on the sofa, reading, of all things in the world, an English Bradshaw's Guide. When I came in he cleared the books and papers from the table, and with him I went into plans and deeds and figures of all sorts. He was interested in everything, and asked me a myriad questions about the place and its surroundings. He clearly had studied beforehand all he could get on the subject of the neighbourhood, for he evidently at the end knew very much more than I did. When I remarked this, he answered.

"Well, but, my friend, is it not needful that I should? When I go there I shall be all alone, and my friend Harker Jonathan, nay, pardon me. I fall into my country's habit of putting your patronymic first, my friend Jonathan Harker will not be by my side to correct and aid me. He will be in Exeter, miles away, probably working at papers of the law with my other friend, Peter Hawkins. So!"

We went thoroughly into the business of the purchase of the estate at Purfleet. When I had told him the facts and got his signature to the necessary papers, and had written a letter with them ready to post to Mr. Hawkins, he began to ask me how I had come across so suitable a place. I read to him the notes which I had made at the time, and which I inscribe here.

"At Purfleet, on a byroad, I came across just such a place as seemed to be required, and where was displayed a dilapidated notice that the place was for sale. It was surrounded by a high wall, of ancient structure, built of heavy stones, and has not been repaired for a large number of years. The closed gates are of heavy old oak and iron, all eaten with rust.

"The estate is called Carfax, no doubt a corruption of the old Quatre Face, as the house is four sided, agreeing with the cardinal points of the compass. It contains in all some twenty acres, quite surrounded by the solid stone wall above mentioned. There are many trees on it, which make it in places gloomy, and there is a deep, dark-looking pond or small lake, evidently fed by some springs, as the water is clear and flows away in a fair-sized stream. The house is very large and of all periods back, I should say, to mediaeval times, for one part is of stone immensely thick, with only a few windows high up and heavily barred with iron. It looks like part of a keep, and is close to an old chapel or church. I could not enter it, as I had not the key of the door leading to it from the house, but I have taken with my Kodak views of it from various points. The house had been added to, but in a very straggling way, and I can only guess at the amount of ground it covers, which must be very great. There are but few houses close at hand, one being a very large house only recently added to and formed into a private lunatic asylum. It is not, however, visible from the grounds."

When I had finished, he said, "I am glad that it is old and big. I myself am of an old family, and to live in a new house would kill me. A house cannot be made habitable in a day, and after all, how few days go to make up a century. I rejoice also that there is a chapel of old times. We Transylvanian nobles love not to think that our bones may lie amongst the common dead. I seek not gaiety nor mirth, not the bright voluptuousness of much sunshine and sparkling waters which please the young and gay. I am no longer young, and my heart, through weary years of mourning over the dead, is not attuned to mirth. Moreover, the walls of my castle are broken. The shadows are many, and the wind breathes cold through the broken battlements and casements. I love the shade and the shadow, and would be alone with my thoughts when I may." Somehow his words and his look did not seem to accord, or else it was that his cast of face made his smile look malignant and saturnine.

Presently, with an excuse, he left me, asking me to pull my papers together. He was some little time away, and I began to look at some of the books around me. One was an atlas, which I found opened naturally to England, as if that map had been much used. On looking at it I found in certain places little rings marked, and on examining these I noticed that one was near London on the east side, manifestly where his new estate was situated. The other two were Exeter, and Whitby on the Yorkshire coast.

It was the better part of an hour when the Count returned. "Aha!" he said. "Still at your books? Good! But you must not work always. Come! I am informed that your supper is ready." He took my arm, and we went into the next room, where I found an excellent supper ready on the table. The Count again excused himself, as he had dined out on his being away from home. But he sat as on the previous night, and chatted whilst I ate. After supper I smoked, as on the last evening, and the Count stayed with me, chatting and asking questions on every conceivable subject, hour after hour. I felt that it was getting very late indeed, but I did not say anything, for I felt under obligation to meet my host's wishes in every way. I was not sleepy, as the long sleep yesterday had fortified me, but I could not help experiencing that chill which comes over one at the coming of the dawn, which is like, in its way, the turn of the tide. They say that people who are near death die generally at the change to dawn or at the turn of the tide. Anyone who has when tired, and tied as it were to his post, experienced this change in the atmosphere can well believe it. All at once we heard the crow of the cock coming up with preternatural shrillness through the clear morning air.

Count Dracula, jumping to his feet, said, "Why there is the morning again! How remiss I am to let you stay up so long. You must make your conversation regarding my dear new country of England less interesting, so that I may not forget how time flies by us," and with a courtly bow, he quickly left me.

I went into my room and drew the curtains, but there was little to notice. My window opened into the courtyard, all I could see was the warm grey of quickening sky. So I pulled the curtains again, and have written of this day.

8 May.--I began to fear as I wrote in this book that I was getting too diffuse. But now I am glad that I went into detail from the first, for there is something so strange about this place and all in it that I cannot but feel uneasy. I wish I were safe out of it, or that I had never come. It may be that this strange night existence is telling on me, but would that that were all! If there were any one to talk to I could bear it, but there is no one. I have only the Count to speak with, and he--I fear I am myself the only living soul within the place. Let me be prosaic so far as facts can be. It will help me to bear up, and imagination must not run riot with me. If it does I am lost. Let me say at once how I stand, or seem to.

I only slept a few hours when I went to bed, and feeling that I could not sleep any more, got up. I had hung my shaving glass by the window, and was just beginning to shave. Suddenly I felt a hand on my shoulder, and heard the Count's voice saying to me, "Good morning." I started, for it amazed me that I had not seen him, since the reflection of the glass covered the whole room behind me. In starting I had cut myself slightly, but did not notice it at the moment. Having answered the Count's salutation, I turned to the glass again to see how I had been mistaken. This time there could be no error, for the man was close to me, and I could see him over my shoulder. But there was no reflection of him in the mirror! The whole room behind me was displayed, but there was no sign of a man in it, except myself.

This was startling, and coming on the top of so many strange things, was beginning to increase that vague feeling of uneasiness which I always have when the Count is near. But at the instant I saw that the cut had bled a little, and the blood was trickling over my chin. I laid down the razor, turning as I did so half round to look for some sticking plaster. When the Count saw my face, his eyes blazed with a sort of demoniac fury, and he suddenly made a grab at my throat. I drew away and his hand touched the string of beads which held the crucifix. It made an instant change in him, for the fury passed so quickly that I could hardly believe that it was ever there.

"Take care," he said, "take care how you cut yourself. It is more dangerous that you think in this country." Then seizing the shaving glass, he went on, "And this is the wretched thing that has done the mischief. It is a foul bauble of man's vanity. Away with it!" And opening the window with one wrench of his terrible hand, he flung out the glass, which was shattered into a thousand pieces on the stones of the courtyard far below. Then he withdrew without a word. It is very annoying, for I do not see how I am to shave, unless in my watch-case or the bottom of the shaving pot, which is fortunately of metal.

When I went into the dining room, breakfast was prepared, but I could not find the Count anywhere. So I breakfasted alone. It is strange that as yet I have not seen the Count eat or drink. He must be a very peculiar man! After breakfast I did a little exploring in the castle. I went out on the stairs, and found a room looking towards the South.

The view was magnificent, and from where I stood there was every opportunity of seeing it. The castle is on the very edge of a terrific precipice. A stone falling from the window would fall a thousand feet without touching anything! As far as the eye can reach is a sea of green tree tops, with occasionally a deep rift where there is a chasm. Here and there are silver threads where the rivers wind in deep gorges through the forests.

But I am not in heart to describe beauty, for when I had seen the view I explored further. Doors, doors, doors everywhere, and all locked and bolted. In no place save from the windows in the castle walls is there an available exit. The castle is a veritable prison, and I am a prisoner!

CHAPTER 3

JONATHAN HARKER'S JOURNAL Continued

When I found that I was a prisoner a sort of wild feeling came over me. I rushed up and down the stairs, trying every door and peering out of every window I could find, but after a little the conviction of my helplessness overpowered all other feelings. When I look back after a few hours I think I must have been mad for the time, for I behaved much as a rat does in a trap. When, however, the conviction had come to me that I was helpless I sat down quietly, as quietly as I have ever done anything in my life, and began to think over what was best to be done. I am thinking still, and as yet have come to no definite conclusion. Of one thing only am I certain. That it is no use making my ideas known to the Count. He knows well that I am imprisoned, and as he has done it himself, and has doubtless his own motives for it, he would only deceive me if I trusted him fully with the facts. So far as I can see, my only plan will be to keep my knowledge and my fears to myself, and my eyes open. I am, I know, either being deceived, like a baby, by my own fears, or else I am in desperate straits, and if the latter be so, I need, and shall need, all my brains to get through.

I had hardly come to this conclusion when I heard the great door below shut, and knew that the Count had returned. He did not come at once into the library, so I went cautiously to my own room and found him making the bed. This was odd, but only confirmed what I had all along thought, that there are no servants in the house. When later I saw him through the chink of the hinges of the door laying the table in the dining room, I was assured of it. For if he does himself all these menial offices, surely it is proof that there is no one else in the castle, it must have been the Count himself who was the driver of the coach that brought me here. This is a terrible thought, for if so, what does it mean that he could control the wolves, as he did, by only holding up his hand for silence? How was it that all the people at Bistritz and on the coach had some terrible fear for me? What meant the giving of the crucifix, of the garlic, of the wild rose, of the mountain ash?

Bless that good, good woman who hung the crucifix round my neck! For it is a comfort and a strength to me whenever I touch it. It is odd that a thing which I have been taught to regard with disfavour and as idolatrous should in a time of loneliness and trouble be of help. Is it that there is something in the essence of the thing itself, or that it is a medium, a tangible help, in conveying memories of sympathy and comfort? Some time, if it may be, I must examine this matter and try to make up my mind about it. In the meantime I must find out all I can about Count Dracula, as it may help me to understand. Tonight he may talk of himself, if I turn the conversation that way. I must be very careful, however, not to awake his suspicion.

Midnight.--I have had a long talk with the Count. I asked him a few questions on Transylvania history, and he warmed up to the subject wonderfully. In his speaking of things and people, and especially of battles, he spoke as if he had been present at them all. This he afterwards explained by saying that to a Boyar the pride of his house and name is his own pride, that their glory is his glory, that their fate is his fate. Whenever he spoke of his house he always said "we", and spoke almost in the plural, like a king speaking. I wish I could put down all he said exactly as he said it, for to me it was most fascinating. It seemed to have in it a whole history of the country. He grew excited as he spoke, and walked about the room pulling his great white moustache and grasping anything on which he laid his hands as though he would crush it by main strength. One thing he said which I shall put down as nearly as I can, for it tells in its way the story of his race.

"We Szekelys have a right to be proud, for in our veins flows the blood of many brave races who fought as the lion fights, for lordship. Here, in the whirlpool of European races, the Ugric tribe bore down from Iceland the fighting spirit which Thor and Wodin gave them, which their Berserkers displayed to such fell intent on the seaboards of Europe, aye, and of Asia and Africa too, till the peoples thought that the werewolves themselves had come. Here, too, when they came, they found the Huns, whose warlike fury had swept the earth like a living flame, till the dying peoples held that in their veins ran the blood of those old witches, who, expelled from Scythia had mated with the devils in the desert. Fools, fools! What devil or what witch was ever so great as Attila, whose blood is in these veins?" He held up his arms. "Is it a wonder that we were a conquering race, that we were proud, that when the Magyar, the Lombard, the Avar, the Bulgar, or the Turk poured his thousands on our frontiers, we drove them back? Is it strange that when Arpad and his legions swept through the Hungarian fatherland he found us here when he reached the frontier, that the Honfoglalas was completed there? And when the Hungarian flood swept eastward, the Szekelys were claimed as kindred by the victorious Magyars, and to us for centuries was trusted the guarding of the frontier of Turkeyland. Aye, and more than that, endless duty of the frontier guard, for as the Turks say, 'water sleeps, and the enemy is sleepless.' Who more gladly than we throughout the Four Nations received the 'bloody sword,' or at its warlike call flocked quicker to the standard of the King? When was redeemed that great shame of my nation, the shame of Cassova, when the flags of the Wallach and the Magyar went down beneath the Crescent? Who was it but one of my own race who as Voivode crossed the Danube and beat the Turk on his own ground? This was a Dracula indeed! Woe was it that his own unworthy brother, when he had fallen, sold his people to the Turk and brought the shame of slavery on them! Was it not this Dracula, indeed, who inspired that other of his race who in a later age again and again brought his forces over the great river into Turkeyland, who, when he was beaten back, came again, and again, though he had to come alone from the bloody field where his troops were being slaughtered, since he knew that he alone could ultimately triumph! They said that he thought only of himself. Bah! What good are peasants without a leader? Where ends the war without a brain and heart to conduct it? Again, when, after the battle of Mohacs, we threw off the Hungarian yoke, we of the Dracula blood were amongst their leaders, for our spirit would not brook that we were not free. Ah, young sir, the Szekelys, and the Dracula as their heart's blood, their brains, and their swords, can boast a record that mushroom growths like the Hapsburgs and the Romanoffs can never reach. The warlike days are over. Blood is too precious a thing in these days of dishonourable peace, and the glories of the great races are as a tale that is told."

It was by this time close on morning, and we went to bed. (Mem., this diary seems horribly like the beginning of the "Arabian Nights," for everything has to break off at cockcrow, or like the ghost of Hamlet's father.)

12 May.--Let me begin with facts, bare, meager facts, verified by books and figures, and of which there can be no doubt. I must not confuse them with experiences which will have to rest on my own observation, or my memory of them. Last evening when the Count came from his room he began by asking me questions on legal matters and on the doing of certain kinds of business. I had spent the day wearily over books, and, simply to keep my mind occupied, went over some of the matters I had been examined in at Lincoln's Inn. There was a certain method in the Count's inquiries, so I shall try to put them down in sequence. The knowledge may somehow or some time be useful to me.

First, he asked if a man in England might have two solicitors or more. I told him he might have a dozen if he wished, but that it would not be wise to have more than one solicitor engaged in one transaction, as only one could act at a time, and that to change would be certain to militate against his interest. He seemed thoroughly to understand, and went on to ask if there would be any practical difficulty in having one man to attend, say, to banking, and another to look after shipping, in case local help were needed in a place far from the home of the banking solicitor. I asked to explain more fully, so that I might not by any chance mislead him, so he said,

"I shall illustrate. Your friend and mine, Mr. Peter Hawkins, from under the shadow of your beautiful cathedral at Exeter, which is far from London, buys for me through your good self my place at London. Good! Now here let me say frankly, lest you should think it strange that I have sought the services of one so far off from London instead of some one resident there, that my motive was that no local interest might be served save my wish only, and as one of London residence might, perhaps, have some purpose of himself or friend to serve, I went thus afield to seek my agent, whose labours should be only to my interest. Now, suppose I, who have much of affairs, wish to ship goods, say, to Newcastle, or Durham, or Harwich, or Dover, might it not be that it could with more ease be done by consigning to one in these ports?"

I answered that certainly it would be most easy, but that we solicitors had a system of agency one for the other, so that local work could be done locally on instruction from any solicitor, so that the client, simply placing himself in the hands of one man, could have his wishes carried out by him without further trouble.

"But," said he, "I could be at liberty to direct myself. Is it not so?"

"Of course," I replied, and "Such is often done by men of business, who do not like the whole of their affairs to be known by any one person."

"Good!" he said, and then went on to ask about the means of making consignments and the forms to be gone through, and of all sorts of difficulties which might arise, but by forethought could be guarded against. I explained all these things to him to the best of my ability, and he certainly left me under the impression that he would have made a wonderful solicitor, for there was nothing that he did not think of or foresee. For a man who was never in the country, and who did not evidently do much in the way of business, his knowledge and acumen were wonderful. When he had satisfied himself on these points of which he had spoken, and I had verified all as well as I could by the books available, he suddenly stood up and said, "Have you written since your first letter to our friend Mr. Peter Hawkins, or to any other?"

It was with some bitterness in my heart that I answered that I had not, that as yet I had not seen any opportunity of sending letters to anybody.

"Then write now, my young friend," he said, laying a heavy hand on my shoulder, "write to our friend and to any other, and say, if it will please you, that you shall stay with me until a month from now."

"Do you wish me to stay so long?" I asked, for my heart grew cold at the thought.

"I desire it much, nay I will take no refusal. When your master, employer, what you will, engaged that someone should come on his behalf, it was understood that my needs only were to be consulted. I have not stinted. Is it not so?"

What could I do but bow acceptance? It was Mr. Hawkins' interest, not mine, and I had to think of him, not myself, and besides, while Count Dracula was speaking, there was that in his eyes and in his bearing which made me remember that I was a prisoner, and that if I wished it I could have no choice. The Count saw his victory in my bow, and his mastery in the trouble of my face, for he began at once to use them, but in his own smooth, resistless way.

"I pray you, my good young friend, that you will not discourse of things other than business in your letters. It will doubtless please your friends to know that you are well, and that you look forward to getting home to them. Is it not so?" As he spoke he handed me three sheets of note paper and three envelopes. They were all of the thinnest foreign post, and looking at them, then at him, and noticing his quiet smile, with the sharp, canine teeth lying over the red underlip, I understood as well as if he had spoken that I should be more careful what I wrote, for he would be able to read it. So I determined to write only formal notes now, but to write fully to Mr. Hawkins in secret, and also to Mina, for to her I could write shorthand, which would puzzle the Count, if he did see it. When I had written my two letters I sat quiet, reading a book whilst the Count wrote several notes, referring as he wrote them to some books on his table. Then he took up my two and placed them with his own, and put by his writing materials, after which, the instant the door had closed behind him, I leaned over and looked at the letters, which were face down on the table. I felt no compunction in doing so for under the circumstances I felt that I should protect myself in every way I could.

One of the letters was directed to Samuel F. Billington, No. 7, The Crescent, Whitby, another to Herr Leutner, Varna. The third was to Coutts & Co., London, and the fourth to Herren Klopstock & Billreuth, bankers, Buda Pesth. The second and fourth were unsealed. I was just about to look at them when I saw the door handle move. I sank back in my seat, having just had time to resume my book before the Count, holding still another letter in his hand, entered the room. He took up the letters on the table and stamped them carefully, and then turning to me, said,

"I trust you will forgive me, but I have much work to do in private this evening. You will, I hope, find all things as you wish." At the door he turned, and after a moment's pause said, "Let me advise you, my dear young friend. Nay, let me warn you with all seriousness, that should you leave these rooms you will not by any chance go to sleep in any other part of the castle. It is old, and has many memories, and there are bad dreams for those who sleep unwisely. Be warned! Should sleep now or ever overcome you, or be like to do, then haste to your own chamber or to these rooms, for your rest will then be safe. But if you be not careful in this respect, then," He finished his speech in a gruesome way, for he motioned with his hands as if he were washing them. I quite understood. My only doubt was as to whether any dream could be more terrible than the unnatural, horrible net of gloom and mystery which seemed closing around me.

Later.--I endorse the last words written, but this time there is no doubt in question. I shall not fear to sleep in any place where he is not. I have placed the crucifix over the head of my bed, I imagine that my rest is thus freer from dreams, and there it shall remain.

When he left me I went to my room. After a little while, not hearing any sound, I came out and went up the stone stair to where I could look out towards the South. There was some sense of freedom in the vast expanse, inaccessible though it was to me, as compared with the narrow darkness of the courtyard. Looking out on this, I felt that I was indeed in prison, and I seemed to want a breath of fresh air, though it were of the night. I am beginning to feel this nocturnal existence tell on me. It is destroying my nerve. I start at my own shadow, and am full of all sorts of horrible imaginings. God knows that there is ground for my terrible fear in this accursed place! I looked out over the beautiful expanse, bathed in soft yellow moonlight till it was almost as light as day. In the soft light the distant hills became melted, and the shadows in the valleys and gorges of velvety blackness. The mere beauty seemed to cheer me. There was peace and comfort in every breath I drew. As I leaned from the window my eye was caught by something moving a storey below me, and somewhat to my left, where I imagined, from the order of the rooms, that the windows of the Count's own room would look out. The window at which I stood was tall and deep, stone-mullioned, and though weatherworn, was still complete. But it was evidently many a day since the case had been there. I drew back behind the stonework, and looked carefully out.

What I saw was the Count's head coming out from the window. I did not see the face, but I knew the man by the neck and the movement of his back and arms. In any case I could not mistake the hands which I had had some many opportunities of studying. I was at first interested and somewhat amused, for it is wonderful how small a matter will interest and amuse a man when he is a prisoner. But my very feelings changed to repulsion and terror when I saw the whole man slowly emerge from the window and begin to crawl down the castle wall over the dreadful abyss, face down with his cloak spreading out around him like great wings. At first I could not believe my eyes. I thought it was some trick of the moonlight, some weird effect of shadow, but I kept looking, and it could be no delusion. I saw the fingers and toes grasp the corners of the stones, worn clear of the mortar by the stress of years, and by thus using every projection and inequality move downwards with considerable speed, just as a lizard moves along a wall.

What manner of man is this, or what manner of creature, is it in the semblance of man? I feel the dread of this horrible place overpowering me. I am in fear, in awful fear, and there is no escape for me. I am encompassed about with terrors that I dare not think of.

15 May.--Once more I have seen the count go out in his lizard fashion. He moved downwards in a sidelong way, some hundred feet down, and a good deal to the left. He vanished into some hole or window. When his head had disappeared, I leaned out to try and see more, but without avail. The distance was too great to allow a proper angle of sight. I knew he had left the castle now, and thought to use the opportunity to explore more than I had dared to do as yet. I went back to the room, and taking a lamp, tried all the doors. They were all locked, as I had expected, and the locks were comparatively new. But I went down the stone stairs to the hall where I had entered originally. I found I could pull back the bolts easily enough and unhook the great chains. But the door was locked, and the key was gone! That key must be in the Count's room. I must watch should his door be unlocked, so that I may get it and escape. I went on to make a thorough examination of the various stairs and passages, and to try the doors that opened from them. One or two small rooms near the hall were open, but there was nothing to see in them except old furniture, dusty with age and moth-eaten. At last, however, I found one door at the top of the stairway which, though it seemed locked, gave a little under pressure. I tried it harder, and found that it was not really locked, but that the resistance came from the fact that the hinges had fallen somewhat, and the heavy door rested on the floor. Here was an opportunity which I might not have again, so I exerted myself, and with many efforts forced it back so that I could enter. I was now in a wing of the castle further to the right than the rooms I knew and a storey lower down. From the windows I could see that the suite of rooms lay along to the south of the castle, the windows of the end room looking out both west and south. On the latter side, as well as to the former, there was a great precipice. The castle was built on the corner of a great rock, so that on three sides it was quite impregnable, and great windows were placed here where sling, or bow, or culverin could not reach, and consequently light and comfort, impossible to a position which had to be guarded, were secured. To the west was a great valley, and then, rising far away, great jagged mountain fastnesses, rising peak on peak, the sheer rock studded with mountain ash and thorn, whose roots clung in cracks and crevices and crannies of the stone. This was evidently the portion of the castle occupied by the ladies in bygone days, for the furniture had more an air of comfort than any I had seen.

The windows were curtainless, and the yellow moonlight, flooding in through the diamond panes, enabled one to see even colours, whilst it softened the wealth of dust which lay over all and disguised in some measure the ravages of time and moth. My lamp seemed to be of little effect in the brilliant moonlight, but I was glad to have it with me, for there was a dread loneliness in the place which chilled my heart and made my nerves tremble. Still, it was better than living alone in the rooms which I had come to hate from the presence of the Count, and after trying a little to school my nerves, I found a soft quietude come over me. Here I am, sitting at a little oak table where in old times possibly some fair lady sat to pen, with much thought and many blushes, her ill-spelt love letter, and writing in my diary in shorthand all that has happened since I closed it last. It is the nineteenth century up-to-date with a vengeance. And yet, unless my senses deceive me, the old centuries had, and have, powers of their own which mere "modernity" cannot kill.

Later: The morning of 16 May.--God preserve my sanity, for to this I am reduced. Safety and the assurance of safety are things of the past. Whilst I live on here there is but one thing to hope for, that I may not go mad, if, indeed, I be not mad already. If I be sane, then surely it is maddening to think that of all the foul things that lurk in this hateful place the Count is the least dreadful to me, that to him alone I can look for safety, even though this be only whilst I can serve his purpose. Great God! Merciful God, let me be calm, for out of that way lies madness indeed. I begin to get new lights on certain things which have puzzled me. Up to now I never quite knew what Shakespeare meant when he made Hamlet say, "My tablets! Quick, my tablets! 'tis meet that I put it down," etc., For now, feeling as though my own brain were unhinged or as if the shock had come which must end in its undoing, I turn to my diary for repose. The habit of entering accurately must help to soothe me.

The Count's mysterious warning frightened me at the time. It frightens me more now when I think of it, for in the future he has a fearful hold upon me. I shall fear to doubt what he may say!

When I had written in my diary and had fortunately replaced the book and pen in my pocket I felt sleepy. The Count's warning came into my mind, but I took pleasure in disobeying it. The sense of sleep was upon me, and with it the obstinacy which sleep brings as outrider. The soft moonlight soothed, and the wide expanse without gave a sense of freedom which refreshed me. I determined not to return tonight to the gloom-haunted rooms, but to sleep here, where, of old, ladies had sat and sung and lived sweet lives whilst their gentle breasts were sad for their menfolk away in the midst of remorseless wars. I drew a great couch out of its place near the corner, so that as I lay, I could look at the lovely view to east and south, and unthinking of and uncaring for the dust, composed myself for sleep. I suppose I must have fallen asleep. I hope so, but I fear, for all that followed was startlingly real, so real that now sitting here in the broad, full sunlight of the morning, I cannot in the least believe that it was all sleep.

I was not alone. The room was the same, unchanged in any way since I came into it. I could see along the floor, in the brilliant moonlight, my own footsteps marked where I had disturbed the long accumulation of dust. In the moonlight opposite me were three young women, ladies by their dress and manner. I thought at the time that I must be dreaming when I saw them, they threw no shadow on the floor. They came close to me, and looked at me for some time, and then whispered together. Two were dark, and had high aquiline noses, like the Count, and great dark, piercing eyes, that seemed to be almost red when contrasted with the pale yellow moon. The other was fair, as fair as can be, with great masses of golden hair and eyes like pale sapphires. I seemed somehow to know her face, and to know it in connection with some dreamy fear, but I could not recollect at the moment how or where. All three had brilliant white teeth that shone like pearls against the ruby of their voluptuous lips. There was something about them that made me uneasy, some longing and at the same time some deadly fear. I felt in my heart a wicked, burning desire that they would kiss me with those red lips. It is not good to note this down, lest some day it should meet Mina's eyes and cause her pain, but it is the truth. They whispered together, and then they all three laughed, such a silvery, musical laugh, but as hard as though the sound never could have come through the softness of human lips. It was like the intolerable, tingling sweetness of water-glasses when played on by a cunning hand. The fair girl shook her head coquettishly, and the other two urged her on.

One said, "Go on! You are first, and we shall follow. Yours is the right to begin."

The other added, "He is young and strong. There are kisses for us all."

I lay quiet, looking out from under my eyelashes in an agony of delightful anticipation. The fair girl advanced and bent over me till I could feel the movement of her breath upon me. Sweet it was in one sense, honey-sweet, and sent the same tingling through the nerves as her voice, but with a bitter underlying the sweet, a bitter offensiveness, as one smells in blood.

I was afraid to raise my eyelids, but looked out and saw perfectly under the lashes. The girl went on her knees, and bent over me, simply gloating. There was a deliberate voluptuousness which was both thrilling and repulsive, and as she arched her neck she actually licked her lips like an animal, till I could see in the moonlight the moisture shining on the scarlet lips and on the red tongue as it lapped the white sharp teeth. Lower and lower went her head as the lips went below the range of my mouth and chin and seemed to fasten on my throat. Then she paused, and I could hear the churning sound of her tongue as it licked her teeth and lips, and I could feel the hot breath on my neck. Then the skin of my throat began to tingle as one's flesh does when the hand that is to tickle it approaches nearer, nearer. I could feel the soft, shivering touch of the lips on the super-sensitive skin of my throat, and the hard dents of two sharp teeth, just touching and pausing there. I closed my eyes in languorous ecstasy and waited, waited with beating heart.

But at that instant, another sensation swept through me as quick as lightning. I was conscious of the presence of the Count, and of his being as if lapped in a storm of fury. As my eyes opened involuntarily I saw his strong hand grasp the slender neck of the fair woman and with giant's power draw it back, the blue eyes transformed with fury, the white teeth champing with rage, and the fair cheeks blazing red with passion. But the Count! Never did I imagine such wrath and fury, even to the demons of the pit. His eyes were positively blazing. The red light in them was lurid, as if the flames of hell fire blazed behind them. His face was deathly pale, and the lines of it were hard like drawn wires. The thick eyebrows that met over the nose now seemed like a heaving bar of white-hot metal. With a fierce sweep of his arm, he hurled the woman from him, and then motioned to the others, as though he were beating them back. It was the same imperious gesture that I had seen used to the wolves. In a voice which, though low and almost in a whisper seemed to cut through the air and then ring in the room he said,

"How dare you touch him, any of you? How dare you cast eyes on him when I had forbidden it? Back, I tell you all! This man belongs to me! Beware how you meddle with him, or you'll have to deal with me."

The fair girl, with a laugh of ribald coquetry, turned to answer him. "You yourself never loved. You never love!" On this the other women joined, and such a mirthless, hard, soulless laughter rang through the room that it almost made me faint to hear. It seemed like the pleasure of fiends.

Then the Count turned, after looking at my face attentively, and said in a soft whisper, "Yes, I too can love. You yourselves can tell it from the past. Is it not so? Well, now I promise you that when I am done with him you shall kiss him at your will. Now go! Go! I must awaken him, for there is work to be done."

"Are we to have nothing tonight?" said one of them, with a low laugh, as she pointed to the bag which he had thrown upon the floor, and which moved as though there were some living thing within it. For answer he nodded his head. One of the women jumped forward and opened it. If my ears did not deceive me there was a gasp and a low wail, as of a half smothered child. The women closed round, whilst I was aghast with horror. But as I looked, they disappeared, and with them the dreadful bag. There was no door near them, and they could not have passed me without my noticing. They simply seemed to fade into the rays of the moonlight and pass out through the window, for I could see outside the dim, shadowy forms for a moment before they entirely faded away.

Then the horror overcame me, and I sank down unconscious.

CHAPTER 4

JONATHAN HARKER'S JOURNAL Continued

I awoke in my own bed. If it be that I had not dreamt, the Count must have carried me here. I tried to satisfy myself on the subject, but could not arrive at any unquestionable result. To be sure, there were certain small evidences, such as that my clothes were folded and laid by in a manner which was not my habit. My watch was still unwound, and I am rigorously accustomed to wind it the last thing before going to bed, and many such details. But these things are no proof, for they may have been evidences that my mind was not as usual, and, for some cause or another, I had certainly been much upset. I must watch for proof. Of one thing I am glad. If it was that the Count carried me here and undressed me, he must have been hurried in his task, for my pockets are intact. I am sure this diary would have been a mystery to him which he would not have brooked. He would have taken or destroyed it. As I look round this room, although it has been to me so full of fear, it is now a sort of sanctuary, for nothing can be more dreadful than those awful women, who were, who are, waiting to suck my blood.

18 May.--I have been down to look at that room again in daylight, for I must know the truth. When I got to the doorway at the top of the stairs I found it closed. It had been so forcibly driven against the jamb that part of the woodwork was splintered. I could see that the bolt of the lock had not been shot, but the door is fastened from the inside. I fear it was no dream, and must act on this surmise.

19 May.--I am surely in the toils. Last night the Count asked me in the suavest tones to write three letters, one saying that my work here was nearly done, and that I should start for home within a few days, another that I was starting on the next morning from the time of the letter, and the third that I had left the castle and arrived at Bistritz. I would fain have rebelled, but felt that in the present state of things it would be madness to quarrel openly with the Count whilst I am so absolutely in his power. And to refuse would be to excite his suspicion and to arouse his anger. He knows that I know too much, and that I must not live, lest I be dangerous to him. My only chance is to prolong my opportunities. Something may occur which will give me a chance to escape. I saw in his eyes something of that gathering wrath which was manifest when he hurled that fair woman from him. He explained to me that posts were few and uncertain, and that my writing now would ensure ease of mind to my friends. And he assured me with so much impressiveness that he would countermand the later letters,

which would be held over at Bistritz until due time in case chance would admit of my prolonging my stay, that to oppose him would have been to create new suspicion. I therefore pretended to fall in with his views, and asked him what dates I should put on the letters.

He calculated a minute, and then said, "The first should be June 12, the second June 19, and the third June 29."

I know now the span of my life. God help me!

28 May.--There is a chance of escape, or at any rate of being able to send word home. A band of Szgany have come to the castle, and are encamped in the courtyard. These are gipsies. I have notes of them in my book. They are peculiar to this part of the world, though allied to the ordinary gipsies all the world over. There are thousands of them in Hungary and Transylvania, who are almost outside all law. They attach themselves as a rule to some great noble or boyar, and call themselves by his name. They are fearless and without religion, save superstition, and they talk only their own varieties of the Romany tongue.

I shall write some letters home, and shall try to get them to have them posted. I have already spoken to them through my window to begin acquaintanceship. They took their hats off and made obeisance and many signs, which however, I could not understand any more than I could their spoken language…

I have written the letters. Mina's is in shorthand, and I simply ask Mr. Hawkins to communicate with her. To her I have explained my situation, but without the horrors which I may only surmise. It would shock and frighten her to death were I to expose my heart to her. Should the letters not carry, then the Count shall not yet know my secret or the extent of my knowledge.…

I have given the letters. I threw them through the bars of my window with a gold piece, and made what signs I could to have them posted. The man who took them pressed them to his heart and bowed, and then put them in his cap. I could do no more. I stole back to the study, and began to read. As the Count did not come in, I have written here…

The Count has come. He sat down beside me, and said in his smoothest voice as he opened two letters, "The Szgany has given me these, of which, though I know not whence they come, I shall, of course, take care. See!"--He must have looked at it.--"One is from you, and to my friend Peter Hawkins. The other,"--here he caught sight of the strange symbols as he opened the envelope, and the dark look came into his face, and his eyes blazed wickedly,--"The other is a vile thing, an outrage upon friendship and hospitality! It is not signed. Well! So it cannot matter to us." And he calmly held letter and envelope in the flame of the lamp till they were consumed.

Then he went on, "The letter to Hawkins, that I shall, of course send on, since it is yours. Your letters are sacred to me. Your pardon, my friend, that unknowingly I did break the seal. Will you not cover it again?" He held out the letter to me, and with a courteous bow handed me a clean envelope.

I could only redirect it and hand it to him in silence. When he went out of the room I could hear the key turn softly. A minute later I went over and tried it, and the door was locked.

When, an hour or two after, the Count came quietly into the room, his coming awakened me, for I had gone to sleep on the sofa. He was very courteous and very cheery in his manner, and seeing that I had been sleeping, he said, "So, my friend, you are tired? Get to bed. There is the surest rest. I may not have the pleasure of talk to-night, since there are many labours to me, but you will sleep, I pray."

I passed to my room and went to bed, and, strange to say, slept without dreaming. Despair has its own calms.

31 May.--This morning when I woke I thought I would provide myself with some papers and envelopes from my bag and keep them in my pocket, so that I might write in case I should get an opportunity, but again a surprise, again a shock!

Every scrap of paper was gone, and with it all my notes, my memoranda, relating to railways and travel, my letter of credit, in fact all that might be useful to me were I once outside the castle. I sat and pondered awhile, and then some thought occurred to me, and I made search of my portmanteau and in the wardrobe where I had placed my clothes.

The suit in which I had travelled was gone, and also my overcoat and rug. I could find no trace of them anywhere. This looked like some new scheme of villainy...

17 June.--This morning, as I was sitting on the edge of my bed cudgelling my brains, I heard without a crackling of whips and pounding and scraping of horses' feet up the rocky path beyond the courtyard. With joy I hurried to the window, and saw drive into the yard two great leiter-wagons, each drawn by eight sturdy horses, and at the head of each pair a Slovak, with his wide hat, great nail-studded belt, dirty sheep-skin, and high boots. They had also their long staves in hand. I ran to the door, intending to descend and try and join them through the main hall, as I thought that way might be opened for them. Again a shock, my door was fastened on the outside.

Then I ran to the window and cried to them. They looked up at me stupidly and pointed, but just then the "hetman" of the Szgany came out, and seeing them pointing to my window, said something, at which they laughed.

Henceforth no effort of mine, no piteous cry or agonized entreaty, would make them even look at me. They resolutely turned away. The leiter-wagons contained great, square boxes, with handles of thick rope. These were evidently empty by the ease with which the Slovaks handled them, and by their resonance as they were roughly moved.

When they were all unloaded and packed in a great heap in one corner of the yard, the Slovaks were given some money by the Szgany, and spitting on it for luck, lazily went each to his horse's head. Shortly afterwards, I heard the cracking of their whips die away in the distance.

24 June.--Last night the Count left me early, and locked himself into his own room. As soon as I dared I ran up the winding stair, and looked out of the window, which opened South. I thought I would watch for the Count, for there is something going on. The Szgany are quartered somewhere in the castle and are doing work of some kind. I know it, for now and then, I hear a far-away muffled sound as of mattock and spade, and, whatever it is, it must be the end of some ruthless villainy.

I had been at the window somewhat less than half an hour, when I saw something coming out of the Count's window. I drew back and watched carefully, and saw the whole man emerge. It was a new shock to me to find that he had on the suit of clothes which I had worn whilst travelling here, and slung over his shoulder the terrible bag which I had seen the women take away. There could be no doubt as to his quest, and in my garb, too! This, then, is his new scheme of evil, that he will allow others to see me, as they think, so that he may both leave evidence that I have been seen in the towns or villages posting my own letters, and that any wickedness which he may do shall by the local people be attributed to me.

It makes me rage to think that this can go on, and whilst I am shut up here, a veritable prisoner, but without that protection of the law which is even a criminal's right and consolation.

I thought I would watch for the Count's return, and for a long time sat doggedly at the window. Then I began to notice that there were some quaint little specks floating in the rays of the moonlight. They were like the tiniest grains of dust, and they whirled round and gathered in clusters in a nebulous sort of way. I watched them with a sense of soothing, and a sort of calm stole over me. I leaned back in the embrasure in a more comfortable position, so that I could enjoy more fully the aerial gambolling.

Something made me start up, a low, piteous howling of dogs somewhere far below in the valley, which was hidden from my sight. Louder it seemed to ring in my ears, and the floating moats of dust to take new shapes to the sound as they danced in the moonlight. I felt myself struggling to awake to some call of my instincts. Nay, my very soul was struggling, and my half-remembered sensibilities were striving to answer the call. I was becoming hypnotised!

Quicker and quicker danced the dust. The moonbeams seemed to quiver as they went by me into the mass of gloom beyond. More and more they gathered till they seemed to take dim phantom shapes. And then I started, broad awake and in full possession of my senses, and ran screaming from the place.

The phantom shapes, which were becoming gradually materialised from the moonbeams, were those three ghostly women to whom I was doomed.

I fled, and felt somewhat safer in my own room, where there was no moonlight, and where the lamp was burning brightly.

When a couple of hours had passed I heard something stirring in the Count's room, something like a sharp wail quickly suppressed. And then there was silence, deep, awful silence, which chilled me. With a beating heart, I tried the door, but I was locked in my prison, and could do nothing. I sat down and simply cried.

As I sat I heard a sound in the courtyard without, the agonised cry of a woman. I rushed to the window, and throwing it up, peered between the bars.

There, indeed, was a woman with dishevelled hair, holding her hands over her heart as one distressed with running. She was leaning against the corner of the gateway. When she saw my face at the window she threw herself forward, and shouted in a voice laden with menace, "Monster, give me my child!"

She threw herself on her knees, and raising up her hands, cried the same words in tones which wrung my heart. Then she tore her hair and beat her breast, and abandoned herself to all the violences of extravagant emotion. Finally, she threw herself forward, and though I could not see her, I could hear the beating of her naked hands against the door.

Somewhere high overhead, probably on the tower, I heard the voice of the Count calling in his harsh, metallic whisper. His call seemed to be answered from far and wide by the howling of wolves. Before many minutes had passed a pack of them poured, like a pent-up dam when liberated, through the wide entrance into the courtyard.

There was no cry from the woman, and the howling of the wolves was but short. Before long they streamed away singly, licking their lips.

I could not pity her, for I knew now what had become of her child, and she was better dead.

What shall I do? What can I do? How can I escape from this dreadful thing of night, gloom, and fear?

25 June.--No man knows till he has suffered from the night how sweet and dear to his heart and eye the morning can be. When the sun grew so high this morning that it struck the top of the great gateway opposite my window, the high spot which it touched seemed to me as if the dove from the ark had lighted there. My fear fell from me as if it had been a vaporous garment which dissolved in the warmth.

I must take action of some sort whilst the courage of the day is upon me. Last night one of my post-dated letters went to post, the first of that fatal series which is to blot out the very traces of my existence from the earth.

Let me not think of it. Action!

It has always been at night-time that I have been molested or threatened, or in some way in danger or in fear. I have not yet seen the Count in the daylight. Can it be that he sleeps when others wake, that he may be awake whilst they sleep? If I could only get into his room! But there is no possible way. The door is always locked, no way for me.

Yes, there is a way, if one dares to take it. Where his body has gone why may not another body go? I have seen him myself crawl from his window. Why should not I imitate him, and go in by his window? The chances are desperate, but my need is more desperate still. I shall risk it. At the worst it can only be death, and a man's death is not a calf's, and the dreaded Hereafter may still be open to me. God help me in my task! Goodbye, Mina, if I fail. Goodbye, my faithful friend and second father. Goodbye, all, and last of all Mina!

Same day, later.--I have made the effort, and God helping me, have come safely back to this room. I must put down every detail in order. I went whilst my courage was fresh straight to the window on the south side, and at once got outside on this side. The stones are big and roughly cut, and the mortar has by process of time been washed away between them. I took off my boots, and ventured out on the desperate way. I looked down once, so as to make sure that a sudden glimpse of the awful depth would not overcome me, but after that kept my eyes away from it. I know pretty well the direction and distance of the Count's window, and made for it as well as I could, having regard to the opportunities available. I did not feel dizzy, I suppose I was too excited, and the time seemed ridiculously short till I found myself standing on the window sill and trying to raise up the sash. I was filled with agitation, however, when I bent down and slid feet foremost in through the window. Then I looked around for the Count, but with surprise and gladness, made a discovery. The room was empty! It was barely furnished with odd things, which seemed to have never been used.

The furniture was something the same style as that in the south rooms, and was covered with dust. I looked for the key, but it was not in the lock, and I could not find it anywhere. The only thing I found was a great heap of gold in one corner, gold of all kinds, Roman, and British, and Austrian, and Hungarian, and Greek and Turkish money, covered with a film of dust, as though it had lain long in the ground. None of it that I noticed was less than three hundred years old. There were also chains and ornaments, some jewelled, but all of them old and stained.

CHAPTER 4

At one corner of the room was a heavy door. I tried it, for, since I could not find the key of the room or the key of the outer door, which was the main object of my search, I must make further examination, or all my efforts would be in vain. It was open, and led through a stone passage to a circular stairway, which went steeply down.

I descended, minding carefully where I went for the stairs were dark, being only lit by loopholes in the heavy masonry. At the bottom there was a dark, tunnel-like passage, through which came a deathly, sickly odour, the odour of old earth newly turned. As I went through the passage the smell grew closer and heavier. At last I pulled open a heavy door which stood ajar, and found myself in an old ruined chapel, which had evidently been used as a graveyard. The roof was broken, and in two places were steps leading to vaults, but the ground had recently been dug over, and the earth placed in great wooden boxes, manifestly those which had been brought by the Slovaks.

There was nobody about, and I made a search over every inch of the ground, so as not to lose a chance. I went down even into the vaults, where the dim light struggled, although to do so was a dread to my very soul. Into two of these I went, but saw nothing except fragments of old coffins and piles of dust. In the third, however, I made a discovery.

There, in one of the great boxes, of which there were fifty in all, on a pile of newly dug earth, lay the Count! He was either dead or asleep. I could not say which, for eyes were open and stony, but without the glassiness of death, and the cheeks had the warmth of life through all their pallor. The lips were as red as ever. But there was no sign of movement, no pulse, no breath, no beating of the heart.

I bent over him, and tried to find any sign of life, but in vain. He could not have lain there long, for the earthy smell would have passed away in a few hours. By the side of the box was its cover, pierced with holes here and there. I thought he might have the keys on him, but when I went to search I saw the dead eyes, and in them dead though they were, such a look of hate, though unconscious of me or my presence, that I fled from the place, and leaving the Count's room by the window, crawled again up the castle wall. Regaining my room, I threw myself panting upon the bed and tried to think.

29 June.--Today is the date of my last letter, and the Count has taken steps to prove that it was genuine, for again I saw him leave the castle by the same window, and in my clothes. As he went down the wall, lizard fashion, I wished I had a gun or some lethal weapon, that I might destroy him. But I fear that no weapon wrought along by man's hand would have any effect on him. I dared not wait to see him return, for I feared to see those weird sisters. I came back to the library, and read there till I fell asleep.

I was awakened by the Count, who looked at me as grimly as a man could look as he said, "Tomorrow, my friend, we must part. You return to your beautiful England, I to some work which may have such an end that we may never meet. Your letter home has been despatched. Tomorrow I shall not be here, but all shall be ready for your journey. In the morning come the Szgany, who have some labours of their own here, and also come some Slovaks. When they have gone, my carriage shall come for you, and shall bear you to the Borgo Pass to meet the diligence from Bukovina to Bistritz. But I am in hopes that I shall see more of you at Castle Dracula."

I suspected him, and determined to test his sincerity. Sincerity! It seems like a profanation of the word to write it in connection with such a monster, so I asked him point-blank, "Why may I not go tonight?"

"Because, dear sir, my coachman and horses are away on a mission."

"But I would walk with pleasure. I want to get away at once."

He smiled, such a soft, smooth, diabolical smile that I knew there was some trick behind his smoothness. He said, "And your baggage?"

"I do not care about it. I can send for it some other time."

The Count stood up, and said, with a sweet courtesy which made me rub my eyes, it seemed so real, "You English have a saying which is close to my heart, for its spirit is that which rules our boyars, 'Welcome the coming, speed the parting guest.' Come with me, my dear young friend. Not an hour shall you wait in my house against your will, though sad am I at your going, and that you so suddenly desire it. Come!" With a stately gravity, he, with the lamp, preceded me down the stairs and along the hall. Suddenly he stopped. "Hark!"

Close at hand came the howling of many wolves. It was almost as if the sound sprang up at the rising of his hand, just as the music of a great orchestra seems to leap under the baton of the conductor. After a pause of a moment, he proceeded, in his stately way, to the door, drew back the ponderous bolts, unhooked the heavy chains, and began to draw it open.

To my intense astonishment I saw that it was unlocked. Suspiciously, I looked all round, but could see no key of any kind.

As the door began to open, the howling of the wolves without grew louder and angrier. Their red jaws, with champing teeth, and their blunt-clawed feet as they leaped, came in through the opening door. I knew than that to struggle at the moment against the Count was useless. With such allies as these at his command, I could do nothing.

But still the door continued slowly to open, and only the Count's body stood in the gap. Suddenly it struck me that this might be the moment and means of my doom. I was to be given to the wolves, and at my own instigation. There was a diabolical wickedness in the idea great enough for the Count, and as the last chance I cried out, "Shut the door! I shall wait till morning." And I covered my face with my hands to hide my tears of bitter disappointment.

With one sweep of his powerful arm, the Count threw the door shut, and the great bolts clanged and echoed through the hall as they shot back into their places.

In silence we returned to the library, and after a minute or two I went to my own room. The last I saw of Count Dracula was his kissing his hand to me, with a red light of triumph in his eyes, and with a smile that Judas in hell might be proud of.

When I was in my room and about to lie down, I thought I heard a whispering at my door. I went to it softly and listened. Unless my ears deceived me, I heard the voice of the Count.

"Back! Back to your own place! Your time is not yet come. Wait! Have patience! Tonight is mine. Tomorrow night is yours!"

There was a low, sweet ripple of laughter, and in a rage I threw open the door, and saw without the three terrible women licking their lips. As I appeared, they all joined in a horrible laugh, and ran away.

I came back to my room and threw myself on my knees. It is then so near the end? Tomorrow! Tomorrow! Lord, help me, and those to whom I am dear!

CHAPTER 4

30 June.--These may be the last words I ever write in this diary. I slept till just before the dawn, and when I woke threw myself on my knees, for I determined that if Death came he should find me ready.

At last I felt that subtle change in the air, and knew that the morning had come. Then came the welcome cockcrow, and I felt that I was safe. With a glad heart, I opened the door and ran down the hall. I had seen that the door was unlocked, and now escape was before me. With hands that trembled with eagerness, I unhooked the chains and threw back the massive bolts.

But the door would not move. Despair seized me. I pulled and pulled at the door, and shook it till, massive as it was, it rattled in its casement. I could see the bolt shot. It had been locked after I left the Count.

Then a wild desire took me to obtain the key at any risk, and I determined then and there to scale the wall again, and gain the Count's room. He might kill me, but death now seemed the happier choice of evils. Without a pause I rushed up to the east window, and scrambled down the wall, as before, into the Count's room. It was empty, but that was as I expected. I could not see a key anywhere, but the heap of gold remained. I went through the door in the corner and down the winding stair and along the dark passage to the old chapel. I knew now well enough where to find the monster I sought.

The great box was in the same place, close against the wall, but the lid was laid on it, not fastened down, but with the nails ready in their places to be hammered home.

I knew I must reach the body for the key, so I raised the lid, and laid it back against the wall. And then I saw something which filled my very soul with horror. There lay the Count, but looking as if his youth had been half restored. For the white hair and moustache were changed to dark iron-grey. The cheeks were fuller, and the white skin seemed ruby-red underneath. The mouth was redder than ever, for on the lips were gouts of fresh blood, which trickled from the corners of the mouth and ran down over the chin and neck. Even the deep, burning eyes seemed set amongst swollen flesh, for the lids and pouches underneath were bloated. It seemed as if the whole awful creature were simply gorged with blood. He lay like a filthy leech, exhausted with his repletion.

I shuddered as I bent over to touch him, and every sense in me revolted at the contact, but I had to search, or I was lost. The coming night might see my own body a banquet in a similar war to those horrid three. I felt all over the body, but no sign could I find of the key. Then I stopped and looked at the Count. There was a mocking smile on the bloated face which seemed to drive me mad. This was the being I was helping to transfer to London, where, perhaps, for centuries to come he might, amongst its teeming millions, satiate his lust for blood, and create a new and ever-widening circle of semi-demons to batten on the helpless.

The very thought drove me mad. A terrible desire came upon me to rid the world of such a monster. There was no lethal weapon at hand, but I seized a shovel which the workmen had been using to fill the cases, and lifting it high, struck, with the edge downward, at the hateful face. But as I did so the head turned, and the eyes fell upon me, with all their blaze of basilisk horror. The sight seemed to paralyze me, and the shovel turned in my hand and glanced from the face, merely making a deep gash above the forehead. The shovel fell from my hand across the box, and as I pulled it away the flange of the blade caught the edge of the lid which fell over again, and hid the horrid thing from my sight. The last glimpse I had was of the bloated face, blood-stained and fixed with a grin of malice which would have held its own in the nethermost hell.

I thought and thought what should be my next move, but my brain seemed on fire, and I waited with a despairing feeling growing over me. As I waited I heard in the distance a gipsy song sung by merry voices coming closer, and through their song the rolling of heavy wheels and the cracking of whips. The Szgany and the Slovaks of whom the Count had spoken were coming. With a last look around and at the box which contained the vile body, I ran from the place and gained the Count's room, determined to rush out at the moment the door should be opened. With strained ears, I listened, and heard downstairs the grinding of the key in the great lock and the falling back of the heavy door. There must have been some other means of entry, or some one had a key for one of the locked doors.

Then there came the sound of many feet tramping and dying away in some passage which sent up a clanging echo. I turned to run down again towards the vault, where I might find the new entrance, but at the moment there seemed to come a violent puff of wind, and the door to the winding stair blew to with a shock that set the dust from the lintels flying. When I ran to push it open, I found that it was hopelessly fast. I was again a prisoner, and the net of doom was closing round me more closely.

As I write there is in the passage below a sound of many tramping feet and the crash of weights being set down heavily, doubtless the boxes, with their freight of earth. There was a sound of hammering. It is the box being nailed down. Now I can hear the heavy feet tramping again along the hall, with many other idle feet coming behind them.

The door is shut, the chains rattle. There is a grinding of the key in the lock. I can hear the key withdrawn, then another door opens and shuts. I hear the creaking of lock and bolt.

Hark! In the courtyard and down the rocky way the roll of heavy wheels, the crack of whips, and the chorus of the Szgany as they pass into the distance.

I am alone in the castle with those horrible women. Faugh! Mina is a woman, and there is nought in common. They are devils of the Pit!

I shall not remain alone with them. I shall try to scale the castle wall farther than I have yet attempted. I shall take some of the gold with me, lest I want it later. I may find a way from this dreadful place.

And then away for home! Away to the quickest and nearest train! Away from the cursed spot, from this cursed land, where the devil and his children still walk with earthly feet!

At least God's mercy is better than that of those monsters, and the precipice is steep and high. At its foot a man may sleep, as a man. Goodbye, all. Mina!

CHAPTER 5

LETTER FROM MISS MINA MURRAY TO MISS LUCY WESTENRA

9 May.

My dearest Lucy,

Forgive my long delay in writing, but I have been simply overwhelmed with work. The life of an assistant schoolmistress is sometimes trying. I am longing to be with you, and by the sea, where we can talk together freely and build our castles in the air. I have been working very hard lately, because I want to keep up with Jonathan's studies, and I have been practicing shorthand very assiduously. When we are married I shall be able to be useful to Jonathan, and if I can stenograph well enough I can take down what he wants to say in this way and write it out for him on the typewriter, at which also I am practicing very hard.

He and I sometimes write letters in shorthand, and he is keeping a stenographic journal of his travels abroad. When I am with you I shall keep a diary in the same way. I don't mean one of those two-pages-to-the-week-with-Sunday-squeezed- in-a-corner diaries, but a sort of journal which I can write in whenever I feel inclined.

I do not suppose there will be much of interest to other people, but it is not intended for them. I may show it to Jonathan some day if there is in it anything worth sharing, but it is really an exercise book. I shall try to do what I see lady journalists do, interviewing and writing descriptions and trying to remember conversations. I am told that, with a little practice, one can remember all that goes on or that one hears said during a day.

However, we shall see. I will tell you of my little plans when we meet. I have just had a few hurried lines from Jonathan from Transylvania. He is well, and will be returning in about a week. I am longing to hear all his news. It must be nice to see strange countries. I wonder if we, I mean Jonathan and I, shall ever see them together. There is the ten o'clock bell ringing. Goodbye.

Your loving

Mina

Tell me all the news when you write. You have not told me anything for a long time. I hear rumours, and especially of a tall, handsome, curly-haired man???

LETTER, LUCY WESTENRA TO MINA MURRAY

17, Chatham Street
Wednesday
My dearest Mina,

I must say you tax me very unfairly with being a bad correspondent. I wrote you twice since we parted, and your last letter was only your second. Besides, I have nothing to tell you. There is really nothing to interest you.

Town is very pleasant just now, and we go a great deal to picture-galleries and for walks and rides in the park. As to the tall, curly-haired man, I suppose it was the one who was with me at the last Pop. Someone has evidently been telling tales.

That was Mr. Holmwood. He often comes to see us, and he and Mamma get on very well together, they have so many things to talk about in common.

We met some time ago a man that would just do for you, if you were not already engaged to Jonathan. He is an excellent *parti*, being handsome, well off, and of good birth. He is a doctor and really clever. Just fancy! He is only nine-and-twenty, and he has an immense lunatic asylum all under his own care. Mr. Holmwood introduced him to me, and he called here to see us, and often comes now. I think he is one of the most resolute men I ever saw, and yet the most calm. He seems absolutely imperturbable. I can fancy what a wonderful power he must have over his patients. He has a curious habit of looking one straight in the face, as if trying to read one's thoughts. He tries this on very much with me, but I flatter myself he has got a tough nut to crack. I know that from my glass.

Do you ever try to read your own face? I do, and I can tell you it is not a bad study, and gives you more trouble than you can well fancy if you have never tried it.

He says that I afford him a curious psychological study, and I humbly think I do. I do not, as you know, take sufficient interest in dress to be able to describe the new fashions. Dress is a bore. That is slang again, but never mind. Arthur says that every day.

There, it is all out, Mina, we have told all our secrets to each other since we were children. We have slept together and eaten together, and laughed and cried together, and now, though I have spoken, I would like to speak more. Oh, Mina, couldn't you guess? I love him. I am blushing as I write, for although I think he loves me, he has not told me so in words. But, oh, Mina, I love him. I love him! There, that does me good.

I wish I were with you, dear, sitting by the fire undressing, as we used to sit, and I would try to tell you what I feel. I do not know how I am writing this even to you. I am afraid to stop, or I should tear up the letter, and I don't want to stop, for I do so want to tell you all. Let me hear from you at once, and tell me all that you think about it. Mina, pray for my happiness.

Lucy

P.S.--I need not tell you this is a secret. Goodnight again. L.

CHAPTER 5

LETTER, LUCY WESTENRA TO MINA MURRAY

24 May

My dearest Mina,

Thanks, and thanks, and thanks again for your sweet letter. It was so nice to be able to tell you and to have your sympathy.

My dear, it never rains but it pours. How true the old proverbs are. Here am I, who shall be twenty in September, and yet I never had a proposal till today, not a real proposal, and today I had three. Just fancy! Three proposals in one day! Isn't it awful! I feel sorry, really and truly sorry, for two of the poor fellows. Oh, Mina, I am so happy that I don't know what to do with myself. And three proposals! But, for goodness' sake, don't tell any of the girls, or they would be getting all sorts of extravagant ideas, and imagining themselves injured and slighted if in their very first day at home they did not get six at least. Some girls are so vain! You and I, Mina dear, who are engaged and are going to settle down soon soberly into old married women, can despise vanity. Well, I must tell you about the three, but you must keep it a secret, dear, from every one except, of course, Jonathan. You will tell him, because I would, if I were in your place, certainly tell Arthur. A woman ought to tell her husband everything. Don't you think so, dear? And I must be fair. Men like women, certainly their wives, to be quite as fair as they are. And women, I am afraid, are not always quite as fair as they should be.

Well, my dear, number One came just before lunch. I told you of him, Dr. John Seward, the lunatic asylum man, with the strong jaw and the good forehead. He was very cool outwardly, but was nervous all the same. He had evidently been schooling himself as to all sorts of little things, and remembered them, but he almost managed to sit down on his silk hat, which men don't generally do when they are cool, and then when he wanted to appear at ease he kept playing with a lancet in a way that made me nearly scream. He spoke to me, Mina, very straightforwardly. He told me how dear I was to him, though he had known me so little, and what his life would be with me to help and cheer him. He was going to tell me how unhappy he would be if I did not care for him, but when he saw me cry he said he was a brute and would not add to my present trouble. Then he broke off and asked if I could love him in time, and when I shook my head his hands trembled, and then with some hesitation he asked me if I cared already for any one else. He put it very nicely, saying that he did not want to wring my confidence from me, but only to know, because if a woman's heart was free a man might have hope. And then, Mina, I felt a sort of duty to tell him that there was some one. I only told him that much, and then he stood up, and he looked very strong and very grave as he took both my hands in his and said he hoped I would be happy, and that If I ever wanted a friend I must count him one of my best.

Oh, Mina dear, I can't help crying, and you must excuse this letter being all blotted. Being proposed to is all very nice and all that sort of thing, but it isn't at all a happy thing when you have to see a poor fellow, whom you know loves you honestly, going away and looking all broken hearted, and to know that, no matter what he may say at the moment, you are passing out of his life. My dear, I must stop here at present, I feel so miserable, though I am so happy.

Evening.

Arthur has just gone, and I feel in better spirits than when I left off, so I can go on telling you about the day.

Well, my dear, number Two came after lunch. He is such a nice fellow, an American from Texas, and he looks so young and so fresh that it seems almost impossible that he has been to so many places and has such adventures. I sympathize with poor Desdemona when she had such a stream poured in her ear, even by a black man. I suppose that we women are such cowards that we think a man will save us from fears, and we marry him. I know now what I would do if I were a man and wanted to make a girl love me. No, I don't, for there was Mr. Morris telling us his stories, and Arthur never told any, and yet…

My dear, I am somewhat previous. Mr. Quincy P. Morris found me alone. It seems that a man always does find a girl alone. No, he doesn't, for Arthur tried twice to make a chance, and I helping him all I could, I am not ashamed to say it now. I must tell you beforehand that Mr. Morris doesn't always speak slang—that is to say, he never does so to strangers or before them, for he is really well educated and has exquisite manners—but he found out that it amused me to hear him talk American slang, and whenever I was present, and there was no one to be shocked, he said such funny things. I am afraid, my dear, he has to invent it all, for it fits exactly into whatever else he has to say. But this is a way slang has. I do not know myself if I shall ever speak slang. I do not know if Arthur likes it, as I have never heard him use any as yet.

Well, Mr. Morris sat down beside me and looked as happy and jolly as he could, but I could see all the same that he was very nervous. He took my hand in his, and said ever so sweetly…

"Miss Lucy, I know I ain't good enough to regulate the fixin's of your little shoes, but I guess if you wait till you find a man that is you will go join them seven young women with the lamps when you quit. Won't you just hitch up alongside of me and let us go down the long road together, driving in double harness?"

Well, he did look so good humoured and so jolly that it didn't seem half so hard to refuse him as it did poor Dr. Seward. So I said, as lightly as I could, that I did not know anything of hitching, and that I wasn't broken to harness at all yet. Then he said that he had spoken in a light manner, and he hoped that if he had made a mistake in doing so on so grave, so momentous, an occasion for him, I would forgive him. He really did look serious when he was saying it, and I couldn't help feeling a bit serious too--I know, Mina, you will think me a horrid flirt--though I couldn't help feeling a sort of exultation that he was number Two in one day. And then, my dear, before I could say a word he began pouring out a perfect torrent of love-making, laying his very heart and soul at my feet. He looked so earnest over it that I shall never again think that a man must be playful always, and never earnest, because he is merry at times. I suppose he saw something in my face which checked him, for he suddenly stopped, and said with a sort of manly fervour that I could have loved him for if I had been free…

"Lucy, you are an honest hearted girl, I know. I should not be here speaking to you as I am now if I did not believe you clean grit, right through to the very depths of your soul. Tell me, like one good fellow to another, is there any one else that you care for?

And if there is I'll never trouble you a hair's breadth again, but will be, if you will let me, a very faithful friend."

My dear Mina, why are men so noble when we women are so little worthy of them? Here was I almost making fun of this great-hearted, true gentleman. I burst into tears—I am afraid, my dear, you will think this a very sloppy letter in more ways than one—and I really felt very badly.

Why can't they let a girl marry three men, or as many as want her, and save all this trouble? But this is heresy, and I must not say it. I am glad to say that, though I was crying, I was able to look into Mr. Morris' brave eyes, and I told him out straight…

"Yes, there is some one I love, though he has not told me yet that he even loves me." I was right to speak to him so frankly, for quite a light came into his face, and he put out both his hands and took mine, I think I put them into his—and said in a hearty way…

"That's my brave girl. It's better worth being late for a chance of winning you than being in time for any other girl in the world. Don't cry, my dear. If it's for me, I'm a hard nut to crack, and I take it standing up. If that other fellow doesn't know his happiness, well, he'd better look for it soon, or he'll have to deal with me. Little girl, your honesty and pluck have made me a friend, and that's rarer than a lover; it's more selfish anyhow. My dear, I'm going to have a pretty lonely walk between this and Kingdom Come. Won't you give me one kiss? It'll be something to keep off the darkness now and then. You can, you know, if you like, for that other good fellow—he must be a good fellow, my dear, and a fine fellow, or you could not love him—hasn't spoken yet."

That quite won me, Mina, for it was brave and sweet of him, and noble too, to a rival—wasn't it?—and he so sad, so I leant over and kissed him.

He stood up with my two hands in his, and as he looked down into my face—I am afraid I was blushing very much, he said, "Little girl, I hold your hand, and you've kissed me, and if these things don't make us friends nothing ever will. Thank you for your sweet honesty to me, and goodbye."

He wrung my hand, and taking up his hat, went straight out of the room without looking back, without a tear or a quiver or a pause, and I am crying like a baby.

Oh, why must a man like that be made unhappy when there are lots of girls about who would worship the very ground he trod on? I know I would if I were free, only I don't want to be free. My dear, this quite upset me, and I feel I cannot write of happiness just at once, after telling you of it, and I don't wish to tell of the number Three until it can be all happy. Ever your loving…

Lucy

P.S.--Oh, about number Three, I needn't tell you of number Three, need I? Besides, it was all so confused. It seemed only a moment from his coming into the room till both his arms were round me, and he was kissing me. I am very, very happy, and I don't know what I have done to deserve it. I must only try in the future to show that I am not ungrateful to God for all His goodness to me in sending to me such a lover, such a husband, and such a friend.

Goodbye.

DR. SEWARD'S DIARY (Kept in phonograph)

25 May.--Ebb tide in appetite today. Cannot eat, cannot rest, so diary instead. Since my rebuff of yesterday I have a sort of empty feeling. Nothing in the world seems of sufficient importance to be worth the doing. As I knew that the only cure for this sort of thing was work, I went amongst the patients. I picked out one who has afforded me a study of much interest. He is so quaint that I am determined to understand him as well as I can. Today I seemed to get nearer than ever before to the heart of his mystery.

I questioned him more fully than I had ever done, with a view to making myself master of the facts of his hallucination. In my manner of doing it there was, I now see, something of cruelty. I seemed to wish to keep him to the point of his madness, a thing which I avoid with the patients as I would the mouth of hell.

(Mem., Under what circumstances would I not avoid the pit of hell?) Omnia Romae venalia sunt. Hell has its price! If there be anything behind this instinct it will be valuable to trace it afterwards accurately, so I had better commence to do so, therefore…

R. M, Renfield, age 59. Sanguine temperament, great physical strength, morbidly excitable, periods of gloom, ending in some fixed idea which I cannot make out. I presume that the sanguine temperament itself and the disturbing influence end in a mentally-accomplished finish, a possibly dangerous man, probably dangerous if unselfish. In selfish men caution is as secure an armour for their foes as for themselves. What I think of on this point is, when self is the fixed point the centripetal force is balanced with the centrifugal. When duty, a cause, etc., is the fixed point, the latter force is paramount, and only accident or a series of accidents can balance it.

LETTER, QUINCEY P. MORRIS TO HON. ARTHUR HOLMOOD

25 May.

My dear Art,

We've told yarns by the campfire in the prairies, and dressed one another's wounds after trying a landing at the Marquesas, and drunk healths on the shore of Titicaca. There are more yarns to be told, and other wounds to be healed, and another health to be drunk. Won't you let this be at my campfire tomorrow night? I have no hesitation in asking you, as I know a certain lady is engaged to a certain dinner party, and that you are free. There will only be one other, our old pal at the Korea, Jack Seward. He's coming, too, and we both want to mingle our weeps over the wine cup, and to drink a health with all our hearts to the happiest man in all the wide world, who has won the noblest heart that God has made and best worth winning. We promise you a hearty welcome, and a loving greeting, and a health as true as your own right hand. We shall both swear to leave you at home if you drink too deep to a certain pair of eyes. Come!

Yours, as ever and always,

Quincey P. Morris

CHAPTER 5

TELEGRAM FROM ARTHUR HOLMWOOD TO QUINCEY P. MORRIS

26 May
Count me in every time. I bear messages which will make both your ears tingle.
Art

CHAPTER 6

MINA MURRAY'S JOURNAL

24 July. Whitby.--Lucy met me at the station, looking sweeter and lovelier than ever, and we drove up to the house at the Crescent in which they have rooms. This is a lovely place. The little river, the Esk, runs through a deep valley, which broadens out as it comes near the harbour. A great viaduct runs across, with high piers, through which the view seems somehow further away than it really is. The valley is beautifully green, and it is so steep that when you are on the high land on either side you look right across it, unless you are near enough to see down. The houses of the old town--the side away from us, are all red-roofed, and seem piled up one over the other anyhow, like the pictures we see of Nuremberg. Right over the town is the ruin of Whitby Abbey, which was sacked by the Danes, and which is the scene of part of "Marmion," where the girl was built up in the wall. It is a most noble ruin, of immense size, and full of beautiful and romantic bits. There is a legend that a white lady is seen in one of the windows. Between it and the town there is another church, the parish one, round which is a big graveyard, all full of tombstones. This is to my mind the nicest spot in Whitby, for it lies right over the town, and has a full view of the harbour and all up the bay to where the headland called Kettleness stretches out into the sea. It descends so steeply over the harbour that part of the bank has fallen away, and some of the graves have been destroyed.

In one place part of the stonework of the graves stretches out over the sandy pathway far below. There are walks, with seats beside them, through the churchyard, and people go and sit there all day long looking at the beautiful view and enjoying the breeze.

I shall come and sit here often myself and work. Indeed, I am writing now, with my book on my knee, and listening to the talk of three old men who are sitting beside me. They seem to do nothing all day but sit here and talk.

The harbour lies below me, with, on the far side, one long granite wall stretching out into the sea, with a curve outwards at the end of it, in the middle of which is a lighthouse. A heavy seawall runs along outside of it. On the near side, the seawall makes an elbow crooked inversely, and its end too has a lighthouse. Between the two piers there is a narrow opening into the harbour, which then suddenly widens.

It is nice at high water, but when the tide is out it shoals away to nothing, and there is merely the stream of the Esk, running between banks of sand, with rocks here and there. Outside the harbour on this side there rises for about half a mile a great reef, the sharp of which runs straight out from behind the south lighthouse. At the end of it is a buoy with a bell, which swings in bad weather, and sends in a mournful sound on the wind.

They have a legend here that when a ship is lost bells are heard out at sea. I must ask the old man about this. He is coming this way...

He is a funny old man. He must be awfully old, for his face is gnarled and twisted like the bark of a tree. He tells me that he is nearly a hundred, and that he was a sailor in the Greenland fishing fleet when Waterloo was fought. He is, I am afraid, a very sceptical person, for when I asked him about the bells at sea and the White Lady at the abbey he said very brusquely,

"I wouldn't fash masel' about them, miss. Them things be all wore out. Mind, I don't say that they never was, but I do say that they wasn't in my time. They be all very well for comers and trippers, an' the like, but not for a nice young lady like you. Them feet-folks from York and Leeds that be always eatin' cured herrin's and drinkin' tea an' lookin' out to buy cheap jet would creed aught. I wonder masel' who'd be bothered tellin' lies to them, even the newspapers, which is full of fool-talk."

I thought he would be a good person to learn interesting things from, so I asked him if he would mind telling me something about the whale fishing in the old days. He was just settling himself to begin when the clock struck six, whereupon he laboured to get up, and said,

"I must gang ageeanwards home now, miss. My grand-daughter doesn't like to be kept waitin' when the tea is ready, for it takes me time to crammle aboon the grees, for there be a many of 'em, and miss, I lack belly-timber sairly by the clock."

He hobbled away, and I could see him hurrying, as well as he could, down the steps. The steps are a great feature on the place. They lead from the town to the church, there are hundreds of them, I do not know how many, and they wind up in a delicate curve. The slope is so gentle that a horse could easily walk up and down them.

I think they must originally have had something to do with the abbey. I shall go home too. Lucy went out, visiting with her mother, and as they were only duty calls, I did not go.

1 August.--I came up here an hour ago with Lucy, and we had a most interesting talk with my old friend and the two others who always come and join him. He is evidently the Sir Oracle of them, and I should think must have been in his time a most dictatorial person.

He will not admit anything, and down faces everybody. If he can't out-argue them he bullies them, and then takes their silence for agreement with his views.

Lucy was looking sweetly pretty in her white lawn frock. She has got a beautiful colour since she has been here.

I noticed that the old men did not lose any time in coming and sitting near her when we sat down. She is so sweet with old people, I think they all fell in love with her on the spot. Even my old man succumbed and did not contradict her, but gave me double share instead. I got him on the subject of the legends, and he went off at once into a sort of sermon. I must try to remember it and put it down.

"It be all fool-talk, lock, stock, and barrel, that's what it be and nowt else. These bans an' wafts an' boh-ghosts an' bar-guests an' bogles an' all anent them is only fit to set bairns an' dizzy women a'belderin'. They be nowt but air-blebs. They, an' all grims an' signs an' warnin's, be all invented by parsons an' illsome berk-bodies an' railway touters to skeer an' scunner hafflin's, an' to get folks to do somethin' that they don't other incline to. It makes me ireful to think o' them. Why, it's them that, not content with printin' lies on paper an' preachin' them out of pulpits, does want to be cuttin' them on the tombstones. Look here all around you in what airt ye will. All them steans, holdin' up their heads as well as they can out of their pride, is acant, simply tumblin' down with the weight o' the lies wrote on them, 'Here lies the body' or 'Sacred to the memory' wrote on all of them, an' yet in nigh half of them there bean't no bodies at all, an' the memories of them bean't cared a pinch of snuff about, much less sacred. Lies all of them, nothin' but lies of one kind or another! My gog, but it'll be a quare scowderment at the Day of Judgment when they come tumblin' up in their death-sarks, all jouped together an' trying' to drag their tombsteans with them to prove how good they was, some of them trimmlin' an' dithering, with their hands that dozzened an' slippery from lyin' in the sea that they can't even keep their gurp o' them."

I could see from the old fellow's self-satisfied air and the way in which he looked round for the approval of his cronies that he was "showing off," so I put in a word to keep him going.

"Oh, Mr. Swales, you can't be serious. Surely these tombstones are not all wrong?"

"Yabblins! There may be a poorish few not wrong, savin' where they make out the people too good, for there be folk that do think a balm-bowl be like the sea, if only it be their own. The whole thing be only lies. Now look you here. You come here a stranger, an' you see this kirkgarth."

I nodded, for I thought it better to assent, though I did not quite understand his dialect. I knew it had something to do with the church.

He went on, "And you consate that all these steans be aboon folk that be haped here, snod an' snog?" I assented again. "Then that be just where the lie comes in. Why, there be scores of these laybeds that be toom as old Dun's 'baccabox on Friday night."

He nudged one of his companions, and they all laughed. "And, my gog! How could they be otherwise? Look at that one, the aftest abaft the bier-bank, read it!"

I went over and read, "Edward Spencelagh, master mariner, murdered by pirates off the coast of Andres, April, 1854, age 30." When I came back Mr. Swales went on,

"Who brought him home, I wonder, to hap him here? Murdered off the coast of Andres! An' you consated his body lay under! Why, I could name ye a dozen whose bones lie in the Greenland seas above," he pointed northwards, "or where the currants may have drifted them. There be the steans around ye. Ye can, with your young eyes, read the small print of the lies from here. This Braithwaite Lowery, I knew his father, lost in the Lively off Greenland in '20, or Andrew Woodhouse, drowned in the same seas in 1777, or John Paxton, drowned off Cape Farewell a year later, or old John Rawlings, whose grandfather sailed with me, drowned in the Gulf of Finland in '50. Do ye think that all these men will have to make a rush to Whitby when the trumpet sounds? I have me antherums aboot it! I tell ye that when they got here they'd be jommlin' and jostlin' one another that way that it 'ud be like a fight up on the ice in the old days, when we'd be at one another from daylight to dark, an' tryin' to tie up our cuts by the aurora borealis." This was evidently local pleasantry, for the old man cackled over it, and his cronies joined in with gusto.

"But," I said, "surely you are not quite correct, for you start on the assumption that all the poor people, or their spirits, will have to take their tombstones with them on the Day of Judgment. Do you think that will be really necessary?"

"Well, what else be they tombstones for? Answer me that, miss!"

"To please their relatives, I suppose."

"To please their relatives, you suppose!" This he said with intense scorn. "How will it pleasure their relatives to know that lies is wrote over them, and that everybody in the place knows that they be lies?"

He pointed to a stone at our feet which had been laid down as a slab, on which the seat was rested, close to the edge of the cliff. "Read the lies on that thruff-stone," he said.

The letters were upside down to me from where I sat, but Lucy was more opposite to them, so she leant over and read, "Sacred to the memory of George Canon, who died, in the hope of a glorious resurrection, on July 29, 1873, falling from the rocks at Kettleness. This tomb was erected by his sorrowing mother to her dearly beloved son. 'He was the only son of his mother, and she was a widow.' Really, Mr. Swales, I don't see anything very funny in that!" She spoke her comment very gravely and somewhat severely.

"Ye don't see aught funny! Ha-ha! But that's because ye don't gawm the sorrowin' mother was a hell-cat that hated him because he was acrewk'd, a regular lamiter he was, an' he hated her so that he committed suicide in order that she mightn't get an insurance she put on his life. He blew nigh the top of his head off with an old musket that they had for scarin' crows with. 'Twarn't for crows then, for it brought the clegs and the dowps to him. That's the way he fell off the rocks. And, as to hopes of a glorious resurrection, I've often heard him say masel' that he hoped he'd go to hell, for his mother was so pious that she'd be sure to go to heaven, an' he didn't want to addle where she was. Now isn't that stean at any rate," he hammered it with his stick as he spoke, "a pack of lies? And won't it make Gabriel keckle when Geordie comes pantin' ut the grees with the tompstean balanced on his hump, and asks to be took as evidence!"

I did not know what to say, but Lucy turned the conversation as she said, rising up, "Oh, why did you tell us of this? It is my favourite seat, and I cannot leave it, and now I find I must go on sitting over the grave of a suicide."

"That won't harm ye, my pretty, an' it may make poor Geordie gladsome to have so trim a lass sittin' on his lap. That won't hurt ye. Why, I've sat here off an' on for nigh twenty years past, an' it hasn't done me no harm. Don't ye fash about them as lies under ye, or that doesn' lie there either! It'll be time for ye to be getting scart when ye see the tombsteans all run away with, and the place as bare as a stubble-field. There's the clock, and I must gang. My service to ye, ladies!" And off he hobbled.

Lucy and I sat awhile, and it was all so beautiful before us that we took hands as we sat, and she told me all over again about Arthur and their coming marriage. That made me just a little heart-sick, for I haven't heard from Jonathan for a whole month.

The same day. I came up here alone, for I am very sad. There was no letter for me. I hope there cannot be anything the matter with Jonathan. The clock has just struck nine. I see the lights scattered all over the town, sometimes in rows where the streets are, and sometimes singly. They run right up the Esk and die away in the curve of the valley. To my left the view is cut off by a black line of roof of the old house next to the abbey. The sheep and lambs are bleating in the fields away behind me, and there is a clatter of donkeys' hoofs up the paved road below. The band on the pier is playing a harsh waltz in good time, and further along the quay there is a Salvation Army meeting in a back street. Neither of the bands hears the other, but up here I hear and see them both. I wonder where Jonathan is and if he is thinking of me! I wish he were here.

DR. SEWARD'S DIARY

5 June.--The case of Renfield grows more interesting the more I get to understand the man. He has certain qualities very largely developed; selfishness, secrecy, and purpose.

I wish I could get at what is the object of the latter. He seems to have some settled scheme of his own, but what it is I do not know. His redeeming quality is a love of animals, though, indeed, he has such curious turns in it that I sometimes imagine he is only abnormally cruel. His pets are of odd sorts.

Just now his hobby is catching flies. He has at present such a quantity that I have had myself to expostulate. To my astonishment, he did not break out into a fury, as I expected, but took the matter in simple seriousness. He thought for a moment, and then said, "May I have three days? I shall clear them away." Of course, I said that would do. I must watch him.

18 June.--He has turned his mind now to spiders, and has got several very big fellows in a box. He keeps feeding them his flies, and the number of the latter is becoming sensibly diminished, although he has used half his food in attracting more flies from outside to his room.

1 July.--His spiders are now becoming as great a nuisance as his flies, and today I told him that he must get rid of them.

He looked very sad at this, so I said that he must some of them, at all events. He cheerfully acquiesced in this, and I gave him the same time as before for reduction.

He disgusted me much while with him, for when a horrid blowfly, bloated with some carrion food, buzzed into the room, he caught it, held it exultantly for a few moments between his finger and thumb, and before I knew what he was going to do, put it in his mouth and ate it.

I scolded him for it, but he argued quietly that it was very good and very wholesome, that it was life, strong life, and gave life to him. This gave me an idea, or the rudiment of one. I must watch how he gets rid of his spiders.

He has evidently some deep problem in his mind, for he keeps a little notebook in which he is always jotting down something. Whole pages of it are filled with masses of figures, generally single numbers added up in batches, and then the totals added in batches again, as though he were focussing some account, as the auditors put it.

8 July.--There is a method in his madness, and the rudimentary idea in my mind is growing. It will be a whole idea soon, and then, oh, unconscious cerebration, you will have to give the wall to your conscious brother.

CHAPTER 6

I kept away from my friend for a few days, so that I might notice if there were any change. Things remain as they were except that he has parted with some of his pets and got a new one.

He has managed to get a sparrow, and has already partially tamed it. His means of taming is simple, for already the spiders have diminished. Those that do remain, however, are well fed, for he still brings in the flies by tempting them with his food.

19 July--We are progressing. My friend has now a whole colony of sparrows, and his flies and spiders are almost obliterated. When I came in he ran to me and said he wanted to ask me a great favour, a very, very great favour. And as he spoke, he fawned on me like a dog.

I asked him what it was, and he said, with a sort of rapture in his voice and bearing, "A kitten, a nice, little, sleek playful kitten, that I can play with, and teach, and feed, and feed, and feed!"

I was not unprepared for this request, for I had noticed how his pets went on increasing in size and vivacity, but I did not care that his pretty family of tame sparrows should be wiped out in the same manner as the flies and spiders. So I said I would see about it, and asked him if he would not rather have a cat than a kitten.

His eagerness betrayed him as he answered, "Oh, yes, I would like a cat! I only asked for a kitten lest you should refuse me a cat. No one would refuse me a kitten, would they?"

I shook my head, and said that at present I feared it would not be possible, but that I would see about it. His face fell, and I could see a warning of danger in it, for there was a sudden fierce, sidelong look which meant killing. The man is an undeveloped homicidal maniac. I shall test him with his present craving and see how it will work out, then I shall know more.

10 pm.--I have visited him again and found him sitting in a corner brooding. When I came in he threw himself on his knees before me and implored me to let him have a cat, that his salvation depended upon it.

I was firm, however, and told him that he could not have it, whereupon he went without a word, and sat down, gnawing his fingers, in the corner where I had found him. I shall see him in the morning early.

20 July.--Visited Renfield very early, before attendant went his rounds. Found him up and humming a tune. He was spreading out his sugar, which he had saved, in the window, and was manifestly beginning his fly catching again, and beginning it cheerfully and with a good grace.

I looked around for his birds, and not seeing them, asked him where they were. He replied, without turning round, that they had all flown away. There were a few feathers about the room and on his pillow a drop of blood. I said nothing, but went and told the keeper to report to me if there were anything odd about him during the day.

11 am.--The attendant has just been to see me to say that Renfield has been very sick and has disgorged a whole lot of feathers. "My belief is, doctor," he said, "that he has eaten his birds, and that he just took and ate them raw!"

11 pm.--I gave Renfield a strong opiate tonight, enough to make even him sleep, and took away his pocketbook to look at it. The thought that has been buzzing about my brain lately is complete, and the theory proved.

My homicidal maniac is of a peculiar kind. I shall have to invent a new classification for him, and call him a zoophagous (life-eating) maniac. What he desires is to absorb as many lives as he can, and he has laid himself out to achieve it in a cumulative way. He gave many flies to one spider and many spiders to one bird, and then wanted a cat to eat the many birds. What would have been his later steps?

It would almost be worth while to complete the experiment. It might be done if there were only a sufficient cause. Men sneered at vivisection, and yet look at its results today! Why not advance science in its most difficult and vital aspect, the knowledge of the brain?

Had I even the secret of one such mind, did I hold the key to the fancy of even one lunatic, I might advance my own branch of science to a pitch compared with which Burdon-Sanderson's physiology or Ferrier's brain knowledge would be as nothing. If only there were a sufficient cause! I must not think too much of this, or I may be tempted. A good cause might turn the scale with me, for may not I too be of an exceptional brain, congenitally?

How well the man reasoned. Lunatics always do within their own scope. I wonder at how many lives he values a man, or if at only one. He has closed the account most accurately, and today begun a new record. How many of us begin a new record with each day of our lives?

To me it seems only yesterday that my whole life ended with my new hope, and that truly I began a new record. So it shall be until the Great Recorder sums me up and closes my ledger account with a balance to profit or loss.

Oh, Lucy, Lucy, I cannot be angry with you, nor can I be angry with my friend whose happiness is yours, but I must only wait on hopeless and work. Work! Work!

If I could have as strong a cause as my poor mad friend there, a good, unselfish cause to make me work, that would be indeed happiness.

MINA MURRAY'S JOURNAL

26 July.--I am anxious, and it soothes me to express myself here. It is like whispering to one's self and listening at the same time. And there is also something about the shorthand symbols that makes it different from writing. I am unhappy about Lucy and about Jonathan. I had not heard from Jonathan for some time, and was very concerned, but yesterday dear Mr. Hawkins, who is always so kind, sent me a letter from him. I had written asking him if he had heard, and he said the enclosed had just been received. It is only a line dated from Castle Dracula, and says that he is just starting for home. That is not like Jonathan. I do not understand it, and it makes me uneasy.

Then, too, Lucy, although she is so well, has lately taken to her old habit of walking in her sleep. Her mother has spoken to me about it, and we have decided that I am to lock the door of our room every night.

Mrs. Westenra has got an idea that sleep-walkers always go out on roofs of houses and along the edges of cliffs and then get suddenly wakened and fall over with a despairing cry that echoes all over the place.

Poor dear, she is naturally anxious about Lucy, and she tells me that her husband, Lucy's father, had the same habit, that he would get up in the night and dress himself and go out, if he were not stopped.

Lucy is to be married in the autumn, and she is already planning out her dresses and how her house is to be arranged. I sympathise with her, for I do the same, only

Jonathan and I will start in life in a very simple way, and shall have to try to make both ends meet.

Mr. Holmwood, he is the Hon. Arthur Holmwood, only son of Lord Godalming, is coming up here very shortly, as soon as he can leave town, for his father is not very well, and I think dear Lucy is counting the moments till he comes.

She wants to take him up in the seat on the churchyard cliff and show him the beauty of Whitby. I daresay it is the waiting which disturbs her. She will be all right when he arrives.

27 July.--No news from Jonathan. I am getting quite uneasy about him, though why I should I do not know, but I do wish that he would write, if it were only a single line.

Lucy walks more than ever, and each night I am awakened by her moving about the room. Fortunately, the weather is so hot that she cannot get cold. But still, the anxiety and the perpetually being awakened is beginning to tell on me, and I am getting nervous and wakeful myself. Thank God, Lucy's health keeps up. Mr. Holmwood has been suddenly called to Ring to see his father, who has been taken seriously ill. Lucy frets at the postponement of seeing him, but it does not touch her looks. She is a trifle stouter, and her cheeks are a lovely rose-pink. She has lost the anemic look which she had. I pray it will all last.

3 August.--Another week gone by, and no news from Jonathan, not even to Mr. Hawkins, from whom I have heard. Oh, I do hope he is not ill. He surely would have written. I look at that last letter of his, but somehow it does not satisfy me. It does not read like him, and yet it is his writing. There is no mistake of that.

Lucy has not walked much in her sleep the last week, but there is an odd concentration about her which I do not understand, even in her sleep she seems to be watching me. She tries the door, and finding it locked, goes about the room searching for the key.

6 August.--Another three days, and no news. This suspense is getting dreadful. If I only knew where to write to or where to go to, I should feel easier. But no one has heard a word of Jonathan since that last letter. I must only pray to God for patience.

Lucy is more excitable than ever, but is otherwise well. Last night was very threatening, and the fishermen say that we are in for a storm. I must try to watch it and learn the weather signs.

Today is a gray day, and the sun as I write is hidden in thick clouds, high over Kettleness. Everything is gray except the green grass, which seems like emerald amongst it, gray earthy rock, gray clouds, tinged with the sunburst at the far edge, hang over the gray sea, into which the sandpoints stretch like gray figures. The sea is tumbling in over the shallows and the sandy flats with a roar, muffled in the sea-mists drifting inland. The horizon is lost in a gray mist. All vastness, the clouds are piled up like giant rocks, and there is a 'brool' over the sea that sounds like some passage of doom. Dark figures are on the beach here and there, sometimes half shrouded in the mist, and seem 'men like trees walking'. The fishing boats are racing for home, and rise and dip in the ground swell as they sweep into the harbour, bending to the scuppers. Here comes old Mr. Swales. He is making straight for me, and I can see, by the way he lifts his hat, that he wants to talk.

I have been quite touched by the change in the poor old man. When he sat down beside me, he said in a very gentle way, "I want to say something to you, miss."

I could see he was not at ease, so I took his poor old wrinkled hand in mine and asked him to speak fully.

So he said, leaving his hand in mine, "I'm afraid, my deary, that I must have shocked you by all the wicked things I've been sayin' about the dead, and such like, for weeks past, but I didn't mean them, and I want ye to remember that when I'm gone. We aud folks that be daffled, and with one foot abaft the krok-hooal, don't altogether like to think of it, and we don't want to feel scart of it, and that's why I've took to makin' light of it, so that I'd cheer up my own heart a bit. But, Lord love ye, miss, I ain't afraid of dyin', not a bit, only I don't want to die if I can help it. My time must be nigh at hand now, for I be aud, and a hundred years is too much for any man to expect. And I'm so nigh it that the Aud Man is already whettin' his scythe. Ye see, I can't get out o' the habit of caffin' about it all at once. The chafts will wag as they be used to. Some day soon the Angel of Death will sound his trumpet for me. But don't ye dooal an' greet, my deary!"--for he saw that I was crying--"if he should come this very night I'd not refuse to answer his call. For life be, after all, only a waitin' for somethin' else than what we're doin', and death be all that we can rightly depend on. But I'm content, for it's comin' to me, my deary, and comin' quick. It may be comin' while we be lookin' and wonderin'. Maybe it's in that wind out over the sea that's bringin' with it loss and wreck, and sore distress, and sad hearts. Look! Look!" he cried suddenly. "There's something in that wind and in the hoast beyont that sounds, and looks, and tastes, and smells like death. It's in the air. I feel it comin'. Lord, make me answer cheerful, when my call comes!" He held up his arms devoutly, and raised his hat. His mouth moved as though he were praying. After a few minutes' silence, he got up, shook hands with me, and blessed me, and said goodbye, and hobbled off. It all touched me, and upset me very much.

I was glad when the coastguard came along, with his spyglass under his arm. He stopped to talk with me, as he always does, but all the time kept looking at a strange ship.

"I can't make her out," he said. "She's a Russian, by the look of her. But she's knocking about in the queerest way. She doesn't know her mind a bit. She seems to see the storm coming, but can't decide whether to run up north in the open, or to put in here. Look there again! She is steered mighty strangely, for she doesn't mind the hand on the wheel, changes about with every puff of wind. We'll hear more of her before this time tomorrow."

CHAPTER 7

CUTTING FROM "THE DAILYGRAPH", 8 AUGUST (PASTED IN MINA MURRAY'S JOURNAL)

From a correspondent.

Whitby.

One of the greatest and suddenest storms on record has just been experienced here, with results both strange and unique. The weather had been somewhat sultry, but not to any degree uncommon in the month of August. Saturday evening was as fine as was ever known, and the great body of holiday-makers laid out yesterday for visits to Mulgrave Woods, Robin Hood's Bay, Rig Mill, Runswick, Staithes, and the various trips in the neighborhood of Whitby. The steamers Emma and Scarborough made trips up and down the coast, and there was an unusual amount of 'tripping' both to and from Whitby. The day was unusually fine till the afternoon, when some of the gossips who frequent the East Cliff churchyard, and from the commanding eminence watch the wide sweep of sea visible to the north and east, called attention to a sudden show of 'mares tails' high in the sky to the northwest. The wind was then blowing from the south-west in the mild degree which in barometrical language is ranked 'No. 2, light breeze.'

The coastguard on duty at once made report, and one old fisherman, who for more than half a century has kept watch on weather signs from the East Cliff, foretold in an emphatic manner the coming of a sudden storm. The approach of sunset was so very beautiful, so grand in its masses of splendidly coloured clouds, that there was quite an assemblage on the walk along the cliff in the old churchyard to enjoy the beauty. Before the sun dipped below the black mass of Kettleness, standing boldly athwart the western sky, its downward way was marked by myriad clouds of every sunset colour, flame, purple, pink, green, violet, and all the tints of gold, with here and there masses not large, but of seemingly absolute blackness, in all sorts of shapes, as well outlined as colossal silhouettes. The experience was not lost on the painters, and doubtless some of the sketches of the 'Prelude to the Great Storm' will grace the R. A and R. I. walls in May next.

More than one captain made up his mind then and there that his 'cobble' or his 'mule', as they term the different classes of boats, would remain in the harbour till the storm had passed. The wind fell away entirely during the evening, and at midnight there was a dead calm, a sultry heat, and that prevailing intensity which, on the approach of thunder, affects persons of a sensitive nature.

There were but few lights in sight at sea, for even the coasting steamers, which usually hug the shore so closely, kept well to seaward, and but few fishing boats were in sight. The only sail noticeable was a foreign schooner with all sails set, which was seemingly going westwards. The foolhardiness or ignorance of her officers was a prolific theme for comment whilst she remained in sight, and efforts were made to signal her to reduce sail in the face of her danger. Before the night shut down she was seen with sails idly flapping as she gently rolled on the undulating swell of the sea.

"As idle as a painted ship upon a painted ocean."

Shortly before ten o'clock the stillness of the air grew quite oppressive, and the silence was so marked that the bleating of a sheep inland or the barking of a dog in the town was distinctly heard, and the band on the pier, with its lively French air, was like a dischord in the great harmony of nature's silence. A little after midnight came a strange sound from over the sea, and high overhead the air began to carry a strange, faint, hollow booming.

Then without warning the tempest broke. With a rapidity which, at the time, seemed incredible, and even afterwards is impossible to realize, the whole aspect of nature at once became convulsed. The waves rose in growing fury, each over-topping its fellow, till in a very few minutes the lately glassy sea was like a roaring and devouring monster. White-crested waves beat madly on the level sands and rushed up the shelving cliffs. Others broke over the piers, and with their spume swept the lanthorns of the lighthouses which rise from the end of either pier of Whitby Harbour.

The wind roared like thunder, and blew with such force that it was with difficulty that even strong men kept their feet, or clung with grim clasp to the iron stanchions. It was found necessary to clear the entire pier from the mass of onlookers, or else the fatalities of the night would have increased manifold. To add to the difficulties and dangers of the time, masses of sea-fog came drifting inland. White, wet clouds, which swept by in ghostly fashion, so dank and damp and cold that it needed but little effort of imagination to think that the spirits of those lost at sea were touching their living brethren with the clammy hands of death, and many a one shuddered as the wreaths of sea-mist swept by.

At times the mist cleared, and the sea for some distance could be seen in the glare of the lightning, which came thick and fast, followed by such peals of thunder that the whole sky overhead seemed trembling under the shock of the footsteps of the storm.

Some of the scenes thus revealed were of immeasurable grandeur and of absorbing interest. The sea, running mountains high, threw skywards with each wave mighty masses of white foam, which the tempest seemed to snatch at and whirl away into space. Here and there a fishing boat, with a rag of sail, running madly for shelter before the blast, now and again the white wings of a storm-tossed seabird. On the summit of the East Cliff the new searchlight was ready for experiment, but had not yet been tried. The officers in charge of it got it into working order, and in the pauses of onrushing mist swept with it the surface of the sea. Once or twice its service was most effective, as when a fishing boat, with gunwale under water, rushed into the harbour, able, by the guidance of the sheltering light, to avoid the danger of dashing against the piers. As each boat achieved the safety of the port there was a shout of joy from the mass of people on the shore, a shout which for a moment seemed to cleave the gale and was then swept away in its rush.

Before long the searchlight discovered some distance away a schooner with all sails set, apparently the same vessel which had been noticed earlier in the evening. The wind had by this time backed to the east, and there was a shudder amongst the watchers on the cliff as they realized the terrible danger in which she now was.

Between her and the port lay the great flat reef on which so many good ships have from time to time suffered, and, with the wind blowing from its present quarter, it would be quite impossible that she should fetch the entrance of the harbour.

It was now nearly the hour of high tide, but the waves were so great that in their troughs the shallows of the shore were almost visible, and the schooner, with all sails set, was rushing with such speed that, in the words of one old salt, "she must fetch up somewhere, if it was only in hell". Then came another rush of sea-fog, greater than any hitherto, a mass of dank mist, which seemed to close on all things like a gray pall, and left available to men only the organ of hearing, for the roar of the tempest, and the crash of the thunder, and the booming of the mighty billows came through the damp oblivion even louder than before. The rays of the searchlight were kept fixed on the harbour mouth across the East Pier, where the shock was expected, and men waited breathless.

The wind suddenly shifted to the northeast, and the remnant of the sea fog melted in the blast. And then, mirabile dictu, between the piers, leaping from wave to wave as it rushed at headlong speed, swept the strange schooner before the blast, with all sail set, and gained the safety of the harbour. The searchlight followed her, and a shudder ran through all who saw her, for lashed to the helm was a corpse, with drooping head, which swung horribly to and fro at each motion of the ship. No other form could be seen on the deck at all.

A great awe came on all as they realised that the ship, as if by a miracle, had found the harbour, unsteered save by the hand of a dead man! However, all took place more quickly than it takes to write these words. The schooner paused not, but rushing across the harbour, pitched herself on that accumulation of sand and gravel washed by many tides and many storms into the southeast corner of the pier jutting under the East Cliff, known locally as Tate Hill Pier.

There was of course a considerable concussion as the vessel drove up on the sand heap. Every spar, rope, and stay was strained, and some of the 'top-hammer' came crashing down. But, strangest of all, the very instant the shore was touched, an immense dog sprang up on deck from below, as if shot up by the concussion, and running forward, jumped from the bow on the sand.

Making straight for the steep cliff, where the churchyard hangs over the laneway to the East Pier so steeply that some of the flat tombstones, thruffsteans or throughstones, as they call them in Whitby vernacular, actually project over where the sustaining cliff has fallen away, it disappeared in the darkness, which seemed intensified just beyond the focus of the searchlight.

It so happened that there was no one at the moment on Tate Hill Pier, as all those whose houses are in close proximity were either in bed or were out on the heights above. Thus the coastguard on duty on the eastern side of the harbour, who at once ran down to the little pier, was the first to climb aboard. The men working the searchlight, after scouring the entrance of the harbour without seeing anything, then turned the light on the derelict and kept it there. The coastguard ran aft, and when he came beside the wheel, bent over to examine it, and recoiled at once as though under some sudden emotion. This seemed to pique general curiosity, and quite a number of people began to run.

It is a good way round from the West Cliff by the Draw-bridge to Tate Hill Pier, but your correspondent is a fairly good runner, and came well ahead of the crowd. When I arrived, however, I found already assembled on the pier a crowd, whom the coastguard and police refused to allow to come on board. By the courtesy of the chief boatman, I was, as your correspondent, permitted to climb on deck, and was one of a small group who saw the dead seaman whilst actually lashed to the wheel.

It was no wonder that the coastguard was surprised, or even awed, for not often can such a sight have been seen. The man was simply fastened by his hands, tied one over the other, to a spoke of the wheel. Between the inner hand and the wood was a crucifix, the set of beads on which it was fastened being around both wrists and wheel, and all kept fast by the binding cords. The poor fellow may have been seated at one time, but the flapping and buffeting of the sails had worked through the rudder of the wheel and had dragged him to and fro, so that the cords with which he was tied had cut the flesh to the bone.

Accurate note was made of the state of things, and a doctor, Surgeon J. M. Caffyn, of 33, East Elliot Place, who came immediately after me, declared, after making examination, that the man must have been dead for quite two days.

In his pocket was a bottle, carefully corked, empty save for a little roll of paper, which proved to be the addendum to the log.

The coastguard said the man must have tied up his own hands, fastening the knots with his teeth. The fact that a coastguard was the first on board may save some complications later on, in the Admiralty Court, for coastguards cannot claim the salvage which is the right of the first civilian entering on a derelict. Already, however, the legal tongues are wagging, and one young law student is loudly asserting that the rights of the owner are already completely sacrificed, his property being held in contravention of the statues of mortmain, since the tiller, as emblemship, if not proof, of delegated possession, is held in a dead hand.

It is needless to say that the dead steersman has been reverently removed from the place where he held his honourable watch and ward till death, a steadfastness as noble as that of the young Casabianca, and placed in the mortuary to await inquest.

Already the sudden storm is passing, and its fierceness is abating. Crowds are scattering backward, and the sky is beginning to redden over the Yorkshire wolds.

I shall send, in time for your next issue, further details of the derelict ship which found her way so miraculously into harbour in the storm.

9 August.--The sequel to the strange arrival of the derelict in the storm last night is almost more startling than the thing itself. It turns out that the schooner is Russian from Varna, and is called the Demeter. She is almost entirely in ballast of silver sand, with only a small amount of cargo, a number of great wooden boxes filled with mould.

This cargo was consigned to a Whitby solicitor, Mr. S.F. Billington, of 7, The Crescent, who this morning went aboard and took formal possession of the goods consigned to him.

The Russian consul, too, acting for the charter-party, took formal possession of the ship, and paid all harbour dues, etc.

Nothing is talked about here today except the strange coincidence. The officials of the Board of Trade have been most exacting in seeing that every compliance has been made with existing regulations. As the matter is to be a 'nine days wonder', they are evidently determined that there shall be no cause of other complaint.

A good deal of interest was abroad concerning the dog which landed when the ship struck, and more than a few of the members of the S.P.C.A., which is very strong in Whitby, have tried to befriend the animal. To the general disappointment, however, it was not to be found. It seems to have disappeared entirely from the town. It may be that it was frightened and made its way on to the moors, where it is still hiding in terror.

There are some who look with dread on such a possibility, lest later on it should in itself become a danger, for it is evidently a fierce brute. Early this morning a large dog, a half-bred mastiff belonging to a coal merchant close to Tate Hill Pier, was found dead in the roadway opposite its master's yard. It had been fighting, and manifestly had had a savage opponent, for its throat was torn away, and its belly was slit open as if with a savage claw.

Later.--By the kindness of the Board of Trade inspector, I have been permitted to look over the log book of the Demeter, which was in order up to within three days, but contained nothing of special interest except as to facts of missing men. The greatest interest, however, is with regard to the paper found in the bottle, which was today produced at the inquest. And a more strange narrative than the two between them unfold it has not been my lot to come across.

As there is no motive for concealment, I am permitted to use them, and accordingly send you a transcript, simply omitting technical details of seamanship and supercargo. It almost seems as though the captain had been seized with some kind of mania before he had got well into blue water, and that this had developed persistently throughout the voyage. Of course my statement must be taken cum grano, since I am writing from the dictation of a clerk of the Russian consul, who kindly translated for me, time being short.

LOG OF THE "DEMETER" Varna to Whitby

Written 18 July, things so strange happening, that I shall keep accurate note henceforth till we land.

On 6 July we finished taking in cargo, silver sand and boxes of earth. At noon set sail. East wind, fresh. Crew, fivehands… two mates, cook, and myself, (captain).

On 11 July at dawn entered Bosphorus. Boarded by Turkish Customs officers. Backsheesh. All correct. Under way at 4 p.m.

On 12 July through Dardanelles. More Customs officers and flagboat of guarding squadron. Backsheesh again. Work of officers thorough, but quick. Want us off soon. At dark passed into Archipelago.

On 13 July passed Cape Matapan. Crew dissatisfied about something. Seemed scared, but would not speak out.

On 14 July was somewhat anxious about crew. Men all steady fellows, who sailed with me before. Mate could not make out what was wrong. They only told him there was SOMETHING, and crossed themselves. Mate lost temper with one of them that day and struck him. Expected fierce quarrel, but all was quiet.

On 16 July mate reported in the morning that one of the crew, Petrofsky, was missing. Could not account for it. Took larboard watch eight bells last night, was relieved by Amramoff, but did not go to bunk. Men more downcast than ever. All said they expected something of the kind, but would not say more than there was SOMETHING aboard. Mate getting very impatient with them. Feared some trouble ahead.

On 17 July, yesterday, one of the men, Olgaren, came to my cabin, and in an awestruck way confided to me that he thought there was a strange man aboard the ship. He said that in his watch he had been sheltering behind the deckhouse, as there was a rain storm, when he saw a tall, thin man, who was not like any of the crew, come up the companionway, and go along the deck forward and disappear. He followed cautiously, but when he got to bows found no one, and the hatchways were all closed. He was in a panic of superstitious fear, and I am afraid the panic may spread. To allay it, I shall today search the entire ship carefully from stem to stern.

Later in the day I got together the whole crew, and told them, as they evidently thought there was some one in the ship, we would search from stem to stern. First mate angry, said it was folly, and to yield to such foolish ideas would demoralise the men, said he would engage to keep them out of trouble with the handspike. I let him take the helm, while the rest began a thorough search, all keeping abreast, with lanterns. We left no corner unsearched. As there were only the big wooden boxes, there were no odd corners where a man could hide. Men much relieved when search over, and went back to work cheerfully. First mate scowled, but said nothing.

22 July.--Rough weather last three days, and all hands busy with sails, no time to be frightened. Men seem to have forgotten their dread. Mate cheerful again, and all on good terms. Praised men for work in bad weather. Passed Gibraltar and out through Straits. All well.

24 July.--There seems some doom over this ship. Already a hand short, and entering the Bay of Biscay with wild weather ahead, and yet last night another man lost, disappeared. Like the first, he came off his watch and was not seen again. Men all in a panic of fear, sent a round robin, asking to have double watch, as they fear to be alone. Mate angry. Fear there will be some trouble, as either he or the men will do some violence.

28 July.--Four days in hell, knocking about in a sort of maelstrom, and the wind a tempest. No sleep for any one. Men all worn out. Hardly know how to set a watch, since no one fit to go on. Second mate volunteered to steer and watch, and let men snatch a few hours sleep. Wind abating, seas still terrific, but feel them less, as ship is steadier.

CHAPTER 7

29 July.--Another tragedy. Had single watch tonight, as crew too tired to double. When morning watch came on deck could find no one except steersman. Raised outcry, and all came on deck. Thorough search, but no one found. Are now without second mate, and crew in a panic. Mate and I agreed to go armed henceforth and wait for any sign of cause.

30 July.--Last night. Rejoiced we are nearing England. Weather fine, all sails set. Retired worn out, slept soundly, awakened by mate telling me that both man of watch and steersman missing. Only self and mate and two hands left to work ship.

1 August.--Two days of fog, and not a sail sighted. Had hoped when in the English Channel to be able to signal for help or get in somewhere. Not having power to work sails, have to run before wind. Dare not lower, as could not raise them again. We seem to be drifting to some terrible doom. Mate now more demoralised than either of men. His stronger nature seems to have worked inwardly against himself. Men are beyond fear, working stolidly and patiently, with minds made up to worst. They are Russian, he Roumanian.

2 August, midnight.--Woke up from few minutes sleep by hearing a cry, seemingly outside my port. Could see nothing in fog. Rushed on deck, and ran against mate. Tells me he heard cry and ran, but no sign of man on watch. One more gone. Lord, help us! Mate says we must be past Straits of Dover, as in a moment of fog lifting he saw North Foreland, just as he heard the man cry out. If so we are now off in the North Sea, and only God can guide us in the fog, which seems to move with us, and God seems to have deserted us.

3 August.--At midnight I went to relieve the man at the wheel and when I got to it found no one there. The wind was steady, and as we ran before it there was no yawing. I dared not leave it, so shouted for the mate. After a few seconds, he rushed up on deck in his flannels. He looked wild-eyed and haggard, and I greatly fear his reason has given way. He came close to me and whispered hoarsely, with his mouth to my ear, as though fearing the very air might hear. "It is here. I know it now. On the watch last night I saw It, like a man, tall and thin, and ghastly pale. It was in the bows, and looking out. I crept behind It, and gave it my knife, but the knife went through It, empty as the air." And as he spoke he took the knife and drove it savagely into space. Then he went on, "But It is here, and I'll find It. It is in the hold, perhaps in one of those boxes. I'll unscrew them one by one and see. You work the helm." And with a warning look and his finger on his lip, he went below. There was springing up a choppy wind, and I could not leave the helm. I saw him come out on deck again with a tool chest and lantern, and go down the forward hatchway. He is mad, stark, raving mad, and it's no use my trying to stop him. He can't hurt those big boxes, they are invoiced as clay, and to pull them about is as harmless a thing as he can do. So here I stay and mind the helm, and write these notes. I can only trust in God and wait till the fog clears. Then, if I can't steer to any har-

bour with the wind that is, I shall cut down sails, and lie by, and signal for help...

It is nearly all over now. Just as I was beginning to hope that the mate would come out calmer, for I heard him knocking away at something in the hold, and work is good for him, there came up the hatchway a sudden, startled scream, which made my blood run cold, and up on the deck he came as if shot from a gun, a raging madman, with his eyes rolling and his face convulsed with fear. "Save me! Save me!" he cried, and then looked round on the blanket of fog. His horror turned to despair, and in a steady voice he said, "You had better come too, captain, before it is too late. He is there! I know the secret now. The sea will save me from Him, and it is all that is left!" Before I could say a word, or move forward to seize him, he sprang on the bulwark and deliberately threw himself into the sea. I suppose I know the secret too, now. It was this madman who had got rid of the men one by one, and now he has followed them himself. God help me! How am I to account for all these horrors when I get to port? When I get to port! Will that ever be?

4 August.--Still fog, which the sunrise cannot pierce, I know there is sunrise because I am a sailor, why else I know not. I dared not go below, I dared not leave the helm, so here all night I stayed, and in the dimness of the night I saw it, Him! God, forgive me, but the mate was right to jump overboard. It was better to die like a man. To die like a sailor in blue water, no man can object. But I am captain, and I must not leave my ship. But I shall baffle this fiend or monster, for I shall tie my hands to the wheel when my strength begins to fail, and along with them I shall tie that which He, It, dare not touch. And then, come good wind or foul, I shall save my soul, and my honour as a captain. I am growing weaker, and the night is coming on. If He can look me in the face again, I may not have time to act. . . If we are wrecked, mayhap this bottle may be found, and those who find it may understand. If not... well, then all men shall know that I have been true to my trust. God and the Blessed Virgin and the Saints help a poor ignorant soul trying to do his duty...

Of course the verdict was an open one. There is no evidence to adduce, and whether or not the man himself committed the murders there is now none to say. The folk here hold almost universally that the captain is simply a hero, and he is to be given a public funeral. Already it is arranged that his body is to be taken with a train of boats up the Esk for a piece and then brought back to Tate Hill Pier and up the abbey steps, for he is to be buried in the churchyard on the cliff. The owners of more than a hundred boats have already given in their names as wishing to follow him to the grave.

No trace has ever been found of the great dog, at which there is much mourning, for, with public opinion in its present state, he would, I believe, be adopted by the town. Tomorrow will see the funeral, and so will end this one more 'mystery of the sea'.

CHAPTER 7

MINA MURRAY'S JOURNAL

8 August.--Lucy was very restless all night, and I too, could not sleep. The storm was fearful, and as it boomed loudly among the chimney pots, it made me shudder. When a sharp puff came it seemed to be like a distant gun. Strangely enough, Lucy did not wake, but she got up twice and dressed herself. Fortunately, each time I awoke in time and managed to undress her without waking her, and got her back to bed. It is a very strange thing, this sleep-walking, for as soon as her will is thwarted in any physical way, her intention, if there be any, disappears, and she yields herself almost exactly to the routine of her life.

Early in the morning we both got up and went down to the harbour to see if anything had happened in the night. There were very few people about, and though the sun was bright, and the air clear and fresh, the big, grim-looking waves, that seemed dark themselves because the foam that topped them was like snow, forced themselves in through the mouth of the harbour, like a bullying man going through a crowd. Somehow I felt glad that Jonathan was not on the sea last night, but on land. But, oh, is he on land or sea? Where is he, and how? I am getting fearfully anxious about him. If I only knew what to do, and could do anything!

10 August.--The funeral of the poor sea captain today was most touching. Every boat in the harbour seemed to be there, and the coffin was carried by captains all the way from Tate Hill Pier up to the churchyard. Lucy came with me, and we went early to our old seat, whilst the cortege of boats went up the river to the Viaduct and came down again. We had a lovely view, and saw the procession nearly all the way. The poor fellow was laid to rest near our seat so that we stood on it, when the time came and saw everything.

Poor Lucy seemed much upset. She was restless and uneasy all the time, and I cannot but think that her dreaming at night is telling on her. She is quite odd in one thing. She will not admit to me that there is any cause for restlessness, or if there be, she does not understand it herself.

There is an additional cause in that poor Mr. Swales was found dead this morning on our seat, his neck being broken. He had evidently, as the doctor said, fallen back in the seat in some sort of fright, for there was a look of fear and horror on his face that the men said made them shudder. Poor dear old man!

Lucy is so sweet and sensitive that she feels influences more acutely than other people do. Just now she was quite upset by a little thing which I did not much heed, though I am myself very fond of animals.

One of the men who came up here often to look for the boats was followed by his dog. The dog is always with him. They are both quiet persons, and I never saw the man angry, nor heard the dog bark. During the service the dog would not come to its master, who was on the seat with us, but kept a few yards off, barking and howling. Its master spoke to it gently, and then harshly, and then angrily. But it would neither come nor cease to make a noise. It was in a fury, with its eyes savage, and all its hair bristling out like a cat's tail when puss is on the war path.

Finally the man too got angry, and jumped down and kicked the dog, and then took it by the scruff of the neck and half dragged and half threw it on the tombstone on which the seat is fixed. The moment it touched the stone the poor thing began to tremble. It did not try to get away, but crouched down, quivering and cowering, and was in such a pitiable state of terror that I tried, though without effect, to comfort it.

Lucy was full of pity, too, but she did not attempt to touch the dog, but looked at it in an agonised sort of way. I greatly fear that she is of too super-sensitive a nature to go through the world without trouble. She will be dreaming of this tonight, I am sure. The whole agglomeration of things, the ship steered into port by a dead man, his attitude, tied to the wheel with a crucifix and beads, the touching funeral, the dog, now furious and now in terror, will all afford material for her dreams.

I think it will be best for her to go to bed tired out physically, so I shall take her for a long walk by the cliffs to Robin Hood's Bay and back. She ought not to have much inclination for sleep-walking then.

CHAPTER 8

MINA MURRAY'S JOURNAL

Same day, 11 o'clock P.M.--Oh, but I am tired! If it were not that I had made my diary a duty I should not open it tonight. We had a lovely walk. Lucy, after a while, was in gay spirits, owing, I think, to some dear cows who came nosing towards us in a field close to the lighthouse, and frightened the wits out of us. I believe we forgot everything, except of course, personal fear, and it seemed to wipe the slate clean and give us a fresh start. We had a capital 'severe tea' at Robin Hood's Bay in a sweet little old-fashioned inn, with a bow window right over the seaweed-covered rocks of the strand. I believe we should have shocked the 'New Woman' with our appetites. Men are more tolerant, bless them! Then we walked home with some, or rather many, stoppages to rest, and with our hearts full of a constant dread of wild bulls.

Lucy was really tired, and we intended to creep off to bed as soon as we could. The young curate came in, however, and Mrs. Westenra asked him to stay for supper. Lucy and I had both a fight for it with the dusty miller. I know it was a hard fight on my part, and I am quite heroic. I think that some day the bishops must get together and see about breeding up a new class of curates, who don't take supper, no matter how hard they may be pressed to, and who will know when girls are tired.

Lucy is asleep and breathing softly. She has more colour in her cheeks than usual, and looks, oh so sweet. If Mr. Holmwood fell in love with her seeing her only in the drawing room, I wonder what he would say if he saw her now. Some of the 'New Women' writers will some day start an idea that men and women should be allowed to see each other asleep before proposing or accepting. But I suppose the 'New Woman' won't condescend in future to accept. She will do the proposing herself. And a nice job she will make of it too! There's some consolation in that. I am so happy tonight, because dear Lucy seems better. I really believe she has turned the corner, and that we are over her troubles with dreaming. I should be quite happy if I only knew if Jonathan... God bless and keep him.

11 August.--Diary again. No sleep now, so I may as well write. I am too agitated to sleep. We have had such an adventure, such an agonizing experience. I fell asleep as soon as I had closed my diary. . . . Suddenly I became broad awake, and sat up, with a horrible sense of fear upon me, and of some feeling of emptiness around me. The room was dark, so I could not see Lucy's bed. I stole across and felt for her. The bed was empty. I lit a match and found that she was not in the room. The door was

shut, but not locked, as I had left it. I feared to wake her mother, who has been more than usually ill lately, so threw on some clothes and got ready to look for her. As I was leaving the room it struck me that the clothes she wore might give me some clue to her dreaming intention. Dressing-gown would mean house, dress outside. Dressing-gown and dress were both in their places. "Thank God," I said to myself, "she cannot be far, as she is only in her nightdress."

I ran downstairs and looked in the sitting room. Not there! Then I looked in all the other rooms of the house, with an ever-growing fear chilling my heart. Finally, I came to the hall door and found it open. It was not wide open, but the catch of the lock had not caught. The people of the house are careful to lock the door every night, so I feared that Lucy must have gone out as she was. There was no time to think of what might happen. A vague over-mastering fear obscured all details.

I took a big, heavy shawl and ran out. The clock was striking one as I was in the Crescent, and there was not a soul in sight. I ran along the North Terrace, but could see no sign of the white figure which I expected. At the edge of the West Cliff above the pier I looked across the harbour to the East Cliff, in the hope or fear, I don't know which, of seeing Lucy in our favourite seat.

There was a bright full moon, with heavy black, driving clouds, which threw the whole scene into a fleeting diorama of light and shade as they sailed across. For a moment or two I could see nothing, as the shadow of a cloud obscured St. Mary's Church and all around it. Then as the cloud passed I could see the ruins of the abbey coming into view, and as the edge of a narrow band of light as sharp as a sword-cut moved along, the church and churchyard became gradually visible. Whatever my expectation was, it was not disappointed, for there, on our favourite seat, the silver light of the moon struck a half-reclining figure, snowy white. The coming of the cloud was too quick for me to see much, for shadow shut down on light almost immediately, but it seemed to me as though something dark stood behind the seat where the white figure shone, and bent over it. What it was, whether man or beast, I could not tell.

I did not wait to catch another glance, but flew down the steep steps to the pier and along by the fish-market to the bridge, which was the only way to reach the East Cliff. The town seemed as dead, for not a soul did I see. I rejoiced that it was so, for I wanted no witness of poor Lucy's condition. The time and distance seemed endless, and my knees trembled and my breath came laboured as I toiled up the endless steps to the abbey. I must have gone fast, and yet it seemed to me as if my feet were weighted with lead, and as though every joint in my body were rusty.

When I got almost to the top I could see the seat and the white figure, for I was now close enough to distinguish it even through the spells of shadow. There was undoubtedly something, long and black, bending over the half-reclining white figure. I called in fright, "Lucy! Lucy!" and something raised a head, and from where I was I could see a white face and red, gleaming eyes.

Lucy did not answer, and I ran on to the entrance of the churchyard. As I entered, the church was between me and the seat, and for a minute or so I lost sight of her. When I came in view again the cloud had passed, and the moonlight struck so brilliantly that I could see Lucy half reclining with her head lying over the back of the seat. She was quite alone, and there was not a sign of any living thing about.

When I bent over her I could see that she was still asleep. Her lips were parted, and she was breathing, not softly as usual with her, but in long, heavy gasps, as though striving to get her lungs full at every breath. As I came close, she put up her hand in her sleep and pulled the collar of her nightdress close around her, as though she felt the cold. I flung the warm shawl over her, and drew the edges tight around her neck, for I dreaded lest she should get some deadly chill from the night air, unclad as she was. I feared to wake her all at once, so, in order to have my hands free to help her, I fastened the shawl at her throat with a big safety pin. But I must have been clumsy in my anxiety and pinched or pricked her with it, for by-and-by, when her breathing became quieter, she put her hand to her throat again and moaned. When I had her carefully wrapped up I put my shoes on her feet, and then began very gently to wake her.

At first she did not respond, but gradually she became more and more uneasy in her sleep, moaning and sighing occasionally. At last, as time was passing fast, and for many other reasons, I wished to get her home at once, I shook her forcibly, till finally she opened her eyes and awoke. She did not seem surprised to see me, as, of course, she did not realize all at once where she was.

Lucy always wakes prettily, and even at such a time, when her body must have been chilled with cold, and her mind somewhat appalled at waking unclad in a churchyard at night, she did not lose her grace. She trembled a little, and clung to me. When I told her to come at once with me home, she rose without a word, with the obedience of a child. As we passed along, the gravel hurt my feet, and Lucy noticed me wince. She stopped and wanted to insist upon my taking my shoes, but I would not. However, when we got to the pathway outside the churchyard, where there was a puddle of water, remaining from the storm, I daubed my feet with mud, using each foot in turn on the other, so that as we went home, no one, in case we should meet any one, should notice my bare feet.

Fortune favoured us, and we got home without meeting a soul. Once we saw a man, who seemed not quite sober, passing along a street in front of us. But we hid in a door till he had disappeared up an opening such as there are here, steep little closes, or 'wynds', as they call them in Scotland. My heart beat so loud all the time sometimes I thought I should faint. I was filled with anxiety about Lucy, not only for her health, lest she should suffer from the exposure, but for her reputation in case the story should get wind. When we got in, and had washed our feet, and had said a prayer of thankfulness together, I tucked her into bed. Before falling asleep she asked, even implored, me not to say a word to any one, even her mother, about her sleep-walking adventure.

I hesitated at first, to promise, but on thinking of the state of her mother's health, and how the knowledge of such a thing would fret her, and think too, of how such a story might become distorted, nay, infallibly would, in case it should leak out, I thought it wiser to do so. I hope I did right. I have locked the door, and the key is tied to my wrist, so perhaps I shall not be again disturbed. Lucy is sleeping soundly. The reflex of the dawn is high and far over the sea…

Same day, noon.--All goes well. Lucy slept till I woke her and seemed not to have even changed her side. The adventure of the night does not seem to have harmed her, on the contrary, it has benefited her, for she looks better this morning than she has done for weeks. I was sorry to notice that my clumsiness with the safety-pin hurt her. Indeed, it might have been serious, for the skin of her throat was pierced. I must have pinched up a piece of loose skin and have transfixed it, for there are two little red points like pin-pricks, and on the band of her nightdress was a drop of blood. When I apologised and was concerned about it, she laughed and petted me, and said she did not even feel it. Fortunately it cannot leave a scar, as it is so tiny.

Same day, night.--We passed a happy day. The air was clear, and the sun bright, and there was a cool breeze. We took our lunch to Mulgrave Woods, Mrs. Westenra driving by the road and Lucy and I walking by the cliff-path and joining her at the gate. I felt a little sad myself, for I could not but feel how absolutely happy it would have been had Jonathan been with me. But there! I must only be patient. In the evening we strolled in the Casino Terrace, and heard some good music by Spohr and Mackenzie, and went to bed early. Lucy seems more restful than she has been for some time, and fell asleep at once. I shall lock the door and secure the key the same as before, though I do not expect any trouble tonight.

12 August.--My expectations were wrong, for twice during the night I was wakened by Lucy trying to get out. She seemed, even in her sleep, to be a little impatient at finding the door shut, and went back to bed under a sort of protest. I woke with the dawn, and heard the birds chirping outside of the window. Lucy woke, too, and I was glad to see, was even better than on the previous morning. All her old gaiety of manner seemed to have come back, and she came and snuggled in beside me and told me all about Arthur. I told her how anxious I was about Jonathan, and then she tried to comfort me. Well, she succeeded somewhat, for, though sympathy can't alter facts, it can make them more bearable.

13 August.--Another quiet day, and to bed with the key on my wrist as before. Again I awoke in the night, and found Lucy sitting up in bed, still asleep, pointing to the window. I got up quietly, and pulling aside the blind, looked out. It was brilliant moonlight, and the soft effect of the light over the sea and sky, merged together in one great silent mystery, was beautiful beyond words. Between me and the moonlight flitted a great bat, coming and going in great whirling circles. Once or twice it came quite close, but was, I suppose, frightened at seeing me, and flitted away across the harbour towards the abbey. When I came back from the window Lucy had lain down again, and was sleeping peacefully. She did not stir again all night.

14 August.--On the East Cliff, reading and writing all day. Lucy seems to have become as much in love with the spot as I am, and it is hard to get her away from it when it is time to come home for lunch or tea or dinner. This afternoon she made a funny remark. We were coming home for dinner, and had come to the top of the steps up from the West Pier and stopped to look at the view, as we generally do. The setting sun, low down in the sky, was just dropping behind Kettleness. The red light was thrown over on the East Cliff and the old abbey, and seemed to bathe everything in a beautiful rosy glow. We were silent for a while, and suddenly Lucy murmured as if to herself...

"His red eyes again! They are just the same." It was such an odd expression, coming apropos of nothing, that it quite startled me. I slewed round a little, so as to see Lucy well without seeming to stare at her, and saw that she was in a half dreamy state, with an odd look on her face that I could not quite make out, so I said nothing, but followed her eyes. She appeared to be looking over at our own seat, whereon was a dark figure seated alone. I was quite a little startled myself, for it seemed for an instant as if the stranger had great eyes like burning flames, but a second look dispelled the illusion. The red sunlight was shining on the windows of St. Mary's Church behind our seat, and as the sun dipped there was just sufficient change in the refraction and reflection to make it appear as if the light moved. I called Lucy's attention to the peculiar effect, and she became herself with a start, but she looked sad all the same. It may have been that she was thinking of that terrible night up there. We never refer to it, so I said nothing, and we went home to dinner. Lucy had a headache and went early to bed. I saw her asleep, and went out for a little stroll myself.

I walked along the cliffs to the westward, and was full of sweet sadness, for I was thinking of Jonathan. When coming home, it was then bright moonlight, so bright that, though the front of our part of the Crescent was in shadow, everything could be well seen, I threw a glance up at our window, and saw Lucy's head leaning out. I opened my handkerchief and waved it. She did not notice or make any movement whatever. Just then, the moonlight crept round an angle of the building, and the light fell on the window. There distinctly was Lucy with her head lying up against the side of the window sill and her eyes shut. She was fast asleep, and by her, seated on the window sill, was something that looked like a good-sized bird. I was afraid she might get a chill, so I ran upstairs, but as I came into the room she was moving back to her bed, fast asleep, and breathing heavily. She was holding her hand to her throat, as though to protect it from the cold.

I did not wake her, but tucked her up warmly. I have taken care that the door is locked and the window securely fastened.

She looks so sweet as she sleeps, but she is paler than is her wont, and there is a drawn, haggard look under her eyes which I do not like. I fear she is fretting about something. I wish I could find out what it is.

15 August.--Rose later than usual. Lucy was languid and tired, and slept on after we had been called. We had a happy surprise at breakfast. Arthur's father is better, and wants the marriage to come off soon. Lucy is full of quiet joy, and her mother is glad and sorry at once. Later on in the day she told me the cause. She is grieved to lose Lucy as her very own, but she is rejoiced that she is soon to have some one to protect her. Poor dear, sweet lady! She confided to me that she has got her death warrant. She has not told Lucy, and made me promise secrecy. Her doctor told her that within a few months, at most, she must die, for her heart is weakening. At any time, even now, a sudden shock would be almost sure to kill her. Ah, we were wise to keep from her the affair of the dreadful night of Lucy's sleep-walking.

17 August.--No diary for two whole days. I have not had the heart to write. Some sort of shadowy pall seems to be coming over our happiness. No news from Jonathan, and Lucy seems to be growing weaker, whilst her mother's hours are numbering to a close. I do not understand Lucy's fading away as she is doing. She eats well and sleeps well, and enjoys the fresh air, but all the time the roses in her cheeks are fading, and she gets weaker and more languid day by day. At night I hear her gasping as if for air.

I keep the key of our door always fastened to my wrist at night, but she gets up and walks about the room, and sits at the open window. Last night I found her leaning out when I woke up, and when I tried to wake her I could not.

She was in a faint. When I managed to restore her, she was weak as water, and cried silently between long, painful struggles for breath. When I asked her how she came to be at the window she shook her head and turned away.

I trust her feeling ill may not be from that unlucky prick of the safety-pin. I looked at her throat just now as she lay asleep, and the tiny wounds seem not to have healed. They are still open, and, if anything, larger than before, and the edges of them are faintly white. They are like little white dots with red centres. Unless they heal within a day or two, I shall insist on the doctor seeing about them.

LETTER, SAMUEL F. BILLINGTON & SON, SOLICITORS WHITBY, TO MESSRS. CARTER, PATERSON & CO., LONDON.

17 August

"Dear Sirs,--Herewith please receive invoice of goods sent by Great Northern Railway. Same are to be delivered at Carfax, near Purfleet, immediately on receipt at goods station King's Cross. The house is at present empty, but enclosed please find keys, all of which are labelled.

"You will please deposit the boxes, fifty in number, which form the consignment, in the partially ruined building forming part of the house and marked 'A' on rough diagrams enclosed. Your agent will easily recognize the locality, as it is the ancient chapel of the mansion. The goods leave by the train at 9:30 tonight, and will be due at King's Cross at 4:30 tomorrow afternoon. As our client wishes the delivery made as soon as possible, we shall be obliged by your having teams ready at King's Cross at the time named and forthwith conveying the goods to destination. In order to obviate any delays possible through any routine requirements as to payment in your departments, we enclose cheque herewith for ten pounds, receipt of which please acknowledge. Should the charge be less than this amount, you can return balance, if greater, we shall at once send cheque for difference on hearing from you. You are to leave the keys on coming away in the main hall of the house, where the proprietor may get them on his entering the house by means of his duplicate key.

"Pray do not take us as exceeding the bounds of business courtesy in pressing you in all ways to use the utmost expedition.

"We are, dear Sirs, Faithfully yours, SAMUEL F. BILLINGTON & SON"

LETTER, MESSRS. CARTER, PATERSON & CO., LONDON, TO MESSRS. BILLINGTON & SON, WHITBY.

21 August.

"Dear Sirs,--We beg to acknowledge 10 pounds received and to return cheque of 1 pound, 17s, 9d, amount of overplus, as shown in receipted account herewith. Goods are delivered in exact accordance with instructions, and keys left in parcel in main hall, as directed.

"We are, dear Sirs, Yours respectfully, Pro CARTER, PATERSON & CO."

MINA MURRAY'S JOURNAL.

18 August.--I am happy today, and write sitting on the seat in the churchyard. Lucy is ever so much better. Last night she slept well all night, and did not disturb me once.

CHAPTER 8

The roses seem coming back already to her cheeks, though she is still sadly pale and wan-looking. If she were in any way anemic I could understand it, but she is not. She is in gay spirits and full of life and cheerfulness. All the morbid reticence seems to have passed from her, and she has just reminded me, as if I needed any reminding, of that night, and that it was here, on this very seat, I found her asleep.

As she told me she tapped playfully with the heel of her boot on the stone slab and said,

"My poor little feet didn't make much noise then! I daresay poor old Mr. Swales would have told me that it was because I didn't want to wake up Geordie."

As she was in such a communicative humour, I asked her if she had dreamed at all that night.

Before she answered, that sweet, puckered look came into her forehead, which Arthur, I call him Arthur from her habit, says he loves, and indeed, I don't wonder that he does. Then she went on in a half-dreaming kind of way, as if trying to recall it to herself.

"I didn't quite dream, but it all seemed to be real. I only wanted to be here in this spot. I don't know why, for I was afraid of something, I don't know what. I remember, though I suppose I was asleep, passing through the streets and over the bridge. A fish leaped as I went by, and I leaned over to look at it, and I heard a lot of dogs howling. The whole town seemed as if it must be full of dogs all howling at once, as I went up the steps. Then I had a vague memory of something long and dark with red eyes, just as we saw in the sunset, and something very sweet and very bitter all around me at once. And then I seemed sinking into deep green water, and there was a singing in my ears, as I have heard there is to drowning men, and then everything seemed passing away from me. My soul seemed to go out from my body and float about the air. I seem to remember that once the West Lighthouse was right under me, and then there was a sort of agonizing feeling, as if I were in an earthquake, and I came back and found you shaking my body. I saw you do it before I felt you."

Then she began to laugh. It seemed a little uncanny to me, and I listened to her breathlessly. I did not quite like it, and thought it better not to keep her mind on the subject, so we drifted on to another subject, and Lucy was like her old self again. When we got home the fresh breeze had braced her up, and her pale cheeks were really more rosy. Her mother rejoiced when she saw her, and we all spent a very happy evening together.

19 August.--Joy, joy, joy! Although not all joy. At last, news of Jonathan. The dear fellow has been ill, that is why he did not write. I am not afraid to think it or to say it, now that I know. Mr. Hawkins sent me on the letter, and wrote himself, oh so kindly. I am to leave in the morning and go over to Jonathan, and to help to nurse him if necessary, and to bring him home. Mr. Hawkins says it would not be a bad thing if we were to be married out there. I have cried over the good Sister's letter till I can feel it wet against my bosom, where it lies. It is of Jonathan, and must be near my heart, for he is in my heart. My journey is all mapped out, and my luggage ready. I am only taking one change of dress. Lucy will bring my trunk to London and keep it till I send for it, for it may be that… I must write no more. I must keep it to say to Jonathan, my husband. The letter that he has seen and touched must comfort me till we meet.

LETTER, SISTER AGATHA, HOSPITAL OF ST. JOSEPH AND STE. MARY BUDA-PESTH, TO MISS WILLHELMINA MURRAY

12 August,

"Dear Madam.

"I write by desire of Mr. Jonathan Harker, who is himself not strong enough to write, though progressing well, thanks to God and St. Joseph and Ste. Mary. He has been under our care for nearly six weeks, suffering from a violent brain fever. He wishes me to convey his love, and to say that by this post I write for him to Mr. Peter Hawkins, Exeter, to say, with his dutiful respects, that he is sorry for his delay, and that all of his work is completed. He will require some few weeks' rest in our sanatorium in the hills, but will then return. He wishes me to say that he has not sufficient money with him, and that he would like to pay for his staying here, so that others who need shall not be wanting for help.

"Believe me,

"Yours, with sympathy and all blessings. Sister Agatha

"P.S.--My patient being asleep, I open this to let you know something more. He has told me all about you, and that you are shortly to be his wife. All blessings to you both! He has had some fearful shock, so says our doctor, and in his delirium his ravings have been dreadful, of wolves and poison and blood, of ghosts and demons, and I fear to say of what. Be careful of him always that there may be nothing to excite him of this kind for a long time to come. The traces of such an illness as his do not lightly die away. We should have written long ago, but we knew nothing of his friends, and there was nothing on him, nothing that anyone could understand. He came in the train from Klausenburg, and the guard was told by the station master there that he rushed into the station shouting for a ticket for home. Seeing from his violent demeanour that he was English, they gave him a ticket for the furthest station on the way thither that the train reached.

"Be assured that he is well cared for. He has won all hearts by his sweetness and gentleness. He is truly getting on well, and I have no doubt will in a few weeks be all himself. But be careful of him for safety's sake. There are, I pray God and St. Joseph and Ste. Mary, many, many, happy years for you both."

DR. SEWARD'S DIARY

19 August.--Strange and sudden change in Renfield last night. About eight o'clock he began to get excited and sniff about as a dog does when setting. The attendant was struck by his manner, and knowing my interest in him, encouraged him to talk. He is usually respectful to the attendant and at times servile, but tonight, the man tells me, he was quite haughty. Would not condescend to talk with him at all.

All he would say was, "I don't want to talk to you. You don't count now. The master is at hand."

The attendant thinks it is some sudden form of religious mania which has seized him. If so, we must look out for squalls, for a strong man with homicidal and religious mania at once might be dangerous. The combination is a dreadful one.

CHAPTER 8

At nine o'clock I visited him myself. His attitude to me was the same as that to the attendant. In his sublime self-feeling the difference between myself and the attendant seemed to him as nothing. It looks like religious mania, and he will soon think that he himself is God.

These infinitesimal distinctions between man and man are too paltry for an Omnipotent Being. How these madmen give themselves away! The real God taketh heed lest a sparrow fall. But the God created from human vanity sees no difference between an eagle and a sparrow. Oh, if men only knew!

For half an hour or more Renfield kept getting excited in greater and greater degree. I did not pretend to be watching him, but I kept strict observation all the same. All at once that shifty look came into his eyes which we always see when a madman has seized an idea, and with it the shifty movement of the head and back which asylum attendants come to know so well. He became quite quiet, and went and sat on the edge of his bed resignedly, and looked into space with lack-luster eyes.

I thought I would find out if his apathy were real or only assumed, and tried to lead him to talk of his pets, a theme which had never failed to excite his attention.

At first he made no reply, but at length said testily, "Bother them all! I don't care a pin about them."

"What?" I said. "You don't mean to tell me you don't care about spiders?" (Spiders at present are his hobby and the notebook is filling up with columns of small figures.)

To this he answered enigmatically, "The bride-maidens rejoice the eyes that wait the coming of the bride. But when the bride draweth nigh, then the maidens shine not to the eyes that are filled."

He would not explain himself, but remained obstinately seated on his bed all the time I remained with him.

I am weary tonight and low in spirits. I cannot but think of Lucy, and how different things might have been. If I don't sleep at once, chloral, the modern Morpheus! I must be careful not to let it grow into a habit. No, I shall take none tonight! I have thought of Lucy, and I shall not dishonour her by mixing the two. If need be, tonight shall be sleepless.

Later.--Glad I made the resolution, gladder that I kept to it. I had lain tossing about, and had heard the clock strike only twice, when the night watchman came to me, sent up from the ward, to say that Renfield had escaped. I threw on my clothes and ran down at once. My patient is too dangerous a person to be roaming about. Those ideas of his might work out dangerously with strangers.

The attendant was waiting for me. He said he had seen him not ten minutes before, seemingly asleep in his bed, when he had looked through the observation trap in the door. His attention was called by the sound of the window being wrenched out. He ran back and saw his feet disappear through the window, and had at once sent up for me. He was only in his night gear, and cannot be far off.

The attendant thought it would be more useful to watch where he should go than to follow him, as he might lose sight of him whilst getting out of the building by the door. He is a bulky man, and couldn't get through the window.

I am thin, so, with his aid, I got out, but feet foremost, and as we were only a few feet above ground landed unhurt.

The attendant told me the patient had gone to the left, and had taken a straight line, so I ran as quickly as I could. As I got through the belt of trees I saw a white figure scale the high wall which separates our grounds from those of the deserted house.

I ran back at once, told the watchman to get three or four men immediately and follow me into the grounds of Carfax, in case our friend might be dangerous. I got a ladder myself, and crossing the wall, dropped down on the other side. I could see Renfield's figure just disappearing behind the angle of the house, so I ran after him. On the far side of the house I found him pressed close against the old iron-bound oak door of the chapel.

He was talking, apparently to some one, but I was afraid to go near enough to hear what he was saying, lest I might frighten him, and he should run off.

Chasing an errant swarm of bees is nothing to following a naked lunatic, when the fit of escaping is upon him! After a few minutes, however, I could see that he did not take note of anything around him, and so ventured to draw nearer to him, the more so as my men had now crossed the wall and were closing him in. I heard him say…

"I am here to do your bidding, Master. I am your slave, and you will reward me, for I shall be faithful. I have worshipped you long and afar off. Now that you are near, I await your commands, and you will not pass me by, will you, dear Master, in your distribution of good things?"

He is a selfish old beggar anyhow. He thinks of the loaves and fishes even when he believes he is in a real Presence. His manias make a startling combination. When we closed in on him he fought like a tiger. He is immensely strong, for he was more like a wild beast than a man.

I never saw a lunatic in such a paroxysm of rage before, and I hope I shall not again. It is a mercy that we have found out his strength and his danger in good time. With strength and determination like his, he might have done wild work before he was caged.

He is safe now, at any rate. Jack Sheppard himself couldn't get free from the strait waistcoat that keeps him restrained, and he's chained to the wall in the padded room.

His cries are at times awful, but the silences that follow are more deadly still, for he means murder in every turn and movement.

Just now he spoke coherent words for the first time. "I shall be patient, Master. It is coming, coming, coming!"

So I took the hint, and came too. I was too excited to sleep, but this diary has quieted me, and I feel I shall get some sleep tonight.

CHAPTER 9

LETTER, MINA HARKER TO LUCY WESTENRA

Buda-Pesth, 24 August.

"My dearest Lucy,

"I know you will be anxious to hear all that has happened since we parted at the railway station at Whitby.

"Well, my dear, I got to Hull all right, and caught the boat to Hamburg, and then the train on here. I feel that I can hardly recall anything of the journey, except that I knew I was coming to Jonathan, and that as I should have to do some nursing, I had better get all the sleep I could. I found my dear one, oh, so thin and pale and weak-looking. All the resolution has gone out of his dear eyes, and that quiet dignity which I told you was in his face has vanished. He is only a wreck of himself, and he does not remember anything that has happened to him for a long time past. At least, he wants me to believe so, and I shall never ask.

"He has had some terrible shock, and I fear it might tax his poor brain if he were to try to recall it. Sister Agatha, who is a good creature and a born nurse, tells me that he wanted her to tell me what they were, but she would only cross herself, and say she would never tell; that the ravings of the sick were the secrets of God, and that if a nurse through her vocation should hear them, she should respect her trust.

"She is a sweet, good soul, and the next day, when she saw I was troubled, she opened up the subject again, and after saying that she could never mention what my poor dear raved about, added: 'I can tell you this much, my dear: that it was not about anything which he has done wrong himself; and you, as his wife to be, have no cause to be concerned. He has not forgotten you or what he owes to you. His fear was of great and terrible things, which no mortal can treat of.'

"I do believe the dear soul thought I might be jealous lest my poor dear should have fallen in love with any other girl. The idea of my being jealous about Jonathan! And yet, my dear, let me whisper, I felt a thrill of joy through me when I knew that no other woman was a cause for trouble. I am now sitting by his bedside, where I can see his face while he sleeps. He is waking!

"When he woke he asked me for his coat, as he wanted to get something from the pocket. I asked Sister Agatha, and she brought all his things. I saw amongst them was his notebook, and was going to ask him to let me look at it, for I knew that I might find some clue to his trouble, but I suppose he must have seen my wish in my eyes, for he sent me over to the window, saying he wanted to be quite alone for a moment.

"Then he called me back, and he said to me very solemnly, 'Wilhelmina', I knew then that he was in deadly earnest, for he has never called me by that name since he asked me to marry him, 'You know, dear, my ideas of the trust between husband and wife. There should be no secret, no concealment. I have had a great shock, and when I try to think of what it is I feel my head spin round, and I do not know if it was real of the dreaming of a madman. You know I had brain fever, and that is to be mad. The secret is here, and I do not want to know it. I want to take up my life here, with our marriage.' For, my dear, we had decided to be married as soon as the formalities are complete. 'Are you willing, Wilhelmina, to share my ignorance? Here is the book. Take it and keep it, read it if you will, but never let me know unless, indeed, some solemn duty should come upon me to go back to the bitter hours, asleep or awake, sane or mad, recorded here.' He fell back exhausted, and I put the book under his pillow, and kissed him. I have asked Sister Agatha to beg the Superior to let our wedding be this afternoon, and am waiting her reply..."

"She has come and told me that the Chaplain of the English mission church has been sent for. We are to be married in an hour, or as soon after as Jonathan awakes."

"Lucy, the time has come and gone. I feel very solemn, but very, very happy. Jonathan woke a little after the hour, and all was ready, and he sat up in bed, propped up with pillows. He answered his 'I will' firmly and strong. I could hardly speak. My heart was so full that even those words seemed to choke me.

"The dear sisters were so kind. Please, God, I shall never, never forget them, nor the grave and sweet responsibilities I have taken upon me. I must tell you of my wedding present. When the chaplain and the sisters had left me alone with my husband--oh, Lucy, it is the first time I have written the words 'my husband'--left me alone with my husband, I took the book from under his pillow, and wrapped it up in white paper, and tied it with a little bit of pale blue ribbon which was round my neck, and sealed it over the knot with sealing wax, and for my seal I used my wedding ring. Then I kissed it and showed it to my husband, and told him that I would keep it so, and then it would be an outward and visible sign for us all our lives that we trusted each other, that I would never open it unless it were for his own dear sake or for the sake of some stern duty. Then he took my hand in his, and oh, Lucy, it was the first time he took his wife's hand, and said that it was the dearest thing in all the wide world, and that he would go through all the past again to win it, if need be. The poor dear meant to have said a part of the past, but he cannot think of time yet, and I shall not wonder if at first he mixes up not only the month, but the year.

"Well, my dear, what could I say? I could only tell him that I was the happiest woman in all the wide world, and that I had nothing to give him except myself, my life, and my trust, and that with these went my love and duty for all the days of my life. And, my dear, when he kissed me, and drew me to him with his poor weak hands, it was like a solemn pledge between us.

"Lucy dear, do you know why I tell you all this? It is not only because it is all sweet to me, but because you have been, and are, very dear to me. It was my privilege to be your friend and guide when you came from the schoolroom to prepare for the world of life. I want you to see now, and with the eyes of a very happy wife, whither duty has led me, so that in your own married life you too may be all happy, as I am.

My dear, please Almighty God, your life may be all it promises, a long day of sunshine, with no harsh wind, no forgetting duty, no distrust. I must not wish you no pain, for that can never be, but I do hope you will be always as happy as I am now. Goodbye, my dear. I shall post this at once, and perhaps, write you very soon again. I must stop, for Jonathan is waking. I must attend my husband!

"Your ever-loving Mina Harker."

LETTER, LUCY WESTENRA TO MINA HARKER.

Whitby, 30 August.

"My dearest Mina,

"Oceans of love and millions of kisses, and may you soon be in your own home with your husband. I wish you were coming home soon enough to stay with us here. The strong air would soon restore Jonathan. It has quite restored me. I have an appetite like a cormorant, am full of life, and sleep well. You will be glad to know that I have quite given up walking in my sleep. I think I have not stirred out of my bed for a week, that is when I once got into it at night. Arthur says I am getting fat. By the way, I forgot to tell you that Arthur is here. We have such walks and drives, and rides, and rowing, and tennis, and fishing together, and I love him more than ever. He tells me that he loves me more, but I doubt that, for at first he told me that he couldn't love me more than he did then. But this is nonsense. There he is, calling to me. So no more just at present from your loving,

"Lucy.

"P.S.--Mother sends her love. She seems better, poor dear.

"P.P.S.--We are to be married on 28 September."

DR. SEWARDS DIARY

20 August.--The case of Renfield grows even more interesting. He has now so far quieted that there are spells of cessation from his passion. For the first week after his attack he was perpetually violent. Then one night, just as the moon rose, he grew quiet, and kept murmuring to himself. "Now I can wait. Now I can wait."

The attendant came to tell me, so I ran down at once to have a look at him. He was still in the strait waistcoat and in the padded room, but the suffused look had gone from his face, and his eyes had something of their old pleading. I might almost say, "cringing", softness. I was satisfied with his present condition, and directed him to be relieved. The attendants hesitated, but finally carried out my wishes without protest.

It was a strange thing that the patient had humour enough to see their distrust, for, coming close to me, he said in a whisper, all the while looking furtively at them, "They think I could hurt you! Fancy me hurting you! The fools!"

It was soothing, somehow, to the feelings to find myself disassociated even in the mind of this poor madman from the others, but all the same I do not follow his thought. Am I to take it that I have anything in common with him, so that we are, as it were, to stand together. Or has he to gain from me some good so stupendous that my well being is needful to him? I must find out later on. Tonight he will not speak. Even the offer of a kitten or even a full-grown cat will not tempt him.

He will only say, "I don't take any stock in cats. I have more to think of now, and I can wait. I can wait."

After a while I left him. The attendant tells me that he was quiet until just before dawn, and that then he began to get uneasy, and at length violent, until at last he fell into a paroxysm which exhausted him so that he swooned into a sort of coma.

. . . Three nights has the same thing happened, violent all day then quiet from moonrise to sunrise. I wish I could get some clue to the cause. It would almost seem as if there was some influence which came and went. Happy thought! We shall tonight play sane wits against mad ones. He escaped before without our help. Tonight he shall escape with it. We shall give him a chance, and have the men ready to follow in case they are required.

23 August.--"The expected always happens." How well Disraeli knew life. Our bird when he found the cage open would not fly, so all our subtle arrangements were for nought. At any rate, we have proved one thing, that the spells of quietness last a reasonable time. We shall in future be able to ease his bonds for a few hours each day. I have given orders to the night attendant merely to shut him in the padded room, when once he is quiet, until the hour before sunrise. The poor soul's body will enjoy the relief even if his mind cannot appreciate it. Hark! The unexpected again! I am called. The patient has once more escaped.

Later.--Another night adventure. Renfield artfully waited until the attendant was entering the room to inspect. Then he dashed out past him and flew down the passage. I sent word for the attendants to follow. Again he went into the grounds of the deserted house, and we found him in the same place, pressed against the old chapel door. When he saw me he became furious, and had not the attendants seized him in time, he would have tried to kill me. As we were holding him a strange thing happened. He suddenly redoubled his efforts, and then as suddenly grew calm. I looked round instinctively, but could see nothing. Then I caught the patient's eye and followed it, but could trace nothing as it looked into the moonlight sky, except a big bat, which was flapping its silent and ghostly way to the west. Bats usually wheel about, but this one seemed to go straight on, as if it knew where it was bound for or had some intention of its own.

The patient grew calmer every instant, and presently said, "You needn't tie me. I shall go quietly!" Without trouble, we came back to the house. I feel there is something ominous in his calm, and shall not forget this night.

LUCY WESTENRA'S DIARY

Hillingham, 24 August.--I must imitate Mina, and keep writing things down. Then we can have long talks when we do meet. I wonder when it will be. I wish she were with me again, for I feel so unhappy. Last night I seemed to be dreaming again just as I was at Whitby. Perhaps it is the change of air, or getting home again. It is all dark and horrid to me, for I can remember nothing. But I am full of vague fear, and I feel so weak and worn out. When Arthur came to lunch he looked quite grieved when he saw me, and I hadn't the spirit to try to be cheerful. I wonder if I could sleep in mother's room tonight. I shall make an excuse to try.

25 August.--Another bad night. Mother did not seem to take to my proposal. She seems not too well herself, and doubtless she fears to worry me. I tried to keep awake,

and succeeded for a while, but when the clock struck twelve it waked me from a doze, so I must have been falling asleep. There was a sort of scratching or flapping at the window, but I did not mind it, and as I remember no more, I suppose I must have fallen asleep. More bad dreams. I wish I could remember them. This morning I am horribly weak. My face is ghastly pale, and my throat pains me. It must be something wrong with my lungs, for I don't seem to be getting air enough. I shall try to cheer up when Arthur comes, or else I know he will be miserable to see me so.

LETTER, ARTHUR TO DR. SEWARD

"Albemarle Hotel, 31 August

"My dear Jack,

"I want you to do me a favour. Lucy is ill, that is she has no special disease, but she looks awful, and is getting worse every day. I have asked her if there is any cause, I not dare to ask her mother, for to disturb the poor lady's mind about her daughter in her present state of health would be fatal. Mrs. Westenra has confided to me that her doom is spoken, disease of the heart, though poor Lucy does not know it yet. I am sure that there is something preying on my dear girl's mind. I am almost distracted when I think of her. To look at her gives me a pang. I told her I should ask you to see her, and though she demurred at first-I know why, old fellow-she finally consented. It will be a painful task for you, I know, old friend, but it is for *her* sake, and I must not hesitate to ask, or you to act. You are to come to lunch at Hillingham tomorrow, two o'clock, so as not to arouse any suspicion in Mrs. Westenra, and after lunch Lucy will take an opportunity of being alone with you. I am filled with anxiety, and want to consult with you alone as soon as I can after you have seen her. Do not fail!

"Arthur."

TELEGRAM, ARTHUR HOLMWOOD TO SEWARD

1 September

"Am summoned to see my father, who is worse. Am writing. Write me fully by tonight's post to Ring. Wire me if necessary."

LETTER FROM DR. SEWARD TO ARTHUR HOLMWOOD

2 September

"My dear old fellow,

"With regard to Miss Westenra's health I hasten to let you know at once that in my opinion there is not any functional disturbance or any malady that I know of. At the same time, I am not by any means satisfied with her appearance. She is woefully different from what she was when I saw her last. Of course you must bear in mind that I did not have full opportunity of examination such as I should wish. Our very friendship makes a little difficulty which not even medical science or custom can bridge over. I had better tell you exactly what happened, leaving you to draw, in a measure, your own conclusions. I shall then say what I have done and propose doing.

"I found Miss Westenra in seemingly gay spirits. Her mother was present, and in a few seconds I made up my mind that she was trying all she knew to mislead her mother and prevent her from being anxious. I have no doubt she guesses, if she does not know, what need of caution there is.

"We lunched alone, and as we all exerted ourselves to be cheerful, we got, as some kind of reward for our labours, some real cheerfulness amongst us. Then Mrs. Westenra went to lie down, and Lucy was left with me. We went into her boudoir, and till we got there her gaiety remained, for the servants were coming and going.

"As soon as the door was closed, however, the mask fell from her face, and she sank down into a chair with a great sigh, and hid her eyes with her hand. When I saw that her high spirits had failed, I at once took advantage of her reaction to make a diagnosis.

"She said to me very sweetly, 'I cannot tell you how I loathe talking about myself.' I reminded her that a doctor's confidence was sacred, but that you were grievously anxious about her. She caught on to my meaning at once, and settled that matter in a word. 'Tell Arthur everything you choose. I do not care for myself, but for him!' So I am quite free.

"I could easily see that she was somewhat bloodless, but I could not see the usual anemic signs, and by the chance, I was able to test the actual quality of her blood, for in opening a window which was stiff a cord gave way, and she cut her hand slightly with broken glass. It was a slight matter in itself, but it gave me an evident chance, and I secured a few drops of the blood and have analysed them.

"The qualitative analysis give a quite normal condition, and shows, I should infer, in itself a vigorous state of health. In other physical matters I was quite satisfied that there is no need for anxiety, but as there must be a cause somewhere, I have come to the conclusion that it must be something mental.

"She complains of difficulty breathing satisfactorily at times, and of heavy, lethargic sleep, with dreams that frighten her, but regarding which she can remember nothing. She says that as a child, she used to walk in her sleep, and that when in Whitby the habit came back, and that once she walked out in the night and went to East Cliff, where Miss Murray found her. But she assures me that of late the habit has not returned.

"I am in doubt, and so have done the best thing I know of. I have written to my old friend and master, Professor Van Helsing, of Amsterdam, who knows as much about obscure diseases as any one in the world. I have asked him to come over, and as you told me that all things were to be at your charge, I have mentioned to him who you are and your relations to Miss Westenra. This, my dear fellow, is in obedience to your wishes, for I am only too proud and happy to do anything I can for her.

"Van Helsing would, I know, do anything for me for a personal reason, so no matter on what ground he comes, we must accept his wishes. He is a seemingly arbitrary man, this is because he knows what he is talking about better than any one else. He is a philosopher and a metaphysician, and one of the most advanced scientists of his day, and he has, I believe, an absolutely open mind. This, with an iron nerve, a temper of the ice-brook, and indomitable resolution, self-command, and toleration exalted from virtues to blessings, and the kindliest and truest heart that beats, these form his equipment for the noble work that he is doing for mankind, work both in theory and practice, for his views are as wide as his all-embracing sympathy. I tell you these facts that you may know why I have such confidence in him. I have asked him to come at once. I shall see Miss Westenra tomorrow again. She is to meet me at the Stores, so that I may not alarm her mother by too early a repetition of my call.

"Yours always."

John Seward

LETTER, ABRAHAM VAN HELSING, MD, DPh, D. Lit, ETC, ETC, TO DR. SEWARD

2 September.

"My good Friend,

"When I received your letter I am already coming to you. By good fortune I can leave just at once, without wrong to any of those who have trusted me. Were fortune other, then it were bad for those who have trusted, for I come to my friend when he call me to aid those he holds dear. Tell your friend that when that time you suck from my wound so swiftly the poison of the gangrene from that knife that our other friend, too nervous, let slip, you did more for him when he wants my aids and you call for them than all his great fortune could do. But it is pleasure added to do for him, your friend, it is to you that I come. Have near at hand, and please it so arrange that we may see the young lady not too late on tomorrow, for it is likely that I may have to return here that night. But if need be I shall come again in three days, and stay longer if it must. Till then goodbye, my friend John.

"Van Helsing."

LETTER, DR. SEWARD TO HON. ARTHUR HOLMWOOD

3 September

"My dear Art,

"Van Helsing has come and gone. He came on with me to Hillingham, and found that, by Lucy's discretion, her mother was lunching out, so that we were alone with her.

"Van Helsing made a very careful examination of the patient. He is to report to me, and I shall advise you, for of course I was not present all the time. He is, I fear, much concerned, but says he must think. When I told him of our friendship and how you trust to me in the matter, he said, 'You must tell him all you think. Tell him what I think, if you can guess it, if you will. Nay, I am not jesting. This is no jest, but life and death, perhaps more.' I asked what he meant by that, for he was very serious. This was when we had come back to town, and he was having a cup of tea before starting on his return to Amsterdam. He would not give me any further clue. You must not be angry with me, Art, because his very reticence means that all his brains are working for her good. He will speak plainly enough when the time comes, be sure. So I told him I would simply write an account of our visit, just as if I were doing a descriptive special article for THE DAILY TELEGRAPH. He seemed not to notice, but remarked that the smuts of London were not quite so bad as they used to be when he was a student here. I am to get his report tomorrow if he can possibly make it. In any case I am to have a letter.

"Well, as to the visit, Lucy was more cheerful than on the day I first saw her, and certainly looked better. She had lost something of the ghastly look that so upset you, and her breathing was normal. She was very sweet to the Professor (as she always is), and tried to make him feel at ease, though I could see the poor girl was making a hard struggle for it.

"I believe Van Helsing saw it, too, for I saw the quick look under his bushy brows that I knew of old. Then he began to chat of all things except ourselves and diseases and with such an infinite geniality that I could see poor Lucy's pretense of animation merge into reality. Then, without any seeming change, he brought the conversation gently round to his visit, and suavely said,

"'My dear young miss, I have the so great pleasure because you are so much beloved. That is much, my dear, even were there that which I do not see. They told me you were down in the spirit, and that you were of a ghastly pale. To them I say "Pouf!"' And he snapped his fingers at me and went on. 'But you and I shall show them how wrong they are. How can he,' and he pointed at me with the same look and gesture as that with which he pointed me out in his class, on, or rather after, a particular occasion which he never fails to remind me of, 'know anything of a young ladies? He has his madmen to play with, and to bring them back to happiness, and to those that love them. It is much to do, and, oh, but there are rewards in that we can bestow such happiness. But the young ladies! He has no wife nor daughter, and the young do not tell themselves to the young, but to the old, like me, who have known so many sorrows and the causes of them. So, my dear, we will send him away to smoke the cigarette in the garden, whiles you and I have little talk all to ourselves.' I took the hint, and strolled about, and presently the professor came to the window and called me in. He looked grave, but said, 'I have made careful examination, but there is no functional cause. With you I agree that there has been much blood lost, it has been but is not. But the conditions of her are in no way anemic. I have asked her to send me her maid, that I may ask just one or two questions, that so I may not chance to miss nothing. I know well what she will say. And yet there is cause. There is always cause for everything. I must go back home and think. You must send me the telegram every day, and if there be cause I shall come again. The disease, for not to be well is a disease, interest me, and the sweet, young dear, she interest me too. She charm me, and for her, if not for you or disease, I come.'

"As I tell you, he would not say a word more, even when we were alone. And so now, Art, you know all I know. I shall keep stern watch. I trust your poor father is rallying. It must be a terrible thing to you, my dear old fellow, to be placed in such a position between two people who are both so dear to you. I know your idea of duty to your father, and you are right to stick to it. But if need be, I shall send you word to come at once to Lucy, so do not be over-anxious unless you hear from me."

DR. SEWARD'S DIARY

4 September.--Zoophagous patient still keeps up our interest in him. He had only one outburst and that was yesterday at an unusual time. Just before the stroke of noon he began to grow restless. The attendant knew the symptoms, and at once summoned aid. Fortunately the men came at a run, and were just in time, for at the stroke of noon he became so violent that it took all their strength to hold him. In about five minutes,

however, he began to get more quiet, and finally sank into a sort of melancholy, in which state he has remained up to now. The attendant tells me that his screams whilst in the paroxysm were really appalling. I found my hands full when I got in, attending to some of the other patients who were frightened by him. Indeed, I can quite understand the effect, for the sounds disturbed even me, though I was some distance away. It is now after the dinner hour of the asylum, and as yet my patient sits in a corner brooding, with a dull, sullen, woe-begone look in his face, which seems rather to indicate than to show something directly. I cannot quite understand it.

Later.--Another change in my patient. At five o'clock I looked in on him, and found him seemingly as happy and contented as he used to be. He was catching flies and eating them, and was keeping note of his capture by making nailmarks on the edge of the door between the ridges of padding. When he saw me, he came over and apologized for his bad conduct, and asked me in a very humble, cringing way to be led back to his own room, and to have his notebook again. I thought it well to humour him, so he is back in his room with the window open. He has the sugar of his tea spread out on the window sill, and is reaping quite a harvest of flies. He is not now eating them, but putting them into a box, as of old, and is already examining the corners of his room to find a spider. I tried to get him to talk about the past few days, for any clue to his thoughts would be of immense help to me, but he would not rise. For a moment or two he looked very sad, and said in a sort of far away voice, as though saying it rather to himself than to me.

"All over! All over! He has deserted me. No hope for me now unless I do it myself!" Then suddenly turning to me in a resolute way, he said, "Doctor, won't you be very good to me and let me have a little more sugar? I think it would be very good for me."

"And the flies?" I said.

"Yes! The flies like it, too, and I like the flies, therefore I like it." And there are people who know so little as to think that madmen do not argue. I procured him a double supply, and left him as happy a man as, I suppose, any in the world. I wish I could fathom his mind.

Midnight.--Another change in him. I had been to see Miss Westenra, whom I found much better, and had just returned, and was standing at our own gate looking at the sunset, when once more I heard him yelling. As his room is on this side of the house, I could hear it better than in the morning. It was a shock to me to turn from the wonderful smoky beauty of a sunset over London, with its lurid lights and inky shadows and all the marvellous tints that come on foul clouds even as on foul water, and to realize all the grim sternness of my own cold stone building, with its wealth of breathing misery, and my own desolate heart to endure it all. I reached him just as the sun was going down, and from his window saw the red disc sink. As it sank he became less and less frenzied, and just as it dipped he slid from the hands that held him, an inert mass, on the floor. It is wonderful, however, what intellectual recuperative power lunatics have, for within a few minutes he stood up quite calmly and looked around him. I signalled to the attendants not to hold him, for I was anxious to see what he would do. He went straight over to the window and brushed out the crumbs of sugar. Then he took his fly box, and emptied it outside, and threw away the box. Then he shut the window, and crossing over, sat down on his bed. All this surprised me, so I asked him, "Are you going to keep flies any more?"

"No," said he. "I am sick of all that rubbish!" He certainly is a wonderfully interesting study. I wish I could get some glimpse of his mind or of the cause of his sudden passion. Stop. There may be a clue after all, if we can find why today his paroxysms came on at high noon and at sunset. Can it be that there is a malign influence of the sun at periods which affects certain natures, as at times the moon does others? We shall see.

TELEGRAM. SEWARD, LONDON, TO VAN HELSING, AMSTERDAM

"4 September.--Patient still better today."

TELEGRAM, SEWARD, LONDON, TO VAN HELSING, AMSTERDAM

"5 September.--Patient greatly improved. Good appetite, sleeps naturally, good spirits, colour coming back."

TELEGRAM, SEWARD, LONDON, TO VAN HELSING, AMSTERDAM

"6 September.--Terrible change for the worse. Come at once. Do not lose an hour. I hold over telegram to Holmwood till have seen you."

CHAPTER 10

LETTER, DR. SEWARD TO HON. ARTHUR HOLMWOOD

6 September
"My dear Art,
"My news today is not so good. Lucy this morning had gone back a bit. There is, however, one good thing which has arisen from it. Mrs. Westenra was naturally anxious concerning Lucy, and has consulted me professionally about her. I took advantage of the opportunity, and told her that my old master, Van Helsing, the great specialist, was coming to stay with me, and that I would put her in his charge conjointly with myself. So now we can come and go without alarming her unduly, for a shock to her would mean sudden death, and this, in Lucy's weak condition, might be disastrous to her. We are hedged in with difficulties, all of us, my poor fellow, but, please God, we shall come through them all right. If any need I shall write, so that, if you do not hear from me, take it for granted that I am simply waiting for news, In haste,
"Yours ever,"
John Seward

DR. SEWARD'S DIARY

7 September.--The first thing Van Helsing said to me when we met at Liverpool Street was, "Have you said anything to our young friend, to lover of her?"

"No," I said. "I waited till I had seen you, as I said in my telegram. I wrote him a letter simply telling him that you were coming, as Miss Westenra was not so well, and that I should let him know if need be."

"Right, my friend," he said. "Quite right! Better he not know as yet. Perhaps he will never know. I pray so, but if it be needed, then he shall know all. And, my good friend John, let me caution you. You deal with the madmen. All men are mad in some way or the other, and inasmuch as you deal discreetly with your madmen, so deal with God's madmen too, the rest of the world. You tell not your madmen what you do nor why you do it. You tell them not what you think. So you shall keep knowledge in its place, where it may rest, where it may gather its kind around it and breed. You and I shall keep as yet what we know here, and here." He touched me on the heart and on the forehead, and then touched himself the same way. "I have for myself thoughts at the present. Later I shall unfold to you."

"Why not now?" I asked. "It may do some good. We may arrive at some decision." He looked at me and said, "My friend John, when the corn is grown, even before it has ripened, while the milk of its mother earth is in him, and the sunshine has not yet begun to paint him with his gold, the husbandman he pull the ear and rub him between his rough hands, and blow away the green chaff, and say to you, 'Look! He's good corn, he will make a good crop when the time comes.'"

I did not see the application and told him so. For reply he reached over and took my ear in his hand and pulled it playfully, as he used long ago to do at lectures, and said, "The good husbandman tell you so then because he knows, but not till then. But you do not find the good husbandman dig up his planted corn to see if he grow. That is for the children who play at husbandry, and not for those who take it as of the work of their life. See you now, friend John? I have sown my corn, and Nature has her work to do in making it sprout, if he sprout at all, there's some promise, and I wait till the ear begins to swell." He broke off, for he evidently saw that I understood. Then he went on gravely, "You were always a careful student, and your case book was ever more full than the rest. And I trust that good habit have not fail. Remember, my friend, that knowledge is stronger than memory, and we should not trust the weaker. Even if you have not kept the good practice, let me tell you that this case of our dear miss is one that may be, mind, I say may be, of such interest to us and others that all the rest may not make him kick the beam, as your people say. Take then good note of it. Nothing is too small. I counsel you, put down in record even your doubts and surmises. Hereafter it may be of interest to you to see how true you guess. We learn from failure, not from success!"

When I described Lucy's symptoms, the same as before, but infinitely more marked, he looked very grave, but said nothing. He took with him a bag in which were many instruments and drugs, "the ghastly paraphernalia of our beneficial trade," as he once called, in one of his lectures, the equipment of a professor of the healing craft.

When we were shown in, Mrs. Westenra met us. She was alarmed, but not nearly so much as I expected to find her. Nature in one of her beneficient moods has ordained that even death has some antidote to its own terrors. Here, in a case where any shock may prove fatal, matters are so ordered that, from some cause or other, the things not personal, even the terrible change in her daughter to whom she is so attached, do not seem to reach her. It is something like the way dame Nature gathers round a foreign body an envelope of some insensitive tissue which can protect from evil that which it would otherwise harm by contact. If this be an ordered selfishness, then we should pause before we condemn any one for the vice of egoism, for there may be deeper root for its causes than we have knowledge of.

I used my knowledge of this phase of spiritual pathology, and set down a rule that she should not be present with Lucy, or think of her illness more than was absolutely required. She assented readily, so readily that I saw again the hand of Nature fighting for life. Van Helsing and I were shown up to Lucy's room. If I was shocked when I saw her yesterday, I was horrified when I saw her today.

She was ghastly, chalkily pale. The red seemed to have gone even from her lips and gums, and the bones of her face stood out prominently. Her breathing was painful to see or hear. Van Helsing's face grew set as marble, and his eyebrows converged till they almost touched over his nose. Lucy lay motionless, and did not seem to have strength to speak, so for a while we were all silent. Then Van Helsing beckoned to me, and we went gently out of the room. The instant we had closed the door he stepped quickly along the passage to the next door, which was open. Then he pulled me quickly in with him and closed the door. "My god!" he said. "This is dreadful. There is not time to be lost. She will die for sheer want of blood to keep the heart's action as it should be. There must be a transfusion of blood at once. Is it you or me?"

"I am younger and stronger, Professor. It must be me."

"Then get ready at once. I will bring up my bag. I am prepared."

I went downstairs with him, and as we were going there was a knock at the hall door. When we reached the hall, the maid had just opened the door, and Arthur was stepping quickly in. He rushed up to me, saying in an eager whisper,

"Jack, I was so anxious. I read between the lines of your letter, and have been in an agony. The dad was better, so I ran down here to see for myself. Is not that gentleman Dr. Van Helsing? I am so thankful to you, sir, for coming."

When first the Professor's eye had lit upon him, he had been angry at his interruption at such a time, but now, as he took in his stalwart proportions and recognized the strong young manhood which seemed to emanate from him, his eyes gleamed. Without a pause he said to him as he held out his hand,

"Sir, you have come in time. You are the lover of our dear miss. She is bad, very, very bad. Nay, my child, do not go like that." For he suddenly grew pale and sat down in a chair almost fainting. "You are to help her. You can do more than any that live, and your courage is your best help."

"What can I do?" asked Arthur hoarsely. "Tell me, and I shall do it. My life is hers, and I would give the last drop of blood in my body for her."

The Professor has a strongly humorous side, and I could from old knowledge detect a trace of its origin in his answer.

"My young sir, I do not ask so much as that, not the last!"

"What shall I do?" There was fire in his eyes, and his open nostrils quivered with intent. Van Helsing slapped him on the shoulder.

"Come!" he said. "You are a man, and it is a man we want. You are better than me, better than my friend John." Arthur looked bewildered, and the Professor went on by explaining in a kindly way.

"Young miss is bad, very bad. She wants blood, and blood she must have or die. My friend John and I have consulted, and we are about to perform what we call transfusion of blood, to transfer from full veins of one to the empty veins which pine for him. John was to give his blood, as he is the more young and strong than me."--Here Arthur took my hand and wrung it hard in silence.--"But now you are here, you are more good than us, old or young, who toil much in the world of thought. Our nerves are not so calm and our blood so bright than yours!"

Arthur turned to him and said, "If you only knew how gladly I would die for her you would understand..." He stopped with a sort of choke in his voice.

"Good boy!" said Van Helsing. "In the not-so-far-off you will be happy that you have done all for her you love. Come now and be silent. You shall kiss her once before it is done, but then you must go, and you must leave at my sign. Say no word to

Madame. You know how it is with her. There must be no shock, any knowledge of this would be one. Come!"

We all went up to Lucy's room. Arthur by direction remained outside. Lucy turned her head and looked at us, but said nothing. She was not asleep, but she was simply too weak to make the effort. Her eyes spoke to us, that was all.

Van Helsing took some things from his bag and laid them on a little table out of sight. Then he mixed a narcotic, and coming over to the bed, said cheerily, "Now, little miss, here is your medicine. Drink it off, like a good child. See, I lift you so that to swallow is easy. Yes." She had made the effort with success.

It astonished me how long the drug took to act. This, in fact, marked the extent of her weakness. The time seemed endless until sleep began to flicker in her eyelids. At last, however, the narcotic began to manifest its potency, and she fell into a deep sleep. When the Professor was satisfied, he called Arthur into the room, and bade him strip off his coat. Then he added, "You may take that one little kiss whiles I bring over the table. Friend John, help to me!" So neither of us looked whilst he bent over her.

Van Helsing, turning to me, said, "He is so young and strong, and of blood so pure that we need not defibrinate it."

Then with swiftness, but with absolute method, Van Helsing performed the operation. As the transfusion went on, something like life seemed to come back to poor Lucy's cheeks, and through Arthur's growing pallor the joy of his face seemed absolutely to shine. After a bit I began to grow anxious, for the loss of blood was telling on Arthur, strong man as he was. It gave me an idea of what a terrible strain Lucy's system must have undergone that what weakened Arthur only partially restored her.

But the Professor's face was set, and he stood watch in hand, and with his eyes fixed now on the patient and now on Arthur. I could hear my own heart beat. Presently, he said in a soft voice, "Do not stir an instant. It is enough. You attend him. I will look to her."

When all was over, I could see how much Arthur was weakened. I dressed the wound and took his arm to bring him away, when Van Helsing spoke without turning round, the man seems to have eyes in the back of his head, "The brave lover, I think, deserve another kiss, which he shall have presently." And as he had now finished his operation, he adjusted the pillow to the patient's head. As he did so the narrow black velvet band which she seems always to wear round her throat, buckled with an old diamond buckle which her lover had given her, was dragged a little up, and showed a red mark on her throat.

Arthur did not notice it, but I could hear the deep hiss of indrawn breath which is one of Van Helsing's ways of betraying emotion. He said nothing at the moment, but turned to me, saying, "Now take down our brave young lover, give him of the port wine, and let him lie down a while. He must then go home and rest, sleep much and eat much, that he may be recruited of what he has so given to his love. He must not stay here. Hold a moment! I may take it, sir, that you are anxious of result. Then bring it with you, that in all ways the operation is successful. You have saved her life this time, and you can go home and rest easy in mind that all that can be is. I shall tell her all when she is well. She shall love you none the less for what you have done. Goodbye."

CHAPTER 10

When Arthur had gone I went back to the room. Lucy was sleeping gently, but her breathing was stronger. I could see the counterpane move as her breast heaved. By the bedside sat Van Helsing, looking at her intently. The velvet band again covered the red mark. I asked the Professor in a whisper, "What do you make of that mark on her throat?"

"What do you make of it?"

"I have not examined it yet," I answered, and then and there proceeded to loose the band. Just over the external jugular vein there were two punctures, not large, but not wholesome looking. There was no sign of disease, but the edges were white and worn looking, as if by some trituration. It at once occurred to me that that this wound, or whatever it was, might be the means of that manifest loss of blood. But I abandoned the idea as soon as it formed, for such a thing could not be. The whole bed would have been drenched to a scarlet with the blood which the girl must have lost to leave such a pallor as she had before the transfusion.

"Well?" said Van Helsing.

"Well," said I. "I can make nothing of it."

The Professor stood up. "I must go back to Amsterdam tonight," he said "There are books and things there which I want. You must remain here all night, and you must not let your sight pass from her."

"Shall I have a nurse?" I asked.

"We are the best nurses, you and I. You keep watch all night. See that she is well fed, and that nothing disturbs her. You must not sleep all the night. Later on we can sleep, you and I. I shall be back as soon as possible. And then we may begin."

"May begin?" I said. "What on earth do you mean?"

"We shall see!" he answered, as he hurried out. He came back a moment later and put his head inside the door and said with a warning finger held up, "Remember, she is your charge. If you leave her, and harm befall, you shall not sleep easy hereafter!"

DR. SEWARD'S DIARY--CONTINUED

8 September.--I sat up all night with Lucy. The opiate worked itself off towards dusk, and she waked naturally. She looked a different being from what she had been before the operation. Her spirits even were good, and she was full of a happy vivacity, but I could see evidences of the absolute prostration which she had undergone. When I told Mrs. Westenra that Dr. Van Helsing had directed that I should sit up with her, she almost pooh-poohed the idea, pointing out her daughter's renewed strength and excellent spirits. I was firm, however, and made preparations for my long vigil. When her maid had prepared her for the night I came in, having in the meantime had supper, and took a seat by the bedside.

She did not in any way make objection, but looked at me gratefully whenever I caught her eye. After a long spell she seemed sinking off to sleep, but with an effort seemed to pull herself together and shook it off. It was apparent that she did not want to sleep, so I tackled the subject at once.

"You do not want to sleep?"

"No. I am afraid."

"Afraid to go to sleep! Why so? It is the boon we all crave for."

"Ah, not if you were like me, if sleep was to you a presage of horror!"

"A presage of horror! What on earth do you mean?"

"I don't know. Oh, I don't know. And that is what is so terrible. All this weakness comes to me in sleep, until I dread the very thought."

"But, my dear girl, you may sleep tonight. I am here watching you, and I can promise that nothing will happen."

"Ah, I can trust you!" she said.

I seized the opportunity, and said, "I promise that if I see any evidence of bad dreams I will wake you at once."

"You will? Oh, will you really? How good you are to me. Then I will sleep!" And almost at the word she gave a deep sigh of relief, and sank back, asleep.

All night long I watched by her. She never stirred, but slept on and on in a deep, tranquil, life-giving, health-giving sleep. Her lips were slightly parted, and her breast rose and fell with the regularity of a pendulum. There was a smile on her face, and it was evident that no bad dreams had come to disturb her peace of mind.

In the early morning her maid came, and I left her in her care and took myself back home, for I was anxious about many things. I sent a short wire to Van Helsing and to Arthur, telling them of the excellent result of the operation. My own work, with its manifold arrears, took me all day to clear off. It was dark when I was able to inquire about my zoophagous patient. The report was good. He had been quite quiet for the past day and night. A telegram came from Van Helsing at Amsterdam whilst I was at dinner, suggesting that I should be at Hillingham tonight, as it might be well to be at hand, and stating that he was leaving by the night mail and would join me early in the morning.

9 September.--I was pretty tired and worn out when I got to Hillingham. For two nights I had hardly had a wink of sleep, and my brain was beginning to feel that numbness which marks cerebral exhaustion. Lucy was up and in cheerful spirits. When she shook hands with me she looked sharply in my face and said,

"No sitting up tonight for you. You are worn out. I am quite well again. Indeed, I am, and if there is to be any sitting up, it is I who will sit up with you."

I would not argue the point, but went and had my supper. Lucy came with me, and, enlivened by her charming presence, I made an excellent meal, and had a couple of glasses of the more than excellent port. Then Lucy took me upstairs, and showed me a room next her own, where a cozy fire was burning.

"Now," she said. "You must stay here. I shall leave this door open and my door too. You can lie on the sofa for I know that nothing would induce any of you doctors to go to bed whilst there is a patient above the horizon. If I want anything I shall call out, and you can come to me at once."

I could not but acquiesce, for I was dog tired, and could not have sat up had I tried. So, on her renewing her promise to call me if she should want anything, I lay on the sofa, and forgot all about everything.

LUCY WESTENRA'S DIARY

9 September.--I feel so happy tonight. I have been so miserably weak, that to be able to think and move about is like feeling sunshine after a long spell of east wind out of a steel sky. Somehow Arthur feels very, very close to me. I seem to feel his presence warm about me. I suppose it is that sickness and weakness are selfish things

and turn our inner eyes and sympathy on ourselves, whilst health and strength give love rein, and in thought and feeling he can wander where he wills. I know where my thoughts are. If only Arthur knew! My dear, my dear, your ears must tingle as you sleep, as mine do waking. Oh, the blissful rest of last night! How I slept, with that dear, good Dr. Seward watching me. And tonight I shall not fear to sleep, since he is close at hand and within call. Thank everybody for being so good to me. Thank God! Goodnight Arthur.

DR. SEWARD'S DIARY

10 September.--I was conscious of the Professor's hand on my head, and started awake all in a second. That is one of the things that we learn in an asylum, at any rate.

"And how is our patient?"

"Well, when I left her, or rather when she left me," I answered.

"Come, let us see," he said. And together we went into the room.

The blind was down, and I went over to raise it gently, whilst Van Helsing stepped, with his soft, cat-like tread, over to the bed.

As I raised the blind, and the morning sunlight flooded the room, I heard the Professor's low hiss of inspiration, and knowing its rarity, a deadly fear shot through my heart. As I passed over he moved back, and his exclamation of horror, "Gott in Himmel!" needed no enforcement from his agonized face. He raised his hand and pointed to the bed, and his iron face was drawn and ashen white. I felt my knees begin to tremble.

There on the bed, seemingly in a swoon, lay poor Lucy, more horribly white and wan-looking than ever. Even the lips were white, and the gums seemed to have shrunken back from the teeth, as we sometimes see in a corpse after a prolonged illness.

Van Helsing raised his foot to stamp in anger, but the instinct of his life and all the long years of habit stood to him, and he put it down again softly.

"Quick!" he said. "Bring the brandy."

I flew to the dining room, and returned with the decanter. He wetted the poor white lips with it, and together we rubbed palm and wrist and heart. He felt her heart, and after a few moments of agonizing suspense said,

"It is not too late. It beats, though but feebly. All our work is undone. We must begin again. There is no young Arthur here now. I have to call on you yourself this time, friend John." As he spoke, he was dipping into his bag, and producing the instruments of transfusion. I had taken off my coat and rolled up my shirt sleeve. There was no possibility of an opiate just at present, and no need of one; and so, without a moment's delay, we began the operation.

After a time, it did not seem a short time either, for the draining away of one's blood, no matter how willingly it be given, is a terrible feeling, Van Helsing held up a warning finger. "Do not stir," he said. "But I fear that with growing strength she may wake, and that would make danger, oh, so much danger. But I shall precaution take. I shall give hypodermic injection of morphia." He proceeded then, swiftly and deftly, to carry out his intent.

The effect on Lucy was not bad, for the faint seemed to merge subtly into the narcotic sleep. It was with a feeling of personal pride that I could see a faint tinge of colour steal back into the pallid cheeks and lips. No man knows, till he experiences it, what it is to feel his own lifeblood drawn away into the veins of the woman he loves.

The Professor watched me critically. "That will do," he said. "Already?" I remonstrated. "You took a great deal more from Art." To which he smiled a sad sort of smile as he replied,

"He is her lover, her fiance. You have work, much work to do for her and for others, and the present will suffice."

When we stopped the operation, he attended to Lucy, whilst I applied digital pressure to my own incision. I laid down, while I waited his leisure to attend to me, for I felt faint and a little sick. By and by he bound up my wound, and sent me downstairs to get a glass of wine for myself. As I was leaving the room, he came after me, and half whispered.

"Mind, nothing must be said of this. If our young lover should turn up unexpected, as before, no word to him. It would at once frighten him and enjealous him, too. There must be none. So!"

When I came back he looked at me carefully, and then said, "You are not much the worse. Go into the room, and lie on your sofa, and rest awhile, then have much breakfast and come here to me."

I followed out his orders, for I knew how right and wise they were. I had done my part, and now my next duty was to keep up my strength. I felt very weak, and in the weakness lost something of the amazement at what had occurred. I fell asleep on the sofa, however, wondering over and over again how Lucy had made such a retrograde movement, and how she could have been drained of so much blood with no sign any where to show for it. I think I must have continued my wonder in my dreams, for, sleeping and waking my thoughts always came back to the little punctures in her throat and the ragged, exhausted appearance of their edges, tiny though they were.

Lucy slept well into the day, and when she woke she was fairly well and strong, though not nearly so much so as the day before. When Van Helsing had seen her, he went out for a walk, leaving me in charge, with strict injunctions that I was not to leave her for a moment. I could hear his voice in the hall, asking the way to the nearest telegraph office.

Lucy chatted with me freely, and seemed quite unconscious that anything had happened. I tried to keep her amused and interested. When her mother came up to see her, she did not seem to notice any change whatever, but said to me gratefully,

"We owe you so much, Dr. Seward, for all you have done, but you really must now take care not to overwork yourself. You are looking pale yourself. You want a wife to nurse and look after you a bit, that you do!" As she spoke, Lucy turned crimson, though it was only momentarily, for her poor wasted veins could not stand for long an unwonted drain to the head. The reaction came in excessive pallor as she turned imploring eyes on me. I smiled and nodded, and laid my finger on my lips. With a sigh, she sank back amid her pillows.

Van Helsing returned in a couple of hours, and presently said to me: "Now you go home, and eat much and drink enough. Make yourself strong. I stay here tonight, and I shall sit up with little miss myself. You and I must watch the case, and we must have none other to know. I have grave reasons. No, do not ask me. Think what you will. Do not fear to think even the most not-improbable. Goodnight."

CHAPTER 10

In the hall two of the maids came to me, and asked if they or either of them might not sit up with Miss Lucy. They implored me to let them, and when I said it was Dr. Van Helsing's wish that either he or I should sit up, they asked me quite piteously to intercede with the 'foreign gentleman'. I was much touched by their kindness. Perhaps it is because I am weak at present, and perhaps because it was on Lucy's account, that their devotion was manifested. For over and over again have I seen similar instances of woman's kindness. I got back here in time for a late dinner, went my rounds, all well, and set this down whilst waiting for sleep. It is coming.

11 September.--This afternoon I went over to Hillingham. Found Van Helsing in excellent spirits, and Lucy much better. Shortly after I had arrived, a big parcel from abroad came for the Professor. He opened it with much impressment, assumed, of course, and showed a great bundle of white flowers.

"These are for you, Miss Lucy," he said.

"For me? Oh, Dr. Van Helsing!"

"Yes, my dear, but not for you to play with. These are medicines." Here Lucy made a wry face. "Nay, but they are not to take in a decoction or in nauseous form, so you need not snub that so charming nose, or I shall point out to my friend Arthur what woes he may have to endure in seeing so much beauty that he so loves so much distort. Aha, my pretty miss, that bring the so nice nose all straight again. This is medicinal, but you do not know how. I put him in your window, I make pretty wreath, and hang him round your neck, so you sleep well. Oh, yes! They, like the lotus flower, make your trouble forgotten. It smell so like the waters of Lethe, and of that fountain of youth that the Conquistadores sought for in the Floridas, and find him all too late."

Whilst he was speaking, Lucy had been examining the flowers and smelling them. Now she threw them down saying, with half laughter, and half disgust,

"Oh, Professor, I believe you are only putting up a joke on me. Why, these flowers are only common garlic."

To my surprise, Van Helsing rose up and said with all his sternness, his iron jaw set and his bushy eyebrows meeting,

"No trifling with me! I never jest! There is grim purpose in what I do, and I warn you that you do not thwart me. Take care, for the sake of others if not for your own." Then seeing poor Lucy scared, as she might well be, he went on more gently, "Oh, little miss, my dear, do not fear me. I only do for your good, but there is much virtue to you in those so common flowers. See, I place them myself in your room. I make myself the wreath that you are to wear. But hush! No telling to others that make so inquisitive questions. We must obey, and silence is a part of obedience, and obedience is to bring you strong and well into loving arms that wait for you. Now sit still a while. Come with me, friend John, and you shall help me deck the room with my garlic, which is all the way from Haarlem, where my friend Vanderpool raise herb in his glass houses all the year. I had to telegraph yesterday, or they would not have been here."

We went into the room, taking the flowers with us. The Professor's actions were certainly odd and not to be found in any pharmacopeia that I ever heard of. First he fastened up the windows and latched them securely. Next, taking a handful of the flowers, he rubbed them all over the sashes, as though to ensure that every whiff of air that might get in would be laden with the garlic smell. Then with the wisp he rubbed all over the jamb of the door, above, below, and at each side, and round the fireplace in the same way. It all seemed grotesque to me, and presently I said, "Well, Professor, I know you always have a reason for what you do, but this certainly puzzles me. It is well we have no sceptic here, or he would say that you were working some spell to keep out an evil spirit."

"Perhaps I am!" he answered quietly as he began to make the wreath which Lucy was to wear round her neck.

We then waited whilst Lucy made her toilet for the night, and when she was in bed he came and himself fixed the wreath of garlic round her neck. The last words he said to her were,

"Take care you do not disturb it, and even if the room feel close, do not tonight open the window or the door."

"I promise," said Lucy. "And thank you both a thousand times for all your kindness to me! Oh, what have I done to be blessed with such friends?"

As we left the house in my fly, which was waiting, Van Helsing said, "Tonight I can sleep in peace, and sleep I want, two nights of travel, much reading in the day between, and much anxiety on the day to follow, and a night to sit up, without to wink. Tomorrow in the morning early you call for me, and we come together to see our pretty miss, so much more strong for my 'spell' which I have work. Ho, ho!"

He seemed so confident that I, remembering my own confidence two nights before and with the baneful result, felt awe and vague terror. It must have been my weakness that made me hesitate to tell it to my friend, but I felt it all the more, like unshed tears.

CHAPTER 11

LUCY WESTENRA'S DIARY

12 September.--How good they all are to me. I quite love that dear Dr. Van Helsing. I wonder why he was so anxious about these flowers. He positively frightened me, he was so fierce. And yet he must have been right, for I feel comfort from them already. Somehow, I do not dread being alone tonight, and I can go to sleep without fear. I shall not mind any flapping outside the window. Oh, the terrible struggle that I have had against sleep so often of late, the pain of sleeplessness, or the pain of the fear of sleep, and with such unknown horrors as it has for me! How blessed are some people, whose lives have no fears, no dreads, to whom sleep is a blessing that comes nightly, and brings nothing but sweet dreams. Well, here I am tonight, hoping for sleep, and lying like Ophelia in the play, with 'virgin crants and maiden strewments.' I never liked garlic before, but tonight it is delightful! There is peace in its smell. I feel sleep coming already. Goodnight, everybody.

DR. SEWARD'S DIARY

13 September.--Called at the Berkeley and found Van Helsing, as usual, up to time. The carriage ordered from the hotel was waiting. The Professor took his bag, which he always brings with him now.

Let all be put down exactly. Van Helsing and I arrived at Hillingham at eight o'clock. It was a lovely morning. The bright sunshine and all the fresh feeling of early autumn seemed like the completion of nature's annual work. The leaves were turning to all kinds of beautiful colours, but had not yet begun to drop from the trees. When we entered we met Mrs. Westenra coming out of the morning room. She is always an early riser. She greeted us warmly and said,

"You will be glad to know that Lucy is better. The dear child is still asleep. I looked into her room and saw her, but did not go in, lest I should disturb her." The Professor smiled, and looked quite jubilant. He rubbed his hands together, and said, "Aha! I thought I had diagnosed the case. My treatment is working."

To which she replied, "You must not take all the credit to yourself, doctor. Lucy's state this morning is due in part to me."

"How do you mean, ma'am?" asked the Professor.

"Well, I was anxious about the dear child in the night, and went into her room. She was sleeping soundly, so soundly that even my coming did not wake her. But the room was awfully stuffy. There were a lot of those horrible, strong-smelling flowers about everywhere, and she had actually a bunch of them round her neck. I feared that the heavy odour would be too much for the dear child in her weak state, so I took them all away and opened a bit of the window to let in a little fresh air. You will be pleased with her, I am sure."

She moved off into her boudoir, where she usually breakfasted early. As she had spoken, I watched the Professor's face, and saw it turn ashen gray. He had been able to retain his self-command whilst the poor lady was present, for he knew her state and how mischievous a shock would be. He actually smiled on her as he held open the door for her to pass into her room. But the instant she had disappeared he pulled me, suddenly and forcibly, into the dining room and closed the door.

Then, for the first time in my life, I saw Van Helsing break down. He raised his hands over his head in a sort of mute despair, and then beat his palms together in a helpless way. Finally he sat down on a chair, and putting his hands before his face, began to sob, with loud, dry sobs that seemed to come from the very racking of his heart.

Then he raised his arms again, as though appealing to the whole universe. "God! God! God!" he said. "What have we done, what has this poor thing done, that we are so sore beset? Is there fate amongst us still, send down from the pagan world of old, that such things must be, and in such way? This poor mother, all unknowing, and all for the best as she think, does such thing as lose her daughter body and soul, and we must not tell her, we must not even warn her, or she die, then both die. Oh, how we are beset! How are all the powers of the devils against us!"

Suddenly he jumped to his feet. "Come," he said, "come, we must see and act. Devils or no devils, or all the devils at once, it matters not. We must fight him all the same." He went to the hall door for his bag, and together we went up to Lucy's room.

Once again I drew up the blind, whilst Van Helsing went towards the bed. This time he did not start as he looked on the poor face with the same awful, waxen pallor as before. He wore a look of stern sadness and infinite pity.

"As I expected," he murmured, with that hissing inspiration of his which meant so much. Without a word he went and locked the door, and then began to set out on the little table the instruments for yet another operation of transfusion of blood. I had long ago recognized the necessity, and begun to take off my coat, but he stopped me with a warning hand. "No!" he said. "Today you must operate. I shall provide. You are weakened already." As he spoke he took off his coat and rolled up his shirtsleeve.

Again the operation. Again the narcotic. Again some return of colour to the ashy cheeks, and the regular breathing of healthy sleep. This time I watched whilst Van Helsing recruited himself and rested.

Presently he took an opportunity of telling Mrs. Westenra that she must not remove anything from Lucy's room without consulting him. That the flowers were of medicinal value, and that the breathing of their odour was a part of the system of cure. Then he took over the care of the case himself, saying that he would watch this night and the next, and would send me word when to come.

After another hour Lucy waked from her sleep, fresh and bright and seemingly not much the worse for her terrible ordeal.

What does it all mean? I am beginning to wonder if my long habit of life amongst the insane is beginning to tell upon my own brain.

LUCY WESTENRA'S DIARY

17 September.--Four days and nights of peace. I am getting so strong again that I hardly know myself. It is as if I had passed through some long nightmare, and had just awakened to see the beautiful sunshine and feel the fresh air of the morning around me. I have a dim half remembrance of long, anxious times of waiting and fearing, darkness in which there was not even the pain of hope to make present distress more poignant. And then long spells of oblivion, and the rising back to life as a diver coming up through a great press of water. Since, however, Dr. Van Helsing has been with me, all this bad dreaming seems to have passed away. The noises that used to frighten me out of my wits, the flapping against the windows, the distant voices which seemed so close to me, the harsh sounds that came from I know not where and commanded me to do I know not what, have all ceased. I go to bed now without any fear of sleep. I do not even try to keep awake. I have grown quite fond of the garlic, and a boxful arrives for me every day from Haarlem. Tonight Dr. Van Helsing is going away, as he has to be for a day in Amsterdam. But I need not be watched. I am well enough to be left alone.

Thank God for Mother's sake, and dear Arthur's, and for all our friends who have been so kind! I shall not even feel the change, for last night Dr. Van Helsing slept in his chair a lot of the time. I found him asleep twice when I awoke. But I did not fear to go to sleep again, although the boughs or bats or something flapped almost angrily against the window panes.

THE PALL MALL GAZETTE 18 September.

THE ESCAPED WOLF PERILOUS ADVENTURE OF OUR INTERVIEWER

INTERVIEW WITH THE KEEPER IN THE ZOOLOGICAL GARDENS

After many inquiries and almost as many refusals, and perpetually using the words 'PALL MALL GAZETTE' as a sort of talisman, I managed to find the keeper of the section of the Zoological Gardens in which the wolf department is included. Thomas Bilder lives in one of the cottages in the enclosure behind the elephant house, and was just sitting down to his tea when I found him. Thomas and his wife are hospitable folk, elderly, and without children, and if the specimen I enjoyed of their hospitality be of the average kind, their lives must be pretty comfortable. The keeper would not enter on what he called business until the supper was over, and we were all satisfied. Then when the table was cleared, and he had lit his pipe, he said,

"Now, Sir, you can go on and arsk me what you want. You'll excoose me refoosin' to talk of perfeshunal subjucts afore meals. I gives the wolves and the jackals and the hyenas in all our section their tea afore I begins to arsk them questions."

"How do you mean, ask them questions?" I queried, wishful to get him into a talkative humor.

"'Ittin' of them over the 'ead with a pole is one way. Scratchin' of their ears in another, when gents as is flush wants a bit of a show-orf to their gals. I don't so much mind the fust, the 'ittin of the pole part afore I chucks in their dinner, but I waits till they've 'ad their sherry and kawffee, so to speak, afore I tries on with the ear scratchin'. Mind you," he added philosophically, "there's a deal of the same nature in us as in them theer animiles. Here's you a-comin' and arskin' of me questions about my business, and I that grump-like that only for your bloomin' 'arf-quid I'd 'a' seen you blowed fust 'fore I'd answer. Not even when you arsked me sarcastic like if I'd like you to arsk the Superintendent if you might arsk me questions. Without offence did I tell yer to go to 'ell?"

"You did."

"An' when you said you'd report me for usin' obscene language that was 'ittin' me over the 'ead. But the 'arf-quid made that all right. I weren't a-goin' to fight, so I waited for the food, and did with my 'owl as the wolves and lions and tigers does. But, lor' love yer 'art, now that the old 'ooman has stuck a chunk of her tea-cake in me, an' rinsed me out with her bloomin' old teapot, and I've lit hup, you may scratch my ears for all you're worth, and won't even get a growl out of me. Drive along with your questions. I know what yer a-comin' at, that 'ere escaped wolf."

"Exactly. I want you to give me your view of it. Just tell me how it happened, and when I know the facts I'll get you to say what you consider was the cause of it, and how you think the whole affair will end."

"All right, guv'nor. This 'ere is about the 'ole story. That 'ere wolf what we called Bersicker was one of three gray ones that came from Norway to Jamrach's, which we bought off him four years ago. He was a nice well-behaved wolf, that never gave no trouble to talk of. I'm more surprised at 'im for wantin' to get out nor any other animile in the place. But, there, you can't trust wolves no more nor women."

"Don't you mind him, Sir!" broke in Mrs. Tom, with a cheery laugh. "'E's got mindin' the animiles so long that blest if he ain't like a old wolf 'isself! But there ain't no 'arm in 'im."

"Well, Sir, it was about two hours after feedin' yesterday when I first hear my disturbance. I was makin' up a litter in the monkey house for a young puma which is ill. But when I heard the yelpin' and 'owlin' I kem away straight. There was Bersicker a-tearin' like a mad thing at the bars as if he wanted to get out. There wasn't much people about that day, and close at hand was only one man, a tall, thin chap, with a 'ook nose and a pointed beard, with a few white hairs runnin' through it. He had a 'ard, cold look and red eyes, and I took a sort of mislike to him, for it seemed as if it was 'im as they was hirritated at. He 'ad white kid gloves on 'is 'ands, and he pointed out the animiles to me and says, 'Keeper, these wolves seem upset at something.'

"'Maybe it's you,' says I, for I did not like the airs as he give 'isself. He didn't get angry, as I 'oped he would, but he smiled a kind of insolent smile, with a mouth full of white, sharp teeth. 'Oh no, they wouldn't like me,' 'e says.

"'Ow yes, they would,' says I, a-imitatin' of him. 'They always like a bone or two to clean their teeth on about tea time, which you 'as a bagful.'

"Well, it was a odd thing, but when the animiles see us a-talkin' they lay down, and when I went over to Bersicker he let me stroke his ears same as ever. That there man kem over, and blessed but if he didn't put in his hand and stroke the old wolf's ears too!

"'Tyke care,' says I. 'Bersicker is quick.'

"'Never mind,' he says. I'm used to 'em!'

"'Are you in the business yourself?' I says, tyking off my 'at, for a man what trades in wolves, anceterer, is a good friend to keepers.

"'Nom,' says he, 'not exactly in the business, but I 'ave made pets of several.' And with that he lifts his 'at as perlite as a lord, and walks away. Old Bersicker kep' a-lookin' arter 'im till 'e was out of sight, and then went and lay down in a corner and wouldn't come hout the 'ole hevening. Well, larst night, so soon as the moon was hup, the wolves here all began a-'owling. There warn't nothing for them to 'owl at. There warn't no one near, except some one that was evidently a-callin' a dog somewheres out back of the gardings in the Park road. Once or twice I went out to see that all was right, and it was, and then the 'owling stopped. Just before twelve o'clock I just took a look round afore turnin' in, an', bust me, but when I kem opposite to old Bersicker's cage I see the rails broken and twisted about and the cage empty. And that's all I know for certing."

"Did any one else see anything?"

"One of our gard'ners was a-comin' 'ome about that time from a 'armony, when he sees a big gray dog comin' out through the garding 'edges. At least, so he says, but I don't give much for it myself, for if he did 'e never said a word about it to his missis when 'e got 'ome, and it was only after the escape of the wolf was made known, and we had been up all night a-huntin' of the Park for Bersicker, that he remembered seein' anything. My own belief was that the 'armony 'ad got into his 'ead."

"Now, Mr. Bilder, can you account in any way for the escape of the wolf?"

"Well, Sir," he said, with a suspicious sort of modesty, "I think I can, but I don't know as 'ow you'd be satisfied with the theory."

"Certainly I shall. If a man like you, who knows the animals from experience, can't hazard a good guess at any rate, who is even to try?"

"Well then, Sir, I accounts for it this way. It seems to me that 'ere wolf escaped--simply because he wanted to get out."

From the hearty way that both Thomas and his wife laughed at the joke I could see that it had done service before, and that the whole explanation was simply an elaborate sell. I couldn't cope in badinage with the worthy Thomas, but I thought I knew a surer way to his heart, so I said, "Now, Mr. Bilder, we'll consider that first half-sovereign worked off, and this brother of his is waiting to be claimed when you've told me what you think will happen."

"Right y'are, Sir," he said briskly. "Ye'll excoose me, I know, for a-chaffin' of ye, but the old woman here winked at me, which was as much as telling me to go on."

"Well, I never!" said the old lady.

"My opinion is this: that 'ere wolf is a'idin' of, somewheres. The gard'ner wot didn't remember said he was a-gallopin' northward faster than a horse could go, but I don't believe him, for, yer see, Sir, wolves don't gallop no more nor dogs does, they not bein' built that way. Wolves is fine things in a storybook, and I dessay when they gets in packs and does be chivyin' somethin' that's more afeared than they is they can make a devil of a noise and chop it up, whatever it is. But, Lor' bless you, in real life a wolf is only a low creature, not half so clever or bold as a good dog, and not half a quarter so much fight in 'im. This one ain't been used to fightin' or even to providin' for hisself, and more like he's somewhere round the Park a'hidin' an' a'shiverin' of, and if he thinks at all, wonderin' where he is to get his breakfast from. Or maybe he's got down some area and is in a coal cellar. My eye, won't some cook get a rum start when she sees his green eyes a-shinin' at her out of the dark! If he can't get food he's bound to look for it, and mayhap he may chance to light on a butcher's shop in time. If he doesn't, and some nursemaid goes out walkin' or orf with a soldier, leavin' of the hinfant in the perambulator--well, then I shouldn't be surprised if the census is one babby the less. That's all."

I was handing him the half-sovereign, when something came bobbing up against the window, and Mr. Bilder's face doubled its natural length with surprise.

"God bless me!" he said. "If there ain't old Bersicker come back by 'isself!"

He went to the door and opened it, a most unnecessary proceeding it seemed to me. I have always thought that a wild animal never looks so well as when some obstacle of pronounced durability is between us. A personal experience has intensified rather than diminished that idea.

After all, however, there is nothing like custom, for neither Bilder nor his wife thought any more of the wolf than I should of a dog. The animal itself was a peaceful and well-behaved as that father of all picture-wolves, Red Riding Hood's quondam friend, whilst moving her confidence in masquerade.

The whole scene was a unutterable mixture of comedy and pathos. The wicked wolf that for a half a day had paralyzed London and set all the children in town shivering in their shoes, was there in a sort of penitent mood, and was received and petted like a sort of vulpine prodigal son. Old Bilder examined him all over with most tender solicitude, and when he had finished with his penitent said,

"There, I knew the poor old chap would get into some kind of trouble. Didn't I say it all along? Here's his head all cut and full of broken glass. 'E's been a-gettin' over some bloomin' wall or other. It's a shyme that people are allowed to top their walls with broken bottles. This 'ere's what comes of it. Come along, Bersicker."

He took the wolf and locked him up in a cage, with a piece of meat that satisfied, in quantity at any rate, the elementary conditions of the fatted calf, and went off to report.

I came off too, to report the only exclusive information that is given today regarding the strange escapade at the Zoo.

DR. SEWARD'S DIARY

17 September.--I was engaged after dinner in my study posting up my books, which, through press of other work and the many visits to Lucy, had fallen sadly into arrear. Suddenly the door was burst open, and in rushed my patient, with his face distorted with passion. I was thunderstruck, for such a thing as a patient getting of his own accord into the Superintendent's study is almost unknown.

Without an instant's notice he made straight at me. He had a dinner knife in his hand, and as I saw he was dangerous, I tried to keep the table between us. He was too quick and too strong for me, however, for before I could get my balance he had struck at me and cut my left wrist rather severely.

Before he could strike again, however, I got in my right hand and he was sprawling on his back on the floor. My wrist bled freely, and quite a little pool trickled on to the carpet. I saw that my friend was not intent on further effort, and occupied myself binding up my wrist, keeping a wary eye on the prostrate figure all the time. When the attendants rushed in, and we turned our attention to him, his employment positively sickened me. He was lying on his belly on the floor licking up, like a dog, the blood which had fallen from my wounded wrist. He was easily secured, and to my surprise, went with the attendants quite placidly, simply repeating over and over again, "The blood is the life! The blood is the life!"

I cannot afford to lose blood just at present. I have lost too much of late for my physical good, and then the prolonged strain of Lucy's illness and its horrible phases is telling on me. I am over excited and weary, and I need rest, rest, rest. Happily Van Helsing has not summoned me, so I need not forego my sleep. Tonight I could not well do without it.

TELEGRAM, VAN HELSING, ANTWERP, TO SEWARD, CARFAX

(Sent to Carfax, Sussex, as no county given, delivered late by twenty-two hours.)

17 September.--Do not fail to be at Hilllingham tonight. If not watching all the time, frequently visit and see that flowers are as placed, very important, do not fail. Shall be with you as soon as possible after arrival.

DR. SEWARD'S DIARY

18 September.--Just off train to London. The arrival of Van Helsing's telegram filled me with dismay. A whole night lost, and I know by bitter experience what may happen in a night. Of course it is possible that all may be well, but what may have happened? Surely there is some horrible doom hanging over us that every possible accident should thwart us in all we try to do. I shall take this cylinder with me, and then I can complete my entry on Lucy's phonograph.

MEMORANDUM LEFT BY LUCY WESTENRA

17 September, Night.--I write this and leave it to be seen, so that no one may by any chance get into trouble through me. This is an exact record of what took place tonight. I feel I am dying of weakness, and have barely strength to write, but it must be done if I die in the doing.

I went to bed as usual, taking care that the flowers were placed as Dr. Van Helsing directed, and soon fell asleep.

I was waked by the flapping at the window, which had begun after that sleep-walking on the cliff at Whitby when Mina saved me, and which now I know so well. I was not afraid, but I did wish that Dr. Seward was in the next room, as Dr. Van Helsing said he would be, so that I might have called him. I tried to sleep, but I could not. Then there came to me the old fear of sleep, and I determined to keep awake. Perversely sleep would try to come then when I did not want it. So, as I feared to be alone, I opened my door and called out, "Is there anybody there?" There was no answer. I was afraid to wake mother, and so closed my door again. Then outside in the shrubbery I heard a sort of howl like a dog's, but more fierce and deeper. I went to the window and looked out, but could see nothing, except a big bat, which had evidently been buffeting its wings against the window. So I went back to bed again, but determined not to go to sleep. Presently the door opened, and mother looked in. Seeing by my moving that I was not asleep, she came in and sat by me. She said to me even more sweetly and softly than her wont,

"I was uneasy about you, darling, and came in to see that you were all right."

I feared she might catch cold sitting there, and asked her to come in and sleep with me, so she came into bed, and lay down beside me. She did not take off her dressing gown, for she said she would only stay a while and then go back to her own bed. As she lay there in my arms, and I in hers the flapping and buffeting came to the window again. She was startled and a little frightened, and cried out, "What is that?"

I tried to pacify her, and at last succeeded, and she lay quiet. But I could hear her poor dear heart still beating terribly. After a while there was the howl again out in the shrubbery, and shortly after there was a crash at the window, and a lot of broken glass was hurled on the floor. The window blind blew back with the wind that rushed in, and in the aperture of the broken panes there was the head of a great, gaunt gray wolf.

Mother cried out in a fright, and struggled up into a sitting posture, and clutched wildly at anything that would help her. Amongst other things, she clutched the wreath of flowers that Dr. Van Helsing insisted on my wearing round my neck, and tore it away from me. For a second or two she sat up, pointing at the wolf, and there was a strange and horrible gurgling in her throat. Then she fell over, as if struck with lightning, and her head hit my forehead and made me dizzy for a moment or two.

The room and all round seemed to spin round. I kept my eyes fixed on the window, but the wolf drew his head back, and a whole myriad of little specks seems to come blowing in through the broken window, and wheeling and circling round like the pillar of dust that travellers describe when there is a simoon in the desert. I tried to stir, but there was some spell upon me, and dear Mother's poor body, which seemed to grow cold already, for her dear heart had ceased to beat, weighed me down, and I remembered no more for a while.

The time did not seem long, but very, very awful, till I recovered consciousness again. Somewhere near, a passing bell was tolling. The dogs all round the neighbourhood were howling, and in our shrubbery, seemingly just outside, a nightingale was singing. I was dazed and stupid with pain and terror and weakness, but the sound of the nightingale seemed like the voice of my dead mother come back to comfort me. The sounds seemed to have awakened the maids, too, for I could hear their bare feet pattering outside my door. I called to them, and they came in, and when they saw what had happened, and what it was that lay over me on the bed, they screamed out. The wind rushed in through the broken window, and the door slammed to. They lifted off the body of my dear mother, and laid her, covered up with a sheet, on the bed after I had got up. They were all so frightened and nervous that I directed them to go to the dining room and each have a glass of wine. The door flew open for an instant and closed again. The maids shrieked, and then went in a body to the dining room, and I laid what flowers I had on my dear mother's breast. When they were there I remembered what Dr. Van Helsing had told me, but I didn't like to remove them, and besides, I would have some of the servants to sit up with me now. I was surprised that the maids did not come back. I called them, but got no answer, so I went to the dining room to look for them.

My heart sank when I saw what had happened. They all four lay helpless on the floor, breathing heavily. The decanter of sherry was on the table half full, but there was a queer, acrid smell about. I was suspicious, and examined the decanter. It smelt of laudanum, and looking on the sideboard, I found that the bottle which Mother's doctor uses for her--oh! did use--was empty. What am I to do? What am I to do? I am back in the room with Mother. I cannot leave her, and I am alone, save for the sleeping servants, whom some one has drugged. Alone with the dead! I dare not go out, for I can hear the low howl of the wolf through the broken window.

The air seems full of specks, floating and circling in the draught from the window, and the lights burn blue and dim. What am I to do? God shield me from harm this night! I shall hide this paper in my breast, where they shall find it when they come to lay me out. My dear mother gone! It is time that I go too. Goodbye, dear Arthur, if I should not survive this night. God keep you, dear, and God help me!

CHAPTER 12

DR. SEWARD'S DIARY

18 September.--I drove at once to Hillingham and arrived early. Keeping my cab at the gate, I went up the avenue alone. I knocked gently and rang as quietly as possible, for I feared to disturb Lucy or her mother, and hoped to only bring a servant to the door. After a while, finding no response, I knocked and rang again, still no answer. I cursed the laziness of the servants that they should lie abed at such an hour, for it was now ten o'clock, and so rang and knocked again, but more impatiently, but still without response. Hitherto I had blamed only the servants, but now a terrible fear began to assail me. Was this desolation but another link in the chain of doom which seemed drawing tight round us? Was it indeed a house of death to which I had come, too late? I know that minutes, even seconds of delay, might mean hours of danger to Lucy, if she had had again one of those frightful relapses, and I went round the house to try if I could find by chance an entry anywhere.

I could find no means of ingress. Every window and door was fastened and locked, and I returned baffled to the porch. As I did so, I heard the rapid pit-pat of a swiftly driven horse's feet. They stopped at the gate, and a few seconds later I met Van Helsing running up the avenue. When he saw me, he gasped out, "Then it was you, and just arrived. How is she? Are we too late? Did you not get my telegram?"

I answered as quickly and coherently as I could that I had only got his telegram early in the morning, and had not a minute in coming here, and that I could not make any one in the house hear me. He paused and raised his hat as he said solemnly, "Then I fear we are too late. God's will be done!"

With his usual recuperative energy, he went on, "Come. If there be no way open to get in, we must make one. Time is all in all to us now."

We went round to the back of the house, where there was a kitchen window. The Professor took a small surgical saw from his case, and handing it to me, pointed to the iron bars which guarded the window. I attacked them at once and had very soon cut through three of them. Then with a long, thin knife we pushed back the fastening of the sashes and opened the window. I helped the Professor in, and followed him. There was no one in the kitchen or in the servants' rooms, which were close at hand. We tried all the rooms as we went along, and in the dining room, dimly lit by rays of light through the shutters, found four servant women lying on the floor. There was no need to think them dead, for their stertorous breathing and the acrid smell of laudanum in the room left no doubt as to their condition.

Van Helsing and I looked at each other, and as we moved away he said, "We can attend to them later." Then we ascended to Lucy's room. For an instant or two we paused at the door to listen, but there was no sound that we could hear. With white faces and trembling hands, we opened the door gently, and entered the room.

How shall I describe what we saw? On the bed lay two women, Lucy and her mother. The latter lay farthest in, and she was covered with a white sheet, the edge of which had been blown back by the drought through the broken window, showing the drawn, white, face, with a look of terror fixed upon it. By her side lay Lucy, with face white and still more drawn. The flowers which had been round her neck we found upon her mother's bosom, and her throat was bare, showing the two little wounds which we had noticed before, but looking horribly white and mangled. Without a word the Professor bent over the bed, his head almost touching poor Lucy's breast. Then he gave a quick turn of his head, as of one who listens, and leaping to his feet, he cried out to me, "It is not yet too late! Quick! Quick! Bring the brandy!"

I flew downstairs and returned with it, taking care to smell and taste it, lest it, too, were drugged like the decanter of sherry which I found on the table. The maids were still breathing, but more restlessly, and I fancied that the narcotic was wearing off. I did not stay to make sure, but returned to Van Helsing. He rubbed the brandy, as on another occasion, on her lips and gums and on her wrists and the palms of her hands. He said to me, "I can do this, all that can be at the present. You go wake those maids. Flick them in the face with a wet towel, and flick them hard. Make them get heat and fire and a warm bath. This poor soul is nearly as cold as that beside her. She will need be heated before we can do anything more."

I went at once, and found little difficulty in waking three of the women. The fourth was only a young girl, and the drug had evidently affected her more strongly so I lifted her on the sofa and let her sleep.

The others were dazed at first, but as remembrance came back to them they cried and sobbed in a hysterical manner. I was stern with them, however, and would not let them talk. I told them that one life was bad enough to lose, and if they delayed they would sacrifice Miss Lucy. So, sobbing and crying they went about their way, half clad as they were, and prepared fire and water. Fortunately, the kitchen and boiler fires were still alive, and there was no lack of hot water. We got a bath and carried Lucy out as she was and placed her in it. Whilst we were busy chafing her limbs there was a knock at the hall door. One of the maids ran off, hurried on some more clothes, and opened it. Then she returned and whispered to us that there was a gentleman who had come with a message from Mr. Holmwood. I bade her simply tell him that he must wait, for we could see no one now. She went away with the message, and, engrossed with our work, I clean forgot all about him.

I never saw in all my experience the Professor work in such deadly earnest. I knew, as he knew, that it was a stand-up fight with death, and in a pause told him so. He answered me in a way that I did not understand, but with the sternest look that his face could wear.

"If that were all, I would stop here where we are now, and let her fade away into peace, for I see no light in life over her horizon." He went on with his work with, if possible, renewed and more frenzied vigour.

Presently we both began to be conscious that the heat was beginning to be of some effect. Lucy's heart beat a trifle more audibly to the stethoscope, and her lungs had a perceptible movement. Van Helsing's face almost beamed, and as we lifted her from the bath and rolled her in a hot sheet to dry her he said to me, "The first gain is ours! Check to the King!"

We took Lucy into another room, which had by now been prepared, and laid her in bed and forced a few drops of brandy down her throat. I noticed that Van Helsing tied a soft silk handkerchief round her throat. She was still unconscious, and was quite as bad as, if not worse than, we had ever seen her.

Van Helsing called in one of the women, and told her to stay with her and not to take her eyes off her till we returned, and then beckoned me out of the room.

"We must consult as to what is to be done," he said as we descended the stairs. In the hall he opened the dining room door, and we passed in, he closing the door carefully behind him. The shutters had been opened, but the blinds were already down, with that obedience to the etiquette of death which the British woman of the lower classes always rigidly observes. The room was, therefore, dimly dark. It was, however, light enough for our purposes. Van Helsing's sternness was somewhat relieved by a look of perplexity. He was evidently torturing his mind about something, so I waited for an instant, and he spoke.

"What are we to do now? Where are we to turn for help? We must have another transfusion of blood, and that soon, or that poor girl's life won't be worth an hour's purchase. You are exhausted already. I am exhausted too. I fear to trust those women, even if they would have courage to submit. What are we to do for some one who will open his veins for her?"

"What's the matter with me, anyhow?"

The voice came from the sofa across the room, and its tones brought relief and joy to my heart, for they were those of Quincey Morris.

Van Helsing started angrily at the first sound, but his face softened and a glad look came into his eyes as I cried out, "Quincey Morris!" and rushed towards him with outstretched hands.

"What brought you here?" I cried as our hands met.

"I guess Art is the cause."

He handed me a telegram.--'Have not heard from Seward for three days, and am terribly anxious. Cannot leave. Father still in same condition. Send me word how Lucy is. Do not delay.--Holmwood.'

"I think I came just in the nick of time. You know you have only to tell me what to do."

Van Helsing strode forward, and took his hand, looking him straight in the eyes as he said, "A brave man's blood is the best thing on this earth when a woman is in trouble. You're a man and no mistake. Well, the devil may work against us for all he's worth, but God sends us men when we want them."

Once again we went through that ghastly operation. I have not the heart to go through with the details. Lucy had got a terrible shock and it told on her more than before, for though plenty of blood went into her veins, her body did not respond to the treatment as well as on the other occasions. Her struggle back into life was something frightful to see and hear. However, the action of both heart and lungs improved, and Van Helsing made a sub-cutaneous injection of morphia, as before, and with good effect. Her faint became a profound slumber. The Professor watched whilst I went downstairs with Quincey Morris, and sent one of the maids to pay off one of the cabmen who were waiting.

I left Quincey lying down after having a glass of wine, and told the cook to get ready a good breakfast. Then a thought struck me, and I went back to the room where Lucy now was. When I came softly in, I found Van Helsing with a sheet or two of note paper in his hand. He had evidently read it, and was thinking it over as he sat with his hand to his brow. There was a look of grim satisfaction in his face, as of one who has had a doubt solved. He handed me the paper saying only, "It dropped from Lucy's breast when we carried her to the bath."

When I had read it, I stood looking at the Professor, and after a pause asked him, "In God's name, what does it all mean? Was she, or is she, mad, or what sort of horrible danger is it?" I was so bewildered that I did not know what to say more. Van Helsing put out his hand and took the paper, saying,

"Do not trouble about it now. Forget it for the present. You shall know and understand it all in good time, but it will be later. And now what is it that you came to me to say?" This brought me back to fact, and I was all myself again.

"I came to speak about the certificate of death. If we do not act properly and wisely, there may be an inquest, and that paper would have to be produced. I am in hopes that we need have no inquest, for if we had it would surely kill poor Lucy, if nothing else did. I know, and you know, and the other doctor who attended her knows, that Mrs. Westenra had disease of the heart, and we can certify that she died of it. Let us fill up the certificate at once, and I shall take it myself to the registrar and go on to the undertaker."

"Good, oh my friend John! Well thought of! Truly Miss Lucy, if she be sad in the foes that beset her, is at least happy in the friends that love her. One, two, three, all open their veins for her, besides one old man. Ah, yes, I know, friend John. I am not blind! I love you all the more for it! Now go."

In the hall I met Quincey Morris, with a telegram for Arthur telling him that Mrs. Westenra was dead, that Lucy also had been ill, but was now going on better, and that Van Helsing and I were with her. I told him where I was going, and he hurried me out, but as I was going said,

"When you come back, Jack, may I have two words with you all to ourselves?" I nodded in reply and went out. I found no difficulty about the registration, and arranged with the local undertaker to come up in the evening to measure for the coffin and to make arrangements.

When I got back Quincey was waiting for me. I told him I would see him as soon as I knew about Lucy, and went up to her room. She was still sleeping, and the Professor seemingly had not moved from his seat at her side. From his putting his finger to his lips, I gathered that he expected her to wake before long and was afraid of forestalling nature. So I went down to Quincey and took him into the breakfast room, where the blinds were not drawn down, and which was a little more cheerful, or rather less cheerless, than the other rooms.

When we were alone, he said to me, "Jack Seward, I don't want to shove myself in anywhere where I've no right to be, but this is no ordinary case. You know I loved that girl and wanted to marry her, but although that's all past and gone, I can't help feeling anxious about her all the same. What is it that's wrong with her? The Dutchman, and a fine old fellow he is, I can see that, said that time you two came into the room, that you must have another transfusion of blood, and that both you and he were exhausted. Now I know well that you medical men speak in camera, and that a man must not expect to know what they consult about in private. But this is no common matter, and whatever it is, I have done my part. Is not that so?"

"That's so," I said, and he went on.

"I take it that both you and Van Helsing had done already what I did today. Is not that so?"

"That's so."

"And I guess Art was in it too. When I saw him four days ago down at his own place he looked queer. I have not seen anything pulled down so quick since I was on the Pampas and had a mare that I was fond of go to grass all in a night. One of those big bats that they call vampires had got at her in the night, and what with his gorge and the vein left open, there wasn't enough blood in her to let her stand up, and I had to put a bullet through her as she lay. Jack, if you may tell me without betraying confidence, Arthur was the first, is not that so?"

As he spoke the poor fellow looked terribly anxious. He was in a torture of suspense regarding the woman he loved, and his utter ignorance of the terrible mystery which seemed to surround her intensified his pain. His very heart was bleeding, and it took all the manhood of him, and there was a royal lot of it, too, to keep him from breaking down. I paused before answering, for I felt that I must not betray anything which the Professor wished kept secret, but already he knew so much, and guessed so much, that there could be no reason for not answering, so I answered in the same phrase.

"That's so."

"And how long has this been going on?"

"About ten days."

"Ten days! Then I guess, Jack Seward, that that poor pretty creature that we all love has had put into her veins within that time the blood of four strong men. Man alive, her whole body wouldn't hold it." Then coming close to me, he spoke in a fierce half-whisper. "What took it out?"

I shook my head. "That," I said, "is the crux. Van Helsing is simply frantic about it, and I am at my wits' end. I can't even hazard a guess. There has been a series of little circumstances which have thrown out all our calculations as to Lucy being properly watched. But these shall not occur again. Here we stay until all be well, or ill."

Quincey held out his hand. "Count me in," he said. "You and the Dutchman will tell me what to do, and I'll do it."

When she woke late in the afternoon, Lucy's first movement was to feel in her breast, and to my surprise, produced the paper which Van Helsing had given me to read. The careful Professor had replaced it where it had come from, lest on waking she should be alarmed. Her eyes then lit on Van Helsing and on me too, and gladdened. Then she looked round the room, and seeing where she was, shuddered. She gave a loud cry, and put her poor thin hands before her pale face.

We both understood what was meant, that she had realized to the full her mother's death. So we tried what we could to comfort her. Doubtless sympathy eased her somewhat, but she was very low in thought and spirit, and wept silently and weakly for a long time. We told her that either or both of us would now remain with her all the time, and that seemed to comfort her. Towards dusk she fell into a doze. Here a very odd thing occurred. Whilst still asleep she took the paper from her breast and tore it in two. Van Helsing stepped over and took the pieces from her. All the same, however, she went on with the action of tearing, as though the material were still in her hands. Finally she lifted her hands and opened them as though scattering the fragments. Van Helsing seemed surprised, and his brows gathered as if in thought, but he said nothing.

19 September.--All last night she slept fitfully, being always afraid to sleep, and something weaker when she woke from it. The Professor and I took in turns to watch, and we never left her for a moment unattended. Quincey Morris said nothing about his intention, but I knew that all night long he patrolled round and round the house.

When the day came, its searching light showed the ravages in poor Lucy's strength. She was hardly able to turn her head, and the little nourishment which she could take seemed to do her no good. At times she slept, and both Van Helsing and I noticed the difference in her, between sleeping and waking. Whilst asleep she looked stronger, although more haggard, and her breathing was softer. Her open mouth showed the pale gums drawn back from the teeth, which looked positively longer and sharper than usual. When she woke the softness of her eyes evidently changed the expression, for she looked her own self, although a dying one. In the afternoon she asked for Arthur, and we telegraphed for him. Quincey went off to meet him at the station.

When he arrived it was nearly six o'clock, and the sun was setting full and warm, and the red light streamed in through the window and gave more colour to the pale cheeks. When he saw her, Arthur was simply choking with emotion, and none of us could speak. In the hours that had passed, the fits of sleep, or the comatose condition that passed for it, had grown more frequent, so that the pauses when conversation was possible were shortened. Arthur's presence, however, seemed to act as a stimulant. She rallied a little, and spoke to him more brightly than she had done since we arrived. He too pulled himself together, and spoke as cheerily as he could, so that the best was made of everything.

It is now nearly one o'clock, and he and Van Helsing are sitting with her. I am to relieve them in a quarter of an hour, and I am entering this on Lucy's phonograph. Until six o'clock they are to try to rest. I fear that tomorrow will end our watching, for the shock has been too great. The poor child cannot rally. God help us all.

LETTER MINA HARKER TO LUCY WESTENRA

(Unopened by her)

17 September

My dearest Lucy,

"It seems an age since I heard from you, or indeed since I wrote. You will pardon me, I know, for all my faults when you have read all my budget of news. Well, I got my husband back all right. When we arrived at Exeter there was a carriage waiting for us, and in it, though he had an attack of gout, Mr. Hawkins. He took us to his house, where there were rooms for us all nice and comfortable, and we dined together. After dinner Mr. Hawkins said,

"'My dears, I want to drink your health and prosperity, and may every blessing attend you both. I know you both from children, and have, with love and pride, seen you grow up. Now I want you to make your home here with me. I have left to me neither chick nor child. All are gone, and in my will I have left you everything.' I cried, Lucy dear, as Jonathan and the old man clasped hands. Our evening was a very, very happy one.

"So here we are, installed in this beautiful old house, and from both my bedroom and the drawing room I can see the great elms of the cathedral close, with their great black stems standing out against the old yellow stone of the cathedral, and I can hear the rooks overhead cawing and cawing and chattering and chattering and gossiping all day, after the manner of rooks--and humans. I am busy, I need not tell you, arranging things and housekeeping. Jonathan and Mr. Hawkins are busy all day, for now that Jonathan is a partner, Mr. Hawkins wants to tell him all about the clients.

"How is your dear mother getting on? I wish I could run up to town for a day or two to see you, dear, but I dare not go yet, with so much on my shoulders, and Jonathan wants looking after still. He is beginning to put some flesh on his bones again, but he was terribly weakened by the long illness. Even now he sometimes starts out of his sleep in a sudden way and awakes all trembling until I can coax him back to his usual placidity. However, thank God, these occasions grow less frequent as the days go on, and they will in time pass away altogether, I trust. And now I have told you my news, let me ask yours. When are you to be married, and where, and who is to perform the ceremony, and what are you to wear, and is it to be a public or private wedding? Tell me all about it, dear, tell me all about everything, for there is nothing which interests you which will not be dear to me. Jonathan asks me to send his 'respectful duty', but I do not think that is good enough from the junior partner of the important firm Hawkins & Harker. And so, as you love me, and he loves me, and I love you with all the moods and tenses of the verb, I send you simply his 'love' instead. Goodbye, my dearest Lucy, and blessings on you.

"Yours,

"Mina Harker"

REPORT FROM PATRICK HENNESSEY, MD, MRCSLK, QCPI, ETC, ETC, TO JOHN SEWARD, MD

20 September

My dear Sir:

"In accordance with your wishes, I enclose report of the conditions of everything left in my charge. With regard to patient, Renfield, there is more to say. He has had another outbreak, which might have had a dreadful ending, but which, as it fortunately happened, was unattended with any unhappy results. This afternoon a carrier's cart with two men made a call at the empty house whose grounds abut on ours, the house to which, you will remember, the patient twice ran away. The men stopped at our gate to ask the porter their way, as they were strangers.

"I was myself looking out of the study window, having a smoke after dinner, and saw one of them come up to the house. As he passed the window of Renfield's room, the patient began to rate him from within, and called him all the foul names he could lay his tongue to. The man, who seemed a decent fellow enough, contented himself by telling him to 'shut up for a foul-mouthed beggar', whereon our man accused him of robbing him and wanting to murder him and said that he would hinder him if he were to swing for it. I opened the window and signed to the man not to notice, so he contented himself after looking the place over and making up his mind as to what kind of place he had got to by saying, 'Lor' bless yer, sir, I wouldn't mind what was said to me in a bloomin' madhouse. I pity ye and the guv'nor for havin' to live in the house with a wild beast like that.'

"Then he asked his way civilly enough, and I told him where the gate of the empty house was. He went away followed by threats and curses and revilings from our man. I went down to see if I could make out any cause for his anger, since he is usually such a well-behaved man, and except his violent fits nothing of the kind had ever occurred. I found him, to my astonishment, quite composed and most genial in his manner. I tried to get him to talk of the incident, but he blandly asked me questions as to what I meant, and led me to believe that he was completely oblivious of the affair. It was, I am sorry to say, however, only another instance of his cunning, for within half an hour I heard of him again. This time he had broken out through the window of his room, and was running down the avenue. I called to the attendants to follow me, and ran after him, for I feared he was intent on some mischief. My fear was justified when I saw the same cart which had passed before coming down the road, having on it some great wooden boxes. The men were wiping their foreheads, and were flushed in the face, as if with violent exercise. Before I could get up to him, the patient rushed at them, and pulling one of them off the cart, began to knock his head against the ground. If I had not seized him just at the moment, I believe he would have killed the man there and then. The other fellow jumped down and struck him over the head with the butt end of his heavy whip. It was a horrible blow, but he did not seem to mind it, but seized him also, and struggled with the three of us, pulling us to and fro as if we were kittens. You know I am no lightweight, and the others were both burly men. At first he was silent in his fighting, but as we began to master him, and the attendants were putting a strait waistcoat on him, he began to shout, 'I'll frustrate them! They shan't rob me! They shan't murder me by inches! I'll fight for my Lord and Master!' and all sorts of similar incoherent ravings. It was with very considerable difficulty that they got him back to the house and put him in the padded room. One of the attendants, Hardy, had a finger broken. However, I set it all right, and he is going on well.

"The two carriers were at first loud in their threats of actions for damages, and promised to rain all the penalties of the law on us. Their threats were, however, mingled with some sort of indirect apology for the defeat of the two of them by a feeble madman. They said that if it had not been for the way their strength had been spent in carrying and raising the heavy boxes to the cart they would have made short work of him. They gave as another reason for their defeat the extraordinary state of drouth to which they had been reduced by the dusty nature of their occupation and the reprehensible distance from the scene of their labors of any place of public entertainment. I quite understood their drift, and after a stiff glass of strong grog, or rather more of the same, and with each a sovereign in hand, they made light of the attack, and swore that they would encounter a worse madman any day for the pleasure of meeting so 'bloomin' good a bloke' as your correspondent. I took their names and addresses, in case they might be needed. They are as follows: Jack Smollet, of Dudding's Rents, King George's Road, Great Walworth, and Thomas Snelling, Peter Farley's Row, Guide Court, Bethnal Green. They are both in the employment of Harris & Sons, Moving and Shipment Company, Orange Master's Yard, Soho.

"I shall report to you any matter of interest occurring here, and shall wire you at once if there is anything of importance.

"Believe me, dear Sir,

"Yours faithfully,

"Patrick Hennessey."

LETTER, MINA HARKER TO LUCY WESTENRA (Unopened by her)

18 September

"My dearest Lucy,

"Such a sad blow has befallen us. Mr. Hawkins has died very suddenly. Some may not think it so sad for us, but we had both come to so love him that it really seems as though we had lost a father. I never knew either father or mother, so that the dear old man's death is a real blow to me. Jonathan is greatly distressed. It is not only that he feels sorrow, deep sorrow, for the dear, good man who has befriended him all his life, and now at the end has treated him like his own son and left him a fortune which to people of our modest bringing up is wealth beyond the dream of avarice, but Jonathan feels it on another account. He says the amount of responsibility which it puts upon him makes him nervous. He begins to doubt himself. I try to cheer him up, and my belief in him helps him to have a belief in himself. But it is here that the grave shock that he experienced tells upon him the most. Oh, it is too hard that a sweet, simple, noble, strong nature such as his, a nature which enabled him by our dear, good friend's aid to rise from clerk to master in a few years, should be so injured that the very essence of its strength is gone. Forgive me, dear, if I worry you with my troubles in the midst of your own happiness, but Lucy dear, I must tell someone, for the strain of keeping up a brave and cheerful appearance to Jonathan tries me, and I have no one here that I can confide in. I dread coming up to London, as we must do that day after tomorrow, for poor Mr. Hawkins left in his will that he was to be buried in the grave with his father. As there are no relations at all, Jonathan will have to be chief mourner. I shall try to run over to see you, dearest, if only for a few minutes. Forgive me for troubling you. With all blessings,

"Your loving

"Mina Harker"

DR. SEWARD'S DIARY

20 September.--Only resolution and habit can let me make an entry tonight. I am too miserable, too low spirited, too sick of the world and all in it, including life itself, that I would not care if I heard this moment the flapping of the wings of the angel of death. And he has been flapping those grim wings to some purpose of late, Lucy's mother and Arthur's father, and now... Let me get on with my work.

CHAPTER 12

I duly relieved Van Helsing in his watch over Lucy. We wanted Arthur to go to rest also, but he refused at first. It was only when I told him that we should want him to help us during the day, and that we must not all break down for want of rest, lest Lucy should suffer, that he agreed to go.

Van Helsing was very kind to him. "Come, my child," he said. "Come with me. You are sick and weak, and have had much sorrow and much mental pain, as well as that tax on your strength that we know of. You must not be alone, for to be alone is to be full of fears and alarms. Come to the drawing room, where there is a big fire, and there are two sofas. You shall lie on one, and I on the other, and our sympathy will be comfort to each other, even though we do not speak, and even if we sleep."

Arthur went off with him, casting back a longing look on Lucy's face, which lay in her pillow, almost whiter than the lawn. She lay quite still, and I looked around the room to see that all was as it should be. I could see that the Professor had carried out in this room, as in the other, his purpose of using the garlic. The whole of the window sashes reeked with it, and round Lucy's neck, over the silk handkerchief which Van Helsing made her keep on, was a rough chaplet of the same odorous flowers.

Lucy was breathing somewhat stertorously, and her face was at its worst, for the open mouth showed the pale gums. Her teeth, in the dim, uncertain light, seemed longer and sharper than they had been in the morning. In particular, by some trick of the light, the canine teeth looked longer and sharper than the rest.

I sat down beside her, and presently she moved uneasily. At the same moment there came a sort of dull flapping or buffeting at the window. I went over to it softly, and peeped out by the corner of the blind. There was a full moonlight, and I could see that the noise was made by a great bat, which wheeled around, doubtless attracted by the light, although so dim, and every now and again struck the window with its wings. When I came back to my seat, I found that Lucy had moved slightly, and had torn away the garlic flowers from her throat. I replaced them as well as I could, and sat watching her.

Presently she woke, and I gave her food, as Van Helsing had prescribed. She took but a little, and that languidly. There did not seem to be with her now the unconscious struggle for life and strength that had hitherto so marked her illness. It struck me as curious that the moment she became conscious she pressed the garlic flowers close to her. It was certainly odd that whenever she got into that lethargic state, with the stertorous breathing, she put the flowers from her, but that when she waked she clutched them close. There was no possibility of making any mistake about this, for in the long hours that followed, she had many spells of sleeping and waking and repeated both actions many times.

At six o'clock Van Helsing came to relieve me. Arthur had then fallen into a doze, and he mercifully let him sleep on. When he saw Lucy's face I could hear the hissing indraw of breath, and he said to me in a sharp whisper. "Draw up the blind. I want light!" Then he bent down, and, with his face almost touching Lucy's, examined her carefully. He removed the flowers and lifted the silk handkerchief from her throat. As he did so he started back and I could hear his ejaculation, "Mein Gott!" as it was smothered in his throat. I bent over and looked, too, and as I noticed some queer chill came over me. The wounds on the throat had absolutely disappeared.

For fully five minutes Van Helsing stood looking at her, with his face at its sternest. Then he turned to me and said calmly, "She is dying. It will not be long now. It will be much difference, mark me, whether she dies conscious or in her sleep. Wake that poor boy, and let him come and see the last. He trusts us, and we have promised him."

I went to the dining room and waked him. He was dazed for a moment, but when he saw the sunlight streaming in through the edges of the shutters he thought he was late, and expressed his fear. I assured him that Lucy was still asleep, but told him as gently as I could that both Van Helsing and I feared that the end was near. He covered his face with his hands, and slid down on his knees by the sofa, where he remained, perhaps a minute, with his head buried, praying, whilst his shoulders shook with grief. I took him by the hand and raised him up. "Come," I said, "my dear old fellow, summon all your fortitude. It will be best and easiest for her."

When we came into Lucy's room I could see that Van Helsing had, with his usual forethought, been putting matters straight and making everything look as pleasing as possible. He had even brushed Lucy's hair, so that it lay on the pillow in its usual sunny ripples. When we came into the room she opened her eyes, and seeing him, whispered softly, "Arthur! Oh, my love, I am so glad you have come!"

He was stooping to kiss her, when Van Helsing motioned him back. "No," he whispered, "not yet! Hold her hand, it will comfort her more."

So Arthur took her hand and knelt beside her, and she looked her best, with all the soft lines matching the angelic beauty of her eyes. Then gradually her eyes closed, and she sank to sleep. For a little bit her breast heaved softly, and her breath came and went like a tired child's.

And then insensibly there came the strange change which I had noticed in the night. Her breathing grew stertorous, the mouth opened, and the pale gums, drawn back, made the teeth look longer and sharper than ever. In a sort of sleep-waking, vague, unconscious way she opened her eyes, which were now dull and hard at once, and said in a soft, voluptuous voice, such as I had never heard from her lips, "Arthur! Oh, my love, I am so glad you have come! Kiss me!"

Arthur bent eagerly over to kiss her, but at that instant Van Helsing, who, like me, had been startled by her voice, swooped upon him, and catching him by the neck with both hands, dragged him back with a fury of strength which I never thought he could have possessed, and actually hurled him almost across the room.

"Not on your life!" he said, "not for your living soul and hers!" And he stood between them like a lion at bay.

Arthur was so taken aback that he did not for a moment know what to do or say, and before any impulse of violence could seize him he realized the place and the occasion, and stood silent, waiting.

I kept my eyes fixed on Lucy, as did Van Helsing, and we saw a spasm as of rage flit like a shadow over her face. The sharp teeth clamped together. Then her eyes closed, and she breathed heavily.

Very shortly after she opened her eyes in all their softness, and putting out her poor, pale, thin hand, took Van Helsing's great brown one, drawing it close to her, she kissed it. "My true friend," she said, in a faint voice, but with untellable pathos, "My true friend, and his! Oh, guard him, and give me peace!"

"I swear it!" he said solemnly, kneeling beside her and holding up his hand, as one who registers an oath. Then he turned to Arthur, and said to him, "Come, my child, take her hand in yours, and kiss her on the forehead, and only once."

CHAPTER 12

Their eyes met instead of their lips, and so they parted. Lucy's eyes closed, and Van Helsing, who had been watching closely, took Arthur's arm, and drew him away.

And then Lucy's breathing became stertorous again, and all at once it ceased.

"It is all over," said Van Helsing. "She is dead!"

I took Arthur by the arm, and led him away to the drawing room, where he sat down, and covered his face with his hands, sobbing in a way that nearly broke me down to see.

I went back to the room, and found Van Helsing looking at poor Lucy, and his face was sterner than ever. Some change had come over her body. Death had given back part of her beauty, for her brow and cheeks had recovered some of their flowing lines. Even the lips had lost their deadly pallor. It was as if the blood, no longer needed for the working of the heart, had gone to make the harshness of death as little rude as might be.

"We thought her dying whilst she slept, and sleeping when she died."

I stood beside Van Helsing, and said, "Ah well, poor girl, there is peace for her at last. It is the end!"

He turned to me, and said with grave solemnity, "Not so, alas! Not so. It is only the beginning!"

When I asked him what he meant, he only shook his head and answered, "We can do nothing as yet. Wait and see."

CHAPTER 13

DR. SEWARD'S DIARY--cont.

The funeral was arranged for the next succeeding day, so that Lucy and her mother might be buried together. I attended to all the ghastly formalities, and the urbane undertaker proved that his staff was afflicted, or blessed, with something of his own obsequious suavity. Even the woman who performed the last offices for the dead remarked to me, in a confidential, brother-professional way, when she had come out from the death chamber,

"She makes a very beautiful corpse, sir. It's quite a privilege to attend on her. It's not too much to say that she will do credit to our establishment!"

I noticed that Van Helsing never kept far away. This was possible from the disordered state of things in the household. There were no relatives at hand, and as Arthur had to be back the next day to attend at his father's funeral, we were unable to notify any one who should have been bidden. Under the circumstances, Van Helsing and I took it upon ourselves to examine papers, etc. He insisted upon looking over Lucy's papers himself. I asked him why, for I feared that he, being a foreigner, might not be quite aware of English legal requirements, and so might in ignorance make some unnecessary trouble.

He answered me, "I know, I know. You forget that I am a lawyer as well as a doctor. But this is not altogether for the law. You knew that, when you avoided the coroner. I have more than him to avoid. There may be papers more, such as this."

As he spoke he took from his pocket book the memorandum which had been in Lucy's breast, and which she had torn in her sleep.

"When you find anything of the solicitor who is for the late Mrs. Westenra, seal all her papers, and write him tonight. For me, I watch here in the room and in Miss Lucy's old room all night, and I myself search for what may be. It is not well that her very thoughts go into the hands of strangers."

I went on with my part of the work, and in another half hour had found the name and address of Mrs. Westenra's solicitor and had written to him. All the poor lady's papers were in order. Explicit directions regarding the place of burial were given. I had hardly sealed the letter, when, to my surprise, Van Helsing walked into the room, saying,

"Can I help you friend John? I am free, and if I may, my service is to you."

"Have you got what you looked for?" I asked.

To which he replied, "I did not look for any specific thing. I only hoped to find, and find I have, all that there was, only some letters and a few memoranda, and a diary new begun. But I have them here, and we shall for the present say nothing of them. I shall see that poor lad tomorrow evening, and, with his sanction, I shall use some."

When we had finished the work in hand, he said to me, "And now, friend John, I think we may to bed. We want sleep, both you and I, and rest to recuperate. Tomorrow we shall have much to do, but for the tonight there is no need of us. Alas!"

Before turning in we went to look at poor Lucy. The undertaker had certainly done his work well, for the room was turned into a small chapelle ardente. There was a wilderness of beautiful white flowers, and death was made as little repulsive as might be. The end of the winding sheet was laid over the face. When the Professor bent over and turned it gently back, we both started at the beauty before us. The tall wax candles showing a sufficient light to note it well. All Lucy's loveliness had come back to her in death, and the hours that had passed, instead of leaving traces of 'decay's effacing fingers', had but restored the beauty of life, till positively I could not believe my eyes that I was looking at a corpse.

The Professor looked sternly grave. He had not loved her as I had, and there was no need for tears in his eyes. He said to me, "Remain till I return," and left the room. He came back with a handful of wild garlic from the box waiting in the hall, but which had not been opened, and placed the flowers amongst the others on and around the bed. Then he took from his neck, inside his collar, a little gold crucifix, and placed it over the mouth. He restored the sheet to its place, and we came away.

I was undressing in my own room, when, with a premonitory tap at the door, he entered, and at once began to speak.

"Tomorrow I want you to bring me, before night, a set of post-mortem knives."

"Must we make an autopsy?" I asked.

"Yes and no. I want to operate, but not what you think. Let me tell you now, but not a word to another. I want to cut off her head and take out her heart. Ah! You a surgeon, and so shocked! You, whom I have seen with no tremble of hand or heart, do operations of life and death that make the rest shudder. Oh, but I must not forget, my dear friend John, that you loved her, and I have not forgotten it for is I that shall operate, and you must not help. I would like to do it tonight, but for Arthur I must not. He will be free after his father's funeral tomorrow, and he will want to see her, to see it. Then, when she is coffined ready for the next day, you and I shall come when all sleep. We shall unscrew the coffin lid, and shall do our operation, and then replace all, so that none know, save we alone."

"But why do it at all? The girl is dead. Why mutilate her poor body without need? And if there is no necessity for a post-mortem and nothing to gain by it, no good to her, to us, to science, to human knowledge, why do it? Without such it is monstrous."

For answer he put his hand on my shoulder, and said, with infinite tenderness, "Friend John, I pity your poor bleeding heart, and I love you the more because it does so bleed. If I could, I would take on myself the burden that you do bear. But there are things that you know not, but that you shall know, and bless me for knowing, though they are not pleasant things. John, my child, you have been my friend now many years, and yet did you ever know me to do any without good cause? I may err, I am but man, but I believe in all I do. Was it not for these causes that you send for me when the great trouble came? Yes! Were you not amazed, nay horrified, when I would not let Arthur kiss his love, though she was dying, and snatched him away by all my strength? Yes! And yet you saw how she thanked me, with her so beautiful dying eyes, her voice, too, so weak, and she kiss my rough old hand and bless me? Yes! And did you not hear me swear promise to her, that so she closed her eyes grateful? Yes!

"Well, I have good reason now for all I want to do. You have for many years trust me. You have believe me weeks past, when there be things so strange that you might have well doubt. Believe me yet a little, friend John. If you trust me not, then I must tell what I think, and that is not perhaps well. And if I work, as work I shall, no matter trust or no trust, without my friend trust in me, I work with heavy heart and feel oh so lonely when I want all help and courage that may be!" He paused a moment and went on solemnly, "Friend John, there are strange and terrible days before us. Let us not be two, but one, that so we work to a good end. Will you not have faith in me?"

I took his hand, and promised him. I held my door open as he went away, and watched him go to his room and close the door. As I stood without moving, I saw one of the maids pass silently along the passage, she had her back to me, so did not see me, and go into the room where Lucy lay. The sight touched me. Devotion is so rare, and we are so grateful to those who show it unasked to those we love. Here was a poor girl putting aside the terrors which she naturally had of death to go watch alone by the bier of the mistress whom she loved, so that the poor clay might not be lonely till laid to eternal rest.

I must have slept long and soundly, for it was broad daylight when Van Helsing waked me by coming into my room. He came over to my bedside and said, "You need not trouble about the knives. We shall not do it."

"Why not?" I asked. For his solemnity of the night before had greatly impressed me.

"Because," he said sternly, "it is too late, or too early. See!" Here he held up the little golden crucifix.

"This was stolen in the night."

"How stolen," I asked in wonder, "since you have it now?"

"Because I get it back from the worthless wretch who stole it, from the woman who robbed the dead and the living. Her punishment will surely come, but not through me. She knew not altogether what she did, and thus unknowing, she only stole. Now we must wait." He went away on the word, leaving me with a new mystery to think of, a new puzzle to grapple with.

The forenoon was a dreary time, but at noon the solicitor came, Mr. Marquand, of Wholeman, Sons, Marquand & Lidderdale. He was very genial and very appreciative of what we had done, and took off our hands all cares as to details. During lunch he told us that Mrs. Westenra had for some time expected sudden death from her heart, and had put her affairs in absolute order. He informed us that, with the exception of a certain entailed property of Lucy's father which now, in default of direct issue, went back to a distant branch of the family, the whole estate, real and personal, was left absolutely to Arthur Holmwood. When he had told us so much he went on,

"Frankly we did our best to prevent such a testamentary disposition, and pointed out certain contingencies that might leave her daughter either penniless or not so free as she should be to act regarding a matrimonial alliance. Indeed, we pressed the matter so far that we almost came into collision, for she asked us if we were or were not prepared to carry out her wishes. Of course, we had then no alternative but to accept. We were right in principle, and ninety-nine times out of a hundred we should have proved, by the logic of events, the accuracy of our judgment.

"Frankly, however, I must admit that in this case any other form of disposition would have rendered impossible the carrying out of her wishes. For by her predeceasing her daughter the latter would have come into possession of the property, and, even had she only survived her mother by five minutes, her property would, in case there were no will, and a will was a practical impossibility in such a case, have been treated at her decease as under intestacy. In which case Lord Godalming, though so dear a friend, would have had no claim in the world. And the inheritors, being remote, would not be likely to abandon their just rights, for sentimental reasons regarding an entire stranger. I assure you, my dear sirs, I am rejoiced at the result, perfectly rejoiced."

He was a good fellow, but his rejoicing at the one little part, in which he was officially interested, of so great a tragedy, was an object-lesson in the limitations of sympathetic understanding.

He did not remain long, but said he would look in later in the day and see Lord Godalming. His coming, however, had been a certain comfort to us, since it assured us that we should not have to dread hostile criticism as to any of our acts. Arthur was expected at five o'clock, so a little before that time we visited the death chamber. It was so in very truth, for now both mother and daughter lay in it. The undertaker, true to his craft, had made the best display he could of his goods, and there was a mortuary air about the place that lowered our spirits at once.

Van Helsing ordered the former arrangement to be adhered to, explaining that, as Lord Godalming was coming very soon, it would be less harrowing to his feelings to see all that was left of his fiancee quite alone.

The undertaker seemed shocked at his own stupidity and exerted himself to restore things to the condition in which we left them the night before, so that when Arthur came such shocks to his feelings as we could avoid were saved.

Poor fellow! He looked desperately sad and broken. Even his stalwart manhood seemed to have shrunk somewhat under the strain of his much-tried emotions. He had, I knew, been very genuinely and devotedly attached to his father, and to lose him, and at such a time, was a bitter blow to him. With me he was warm as ever, and to Van Helsing he was sweetly courteous. But I could not help seeing that there was some constraint with him. The professor noticed it too, and motioned me to bring him upstairs. I did so, and left him at the door of the room, as I felt he would like to be quite alone with her, but he took my arm and led me in, saying huskily,

"You loved her too, old fellow. She told me all about it, and there was no friend had a closer place in her heart than you. I don't know how to thank you for all you have done for her. I can't think yet..."

Here he suddenly broke down, and threw his arms round my shoulders and laid his head on my breast, crying, "Oh, Jack! Jack! What shall I do? The whole of life seems gone from me all at once, and there is nothing in the wide world for me to live for."

I comforted him as well as I could. In such cases men do not need much expression. A grip of the hand, the tightening of an arm over the shoulder, a sob in unison, are expressions of sympathy dear to a man's heart. I stood still and silent till his sobs died away, and then I said softly to him, "Come and look at her."

Together we moved over to the bed, and I lifted the lawn from her face. God! How beautiful she was. Every hour seemed to be enhancing her loveliness. It frightened and amazed me somewhat. And as for Arthur, he fell to trembling, and finally was shaken with doubt as with an ague. At last, after a long pause, he said to me in a faint whisper, "Jack, is she really dead?"

I assured him sadly that it was so, and went on to suggest, for I felt that such a horrible doubt should not have life for a moment longer than I could help, that it often happened that after death faces become softened and even resolved into their youthful beauty, that this was especially so when death had been preceded by any acute or prolonged suffering. I seemed to quite do away with any doubt, and after kneeling beside the couch for a while and looking at her lovingly and long, he turned aside. I told him that that must be goodbye, as the coffin had to be prepared, so he went back and took her dead hand in his and kissed it, and bent over and kissed her forehead. He came away, fondly looking back over his shoulder at her as he came.

I left him in the drawing room, and told Van Helsing that he had said goodbye, so the latter went to the kitchen to tell the undertaker's men to proceed with the preparations and to screw up the coffin. When he came out of the room again I told him of Arthur's question, and he replied, "I am not surprised. Just now I doubted for a moment myself!"

We all dined together, and I could see that poor Art was trying to make the best of things. Van Helsing had been silent all dinner time, but when we had lit our cigars he said, "Lord..." but Arthur interrupted him.

"No, no, not that, for God's sake! Not yet at any rate. Forgive me, sir. I did not mean to speak offensively. It is only because my loss is so recent."

The Professor answered very sweetly, "I only used that name because I was in doubt. I must not call you 'Mr.' and I have grown to love you, yes, my dear boy, to love you, as Arthur."

Arthur held out his hand, and took the old man's warmly. "Call me what you will," he said. "I hope I may always have the title of a friend. And let me say that I am at a loss for words to thank you for your goodness to my poor dear." He paused a moment, and went on, "I know that she understood your goodness even better than I do. And if I was rude or in any way wanting at that time you acted so, you remember"--the Professor nodded--"you must forgive me."

He answered with a grave kindness, "I know it was hard for you to quite trust me then, for to trust such violence needs to understand, and I take it that you do not, that you cannot, trust me now, for you do not yet understand. And there may be more times when I shall want you to trust when you cannot, and may not, and must not yet understand. But the time will come when your trust shall be whole and complete in me, and when you shall understand as though the sunlight himself shone through. Then you shall bless me from first to last for your own sake, and for the sake of others, and for her dear sake to whom I swore to protect."

"And indeed, indeed, sir," said Arthur warmly. "I shall in all ways trust you. I know and believe you have a very noble heart, and you are Jack's friend, and you were hers. You shall do what you like."

The Professor cleared his throat a couple of times, as though about to speak, and finally said, "May I ask you something now?"

"Certainly."

"You know that Mrs. Westenra left you all her property?"

"No, poor dear. I never thought of it."

"And as it is all yours, you have a right to deal with it as you will. I want you to give me permission to read all Miss Lucy's papers and letters. Believe me, it is no idle curiosity. I have a motive of which, be sure, she would have approved. I have them all here. I took them before we knew that all was yours, so that no strange hand might touch them, no strange eye look through words into her soul. I shall keep them, if I may. Even you may not see them yet, but I shall keep them safe. No word shall be lost, and in the good time I shall give them back to you. It is a hard thing that I ask, but you will do it, will you not, for Lucy's sake?"

Arthur spoke out heartily, like his old self, "Dr. Van Helsing, you may do what you will. I feel that in saying this I am doing what my dear one would have approved. I shall not trouble you with questions till the time comes."

The old Professor stood up as he said solemnly, "And you are right. There will be pain for us all, but it will not be all pain, nor will this pain be the last. We and you too, you most of all, dear boy, will have to pass through the bitter water before we reach the sweet. But we must be brave of heart and unselfish, and do our duty, and all will be well!"

I slept on a sofa in Arthur's room that night. Van Helsing did not go to bed at all. He went to and fro, as if patroling the house, and was never out of sight of the room where Lucy lay in her coffin, strewn with the wild garlic flowers, which sent through the odour of lily and rose, a heavy, overpowering smell into the night.

MINA HARKER'S JOURNAL

22 September.--In the train to Exeter. Jonathan sleeping. It seems only yesterday that the last entry was made, and yet how much between then, in Whitby and all the world before me, Jonathan away and no news of him, and now, married to Jonathan, Jonathan a solicitor, a partner, rich, master of his business, Mr. Hawkins dead and buried, and Jonathan with another attack that may harm him. Some day he may ask me about it. Down it all goes. I am rusty in my shorthand, see what unexpected prosperity does for us, so it may be as well to freshen it up again with an exercise anyhow.

The service was very simple and very solemn. There were only ourselves and the servants there, one or two old friends of his from Exeter, his London agent, and a gentleman representing Sir John Paxton, the President of the Incorporated Law Society. Jonathan and I stood hand in hand, and we felt that our best and dearest friend was gone from us.

We came back to town quietly, taking a bus to Hyde Park Corner. Jonathan thought it would interest me to go into the Row for a while, so we sat down. But there were very few people there, and it was sad-looking and desolate to see so many empty chairs. It made us think of the empty chair at home. So we got up and walked down Piccadilly. Jonathan was holding me by the arm, the way he used to in the old days before I went to school. I felt it very improper, for you can't go on for some years teaching etiquette and decorum to other girls without the pedantry of it biting into yourself a bit. But it was Jonathan, and he was my husband, and we didn't know anybody who saw us, and we didn't care if they did, so on we walked. I was looking at a very beautiful girl, in a big cart-wheel hat, sitting in a victoria outside Guiliano's, when I felt Jonathan clutch my arm so tight that he hurt me, and he said under his breath, "My God!"

I am always anxious about Jonathan, for I fear that some nervous fit may upset him again. So I turned to him quickly, and asked him what it was that disturbed him.

He was very pale, and his eyes seemed bulging out as, half in terror and half in amazement, he gazed at a tall, thin man, with a beaky nose and black moustache and pointed beard, who was also observing the pretty girl. He was looking at her so hard that he did not see either of us, and so I had a good view of him. His face was not a good face. It was hard, and cruel, and sensual, and big white teeth, that looked all the whiter because his lips were so red, were pointed like an animal's. Jonathan kept staring at him, till I was afraid he would notice. I feared he might take it ill, he looked so fierce and nasty. I asked Jonathan why he was disturbed, and he answered, evidently thinking that I knew as much about it as he did, "Do you see who it is?"

"No, dear," I said. "I don't know him, who is it?" His answer seemed to shock and thrill me, for it was said as if he did not know that it was me, Mina, to whom he was speaking. "It is the man himself!"

The poor dear was evidently terrified at something, very greatly terrified. I do believe that if he had not had me to lean on and to support him he would have sunk down. He kept staring. A man came out of the shop with a small parcel, and gave it to the lady, who then drove off. The dark man kept his eyes fixed on her, and when the carriage moved up Piccadilly he followed in the same direction, and hailed a hansom. Jonathan kept looking after him, and said, as if to himself,

"I believe it is the Count, but he has grown young. My God, if this be so! Oh, my God! My God! If only I knew! If only I knew!" He was distressing himself so much that I feared to keep his mind on the subject by asking him any questions, so I remained silent. I drew away quietly, and he, holding my arm, came easily. We walked a little further, and then went in and sat for a while in the Green Park. It was a hot day for autumn, and there was a comfortable seat in a shady place. After a few minutes' staring at nothing, Jonathan's eyes closed, and he went quickly into a sleep, with his head on my shoulder. I thought it was the best thing for him, so did not disturb him. In about twenty minutes he woke up, and said to me quite cheerfully,

"Why, Mina, have I been asleep! Oh, do forgive me for being so rude. Come, and we'll have a cup of tea somewhere."

He had evidently forgotten all about the dark stranger, as in his illness he had forgotten all that this episode had reminded him of. I don't like this lapsing into forgetfulness. It may make or continue some injury to the brain. I must not ask him, for fear I shall do more harm than good, but I must somehow learn the facts of his journey abroad. The time is come, I fear, when I must open the parcel, and know what is written. Oh, Jonathan, you will, I know, forgive me if I do wrong, but it is for your own dear sake.

Later.--A sad homecoming in every way, the house empty of the dear soul who was so good to us. Jonathan still pale and dizzy under a slight relapse of his malady, and now a telegram from Van Helsing, whoever he may be. "You will be grieved to hear that Mrs. Westenra died five days ago, and that Lucy died the day before yesterday. They were both buried today."

Oh, what a wealth of sorrow in a few words! Poor Mrs. Westenra! Poor Lucy! Gone, gone, never to return to us! And poor, poor Arthur, to have lost such a sweetness out of his life! God help us all to bear our troubles.

DR. SEWARD'S DIARY-CONT.

22 September.--It is all over. Arthur has gone back to Ring, and has taken Quincey Morris with him. What a fine fellow is Quincey! I believe in my heart of hearts that he suffered as much about Lucy's death as any of us, but he bore himself through it like a moral Viking. If America can go on breeding men like that, she will be a power in the world indeed. Van Helsing is lying down, having a rest preparatory to his journey. He goes to Amsterdam tonight, but says he returns tomorrow night, that he only wants to make some arrangements which can only be made personally. He is to stop with me then, if he can. He says he has work to do in London which may take him some time. Poor old fellow! I fear that the strain of the past week has broken down even his iron strength. All the time of the burial he was, I could see, putting some terrible restraint on himself. When it was all over, we were standing beside Arthur, who, poor fellow, was speaking of his part in the operation where his blood had been transfused to his Lucy's veins. I could see Van Helsing's face grow white and purple by turns. Arthur was saying that he felt since then as if they two had been really married, and that she was his wife in the sight of God. None of us said a word of the other operations, and none of us ever shall. Arthur and Quincey went away together to the station, and Van Helsing and I came on here. The moment we were alone in the carriage he gave way to a regular fit of hysterics. He has denied to me since that it was hysterics, and insisted that it was only his sense of humor asserting itself under very terrible conditions. He laughed till he cried, and I had to draw down the blinds lest any one should see us and misjudge. And then he cried, till he laughed again, and laughed and cried together, just as a woman does. I tried to be stern with him, as one is to a woman under the circumstances, but it had no effect. Men and women are so different in manifestations of nervous strength or weakness! Then when his face grew grave and stern again I asked him why his mirth, and why at such a time. His reply was in a way characteristic of him, for it was logical and forceful and mysterious. He said,

"Ah, you don't comprehend, friend John. Do not think that I am not sad, though I laugh. See, I have cried even when the laugh did choke me. But no more think that I am all sorry when I cry, for the laugh he come just the same. Keep it always with you that laughter who knock at your door and say, 'May I come in?' is not true laughter. No! He is a king, and he come when and how he like. He ask no person, he choose no time of suitability. He say, 'I am here.' Behold, in example I grieve my heart out for that so sweet young girl. I give my blood for her, though I am old and worn. I give my time, my skill, my sleep. I let my other sufferers want that she may have all. And yet I can laugh at her very grave, laugh when the clay from the spade of the sexton drop upon her coffin and say 'Thud, thud!' to my heart, till it send back the blood from my cheek. My heart bleed for that poor boy, that dear boy, so of the age of mine own boy had I been so blessed that he live, and with his hair and eyes the same.

"There, you know now why I love him so. And yet when he say things that touch my husband-heart to the quick, and make my father-heart yearn to him as to no other man, not even you, friend John, for we are more level in experiences than father and son, yet even at such a moment King Laugh he come to me and shout and bellow in my ear, 'Here I am! Here I am!' till the blood come dance back and bring some of the sunshine that he carry with him to my cheek. Oh, friend John, it is a strange world, a sad world, a world full of miseries, and woes, and troubles. And yet when King Laugh come, he make them all dance to the tune he play. Bleeding hearts, and dry bones of the churchyard, and tears that burn as they fall, all dance together to the music that he make with that smileless mouth of him. And believe me, friend John, that he is good to come, and kind. Ah, we men and women are like ropes drawn tight with strain that pull us different ways. Then tears come, and like the rain on the ropes, they brace us up, until perhaps the strain become too great, and we break. But King Laugh he come like the sunshine, and he ease off the strain again, and we bear to go on with our labor, what it may be."

I did not like to wound him by pretending not to see his idea, but as I did not yet understand the cause of his laughter, I asked him. As he answered me his face grew stern, and he said in quite a different tone,

"Oh, it was the grim irony of it all, this so lovely lady garlanded with flowers, that looked so fair as life, till one by one we wondered if she were truly dead, she laid in that so fine marble house in that lonely churchyard, where rest so many of her kin, laid there with the mother who loved her, and whom she loved, and that sacred bell going 'Toll! Toll! Toll!' so sad and slow, and those holy men, with the white garments of the angel, pretending to read books, and yet all the time their eyes never on the page, and all of us with the bowed head. And all for what? She is dead, so! Is it not?"

"Well, for the life of me, Professor," I said, "I can't see anything to laugh at in all that. Why, your expression makes it a harder puzzle than before. But even if the burial service was comic, what about poor Art and his trouble? Why his heart was simply breaking."

"Just so. Said he not that the transfusion of his blood to her veins had made her truly his bride?"

"Yes, and it was a sweet and comforting idea for him."

"Quite so. But there was a difficulty, friend John. If so that, then what about the others? Ho, ho! Then this so sweet maid is a polyandrist, and me, with my poor wife dead to me, but alive by Church's law, though no wits, all gone, even I, who am faithful husband to this now-no-wife, am bigamist."

"I don't see where the joke comes in there either!" I said, and I did not feel particularly pleased with him for saying such things. He laid his hand on my arm, and said,

"Friend John, forgive me if I pain. I showed not my feeling to others when it would wound, but only to you, my old friend, whom I can trust. If you could have looked into my heart then when I want to laugh, if you could have done so when the laugh arrived, if you could do so now, when King Laugh have pack up his crown, and all that is to him, for he go far, far away from me, and for a long, long time, maybe you would perhaps pity me the most of all."

I was touched by the tenderness of his tone, and asked why.

"Because I know!"

And now we are all scattered, and for many a long day loneliness will sit over our roofs with brooding wings. Lucy lies in the tomb of her kin, a lordly death house in a lonely churchyard, away from teeming London, where the air is fresh, and the sun rises over Hampstead Hill, and where wild flowers grow of their own accord.

So I can finish this diary, and God only knows if I shall ever begin another. If I do, or if I even open this again, it will be to deal with different people and different themes, for here at the end, where the romance of my life is told, ere I go back to take up the thread of my life-work, I say sadly and without hope, "FINIS".

THE WESTMINSTER GAZETTE, 25 SEPTEMBER A HAMPSTEAD MYSTERY

The neighborhood of Hampstead is just at present exercised with a series of events which seem to run on lines parallel to those of what was known to the writers of headlines as "The Kensington Horror," or "The Stabbing Woman," or "The Woman in Black." During the past two or three days several cases have occurred of young children straying from home or neglecting to return from their playing on the Heath. In all these cases the children were too young to give any properly intelligible account of themselves, but the consensus of their excuses is that they had been with a "bloofer lady." It has always been late in the evening when they have been missed, and on two occasions the children have not been found until early in the following morning. It is generally supposed in the neighborhood that, as the first child missed gave as his reason for being away that a "bloofer lady" had asked him to come for a walk, the others had picked up the phrase and used it as occasion served. This is the more natural as the favourite game of the little ones at present is luring each other away by wiles. A correspondent writes us that to see some of the tiny tots pretending to be the "bloofer lady" is supremely funny. Some of our caricaturists might, he says, take a lesson in the irony of grotesque by comparing the reality and the picture. It is only in accordance with general principles of human nature that the "bloofer lady" should be the popular role at these al fresco performances. Our correspondent naively says that even Ellen Terry could not be so winningly attractive as some of these grubby-faced little children pretend, and even imagine themselves, to be.

There is, however, possibly a serious side to the question, for some of the children, indeed all who have been missed at night, have been slightly torn or wounded in the throat. The wounds seem such as might be made by a rat or a small dog, and although of not much importance individually, would tend to show that whatever animal inflicts them has a system or method of its own. The police of the division have been instructed to keep a sharp lookout for straying children, especially when very young, in and around Hampstead Heath, and for any stray dog which may be about.

THE WESTMINSTER GAZETTE, 25 SEPTEMBER EXTRA SPECIAL

THE HAMPSTEAD HORROR
ANOTHER CHILD INJURED
THE "BLOOFER LADY"

We have just received intelligence that another child, missed last night, was only discovered late in the morning under a furze bush at the Shooter's Hill side of Hampstead Heath, which is perhaps, less frequented than the other parts. It has the same tiny wound in the throat as has been noticed in other cases. It was terribly weak, and looked quite emaciated. It too, when partially restored, had the common story to tell of being lured away by the "bloofer lady".

CHAPTER 14

MINA HARKER'S JOURNAL

23 September.--Jonathan is better after a bad night. I am so glad that he has plenty of work to do, for that keeps his mind off the terrible things, and oh, I am rejoiced that he is not now weighed down with the responsibility of his new position. I knew he would be true to himself, and now how proud I am to see my Jonathan rising to the height of his advancement and keeping pace in all ways with the duties that come upon him. He will be away all day till late, for he said he could not lunch at home. My household work is done, so I shall take his foreign journal, and lock myself up in my room and read it.

24 September.--I hadn't the heart to write last night, that terrible record of Jonathan's upset me so. Poor dear! How he must have suffered, whether it be true or only imagination. I wonder if there is any truth in it at all. Did he get his brain fever, and then write all those terrible things, or had he some cause for it all? I suppose I shall never know, for I dare not open the subject to him. And yet that man we saw yesterday! He seemed quite certain of him, poor fellow! I suppose it was the funeral upset him and sent his mind back on some train of thought.

He believes it all himself. I remember how on our wedding day he said "Unless some solemn duty come upon me to go back to the bitter hours, asleep or awake, mad or sane…" There seems to be through it all some thread of continuity. That fearful Count was coming to London. If it should be, and he came to London, with its teeming millions… There may be a solemn duty, and if it come we must not shrink from it. I shall be prepared. I shall get my typewriter this very hour and begin transcribing. Then we shall be ready for other eyes if required. And if it be wanted, then, perhaps, if I am ready, poor Jonathan may not be upset, for I can speak for him and never let him be troubled or worried with it at all. If ever Jonathan quite gets over the nervousness he may want to tell me of it all, and I can ask him questions and find out things, and see how I may comfort him.

LETTER, VAN HELSING TO MRS. HARKER

24 September
(Confidence)
"Dear Madam,

"I pray you to pardon my writing, in that I am so far friend as that I sent to you sad news of Miss Lucy Westenra's death. By the kindness of Lord Godalming, I am empowered to read her letters and papers, for I am deeply concerned about certain matters vitally important. In them I find some letters from you, which show how great friends you were and how you love her. Oh, Madam Mina, by that love, I implore you, help me. It is for others' good that I ask, to redress great wrong, and to lift much and terrible troubles, that may be more great than you can know. May it be that I see you? You can trust me. I am friend of Dr. John Seward and of Lord Godalming (that was Arthur of Miss Lucy). I must keep it private for the present from all. I should come to Exeter to see you at once if you tell me I am privilege to come, and where and when. I implore your pardon, Madam. I have read your letters to poor Lucy, and know how good you are and how your husband suffer. So I pray you, if it may be, enlighten him not, least it may harm. Again your pardon, and forgive me.

"VAN HELSING"

TELEGRAM, MRS. HARKER TO VAN HELSING

25 September.--Come today by quarter past ten train if you can catch it. Can see you any time you call.

"WILHELMINA HARKER"

MINA HARKER'S JOURNAL

25 September.--I cannot help feeling terribly excited as the time draws near for the visit of Dr. Van Helsing, for somehow I expect that it will throw some light upon Jonathan's sad experience, and as he attended poor dear Lucy in her last illness, he can tell me all about her. That is the reason of his coming. It is concerning Lucy and her sleep-walking, and not about Jonathan. Then I shall never know the real truth now! How silly I am. That awful journal gets hold of my imagination and tinges everything with something of its own colour. Of course it is about Lucy. That habit came back to the poor dear, and that awful night on the cliff must have made her ill. I had almost forgotten in my own affairs how ill she was afterwards. She must have told him of her sleep-walking adventure on the cliff, and that I knew all about it, and now he wants me to tell him what I know, so that he may understand. I hope I did right in not saying anything of it to Mrs. Westenra. I should never forgive myself if any act of mine, were it even a negative one, brought harm on poor dear Lucy. I hope too, Dr. Van Helsing will not blame me. I have had so much trouble and anxiety of late that I feel I cannot bear more just at present.

I suppose a cry does us all good at times, clears the air as other rain does. Perhaps it was reading the journal yesterday that upset me, and then Jonathan went away this morning to stay away from me a whole day and night, the first time we have been parted since our marriage. I do hope the dear fellow will take care of himself, and that nothing will occur to upset him. It is two o'clock, and the doctor will be here soon now. I shall say nothing of Jonathan's journal unless he asks me. I am so glad I have typewritten out my own journal, so that, in case he asks about Lucy, I can hand it to him. It will save much questioning.

CHAPTER 14

Later.--He has come and gone. Oh, what a strange meeting, and how it all makes my head whirl round. I feel like one in a dream. Can it be all possible, or even a part of it? If I had not read Jonathan's journal first, I should never have accepted even a possibility. Poor, poor, dear Jonathan! How he must have suffered. Please the good God, all this may not upset him again. I shall try to save him from it. But it may be even a consolation and a help to him, terrible though it be and awful in its consequences, to know for certain that his eyes and ears and brain did not deceive him, and that it is all true. It may be that it is the doubt which haunts him, that when the doubt is removed, no matter which, waking or dreaming, may prove the truth, he will be more satisfied and better able to bear the shock. Dr. Van Helsing must be a good man as well as a clever one if he is Arthur's friend and Dr. Seward's, and if they brought him all the way from Holland to look after Lucy. I feel from having seen him that he is good and kind and of a noble nature. When he comes tomorrow I shall ask him about Jonathan. And then, please God, all this sorrow and anxiety may lead to a good end. I used to think I would like to practice interviewing. Jonathan's friend on "The Exeter News" told him that memory is everything in such work, that you must be able to put down exactly almost every word spoken, even if you had to refine some of it afterwards. Here was a rare interview. I shall try to record it verbatim.

It was half-past two o'clock when the knock came. I took my courage a deux mains and waited. In a few minutes Mary opened the door, and announced "Dr. Van Helsing".

I rose and bowed, and he came towards me, a man of medium weight, strongly built, with his shoulders set back over a broad, deep chest and a neck well balanced on the trunk as the head is on the neck. The poise of the head strikes me at once as indicative of thought and power. The head is noble, well-sized, broad, and large behind the ears. The face, clean-shaven, shows a hard, square chin, a large resolute, mobile mouth, a good-sized nose, rather straight, but with quick, sensitive nostrils, that seem to broaden as the big bushy brows come down and the mouth tightens. The forehead is broad and fine, rising at first almost straight and then sloping back above two bumps or ridges wide apart, such a forehead that the reddish hair cannot possibly tumble over it, but falls naturally back and to the sides. Big, dark blue eyes are set widely apart, and are quick and tender or stern with the man's moods. He said to me,

"Mrs. Harker, is it not?" I bowed assent.

"That was Miss Mina Murray?" Again I assented.

"It is Mina Murray that I came to see that was friend of that poor dear child Lucy Westenra. Madam Mina, it is on account of the dead that I come."

"Sir," I said, "you could have no better claim on me than that you were a friend and helper of Lucy Westenra." And I held out my hand. He took it and said tenderly,

"Oh, Madam Mina, I know that the friend of that poor little girl must be good, but I had yet to learn..." He finished his speech with a courtly bow. I asked him what it was that he wanted to see me about, so he at once began.

"I have read your letters to Miss Lucy. Forgive me, but I had to begin to inquire somewhere, and there was none to ask. I know that you were with her at Whitby. She sometimes kept a diary, you need not look surprised, Madam Mina. It was begun after you had left, and was an imitation of you, and in that diary she traces by inference certain things to a sleep-walking in which she puts down that you saved her. In great perplexity then I come to you, and ask you out of your so much kindness to tell me all of it that you can remember."

"I can tell you, I think, Dr. Van Helsing, all about it."

"Ah, then you have good memory for facts, for details? It is not always so with young ladies."

"No, doctor, but I wrote it all down at the time. I can show it to you if you like."

"Oh, Madam Mina, I well be grateful. You will do me much favour."

I could not resist the temptation of mystifying him a bit, I suppose it is some taste of the original apple that remains still in our mouths, so I handed him the shorthand diary. He took it with a grateful bow, and said, "May I read it?"

"If you wish," I answered as demurely as I could. He opened it, and for an instant his face fell. Then he stood up and bowed.

"Oh, you so clever woman!" he said. "I knew long that Mr. Jonathan was a man of much thankfulness, but see, his wife have all the good things. And will you not so much honour me and so help me as to read it for me? Alas! I know not the shorthand."

By this time my little joke was over, and I was almost ashamed. So I took the typewritten copy from my work basket and handed it to him.

"Forgive me," I said. "I could not help it, but I had been thinking that it was of dear Lucy that you wished to ask, and so that you might not have time to wait, not on my account, but because I know your time must be precious, I have written it out on the typewriter for you."

He took it and his eyes glistened. "You are so good," he said. "And may I read it now? I may want to ask you some things when I have read."

"By all means," I said, "read it over whilst I order lunch, and then you can ask me questions whilst we eat."

He bowed and settled himself in a chair with his back to the light, and became so absorbed in the papers, whilst I went to see after lunch chiefly in order that he might not be disturbed. When I came back, I found him walking hurriedly up and down the room, his face all ablaze with excitement. He rushed up to me and took me by both hands.

"Oh, Madam Mina," he said, "how can I say what I owe to you? This paper is as sunshine. It opens the gate to me. I am dazed, I am dazzled, with so much light, and yet clouds roll in behind the light every time. But that you do not, cannot comprehend. Oh, but I am grateful to you, you so clever woman. Madame," he said this very solemnly, "if ever Abraham Van Helsing can do anything for you or yours, I trust you will let me know. It will be pleasure and delight if I may serve you as a friend, as a friend, but all I have ever learned, all I can ever do, shall be for you and those you love. There are darknesses in life, and there are lights. You are one of the lights. You will have a happy life and a good life, and your husband will be blessed in you."

"But, doctor, you praise me too much, and you do not know me."

"Not know you, I, who am old, and who have studied all my life men and women, I who have made my specialty the brain and all that belongs to him and all that follow from him! And I have read your diary that you have so goodly written for me, and which breathes out truth in every line. I, who have read your so sweet letter to poor Lucy of your marriage and your trust, not know you! Oh, Madam Mina, good women tell all their lives, and by day and by hour and by minute, such things that angels can read. And we men who wish to know have in us something of angels' eyes. Your husband is noble nature, and you are noble too, for you trust, and trust cannot be where there is mean nature. And your husband, tell me of him. Is he quite well? Is all that fever gone, and is he strong and hearty?"

I saw here an opening to ask him about Jonathan, so I said, "He was almost recovered, but he has been greatly upset by Mr. Hawkins death."

He interrupted, "Oh, yes. I know. I know. I have read your last two letters."

I went on, "I suppose this upset him, for when we were in town on Thursday last he had a sort of shock."

"A shock, and after brain fever so soon! That is not good. What kind of shock was it?"

"He thought he saw some one who recalled something terrible, something which led to his brain fever." And here the whole thing seemed to overwhelm me in a rush. The pity for Jonathan, the horror which he experienced, the whole fearful mystery of his diary, and the fear that has been brooding over me ever since, all came in a tumult. I suppose I was hysterical, for I threw myself on my knees and held up my hands to him, and implored him to make my husband well again. He took my hands and raised me up, and made me sit on the sofa, and sat by me. He held my hand in his, and said to me with, oh, such infinite sweetness,

"My life is a barren and lonely one, and so full of work that I have not had much time for friendships, but since I have been summoned to here by my friend John Seward I have known so many good people and seen such nobility that I feel more than ever, and it has grown with my advancing years, the loneliness of my life. Believe me, then, that I come here full of respect for you, and you have given me hope, hope, not in what I am seeking of, but that there are good women still left to make life happy, good women, whose lives and whose truths may make good lesson for the children that are to be. I am glad, glad, that I may here be of some use to you. For if your husband suffer, he suffer within the range of my study and experience. I promise you that I will gladly do all for him that I can, all to make his life strong and manly, and your life a happy one. Now you must eat. You are overwrought and perhaps overanxious. Husband Jonathan would not like to see you so pale, and what he like not where he love, is not to his good. Therefore for his sake you must eat and smile. You have told me about Lucy, and so now we shall not speak of it, lest it distress. I shall stay in Exeter tonight, for I want to think much over what you have told me, and when I have thought I will ask you questions, if I may. And then too, you will tell me of husband Jonathan's trouble so far as you can, but not yet. You must eat now, afterwards you shall tell me all."

After lunch, when we went back to the drawing room, he said to me, "And now tell me all about him."

When it came to speaking to this great learned man, I began to fear that he would think me a weak fool, and Jonathan a madman, that journal is all so strange, and I hesitated to go on. But he was so sweet and kind, and he had promised to help, and I trusted him, so I said,

"Dr. Van Helsing, what I have to tell you is so queer that you must not laugh at me or at my husband. I have been since yesterday in a sort of fever of doubt. You must be kind to me, and not think me foolish that I have even half believed some very strange things."

He reassured me by his manner as well as his words when he said, "Oh, my dear, if you only know how strange is the matter regarding which I am here, it is you who would laugh. I have learned not to think little of any one's belief, no matter how strange it may be. I have tried to keep an open mind, and it is not the ordinary things of life that could close it, but the strange things, the extraordinary things, the things that make one doubt if they be mad or sane."

"Thank you, thank you a thousand times! You have taken a weight off my mind. If you will let me, I shall give you a paper to read. It is long, but I have typewritten it out. It will tell you my trouble and Jonathan's. It is the copy of his journal when abroad, and all that happened. I dare not say anything of it. You will read for yourself and judge. And then when I see you, perhaps, you will be very kind and tell me what you think."

"I promise," he said as I gave him the papers. "I shall in the morning, as soon as I can, come to see you and your husband, if I may."

"Jonathan will be here at half-past eleven, and you must come to lunch with us and see him then. You could catch the quick 3:34 train, which will leave you at Paddington before eight." He was surprised at my knowledge of the trains offhand, but he does not know that I have made up all the trains to and from Exeter, so that I may help Jonathan in case he is in a hurry.

So he took the papers with him and went away, and I sit here thinking, thinking I don't know what.

LETTER (by hand), VAN HELSING TO MRS. HARKER

25 September, 6 o'clock

"Dear Madam Mina,

"I have read your husband's so wonderful diary. You may sleep without doubt. Strange and terrible as it is, it is true! I will pledge my life on it. It may be worse for others, but for him and you there is no dread. He is a noble fellow, and let me tell you from experience of men, that one who would do as he did in going down that wall and to that room, aye, and going a second time, is not one to be injured in permanence by a shock. His brain and his heart are all right, this I swear, before I have even seen him, so be at rest. I shall have much to ask him of other things. I am blessed that today I come to see you, for I have learn all at once so much that again I am dazzled, dazzled more than ever, and I must think.

"Yours the most faithful,

"Abraham Van Helsing."

LETTER, MRS. HARKER TO VAN HELSING

25 September, 6:30 P.M.

"My dear Dr. Van Helsing,

"A thousand thanks for your kind letter, which has taken a great weight off my mind. And yet, if it be true, what terrible things there are in the world, and what an awful thing if that man, that monster, be really in London! I fear to think. I have this moment, whilst writing, had a wire from Jonathan, saying that he leaves by the 6:25

tonight from Launceston and will be here at 10:18, so that I shall have no fear tonight. Will you, therefore, instead of lunching with us, please come to breakfast at eight o'clock, if this be not too early for you? You can get away, if you are in a hurry, by the 10:30 train, which will bring you to Paddington by 2:35. Do not answer this, as I shall take it that, if I do not hear, you will come to breakfast.

"Believe me,

"Your faithful and grateful friend,

"Mina Harker."

JONATHAN HARKER'S JOURNAL

26 September.--I thought never to write in this diary again, but the time has come. When I got home last night Mina had supper ready, and when we had supped she told me of Van Helsing's visit, and of her having given him the two diaries copied out, and of how anxious she has been about me. She showed me in the doctor's letter that all I wrote down was true. It seems to have made a new man of me. It was the doubt as to the reality of the whole thing that knocked me over. I felt impotent, and in the dark, and distrustful. But, now that I know, I am not afraid, even of the Count. He has succeeded after all, then, in his design in getting to London, and it was he I saw. He has got younger, and how? Van Helsing is the man to unmask him and hunt him out, if he is anything like what Mina says. We sat late, and talked it over. Mina is dressing, and I shall call at the hotel in a few minutes and bring him over.

He was, I think, surprised to see me. When I came into the room where he was, and introduced myself, he took me by the shoulder, and turned my face round to the light, and said, after a sharp scrutiny,

"But Madam Mina told me you were ill, that you had had a shock."

It was so funny to hear my wife called 'Madam Mina' by this kindly, strong-faced old man. I smiled, and said, "I was ill, I have had a shock, but you have cured me already."

"And how?"

"By your letter to Mina last night. I was in doubt, and then everything took a hue of unreality, and I did not know what to trust, even the evidence of my own senses. Not knowing what to trust, I did not know what to do, and so had only to keep on working in what had hitherto been the groove of my life. The groove ceased to avail me, and I mistrusted myself. Doctor, you don't know what it is to doubt everything, even yourself. No, you don't, you couldn't with eyebrows like yours."

He seemed pleased, and laughed as he said, "So! You are a physiognomist. I learn more here with each hour. I am with so much pleasure coming to you to breakfast, and, oh, sir, you will pardon praise from an old man, but you are blessed in your wife."

I would listen to him go on praising Mina for a day, so I simply nodded and stood silent.

"She is one of God's women, fashioned by His own hand to show us men and other women that there is a heaven where we can enter, and that its light can be here on earth. So true, so sweet, so noble, so little an egoist, and that, let me tell you, is much in this age, so sceptical and selfish. And you, sir… I have read all the letters to poor Miss Lucy, and some of them speak of you, so I know you since some days from the knowing of others, but I have seen your true self since last night. You will give me your hand, will you not? And let us be friends for all our lives."

We shook hands, and he was so earnest and so kind that it made me quite choky.

"And now," he said, "may I ask you for some more help? I have a great task to do, and at the beginning it is to know. You can help me here. Can you tell me what went before your going to Transylvania? Later on I may ask more help, and of a different kind, but at first this will do."

"Look here, Sir," I said, "does what you have to do concern the Count?"

"It does," he said solemnly.

"Then I am with you heart and soul. As you go by the 10:30 train, you will not have time to read them, but I shall get the bundle of papers. You can take them with you and read them in the train."

After breakfast I saw him to the station. When we were parting he said, "Perhaps you will come to town if I send for you, and take Madam Mina too."

"We shall both come when you will," I said.

I had got him the morning papers and the London papers of the previous night, and while we were talking at the carriage window, waiting for the train to start, he was turning them over. His eyes suddenly seemed to catch something in one of them, "The Westminster Gazette", I knew it by the colour, and he grew quite white. He read something intently, groaning to himself, "Mein Gott! Mein Gott! So soon! So soon!" I do not think he remembered me at the moment. Just then the whistle blew, and the train moved off. This recalled him to himself, and he leaned out of the window and waved his hand, calling out, "Love to Madam Mina. I shall write so soon as ever I can."

DR. SEWARD'S DIARY

26 September.--Truly there is no such thing as finality. Not a week since I said "Finis," and yet here I am starting fresh again, or rather going on with the record. Until this afternoon I had no cause to think of what is done. Renfield had become, to all intents, as sane as he ever was. He was already well ahead with his fly business, and he had just started in the spider line also, so he had not been of any trouble to me. I had a letter from Arthur, written on Sunday, and from it I gather that he is bearing up wonderfully well. Quincey Morris is with him, and that is much of a help, for he himself is a bubbling well of good spirits. Quincey wrote me a line too, and from him I hear that Arthur is beginning to recover something of his old buoyancy, so as to them all my mind is at rest. As for myself, I was settling down to my work with the enthusiasm which I used to have for it, so that I might fairly have said that the wound which poor Lucy left on me was becoming cicatrised.

Everything is, however, now reopened, and what is to be the end God only knows. I have an idea that Van Helsing thinks he knows, too, but he will only let out enough at a time to whet curiosity. He went to Exeter yesterday, and stayed there all night. Today he came back, and almost bounded into the room at about half-past five o'clock, and thrust last night's "Westminster Gazette" into my hand.

"What do you think of that?" he asked as he stood back and folded his arms.

I looked over the paper, for I really did not know what he meant, but he took it from me and pointed out a paragraph about children being decoyed away at Hampstead. It did not convey much to me, until I reached a passage where it described small puncture wounds on their throats. An idea struck me, and I looked up.

"Well?" he said.

"It is like poor Lucy's."

"And what do you make of it?"

"Simply that there is some cause in common. Whatever it was that injured her has injured them." I did not quite understand his answer.

"That is true indirectly, but not directly."

"How do you mean, Professor?" I asked. I was a little inclined to take his seriousness lightly, for, after all, four days of rest and freedom from burning, harrowing, anxiety does help to restore one's spirits, but when I saw his face, it sobered me. Never, even in the midst of our despair about poor Lucy, had he looked more stern.

"Tell me!" I said. "I can hazard no opinion. I do not know what to think, and I have no data on which to found a conjecture."

"Do you mean to tell me, friend John, that you have no suspicion as to what poor Lucy died of, not after all the hints given, not only by events, but by me?"

"Of nervous prostration following a great loss or waste of blood."

"And how was the blood lost or wasted?" I shook my head.

He stepped over and sat down beside me, and went on, "You are a clever man, friend John. You reason well, and your wit is bold, but you are too prejudiced. You do not let your eyes see nor your ears hear, and that which is outside your daily life is not of account to you. Do you not think that there are things which you cannot understand, and yet which are, that some people see things that others cannot? But there are things old and new which must not be contemplated by men's eyes, because they know, or think they know, some things which other men have told them. Ah, it is the fault of our science that it wants to explain all, and if it explain not, then it says there is nothing to explain. But yet we see around us every day the growth of new beliefs, which think themselves new, and which are yet but the old, which pretend to be young, like the fine ladies at the opera. I suppose now you do not believe in corporeal transference. No? Nor in materialization. No? Nor in astral bodies. No? Nor in the reading of thought. No? Nor in hypnotism..."

"Yes," I said. "Charcot has proved that pretty well."

He smiled as he went on, "Then you are satisfied as to it. Yes? And of course then you understand how it act, and can follow the mind of the great Charcot, alas that he is no more, into the very soul of the patient that he influence. No? Then, friend John, am I to take it that you simply accept fact, and are satisfied to let from premise to conclusion be a blank? No? Then tell me, for I am a student of the brain, how you accept hypnotism and reject the thought reading. Let me tell you, my friend, that there are things done today in electrical science which would have been deemed unholy by the very man who discovered electricity, who would themselves not so long before been burned as wizards. There are always mysteries in life. Why was it that Methuselah lived nine hundred years, and 'Old Parr' one hundred and sixty-nine, and yet that poor Lucy, with four men's blood in her poor veins, could not live even one day? For, had she live one more day, we could save her. Do you know all the mystery of life and death? Do you know the altogether of comparative anatomy and can say wherefore the qualities of brutes are in some men, and not in others? Can you tell me why, when other spiders die small and soon, that one great spider lived for centuries in the tower of the old Spanish church and grew and grew, till, on descending, he could drink the oil of all the church lamps? Can you tell me why in the Pampas, ay and elsewhere, there are bats that come out at night and open the veins of cattle and horses and suck dry their veins, how in some islands of the Western seas there are bats which hang on the trees all day, and those who have seen describe as like giant nuts or pods, and that when the sailors sleep on the deck, because that it is hot, flit down on them and then, and then in the morning are found dead men, white as even Miss Lucy was?"

"Good God, Professor!" I said, starting up. "Do you mean to tell me that Lucy was bitten by such a bat, and that such a thing is here in London in the nineteenth century?"

He waved his hand for silence, and went on, "Can you tell me why the tortoise lives more long than generations of men, why the elephant goes on and on till he have sees dynasties, and why the parrot never die only of bite of cat of dog or other complaint? Can you tell me why men believe in all ages and places that there are men and women who cannot die? We all know, because science has vouched for the fact, that there have been toads shut up in rocks for thousands of years, shut in one so small hole that only hold him since the youth of the world. Can you tell me how the Indian fakir can make himself to die and have been buried, and his grave sealed and corn sowed on it, and the corn reaped and be cut and sown and reaped and cut again, and then men come and take away the unbroken seal and that there lie the Indian fakir, not dead, but that rise up and walk amongst them as before?"

Here I interrupted him. I was getting bewildered. He so crowded on my mind his list of nature's eccentricities and possible impossibilities that my imagination was getting fired. I had a dim idea that he was teaching me some lesson, as long ago he used to do in his study at Amsterdam. But he used them to tell me the thing, so that I could have the object of thought in mind all the time. But now I was without his help, yet I wanted to follow him, so I said,

"Professor, let me be your pet student again. Tell me the thesis, so that I may apply your knowledge as you go on. At present I am going in my mind from point to point as a madman, and not a sane one, follows an idea. I feel like a novice lumbering through a bog in a midst, jumping from one tussock to another in the mere blind effort to move on without knowing where I am going."

"That is a good image," he said. "Well, I shall tell you. My thesis is this, I want you to believe."

"To believe what?"

"To believe in things that you cannot. Let me illustrate. I heard once of an American who so defined faith, 'that faculty which enables us to believe things which we know to be untrue.' For one, I follow that man. He meant that we shall have an open mind, and not let a little bit of truth check the rush of the big truth, like a small rock does a railway truck. We get the small truth first. Good! We keep him, and we value him, but all the same we must not let him think himself all the truth in the universe."

"Then you want me not to let some previous conviction inure the receptivity of my mind with regard to some strange matter. Do I read your lesson aright?"

"Ah, you are my favourite pupil still. It is worth to teach you. Now that you are willing to understand, you have taken the first step to understand. You think then that those so small holes in the children's throats were made by the same that made the holes in Miss Lucy?"

"I suppose so."

He stood up and said solemnly, "Then you are wrong. Oh, would it were so! But alas! No. It is worse, far, far worse."

"In God's name, Professor Van Helsing, what do you mean?" I cried.

He threw himself with a despairing gesture into a chair, and placed his elbows on the table, covering his face with his hands as he spoke.

"They were made by Miss Lucy!"

CHAPTER 15

DR. SEWARD'S DIARY--cont.

For a while sheer anger mastered me. It was as if he had during her life struck Lucy on the face. I smote the table hard and rose up as I said to him, "Dr. Van Helsing, are you mad?"

He raised his head and looked at me, and somehow the tenderness of his face calmed me at once. "Would I were!" he said. "Madness were easy to bear compared with truth like this. Oh, my friend, why, think you, did I go so far round, why take so long to tell so simple a thing? Was it because I hate you and have hated you all my life? Was it because I wished to give you pain? Was it that I wanted, now so late, revenge for that time when you saved my life, and from a fearful death? Ah no!"

"Forgive me," said I.

He went on, "My friend, it was because I wished to be gentle in the breaking to you, for I know you have loved that so sweet lady. But even yet I do not expect you to believe. It is so hard to accept at once any abstract truth, that we may doubt such to be possible when we have always believed the 'no' of it. It is more hard still to accept so sad a concrete truth, and of such a one as Miss Lucy. Tonight I go to prove it. Dare you come with me?"

This staggered me. A man does not like to prove such a truth, Byron excepted from the category, jealousy.

"And prove the very truth he most abhorred."

He saw my hesitation, and spoke, "The logic is simple, no madman's logic this time, jumping from tussock to tussock in a misty bog. If it not be true, then proof will be relief. At worst it will not harm. If it be true! Ah, there is the dread. Yet every dread should help my cause, for in it is some need of belief. Come, I tell you what I propose. First, that we go off now and see that child in the hospital. Dr. Vincent, of the North Hospital, where the papers say the child is, is a friend of mine, and I think of yours since you were in class at Amsterdam. He will let two scientists see his case, if he will not let two friends. We shall tell him nothing, but only that we wish to learn. And then..."

"And then?"

He took a key from his pocket and held it up. "And then we spend the night, you and I, in the churchyard where Lucy lies. This is the key that lock the tomb. I had it from the coffin man to give to Arthur."

CHAPTER 15

My heart sank within me, for I felt that there was some fearful ordeal before us. I could do nothing, however, so I plucked up what heart I could and said that we had better hasten, as the afternoon was passing.

We found the child awake. It had had a sleep and taken some food, and altogether was going on well. Dr. Vincent took the bandage from its throat, and showed us the punctures. There was no mistaking the similarity to those which had been on Lucy's throat. They were smaller, and the edges looked fresher, that was all. We asked Vincent to what he attributed them, and he replied that it must have been a bite of some animal, perhaps a rat, but for his own part, he was inclined to think it was one of the bats which are so numerous on the northern heights of London. "Out of so many harmless ones," he said, "there may be some wild specimen from the South of a more malignant species. Some sailor may have brought one home, and it managed to escape, or even from the Zoological Gardens a young one may have got loose, or one be bred there from a vampire. These things do occur, you, know. Only ten days ago a wolf got out, and was, I believe, traced up in this direction. For a week after, the children were playing nothing but Red Riding Hood on the Heath and in every alley in the place until this 'bloofer lady' scare came along, since then it has been quite a gala time with them. Even this poor little mite, when he woke up today, asked the nurse if he might go away. When she asked him why he wanted to go, he said he wanted to play with the 'bloofer lady'."

"I hope," said Van Helsing, "that when you are sending the child home you will caution its parents to keep strict watch over it. These fancies to stray are most dangerous, and if the child were to remain out another night, it would probably be fatal. But in any case I suppose you will not let it away for some days?"

"Certainly not, not for a week at least, longer if the wound is not healed."

Our visit to the hospital took more time than we had reckoned on, and the sun had dipped before we came out. When Van Helsing saw how dark it was, he said,

"There is not hurry. It is more late than I thought. Come, let us seek somewhere that we may eat, and then we shall go on our way."

We dined at 'Jack Straw's Castle' along with a little crowd of bicyclists and others who were genially noisy. About ten o'clock we started from the inn. It was then very dark, and the scattered lamps made the darkness greater when we were once outside their individual radius. The Professor had evidently noted the road we were to go, for he went on unhesitatingly, but, as for me, I was in quite a mixup as to locality. As we went further, we met fewer and fewer people, till at last we were somewhat surprised when we met even the patrol of horse police going their usual suburban round. At last we reached the wall of the churchyard, which we climbed over. With some little difficulty, for it was very dark, and the whole place seemed so strange to us, we found the Westenra tomb. The Professor took the key, opened the creaky door, and standing back, politely, but quite unconsciously, motioned me to precede him. There was a delicious irony in the offer, in the courtliness of giving preference on such a ghastly occasion. My companion followed me quickly, and cautiously drew the door to, after carefully ascertaining that the lock was a falling, and not a spring one. In the latter case we should have been in a bad plight. Then he fumbled in his bag, and taking out a matchbox and a piece of candle, proceeded to make a light. The tomb in the daytime, and when wreathed with fresh flowers, had looked grim and gruesome enough, but now, some days afterwards, when the flowers hung lank and dead, their whites turning to rust and their greens to browns, when the spider and the beetle had resumed their accustomed dominance, when the time-discoloured stone, and dust-encrusted mortar, and rusty, dank iron, and tarnished brass, and clouded silver-plating gave back the feeble glimmer of a candle, the effect was more miserable and sordid than could have been imagined. It conveyed irresistibly the idea that life, animal life, was not the only thing which could pass away.

Van Helsing went about his work systematically. Holding his candle so that he could read the coffin plates, and so holding it that the sperm dropped in white patches which congealed as they touched the metal, he made assurance of Lucy's coffin. Another search in his bag, and he took out a turnscrew.

"What are you going to do?" I asked.

"To open the coffin. You shall yet be convinced."

Straightway he began taking out the screws, and finally lifted off the lid, showing the casing of lead beneath. The sight was almost too much for me. It seemed to be as much an affront to the dead as it would have been to have stripped off her clothing in her sleep whilst living. I actually took hold of his hand to stop him.

He only said, "You shall see," and again fumbling in his bag took out a tiny fret saw. Striking the turnscrew through the lead with a swift downward stab, which made me wince, he made a small hole, which was, however, big enough to admit the point of the saw. I had expected a rush of gas from the week-old corpse. We doctors, who have had to study our dangers, have to become accustomed to such things, and I drew back towards the door. But the Professor never stopped for a moment. He sawed down a couple of feet along one side of the lead coffin, and then across, and down the other side. Taking the edge of the loose flange, he bent it back towards the foot of the coffin, and holding up the candle into the aperture, motioned to me to look.

I drew near and looked. The coffin was empty. It was certainly a surprise to me, and gave me a considerable shock, but Van Helsing was unmoved. He was now more sure than ever of his ground, and so emboldened to proceed in his task. "Are you satisfied now, friend John?" he asked.

I felt all the dogged argumentativeness of my nature awake within me as I answered him, "I am satisfied that Lucy's body is not in that coffin, but that only proves one thing."

"And what is that, friend John?"

"That it is not there."

"That is good logic," he said, "so far as it goes. But how do you, how can you, account for it not being there?"

"Perhaps a body-snatcher," I suggested. "Some of the undertaker's people may have stolen it." I felt that I was speaking folly, and yet it was the only real cause which I could suggest.

The Professor sighed. "Ah well!" he said, "we must have more proof. Come with me."

He put on the coffin lid again, gathered up all his things and placed them in the bag, blew out the light, and placed the candle also in the bag. We opened the door, and went out. Behind us he closed the door and locked it. He handed me the key, saying, "Will you keep it? You had better be assured."

CHAPTER 15

I laughed, it was not a very cheerful laugh, I am bound to say, as I motioned him to keep it. "A key is nothing," I said, "there are many duplicates, and anyhow it is not difficult to pick a lock of this kind."

He said nothing, but put the key in his pocket. Then he told me to watch at one side of the churchyard whilst he would watch at the other.

I took up my place behind a yew tree, and I saw his dark figure move until the intervening headstones and trees hid it from my sight.

It was a lonely vigil. Just after I had taken my place I heard a distant clock strike twelve, and in time came one and two. I was chilled and unnerved, and angry with the Professor for taking me on such an errand and with myself for coming. I was too cold and too sleepy to be keenly observant, and not sleepy enough to betray my trust, so altogether I had a dreary, miserable time.

Suddenly, as I turned round, I thought I saw something like a white streak, moving between two dark yew trees at the side of the churchyard farthest from the tomb. At the same time a dark mass moved from the Professor's side of the ground, and hurriedly went towards it. Then I too moved, but I had to go round headstones and railed-off tombs, and I stumbled over graves. The sky was overcast, and somewhere far off an early cock crew. A little ways off, beyond a line of scattered juniper trees, which marked the pathway to the church, a white dim figure flitted in the direction of the tomb. The tomb itself was hidden by trees, and I could not see where the figure had disappeared. I heard the rustle of actual movement where I had first seen the white figure, and coming over, found the Professor holding in his arms a tiny child. When he saw me he held it out to me, and said, "Are you satisfied now?"

"No," I said, in a way that I felt was aggressive.

"Do you not see the child?"

"Yes, it is a child, but who brought it here? And is it wounded?"

"We shall see," said the Professor, and with one impulse we took our way out of the churchyard, he carrying the sleeping child.

When we had got some little distance away, we went into a clump of trees, and struck a match, and looked at the child's throat. It was without a scratch or scar of any kind.

"Was I right?" I asked triumphantly.

"We were just in time," said the Professor thankfully.

We had now to decide what we were to do with the child, and so consulted about it. If we were to take it to a police station we should have to give some account of our movements during the night. At least, we should have had to make some statement as to how we had come to find the child. So finally we decided that we would take it to the Heath, and when we heard a policeman coming, would leave it where he could not fail to find it. We would then seek our way home as quickly as we could. All fell out well. At the edge of Hampstead Heath we heard a policeman's heavy tramp, and laying the child on the pathway, we waited and watched until he saw it as he flashed his lantern to and fro. We heard his exclamation of astonishment, and then we went away silently. By good chance we got a cab near the 'Spainiards,' and drove to town.

I cannot sleep, so I make this entry. But I must try to get a few hours' sleep, as Van Helsing is to call for me at noon. He insists that I go with him on another expedition.

27 September.--It was two o'clock before we found a suitable opportunity for our attempt. The funeral held at noon was all completed, and the last stragglers of the

mourners had taken themselves lazily away, when, looking carefully from behind a clump of alder trees, we saw the sexton lock the gate after him. We knew that we were safe till morning did we desire it, but the Professor told me that we should not want more than an hour at most. Again I felt that horrid sense of the reality of things, in which any effort of imagination seemed out of place, and I realized distinctly the perils of the law which we were incurring in our unhallowed work. Besides, I felt it was all so useless. Outrageous as it was to open a leaden coffin, to see if a woman dead nearly a week were really dead, it now seemed the height of folly to open the tomb again, when we knew, from the evidence of our own eyesight, that the coffin was empty. I shrugged my shoulders, however, and rested silent, for Van Helsing had a way of going on his own road, no matter who remonstrated. He took the key, opened the vault, and again courteously motioned me to precede. The place was not so gruesome as last night, but oh, how unutterably mean looking when the sunshine streamed in. Van Helsing walked over to Lucy's coffin, and I followed. He bent over and again forced back the leaden flange, and a shock of surprise and dismay shot through me.

There lay Lucy, seemingly just as we had seen her the night before her funeral. She was, if possible, more radiantly beautiful than ever, and I could not believe that she was dead. The lips were red, nay redder than before, and on the cheeks was a delicate bloom.

"Is this a juggle?" I said to him.

"Are you convinced now?" said the Professor, in response, and as he spoke he put over his hand, and in a way that made me shudder, pulled back the dead lips and showed the white teeth. "See," he went on, "they are even sharper than before. With this and this," and he touched one of the canine teeth and that below it, "the little children can be bitten. Are you of belief now, friend John?"

Once more argumentative hostility woke within me. I could not accept such an overwhelming idea as he suggested. So, with an attempt to argue of which I was even at the moment ashamed, I said, "She may have been placed here since last night."

"Indeed? That is so, and by whom?"

"I do not know. Someone has done it."

"And yet she has been dead one week. Most peoples in that time would not look so."

I had no answer for this, so was silent. Van Helsing did not seem to notice my silence. At any rate, he showed neither chagrin nor triumph. He was looking intently at the face of the dead woman, raising the eyelids and looking at the eyes, and once more opening the lips and examining the teeth. Then he turned to me and said,

"Here, there is one thing which is different from all recorded. Here is some dual life that is not as the common. She was bitten by the vampire when she was in a trance, sleep-walking, oh, you start. You do not know that, friend John, but you shall know it later, and in trance could he best come to take more blood. In trance she dies, and in trance she is UnDead, too. So it is that she differ from all other. Usually when the UnDead sleep at home," as he spoke he made a comprehensive sweep of his arm to designate what to a vampire was 'home', "their face show what they are, but this so sweet that was when she not UnDead she go back to the nothings of the common dead. There is no malign there, see, and so it make hard that I must kill her in her sleep."

CHAPTER 15

This turned my blood cold, and it began to dawn upon me that I was accepting Van Helsing's theories. But if she were really dead, what was there of terror in the idea of killing her?

He looked up at me, and evidently saw the change in my face, for he said almost joyously, "Ah, you believe now?"

I answered, "Do not press me too hard all at once. I am willing to accept. How will you do this bloody work?"

"I shall cut off her head and fill her mouth with garlic, and I shall drive a stake through her body."

It made me shudder to think of so mutilating the body of the woman whom I had loved. And yet the feeling was not so strong as I had expected. I was, in fact, beginning to shudder at the presence of this being, this UnDead, as Van Helsing called it, and to loathe it. Is it possible that love is all subjective, or all objective?

I waited a considerable time for Van Helsing to begin, but he stood as if wrapped in thought. Presently he closed the catch of his bag with a snap, and said,

"I have been thinking, and have made up my mind as to what is best. If I did simply follow my inclining I would do now, at this moment, what is to be done. But there are other things to follow, and things that are thousand times more difficult in that them we do not know. This is simple. She have yet no life taken, though that is of time, and to act now would be to take danger from her forever. But then we may have to want Arthur, and how shall we tell him of this? If you, who saw the wounds on Lucy's throat, and saw the wounds so similar on the child's at the hospital, if you, who saw the coffin empty last night and full today with a woman who have not change only to be more rose and more beautiful in a whole week, after she die, if you know of this and know of the white figure last night that brought the child to the churchyard, and yet of your own senses you did not believe, how then, can I expect Arthur, who know none of those things, to believe?

"He doubted me when I took him from her kiss when she was dying. I know he has forgiven me because in some mistaken idea I have done things that prevent him say goodbye as he ought, and he may think that in some more mistaken idea this woman was buried alive, and that in most mistake of all we have killed her. He will then argue back that it is we, mistaken ones, that have killed her by our ideas, and so he will be much unhappy always. Yet he never can be sure, and that is the worst of all. And he will sometimes think that she he loved was buried alive, and that will paint his dreams with horrors of what she must have suffered, and again, he will think that we may be right, and that his so beloved was, after all, an UnDead. No! I told him once, and since then I learn much. Now, since I know it is all true, a hundred thousand times more do I know that he must pass through the bitter waters to reach the sweet. He, poor fellow, must have one hour that will make the very face of heaven grow black to him, then we can act for good all round and send him peace. My mind is made up. Let us go. You return home for tonight to your asylum, and see that all be well. As for me, I shall spend the night here in this churchyard in my own way. Tomorrow night you will come to me to the Berkeley Hotel at ten of the clock. I shall send for Arthur to come too, and also that so fine young man of America that gave his blood. Later we shall all have work to do. I come with you so far as Piccadilly and there dine, for I must be back here before the sun set."

So we locked the tomb and came away, and got over the wall of the churchyard, which was not much of a task, and drove back to Piccadilly.

NOTE LEFT BY VAN HELSING IN HIS PORTMANTEAU, BERKELEY HOTEL DIRECTED TO JOHN SEWARD, M. D. (Not Delivered)

27 September

"Friend John,

"I write this in case anything should happen. I go alone to watch in that churchyard. It pleases me that the UnDead, Miss Lucy, shall not leave tonight, that so on the morrow night she may be more eager. Therefore I shall fix some things she like not, garlic and a crucifix, and so seal up the door of the tomb. She is young as UnDead, and will heed. Moreover, these are only to prevent her coming out. They may not prevail on her wanting to get in, for then the UnDead is desperate, and must find the line of least resistance, whatsoever it may be. I shall be at hand all the night from sunset till after sunrise, and if there be aught that may be learned I shall learn it. For Miss Lucy or from her, I have no fear, but that other to whom is there that she is UnDead, he have not the power to seek her tomb and find shelter. He is cunning, as I know from Mr. Jonathan and from the way that all along he have fooled us when he played with us for Miss Lucy's life, and we lost, and in many ways the UnDead are strong. He have always the strength in his hand of twenty men, even we four who gave our strength to Miss Lucy it also is all to him. Besides, he can summon his wolf and I know not what. So if it be that he came thither on this night he shall find me. But none other shall, until it be too late. But it may be that he will not attempt the place. There is no reason why he should. His hunting ground is more full of game than the churchyard where the UnDead woman sleeps, and the one old man watch.

"Therefore I write this in case... Take the papers that are with this, the diaries of Harker and the rest, and read them, and then find this great UnDead, and cut off his head and burn his heart or drive a stake through it, so that the world may rest from him.

"If it be so, farewell.

"VAN HELSING."

DR. SEWARD'S DIARY

28 September.--It is wonderful what a good night's sleep will do for one. Yesterday I was almost willing to accept Van Helsing's monstrous ideas, but now they seem to start out lurid before me as outrages on common sense. I have no doubt that he believes it all. I wonder if his mind can have become in any way unhinged. Surely there must be some rational explanation of all these mysterious things. Is it possible that the Professor can have done it himself? He is so abnormally clever that if he went off his head he would carry out his intent with regard to some fixed idea in a wonderful way. I am loathe to think it, and indeed it would be almost as great a marvel as the other to find that Van Helsing was mad, but anyhow I shall watch him carefully. I may get some light on the mystery.

CHAPTER 15

29 September.--Last night, at a little before ten o'clock, Arthur and Quincey came into Van Helsing's room. He told us all what he wanted us to do, but especially addressing himself to Arthur, as if all our wills were centred in his. He began by saying that he hoped we would all come with him too, "for," he said, "there is a grave duty to be done there. You were doubtless surprised at my letter?" This query was directly addressed to Lord Godalming.

"I was. It rather upset me for a bit. There has been so much trouble around my house of late that I could do without any more. I have been curious, too, as to what you mean.

"Quincey and I talked it over, but the more we talked, the more puzzled we got, till now I can say for myself that I'm about up a tree as to any meaning about anything."

"Me too," said Quincey Morris laconically.

"Oh," said the Professor, "then you are nearer the beginning, both of you, than friend John here, who has to go a long way back before he can even get so far as to begin."

It was evident that he recognized my return to my old doubting frame of mind without my saying a word. Then, turning to the other two, he said with intense gravity,

"I want your permission to do what I think good this night. It is, I know, much to ask, and when you know what it is I propose to do you will know, and only then how much. Therefore may I ask that you promise me in the dark, so that afterwards, though you may be angry with me for a time, I must not disguise from myself the possibility that such may be, you shall not blame yourselves for anything."

"That's frank anyhow," broke in Quincey. "I'll answer for the Professor. I don't quite see his drift, but I swear he's honest, and that's good enough for me."

"I thank you, Sir," said Van Helsing proudly. "I have done myself the honour of counting you one trusting friend, and such endorsement is dear to me." He held out a hand, which Quincey took.

Then Arthur spoke out, "Dr. Van Helsing, I don't quite like to 'buy a pig in a poke', as they say in Scotland, and if it be anything in which my honour as a gentleman or my faith as a Christian is concerned, I cannot make such a promise. If you can assure me that what you intend does not violate either of these two, then I give my consent at once, though for the life of me, I cannot understand what you are driving at."

"I accept your limitation," said Van Helsing, "and all I ask of you is that if you feel it necessary to condemn any act of mine, you will first consider it well and be satisfied that it does not violate your reservations."

"Agreed!" said Arthur. "That is only fair. And now that the pourparlers are over, may I ask what it is we are to do?"

"I want you to come with me, and to come in secret, to the churchyard at Kingstead."

Arthur's face fell as he said in an amazed sort of way,

"Where poor Lucy is buried?"

The Professor bowed.

Arthur went on, "And when there?"

"To enter the tomb!"

Arthur stood up. "Professor, are you in earnest, or is it some monstrous joke? Pardon me, I see that you are in earnest." He sat down again, but I could see that he sat firmly and proudly, as one who is on his dignity. There was silence until he asked again, "And when in the tomb?"

"To open the coffin."

"This is too much!" he said, angrily rising again. "I am willing to be patient in all things that are reasonable, but in this, this desecration of the grave, of one who…" He fairly choked with indignation.

The Professor looked pityingly at him. "If I could spare you one pang, my poor friend," he said, "God knows I would. But this night our feet must tread in thorny paths, or later, and for ever, the feet you love must walk in paths of flame!"

Arthur looked up with set white face and said, "Take care, sir, take care!"

"Would it not be well to hear what I have to say?" said Van Helsing. "And then you will at least know the limit of my purpose. Shall I go on?"

"That's fair enough," broke in Morris.

After a pause Van Helsing went on, evidently with an effort, "Miss Lucy is dead, is it not so? Yes! Then there can be no wrong to her. But if she be not dead…"

Arthur jumped to his feet, "Good God!" he cried. "What do you mean? Has there been any mistake, has she been buried alive?" He groaned in anguish that not even hope could soften.

"I did not say she was alive, my child. I did not think it. I go no further than to say that she might be UnDead."

"UnDead! Not alive! What do you mean? Is this all a nightmare, or what is it?"

"There are mysteries which men can only guess at, which age by age they may solve only in part. Believe me, we are now on the verge of one. But I have not done. May I cut off the head of dead Miss Lucy?"

"Heavens and earth, no!" cried Arthur in a storm of passion. "Not for the wide world will I consent to any mutilation of her dead body. Dr. Van Helsing, you try me too far. What have I done to you that you should torture me so? What did that poor, sweet girl do that you should want to cast such dishonour on her grave? Are you mad, that you speak of such things, or am I mad to listen to them? Don't dare think more of such a desecration. I shall not give my consent to anything you do. I have a duty to do in protecting her grave from outrage, and by God, I shall do it!"

Van Helsing rose up from where he had all the time been seated, and said, gravely and sternly, "My Lord Godalming, I too, have a duty to do, a duty to others, a duty to you, a duty to the dead, and by God, I shall do it! All I ask you now is that you come with me, that you look and listen, and if when later I make the same request you do not be more eager for its fulfillment even than I am, then, I shall do my duty, whatever it may seem to me. And then, to follow your Lordship's wishes I shall hold myself at your disposal to render an account to you, when and where you will." His voice broke a little, and he went on with a voice full of pity.

"But I beseech you, do not go forth in anger with me. In a long life of acts which were often not pleasant to do, and which sometimes did wring my heart, I have never had so heavy a task as now. Believe me that if the time comes for you to change your mind towards me, one look from you will wipe away all this so sad hour, for I would do what a man can to save you from sorrow. Just think. For why should I give myself so much labor and so much of sorrow? I have come here from my own land to do what I can of good, at the first to please my friend John, and then to help a sweet young lady, whom too, I come to love. For her, I am ashamed to say so much, but I say it in kindness, I gave what you gave, the blood of my veins. I gave it, I who was not, like you, her lover, but only her physician and her friend. I gave her my nights and days, before death, after death, and if my death can do her good even now, when she is the dead UnDead, she shall have it freely." He said this with a very grave, sweet pride, and Arthur was much affected by it.

He took the old man's hand and said in a broken voice, "Oh, it is hard to think of it, and I cannot understand, but at least I shall go with you and wait."

CHAPTER 16

DR. SEWARD'S DIARY--cont.

It was just a quarter before twelve o'clock when we got into the churchyard over the low wall. The night was dark with occasional gleams of moonlight between the dents of the heavy clouds that scudded across the sky. We all kept somehow close together, with Van Helsing slightly in front as he led the way. When we had come close to the tomb I looked well at Arthur, for I feared the proximity to a place laden with so sorrowful a memory would upset him, but he bore himself well. I took it that the very mystery of the proceeding was in some way a counteractant to his grief. The Professor unlocked the door, and seeing a natural hesitation amongst us for various reasons, solved the difficulty by entering first himself. The rest of us followed, and he closed the door. He then lit a dark lantern and pointed to a coffin. Arthur stepped forward hesitatingly. Van Helsing said to me, "You were with me here yesterday. Was the body of Miss Lucy in that coffin?"

"It was."

The Professor turned to the rest saying, "You hear, and yet there is no one who does not believe with me."

He took his screwdriver and again took off the lid of the coffin. Arthur looked on, very pale but silent. When the lid was removed he stepped forward. He evidently did not know that there was a leaden coffin, or at any rate, had not thought of it. When he saw the rent in the lead, the blood rushed to his face for an instant, but as quickly fell away again, so that he remained of a ghastly whiteness. He was still silent. Van Helsing forced back the leaden flange, and we all looked in and recoiled.

The coffin was empty!

For several minutes no one spoke a word. The silence was broken by Quincey Morris, "Professor, I answered for you. Your word is all I want. I wouldn't ask such a thing ordinarily, I wouldn't so dishonour you as to imply a doubt, but this is a mystery that goes beyond any honour or dishonour. Is this your doing?"

"I swear to you by all that I hold sacred that I have not removed or touched her. What happened was this. Two nights ago my friend Seward and I came here, with good purpose, believe me. I opened that coffin, which was then sealed up, and we found it as now, empty. We then waited, and saw something white come through the trees. The next day we came here in daytime and she lay there. Did she not, friend John?

"Yes."

"That night we were just in time. One more so small child was missing, and we find it, thank God, unharmed amongst the graves. Yesterday I came here before sundown, for at sundown the UnDead can move. I waited here all night till the sun rose, but I saw nothing. It was most probable that it was because I had laid over the clamps of those doors garlic, which the UnDead cannot bear, and other things which they shun. Last night there was no exodus, so tonight before the sundown I took away my garlic and other things. And so it is we find this coffin empty. But bear with me. So far there is much that is strange. Wait you with me outside, unseen and unheard, and things much stranger are yet to be. So," here he shut the dark slide of his lantern, "now to the outside." He opened the door, and we filed out, he coming last and locking the door behind him.

Oh! But it seemed fresh and pure in the night air after the terror of that vault. How sweet it was to see the clouds race by, and the passing gleams of the moonlight between the scudding clouds crossing and passing, like the gladness and sorrow of a man's life. How sweet it was to breathe the fresh air, that had no taint of death and decay. How humanizing to see the red lighting of the sky beyond the hill, and to hear far away the muffled roar that marks the life of a great city. Each in his own way was solemn and overcome. Arthur was silent, and was, I could see, striving to grasp the purpose and the inner meaning of the mystery. I was myself tolerably patient, and half inclined again to throw aside doubt and to accept Van Helsing's conclusions. Quincey Morris was phlegmatic in the way of a man who accepts all things, and accepts them in the spirit of cool bravery, with hazard of all he has at stake. Not being able to smoke, he cut himself a good-sized plug of tobacco and began to chew. As to Van Helsing, he was employed in a definite way. First he took from his bag a mass of what looked like thin, wafer-like biscuit, which was carefully rolled up in a white napkin. Next he took out a double handful of some whitish stuff, like dough or putty. He crumbled the wafer up fine and worked it into the mass between his hands. This he then took, and rolling it into thin strips, began to lay them into the crevices between the door and its setting in the tomb. I was somewhat puzzled at this, and being close, asked him what it was that he was doing. Arthur and Quincey drew near also, as they too were curious.

He answered, "I am closing the tomb so that the UnDead may not enter."

"And is that stuff you have there going to do it?"

"It is."

"What is that which you are using?" This time the question was by Arthur. Van Helsing reverently lifted his hat as he answered.

"The Host. I brought it from Amsterdam. I have an Indulgence."

It was an answer that appalled the most sceptical of us, and we felt individually that in the presence of such earnest purpose as the Professor's, a purpose which could thus use the to him most sacred of things, it was impossible to distrust. In respectful silence we took the places assigned to us close round the tomb, but hidden from the sight of any one approaching. I pitied the others, especially Arthur. I had myself been apprenticed by my former visits to this watching horror, and yet I, who had up to an hour ago repudiated the proofs, felt my heart sink within me. Never did tombs look so ghastly white. Never did cypress, or yew, or juniper so seem the embodiment of funeral gloom. Never did tree or grass wave or rustle so ominously. Never did bough creak so mysteriously, and never did the far-away howling of dogs send such a woeful presage through the night.

There was a long spell of silence, big, aching, void, and then from the Professor a keen "S-s-s-s!" He pointed, and far down the avenue of yews we saw a white figure advance, a dim white figure, which held something dark at its breast. The figure stopped, and at the moment a ray of moonlight fell upon the masses of driving clouds, and showed in startling prominence a dark-haired woman, dressed in the cerements of the grave. We could not see the face, for it was bent down over what we saw to be a fair-haired child. There was a pause and a sharp little cry, such as a child gives in sleep, or a dog as it lies before the fire and dreams. We were starting forward, but the Professor's warning hand, seen by us as he stood behind a yew tree, kept us back. And then as we looked the white figure moved forwards again. It was now near enough for us to see clearly, and the moonlight still held. My own heart grew cold as ice, and I could hear the gasp of Arthur, as we recognized the features of Lucy Westenra. Lucy Westenra, but yet how changed. The sweetness was turned to adamantine, heartless cruelty, and the purity to voluptuous wantonness.

Van Helsing stepped out, and obedient to his gesture, we all advanced too. The four of us ranged in a line before the door of the tomb. Van Helsing raised his lantern and drew the slide. By the concentrated light that fell on Lucy's face we could see that the lips were crimson with fresh blood, and that the stream had trickled over her chin and stained the purity of her lawn death-robe.

We shuddered with horror. I could see by the tremulous light that even Van Helsing's iron nerve had failed. Arthur was next to me, and if I had not seized his arm and held him up, he would have fallen.

When Lucy, I call the thing that was before us Lucy because it bore her shape, saw us she drew back with an angry snarl, such as a cat gives when taken unawares, then her eyes ranged over us. Lucy's eyes in form and colour, but Lucy's eyes unclean and full of hell fire, instead of the pure, gentle orbs we knew. At that moment the remnant of my love passed into hate and loathing. Had she then to be killed, I could have done it with savage delight. As she looked, her eyes blazed with unholy light, and the face became wreathed with a voluptuous smile. Oh, God, how it made me shudder to see it! With a careless motion, she flung to the ground, callous as a devil, the child that up to now she had clutched strenuously to her breast, growling over it as a dog growls over a bone. The child gave a sharp cry, and lay there moaning. There was a cold-bloodedness in the act which wrung a groan from Arthur. When she advanced to him with outstretched arms and a wanton smile he fell back and hid his face in his hands.

She still advanced, however, and with a languorous, voluptuous grace, said, "Come to me, Arthur. Leave these others and come to me. My arms are hungry for you. Come, and we can rest together. Come, my husband, come!"

There was something diabolically sweet in her tones, something of the tinkling of glass when struck, which rang through the brains even of us who heard the words addressed to another.

As for Arthur, he seemed under a spell, moving his hands from his face, he opened wide his arms. She was leaping for them, when Van Helsing sprang forward and held between them his little golden crucifix. She recoiled from it, and, with a suddenly distorted face, full of rage, dashed past him as if to enter the tomb.

CHAPTER 16

When within a foot or two of the door, however, she stopped, as if arrested by some irresistible force. Then she turned, and her face was shown in the clear burst of moonlight and by the lamp, which had now no quiver from Van Helsing's nerves. Never did I see such baffled malice on a face, and never, I trust, shall such ever be seen again by mortal eyes. The beautiful colour became livid, the eyes seemed to throw out sparks of hell fire, the brows were wrinkled as though the folds of flesh were the coils of Medusa's snakes, and the lovely, blood-stained mouth grew to an open square, as in the passion masks of the Greeks and Japanese. If ever a face meant death, if looks could kill, we saw it at that moment.

And so for full half a minute, which seemed an eternity, she remained between the lifted crucifix and the sacred closing of her means of entry.

Van Helsing broke the silence by asking Arthur, "Answer me, oh my friend! Am I to proceed in my work?"

"Do as you will, friend. Do as you will. There can be no horror like this ever any more." And he groaned in spirit.

Quincey and I simultaneously moved towards him, and took his arms. We could hear the click of the closing lantern as Van Helsing held it down. Coming close to the tomb, he began to remove from the chinks some of the sacred emblem which he had placed there. We all looked on with horrified amazement as we saw, when he stood back, the woman, with a corporeal body as real at that moment as our own, pass through the interstice where scarce a knife blade could have gone. We all felt a glad sense of relief when we saw the Professor calmly restoring the strings of putty to the edges of the door.

When this was done, he lifted the child and said, "Come now, my friends. We can do no more till tomorrow. There is a funeral at noon, so here we shall all come before long after that. The friends of the dead will all be gone by two, and when the sexton locks the gate we shall remain. Then there is more to do, but not like this of tonight. As for this little one, he is not much harmed, and by tomorrow night he shall be well. We shall leave him where the police will find him, as on the other night, and then to home."

Coming close to Arthur, he said, "My friend Arthur, you have had a sore trial, but after, when you look back, you will see how it was necessary. You are now in the bitter waters, my child. By this time tomorrow you will, please God, have passed them, and have drunk of the sweet waters. So do not mourn over-much. Till then I shall not ask you to forgive me."

Arthur and Quincey came home with me, and we tried to cheer each other on the way. We had left behind the child in safety, and were tired. So we all slept with more or less reality of sleep.

29 September, night.--A little before twelve o'clock we three, Arthur, Quincey Morris, and myself, called for the Professor. It was odd to notice that by common consent we had all put on black clothes. Of course, Arthur wore black, for he was in deep mourning, but the rest of us wore it by instinct. We got to the graveyard by half-past one, and strolled about, keeping out of official observation, so that when the gravediggers had completed their task and the sexton, under the belief that every one had gone, had locked the gate, we had the place all to ourselves. Van Helsing, instead of his little black bag, had with him a long leather one, something like a cricketing bag. It was manifestly of fair weight.

When we were alone and had heard the last of the footsteps die out up the road, we silently, and as if by ordered intention, followed the Professor to the tomb. He unlocked the door, and we entered, closing it behind us. Then he took from his bag the lantern, which he lit, and also two wax candles, which, when lighted, he stuck by melting their own ends, on other coffins, so that they might give light sufficient to work by. When he again lifted the lid off Lucy's coffin we all looked, Arthur trembling like an aspen, and saw that the corpse lay there in all its death beauty. But there was no love in my own heart, nothing but loathing for the foul Thing which had taken Lucy's shape without her soul. I could see even Arthur's face grow hard as he looked. Presently he said to Van Helsing, "Is this really Lucy's body, or only a demon in her shape?"

"It is her body, and yet not it. But wait a while, and you shall see her as she was, and is."

She seemed like a nightmare of Lucy as she lay there, the pointed teeth, the blood stained, voluptuous mouth, which made one shudder to see, the whole carnal and unspirited appearance, seeming like a devilish mockery of Lucy's sweet purity. Van Helsing, with his usual methodicalness, began taking the various contents from his bag and placing them ready for use. First he took out a soldering iron and some plumbing solder, and then small oil lamp, which gave out, when lit in a corner of the tomb, gas which burned at a fierce heat with a blue flame, then his operating knives, which he placed to hand, and last a round wooden stake, some two and a half or three inches thick and about three feet long. One end of it was hardened by charring in the fire, and was sharpened to a fine point. With this stake came a heavy hammer, such as in households is used in the coal cellar for breaking the lumps. To me, a doctor's preparations for work of any kind are stimulating and bracing, but the effect of these things on both Arthur and Quincey was to cause them a sort of consternation. They both, however, kept their courage, and remained silent and quiet.

When all was ready, Van Helsing said, "Before we do anything, let me tell you this. It is out of the lore and experience of the ancients and of all those who have studied the powers of the UnDead. When they become such, there comes with the change the curse of immortality. They cannot die, but must go on age after age adding new victims and multiplying the evils of the world. For all that die from the preying of the Undead become themselves Undead, and prey on their kind. And so the circle goes on ever widening, like as the ripples from a stone thrown in the water. Friend Arthur, if you had met that kiss which you know of before poor Lucy die, or again, last night when you open your arms to her, you would in time, when you had died, have become nosferatu, as they call it in Eastern Europe, and would for all time make more of those Un-Deads that so have filled us with horror. The career of this so unhappy dear lady is but just begun. Those children whose blood she sucked are not as yet so much the worse, but if she lives on, UnDead, more and more they lose their blood and by her power over them they come to her, and so she draw their blood with that so wicked mouth. But if she die in truth, then all cease. The tiny wounds of the throats disappear, and they go back to their play unknowing ever of what has been. But of the most blessed of all, when this now UnDead be made to rest as true dead, then the soul of the poor lady whom we love shall again be free. Instead of working wickedness by night and growing more debased in the assimilating of it by day, she shall take her place with the other Angels. So that, my friend, it will be a blessed hand for her that shall strike the blow that sets her free. To this I am willing, but is there none amongst us who has a better right? Will it be no joy to think of hereafter in the silence of the night when sleep is not, 'It was my hand that sent her to the stars. It was the hand of him that loved her best, the hand that of all she would herself have chosen, had it been to her to choose?' Tell me if there be such a one amongst us?"

We all looked at Arthur. He saw too, what we all did, the infinite kindness which suggested that his should be the hand which would restore Lucy to us as a holy, and not an unholy, memory. He stepped forward and said bravely, though his hand trembled, and his face was as pale as snow, "My true friend, from the bottom of my broken heart I thank you. Tell me what I am to do, and I shall not falter!"

Van Helsing laid a hand on his shoulder, and said, "Brave lad! A moment's courage, and it is done. This stake must be driven through her. It well be a fearful ordeal, be not deceived in that, but it will be only a short time, and you will then rejoice more than your pain was great. From this grim tomb you will emerge as though you tread on air. But you must not falter when once you have begun. Only think that we, your true friends, are round you, and that we pray for you all the time."

"Go on," said Arthur hoarsely. "Tell me what I am to do."

"Take this stake in your left hand, ready to place to the point over the heart, and the hammer in your right. Then when we begin our prayer for the dead, I shall read him, I have here the book, and the others shall follow, strike in God's name, that so all may be well with the dead that we love and that the UnDead pass away."

Arthur took the stake and the hammer, and when once his mind was set on action his hands never trembled nor even quivered. Van Helsing opened his missal and began to read, and Quincey and I followed as well as we could.

Arthur placed the point over the heart, and as I looked I could see its dint in the white flesh. Then he struck with all his might.

The thing in the coffin writhed, and a hideous, blood-curdling screech came from the opened red lips. The body shook and quivered and twisted in wild contortions. The sharp white teeth champed together till the lips were cut, and the mouth was smeared with a crimson foam. But Arthur never faltered. He looked like a figure of Thor as his untrembling arm rose and fell, driving deeper and deeper the mercy-bearing stake, whilst the blood from the pierced heart welled and spurted up around it. His face was set, and high duty seemed to shine through it. The sight of it gave us courage so that our voices seemed to ring through the little vault.

And then the writhing and quivering of the body became less, and the teeth seemed to champ, and the face to quiver. Finally it lay still. The terrible task was over.

The hammer fell from Arthur's hand. He reeled and would have fallen had we not caught him. The great drops of sweat sprang from his forehead, and his breath came in broken gasps. It had indeed been an awful strain on him, and had he not been forced to his task by more than human considerations he could never have gone through with it. For a few minutes we were so taken up with him that we did not look towards the coffin. When we did, however, a murmur of startled surprise ran from one to the other of us. We gazed so eagerly that Arthur rose, for he had been seated on the ground, and came and looked too, and then a glad strange light broke over his face and dispelled altogether the gloom of horror that lay upon it.

There, in the coffin lay no longer the foul Thing that we had so dreaded and grown to hate that the work of her destruction was yielded as a privilege to the one best entitled to it, but Lucy as we had seen her in life, with her face of unequalled sweetness and purity. True that there were there, as we had seen them in life, the traces of care and pain and waste. But these were all dear to us, for they marked her truth to what we knew. One and all we felt that the holy calm that lay like sunshine over the wasted face and form was only an earthly token and symbol of the calm that was to reign for ever.

Van Helsing came and laid his hand on Arthur's shoulder, and said to him, "And now, Arthur my friend, dear lad, am I not forgiven?"

The reaction of the terrible strain came as he took the old man's hand in his, and raising it to his lips, pressed it, and said, "Forgiven! God bless you that you have given my dear one her soul again, and me peace." He put his hands on the Professor's shoulder, and laying his head on his breast, cried for a while silently, whilst we stood unmoving.

When he raised his head Van Helsing said to him, "And now, my child, you may kiss her. Kiss her dead lips if you will, as she would have you to, if for her to choose. For she is not a grinning devil now, not any more a foul Thing for all eternity. No longer she is the devil's UnDead. She is God's true dead, whose soul is with Him!"

Arthur bent and kissed her, and then we sent him and Quincey out of the tomb. The Professor and I sawed the top off the stake, leaving the point of it in the body. Then we cut off the head and filled the mouth with garlic. We soldered up the leaden coffin, screwed on the coffin lid, and gathering up our belongings, came away. When the Professor locked the door he gave the key to Arthur.

Outside the air was sweet, the sun shone, and the birds sang, and it seemed as if all nature were tuned to a different pitch. There was gladness and mirth and peace everywhere, for we were at rest ourselves on one account, and we were glad, though it was with a tempered joy.

Before we moved away Van Helsing said, "Now, my friends, one step of our work is done, one the most harrowing to ourselves. But there remains a greater task: to find out the author of all this our sorrow and to stamp him out. I have clues which we can follow, but it is a long task, and a difficult one, and there is danger in it, and pain. Shall you not all help me? We have learned to believe, all of us, is it not so? And since so, do we not see our duty? Yes! And do we not promise to go on to the bitter end?"

Each in turn, we took his hand, and the promise was made. Then said the Professor as we moved off, "Two nights hence you shall meet with me and dine together at seven of the clock with friend John. I shall entreat two others, two that you know not as yet, and I shall be ready to all our work show and our plans unfold. Friend John, you come with me home, for I have much to consult you about, and you can help me. Tonight I leave for Amsterdam, but shall return tomorrow night. And then begins our great quest. But first I shall have much to say, so that you may know what to do and to dread. Then our promise shall be made to each other anew. For there is a terrible task before us, and once our feet are on the ploughshare we must not draw back."

CHAPTER 17

DR. SEWARD'S DIARY--cont.

When we arrived at the Berkely Hotel, Van Helsing found a telegram waiting for him.

"Am coming up by train. Jonathan at Whitby. Important news. Mina Harker."

The Professor was delighted. "Ah, that wonderful Madam Mina," he said, "pearl among women! She arrive, but I cannot stay. She must go to your house, friend John. You must meet her at the station. Telegraph her en route so that she may be prepared."

When the wire was dispatched he had a cup of tea. Over it he told me of a diary kept by Jonathan Harker when abroad, and gave me a typewritten copy of it, as also of Mrs. Harker's diary at Whitby. "Take these," he said, "and study them well. When I have returned you will be master of all the facts, and we can then better enter on our inquisition. Keep them safe, for there is in them much of treasure. You will need all your faith, even you who have had such an experience as that of today. What is here told," he laid his hand heavily and gravely on the packet of papers as he spoke, "may be the beginning of the end to you and me and many another, or it may sound the knell of the UnDead who walk the earth. Read all, I pray you, with the open mind, and if you can add in any way to the story here told do so, for it is all important. You have kept a diary of all these so strange things, is it not so? Yes! Then we shall go through all these together when we meet." He then made ready for his departure and shortly drove off to Liverpool Street. I took my way to Paddington, where I arrived about fifteen minutes before the train came in.

The crowd melted away, after the bustling fashion common to arrival platforms, and I was beginning to feel uneasy, lest I might miss my guest, when a sweet-faced, dainty looking girl stepped up to me, and after a quick glance said, "Dr. Seward, is it not?"

"And you are Mrs. Harker!" I answered at once, whereupon she held out her hand.

"I knew you from the description of poor dear Lucy, but..." She stopped suddenly, and a quick blush overspread her face.

The blush that rose to my own cheeks somehow set us both at ease, for it was a tacit answer to her own. I got her luggage, which included a typewriter, and we took the Underground to Fenchurch Street, after I had sent a wire to my housekeeper to have a sitting room and a bedroom prepared at once for Mrs. Harker.

In due time we arrived. She knew, of course, that the place was a lunatic asylum, but I could see that she was unable to repress a shudder when we entered.

She told me that, if she might, she would come presently to my study, as she had much to say. So here I am finishing my entry in my phonograph diary whilst I await her. As yet I have not had the chance of looking at the papers which Van Helsing left with me, though they lie open before me. I must get her interested in something, so that I may have an opportunity of reading them. She does not know how precious time is, or what a task we have in hand. I must be careful not to frighten her. Here she is!

MINA HARKER'S JOURNAL

29 September.--After I had tidied myself, I went down to Dr. Seward's study. At the door I paused a moment, for I thought I heard him talking with some one. As, however, he had pressed me to be quick, I knocked at the door, and on his calling out, "Come in," I entered.

To my intense surprise, there was no one with him. He was quite alone, and on the table opposite him was what I knew at once from the description to be a phonograph. I had never seen one, and was much interested.

"I hope I did not keep you waiting," I said, "but I stayed at the door as I heard you talking, and thought there was someone with you."

"Oh," he replied with a smile, "I was only entering my diary."

"Your diary?" I asked him in surprise.

"Yes," he answered. "I keep it in this." As he spoke he laid his hand on the phonograph. I felt quite excited over it, and blurted out, "Why, this beats even shorthand! May I hear it say something?"

"Certainly," he replied with alacrity, and stood up to put it in train for speaking. Then he paused, and a troubled look overspread his face.

"The fact is," he began awkwardly, "I only keep my diary in it, and as it is entirely, almost entirely, about my cases it may be awkward, that is, I mean..." He stopped, and I tried to help him out of his embarrassment.

"You helped to attend dear Lucy at the end. Let me hear how she died, for all that I know of her, I shall be very grateful. She was very, very dear to me."

To my surprise, he answered, with a horrorstruck look in his face, "Tell you of her death? Not for the wide world!"

"Why not?" I asked, for some grave, terrible feeling was coming over me.

Again he paused, and I could see that he was trying to invent an excuse. At length, he stammered out, "You see, I do not know how to pick out any particular part of the diary."

Even while he was speaking an idea dawned upon him, and he said with unconscious simplicity, in a different voice, and with the naivete of a child, "that's quite true, upon my honour. Honest Indian!"

I could not but smile, at which he grimaced. "I gave myself away that time!" he said. "But do you know that, although I have kept the diary for months past, it never once struck me how I was going to find any particular part of it in case I wanted to look it up?"

CHAPTER 17

By this time my mind was made up that the diary of a doctor who attended Lucy might have something to add to the sum of our knowledge of that terrible Being, and I said boldly, "Then, Dr. Seward, you had better let me copy it out for you on my typewriter."

He grew to a positively deathly pallor as he said, "No! No! No! For all the world. I wouldn't let you know that terrible story!"

Then it was terrible. My intuition was right! For a moment, I thought, and as my eyes ranged the room, unconsciously looking for something or some opportunity to aid me, they lit on a great batch of typewriting on the table. His eyes caught the look in mine, and without his thinking, followed their direction. As they saw the parcel he realized my meaning.

"You do not know me," I said. "When you have read those papers, my own diary and my husband's also, which I have typed, you will know me better. I have not faltered in giving every thought of my own heart in this cause. But, of course, you do not know me, yet, and I must not expect you to trust me so far."

He is certainly a man of noble nature. Poor dear Lucy was right about him. He stood up and opened a large drawer, in which were arranged in order a number of hollow cylinders of metal covered with dark wax, and said,

"You are quite right. I did not trust you because I did not know you. But I know you now, and let me say that I should have known you long ago. I know that Lucy told you of me. She told me of you too. May I make the only atonement in my power? Take the cylinders and hear them. The first half-dozen of them are personal to me, and they will not horrify you. Then you will know me better. Dinner will by then be ready. In the meantime I shall read over some of these documents, and shall be better able to understand certain things."

He carried the phonograph himself up to my sitting room and adjusted it for me. Now I shall learn something pleasant, I am sure. For it will tell me the other side of a true love episode of which I know one side already.

DR. SEWARD'S DIARY

29 September.--I was so absorbed in that wonderful diary of Jonathan Harker and that other of his wife that I let the time run on without thinking. Mrs. Harker was not down when the maid came to announce dinner, so I said, "She is possibly tired. Let dinner wait an hour," and I went on with my work. I had just finished Mrs. Harker's diary, when she came in. She looked sweetly pretty, but very sad, and her eyes were flushed with crying. This somehow moved me much. Of late I have had cause for tears, God knows! But the relief of them was denied me, and now the sight of those sweet eyes, brightened by recent tears, went straight to my heart. So I said as gently as I could, "I greatly fear I have distressed you."

"Oh, no, not distressed me," she replied. "But I have been more touched than I can say by your grief. That is a wonderful machine, but it is cruelly true. It told me, in its very tones, the anguish of your heart. It was like a soul crying out to Almighty God. No one must hear them spoken ever again! See, I have tried to be useful. I have copied out the words on my typewriter, and none other need now hear your heart beat, as I did."

"No one need ever know, shall ever know," I said in a low voice. She laid her hand on mine and said very gravely, "Ah, but they must!"

"Must! But why?" I asked.

"Because it is a part of the terrible story, a part of poor Lucy's death and all that led to it. Because in the struggle which we have before us to rid the earth of this terrible monster we must have all the knowledge and all the help which we can get. I think that the cylinders which you gave me contained more than you intended me to know. But I can see that there are in your record many lights to this dark mystery. You will let me help, will you not? I know all up to a certain point, and I see already, though your diary only took me to 7 September, how poor Lucy was beset, and how her terrible doom was being wrought out. Jonathan and I have been working day and night since Professor Van Helsing saw us. He is gone to Whitby to get more information, and he will be here tomorrow to help us. We need have no secrets amongst us. Working together and with absolute trust, we can surely be stronger than if some of us were in the dark."

She looked at me so appealingly, and at the same time manifested such courage and resolution in her bearing, that I gave in at once to her wishes. "You shall," I said, "do as you like in the matter. God forgive me if I do wrong! There are terrible things yet to learn of, but if you have so far traveled on the road to poor Lucy's death, you will not be content, I know, to remain in the dark. Nay, the end, the very end, may give you a gleam of peace. Come, there is dinner. We must keep one another strong for what is before us. We have a cruel and dreadful task. When you have eaten you shall learn the rest, and I shall answer any questions you ask, if there be anything which you do not understand, though it was apparent to us who were present."

MINA HARKER'S JOURNAL

29 September.--After dinner I came with Dr. Seward to his study. He brought back the phonograph from my room, and I took a chair, and arranged the phonograph so that I could touch it without getting up, and showed me how to stop it in case I should want to pause. Then he very thoughtfully took a chair, with his back to me, so that I might be as free as possible, and began to read. I put the forked metal to my ears and listened.

When the terrible story of Lucy's death, and all that followed, was done, I lay back in my chair powerless. Fortunately I am not of a fainting disposition. When Dr. Seward saw me he jumped up with a horrified exclamation, and hurriedly taking a case bottle from the cupboard, gave me some brandy, which in a few minutes somewhat restored me. My brain was all in a whirl, and only that there came through all the multitude of horrors, the holy ray of light that my dear Lucy was at last at peace, I do not think I could have borne it without making a scene. It is all so wild and mysterious, and strange that if I had not known Jonathan's experience in Transylvania I could not have believed. As it was, I didn't know what to believe, and so got out of my difficulty by attending to something else. I took the cover off my typewriter, and said to Dr. Seward,

"Let me write this all out now. We must be ready for Dr. Van Helsing when he comes. I have sent a telegram to Jonathan to come on here when he arrives in London from Whitby. In this matter dates are everything, and I think that if we get all of our material ready, and have every item put in chronological order, we shall have done much.

"You tell me that Lord Godalming and Mr. Morris are coming too. Let us be able to tell them when they come."

He accordingly set the phonograph at a slow pace, and I began to typewrite from the beginning of the seventeenth cylinder. I used manifold, and so took three copies of the diary, just as I had done with the rest. It was late when I got through, but Dr. Seward went about his work of going his round of the patients. When he had finished he came back and sat near me, reading, so that I did not feel too lonely whilst I worked. How good and thoughtful he is. The world seems full of good men, even if there are monsters in it.

Before I left him I remembered what Jonathan put in his diary of the Professor's perturbation at reading something in an evening paper at the station at Exeter, so, seeing that Dr. Seward keeps his newspapers, I borrowed the files of 'The Westminster Gazette' and 'The Pall Mall Gazette' and took them to my room. I remember how much the 'Dailygraph' and 'The Whitby Gazette', of which I had made cuttings, had helped us to understand the terrible events at Whitby when Count Dracula landed, so I shall look through the evening papers since then, and perhaps I shall get some new light. I am not sleepy, and the work will help to keep me quiet.

DR. SEWARD'S DIARY

30 September.--Mr. Harker arrived at nine o'clock. He got his wife's wire just before starting. He is uncommonly clever, if one can judge from his face, and full of energy. If this journal be true, and judging by one's own wonderful experiences, it must be, he is also a man of great nerve. That going down to the vault a second time was a remarkable piece of daring. After reading his account of it I was prepared to meet a good specimen of manhood, but hardly the quiet, businesslike gentleman who came here today.

LATER.--After lunch Harker and his wife went back to their own room, and as I passed a while ago I heard the click of the typewriter. They are hard at it. Mrs. Harker says that they are knitting together in chronological order every scrap of evidence they have. Harker has got the letters between the consignee of the boxes at Whitby and the carriers in London who took charge of them. He is now reading his wife's transcript of my diary. I wonder what they make out of it. Here it is…

Strange that it never struck me that the very next house might be the Count's hiding place! Goodness knows that we had enough clues from the conduct of the patient Renfield! The bundle of letters relating to the purchase of the house were with the transcript. Oh, if we had only had them earlier we might have saved poor Lucy! Stop! That way madness lies! Harker has gone back, and is again collecting material. He says that by dinner time they will be able to show a whole connected narrative. He thinks that in the meantime I should see Renfield, as hitherto he has been a sort of index to the coming and going of the Count. I hardly see this yet, but when I get at the dates I suppose I shall. What a good thing that Mrs. Harker put my cylinders into type! We never could have found the dates otherwise.

I found Renfield sitting placidly in his room with his hands folded, smiling benignly. At the moment he seemed as sane as any one I ever saw. I sat down and talked with him on a lot of subjects, all of which he treated naturally. He then, of his own accord, spoke of going home, a subject he has never mentioned to my knowledge during his sojourn here. In fact, he spoke quite confidently of getting his discharge at once. I believe that, had I not had the chat with Harker and read the letters and the dates of his outbursts, I should have been prepared to sign for him after a brief time of observation. As it is, I am darkly suspicious. All those out-breaks were in some way linked with the proximity of the Count. What then does this absolute content mean? Can it be that his instinct is satisfied as to the vampire's ultimate triumph? Stay. He is himself zoophagous, and in his wild ravings outside the chapel door of the deserted house he always spoke of 'master'. This all seems confirmation of our idea. However, after a while I came away. My friend is just a little too sane at present to make it safe to probe him too deep with questions. He might begin to think, and then... So I came away. I mistrust these quiet moods of his, so I have given the attendant a hint to look closely after him, and to have a strait waistcoat ready in case of need.

JOHNATHAN HARKER'S JOURNAL

29 September, in train to London.--When I received Mr. Billington's courteous message that he would give me any information in his power I thought it best to go down to Whitby and make, on the spot, such inquiries as I wanted. It was now my object to trace that horrid cargo of the Count's to its place in London. Later, we may be able to deal with it. Billington junior, a nice lad, met me at the station, and brought me to his father's house, where they had decided that I must spend the night. They are hospitable, with true Yorkshire hospitality, give a guest everything and leave him to do as he likes. They all knew that I was busy, and that my stay was short, and Mr. Billington had ready in his office all the papers concerning the consignment of boxes. It gave me almost a turn to see again one of the letters which I had seen on the Count's table before I knew of his diabolical plans. Everything had been carefully thought out, and done systematically and with precision. He seemed to have been prepared for every obstacle which might be placed by accident in the way of his intentions being carried out. To use an Americanism, he had 'taken no chances', and the absolute accuracy with which his instructions were fulfilled was simply the logical result of his care. I saw the invoice, and took note of it. 'Fifty cases of common earth, to be used for experimental purposes'. Also the copy of the letter to Carter Paterson, and their reply. Of both these I got copies. This was all the information Mr. Billington could give me, so I went down to the port and saw the coastguards, the Customs Officers and the harbour master, who kindly put me in communication with the men who had actually received the boxes. Their tally was exact with the list, and they had nothing to add to the simple description 'fifty cases of common earth', except that the boxes were 'main and mortal heavy', and that shifting them was dry work. One of them added that it was hard lines that there wasn't any gentleman 'such like as like yourself, squire', to show some sort of appreciation of their efforts in a liquid form. Another put in a rider that the thirst then generated was such that even the time which had elapsed had not completely allayed it. Needless to add, I took care before leaving to lift, forever and adequately, this source of reproach.

30 September.--The station master was good enough to give me a line to his old companion the station master at King's Cross, so that when I arrived there in the

morning I was able to ask him about the arrival of the boxes. He, too put me at once in communication with the proper officials, and I saw that their tally was correct with the original invoice. The opportunities of acquiring an abnormal thirst had been here limited. A noble use of them had, however, been made, and again I was compelled to deal with the result in ex post facto manner.

From thence I went to Carter Paterson's central office, where I met with the utmost courtesy. They looked up the transaction in their day book and letter book, and at once telephoned to their King's Cross office for more details. By good fortune, the men who did the teaming were waiting for work, and the official at once sent them over, sending also by one of them the way-bill and all the papers connected with the delivery of the boxes at Carfax. Here again I found the tally agreeing exactly. The carriers' men were able to supplement the paucity of the written words with a few more details. These were, I shortly found, connected almost solely with the dusty nature of the job, and the consequent thirst engendered in the operators. On my affording an opportunity, through the medium of the currency of the realm, of the allaying, at a later period, this beneficial evil, one of the men remarked,

"That 'ere 'ouse, guv'nor, is the rummiest I ever was in. Blyme! But it ain't been touched sence a hundred years. There was dust that thick in the place that you might have slep' on it without 'urtin' of yer bones. An' the place was that neglected that yer might 'ave smelled ole Jerusalem in it. But the old chapel, that took the cike, that did! Me and my mate, we thort we wouldn't never git out quick enough. Lor', I wouldn't take less nor a quid a moment to stay there arter dark."

Having been in the house, I could well believe him, but if he knew what I know, he would, I think have raised his terms.

Of one thing I am now satisfied. That all those boxes which arrived at Whitby from Varna in the Demeter were safely deposited in the old chapel at Carfax. There should be fifty of them there, unless any have since been removed, as from Dr. Seward's diary I fear.

Later.--Mina and I have worked all day, and we have put all the papers into order.

MINA HARKER'S JOURNAL

30 September.--I am so glad that I hardly know how to contain myself. It is, I suppose, the reaction from the haunting fear which I have had, that this terrible affair and the reopening of his old wound might act detrimentally on Jonathan. I saw him leave for Whitby with as brave a face as could, but I was sick with apprehension. The effort has, however, done him good. He was never so resolute, never so strong, never so full of volcanic energy, as at present. It is just as that dear, good Professor Van Helsing said, he is true grit, and he improves under strain that would kill a weaker nature. He came back full of life and hope and determination. We have got everything in order for tonight. I feel myself quite wild with excitement. I suppose one ought to pity anything so hunted as the Count. That is just it. This thing is not human, not even a beast. To read Dr. Seward's account of poor Lucy's death, and what followed, is enough to dry up the springs of pity in one's heart.

Later.--Lord Godalming and Mr. Morris arrived earlier than we expected. Dr. Seward was out on business, and had taken Jonathan with him, so I had to see them. It was to me a painful meeting, for it brought back all poor dear Lucy's hopes of only a few months ago. Of course they had heard Lucy speak of me, and it seemed that Dr. Van Helsing, too, had been quite 'blowing my trumpet', as Mr. Morris expressed it. Poor fellows, neither of them is aware that I know all about the proposals they made to Lucy. They did not quite know what to say or do, as they were ignorant of the amount of my knowledge. So they had to keep on neutral subjects. However, I thought the matter over, and came to the conclusion that the best thing I could do would be to post them on affairs right up to date. I knew from Dr. Seward's diary that they had been at Lucy's death, her real death, and that I need not fear to betray any secret before the time. So I told them, as well as I could, that I had read all the papers and diaries, and that my husband and I, having typewritten them, had just finished putting them in order. I gave them each a copy to read in the library. When Lord Godalming got his and turned it over, it does make a pretty good pile, he said, "Did you write all this, Mrs. Harker?"

I nodded, and he went on.

"I don't quite see the drift of it, but you people are all so good and kind, and have been working so earnestly and so energetically, that all I can do is to accept your ideas blindfold and try to help you. I have had one lesson already in accepting facts that should make a man humble to the last hour of his life. Besides, I know you loved my Lucy…"

Here he turned away and covered his face with his hands. I could hear the tears in his voice. Mr. Morris, with instinctive delicacy, just laid a hand for a moment on his shoulder, and then walked quietly out of the room. I suppose there is something in a woman's nature that makes a man free to break down before her and express his feelings on the tender or emotional side without feeling it derogatory to his manhood. For when Lord Godalming found himself alone with me he sat down on the sofa and gave way utterly and openly. I sat down beside him and took his hand. I hope he didn't think it forward of me, and that if he ever thinks of it afterwards he never will have such a thought. There I wrong him. I know he never will. He is too true a gentleman. I said to him, for I could see that his heart was breaking, "I loved dear Lucy, and I know what she was to you, and what you were to her. She and I were like sisters, and now she is gone, will you not let me be like a sister to you in your trouble? I know what sorrows you have had, though I cannot measure the depth of them. If sympathy and pity can help in your affliction, won't you let me be of some little service, for Lucy's sake?"

In an instant the poor dear fellow was overwhelmed with grief. It seemed to me that all that he had of late been suffering in silence found a vent at once. He grew quite hysterical, and raising his open hands, beat his palms together in a perfect agony of grief. He stood up and then sat down again, and the tears rained down his cheeks. I felt an infinite pity for him, and opened my arms unthinkingly. With a sob he laid his head on my shoulder and cried like a wearied child, whilst he shook with emotion.

We women have something of the mother in us that makes us rise above smaller matters when the mother spirit is invoked. I felt this big sorrowing man's head resting on me, as though it were that of a baby that some day may lie on my bosom, and I stroked his hair as though he were my own child. I never thought at the time how strange it all was.

After a little bit his sobs ceased, and he raised himself with an apology, though he made no disguise of his emotion. He told me that for days and nights past, weary days and sleepless nights, he had been unable to speak with any one, as a man must speak in his time of sorrow. There was no woman whose sympathy could be given to him, or with whom, owing to the terrible circumstance with which his sorrow was surrounded, he could speak freely.

"I know now how I suffered," he said, as he dried his eyes, "but I do not know even yet, and none other can ever know, how much your sweet sympathy has been to me today. I shall know better in time, and believe me that, though I am not ungrateful now, my gratitude will grow with my understanding. You will let me be like a brother, will you not, for all our lives, for dear Lucy's sake?"

"For dear Lucy's sake," I said as we clasped hands. "Ay, and for your own sake," he added, "for if a man's esteem and gratitude are ever worth the winning, you have won mine today. If ever the future should bring to you a time when you need a man's help, believe me, you will not call in vain. God grant that no such time may ever come to you to break the sunshine of your life, but if it should ever come, promise me that you will let me know."

He was so earnest, and his sorrow was so fresh, that I felt it would comfort him, so I said, "I promise."

As I came along the corridor I saw Mr. Morris looking out of a window. He turned as he heard my footsteps. "How is Art?" he said. Then noticing my red eyes, he went on, "Ah, I see you have been comforting him. Poor old fellow! He needs it. No one but a woman can help a man when he is in trouble of the heart, and he had no one to comfort him."

He bore his own trouble so bravely that my heart bled for him. I saw the manuscript in his hand, and I knew that when he read it he would realize how much I knew, so I said to him, "I wish I could comfort all who suffer from the heart. Will you let me be your friend, and will you come to me for comfort if you need it? You will know later why I speak."

He saw that I was in earnest, and stooping, took my hand, and raising it to his lips, kissed it. It seemed but poor comfort to so brave and unselfish a soul, and impulsively I bent over and kissed him. The tears rose in his eyes, and there was a momentary choking in his throat. He said quite calmly, "Little girl, you will never forget that true hearted kindness, so long as ever you live!" Then he went into the study to his friend.

"Little girl!" The very words he had used to Lucy, and, oh, but he proved himself a friend.

CHAPTER 18

DR. SEWARD'S DIARY

30 September.--I got home at five o'clock, and found that Godalming and Morris had not only arrived, but had already studied the transcript of the various diaries and letters which Harker had not yet returned from his visit to the carriers' men, of whom Dr. Hennessey had written to me. Mrs. Harker gave us a cup of tea, and I can honestly say that, for the first time since I have lived in it, this old house seemed like home. When we had finished, Mrs. Harker said,

"Dr. Seward, may I ask a favour? I want to see your patient, Mr. Renfield. Do let me see him. What you have said of him in your diary interests me so much!"

She looked so appealing and so pretty that I could not refuse her, and there was no possible reason why I should, so I took her with me. When I went into the room, I told the man that a lady would like to see him, to which he simply answered, "Why?"

"She is going through the house, and wants to see every one in it," I answered.

"Oh, very well," he said, "let her come in, by all means, but just wait a minute till I tidy up the place."

His method of tidying was peculiar, he simply swallowed all the flies and spiders in the boxes before I could stop him. It was quite evident that he feared, or was jealous of, some interference. When he had got through his disgusting task, he said cheerfully, "Let the lady come in," and sat down on the edge of his bed with his head down, but with his eyelids raised so that he could see her as she entered. For a moment I thought that he might have some homicidal intent. I remembered how quiet he had been just before he attacked me in my own study, and I took care to stand where I could seize him at once if he attempted to make a spring at her.

She came into the room with an easy gracefulness which would at once command the respect of any lunatic, for easiness is one of the qualities mad people most respect. She walked over to him, smiling pleasantly, and held out her hand.

"Good evening, Mr. Renfield," said she. "You see, I know you, for Dr. Seward has told me of you." He made no immediate reply, but eyed her all over intently with a set frown on his face. This look gave way to one of wonder, which merged in doubt, then to my intense astonishment he said, "You're not the girl the doctor wanted to marry, are you? You can't be, you know, for she's dead."

Mrs. Harker smiled sweetly as she replied, "Oh no! I have a husband of my own, to whom I was married before I ever saw Dr. Seward, or he me. I am Mrs. Harker."

"Then what are you doing here?"

"My husband and I are staying on a visit with Dr. Seward."

"Then don't stay."

"But why not?"

I thought that this style of conversation might not be pleasant to Mrs. Harker, any more than it was to me, so I joined in, "How did you know I wanted to marry anyone?"

His reply was simply contemptuous, given in a pause in which he turned his eyes from Mrs. Harker to me, instantly turning them back again, "What an asinine question!"

"I don't see that at all, Mr. Renfield," said Mrs. Harker, at once championing me.

He replied to her with as much courtesy and respect as he had shown contempt to me, "You will, of course, understand, Mrs. Harker, that when a man is so loved and honoured as our host is, everything regarding him is of interest in our little community. Dr. Seward is loved not only by his household and his friends, but even by his patients, who, being some of them hardly in mental equilibrium, are apt to distort causes and effects. Since I myself have been an inmate of a lunatic asylum, I cannot but notice that the sophistic tendencies of some of its inmates lean towards the errors of non causa and ignoratio elenche."

I positively opened my eyes at this new development. Here was my own pet lunatic, the most pronounced of his type that I had ever met with, talking elemental philosophy, and with the manner of a polished gentleman. I wonder if it was Mrs. Harker's presence which had touched some chord in his memory. If this new phase was spontaneous, or in any way due to her unconscious influence, she must have some rare gift or power.

We continued to talk for some time, and seeing that he was seemingly quite reasonable, she ventured, looking at me questioningly as she began, to lead him to his favourite topic. I was again astonished, for he addressed himself to the question with the impartiality of the completest sanity. He even took himself as an example when he mentioned certain things.

"Why, I myself am an instance of a man who had a strange belief. Indeed, it was no wonder that my friends were alarmed, and insisted on my being put under control. I used to fancy that life was a positive and perpetual entity, and that by consuming a multitude of live things, no matter how low in the scale of creation, one might indefinitely prolong life. At times I held the belief so strongly that I actually tried to take human life. The doctor here will bear me out that on one occasion I tried to kill him for the purpose of strengthening my vital powers by the assimilation with my own body of his life through the medium of his blood, relying of course, upon the Scriptural phrase, 'For the blood is the life.' Though, indeed, the vendor of a certain nostrum has vulgarized the truism to the very point of contempt. Isn't that true, doctor?"

I nodded assent, for I was so amazed that I hardly knew what to either think or say, it was hard to imagine that I had seen him eat up his spiders and flies not five minutes before. Looking at my watch, I saw that I should go to the station to meet Van Helsing, so I told Mrs. Harker that it was time to leave.

She came at once, after saying pleasantly to Mr. Renfield, "Goodbye, and I hope I may see you often, under auspices pleasanter to yourself."

To which, to my astonishment, he replied, "Goodbye, my dear. I pray God I may never see your sweet face again. May He bless and keep you!"

When I went to the station to meet Van Helsing I left the boys behind me. Poor Art seemed more cheerful than he has been since Lucy first took ill, and Quincey is more like his own bright self than he has been for many a long day.

Van Helsing stepped from the carriage with the eager nimbleness of a boy. He saw me at once, and rushed up to me, saying, "Ah, friend John, how goes all? Well? So! I have been busy, for I come here to stay if need be. All affairs are settled with me, and I have much to tell. Madam Mina is with you? Yes. And her so fine husband? And Arthur and my friend Quincey, they are with you, too? Good!"

As I drove to the house I told him of what had passed, and of how my own diary had come to be of some use through Mrs. Harker's suggestion, at which the Professor interrupted me.

"Ah, that wonderful Madam Mina! She has man's brain, a brain that a man should have were he much gifted, and a woman's heart. The good God fashioned her for a purpose, believe me, when He made that so good combination. Friend John, up to now fortune has made that woman of help to us, after tonight she must not have to do with this so terrible affair. It is not good that she run a risk so great. We men are determined, nay, are we not pledged, to destroy this monster? But it is no part for a woman. Even if she be not harmed, her heart may fail her in so much and so many horrors and hereafter she may suffer, both in waking, from her nerves, and in sleep, from her dreams. And, besides, she is young woman and not so long married, there may be other things to think of some time, if not now. You tell me she has wrote all, then she must consult with us, but tomorrow she say goodbye to this work, and we go alone."

I agreed heartily with him, and then I told him what we had found in his absence, that the house which Dracula had bought was the very next one to my own. He was amazed, and a great concern seemed to come on him.

"Oh that we had known it before!" he said, "for then we might have reached him in time to save poor Lucy. However, 'the milk that is spilt cries not out afterwards,' as you say. We shall not think of that, but go on our way to the end." Then he fell into a silence that lasted till we entered my own gateway. Before we went to prepare for dinner he said to Mrs. Harker, "I am told, Madam Mina, by my friend John that you and your husband have put up in exact order all things that have been, up to this moment."

"Not up to this moment, Professor," she said impulsively, "but up to this morning."

"But why not up to now? We have seen hitherto how good light all the little things have made. We have told our secrets, and yet no one who has told is the worse for it."

Mrs. Harker began to blush, and taking a paper from her pockets, she said, "Dr. Van Helsing, will you read this, and tell me if it must go in. It is my record of today. I too have seen the need of putting down at present everything, however trivial, but there is little in this except what is personal. Must it go in?"

The Professor read it over gravely, and handed it back, saying, "It need not go in if you do not wish it, but I pray that it may. It can but make your husband love you the more, and all us, your friends, more honour you, as well as more esteem and love." She took it back with another blush and a bright smile.

CHAPTER 18

And so now, up to this very hour, all the records we have are complete and in order. The Professor took away one copy to study after dinner, and before our meeting, which is fixed for nine o'clock. The rest of us have already read everything, so when we meet in the study we shall all be informed as to facts, and can arrange our plan of battle with this terrible and mysterious enemy.

MINA HARKER'S JOURNAL

30 September.--When we met in Dr. Seward's study two hours after dinner, which had been at six o'clock, we unconsciously formed a sort of board or committee. Professor Van Helsing took the head of the table, to which Dr. Seward motioned him as he came into the room. He made me sit next to him on his right, and asked me to act as secretary. Jonathan sat next to me. Opposite us were Lord Godalming, Dr. Seward, and Mr. Morris, Lord Godalming being next the Professor, and Dr. Seward in the centre.

The Professor said, "I may, I suppose, take it that we are all acquainted with the facts that are in these papers." We all expressed assent, and he went on, "Then it were, I think, good that I tell you something of the kind of enemy with which we have to deal. I shall then make known to you something of the history of this man, which has been ascertained for me. So we then can discuss how we shall act, and can take our measure according.

"There are such beings as vampires, some of us have evidence that they exist. Even had we not the proof of our own unhappy experience, the teachings and the records of the past give proof enough for sane peoples. I admit that at the first I was sceptic. Were it not that through long years I have trained myself to keep an open mind, I could not have believed until such time as that fact thunder on my ear. 'See! See! I prove, I prove.' Alas! Had I known at first what now I know, nay, had I even guess at him, one so precious life had been spared to many of us who did love her. But that is gone, and we must so work, that other poor souls perish not, whilst we can save. The nosferatu do not die like the bee when he sting once. He is only stronger, and being stronger, have yet more power to work evil. This vampire which is amongst us is of himself so strong in person as twenty men, he is of cunning more than mortal, for his cunning be the growth of ages, he have still the aids of necromancy, which is, as his etymology imply, the divination by the dead, and all the dead that he can come nigh to are for him at command; he is brute, and more than brute; he is devil in callous, and the heart of him is not; he can, within his range, direct the elements, the storm, the fog, the thunder; he can command all the meaner things, the rat, and the owl, and the bat, the moth, and the fox, and the wolf, he can grow and become small; and he can at times vanish and come unknown. How then are we to begin our strike to destroy him? How shall we find his where, and having found it, how can we destroy? My friends, this is much, it is a terrible task that we undertake, and there may be consequence to make the brave shudder. For if we fail in this our fight he must surely win, and then where end we? Life is nothings, I heed him not. But to fail here, is not mere life or death. It is that we become as him, that we henceforward become foul things of the night like him, without heart or conscience, preying on the bodies and the souls of those we love best. To us forever are the gates of heaven shut, for who shall open them to us again? We go on for all time abhorred by all, a blot on the face of God's sunshine, an arrow in the side of Him who died for man. But we are face to face with duty, and in such case must we shrink? For me, I say no, but then I am old, and life, with his sunshine, his fair places, his song of birds, his music and his love, lie far behind. You others are young. Some have seen sorrow, but there are fair days yet in store. What say you?"

Whilst he was speaking, Jonathan had taken my hand. I feared, oh so much, that the appalling nature of our danger was overcoming him when I saw his hand stretch out, but it was life to me to feel its touch, so strong, so self reliant, so resolute. A brave man's hand can speak for itself, it does not even need a woman's love to hear its music.

When the Professor had done speaking my husband looked in my eyes, and I in his, there was no need for speaking between us.

"I answer for Mina and myself," he said.

"Count me in, Professor," said Mr. Quincey Morris, laconically as usual.

"I am with you," said Lord Godalming, "for Lucy's sake, if for no other reason."

Dr. Seward simply nodded.

The Professor stood up and, after laying his golden crucifix on the table, held out his hand on either side. I took his right hand, and Lord Godalming his left, Jonathan held my right with his left and stretched across to Mr. Morris. So as we all took hands our solemn compact was made. I felt my heart icy cold, but it did not even occur to me to draw back. We resumed our places, and Dr. Van Helsing went on with a sort of cheerfulness which showed that the serious work had begun. It was to be taken as gravely, and in as businesslike a way, as any other transaction of life.

"Well, you know what we have to contend against, but we too, are not without strength. We have on our side power of combination, a power denied to the vampire kind, we have sources of science, we are free to act and think, and the hours of the day and the night are ours equally. In fact, so far as our powers extend, they are unfettered, and we are free to use them. We have self devotion in a cause and an end to achieve which is not a selfish one. These things are much.

"Now let us see how far the general powers arrayed against us are restrict, and how the individual cannot. In fine, let us consider the limitations of the vampire in general, and of this one in particular.

"All we have to go upon are traditions and superstitions. These do not at the first appear much, when the matter is one of life and death, nay of more than either life or death. Yet must we be satisfied, in the first place because we have to be, no other means is at our control, and secondly, because, after all these things, tradition and superstition, are everything. Does not the belief in vampires rest for others, though not, alas! for us, on them? A year ago which of us would have received such a possibility, in the midst of our scientific, sceptical, matter-of-fact nineteenth century? We even scouted a belief that we saw justified under our very eyes. Take it, then, that the vampire, and the belief in his limitations and his cure, rest for the moment on the same base. For, let me tell you, he is known everywhere that men have been. In old Greece, in old Rome, he flourish in Germany all over, in France, in India, even in the Chermosese, and in China, so far from us in all ways, there even is he, and the peoples for him at this day. He have follow the wake of the berserker Icelander, the devil-begotten Hun, the Slav, the Saxon, the Magyar.

CHAPTER 18

"So far, then, we have all we may act upon, and let me tell you that very much of the beliefs are justified by what we have seen in our own so unhappy experience. The vampire live on, and cannot die by mere passing of the time, he can flourish when that he can fatten on the blood of the living. Even more, we have seen amongst us that he can even grow younger, that his vital faculties grow strenuous, and seem as though they refresh themselves when his special pabulum is plenty.

"But he cannot flourish without this diet, he eat not as others. Even friend Jonathan, who lived with him for weeks, did never see him eat, never! He throws no shadow, he make in the mirror no reflect, as again Jonathan observe. He has the strength of many of his hand, witness again Jonathan when he shut the door against the wolves, and when he help him from the diligence too. He can transform himself to wolf, as we gather from the ship arrival in Whitby, when he tear open the dog, he can be as bat, as Madam Mina saw him on the window at Whitby, and as friend John saw him fly from this so near house, and as my friend Quincey saw him at the window of Miss Lucy.

"He can come in mist which he create, that noble ship's captain proved him of this, but, from what we know, the distance he can make this mist is limited, and it can only be round himself.

"He come on moonlight rays as elemental dust, as again Jonathan saw those sisters in the castle of Dracula. He become so small, we ourselves saw Miss Lucy, ere she was at peace, slip through a hairbreadth space at the tomb door. He can, when once he find his way, come out from anything or into anything, no matter how close it be bound or even fused up with fire, solder you call it. He can see in the dark, no small power this, in a world which is one half shut from the light. Ah, but hear me through.

"He can do all these things, yet he is not free. Nay, he is even more prisoner than the slave of the galley, than the madman in his cell. He cannot go where he lists, he who is not of nature has yet to obey some of nature's laws, why we know not. He may not enter anywhere at the first, unless there be some one of the household who bid him to come, though afterwards he can come as he please. His power ceases, as does that of all evil things, at the coming of the day.

"Only at certain times can he have limited freedom. If he be not at the place whither he is bound, he can only change himself at noon or at exact sunrise or sunset. These things we are told, and in this record of ours we have proof by inference. Thus, whereas he can do as he will within his limit, when he have his earth-home, his coffin-home, his hell-home, the place unhallowed, as we saw when he went to the grave of the suicide at Whitby, still at other time he can only change when the time come. It is said, too, that he can only pass running water at the slack or the flood of the tide. Then there are things which so afflict him that he has no power, as the garlic that we know of, and as for things sacred, as this symbol, my crucifix, that was amongst us even now when we resolve, to them he is nothing, but in their presence he take his place far off and silent with respect. There are others, too, which I shall tell you of, lest in our seeking we may need them.

"The branch of wild rose on his coffin keep him that he move not from it, a sacred bullet fired into the coffin kill him so that he be true dead, and as for the stake through him, we know already of its peace, or the cut off head that giveth rest. We have seen it with our eyes.

"Thus when we find the habitation of this man-that-was, we can confine him to his coffin and destroy him, if we obey what we know. But he is clever. I have asked my friend Arminius, of Buda-Pesth University, to make his record, and from all the means that are, he tell me of what he has been. He must, indeed, have been that Voivode Dracula who won his name against the Turk, over the great river on the very frontier of Turkeyland. If it be so, then was he no common man, for in that time, and for centuries after, he was spoken of as the cleverest and the most cunning, as well as the bravest of the sons of the 'land beyond the forest.' That mighty brain and that iron resolution went with him to his grave, and are even now arrayed against us. The Draculas were, says Arminius, a great and noble race, though now and again were scions who were held by their coevals to have had dealings with the Evil One. They learned his secrets in the Scholomance, amongst the mountains over Lake Hermanstadt, where the devil claims the tenth scholar as his due. In the records are such words as 'stregoica' witch, 'ordog' and 'pokol' Satan and hell, and in one manuscript this very Dracula is spoken of as 'wampyr,' which we all understand too well. There have been from the loins of this very one great men and good women, and their graves make sacred the earth where alone this foulness can dwell. For it is not the least of its terrors that this evil thing is rooted deep in all good, in soil barren of holy memories it cannot rest."

Whilst they were talking Mr. Morris was looking steadily at the window, and he now got up quietly, and went out of the room. There was a little pause, and then the Professor went on.

"And now we must settle what we do. We have here much data, and we must proceed to lay out our campaign. We know from the inquiry of Jonathan that from the castle to Whitby came fifty boxes of earth, all of which were delivered at Carfax, we also know that at least some of these boxes have been removed. It seems to me, that our first step should be to ascertain whether all the rest remain in the house beyond that wall where we look today, or whether any more have been removed. If the latter, we must trace…"

Here we were interrupted in a very startling way. Outside the house came the sound of a pistol shot, the glass of the window was shattered with a bullet, which ricochetting from the top of the embrasure, struck the far wall of the room. I am afraid I am at heart a coward, for I shrieked out. The men all jumped to their feet, Lord Godalming flew over to the window and threw up the sash. As he did so we heard Mr. Morris' voice without, "Sorry! I fear I have alarmed you. I shall come in and tell you about it."

A minute later he came in and said, "It was an idiotic thing of me to do, and I ask your pardon, Mrs. Harker, most sincerely, I fear I must have frightened you terribly. But the fact is that whilst the Professor was talking there came a big bat and sat on the window sill. I have got such a horror of the damned brutes from recent events that I cannot stand them, and I went out to have a shot, as I have been doing of late of evenings, whenever I have seen one. You used to laugh at me for it then, Art."

"Did you hit it?" asked Dr. Van Helsing.

"I don't know, I fancy not, for it flew away into the wood." Without saying any more he took his seat, and the Professor began to resume his statement.

"We must trace each of these boxes, and when we are ready, we must either capture or kill this monster in his lair, or we must, so to speak, sterilize the earth, so that no more he can seek safety in it. Thus in the end we may find him in his form of man between the hours of noon and sunset, and so engage with him when he is at his most weak.

"And now for you, Madam Mina, this night is the end until all be well. You are too precious to us to have such risk. When we part tonight, you no more must question. We shall tell you all in good time. We are men and are able to bear, but you must be our star and our hope, and we shall act all the more free that you are not in the danger, such as we are."

All the men, even Jonathan, seemed relieved, but it did not seem to me good that they should brave danger and, perhaps lessen their safety, strength being the best safety, through care of me, but their minds were made up, and though it was a bitter pill for me to swallow, I could say nothing, save to accept their chivalrous care of me.

Mr. Morris resumed the discussion, "As there is no time to lose, I vote we have a look at his house right now. Time is everything with him, and swift action on our part may save another victim."

I own that my heart began to fail me when the time for action came so close, but I did not say anything, for I had a greater fear that if I appeared as a drag or a hindrance to their work, they might even leave me out of their counsels altogether. They have now gone off to Carfax, with means to get into the house.

Manlike, they had told me to go to bed and sleep, as if a woman can sleep when those she loves are in danger! I shall lie down, and pretend to sleep, lest Jonathan have added anxiety about me when he returns.

DR. SEWARD'S DIARY

1 October, 4 A.M.--Just as we were about to leave the house, an urgent message was brought to me from Renfield to know if I would see him at once, as he had something of the utmost importance to say to me. I told the messenger to say that I would attend to his wishes in the morning, I was busy just at the moment.

The attendant added, "He seems very importunate, sir. I have never seen him so eager. I don't know but what, if you don't see him soon, he will have one of his violent fits." I knew the man would not have said this without some cause, so I said, "All right, I'll go now," and I asked the others to wait a few minutes for me, as I had to go and see my patient.

"Take me with you, friend John," said the Professor. "His case in your diary interest me much, and it had bearing, too, now and again on our case. I should much like to see him, and especial when his mind is disturbed."

"May I come also?" asked Lord Godalming.

"Me too?" said Quincey Morris. "May I come?" said Harker. I nodded, and we all went down the passage together.

We found him in a state of considerable excitement, but far more rational in his speech and manner than I had ever seen him. There was an unusual understanding of himself, which was unlike anything I had ever met with in a lunatic, and he took it for granted that his reasons would prevail with others entirely sane. We all five went into the room, but none of the others at first said anything. His request was that I would at once release him from the asylum and send him home. This he backed up with arguments regarding his complete recovery, and adduced his own existing sanity.

"I appeal to your friends," he said, "they will, perhaps, not mind sitting in judgement on my case. By the way, you have not introduced me."

I was so much astonished, that the oddness of introducing a madman in an asylum did not strike me at the moment, and besides, there was a certain dignity in the man's manner, so much of the habit of equality, that I at once made the introduction, "Lord Godalming, Professor Van Helsing, Mr. Quincey Morris, of Texas, Mr. Jonathan Harker, Mr. Renfield."

He shook hands with each of them, saying in turn, "Lord Godalming, I had the honour of seconding your father at the Windham; I grieve to know, by your holding the title, that he is no more. He was a man loved and honoured by all who knew him, and in his youth was, I have heard, the inventor of a burnt rum punch, much patronized on Derby night. Mr. Morris, you should be proud of your great state. Its reception into the Union was a precedent which may have far-reaching effects hereafter, when the Pole and the Tropics may hold alliance to the Stars and Stripes. The power of Treaty may yet prove a vast engine of enlargement, when the Monroe doctrine takes its true place as a political fable. What shall any man say of his pleasure at meeting Van Helsing? Sir, I make no apology for dropping all forms of conventional prefix. When an individual has revolutionized therapeutics by his discovery of the continuous evolution of brain matter, conventional forms are unfitting, since they would seem to limit him to one of a class. You, gentlemen, who by nationality, by heredity, or by the possession of natural gifts, are fitted to hold your respective places in the moving world, I take to witness that I am as sane as at least the majority of men who are in full possession of their liberties. And I am sure that you, Dr. Seward, humanitarian and medico-jurist as well as scientist, will deem it a moral duty to deal with me as one to be considered as under exceptional circumstances." He made this last appeal with a courtly air of conviction which was not without its own charm.

I think we were all staggered. For my own part, I was under the conviction, despite my knowledge of the man's character and history, that his reason had been restored, and I felt under a strong impulse to tell him that I was satisfied as to his sanity, and would see about the necessary formalities for his release in the morning. I thought it better to wait, however, before making so grave a statement, for of old I knew the sudden changes to which this particular patient was liable. So I contented myself with making a general statement that he appeared to be improving very rapidly, that I would have a longer chat with him in the morning, and would then see what I could do in the direction of meeting his wishes.

This did not at all satisfy him, for he said quickly, "But I fear, Dr. Seward, that you hardly apprehend my wish. I desire to go at once, here, now, this very hour, this very moment, if I may. Time presses, and in our implied agreement with the old scytheman it is of the essence of the contract. I am sure it is only necessary to put before so admirable a practitioner as Dr. Seward so simple, yet so momentous a wish, to ensure its fulfilment."

He looked at me keenly, and seeing the negative in my face, turned to the others, and scrutinized them closely. Not meeting any sufficient response, he went on, "Is it possible that I have erred in my supposition?"

"You have," I said frankly, but at the same time, as I felt, brutally.

There was a considerable pause, and then he said slowly, "Then I suppose I must only shift my ground of request. Let me ask for this concession, boon, privilege, what you will. I am content to implore in such a case, not on personal grounds, but for the sake of others. I am not at liberty to give you the whole of my reasons, but you may, I assure you, take it from me that they are good ones, sound and unselfish, and spring from the highest sense of duty.

"Could you look, sir, into my heart, you would approve to the full the sentiments which animate me. Nay, more, you would count me amongst the best and truest of your friends."

Again he looked at us all keenly. I had a growing conviction that this sudden change of his entire intellectual method was but yet another phase of his madness, and so determined to let him go on a little longer, knowing from experience that he would, like all lunatics, give himself away in the end. Van Helsing was gazing at him with a look of utmost intensity, his bushy eyebrows almost meeting with the fixed concentration of his look. He said to Renfield in a tone which did not surprise me at the time, but only when I thought of it afterwards, for it was as of one addressing an equal, "Can you not tell frankly your real reason for wishing to be free tonight? I will undertake that if you will satisfy even me, a stranger, without prejudice, and with the habit of keeping an open mind, Dr. Seward will give you, at his own risk and on his own responsibility, the privilege you seek."

He shook his head sadly, and with a look of poignant regret on his face. The Professor went on, "Come, sir, bethink yourself. You claim the privilege of reason in the highest degree, since you seek to impress us with your complete reasonableness. You do this, whose sanity we have reason to doubt, since you are not yet released from medical treatment for this very defect. If you will not help us in our effort to choose the wisest course, how can we perform the duty which you yourself put upon us? Be wise, and help us, and if we can we shall aid you to achieve your wish."

He still shook his head as he said, "Dr. Van Helsing, I have nothing to say. Your argument is complete, and if I were free to speak I should not hesitate a moment, but I am not my own master in the matter. I can only ask you to trust me. If I am refused, the responsibility does not rest with me."

I thought it was now time to end the scene, which was becoming too comically grave, so I went towards the door, simply saying, "Come, my friends, we have work to do. Goodnight."

As, however, I got near the door, a new change came over the patient. He moved towards me so quickly that for the moment I feared that he was about to make another homicidal attack. My fears, however, were groundless, for he held up his two hands imploringly, and made his petition in a moving manner. As he saw that the very excess of his emotion was militating against him, by restoring us more to our old relations, he became still more demonstrative. I glanced at Van Helsing, and saw my conviction reflected in his eyes, so I became a little more fixed in my manner, if not more stern, and motioned to him that his efforts were unavailing. I had previously seen something of the same constantly growing excitement in him when he had to make some request of which at the time he had thought much, such for instance, as when he wanted a cat, and I was prepared to see the collapse into the same sullen acquiescence on this occasion.

My expectation was not realized, for when he found that his appeal would not be successful, he got into quite a frantic condition. He threw himself on his knees, and held up his hands, wringing them in plaintive supplication, and poured forth a torrent of entreaty, with the tears rolling down his cheeks, and his whole face and form expressive of the deepest emotion.

"Let me entreat you, Dr. Seward, oh, let me implore you, to let me out of this house at once. Send me away how you will and where you will, send keepers with me with whips and chains, let them take me in a strait waistcoat, manacled and leg-ironed, even to gaol, but let me go out of this. You don't know what you do by keeping me here. I am speaking from the depths of my heart, of my very soul. You don't know whom you wrong, or how, and I may not tell. Woe is me! I may not tell. By all you hold sacred, by all you hold dear, by your love that is lost, by your hope that lives, for the sake of the Almighty, take me out of this and save my soul from guilt! Can't you hear me, man? Can't you understand? Will you never learn? Don't you know that I am sane and earnest now, that I am no lunatic in a mad fit, but a sane man fighting for his soul? Oh, hear me! Hear me! Let me go, let me go, let me go!"

I thought that the longer this went on the wilder he would get, and so would bring on a fit, so I took him by the hand and raised him up.

"Come," I said sternly, "no more of this, we have had quite enough already. Get to your bed and try to behave more discreetly."

He suddenly stopped and looked at me intently for several moments. Then, without a word, he rose and moving over, sat down on the side of the bed. The collapse had come, as on former occasions, just as I had expected.

When I was leaving the room, last of our party, he said to me in a quiet, well-bred voice, "You will, I trust, Dr. Seward, do me the justice to bear in mind, later on, that I did what I could to convince you tonight."

CHAPTER 19

JONATHAN HARKER'S JOURNAL

1 October, 5 A.M.--I went with the party to the search with an easy mind, for I think I never saw Mina so absolutely strong and well. I am so glad that she consented to hold back and let us men do the work. Somehow, it was a dread to me that she was in this fearful business at all, but now that her work is done, and that it is due to her energy and brains and foresight that the whole story is put together in such a way that every point tells, she may well feel that her part is finished, and that she can henceforth leave the rest to us. We were, I think, all a little upset by the scene with Mr. Renfield. When we came away from his room we were silent till we got back to the study.

Then Mr. Morris said to Dr. Seward, "Say, Jack, if that man wasn't attempting a bluff, he is about the sanest lunatic I ever saw. I'm not sure, but I believe that he had some serious purpose, and if he had, it was pretty rough on him not to get a chance."

Lord Godalming and I were silent, but Dr. Van Helsing added, "Friend John, you know more lunatics than I do, and I'm glad of it, for I fear that if it had been to me to decide I would before that last hysterical outburst have given him free. But we live and learn, and in our present task we must take no chance, as my friend Quincey would say. All is best as they are."

Dr. Seward seemed to answer them both in a dreamy kind of way, "I don't know but that I agree with you. If that man had been an ordinary lunatic I would have taken my chance of trusting him, but he seems so mixed up with the Count in an indexy kind of way that I am afraid of doing anything wrong by helping his fads. I can't forget how he prayed with almost equal fervor for a cat, and then tried to tear my throat out with his teeth. Besides, he called the Count 'lord and master', and he may want to get out to help him in some diabolical way. That horrid thing has the wolves and the rats and his own kind to help him, so I suppose he isn't above trying to use a respectable lunatic. He certainly did seem earnest, though. I only hope we have done what is best. These things, in conjunction with the wild work we have in hand, help to unnerve a man."

The Professor stepped over, and laying his hand on his shoulder, said in his grave, kindly way, "Friend John, have no fear. We are trying to do our duty in a very sad and terrible case, we can only do as we deem best. What else have we to hope for, except the pity of the good God?"

Lord Godalming had slipped away for a few minutes, but now he returned. He held up a little silver whistle as he remarked, "That old place may be full of rats, and if so, I've got an antidote on call."

Having passed the wall, we took our way to the house, taking care to keep in the shadows of the trees on the lawn when the moonlight shone out. When we got to the porch the Professor opened his bag and took out a lot of things, which he laid on the step, sorting them into four little groups, evidently one for each. Then he spoke.

"My friends, we are going into a terrible danger, and we need arms of many kinds. Our enemy is not merely spiritual. Remember that he has the strength of twenty men, and that, though our necks or our windpipes are of the common kind, and therefore breakable or crushable, his are not amenable to mere strength. A stronger man, or a body of men more strong in all than him, can at certain times hold him, but they cannot hurt him as we can be hurt by him. We must, therefore, guard ourselves from his touch. Keep this near your heart." As he spoke he lifted a little silver crucifix and held it out to me, I being nearest to him, "put these flowers round your neck," here he handed to me a wreath of withered garlic blossoms, "for other enemies more mundane, this revolver and this knife, and for aid in all, these so small electric lamps, which you can fasten to your breast, and for all, and above all at the last, this, which we must not desecrate needless."

This was a portion of Sacred Wafer, which he put in an envelope and handed to me. Each of the others was similarly equipped.

"Now," he said, "friend John, where are the skeleton keys? If so that we can open the door, we need not break house by the window, as before at Miss Lucy's."

Dr. Seward tried one or two skeleton keys, his mechanical dexterity as a surgeon standing him in good stead. Presently he got one to suit, after a little play back and forward the bolt yielded, and with a rusty clang, shot back. We pressed on the door, the rusty hinges creaked, and it slowly opened. It was startlingly like the image conveyed to me in Dr. Seward's diary of the opening of Miss Westenra's tomb, I fancy that the same idea seemed to strike the others, for with one accord they shrank back. The Professor was the first to move forward, and stepped into the open door.

"In manus tuas, Domine!" he said, crossing himself as he passed over the threshold. We closed the door behind us, lest when we should have lit our lamps we should possibly attract attention from the road. The Professor carefully tried the lock, lest we might not be able to open it from within should we be in a hurry making our exit. Then we all lit our lamps and proceeded on our search.

The light from the tiny lamps fell in all sorts of odd forms, as the rays crossed each other, or the opacity of our bodies threw great shadows. I could not for my life get away from the feeling that there was someone else amongst us. I suppose it was the recollection, so powerfully brought home to me by the grim surroundings, of that terrible experience in Transylvania. I think the feeling was common to us all, for I noticed that the others kept looking over their shoulders at every sound and every new shadow, just as I felt myself doing.

The whole place was thick with dust. The floor was seemingly inches deep, except where there were recent footsteps, in which on holding down my lamp I could see marks of hobnails where the dust was cracked. The walls were fluffy and heavy with dust, and in the corners were masses of spider's webs, whereon the dust had gathered till they looked like old tattered rags as the weight had torn them partly down. On a table in the hall was a great bunch of keys, with a time-yellowed label on each. They had been used several times, for on the table were several similar rents in the blanket of dust, similar to that exposed when the Professor lifted them.

He turned to me and said, "You know this place, Jonathan. You have copied maps of it, and you know it at least more than we do. Which is the way to the chapel?"

I had an idea of its direction, though on my former visit I had not been able to get admission to it, so I led the way, and after a few wrong turnings found myself opposite a low, arched oaken door, ribbed with iron bands.

"This is the spot," said the Professor as he turned his lamp on a small map of the house, copied from the file of my original correspondence regarding the purchase. With a little trouble we found the key on the bunch and opened the door. We were prepared for some unpleasantness, for as we were opening the door a faint, malodorous air seemed to exhale through the gaps, but none of us ever expected such an odour as we encountered. None of the others had met the Count at all at close quarters, and when I had seen him he was either in the fasting stage of his existence in his rooms or, when he was bloated with fresh blood, in a ruined building open to the air, but here the place was small and close, and the long disuse had made the air stagnant and foul. There was an earthy smell, as of some dry miasma, which came through the fouler air. But as to the odour itself, how shall I describe it? It was not alone that it was composed of all the ills of mortality and with the pungent, acrid smell of blood, but it seemed as though corruption had become itself corrupt. Faugh! It sickens me to think of it. Every breath exhaled by that monster seemed to have clung to the place and intensified its loathsomeness.

Under ordinary circumstances such a stench would have brought our enterprise to an end, but this was no ordinary case, and the high and terrible purpose in which we were involved gave us a strength which rose above merely physical considerations. After the involuntary shrinking consequent on the first nauseous whiff, we one and all set about our work as though that loathsome place were a garden of roses.

We made an accurate examination of the place, the Professor saying as we began, "The first thing is to see how many of the boxes are left, we must then examine every hole and corner and cranny and see if we cannot get some clue as to what has become of the rest."

A glance was sufficient to show how many remained, for the great earth chests were bulky, and there was no mistaking them.

There were only twenty-nine left out of the fifty! Once I got a fright, for, seeing Lord Godalming suddenly turn and look out of the vaulted door into the dark passage beyond, I looked too, and for an instant my heart stood still. Somewhere, looking out from the shadow, I seemed to see the high lights of the Count's evil face, the ridge of the nose, the red eyes, the red lips, the awful pallor. It was only for a moment, for, as Lord Godalming said, "I thought I saw a face, but it was only the shadows," and resumed his inquiry, I turned my lamp in the direction, and stepped into the passage. There was no sign of anyone, and as there were no corners, no doors, no aperture of any kind, but only the solid walls of the passage, there could be no hiding place even for him. I took it that fear had helped imagination, and said nothing.

A few minutes later I saw Morris step suddenly back from a corner, which he was examining. We all followed his movements with our eyes, for undoubtedly some nervousness was growing on us, and we saw a whole mass of phosphorescence, which twinkled like stars. We all instinctively drew back. The whole place was becoming alive with rats.

For a moment or two we stood appalled, all save Lord Godalming, who was seemingly prepared for such an emergency. Rushing over to the great iron-bound oaken door, which Dr. Seward had described from the outside, and which I had seen myself, he turned the key in the lock, drew the huge bolts, and swung the door open. Then, taking his little silver whistle from his pocket, he blew a low, shrill call. It was answered from behind Dr. Seward's house by the yelping of dogs, and after about a minute three terriers came dashing round the corner of the house. Unconsciously we had all moved towards the door, and as we moved I noticed that the dust had been much disturbed. The boxes which had been taken out had been brought this way. But even in the minute that had elapsed the number of the rats had vastly increased. They seemed to swarm over the place all at once, till the lamplight, shining on their moving dark bodies and glittering, baleful eyes, made the place look like a bank of earth set with fireflies. The dogs dashed on, but at the threshold suddenly stopped and snarled, and then, simultaneously lifting their noses, began to howl in most lugubrious fashion. The rats were multiplying in thousands, and we moved out.

Lord Godalming lifted one of the dogs, and carrying him in, placed him on the floor. The instant his feet touched the ground he seemed to recover his courage, and rushed at his natural enemies. They fled before him so fast that before he had shaken the life out of a score, the other dogs, who had by now been lifted in the same manner, had but small prey ere the whole mass had vanished.

With their going it seemed as if some evil presence had departed, for the dogs frisked about and barked merrily as they made sudden darts at their prostrate foes, and turned them over and over and tossed them in the air with vicious shakes. We all seemed to find our spirits rise. Whether it was the purifying of the deadly atmosphere by the opening of the chapel door, or the relief which we experienced by finding ourselves in the open I know not, but most certainly the shadow of dread seemed to slip from us like a robe, and the occasion of our coming lost something of its grim significance, though we did not slacken a whit in our resolution. We closed the outer door and barred and locked it, and bringing the dogs with us, began our search of the house. We found nothing throughout except dust in extraordinary proportions, and all untouched save for my own footsteps when I had made my first visit. Never once did the dogs exhibit any symptom of uneasiness, and even when we returned to the chapel they frisked about as though they had been rabbit hunting in a summer wood.

The morning was quickening in the east when we emerged from the front. Dr. Van Helsing had taken the key of the hall door from the bunch, and locked the door in orthodox fashion, putting the key into his pocket when he had done.

"So far," he said, "our night has been eminently successful. No harm has come to us such as I feared might be and yet we have ascertained how many boxes are missing. More than all do I rejoice that this, our first, and perhaps our most difficult and dangerous, step has been accomplished without the bringing thereinto our most sweet Madam Mina or troubling her waking or sleeping thoughts with sights and sounds and smells of horror which she might never forget. One lesson, too, we have learned, if it be allowable to argue a particulari, that the brute beasts which are to the Count's command are yet themselves not amenable to his spiritual power, for look, these rats that would come to his call, just as from his castle top he summon the wolves to your going and to that poor mother's cry, though they come to him, they run pell-mell from the so little dogs of my friend Arthur. We have other matters before us, other dangers, other fears, and that monster... He has not used his power over the brute world for the only or the last time tonight. So be it that he has gone elsewhere. Good! It has given us opportunity to cry 'check' in some ways in this chess game, which we play for the stake of human souls. And now let us go home. The dawn is close at hand, and we have reason to be content with our first night's work. It may be ordained that we have many nights and days to follow, if full of peril, but we must go on, and from no danger shall we shrink."

The house was silent when we got back, save for some poor creature who was screaming away in one of the distant wards, and a low, moaning sound from Renfield's room. The poor wretch was doubtless torturing himself, after the manner of the insane, with needless thoughts of pain.

I came tiptoe into our own room, and found Mina asleep, breathing so softly that I had to put my ear down to hear it. She looks paler than usual. I hope the meeting tonight has not upset her. I am truly thankful that she is to be left out of our future work, and even of our deliberations. It is too great a strain for a woman to bear. I did not think so at first, but I know better now. Therefore I am glad that it is settled. There may be things which would frighten her to hear, and yet to conceal them from her might be worse than to tell her if once she suspected that there was any concealment. Henceforth our work is to be a sealed book to her, till at least such time as we can tell her that all is finished, and the earth free from a monster of the nether world. I daresay it will be difficult to begin to keep silence after such confidence as ours, but I must be resolute, and tomorrow I shall keep dark over tonight's doings, and shall refuse to speak of anything that has happened. I rest on the sofa, so as not to disturb her.

1 October, later.--I suppose it was natural that we should have all overslept ourselves, for the day was a busy one, and the night had no rest at all. Even Mina must have felt its exhaustion, for though I slept till the sun was high, I was awake before her, and had to call two or three times before she awoke. Indeed, she was so sound asleep that for a few seconds she did not recognize me, but looked at me with a sort of blank terror, as one looks who has been waked out of a bad dream. She complained a little of being tired, and I let her rest till later in the day. We now know of twenty-one boxes having been removed, and if it be that several were taken in any of these removals we may be able to trace them all. Such will, of course, immensely simplify our labor, and the sooner the matter is attended to the better. I shall look up Thomas Snelling today.

DR. SEWARD'S DIARY

1 October.--It was towards noon when I was awakened by the Professor walking into my room. He was more jolly and cheerful than usual, and it is quite evident that last night's work has helped to take some of the brooding weight off his mind.

After going over the adventure of the night he suddenly said, "Your patient interests me much. May it be that with you I visit him this morning? Or if that you are too occupy, I can go alone if it may be. It is a new experience to me to find a lunatic who talk philosophy, and reason so sound."

I had some work to do which pressed, so I told him that if he would go alone I would be glad, as then I should not have to keep him waiting, so I called an attendant and gave him the necessary instructions. Before the Professor left the room I cautioned him against getting any false impression from my patient.

"But," he answered, "I want him to talk of himself and of his delusion as to consuming live things. He said to Madam Mina, as I see in your diary of yesterday, that he had once had such a belief. Why do you smile, friend John?"

"Excuse me," I said, "but the answer is here." I laid my hand on the typewritten matter. "When our sane and learned lunatic made that very statement of how he used to consume life, his mouth was actually nauseous with the flies and spiders which he had eaten just before Mrs. Harker entered the room."

Van Helsing smiled in turn. "Good!" he said. "Your memory is true, friend John. I should have remembered. And yet it is this very obliquity of thought and memory which makes mental disease such a fascinating study. Perhaps I may gain more knowledge out of the folly of this madman than I shall from the teaching of the most wise. Who knows?"

I went on with my work, and before long was through that in hand. It seemed that the time had been very short indeed, but there was Van Helsing back in the study.

"Do I interrupt?" he asked politely as he stood at the door.

"Not at all," I answered. "Come in. My work is finished, and I am free. I can go with you now, if you like."

"It is needless, I have seen him!"

"Well?"

"I fear that he does not appraise me at much. Our interview was short. When I entered his room he was sitting on a stool in the centre, with his elbows on his knees, and his face was the picture of sullen discontent. I spoke to him as cheerfully as I could, and with such a measure of respect as I could assume. He made no reply whatever. 'Don't you know me?' I asked. His answer was not reassuring: 'I know you well enough; you are the old fool Van Helsing. I wish you would take yourself and your idiotic brain theories somewhere else. Damn all thick-headed Dutchmen!' Not a word more would he say, but sat in his implacable sullenness as indifferent to me as though I had not been in the room at all. Thus departed for this time my chance of much learning from this so clever lunatic, so I shall go, if I may, and cheer myself with a few happy words with that sweet soul Madam Mina. Friend John, it does rejoice me unspeakable that she is no more to be pained, no more to be worried with our terrible things. Though we shall much miss her help, it is better so."

"I agree with you with all my heart," I answered earnestly, for I did not want him to weaken in this matter. "Mrs. Harker is better out of it. Things are quite bad enough for us, all men of the world, and who have been in many tight places in our time, but it is no place for a woman, and if she had remained in touch with the affair, it would in time infallibly have wrecked her."

So Van Helsing has gone to confer with Mrs. Harker and Harker, Quincey and Art are all out following up the clues as to the earth boxes. I shall finish my round of work and we shall meet tonight.

CHAPTER 19

MINA HARKER'S JOURNAL

1 October.--It is strange to me to be kept in the dark as I am today, after Jonathan's full confidence for so many years, to see him manifestly avoid certain matters, and those the most vital of all. This morning I slept late after the fatigues of yesterday, and though Jonathan was late too, he was the earlier. He spoke to me before he went out, never more sweetly or tenderly, but he never mentioned a word of what had happened in the visit to the Count's house. And yet he must have known how terribly anxious I was. Poor dear fellow! I suppose it must have distressed him even more than it did me. They all agreed that it was best that I should not be drawn further into this awful work, and I acquiesced. But to think that he keeps anything from me! And now I am crying like a silly fool, when I know it comes from my husband's great love and from the good, good wishes of those other strong men.

That has done me good. Well, some day Jonathan will tell me all. And lest it should ever be that he should think for a moment that I kept anything from him, I still keep my journal as usual. Then if he has feared of my trust I shall show it to him, with every thought of my heart put down for his dear eyes to read. I feel strangely sad and low-spirited today. I suppose it is the reaction from the terrible excitement.

Last night I went to bed when the men had gone, simply because they told me to. I didn't feel sleepy, and I did feel full of devouring anxiety. I kept thinking over everything that has been ever since Jonathan came to see me in London, and it all seems like a horrible tragedy, with fate pressing on relentlessly to some destined end. Everything that one does seems, no matter how right it may be, to bring on the very thing which is most to be deplored. If I hadn't gone to Whitby, perhaps poor dear Lucy would be with us now. She hadn't taken to visiting the churchyard till I came, and if she hadn't come there in the day time with me she wouldn't have walked in her sleep. And if she hadn't gone there at night and asleep, that monster couldn't have destroyed her as he did. Oh, why did I ever go to Whitby? There now, crying again! I wonder what has come over me today. I must hide it from Jonathan, for if he knew that I had been crying twice in one morning… I, who never cried on my own account, and whom he has never caused to shed a tear, the dear fellow would fret his heart out. I shall put a bold face on, and if I do feel weepy, he shall never see it. I suppose it is just one of the lessons that we poor women have to learn…

I can't quite remember how I fell asleep last night. I remember hearing the sudden barking of the dogs and a lot of queer sounds, like praying on a very tumultuous scale, from Mr. Renfield's room, which is somewhere under this. And then there was silence over everything, silence so profound that it startled me, and I got up and looked out of the window. All was dark and silent, the black shadows thrown by the moonlight seeming full of a silent mystery of their own. Not a thing seemed to be stirring, but all to be grim and fixed as death or fate, so that a thin streak of white mist, that crept with almost imperceptible slowness across the grass towards the house, seemed to have a sentience and a vitality of its own. I think that the digression of my thoughts must have done me good, for when I got back to bed I found a lethargy creeping over me. I lay a while, but could not quite sleep, so I got out and looked out of the window again. The mist was spreading, and was now close up to the house, so that I could see it lying thick against the wall, as though it were stealing up to the windows. The poor man was more loud than ever, and though I could not distinguish a word he said, I could in some way recognize in his tones some passionate entreaty on his part. Then there was the sound of a struggle, and I knew that the attendants were dealing with him. I was so frightened that I crept into bed, and pulled the clothes over my head, putting my fingers in my ears. I was not then a bit sleepy, at least so I thought, but I must have fallen asleep, for except dreams, I do not remember anything until the morning, when Jonathan woke me. I think that it took me an effort and a little time to realize where I was, and that it was Jonathan who was bending over me. My dream was very peculiar, and was almost typical of the way that waking thoughts become merged in, or continued in, dreams.

I thought that I was asleep, and waiting for Jonathan to come back. I was very anxious about him, and I was powerless to act, my feet, and my hands, and my brain were weighted, so that nothing could proceed at the usual pace. And so I slept uneasily and thought. Then it began to dawn upon me that the air was heavy, and dank, and cold. I put back the clothes from my face, and found, to my surprise, that all was dim around. The gaslight which I had left lit for Jonathan, but turned down, came only like a tiny red spark through the fog, which had evidently grown thicker and poured into the room. Then it occurred to me that I had shut the window before I had come to bed. I would have got out to make certain on the point, but some leaden lethargy seemed to chain my limbs and even my will. I lay still and endured, that was all. I closed my eyes, but could still see through my eyelids. (It is wonderful what tricks our dreams play us, and how conveniently we can imagine.) The mist grew thicker and thicker and I could see now how it came in, for I could see it like smoke, or with the white energy of boiling water, pouring in, not through the window, but through the joinings of the door. It got thicker and thicker, till it seemed as if it became concentrated into a sort of pillar of cloud in the room, through the top of which I could see the light of the gas shining like a red eye. Things began to whirl through my brain just as the cloudy column was now whirling in the room, and through it all came the scriptural words "a pillar of cloud by day and of fire by night." Was it indeed such spiritual guidance that was coming to me in my sleep? But the pillar was composed of both the day and the night guiding, for the fire was in the red eye, which at the thought got a new fascination for me, till, as I looked, the fire divided, and seemed to shine on me through the fog like two red eyes, such as Lucy told me of in her momentary mental wandering when, on the cliff, the dying sunlight struck the windows of St. Mary's Church. Suddenly the horror burst upon me that it was thus that Jonathan had seen those awful women growing into reality through the whirling mist in the moonlight, and in my dream I must have fainted, for all became black darkness. The last conscious effort which imagination made was to show me a livid white face bending over me out of the mist.

I must be careful of such dreams, for they would unseat one's reason if there were too much of them. I would get Dr. Van Helsing or Dr. Seward to prescribe something for me which would make me sleep, only that I fear to alarm them. Such a dream at the present time would become woven into their fears for me. Tonight I shall strive hard to sleep naturally. If I do not, I shall tomorrow night get them to give me a dose of chloral, that cannot hurt me for once, and it will give me a good night's sleep. Last night tired me more than if I had not slept at all.

2 October 10 P.M.--Last night I slept, but did not dream. I must have slept soundly, for I was not waked by Jonathan coming to bed, but the sleep has not refreshed

me, for today I feel terribly weak and spiritless. I spent all yesterday trying to read, or lying down dozing. In the afternoon, Mr. Renfield asked if he might see me. Poor man, he was very gentle, and when I came away he kissed my hand and bade God bless me. Some way it affected me much. I am crying when I think of him. This is a new weakness, of which I must be careful. Jonathan would be miserable if he knew I had been crying. He and the others were out till dinner time, and they all came in tired. I did what I could to brighten them up, and I suppose that the effort did me good, for I forgot how tired I was. After dinner they sent me to bed, and all went off to smoke together, as they said, but I knew that they wanted to tell each other of what had occurred to each during the day. I could see from Jonathan's manner that he had something important to communicate. I was not so sleepy as I should have been, so before they went I asked Dr. Seward to give me a little opiate of some kind, as I had not slept well the night before. He very kindly made me up a sleeping draught, which he gave to me, telling me that it would do me no harm, as it was very mild… I have taken it, and am waiting for sleep, which still keeps aloof. I hope I have not done wrong, for as sleep begins to flirt with me, a new fear comes: that I may have been foolish in thus depriving myself of the power of waking. I might want it. Here comes sleep. Goodnight.

CHAPTER 20

JONATHAN HARKER'S JOURNAL

1 October, evening.--I found Thomas Snelling in his house at Bethnal Green, but unhappily he was not in a condition to remember anything. The very prospect of beer which my expected coming had opened to him had proved too much, and he had begun too early on his expected debauch. I learned, however, from his wife, who seemed a decent, poor soul, that he was only the assistant of Smollet, who of the two mates was the responsible person. So off I drove to Walworth, and found Mr. Joseph Smollet at home and in his shirtsleeves, taking a late tea out of a saucer. He is a decent, intelligent fellow, distinctly a good, reliable type of workman, and with a headpiece of his own. He remembered all about the incident of the boxes, and from a wonderful dog-eared notebook, which he produced from some mysterious receptacle about the seat of his trousers, and which had hieroglyphical entries in thick, half-obliterated pencil, he gave me the destinations of the boxes. There were, he said, six in the cartload which he took from Carfax and left at 197 Chicksand Street, Mile End New Town, and another six which he deposited at Jamaica Lane, Bermondsey. If then the Count meant to scatter these ghastly refuges of his over London, these places were chosen as the first of delivery, so that later he might distribute more fully. The systematic manner in which this was done made me think that he could not mean to confine himself to two sides of London. He was now fixed on the far east on the northern shore, on the east of the southern shore, and on the south. The north and west were surely never meant to be left out of his diabolical scheme, let alone the City itself and the very heart of fashionable London in the south-west and west. I went back to Smollet, and asked him if he could tell us if any other boxes had been taken from Carfax.

He replied, "Well guv'nor, you've treated me very 'an'some", I had given him half a sovereign, "an I'll tell yer all I know. I heard a man by the name of Bloxam say four nights ago in the 'Are an' 'Ounds, in Pincher's Alley, as 'ow he an' his mate 'ad 'ad a rare dusty job in a old 'ouse at Purfleet. There ain't a many such jobs as this 'ere, an' I'm thinkin' that maybe Sam Bloxam could tell ye summut."

I asked if he could tell me where to find him. I told him that if he could get me the address it would be worth another half sovereign to him. So he gulped down the rest of his tea and stood up, saying that he was going to begin the search then and there.

At the door he stopped, and said, "Look 'ere, guv'nor, there ain't no sense in me a keepin' you 'ere. I may find Sam soon, or I mayn't, but anyhow he ain't like to be in a way to tell ye much tonight. Sam is a rare one when he starts on the booze. If you can give me a envelope with a stamp on it, and put yer address on it, I'll find out where Sam is to be found and post it ye tonight. But ye'd better be up arter 'im soon in the mornin', never mind the booze the night afore."

This was all practical, so one of the children went off with a penny to buy an envelope and a sheet of paper, and to keep the change. When she came back, I addressed the envelope and stamped it, and when Smollet had again faithfully promised to post the address when found, I took my way to home. We're on the track anyhow. I am tired tonight, and I want to sleep. Mina is fast asleep, and looks a little too pale. Her eyes look as though she had been crying. Poor dear, I've no doubt it frets her to be kept in the dark, and it may make her doubly anxious about me and the others. But it is best as it is. It is better to be disappointed and worried in such a way now than to have her nerve broken. The doctors were quite right to insist on her being kept out of this dreadful business. I must be firm, for on me this particular burden of silence must rest. I shall not ever enter on the subject with her under any circumstances. Indeed, It may not be a hard task, after all, for she herself has become reticent on the subject, and has not spoken of the Count or his doings ever since we told her of our decision.

2 October, evening--A long and trying and exciting day. By the first post I got my directed envelope with a dirty scrap of paper enclosed, on which was written with a carpenter's pencil in a sprawling hand, "Sam Bloxam, Korkrans, 4 Poters Cort, Bartel Street, Walworth. Arsk for the depite."

I got the letter in bed, and rose without waking Mina. She looked heavy and sleepy and pale, and far from well. I determined not to wake her, but that when I should return from this new search, I would arrange for her going back to Exeter. I think she would be happier in our own home, with her daily tasks to interest her, than in being here amongst us and in ignorance. I only saw Dr. Seward for a moment, and told him where I was off to, promising to come back and tell the rest so soon as I should have found out anything. I drove to Walworth and found, with some difficulty, Potter's Court. Mr. Smollet's spelling misled me, as I asked for Poter's Court instead of Potter's Court. However, when I had found the court, I had no difficulty in discovering Corcoran's lodging house.

When I asked the man who came to the door for the "depite," he shook his head, and said, "I dunno 'im. There ain't no such a person 'ere. I never 'eard of 'im in all my bloomin' days. Don't believe there ain't nobody of that kind livin' 'ere or anywheres."

I took out Smollet's letter, and as I read it it seemed to me that the lesson of the spelling of the name of the court might guide me. "What are you?" I asked.

"I'm the depity," he answered.

I saw at once that I was on the right track. Phonetic spelling had again misled me. A half crown tip put the deputy's knowledge at my disposal, and I learned that Mr. Bloxam, who had slept off the remains of his beer on the previous night at Corcoran's, had left for his work at Poplar at five o'clock that morning. He could not tell me where the place of work was situated, but he had a vague idea that it was some kind of a "new-fangled ware'us," and with this slender clue I had to start for Poplar. It was twelve o'clock before I got any satisfactory hint of such a building, and this I got at a coffee shop, where some workmen were having their dinner. One of them suggested that there was being erected at Cross Angel Street a new "cold storage" building, and as this suited the condition of a "new-fangled ware'us," I at once drove to it. An interview with a surly gatekeeper and a surlier foreman, both of whom were appeased with the coin of the realm, put me on the track of Bloxam. He was sent for on my suggestion that I was willing to pay his days wages to his foreman for the privilege of asking him a few questions on a private matter. He was a smart enough fellow, though rough of speech and bearing. When I had promised to pay for his information and given him an earnest, he told me that he had made two journeys between Carfax and a house in Piccadilly, and had taken from this house to the latter nine great boxes, "main heavy ones," with a horse and cart hired by him for this purpose.

I asked him if he could tell me the number of the house in Piccadilly, to which he replied, "Well, guv'nor, I forgits the number, but it was only a few door from a big white church, or somethink of the kind, not long built. It was a dusty old 'ouse, too, though nothin' to the dustiness of the 'ouse we tooked the bloomin' boxes from."

"How did you get in if both houses were empty?"

"There was the old party what engaged me a waitin' in the 'ouse at Purfleet. He 'elped me to lift the boxes and put them in the dray. Curse me, but he was the strongest chap I ever struck, an' him a old feller, with a white moustache, one that thin you would think he couldn't throw a shadder."

How this phrase thrilled through me!

"Why, 'e took up 'is end o' the boxes like they was pounds of tea, and me a puffin' an' a blowin' afore I could upend mine anyhow, an' I'm no chicken, neither."

"How did you get into the house in Piccadilly?" I asked.

"He was there too. He must 'a started off and got there afore me, for when I rung of the bell he kem an' opened the door 'isself an' 'elped me carry the boxes into the 'all."

"The whole nine?" I asked.

"Yus, there was five in the first load an' four in the second. It was main dry work, an' I don't so well remember 'ow I got 'ome."

I interrupted him, "Were the boxes left in the hall?"

"Yus, it was a big 'all, an' there was nothin' else in it."

I made one more attempt to further matters. "You didn't have any key?"

"Never used no key nor nothink. The old gent, he opened the door 'isself an' shut it again when I druv off. I don't remember the last time, but that was the beer."

"And you can't remember the number of the house?"

"No, sir. But ye needn't have no difficulty about that. It's a 'igh 'un with a stone front with a bow on it, an' 'igh steps up to the door. I know them steps, 'avin' 'ad to carry the boxes up with three loafers what come round to earn a copper. The old gent give them shillin's, an' they seein' they got so much, they wanted more. But 'e took one of them by the shoulder and was like to throw 'im down the steps, till the lot of them went away cussin'."

I thought that with this description I could find the house, so having paid my friend for his information, I started off for Piccadilly. I had gained a new painful experience. The Count could, it was evident, handle the earth boxes himself. If so, time was precious, for now that he had achieved a certain amount of distribution, he could, by choosing his own time, complete the task unobserved. At Piccadilly Circus I discharged my cab, and walked westward. Beyond the Junior Constitutional I came across the house described and was satisfied that this was the next of the lairs arranged by Dracula. The house looked as though it had been long untenanted. The windows were encrusted with dust, and the shutters were up. All the framework was black with time, and from the iron the paint had mostly scaled away. It was evident that up to lately there had been a large notice board in front of the balcony. It had, however, been roughly torn away, the uprights which had supported it still remaining. Behind the rails of the balcony I saw there were some loose boards, whose raw edges looked white. I would have given a good deal to have been able to see the notice board intact, as it would, perhaps, have given some clue to the ownership of the house. I remembered my experience of the investigation and purchase of Carfax, and I could not but feel that if I could find the former owner there might be some means discovered of gaining access to the house.

There was at present nothing to be learned from the Piccadilly side, and nothing could be done, so I went around to the back to see if anything could be gathered from this quarter. The mews were active, the Piccadilly houses being mostly in occupation. I asked one or two of the grooms and helpers whom I saw around if they could tell me anything about the empty house. One of them said that he heard it had lately been taken, but he couldn't say from whom. He told me, however, that up to very lately there had been a notice board of "For Sale" up, and that perhaps Mitchell, Sons, & Candy the house agents could tell me something, as he thought he remembered seeing the name of that firm on the board. I did not wish to seem too eager, or to let my informant know or guess too much, so thanking him in the usual manner, I strolled away. It was now growing dusk, and the autumn night was closing in, so I did not lose any time. Having learned the address of Mitchell, Sons, & Candy from a directory at the Berkeley, I was soon at their office in Sackville Street.

The gentleman who saw me was particularly suave in manner, but uncommunicative in equal proportion. Having once told me that the Piccadilly house, which throughout our interview he called a "mansion," was sold, he considered my business as concluded. When I asked who had purchased it, he opened his eyes a thought wider, and paused a few seconds before replying, "It is sold, sir."

"Pardon me," I said, with equal politeness, "but I have a special reason for wishing to know who purchased it."

Again he paused longer, and raised his eyebrows still more. "It is sold, sir," was again his laconic reply.

"Surely," I said, "you do not mind letting me know so much."

"But I do mind," he answered. "The affairs of their clients are absolutely safe in the hands of Mitchell, Sons, & Candy."

This was manifestly a prig of the first water, and there was no use arguing with him. I thought I had best meet him on his own ground, so I said, "Your clients, sir, are happy in having so resolute a guardian of their confidence. I am myself a professional man."

Here I handed him my card. "In this instance I am not prompted by curiosity, I act on the part of Lord Godalming, who wishes to know something of the property which was, he understood, lately for sale."

These words put a different complexion on affairs. He said, "I would like to oblige you if I could, Mr. Harker, and especially would I like to oblige his lordship. We once carried out a small matter of renting some chambers for him when he was the honourable Arthur Holmwood. If you will let me have his lordship's address I will consult the House on the subject, and will, in any case, communicate with his lordship by tonight's post. It will be a pleasure if we can so far deviate from our rules as to give the required information to his lordship."

I wanted to secure a friend, and not to make an enemy, so I thanked him, gave the address at Dr. Seward's and came away. It was now dark, and I was tired and hungry. I got a cup of tea at the Aerated Bread Company and came down to Purfleet by the next train.

I found all the others at home. Mina was looking tired and pale, but she made a gallant effort to be bright and cheerful. It wrung my heart to think that I had had to keep anything from her and so caused her inquietude. Thank God, this will be the last night of her looking on at our conferences, and feeling the sting of our not showing our confidence. It took all my courage to hold to the wise resolution of keeping her out of our grim task. She seems somehow more reconciled, or else the very subject seems to have become repugnant to her, for when any accidental allusion is made she actually shudders. I am glad we made our resolution in time, as with such a feeling as this, our growing knowledge would be torture to her.

I could not tell the others of the day's discovery till we were alone, so after dinner, followed by a little music to save appearances even amongst ourselves, I took Mina to her room and left her to go to bed. The dear girl was more affectionate with me than ever, and clung to me as though she would detain me, but there was much to be talked of and I came away. Thank God, the ceasing of telling things has made no difference between us.

When I came down again I found the others all gathered round the fire in the study. In the train I had written my diary so far, and simply read it off to them as the best means of letting them get abreast of my own information.

When I had finished Van Helsing said, "This has been a great day's work, friend Jonathan. Doubtless we are on the track of the missing boxes. If we find them all in that house, then our work is near the end. But if there be some missing, we must search until we find them. Then shall we make our final coup, and hunt the wretch to his real death."

We all sat silent awhile and all at once Mr. Morris spoke, "Say! How are we going to get into that house?"

"We got into the other," answered Lord Godalming quickly.

"But, Art, this is different. We broke house at Carfax, but we had night and a walled park to protect us. It will be a mighty different thing to commit burglary in Piccadilly, either by day or night. I confess I don't see how we are going to get in unless that agency duck can find us a key of some sort."

Lord Godalming's brows contracted, and he stood up and walked about the room. By-and-by he stopped and said, turning from one to another of us, "Quincey's head is level. This burglary business is getting serious. We got off once all right, but we have now a rare job on hand. Unless we can find the Count's key basket."

As nothing could well be done before morning, and as it would be at least advisable to wait till Lord Godalming should hear from Mitchell's, we decided not to take any active step before breakfast time. For a good while we sat and smoked, discussing the matter in its various lights and bearings. I took the opportunity of bringing this diary right up to the moment. I am very sleepy and shall go to bed...

Just a line. Mina sleeps soundly and her breathing is regular. Her forehead is puckered up into little wrinkles, as though she thinks even in her sleep. She is still too pale, but does not look so haggard as she did this morning. Tomorrow will, I hope, mend all this. She will be herself at home in Exeter. Oh, but I am sleepy!

DR. SEWARD'S DIARY

1 October.--I am puzzled afresh about Renfield. His moods change so rapidly that I find it difficult to keep touch of them, and as they always mean something more than his own well-being, they form a more than interesting study. This morning, when I went to see him after his repulse of Van Helsing, his manner was that of a man commanding destiny. He was, in fact, commanding destiny, subjectively. He did not really care for any of the things of mere earth, he was in the clouds and looked down on all the weaknesses and wants of us poor mortals.

I thought I would improve the occasion and learn something, so I asked him, "What about the flies these times?"

He smiled on me in quite a superior sort of way, such a smile as would have become the face of Malvolio, as he answered me, "The fly, my dear sir, has one striking feature. Its wings are typical of the aerial powers of the psychic faculties. The ancients did well when they typified the soul as a butterfly!"

I thought I would push his analogy to its utmost logically, so I said quickly, "Oh, it is a soul you are after now, is it?"

His madness foiled his reason, and a puzzled look spread over his face as, shaking his head with a decision which I had but seldom seen in him.

He said, "Oh, no, oh no! I want no souls. Life is all I want." Here he brightened up. "I am pretty indifferent about it at present. Life is all right. I have all I want. You must get a new patient, doctor, if you wish to study zoophagy!"

This puzzled me a little, so I drew him on. "Then you command life. You are a god, I suppose?"

He smiled with an ineffably benign superiority. "Oh no! Far be it from me to arrogate to myself the attributes of the Deity. I am not even concerned in His especially spiritual doings. If I may state my intellectual position I am, so far as concerns things purely terrestrial, somewhat in the position which Enoch occupied spiritually!"

This was a poser to me. I could not at the moment recall Enoch's appositeness, so I had to ask a simple question, though I felt that by so doing I was lowering myself in the eyes of the lunatic. "And why with Enoch?"

"Because he walked with God."

I could not see the analogy, but did not like to admit it, so I harked back to what he had denied. "So you don't care about life and you don't want souls. Why not?" I put my question quickly and somewhat sternly, on purpose to disconcert him.

The effort succeeded, for an instant he unconsciously relapsed into his old servile manner, bent low before me, and actually fawned upon me as he replied. "I don't want any souls, indeed, indeed! I don't. I couldn't use them if I had them. They would be no manner of use to me. I couldn't eat them or…"

He suddenly stopped and the old cunning look spread over his face, like a wind sweep on the surface of the water.

"And doctor, as to life, what is it after all? When you've got all you require, and you know that you will never want, that is all. I have friends, good friends, like you, Dr. Seward." This was said with a leer of inexpressible cunning. "I know that I shall never lack the means of life!"

I think that through the cloudiness of his insanity he saw some antagonism in me, for he at once fell back on the last refuge of such as he, a dogged silence. After a short time I saw that for the present it was useless to speak to him. He was sulky, and so I came away.

Later in the day he sent for me. Ordinarily I would not have come without special reason, but just at present I am so interested in him that I would gladly make an effort. Besides, I am glad to have anything to help pass the time. Harker is out, following up clues, and so are Lord Godalming and Quincey. Van Helsing sits in my study poring over the record prepared by the Harkers. He seems to think that by accurate knowledge of all details he will light up on some clue. He does not wish to be disturbed in the work, without cause. I would have taken him with me to see the patient, only I thought that after his last repulse he might not care to go again. There was also another reason. Renfield might not speak so freely before a third person as when he and I were alone.

I found him sitting in the middle of the floor on his stool, a pose which is generally indicative of some mental energy on his part. When I came in, he said at once, as though the question had been waiting on his lips. "What about souls?"

It was evident then that my surmise had been correct. Unconscious cerebration was doing its work, even with the lunatic. I determined to have the matter out.

"What about them yourself?" I asked.

He did not reply for a moment but looked all around him, and up and down, as though he expected to find some inspiration for an answer.

"I don't want any souls!" he said in a feeble, apologetic way. The matter seemed preying on his mind, and so I determined to use it, to "be cruel only to be kind." So I said, "You like life, and you want life?"

"Oh yes! But that is all right. You needn't worry about that!"

"But," I asked, "how are we to get the life without getting the soul also?"

This seemed to puzzle him, so I followed it up, "A nice time you'll have some time when you're flying out here, with the souls of thousands of flies and spiders and birds and cats buzzing and twittering and moaning all around you. You've got their lives, you know, and you must put up with their souls!"

Something seemed to affect his imagination, for he put his fingers to his ears and shut his eyes, screwing them up tightly just as a small boy does when his face is being soaped. There was something pathetic in it that touched me. It also gave me a lesson, for it seemed that before me was a child, only a child, though the features were worn, and the stubble on the jaws was white. It was evident that he was undergoing some process of mental disturbance, and knowing how his past moods had interpreted things seemingly foreign to himself, I thought I would enter into his mind as well as I could and go with him.

The first step was to restore confidence, so I asked him, speaking pretty loud so that he would hear me through his closed ears, "Would you like some sugar to get your flies around again?"

He seemed to wake up all at once, and shook his head. With a laugh he replied, "Not much! Flies are poor things, after all!" After a pause he added, "But I don't want their souls buzzing round me, all the same."

"Or spiders?" I went on.

"Blow spiders! What's the use of spiders? There isn't anything in them to eat or..." He stopped suddenly as though reminded of a forbidden topic.

"So, so!" I thought to myself, "this is the second time he has suddenly stopped at the word 'drink'. What does it mean?"

Renfield seemed himself aware of having made a lapse, for he hurried on, as though to distract my attention from it, "I don't take any stock at all in such matters. 'Rats and mice and such small deer,' as Shakespeare has it, 'chicken feed of the larder' they might be called. I'm past all that sort of nonsense. You might as well ask a man to eat molecules with a pair of chopsticks, as to try to interest me about the less carnivora, when I know of what is before me."

"I see," I said. "You want big things that you can make your teeth meet in? How would you like to breakfast on an elephant?"

"What ridiculous nonsense you are talking?" He was getting too wide awake, so I thought I would press him hard.

"I wonder," I said reflectively, "what an elephant's soul is like!"

The effect I desired was obtained, for he at once fell from his high-horse and became a child again.

"I don't want an elephant's soul, or any soul at all!" he said. For a few moments he sat despondently. Suddenly he jumped to his feet, with his eyes blazing and all the signs of intense cerebral excitement. "To hell with you and your souls!" he shouted. "Why do you plague me about souls? Haven't I got enough to worry, and pain, to distract me already, without thinking of souls?"

He looked so hostile that I thought he was in for another homicidal fit, so I blew my whistle.

The instant, however, that I did so he became calm, and said apologetically, "Forgive me, Doctor. I forgot myself. You do not need any help. I am so worried in my mind that I am apt to be irritable. If you only knew the problem I have to face, and that I am working out, you would pity, and tolerate, and pardon me. Pray do not put me in a strait waistcoat. I want to think and I cannot think freely when my body is confined. I am sure you will understand!"

He had evidently self-control, so when the attendants came I told them not to mind, and they withdrew. Renfield watched them go. When the door was closed he said with considerable dignity and sweetness, "Dr. Seward, you have been very considerate towards me. Believe me that I am very, very grateful to you!"

I thought it well to leave him in this mood, and so I came away. There is certainly something to ponder over in this man's state. Several points seem to make what the American interviewer calls "a story," if one could only get them in proper order. Here they are:

Will not mention "drinking."

Fears the thought of being burdened with the "soul" of anything.

Has no dread of wanting "life" in the future.

Despises the meaner forms of life altogether, though he dreads
being haunted by their souls.

Logically all these things point one way! He has assurance of
some kind that he will acquire some higher life.
He dreads the consequence, the burden of a soul. Then it is a
human life he looks to!
And the assurance…?

Merciful God! The Count has been to him, and there is some new scheme of terror afoot!

Later.--I went after my round to Van Helsing and told him my suspicion. He grew very grave, and after thinking the matter over for a while asked me to take him to Renfield. I did so. As we came to the door we heard the lunatic within singing gaily, as he used to do in the time which now seems so long ago.

When we entered we saw with amazement that he had spread out his sugar as of old. The flies, lethargic with the autumn, were beginning to buzz into the room. We tried to make him talk of the subject of our previous conversation, but he would not attend. He went on with his singing, just as though we had not been present. He had got a scrap of paper and was folding it into a notebook. We had to come away as ignorant as we went in.

His is a curious case indeed. We must watch him tonight.

LETTER, MITCHELL, SONS & CANDY TO LORD GODALMING.

"1 October.

"My Lord,

"We are at all times only too happy to meet your wishes. We beg, with regard to the desire of your Lordship, expressed by Mr. Harker on your behalf, to supply the following information concerning the sale and purchase of No. 347, Piccadilly. The original vendors are the executors of the late Mr. Archibald Winter-Suffield. The purchaser is a foreign nobleman, Count de Ville, who effected the purchase himself paying the purchase money in notes 'over the counter,' if your Lordship will pardon us using so vulgar an expression. Beyond this we know nothing whatever of him.

"We are, my Lord,

"Your Lordship's humble servants,

"MITCHELL, SONS & CANDY."

DR. SEWARD'S DIARY

2 October.--I placed a man in the corridor last night, and told him to make an accurate note of any sound he might hear from Renfield's room, and gave him instructions that if there should be anything strange he was to call me. After dinner, when we had all gathered round the fire in the study, Mrs. Harker having gone to bed, we discussed the attempts and discoveries of the day. Harker was the only one who had any result, and we are in great hopes that his clue may be an important one.

Before going to bed I went round to the patient's room and looked in through the observation trap. He was sleeping soundly, his heart rose and fell with regular respiration.

CHAPTER 20

This morning the man on duty reported to me that a little after midnight he was restless and kept saying his prayers somewhat loudly. I asked him if that was all. He replied that it was all he heard. There was something about his manner, so suspicious that I asked him point blank if he had been asleep. He denied sleep, but admitted to having "dozed" for a while. It is too bad that men cannot be trusted unless they are watched.

Today Harker is out following up his clue, and Art and Quincey are looking after horses. Godalming thinks that it will be well to have horses always in readiness, for when we get the information which we seek there will be no time to lose. We must sterilize all the imported earth between sunrise and sunset. We shall thus catch the Count at his weakest, and without a refuge to fly to. Van Helsing is off to the British Museum looking up some authorities on ancient medicine. The old physicians took account of things which their followers do not accept, and the Professor is searching for witch and demon cures which may be useful to us later.

I sometimes think we must be all mad and that we shall wake to sanity in strait waistcoats.

Later.--We have met again. We seem at last to be on the track, and our work of tomorrow may be the beginning of the end. I wonder if Renfield's quiet has anything to do with this. His moods have so followed the doings of the Count, that the coming destruction of the monster may be carried to him some subtle way. If we could only get some hint as to what passed in his mind, between the time of my argument with him today and his resumption of fly-catching, it might afford us a valuable clue. He is now seemingly quiet for a spell… Is he? That wild yell seemed to come from his room…

The attendant came bursting into my room and told me that Renfield had somehow met with some accident. He had heard him yell, and when he went to him found him lying on his face on the floor, all covered with blood. I must go at once…

CHAPTER 21

DR. SEWARD'S DIARY

3 October.--Let me put down with exactness all that happened, as well as I can remember, since last I made an entry. Not a detail that I can recall must be forgotten. In all calmness I must proceed.

When I came to Renfield's room I found him lying on the floor on his left side in a glittering pool of blood. When I went to move him, it became at once apparent that he had received some terrible injuries. There seemed none of the unity of purpose between the parts of the body which marks even lethargic sanity. As the face was exposed I could see that it was horribly bruised, as though it had been beaten against the floor. Indeed it was from the face wounds that the pool of blood originated.

The attendant who was kneeling beside the body said to me as we turned him over, "I think, sir, his back is broken. See, both his right arm and leg and the whole side of his face are paralysed." How such a thing could have happened puzzled the attendant beyond measure. He seemed quite bewildered, and his brows were gathered in as he said, "I can't understand the two things. He could mark his face like that by beating his own head on the floor. I saw a young woman do it once at the Eversfield Asylum before anyone could lay hands on her. And I suppose he might have broken his neck by falling out of bed, if he got in an awkward kink. But for the life of me I can't imagine how the two things occurred. If his back was broke, he couldn't beat his head, and if his face was like that before the fall out of bed, there would be marks of it."

I said to him, "Go to Dr. Van Helsing, and ask him to kindly come here at once. I want him without an instant's delay."

The man ran off, and within a few minutes the Professor, in his dressing gown and slippers, appeared. When he saw Renfield on the ground, he looked keenly at him a moment, and then turned to me. I think he recognized my thought in my eyes, for he said very quietly, manifestly for the ears of the attendant, "Ah, a sad accident! He will need very careful watching, and much attention. I shall stay with you myself, but I shall first dress myself. If you will remain I shall in a few minutes join you."

The patient was now breathing stertorously and it was easy to see that he had suffered some terrible injury.

Van Helsing returned with extraordinary celerity, bearing with him a surgical case. He had evidently been thinking and had his mind made up, for almost before he looked at the patient, he whispered to me, "Send the attendant away. We must be alone with him when he becomes conscious, after the operation."

I said, "I think that will do now, Simmons. We have done all that we can at present. You had better go your round, and Dr. Van Helsing will operate. Let me know instantly if there be anything unusual anywhere."

The man withdrew, and we went into a strict examination of the patient. The wounds of the face were superficial. The real injury was a depressed fracture of the skull, extending right up through the motor area.

The Professor thought a moment and said, "We must reduce the pressure and get back to normal conditions, as far as can be. The rapidity of the suffusion shows the terrible nature of his injury. The whole motor area seems affected. The suffusion of the brain will increase quickly, so we must trephine at once or it may be too late."

As he was speaking there was a soft tapping at the door. I went over and opened it and found in the corridor without, Arthur and Quincey in pajamas and slippers; the former spoke, "I heard your man call up Dr. Van Helsing and tell him of an accident. So I woke Quincey or rather called for him as he was not asleep. Things are moving too quickly and too strangely for sound sleep for any of us these times. I've been thinking that tomorrow night will not see things as they have been. We'll have to look back, and forward a little more than we have done. May we come in?"

I nodded, and held the door open till they had entered, then I closed it again. When Quincey saw the attitude and state of the patient, and noted the horrible pool on the floor, he said softly, "My God! What has happened to him? Poor, poor devil!"

I told him briefly, and added that we expected he would recover consciousness after the operation, for a short time, at all events. He went at once and sat down on the edge of the bed, with Godalming beside him. We all watched in patience.

"We shall wait," said Van Helsing, "just long enough to fix the best spot for trephining, so that we may most quickly and perfectly remove the blood clot, for it is evident that the haemorrhage is increasing."

The minutes during which we waited passed with fearful slowness. I had a horrible sinking in my heart, and from Van Helsing's face I gathered that he felt some fear or apprehension as to what was to come. I dreaded the words Renfield might speak. I was positively afraid to think. But the conviction of what was coming was on me, as I have read of men who have heard the death watch. The poor man's breathing came in uncertain gasps. Each instant he seemed as though he would open his eyes and speak, but then would follow a prolonged stertorous breath, and he would relapse into a more fixed insensibility. Inured as I was to sick beds and death, this suspense grew and grew upon me. I could almost hear the beating of my own heart, and the blood surging through my temples sounded like blows from a hammer. The silence finally became agonizing. I looked at my companions, one after another, and saw from their flushed faces and damp brows that they were enduring equal torture. There was a nervous suspense over us all, as though overhead some dread bell would peal out powerfully when we should least expect it.

At last there came a time when it was evident that the patient was sinking fast. He might die at any moment. I looked up at the Professor and caught his eyes fixed on mine. His face was sternly set as he spoke, "There is no time to lose. His words may be worth many lives. I have been thinking so, as I stood here. It may be there is a soul at stake! We shall operate just above the ear."

Without another word he made the operation. For a few moments the breathing continued to be stertorous. Then there came a breath so prolonged that it seemed as though it would tear open his chest. Suddenly his eyes opened, and became fixed in a wild, helpless stare. This was continued for a few moments, then it was softened into a glad surprise, and from his lips came a sigh of relief. He moved convulsively, and as he did so, said, "I'll be quiet, Doctor. Tell them to take off the strait waistcoat. I have had a terrible dream, and it has left me so weak that I cannot move. What's wrong with my face? It feels all swollen, and it smarts dreadfully."

He tried to turn his head, but even with the effort his eyes seemed to grow glassy again so I gently put it back. Then Van Helsing said in a quiet grave tone, "Tell us your dream, Mr. Renfield."

As he heard the voice his face brightened, through its mutilation, and he said, "That is Dr. Van Helsing. How good it is of you to be here. Give me some water, my lips are dry, and I shall try to tell you. I dreamed…"

He stopped and seemed fainting. I called quietly to Quincey, "The brandy, it is in my study, quick!" He flew and returned with a glass, the decanter of brandy and a carafe of water. We moistened the parched lips, and the patient quickly revived.

It seemed, however, that his poor injured brain had been working in the interval, for when he was quite conscious, he looked at me piercingly with an agonized confusion which I shall never forget, and said, "I must not deceive myself. It was no dream, but all a grim reality." Then his eyes roved round the room. As they caught sight of the two figures sitting patiently on the edge of the bed he went on, "If I were not sure already, I would know from them."

For an instant his eyes closed, not with pain or sleep but voluntarily, as though he were bringing all his faculties to bear. When he opened them he said, hurriedly, and with more energy than he had yet displayed, "Quick, Doctor, quick, I am dying! I feel that I have but a few minutes, and then I must go back to death, or worse! Wet my lips with brandy again. I have something that I must say before I die. Or before my poor crushed brain dies anyhow. Thank you! It was that night after you left me, when I implored you to let me go away. I couldn't speak then, for I felt my tongue was tied. But I was as sane then, except in that way, as I am now. I was in an agony of despair for a long time after you left me, it seemed hours. Then there came a sudden peace to me. My brain seemed to become cool again, and I realized where I was. I heard the dogs bark behind our house, but not where He was!"

As he spoke, Van Helsing's eyes never blinked, but his hand came out and met mine and gripped it hard. He did not, however, betray himself. He nodded slightly and said, "Go on," in a low voice.

Renfield proceeded. "He came up to the window in the mist, as I had seen him often before, but he was solid then, not a ghost, and his eyes were fierce like a man's when angry. He was laughing with his red mouth, the sharp white teeth glinted in the moonlight when he turned to look back over the belt of trees, to where the dogs were barking. I wouldn't ask him to come in at first, though I knew he wanted to, just as he had wanted all along. Then he began promising me things, not in words but by doing them."

He was interrupted by a word from the Professor, "How?"

"By making them happen. Just as he used to send in the flies when the sun was shining. Great big fat ones with steel and sapphire on their wings. And big moths, in the night, with skull and cross-bones on their backs."

Van Helsing nodded to him as he whispered to me unconsciously, "The Acherontia Atropos of the Sphinges, what you call the 'Death's-head Moth'?"

The patient went on without stopping, "Then he began to whisper. 'Rats, rats, rats! Hundreds, thousands, millions of them, and every one a life. And dogs to eat them, and cats too. All lives! All red blood, with years of life in it, and not merely buzzing flies!' I laughed at him, for I wanted to see what he could do. Then the dogs howled, away beyond the dark trees in His house. He beckoned me to the window. I got up and looked out, and He raised his hands, and seemed to call out without using any words. A dark mass spread over the grass, coming on like the shape of a flame of fire. And then He moved the mist to the right and left, and I could see that there were thousands of rats with their eyes blazing red, like His only smaller. He held up his hand, and they all stopped, and I thought he seemed to be saying, 'All these lives will I give you, ay, and many more and greater, through countless ages, if you will fall down and worship me!' And then a red cloud, like the colour of blood, seemed to close over my eyes, and before I knew what I was doing, I found myself opening the sash and saying to Him, 'Come in, Lord and Master!' The rats were all gone, but He slid into the room through the sash, though it was only open an inch wide, just as the Moon herself has often come in through the tiniest crack and has stood before me in all her size and splendour."

His voice was weaker, so I moistened his lips with the brandy again, and he continued, but it seemed as though his memory had gone on working in the interval for his story was further advanced. I was about to call him back to the point, but Van Helsing whispered to me, "Let him go on. Do not interrupt him. He cannot go back, and maybe could not proceed at all if once he lost the thread of his thought."

He proceeded, "All day I waited to hear from him, but he did not send me anything, not even a blowfly, and when the moon got up I was pretty angry with him. When he did slide in through the window, though it was shut, and did not even knock, I got mad with him. He sneered at me, and his white face looked out of the mist with his red eyes gleaming, and he went on as though he owned the whole place, and I was no one. He didn't even smell the same as he went by me. I couldn't hold him. I thought that, somehow, Mrs. Harker had come into the room."

The two men sitting on the bed stood up and came over, standing behind him so that he could not see them, but where they could hear better. They were both silent, but the Professor started and quivered. His face, however, grew grimmer and sterner still. Renfield went on without noticing, "When Mrs. Harker came in to see me this afternoon she wasn't the same. It was like tea after the teapot has been watered." Here we all moved, but no one said a word.

He went on, "I didn't know that she was here till she spoke, and she didn't look the same. I don't care for the pale people. I like them with lots of blood in them, and hers all seemed to have run out. I didn't think of it at the time, but when she went away I began to think, and it made me mad to know that He had been taking the life out of her." I could feel that the rest quivered, as I did; but we remained otherwise still. "So when He came tonight I was ready for Him. I saw the mist stealing in, and I grabbed it tight. I had heard that madmen have unnatural strength. And as I knew I was a madman, at times anyhow, I resolved to use my power. Ay, and He felt it too, for He had to come out of the mist to struggle with me. I held tight, and I thought I was going to win, for I didn't mean Him to take any more of her life, till I saw His eyes. They burned into me, and my strength became like water. He slipped through it, and when I tried to cling to Him, He raised me up and flung me down. There was a red cloud before me, and a noise like thunder, and the mist seemed to steal away under the door."

His voice was becoming fainter and his breath more stertorous. Van Helsing stood up instinctively.

"We know the worst now," he said. "He is here, and we know his purpose. It may not be too late. Let us be armed, the same as we were the other night, but lose no time, there is not an instant to spare."

There was no need to put our fear, nay our conviction, into words, we shared them in common. We all hurried and took from our rooms the same things that we had when we entered the Count's house. The Professor had his ready, and as we met in the corridor he pointed to them significantly as he said, "They never leave me, and they shall not till this unhappy business is over. Be wise also, my friends. It is no common enemy that we deal with Alas! Alas! That dear Madam Mina should suffer!" He stopped, his voice was breaking, and I do not know if rage or terror predominated in my own heart.

Outside the Harkers' door we paused. Art and Quincey held back, and the latter said, "Should we disturb her?"

"We must," said Van Helsing grimly. "If the door be locked, I shall break it in."

"May it not frighten her terribly? It is unusual to break into a lady's room!"

Van Helsing said solemnly, "You are always right. But this is life and death. All chambers are alike to the doctor. And even were they not they are all as one to me tonight. Friend John, when I turn the handle, if the door does not open, do you put your shoulder down and shove; and you too, my friends. Now!"

He turned the handle as he spoke, but the door did not yield. We threw ourselves against it. With a crash it burst open, and we almost fell headlong into the room. The Professor did actually fall, and I saw across him as he gathered himself up from hands and knees. What I saw appalled me. I felt my hair rise like bristles on the back of my neck, and my heart seemed to stand still.

The moonlight was so bright that through the thick yellow blind the room was light enough to see. On the bed beside the window lay Jonathan Harker, his face flushed and breathing heavily as though in a stupor. Kneeling on the near edge of the bed facing outwards was the white-clad figure of his wife. By her side stood a tall, thin man, clad in black. His face was turned from us, but the instant we saw we all recognized the Count, in every way, even to the scar on his forehead. With his left hand he held both Mrs. Harker's hands, keeping them away with her arms at full tension. His right hand gripped her by the back of the neck, forcing her face down on his bosom. Her white nightdress was smeared with blood, and a thin stream trickled down the man's bare chest which was shown by his torn-open dress. The attitude of the two had a terrible resemblance to a child forcing a kitten's nose into a saucer of milk to compel it to drink. As we burst into the room, the Count turned his face, and the hellish look that I had heard described seemed to leap into it. His eyes flamed red with devilish passion. The great nostrils of the white aquiline nose opened wide and quivered at the edge, and the white sharp teeth, behind the full lips of the blood dripping mouth, clamped together like those of a wild beast. With a wrench, which threw his victim back upon the bed as though hurled from a height, he turned and sprang at us. But by this time the Professor had gained his feet, and was holding towards him the envelope which contained the Sacred Wafer. The Count suddenly stopped, just as poor Lucy had done outside the tomb, and cowered back. Further and further back he cowered, as we, lifting our crucifixes, advanced. The moonlight suddenly failed, as a great black cloud sailed across the sky. And when the gaslight sprang up under Quincey's match, we saw nothing but a faint vapour. This, as we looked, trailed under the door, which with the recoil from its bursting open, had swung back to its old position. Van Helsing, Art, and I moved forward to Mrs. Harker, who by this time had drawn her breath and with it had given a scream so wild, so ear-piercing, so despairing that it seems to me now that it will ring in my ears till my dying day. For a few seconds she lay in her helpless attitude and disarray. Her face was ghastly, with a pallor which was accentuated by the blood which smeared her lips and cheeks and chin. From her throat trickled a thin stream of blood. Her eyes were mad with terror. Then she put before her face her poor crushed hands, which bore on their whiteness the red mark of the Count's terrible grip, and from behind them came a low desolate wail which made the terrible scream seem only the quick expression of an endless grief. Van Helsing stepped forward and drew the coverlet gently over her body, whilst Art, after looking at her face for an instant despairingly, ran out of the room.

Van Helsing whispered to me, "Jonathan is in a stupor such as we know the Vampire can produce. We can do nothing with poor Madam Mina for a few moments till she recovers herself. I must wake him!"

He dipped the end of a towel in cold water and with it began to flick him on the face, his wife all the while holding her face between her hands and sobbing in a way that was heart breaking to hear. I raised the blind, and looked out of the window. There was much moonshine, and as I looked I could see Quincey Morris run across the lawn and hide himself in the shadow of a great yew tree. It puzzled me to think why he was doing this. But at the instant I heard Harker's quick exclamation as he woke to partial consciousness, and turned to the bed. On his face, as there might well be, was a look of wild amazement. He seemed dazed for a few seconds, and then full consciousness seemed to burst upon him all at once, and he started up.

His wife was aroused by the quick movement, and turned to him with her arms stretched out, as though to embrace him. Instantly, however, she drew them in again, and putting her elbows together, held her hands before her face, and shuddered till the bed beneath her shook.

"In God's name what does this mean?" Harker cried out. "Dr. Seward, Dr. Van Helsing, what is it? What has happened? What is wrong? Mina, dear what is it? What does that blood mean? My God, my God! Has it come to this!" And, raising himself to his knees, he beat his hands wildly together. "Good God help us! Help her! Oh, help her!"

With a quick movement he jumped from bed, and began to pull on his clothes, all the man in him awake at the need for instant exertion. "What has happened? Tell me all about it!" he cried without pausing. "Dr. Van Helsing, you love Mina, I know. Oh, do something to save her. It cannot have gone too far yet. Guard her while I look for him!"

His wife, through her terror and horror and distress, saw some sure danger to him. Instantly forgetting her own grief, she seized hold of him and cried out.

"No! No! Jonathan, you must not leave me. I have suffered enough tonight, God knows, without the dread of his harming you. You must stay with me. Stay with these friends who will watch over you!" Her expression became frantic as she spoke. And, he yielding to her, she pulled him down sitting on the bedside, and clung to him fiercely.

Van Helsing and I tried to calm them both. The Professor held up his golden crucifix, and said with wonderful calmness, "Do not fear, my dear. We are here, and whilst this is close to you no foul thing can approach. You are safe for tonight, and we must be calm and take counsel together."

She shuddered and was silent, holding down her head on her husband's breast. When she raised it, his white nightrobe was stained with blood where her lips had touched, and where the thin open wound in the neck had sent forth drops. The instant she saw it she drew back, with a low wail, and whispered, amidst choking sobs.

"Unclean, unclean! I must touch him or kiss him no more. Oh, that it should be that it is I who am now his worst enemy, and whom he may have most cause to fear."

To this he spoke out resolutely, "Nonsense, Mina. It is a shame to me to hear such a word. I would not hear it of you. And I shall not hear it from you. May God judge me by my deserts, and punish me with more bitter suffering than even this hour, if by any act or will of mine anything ever come between us!"

He put out his arms and folded her to his breast. And for a while she lay there sobbing. He looked at us over her bowed head, with eyes that blinked damply above his quivering nostrils. His mouth was set as steel.

After a while her sobs became less frequent and more faint, and then he said to me, speaking with a studied calmness which I felt tried his nervous power to the utmost.

"And now, Dr. Seward, tell me all about it. Too well I know the broad fact. Tell me all that has been."

I told him exactly what had happened and he listened with seeming impassiveness, but his nostrils twitched and his eyes blazed as I told how the ruthless hands of the Count had held his wife in that terrible and horrid position, with her mouth to the open wound in his breast. It interested me, even at that moment, to see that whilst the face of white set passion worked convulsively over the bowed head, the hands tenderly and lovingly stroked the ruffled hair. Just as I had finished, Quincey and Godalming knocked at the door. They entered in obedience to our summons. Van Helsing looked at me questioningly. I understood him to mean if we were to take advantage of their coming to divert if possible the thoughts of the unhappy husband and wife from each other and from themselves. So on nodding acquiescence to him he asked them what they had seen or done. To which Lord Godalming answered.

"I could not see him anywhere in the passage, or in any of our rooms. I looked in the study but, though he had been there, he had gone. He had, however..." He stopped suddenly, looking at the poor drooping figure on the bed.

Van Helsing said gravely, "Go on, friend Arthur. We want here no more concealments. Our hope now is in knowing all. Tell freely!"

So Art went on, "He had been there, and though it could only have been for a few seconds, he made rare hay of the place. All the manuscript had been burned, and the blue flames were flickering amongst the white ashes. The cylinders of your phonograph too were thrown on the fire, and the wax had helped the flames."

Here I interrupted. "Thank God there is the other copy in the safe!"

His face lit for a moment, but fell again as he went on. "I ran downstairs then, but could see no sign of him. I looked into Renfield's room, but there was no trace there except…" Again he paused.

"Go on," said Harker hoarsely. So he bowed his head and moistening his lips with his tongue, added, "except that the poor fellow is dead."

Mrs. Harker raised her head, looking from one to the other of us she said solemnly, "God's will be done!"

I could not but feel that Art was keeping back something. But, as I took it that it was with a purpose, I said nothing.

Van Helsing turned to Morris and asked, "And you, friend Quincey, have you any to tell?"

"A little," he answered. "It may be much eventually, but at present I can't say. I thought it well to know if possible where the Count would go when he left the house. I did not see him, but I saw a bat rise from Renfield's window, and flap westward. I expected to see him in some shape go back to Carfax, but he evidently sought some other lair. He will not be back tonight, for the sky is reddening in the east, and the dawn is close. We must work tomorrow!"

He said the latter words through his shut teeth. For a space of perhaps a couple of minutes there was silence, and I could fancy that I could hear the sound of our hearts beating.

Then Van Helsing said, placing his hand tenderly on Mrs. Harker's head, "And now, Madam Mina, poor dear, dear, Madam Mina, tell us exactly what happened. God knows that I do not want that you be pained, but it is need that we know all. For now more than ever has all work to be done quick and sharp, and in deadly earnest. The day is close to us that must end all, if it may be so, and now is the chance that we may live and learn."

The poor dear lady shivered, and I could see the tension of her nerves as she clasped her husband closer to her and bent her head lower and lower still on his breast. Then she raised her head proudly, and held out one hand to Van Helsing who took it in his, and after stooping and kissing it reverently, held it fast. The other hand was locked in that of her husband, who held his other arm thrown round her protectingly. After a pause in which she was evidently ordering her thoughts, she began.

"I took the sleeping draught which you had so kindly given me, but for a long time it did not act. I seemed to become more wakeful, and myriads of horrible fancies began to crowd in upon my mind. All of them connected with death, and vampires, with blood, and pain, and trouble." Her husband involuntarily groaned as she turned to him and said lovingly, "Do not fret, dear. You must be brave and strong, and help me through the horrible task. If you only knew what an effort it is to me to tell of this fearful thing at all, you would understand how much I need your help. Well, I saw I must try to help the medicine to its work with my will, if it was to do me any good, so I resolutely set myself to sleep. Sure enough sleep must soon have come to me, for I remember no more. Jonathan coming in had not waked me, for he lay by my side when next I remember. There was in the room the same thin white mist that I had before noticed. But I forget now if you know of this. You will find it in my diary which

I shall show you later. I felt the same vague terror which had come to me before and the same sense of some presence. I turned to wake Jonathan, but found that he slept so soundly that it seemed as if it was he who had taken the sleeping draught, and not I. I tried, but I could not wake him. This caused me a great fear, and I looked around terrified. Then indeed, my heart sank within me. Beside the bed, as if he had stepped out of the mist, or rather as if the mist had turned into his figure, for it had entirely disappeared, stood a tall, thin man, all in black. I knew him at once from the description of the others. The waxen face, the high aquiline nose, on which the light fell in a thin white line, the parted red lips, with the sharp white teeth showing between, and the red eyes that I had seemed to see in the sunset on the windows of St. Mary's Church at Whitby. I knew, too, the red scar on his forehead where Jonathan had struck him. For an instant my heart stood still, and I would have screamed out, only that I was paralyzed. In the pause he spoke in a sort of keen, cutting whisper, pointing as he spoke to Jonathan.

"'Silence! If you make a sound I shall take him and dash his brains out before your very eyes.' I was appalled and was too bewildered to do or say anything. With a mocking smile, he placed one hand upon my shoulder and, holding me tight, bared my throat with the other, saying as he did so, 'First, a little refreshment to reward my exertions. You may as well be quiet. It is not the first time, or the second, that your veins have appeased my thirst!' I was bewildered, and strangely enough, I did not want to hinder him. I suppose it is a part of the horrible curse that such is, when his touch is on his victim. And oh, my God, my God, pity me! He placed his reeking lips upon my throat!" Her husband groaned again. She clasped his hand harder, and looked at him pityingly, as if he were the injured one, and went on.

"I felt my strength fading away, and I was in a half swoon. How long this horrible thing lasted I know not, but it seemed that a long time must have passed before he took his foul, awful, sneering mouth away. I saw it drip with the fresh blood!" The remembrance seemed for a while to overpower her, and she drooped and would have sunk down but for her husband's sustaining arm. With a great effort she recovered herself and went on.

"Then he spoke to me mockingly, 'And so you, like the others, would play your brains against mine. You would help these men to hunt me and frustrate me in my design! You know now, and they know in part already, and will know in full before long, what it is to cross my path. They should have kept their energies for use closer to home. Whilst they played wits against me, against me who commanded nations, and intrigued for them, and fought for them, hundreds of years before they were born, I was countermining them. And you, their best beloved one, are now to me, flesh of my flesh, blood of my blood, kin of my kin, my bountiful wine-press for a while, and shall be later on my companion and my helper. You shall be avenged in turn, for not one of them but shall minister to your needs. But as yet you are to be punished for what you have done. You have aided in thwarting me. Now you shall come to my call. When my brain says "Come!" to you, you shall cross land or sea to do my bidding. And to that end this!'

"With that he pulled open his shirt, and with his long sharp nails opened a vein in his breast. When the blood began to spurt out, he took my hands in one of his, holding them tight, and with the other seized my neck and pressed my mouth to the wound, so that I must either suffocate or swallow some to the... Oh, my God! My God! What have I done? What have I done to deserve such a fate, I who have tried to walk in meekness and righteousness all my days. God pity me! Look down on a poor soul in worse than mortal peril. And in mercy pity those to whom she is dear!" Then she began to rub her lips as though to cleanse them from pollution.

As she was telling her terrible story, the eastern sky began to quicken, and everything became more and more clear. Harker was still and quiet; but over his face, as the awful narrative went on, came a grey look which deepened and deepened in the morning light, till when the first red streak of the coming dawn shot up, the flesh stood darkly out against the whitening hair.

We have arranged that one of us is to stay within call of the unhappy pair till we can meet together and arrange about taking action.

Of this I am sure. The sun rises today on no more miserable house in all the great round of its daily course.

CHAPTER 22

JONATHAN HARKER'S JOURNAL

3 October.--As I must do something or go mad, I write this diary. It is now six o'clock, and we are to meet in the study in half an hour and take something to eat, for Dr. Van Helsing and Dr. Seward are agreed that if we do not eat we cannot work our best. Our best will be, God knows, required today. I must keep writing at every chance, for I dare not stop to think. All, big and little, must go down. Perhaps at the end the little things may teach us most. The teaching, big or little, could not have landed Mina or me anywhere worse than we are today. However, we must trust and hope. Poor Mina told me just now, with the tears running down her dear cheeks, that it is in trouble and trial that our faith is tested. That we must keep on trusting, and that God will aid us up to the end. The end! Oh my God! What end?... To work! To work!

When Dr. Van Helsing and Dr. Seward had come back from seeing poor Renfield, we went gravely into what was to be done. First, Dr. Seward told us that when he and Dr. Van Helsing had gone down to the room below they had found Renfield lying on the floor, all in a heap. His face was all bruised and crushed in, and the bones of the neck were broken.

Dr. Seward asked the attendant who was on duty in the passage if he had heard anything. He said that he had been sitting down, he confessed to half dozing, when he heard loud voices in the room, and then Renfield had called out loudly several times, "God! God! God!" After that there was a sound of falling, and when he entered the room he found him lying on the floor, face down, just as the doctors had seen him. Van Helsing asked if he had heard "voices" or "a voice," and he said he could not say. That at first it had seemed to him as if there were two, but as there was no one in the room it could have been only one. He could swear to it, if required, that the word "God" was spoken by the patient.

Dr. Seward said to us, when we were alone, that he did not wish to go into the matter. The question of an inquest had to be considered, and it would never do to put forward the truth, as no one would believe it. As it was, he thought that on the attendant's evidence he could give a certificate of death by misadventure in falling from bed. In case the coroner should demand it, there would be a formal inquest, necessarily to the same result.

When the question began to be discussed as to what should be our next step, the very first thing we decided was that Mina should be in full confidence. That nothing of any sort, no matter how painful, should be kept from her. She herself agreed as to its wisdom, and it was pitiful to see her so brave and yet so sorrowful, and in such a depth of despair.

"There must be no concealment," she said. "Alas! We have had too much already. And besides there is nothing in all the world that can give me more pain than I have already endured, than I suffer now! Whatever may happen, it must be of new hope or of new courage to me!"

Van Helsing was looking at her fixedly as she spoke, and said, suddenly but quietly, "But dear Madam Mina, are you not afraid. Not for yourself, but for others from yourself, after what has happened?"

Her face grew set in its lines, but her eyes shone with the devotion of a martyr as she answered, "Ah no! For my mind is made up!"

"To what?" he asked gently, whilst we were all very still, for each in our own way we had a sort of vague idea of what she meant.

Her answer came with direct simplicity, as though she was simply stating a fact, "Because if I find in myself, and I shall watch keenly for it, a sign of harm to any that I love, I shall die!"

"You would not kill yourself?" he asked, hoarsely.

"I would. If there were no friend who loved me, who would save me such a pain, and so desperate an effort!" She looked at him meaningly as she spoke.

He was sitting down, but now he rose and came close to her and put his hand on her head as he said solemnly. "My child, there is such an one if it were for your good. For myself I could hold it in my account with God to find such an euthanasia for you, even at this moment if it were best. Nay, were it safe! But my child..."

For a moment he seemed choked, and a great sob rose in his throat. He gulped it down and went on, "There are here some who would stand between you and death. You must not die. You must not die by any hand, but least of all your own. Until the other, who has fouled your sweet life, is true dead you must not die. For if he is still with the quick Undead, your death would make you even as he is. No, you must live! You must struggle and strive to live, though death would seem a boon unspeakable. You must fight Death himself, though he come to you in pain or in joy. By the day, or the night, in safety or in peril! On your living soul I charge you that you do not die. Nay, nor think of death, till this great evil be past."

The poor dear grew white as death, and shook and shivered, as I have seen a quicksand shake and shiver at the incoming of the tide. We were all silent. We could do nothing. At length she grew more calm and turning to him said sweetly, but oh so sorrowfully, as she held out her hand, "I promise you, my dear friend, that if God will let me live, I shall strive to do so. Till, if it may be in His good time, this horror may have passed away from me."

She was so good and brave that we all felt that our hearts were strengthened to work and endure for her, and we began to discuss what we were to do. I told her that she was to have all the papers in the safe, and all the papers or diaries and phonographs we might hereafter use, and was to keep the record as she had done before. She was pleased with the prospect of anything to do, if "pleased" could be used in connection with so grim an interest.

As usual Van Helsing had thought ahead of everyone else, and was prepared with an exact ordering of our work.

"It is perhaps well," he said, "that at our meeting after our visit to Carfax we decided not to do anything with the earth boxes that lay there. Had we done so, the Count must have guessed our purpose, and would doubtless have taken measures in advance to frustrate such an effort with regard to the others. But now he does not know our intentions. Nay, more, in all probability, he does not know that such a power exists to us as can sterilize his lairs, so that he cannot use them as of old.

"We are now so much further advanced in our knowledge as to their disposition that, when we have examined the house in Piccadilly, we may track the very last of them. Today then, is ours, and in it rests our hope. The sun that rose on our sorrow this morning guards us in its course. Until it sets tonight, that monster must retain whatever form he now has. He is confined within the limitations of his earthly envelope. He cannot melt into thin air nor disappear through cracks or chinks or crannies. If he go through a doorway, he must open the door like a mortal. And so we have this day to hunt out all his lairs and sterilize them. So we shall, if we have not yet catch him and destroy him, drive him to bay in some place where the catching and the destroying shall be, in time, sure."

Here I started up for I could not contain myself at the thought that the minutes and seconds so preciously laden with Mina's life and happiness were flying from us, since whilst we talked action was impossible. But Van Helsing held up his hand warningly.

"Nay, friend Jonathan," he said, "in this, the quickest way home is the longest way, so your proverb say. We shall all act and act with desperate quick, when the time has come. But think, in all probable the key of the situation is in that house in Piccadilly. The Count may have many houses which he has bought. Of them he will have deeds of purchase, keys and other things. He will have paper that he write on. He will have his book of cheques. There are many belongings that he must have somewhere. Why not in this place so central, so quiet, where he come and go by the front or the back at all hours, when in the very vast of the traffic there is none to notice. We shall go there and search that house. And when we learn what it holds, then we do what our friend Arthur call, in his phrases of hunt 'stop the earths' and so we run down our old fox, so? Is it not?"

"Then let us come at once," I cried, "we are wasting the precious, precious time!"

The Professor did not move, but simply said, "And how are we to get into that house in Piccadilly?"

"Any way!" I cried. "We shall break in if need be."

"And your police? Where will they be, and what will they say?"

I was staggered, but I knew that if he wished to delay he had a good reason for it. So I said, as quietly as I could, "Don't wait more than need be. You know, I am sure, what torture I am in."

"Ah, my child, that I do. And indeed there is no wish of me to add to your anguish. But just think, what can we do, until all the world be at movement. Then will come our time. I have thought and thought, and it seems to me that the simplest way is the best of all. Now we wish to get into the house, but we have no key. Is it not so?" I nodded.

"Now suppose that you were, in truth, the owner of that house, and could not still get in. And think there was to you no conscience of the housebreaker, what would you do?"

"I should get a respectable locksmith, and set him to work to pick the lock for me."

"And your police, they would interfere, would they not?"

"Oh no! Not if they knew the man was properly employed."

"Then," he looked at me as keenly as he spoke, "all that is in doubt is the conscience of the employer, and the belief of your policemen as to whether or not that employer has a good conscience or a bad one. Your police must indeed be zealous men and clever, oh so clever, in reading the heart, that they trouble themselves in such matter. No, no, my friend Jonathan, you go take the lock off a hundred empty houses in this your London, or of any city in the world, and if you do it as such things are rightly done, and at the time such things are rightly done, no one will interfere. I have read of a gentleman who owned a so fine house in London, and when he went for months of summer to Switzerland and lock up his house, some burglar come and broke window at back and got in. Then he went and made open the shutters in front and walk out and in through the door, before the very eyes of the police. Then he have an auction in that house, and advertise it, and put up big notice. And when the day come he sell off by a great auctioneer all the goods of that other man who own them. Then he go to a builder, and he sell him that house, making an agreement that he pull it down and take all away within a certain time. And your police and other authority help him all they can. And when that owner come back from his holiday in Switzerland he find only an empty hole where his house had been. This was all done en regle, and in our work we shall be en regle too. We shall not go so early that the policemen who have then little to think of, shall deem it strange. But we shall go after ten o'clock, when there are many about, and such things would be done were we indeed owners of the house."

I could not but see how right he was and the terrible despair of Mina's face became relaxed in thought. There was hope in such good counsel.

Van Helsing went on, "When once within that house we may find more clues. At any rate some of us can remain there whilst the rest find the other places where there be more earth boxes, at Bermondsey and Mile End."

Lord Godalming stood up. "I can be of some use here," he said. "I shall wire to my people to have horses and carriages where they will be most convenient."

"Look here, old fellow," said Morris, "it is a capital idea to have all ready in case we want to go horse backing, but don't you think that one of your snappy carriages with its heraldic adornments in a byway of Walworth or Mile End would attract too much attention for our purpose? It seems to me that we ought to take cabs when we go south or east. And even leave them somewhere near the neighbourhood we are going to."

"Friend Quincey is right!" said the Professor. "His head is what you call in plane with the horizon. It is a difficult thing that we go to do, and we do not want no peoples to watch us if so it may."

Mina took a growing interest in everything and I was rejoiced to see that the exigency of affairs was helping her to forget for a time the terrible experience of the night. She was very, very pale, almost ghastly, and so thin that her lips were drawn away, showing her teeth in somewhat of prominence. I did not mention this last, lest it should give her needless pain, but it made my blood run cold in my veins to think of what had occurred with poor Lucy when the Count had sucked her blood. As yet there was no sign of the teeth growing sharper, but the time as yet was short, and there was time for fear.

When we came to the discussion of the sequence of our efforts and of the disposition of our forces, there were new sources of doubt. It was finally agreed that before starting for Piccadilly we should destroy the Count's lair close at hand. In case he should find it out too soon, we should thus be still ahead of him in our work of destruction. And his presence in his purely material shape, and at his weakest, might give us some new clue.

As to the disposal of forces, it was suggested by the Professor that, after our visit to Carfax, we should all enter the house in Piccadilly. That the two doctors and I should remain there, whilst Lord Godalming and Quincey found the lairs at Walworth and Mile End and destroyed them. It was possible, if not likely, the Professor urged, that the Count might appear in Piccadilly during the day, and that if so we might be able to cope with him then and there. At any rate, we might be able to follow him in force. To this plan I strenuously objected, and so far as my going was concerned, for I said that I intended to stay and protect Mina. I thought that my mind was made up on the subject, but Mina would not listen to my objection. She said that there might be some law matter in which I could be useful. That amongst the Count's papers might be some clue which I could understand out of my experience in Transylvania. And that, as it was, all the strength we could muster was required to cope with the Count's extraordinary power. I had to give in, for Mina's resolution was fixed. She said that it was the last hope for her that we should all work together.

"As for me," she said, "I have no fear. Things have been as bad as they can be. And whatever may happen must have in it some element of hope or comfort. Go, my husband! God can, if He wishes it, guard me as well alone as with any one present."

So I started up crying out, "Then in God's name let us come at once, for we are losing time. The Count may come to Piccadilly earlier than we think."

"Not so!" said Van Helsing, holding up his hand.

"But why?" I asked.

"Do you forget," he said, with actually a smile, "that last night he banqueted heavily, and will sleep late?"

Did I forget! Shall I ever… can I ever! Can any of us ever forget that terrible scene! Mina struggled hard to keep her brave countenance, but the pain overmastered her and she put her hands before her face, and shuddered whilst she moaned. Van Helsing had not intended to recall her frightful experience. He had simply lost sight of her and her part in the affair in his intellectual effort.

When it struck him what he said, he was horrified at his thoughtlessness and tried to comfort her.

"Oh, Madam Mina," he said, "dear, dear, Madam Mina, alas! That I of all who so reverence you should have said anything so forgetful. These stupid old lips of mine and this stupid old head do not deserve so, but you will forget it, will you not?" He bent low beside her as he spoke.

She took his hand, and looking at him through her tears, said hoarsely, "No, I shall not forget, for it is well that I remember. And with it I have so much in memory of you that is sweet, that I take it all together. Now, you must all be going soon. Breakfast is ready, and we must all eat that we may be strong."

Breakfast was a strange meal to us all. We tried to be cheerful and encourage each other, and Mina was the brightest and most cheerful of us. When it was over, Van Helsing stood up and said, "Now, my dear friends, we go forth to our terrible enterprise. Are we all armed, as we were on that night when first we visited our enemy's lair. Armed against ghostly as well as carnal attack?"

We all assured him.

"Then it is well. Now, Madam Mina, you are in any case quite safe here until the sunset. And before then we shall return... if... We shall return! But before we go let me see you armed against personal attack. I have myself, since you came down, prepared your chamber by the placing of things of which we know, so that He may not enter. Now let me guard yourself. On your forehead I touch this piece of Sacred Wafer in the name of the Father, the Son, and..."

There was a fearful scream which almost froze our hearts to hear. As he had placed the Wafer on Mina's forehead, it had seared it... had burned into the flesh as though it had been a piece of white-hot metal. My poor darling's brain had told her the significance of the fact as quickly as her nerves received the pain of it, and the two so overwhelmed her that her overwrought nature had its voice in that dreadful scream.

But the words to her thought came quickly. The echo of the scream had not ceased to ring on the air when there came the reaction, and she sank on her knees on the floor in an agony of abasement. Pulling her beautiful hair over her face, as the leper of old his mantle, she wailed out.

"Unclean! Unclean! Even the Almighty shuns my polluted flesh! I must bear this mark of shame upon my forehead until the Judgement Day."

They all paused. I had thrown myself beside her in an agony of helpless grief, and putting my arms around held her tight. For a few minutes our sorrowful hearts beat together, whilst the friends around us turned away their eyes that ran tears silently. Then Van Helsing turned and said gravely. So gravely that I could not help feeling that he was in some way inspired, and was stating things outside himself.

"It may be that you may have to bear that mark till God himself see fit, as He most surely shall, on the Judgement Day, to redress all wrongs of the earth and of His children that He has placed thereon. And oh, Madam Mina, my dear, my dear, may we who love you be there to see, when that red scar, the sign of God's knowledge of what has been, shall pass away, and leave your forehead as pure as the heart we know. For so surely as we live, that scar shall pass away when God sees right to lift the burden that is hard upon us. Till then we bear our Cross, as His Son did in obedience to His Will. It may be that we are chosen instruments of His good pleasure, and that we ascend to His bidding as that other through stripes and shame. Through tears and blood. Through doubts and fear, and all that makes the difference between God and man."

There was hope in his words, and comfort. And they made for resignation. Mina and I both felt so, and simultaneously we each took one of the old man's hands and bent over and kissed it. Then without a word we all knelt down together, and all holding hands, swore to be true to each other. We men pledged ourselves to raise the veil of sorrow from the head of her whom, each in his own way, we loved. And we prayed for help and guidance in the terrible task which lay before us. It was then time to start. So I said farewell to Mina, a parting which neither of us shall forget to our dying day, and we set out.

To one thing I have made up my mind. If we find out that Mina must be a vampire in the end, then she shall not go into that unknown and terrible land alone. I suppose it is thus that in old times one vampire meant many. Just as their hideous bodies could only rest in sacred earth, so the holiest love was the recruiting sergeant for their ghastly ranks.

We entered Carfax without trouble and found all things the same as on the first occasion. It was hard to believe that amongst so prosaic surroundings of neglect and dust and decay there was any ground for such fear as already we knew. Had not our minds been made up, and had there not been terrible memories to spur us on, we could hardly have proceeded with our task. We found no papers, or any sign of use in the house. And in the old chapel the great boxes looked just as we had seen them last.

Dr. Van Helsing said to us solemnly as we stood before him, "And now, my friends, we have a duty here to do. We must sterilize this earth, so sacred of holy memories, that he has brought from a far distant land for such fell use. He has chosen this earth because it has been holy. Thus we defeat him with his own weapon, for we make it more holy still. It was sanctified to such use of man, now we sanctify it to God."

As he spoke he took from his bag a screwdriver and a wrench, and very soon the top of one of the cases was thrown open. The earth smelled musty and close, but we did not somehow seem to mind, for our attention was concentrated on the Professor. Taking from his box a piece of the Sacred Wafer he laid it reverently on the earth, and then shutting down the lid began to screw it home, we aiding him as he worked.

One by one we treated in the same way each of the great boxes, and left them as we had found them to all appearance. But in each was a portion of the Host. When we closed the door behind us, the Professor said solemnly, "So much is already done. It may be that with all the others we can be so successful, then the sunset of this evening may shine of Madam Mina's forehead all white as ivory and with no stain!"

As we passed across the lawn on our way to the station to catch our train we could see the front of the asylum. I looked eagerly, and in the window of my own room saw Mina. I waved my hand to her, and nodded to tell that our work there was successfully accomplished. She nodded in reply to show that she understood. The last I saw, she was waving her hand in farewell. It was with a heavy heart that we sought the station and just caught the train, which was steaming in as we reached the platform. I have written this in the train.

Piccadilly, 12:30 o'clock.--Just before we reached Fenchurch Street Lord Godalming said to me, "Quincey and I will find a locksmith. You had better not come with us in case there should be any difficulty. For under the circumstances it wouldn't seem so bad for us to break into an empty house. But you are a solicitor and the Incorporated Law Society might tell you that you should have known better."

I demurred as to my not sharing any danger even of odium, but he went on, "Besides, it will attract less attention if there are not too many of us. My title will make it all right with the locksmith, and with any policeman that may come along. You had better go with Jack and the Professor and stay in the Green Park. Somewhere in sight of the house, and when you see the door opened and the smith has gone away, do you all come across. We shall be on the lookout for you, and shall let you in."

"The advice is good!" said Van Helsing, so we said no more. Godalming and Morris hurried off in a cab, we following in another. At the corner of Arlington Street our contingent got out and strolled into the Green Park. My heart beat as I saw the house on which so much of our hope was centred, looming up grim and silent in its deserted condition amongst its more lively and spruce-looking neighbours. We sat down on a bench within good view, and began to smoke cigars so as to attract as little attention as possible. The minutes seemed to pass with leaden feet as we waited for the coming of the others.

At length we saw a four-wheeler drive up. Out of it, in leisurely fashion, got Lord Godalming and Morris. And down from the box descended a thick-set working man with his rush-woven basket of tools. Morris paid the cabman, who touched his hat and drove away. Together the two ascended the steps, and Lord Godalming pointed out what he wanted done. The workman took off his coat leisurely and hung it on one of the spikes of the rail, saying something to a policeman who just then sauntered along. The policeman nodded acquiescence, and the man kneeling down placed his bag beside him. After searching through it, he took out a selection of tools which he proceeded to lay beside him in orderly fashion. Then he stood up, looked in the keyhole, blew into it, and turning to his employers, made some remark. Lord Godalming smiled, and the man lifted a good sized bunch of keys. Selecting one of them, he began to probe the lock, as if feeling his way with it. After fumbling about for a bit he tried a second, and then a third. All at once the door opened under a slight push from him, and he and the two others entered the hall. We sat still. My own cigar burnt furiously, but Van Helsing's went cold altogether. We waited patiently as we saw the workman come out and bring his bag. Then he held the door partly open, steadying it with his knees, whilst he fitted a key to the lock. This he finally handed to Lord Godalming, who took out his purse and gave him something. The man touched his hat, took his bag, put on his coat and departed. Not a soul took the slightest notice of the whole transaction.

When the man had fairly gone, we three crossed the street and knocked at the door. It was immediately opened by Quincey Morris, beside whom stood Lord Godalming lighting a cigar.

"The place smells so vilely," said the latter as we came in. It did indeed smell vilely—like the old chapel at Carfax—and with our previous experience it was plain to us that the Count had been using the place pretty freely. We moved to explore the house, all keeping together in case of attack, for we knew we had a strong and wily enemy to deal with, and as yet we did not know whether the Count might not be in the house.

In the dining room, which lay at the back of the hall, we found eight boxes of earth. Eight boxes only out of the nine which we sought! Our work was not over, and would never be until we should have found the missing box.

First we opened the shutters of the window which looked out across a narrow stone flagged yard at the blank face of a stable, pointed to look like the front of a miniature house. There were no windows in it, so we were not afraid of being overlooked. We did not lose any time in examining the chests. With the tools which we had brought with us we opened them, one by one, and treated them as we had treated those others in the old chapel. It was evident to us that the Count was not at present in the house, and we proceeded to search for any of his effects.

After a cursory glance at the rest of the rooms, from basement to attic, we came to the conclusion that the dining room contained any effects which might belong to the Count. And so we proceeded to minutely examine them. They lay in a sort of orderly disorder on the great dining room table.

There were title deeds of the Piccadilly house in a great bundle, deeds of the purchase of the houses at Mile End and Bermondsey, notepaper, envelopes, and pens and ink. All were covered up in thin wrapping paper to keep them from the dust. There were also a clothes brush, a brush and comb, and a jug and basin. The latter containing dirty water which was reddened as if with blood. Last of all was a little heap of keys of all sorts and sizes, probably those belonging to the other houses.

When we had examined this last find, Lord Godalming and Quincey Morris taking accurate notes of the various addresses of the houses in the East and the South, took with them the keys in a great bunch, and set out to destroy the boxes in these places. The rest of us are, with what patience we can, waiting their return, or the coming of the Count.

CHAPTER 23

DR. SEWARD'S DIARY

3 October.--The time seemed terribly long whilst we were waiting for the coming of Godalming and Quincey Morris. The Professor tried to keep our minds active by using them all the time. I could see his beneficent purpose, by the side glances which he threw from time to time at Harker. The poor fellow is overwhelmed in a misery that is appalling to see. Last night he was a frank, happy-looking man, with strong, youthful face, full of energy, and with dark brown hair. Today he is a drawn, haggard old man, whose white hair matches well with the hollow burning eyes and grief-written lines of his face. His energy is still intact. In fact, he is like a living flame. This may yet be his salvation, for if all go well, it will tide him over the despairing period. He will then, in a kind of way, wake again to the realities of life. Poor fellow, I thought my own trouble was bad enough, but his… !

The Professor knows this well enough, and is doing his best to keep his mind active. What he has been saying was, under the circumstances, of absorbing interest. So well as I can remember, here it is:

"I have studied, over and over again since they came into my hands, all the papers relating to this monster, and the more I have studied, the greater seems the necessity to utterly stamp him out. All through there are signs of his advance. Not only of his power, but of his knowledge of it. As I learned from the researches of my friend Arminius of Buda-Pesth, he was in life a most wonderful man. Soldier, statesman, and alchemist--which latter was the highest development of the science knowledge of his time. He had a mighty brain, a learning beyond compare, and a heart that knew no fear and no remorse. He dared even to attend the Scholomance, and there was no branch of knowledge of his time that he did not essay.

"Well, in him the brain powers survived the physical death. Though it would seem that memory was not all complete. In some faculties of mind he has been, and is, only a child. But he is growing, and some things that were childish at the first are now of man's stature. He is experimenting, and doing it well. And if it had not been that we have crossed his path he would be yet, he may be yet if we fail, the father or furtherer of a new order of beings, whose road must lead through Death, not Life."

Harker groaned and said, "And this is all arrayed against my darling! But how is he experimenting? The knowledge may help us to defeat him!"

"He has all along, since his coming, been trying his power, slowly but surely. That big child-brain of his is working. Well for us, it is as yet a child-brain. For had he dared, at the first, to attempt certain things he would long ago have been beyond our power. However, he means to succeed, and a man who has centuries before him can afford to wait and to go slow. Festina lente may well be his motto."

"I fail to understand," said Harker wearily. "Oh, do be more plain to me! Perhaps grief and trouble are dulling my brain."

The Professor laid his hand tenderly on his shoulder as he spoke, "Ah, my child, I will be plain. Do you not see how, of late, this monster has been creeping into knowledge experimentally. How he has been making use of the zoophagous patient to effect his entry into friend John's home. For your Vampire, though in all afterwards he can come when and how he will, must at the first make entry only when asked thereto by an inmate. But these are not his most important experiments. Do we not see how at the first all these so great boxes were moved by others. He knew not then but that must be so. But all the time that so great child-brain of his was growing, and he began to consider whether he might not himself move the box. So he began to help. And then, when he found that this be all right, he try to move them all alone. And so he progress, and he scatter these graves of him. And none but he know where they are hidden.

"He may have intend to bury them deep in the ground. So that only he use them in the night, or at such time as he can change his form, they do him equal well, and none may know these are his hiding place! But, my child, do not despair, this knowledge came to him just too late! Already all of his lairs but one be sterilize as for him. And before the sunset this shall be so. Then he have no place where he can move and hide. I delayed this morning that so we might be sure. Is there not more at stake for us than for him? Then why not be more careful than him? By my clock it is one hour and already, if all be well, friend Arthur and Quincey are on their way to us. Today is our day, and we must go sure, if slow, and lose no chance. See! There are five of us when those absent ones return."

Whilst we were speaking we were startled by a knock at the hall door, the double postman's knock of the telegraph boy. We all moved out to the hall with one impulse, and Van Helsing, holding up his hand to us to keep silence, stepped to the door and opened it. The boy handed in a dispatch. The Professor closed the door again, and after looking at the direction, opened it and read aloud.

"Look out for D. He has just now, 12:45, come from Carfax hurriedly and hastened towards the South. He seems to be going the round and may want to see you: Mina."

There was a pause, broken by Jonathan Harker's voice, "Now, God be thanked, we shall soon meet!"

Van Helsing turned to him quickly and said, "God will act in His own way and time. Do not fear, and do not rejoice as yet. For what we wish for at the moment may be our own undoings."

"I care for nothing now," he answered hotly, "except to wipe out this brute from the face of creation. I would sell my soul to do it!"

"Oh, hush, hush, my child!" said Van Helsing. "God does not purchase souls in this wise, and the Devil, though he may purchase, does not keep faith. But God is merciful and just, and knows your pain and your devotion to that dear Madam Mina.

Think you, how her pain would be doubled, did she but hear your wild words. Do not fear any of us, we are all devoted to this cause, and today shall see the end. The time is coming for action. Today this Vampire is limit to the powers of man, and till sunset he may not change. It will take him time to arrive here, see it is twenty minutes past one, and there are yet some times before he can hither come, be he never so quick. What we must hope for is that my Lord Arthur and Quincey arrive first."

About half an hour after we had received Mrs. Harker's telegram, there came a quiet, resolute knock at the hall door. It was just an ordinary knock, such as is given hourly by thousands of gentlemen, but it made the Professor's heart and mine beat loudly. We looked at each other, and together moved out into the hall. We each held ready to use our various armaments, the spiritual in the left hand, the mortal in the right. Van Helsing pulled back the latch, and holding the door half open, stood back, having both hands ready for action. The gladness of our hearts must have shown upon our faces when on the step, close to the door, we saw Lord Godalming and Quincey Morris. They came quickly in and closed the door behind them, the former saying, as they moved along the hall:

"It is all right. We found both places. Six boxes in each and we destroyed them all."

"Destroyed?" asked the Professor.

"For him!" We were silent for a minute, and then Quincey said, "There's nothing to do but to wait here. If, however, he doesn't turn up by five o'clock, we must start off. For it won't do to leave Mrs. Harker alone after sunset."

"He will be here before long now," said Van Helsing, who had been consulting his pocketbook. "Nota bene, in Madam's telegram he went south from Carfax. That means he went to cross the river, and he could only do so at slack of tide, which should be something before one o'clock. That he went south has a meaning for us. He is as yet only suspicious, and he went from Carfax first to the place where he would suspect interference least. You must have been at Bermondsey only a short time before him. That he is not here already shows that he went to Mile End next. This took him some time, for he would then have to be carried over the river in some way. Believe me, my friends, we shall not have long to wait now. We should have ready some plan of attack, so that we may throw away no chance. Hush, there is no time now. Have all your arms! Be ready!" He held up a warning hand as he spoke, for we all could hear a key softly inserted in the lock of the hall door.

I could not but admire, even at such a moment, the way in which a dominant spirit asserted itself. In all our hunting parties and adventures in different parts of the world, Quincey Morris had always been the one to arrange the plan of action, and Arthur and I had been accustomed to obey him implicitly. Now, the old habit seemed to be renewed instinctively. With a swift glance around the room, he at once laid out our plan of attack, and without speaking a word, with a gesture, placed us each in position. Van Helsing, Harker, and I were just behind the door, so that when it was opened the Professor could guard it whilst we two stepped between the incomer and the door. Godalming behind and Quincey in front stood just out of sight ready to move in front of the window. We waited in a suspense that made the seconds pass with nightmare slowness. The slow, careful steps came along the hall. The Count was evidently prepared for some surprise, at least he feared it.

Suddenly with a single bound he leaped into the room. Winning a way past us before any of us could raise a hand to stay him. There was something so pantherlike in the movement, something so unhuman, that it seemed to sober us all from the shock of his coming. The first to act was Harker, who with a quick movement, threw himself before the door leading into the room in the front of the house. As the Count saw us, a horrible sort of snarl passed over his face, showing the eyeteeth long and pointed. But the evil smile as quickly passed into a cold stare of lion-like disdain. His expression again changed as, with a single impulse, we all advanced upon him. It was a pity that we had not some better organized plan of attack, for even at the moment I wondered what we were to do. I did not myself know whether our lethal weapons would avail us anything.

Harker evidently meant to try the matter, for he had ready his great Kukri knife and made a fierce and sudden cut at him. The blow was a powerful one; only the diabolical quickness of the Count's leap back saved him. A second less and the trenchant blade had shorn through his heart. As it was, the point just cut the cloth of his coat, making a wide gap whence a bundle of bank notes and a stream of gold fell out. The expression of the Count's face was so hellish, that for a moment I feared for Harker, though I saw him throw the terrible knife aloft again for another stroke. Instinctively I moved forward with a protective impulse, holding the Crucifix and Wafer in my left hand. I felt a mighty power fly along my arm, and it was without surprise that I saw the monster cower back before a similar movement made spontaneously by each one of us. It would be impossible to describe the expression of hate and baffled malignity, of anger and hellish rage, which came over the Count's face. His waxen hue became greenish-yellow by the contrast of his burning eyes, and the red scar on the forehead showed on the pallid skin like a palpitating wound. The next instant, with a sinuous dive he swept under Harker's arm, ere his blow could fall, and grasping a handful of the money from the floor, dashed across the room, threw himself at the window. Amid the crash and glitter of the falling glass, he tumbled into the flagged area below. Through the sound of the shivering glass I could hear the "ting" of the gold, as some of the sovereigns fell on the flagging.

We ran over and saw him spring unhurt from the ground. He, rushing up the steps, crossed the flagged yard, and pushed open the stable door. There he turned and spoke to us.

"You think to baffle me, you with your pale faces all in a row, like sheep in a butcher's. You shall be sorry yet, each one of you! You think you have left me without a place to rest, but I have more. My revenge is just begun! I spread it over centuries, and time is on my side. Your girls that you all love are mine already. And through them you and others shall yet be mine, my creatures, to do my bidding and to be my jackals when I want to feed. Bah!"

With a contemptuous sneer, he passed quickly through the door, and we heard the rusty bolt creak as he fastened it behind him. A door beyond opened and shut. The first of us to speak was the Professor. Realizing the difficulty of following him through the stable, we moved toward the hall.

"We have learnt something... much! Notwithstanding his brave words, he fears us. He fears time, he fears want! For if not, why he hurry so? His very tone betray him, or my ears deceive. Why take that money? You follow quick. You are hunters of the wild beast, and understand it so. For me, I make sure that nothing here may be of use to him, if so that he returns."

As he spoke he put the money remaining in his pocket, took the title deeds in the bundle as Harker had left them, and swept the remaining things into the open fireplace, where he set fire to them with a match.

Godalming and Morris had rushed out into the yard, and Harker had lowered himself from the window to follow the Count. He had, however, bolted the stable door, and by the time they had forced it open there was no sign of him. Van Helsing and I tried to make inquiry at the back of the house. But the mews was deserted and no one had seen him depart.

It was now late in the afternoon, and sunset was not far off. We had to recognize that our game was up. With heavy hearts we agreed with the Professor when he said, "Let us go back to Madam Mina. Poor, poor dear Madam Mina. All we can do just now is done, and we can there, at least, protect her. But we need not despair. There is but one more earth box, and we must try to find it. When that is done all may yet be well."

I could see that he spoke as bravely as he could to comfort Harker. The poor fellow was quite broken down, now and again he gave a low groan which he could not suppress. He was thinking of his wife.

With sad hearts we came back to my house, where we found Mrs. Harker waiting us, with an appearance of cheerfulness which did honour to her bravery and unselfishness. When she saw our faces, her own became as pale as death. For a second or two her eyes were closed as if she were in secret prayer.

And then she said cheerfully, "I can never thank you all enough. Oh, my poor darling!"

As she spoke, she took her husband's grey head in her hands and kissed it.

"Lay your poor head here and rest it. All will yet be well, dear! God will protect us if He so will it in His good intent." The poor fellow groaned. There was no place for words in his sublime misery.

We had a sort of perfunctory supper together, and I think it cheered us all up somewhat. It was, perhaps, the mere animal heat of food to hungry people, for none of us had eaten anything since breakfast, or the sense of companionship may have helped us, but anyhow we were all less miserable, and saw the morrow as not altogether without hope.

True to our promise, we told Mrs. Harker everything which had passed. And although she grew snowy white at times when danger had seemed to threaten her husband, and red at others when his devotion to her was manifested, she listened bravely and with calmness. When we came to the part where Harker had rushed at the Count so recklessly, she clung to her husband's arm, and held it tight as though her clinging could protect him from any harm that might come. She said nothing, however, till the narration was all done, and matters had been brought up to the present time.

Then without letting go her husband's hand she stood up amongst us and spoke. Oh, that I could give any idea of the scene. Of that sweet, sweet, good, good woman in all the radiant beauty of her youth and animation, with the red scar on her forehead, of which she was conscious, and which we saw with grinding of our teeth, remembering whence and how it came. Her loving kindness against our grim hate. Her tender faith against all our fears and doubting. And we, knowing that so far as symbols went, she with all her goodness and purity and faith, was outcast from God.

"Jonathan," she said, and the word sounded like music on her lips it was so full of love and tenderness, "Jonathan dear, and you all my true, true friends, I want you to bear something in mind through all this dreadful time. I know that you must fight. That you must destroy even as you destroyed the false Lucy so that the true Lucy might live hereafter. But it is not a work of hate. That poor soul who has wrought all this misery is the saddest case of all. Just think what will be his joy when he, too, is destroyed in his worser part that his better part may have spiritual immortality. You must be pitiful to him, too, though it may not hold your hands from his destruction."

As she spoke I could see her husband's face darken and draw together, as though the passion in him were shriveling his being to its core. Instinctively the clasp on his wife's hand grew closer, till his knuckles looked white. She did not flinch from the pain which I knew she must have suffered, but looked at him with eyes that were more appealing than ever.

As she stopped speaking he leaped to his feet, almost tearing his hand from hers as he spoke.

"May God give him into my hand just for long enough to destroy that earthly life of him which we are aiming at. If beyond it I could send his soul forever and ever to burning hell I would do it!"

"Oh, hush! Oh, hush in the name of the good God. Don't say such things, Jonathan, my husband, or you will crush me with fear and horror. Just think, my dear... I have been thinking all this long, long day of it... that... perhaps... some day... I, too, may need such pity, and that some other like you, and with equal cause for anger, may deny it to me! Oh, my husband! My husband, indeed I would have spared you such a thought had there been another way. But I pray that God may not have treasured your wild words, except as the heart-broken wail of a very loving and sorely stricken man. Oh, God, let these poor white hairs go in evidence of what he has suffered, who all his life has done no wrong, and on whom so many sorrows have come."

We men were all in tears now. There was no resisting them, and we wept openly. She wept, too, to see that her sweeter counsels had prevailed. Her husband flung himself on his knees beside her, and putting his arms round her, hid his face in the folds of her dress. Van Helsing beckoned to us and we stole out of the room, leaving the two loving hearts alone with their God.

Before they retired the Professor fixed up the room against any coming of the Vampire, and assured Mrs. Harker that she might rest in peace. She tried to school herself to the belief, and manifestly for her husband's sake, tried to seem content. It was a brave struggle, and was, I think and believe, not without its reward. Van Helsing had placed at hand a bell which either of them was to sound in case of any emergency. When they had retired, Quincey, Godalming, and I arranged that we should sit up, dividing the night between us, and watch over the safety of the poor stricken lady. The first watch falls to Quincey, so the rest of us shall be off to bed as soon as we can.

Godalming has already turned in, for his is the second watch. Now that my work is done I, too, shall go to bed.

CHAPTER 23

JONATHAN HARKER'S JOURNAL

3-4 October, close to midnight.--I thought yesterday would never end. There was over me a yearning for sleep, in some sort of blind belief that to wake would be to find things changed, and that any change must now be for the better. Before we parted, we discussed what our next step was to be, but we could arrive at no result. All we knew was that one earth box remained, and that the Count alone knew where it was. If he chooses to lie hidden, he may baffle us for years. And in the meantime, the thought is too horrible, I dare not think of it even now. This I know, that if ever there was a woman who was all perfection, that one is my poor wronged darling. I loved her a thousand times more for her sweet pity of last night, a pity that made my own hate of the monster seem despicable. Surely God will not permit the world to be the poorer by the loss of such a creature. This is hope to me. We are all drifting reefwards now, and faith is our only anchor. Thank God! Mina is sleeping, and sleeping without dreams. I fear what her dreams might be like, with such terrible memories to ground them in. She has not been so calm, within my seeing, since the sunset. Then, for a while, there came over her face a repose which was like spring after the blasts of March. I thought at the time that it was the softness of the red sunset on her face, but somehow now I think it has a deeper meaning. I am not sleepy myself, though I am weary... weary to death. However, I must try to sleep. For there is tomorrow to think of, and there is no rest for me until...

Later--I must have fallen asleep, for I was awakened by Mina, who was sitting up in bed, with a startled look on her face. I could see easily, for we did not leave the room in darkness. She had placed a warning hand over my mouth, and now she whispered in my ear, "Hush! There is someone in the corridor!" I got up softly, and crossing the room, gently opened the door.

Just outside, stretched on a mattress, lay Mr. Morris, wide awake. He raised a warning hand for silence as he whispered to me, "Hush! Go back to bed. It is all right. One of us will be here all night. We don't mean to take any chances!"

His look and gesture forbade discussion, so I came back and told Mina. She sighed and positively a shadow of a smile stole over her poor, pale face as she put her arms round me and said softly, "Oh, thank God for good brave men!" With a sigh she sank back again to sleep. I write this now as I am not sleepy, though I must try again.

4 October, morning.--Once again during the night I was wakened by Mina. This time we had all had a good sleep, for the grey of the coming dawn was making the windows into sharp oblongs, and the gas flame was like a speck rather than a disc of light.

She said to me hurriedly, "Go, call the Professor. I want to see him at once."

"Why?" I asked.

"I have an idea. I suppose it must have come in the night, and matured without my knowing it. He must hypnotize me before the dawn, and then I shall be able to speak. Go quick, dearest, the time is getting close."

I went to the door. Dr. Seward was resting on the mattress, and seeing me, he sprang to his feet.

"Is anything wrong?" he asked, in alarm.

"No," I replied. "But Mina wants to see Dr. Van Helsing at once."

"I will go," he said, and hurried into the Professor's room.

Two or three minutes later Van Helsing was in the room in his dressing gown, and Mr. Morris and Lord Godalming were with Dr. Seward at the door asking questions. When the Professor saw Mina a smile, a positive smile ousted the anxiety of his face.

He rubbed his hands as he said, "Oh, my dear Madam Mina, this is indeed a change. See! Friend Jonathan, we have got our dear Madam Mina, as of old, back to us today!" Then turning to her, he said cheerfully, "And what am I to do for you? For at this hour you do not want me for nothing."

"I want you to hypnotize me!" she said. "Do it before the dawn, for I feel that then I can speak, and speak freely. Be quick, for the time is short!" Without a word he motioned her to sit up in bed.

Looking fixedly at her, he commenced to make passes in front of her, from over the top of her head downward, with each hand in turn. Mina gazed at him fixedly for a few minutes, during which my own heart beat like a trip hammer, for I felt that some crisis was at hand. Gradually her eyes closed, and she sat, stock still. Only by the gentle heaving of her bosom could one know that she was alive. The Professor made a few more passes and then stopped, and I could see that his forehead was covered with great beads of perspiration. Mina opened her eyes, but she did not seem the same woman. There was a far-away look in her eyes, and her voice had a sad dreaminess which was new to me. Raising his hand to impose silence, the Professor motioned to me to bring the others in. They came on tiptoe, closing the door behind them, and stood at the foot of the bed, looking on. Mina appeared not to see them. The stillness was broken by Van Helsing's voice speaking in a low level tone which would not break the current of her thoughts.

"Where are you?" The answer came in a neutral way.

"I do not know. Sleep has no place it can call its own." For several minutes there was silence. Mina sat rigid, and the Professor stood staring at her fixedly.

The rest of us hardly dared to breathe. The room was growing lighter. Without taking his eyes from Mina's face, Dr. Van Helsing motioned me to pull up the blind. I did so, and the day seemed just upon us. A red streak shot up, and a rosy light seemed to diffuse itself through the room. On the instant the Professor spoke again.

"Where are you now?"

The answer came dreamily, but with intention. It were as though she were interpreting something. I have heard her use the same tone when reading her shorthand notes.

"I do not know. It is all strange to me!"

"What do you see?"

"I can see nothing. It is all dark."

"What do you hear?" I could detect the strain in the Professor's patient voice.

"The lapping of water. It is gurgling by, and little waves leap. I can hear them on the outside."

"Then you are on a ship?'"

We all looked at each other, trying to glean something each from the other. We were afraid to think.

The answer came quick, "Oh, yes!"

"What else do you hear?"

"The sound of men stamping overhead as they run about. There is the creaking of a chain, and the loud tinkle as the check of the capstan falls into the ratchet."

"What are you doing?"

"I am still, oh so still. It is like death!" The voice faded away into a deep breath as of one sleeping, and the open eyes closed again.

By this time the sun had risen, and we were all in the full light of day. Dr. Van Helsing placed his hands on Mina's shoulders, and laid her head down softly on her pillow. She lay like a sleeping child for a few moments, and then, with a long sigh, awoke and stared in wonder to see us all around her.

"Have I been talking in my sleep?" was all she said. She seemed, however, to know the situation without telling, though she was eager to know what she had told. The Professor repeated the conversation, and she said, "Then there is not a moment to lose. It may not be yet too late!"

Mr. Morris and Lord Godalming started for the door but the Professor's calm voice called them back.

"Stay, my friends. That ship, wherever it was, was weighing anchor at the moment in your so great Port of London. Which of them is it that you seek? God be thanked that we have once again a clue, though whither it may lead us we know not. We have been blind somewhat. Blind after the manner of men, since we can look back we see what we might have seen looking forward if we had been able to see what we might have seen! Alas, but that sentence is a puddle, is it not? We can know now what was in the Count's mind, when he seize that money, though Jonathan's so fierce knife put him in the danger that even he dread. He meant escape. Hear me, ESCAPE! He saw that with but one earth box left, and a pack of men following like dogs after a fox, this London was no place for him. He have take his last earth box on board a ship, and he leave the land. He think to escape, but no! We follow him. Tally Ho! As friend Arthur would say when he put on his red frock! Our old fox is wily. Oh! So wily, and we must follow with wile. I, too, am wily and I think his mind in a little while. In meantime we may rest and in peace, for there are between us which he do not want to pass, and which he could not if he would. Unless the ship were to touch the land, and then only at full or slack tide. See, and the sun is just rose, and all day to sunset is us. Let us take bath, and dress, and have breakfast which we all need, and which we can eat comfortably since he be not in the same land with us."

Mina looked at him appealingly as she asked, "But why need we seek him further, when he is gone away from us?"

He took her hand and patted it as he replied, "Ask me nothing as yet. When we have breakfast, then I answer all questions." He would say no more, and we separated to dress.

After breakfast Mina repeated her question. He looked at her gravely for a minute and then said sorrowfully, "Because my dear, dear Madam Mina, now more than ever must we find him even if we have to follow him to the jaws of Hell!"

She grew paler as she asked faintly, "Why?"

"Because," he answered solemnly, "he can live for centuries, and you are but mortal woman. Time is now to be dreaded, since once he put that mark upon your throat."

I was just in time to catch her as she fell forward in a faint.

CHAPTER 24

DR. SEWARD'S PHONOGRAPH DIARY SPOKEN BY VAN HELSING

This to Jonathan Harker.

You are to stay with your dear Madam Mina. We shall go to make our search, if I can call it so, for it is not search but knowing, and we seek confirmation only. But do you stay and take care of her today. This is your best and most holiest office. This day nothing can find him here.

Let me tell you that so you will know what we four know already, for I have tell them. He, our enemy, have gone away. He have gone back to his Castle in Transylvania. I know it so well, as if a great hand of fire wrote it on the wall. He have prepare for this in some way, and that last earth box was ready to ship somewheres. For this he took the money. For this he hurry at the last, lest we catch him before the sun go down. It was his last hope, save that he might hide in the tomb that he think poor Miss Lucy, being as he thought like him, keep open to him. But there was not of time. When that fail he make straight for his last resource, his last earth-work I might say did I wish double entente. He is clever, oh so clever! He know that his game here was finish. And so he decide he go back home. He find ship going by the route he came, and he go in it.

We go off now to find what ship, and whither bound. When we have discover that, we come back and tell you all. Then we will comfort you and poor Madam Mina with new hope. For it will be hope when you think it over, that all is not lost. This very creature that we pursue, he take hundreds of years to get so far as London. And yet in one day, when we know of the disposal of him we drive him out. He is finite, though he is powerful to do much harm and suffers not as we do. But we are strong, each in our purpose, and we are all more strong together. Take heart afresh, dear husband of Madam Mina. This battle is but begun and in the end we shall win. So sure as that God sits on high to watch over His children. Therefore be of much comfort till we return.

VAN HELSING.

CHAPTER 24

JONATHAN HARKER'S JOURNAL

4 October.--When I read to Mina, Van Helsing's message in the phonograph, the poor girl brightened up considerably. Already the certainty that the Count is out of the country has given her comfort. And comfort is strength to her. For my own part, now that his horrible danger is not face to face with us, it seems almost impossible to believe in it. Even my own terrible experiences in Castle Dracula seem like a long forgotten dream. Here in the crisp autumn air in the bright sunlight.

Alas! How can I disbelieve! In the midst of my thought my eye fell on the red scar on my poor darling's white forehead. Whilst that lasts, there can be no disbelief. Mina and I fear to be idle, so we have been over all the diaries again and again. Somehow, although the reality seem greater each time, the pain and the fear seem less. There is something of a guiding purpose manifest throughout, which is comforting. Mina says that perhaps we are the instruments of ultimate good. It may be! I shall try to think as she does. We have never spoken to each other yet of the future. It is better to wait till we see the Professor and the others after their investigations.

The day is running by more quickly than I ever thought a day could run for me again. It is now three o'clock.

MINA HARKER'S JOURNAL

5 October, 5 P.M.--Our meeting for report. Present: Professor Van Helsing, Lord Godalming, Dr. Seward, Mr. Quincey Morris, Jonathan Harker, Mina Harker.

Dr. Van Helsing described what steps were taken during the day to discover on what boat and whither bound Count Dracula made his escape.

"As I knew that he wanted to get back to Transylvania, I felt sure that he must go by the Danube mouth, or by somewhere in the Black Sea, since by that way he come. It was a dreary blank that was before us. *Omne ignotum pro magnifico*; and so with heavy hearts we start to find what ships leave for the Black Sea last night. He was in sailing ship, since Madam Mina tell of sails being set. These not so important as to go in your list of the shipping in the Times, and so we go, by suggestion of Lord Godalming, to your Lloyd's, where are note of all ships that sail, however so small. There we find that only one Black Sea bound ship go out with the tide. She is the Czarina Catherine, and she sail from Doolittle's Wharf for Varna, and thence to other ports and up the Danube. 'So!' said I, 'this is the ship whereon is the Count.' So off we go to Doolittle's Wharf, and there we find a man in an office. From him we inquire of the goings of the Czarina Catherine. He swear much, and he red face and loud of voice, but he good fellow all the same. And when Quincey give him something from his pocket which crackle as he roll it up, and put it in a so small bag which he have hid deep in his clothing, he still better fellow and humble servant to us. He come with us, and ask many men who are rough and hot. These be better fellows too when they have been no more thirsty. They say much of blood and bloom, and of others which I comprehend not, though I guess what they mean. But nevertheless they tell us all things which we want to know.

"They make known to us among them, how last afternoon at about five o'clock comes a man so hurry. A tall man, thin and pale, with high nose and teeth so white, and eyes that seem to be burning. That he be all in black, except that he have a hat of straw which suit not him or the time. That he scatter his money in making quick inquiry as to what ship sails for the Black Sea and for where. Some took him to the office and then to the ship, where he will not go aboard but halt at shore end of gangplank, and ask that the captain come to him. The captain come, when told that he will be pay well, and though he swear much at the first he agree to term. Then the thin man go and some one tell him where horse and cart can be hired. He go there and soon he come again, himself driving cart on which a great box. This he himself lift down, though it take several to put it on truck for the ship. He give much talk to captain as to how and where his box is to be place. But the captain like it not and swear at him in many tongues, and tell him that if he like he can come and see where it shall be. But he say 'no,' that he come not yet, for that he have much to do. Whereupon the captain tell him that he had better be quick, with blood, for that his ship will leave the place, of blood, before the turn of the tide, with blood. Then the thin man smile and say that of course he must go when he think fit, but he will be surprise if he go quite so soon. The captain swear again, polyglot, and the thin man make him bow, and thank him, and say that he will so far intrude on his kindness as to come aboard before the sailing. Final the captain, more red than ever, and in more tongues, tell him that he doesn't want no Frenchmen, with bloom upon them and also with blood, in his ship, with blood on her also. And so, after asking where he might purchase ship forms, he departed.

"No one knew where he went 'or bloomin' well cared' as they said, for they had something else to think of, well with blood again. For it soon became apparent to all that the Czarina Catherine would not sail as was expected. A thin mist began to creep up from the river, and it grew, and grew. Till soon a dense fog enveloped the ship and all around her. The captain swore polyglot, very polyglot, polyglot with bloom and blood, but he could do nothing. The water rose and rose, and he began to fear that he would lose the tide altogether. He was in no friendly mood, when just at full tide, the thin man came up the gangplank again and asked to see where his box had been stowed. Then the captain replied that he wished that he and his box, old and with much bloom and blood, were in hell. But the thin man did not be offend, and went down with the mate and saw where it was place, and came up and stood awhile on deck in fog. He must have come off by himself, for none notice him. Indeed they thought not of him, for soon the fog begin to melt away, and all was clear again. My friends of the thirst and the language that was of bloom and blood laughed, as they told how the captain's swears exceeded even his usual polyglot, and was more than ever full of picturesque, when on questioning other mariners who were on movement up and down the river that hour, he found that few of them had seen any of fog at all, except where it lay round the wharf. However, the ship went out on the ebb tide, and was doubtless by morning far down the river mouth. She was then, when they told us, well out to sea.

"And so, my dear Madam Mina, it is that we have to rest for a time, for our enemy is on the sea, with the fog at his command, on his way to the Danube mouth. To sail a ship takes time, go she never so quick. And when we start to go on land more quick, and we meet him there. Our best hope is to come on him when in the box between sunrise and sunset. For then he can make no struggle, and we may deal with him as we should. There are days for us, in which we can make ready our plan. We know all about where he go. For we have seen the owner of the ship, who have shown us invoices and all papers that can be. The box we seek is to be landed in Varna, and to be given to an agent, one Ristics who will there present his credentials. And so our merchant friend will have done his part. When he ask if there be any wrong, for that so, he can telegraph and have inquiry made at Varna, we say 'no,' for what is to be done is not for police or of the customs. It must be done by us alone and in our own way."

When Dr. Van Helsing had done speaking, I asked him if he were certain that the Count had remained on board the ship. He replied, "We have the best proof of that, your own evidence, when in the hypnotic trance this morning."

I asked him again if it were really necessary that they should pursue the Count, for oh! I dread Jonathan leaving me, and I know that he would surely go if the others went. He answered in growing passion, at first quietly. As he went on, however, he grew more angry and more forceful, till in the end we could not but see wherein was at least some of that personal dominance which made him so long a master amongst men.

"Yes, it is necessary, necessary, necessary! For your sake in the first, and then for the sake of humanity. This monster has done much harm already, in the narrow scope where he find himself, and in the short time when as yet he was only as a body groping his so small measure in darkness and not knowing. All this have I told these others. You, my dear Madam Mina, will learn it in the phonograph of my friend John, or in that of your husband. I have told them how the measure of leaving his own barren land, barren of peoples, and coming to a new land where life of man teems till they are like the multitude of standing corn, was the work of centuries. Were another of the Undead, like him, to try to do what he has done, perhaps not all the centuries of the world that have been, or that will be, could aid him. With this one, all the forces of nature that are occult and deep and strong must have worked together in some wonderous way. The very place, where he have been alive, Undead for all these centuries, is full of strangeness of the geologic and chemical world. There are deep caverns and fissures that reach none know whither. There have been volcanoes, some of whose openings still send out waters of strange properties, and gases that kill or make to vivify. Doubtless, there is something magnetic or electric in some of these combinations of occult forces which work for physical life in strange way, and in himself were from the first some great qualities. In a hard and warlike time he was celebrate that he have more iron nerve, more subtle brain, more braver heart, than any man. In him some vital principle have in strange way found their utmost. And as his body keep strong and grow and thrive, so his brain grow too. All this without that diabolic aid which is surely to him. For it have to yield to the powers that come from, and are, symbolic of good. And now this is what he is to us. He have infect you, oh forgive me, my dear, that I must say such, but it is for good of you that I speak. He infect you in such wise, that even if he do no more, you have only to live, to live in your own old, sweet way, and so in time, death, which is of man's common lot and with God's sanction, shall make you like to him. This must not be! We have sworn together that it must not. Thus are we ministers of God's own wish. That the world, and men for whom His Son die, will not be given over to monsters, whose very existence would defame Him. He have allowed us to redeem one soul already, and we go out as the old knights of the Cross to redeem more. Like them we shall travel towards the sunrise. And like them, if we fall, we fall in good cause."

He paused and I said, "But will not the Count take his rebuff wisely? Since he has been driven from England, will he not avoid it, as a tiger does the village from which he has been hunted?"

"Aha!" he said, "your simile of the tiger good, for me, and I shall adopt him. Your maneater, as they of India call the tiger who has once tasted blood of the human, care no more for the other prey, but prowl unceasing till he get him. This that we hunt from our village is a tiger, too, a maneater, and he never cease to prowl. Nay, in himself he is not one to retire and stay afar. In his life, his living life, he go over the Turkey frontier and attack his enemy on his own ground. He be beaten back, but did he stay? No! He come again, and again, and again. Look at his persistence and endurance. With the child-brain that was to him he have long since conceive the idea of coming to a great city. What does he do? He find out the place of all the world most of promise for him. Then he deliberately set himself down to prepare for the task. He find in patience just how is his strength, and what are his powers. He study new tongues. He learn new social life, new environment of old ways, the politics, the law, the finance, the science, the habit of a new land and a new people who have come to be since he was. His glimpse that he have had, whet his appetite only and enkeen his desire. Nay, it help him to grow as to his brain. For it all prove to him how right he was at the first in his surmises. He have done this alone, all alone! From a ruin tomb in a forgotten land. What more may he not do when the greater world of thought is open to him. He that can smile at death, as we know him. Who can flourish in the midst of diseases that kill off whole peoples. Oh! If such an one was to come from God, and not the Devil, what a force for good might he not be in this old world of ours. But we are pledged to set the world free. Our toil must be in silence, and our efforts all in secret. For in this enlightened age, when men believe not even what they see, the doubting of wise men would be his greatest strength. It would be at once his sheath and his armor, and his weapons to destroy us, his enemies, who are willing to peril even our own souls for the safety of one we love. For the good of mankind, and for the honour and glory of God."

After a general discussion it was determined that for tonight nothing be definitely settled. That we should all sleep on the facts, and try to think out the proper conclusions. Tomorrow, at breakfast, we are to meet again, and after making our conclusions known to one another, we shall decide on some definite cause of action…

I feel a wonderful peace and rest tonight. It is as if some haunting presence were removed from me. Perhaps…

My surmise was not finished, could not be, for I caught sight in the mirror of the red mark upon my forehead, and I knew that I was still unclean.

DR. SEWARD'S DIARY

5 October.--We all arose early, and I think that sleep did much for each and all of us. When we met at early breakfast there was more general cheerfulness than any of us had ever expected to experience again.

It is really wonderful how much resilience there is in human nature. Let any obstructing cause, no matter what, be removed in any way, even by death, and we fly back to first principles of hope and enjoyment. More than once as we sat around the table, my eyes opened in wonder whether the whole of the past days had not been a dream. It was only when I caught sight of the red blotch on Mrs. Harker's forehead that I was brought back to reality. Even now, when I am gravely revolving the matter, it is almost impossible to realize that the cause of all our trouble is still existent. Even Mrs. Harker seems to lose sight of her trouble for whole spells. It is only now and again, when something recalls it to her mind, that she thinks of her terrible scar. We are to meet here in my study in half an hour and decide on our course of action. I see only one immediate difficulty, I know it by instinct rather than reason. We shall all have to speak frankly. And yet I fear that in some mysterious way poor Mrs. Harker's tongue is tied. I know that she forms conclusions of her own, and from all that has been I can guess how brilliant and how true they must be. But she will not, or cannot, give them utterance. I have mentioned this to Van Helsing, and he and I are to talk it over when we are alone. I suppose it is some of that horrid poison which has got into her veins beginning to work. The Count had his own purposes when he gave her what Van Helsing called "the Vampire's baptism of blood." Well, there may be a poison that distills itself out of good things. In an age when the existence of ptomaines is a mystery we should not wonder at anything! One thing I know, that if my instinct be true regarding poor Mrs. Harker's silences, then there is a terrible difficulty, an unknown danger, in the work before us. The same power that compels her silence may compel her speech. I dare not think further, for so I should in my thoughts dishonour a noble woman!

Later.--When the Professor came in, we talked over the state of things. I could see that he had something on his mind, which he wanted to say, but felt some hesitancy about broaching the subject. After beating about the bush a little, he said, "Friend John, there is something that you and I must talk of alone, just at the first at any rate. Later, we may have to take the others into our confidence."

Then he stopped, so I waited. He went on, "Madam Mina, our poor, dear Madam Mina is changing."

A cold shiver ran through me to find my worst fears thus endorsed. Van Helsing continued.

"With the sad experience of Miss Lucy, we must this time be warned before things go too far. Our task is now in reality more difficult than ever, and this new trouble makes every hour of the direst importance. I can see the characteristics of the vampire coming in her face. It is now but very, very slight. But it is to be seen if we have eyes to notice without prejudge. Her teeth are sharper, and at times her eyes are more hard. But these are not all, there is to her the silence now often, as so it was with Miss Lucy. She did not speak, even when she wrote that which she wished to be known later. Now my fear is this. If it be that she can, by our hypnotic trance, tell what the Count see and hear, is it not more true that he who have hypnotize her first, and who have drink of her very blood and make her drink of his, should if he will, compel her mind to disclose to him that which she know?"

I nodded acquiescence. He went on, "Then, what we must do is to prevent this. We must keep her ignorant of our intent, and so she cannot tell what she know not. This is a painful task! Oh, so painful that it heartbreak me to think of it, but it must be. When today we meet, I must tell her that for reason which we will not to speak she must not more be of our council, but be simply guarded by us."

He wiped his forehead, which had broken out in profuse perspiration at the thought of the pain which he might have to inflict upon the poor soul already so tortured. I knew that it would be some sort of comfort to him if I told him that I also had come to the same conclusion. For at any rate it would take away the pain of doubt. I told him, and the effect was as I expected.

It is now close to the time of our general gathering. Van Helsing has gone away to prepare for the meeting, and his painful part of it. I really believe his purpose is to be able to pray alone.

Later.--At the very outset of our meeting a great personal relief was experienced by both Van Helsing and myself. Mrs. Harker had sent a message by her husband to say that she would not join us at present, as she thought it better that we should be free to discuss our movements without her presence to embarrass us. The Professor and I looked at each other for an instant, and somehow we both seemed relieved. For my own part, I thought that if Mrs. Harker realized the danger herself, it was much pain as well as much danger averted. Under the circumstances we agreed, by a questioning look and answer, with finger on lip, to preserve silence in our suspicions, until we should have been able to confer alone again. We went at once into our Plan of Campaign.

Van Helsing roughly put the facts before us first, "The Czarina Catherine left the Thames yesterday morning. It will take her at the quickest speed she has ever made at least three weeks to reach Varna. But we can travel overland to the same place in three days. Now, if we allow for two days less for the ship's voyage, owing to such weather influences as we know that the Count can bring to bear, and if we allow a whole day and night for any delays which may occur to us, then we have a margin of nearly two weeks.

"Thus, in order to be quite safe, we must leave here on 17th at latest. Then we shall at any rate be in Varna a day before the ship arrives, and able to make such preparations as may be necessary. Of course we shall all go armed, armed against evil things, spiritual as well as physical."

Here Quincey Morris added, "I understand that the Count comes from a wolf country, and it may be that he shall get there before us. I propose that we add Winchesters to our armament. I have a kind of belief in a Winchester when there is any trouble of that sort around. Do you remember, Art, when we had the pack after us at Tobolsk? What wouldn't we have given then for a repeater apiece!"

"Good!" said Van Helsing, "Winchesters it shall be. Quincey's head is level at times, but most so when there is to hunt, metaphor be more dishonour to science than wolves be of danger to man. In the meantime we can do nothing here. And as I think that Varna is not familiar to any of us, why not go there more soon? It is as long to wait here as there. Tonight and tomorrow we can get ready, and then if all be well, we four can set out on our journey."

"We four?" said Harker interrogatively, looking from one to another of us.

"Of course!" answered the Professor quickly. "You must remain to take care of your so sweet wife!"

Harker was silent for awhile and then said in a hollow voice, "Let us talk of that part of it in the morning. I want to consult with Mina."

I thought that now was the time for Van Helsing to warn him not to disclose our plan to her, but he took no notice. I looked at him significantly and coughed. For answer he put his finger to his lips and turned away.

CHAPTER 24

JONATHAN HARKER'S JOURNAL

5 October, afternoon.--For some time after our meeting this morning I could not think. The new phases of things leave my mind in a state of wonder which allows no room for active thought. Mina's determination not to take any part in the discussion set me thinking. And as I could not argue the matter with her, I could only guess. I am as far as ever from a solution now. The way the others received it, too puzzled me. The last time we talked of the subject we agreed that there was to be no more concealment of anything amongst us. Mina is sleeping now, calmly and sweetly like a little child. Her lips are curved and her face beams with happiness. Thank God, there are such moments still for her.

Later.--How strange it all is. I sat watching Mina's happy sleep, and I came as near to being happy myself as I suppose I shall ever be. As the evening drew on, and the earth took its shadows from the sun sinking lower, the silence of the room grew more and more solemn to me.

All at once Mina opened her eyes, and looking at me tenderly said, "Jonathan, I want you to promise me something on your word of honour. A promise made to me, but made holily in God's hearing, and not to be broken though I should go down on my knees and implore you with bitter tears. Quick, you must make it to me at once."

"Mina," I said, "a promise like that, I cannot make at once. I may have no right to make it."

"But, dear one," she said, with such spiritual intensity that her eyes were like pole stars, "it is I who wish it. And it is not for myself. You can ask Dr. Van Helsing if I am not right. If he disagrees you may do as you will. Nay, more if you all agree, later you are absolved from the promise."

"I promise!" I said, and for a moment she looked supremely happy. Though to me all happiness for her was denied by the red scar on her forehead.

She said, "Promise me that you will not tell me anything of the plans formed for the campaign against the Count. Not by word, or inference, or implication, not at any time whilst this remains to me!" And she solemnly pointed to the scar. I saw that she was in earnest, and said solemnly, "I promise!" and as I said it I felt that from that instant a door had been shut between us.

Later, midnight.--Mina has been bright and cheerful all the evening. So much so that all the rest seemed to take courage, as if infected somewhat with her gaiety. As a result even I myself felt as if the pall of gloom which weighs us down were somewhat lifted. We all retired early. Mina is now sleeping like a little child. It is wonderful thing that her faculty of sleep remains to her in the midst of her terrible trouble. Thank God for it, for then at least she can forget her care. Perhaps her example may affect me as her gaiety did tonight. I shall try it. Oh! For a dreamless sleep.

6 October, morning.--Another surprise. Mina woke me early, about the same time as yesterday, and asked me to bring Dr. Van Helsing. I thought that it was another occasion for hypnotism, and without question went for the Professor. He had evidently expected some such call, for I found him dressed in his room. His door was ajar, so that he could hear the opening of the door of our room. He came at once. As he passed into the room, he asked Mina if the others might come, too.

"No," she said quite simply, "it will not be necessary. You can tell them just as well. I must go with you on your journey."

Dr. Van Helsing was as startled as I was. After a moment's pause he asked, "But why?"

"You must take me with you. I am safer with you, and you shall be safer, too."

"But why, dear Madam Mina? You know that your safety is our solemnest duty. We go into danger, to which you are, or may be, more liable than any of us from… from circumstances… things that have been." He paused embarrassed.

As she replied, she raised her finger and pointed to her forehead. "I know. That is why I must go. I can tell you now, whilst the sun is coming up. I may not be able again. I know that when the Count wills me I must go. I know that if he tells me to come in secret, I must by wile. By any device to hoodwink, even Jonathan." God saw the look that she turned on me as she spoke, and if there be indeed a Recording Angel that look is noted to her ever-lasting honour. I could only clasp her hand. I could not speak. My emotion was too great for even the relief of tears.

She went on. "You men are brave and strong. You are strong in your numbers, for you can defy that which would break down the human endurance of one who had to guard alone. Besides, I may be of service, since you can hypnotize me and so learn that which even I myself do not know."

Dr. Van Helsing said gravely, "Madam Mina, you are, as always, most wise. You shall with us come. And together we shall do that which we go forth to achieve."

When he had spoken, Mina's long spell of silence made me look at her. She had fallen back on her pillow asleep. She did not even wake when I had pulled up the blind and let in the sunlight which flooded the room. Van Helsing motioned to me to come with him quietly. We went to his room, and within a minute Lord Godalming, Dr. Seward, and Mr. Morris were with us also.

He told them what Mina had said, and went on. "In the morning we shall leave for Varna. We have now to deal with a new factor, Madam Mina. Oh, but her soul is true. It is to her an agony to tell us so much as she has done. But it is most right, and we are warned in time. There must be no chance lost, and in Varna we must be ready to act the instant when that ship arrives."

"What shall we do exactly?" asked Mr. Morris laconically.

The Professor paused before replying, "We shall at the first board that ship. Then, when we have identified the box, we shall place a branch of the wild rose on it. This we shall fasten, for when it is there none can emerge, so that at least says the superstition. And to superstition must we trust at the first. It was man's faith in the early, and it have its root in faith still. Then, when we get the opportunity that we seek, when none are near to see, we shall open the box, and… and all will be well."

"I shall not wait for any opportunity," said Morris. "When I see the box I shall open it and destroy the monster, though there were a thousand men looking on, and if I am to be wiped out for it the next moment!" I grasped his hand instinctively and found it as firm as a piece of steel. I think he understood my look. I hope he did.

"Good boy," said Dr. Van Helsing. "Brave boy. Quincey is all man. God bless him for it. My child, believe me none of us shall lag behind or pause from any fear. I do but say what we may do… what we must do. But, indeed, indeed we cannot say what we may do. There are so many things which may happen, and their ways and their ends are so various that until the moment we may not say. We shall all be armed, in all ways. And when the time for the end has come, our effort shall not be lack. Now let us today put all our affairs in order. Let all things which touch on others dear to us, and who on us depend, be complete. For none of us can tell what, or when, or how, the end may be. As for me, my own affairs are regulate, and as I have nothing else to do, I shall go make arrangements for the travel. I shall have all tickets and so forth for our journey."

There was nothing further to be said, and we parted. I shall now settle up all my affairs of earth, and be ready for whatever may come.

Later.--It is done. My will is made, and all complete. Mina if she survive is my sole heir. If it should not be so, then the others who have been so good to us shall have remainder.

It is now drawing towards the sunset. Mina's uneasiness calls my attention to it. I am sure that there is something on her mind which the time of exact sunset will reveal. These occasions are becoming harrowing times for us all. For each sunrise and sunset opens up some new danger, some new pain, which however, may in God's will be means to a good end. I write all these things in the diary since my darling must not hear them now. But if it may be that she can see them again, they shall be ready. She is calling to me.

CHAPTER 25

DR. SEWARD'S DIARY

11 October, Evening.--Jonathan Harker has asked me to note this, as he says he is hardly equal to the task, and he wants an exact record kept.

I think that none of us were surprised when we were asked to see Mrs. Harker a little before the time of sunset. We have of late come to understand that sunrise and sunset are to her times of peculiar freedom. When her old self can be manifest without any controlling force subduing or restraining her, or inciting her to action. This mood or condition begins some half hour or more before actual sunrise or sunset, and lasts till either the sun is high, or whilst the clouds are still aglow with the rays streaming above the horizon. At first there is a sort of negative condition, as if some tie were loosened, and then the absolute freedom quickly follows. When, however, the freedom ceases the change back or relapse comes quickly, preceded only by a spell of warning silence.

Tonight, when we met, she was somewhat constrained, and bore all the signs of an internal struggle. I put it down myself to her making a violent effort at the earliest instant she could do so.

A very few minutes, however, gave her complete control of herself. Then, motioning her husband to sit beside her on the sofa where she was half reclining, she made the rest of us bring chairs up close.

Taking her husband's hand in hers, she began, "We are all here together in freedom, for perhaps the last time! I know that you will always be with me to the end." This was to her husband whose hand had, as we could see, tightened upon her. "In the morning we go out upon our task, and God alone knows what may be in store for any of us. You are going to be so good to me to take me with you. I know that all that brave earnest men can do for a poor weak woman, whose soul perhaps is lost, no, no, not yet, but is at any rate at stake, you will do. But you must remember that I am not as you are. There is a poison in my blood, in my soul, which may destroy me, which must destroy me, unless some relief comes to us. Oh, my friends, you know as well as I do, that my soul is at stake. And though I know there is one way out for me, you must not and I must not take it!" She looked appealingly to us all in turn, beginning and ending with her husband.

"What is that way?" asked Van Helsing in a hoarse voice. "What is that way, which we must not, may not, take?"

CHAPTER 25

"That I may die now, either by my own hand or that of another, before the greater evil is entirely wrought. I know, and you know, that were I once dead you could and would set free my immortal spirit, even as you did my poor Lucy's. Were death, or the fear of death, the only thing that stood in the way I would not shrink to die here now, amidst the friends who love me. But death is not all. I cannot believe that to die in such a case, when there is hope before us and a bitter task to be done, is God's will. Therefore, I on my part, give up here the certainty of eternal rest, and go out into the dark where may be the blackest things that the world or the nether world holds!"

We were all silent, for we knew instinctively that this was only a prelude. The faces of the others were set, and Harker's grew ashen grey. Perhaps, he guessed better than any of us what was coming.

She continued, "This is what I can give into the hotch-pot." I could not but note the quaint legal phrase which she used in such a place, and with all seriousness. "What will each of you give? Your lives I know," she went on quickly, "that is easy for brave men. Your lives are God's, and you can give them back to Him, but what will you give to me?" She looked again questioningly, but this time avoided her husband's face. Quincey seemed to understand, he nodded, and her face lit up. "Then I shall tell you plainly what I want, for there must be no doubtful matter in this connection between us now. You must promise me, one and all, even you, my beloved husband, that should the time come, you will kill me."

"What is that time?" The voice was Quincey's, but it was low and strained.

"When you shall be convinced that I am so changed that it is better that I die that I may live. When I am thus dead in the flesh, then you will, without a moment's delay, drive a stake through me and cut off my head, or do whatever else may be wanting to give me rest!"

Quincey was the first to rise after the pause. He knelt down before her and taking her hand in his said solemnly, "I'm only a rough fellow, who hasn't, perhaps, lived as a man should to win such a distinction, but I swear to you by all that I hold sacred and dear that, should the time ever come, I shall not flinch from the duty that you have set us. And I promise you, too, that I shall make all certain, for if I am only doubtful I shall take it that the time has come!"

"My true friend!" was all she could say amid her fast-falling tears, as bending over, she kissed his hand.

"I swear the same, my dear Madam Mina!" said Van Helsing. "And I!" said Lord Godalming, each of them in turn kneeling to her to take the oath. I followed, myself.

Then her husband turned to her wan-eyed and with a greenish pallor which subdued the snowy whiteness of his hair, and asked, "And must I, too, make such a promise, oh, my wife?"

"You too, my dearest," she said, with infinite yearning of pity in her voice and eyes. "You must not shrink. You are nearest and dearest and all the world to me. Our souls are knit into one, for all life and all time. Think, dear, that there have been times when brave men have killed their wives and their womenkind, to keep them from falling into the hands of the enemy. Their hands did not falter any the more because those that they loved implored them to slay them. It is men's duty towards those whom they love, in such times of sore trial! And oh, my dear, if it is to be that I must meet death at any hand, let it be at the hand of him that loves me best. Dr. Van Helsing, I have not forgotten your mercy in poor Lucy's case to him who loved." She stopped with a flying blush, and changed her phrase, "to him who had best right to give her peace. If that time shall come again, I look to you to make it a happy memory of my husband's life that it was his loving hand which set me free from the awful thrall upon me."

"Again I swear!" came the Professor's resonant voice.

Mrs. Harker smiled, positively smiled, as with a sigh of relief she leaned back and said, "And now one word of warning, a warning which you must never forget. This time, if it ever come, may come quickly and unexpectedly, and in such case you must lose no time in using your opportunity. At such a time I myself might be… nay! If the time ever come, shall be, leagued with your enemy against you.

"One more request," she became very solemn as she said this, "it is not vital and necessary like the other, but I want you to do one thing for me, if you will."

We all acquiesced, but no one spoke. There was no need to speak.

"I want you to read the Burial Service." She was interrupted by a deep groan from her husband. Taking his hand in hers, she held it over her heart, and continued. "You must read it over me some day. Whatever may be the issue of all this fearful state of things, it will be a sweet thought to all or some of us. You, my dearest, will I hope read it, for then it will be in your voice in my memory forever, come what may!"

"But oh, my dear one," he pleaded, "death is afar off from you."

"Nay," she said, holding up a warning hand. "I am deeper in death at this moment than if the weight of an earthly grave lay heavy upon me!"

"Oh, my wife, must I read it?" he said, before he began.

"It would comfort me, my husband!" was all she said, and he began to read when she had got the book ready.

How can I, how could anyone, tell of that strange scene, its solemnity, its gloom, its sadness, its horror, and withal, its sweetness. Even a sceptic, who can see nothing but a travesty of bitter truth in anything holy or emotional, would have been melted to the heart had he seen that little group of loving and devoted friends kneeling round that stricken and sorrowing lady; or heard the tender passion of her husband's voice, as in tones so broken and emotional that often he had to pause, he read the simple and beautiful service from the Burial of the Dead. I cannot go on… words… and v-voices… f-fail m-me!

She was right in her instinct. Strange as it was, bizarre as it may hereafter seem even to us who felt its potent influence at the time, it comforted us much. And the silence, which showed Mrs. Harker's coming relapse from her freedom of soul, did not seem so full of despair to any of us as we had dreaded.

JONATHAN HARKER'S JOURNAL

15 October, Varna.--We left Charing Cross on the morning of the 12th, got to Paris the same night, and took the places secured for us in the Orient Express. We traveled night and day, arriving here at about five o'clock. Lord Godalming went to the Consulate to see if any telegram had arrived for him, whilst the rest of us came on to this hotel, "the Odessus." The journey may have had incidents. I was, however, too eager to get on, to care for them. Until the Czarina Catherine comes into port there will be no interest for me in anything in the wide world. Thank God! Mina is well, and looks to be getting stronger. Her colour is coming back. She sleeps a great deal. Throughout the journey she slept nearly all the time. Before sunrise and sunset, how-

ever, she is very wakeful and alert. And it has become a habit for Van Helsing to hypnotize her at such times. At first, some effort was needed, and he had to make many passes. But now, she seems to yield at once, as if by habit, and scarcely any action is needed. He seems to have power at these particular moments to simply will, and her thoughts obey him. He always asks her what she can see and hear.

She answers to the first, "Nothing, all is dark."

And to the second, "I can hear the waves lapping against the ship, and the water rushing by. Canvas and cordage strain and masts and yards creak. The wind is high... I can hear it in the shrouds, and the bow throws back the foam."

It is evident that the Czarina Catherine is still at sea, hastening on her way to Varna. Lord Godalming has just returned. He had four telegrams, one each day since we started, and all to the same effect. That the Czarina Catherine had not been reported to Lloyd's from anywhere. He had arranged before leaving London that his agent should send him every day a telegram saying if the ship had been reported. He was to have a message even if she were not reported, so that he might be sure that there was a watch being kept at the other end of the wire.

We had dinner and went to bed early. Tomorrow we are to see the Vice Consul, and to arrange, if we can, about getting on board the ship as soon as she arrives. Van Helsing says that our chance will be to get on the boat between sunrise and sunset. The Count, even if he takes the form of a bat, cannot cross the running water of his own volition, and so cannot leave the ship. As he dare not change to man's form without suspicion, which he evidently wishes to avoid, he must remain in the box. If, then, we can come on board after sunrise, he is at our mercy, for we can open the box and make sure of him, as we did of poor Lucy, before he wakes. What mercy he shall get from us all will not count for much. We think that we shall not have much trouble with officials or the seamen. Thank God! This is the country where bribery can do anything, and we are well supplied with money. We have only to make sure that the ship cannot come into port between sunset and sunrise without our being warned, and we shall be safe. Judge Moneybag will settle this case, I think!

16 October.--Mina's report still the same. Lapping waves and rushing water, darkness and favouring winds. We are evidently in good time, and when we hear of the Czarina Catherine we shall be ready. As she must pass the Dardanelles we are sure to have some report.

17 October.--Everything is pretty well fixed now, I think, to welcome the Count on his return from his tour. Godalming told the shippers that he fancied that the box sent aboard might contain something stolen from a friend of his, and got a half consent that he might open it at his own risk. The owner gave him a paper telling the Captain to give him every facility in doing whatever he chose on board the ship, and also a similar authorization to his agent at Varna. We have seen the agent, who was much impressed with Godalming's kindly manner to him, and we are all satisfied that whatever he can do to aid our wishes will be done.

We have already arranged what to do in case we get the box open. If the Count is there, Van Helsing and Seward will cut off his head at once and drive a stake through his heart. Morris and Godalming and I shall prevent interference, even if we have to use the arms which we shall have ready. The Professor says that if we can so treat the Count's body, it will soon after fall into dust. In such case there would be no evidence against us, in case any suspicion of murder were aroused. But even if it were not, we should stand or fall by our act, and perhaps some day this very script may be evidence to come between some of us and a rope. For myself, I should take the chance only too thankfully if it were to come. We mean to leave no stone unturned to carry out our intent. We have arranged with certain officials that the instant the Czarina Catherine is seen, we are to be informed by a special messenger.

24 October.--A whole week of waiting. Daily telegrams to Godalming, but only the same story. "Not yet reported." Mina's morning and evening hypnotic answer is unvaried. Lapping waves, rushing water, and creaking masts.

TELEGRAM, OCTOBER 24TH RUFUS SMITH, LLOYD'S, LONDON, TO LORD GODALMING, CARE OF H. B. M. VICE CONSUL, VARNA

"Czarina Catherine reported this morning from Dardanelles."

DR. SEWARD'S DIARY

25 October.--How I miss my phonograph! To write a diary with a pen is irksome to me! But Van Helsing says I must. We were all wild with excitement yesterday when Godalming got his telegram from Lloyd's. I know now what men feel in battle when the call to action is heard. Mrs. Harker, alone of our party, did not show any signs of emotion. After all, it is not strange that she did not, for we took special care not to let her know anything about it, and we all tried not to show any excitement when we were in her presence. In old days she would, I am sure, have noticed, no matter how we might have tried to conceal it. But in this way she is greatly changed during the past three weeks. The lethargy grows upon her, and though she seems strong and well, and is getting back some of her colour, Van Helsing and I are not satisfied. We talk of her often. We have not, however, said a word to the others. It would break poor Harker's heart, certainly his nerve, if he knew that we had even a suspicion on the subject. Van Helsing examines, he tells me, her teeth very carefully, whilst she is in the hypnotic condition, for he says that so long as they do not begin to sharpen there is no active danger of a change in her. If this change should come, it would be necessary to take steps! We both know what those steps would have to be, though we do not mention our thoughts to each other. We should neither of us shrink from the task, awful though it be to contemplate. "Euthanasia" is an excellent and a comforting word! I am grateful to whoever invented it.

It is only about 24 hours' sail from the Dardanelles to here, at the rate the Czarina Catherine has come from London. She should therefore arrive some time in the morning, but as she cannot possibly get in before noon, we are all about to retire early. We shall get up at one o'clock, so as to be ready.

25 October, Noon.--No news yet of the ship's arrival. Mrs. Harker's hypnotic report this morning was the same as usual, so it is possible that we may get news at any moment. We men are all in a fever of excitement, except Harker, who is calm. His hands are cold as ice, and an hour ago I found him whetting the edge of the great Ghoorka knife which he now always carries with him. It will be a bad lookout for the

Count if the edge of that "Kukri" ever touches his throat, driven by that stern, ice-cold hand!

Van Helsing and I were a little alarmed about Mrs. Harker today. About noon she got into a sort of lethargy which we did not like. Although we kept silence to the others, we were neither of us happy about it. She had been restless all the morning, so that we were at first glad to know that she was sleeping. When, however, her husband mentioned casually that she was sleeping so soundly that he could not wake her, we went to her room to see for ourselves. She was breathing naturally and looked so well and peaceful that we agreed that the sleep was better for her than anything else. Poor girl, she has so much to forget that it is no wonder that sleep, if it brings oblivion to her, does her good.

Later.--Our opinion was justified, for when after a refreshing sleep of some hours she woke up, she seemed brighter and better than she had been for days. At sunset she made the usual hypnotic report. Wherever he may be in the Black Sea, the Count is hurrying to his destination. To his doom, I trust!

26 October.--Another day and no tidings of the Czarina Catherine. She ought to be here by now. That she is still journeying somewhere is apparent, for Mrs. Harker's hypnotic report at sunrise was still the same. It is possible that the vessel may be lying by, at times, for fog. Some of the steamers which came in last evening reported patches of fog both to north and south of the port. We must continue our watching, as the ship may now be signalled any moment.

27 October, Noon.--Most strange. No news yet of the ship we wait for. Mrs. Harker reported last night and this morning as usual. "Lapping waves and rushing water," though she added that "the waves were very faint." The telegrams from London have been the same, "no further report." Van Helsing is terribly anxious, and told me just now that he fears the Count is escaping us.

He added significantly, "I did not like that lethargy of Madam Mina's. Souls and memories can do strange things during trance." I was about to ask him more, but Harker just then came in, and he held up a warning hand. We must try tonight at sunset to make her speak more fully when in her hypnotic state.

28 October.--Telegram. Rufus Smith, London, to Lord Godalming, care H. B. M. Vice Consul, Varna

"Czarina Catherine reported entering Galatz at one o'clock today."

DR. SEWARD'S DIARY

28 October.--When the telegram came announcing the arrival in Galatz I do not think it was such a shock to any of us as might have been expected. True, we did not know whence, or how, or when, the bolt would come. But I think we all expected that something strange would happen. The day of arrival at Varna made us individually satisfied that things would not be just as we had expected. We only waited to learn where the change would occur. None the less, however, it was a surprise. I suppose that nature works on such a hopeful basis that we believe against ourselves that things will be as they ought to be, not as we should know that they will be. Transcendentalism is a beacon to the angels, even if it be a will-o'-the-wisp to man. Van Helsing raised his hand over his head for a moment, as though in remonstrance with the Al-

mighty. But he said not a word, and in a few seconds stood up with his face sternly set.

Lord Godalming grew very pale, and sat breathing heavily. I was myself half stunned and looked in wonder at one after another. Quincey Morris tightened his belt with that quick movement which I knew so well. In our old wandering days it meant "action." Mrs. Harker grew ghastly white, so that the scar on her forehead seemed to burn, but she folded her hands meekly and looked up in prayer. Harker smiled, actually smiled, the dark, bitter smile of one who is without hope, but at the same time his action belied his words, for his hands instinctively sought the hilt of the great Kukri knife and rested there.

"When does the next train start for Galatz?" said Van Helsing to us generally.

"At 6:30 tomorrow morning!" We all started, for the answer came from Mrs. Harker.

"How on earth do you know?" said Art.

"You forget, or perhaps you do not know, though Jonathan does and so does Dr. Van Helsing, that I am the train fiend. At home in Exeter I always used to make up the time tables, so as to be helpful to my husband. I found it so useful sometimes, that I always make a study of the time tables now. I knew that if anything were to take us to Castle Dracula we should go by Galatz, or at any rate through Bucharest, so I learned the times very carefully. Unhappily there are not many to learn, as the only train tomorrow leaves as I say."

"Wonderful woman!" murmured the Professor.

"Can't we get a special?" asked Lord Godalming.

Van Helsing shook his head, "I fear not. This land is very different from yours or mine. Even if we did have a special, it would probably not arrive as soon as our regular train. Moreover, we have something to prepare. We must think. Now let us organize. You, friend Arthur, go to the train and get the tickets and arrange that all be ready for us to go in the morning. Do you, friend Jonathan, go to the agent of the ship and get from him letters to the agent in Galatz, with authority to make a search of the ship just as it was here. Quincey Morris, you see the Vice Consul, and get his aid with his fellow in Galatz and all he can do to make our way smooth, so that no times be lost when over the Danube. John will stay with Madam Mina and me, and we shall consult. For so if time be long you may be delayed. And it will not matter when the sun set, since I am here with Madam to make report."

"And I," said Mrs. Harker brightly, and more like her old self than she had been for many a long day, "shall try to be of use in all ways, and shall think and write for you as I used to do. Something is shifting from me in some strange way, and I feel freer than I have been of late!"

The three younger men looked happier at the moment as they seemed to realize the significance of her words. But Van Helsing and I, turning to each other, met each a grave and troubled glance. We said nothing at the time, however.

When the three men had gone out to their tasks Van Helsing asked Mrs. Harker to look up the copy of the diaries and find him the part of Harker's journal at the Castle. She went away to get it.

When the door was shut upon her he said to me, "We mean the same! Speak out!"

"Here is some change. It is a hope that makes me sick, for it may deceive us."

"Quite so. Do you know why I asked her to get the manuscript?"

"No!" said I, "unless it was to get an opportunity of seeing me alone."

"You are in part right, friend John, but only in part. I want to tell you something. And oh, my friend, I am taking a great, a terrible, risk. But I believe it is right. In the moment when Madam Mina said those words that arrest both our understanding, an inspiration came to me. In the trance of three days ago the Count sent her his spirit to read her mind. Or more like he took her to see him in his earth box in the ship with water rushing, just as it go free at rise and set of sun. He learn then that we are here, for she have more to tell in her open life with eyes to see ears to hear than he, shut as he is, in his coffin box. Now he make his most effort to escape us. At present he want her not.

"He is sure with his so great knowledge that she will come at his call. But he cut her off, take her, as he can do, out of his own power, that so she come not to him. Ah! There I have hope that our man brains that have been of man so long and that have not lost the grace of God, will come higher than his child-brain that lie in his tomb for centuries, that grow not yet to our stature, and that do only work selfish and therefore small. Here comes Madam Mina. Not a word to her of her trance! She knows it not, and it would overwhelm her and make despair just when we want all her hope, all her courage, when most we want all her great brain which is trained like man's brain, but is of sweet woman and have a special power which the Count give her, and which he may not take away altogether, though he think not so. Hush! Let me speak, and you shall learn. Oh, John, my friend, we are in awful straits. I fear, as I never feared before. We can only trust the good God. Silence! Here she comes!"

I thought that the Professor was going to break down and have hysterics, just as he had when Lucy died, but with a great effort he controlled himself and was at perfect nervous poise when Mrs. Harker tripped into the room, bright and happy looking and, in the doing of work, seemingly forgetful of her misery. As she came in, she handed a number of sheets of typewriting to Van Helsing. He looked over them gravely, his face brightening up as he read.

Then holding the pages between his finger and thumb he said, "Friend John, to you with so much experience already, and you too, dear Madam Mina, that are young, here is a lesson. Do not fear ever to think. A half thought has been buzzing often in my brain, but I fear to let him loose his wings. Here now, with more knowledge, I go back to where that half thought come from and I find that he be no half thought at all. That be a whole thought, though so young that he is not yet strong to use his little wings. Nay, like the 'Ugly Duck' of my friend Hans Andersen, he be no duck thought at all, but a big swan thought that sail nobly on big wings, when the time come for him to try them. See I read here what Jonathan have written.

"That other of his race who, in a later age, again and again, brought his forces over The Great River into Turkey Land, who when he was beaten back, came again, and again, and again, though he had to come alone from the bloody field where his troops were being slaughtered, since he knew that he alone could ultimately triumph.

"What does this tell us? Not much? No! The Count's child thought see nothing, therefore he speak so free. Your man thought see nothing. My man thought see nothing, till just now. No! But there comes another word from some one who speak without thought because she, too, know not what it mean, what it might mean. Just as there are elements which rest, yet when in nature's course they move on their way and they touch, the pouf! And there comes a flash of light, heaven wide, that blind and kill and destroy some. But that show up all earth below for leagues and leagues. Is it not so? Well, I shall explain. To begin, have you ever study the philosophy of crime? 'Yes' and 'No.' You, John, yes, for it is a study of insanity. You, no, Madam Mina, for crime touch you not, not but once. Still, your mind works true, and argues not a particulari ad universale. There is this peculiarity in criminals. It is so constant, in all countries and at all times, that even police, who know not much from philosophy, come to know it empirically, that it is. That is to be empiric. The criminal always work at one crime, that is the true criminal who seems predestinate to crime, and who will of none other. This criminal has not full man brain. He is clever and cunning and resourceful, but he be not of man stature as to brain. He be of child brain in much. Now this criminal of ours is predestinate to crime also. He, too, have child brain, and it is of the child to do what he have done. The little bird, the little fish, the little animal learn not by principle, but empirically. And when he learn to do, then there is to him the ground to start from to do more. 'Dos pou sto,' said Archimedes. 'Give me a fulcrum, and I shall move the world!' To do once, is the fulcrum whereby child brain become man brain. And until he have the purpose to do more, he continue to do the same again every time, just as he have done before! Oh, my dear, I see that your eyes are opened, and that to you the lightning flash show all the leagues," for Mrs. Harker began to clap her hands and her eyes sparkled.

He went on, "Now you shall speak. Tell us two dry men of science what you see with those so bright eyes." He took her hand and held it whilst he spoke. His finger and thumb closed on her pulse, as I thought instinctively and unconsciously, as she spoke.

"The Count is a criminal and of criminal type. Nordau and Lombroso would so classify him, and qua criminal he is of an imperfectly formed mind. Thus, in a difficulty he has to seek resource in habit. His past is a clue, and the one page of it that we know, and that from his own lips, tells that once before, when in what Mr. Morris would call a 'tight place,' he went back to his own country from the land he had tried to invade, and thence, without losing purpose, prepared himself for a new effort. He came again better equipped for his work, and won. So he came to London to invade a new land. He was beaten, and when all hope of success was lost, and his existence in danger, he fled back over the sea to his home. Just as formerly he had fled back over the Danube from Turkey Land."

"Good, good! Oh, you so clever lady!" said Van Helsing, enthusiastically, as he stooped and kissed her hand. A moment later he said to me, as calmly as though we had been having a sick room consultation, "Seventy-two only, and in all this excitement. I have hope."

Turning to her again, he said with keen expectation, "But go on. Go on! There is more to tell if you will. Be not afraid. John and I know. I do in any case, and shall tell you if you are right. Speak, without fear!"

"I will try to. But you will forgive me if I seem too egotistical."

"Nay! Fear not, you must be egotist, for it is of you that we think."

"Then, as he is criminal he is selfish. And as his intellect is small and his action is based on selfishness, he confines himself to one purpose. That purpose is remorseless. As he fled back over the Danube, leaving his forces to be cut to pieces, so now he is intent on being safe, careless of all. So his own selfishness frees my soul somewhat from the terrible power which he acquired over me on that dreadful night. I felt it! Oh,

I felt it! Thank God, for His great mercy! My soul is freer than it has been since that awful hour. And all that haunts me is a fear lest in some trance or dream he may have used my knowledge for his ends."

The Professor stood up, "He has so used your mind, and by it he has left us here in Varna, whilst the ship that carried him rushed through enveloping fog up to Galatz, where, doubtless, he had made preparation for escaping from us. But his child mind only saw so far. And it may be that as ever is in God's Providence, the very thing that the evil doer most reckoned on for his selfish good, turns out to be his chiefest harm. The hunter is taken in his own snare, as the great Psalmist says. For now that he think he is free from every trace of us all, and that he has escaped us with so many hours to him, then his selfish child brain will whisper him to sleep. He think, too, that as he cut himself off from knowing your mind, there can be no knowledge of him to you. There is where he fail! That terrible baptism of blood which he give you makes you free to go to him in spirit, as you have as yet done in your times of freedom, when the sun rise and set. At such times you go by my volition and not by his. And this power to good of you and others, you have won from your suffering at his hands. This is now all more precious that he know it not, and to guard himself have even cut himself off from his knowledge of our where. We, however, are not selfish, and we believe that God is with us through all this blackness, and these many dark hours. We shall follow him, and we shall not flinch, even if we peril ourselves that we become like him. Friend John, this has been a great hour, and it have done much to advance us on our way. You must be scribe and write him all down, so that when the others return from their work you can give it to them, then they shall know as we do."

And so I have written it whilst we wait their return, and Mrs. Harker has written with the typewriter all since she brought the MS to us.

CHAPTER 26

DR. SEWARD'S DIARY

29 October.--This is written in the train from Varna to Galatz. Last night we all assembled a little before the time of sunset. Each of us had done his work as well as he could, so far as thought, and endeavour, and opportunity go, we are prepared for the whole of our journey, and for our work when we get to Galatz. When the usual time came round Mrs. Harker prepared herself for her hypnotic effort, and after a longer and more serious effort on the part of Van Helsing than has been usually necessary, she sank into the trance. Usually she speaks on a hint, but this time the Professor had to ask her questions, and to ask them pretty resolutely, before we could learn anything. At last her answer came.

"I can see nothing. We are still. There are no waves lapping, but only a steady swirl of water softly running against the hawser. I can hear men's voices calling, near and far, and the roll and creak of oars in the rowlocks. A gun is fired somewhere, the echo of it seems far away. There is tramping of feet overhead, and ropes and chains are dragged along. What is this? There is a gleam of light. I can feel the air blowing upon me."

Here she stopped. She had risen, as if impulsively, from where she lay on the sofa, and raised both her hands, palms upwards, as if lifting a weight. Van Helsing and I looked at each other with understanding. Quincey raised his eyebrows slightly and looked at her intently, whilst Harker's hand instinctively closed round the hilt of his Kukri. There was a long pause. We all knew that the time when she could speak was passing, but we felt that it was useless to say anything.

Suddenly she sat up, and as she opened her eyes said sweetly, "Would none of you like a cup of tea? You must all be so tired!"

We could only make her happy, and so acquiesced. She bustled off to get tea. When she had gone Van Helsing said, "You see, my friends. He is close to land. He has left his earth chest. But he has yet to get on shore. In the night he may lie hidden somewhere, but if he be not carried on shore, or if the ship do not touch it, he cannot achieve the land. In such case he can, if it be in the night, change his form and jump or fly on shore, then, unless he be carried he cannot escape. And if he be carried, then the customs men may discover what the box contain. Thus, in fine, if he escape not on shore tonight, or before dawn, there will be the whole day lost to him. We may then arrive in time. For if he escape not at night we shall come on him in daytime, boxed up and at our mercy. For he dare not be his true self, awake and visible, lest he be discovered."

There was no more to be said, so we waited in patience until the dawn, at which time we might learn more from Mrs. Harker.

Early this morning we listened, with breathless anxiety, for her response in her trance. The hypnotic stage was even longer in coming than before, and when it came the time remaining until full sunrise was so short that we began to despair. Van Helsing seemed to throw his whole soul into the effort. At last, in obedience to his will she made reply.

"All is dark. I hear lapping water, level with me, and some creaking as of wood on wood." She paused, and the red sun shot up. We must wait till tonight.

And so it is that we are travelling towards Galatz in an agony of expectation. We are due to arrive between two and three in the morning. But already, at Bucharest, we are three hours late, so we cannot possibly get in till well after sunup. Thus we shall have two more hypnotic messages from Mrs. Harker! Either or both may possibly throw more light on what is happening.

Later.--Sunset has come and gone. Fortunately it came at a time when there was no distraction. For had it occurred whilst we were at a station, we might not have secured the necessary calm and isolation. Mrs. Harker yielded to the hypnotic influence even less readily than this morning. I am in fear that her power of reading the Count's sensations may die away, just when we want it most. It seems to me that her imagination is beginning to work. Whilst she has been in the trance hitherto she has confined herself to the simplest of facts. If this goes on it may ultimately mislead us. If I thought that the Count's power over her would die away equally with her power of knowledge it would be a happy thought. But I am afraid that it may not be so.

When she did speak, her words were enigmatical, "Something is going out. I can feel it pass me like a cold wind. I can hear, far off, confused sounds, as of men talking in strange tongues, fierce falling water, and the howling of wolves." She stopped and a shudder ran through her, increasing in intensity for a few seconds, till at the end, she shook as though in a palsy. She said no more, even in answer to the Professor's imperative questioning. When she woke from the trance, she was cold, and exhausted, and languid, but her mind was all alert. She could not remember anything, but asked what she had said. When she was told, she pondered over it deeply for a long time and in silence.

30 October, 7 A.M.--We are near Galatz now, and I may not have time to write later. Sunrise this morning was anxiously looked for by us all. Knowing of the increasing difficulty of procuring the hypnotic trance, Van Helsing began his passes earlier than usual. They produced no effect, however, until the regular time, when she yielded with a still greater difficulty, only a minute before the sun rose. The Professor lost no time in his questioning.

Her answer came with equal quickness, "All is dark. I hear water swirling by, level with my ears, and the creaking of wood on wood. Cattle low far off. There is another sound, a queer one like…" She stopped and grew white, and whiter still.

"Go on, go on! Speak, I command you!" said Van Helsing in an agonized voice. At the same time there was despair in his eyes, for the risen sun was reddening even Mrs. Harker's pale face. She opened her eyes, and we all started as she said, sweetly and seemingly with the utmost unconcern.

"Oh, Professor, why ask me to do what you know I can't? I don't remember anything." Then, seeing the look of amazement on our faces, she said, turning from one to the other with a troubled look, "What have I said? What have I done? I know nothing, only that I was lying here, half asleep, and heard you say 'go on! speak, I command you!' It seemed so funny to hear you order me about, as if I were a bad child!"

"Oh, Madam Mina," he said, sadly, "it is proof, if proof be needed, of how I love and honour you, when a word for your good, spoken more earnest than ever, can seem so strange because it is to order her whom I am proud to obey!"

The whistles are sounding. We are nearing Galatz. We are on fire with anxiety and eagerness.

MINA HARKER'S JOURNAL

30 October.--Mr. Morris took me to the hotel where our rooms had been ordered by telegraph, he being the one who could best be spared, since he does not speak any foreign language. The forces were distributed much as they had been at Varna, except that Lord Godalming went to the Vice Consul, as his rank might serve as an immediate guarantee of some sort to the official, we being in extreme hurry. Jonathan and the two doctors went to the shipping agent to learn particulars of the arrival of the Czarina Catherine.

Later.--Lord Godalming has returned. The Consul is away, and the Vice Consul sick. So the routine work has been attended to by a clerk. He was very obliging, and offered to do anything in his power.

JONATHAN HARKER'S JOURNAL

30 October.--At nine o'clock Dr. Van Helsing, Dr. Seward, and I called on Messrs. Mackenzie & Steinkoff, the agents of the London firm of Hapgood. They had received a wire from London, in answer to Lord Godalming's telegraphed request, asking them to show us any civility in their power. They were more than kind and courteous, and took us at once on board the Czarina Catherine, which lay at anchor out in the river harbor. There we saw the Captain, Donelson by name, who told us of his voyage. He said that in all his life he had never had so favourable a run.

"Man!" he said, "but it made us afeard, for we expect it that we should have to pay for it wi' some rare piece o' ill luck, so as to keep up the average. It's no canny to run frae London to the Black Sea wi' a wind ahint ye, as though the Deil himself were blawin' on yer sail for his ain purpose. An' a' the time we could no speer a thing. Gin we were nigh a ship, or a port, or a headland, a fog fell on us and travelled wi' us, till when after it had lifted and we looked out, the deil a thing could we see. We ran by Gibraltar wi' oot bein' able to signal. An' til we came to the Dardanelles and had to wait to get our permit to pass, we never were within hail o' aught. At first I inclined to slack off sail and beat about till the fog was lifted. But whiles, I thocht that if the Deil was minded to get us into the Black Sea quick, he was like to do it whether we would or no. If we had a quick voyage it would be no to our miscredit wi' the owners, or no hurt to our traffic, an' the Old Mon who had served his ain purpose wad be decently grateful to us for no hinderin' him."

This mixture of simplicity and cunning, of superstition and commercial reasoning, aroused Van Helsing, who said, "Mine friend, that Devil is more clever than he is thought by some, and he know when he meet his match!"

The skipper was not displeased with the compliment, and went on, "When we got past the Bosphorus the men began to grumble. Some o' them, the Roumanians, came and asked me to heave overboard a big box which had been put on board by a queer lookin' old man just before we had started frae London. I had seen them speer at the fellow, and put out their twa fingers when they saw him, to guard them against the evil eye. Man! but the supersteetion of foreigners is pairfectly rideeculous! I sent them aboot their business pretty quick, but as just after a fog closed in on us I felt a wee bit as they did anent something, though I wouldn't say it was again the big box. Well, on we went, and as the fog didn't let up for five days I joost let the wind carry us, for if the Deil wanted to get somewheres, well, he would fetch it up a'reet. An' if he didn't, well, we'd keep a sharp lookout anyhow. Sure eneuch, we had a fair way and deep water all the time. And two days ago, when the mornin' sun came through the fog, we found ourselves just in the river opposite Galatz. The Roumanians were wild, and wanted me right or wrong to take out the box and fling it in the river. I had to argy wi' them aboot it wi' a handspike. An' when the last o' them rose off the deck wi' his head in his hand, I had convinced them that, evil eye or no evil eye, the property and the trust of my owners were better in my hands than in the river Danube. They had, mind ye, taken the box on the deck ready to fling in, and as it was marked Galatz via Varna, I thocht I'd let it lie till we discharged in the port an' get rid o't althegither. We didn't do much clearin' that day, an' had to remain the nicht at anchor. But in the mornin', braw an' airly, an hour before sunup, a man came aboard wi' an order, written to him from England, to receive a box marked for one Count Dracula. Sure eneuch the matter was one ready to his hand. He had his papers a' reet, an' glad I was to be rid o' the dam' thing, for I was beginnin' masel' to feel uneasy at it. If the Deil did have any luggage aboord the ship, I'm thinkin' it was nane ither than that same!"

"What was the name of the man who took it?" asked Dr. Van Helsing with restrained eagerness.

"I'll be tellin' ye quick!" he answered, and stepping down to his cabin, produced a receipt signed "Immanuel Hildesheim." Burgen-strasse 16 was the address. We found out that this was all the Captain knew, so with thanks we came away.

We found Hildesheim in his office, a Hebrew of rather the Adelphi Theatre type, with a nose like a sheep, and a fez. His arguments were pointed with specie, we doing the punctuation, and with a little bargaining he told us what he knew. This turned out to be simple but important. He had received a letter from Mr. de Ville of London, telling him to receive, if possible before sunrise so as to avoid customs, a box which would arrive at Galatz in the Czarina Catherine. This he was to give in charge to a certain Petrof Skinsky, who dealt with the Slovaks who traded down the river to the port. He had been paid for his work by an English bank note, which had been duly cashed for gold at the Danube International Bank. When Skinsky had come to him, he had taken him to the ship and handed over the box, so as to save porterage. That was all he knew.

We then sought for Skinsky, but were unable to find him. One of his neighbors, who did not seem to bear him any affection, said that he had gone away two days before, no one knew whither. This was corroborated by his landlord, who had received by messenger the key of the house together with the rent due, in English money. This had been between ten and eleven o'clock last night. We were at a standstill again.

Whilst we were talking one came running and breathlessly gasped out that the body of Skinsky had been found inside the wall of the churchyard of St. Peter, and that the throat had been torn open as if by some wild animal. Those we had been speaking with ran off to see the horror, the women crying out. "This is the work of a Slovak!" We hurried away lest we should have been in some way drawn into the affair, and so detained.

As we came home we could arrive at no definite conclusion. We were all convinced that the box was on its way, by water, to somewhere, but where that might be we would have to discover. With heavy hearts we came home to the hotel to Mina.

When we met together, the first thing was to consult as to taking Mina again into our confidence. Things are getting desperate, and it is at least a chance, though a hazardous one. As a preliminary step, I was released from my promise to her.

MINA HARKER'S JOURNAL

30 October, evening.--They were so tired and worn out and dispirited that there was nothing to be done till they had some rest, so I asked them all to lie down for half an hour whilst I should enter everything up to the moment. I feel so grateful to the man who invented the "Traveller's" typewriter, and to Mr. Morris for getting this one for me. I should have felt quite astray doing the work if I had to write with a pen…

It is all done. Poor dear, dear Jonathan, what he must have suffered, what he must be suffering now. He lies on the sofa hardly seeming to breathe, and his whole body appears in collapse. His brows are knit. His face is drawn with pain. Poor fellow, maybe he is thinking, and I can see his face all wrinkled up with the concentration of his thoughts. Oh! if I could only help at all. I shall do what I can.

I have asked Dr. Van Helsing, and he has got me all the papers that I have not yet seen. Whilst they are resting, I shall go over all carefully, and perhaps I may arrive at some conclusion. I shall try to follow the Professor's example, and think without prejudice on the facts before me…

I do believe that under God's providence I have made a discovery. I shall get the maps and look over them.

I am more than ever sure that I am right. My new conclusion is ready, so I shall get our party together and read it. They can judge it. It is well to be accurate, and every minute is precious.

MINA HARKER'S MEMORANDUM (ENTERED IN HER JOURNAL)

Ground of inquiry.--Count Dracula's problem is to get back to his own place.

(a) He must be brought back by some one. This is evident; for had he power to move himself as he wished he could go either as man, or wolf, or bat, or in some other way. He evidently fears discovery or interference, in the state of helplessness in which he must be, confined as he is between dawn and sunset in his wooden box.

(b) How is he to be taken?--Here a process of exclusions may help us. By road, by rail, by water?

1. By Road.--There are endless difficulties, especially in leaving the city.

(x) There are people. And people are curious, and investigate. A hint, a surmise, a doubt as to what might be in the box, would destroy him.

(y) There are, or there may be, customs and octroi officers to pass.

(z) His pursuers might follow. This is his highest fear. And in order to prevent his being betrayed he has repelled, so far as he can, even his victim, me!

2. By Rail.--There is no one in charge of the box. It would have to take its chance of being delayed, and delay would be fatal, with enemies on the track. True, he might escape at night. But what would he be, if left in a strange place with no refuge that he could fly to? This is not what he intends, and he does not mean to risk it.

3. By Water.--Here is the safest way, in one respect, but with most danger in another. On the water he is powerless except at night. Even then he can only summon fog and storm and snow and his wolves. But were he wrecked, the living water would engulf him, helpless, and he would indeed be lost. He could have the vessel drive to land, but if it were unfriendly land, wherein he was not free to move, his position would still be desperate.

We know from the record that he was on the water, so what we have to do is to ascertain what water.

The first thing is to realize exactly what he has done as yet. We may, then, get a light on what his task is to be.

Firstly.--We must differentiate between what he did in London as part of his general plan of action, when he was pressed for moments and had to arrange as best he could.

Secondly.--We must see, as well as we can surmise it from the facts we know of, what he has done here.

As to the first, he evidently intended to arrive at Galatz, and sent invoice to Varna to deceive us lest we should ascertain his means of exit from England. His immediate and sole purpose then was to escape. The proof of this, is the letter of instructions sent to Immanuel Hildesheim to clear and take away the box before sunrise. There is also the instruction to Petrof Skinsky. These we must only guess at, but there must have been some letter or message, since Skinsky came to Hildesheim.

That, so far, his plans were successful we know. The Czarina Catherine made a phenomenally quick journey. So much so that Captain Donelson's suspicions were aroused. But his superstition united with his canniness played the Count's game for him, and he ran with his favouring wind through fogs and all till he brought up blindfold at Galatz. That the Count's arrangements were well made, has been proved. Hildesheim cleared the box, took it off, and gave it to Skinsky. Skinsky took it, and here we lose the trail. We only know that the box is somewhere on the water, moving along. The customs and the octroi, if there be any, have been avoided.

Now we come to what the Count must have done after his arrival, on land, at Galatz.

The box was given to Skinsky before sunrise. At sunrise the Count could appear in his own form. Here, we ask why Skinsky was chosen at all to aid in the work? In my husband's diary, Skinsky is mentioned as dealing with the Slovaks who trade down the river to the port. And the man's remark, that the murder was the work of a Slovak, showed the general feeling against his class. The Count wanted isolation.

My surmise is this, that in London the Count decided to get back to his castle by water, as the most safe and secret way. He was brought from the castle by Szgany, and probably they delivered their cargo to Slovaks who took the boxes to Varna, for there they were shipped to London. Thus the Count had knowledge of the persons who could arrange this service. When the box was on land, before sunrise or after sunset, he came out from his box, met Skinsky and instructed him what to do as to arranging the carriage of the box up some river. When this was done, and he knew that all was in train, he blotted out his traces, as he thought, by murdering his agent.

I have examined the map and find that the river most suitable for the Slovaks to have ascended is either the Pruth or the Sereth. I read in the typescript that in my trance I heard cows low and water swirling level with my ears and the creaking of wood. The Count in his box, then, was on a river in an open boat, propelled probably either by oars or poles, for the banks are near and it is working against stream. There would be no such if floating down stream.

Of course it may not be either the Sereth or the Pruth, but we may possibly investigate further. Now of these two, the Pruth is the more easily navigated, but the Sereth is, at Fundu, joined by the Bistritza which runs up round the Borgo Pass. The loop it makes is manifestly as close to Dracula's castle as can be got by water.

MINA HARKER'S JOURNAL--CONTINUED

When I had done reading, Jonathan took me in his arms and kissed me. The others kept shaking me by both hands, and Dr. Van Helsing said, "Our dear Madam Mina is once more our teacher. Her eyes have been where we were blinded. Now we are on the track once again, and this time we may succeed. Our enemy is at his most helpless. And if we can come on him by day, on the water, our task will be over. He has a start, but he is powerless to hasten, as he may not leave this box lest those who carry him may suspect. For them to suspect would be to prompt them to throw him in the stream where he perish. This he knows, and will not. Now men, to our Council of War, for here and now, we must plan what each and all shall do."

"I shall get a steam launch and follow him," said Lord Godalming.

"And I, horses to follow on the bank lest by chance he land," said Mr. Morris.

"Good!" said the Professor, "both good. But neither must go alone. There must be force to overcome force if need be. The Slovak is strong and rough, and he carries rude arms." All the men smiled, for amongst them they carried a small arsenal.

Said Mr. Morris, "I have brought some Winchesters. They are pretty handy in a crowd, and there may be wolves. The Count, if you remember, took some other precautions. He made some requisitions on others that Mrs. Harker could not quite hear or understand. We must be ready at all points."

Dr. Seward said, "I think I had better go with Quincey. We have been accustomed to hunt together, and we two, well armed, will be a match for whatever may come along. You must not be alone, Art. It may be necessary to fight the Slovaks, and a chance thrust, for I don't suppose these fellows carry guns, would undo all our plans.

There must be no chances, this time. We shall not rest until the Count's head and body have been separated, and we are sure that he cannot reincarnate."

He looked at Jonathan as he spoke, and Jonathan looked at me. I could see that the poor dear was torn about in his mind. Of course he wanted to be with me. But then the boat service would, most likely, be the one which would destroy the... the... Vampire. (Why did I hesitate to write the word?)

He was silent awhile, and during his silence Dr. Van Helsing spoke, "Friend Jonathan, this is to you for twice reasons. First, because you are young and brave and can fight, and all energies may be needed at the last. And again that it is your right to destroy him. That, which has wrought such woe to you and yours. Be not afraid for Madam Mina. She will be my care, if I may. I am old. My legs are not so quick to run as once. And I am not used to ride so long or to pursue as need be, or to fight with lethal weapons. But I can be of other service. I can fight in other way. And I can die, if need be, as well as younger men. Now let me say that what I would is this. While you, my Lord Godalming and friend Jonathan go in your so swift little steamboat up the river, and whilst John and Quincey guard the bank where perchance he might be landed, I will take Madam Mina right into the heart of the enemy's country. Whilst the old fox is tied in his box, floating on the running stream whence he cannot escape to land, where he dares not raise the lid of his coffin box lest his Slovak carriers should in fear leave him to perish, we shall go in the track where Jonathan went, from Bistritz over the Borgo, and find our way to the Castle of Dracula. Here, Madam Mina's hypnotic power will surely help, and we shall find our way, all dark and unknown otherwise, after the first sunrise when we are near that fateful place. There is much to be done, and other places to be made sanctify, so that that nest of vipers be obliterated."

Here Jonathan interrupted him hotly, "Do you mean to say, Professor Van Helsing, that you would bring Mina, in her sad case and tainted as she is with that devil's illness, right into the jaws of his deathtrap? Not for the world! Not for Heaven or Hell!"

He became almost speechless for a minute, and then went on, "Do you know what the place is? Have you seen that awful den of hellish infamy, with the very moonlight alive with grisly shapes, and every speck of dust that whirls in the wind a devouring monster in embryo? Have you felt the Vampire's lips upon your throat?"

Here he turned to me, and as his eyes lit on my forehead he threw up his arms with a cry, "Oh, my God, what have we done to have this terror upon us?" and he sank down on the sofa in a collapse of misery.

The Professor's voice, as he spoke in clear, sweet tones, which seemed to vibrate in the air, calmed us all.

"Oh, my friend, it is because I would save Madam Mina from that awful place that I would go. God forbid that I should take her into that place. There is work, wild work, to be done before that place can be purify. Remember that we are in terrible straits. If the Count escape us this time, and he is strong and subtle and cunning, he may choose to sleep him for a century, and then in time our dear one," he took my hand, "would come to him to keep him company, and would be as those others that you, Jonathan, saw. You have told us of their gloating lips. You heard their ribald laugh as they clutched the moving bag that the Count threw to them. You shudder, and well may it be. Forgive me that I make you so much pain, but it is necessary. My friend, is it not a dire need for that which I am giving, possibly my life? If it were that any one went into that place to stay, it is I who would have to go to keep them company."

"Do as you will," said Jonathan, with a sob that shook him all over, "we are in the hands of God!"

Later.--Oh, it did me good to see the way that these brave men worked. How can women help loving men when they are so earnest, and so true, and so brave! And, too, it made me think of the wonderful power of money! What can it not do when basely used. I felt so thankful that Lord Godalming is rich, and both he and Mr. Morris, who also has plenty of money, are willing to spend it so freely. For if they did not, our little expedition could not start, either so promptly or so well equipped, as it will within another hour. It is not three hours since it was arranged what part each of us was to do. And now Lord Godalming and Jonathan have a lovely steam launch, with steam up ready to start at a moment's notice. Dr. Seward and Mr. Morris have half a dozen good horses, well appointed. We have all the maps and appliances of various kinds that can be had. Professor Van Helsing and I are to leave by the 11:40 train tonight for Veresti, where we are to get a carriage to drive to the Borgo Pass. We are bringing a good deal of ready money, as we are to buy a carriage and horses. We shall drive ourselves, for we have no one whom we can trust in the matter. The Professor knows something of a great many languages, so we shall get on all right. We have all got arms, even for me a large bore revolver. Jonathan would not be happy unless I was armed like the rest. Alas! I cannot carry one arm that the rest do, the scar on my forehead forbids that. Dear Dr. Van Helsing comforts me by telling me that I am fully armed as there may be wolves. The weather is getting colder every hour, and there are snow flurries which come and go as warnings.

Later.--It took all my courage to say goodbye to my darling. We may never meet again. Courage, Mina! The Professor is looking at you keenly. His look is a warning. There must be no tears now, unless it may be that God will let them fall in gladness.

JONATHAN HARKER'S JOURNAL

30 October, night.--I am writing this in the light from the furnace door of the steam launch. Lord Godalming is firing up. He is an experienced hand at the work, as he has had for years a launch of his own on the Thames, and another on the Norfolk Broads. Regarding our plans, we finally decided that Mina's guess was correct, and that if any waterway was chosen for the Count's escape back to his Castle, the Sereth and then the Bistritza at its junction, would be the one. We took it, that somewhere about the 47th degree, north latitude, would be the place chosen for crossing the country between the river and the Carpathians. We have no fear in running at good speed up the river at night. There is plenty of water, and the banks are wide enough apart to make steaming, even in the dark, easy enough. Lord Godalming tells me to sleep for a while, as it is enough for the present for one to be on watch. But I cannot sleep, how can I with the terrible danger hanging over my darling, and her going out into that awful place...

My only comfort is that we are in the hands of God. Only for that faith it would be easier to die than to live, and so be quit of all the trouble. Mr. Morris and Dr. Seward were off on their long ride before we started. They are to keep up the right bank, far enough off to get on higher lands where they can see a good stretch of river and avoid the following of its curves. They have, for the first stages, two men to ride and lead their spare horses, four in all, so as not to excite curiosity. When they dismiss the men, which shall be shortly, they shall themselves look after the horses. It may be necessary for us to join forces. If so they can mount our whole party. One of the saddles has a moveable horn, and can be easily adapted for Mina, if required.

It is a wild adventure we are on. Here, as we are rushing along through the darkness, with the cold from the river seeming to rise up and strike us, with all the mysterious voices of the night around us, it all comes home. We seem to be drifting into unknown places and unknown ways. Into a whole world of dark and dreadful things. Godalming is shutting the furnace door…

31 October.--Still hurrying along. The day has come, and Godalming is sleeping. I am on watch. The morning is bitterly cold, the furnace heat is grateful, though we have heavy fur coats. As yet we have passed only a few open boats, but none of them had on board any box or package of anything like the size of the one we seek. The men were scared every time we turned our electric lamp on them, and fell on their knees and prayed.

1 November, evening.--No news all day. We have found nothing of the kind we seek. We have now passed into the Bistritza, and if we are wrong in our surmise our chance is gone. We have overhauled every boat, big and little. Early this morning, one crew took us for a Government boat, and treated us accordingly. We saw in this a way of smoothing matters, so at Fundu, where the Bistritza runs into the Sereth, we got a Roumanian flag which we now fly conspicuously. With every boat which we have overhauled since then this trick has succeeded. We have had every deference shown to us, and not once any objection to whatever we chose to ask or do. Some of the Slovaks tell us that a big boat passed them, going at more than usual speed as she had a double crew on board. This was before they came to Fundu, so they could not tell us whether the boat turned into the Bistritza or continued on up the Sereth. At Fundu we could not hear of any such boat, so she must have passed there in the night. I am feeling very sleepy. The cold is perhaps beginning to tell upon me, and nature must have rest some time. Godalming insists that he shall keep the first watch. God bless him for all his goodness to poor dear Mina and me.

2 November, morning.--It is broad daylight. That good fellow would not wake me. He says it would have been a sin to, for I slept peacefully and was forgetting my trouble. It seems brutally selfish to me to have slept so long, and let him watch all night, but he was quite right. I am a new man this morning. And, as I sit here and watch him sleeping, I can do all that is necessary both as to minding the engine, steering, and keeping watch. I can feel that my strength and energy are coming back to me. I wonder where Mina is now, and Van Helsing. They should have got to Veresti about noon on Wednesday. It would take them some time to get the carriage and horses. So if they had started and travelled hard, they would be about now at the Borgo Pass. God guide and help them! I am afraid to think what may happen. If we could only go faster. But we cannot. The engines are throbbing and doing their utmost. I wonder how Dr. Seward and Mr. Morris are getting on. There seem to be endless streams running down the mountains into this river, but as none of them are very large, at present, at all events, though they are doubtless terrible in winter and when the snow melts, the horsemen may not have met much obstruction. I hope that before we get to Strasba

we may see them. For if by that time we have not overtaken the Count, it may be necessary to take counsel together what to do next.

DR. SEWARD'S DIARY

2 November.--Three days on the road. No news, and no time to write it if there had been, for every moment is precious. We have had only the rest needful for the horses. But we are both bearing it wonderfully. Those adventurous days of ours are turning up useful. We must push on. We shall never feel happy till we get the launch in sight again.

3 November.--We heard at Fundu that the launch had gone up the Bistritza. I wish it wasn't so cold. There are signs of snow coming. And if it falls heavy it will stop us. In such case we must get a sledge and go on, Russian fashion.

4 November.--Today we heard of the launch having been detained by an accident when trying to force a way up the rapids. The Slovak boats get up all right, by aid of a rope and steering with knowledge. Some went up only a few hours before. Godalming is an amateur fitter himself, and evidently it was he who put the launch in trim again.

Finally, they got up the rapids all right, with local help, and are off on the chase afresh. I fear that the boat is not any better for the accident, the peasantry tell us that after she got upon smooth water again, she kept stopping every now and again so long as she was in sight. We must push on harder than ever. Our help may be wanted soon.

MINA HARKER'S JOURNAL

31 October.--Arrived at Veresti at noon. The Professor tells me that this morning at dawn he could hardly hypnotize me at all, and that all I could say was, "dark and quiet." He is off now buying a carriage and horses. He says that he will later on try to buy additional horses, so that we may be able to change them on the way. We have something more than 70 miles before us. The country is lovely, and most interesting. If only we were under different conditions, how delightful it would be to see it all. If Jonathan and I were driving through it alone what a pleasure it would be. To stop and see people, and learn something of their life, and to fill our minds and memories with all the colour and picturesqueness of the whole wild, beautiful country and the quaint people! But, alas!

Later.--Dr. Van Helsing has returned. He has got the carriage and horses. We are to have some dinner, and to start in an hour. The landlady is putting us up a huge basket of provisions. It seems enough for a company of soldiers. The Professor encourages her, and whispers to me that it may be a week before we can get any food again. He has been shopping too, and has sent home such a wonderful lot of fur coats and wraps, and all sorts of warm things. There will not be any chance of our being cold.

We shall soon be off. I am afraid to think what may happen to us. We are truly in the hands of God. He alone knows what may be, and I pray Him, with all the strength of my sad and humble soul, that He will watch over my beloved husband. That whatever may happen, Jonathan may know that I loved him and honoured him more than I can say, and that my latest and truest thought will be always for him.

CHAPTER 27

MINA HARKER'S JOURNAL

1 November.--All day long we have travelled, and at a good speed. The horses seem to know that they are being kindly treated, for they go willingly their full stage at best speed. We have now had so many changes and find the same thing so constantly that we are encouraged to think that the journey will be an easy one. Dr. Van Helsing is laconic, he tells the farmers that he is hurrying to Bistritz, and pays them well to make the exchange of horses. We get hot soup, or coffee, or tea, and off we go. It is a lovely country. Full of beauties of all imaginable kinds, and the people are brave, and strong, and simple, and seem full of nice qualities. They are very, very superstitious. In the first house where we stopped, when the woman who served us saw the scar on my forehead, she crossed herself and put out two fingers towards me, to keep off the evil eye. I believe they went to the trouble of putting an extra amount of garlic into our food, and I can't abide garlic. Ever since then I have taken care not to take off my hat or veil, and so have escaped their suspicions. We are travelling fast, and as we have no driver with us to carry tales, we go ahead of scandal. But I daresay that fear of the evil eye will follow hard behind us all the way. The Professor seems tireless. All day he would not take any rest, though he made me sleep for a long spell. At sunset time he hypnotized me, and he says I answered as usual, "darkness, lapping water and creaking wood." So our enemy is still on the river. I am afraid to think of Jonathan, but somehow I have now no fear for him, or for myself. I write this whilst we wait in a farmhouse for the horses to be ready. Dr. Van Helsing is sleeping. Poor dear, he looks very tired and old and grey, but his mouth is set as firmly as a conqueror's. Even in his sleep he is intense with resolution. When we have well started I must make him rest whilst I drive. I shall tell him that we have days before us, and he must not break down when most of all his strength will be needed... All is ready. We are off shortly.

2 November, morning.--I was successful, and we took turns driving all night. Now the day is on us, bright though cold. There is a strange heaviness in the air. I say heaviness for want of a better word. I mean that it oppresses us both. It is very cold, and only our warm furs keep us comfortable. At dawn Van Helsing hypnotized me. He says I answered "darkness, creaking wood and roaring water," so the river is changing as they ascend. I do hope that my darling will not run any chance of danger, more than need be, but we are in God's hands.

2 November, night.--All day long driving. The country gets wilder as we go, and the great spurs of the Carpathians, which at Veresti seemed so far from us and so low on the horizon, now seem to gather round us and tower in front. We both seem in good spirits. I think we make an effort each to cheer the other, in the doing so we cheer ourselves. Dr. Van Helsing says that by morning we shall reach the Borgo Pass. The houses are very few here now, and the Professor says that the last horse we got will have to go on with us, as we may not be able to change. He got two in addition to the two we changed, so that now we have a rude four-in-hand. The dear horses are patient and good, and they give us no trouble. We are not worried with other travellers, and so even I can drive. We shall get to the Pass in daylight. We do not want to arrive before. So we take it easy, and have each a long rest in turn. Oh, what will tomorrow bring to us? We go to seek the place where my poor darling suffered so much. God grant that we may be guided aright, and that He will deign to watch over my husband and those dear to us both, and who are in such deadly peril. As for me, I am not worthy in His sight. Alas! I am unclean to His eyes, and shall be until He may deign to let me stand forth in His sight as one of those who have not incurred His wrath.

MEMORANDUM BY ABRAHAM VAN HELSING

4 November.--This to my old and true friend John Seward, M.D., of Purfleet, London, in case I may not see him. It may explain. It is morning, and I write by a fire which all the night I have kept alive, Madam Mina aiding me. It is cold, cold. So cold that the grey heavy sky is full of snow, which when it falls will settle for all winter as the ground is hardening to receive it. It seems to have affected Madam Mina. She has been so heavy of head all day that she was not like herself. She sleeps, and sleeps, and sleeps! She who is usual so alert, have done literally nothing all the day. She even have lost her appetite. She make no entry into her little diary, she who write so faithful at every pause. Something whisper to me that all is not well. However, tonight she is more *vif*. Her long sleep all day have refresh and restore her, for now she is all sweet and bright as ever. At sunset I try to hypnotize her, but alas! with no effect. The power has grown less and less with each day, and tonight it fail me altogether. Well, God's will be done, whatever it may be, and whithersoever it may lead!

Now to the historical, for as Madam Mina write not in her stenography, I must, in my cumbrous old fashion, that so each day of us may not go unrecorded.

We got to the Borgo Pass just after sunrise yesterday morning. When I saw the signs of the dawn I got ready for the hypnotism. We stopped our carriage, and got down so that there might be no disturbance. I made a couch with furs, and Madam Mina, lying down, yield herself as usual, but more slow and more short time than ever, to the hypnotic sleep. As before, came the answer, "darkness and the swirling of water." Then she woke, bright and radiant and we go on our way and soon reach the Pass. At this time and place, she become all on fire with zeal. Some new guiding power be in her manifested, for she point to a road and say, "This is the way."

"How know you it?" I ask.

"Of course I know it," she answer, and with a pause, add, "Have not my Jonathan travelled it and wrote of his travel?"

CHAPTER 27

At first I think somewhat strange, but soon I see that there be only one such by-road. It is used but little, and very different from the coach road from the Bukovina to Bistritz, which is more wide and hard, and more of use.

So we came down this road. When we meet other ways, not always were we sure that they were roads at all, for they be neglect and light snow have fallen, the horses know and they only. I give rein to them, and they go on so patient. By and by we find all the things which Jonathan have note in that wonderful diary of him. Then we go on for long, long hours and hours. At the first, I tell Madam Mina to sleep. She try, and she succeed. She sleep all the time, till at the last, I feel myself to suspicious grow, and attempt to wake her. But she sleep on, and I may not wake her though I try. I do not wish to try too hard lest I harm her. For I know that she have suffer much, and sleep at times be all-in-all to her. I think I drowse myself, for all of sudden I feel guilt, as though I have done something. I find myself bolt up, with the reins in my hand, and the good horses go along jog, jog, just as ever. I look down and find Madam Mina still asleep. It is now not far off sunset time, and over the snow the light of the sun flow in big yellow flood, so that we throw great long shadow on where the mountain rise so steep. For we are going up, and up, and all is oh so wild and rocky, as though it were the end of the world.

Then I arouse Madam Mina. This time she wake with not much trouble, and then I try to put her to hypnotic sleep. But she sleep not, being as though I were not. Still I try and try, till all at once I find her and myself in dark, so I look round, and find that the sun have gone down. Madam Mina laugh, and I turn and look at her. She is now quite awake, and look so well as I never saw her since that night at Carfax when we first enter the Count's house. I am amaze, and not at ease then. But she is so bright and tender and thoughtful for me that I forget all fear. I light a fire, for we have brought supply of wood with us, and she prepare food while I undo the horses and set them, tethered in shelter, to feed. Then when I return to the fire she have my supper ready. I go to help her, but she smile, and tell me that she have eat already. That she was so hungry that she would not wait. I like it not, and I have grave doubts. But I fear to affright her, and so I am silent of it. She help me and I eat alone, and then we wrap in fur and lie beside the fire, and I tell her to sleep while I watch. But presently I forget all of watching. And when I sudden remember that I watch, I find her lying quiet, but awake, and looking at me with so bright eyes. Once, twice more the same occur, and I get much sleep till before morning. When I wake I try to hypnotize her, but alas! though she shut her eyes obedient, she may not sleep. The sun rise up, and up, and up, and then sleep come to her too late, but so heavy that she will not wake. I have to lift her up, and place her sleeping in the carriage when I have harnessed the horses and made all ready. Madam still sleep, and she look in her sleep more healthy and more redder than before. And I like it not. And I am afraid, afraid, afraid! I am afraid of all things, even to think but I must go on my way. The stake we play for is life and death, or more than these, and we must not flinch.

5 November, morning.--Let me be accurate in everything, for though you and I have seen some strange things together, you may at the first think that I, Van Helsing, am mad. That the many horrors and the so long strain on nerves has at the last turn my brain.

All yesterday we travel, always getting closer to the mountains, and moving into a more and more wild and desert land. There are great, frowning precipices and much falling water, and Nature seem to have held sometime her carnival. Madam Mina still sleep and sleep. And though I did have hunger and appeased it, I could not waken her, even for food. I began to fear that the fatal spell of the place was upon her, tainted as she is with that Vampire baptism. "Well," said I to myself, "if it be that she sleep all the day, it shall also be that I do not sleep at night." As we travel on the rough road, for a road of an ancient and imperfect kind there was, I held down my head and slept.

Again I waked with a sense of guilt and of time passed, and found Madam Mina still sleeping, and the sun low down. But all was indeed changed. The frowning mountains seemed further away, and we were near the top of a steep rising hill, on summit of which was such a castle as Jonathan tell of in his diary. At once I exulted and feared. For now, for good or ill, the end was near.

I woke Madam Mina, and again tried to hypnotize her, but alas! unavailing till too late. Then, ere the great dark came upon us, for even after down sun the heavens reflected the gone sun on the snow, and all was for a time in a great twilight. I took out the horses and fed them in what shelter I could. Then I make a fire, and near it I make Madam Mina, now awake and more charming than ever, sit comfortable amid her rugs. I got ready food, but she would not eat, simply saying that she had not hunger. I did not press her, knowing her unavailingness. But I myself eat, for I must needs now be strong for all. Then, with the fear on me of what might be, I drew a ring so big for her comfort, round where Madam Mina sat. And over the ring I passed some of the wafer, and I broke it fine so that all was well guarded. She sat still all the time, so still as one dead. And she grew whiter and even whiter till the snow was not more pale, and no word she said. But when I drew near, she clung to me, and I could know that the poor soul shook her from head to feet with a tremor that was pain to feel.

I said to her presently, when she had grown more quiet, "Will you not come over to the fire?" for I wished to make a test of what she could. She rose obedient, but when she have made a step she stopped, and stood as one stricken.

"Why not go on?" I asked. She shook her head, and coming back, sat down in her place. Then, looking at me with open eyes, as of one waked from sleep, she said simply, "I cannot!" and remained silent. I rejoiced, for I knew that what she could not, none of those that we dreaded could. Though there might be danger to her body, yet her soul was safe!

Presently the horses began to scream, and tore at their tethers till I came to them and quieted them. When they did feel my hands on them, they whinnied low as in joy, and licked at my hands and were quiet for a time. Many times through the night did I come to them, till it arrive to the cold hour when all nature is at lowest, and every time my coming was with quiet of them. In the cold hour the fire began to die, and I was about stepping forth to replenish it, for now the snow came in flying sweeps and with it a chill mist. Even in the dark there was a light of some kind, as there ever is over snow, and it seemed as though the snow flurries and the wreaths of mist took shape as of women with trailing garments. All was in dead, grim silence only that the horses whinnied and cowered, as if in terror of the worst. I began to fear, horrible fears. But then came to me the sense of safety in that ring wherein I stood. I began too, to think that my imaginings were of the night, and the gloom, and the unrest that I have gone through, and all the terrible anxiety. It was as though my memories of all Jonathan's horrid experience were befooling me. For the snow flakes and the mist began to wheel and circle round, till I could get as though a shadowy glimpse of those women that would have kissed him. And then the horses cowered lower and lower, and moaned in terror as men do in pain. Even the madness of fright was not to them, so that they could break away. I feared for my dear Madam Mina when these weird figures drew near and circled round. I looked at her, but she sat calm, and smiled at me. When I would have stepped to the fire to replenish it, she caught me and held me back, and whispered, like a voice that one hears in a dream, so low it was.

"No! No! Do not go without. Here you are safe!"

I turned to her, and looking in her eyes said, "But you? It is for you that I fear!"

Whereat she laughed, a laugh low and unreal, and said, "Fear for me! Why fear for me? None safer in all the world from them than I am," and as I wondered at the meaning of her words, a puff of wind made the flame leap up, and I see the red scar on her forehead. Then, alas! I knew. Did I not, I would soon have learned, for the wheeling figures of mist and snow came closer, but keeping ever without the Holy circle. Then they began to materialize till, if God have not taken away my reason, for I saw it through my eyes. There were before me in actual flesh the same three women that Jonathan saw in the room, when they would have kissed his throat. I knew the swaying round forms, the bright hard eyes, the white teeth, the ruddy colour, the voluptuous lips. They smiled ever at poor dear Madam Mina. And as their laugh came through the silence of the night, they twined their arms and pointed to her, and said in those so sweet tingling tones that Jonathan said were of the intolerable sweetness of the water glasses, "Come, sister. Come to us. Come!"

In fear I turned to my poor Madam Mina, and my heart with gladness leapt like flame. For oh! the terror in her sweet eyes, the repulsion, the horror, told a story to my heart that was all of hope. God be thanked she was not, yet, of them. I seized some of the firewood which was by me, and holding out some of the Wafer, advanced on them towards the fire. They drew back before me, and laughed their low horrid laugh. I fed the fire, and feared them not. For I knew that we were safe within the ring, which she could not leave no more than they could enter. The horses had ceased to moan, and lay still on the ground. The snow fell on them softly, and they grew whiter. I knew that there was for the poor beasts no more of terror.

And so we remained till the red of the dawn began to fall through the snow gloom. I was desolate and afraid, and full of woe and terror. But when that beautiful sun began to climb the horizon life was to me again. At the first coming of the dawn the horrid figures melted in the whirling mist and snow. The wreaths of transparent gloom moved away towards the castle, and were lost.

Instinctively, with the dawn coming, I turned to Madam Mina, intending to hypnotize her. But she lay in a deep and sudden sleep, from which I could not wake her. I tried to hypnotize through her sleep, but she made no response, none at all, and the day broke. I fear yet to stir. I have made my fire and have seen the horses, they are all dead. Today I have much to do here, and I keep waiting till the sun is up high. For there may be places where I must go, where that sunlight, though snow and mist obscure it, will be to me a safety.

I will strengthen me with breakfast, and then I will do my terrible work. Madam Mina still sleeps, and God be thanked! She is calm in her sleep…

JONATHAN HARKER'S JOURNAL

4 November, evening.--The accident to the launch has been a terrible thing for us. Only for it we should have overtaken the boat long ago, and by now my dear Mina would have been free. I fear to think of her, off on the wolds near that horrid place. We have got horses, and we follow on the track. I note this whilst Godalming is getting ready. We have our arms. The Szgany must look out if they mean to fight. Oh, if only Morris and Seward were with us. We must only hope! If I write no more Goodby Mina! God bless and keep you.

DR. SEWARD'S DIARY

5 November.--With the dawn we saw the body of Szgany before us dashing away from the river with their leiter wagon. They surrounded it in a cluster, and hurried along as though beset. The snow is falling lightly and there is a strange excitement in the air. It may be our own feelings, but the depression is strange. Far off I hear the howling of wolves. The snow brings them down from the mountains, and there are dangers to all of us, and from all sides. The horses are nearly ready, and we are soon off. We ride to death of some one. God alone knows who, or where, or what, or when, or how it may be…

DR. VAN HELSING'S MEMORANDUM

5 November, afternoon.--I am at least sane. Thank God for that mercy at all events, though the proving it has been dreadful. When I left Madam Mina sleeping within the Holy circle, I took my way to the castle. The blacksmith hammer which I took in the carriage from Veresti was useful, though the doors were all open I broke them off the rusty hinges, lest some ill intent or ill chance should close them, so that being entered I might not get out. Jonathan's bitter experience served me here. By memory of his diary I found my way to the old chapel, for I knew that here my work lay. The air was oppressive. It seemed as if there was some sulphurous fume, which at times made me dizzy. Either there was a roaring in my ears or I heard afar off the howl of wolves. Then I bethought me of my dear Madam Mina, and I was in terrible plight. The dilemma had me between his horns.

Her, I had not dare to take into this place, but left safe from the Vampire in that Holy circle. And yet even there would be the wolf! I resolve me that my work lay here, and that as to the wolves we must submit, if it were God's will. At any rate it was only death and freedom beyond. So did I choose for her. Had it but been for myself the choice had been easy, the maw of the wolf were better to rest in than the grave of the Vampire! So I make my choice to go on with my work.

I knew that there were at least three graves to find, graves that are inhabit. So I search, and search, and I find one of them. She lay in her Vampire sleep, so full of life and voluptuous beauty that I shudder as though I have come to do murder. Ah, I doubt not that in the old time, when such things were, many a man who set forth to do such a task as mine, found at the last his heart fail him, and then his nerve. So he delay, and delay, and delay, till the mere beauty and the fascination of the wanton Undead have hypnotize him. And he remain on and on, till sunset come, and the Vampire sleep be over. Then the beautiful eyes of the fair woman open and look love, and the voluptuous mouth present to a kiss, and the man is weak. And there remain one more victim in the Vampire fold. One more to swell the grim and grisly ranks of the Undead!...

There is some fascination, surely, when I am moved by the mere presence of such an one, even lying as she lay in a tomb fretted with age and heavy with the dust of centuries, though there be that horrid odour such as the lairs of the Count have had. Yes, I was moved. I, Van Helsing, with all my purpose and with my motive for hate. I was moved to a yearning for delay which seemed to paralyze my faculties and to clog my very soul. It may have been that the need of natural sleep, and the strange oppression of the air were beginning to overcome me. Certain it was that I was lapsing into sleep, the open eyed sleep of one who yields to a sweet fascination, when there came through the snow-stilled air a long, low wail, so full of woe and pity that it woke me like the sound of a clarion. For it was the voice of my dear Madam Mina that I heard.

Then I braced myself again to my horrid task, and found by wrenching away tomb tops one other of the sisters, the other dark one. I dared not pause to look on her as I had on her sister, lest once more I should begin to be enthrall. But I go on searching until, presently, I find in a high great tomb as if made to one much beloved that other fair sister which, like Jonathan I had seen to gather herself out of the atoms of the mist. She was so fair to look on, so radiantly beautiful, so exquisitely voluptuous, that the very instinct of man in me, which calls some of my sex to love and to protect one of hers, made my head whirl with new emotion. But God be thanked, that soul wail of my dear Madam Mina had not died out of my ears. And, before the spell could be wrought further upon me, I had nerved myself to my wild work. By this time I had searched all the tombs in the chapel, so far as I could tell. And as there had been only three of these Undead phantoms around us in the night, I took it that there were no more of active Undead existent. There was one great tomb more lordly than all the rest. Huge it was, and nobly proportioned. On it was but one word.

DRACULA

This then was the Undead home of the King Vampire, to whom so many more were due. Its emptiness spoke eloquent to make certain what I knew. Before I began to restore these women to their dead selves through my awful work, I laid in Dracula's tomb some of the Wafer, and so banished him from it, Undead, for ever.

Then began my terrible task, and I dreaded it. Had it been but one, it had been easy, comparative. But three! To begin twice more after I had been through a deed of horror. For it was terrible with the sweet Miss Lucy, what would it not be with these strange ones who had survived through centuries, and who had been strengthened by the passing of the years. Who would, if they could, have fought for their foul lives...

Oh, my friend John, but it was butcher work. Had I not been nerved by thoughts of other dead, and of the living over whom hung such a pall of fear, I could not have gone on. I tremble and tremble even yet, though till all was over, God be thanked, my nerve did stand. Had I not seen the repose in the first place, and the gladness that stole over it just ere the final dissolution came, as realization that the soul had been won, I could not have gone further with my butchery. I could not have endured the horrid screeching as the stake drove home, the plunging of writhing form, and lips of bloody foam. I should have fled in terror and left my work undone. But it is over! And the poor souls, I can pity them now and weep, as I think of them placid each in her full sleep of death for a short moment ere fading. For, friend John, hardly had my knife severed the head of each, before the whole body began to melt away and crumble into its native dust, as though the death that should have come centuries ago had at last assert himself and say at once and loud, "I am here!"

Before I left the castle I so fixed its entrances that never more can the Count enter there Undead.

When I stepped into the circle where Madam Mina slept, she woke from her sleep and, seeing me, cried out in pain that I had endured too much.

"Come!" she said, "come away from this awful place! Let us go to meet my husband who is, I know, coming towards us." She was looking thin and pale and weak. But her eyes were pure and glowed with fervour. I was glad to see her paleness and her illness, for my mind was full of the fresh horror of that ruddy vampire sleep.

And so with trust and hope, and yet full of fear, we go eastward to meet our friends, and him, whom Madam Mina tell me that she know are coming to meet us.

MINA HARKER'S JOURNAL

6 November.--It was late in the afternoon when the Professor and I took our way towards the east whence I knew Jonathan was coming. We did not go fast, though the way was steeply downhill, for we had to take heavy rugs and wraps with us. We dared not face the possibility of being left without warmth in the cold and the snow. We had to take some of our provisions too, for we were in a perfect desolation, and so far as we could see through the snowfall, there was not even the sign of habitation. When we had gone about a mile, I was tired with the heavy walking and sat down to rest. Then we looked back and saw where the clear line of Dracula's castle cut the sky. For we were so deep under the hill whereon it was set that the angle of perspective of the Carpathian mountains was far below it. We saw it in all its grandeur, perched a thousand feet on the summit of a sheer precipice, and with seemingly a great gap between it and the steep of the adjacent mountain on any side. There was something wild and uncanny about the place. We could hear the distant howling of wolves. They were far off, but the sound, even though coming muffled through the deadening snowfall, was full of terror. I knew from the way Dr. Van Helsing was searching about that he was trying to seek some strategic point, where we would be less exposed in case of attack. The rough roadway still led downwards. We could trace it through the drifted snow.

In a little while the Professor signalled to me, so I got up and joined him. He had found a wonderful spot, a sort of natural hollow in a rock, with an entrance like a doorway between two boulders. He took me by the hand and drew me in.

"See!" he said, "here you will be in shelter. And if the wolves do come I can meet them one by one."

He brought in our furs, and made a snug nest for me, and got out some provisions and forced them upon me. But I could not eat, to even try to do so was repulsive to me, and much as I would have liked to please him, I could not bring myself to the attempt. He looked very sad, but did not reproach me. Taking his field glasses from the case, he stood on the top of the rock, and began to search the horizon.

Suddenly he called out, "Look! Madam Mina, look! Look!"

I sprang up and stood beside him on the rock. He handed me his glasses and pointed. The snow was now falling more heavily, and swirled about fiercely, for a high wind was beginning to blow. However, there were times when there were pauses between the snow flurries and I could see a long way round. From the height where we were it was possible to see a great distance. And far off, beyond the white waste of snow, I could see the river lying like a black ribbon in kinks and curls as it wound its way. Straight in front of us and not far off, in fact so near that I wondered we had not noticed before, came a group of mounted men hurrying along. In the midst of them was a cart, a long leiter wagon which swept from side to side, like a dog's tail wagging, with each stern inequality of the road. Outlined against the snow as they were, I could see from the men's clothes that they were peasants or gypsies of some kind.

On the cart was a great square chest. My heart leaped as I saw it, for I felt that the end was coming. The evening was now drawing close, and well I knew that at sunset the Thing, which was till then imprisoned there, would take new freedom and could in any of many forms elude pursuit. In fear I turned to the Professor. To my consternation, however, he was not there. An instant later, I saw him below me. Round the rock he had drawn a circle, such as we had found shelter in last night.

When he had completed it he stood beside me again saying, "At least you shall be safe here from him!" He took the glasses from me, and at the next lull of the snow swept the whole space below us. "See," he said, "they come quickly. They are flogging the horses, and galloping as hard as they can."

He paused and went on in a hollow voice, "They are racing for the sunset. We may be too late. God's will be done!" Down came another blinding rush of driving snow, and the whole landscape was blotted out. It soon passed, however, and once more his glasses were fixed on the plain.

Then came a sudden cry, "Look! Look! Look! See, two horsemen follow fast, coming up from the south. It must be Quincey and John. Take the glass. Look before the snow blots it all out!" I took it and looked. The two men might be Dr. Seward and Mr. Morris. I knew at all events that neither of them was Jonathan. At the same time I knew that Jonathan was not far off. Looking around I saw on the north side of the coming party two other men, riding at breakneck speed. One of them I knew was Jonathan, and the other I took, of course, to be Lord Godalming. They too, were pursuing the party with the cart. When I told the Professor he shouted in glee like a schoolboy, and after looking intently till a snow fall made sight impossible, he laid his Winchester rifle ready for use against the boulder at the opening of our shelter.

"They are all converging," he said. "When the time comes we shall have gypsies on all sides." I got out my revolver ready to hand, for whilst we were speaking the howling of wolves came louder and closer. When the snow storm abated a moment we looked again. It was strange to see the snow falling in such heavy flakes close to us, and beyond, the sun shining more and more brightly as it sank down towards the far mountain tops. Sweeping the glass all around us I could see here and there dots moving singly and in twos and threes and larger numbers. The wolves were gathering for their prey.

Every instant seemed an age whilst we waited. The wind came now in fierce bursts, and the snow was driven with fury as it swept upon us in circling eddies. At times we could not see an arm's length before us. But at others, as the hollow sounding wind swept by us, it seemed to clear the air space around us so that we could see afar off. We had of late been so accustomed to watch for sunrise and sunset, that we knew with fair accuracy when it would be. And we knew that before long the sun would set. It was hard to believe that by our watches it was less than an hour that we waited in that rocky shelter before the various bodies began to converge close upon us. The wind came now with fiercer and more bitter sweeps, and more steadily from the north. It seemingly had driven the snow clouds from us, for with only occasional bursts, the snow fell. We could distinguish clearly the individuals of each party, the pursued and the pursuers. Strangely enough those pursued did not seem to realize, or at least to care, that they were pursued. They seemed, however, to hasten with redoubled speed as the sun dropped lower and lower on the mountain tops.

Closer and closer they drew. The Professor and I crouched down behind our rock, and held our weapons ready. I could see that he was determined that they should not pass. One and all were quite unaware of our presence.

All at once two voices shouted out to "Halt!" One was my Jonathan's, raised in a high key of passion. The other Mr. Morris' strong resolute tone of quiet command. The gypsies may not have known the language, but there was no mistaking the tone, in whatever tongue the words were spoken. Instinctively they reined in, and at the instant Lord Godalming and Jonathan dashed up at one side and Dr. Seward and Mr. Morris on the other. The leader of the gypsies, a splendid looking fellow who sat his horse like a centaur, waved them back, and in a fierce voice gave to his companions some word to proceed. They lashed the horses which sprang forward. But the four men raised their Winchester rifles, and in an unmistakable way commanded them to stop. At the same moment Dr. Van Helsing and I rose behind the rock and pointed our weapons at them. Seeing that they were surrounded the men tightened their reins and drew up. The leader turned to them and gave a word at which every man of the gypsy party drew what weapon he carried, knife or pistol, and held himself in readiness to attack. Issue was joined in an instant.

The leader, with a quick movement of his rein, threw his horse out in front, and pointed first to the sun, now close down on the hill tops, and then to the castle, said something which I did not understand. For answer, all four men of our party threw themselves from their horses and dashed towards the cart. I should have felt terrible fear at seeing Jonathan in such danger, but that the ardor of battle must have been upon me as well as the rest of them. I felt no fear, but only a wild, surging desire to do something. Seeing the quick movement of our parties, the leader of the gypsies gave a command. His men instantly formed round the cart in a sort of undisciplined endeavour, each one shouldering and pushing the other in his eagerness to carry out the order.

In the midst of this I could see that Jonathan on one side of the ring of men, and Quincey on the other, were forcing a way to the cart. It was evident that they were bent on finishing their task before the sun should set. Nothing seemed to stop or even to hinder them. Neither the levelled weapons nor the flashing knives of the gypsies in front, nor the howling of the wolves behind, appeared to even attract their attention. Jonathan's impetuosity, and the manifest singleness of his purpose, seemed to overawe those in front of him. Instinctively they cowered aside and let him pass. In an instant he had jumped upon the cart, and with a strength which seemed incredible, raised the great box, and flung it over the wheel to the ground. In the meantime, Mr. Morris had had to use force to pass through his side of the ring of Szgany. All the time I had been breathlessly watching Jonathan I had, with the tail of my eye, seen him pressing desperately forward, and had seen the knives of the gypsies flash as he won a way through them, and they cut at him. He had parried with his great bowie knife, and at first I thought that he too had come through in safety. But as he sprang beside Jonathan, who had by now jumped from the cart, I could see that with his left hand he was clutching at his side, and that the blood was spurting through his fingers. He did not delay notwithstanding this, for as Jonathan, with desperate energy, attacked one end of the chest, attempting to prize off the lid with his great Kukri knife, he attacked the other frantically with his bowie. Under the efforts of both men the lid began to yield. The nails drew with a screeching sound, and the top of the box was thrown back.

By this time the gypsies, seeing themselves covered by the Winchesters, and at the mercy of Lord Godalming and Dr. Seward, had given in and made no further resistance. The sun was almost down on the mountain tops, and the shadows of the whole group fell upon the snow. I saw the Count lying within the box upon the earth, some of which the rude falling from the cart had scattered over him. He was deathly pale, just like a waxen image, and the red eyes glared with the horrible vindictive look which I knew so well.

As I looked, the eyes saw the sinking sun, and the look of hate in them turned to triumph.

But, on the instant, came the sweep and flash of Jonathan's great knife. I shrieked as I saw it shear through the throat. Whilst at the same moment Mr. Morris's bowie knife plunged into the heart.

It was like a miracle, but before our very eyes, and almost in the drawing of a breath, the whole body crumbled into dust and passed from our sight.

I shall be glad as long as I live that even in that moment of final dissolution, there was in the face a look of peace, such as I never could have imagined might have rested there.

The Castle of Dracula now stood out against the red sky, and every stone of its broken battlements was articulated against the light of the setting sun.

The gypsies, taking us as in some way the cause of the extraordinary disappearance of the dead man, turned, without a word, and rode away as if for their lives. Those who were unmounted jumped upon the leiter wagon and shouted to the horsemen not to desert them. The wolves, which had withdrawn to a safe distance, followed in their wake, leaving us alone.

Mr. Morris, who had sunk to the ground, leaned on his elbow, holding his hand pressed to his side. The blood still gushed through his fingers. I flew to him, for the Holy circle did not now keep me back; so did the two doctors. Jonathan knelt behind him and the wounded man laid back his head on his shoulder. With a sigh he took, with a feeble effort, my hand in that of his own which was unstained.

He must have seen the anguish of my heart in my face, for he smiled at me and said, "I am only too happy to have been of service! Oh, God!" he cried suddenly, struggling to a sitting posture and pointing to me. "It was worth for this to die! Look! Look!"

The sun was now right down upon the mountain top, and the red gleams fell upon my face, so that it was bathed in rosy light. With one impulse the men sank on their knees and a deep and earnest "Amen" broke from all as their eyes followed the pointing of his finger.

The dying man spoke, "Now God be thanked that all has not been in vain! See! The snow is not more stainless than her forehead! The curse has passed away!"

And, to our bitter grief, with a smile and in silence, he died, a gallant gentleman.

NOTE

Seven years ago we all went through the flames. And the happiness of some of us since then is, we think, well worth the pain we endured. It is an added joy to Mina and to me that our boy's birthday is the same day as that on which Quincey Morris died. His mother holds, I know, the secret belief that some of our brave friend's spirit has passed into him. His bundle of names links all our little band of men together. But we call him Quincey.

In the summer of this year we made a journey to Transylvania, and went over the old ground which was, and is, to us so full of vivid and terrible memories. It was almost impossible to believe that the things which we had seen with our own eyes and heard with our own ears were living truths. Every trace of all that had been was blotted out. The castle stood as before, reared high above a waste of desolation.

When we got home we were talking of the old time, which we could all look back on without despair, for Godalming and Seward are both happily married. I took the papers from the safe where they had been ever since our return so long ago. We were struck with the fact, that in all the mass of material of which the record is composed, there is hardly one authentic document. Nothing but a mass of typewriting, except the later notebooks of Mina and Seward and myself, and Van Helsing's memorandum. We could hardly ask any one, even did we wish to, to accept these as proofs of so wild a story. Van Helsing summed it all up as he said, with our boy on his knee.

"We want no proofs. We ask none to believe us! This boy will some day know what a brave and gallant woman his mother is. Already he knows her sweetness and loving care. Later on he will understand how some men so loved her, that they did dare much for her sake."

JONATHAN HARKER

THE JEWEL OF SEVEN STARS

To Eleanor and Constance Hoyt

Chapter I - A Summons in the Night

It all seemed so real that I could hardly imagine that it had ever occurred before; and yet each episode came, not as a fresh step in the logic of things, but as something expected. It is in such a wise that memory plays its pranks for good or ill; for pleasure or pain; for weal or woe. It is thus that life is bittersweet, and that which has been done becomes eternal.

Again, the light skiff, ceasing to shoot through the lazy water as when the oars flashed and dripped, glided out of the fierce July sunlight into the cool shade of the great drooping willow branches—I standing up in the swaying boat, she sitting still and with deft fingers guarding herself from stray twigs or the freedom of the resilience of moving boughs. Again, the water looked golden-brown under the canopy of translucent green; and the grassy bank was of emerald hue. Again, we sat in the cool shade, with the myriad noises of nature both without and within our bower merging into that drowsy hum in whose sufficing environment the great world with its disturbing trouble, and its more disturbing joys, can be effectually forgotten. Again, in that blissful solitude the young girl lost the convention of her prim, narrow upbringing, and told me in a natural, dreamy way of the loneliness of her new life. With an undertone of sadness she made me feel how in that spacious home each one of the household was isolated by the personal magnificence of her father and herself; that there confidence had no altar, and sympathy no shrine; and that there even her father's face was as distant as the old country life seemed now. Once more, the wisdom of my manhood and the experience of my years laid themselves at the girl's feet. It was seemingly their own doing; for the individual "I" had no say in the matter, but only just obeyed imperative orders. And once again the flying seconds multiplied themselves endlessly. For it is in the arcana of dreams that existences merge and renew themselves, change and yet keep the same—like the soul of a musician in a fugue. And so memory swooned, again and again, in sleep.

It seems that there is never to be any perfect rest. Even in Eden the snake rears its head among the laden boughs of the Tree of Knowledge. The silence of the dreamless night is broken by the roar of the avalanche; the hissing of sudden floods; the clanging of the engine bell marking its sweep through a sleeping American town; the clanking of distant paddles over the sea.... Whatever it is, it is breaking the charm of my Eden. The canopy of greenery above us, starred with diamond-points of light, seems to quiver in the ceaseless beat of paddles; and the restless bell seems as though it would never cease....

All at once the gates of Sleep were thrown wide open, and my waking ears took in the cause of the disturbing sounds. Waking existence is prosaic enough—there was somebody knocking and ringing at someone's street door.

I was pretty well accustomed in my Jermyn Street chambers to passing sounds; usually I did not concern myself, sleeping or waking, with the doings, however noisy, of my neighbours. But this noise was too continuous, too insistent, too imperative to be ignored. There was some active intelligence behind that ceaseless sound; and some stress or need behind the intelligence. I was not altogether selfish, and at the thought of someone's need I was, without premeditation, out of bed. Instinctively I looked at my watch. It was just three o'clock; there was a faint edging of grey round the green blind which darkened my room. It was evident that the knocking and ringing were at the door of our own house; and it was evident, too, that there was no one awake to answer the call. I slipped on my dressing-gown and slippers, and went down to the hall door. When I opened it there stood a dapper groom, with one hand pressed unflinchingly on the electric bell whilst with the other he raised a ceaseless clangour with the knocker. The instant he saw me the noise ceased; one hand went up instinctively to the brim of his hat, and the other produced a letter from his pocket. A neat brougham was opposite the door, the horses were breathing heavily as though they had come fast. A policeman, with his night lantern still alight at his belt, stood by, attracted to the spot by the noise.

"Beg pardon, sir, I'm sorry for disturbing you, but my orders was imperative; I was not to lose a moment, but to knock and ring till someone came. May I ask you, sir, if Mr. Malcolm Ross lives here?"

"I am Mr. Malcolm Ross."

"Then this letter is for you, sir, and the bro'am is for you too, sir!"

I took, with a strange curiosity, the letter which he handed to me. As a barrister I had had, of course, odd experiences now and then, including sudden demands upon my time; but never anything like this. I stepped back into the hall, closing the door to, but leaving it ajar; then I switched on the electric light. The letter was directed in a strange hand, a woman's. It began at once without "dear sir" or any such address:

"You said you would like to help me if I needed it; and I believe you meant what you said. The time has come sooner than I expected. I am in dreadful trouble, and do not know where to turn, or to whom to apply. An attempt has, I fear, been made to murder my Father; though, thank God, he still lives. But he is quite unconscious. The doctors and police have been sent for; but there is no one here whom I can depend on. Come at once if you are able to; and forgive me if you can. I suppose I shall realise later what I have done in asking such a favour; but at present I cannot think. Come! Come at once! MARGARET TRELAWNY."

Pain and exultation struggled in my mind as I read; but the mastering thought was that she was in trouble and had called on me—me! My dreaming of her, then, was not altogether without a cause. I called out to the groom:

"Wait! I shall be with you in a minute!" Then I flew upstairs.

A very few minutes sufficed to wash and dress; and we were soon driving through the streets as fast as the horses could go. It was market morning, and when we got out on Piccadilly there was an endless stream of carts coming from the west; but for the rest the roadway was clear, and we went quickly. I had told the groom to come into the brougham with me so that he could tell me what had happened as we went along. He sat awkwardly, with his hat on his knees as he spoke.

"Miss Trelawny, sir, sent a man to tell us to get out a carriage at once; and when we was ready she come herself and gave me the letter and told Morgan—the coachman, sir—to fly. She said as I was to lose not a second, but to keep knocking till someone come."

"Yes, I know, I know—you told me! What I want to know is, why she sent for me. What happened in the house?"

"I don't quite know myself, sir; except that master was found in his room senseless, with the sheets all bloody, and a wound on his head. He couldn't be waked nohow. Twas Miss Trelawny herself as found him."

"How did she come to find him at such an hour? It was late in the night, I suppose?"

"I don't know, sir; I didn't hear nothing at all of the details."

As he could tell me no more, I stopped the carriage for a moment to let him get out on the box; then I turned the matter over in my mind as I sat alone. There were many things which I could have asked the servant; and for a few moments after he had gone I was angry with myself for not having used my opportunity. On second thought, however, I was glad the temptation was gone. I felt that it would be more delicate to learn what I wanted to know of Miss Trelawny's surroundings from herself, rather than from her servants.

We bowled swiftly along Knightsbridge, the small noise of our well-appointed vehicle sounding hollowly in the morning air. We turned up the Kensington Palace Road and presently stopped opposite a great house on the left-hand side, nearer, so far as I could judge, the Notting Hill than the Kensington end of the avenue. It was a truly fine house, not only with regard to size but to architecture. Even in the dim grey light of the morning, which tends to diminish the size of things, it looked big.

Miss Trelawny met me in the hall. She was not in any way shy. She seemed to rule all around her with a sort of high-bred dominance, all the more remarkable as she was greatly agitated and as pale as snow. In the great hall were several servants, the men standing together near the hall door, and the women clinging together in the further corners and doorways. A police superintendent had been talking to Miss Trelawny; two men in uniform and one plain-clothes man stood near him. As she took my hand impulsively there was a look of relief in her eyes, and she gave a gentle sigh of relief. Her salutation was simple.

"I knew you would come!"

The clasp of the hand can mean a great deal, even when it is not intended to mean anything especially. Miss Trelawny's hand somehow became lost in my own. It was not that it was a small hand; it was fine and flexible, with long delicate fingers—a rare and beautiful hand; it was the unconscious self-surrender. And though at the moment I could not dwell on the cause of the thrill which swept me, it came back to me later.

She turned and said to the police superintendent:

"This is Mr. Malcolm Ross." The police officer saluted as he answered:

"I know Mr. Malcolm Ross, miss. Perhaps he will remember I had the honour of working with him in the Brixton Coining case." I had not at first glance noticed who it was, my whole attention having been taken with Miss Trelawny.

"Of course, Superintendent Dolan, I remember very well!" I said as we shook hands. I could not but note that the acquaintanceship seemed a relief to Miss Trelawny. There was a certain vague uneasiness in her manner which took my attention; instinctively I felt that it would be less embarrassing for her to speak with me alone. So I said to the Superintendent:

"Perhaps it will be better if Miss Trelawny will see me alone for a few minutes. You, of course, have already heard all she knows; and I shall understand better how things are if I may ask some questions. I will then talk the matter over with you if I may."

"I shall be glad to be of what service I can, sir," he answered heartily.

Following Miss Trelawny, I moved over to a dainty room which opened from the hall and looked out on the garden at the back of the house. When we had entered and I had closed the door she said:

"I will thank you later for your goodness in coming to me in my trouble; but at present you can best help me when you know the facts."

"Go on," I said. "Tell me all you know and spare no detail, however trivial it may at the present time seem to be." She went on at once:

"I was awakened by some sound; I do not know what. I only know that it came through my sleep; for all at once I found myself awake, with my heart beating wildly, listening anxiously for some sound from my Father's room. My room is next Father's, and I can often hear him moving about before I fall asleep. He works late at night, sometimes very late indeed; so that when I wake early, as I do occasionally, or in the grey of the dawn, I hear him still moving. I tried once to remonstrate with him about staying up so late, as it cannot be good for him; but I never ventured to repeat the experiment. You know how stern and cold he can be—at least you may remember what I told you about him; and when he is polite in this mood he is dreadful. When he is angry I can bear it much better; but when he is slow and deliberate, and the side of his mouth lifts up to show the sharp teeth, I think I feel—well, I don't know how! Last night I got up softly and stole to the door, for I really feared to disturb him. There was not any noise of moving, and no kind of cry at all; but there was a queer kind of dragging sound, and a slow, heavy breathing. Oh! it was dreadful, waiting there in the dark and the silence, and fearing—fearing I did not know what!

"At last I took my courage a deux mains, and turning the handle as softly as I could, I opened the door a tiny bit. It was quite dark within; I could just see the outline of the windows. But in the darkness the sound of breathing, becoming more distinct, was appalling. As I listened, this continued; but there was no other sound. I pushed the door open all at once. I was afraid to open it slowly; I felt as if there might be some dreadful thing behind it ready to pounce out on me! Then I switched on the electric light, and stepped into the room. I looked first at the bed. The sheets were all crumpled up, so that I knew Father had been in bed; but there was a great dark red patch in the centre of the bed, and spreading to the edge of it, that made my heart stand still. As I was gazing at it the sound of the breathing came across the room, and my eyes followed to it. There was Father on his right side with the other arm under him, just as if his dead body had been thrown there all in a heap. The track of blood went across the room up to the bed, and there was a pool all around him which looked terribly red and glittering as I bent over to examine him. The place where he lay was right in front of the big safe. He was in his pyjamas. The left sleeve was torn, showing his bare arm, and stretched out toward the safe. It looked—oh! so terrible, patched all with blood, and with the flesh torn or cut all around a gold chain bangle on his wrist. I did not know he wore such a thing, and it seemed to give me a new shock of surprise."

She paused a moment; and as I wished to relieve her by a moment's divergence of thought, I said:

"Oh, that need not surprise you. You will see the most unlikely men wearing bangles. I have seen a judge condemn a man to death, and the wrist of the hand he held up had a gold bangle." She did not seem to heed much the words or the idea; the pause, however, relieved her somewhat, and she went on in a steadier voice:

"I did not lose a moment in summoning aid, for I feared he might bleed to death. I rang the bell, and then went out and called for help as loudly as I could. In what must have been a very short time—though it seemed an incredibly long one to me—some of the servants came running up; and then others, till the room seemed full of staring eyes, and dishevelled hair, and night clothes of all sorts.

"We lifted Father on a sofa; and the housekeeper, Mrs. Grant, who seemed to have her wits about her more than any of us, began to look where the flow of blood came from. In a few seconds it became apparent that it came from the arm which was bare. There was a deep wound—not clean-cut as with a knife, but like a jagged rent or tear—close to the wrist, which seemed to have cut into the vein. Mrs. Grant tied a handkerchief round the cut, and screwed it up tight with a silver paper-cutter; and the flow of blood seemed to be checked at once. By this time I had come to my senses—or such of them as remained; and I sent off one man for the doctor and another for the police. When they had gone, I felt that, except for the servants, I was all alone in the house, and that I knew nothing—of my Father or anything else; and a great longing came to me to have someone with me who could help me. Then I thought of you and your kind offer in the boat under the willow-tree; and, without waiting to think, I told the men to get a carriage ready at once, and I scribbled a note and sent it on to you."

She paused. I did not like to say just then anything of how I felt. I looked at her; I think she understood, for her eyes were raised to mine for a moment and then fell, leaving her cheeks as red as peony roses. With a manifest effort she went on with her story:

"The Doctor was with us in an incredibly short time. The groom had met him letting himself into his house with his latchkey, and he came here running. He made a proper tourniquet for poor Father's arm, and then went home to get some appliances. I dare say he will be back almost immediately. Then a policeman came, and sent a message to the station; and very soon the Superintendent was here. Then you came."

There was a long pause, and I ventured to take her hand for an instant. Without a word more we opened the door, and joined the Superintendent in the hall. He hurried up to us, saying as he came:

"I have been examining everything myself, and have sent off a message to Scotland Yard. You see, Mr. Ross, there seemed so much that was odd about the case that I thought we had better have the best man of the Criminal Investigation Department that we could get. So I sent a note asking to have Sergeant Daw sent at once. You remember him, sir, in that American poisoning case at Hoxton."

"Oh yes," I said, "I remember him well; in that and other cases, for I have benefited several times by his skill and acumen. He has a mind that works as truly as any that I know. When I have been for the defence, and believed my man was innocent, I was glad to have him against us!"

"That is high praise, sir!" said the Superintendent gratified: "I am glad you approve of my choice; that I did well in sending for him."

I answered heartily:

"Could not be better. I do not doubt that between you we shall get at the facts—and what lies behind them!"

We ascended to Mr. Trelawny's room, where we found everything exactly as his daughter had described.

There came a ring at the house bell, and a minute later a man was shown into the room. A young man with aquiline features, keen grey eyes, and a forehead that stood out square and broad as that of a thinker. In his hand he had a black bag which he at once opened. Miss Trelawny introduced us: "Doctor Winchester, Mr. Ross, Superintendent Dolan." We bowed mutually, and he, without a moment's delay, began his work. We all waited, and eagerly watched him as he proceeded to dress the wound. As he went on he turned now and again to call the Superintendent's attention to some point about the wound, the latter proceeding to enter the fact at once in his notebook.

"See! several parallel cuts or scratches beginning on the left side of the wrist and in some places endangering the radial artery.

"These small wounds here, deep and jagged, seem as if made with a blunt instrument. This in particular would seem as if made with some kind of sharp wedge; the flesh round it seems torn as if with lateral pressure."

Turning to Miss Trelawny he said presently:

"Do you think we might remove this bangle? It is not absolutely necessary, as it will fall lower on the wrist where it can hang loosely; but it might add to the patient's comfort later on." The poor girl flushed deeply as she answered in a low voice:

"I do not know. I—I have only recently come to live with my Father; and I know so little of his life or his ideas that I fear I can hardly judge in such a matter. The Doctor, after a keen glance at her, said in a very kindly way:

"Forgive me! I did not know. But in any case you need not be distressed. It is not required at present to move it. Were it so I should do so at once on my own responsibility. If it be necessary later on, we can easily remove it with a file. Your Father doubtless has some object in keeping it as it is. See! there is a tiny key attached to it...." As he was speaking he stopped and bent lower, taking from my hand the candle which I held and lowering it till its light fell on the bangle. Then motioning me to hold the candle in the same position, he took from his pocket a magnifying-glass which he adjusted. When he had made a careful examination he stood up and handed the magnifying-glass to Dolan, saying as he did so:

"You had better examine it yourself. That is no ordinary bangle. The gold is wrought over triple steel links; see where it is worn away. It is manifestly not meant to be removed lightly; and it would need more than an ordinary file to do it."

The Superintendent bent his great body; but not getting close enough that way knelt down by the sofa as the Doctor had done. He examined the bangle minutely, turning it slowly round so that no particle of it escaped observation. Then he stood up and handed the magnifying-glass to me. "When you have examined it yourself," he said, "let the lady look at it if she will," and he commenced to write at length in his notebook.

I made a simple alteration in his suggestion. I held out the glass toward Miss Trelawny, saying:

"Had you not better examine it first?" She drew back, slightly raising her hand in disclaimer, as she said impulsively:

"Oh no! Father would doubtless have shown it to me had he wished me to see it. I would not like to without his consent." Then she added, doubtless fearing lest her delicacy of view should give offence to the rest of us:

"Of course it is right that you should see it. You have to examine and consider everything; and indeed—indeed I am grateful to you..."

She turned away; I could see that she was crying quietly. It was evident to me that even in the midst of her trouble and anxiety there was a chagrin that she knew so little of her father; and that her ignorance had to be shown at such a time and amongst so many strangers. That they were all men did not make the shame more easy to bear, though there was a certain relief in it. Trying to interpret her feelings I could not but think that she must have been glad that no woman's eyes—of understanding greater than man's—were upon her in that hour.

When I stood up from my examination, which verified to me that of the Doctor, the latter resumed his place beside the couch and went on with his ministrations. Superintendent Dolan said to me in a whisper:

"I think we are fortunate in our doctor!" I nodded, and was about to add something in praise of his acumen, when there came a low tapping at the door.

Chapter II - Strange Instructions

Superintendent Dolan went quietly to the door; by a sort of natural understanding he had taken possession of affairs in the room. The rest of us waited. He opened the door a little way; and then with a gesture of manifest relief threw it wide, and a young man stepped in. A young man clean-shaven, tall and slight; with an eagle face and bright, quick eyes that seemed to take in everything around him at a glance. As he came in, the Superintendent held out his hand; the two men shook hands warmly.

"I came at once, sir, the moment I got your message. I am glad I still have your confidence."

"That you'll always have," said the Superintendent heartily. "I have not forgotten our old Bow Street days, and I never shall!" Then, without a word of preliminary, he began to tell everything he knew up to the moment of the newcomer's entry. Sergeant Daw asked a few questions—a very few—when it was necessary for his understanding of circumstances or the relative positions of persons; but as a rule Dolan, who knew his work thoroughly, forestalled every query, and explained all necessary matters as he went on. Sergeant Daw threw occasionally swift glances round him; now at one of us; now at the room or some part of it; now at the wounded man lying senseless on the sofa.

When the Superintendent had finished, the Sergeant turned to me and said:

"Perhaps you remember me, sir. I was with you in that Hoxton case."

"I remember you very well," I said as I held out my hand. The Superintendent spoke again:

"You understand, Sergeant Daw, that you are put in full charge of this case."

"Under you I hope, sir," he interrupted. The other shook his head and smiled as he said:

"It seems to me that this is a case that will take all a man's time and his brains. I have other work to do; but I shall be more than interested, and if I can help in any possible way I shall be glad to do so!"

"All right, sir," said the other, accepting his responsibility with a sort of modified salute; straightway he began his investigation.

First he came over to the Doctor and, having learned his name and address, asked him to write a full report which he could use, and which he could refer to headquarters if necessary. Doctor Winchester bowed gravely as he promised. Then the Sergeant approached me and said sotto voce:

"I like the look of your doctor. I think we can work together!" Turning to Miss Trelawny he asked:

"Please let me know what you can of your Father; his ways of life, his history—in fact of anything of whatsoever kind which interests him, or in which he may be concerned." I was about to interrupt to tell him what she had already said of her ignorance in all matters of her father and his ways, but her warning hand was raised to me pointedly and she spoke herself.

"Alas! I know little or nothing. Superintendent Dolan and Mr. Ross know already all I can say."

"Well, ma'am, we must be content to do what we can," said the officer genially. "I'll begin by making a minute examination. You say that you were outside the door when you heard the noise?"

"I was in my room when I heard the queer sound—indeed it must have been the early part of whatever it was which woke me. I came out of my room at once. Father's door was shut, and I could see the whole landing and the upper slopes of the staircase. No one could have left by the door unknown to me, if that is what you mean!"

"That is just what I do mean, miss. If every one who knows anything will tell me as well as that, we shall soon get to the bottom of this."

He then went over to the bed, looked at it carefully, and asked:

"Has the bed been touched?"

"Not to my knowledge," said Miss Trelawny, "but I shall ask Mrs. Grant—the housekeeper," she added as she rang the bell. Mrs. Grant answered it in person. "Come in," said Miss Trelawny. "These gentlemen want to know, Mrs. Grant, if the bed has been touched."

"Not by me, ma'am."

"Then," said Miss Trelawny, turning to Sergeant Daw, "it cannot have been touched by any one. Either Mrs. Grant or I myself was here all the time, and I do not think any of the servants who came when I gave the alarm were near the bed at all. You see, Father lay here just under the great safe, and every one crowded round him. We sent them all away in a very short time." Daw, with a motion of his hand, asked us all to stay at the other side of the room whilst with a magnifying-glass he examined the bed, taking care as he moved each fold of the bed-clothes to replace it in exact position. Then he examined with his magnifying-glass the floor beside it, taking especial pains where the blood had trickled over the side of the bed, which was of heavy red wood handsomely carved. Inch by inch, down on his knees, carefully avoiding any touch with the stains on the floor, he followed the blood-marks over to the spot, close under the great safe, where the body had lain. All around and about this spot he went for a radius of some yards; but seemingly did not meet with anything to arrest special attention. Then he examined the front of the safe; round the lock, and along the bottom and top of the double doors, more especially at the places of their touching in front.

Next he went to the windows, which were fastened down with the hasps.

"Were the shutters closed?" he asked Miss Trelawny in a casual way as though he expected the negative answer, which came.

All this time Doctor Winchester was attending to his patient; now dressing the wounds in the wrist or making minute examination all over the head and throat, and over the heart. More than once he put his nose to the mouth of the senseless man and sniffed. Each time he did so he finished up by unconsciously looking round the room, as though in search of something.

Then we heard the deep strong voice of the Detective:

"So far as I can see, the object was to bring that key to the lock of the safe. There seems to be some secret in the mechanism that I am unable to guess at, though I served a year in Chubb's before I joined the police. It is a combination lock of seven letters; but there seems to be a way of locking even the combination. It is one of Chatwood's; I shall call at their place and find out something about it." Then turning to the Doctor, as though his own work were for the present done, he said:

"Have you anything you can tell me at once, Doctor, which will not interfere with your full report? If there is any doubt I can wait, but the sooner I know something definite the better." Doctor Winchester answered at once:

"For my own part I see no reason in waiting. I shall make a full report of course. But in the meantime I shall tell you all I know—which is after all not very much, and all I think—which is less definite. There is no wound on the head which could account for the state of stupor in which the patient continues. I must, therefore, take it that either he has been drugged or is under some hypnotic influence. So far as I can judge, he has not been drugged—at least by means of any drug of whose qualities I am aware. Of course, there is ordinarily in this room so much of a mummy smell that it is difficult to be certain about anything having a delicate aroma. I dare say that you have noticed the peculiar Egyptians scents, bitumen, nard, aromatic gums and spices, and so forth. It is quite possible that somewhere in this room, amongst the curios and hidden by stronger scents, is some substance or liquid which may have the effect we see. It is possible that the patient has taken some drug, and that he may in some sleeping phase have injured himself. I do not think this is likely; and circumstances, other than those which I have myself been investigating, may prove that this surmise is not correct. But in the meantime it is possible; and must, till it be disproved, be kept within our purview." Here Sergeant Daw interrupted:

"That may be, but if so, we should be able to find the instrument with which the wrist was injured. There would be marks of blood somewhere."

"Exactly so!" said the Doctor, fixing his glasses as though preparing for an argument. "But if it be that the patient has used some strange drug, it may be one that does not take effect at once. As we are as yet ignorant of its potentialities—if, indeed, the whole surmise is correct at all—we must be prepared at all points."

Here Miss Trelawny joined in the conversation:

"That would be quite right, so far as the action of the drug was concerned; but according to the second part of your surmise the wound may have been self-inflicted, and this after the drug had taken effect."

"True!" said the Detective and the Doctor simultaneously. She went on:

"As however, Doctor, your guess does not exhaust the possibilities, we must bear in mind that some other variant of the same root-idea may be correct. I take it, therefore, that our first search, to be made on this assumption, must be for the weapon with which the injury was done to my Father's wrist."

"Perhaps he put the weapon in the safe before he became quite unconscious," said I, giving voice foolishly to a half-formed thought.

"That could not be," said the Doctor quickly. "At least I think it could hardly be," he added cautiously, with a brief bow to me. "You see, the left hand is covered with blood; but there is no blood mark whatever on the safe."

"Quite right!" I said, and there was a long pause.

The first to break the silence was the Doctor.

"We shall want a nurse here as soon as possible; and I know the very one to suit. I shall go at once to get her if I can. I must ask that till I return some of you will remain constantly with the patient. It may be necessary to remove him to another room later on; but in the meantime he is best left here. Miss Trelawny, may I take it that either you or Mrs. Grant will remain here—not merely in the room, but close to the patient and watchful of him—till I return?"

She bowed in reply, and took a seat beside the sofa. The Doctor gave her some directions as to what she should do in case her father should become conscious before his return.

The next to move was Superintendent Dolan, who came close to Sergeant Daw as he said:

"I had better return now to the station—unless, of course, you should wish me to remain for a while."

He answered, "Is Johnny Wright still in your division?"

"Yes! Would you like him to be with you?" The other nodded reply. "Then I will send him on to you as soon as can be arranged. He shall then stay with you as long as you wish. I will tell him that he is to take his instructions entirely from you."

The Sergeant accompanied him to the door, saying as he went:

"Thank you, sir; you are always thoughtful for men who are working with you. It is a pleasure to me to be with you again. I shall go back to Scotland Yard and report to my chief. Then I shall call at Chatwood's; and I shall return here as soon as possible. I suppose I may take it, miss, that I may put up here for a day or two, if required. It may be some help, or possibly some comfort to you, if I am about, until we unravel this mystery."

"I shall be very grateful to you." He looked keenly at her for a few seconds before he spoke again.

"Before I go have I permission to look about your Father's table and desk? There might be something which would give us a clue—or a lead at all events." Her answer was so unequivocal as almost to surprise him.

"You have the fullest possible permission to do anything which may help us in this dreadful trouble—to discover what it is that is wrong with my Father, or which may shield him in the future!"

He began at once a systematic search of the dressing-table, and after that of the writing-table in the room. In one of the drawers he found a letter sealed; this he brought at once across the room and handed to Miss Trelawny.

"A letter—directed to me—and in my Father's hand!" she said as she eagerly opened it. I watched her face as she began to read; but seeing at once that Sergeant Daw kept his keen eyes on her face, unflinchingly watching every flitting expression, I kept my eyes henceforth fixed on his. When Miss Trelawny had read her letter through, I had in my mind a conviction, which, however, I kept locked in my own heart. Amongst the suspicions in the mind of the Detective was one, rather perhaps potential than definite, of Miss Trelawny herself.

For several minutes Miss Trelawny held the letter in her hand with her eyes downcast, thinking. Then she read it carefully again; this time the varying expressions were intensified, and I thought I could easily follow them. When she had finished the second reading, she paused again. Then, though with some reluctance, she handed the letter to the Detective. He read it eagerly but with unchanging face; read it a second time, and then handed it back with a bow. She paused a little again, and then handed it to me. As she did so she raised her eyes to mine for a single moment appealingly; a swift blush spread over her pale cheeks and forehead.

With mingled feelings I took it, but, all said, I was glad. She did not show any perturbation in giving the letter to the Detective—she might not have shown any to anyone else. But to me... I feared to follow the thought further; but read on, conscious that the eyes of both Miss Trelawny and the Detective were fixed on me.

> "MY DEAR DAUGHTER, I want you to take this letter as an instruction—absolute and imperative, and admitting of no deviation whatever—in case anything untoward or unexpected by you or by others should happen to me. If I should be suddenly and mysteriously stricken down—either by sickness, accident or attack—you must follow these directions implicitly. If I am not already in my bedroom when you are made cognisant of my state, I am to be brought there as quickly as possible. Even should I be dead, my body is to be brought there. Thenceforth, until I am either conscious and able to give instructions on my own account, or buried, I am never to be left alone—not for a single instant. From nightfall to sunrise at least two persons must remain in the room. It will be well that a trained nurse be in the room from time to time, and will note any symptoms, either permanent or changing, which may strike her. My solicitors, Marvin & Jewkes, of 27B Lincoln's Inn, have full instructions in case of my death; and Mr. Marvin has himself undertaken to see personally my wishes carried out. I should advise you, my dear Daughter, seeing that you have no relative to apply to, to get some friend whom you can trust to either remain within the house where instant communication can be made, or to come nightly to aid in the watching, or to be within call. Such friend may be either male or female; but, whichever it may be, there should be added one other watcher or attendant at hand of the opposite sex. Understand, that it is of the very essence of my wish that there should be, awake and exercising themselves to my purposes, both masculine and feminine intelligences. Once more, my dear Margaret, let me impress on you the need for observation and just reasoning to conclusions, howsoever strange. If I am taken ill or injured, this will be no ordinary occasion; and I wish to warn you, so that your guarding may be complete.
>
> "Nothing in my room—I speak of the curios—must be removed or displaced in any way, or for any cause whatever. I have a special reason and a special purpose in the placing of each; so that any moving of them would thwart my plans.

"Should you want money or counsel in anything, Mr. Marvin will carry out your wishes; to the which he has my full instructions."
"ABEL TRELAWNY."

I read the letter a second time before speaking, for I feared to betray myself. The choice of a friend might be a momentous occasion for me. I had already ground for hope, that she had asked me to help her in the first throe of her trouble; but love makes its own doubtings, and I feared. My thoughts seemed to whirl with lightning rapidity, and in a few seconds a whole process of reasoning became formulated. I must not volunteer to be the friend that the father advised his daughter to have to aid her in her vigil; and yet that one glance had a lesson which I must not ignore. Also, did not she, when she wanted help, send to me—to me a stranger, except for one meeting at a dance and one brief afternoon of companionship on the river? Would it not humiliate her to make her ask me twice? Humiliate her! No! that pain I could at all events save her; it is not humiliation to refuse. So, as I handed her back the letter, I said:

"I know you will forgive me, Miss Trelawny, if I presume too much; but if you will permit me to aid in the watching I shall be proud. Though the occasion is a sad one, I shall be so far happy to be allowed the privilege."

Despite her manifest and painful effort at self-control, the red tide swept her face and neck. Even her eyes seemed suffused, and in stern contrast with her pale cheeks when the tide had rolled back. She answered in a low voice:

"I shall be very grateful for your help!" Then in an afterthought she added:

"But you must not let me be selfish in my need! I know you have many duties to engage you; and though I shall value your help highly—most highly—it would not be fair to monopolise your time."

"As to that," I answered at once, "my time is yours. I can for today easily arrange my work so that I can come here in the afternoon and stay till morning. After that, if the occasion still demands it, I can so arrange my work that I shall have more time still at my disposal."

She was much moved. I could see the tears gather in her eyes, and she turned away her head. The Detective spoke:

"I am glad you will be here, Mr. Ross. I shall be in the house myself, as Miss Trelawny will allow me, if my people in Scotland Yard will permit. That letter seems to put a different complexion on everything; though the mystery remains greater than ever. If you can wait here an hour or two I shall go to headquarters, and then to the safe-makers. After that I shall return; and you can go away easier in your mind, for I shall be here."

When he had gone, we two, Miss Trelawny and I, remained in silence. At last she raised her eyes and looked at me for a moment; after that I would not have exchanged places with a king. For a while she busied herself round the extemporised bedside of her father. Then, asking me to be sure not to take my eyes off him till she returned, she hurried out.

In a few minutes she came back with Mrs. Grant and two maids and a couple of men, who bore the entire frame and furniture of a light iron bed. This they proceeded to put together and to make. When the work was completed, and the servants had withdrawn, she said to me:

"It will be well to be all ready when the Doctor returns. He will surely want to have Father put to bed; and a proper bed will be better for him than the sofa." She then got a chair close beside her father, and sat down watching him.

I went about the room, taking accurate note of all I saw. And truly there were enough things in the room to evoke the curiosity of any man—even though the attendant circumstances were less strange. The whole place, excepting those articles of furniture necessary to a well-furnished bedroom, was filled with magnificent curios, chiefly Egyptian. As the room was of immense size there was opportunity for the placing of a large number of them, even if, as with these, they were of huge proportions.

Whilst I was still investigating the room there came the sound of wheels on the gravel outside the house. There was a ring at the hall door, and a few minutes later, after a preliminary tap at the door and an answering "Come in!" Doctor Winchester entered, followed by a young woman in the dark dress of a nurse.

"I have been fortunate!" he said as he came in. "I found her at once and free. Miss Trelawny, this is Nurse Kennedy!"

Chapter III - The Watchers

I was struck by the way the two young women looked at each other. I suppose I have been so much in the habit of weighing up in my own mind the personality of witnesses and of forming judgment by their unconscious action and mode of bearing themselves, that the habit extends to my life outside as well as within the court-house. At this moment of my life anything that interested Miss Trelawny interested me; and as she had been struck by the newcomer I instinctively weighed her up also. By comparison of the two I seemed somehow to gain a new knowledge of Miss Trelawny. Certainly, the two women made a good contrast. Miss Trelawny was of fine figure; dark, straight-featured. She had marvellous eyes; great, wide-open, and as black and soft as velvet, with a mysterious depth. To look in them was like gazing at a black mirror such as Doctor Dee used in his wizard rites. I heard an old gentleman at the picnic, a great oriental traveller, describe the effect of her eyes "as looking at night at the great distant lamps of a mosque through the open door." The eyebrows were typical. Finely arched and rich in long curling hair, they seemed like the proper architectural environment of the deep, splendid eyes. Her hair was black also, but was as fine as silk. Generally black hair is a type of animal strength and seems as if some strong expression of the forces of a strong nature; but in this case there could be no such thought. There were refinement and high breeding; and though there was no suggestion of weakness, any sense of power there was, was rather spiritual than animal. The whole harmony of her being seemed complete. Carriage, figure, hair, eyes; the mobile, full mouth, whose scarlet lips and white teeth seemed to light up the lower part of the face—as the eyes did the upper; the wide sweep of the jaw from chin to ear; the long, fine fingers; the hand which seemed to move from the wrist as though it had a sentience of its own. All these perfections went to make up a personality that dominated either by its grace, its sweetness, its beauty, or its charm.

Nurse Kennedy, on the other hand, was rather under than over a woman's average height. She was firm and thickset, with full limbs and broad, strong, capable hands. Her colour was in the general effect that of an autumn leaf. The yellow-brown hair was thick and long, and the golden-brown eyes sparkled from the freckled, sunburnt skin. Her rosy cheeks gave a general idea of rich brown. The red lips and white teeth did not alter the colour scheme, but only emphasized it. She had a snub nose—there was no possible doubt about it; but like such noses in general it showed a nature generous, untiring, and full of good-nature. Her broad white forehead, which even the freckles had spared, was full of forceful thought and reason.

Doctor Winchester had on their journey from the hospital, coached her in the necessary particulars, and without a word she took charge of the patient and set to work. Having examined the new-made bed and shaken the pillows, she spoke to the Doctor, who gave instructions; presently we all four, stepping together, lifted the unconscious man from the sofa.

Early in the afternoon, when Sergeant Daw had returned, I called at my rooms in Jermyn Street, and sent out such clothes, books and papers as I should be likely to want within a few days. Then I went on to keep my legal engagements.

The Court sat late that day as an important case was ending; it was striking six as I drove in at the gate of the Kensington Palace Road. I found myself installed in a large room close to the sick chamber.

That night we were not yet regularly organised for watching, so that the early part of the evening showed an unevenly balanced guard. Nurse Kennedy, who had been on duty all day, was lying down, as she had arranged to come on again by twelve o'clock. Doctor Winchester, who was dining in the house, remained in the room until dinner was announced; and went back at once when it was over. During dinner Mrs. Grant remained in the room, and with her Sergeant Daw, who wished to complete a minute examination which he had undertaken of everything in the room and near it. At nine o'clock Miss Trelawny and I went in to relieve the Doctor. She had lain down for a few hours in the afternoon so as to be refreshed for her work at night. She told me that she had determined that for this night at least she would sit up and watch. I did not try to dissuade her, for I knew that her mind was made up. Then and there I made up my mind that I would watch with her—unless, of course, I should see that she really did not wish it. I said nothing of my intentions for the present. We came in on tiptoe, so silently that the Doctor, who was bending over the bed, did not hear us, and seemed a little startled when suddenly looking up he saw our eyes upon him. I felt that the mystery of the whole thing was getting on his nerves, as it had already got on the nerves of some others of us. He was, I fancied, a little annoyed with himself for having been so startled, and at once began to talk in a hurried manner as though to get over our idea of his embarrassment:

"I am really and absolutely at my wits' end to find any fit cause for this stupor. I have made again as accurate an examination as I know how, and I am satisfied that there is no injury to the brain, that is, no external injury. Indeed, all his vital organs seem unimpaired. I have given him, as you know, food several times and it has manifestly done him good. His breathing is strong and regular, and his pulse is slower and stronger than it was this morning. I cannot find evidence of any known drug, and his unconsciousness does not resemble any of the many cases of hypnotic sleep which I saw in the Charcot Hospital in Paris. And as to these wounds"—he laid his finger gently on the bandaged wrist which lay outside the coverlet as he spoke, "I do not know what to make of them. They might have been made by a carding-machine; but that supposition is untenable. It is within the bounds of possibility that they might have been made by a wild animal if it had taken care to sharpen its claws. That too is, I take it, impossible. By the way, have you any strange pets here in the house; anything of an exceptional kind, such as a tiger-cat or anything out of the common?" Miss Trelawny smiled a sad smile which made my heart ache, as she made answer:

"Oh no! Father does not like animals about the house, unless they are dead and mummied." This was said with a touch of bitterness—or jealousy, I could hardly tell which. "Even my poor kitten was only allowed in the house on sufferance; and though he is the dearest and best-conducted cat in the world, he is now on a sort of parole, and is not allowed into this room."

As she was speaking a faint rattling of the door handle was heard. Instantly Miss Trelawny's face brightened. She sprang up and went over to the door, saying as she went:

"There he is! That is my Silvio. He stands on his hind legs and rattles the door handle when he wants to come into a room." She opened the door, speaking to the cat as though he were a baby: "Did him want his movver? Come then; but he must stay with her!" She lifted the cat, and came back with him in her arms. He was certainly a magnificent animal. A chinchilla grey Persian with long silky hair; a really lordly animal with a haughty bearing despite his gentleness; and with great paws which spread out as he placed them on the ground. Whilst she was fondling him, he suddenly gave a wriggle like an eel and slipped out of her arms. He ran across the room and stood opposite a low table on which stood the mummy of an animal, and began to mew and snarl. Miss Trelawny was after him in an instant and lifted him in her arms, kicking and struggling and wriggling to get away; but not biting or scratching, for evidently he loved his beautiful mistress. He ceased to make a noise the moment he was in her arms; in a whisper she admonished him:

"O you naughty Silvio! You have broken your parole that mother gave for you. Now, say goodnight to the gentlemen, and come away to mother's room!" As she was speaking she held out the cat's paw to me to shake. As I did so I could not but admire its size and beauty. "Why," said I, "his paw seems like a little boxing-glove full of claws." She smiled:

"So it ought to. Don't you notice that my Silvio has seven toes, see!" she opened the paw; and surely enough there were seven separate claws, each of them sheathed in a delicate, fine, shell-like case. As I gently stroked the foot the claws emerged and one of them accidentally—there was no anger now and the cat was purring—stuck into my hand. Instinctively I said as I drew back:

"Why, his claws are like razors!"

Doctor Winchester had come close to us and was bending over looking at the cat's claws; as I spoke he said in a quick, sharp way:

"Eh!" I could hear the quick intake of his breath. Whilst I was stroking the now quiescent cat, the Doctor went to the table and tore off a piece of blotting-paper from the writing-pad and came back. He laid the paper on his palm and, with a simple "pardon me!" to Miss Trelawny, placed the cat's paw on it and pressed it down with his other hand. The haughty cat seemed to resent somewhat the familiarity, and tried to draw its foot away. This was plainly what the Doctor wanted, for in the act the cat opened the sheaths of its claws and made several reefs in the soft paper. Then Miss Trelawny took her pet away. She returned in a couple of minutes; as she came in she said:

"It is most odd about that mummy! When Silvio came into the room first—indeed I took him in as a kitten to show to Father—he went on just the same way. He jumped up on the table, and tried to scratch and bite the mummy. That was what made Father so angry, and brought the decree of banishment on poor Silvio. Only his parole, given through me, kept him in the house."

Whilst she had been gone, Doctor Winchester had taken the bandage from her father's wrist. The wound was now quite clear, as the separate cuts showed out in fierce red lines. The Doctor folded the blotting-paper across the line of punctures made by the cat's claws, and held it down close to the wound. As he did so, he looked up triumphantly and beckoned us over to him.

The cuts in the paper corresponded with the wounds in the wrist! No explanation was needed, as he said:

"It would have been better if master Silvio had not broken his parole!"

We were all silent for a little while. Suddenly Miss Trelawny said:

"But Silvio was not in here last night!"

"Are you sure? Could you prove that if necessary?" She hesitated before replying:

"I am certain of it; but I fear it would be difficult to prove. Silvio sleeps in a basket in my room. I certainly put him to bed last night; I remember distinctly laying his little blanket over him, and tucking him in. This morning I took him out of the basket myself. I certainly never noticed him in here; though, of course, that would not mean much, for I was too concerned about poor father, and too much occupied with him, to notice even Silvio."

The Doctor shook his head as he said with a certain sadness:

"Well, at any rate it is no use trying to prove anything now. Any cat in the world would have cleaned blood-marks—did any exist—from his paws in a hundredth part of the time that has elapsed."

Again we were all silent; and again the silence was broken by Miss Trelawny:

"But now that I think of it, it could not have been poor Silvio that injured Father. My door was shut when I first heard the sound; and Father's was shut when I listened at it. When I went in, the injury had been done; so that it must have been before Silvio could possibly have got in." This reasoning commended itself, especially to me as a barrister, for it was proof to satisfy a jury. It gave me a distinct pleasure to have Silvio acquitted of the crime—possibly because he was Miss Trelawny's cat and was loved by her. Happy cat! Silvio's mistress was manifestly pleased as I said:

"Verdict, 'not guilty!'" Doctor Winchester after a pause observed:

"My apologies to master Silvio on this occasion; but I am still puzzled to know why he is so keen against that mummy. Is he the same toward the other mummies in the house? There are, I suppose, a lot of them. I saw three in the hall as I came in."

"There are lots of them," she answered. "I sometimes don't know whether I am in a private house or the British Museum. But Silvio never concerns himself about any of them except that particular one. I suppose it must be because it is of an animal, not a man or a woman."

"Perhaps it is of a cat!" said the Doctor as he started up and went across the room to look at the mummy more closely. "Yes," he went on, "it is the mummy of a cat; and a very fine one, too. If it hadn't been a special favourite of some very special person it would never have received so much honour. See! A painted case and obsidian eyes—just like a human mummy. It is an extraordinary thing, that knowledge of kind to kind. Here is a dead cat—that is all; it is perhaps four or five thousand years old—and another cat of another breed, in what is practically another world, is ready to fly at it, just as it would if it were not dead. I should like to experiment a bit about that cat if you don't mind, Miss Trelawny." She hesitated before replying:

"Of course, do anything you may think necessary or wise; but I hope it will not be anything to hurt or worry my poor Silvio." The Doctor smiled as he answered:

"Oh, Silvio would be all right: it is the other one that my sympathies would be reserved for."

"How do you mean?"

"Master Silvio will do the attacking; the other one will do the suffering."

"Suffering?" There was a note of pain in her voice. The Doctor smiled more broadly:

"Oh, please make your mind easy as to that. The other won't suffer as we understand it; except perhaps in his structure and outfit."

"What on earth do you mean?"

"Simply this, my dear young lady, that the antagonist will be a mummy cat like this one. There are, I take it, plenty of them to be had in Museum Street. I shall get one and place it here instead of that one—you won't think that a temporary exchange will violate your Father's instructions, I hope. We shall then find out, to begin with, whether Silvio objects to all mummy cats, or only to this one in particular."

"I don't know," she said doubtfully. "Father's instructions seem very uncompromising." Then after a pause she went on: "But of course under the circumstances anything that is to be ultimately for his good must be done. I suppose there can't be anything very particular about the mummy of a cat."

Doctor Winchester said nothing. He sat rigid, with so grave a look on his face that his extra gravity passed on to me; and in its enlightening perturbation I began to realise more than I had yet done the strangeness of the case in which I was now so deeply concerned. When once this thought had begun there was no end to it. Indeed it grew, and blossomed, and reproduced itself in a thousand different ways. The room and all in it gave grounds for strange thoughts. There were so many ancient relics that unconsciously one was taken back to strange lands and strange times. There were so many mummies or mummy objects, round which there seemed to cling for ever the penetrating odours of bitumen, and spices and gums—"Nard and Circassia's balmy smells"—that one was unable to forget the past. Of course, there was but little light in the room, and that carefully shaded; so that there was no glare anywhere. None of that direct light which can manifest itself as a power or an entity, and so make for companionship. The room was a large one, and lofty in proportion to its size. In its vastness was place for a multitude of things not often found in a bedchamber. In far corners of the room were shadows of uncanny shape. More than once as I thought, the multitudinous presence of the dead and the past took such hold on me that I caught myself looking round fearfully as though some strange personality or influence was present. Even the manifest presence of Doctor Winchester and Miss Trelawny could not altogether comfort or satisfy me at such moments. It was with a distinct sense of relief that I saw a new personality in the room in the shape of Nurse Kennedy. There was no doubt that that business-like, self-reliant, capable young woman added an element of security to such wild imaginings as my own. She had a quality of common sense that seemed to pervade everything around her, as though it were some kind of emanation. Up to that moment I had been building fancies around the sick man; so that finally all about him, including myself, had become involved in them, or enmeshed, or saturated, or... But now that she had come, he relapsed into his proper perspective as a patient; the room was a sick-room, and the shadows lost their fearsome quality. The only thing which it could not altogether abrogate was the strange Egyptian smell. You may put a mummy in a glass case and hermetically seal it so that no corroding air can get within; but all the same it will exhale its odour. One might think that four or five thousand years would exhaust the olfactory qualities of anything; but experience teaches us that these smells remain, and that their secrets are unknown to us. Today they are as much mysteries as they were when the embalmers put the body in the bath of natron...

All at once I sat up. I had become lost in an absorbing reverie. The Egyptian smell had seemed to get on my nerves—on my memory—on my very will.

At that moment I had a thought which was like an inspiration. If I was influenced in such a manner by the smell, might it not be that the sick man, who lived half his life or more in the atmosphere, had gradually and by slow but sure process taken into his system something which had permeated him to such degree that it had a new power derived from quantity—or strength—or...

I was becoming lost again in a reverie. This would not do. I must take such precaution that I could remain awake, or free from such entrancing thought. I had had but half a night's sleep last night; and this night I must remain awake. Without stating my intention, for I feared that I might add to the trouble and uneasiness of Miss Trelawny, I went downstairs and out of the house. I soon found a chemist's shop, and came away with a respirator. When I got back, it was ten o'clock; the Doctor was going for the night. The Nurse came with him to the door of the sick-room, taking her last instructions. Miss Trelawny sat still beside the bed. Sergeant Daw, who had entered as the Doctor went out, was some little distance off.

When Nurse Kennedy joined us, we arranged that she should sit up till two o'clock, when Miss Trelawny would relieve her. Thus, in accordance with Mr. Trelawny's instructions, there would always be a man and a woman in the room; and each one of us would overlap, so that at no time would a new set of watchers come on duty without some one to tell of what—if anything—had occurred. I lay down on a sofa in my own room, having arranged that one of the servants should call me a little before twelve. In a few moments I was asleep.

When I was waked, it took me several seconds to get back my thoughts so as to recognise my own identity and surroundings. The short sleep had, however, done me good, and I could look on things around me in a more practical light than I had been able to do earlier in the evening. I bathed my face, and thus refreshed went into the sick-room. I moved very softly. The Nurse was sitting by the bed, quiet and alert; the Detective sat in an arm-chair across the room in deep shadow. He did not move when I crossed, until I got close to him, when he said in a dull whisper:

"It is all right; I have not been asleep!" An unnecessary thing to say, I thought—it always is, unless it be untrue in spirit. When I told him that his watch was over; that he might go to bed till I should call him at six o'clock, he seemed relieved and went with alacrity. At the door he turned and, coming back to me, said in a whisper:

"I sleep lightly and I shall have my pistols with me. I won't feel so heavy-headed when I get out of this mummy smell."

He too, then, had shared my experience of drowsiness!

I asked the Nurse if she wanted anything. I noticed that she had a vinaigrette in her lap. Doubtless she, too, had felt some of the influence which had so affected me. She said that she had all she required, but that if she should want anything she would at once let me know. I wished to keep her from noticing my respirator, so I went to the chair in the shadow where her back was toward me. Here I quietly put it on, and made myself comfortable.

For what seemed a long time, I sat and thought and thought. It was a wild medley of thoughts, as might have been expected from the experiences of the previous day and night. Again I found myself thinking of the Egyptian smell; and I remember that I felt a delicious satisfaction that I did not experience it as I had done. The respirator was doing its work.

It must have been that the passing of this disturbing thought made for repose of mind, which is the corollary of bodily rest, for, though I really cannot remember being asleep or waking from it, I saw a vision—I dreamed a dream, I scarcely know which.

I was still in the room, seated in the chair. I had on my respirator and knew that I breathed freely. The Nurse sat in her chair with her back toward me. She sat quite still. The sick man lay as still as the dead. It was rather like the picture of a scene than the reality; all were still and silent; and the stillness and silence were continuous. Outside, in the distance I could hear the sounds of a city, the occasional roll of wheels, the shout of a reveller, the far-away echo of whistles and the rumbling of trains. The light was very, very low; the reflection of it under the green-shaded lamp was a dim relief to the darkness, rather than light. The green silk fringe of the lamp had merely the colour of an emerald seen in the moonlight. The room, for all its darkness, was full of shadows. It seemed in my whirling thoughts as though all the real things had become shadows—shadows which moved, for they passed the dim outline of the high windows. Shadows which had sentience. I even thought there was sound, a faint sound as of the mew of a cat—the rustle of drapery and a metallic clink as of metal faintly touching metal. I sat as one entranced. At last I felt, as in nightmare, that this was sleep, and that in the passing of its portals all my will had gone.

All at once my senses were full awake. A shriek rang in my ears. The room was filled suddenly with a blaze of light. There was the sound of pistol shots—one, two; and a haze of white smoke in the room. When my waking eyes regained their power, I could have shrieked with horror myself at what I saw before me.

Chapter IV - The Second Attempt

The sight which met my eyes had the horror of a dream within a dream, with the certainty of reality added. The room was as I had seen it last; except that the shadowy look had gone in the glare of the many lights, and every article in it stood stark and solidly real.

By the empty bed sat Nurse Kennedy, as my eyes had last seen her, sitting bolt upright in the arm-chair beside the bed. She had placed a pillow behind her, so that her back might be erect; but her neck was fixed as that of one in a cataleptic trance. She was, to all intents and purposes, turned into stone. There was no special expression on her face—no fear, no horror; nothing such as might be expected of one in such a condition. Her open eyes showed neither wonder nor interest. She was simply a negative existence, warm, breathing, placid; but absolutely unconscious of the world around her. The bedclothes were disarranged, as though the patient had been drawn from under them without throwing them back. The corner of the upper sheet hung upon the floor; close by it lay one of the bandages with which the Doctor had dressed the wounded wrist. Another and another lay further along the floor, as though forming a clue to where the sick man now lay. This was almost exactly where he had been found on the previous night, under the great safe. Again, the left arm lay toward the safe. But there had been a new outrage, an attempt had been made to sever the arm close to the bangle which held the tiny key. A heavy "kukri" knife—one of the leaf-shaped knives which the Gurkhas and others of the hill tribes of India use with such effect—had been taken from its place on the wall, and with it the attempt had been made. It was manifest that just at the moment of striking, the blow had been arrested, for only the point of the knife and not the edge of the blade had struck the flesh. As it was, the outer side of the arm had been cut to the bone and the blood was pouring out. In addition, the former wound in front of the arm had been cut or torn about terribly, one of the cuts seemed to jet out blood as if with each pulsation of the heart. By the side of her father knelt Miss Trelawny, her white nightdress stained with the blood in which she knelt. In the middle of the room Sergeant Daw, in his shirt and trousers and stocking feet, was putting fresh cartridges into his revolver in a dazed mechanical kind of way. His eyes were red and heavy, and he seemed only half awake, and less than half conscious of what was going on around him. Several servants, bearing lights of various kinds, were clustered round the doorway.

As I rose from my chair and came forward, Miss Trelawny raised her eyes toward me. When she saw me she shrieked and started to her feet, pointing towards me. Never shall I forget the strange picture she made, with her white drapery all smeared with blood which, as she rose from the pool, ran in streaks toward her bare feet. I believe that I had only been asleep; that whatever influence had worked on Mr. Trelawny and Nurse Kennedy—and in less degree on Sergeant Daw—had not touched me. The respirator had been of some service, though it had not kept off the tragedy whose dire evidences were before me. I can understand now—I could understand even then—the fright, added to that which had gone before, which my appearance must have evoked. I had still on the respirator, which covered mouth and nose; my hair had been tossed in my sleep. Coming suddenly forward, thus enwrapped and dishevelled, in that horrified crowd, I must have had, in the strange mixture of lights, an extraordinary and terrifying appearance. It was well that I recognised all this in time to avert another catastrophe; for the half-dazed, mechanically-acting Detective put in the cartridges and had raised his revolver to shoot at me when I succeeded in wrenching off the respirator and shouting to him to hold his hand. In this also he acted mechanically; the red, half-awake eyes had not in them even then the intention of conscious action. The danger, however, was averted. The relief of the situation, strangely enough, came in a simple fashion. Mrs. Grant, seeing that her young mistress had on only her nightdress, had gone to fetch a dressing-gown, which she now threw over her. This simple act brought us all back to the region of fact. With a long breath, one and all seemed to devote themselves to the most pressing matter before us, that of staunching the flow of blood from the arm of the wounded man. Even as the thought of action came, I rejoiced; for the bleeding was very proof that Mr. Trelawny still lived.

Last night's lesson was not thrown away. More than one of those present knew now what to do in such an emergency, and within a few seconds willing hands were at work on a tourniquet. A man was at once despatched for the doctor, and several of the servants disappeared to make themselves respectable. We lifted Mr. Trelawny on to the sofa where he had lain yesterday; and, having done what we could for him, turned our attention to the Nurse. In all the turmoil she had not stirred; she sat there as before, erect and rigid, breathing softly and naturally and with a placid smile. As it was manifestly of no use to attempt anything with her till the doctor had come, we began to think of the general situation.

Mrs. Grant had by this time taken her mistress away and changed her clothes; for she was back presently in a dressing-gown and slippers, and with the traces of blood removed from her hands. She was now much calmer, though she trembled sadly; and her face was ghastly white. When she had looked at her father's wrist, I holding the tourniquet, she turned her eyes round the room, resting them now and again on each one of us present in turn, but seeming to find no comfort. It was so apparent to me that she did not know where to begin or whom to trust that, to reassure her, I said:

"I am all right now; I was only asleep." Her voice had a gulp in it as she said in a low voice:

"Asleep! You! and my Father in danger! I thought you were on the watch!" I felt the sting of justice in the reproach; but I really wanted to help her, so I answered:

"Only asleep. It is bad enough, I know; but there is something more than an "only" round us here. Had it not been that I took a definite precaution I might have been like the Nurse there." She turned her eyes swiftly on the weird figure, sitting grimly upright like a painted statue; and then her face softened. With the action of habitual courtesy she said:

"Forgive me! I did not mean to be rude. But I am in such distress and fear that I hardly know what I am saying. Oh, it is dreadful! I fear for fresh trouble and horror and mystery every moment." This cut me to the very heart, and out of the heart's fulness I spoke:

"Don't give me a thought! I don't deserve it. I was on guard, and yet I slept. All that I can say is that I didn't mean to, and I tried to avoid it; but it was over me before I knew it. Anyhow, it is done now; and can't be undone. Probably some day we may understand it all; but now let us try to get at some idea of what has happened. Tell me what you remember!" The effort to recollect seemed to stimulate her; she became calmer as she spoke:

"I was asleep, and woke suddenly with the same horrible feeling on me that Father was in great and immediate danger. I jumped up and ran, just as I was, into his room. It was nearly pitch dark, but as I opened the door there was light enough to see Father's nightdress as he lay on the floor under the safe, just as on that first awful night. Then I think I must have gone mad for a moment." She stopped and shuddered. My eyes lit on Sergeant Daw, still fiddling in an aimless way with the revolver. Mindful of my work with the tourniquet, I said calmly:

"Now tell us, Sergeant Daw, what did you fire at?" The policeman seemed to pull himself together with the habit of obedience. Looking around at the servants remaining in the room, he said with that air of importance which, I take it, is the regulation attitude of an official of the law before strangers:

"Don't you think, sir, that we can allow the servants to go away? We can then better go into the matter." I nodded approval; the servants took the hint and withdrew, though unwillingly, the last one closing the door behind him. Then the Detective went on:

"I think I had better tell you my impressions, sir, rather than recount my actions. That is, so far as I remember them." There was a mortified deference now in his manner, which probably arose from his consciousness of the awkward position in which he found himself. "I went to sleep half-dressed—as I am now, with a revolver under my pillow. It was the last thing I remember thinking of. I do not know how long I slept. I had turned off the electric light, and it was quite dark. I thought I heard a scream; but I can't be sure, for I felt thick-headed as a man does when he is called too soon after an extra long stretch of work. Not that such was the case this time. Anyhow my thoughts flew to the pistol. I took it out, and ran on to the landing. Then I heard a sort of scream, or rather a call for help, and ran into this room. The room was dark, for the lamp beside the Nurse was out, and the only light was that from the landing, coming through the open door. Miss Trelawny was kneeling on the floor beside her father, and was screaming. I thought I saw something move between me and the window; so, without thinking, and being half dazed and only half awake, I shot at it. It moved a little more to the right between the windows, and I shot again. Then you came up out of the big chair with all that muffling on your face. It seemed to me, being as I say half dazed and half awake—I know, sir, you will take this into account—as if it had been you, being in the same direction as the thing I had fired at. And so I was about to fire again when you pulled off the wrap." Here I asked him—I was cross-examining now and felt at home:

"You say you thought I was the thing you fired at. What thing?" The man scratched his head, but made no reply.

"Come, sir," I said, "what thing; what was it like?" The answer came in a low voice:

"I don't know, sir. I thought there was something; but what it was, or what it was like, I haven't the faintest notion. I suppose it was because I had been thinking of the pistol before I went to sleep, and because when I came in here I was half dazed and only half awake—which I hope you will in future, sir, always remember." He clung to that formula of excuse as though it were his sheet-anchor. I did not want to antagonise the man; on the contrary I wanted to have him with us. Besides, I had on me at that time myself the shadow of my own default; so I said as kindly as I knew how:

"Quite right! Sergeant. Your impulse was correct; though of course in the half-somnolent condition in which you were, and perhaps partly affected by the same influence—whatever it may be—which made me sleep and which has put the Nurse in that cataleptic trance, it could not be expected that you would paused to weigh matters. But now, whilst the matter is fresh, let me see exactly where you stood and where I sat. We shall be able to trace the course of your bullets." The prospect of action and the exercise of his habitual skill seemed to brace him at once; he seemed a different man as he set about his work. I asked Mrs. Grant to hold the tourniquet, and went and stood where he had stood and looked where, in the darkness, he had pointed. I could not but notice the mechanical exactness of his mind, as when he showed me where he had stood, or drew, as a matter of course, the revolver from his pistol pocket, and pointed with it. The chair from which I had risen still stood in its place. Then I asked him to point with his hand only, as I wished to move in the track of his shot.

Just behind my chair, and a little back of it, stood a high buhl cabinet. The glass door was shattered. I asked:

"Was this the direction of your first shot or your second?" The answer came promptly.

"The second; the first was over there!"

He turned a little to the left, more toward the wall where the great safe stood, and pointed. I followed the direction of his hand and came to the low table whereon rested, amongst other curios, the mummy of the cat which had raised Silvio's ire. I got a candle and easily found the mark of the bullet. It had broken a little glass vase and a tazza of black basalt, exquisitely engraved with hieroglyphics, the graven lines being filled with some faint green cement and the whole thing being polished to an equal surface. The bullet, flattened against the wall, lay on the table.

I then went to the broken cabinet. It was evidently a receptacle for valuable curios; for in it were some great scarabs of gold, agate, green jasper, amethyst, lapis lazuli, opal, granite, and blue-green china. None of these things happily were touched. The bullet had gone through the back of the cabinet; but no other damage, save the shattering of the glass, had been done. I could not but notice the strange arrangement of the curios on the shelf of the cabinet. All the scarabs, rings, amulets, &c. were arranged in an uneven oval round an exquisitely-carved golden miniature figure of a hawk-headed God crowned with a disk and plumes. I did not wait to look further at present, for my attention was demanded by more pressing things; but I determined to make a more minute examination when I should have time. It was evident that some of the strange Egyptian smell clung to these old curios; through the broken glass came an added whiff of spice and gum and bitumen, almost stronger than those I had already noticed as coming from others in the room.

All this had really taken but a few minutes. I was surprised when my eye met, through the chinks between the dark window blinds and the window cases, the brighter light of the coming dawn. When I went back to the sofa and took the tourniquet from Mrs. Grant, she went over and pulled up the blinds.

It would be hard to imagine anything more ghastly than the appearance of the room with the faint grey light of early morning coming in upon it. As the windows faced north, any light that came was a fixed grey light without any of the rosy possibility of dawn which comes in the eastern quarter of heaven. The electric lights seemed dull and yet glaring; and every shadow was of a hard intensity. There was nothing of morning freshness; nothing of the softness of night. All was hard and cold and inexpressibly dreary. The face of the senseless man on the sofa seemed of a ghastly yellow; and the Nurse's face had taken a suggestion of green from the shade of the lamp near her. Only Miss Trelawny's face looked white; and it was of a pallor which made my heart ache. It looked as if nothing on God's earth could ever again bring back to it the colour of life and happiness.

It was a relief to us all when Doctor Winchester came in, breathless with running. He only asked one question:

"Can anyone tell me anything of how this wound was gotten?" On seeing the headshake which went round us under his glance, he said no more, but applied himself to his surgical work. For an instant he looked up at the Nurse sitting so still; but then bent himself to his task, a grave frown contracting his brows. It was not till the arteries were tied and the wounds completely dressed that he spoke again, except, of course, when he had asked for anything to be handed to him or to be done for him. When Mr. Trelawny's wounds had been thoroughly cared for, he said to Miss Trelawny:

"What about Nurse Kennedy?" She answered at once:

"I really do not know. I found her when I came into the room at half-past two o'clock, sitting exactly as she does now. We have not moved her, or changed her position. She has not wakened since. Even Sergeant Daw's pistol-shots did not disturb her."

"Pistol-shots? Have you then discovered any cause for this new outrage?" The rest were silent, so I answered:

"We have discovered nothing. I was in the room watching with the Nurse. Earlier in the evening I fancied that the mummy smells were making me drowsy, so I went out and got a respirator. I had it on when I came on duty; but it did not keep me from going to sleep. I awoke to see the room full of people; that is, Miss Trelawny and Sergeant Daw, being only half awake and still stupefied by the same scent or influence which had affected us, fancied that he saw something moving through the shadowy darkness of the room, and fired twice. When I rose out of my chair, with my face swathed in the respirator, he took me for the cause of the trouble. Naturally enough, he was about to fire again, when I was fortunately in time to manifest my identity. Mr. Trelawny was lying beside the safe, just as he was found last night; and was bleeding profusely from the new wound in his wrist. We lifted him on the sofa, and made a tourniquet. That is, literally and absolutely, all that any of us know as yet. We have not touched the knife, which you see lies close by the pool of blood. Look!" I said, going over and lifting it. "The point is red with the blood which has dried."

Doctor Winchester stood quite still a few minutes before speaking:

"Then the doings of this night are quite as mysterious as those of last night?"

"Quite!" I answered. He said nothing in reply, but turning to Miss Trelawny said:

"We had better take Nurse Kennedy into another room. I suppose there is nothing to prevent it?"

"Nothing! Please, Mrs. Grant, see that Nurse Kennedy's room is ready; and ask two of the men to come and carry her in." Mrs. Grant went out immediately; and in a few minutes came back saying:

"The room is quite ready; and the men are here." By her direction two footmen came into the room and, lifting up the rigid body of Nurse Kennedy under the supervision of the Doctor, carried her out of the room. Miss Trelawny remained with me in the sick chamber, and Mrs. Grant went with the Doctor into the Nurse's room.

When we were alone Miss Trelawny came over to me, and taking both my hands in hers, said:

"I hope you won't remember what I said. I did not mean it, and I was distraught." I did not make reply; but I held her hands and kissed them. There are different ways of kissing a lady's hands. This way was intended as homage and respect; and it was accepted as such in the high-bred, dignified way which marked Miss Trelawny's bearing and every movement. I went over to the sofa and looked down at the senseless man. The dawn had come much nearer in the last few minutes, and there was something of the clearness of day in the light. As I looked at the stern, cold, set face, now as white as a marble monument in the pale grey light, I could not but feel that there was some deep mystery beyond all that had happened within the last twenty-six hours. Those beetling brows screened some massive purpose; that high, broad forehead held some finished train of reasoning, which the broad chin and massive jaw would help to carry into effect. As I looked and wondered, there began to steal over me again that phase of wandering thought which had last night heralded the approach of sleep. I resisted it, and held myself sternly to the present. This was easier to do when Miss Trelawny came close to me, and, leaning her forehead against my shoulder, began to cry silently. Then all the manhood in me woke, and to present purpose. It was of little use trying to speak; words were inadequate to thought. But we understood each other; she did not draw away when I put arm protectingly over her shoulder as I used to do with my little sister long ago when in her childish trouble she would come to her big brother to be comforted. That very act or attitude of protection made me more resolute in my purpose, and seemed to clear my brain of idle, dreamy wandering in thought. With an instinct of greater protection, however, I took away my arm as I heard the Doctor's footstep outside the door.

When Doctor Winchester came in he looked intently at the patient before speaking. His brows were set, and his mouth was a thin, hard line. Presently he said:

"There is much in common between the sleep of your Father and Nurse Kennedy. Whatever influence has brought it about has probably worked the same way in both cases. In Kennedy's case the coma is less marked. I cannot but feel, however, that with her we may be able to do more and more quickly than with this patient, as our hands are not tied. I have placed her in a draught; and already she shows some signs, though very faint ones, of ordinary unconsciousness. The rigidity of her limbs is less, and her skin seems more sensitive—or perhaps I should say less insensitive—to pain."

"How is it, then," I asked, "that Mr. Trelawny is still in this state of insensibility; and yet, so far as we know, his body has not had such rigidity at all?"

"That I cannot answer. The problem is one which we may solve in a few hours; or it may need a few days. But it will be a useful lesson in diagnosis to us all; and perhaps to many and many others after us, who knows!" he added, with the genuine fire of an enthusiast.

As the morning wore on, he flitted perpetually between the two rooms, watching anxiously over both patients. He made Mrs. Grant remain with the Nurse, but either Miss Trelawny or I, generally both of us, remained with the wounded man. We each managed, however, to get bathed and dressed; the Doctor and Mrs. Grant remained with Mr. Trelawny whilst we had breakfast.

Sergeant Daw went off to report at Scotland Yard the progress of the night; and then to the local station to arrange for the coming of his comrade, Wright, as fixed with Superintendent Dolan. When he returned I could not but think that he had been hauled over the coals for shooting in a sick-room; or perhaps for shooting at all without certain and proper cause. His remark to me enlightened me in the matter:

"A good character is worth something, sir, in spite of what some of them say. See! I've still got leave to carry my revolver."

That day was a long and anxious one. Toward nightfall Nurse Kennedy so far improved that the rigidity of her limbs entirely disappeared. She still breathed quietly and regularly; but the fixed expression of her face, though it was a calm enough expression, gave place to fallen eyelids and the negative look of sleep. Doctor Winchester had, towards evening, brought two more nurses, one of whom was to remain with Nurse Kennedy and the other to share in the watching with Miss Trelawny, who had insisted on remaining up herself. She had, in order to prepare for the duty, slept for several hours in the afternoon. We had all taken counsel together, and had arranged thus for the watching in Mr. Trelawny's room. Mrs. Grant was to remain beside the patient till twelve, when Miss Trelawny would relieve her. The new nurse was to sit in Miss Trelawny's room, and to visit the sick chamber each quarter of an hour. The Doctor would remain till twelve; when I was to relieve him. One or other of the detectives was to remain within hail of the room all night; and to pay periodical visits to see that all was well. Thus, the watchers would be watched; and the possibility of such events as last night, when the watchers were both overcome, would be avoided.

When the sun set, a strange and grave anxiety fell on all of us; and in our separate ways we prepared for the vigil. Doctor Winchester had evidently been thinking of my respirator, for he told me he would go out and get one. Indeed, he took to the idea so kindly that I persuaded Miss Trelawny also to have one which she could put on when her time for watching came.

And so the night drew on.

Chapter V - More Strange Instructions

When I came from my room at half-past eleven o'clock I found all well in the sick-room. The new nurse, prim, neat, and watchful, sat in the chair by the bedside where Nurse Kennedy had sat last night. A little way off, between the bed and the safe, sat Dr. Winchester alert and wakeful, but looking strange and almost comic with the respirator over mouth and nose. As I stood in the doorway looking at them I heard a slight sound; turning round I saw the new detective, who nodded, held up the finger of silence and withdrew quietly. Hitherto no one of the watchers was overcome by sleep.

I took a chair outside the door. As yet there was no need for me to risk coming again under the subtle influence of last night. Naturally my thoughts went revolving round the main incidents of the last day and night, and I found myself arriving at strange conclusions, doubts, conjectures; but I did not lose myself, as on last night, in trains of thought. The sense of the present was ever with me, and I really felt as should a sentry on guard. Thinking is not a slow process; and when it is earnest the time can pass quickly. It seemed a very short time indeed till the door, usually left ajar, was pulled open and Dr. Winchester emerged, taking off his respirator as he came. His act, when he had it off, was demonstrative of his keenness. He turned up the outside of the wrap and smelled it carefully.

"I am going now," he said. "I shall come early in the morning; unless, of course, I am sent for before. But all seems well tonight."

The next to appear was Sergeant Daw, who went quietly into the room and took the seat vacated by the Doctor. I still remained outside; but every few minutes looked into the room. This was rather a form than a matter of utility, for the room was so dark that coming even from the dimly-lighted corridor it was hard to distinguish anything.

A little before twelve o'clock Miss Trelawny came from her room. Before coming to her father's she went into that occupied by Nurse Kennedy. After a couple of minutes she came out, looking, I thought, a trifle more cheerful. She had her respirator in her hand, but before putting it on, asked me if anything special had occurred since she had gone to lie down. I answered in a whisper—there was no loud talking in the house tonight—that all was safe, was well. She then put on her respirator, and I mine; and we entered the room. The Detective and the Nurse rose up, and we took their places. Sergeant Daw was the last to go out; he closed the door behind him as we had arranged.

For a while I sat quiet, my heart beating. The place was grimly dark. The only light was a faint one from the top of the lamp which threw a white circle on the high ceiling, except the emerald sheen of the shade as the light took its under edges. Even the light only seemed to emphasize the blackness of the shadows. These presently began to seem, as on last night, to have a sentience of their own. I did not myself feel in the least sleepy; and each time I went softly over to look at the patient, which I did about every ten minutes, I could see that Miss Trelawny was keenly alert. Every quarter of an hour one or other of the policemen looked in through the partly opened door. Each time both Miss Trelawny and I said through our mufflers, "all right," and the door was closed again.

As the time wore on, the silence and the darkness seemed to increase. The circle of light on the ceiling was still there, but it seemed less brilliant than at first. The green edging of the lamp-shade became like Maori greenstone rather than emerald. The sounds of the night without the house, and the starlight spreading pale lines along the edges of the window-cases, made the pall of black within more solemn and more mysterious.

We heard the clock in the corridor chiming the quarters with its silver bell till two o'clock; and then a strange feeling came over me. I could see from Miss Trelawny's movement as she looked round, that she also had some new sensation. The new detective had just looked in; we two were alone with the unconscious patient for another quarter of an hour.

My heart began to beat wildly. There was a sense of fear over me. Not for myself; my fear was impersonal. It seemed as though some new person had entered the room, and that a strong intelligence was awake close to me. Something brushed against my leg. I put my hand down hastily and touched the furry coat of Silvio. With a very faint far-away sound of a snarl he turned and scratched at me. I felt blood on my hand. I rose gently and came over to the bedside. Miss Trelawny, too, had stood up and was looking behind her, as though there was something close to her. Her eyes were wild, and her breast rose and fell as though she were fighting for air. When I touched her she did not seem to feel me; she worked her hands in front of her, as though she was fending off something.

There was not an instant to lose. I seized her in my arms and rushed over to the door, threw it open, and strode into the passage, calling loudly:

"Help! Help!"

In an instant the two Detectives, Mrs. Grant, and the Nurse appeared on the scene. Close on their heels came several of the servants, both men and women. Immediately Mrs. Grant came near enough, I placed Miss Trelawny in her arms, and rushed back into the room, turning up the electric light as soon as I could lay my hand on it. Sergeant Daw and the Nurse followed me.

We were just in time. Close under the great safe, where on the two successive nights he had been found, lay Mr. Trelawny with his left arm, bare save for the bandages, stretched out. Close by his side was a leaf-shaped Egyptian knife which had lain amongst the curios on the shelf of the broken cabinet. Its point was stuck in the parquet floor, whence had been removed the blood-stained rug.

But there was no sign of disturbance anywhere; nor any sign of any one or anything unusual. The Policemen and I searched the room accurately, whilst the Nurse and two of the servants lifted the wounded man back to bed; but no sign or clue could we get. Very soon Miss Trelawny returned to the room. She was pale but collected. When she came close to me she said in a low voice:

"I felt myself fainting. I did not know why; but I was afraid!"

The only other shock I had was when Miss Trelawny cried out to me, as I placed my hand on the bed to lean over and look carefully at her father:

"You are wounded. Look! look! your hand is bloody. There is blood on the sheets!" I had, in the excitement, quite forgotten Silvio's scratch. As I looked at it, the recollection came back to me; but before I could say a word Miss Trelawny had caught hold of my hand and lifted it up. When she saw the parallel lines of the cuts she cried out again:

"It is the same wound as Father's!" Then she laid my hand down gently but quickly, and said to me and to Sergeant Daw:

"Come to my room! Silvio is there in his basket." We followed her, and found Silvio sitting in his basket awake. He was licking his paws. The Detective said:

"He is there sure enough; but why licking his paws?"

Margaret—Miss Trelawny—gave a moan as she bent over and took one of the forepaws in her hand; but the cat seemed to resent it and snarled. At that Mrs. Grant came into the room. When she saw that we were looking at the cat she said:

"The Nurse tells me that Silvio was asleep on Nurse Kennedy's bed ever since you went to your Father's room until a while ago. He came there just after you had gone to master's room. Nurse says that Nurse Kennedy is moaning and muttering in her sleep as though she had a nightmare. I think we should send for Dr. Winchester."

"Do so at once, please!" said Miss Trelawny; and we went back to the room.

For a while Miss Trelawny stood looking at her father, with her brows wrinkled. Then, turning to me, as though her mind were made up, she said:

"Don't you think we should have a consultation on Father? Of course I have every confidence in Doctor Winchester; he seems an immensely clever young man. But he is a young man; and there must be men who have devoted themselves to this branch of science. Such a man would have more knowledge and more experience; and his knowledge and experience might help to throw light on poor Father's case. As it is, Doctor Winchester seems to be quite in the dark. Oh! I don't know what to do. It is all so terrible!" Here she broke down a little and cried; and I tried to comfort her.

Doctor Winchester arrived quickly. His first thought was for his patient; but when he found him without further harm, he visited Nurse Kennedy. When he saw her, a hopeful look came into his eyes. Taking a towel, he dipped a corner of it in cold water and flicked on the face. The skin coloured, and she stirred slightly. He said to the new nurse—Sister Doris he called her:

"She is all right. She will wake in a few hours at latest. She may be dizzy and distraught at first, or perhaps hysterical. If so, you know how to treat her."

"Yes, sir!" answered Sister Doris demurely; and we went back to Mr. Trelawny's room. As soon as we had entered, Mrs. Grant and the Nurse went out so that only Doctor Winchester, Miss Trelawny, and myself remained in the room. When the door had been closed Doctor Winchester asked me as to what had occurred. I told him fully, giving exactly every detail so far as I could remember. Throughout my narrative, which did not take long, however, he kept asking me questions as to who had been present and the order in which each one had come into the room. He asked other things, but nothing of any importance; these were all that took my attention, or remained in my memory. When our conversation was finished, he said in a very decided way indeed, to Miss Trelawny:

"I think, Miss Trelawny, that we had better have a consultation on this case." She answered at once, seemingly a little to his surprise:

"I am glad you have mentioned it. I quite agree. Who would you suggest?"

"Have you any choice yourself?" he asked. "Any one to whom your Father is known? Has he ever consulted any one?"

"Not to my knowledge. But I hope you will choose whoever you think would be best. My dear Father should have all the help that can be had; and I shall be deeply obliged by your choosing. Who is the best man in London—anywhere else—in such a case?"

"There are several good men; but they are scattered all over the world. Somehow, the brain specialist is born, not made; though a lot of hard work goes to the completing of him and fitting him for his work. He comes from no country. The most daring investigator up to the present is Chiuni, the Japanese; but he is rather a surgical experimentalist than a practitioner. Then there is Zammerfest of Uppsala, and Fenelon of the University of Paris, and Morfessi of Naples. These, of course, are in addition to our own men, Morrison of Aberdeen and Richardson of Birmingham. But before them all I would put Frere of King's College. Of all that I have named he best unites theory and practice. He has no hobbies—that have been discovered at all events; and his experience is immense. It is the regret of all of us who admire him that the nerve so firm and the hand so dexterous must yield to time. For my own part I would rather have Frere than any one living."

"Then," said Miss Trelawny decisively, "let us have Doctor Frere—by the way, is he 'Doctor' or 'Mister'?—as early as we can get him in the morning!"

A weight seemed removed from him, and he spoke with greater ease and geniality than he had yet shown:

"He is Sir James Frere. I shall go to him myself as early as it is possibly to see him, and shall ask him to come here at once." Then turning to me he said:

"You had better let me dress your hand."

"It is nothing," I said.

"Nevertheless it should be seen to. A scratch from any animal might turn out dangerous; there is nothing like being safe." I submitted; forthwith he began to dress my hand. He examined with a magnifying-glass the several parallel wounds, and compared them with the slip of blotting-paper, marked with Silvio's claws, which he took from his pocket-book. He put back the paper, simply remarking:

"It's a pity that Silvio slips in—and out—just when he shouldn't."

The morning wore slowly on. By ten o'clock Nurse Kennedy had so far recovered that she was able to sit up and talk intelligibly. But she was still hazy in her thoughts; and could not remember anything that had happened on the previous night, after her taking her place by the sick-bed. As yet she seemed neither to know nor care what had happened.

It was nearly eleven o'clock when Doctor Winchester returned with Sir James Frere. Somehow I felt my heart sink when from the landing I saw them in the hall below; I knew that Miss Trelawny was to have the pain of telling yet another stranger of her ignorance of her father's life.

Chapter V - More Strange Instructions

Sir James Frere was a man who commanded attention followed by respect. He knew so thoroughly what he wanted himself, that he placed at once on one side all wishes and ideas of less definite persons. The mere flash of his piercing eyes, or the set of his resolute mouth, or the lowering of his great eyebrows, seemed to compel immediate and willing obedience to his wishes. Somehow, when we had all been introduced and he was well amongst us, all sense of mystery seemed to melt away. It was with a hopeful spirit that I saw him pass into the sick-room with Doctor Winchester.

They remained in the room a long time; once they sent for the Nurse, the new one, Sister Doris, but she did not remain long. Again they both went into Nurse Kennedy's room. He sent out the nurse attendant on her. Doctor Winchester told me afterward that Nurse Kennedy, though she was ignorant of later matters, gave full and satisfactory answers to all Doctor Frere's questions relating to her patient up to the time she became unconscious. Then they went to the study, where they remained so long, and their voices raised in heated discussion seemed in such determined opposition, that I began to feel uneasy. As for Miss Trelawny, she was almost in a state of collapse from nervousness before they joined us. Poor girl! she had had a sadly anxious time of it, and her nervous strength had almost broken down.

They came out at last, Sir James first, his grave face looking as unenlightening as that of the sphinx. Doctor Winchester followed him closely; his face was pale, but with that kind of pallor which looked like a reaction. It gave me the idea that it had been red not long before. Sir James asked that Miss Trelawny would come into the study. He suggested that I should come also. When we had entered, Sir James turned to me and said:

"I understand from Doctor Winchester that you are a friend of Miss Trelawny, and that you have already considerable knowledge of this case. Perhaps it will be well that you should be with us. I know you already as a keen lawyer, Mr. Ross, though I never had the pleasure of meeting you. As Doctor Winchester tells me that there are some strange matters outside this case which seem to puzzle him—and others—and in which he thinks you may yet be specially interested, it might be as well that you should know every phase of the case. For myself I do not take much account of mysteries—except those of science; and as there seems to be some idea of an attempt at assassination or robbery, all I can say is that if assassins were at work they ought to take some elementary lessons in anatomy before their next job, for they seem thoroughly ignorant. If robbery were their purpose, they seem to have worked with marvellous inefficiency. That, however, is not my business." Here he took a big pinch of snuff, and turning to Miss Trelawny, went on: "Now as to the patient. Leaving out the cause of his illness, all we can say at present is that he appears to be suffering from a marked attack of catalepsy. At present nothing can be done, except to sustain his strength. The treatment of my friend Doctor Winchester is mainly such as I approve of; and I am confident that should any slight change arise he will be able to deal with it satisfactorily. It is an interesting case—most interesting; and should any new or abnormal development arise I shall be happy to come at any time. There is just one thing to which I wish to call your attention; and I put it to you, Miss Trelawny, directly, since it is your responsibility. Doctor Winchester informs me that you are not yourself free in the matter, but are bound by an instruction given by your Father in case just such a condition of things should arise. I would strongly advise that the patient be removed to another room; or, as an alternative, that those mummies and all such things should be removed from his chamber. Why, it's enough to put any man into an abnormal condition, to have such an assemblage of horrors round him, and to breathe the atmosphere which they exhale. You have evidence already of how such mephitic odour may act. That nurse—Kennedy, I think you said, Doctor—isn't yet out of her state of catalepsy; and you, Mr. Ross, have, I am told, experienced something of the same effects. I know this"—here his eyebrows came down more than ever, and his mouth hardened—"if I were in charge here I should insist on the patient having a different atmosphere; or I would throw up the case. Doctor Winchester already knows that I can only be again consulted on this condition being fulfilled. But I trust that you will see your way, as a good daughter to my mind should, to looking to your Father's health and sanity rather than to any whim of his—whether supported or not by a foregoing fear, or by any number of "penny dreadful" mysteries. The day has hardly come yet, I am glad to say, when the British Museum and St. Thomas's Hospital have exchanged their normal functions. Good-day, Miss Trelawny. I earnestly hope that I may soon see your Father restored. Remember, that should you fulfil the elementary condition which I have laid down, I am at your service day or night. Good-morning, Mr. Ross. I hope you will be able to report to me soon, Doctor Winchester."

When he had gone we stood silent, till the rumble of his carriage wheels died away. The first to speak was Doctor Winchester:

"I think it well to say that to my mind, speaking purely as a physician, he is quite right. I feel as if I could have assaulted him when he made it a condition of not giving up the case; but all the same he is right as to treatment. He does not understand that there is something odd about this special case; and he will not realise the knot that we are all tied up in by Mr. Trelawny's instructions. Of course—" He was interrupted by Miss Trelawny:

"Doctor Winchester, do you, too, wish to give up the case; or are you willing to continue it under the conditions you know?"

"Give it up! Less now than ever. Miss Trelawny, I shall never give it up, so long as life is left to him or any of us!" She said nothing, but held out her hand, which he took warmly.

"Now," said she, "if Sir James Frere is a type of the cult of Specialists, I want no more of them. To start with, he does not seem to know any more than you do about my Father's condition; and if he were a hundredth part as much interested in it as you are, he would not stand on such punctilio. Of course, I am only too anxious about my poor Father; and if I can see a way to meet either of Sir James Frere's conditions, I shall do so. I shall ask Mr. Marvin to come here today, and advise me as to the limit of Father's wishes. If he thinks I am free to act in any way on my own responsibility, I shall not hesitate to do so." Then Doctor Winchester took his leave.

Miss Trelawny sat down and wrote a letter to Mr. Marvin, telling him of the state of affairs, and asking him to come and see her and to bring with him any papers which might throw any light on the subject. She sent the letter off with a carriage to bring back the solicitor; we waited with what patience we could for his coming.

It is not a very long journey for oneself from Kensington Palace Gardens to Lincoln's Inn Fields; but it seemed endlessly long when waiting for someone else to take it. All things, however, are amenable to Time; it was less than an hour all told when Mr. Marvin was with us.

He recognised Miss Trelawny's impatience, and when he had learned sufficient of her father's illness, he said to her:

"Whenever you are ready I can go with you into particulars regarding your Father's wishes."

"Whenever you like," she said, with an evident ignorance of his meaning. "Why not now?" He looked at me, as to a fellow man of business, and stammered out:

"We are not alone."

"I have brought Mr. Ross here on purpose," she answered. "He knows so much at present, that I want him to know more." The solicitor was a little disconcerted, a thing which those knowing him only in courts would hardly have believed. He answered, however, with some hesitation:

"But, my dear young lady—Your Father's wishes!—Confidence between father and child—"

Here she interrupted him; there was a tinge of red in her pale cheeks as she did so:

"Do you really think that applies to the present circumstances, Mr. Marvin? My Father never told me anything of his affairs; and I can now, in this sad extremity, only learn his wishes through a gentleman who is a stranger to me and of whom I never even heard till I got my Father's letter, written to be shown to me only in extremity. Mr. Ross is a new friend; but he has all my confidence, and I should like him to be present. Unless, of course," she added, "such a thing is forbidden by my Father. Oh! forgive me, Mr. Marvin, if I seem rude; but I have been in such dreadful trouble and anxiety lately, that I have hardly command of myself." She covered her eyes with her hand for a few seconds; we two men looked at each other and waited, trying to appear unmoved. She went on more firmly; she had recovered herself:

"Please! please do not think I am ungrateful to you for your kindness in coming here and so quickly. I really am grateful; and I have every confidence in your judgment. If you wish, or think it best, we can be alone." I stood up; but Mr. Marvin made a dissentient gesture. He was evidently pleased with her attitude; there was geniality in his voice and manner as he spoke:

"Not at all! Not at all! There is no restriction on your Father's part; and on my own I am quite willing. Indeed, all told, it may be better. From what you have said of Mr. Trelawny's illness, and the other—incidental—matters, it will be well in case of any grave eventuality, that it was understood from the first, that circumstances were ruled by your Father's own imperative instructions. For, please understand me, his instructions are imperative—most imperative. They are so unyielding that he has given me a Power of Attorney, under which I have undertaken to act, authorising me to see his written wishes carried out. Please believe me once for all, that he intended fully everything mentioned in that letter to you! Whilst he is alive he is to remain in his own room; and none of his property is to be removed from it under any circumstances whatever. He has even given an inventory of the articles which are not to be displaced."

Miss Trelawny was silent. She looked somewhat distressed; so, thinking that I understood the immediate cause, I asked:

"May we see the list?" Miss Trelawny's face at once brightened; but it fell again as the lawyer answered promptly—he was evidently prepared for the question:

"Not unless I am compelled to take action on the Power of Attorney. I have brought that instrument with me. You will recognise, Mr. Ross"—he said this with a sort of business conviction which I had noticed in his professional work, as he handed me the deed—"how strongly it is worded, and how the grantor made his wishes apparent in such a way as to leave no loophole. It is his own wording, except for certain legal formalities; and I assure you I have seldom seen a more iron-clad document. Even I myself have no power to make the slightest relaxation of the instructions, without committing a distinct breach of faith. And that, I need not tell you, is impossible." He evidently added the last words in order to prevent an appeal to his personal consideration. He did not like the seeming harshness of his words, however, for he added:

"I do hope, Miss Trelawny, that you understand that I am willing—frankly and unequivocally willing—to do anything I can, within the limits of my power, to relieve your distress. But your Father had, in all his doings, some purpose of his own which he did not disclose to me. So far as I can see, there is not a word of his instructions that he had not thought over fully. Whatever idea he had in his mind was the idea of a lifetime; he had studied it in every possible phase, and was prepared to guard it at every point.

"Now I fear I have distressed you, and I am truly sorry for it; for I see you have much—too much—to bear already. But I have no alternative. If you want to consult me at any time about anything, I promise you I will come without a moment's delay, at any hour of the day or night. There is my private address," he scribbled in his pocket-book as he spoke, "and under it the address of my club, where I am generally to be found in the evening." He tore out the paper and handed it to her. She thanked him. He shook hands with her and with me and withdrew.

As soon as the hall door was shut on him, Mrs. Grant tapped at the door and came in. There was such a look of distress in her face that Miss Trelawny stood up, deadly white, and asked her:

"What is it, Mrs. Grant? What is it? Any new trouble?"

"I grieve to say, miss, that the servants, all but two, have given notice and want to leave the house today. They have talked the matter over among themselves; the butler has spoken for the rest. He says as how they are willing to forego their wages, and even to pay their legal obligations instead of notice; but that go today they must."

"What reason do they give?"

"None, miss. They say as how they're sorry, but that they've nothing to say. I asked Jane, the upper housemaid, miss, who is not with the rest but stops on; and she tells me confidential that they've got some notion in their silly heads that the house is haunted!"

We ought to have laughed, but we didn't. I could not look in Miss Trelawny's face and laugh. The pain and horror there showed no sudden paroxysm of fear; there was a fixed idea of which this was a confirmation. For myself, it seemed as if my brain had found a voice. But the voice was not complete; there was some other thought, darker and deeper, which lay behind it, whose voice had not sounded as yet.

Chapter VI - Suspicions

The first to get full self-command was Miss Trelawny. There was a haughty dignity in her bearing as she said:

"Very well, Mrs. Grant; let them go! Pay them up to today, and a month's wages. They have hitherto been very good servants; and the occasion of their leaving is not an ordinary one. We must not expect much faithfulness from any one who is beset with fears. Those who remain are to have in future double wages; and please send these to me presently when I send word." Mrs. Grant bristled with smothered indignation; all the housekeeper in her was outraged by such generous treatment of servants who had combined to give notice:

"They don't deserve it, miss; them to go on so, after the way they have been treated here. Never in my life have I seen servants so well treated or anyone so good to them and gracious to them as you have been. They might be in the household of a King for treatment. And now, just as there is trouble, to go and act like this. It's abominable, that's what it is!"

Miss Trelawny was very gentle with her, and smothered her ruffled dignity; so that presently she went away with, in her manner, a lesser measure of hostility to the undeserving. In quite a different frame of mind she returned presently to ask if her mistress would like her to engage a full staff of other servants, or at any rate try to do so. "For you know, ma'am," she went on, "when once a scare has been established in the servants' hall, it's wellnigh impossible to get rid of it. Servants may come; but they go away just as quick. There's no holding them. They simply won't stay; or even if they work out their month's notice, they lead you that life that you wish every hour of the day that you hadn't kept them. The women are bad enough, the huzzies; but the men are worse!" There was neither anxiety nor indignation in Miss Trelawny's voice or manner as she said:

"I think, Mrs. Grant, we had better try to do with those we have. Whilst my dear Father is ill we shall not be having any company, so that there will be only three now in the house to attend to. If those servants who are willing to stay are not enough, I should only get sufficient to help them to do the work. It will not, I should think, be difficult to get a few maids; perhaps some that you know already. And please bear in mind, that those whom you get, and who are suitable and will stay, are henceforth to have the same wages as those who are remaining. Of course, Mrs. Grant, you well enough understand that though I do not group you in any way with the servants, the rule of double salary applies to you too." As she spoke she extended her long, fine-shaped hand, which the other took and then, raising it to her lips, kissed it impressively with the freedom of an elder woman to a younger. I could not but admire the generosity of her treatment of her servants. In my mind I endorsed Mrs. Grant's sotto voce remark as she left the room:

"No wonder the house is like a King's house, when the mistress is a Princess!"

"A Princess!" That was it. The idea seemed to satisfy my mind, and to bring back in a wave of light the first moment when she swept across my vision at the ball in Belgrave Square. A queenly figure! tall and slim, bending, swaying, undulating as the lily or the lotos. Clad in a flowing gown of some filmy black material shot with gold. For ornament in her hair she wore an old Egyptian jewel, a tiny crystal disk, set between rising plumes carved in lapis lazuli. On her wrist was a broad bangle or bracelet of antique work, in the shape of a pair of spreading wings wrought in gold, with the feathers made of coloured gems. For all her gracious bearing toward me, when our hostess introduced me, I was then afraid of her. It was only when later, at the picnic on the river, I had come to realise her sweet and gentle, that my awe changed to something else.

For a while she sat, making some notes or memoranda. Then putting them away, she sent for the faithful servants. I thought that she had better have this interview alone, and so left her. When I came back there were traces of tears in her eyes.

The next phase in which I had a part was even more disturbing, and infinitely more painful. Late in the afternoon Sergeant Daw came into the study where I was sitting. After closing the door carefully and looking all round the room to make certain that we were alone, he came close to me.

"What is it?" I asked him. "I see you wish to speak to me privately."

"Quite so, sir! May I speak in absolute confidence?"

"Of course you may. In anything that is for the good of Miss Trelawny—and of course Mr. Trelawny—you may be perfectly frank. I take it that we both want to serve them to the best of our powers." He hesitated before replying:

"Of course you know that I have my duty to do; and I think you know me well enough to know that I will do it. I am a policeman—a detective; and it is my duty to find out the facts of any case I am put on, without fear or favour to anyone. I would rather speak to you alone, in confidence if I may, without reference to any duty of anyone to anyone, except mine to Scotland Yard."

"Of course! of course!" I answered mechanically, my heart sinking, I did not know why. "Be quite frank with me. I assure you of my confidence."

"Thank you, sir. I take it that what I say is not to pass beyond you—not to anyone. Not to Miss Trelawny herself, or even to Mr. Trelawny when he becomes well again."

"Certainly, if you make it a condition!" I said a little more stiffly. The man recognised the change in my voice or manner, and said apologetically:

"Excuse me, sir, but I am going outside my duty in speaking to you at all on the subject. I know you, however, of old; and I feel that I can trust you. Not your word, sir, that is all right; but your discretion!"

I bowed. "Go on!" I said. He began at once:

"I have gone over this case, sir, till my brain begins to reel; but I can't find any ordinary solution of it. At the time of each attempt no one has seemingly come into the house; and certainly no one has got out. What does it strike you is the inference?"

"That the somebody—or the something—was in the house already," I answered, smiling in spite of myself.

"That's just what I think," he said, with a manifest sigh of relief. "Very well! Who can be that someone?"

"'Someone, or something,' was what I said," I answered.

"Let us make it 'someone,' Mr. Ross! That cat, though he might have scratched or bit, never pulled the old gentleman out of bed, and tried to get the bangle with the key off his arm. Such things are all very well in books where your amateur detectives, who know everything before it's done, can fit them into theories; but in Scotland Yard, where the men aren't all idiots either, we generally find that when crime is done, or attempted, it's people, not things, that are at the bottom of it."

"Then make it 'people' by all means, Sergeant."

"We were speaking of 'someone,' sir."

"Quite right. Someone, be it!"

"Did it ever strike you, sir, that on each of the three separate occasions where outrage was effected, or attempted, there was one person who was the first to be present and to give the alarm?"

"Let me see! Miss Trelawny, I believe, gave the alarm on the first occasion. I was present myself, if fast asleep, on the second; and so was Nurse Kennedy. When I woke there were several people in the room; you were one of them. I understand that on that occasion also Miss Trelawny was before you. At the last attempt I was Miss Trelawny fainted. I carried her out and went back. In returning, I was first; and I think you were close behind me."

Sergeant Daw thought for a moment before replying:

"She was present, or first, in the room on all the occasions; there was only damage done in the first and second!"

The inference was one which I, as a lawyer, could not mistake. I thought the best thing to do was to meet it half-way. I have always found that the best way to encounter an inference is to cause it to be turned into a statement.

"You mean," I said, "that as on the only occasions when actual harm was done, Miss Trelawny's being the first to discover it is a proof that she did it; or was in some way connected with the attempt, as well as the discovery?"

"I didn't venture to put it as clear as that; but that is where the doubt which I had leads." Sergeant Daw was a man of courage; he evidently did not shrink from any conclusion of his reasoning on facts.

We were both silent for a while. Fears began crowding in on my own mind. Not doubts of Miss Trelawny, or of any act of hers; but fears lest such acts should be misunderstood. There was evidently a mystery somewhere; and if no solution to it could be found, the doubt would be cast on someone. In such cases the guesses of the majority are bound to follow the line of least resistance; and if it could be proved that any personal gain to anyone could follow Mr. Trelawny's death, should such ensue, it might prove a difficult task for anyone to prove innocence in the face of suspicious facts. I found myself instinctively taking that deferential course which, until the plan of battle of the prosecution is unfolded, is so safe an attitude for the defence. It would never do for me, at this stage, to combat any theories which a detective might form. I could best help Miss Trelawny by listening and understanding. When the time should come for the dissipation and obliteration of the theories, I should be quite willing to use all my militant ardour, and all the weapons at my command.

"You will of course do your duty, I know," I said, "and without fear. What course do you intend to take?"

"I don't know as yet, sir. You see, up to now it isn't with me even a suspicion. If any one else told me that that sweet young lady had a hand in such a matter, I would think him a fool; but I am bound to follow my own conclusions. I know well that just as unlikely persons have been proved guilty, when a whole court—all except the prosecution who knew the facts, and the judge who had taught his mind to wait—would have sworn to innocence. I wouldn't, for all the world, wrong such a young lady; more especial when she has such a cruel weight to bear. And you will be sure that I won't say a word that'll prompt anyone else to make such a charge. That's why I speak to you in confidence, man to man. You are skilled in proofs; that is your profession. Mine only gets so far as suspicions, and what we call our own proofs—which are nothing but ex parte evidence after all. You know Miss Trelawny better than I do; and though I watch round the sick-room, and go where I like about the house and in and out of it, I haven't the same opportunities as you have of knowing the lady and what her life is, or her means are; or of anything else which might give me a clue to her actions. If I were to try to find out from her, it would at once arouse her suspicions. Then, if she were guilty, all possibility of ultimate proof would go; for she would easily find a way to baffle discovery. But if she be innocent, as I hope she is, it would be doing a cruel wrong to accuse her. I have thought the matter over according to my lights before I spoke to you; and if I have taken a liberty, sir, I am truly sorry."

"No liberty in the world, Daw," I said warmly, for the man's courage and honesty and consideration compelled respect. "I am glad you have spoken to me so frankly. We both want to find out the truth; and there is so much about this case that is strange—so strange as to go beyond all experiences—that to aim at truth is our only chance of making anything clear in the long-run—no matter what our views are, or what object we wish to achieve ultimately!" The Sergeant looked pleased as he went on:

"I thought, therefore, that if you had it once in your mind that somebody else held to such a possibility, you would by degrees get proof; or at any rate such ideas as would convince yourself, either for or against it. Then we would come to some conclusion; or at any rate we should so exhaust all other possibilities that the most likely one would remain as the nearest thing to proof, or strong suspicion, that we could get. After that we should have to—"

Just at this moment the door opened and Miss Trelawny entered the room. The moment she saw us she drew back quickly, saying:

"Oh, I beg pardon! I did not know you were here, and engaged." By the time I had stood up, she was about to go back.

"Do come in," I said; "Sergeant Daw and I were only talking matters over."

Whilst she was hesitating, Mrs. Grant appeared, saying as she entered the room: "Doctor Winchester is come, miss, and is asking for you."

I obeyed Miss Trelawny's look; together we left the room.

When the Doctor had made his examination, he told us that there was seemingly no change. He added that nevertheless he would like to stay in the house that night is he might. Miss Trelawny looked glad, and sent word to Mrs. Grant to get a room ready for him. Later in the day, when he and I happened to be alone together, he said suddenly:

"I have arranged to stay here tonight because I want to have a talk with you. And as I wish it to be quite private, I thought the least suspicious way would be to have a cigar together late in the evening when Miss Trelawny is watching her father." We still kept to our arrangement that either the sick man's daughter or I should be on watch all night. We were to share the duty at the early hours of the morning. I was anxious about this, for I knew from our conversation that the Detective would watch in secret himself, and would be particularly alert about that time.

The day passed uneventfully. Miss Trelawny slept in the afternoon; and after dinner went to relieve the Nurse. Mrs. Grant remained with her, Sergeant Daw being on duty in the corridor. Doctor Winchester and I took our coffee in the library. When we had lit our cigars he said quietly:

"Now that we are alone I want to have a confidential talk. We are 'tiled,' of course; for the present at all events?"

"Quite so!" I said, my heart sinking as I thought of my conversation with Sergeant Daw in the morning, and of the disturbing and harrowing fears which it had left in my mind. He went on:

"This case is enough to try the sanity of all of us concerned in it. The more I think of it, the madder I seem to get; and the two lines, each continually strengthened, seem to pull harder in opposite directions."

"What two lines?" He looked at me keenly for a moment before replying. Doctor Winchester's look at such moments was apt to be disconcerting. It would have been so to me had I had a personal part, other than my interest in Miss Trelawny, in the matter. As it was, however, I stood it unruffled. I was now an attorney in the case; an amicus curiae in one sense, in another retained for the defence. The mere thought that in this clever man's mind were two lines, equally strong and opposite, was in itself so consoling as to neutralise my anxiety as to a new attack. As he began to speak, the Doctor's face wore an inscrutable smile; this, however, gave place to a stern gravity as he proceeded:

"Two lines: Fact and—Fancy! In the first there is this whole thing; attacks, attempts at robbery and murder; stupefyings; organised catalepsy which points to either criminal hypnotism and thought suggestion, or some simple form of poisoning unclassified yet in our toxicology. In the other there is some influence at work which is not classified in any book that I know—outside the pages of romance. I never felt in my life so strongly the truth of Hamlet's words:

'There are more things in Heaven and earth...
Than are dreamt of in your philosophy.'

"Let us take the 'Fact' side first. Here we have a man in his home; amidst his own household; plenty of servants of different classes in the house, which forbids the possibility of an organised attempt made from the servants" hall. He is wealthy, learned, clever. From his physiognomy there is no doubting that he is a man of iron will and determined purpose. His daughter—his only child, I take it, a young girl bright and clever—is sleeping in the very next room to his. There is seemingly no possible reason for expecting any attack or disturbance of any kind; and no reasonable opportunity for any outsider to effect it. And yet we have an attack made; a brutal and remorseless attack, made in the middle of the night. Discovery is made quickly; made with that rapidity which in criminal cases generally is found to be not accidental, but of premeditated intent. The attacker, or attackers, are manifestly disturbed before the completion of their work, whatever their ultimate intent may have been. And yet there is no possible sign of their escape; no clue, no disturbance of anything; no open door or window; no sound. Nothing whatever to show who had done the deed, or even that a deed has been done; except the victim, and his surroundings incidental to the deed!

"The next night a similar attempt is made, though the house is full of wakeful people; and though there are on watch in the room and around it a detective officer, a trained nurse, an earnest friend, and the man's own daughter. The nurse is thrown into a catalepsy, and the watching friend—though protected by a respirator—into a deep sleep. Even the detective is so far overcome with some phase of stupor that he fires off his pistol in the sick-room, and can't even tell what he thought he was firing at. That respirator of yours is the only thing that seems to have a bearing on the 'fact' side of the affair. That you did not lose your head as the others did—the effect in such case being in proportion to the amount of time each remained in the room—points to the probability that the stupefying medium was not hypnotic, whatever else it may have been. But again, there is a fact which is contradictory. Miss Trelawny, who was in the room more than any of you—for she was in and out all the time and did her share of permanent watching also—did not seem to be affected at all. This would show that the influence, whatever it is, does not affect generally—unless, of course, it was that she was in some way inured to it. If it should turn out that it be some strange exhalation from some of those Egyptian curios, that might account for it; only, we are then face to face with the fact that Mr. Trelawny, who was most of all in the room—who, in fact, lived more than half his life in it—was affected worst of all. What kind of influence could it be which would account for all these different and contradictory effects? No! the more I think of this form of the dilemma, the more I am bewildered! Why, even if it were that the attack, the physical attack, on Mr. Trelawny had been made by some one residing in the house and not within the sphere of suspicion, the oddness of the stupefyings would still remain a mystery. It is not easy to put anyone into a catalepsy. Indeed, so far as is known yet in science, there is no way to achieve such an object at will. The crux of the whole matter is Miss Trelawny, who seems to be subject to none of the influences, or possibly of the variants of the same influence at work. Through all she goes unscathed, except for that one slight semi-faint. It is most strange!"

I listened with a sinking heart; for, though his manner was not illuminative of distrust, his argument was disturbing. Although it was not so direct as the suspicion of the Detective, it seemed to single out Miss Trelawny as different from all others concerned; and in a mystery to be alone is to be suspected, ultimately if not immediately. I thought it better not to say anything. In such a case silence is indeed golden; and if I said nothing now I might have less to defend, or explain, or take back later. I was, therefore, secretly glad that his form of putting his argument did not require any answer from me—for the present, at all events. Doctor Winchester did not seem to expect any answer—a fact which, when I recognised it, gave my pleasure, I hardly knew why. He paused for a while, sitting with his chin in his hand, his eyes staring at vacancy, whilst his brows were fixed. His cigar was held limp between his fingers; he had apparently forgotten it. In an even voice, as though commencing exactly where he had left off, he resumed his argument:

"The other horn of the dilemma is a different affair altogether; and if we once enter on it we must leave everything in the shape of science and experience behind us. I confess that it has its fascinations for me; though at every new thought I find myself romancing in a way that makes me pull up suddenly and look facts resolutely in the face. I sometimes wonder whether the influence or emanation from the sick-room at times affects me as it did the others—the Detective, for instance. Of course it may be that if it is anything chemical, any drug, for example, in vaporeal form, its effects may be cumulative. But then, what could there be that could produce such an effect? The room is, I know, full of mummy smell; and no wonder, with so many relics from the tomb, let alone the actual mummy of that animal which Silvio attacked. By the way, I am going to test him tomorrow; I have been on the trace of a mummy cat, and am to get possession of it in the morning. When I bring it here we shall find out if it be a fact that racial instinct can survive a few thousand years in the grave. However, to get back to the subject in hand. These very mummy smells arise from the presence of substances, and combinations of substances, which the Egyptian priests, who were the learned men and scientists of their time, found by the experience of centuries to be strong enough to arrest the natural forces of decay. There must be powerful agencies at work to effect such a purpose; and it is possible that we may have here some rare substance or combination whose qualities and powers are not understood in this later and more prosaic age. I wonder if Mr. Trelawny has any knowledge, or even suspicion, of such a kind? I only know this for certain, that a worse atmosphere for a sick chamber could not possibly be imagined; and I admire the courage of Sir James Frere in refusing to have anything to do with a case under such conditions. These instructions of Mr. Trelawny to his daughter, and from what you have told me, the care with which he has protected his wishes through his solicitor, show that he suspected something, at any rate. Indeed, it would almost seem as if he expected something to happen.... I wonder if it would be possible to learn anything about that! Surely his papers would show or suggest something.... It is a difficult matter to tackle; but it might have to be done. His present condition cannot go on for ever; and if anything should happen there would have to be an inquest. In such case full examination would have to be made into everything.... As it stands, the police evidence would show a murderous attack more than once repeated. As no clue is apparent, it would be necessary to seek one in a motive."

He was silent. The last words seemed to come in a lower and lower tone as he went on. It had the effect of hopelessness. It came to me as a conviction that now was my time to find out if he had any definite suspicion; and as if in obedience to some command, I asked:

"Do you suspect anyone?" He seemed in a way startled rather than surprised as he turned his eyes on me:

"Suspect anyone? Any thing, you mean. I certainly suspect that there is some influence; but at present my suspicion is held within such limit. Later on, if there be any sufficiently definite conclusion to my reasoning, or my thinking—for there are not proper data for reasoning—I may suspect; at present however—"

He stopped suddenly and looked at the door. There was a faint sound as the handle turned. My own heart seemed to stand still. There was over me some grim, vague apprehension. The interruption in the morning, when I was talking with the Detective, came back upon me with a rush.

The door opened, and Miss Trelawny entered the room.

When she saw us, she started back; and a deep flush swept her face. For a few seconds she paused; at such a time a few succeeding seconds seem to lengthen in geometrical progression. The strain upon me, and, as I could easily see, on the Doctor also, relaxed as she spoke:

"Oh, forgive me, I did not know that you were engaged. I was looking for you, Doctor Winchester, to ask you if I might go to bed tonight with safety, as you will be here. I feel so tired and worn-out that I fear I may break down; and tonight I would certainly not be of any use." Doctor Winchester answered heartily:

"Do! Do go to bed by all means, and get a good night's sleep. God knows! you want it. I am more than glad you have made the suggestion, for I feared when I saw you tonight that I might have you on my hands a patient next."

She gave a sigh of relief, and the tired look seemed to melt from her face. Never shall I forget the deep, earnest look in her great, beautiful black eyes as she said to me:

"You will guard Father tonight, won't you, with Doctor Winchester? I am so anxious about him that every second brings new fears. But I am really worn-out; and if I don't get a good sleep, I think I shall go mad. I will change my room for tonight. I'm afraid that if I stay so close to Father's room I shall multiply every sound into a new terror. But, of course, you will have me waked if there be any cause. I shall be in the bedroom of the little suite next the boudoir off the hall. I had those rooms when first I came to live with Father, and I had no care then.... It will be easier to rest there; and perhaps for a few hours I may forget. I shall be all right in the morning. Good-night!"

When I had closed the door behind her and come back to the little table at which we had been sitting, Doctor Winchester said:

"That poor girl is overwrought to a terrible degree. I am delighted that she is to get a rest. It will be life to her; and in the morning she will be all right. Her nervous system is on the verge of a breakdown. Did you notice how fearfully disturbed she was, and how red she got when she came in and found us talking? An ordinary thing like that, in her own house with her own guests, wouldn't under normal circumstances disturb her!"

I was about to tell him, as an explanation in her defence, how her entrance was a repetition of her finding the Detective and myself alone together earlier in the day, when I remembered that that conversation was so private that even an allusion to it might be awkward in evoking curiosity. So I remained silent.

We stood up to go to the sick-room; but as we took our way through the dimly-lighted corridor I could not help thinking, again and again, and again—ay, and for many a day after—how strange it was that she had interrupted me on two such occasions when touching on such a theme.

There was certainly some strange web of accidents, in whose meshes we were all involved.

Chapter VII - The Traveller's Loss

That night everything went well. Knowing that Miss Trelawny herself was not on guard, Doctor Winchester and I doubled our vigilance. The Nurses and Mrs. Grant kept watch, and the Detectives made their visit each quarter of an hour. All night the patient remained in his trance. He looked healthy, and his chest rose and fell with the easy breathing of a child. But he never stirred; only for his breathing he might have been of marble. Doctor Winchester and I wore our respirators, and irksome they were on that intolerably hot night. Between midnight and three o'clock I felt anxious, and had once more that creepy feeling to which these last few nights had accustomed me; but the grey of the dawn, stealing round the edges of the blinds, came with inexpressible relief, followed by restfulness, went through the household. During the hot night my ears, strained to every sound, had been almost painfully troubled; as though my brain or sensoria were in anxious touch with them. Every breath of the Nurse or the rustle of her dress; every soft pat of slippered feet, as the Policeman went his rounds; every moment of watching life, seemed to be a new impetus to guardianship. Something of the same feeling must have been abroad in the house; now and again I could hear upstairs the sound of restless feet, and more than once downstairs the opening of a window. With the coming of the dawn, however, all this ceased, and the whole household seemed to rest. Doctor Winchester went home when Sister Doris came to relieve Mrs. Grant. He was, I think, a little disappointed or chagrined that nothing of an exceptional nature had happened during his long night vigil.

At eight o'clock Miss Trelawny joined us, and I was amazed as well as delighted to see how much good her night's sleep had done her. She was fairly radiant; just as I had seen her at our first meeting and at the picnic. There was even a suggestion of colour in her cheeks, which, however, looked startlingly white in contrast with her black brows and scarlet lips. With her restored strength, there seemed to have come a tenderness even exceeding that which she had at first shown to her sick father. I could not but be moved by the loving touches as she fixed his pillows and brushed the hair from his forehead.

I was wearied out myself with my long spell of watching; and now that she was on guard I started off to bed, blinking my tired eyes in the full light and feeling the weariness of a sleepless night on me all at once.

I had a good sleep, and after lunch I was about to start out to walk to Jermyn Street, when I noticed an importunate man at the hall door. The servant in charge was the one called Morris, formerly the "odd man," but since the exodus of the servants promoted to be butler pro tem. The stranger was speaking rather loudly, so that there was no difficulty in understanding his grievance. The servant man was respectful in both words and demeanour; but he stood squarely in front of the great double door, so that the other could not enter. The first words which I heard from the visitor sufficiently explained the situation:

"That's all very well, but I tell you I must see Mr. Trelawny! What is the use of your saying I can't, when I tell you I must. You put me off, and off, and off! I came here at nine; you said then that he was not up, and that as he was not well he could not be disturbed. I came at twelve; and you told me again he was not up. I asked then to see any of his household; you told me that Miss Trelawny was not up. Now I come again at three, and you tell me he is still in bed, and is not awake yet. Where is Miss Trelawny? 'She is occupied and must not be disturbed!' Well, she must be disturbed! Or some one must. I am here about Mr. Trelawny's special business; and I have come from a place where servants always begin by saying No. 'No' isn't good enough for me this time! I've had three years of it, waiting outside doors and tents when it took longer to get in than it did into the tombs; and then you would think, too, the men inside were as dead as the mummies. I've had about enough of it, I tell you. And when I come home, and find the door of the man I've been working for barred, in just the same way and with the same old answers, it stirs me up the wrong way. Did Mr. Trelawny leave orders that he would not see me when I should come?"

He paused and excitedly mopped his forehead. The servant answered very respectfully:

"I am very sorry, sir, if in doing my duty I have given any offence. But I have my orders, and must obey them. If you would like to leave any message, I will give it to Miss Trelawny; and if you will leave your address, she can communicate with you if she wishes." The answer came in such a way that it was easy to see that the speaker was a kind-hearted man, and a just one.

"My good fellow, I have no fault to find with you personally; and I am sorry if I have hurt your feelings. I must be just, even if I am angry. But it is enough to anger any man to find himself in the position I am. Time is pressing. There is not an hour—not a minute—to lose! And yet here I am, kicking my heels for six hours; knowing all the time that your master will be a hundred times angrier than I am, when he hears how the time has been fooled away. He would rather be waked out of a thousand sleeps than not see me just at present—and before it is too late. My God! it's simply dreadful, after all I've gone through, to have my work spoiled at the last and be foiled in the very doorway by a stupid flunkey! Is there no one with sense in the house; or with authority, even if he hasn't got sense? I could mighty soon convince him that your master must be awakened; even if he sleeps like the Seven Sleepers—"

There was no mistaking the man's sincerity, or the urgency and importance of his business; from his point of view at any rate. I stepped forward.

"Morris," I said, "you had better tell Miss Trelawny that this gentleman wants to see her particularly. If she is busy, ask Mrs. Grant to tell her."

"Very good, sir!" he answered in a tone of relief, and hurried away.

I took the stranger into the little boudoir across the hall. As we went he asked me:

"Are you the secretary?"

"No! I am a friend of Miss Trelawny's. My name is Ross."

"Thank you very much, Mr. Ross, for your kindness!" he said. "My name is Corbeck. I would give you my card, but they don't use cards where I've come from. And if I had had any, I suppose they, too, would have gone last night—"

He stopped suddenly, as though conscious that he had said too much. We both remained silent; as we waited I took stock of him. A short, sturdy man, brown as a coffee-berry; possibly inclined to be fat, but now lean exceedingly. The deep wrinkles in his face and neck were not merely from time and exposure; there were those unmistakable signs where flesh or fat has fallen away, and the skin has become loose. The neck was simply an intricate surface of seams and wrinkles, and sun-scarred with the burning of the Desert. The Far East, the Tropic Seasons, and the Desert—each can have its colour mark. But all three are quite different; and an eye which has once known, can thenceforth easily distinguish them. The dusky pallor of one; the fierce red-brown of the other; and of the third, the dark, ingrained burning, as though it had become a permanent colour. Mr. Corbeck had a big head, massive and full; with shaggy, dark red-brown hair, but bald on the temples. His forehead was a fine one, high and broad; with, to use the terms of physiognomy, the frontal sinus boldly marked. The squareness of it showed "ratiocination"; and the fulness under the eyes "language". He had the short, broad nose that marks energy; the square chin—marked despite a thick, unkempt beard—and massive jaw that showed great resolution.

"No bad man for the Desert!" I thought as I looked.

Miss Trelawny came very quickly. When Mr. Corbeck saw her, he seemed somewhat surprised. But his annoyance and excitement had not disappeared; quite enough remained to cover up any such secondary and purely exoteric feeling as surprise. But as she spoke he never took his eyes off her; and I made a mental note that I would find some early opportunity of investigating the cause of his surprise. She began with an apology which quite smoothed down his ruffled feelings:

"Of course, had my Father been well you would not have been kept waiting. Indeed, had not I been on duty in the sick-room when you called the first time, I should have seen you at once. Now will you kindly tell me what is the matter which so presses?" He looked at me and hesitated. She spoke at once:

"You may say before Mr. Ross anything which you can tell me. He has my fullest confidence, and is helping me in my trouble. I do not think you quite understand how serious my Father's condition is. For three days he has not waked, or given any sign of consciousness; and I am in terrible trouble about him. Unhappily I am in great ignorance of my Father and his life. I only came to live with him a year ago; and I know nothing whatever of his affairs. I do not even know who you are, or in what way your business is associated with him." She said this with a little deprecating smile, all conventional and altogether graceful; as though to express in the most genuine way her absurd ignorance.

He looked steadily at her for perhaps a quarter of a minute; then he spoke, beginning at once as though his mind were made up and his confidence established:

"My name is Eugene Corbeck. I am a Master of Arts and Doctor of Laws and Master of Surgery of Cambridge; Doctor of Letters of Oxford; Doctor of Science and Doctor of Languages of London University; Doctor of Philosophy of Berlin; Doctor of Oriental Languages of Paris. I have some other degrees, honorary and otherwise, but I need not trouble you with them. Those I have name will show you that I am sufficiently feathered with diplomas to fly into even a sick-room. Early in life—

fortunately for my interests and pleasures, but unfortunately for my pocket—I fell in with Egyptology. I must have been bitten by some powerful scarab, for I took it bad. I went out tomb-hunting; and managed to get a living of a sort, and to learn some things that you can't get out of books. I was in pretty low water when I met your Father, who was doing some explorations on his own account; and since then I haven't found that I have many unsatisfied wants. He is a real patron of the arts; no mad Egyptologist can ever hope for a better chief!"

He spoke with feeling; and I was glad to see that Miss Trelawny coloured up with pleasure at the praise of her father. I could not help noticing, however, that Mr. Corbeck was, in a measure, speaking as if against time. I took it that he wished, while speaking, to study his ground; to see how far he would be justified in taking into confidence the two strangers before him. As he went on, I could see that his confidence kept increasing. When I thought of it afterward, and remembered what he had said, I realised that the measure of the information which he gave us marked his growing trust.

"I have been several times out on expeditions in Egypt for your Father; and I have always found it a delight to work for him. Many of his treasures—and he has some rare ones, I tell you-he has procured through me, either by my exploration or by purchase—or—or—otherwise. Your Father, Miss Trelawny, has a rare knowledge. He sometimes makes up his mind that he wants to find a particular thing, of whose existence—if it still exists—he has become aware; and he will follow it all over the world till he gets it. I've been on just such a chase now."

He stopped suddenly, as suddenly as thought his mouth had been shut by the jerk of a string. We waited; when he went on he spoke with a caution that was new to him, as though he wished to forestall our asking any questions:

"I am not at liberty to mention anything of my mission; where it was to, what it was for, or anything at all about it. Such matters are in confidence between Mr. Trelawny and myself; I am pledged to absolute secrecy."

He paused, and an embarrassed look crept over his face. Suddenly he said:

"You are sure, Miss Trelawny, your Father is not well enough to see me today?"

A look of wonderment was on her face in turn. But it cleared at once;—she stood up, saying in a tone in which dignity and graciousness were blended:

"Come and see for yourself!" She moved toward her father's room; he followed, and I brought up the rear.

Mr. Corbeck entered the sick-room as though he knew it. There is an unconscious attitude or bearing to persons in new surroundings which there is no mistaking. Even in his anxiety to see his powerful friend, he glanced for a moment round the room, as at a familiar place. Then all his attention became fixed on the bed. I watched him narrowly, for somehow I felt that on this man depended much of our enlightenment regarding the strange matter in which we were involved.

It was not that I doubted him. The man was of transparent honesty; it was this very quality which we had to dread. He was of that courageous, fixed trueness to his undertaking, that if he should deem it his duty to guard a secret he would do it to the last. The case before us was, at least, an unusual one; and it would, consequently, require more liberal recognition of bounds of the duty of secrecy than would hold under ordinary conditions. To us, ignorance was helplessness. If we could learn anything of the past we might at least form some idea of the conditions antecedent to the attack;

and might, so, achieve some means of helping the patient to recovery. There were curios which might be removed.... My thoughts were beginning to whirl once again; I pulled myself up sharply and watched. There was a look of infinite pity on the sun-stained, rugged face as he gazed at his friend, lying so helpless. The sternness of Mr. Trelawny's face had not relaxed in sleep; but somehow it made the helplessness more marked. It would not have troubled one to see a weak or an ordinary face under such conditions; but this purposeful, masterful man, lying before us wrapped in impenetrable sleep, had all the pathos of a great ruin. The sight was not a new one to us; but I could see that Miss Trelawny, like myself, was moved afresh by it in the presence of the stranger. Mr. Corbeck's face grew stern. All the pity died away; and in its stead came a grim, hard look which boded ill for whoever had been the cause of this mighty downfall. This look in turn gave place to one of decision; the volcanic energy of the man was working to some definite purpose. He glanced around at us; and as his eyes lighted on Nurse Kennedy his eyebrows went up a trifle. She noted the look, and glanced interrogatively at Miss Trelawny, who flashed back a reply with a glance. She went quietly from the room, closing the door behind her. Mr. Corbeck looked first at me, with a strong man's natural impulse to learn from a man rather than a woman; then at Miss Trelawny, with a remembrance of the duty of courtesy, and said:

"Tell me all about it. How it began and when!" Miss Trelawny looked at me appeallingly; and forthwith I told him all that I knew. He seemed to make no motion during the whole time; but insensibly the bronze face became steel. When, at the end, I told him of Mr. Marvin's visit and of the Power of Attorney, his look began to brighten. And when, seeing his interest in the matter, I went more into detail as to its terms, he spoke:

"Good! Now I know where my duty lies!"

With a sinking heart I heard him. Such a phrase, coming at such a time, seemed to close the door to my hopes of enlightenment.

"What do you mean?" I asked, feeling that my question was a feeble one.

His answer emphasized my fears:

"Trelawny knows what he is doing. He had some definite purpose in all that he did; and we must not thwart him. He evidently expected something to happen, and guarded himself at all points."

"Not at all points!" I said impulsively. "There must have been a weak spot somewhere, or he wouldn't be lying here like that!" Somehow his impassiveness surprised me. I had expected that he would find a valid argument in my phrase; but it did not move him, at least not in the way I thought. Something like a smile flickered over his swarthy face as he answered me:

"This is not the end! Trelawny did not guard himself to no purpose. Doubtless, he expected this too; or at any rate the possibility of it."

"Do you know what he expected, or from what source?" The questioner was Miss Trelawny.

The answer came at once: "No! I know nothing of either. I can guess..." He stopped suddenly.

"Guess what?" The suppressed excitement in the girl's voice was akin to anguish. The steely look came over the swarthy face again; but there was tenderness and courtesy in both voice and manner as he replied:

"Believe me, I would do anything I honestly could to relieve you anxiety. But in this I have a higher duty."

"What duty?"

"Silence!" As he spoke the word, the strong mouth closed like a steel trap.

We all remained silent for a few minutes. In the intensity of our thinking, the silence became a positive thing; the small sounds of life within and without the house seemed intrusive. The first to break it was Miss Trelawny. I had seen an idea—a hope—flash in her eyes; but she steadied herself before speaking:

"What was the urgent subject on which you wanted to see me, knowing that my Father was—not available?" The pause showed her mastery of her thoughts.

The instantaneous change in Mr. Corbeck was almost ludicrous. His start of surprise, coming close upon his iron-clad impassiveness, was like a pantomimic change. But all idea of comedy was swept away by the tragic earnestness with which he remembered his original purpose.

"My God!" he said, as he raised his hand from the chair back on which it rested, and beat it down with a violence which would in itself have arrested attention. His brows corrugated as he went on: "I quite forgot! What a loss! Now of all times! Just at the moment of success! He lying there helpless, and my tongue tied! Not able to raise hand or foot in my ignorance of his wishes!"

"What is it? Oh, do tell us! I am so anxious about my dear Father! Is it any new trouble? I hope not! oh, I hope not! I have had such anxiety and trouble already! It alarms me afresh to hear you speak so! Won't you tell me something to allay this terrible anxiety and uncertainty?"

He drew his sturdy form up to his full height as he said:

"Alas! I cannot, may not, tell you anything. It is his secret." He pointed to the bed. "And yet—and yet I came here for his advice, his counsel, his assistance. And he lies there helpless.... And time is flying by us! It may soon be too late!"

"What is it? what is it?" broke in Miss Trelawny in a sort of passion of anxiety, her face drawn with pain. "Oh, speak! Say something! This anxiety, and horror, and mystery are killing me!" Mr. Corbeck calmed himself by a great effort.

"I may not tell you details; but I have had a great loss. My mission, in which I have spent three years, was successful. I discovered all that I sought—and more; and brought them home with me safely. Treasures, priceless in themselves, but doubly precious to him by whose wishes and instructions I sought them. I arrived in London only last night, and when I woke this morning my precious charge was stolen. Stolen in some mysterious way. Not a soul in London knew that I was arriving. No one but myself knew what was in the shabby portmanteau that I carried. My room had but one door, and that I locked and bolted. The room was high in the house, five stories up, so that no entrance could have been obtained by the window. Indeed, I had closed the window myself and shut the hasp, for I wished to be secure in every way. This morning the hasp was untouched.... And yet my portmanteau was empty. The lamps were gone! ... There! it is out. I went to Egypt to search for a set of antique lamps which Mr. Trelawny wished to trace. With incredible labour, and through many dangers, I followed them. I brought them safe home.... And now!" He turned away much moved. Even his iron nature was breaking down under the sense of loss.

Miss Trelawny stepped over and laid her hand on his arm. I looked at her in amazement. All the passion and pain which had so moved her seemed to have taken the form of resolution. Her form was erect, her eyes blazed; energy was manifest in every nerve and fibre of her being. Even her voice was full of nervous power as she spoke. It was apparent that she was a marvellously strong woman, and that her strength could answer when called upon.

"We must act at once! My Father's wishes must be carried out if it is possible to us. Mr. Ross, you are a lawyer. We have actually in the house a man whom you consider one of the best detectives in London. Surely we can do something. We can begin at once!" Mr. Corbeck took new life from her enthusiasm.

"Good! You are your Father's daughter!" was all he said. But his admiration for her energy was manifested by the impulsive way in which he took her hand. I moved over to the door. I was going to bring Sergeant Daw; and from her look of approval, I knew that Margaret—Miss Trelawny—understood. I was at the door when Mr. Corbeck called me back.

"One moment," he said, "before we bring a stranger on the scene. It must be borne in mind that he is not to know what you know now, that the lamps were the objects of a prolonged and difficult and dangerous search. All I can tell him, all that he must know from any source, is that some of my property has been stolen. I must describe some of the lamps, especially one, for it is of gold; and my fear is lest the thief, ignorant of its historic worth, may, in order to cover up his crime, have it melted. I would willingly pay ten, twenty, a hundred, a thousand times its intrinsic value rather than have it destroyed. I shall tell him only what is necessary. So, please, let me answer any questions he may ask; unless, of course, I ask you or refer to either of you for the answer." We both nodded acquiescence. Then a thought struck me and I said:

"By the way, if it be necessary to keep this matter quiet it will be better to have it if possible a private job for the Detective. If once a thing gets to Scotland Yard it is out of our power to keep it quiet, and further secrecy may be impossible. I shall sound Sergeant Daw before he comes up. If I say nothing, it will mean that he accepts the task and will deal with it privately." Mr. Corbeck answered at once:

"Secrecy is everything. The one thing I dread is that the lamps, or some of them, may be destroyed at once." To my intense astonishment Miss Trelawny spoke out at once, but quietly, in a decided voice:

"They will not be destroyed; nor any of them!" Mr. Corbeck actually smiled in amazement.

"How on earth do you know?" he asked. Her answer was still more incomprehensible:

"I don't know how I know it; but know it I do. I feel it all through me; as though it were a conviction which has been with me all my life!"

Chapter VIII - The Finding of the Lamps

Sergeant Daw at first made some demur; but finally agreed to advise privately on a matter which might be suggested to him. He added that I was to remember that he only undertook to advise; for if action were required he might have to refer the matter to headquarters. With this understanding I left him in the study, and brought Miss Trelawny and Mr. Corbeck to him. Nurse Kennedy resumed her place at the bedside before we left the room.

I could not but admire the cautious, cool-headed precision with which the traveller stated his case. He did not seem to conceal anything, and yet he gave the least possible description of the objects missing. He did not enlarge on the mystery of the case; he seemed to look on it as an ordinary hotel theft. Knowing, as I did, that his one object was to recover the articles before their identity could be obliterated, I could see the rare intellectual skill with which he gave the necessary matter and held back all else, though without seeming to do so. "Truly," thought I, "this man has learned the lesson of the Eastern bazaars; and with Western intellect has improved upon his masters!" He quite conveyed his idea to the Detective, who, after thinking the matter over for a few moments, said:

"Pot or scale? that is the question."

"What does that mean?" asked the other, keenly alert.

"An old thieves phrase from Birmingham. I thought that in these days of slang everyone knew that. In old times at Brum, which had a lot of small metal industries, the gold- and silver-smiths used to buy metal from almost anyone who came along. And as metal in small quantities could generally be had cheap when they didn't ask where it came from, it got to be a custom to ask only one thing—whether the customer wanted the goods melted, in which case the buyer made the price, and the melting-pot was always on the fire. If it was to be preserved in its present state at the buyer's option, it went into the scale and fetched standard price for old metal.

"There is a good deal of such work done still, and in other places than Brum. When we're looking for stolen watches we often come across the works, and it's not possible to identify wheels and springs out of a heap; but it's not often that we come across cases that are wanted. Now, in the present instance much will depend on whether the thief is a good man—that's what they call a man who knows his work. A first-class crook will know whether a thing is of more value than merely the metal in it; and in such case he would put it with someone who could place it later on—in

America or France, perhaps. By the way, do you think anyone but yourself could identify your lamps?"

"No one but myself!"

"Are there others like them?"

"Not that I know of," answered Mr. Corbeck; "though there may be others that resemble them in many particulars." The Detective paused before asking again: "Would any other skilled person—at the British Museum, for instance, or a dealer, or a collector like Mr. Trelawny, know the value—the artistic value—of the lamps?"

"Certainly! Anyone with a head on his shoulders would see at a glance that the things were valuable."

The Detective's face brightened. "Then there is a chance. If your door was locked and the window shut, the goods were not stolen by the chance of a chambermaid or a boots coming along. Whoever did the job went after it special; and he ain't going to part with his swag without his price. This must be a case of notice to the pawnbrokers. There's one good thing about it, anyhow, that the hue and cry needn't be given. We needn't tell Scotland Yard unless you like; we can work the thing privately. If you wish to keep the thing dark, as you told me at the first, that is our chance." Mr. Corbeck, after a pause, said quietly:

"I suppose you couldn't hazard a suggestion as to how the robbery was effected?" The Policeman smiled the smile of knowledge and experience.

"In a very simple way, I have no doubt, sir. That is how all these mysterious crimes turn out in the long-run. The criminal knows his work and all the tricks of it; and he is always on the watch for chances. Moreover, he knows by experience what these chances are likely to be, and how they usually come. The other person is only careful; he doesn't know all the tricks and pits that may be made for him, and by some little oversight or other he falls into the trap. When we know all about this case, you will wonder that you did not see the method of it all along!" This seemed to annoy Mr. Corbeck a little; there was decided heat in his manner as he answered:

"Look here, my good friend, there is not anything simple about this case—except that the things were taken. The window was closed; the fireplace was bricked up. There is only one door to the room, and that I locked and bolted. There is no transom; I have heard all about hotel robberies through the transom. I never left my room in the night. I looked at the things before going to bed; and I went to look at them again when I woke up. If you can rig up any kind of simple robbery out of these facts you are a clever man. That's all I say; clever enough to go right away and get my things back." Miss Trelawny laid her hand upon his arm in a soothing way, and said quietly:

"Do not distress yourself unnecessarily. I am sure they will turn up." Sergeant Daw turned to her so quickly that I could not help remembering vividly his suspicions of her, already formed, as he said:

"May I ask, miss, on what you base that opinion?"

I dreaded to hear her answer, given to ears already awake to suspicion; but it came to me as a new pain or shock all the same:

"I cannot tell you how I know. But I am sure of it!" The Detective looked at her for some seconds in silence, and then threw a quick glance at me.

Presently he had a little more conversation with Mr. Corbeck as to his own movements, the details of the hotel and the room, and the means of identifying the goods. Then he went away to commence his inquiries, Mr. Corbeck impressing on him the necessity for secrecy lest the thief should get wind of his danger and destroy the lamps. Mr. Corbeck promised, when going away to attend to various matters of his own business, to return early in the evening, and to stay in the house.

All that day Miss Trelawny was in better spirits and looked in better strength than she had yet been, despite the new shock and annoyance of the theft which must ultimately bring so much disappointment to her father.

We spent most of the day looking over the curio treasures of Mr. Trelawny. From what I had heard from Mr. Corbeck I began to have some idea of the vastness of his enterprise in the world of Egyptian research; and with this light everything around me began to have a new interest. As I went on, the interest grew; any lingering doubts which I might have had changed to wonder and admiration. The house seemed to be a veritable storehouse of marvels of antique art. In addition to the curios, big and little, in Mr. Trelawny's own room—from the great sarcophagi down to the scarabs of all kinds in the cabinets—the great hall, the staircase landings, the study, and even the boudoir were full of antique pieces which would have made a collector's mouth water.

Miss Trelawny from the first came with me, and looked with growing interest at everything. After having examined some cabinets of exquisite amulets she said to me in quite a naive way:

"You will hardly believe that I have of late seldom even looked at any of these things. It is only since Father has been ill that I seem to have even any curiosity about them. But now, they grow and grow on me to quite an absorbing degree. I wonder if it is that the collector's blood which I have in my veins is beginning to manifest itself. If so, the strange thing is that I have not felt the call of it before. Of course I know most of the big things, and have examined them more or less; but really, in a sort of way I have always taken them for granted, as though they had always been there. I have noticed the same thing now and again with family pictures, and the way they are taken for granted by the family. If you will let me examine them with you it will be delightful!"

It was a joy to me to hear her talk in such a way; and her last suggestion quite thrilled me. Together we went round the various rooms and passages, examining and admiring the magnificent curios. There was such a bewildering amount and variety of objects that we could only glance at most of them; but as we went along we arranged that we should take them seriatim, day by day, and examine them more closely. In the hall was a sort of big frame of floriated steel work which Margaret said her father used for lifting the heavy stone lids of the sarcophagi. It was not heavy and could be moved about easily enough. By aid of this we raised the covers in turn and looked at the endless series of hieroglyphic pictures cut in most of them. In spite of her profession of ignorance Margaret knew a good deal about them; her year of life with her father had had unconsciously its daily and hourly lesson. She was a remarkably clever and acute-minded girl, and with a prodigious memory; so that her store of knowledge, gathered unthinkingly bit by bit, had grown to proportions that many a scholar might have envied.

And yet it was all so naive and unconscious; so girlish and simple. She was so fresh in her views and ideas, and had so little thought of self, that in her companionship I forgot for the time all the troubles and mysteries which enmeshed the house; and I felt like a boy again....

The most interesting of the sarcophagi were undoubtedly the three in Mr. Trelawny's room. Of these, two were of dark stone, one of porphyry and the other of a sort of ironstone. These were wrought with some hieroglyphs. But the third was strikingly different. It was of some yellow-brown substance of the dominating colour effect of Mexican onyx, which it resembled in many ways, excepting that the natural pattern of its convolutions was less marked. Here and there were patches almost transparent—certainly translucent. The whole chest, cover and all, was wrought with hundreds, perhaps thousands, of minute hieroglyphics, seemingly in an endless series. Back, front, sides, edges, bottom, all had their quota of the dainty pictures, the deep blue of their colouring showing up fresh and sharply edge in the yellow stone. It was very long, nearly nine feet; and perhaps a yard wide. The sides undulated, so that there was no hard line. Even the corners took such excellent curves that they pleased the eye. "Truly," I said, "this must have been made for a giant!"

"Or for a giantess!" said Margaret.

This sarcophagus stood near to one of the windows. It was in one respect different from all the other sarcophagi in the place. All the others in the house, of whatever material—granite, porphyry, ironstone, basalt, slate, or wood—were quite simple in form within. Some of them were plain of interior surface; others were engraved, in whole or part, with hieroglyphics. But each and all of them had no protuberances or uneven surface anywhere. They might have been used for baths; indeed, they resembled in many ways Roman baths of stone or marble which I had seen. Inside this, however, was a raised space, outlined like a human figure. I asked Margaret if she could explain it in any way. For answer she said:

"Father never wished to speak about this. It attracted my attention from the first; but when I asked him about it he said: 'I shall tell you all about it some day, little girl—if I live! But not yet! The story is not yet told, as I hope to tell it to you! Some day, perhaps soon, I shall know all; and then we shall go over it together. And a mighty interesting story you will find it—from first to last!' Once afterward I said, rather lightly I am afraid: 'Is that story of the sarcophagus told yet, Father?' He shook his head, and looked at me gravely as he said: 'Not yet, little girl; but it will be—if I live—if I live!' His repeating that phrase about his living rather frightened me; I never ventured to ask him again."

Somehow this thrilled me. I could not exactly say how or why; but it seemed like a gleam of light at last. There are, I think, moments when the mind accepts something as true; though it can account for neither the course of the thought, nor, if there be more than one thought, the connection between them. Hitherto we had been in such outer darkness regarding Mr. Trelawny, and the strange visitation which had fallen on him, that anything which afforded a clue, even of the faintest and most shadowy kind, had at the outset the enlightening satisfaction of a certainty. Here were two lights of our puzzle. The first that Mr. Trelawny associated with this particular curio a doubt of his own living. The second that he had some purpose or expectation with regard to it, which he would not disclose, even to his daughter, till complete. Again it was to be borne in mind that this sarcophagus differed internally from all the others. What meant that odd raised place? I said nothing to Miss Trelawny, for I feared lest I should either frighten her or buoy her up with future hopes; but I made up my mind that I would take an early opportunity for further investigation.

Close beside the sarcophagus was a low table of green stone with red veins in it, like bloodstone. The feet were fashioned like the paws of a jackal, and round each leg was twined a full-throated snake wrought exquisitely in pure gold. On it rested a strange and very beautiful coffer or casket of stone of a peculiar shape. It was something like a small coffin, except that the longer sides, instead of being cut off square like the upper or level part were continued to a point. Thus it was an irregular septahedron, there being two planes on each of the two sides, one end and a top and bottom. The stone, of one piece of which it was wrought, was such as I had never seen before. At the base it was of a full green, the colour of emerald without, of course, its gleam. It was not by any means dull, however, either in colour or substance, and was of infinite hardness and fineness of texture. The surface was almost that of a jewel. The colour grew lighter as it rose, with gradation so fine as to be imperceptible, changing to a fine yellow almost of the colour of "mandarin" china. It was quite unlike anything I had ever seen, and did not resemble any stone or gem that I knew. I took it to be some unique mother-stone, or matrix of some gem. It was wrought all over, except in a few spots, with fine hieroglyphics, exquisitely done and coloured with the same blue-green cement or pigment that appeared on the sarcophagus. In length it was about two feet and a half; in breadth about half this, and was nearly a foot high. The vacant spaces were irregularly distributed about the top running to the pointed end. These places seemed less opaque than the rest of the stone. I tried to lift up the lid so that I might see if they were translucent; but it was securely fixed. It fitted so exactly that the whole coffer seemed like a single piece of stone mysteriously hollowed from within. On the sides and edges were some odd-looking protuberances wrought just as finely as any other portion of the coffer which had been sculptured by manifest design in the cutting of the stone. They had queer-shaped holes or hollows, different in each; and, like the rest, were covered with the hieroglyphic figures, cut finely and filled in with the same blue-green cement.

On the other side of the great sarcophagus stood another small table of alabaster, exquisitely chased with symbolic figures of gods and the signs of the zodiac. On this table stood a case of about a foot square composed of slabs of rock crystal set in a skeleton of bands of red gold, beautifully engraved with hieroglyphics, and coloured with a blue green, very much the tint of the figures on the sarcophagus and the coffer. The whole work was quite modern.

But if the case was modern what it held was not. Within, on a cushion of cloth of gold as fine as silk, and with the peculiar softness of old gold, rested a mummy hand, so perfect that it startled one to see it. A woman's hand, fine and long, with slim tapering fingers and nearly as perfect as when it was given to the embalmer thousands of years before. In the embalming it had lost nothing of its beautiful shape; even the wrist seemed to maintain its pliability as the gentle curve lay on the cushion. The skin was of a rich creamy or old ivory colour; a dusky fair skin which suggested heat, but heat in shadow. The great peculiarity of it, as a hand, was that it had in all seven fingers, there being two middle and two index fingers. The upper end of the wrist was jagged, as though it had been broken off, and was stained with a red-brown stain. On the cushion near the hand was a small scarab, exquisitely wrought of emerald.

"That is another of Father's mysteries. When I asked him about it he said that it was perhaps the most valuable thing he had, except one. When I asked him what that one was, he refused to tell me, and forbade me to ask him anything concerning it. 'I will tell you,' he said, 'all about it, too, in good time—if I live!'"

"If I live!" the phrase again. These three things grouped together, the Sarcophagus, the Coffer, and the Hand, seemed to make a trilogy of mystery indeed!

At this time Miss Trelawny was sent for on some domestic matter. I looked at the other curios in the room; but they did not seem to have anything like the same charm for me, now that she was away. Later on in the day I was sent for to the boudoir where she was consulting with Mrs. Grant as to the lodgment of Mr. Corbeck. They were in doubt as to whether he should have a room close to Mr. Trelawny's or quite away from it, and had thought it well to ask my advice on the subject. I came to the conclusion that he had better not be too near; for the first at all events, he could easily be moved closer if necessary. When Mrs. Grant had gone, I asked Miss Trelawny how it came that the furniture of this room, the boudoir in which we were, was so different from the other rooms of the house.

"Father's forethought!" she answered. "When I first came, he thought, and rightly enough, that I might get frightened with so many records of death and the tomb everywhere. So he had this room and the little suite off it—that door opens into the sitting-room—where I slept last night, furnished with pretty things. You see, they are all beautiful. That cabinet belonged to the great Napoleon."

"There is nothing Egyptian in these rooms at all then?" I asked, rather to show interest in what she had said than anything else, for the furnishing of the room was apparent. "What a lovely cabinet! May I look at it?"

"Of course! with the greatest pleasure!" she answered, with a smile. "Its finishing, within and without, Father says, is absolutely complete." I stepped over and looked at it closely. It was made of tulip wood, inlaid in patterns; and was mounted in ormolu. I pulled open one of the drawers, a deep one where I could see the work to great advantage. As I pulled it, something rattled inside as though rolling; there was a tinkle as of metal on metal.

"Hullo!" I said. "There is something in here. Perhaps I had better not open it."

"There is nothing that I know of," she answered. "Some of the housemaids may have used it to put something by for the time and forgotten it. Open it by all means!"

I pulled open the drawer; as I did so, both Miss Trelawny and I started back in amazement.

There before our eyes lay a number of ancient Egyptian lamps, of various sizes and of strangely varied shapes.

We leaned over them and looked closely. My own heart was beating like a trip-hammer; and I could see by the heaving of Margaret's bosom that she was strangely excited.

Whilst we looked, afraid to touch and almost afraid to think, there was a ring at the front door; immediately afterwards Mr. Corbeck, followed by Sergeant Daw, came into the hall. The door of the boudoir was open, and when they saw us Mr. Corbeck came running in, followed more slowly by the Detective. There was a sort of chastened joy in his face and manner as he said impulsively:

"Rejoice with me, my dear Miss Trelawny, my luggage has come and all my things are intact!" Then his face fell as he added, "Except the lamps. The lamps that were worth all the rest a thousand times...." He stopped, struck by the strange pallor of her face. Then his eyes, following her look and mine, lit on the cluster of lamps in the drawer. He gave a sort of cry of surprise and joy as he bent over and touched them:

"My lamps! My lamps! Then they are safe—safe—safe! ... But how, in the name of God—of all the Gods—did they come here?"

We all stood silent. The Detective made a deep sound of in-taking breath. I looked at him, and as he caught my glance he turned his eyes on Miss Trelawny whose back was toward him.

There was in them the same look of suspicion which had been there when he had spoken to me of her being the first to find her father on the occasions of the attacks.

Chapter IX - The Need of Knowledge

Mr. Corbeck seemed to go almost off his head at the recovery of the lamps. He took them up one by one and looked them all over tenderly, as though they were things that he loved. In his delight and excitement he breathed so hard that it seemed almost like a cat purring. Sergeant Daw said quietly, his voice breaking the silence like a discord in a melody:

"Are you quite sure those lamps are the ones you had, and that were stolen?"

His answer was in an indignant tone: "Sure! Of course I'm sure. There isn't another set of lamps like these in the world!"

"So far as you know!" The Detective's words were smooth enough, but his manner was so exasperating that I was sure he had some motive in it; so I waited in silence. He went on:

"Of course there may be some in the British Museum; or Mr. Trelawny may have had these already. There's nothing new under the sun, you know, Mr. Corbeck; not even in Egypt. These may be the originals, and yours may have been the copies. Are there any points by which you can identify these as yours?"

Mr. Corbeck was really angry by this time. He forgot his reserve; and in his indignation poured forth a torrent of almost incoherent, but enlightening, broken sentences:

"Identify! Copies of them! British Museum! Rot! Perhaps they keep a set in Scotland Yard for teaching idiot policemen Egyptology! Do I know them? When I have carried them about my body, in the desert, for three months; and lay awake night after night to watch them! When I have looked them over with a magnifying-glass, hour after hour, till my eyes ached; till every tiny blotch, and chip, and dinge became as familiar to me as his chart to a captain; as familiar as they doubtless have been all the time to every thick-headed area-prowler within the bounds of mortality. See here, young man, look at these!" He ranged the lamps in a row on the top of the cabinet. "Did you ever see a set of lamps of these shapes—of any one of these shapes? Look at these dominant figures on them! Did you ever see so complete a set—even in Scotland Yard; even in Bow Street? Look! one on each, the seven forms of Hathor. Look at that figure of the Ka of a Princess of the Two Egypts, standing between Ra and Osiris in the Boat of the Dead, with the Eye of Sleep, supported on legs, bending before her; and Harmochis rising in the north. Will you find that in the British Museum—or Bow Street? Or perhaps your studies in the Gizeh Museum, or the Fitzwilliam, or Paris, or Leyden, or Berlin, have shown you that the episode is common in hieroglyphics; and that this is only a copy. Perhaps you can tell me what that figure of

Ptah-Seker-Ausar holding the Tet wrapped in the Sceptre of Papyrus means? Did you ever see it before; even in the British Museum, or Gizeh, or Scotland Yard?"

He broke off suddenly; and then went on in quite a different way:

"Look here! it seems to me that the thick-headed idiot is myself! I beg your pardon, old fellow, for my rudeness. I quite lost my temper at the suggestion that I do not know these lamps. You don't mind, do you?" The Detective answered heartily:

"Lord, sir, not I. I like to see folks angry when I am dealing with them, whether they are on my side or the other. It is when people are angry that you learn the truth from them. I keep cool; that is my trade! Do you know, you have told me more about those lamps in the past two minutes than when you filled me up with details of how to identify them."

Mr. Corbeck grunted; he was not pleased at having given himself away. All at once he turned to me and said in his natural way:

"Now tell me how you got them back?" I was so surprised that I said without thinking:

"We didn't get them back!" The traveller laughed openly.

"What on earth do you mean?" he asked. "You didn't get them back! Why, there they are before your eyes! We found you looking at them when we came in." By this time I had recovered my surprise and had my wits about me.

"Why, that's just it," I said. "We had only come across them, by accident, that very moment!"

Mr. Corbeck drew back and looked hard at Miss Trelawny and myself; turning his eyes from one to the other as he asked:

"Do you mean to tell me that no one brought them here; that you found them in that drawer? That, so to speak, no one at all brought them back?"

"I suppose someone must have brought them here; they couldn't have come of their own accord. But who it was, or when, or how, neither of us knows. We shall have to make inquiry, and see if any of the servants know anything of it."

We all stood silent for several seconds. It seemed a long time. The first to speak was the Detective, who said in an unconscious way:

"Well, I'm damned! I beg your pardon, miss!" Then his mouth shut like a steel trap.

We called up the servants, one by one, and asked them if they knew anything of some articles placed in a drawer in the boudoir; but none of them could throw any light on the circumstance. We did not tell them what the articles were; or let them see them.

Mr. Corbeck packed the lamps in cotton wool, and placed them in a tin box. This, I may mention incidentally, was then brought up to the detectives' room, where one of the men stood guard over them with a revolver the whole night. Next day we got a small safe into the house, and placed them in it. There were two different keys. One of them I kept myself; the other I placed in my drawer in the Safe Deposit vault. We were all determined that the lamps should not be lost again.

About an hour after we had found the lamps, Doctor Winchester arrived. He had a large parcel with him, which, when unwrapped, proved to be the mummy of a cat. With Miss Trelawny's permission he placed this in the boudoir; and Silvio was brought close to it. To the surprise of us all, however, except perhaps Doctor Winchester, he did not manifest the least annoyance; he took no notice of it whatever. He stood on the table close beside it, purring loudly. Then, following out his plan, the Doctor brought him into Mr. Trelawny's room, we all following. Doctor Winchester was excited; Miss Trelawny anxious. I was more than interested myself, for I began to have a glimmering of the Doctor's idea. The Detective was calmly and coldly superior; but Mr. Corbeck, who was an enthusiast, was full of eager curiosity.

The moment Doctor Winchester got into the room, Silvio began to mew and wriggle; and jumping out of his arms, ran over to the cat mummy and began to scratch angrily at it. Miss Trelawny had some difficulty in taking him away; but so soon as he was out of the room he became quiet. When she came back there was a clamour of comments:

"I thought so!" from the Doctor.

"What can it mean?" from Miss Trelawny.

"That's a very strange thing!" from Mr. Corbeck.

"Odd! but it doesn't prove anything!" from the Detective.

"I suspend my judgment!" from myself, thinking it advisable to say something.

Then by common consent we dropped the theme—for the present.

In my room that evening I was making some notes of what had happened, when there came a low tap on the door. In obedience to my summons Sergeant Daw came in, carefully closing the door behind him.

"Well, Sergeant," said I, "sit down. What is it?"

"I wanted to speak to you, sir, about those lamps." I nodded and waited: he went on: "You know that that room where they were found opens directly into the room where Miss Trelawny slept last night?"

"Yes."

"During the night a window somewhere in that part of the house was opened, and shut again. I heard it, and took a look round; but I could see no sign of anything."

"Yes, I know that!" I said; "I heard a window moved myself."

"Does nothing strike you as strange about it, sir?"

"Strange!" I said; "Strange! why it's all the most bewildering, maddening thing I have ever encountered. It is all so strange that one seems to wonder, and simply waits for what will happen next. But what do you mean by strange?"

The Detective paused, as if choosing his words to begin; and then said deliberately:

"You see, I am not one who believes in magic and such things. I am for facts all the time; and I always find in the long-run that there is a reason and a cause for everything. This new gentleman says these things were stolen out of his room in the hotel. The lamps, I take it from some things he has said, really belong to Mr. Trelawny. His daughter, the lady of the house, having left the room she usually occupies, sleeps that night on the ground floor. A window is heard to open and shut during the night. When we, who have been during the day trying to find a clue to the robbery, come to the house, we find the stolen goods in a room close to where she slept, and opening out of it!"

He stopped. I felt that same sense of pain and apprehension, which I had experienced when he had spoken to me before, creeping, or rather rushing, over me again. I had to face the matter out, however. My relations with her, and the feeling toward her which I now knew full well meant a very deep love and devotion, demanded so much.

I said as calmly as I could, for I knew the keen eyes of the skilful investigator were on me:

"And the inference?"

He answered with the cool audacity of conviction:

"The inference to me is that there was no robbery at all. The goods were taken by someone to this house, where they were received through a window on the ground floor. They were placed in the cabinet, ready to be discovered when the proper time should come!"

Somehow I felt relieved; the assumption was too monstrous. I did not want, however, my relief to be apparent, so I answered as gravely as I could:

"And who do you suppose brought them to the house?"

"I keep my mind open as to that. Possibly Mr. Corbeck himself; the matter might be too risky to trust to a third party."

"Then the natural extension of your inference is that Mr. Corbeck is a liar and a fraud; and that he is in conspiracy with Miss Trelawny to deceive someone or other about those lamps."

"Those are harsh words, Mr. Ross. They're so plain-spoken that they bring a man up standing, and make new doubts for him. But I have to go where my reason points. It may be that there is another party than Miss Trelawny in it. Indeed, if it hadn't been for the other matter that set me thinking and bred doubts of its own about her, I wouldn't dream of mixing her up in this. But I'm safe on Corbeck. Whoever else is in it, he is! The things couldn't have been taken without his connivance—if what he says is true. If it isn't—well! he is a liar anyhow. I would think it a bad job to have him stay in the house with so many valuables, only that it will give me and my mate a chance of watching him. We'll keep a pretty good look-out, too, I tell you. He's up in my room now, guarding those lamps; but Johnny Wright is there too. I go on before he comes off; so there won't be much chance of another house-breaking. Of course, Mr. Ross, all this, too, is between you and me."

"Quite so! You may depend on my silence!" I said; and he went away to keep a close eye on the Egyptologist.

It seemed as though all my painful experiences were to go in pairs, and that the sequence of the previous day was to be repeated; for before long I had another private visit from Doctor Winchester who had now paid his nightly visit to his patient and was on his way home. He took the seat which I proffered and began at once:

"This is a strange affair altogether. Miss Trelawny has just been telling me about the stolen lamps, and of the finding of them in the Napoleon cabinet. It would seem to be another complication of the mystery; and yet, do you know, it is a relief to me. I have exhausted all human and natural possibilities of the case, and am beginning to fall back on superhuman and supernatural possibilities. Here are such strange things that, if I am not going mad, I think we must have a solution before long. I wonder if I might ask some questions and some help from Mr. Corbeck, without making further complications and embarrassing us. He seems to know an amazing amount regarding Egypt and all relating to it. Perhaps he wouldn't mind translating a little bit of hieroglyphic. It is child's play to him. What do you think?"

When I had thought the matter over a few seconds I spoke. We wanted all the help we could get. For myself, I had perfect confidence in both men; and any comparing notes, or mutual assistance, might bring good results. Such could hardly bring evil.

"By all means I should ask him. He seems an extraordinarily learned man in Egyptology; and he seems to me a good fellow as well as an enthusiast. By the way, it will be necessary to be a little guarded as to whom you speak regarding any information which he may give you."

"Of course!" he answered. "Indeed I should not dream of saying anything to anybody, excepting yourself. We have to remember that when Mr. Trelawny recovers he may not like to think that we have been chattering unduly over his affairs."

"Look here!" I said, "why not stay for a while: and I shall ask him to come and have a pipe with us. We can then talk over things."

He acquiesced: so I went to the room where Mr. Corbeck was, and brought him back with me. I thought the detectives were pleased at his going. On the way to my room he said:

"I don't half like leaving those things there, with only those men to guard them. They're a deal sight too precious to be left to the police!"

From which it would appear that suspicion was not confined to Sergeant Daw.

Mr. Corbeck and Doctor Winchester, after a quick glance at each other, became at once on most friendly terms. The traveller professed his willingness to be of any assistance which he could, provided, he added, that it was anything about which he was free to speak. This was not very promising; but Doctor Winchester began at once:

"I want you, if you will, to translate some hieroglyphic for me."

"Certainly, with the greatest pleasure, so far as I can. For I may tell you that hieroglyphic writing is not quite mastered yet; though we are getting at it! We are getting at it! What is the inscription?"

"There are two," he answered. "One of them I shall bring here."

He went out, and returned in a minute with the mummy cat which he had that evening introduced to Silvio. The scholar took it; and, after a short examination, said:

"There is nothing especial in this. It is an appeal to Bast, the Lady of Bubastis, to give her good bread and milk in the Elysian Fields. There may be more inside; and if you will care to unroll it, I will do my best. I do not think, however, that there is anything special. From the method of wrapping I should say it is from the Delta; and of a late period, when such mummy work was common and cheap. What is the other inscription you wish me to see?"

"The inscription on the mummy cat in Mr. Trelawny's room."

Mr. Corbeck's face fell. "No!" he said, "I cannot do that! I am, for the present at all events, practically bound to secrecy regarding any of the things in Mr. Trelawny's room."

Doctor Winchester's comment and my own were made at the same moment. I said only the one word "Checkmate!" from which I think he may have gathered that I guessed more of his idea and purpose than perhaps I had intentionally conveyed to him. He murmured:

"Practically bound to secrecy?"

Mr. Corbeck at once took up the challenge conveyed:

"Do not misunderstand me! I am not bound by any definite pledge of secrecy; but I am bound in honour to respect Mr. Trelawny's confidence, given to me, I may tell you, in a very large measure. Regarding many of the objects in his room he has a definite purpose in view; and it would not be either right or becoming for me, his trusted friend and confidant, to forestall that purpose. Mr. Trelawny, you may know—or rather you do not know or you would not have so construed my remark—is a scholar, a very great scholar. He has worked for years toward a certain end. For this he has spared no labour, no expense, no personal danger or self-denial. He is on the line of a result which will place him amongst the foremost discoverers or investigators of his age. And now, just at the time when any hour might bring him success, he is stricken down!"

He stopped, seemingly overcome with emotion. After a time he recovered himself and went on:

"Again, do not misunderstand me as to another point. I have said that Mr. Trelawny has made much confidence with me; but I do not mean to lead you to believe that I know all his plans, or his aims or objects. I know the period which he has been studying; and the definite historical individual whose life he has been investigating, and whose records he has been following up one by one with infinite patience. But beyond this I know nothing. That he has some aim or object in the completion of this knowledge I am convinced. What it is I may guess; but I must say nothing. Please to remember, gentlemen, that I have voluntarily accepted the position of recipient of a partial confidence. I have respected that; and I must ask any of my friends to do the same."

He spoke with great dignity; and he grew, moment by moment, in the respect and esteem of both Doctor Winchester and myself. We understood that he had not done speaking; so we waited in silence till he continued:

"I have spoken this much, although I know well that even such a hint as either of you might gather from my words might jeopardise the success of his work. But I am convinced that you both wish to help him—and his daughter," he said this looking me fairly between the eyes, "to the best of your power, honestly and unselfishly. He is so stricken down, and the manner of it is so mysterious that I cannot but think that it is in some way a result of his own work. That he calculated on some set-back is manifest to us all. God knows! I am willing to do what I can, and to use any knowledge I have in his behalf. I arrived in England full of exultation at the thought that I had fulfilled the mission with which he had trusted me. I had got what he said were the last objects of his search; and I felt assured that he would now be able to begin the experiment of which he had often hinted to me. It is too dreadful that at just such a time such a calamity should have fallen on him. Doctor Winchester, you are a physician; and, if your face does not belie you, you are a clever and a bold one. Is there no way which you can devise to wake this man from his unnatural stupor?"

There was a pause; then the answer came slowly and deliberately:

"There is no ordinary remedy that I know of. There might possibly be some extraordinary one. But there would be no use in trying to find it, except on one condition."

"And that?"

"Knowledge! I am completely ignorant of Egyptian matters, language, writing, history, secrets, medicines, poisons, occult powers—all that go to make up the mystery of that mysterious land. This disease, or condition, or whatever it may be called, from which Mr. Trelawny is suffering, is in some way connected with Egypt. I have had a suspicion of this from the first; and later it grew into a certainty, though without proof. What you have said tonight confirms my conjecture, and makes me believe that a proof is to be had. I do not think that you quite know all that has gone on in this house since the night of the attack—of the finding of Mr. Trelawny's body. Now I propose that we confide in you. If Mr. Ross agrees, I shall ask him to tell you. He is more skilled than I am in putting facts before other people. He can speak by his brief; and in this case he has the best of all briefs, the experience of his own eyes and ears, and the evidence that he has himself taken on the spot from participators in, or spectators of, what has happened. When you know all, you will, I hope, be in a position to judge as to whether you can best help Mr. Trelawny, and further his secret wishes, by your silence or your speech."

I nodded approval. Mr. Corbeck jumped up, and in his impulsive way held out a hand to each.

"Done!" he said. "I acknowledge the honour of your confidence; and on my part I pledge myself that if I find my duty to Mr. Trelawny's wishes will, in his own interest, allow my lips to open on his affairs, I shall speak so freely as I may."

Accordingly I began, and told him, as exactly as I could, everything that had happened from the moment of my waking at the knocking on the door in Jermyn Street. The only reservations I made were as to my own feeling toward Miss Trelawny and the matters of small import to the main subject which followed it; and my conversations with Sergeant Daw, which were in themselves private, and which would have demanded discretionary silence in any case. As I spoke, Mr. Corbeck followed with breathless interest. Sometimes he would stand up and pace about the room in uncontrollable excitement; and then recover himself suddenly, and sit down again. Sometimes he would be about to speak, but would, with an effort, restrain himself. I think the narration helped me to make up my own mind; for even as I talked, things seemed to appear in a clearer light. Things big and little, in relation of their importance to the case, fell into proper perspective. The story up to date became coherent, except as to its cause, which seemed a greater mystery than ever. This is the merit of entire, or collected, narrative. Isolated facts, doubts, suspicions, conjectures, give way to a homogeneity which is convincing.

That Mr. Corbeck was convinced was evident. He did not go through any process of explanation or limitation, but spoke right out at once to the point, and fearlessly like a man:

"That settles me! There is in activity some Force that needs special care. If we all go on working in the dark we shall get in one another's way, and by hampering each other, undo the good that any or each of us, working in different directions, might do. It seems to me that the first thing we have to accomplish is to get Mr. Trelawny waked out of that unnatural sleep. That he can be waked is apparent from the way the Nurse has recovered; though what additional harm may have been done to him in the time he has been lying in that room I suppose no one can tell. We must chance that, however. He has lain there, and whatever the effect might be, it is there now; and we have, and shall have, to deal with it as a fact. A day more or less won't hurt in the long-run. It is late now; and we shall probably have tomorrow a task before us that will require our energies afresh. You, Doctor, will want to get to your sleep; for I suppose you have other work as well as this to do tomorrow. As for you, Mr. Ross, I understand that you are to have a spell of watching in the sick-room tonight. I shall get you a book which will help to pass the time for you. I shall go and look for it in the library. I know where it was when I was here last; and I don't suppose Mr. Trelawny has used it since. He knew long ago all that was in it which was or might be of interest to him. But it will be necessary, or at least helpful, to understand other things which I shall tell you later. You will be able to tell Doctor Winchester all that would aid him. For I take it that our work will branch out pretty soon. We shall each have our own end to hold up; and it will take each of us all our time and understanding to get through his own tasks. It will not be necessary for you to read the whole book. All that will interest you—with regard to our matter I mean of course, for the whole book is interesting as a record of travel in a country then quite unknown—is the preface, and two or three chapters which I shall mark for you."

He shook hands warmly with Doctor Winchester who had stood up to go.

Whilst he was away I sat lonely, thinking. As I thought, the world around me seemed to be illimitably great. The only little spot in which I was interested seemed like a tiny speck in the midst of a wilderness. Without and around it were darkness and unknown danger, pressing in from every side. And the central figure in our little oasis was one of sweetness and beauty. A figure one could love; could work for; could die for...!

Mr. Corbeck came back in a very short time with the book; he had found it at once in the spot where he had seen it three years before. Having placed in it several slips of paper, marking the places where I was to read, he put it into my hands, saying:

"That is what started Mr. Trelawny; what started me when I read it; and which will, I have no doubt, be to you an interesting beginning to a special study—whatever the end may be. If, indeed, any of us here may ever see the end."

At the door he paused and said:

"I want to take back one thing. That Detective is a good fellow. What you have told me of him puts him in a new light. The best proof of it is that I can go quietly to sleep tonight, and leave the lamps in his care!"

When he had gone I took the book with me, put on my respirator, and went to my spell of duty in the sick-room!

Chapter X - The Valley of the Sorcerer

I placed the book on the little table on which the shaded lamp rested and moved the screen to one side. Thus I could have the light on my book; and by looking up, see the bed, and the Nurse, and the door. I cannot say that the conditions were enjoyable, or calculated to allow of that absorption in the subject which is advisable for effective study. However, I composed myself to the work as well as I could. The book was one which, on the very face of it, required special attention. It was a folio in Dutch, printed in Amsterdam in 1650. Some one had made a literal translation, writing generally the English word under the Dutch, so that the grammatical differences between the two tongues made even the reading of the translation a difficult matter. One had to dodge backward and forward among the words. This was in addition to the difficulty of deciphering a strange handwriting of two hundred years ago. I found, however, that after a short time I got into the habit of following in conventional English the Dutch construction; and, as I became more familiar with the writing, my task became easier.

At first the circumstances of the room, and the fear lest Miss Trelawny should return unexpectedly and find me reading the book, disturbed me somewhat. For we had arranged amongst us, before Doctor Winchester had gone home, that she was not to be brought into the range of the coming investigation. We considered that there might be some shock to a woman's mind in matters of apparent mystery; and further, that she, being Mr. Trelawny's daughter, might be placed in a difficult position with him afterward if she took part in, or even had a personal knowledge of, the disregarding of his expressed wishes. But when I remembered that she did not come on nursing duty till two o'clock, the fear of interruption passed away. I had still nearly three house before me. Nurse Kennedy sat in her chair by the bedside, patient and alert. A clock ticked on the landing; other clocks in the house ticked; the life of the city without manifested itself in the distant hum, now and again swelling into a roar as a breeze floating westward took the concourse of sounds with it. But still the dominant idea was of silence. The light on my book, and the soothing fringe of green silk round the shade intensified, whenever I looked up, the gloom of the sick-room. With every line I read, this seemed to grow deeper and deeper; so that when my eyes came back to the page the light seemed to dazzle me. I stuck to my work, however, and presently began to get sufficiently into the subject to become interested in it.

The book was by one Nicholas van Huyn of Hoorn. In the preface he told how, attracted by the work of John Greaves of Merton College, Pyramidographia, he himself visited Egypt, where he became so interested in its wonders that he devoted some years of his life to visiting strange places, and exploring the ruins of many temples and tombs. He had come across many variants of the story of the building of the Pyramids as told by the Arabian historian, Ibn Abd Alhokin, some of which he set down. These I did not stop to read, but went on to the marked pages.

As soon as I began to read these, however, there grew on me some sense of a disturbing influence. Once or twice I looked to see if the Nurse had moved, for there was a feeling as though some one were near me. Nurse Kennedy sat in her place, as steady and alert as ever; and I came back to my book again.

The narrative went on to tell how, after passing for several days through the mountains to the east of Aswan, the explorer came to a certain place. Here I give his own words, simply putting the translation into modern English:

"Toward evening we came to the entrance of a narrow, deep valley, running east and west. I wished to proceed through this; for the sun, now nearly down on the horizon, showed a wide opening beyond the narrowing of the cliffs. But the fellaheen absolutely refused to enter the valley at such a time, alleging that they might be caught by the night before they could emerge from the other end. At first they would give no reason for their fear. They had hitherto gone anywhere I wished, and at any time, without demur. On being pressed, however, they said that the place was the Valley of the Sorcerer, where none might come in the night. On being asked to tell of the Sorcerer, they refused, saying that there was no name, and that they knew nothing. On the next morning, however, when the sun was up and shining down the valley, their fears had somewhat passed away. Then they told me that a great Sorcerer in ancient days—'millions of millions of years' was the term they used—a King or a Queen, they could not say which, was buried there. They could not give the name, persisting to the last that there was no name; and that anyone who should name it would waste away in life so that at death nothing of him would remain to be raised again in the Other World. In passing through the valley they kept together in a cluster, hurrying on in front of me. None dared to remain behind. They gave, as their reason for so proceeding, that the arms of the Sorcerer were long, and that it was dangerous to be the last. The which was of little comfort to me who of this necessity took that honourable post. In the narrowest part of the valley, on the south side, was a great cliff of rock, rising sheer, of smooth and even surface. Hereon were graven certain cabalistic signs, and many figures of men and animals, fishes, reptiles and birds; suns and stars; and many quaint symbols. Some of these latter were disjointed limbs and features, such as arms and legs, fingers, eyes, noses, ears, and lips. Mysterious symbols which will puzzle the Recording Angel to interpret at the Judgment Day. The cliff faced exactly north. There was something about it so strange, and so different from the other carved rocks which I had visited, that I called a halt and spent the day in examining the rock front as well as I could with my telescope. The Egyptians of my company were terribly afraid, and used every kind of persuasion to induce me to pass on. I stayed till late in the afternoon, by which time I had failed to make out aright the entry of any tomb, for I suspected that such was the purpose of the sculpture of the rock. By this time the men were rebellious; and I had to leave the valley if I did not wish my whole retinue to desert. But I secretly made up my mind to discover the tomb, and explore it. To this end I went further into the mountains, where I met with an Arab Sheik who was willing to take service with me. The Arabs were not bound by the same superstitious fears as the Egyptians; Sheik Abu Some and his following were willing to take a part in the explorations.

"When I returned to the valley with these Bedouins, I made effort to climb the face of the rock, but failed, it being of one impenetrable smoothness. The stone, generally flat and smooth by nature, had been chiselled to completeness. That there had been projecting steps was manifest, for there remained, untouched by the wondrous climate of that strange land, the marks of saw and chisel and mallet where the steps had been cut or broken away.

"Being thus baffled of winning the tomb from below, and being unprovided with ladders to scale, I found a way by much circuitous journeying to the top of the cliff. Thence I caused myself to be lowered by ropes, till I had investigated that portion of the rock face wherein I expected to find the opening. I found that there was an entrance, closed however by a great stone slab. This was cut in the rock more than a hundred feet up, being two-thirds the height of the cliff. The hieroglyphic and cabalistic symbols cut in the rock were so managed as to disguise it. The cutting was deep, and was continued through the rock and the portals of the doorway, and through the great slab which formed the door itself. This was fixed in place with such incredible exactness that no stone chisel or cutting implement which I had with me could find a lodgment in the interstices. I used much force, however; and by many heavy strokes won a way into the tomb, for such I found it to be. The stone door having fallen into the entrance I passed over it into the tomb, noting as I went a long iron chain which hung coiled on a bracket close to the doorway.

"The tomb I found to be complete, after the manner of the finest Egyptian tombs, with chamber and shaft leading down to the corridor, ending in the Mummy Pit. It had the table of pictures, which seems some kind of record—whose meaning is now for ever lost—graven in a wondrous colour on a wondrous stone.

"All the walls of the chamber and the passage were carved with strange writings in the uncanny form mentioned. The huge stone coffin or sarcophagus in the deep pit was marvellously graven throughout with signs. The Arab chief and two others who ventured into the tomb with me, and who were evidently used to such grim explorations, managed to take the cover from the sarcophagus without breaking it. At which they wondered; for such good fortune, they said, did not usually attend such efforts. Indeed they seemed not over careful; and did handle the various furniture of the tomb with such little concern that, only for its great strength and thickness, even the coffin itself might have been injured. Which gave me much concern, for it was very beautifully wrought of rare stone, such as I had no knowledge of. Much I grieved that it were not possible to carry it away. But time and desert journeyings forbade such; I could only take with me such small matters as could be carried on the person.

"Within the sarcophagus was a body, manifestly of a woman, swathed with many wrappings of linen, as is usual with all mummies. From certain embroiderings thereon, I gathered that she was of high rank. Across the breast was one hand, unwrapped. In the mummies which I had seen, the arms and hands are within the wrappings, and certain adornments of wood, shaped and painted to resemble arms and hands, lie outside the enwrapped body.

"But this hand was strange to see, for it was the real hand of her who lay enwrapped there; the arm projecting from the cerements being of flesh, seemingly made as like marble in the process of embalming. Arm and hand were of dusky white, being of the hue of ivory that hath lain long in air. The skin and the nails were complete and whole, as though the body had been placed for burial over night. I touched the hand and moved it, the arm being something flexible as a live arm; though stiff with long disuse, as are the arms of those faqueers which I have seen in the Indees. There was, too, an added wonder that on this ancient hand were no less than seven fingers, the same all being fine and long, and of great beauty. Sooth to say, it made me shudder and my flesh creep to touch that hand that had lain there undisturbed for so many thousands of years, and yet was like unto living flesh. Underneath the hand, as though guarded by it, lay a huge jewel of ruby; a great stone of wondrous bigness, for the ruby is in the main a small jewel. This one was of wondrous colour, being as of fine blood whereon the light shineth. But its wonder lay not in its size or colour, though these were, as I have said, of priceless rarity; but in that the light of it shone from seven stars, each of seven points, as clearly as though the stars were in reality there imprisoned. When that the hand was lifted, the sight of that wondrous stone lying there struck me with a shock almost to momentary paralysis. I stood gazing on it, as did those with me, as though it were that faded head of the Gorgon Medusa with the snakes in her hair, whose sight struck into stone those who beheld. So strong was the feeling that I wanted to hurry away from the place. So, too, those with me; therefore, taking this rare jewel, together with certain amulets of strangeness and richness being wrought of jewel-stones, I made haste to depart. I would have remained longer, and made further research in the wrappings of the mummy, but that I feared so to do. For it came to me all at once that I was in a desert place, with strange men who were with me because they were not over-scrupulous. That we were in a lone cavern of the dead, an hundred feet above the ground, where none could find me were ill done to me, nor would any ever seek. But in secret I determined that I would come again, though with more secure following. Moreover, was I tempted to seek further, as in examining the wrappings I saw many things of strange import in that wondrous tomb; including a casket of eccentric shape made of some strange stone, which methought might have contained other jewels, inasmuch as it had secure lodgment in the great sarcophagus itself. There was in the tomb also another coffer which, though of rare proportion and adornment, was more simply shaped. It was of ironstone of great thickness; but the cover was lightly cemented down with what seemed gum and Paris plaster, as though to insure that no air could penetrate. The Arabs with me so insisted in its opening, thinking that from its thickness much treasure was stored therein, that I consented thereto. But their hope was a false one, as it proved. Within, closely packed, stood four jars finely wrought and carved with various adornments. Of these one was the head of a man, another of a dog, another of a jackal, and another of a hawk. I had before known that such burial urns as these were used to contain the entrails and other organs of the mummied dead; but on opening these, for the fastening of wax, though complete, was thin, and yielded easily, we found that they held but oil. The Bedouins, spilling most of the oil in the process, groped with their hands in the jars lest treasure should have been there concealed. But their searching was of no avail; no treasure was there. I was warned of my danger by seeing in the eyes of the Arabs certain covetous glances. Whereon, in order to hasten their departure, I wrought upon those fears of superstition which even in these callous men were apparent. The chief of the Bedouins ascended from the Pit to give the signal to those above to raise us; and I, not caring to remain with the men whom I mistrusted, followed him immediately. The others did not come at once; from which I feared that they were rifling the tomb afresh on their own account. I refrained to speak of it, however, lest worse should befall. At last they came. One of them, who ascended first, in landing at the top of the cliff lost his foothold and fell below. He was instantly killed. The other followed, but in safety. The chief came next, and I came last. Before coming away I pulled into its place again, as well as I could, the slab of stone that covered the entrance to the tomb. I wished, if possible, to preserve it for my own examination should I come again.

"When we all stood on the hill above the cliff, the burning sun that was bright and full of glory was good to see after the darkness and strange mystery of the tomb. Even was I glad that the poor Arab who fell down the cliff and lay dead below, lay in the sunlight and not in that gloomy cavern. I would fain have gone with my companions to seek him and give him sepulture of some kind; but the Sheik made light of it, and sent two of his men to see to it whilst we went on our way.

"That night as we camped, one of the men only returned, saying that a lion of the desert had killed his companion after that they had buried the dead man in a deep sand without the valley, and had covered the spot where he lay with many great rocks, so that jackals or other preying beasts might not dig him up again as is their wont.

"Later, in the light of the fire round which the men sat or lay, I saw him exhibit to his fellows something white which they seemed to regard with special awe and reverence. So I drew near silently, and saw that it was none other than the white hand of the mummy which had lain protecting the Jewel in the great sarcophagus. I heard the Bedouin tell how he had found it on the body of him who had fallen from the cliff. There was no mistaking it, for there were the seven fingers which I had noted before. This man must have wrenched it off the dead body whilst his chief and I were otherwise engaged; and from the awe of the others I doubted not that he had hoped to use it as an Amulet, or charm. Whereas if powers it had, they were not for him who had taken it from the dead; since his death followed hard upon his theft. Already his Amulet had had an awesome baptism; for the wrist of the dead hand was stained with red as though it had been dipped in recent blood.

"That night I was in certain fear lest there should be some violence done to me; for if the poor dead hand was so valued as a charm, what must be the worth in such wise of the rare Jewel which it had guarded. Though only the chief knew of it, my doubt was perhaps even greater; for he could so order matters as to have me at his mercy when he would. I guarded myself, therefore, with wakefulness so well as I could, determined that at my earliest opportunity I should leave this party, and complete my journeying home, first to the Nile bank, and then down its course to Alexandria; with other guides who knew not what strange matters I had with me.

"At last there came over me a disposition of sleep, so potent that I felt it would be resistless. Fearing attack, or that being searched in my sleep the Bedouin might find the Star Jewel which he had seen me place with others in my dress, I took it out unobserved and held it in my hand. It seemed to give back the light of the flickering fire and the light of the stars—for there was no moon—with equal fidelity; and I could note that on its reverse it was graven deeply with certain signs such as I had seen in the tomb. As I sank into the unconsciousness of sleep, the graven Star Jewel was hidden in the hollow of my clenched hand.

"I waked out of sleep with the light of the morning sun on my face. I sat up and looked around me. The fire was out, and the camp was desolate; save for one figure which lay prone close to me. It was that of the Arab chief, who lay on his back, dead. His face was almost black; and his eyes were open, and staring horribly up at the sky, as though he saw there some dreadful vision. He had evidently been strangled; for on looking, I found on his throat the red marks where fingers had pressed. There seemed so many of these marks that I counted them. There were seven; and all parallel, except the thumb mark, as though made with one hand. This thrilled me as I thought of the mummy hand with the seven fingers.

"Even there, in the open desert, it seemed as if there could be enchantments!

"In my surprise, as I bent over him, I opened my right hand, which up to now I had held shut with the feeling, instinctive even in sleep, of keeping safe that which it held. As I did so, the Star Jewel held there fell out and struck the dead man on the mouth. Mirabile dictu there came forth at once from the dead mouth a great gush of blood, in which the red jewel was for the moment lost. I turned the dead man over to look for it, and found that he lay with his right hand bent under him as though he had fallen on it; and in it he held a great knife, keen of point and edge, such as Arabs carry at the belt. It may have been that he was about to murder me when vengeance came on him, whether from man or God, or the Gods of Old, I know not. Suffice it, that when I found my Ruby Jewel, which shone up as a living star from the mess of blood wherein it lay, I paused not, but fled from the place. I journeyed on alone through the hot desert, till, by God's grace, I came upon an Arab tribe camping by a well, who gave me salt. With them I rested till they had set me on my way.

"I know not what became of the mummy hand, or of those who had it. What strife, or suspicion, or disaster, or greed went with it I know not; but some such cause there must have been, since those who had it fled with it. It doubtless is used as a charm of potence by some desert tribe.

"At the earliest opportunity I made examination of the Star Ruby, as I wished to try to understand what was graven on it. The symbols—whose meaning, however, I could not understand—were as follows..."

Twice, whilst I had been reading this engrossing narrative, I had thought that I had seen across the page streaks of shade, which the weirdness of the subject had made to seem like the shadow of a hand. On the first of these occasions I found that the illusion came from the fringe of green silk around the lamp; but on the second I had looked up, and my eyes had lit on the mummy hand across the room on which the starlight was falling under the edge of the blind. It was of little wonder that I had connected it with such a narrative; for if my eyes told me truly, here, in this room with me, was the very hand of which the traveller Van Huyn had written. I looked over at the bed; and it comforted me to think that the Nurse still sat there, calm and wakeful. At such a time, with such surrounds, during such a narrative, it was well to have assurance of the presence of some living person.

I sat looking at the book on the table before me; and so many strange thoughts crowded on me that my mind began to whirl. It was almost as if the light on the white fingers in front of me was beginning to have some hypnotic effect. All at once, all thoughts seemed to stop; and for an instant the world and time stood still.

There lay a real hand across the book! What was there to so overcome me, as was the case? I knew the hand that I saw on the book—and loved it. Margaret Trelawny's hand was a joy to me to see—to touch; and yet at that moment, coming after other marvellous things, it had a strangely moving effect on me. It was but momentary, however, and had passed even before her voice had reached me.

"What disturbs you? What are you staring at the book for? I thought for an instant that you must have been overcome again!" I jumped up.

"I was reading," I said, "an old book from the library." As I spoke I closed it and put it under my arm. "I shall now put it back, as I understand that your Father wishes all things, especially books, kept in their proper places." My words were intentionally misleading; for I did not wish her to know what I was reading, and thought it best not to wake her curiosity by leaving the book about. I went away, but not to the library; I left the book in my room where I could get it when I had had my sleep in the day. When I returned Nurse Kennedy was ready to go to bed; so Miss Trelawny watched with me in the room. I did not want any book whilst she was present. We sat close together and talked in a whisper whilst the moments flew by. It was with surprise that I noted the edge of the curtains changing from grey to yellow light. What we talked of had nothing to do with the sick man, except in so far that all which concerned his daughter must ultimately concern him. But it had nothing to say to Egypt, or mummies, or the dead, or caves, or Bedouin chiefs. I could well take note in the growing light that Margaret's hand had not seven fingers, but five; for it lay in mine.

When Doctor Winchester arrived in the morning and had made his visit to his patient, he came to see me as I sat in the dining-room having a little meal—breakfast or supper, I hardly knew which it was—before I went to lie down. Mr. Corbeck came in at the same time; and we resumed out conversation where we had left it the night before. I told Mr. Corbeck that I had read the chapter about the finding of the tomb, and that I thought Doctor Winchester should read it, too. The latter said that, if he might, he would take it with him; he had that morning to make a railway journey to Ipswich, and would read it on the train. He said he would bring it back with him when he came again in the evening. I went up to my room to bring it down; but I could not find it anywhere. I had a distinct recollection of having left it on the little table beside my bed, when I had come up after Miss Trelawny's going on duty into the sick-room. It was very strange; for the book was not of a kind that any of the servants would be likely to take. I had to come back and explain to the others that I could not find it.

When Doctor Winchester had gone, Mr. Corbeck, who seemed to know the Dutchman's work by heart, talked the whole matter over with me. I told him that I was interrupted by a change of nurses, just as I had come to the description of the ring. He smiled as he said:

"So far as that is concerned, you need not be disappointed. Not in Van Huyn's time, nor for nearly two centuries later, could the meaning of that engraving have been understood. It was only when the work was taken up and followed by Young and Champollion, by Birch and Lepsius and Rosellini and Salvolini, by Mariette Bey and by Wallis Budge and Flinders Petrie and the other scholars of their times that great results ensued, and that the true meaning of hieroglyphic was known.

"Later, I shall explain to you, if Mr. Trelawny does not explain it himself, or if he does not forbid me to, what it means in that particular place. I think it will be better for you to know what followed Van Huyn's narrative; for with the description of the stone, and the account of his bringing it to Holland at the termination of his travels, the episode ends. Ends so far as his book is concerned. The chief thing about the book is that it sets others thinking—and acting. Amongst them were Mr. Trelawny and myself. Mr. Trelawny is a good linguist of the Orient, but he does not know Northern tongues. As for me I have a faculty for learning languages; and when I was pursuing my studies in Leyden I learned Dutch so that I might more easily make references in the library there. Thus it was, that at the very time when Mr. Trelawny, who, in making his great collection of works on Egypt, had, through a booksellers' catalogue, acquired this volume with the manuscript translation, was studying it, I was reading another copy, in original Dutch, in Leyden. We were both struck by the description of the lonely tomb in the rock; cut so high up as to be inaccessible to ordinary seekers: with all means of reaching it carefully obliterated; and yet with such an elaborate ornamentation of the smoothed surface of the cliff as Van Huyn has described. It also struck us both as an odd thing—for in the years between Van Huyn's time and our own the general knowledge of Egyptian curios and records has increased marvellously—that in the case of such a tomb, made in such a place, and which must have cost an immense sum of money, there was no seeming record or effigy to point out who lay within. Moreover, the very name of the place, 'the Valley of the Sorcerer', had, in a prosaic age, attractions of its own. When we met, which we did through his seeking the assistance of other Egyptologists in his work, we talked over this as we did over many other things; and we determined to make search for the mysterious valley. Whilst we were waiting to start on the travel, for many things were required which Mr. Trelawny undertook to see to himself, I went to Holland to try if I could by any traces verify Van Huyn's narrative. I went straight to Hoorn, and set patiently to work to find the house of the traveller and his descendants, if any. I need not trouble you with details of my seeking—and finding. Hoorn is a place that has not changed much since Van Huyn's time, except that it has lost the place which it held amongst commercial cities. Its externals are such as they had been then; in such a sleepy old place a century or two does not count for much. I found the house, and discovered that none of the descendants were alive. I searched records; but only to one end—death and extinction. Then I set me to work to find what had become of his treasures; for that such a traveller must have had great treasures was apparent. I traced a good many to museums in Leyden, Utrecht, and Amsterdam; and some few to the private houses of rich collectors. At last, in the shop of an old watchmaker and jeweller at Hoorn, I found what he considered his chiefest treasure; a great ruby, carven like a scarab, with seven stars, and engraven with hieroglyphics. The old man did not know hieroglyphic character, and in his old-world, sleepy life, the philological discoveries of recent years had not reached him. He did not know anything of Van Huyn, except that such a person had been, and that his name was, during two centuries, venerated in the town as a great traveller. He valued the jewel as only a rare stone, spoiled in part by the cutting; and though he was at first loth to part with such an unique gem, he became amenable ultimately to commercial reason. I had a full purse, since I bought for Mr. Trelawny, who is, as I suppose you know, immensely wealthy. I was shortly on my way back to London, with the Star Ruby safe in my pocket-book; and in my heart a joy and exultation which knew no bounds.

"For here we were with proof of Van Huyn's wonderful story. The jewel was put in security in Mr. Trelawny's great safe; and we started out on our journey of exploration in full hope.

"Mr. Trelawny was, at the last, loth to leave his young wife whom he dearly loved; but she, who loved him equally, knew his longing to prosecute the search. So keeping to herself, as all good women do, all her anxieties—which in her case were special—she bade him follow out his bent."

Chapter XI - A Queen's Tomb

"Mr. Trelawny's hope was at least as great as my own. He is not so volatile a man as I am, prone to ups and downs of hope and despair; but he has a fixed purpose which crystallises hope into belief. At times I had feared that there might have been two such stones, or that the adventures of Van Huyn were traveller's fictions, based on some ordinary acquisition of the curio in Alexandria or Cairo, or London or Amsterdam. But Mr. Trelawny never faltered in his belief. We had many things to distract our minds from belief or disbelief. This was soon after Arabi Pasha, and Egypt was so safe place for travellers, especially if they were English. But Mr. Trelawny is a fearless man; and I almost come to think at times that I am not a coward myself. We got together a band of Arabs whom one or other of us had known in former trips to the desert, and whom we could trust; that is, we did not distrust them as much as others. We were numerous enough to protect ourselves from chance marauding bands, and we took with us large impedimenta. We had secured the consent and passive co-operation of the officials still friendly to Britain; in the acquiring of which consent I need hardly say that Mr. Trelawny's riches were of chief importance. We found our way in dhahabiyehs to Aswan; whence, having got some Arabs from the Sheik and having given our usual backsheesh, we set out on our journey through the desert.

"Well, after much wandering and trying every winding in the interminable jumble of hills, we came at last at nightfall on just such a valley as Van Huyn had described. A valley with high, steep cliffs; narrowing in the centre, and widening out to the eastern and western ends. At daylight we were opposite the cliff and could easily note the opening high up in the rock, and the hieroglyphic figures which were evidently intended originally to conceal it.

"But the signs which had baffled Van Huyn and those of his time—and later, were no secrets to us. The host of scholars who have given their brains and their lives to this work, had wrested open the mysterious prison-house of Egyptian language. On the hewn face of the rocky cliff we, who had learned the secrets, could read what the Theban priesthood had had there inscribed nearly fifty centuries before.

"For that the external inscription was the work of the priesthood—and a hostile priesthood at that—there could be no living doubt. The inscription on the rock, written in hieroglyphic, ran thus:

"'Hither the Gods come not at any summons. The "Nameless One" has insulted them and is for ever alone. Go not nigh, lest their vengeance wither you away!'

"The warning must have been a terribly potent one at the time it was written and for thousands of years afterwards; even when the language in which it was given had become a dead mystery to the people of the land. The tradition of such a terror lasts longer than its cause. Even in the symbols used there was an added significance of alliteration. 'For ever' is given in the hieroglyphics as 'millions of years'. This symbol was repeated nine times, in three groups of three; and after each group a symbol of the Upper World, the Under World, and the Sky. So that for this Lonely One there could be, through the vengeance of all the Gods, resurrection in neither the World of Sunlight, in the World of the Dead, or for the soul in the region of the Gods.

"Neither Mr. Trelawny nor I dared to tell any of our people what the writing meant. For though they did not believe in the religion whence the curse came, or in the Gods whose vengeance was threatened, yet they were so superstitious that they would probably, had they known of it, have thrown up the whole task and run away.

"Their ignorance, however, and our discretion preserved us. We made an encampment close at hand, but behind a jutting rock a little further along the valley, so that they might not have the inscription always before them. For even that traditional name of the place: 'The Valley of the Sorcerer', had a fear for them; and for us through them. With the timber which we had brought, we made a ladder up the face of the rock. We hung a pulley on a beam fixed to project from the top of the cliff. We found the great slab of rock, which formed the door, placed clumsily in its place and secured by a few stones. Its own weight kept it in safe position. In order to enter, we had to push it in; and we passed over it. We found the great coil of chain which Van Huyn had described fastened into the rock. There were, however, abundant evidences amid the wreckage of the great stone door, which had revolved on iron hinges at top and bottom, that ample provision had been originally made for closing and fastening it from within.

"Mr. Trelawny and I went alone into the tomb. We had brought plenty of lights with us; and we fixed them as we went along. We wished to get a complete survey at first, and then make examination of all in detail. As we went on, we were filled with ever-increasing wonder and delight. The tomb was one of the most magnificent and beautiful which either of us had ever seen. From the elaborate nature of the sculpture and painting, and the perfection of the workmanship, it was evident that the tomb was prepared during the lifetime of her for whose resting-place it was intended. The drawing of the hieroglyphic pictures was fine, and the colouring superb; and in that high cavern, far away from even the damp of the Nile-flood, all was as fresh as when the artists had laid down their palettes. There was one thing which we could not avoid seeing. That although the cutting on the outside rock was the work of the priesthood, the smoothing of the cliff face was probably a part of the tomb-builder's original design. The symbolism of the painting and cutting within all gave the same idea. The outer cavern, partly natural and partly hewn, was regarded architecturally as only an ante-chamber. At the end of it, so that it would face the east, was a pillared portico, hewn out of the solid rock. The pillars were massive and were seven-sided, a thing which we had not come across in any other tomb. Sculptured on the architrave was the Boat of the Moon, containing Hathor, cow-headed and bearing the disk and plumes, and the dog-headed Hapi, the God of the North. It was steered by Harpocrates towards the north, represented by the Pole Star surrounded by Draco and Ursa Major. In the latter the stars that form what we call the 'Plough' were cut larger than any of the other stars; and were filled with gold so that, in the light of torches, they seemed to flame with a special significance. Passing within the portico, we found two of the architectural features of a rock tomb, the Chamber, or Chapel, and the Pit, all complete as Van Huyn had noticed, though in his day the names given to these parts by the Egyptians of old were unknown.

"The Stele, or record, which had its place low down on the western wall, was so remarkable that we examined it minutely, even before going on our way to find the mummy which was the object of our search. This Stele was a great slab of lapis lazuli, cut all over with hieroglyphic figures of small size and of much beauty. The cutting was filled in with some cement of exceeding fineness, and of the colour of pure vermilion. The inscription began:

"'Tera, Queen of the Egypts, daughter of Antef, Monarch of the North and the South.' 'Daughter of the Sun,' 'Queen of the Diadems'.

"It then set out, in full record, the history of her life and reign.

"The signs of sovereignty were given with a truly feminine profusion of adornment. The united Crowns of Upper and Lower Egypt were, in especial, cut with exquisite precision. It was new to us both to find the Hejet and the Desher—the White and the Red crowns of Upper and Lower Egypt—on the Stele of a queen; for it was a rule, without exception in the records, that in ancient Egypt either crown was worn only by a king; though they are to be found on goddesses. Later on we found an explanation, of which I shall say more presently.

"Such an inscription was in itself a matter so startling as to arrest attention from anyone anywhere at any time; but you can have no conception of the effect which it had upon us. Though our eyes were not the first which had seen it, they were the first which could see it with understanding since first the slab of rock was fixed in the cliff opening nearly five thousand years before. To us was given to read this message from the dead. This message of one who had warred against the Gods of Old, and claimed to have controlled them at a time when the hierarchy professed to be the only means of exciting their fears or gaining their good will.

"The walls of the upper chamber of the Pit and the sarcophagus Chamber were profusely inscribed; all the inscriptions, except that on the Stele, being coloured with bluish-green pigment. The effect when seen sideways as the eye caught the green facets, was that of an old, discoloured Indian turquoise.

"We descended the Pit by the aid of the tackle we had brought with us. Trelawny went first. It was a deep pit, more than seventy feet; but it had never been filled up. The passage at the bottom sloped up to the sarcophagus Chamber, and was longer than is usually found. It had not been walled up.

"Within, we found a great sarcophagus of yellow stone. But that I need not describe; you have seen it in Mr. Trelawny's chamber. The cover of it lay on the ground; it had not been cemented, and was just as Van Huyn had described it. Needless to say, we were excited as we looked within. There must, however, be one sense of disappointment. I could not help feeling how different must have been the sight which met the Dutch traveller's eyes when he looked within and found that white hand lying life-like above the shrouding mummy cloths. It is true that a part of the arm was there, white and ivory like.

"But there was a thrill to us which came not to Van Huyn!

"The end of the wrist was covered with dried blood! It was as though the body had bled after death! The jagged ends of the broken wrist were rough with the clotted blood; through this the white bone, sticking out, looked like the matrix of opal. The blood had streamed down and stained the brown wrappings as with rust. Here, then, was full confirmation of the narrative. With such evidence of the narrator's truth before us, we could not doubt the other matters which he had told, such as the blood on the mummy hand, or marks of the seven fingers on the throat of the strangled Sheik.

"I shall not trouble you with details of all we saw, or how we learned all we knew. Part of it was from knowledge common to scholars; part we read on the Stele in the tomb, and in the sculptures and hieroglyphic paintings on the walls.

"Queen Tera was of the Eleventh, or Theban Dynasty of Egyptian Kings which held sway between the twenty-ninth and twenty-fifth centuries before Christ. She succeeded as the only child of her father, Antef. She must have been a girl of extraordinary character as well as ability, for she was but a young girl when her father died. Her youth and sex encouraged the ambitious priesthood, which had then achieved immense power. By their wealth and numbers and learning they dominated all Egypt, more especially the Upper portion. They were then secretly ready to make an effort for the achievement of their bold and long-considered design, that of transferring the governing power from a Kingship to a Hierarchy. But King Antef had suspected some such movement, and had taken the precaution of securing to his daughter the allegiance of the army. He had also had her taught statecraft, and had even made her learned in the lore of the very priests themselves. He had used those of one cult against the other; each being hopeful of some present gain on its own part by the influence of the King, or of some ultimate gain from its own influence over his daughter. Thus, the Princess had been brought up amongst scribes, and was herself no mean artist. Many of these things were told on the walls in pictures or in hieroglyphic writing of great beauty; and we came to the conclusion that not a few of them had been done by the Princess herself. It was not without cause that she was inscribed on the Stele as 'Protector of the Arts'.

"But the King had gone to further lengths, and had had his daughter taught magic, by which she had power over Sleep and Will. This was real magic—"black" magic; not the magic of the temples, which, I may explain, was of the harmless or "white" order, and was intended to impress rather than to effect. She had been an apt pupil; and had gone further than her teachers. Her power and her resources had given her great opportunities, of which she had availed herself to the full. She had won secrets from nature in strange ways; and had even gone to the length of going down into the tomb herself, having been swathed and coffined and left as dead for a whole month. The priests had tried to make out that the real Princess Tera had died in the experiment, and that another girl had been substituted; but she had conclusively proved their error. All this was told in pictures of great merit. It was probably in her time that the impulse was given in the restoring the artistic greatness of the Fourth Dynasty which had found its perfection in the days of Chufu.

"In the Chamber of the sarcophagus were pictures and writings to show that she had achieved victory over Sleep. Indeed, there was everywhere a symbolism, wonderful even in a land and an age of symbolism. Prominence was given to the fact that she, though a Queen, claimed all the privileges of kingship and masculinity. In one place she was pictured in man's dress, and wearing the White and Red Crowns. In the following picture she was in female dress, but still wearing the Crowns of Upper and Lower Egypt, while the discarded male raiment lay at her feet. In every picture where hope, or aim, of resurrection was expressed there was the added symbol of the North; and in many places—always in representations of important events, past, present, or future—was a grouping of the stars of the Plough. She evidently regarded this constellation as in some way peculiarly associated with herself.

"Perhaps the most remarkable statement in the records, both on the Stele and in the mural writings, was that Queen Tera had power to compel the Gods. This, by the way, was not an isolated belief in Egyptian history; but was different in its cause. She had engraved on a ruby, carved like a scarab, and having seven stars of seven points, Master Words to compel all the Gods, both of the Upper and the Under Worlds.

"In the statement it was plainly set forth that the hatred of the priests was, she knew, stored up for her, and that they would after her death try to suppress her name. This was a terrible revenge, I may tell you, in Egyptian mythology; for without a name no one can after death be introduced to the Gods, or have prayers said for him. Therefore, she had intended her resurrection to be after a long time and in a more northern land, under the constellation whose seven stars had ruled her birth. To this end, her hand was to be in the air—'unwrapped'—and in it the Jewel of Seven Stars, so that wherever there was air she might move even as her Ka could move! This, after thinking it over, Mr. Trelawny and I agreed meant that her body could become astral at command, and so move, particle by particle, and become whole again when and where required. Then there was a piece of writing in which allusion was made to a chest or casket in which were contained all the Gods, and Will, and Sleep, the two latter being personified by symbols. The box was mentioned as with seven sides. It was not much of a surprise to us when, underneath the feet of the mummy, we found the seven-sided casket, which you have also seen in Mr. Trelawny's room. On the underneath part of the wrapping—linen of the left foot was painted, in the same vermilion colour as that used in the Stele, the hieroglyphic symbol for much water, and underneath the right foot the symbol of the earth. We made out the symbolism to be that her body, immortal and transferable at will, ruled both the land and water, air and fire—the latter being exemplified by the light of the Jewel Stone, and further by the flint and iron which lay outside the mummy wrappings.

"As we lifted the casket from the sarcophagus, we noticed on its sides the strange protuberances which you have already seen; but we were unable at the time to account for them. There were a few amulets in the sarcophagus, but none of any special worth or significance. We took it that if there were such, they were within the wrappings; or more probably in the strange casket underneath the mummy's feet. This, however, we could not open. There were signs of there being a cover; certainly the upper portion and the lower were each in one piece. The fine line, a little way from the top, appeared to be where the cover was fixed; but it was made with such exquisite fineness and finish that the joining could hardly be seen. Certainly the top could not be moved. We took it, that it was in some way fastened from within. I tell you all this in order that you may understand things with which you may be in contact later. You must suspend your judgment entirely. Such strange things have happened regarding this mummy and all around it, that there is a necessity for new belief somewhere. It is absolutely impossible to reconcile certain things which have happened with the ordinary currents of life or knowledge.

"We stayed around the Valley of the Sorcerer, till we had copied roughly all the drawings and writings on the walls, ceiling and floor. We took with us the Stele of lapis lazuli, whose graven record was coloured with vermilion pigment. We took the sarcophagus and the mummy; the stone chest with the alabaster jars; the tables of bloodstone and alabaster and onyx and carnelian; and the ivory pillow whose arch rested on 'buckles', round each of which was twisted an uraeus wrought in gold. We took all the articles which lay in the Chapel, and the Mummy Pit; the wooden boats with crews and the ushaptiu figures, and the symbolic amulets.

"When coming away we took down the ladders, and at a distance buried them in the sand under a cliff, which we noted so that if necessary we might find them again. Then with our heavy baggage, we set out on our laborious journey back to the Nile. It was no easy task, I tell you, to bring the case with that great sarcophagus over the desert. We had a rough cart and sufficient men to draw it; but the progress seemed terribly slow, for we were anxious to get our treasures into a place of safety. The night was an anxious time with us, for we feared attack from some marauding band. But more still we feared some of those with us. They were, after all, but predatory, unscrupulous men; and we had with us a considerable bulk of precious things. They, or at least the dangerous ones amongst them, did not know why it was so precious; they took it for granted that it was material treasure of some kind that we carried. We had taken the mummy from the sarcophagus, and packed it for safety of travel in a separate case. During the first night two attempts were made to steal things from the cart; and two men were found dead in the morning.

"On the second night there came on a violent storm, one of those terrible simooms of the desert which makes one feel his helplessness. We were overwhelmed with drifting sand. Some of our Bedouins had fled before the storm, hoping to find shelter; the rest of us, wrapped in our bournous, endured with what patience we could. In the morning, when the storm had passed, we recovered from under the piles of sand what we could of our impedimenta. We found the case in which the mummy had been packed all broken, but the mummy itself could nowhere be found. We searched everywhere around, and dug up the sand which had piled around us; but in vain. We did not know what to do, for Trelawny had his heart set on taking home that mummy. We waited a whole day in hopes that the Bedouins, who had fled, would return; we had a blind hope that they might have in some way removed the mummy from the cart, and would restore it. That night, just before dawn, Mr. Trelawny woke me up and whispered in my ear:

"'We must go back to the tomb in the Valley of the Sorcerer. Show no hesitation in the morning when I give the orders! If you ask any questions as to where we are going it will create suspicion, and will defeat our purpose."

"'All right!" I answered. "But why shall we go there?' His answer seemed to thrill through me as though it had struck some chord ready tuned within:

"'We shall find the mummy there! I am sure of it!' Then anticipating doubt or argument he added:

"'Wait, and you shall see!' and he sank back into his blanket again.

"The Arabs were surprised when we retraced our steps; and some of them were not satisfied. There was a good deal of friction, and there were several desertions; so that it was with a diminished following that we took our way eastward again. At first the Sheik did not manifest any curiosity as to our definite destination; but when it became apparent that we were again making for the Valley of the Sorcerer, he too showed concern. This grew as we drew near; till finally at the entrance of the valley he halted and refused to go further. He said he would await our return if we chose to go on alone. That he would wait three days; but if by that time we had not returned he would leave. No offer of money would tempt him to depart from this resolution. The only concession he would make was that he would find the ladders and bring them near the cliff. This he did; and then, with the rest of the troop, he went back to wait at the entrance of the valley.

"Mr. Trelawny and I took ropes and torches, and again ascended to the tomb. It was evident that someone had been there in our absence, for the stone slab which protected the entrance to the tomb was lying flat inside, and a rope was dangling from the cliff summit. Within, there was another rope hanging into the shaft of the Mummy Pit. We looked at each other; but neither said a word. We fixed our own rope, and as arranged Trelawny descended first, I following at once. It was not till we stood together at the foot of the shaft that the thought flashed across me that we might be in some sort of a trap; that someone might descend the rope from the cliff, and by cutting the rope by which we had lowered ourselves into the Pit, bury us there alive. The thought was horrifying; but it was too late to do anything. I remained silent. We both had torches, so that there was ample light as we passed through the passage and entered the Chamber where the sarcophagus had stood. The first thing noticeable was the emptiness of the place. Despite all its magnificent adornment, the tomb was made a desolation by the absence of the great sarcophagus, to hold which it was hewn in the rock; of the chest with the alabaster jars; of the tables which had held the implements and food for the use of the dead, and the ushaptiu figures.

"It was made more infinitely desolate still by the shrouded figure of the mummy of Queen Tera which lay on the floor where the great sarcophagus had stood! Beside it lay, in the strange contorted attitudes of violent death, three of the Arabs who had deserted from our party. Their faces were black, and their hands and necks were smeared with blood which had burst from mouth and nose and eyes.

"On the throat of each were the marks, now blackening, of a hand of seven fingers.

"Trelawny and I drew close, and clutched each other in awe and fear as we looked.

"For, most wonderful of all, across the breast of the mummied Queen lay a hand of seven fingers, ivory white, the wrist only showing a scar like a jagged red line, from which seemed to depend drops of blood."

Chapter XII - The Magic Coffer

"When we recovered our amazement, which seemed to last unduly long, we did not lose any time carrying the mummy through the passage, and hoisting it up the Pit shaft. I went first, to receive it at the top. As I looked down, I saw Mr. Trelawny lift the severed hand and put it in his breast, manifestly to save it from being injured or lost. We left the dead Arabs where they lay. With our ropes we lowered our precious burden to the ground; and then took it to the entrance of the valley where our escort was to wait. To our astonishment we found them on the move. When we remonstrated with the Sheik, he answered that he had fulfilled his contract to the letter; he had waited the three days as arranged. I thought that he was lying to cover up his base intention of deserting us; and I found when we compared notes that Trelawny had the same suspicion. It was not till we arrived at Cairo that we found he was correct. It was the 3rd of November 1884 when we entered the Mummy Pit for the second time; we had reason to remember the date.

"We had lost three whole days of our reckoning—out of our lives—whilst we had stood wondering in that chamber of the dead. Was it strange, then, that we had a superstitious feeling with regard to the dead Queen Tera and all belonging to her? Is it any wonder that it rests with us now, with a bewildering sense of some power outside ourselves or our comprehension? Will it be any wonder if it go down to the grave with us at the appointed time? If, indeed, there be any graves for us who have robbed the dead!" He was silent for quite a minute before he went on:

"We got to Cairo all right, and from there to Alexandria, where we were to take ship by the Messagerie service to Marseilles, and go thence by express to London. But

'The best-laid schemes o' mice and men Gang aft agley.'

At Alexandria, Trelawny found waiting a cable stating that Mrs. Trelawny had died in giving birth to a daughter.

"Her stricken husband hurried off at once by the Orient Express; and I had to bring the treasure alone to the desolate house. I got to London all safe; there seemed to be some special good fortune to our journey. When I got to this house, the funeral had long been over. The child had been put out to nurse, and Mr. Trelawny had so far recovered from the shock of his loss that he had set himself to take up again the broken threads of his life and his work. That he had had a shock, and a bad one, was apparent. The sudden grey in his black hair was proof enough in itself; but in addition, the strong cast of his features had become set and stern. Since he received that cable in the shipping office at Alexandria I have never seen a happy smile on his face.

"Work is the best thing in such a case; and to his work he devoted himself heart and soul. The strange tragedy of his loss and gain—for the child was born after the mother's death—took place during the time that we stood in that trance in the Mummy Pit of Queen Tera. It seemed to have become in some way associated with his Egyptian studies, and more especially with the mysteries connected with the Queen. He told me very little about his daughter; but that two forces struggled in his mind regarding her was apparent. I could see that he loved, almost idolised her. Yet he could never forget that her birth had cost her mother's life. Also, there was something whose existence seemed to wring his father's heart, though he would never tell me what it was. Again, he once said in a moment of relaxation of his purpose of silence:

"'She is unlike her mother; but in both feature and colour she has a marvellous resemblance to the pictures of Queen Tera.'

"He said that he had sent her away to people who would care for her as he could not; and that till she became a woman she should have all the simple pleasures that a young girl might have, and that were best for her. I would often have talked with him about her; but he would never say much. Once he said to me: 'There are reasons why I should not speak more than is necessary. Some day you will know—and understand!' I respected his reticence; and beyond asking after her on my return after a journey, I have never spoken of her again. I had never seen her till I did so in your presence.

"Well, when the treasures which we had—ah!—taken from the tomb had been brought here, Mr. Trelawny arranged their disposition himself. The mummy, all except the severed hand, he placed in the great ironstone sarcophagus in the hall. This was wrought for the Theban High Priest Uni, and is, as you may have remarked, all inscribed with wonderful invocations to the old Gods of Egypt. The rest of the things from the tomb he disposed about his own room, as you have seen. Amongst them he placed, for special reasons of his own, the mummy hand. I think he regards this as the most sacred of his possessions, with perhaps one exception. That is the carven ruby which he calls the 'Jewel of Seven Stars', which he keeps in that great safe which is locked and guarded by various devices, as you know.

"I dare say you find this tedious; but I have had to explain it, so that you should understand all up to the present. It was a long time after my return with the mummy of Queen Tera when Mr. Trelawny re-opened the subject with me. He had been several times to Egypt, sometimes with me and sometimes alone; and I had been several trips, on my own account or for him. But in all that time, nearly sixteen years, he never mentioned the subject, unless when some pressing occasion suggested, if it did not necessitate, a reference.

"One morning early he sent for me in a hurry; I was then studying in the British Museum, and had rooms in Hart Street. When I came, he was all on fire with excitement. I had not seen him in such a glow since before the news of his wife's death. He took me at once into his room. The window blinds were down and the shutters closed; not a ray of daylight came in. The ordinary lights in the room were not lit, but there were a lot of powerful electric lamps, fifty candle-power at least, arranged on one side of the room. The little bloodstone table on which the heptagonal coffer stands was drawn to the centre of the room. The coffer looked exquisite in the glare of light which shone on it. It actually seemed to glow as if lit in some way from within.

"'What do you think of it?' he asked.

"'It is like a jewel,' I answered. 'You may well call it the 'sorcerer's Magic Coffer', if it often looks like that. It almost seems to be alive.'

"'Do you know why it seems so?'

"'From the glare of the light, I suppose?'

"'Light of course,' he answered, 'but it is rather the disposition of light.' As he spoke he turned up the ordinary lights of the room and switched off the special ones. The effect on the stone box was surprising; in a second it lost all its glowing effect. It was still a very beautiful stone, as always; but it was stone and no more.

"'Do you notice anything about the arrangement of the lamps?' he asked.

"'No!'

"'They were in the shape of the stars in the Plough, as the stars are in the ruby!' The statement came to me with a certain sense of conviction. I do not know why, except that there had been so many mysterious associations with the mummy and all belonging to it that any new one seemed enlightening. I listened as Trelawny went on to explain:

"'For sixteen years I have never ceased to think of that adventure, or to try to find a clue to the mysteries which came before us; but never until last night did I seem to find a solution. I think I must have dreamed of it, for I woke all on fire about it. I jumped out of bed with a determination of doing something, before I quite knew what it was that I wished to do. Then, all at once, the purpose was clear before me. There were allusions in the writing on the walls of the tomb to the seven stars of the Great Bear that go to make up the Plough; and the North was again and again emphasized. The same symbols were repeated with regard to the "Magic Box", as we called it. We had already noticed those peculiar translucent spaces in the stone of the box. You remember the hieroglyphic writing had told that the jewel came from the heart of an aerolite, and that the coffer was cut from it also. It might be, I thought, that the light of the seven stars, shining in the right direction, might have some effect on the box, or something within it. I raised the blind and looked out. The Plough was high in the heavens, and both its stars and the Pole Star were straight opposite the window. I pulled the table with the coffer out into the light, and shifted it until the translucent patches were in the direction of the stars. Instantly the box began to glow, as you saw it under the lamps, though but slightly. I waited and waited; but the sky clouded over, and the light died away. So I got wires and lamps—you know how often I use them in experiments—and tried the effect of electric light. It took me some time to get the lamps properly placed, so that they would correspond to the parts of the stone, but the moment I got them right the whole thing began to glow as you have seen it.

"'I could get no further, however. There was evidently something wanting. All at once it came to me that if light could have some effect there should be in the tomb some means of producing light, for there could not be starlight in the Mummy Pit in the cavern. Then the whole thing seemed to become clear. On the bloodstone table, which has a hollow carved in its top, into which the bottom of the coffer fits, I laid the Magic Coffer; and I at once saw that the odd protuberances so carefully wrought in the substance of the stone corresponded in a way to the stars in the constellation. These, then, were to hold lights.

"'Eureka!' I cried. 'All we want now is the lamps.'" I tried placing the electric lights on, or close to, the protuberances. But the glow never came to the stone. So the conviction grew on me that there were special lamps made for the purpose. If we could find them, a step on the road to solving the mystery should be gained.

"'But what about the lamps?' I asked. 'Where are they? When are we to discover them? How are we to know them if we do find them? What—"

"He stopped me at once:

"'One thing at a time!' he said quietly. 'Your first question contains all the rest. Where are these lamps? I shall tell you: In the tomb!'

"'In the tomb!' I repeated in surprise. 'Why you and I searched the place ourselves from end to end; and there was not a sign of a lamp. Not a sign of anything remaining when we came away the first time; or on the second, except the bodies of the Arabs.'

"Whilst I was speaking, he had uncoiled some large sheets of paper which he had brought in his hand from his own room. These he spread out on the great table, keeping their edges down with books and weights. I knew them at a glance; they were the careful copies which he had made of our first transcripts from the writing in the tomb. When he had all ready, he turned to me and said slowly:

"'Do you remember wondering, when we examined the tomb, at the lack of one thing which is usually found in such a tomb?'

"'Yes! There was no serdab.'

"The serdab, I may perhaps explain," said Mr. Corbeck to me, "is a sort of niche built or hewn in the wall of a tomb. Those which have as yet been examined bear no inscriptions, and contain only effigies of the dead for whom the tomb was made." Then he went on with his narrative:

"Trelawny, when he saw that I had caught his meaning, went on speaking with something of his old enthusiasm:

"'I have come to the conclusion that there must be a serdab—a secret one. We were dull not to have thought of it before. We might have known that the maker of such a tomb—a woman, who had shown in other ways such a sense of beauty and completeness, and who had finished every detail with a feminine richness of elaboration—would not have neglected such an architectural feature. Even if it had not its own special significance in ritual, she would have had it as an adornment. Others had had it, and she liked her own work to be complete. Depend upon it, there was—there is—a serdab; and that in it, when it is discovered, we shall find the lamps. Of course, had we known then what we now know or at all events surmise, that there were lamps, we might have suspected some hidden spot, some cachet. I am going to ask you to go out to Egypt again; to seek the tomb; to find the serdab; and to bring back the lamps!'"

"'And if I find there is no serdab; or if discovering it I find no lamps in it, what then?' He smiled grimly with that saturnine smile of his, so rarely seen for years past, as he spoke slowly:

"'Then you will have to hustle till you find them!'

"'Good!' I said. He pointed to one of the sheets.

"'Here are the transcripts from the Chapel at the south and the east. I have been looking over the writings again; and I find that in seven places round this corner are the symbols of the constellation which we call the Plough, which Queen Tera held to rule her birth and her destiny. I have examined them carefully, and I notice that they are all representations of the grouping of the stars, as the constellation appears in different parts of the heavens. They are all astronomically correct; and as in the real sky the Pointers indicate the Pole Star, so these all point to one spot in the wall where usually the serdab is to be found!'

"'Bravo!' I shouted, for such a piece of reasoning demanded applause. He seemed pleased as he went on:

"'When you are in the tomb, examine this spot. There is probably some spring or mechanical contrivance for opening the receptacle. What it may be, there is no use guessing. You will know what best to do, when you are on the spot.'

"I started the next week for Egypt; and never rested till I stood again in the tomb. I had found some of our old following; and was fairly well provided with help. The country was now in a condition very different to that in which it had been sixteen years before; there was no need for troops or armed men.

"I climbed the rock face alone. There was no difficulty, for in that fine climate the woodwork of the ladder was still dependable. It was easy to see that in the years that had elapsed there had been other visitors to the tomb; and my heart sank within me when I thought that some of them might by chance have come across the secret place. It would be a bitter discovery indeed to find that they had forestalled me; and that my journey had been in vain.

"The bitterness was realised when I lit my torches, and passed between the seven-sided columns to the Chapel of the tomb.

"There, in the very spot where I had expected to find it, was the opening of a serdab. And the serdab was empty.

"But the Chapel was not empty; for the dried-up body of a man in Arab dress lay close under the opening, as though he had been stricken down. I examined all round the walls to see if Trelawny's surmise was correct; and I found that in all the positions of the stars as given, the Pointers of the Plough indicated a spot to the left hand, or south side, of the opening of the serdab, where was a single star in gold.

"I pressed this, and it gave way. The stone which had marked the front of the serdab, and which lay back against the wall within, moved slightly. On further examining the other side of the opening, I found a similar spot, indicated by other representations of the constellation; but this was itself a figure of the seven stars, and each was wrought in burnished gold. I pressed each star in turn; but without result. Then it struck me that if the opening spring was on the left, this on the right might have been intended for the simultaneous pressure of all the stars by one hand of seven fingers. By using both my hands, I managed to effect this.

"With a loud click, a metal figure seemed to dart from close to the opening of the serdab; the stone slowly swung back to its place, and shut with a click. The glimpse which I had of the descending figure appalled me for the moment. It was like that grim guardian which, according to the Arabian historian Ibn Abd Alhokin, the builder of the Pyramids, King Saurid Ibn Salhouk placed in the Western Pyramid to defend its treasure: 'A marble figure, upright, with lance in hand; with on his head a serpent wreathed. When any approached, the serpent would bite him on one side, and twining about his throat and killing him, would return again to his place.'

"I knew well that such a figure was not wrought to pleasantry; and that to brave it was no child's play. The dead Arab at my feet was proof of what could be done! So I examined again along the wall; and found here and there chippings as if someone had been tapping with a heavy hammer. This then had been what happened: The grave-robber, more expert at his work than we had been, and suspecting the presence of a hidden serdab, had made essay to find it. He had struck the spring by chance; had released the avenging 'Treasurer', as the Arabian writer designated him. The issue spoke for itself. I got a piece of wood, and, standing at a safe distance, pressed with the end of it upon the star.

"Instantly the stone flew back. The hidden figure within darted forward and thrust out its lance. Then it rose up and disappeared. I thought I might now safely press on the seven stars; and did so. Again the stone rolled back; and the 'Treasurer' flashed by to his hidden lair.

"I repeated both experiments several times; with always the same result. I should have liked to examine the mechanism of that figure of such malignant mobility; but it was not possible without such tools as could not easily be had. It might be necessary to cut into a whole section of the rock. Some day I hope to go back, properly equipped, and attempt it.

"Perhaps you do not know that the entrance to a serdab is almost always very narrow; sometimes a hand can hardly be inserted. Two things I learned from this serdab. The first was that the lamps, if lamps at all there had been, could not have been of large size; and secondly, that they would be in some way associated with Hathor, whose symbol, the hawk in a square with the right top corner forming a smaller square, was cut in relief on the wall within, and coloured the bright vermilion which we had found on the Stele. Hathor is the goddess who in Egyptian mythology answers to Venus of the Greeks, in as far as she is the presiding deity of beauty and pleasure. In the Egyptian mythology, however, each God has many forms; and in some aspects Hathor has to do with the idea of resurrection. There are seven forms or variants of the Goddess; why should not these correspond in some way to the seven lamps! That there had been such lamps, I was convinced. The first grave-robber had met his death; the second had found the contents of the serdab. The first attempt had been made years since; the state of the body proved this. I had no clue to the second attempt. It might have been long ago; or it might have been recently. If, however, others had been to the tomb, it was probable that the lamps had been taken long ago. Well! all the more difficult would be my search; for undertaken it must be!

"That was nearly three years ago; and for all that time I have been like the man in the Arabian Nights, seeking old lamps, not for new, but for cash. I dared not say what I was looking for, or attempt to give any description; for such would have defeated my purpose. But I had in my own mind at the start a vague idea of what I must find. In process of time this grew more and more clear; till at last I almost overshot my mark by searching for something which might have been wrong.

"The disappointments I suffered, and the wild-goose chases I made, would fill a volume; but I persevered. At last, not two months ago, I was shown by an old dealer in Mossul one lamp such as I had looked for. I had been tracing it for nearly a year, always suffering disappointment, but always buoyed up to further endeavour by a growing hope that I was on the track.

"I do not know how I restrained myself when I realised that, at last, I was at least close to success. I was skilled, however, in the finesse of Eastern trade; and the Jew-Arab-Portugee trader met his match. I wanted to see all his stock before buying; and one by one he produced, amongst masses of rubbish, seven different lamps. Each of them had a distinguishing mark; and each and all was some form of the symbol of Hathor. I think I shook the imperturbability of my swarthy friend by the magnitude of my purchases; for in order to prevent him guessing what form of goods I sought, I nearly cleared out his shop. At the end he nearly wept, and said I had ruined him; for now he had nothing to sell. He would have torn his hair had he known what price I should ultimately have given for some of his stock, that perhaps he valued least.

"I parted with most of my merchandise at normal price as I hurried home. I did not dare to give it away, or even lose it, lest I should incur suspicion. My burden was far too precious to be risked by any foolishness now. I got on as fast as it is possible to travel in such countries; and arrived in London with only the lamps and certain portable curios and papyri which I had picked up on my travels.

"Now, Mr. Ross, you know all I know; and I leave it to your discretion how much, if any of it, you will tell Miss Trelawny."

As he finished a clear young voice said behind us:

"What about Miss Trelawny? She is here!"

We turned, startled; and looked at each other inquiringly. Miss Trelawny stood in the doorway. We did not know how long she had been present, or how much she had heard.

Chapter XIII - Awaking From the Trance

The first unexpected words may always startle a hearer; but when the shock is over, the listener's reason has asserted itself, and he can judge of the manner, as well as of the matter, of speech. Thus it was on this occasion. With intelligence now alert, I could not doubt of the simple sincerity of Margaret's next question.

"What have you two men been talking about all this time, Mr. Ross? I suppose, Mr. Corbeck has been telling you all his adventures in finding the lamps. I hope you will tell me too, some day, Mr. Corbeck; but that must not be till my poor Father is better. He would like, I am sure, to tell me all about these things himself; or to be present when I heard them." She glanced sharply from one to the other. "Oh, that was what you were saying as I came in? All right! I shall wait; but I hope it won't be long. The continuance of Father's condition is, I feel, breaking me down. A little while ago I felt that my nerves were giving out; so I determined to go out for a walk in the Park. I am sure it will do me good. I want you, if you will, Mr. Ross, to be with Father whilst I am away. I shall feel secure then."

I rose with alacrity, rejoicing that the poor girl was going out, even for half an hour. She was looking terribly wearied and haggard; and the sight of her pale cheeks made my heart ache. I went to the sick-room; and sat down in my usual place. Mrs. Grant was then on duty; we had not found it necessary to have more than one person in the room during the day. When I came in, she took occasion to go about some household duty. The blinds were up, but the north aspect of the room softened the hot glare of the sunlight without.

I sat for a long time thinking over all that Mr. Corbeck had told me; and weaving its wonders into the tissue of strange things which had come to pass since I had entered the house. At times I was inclined to doubt; to doubt everything and every one; to doubt even the evidences of my own five senses. The warnings of the skilled detective kept coming back to my mind. He had put down Mr. Corbeck as a clever liar, and a confederate of Miss Trelawny. Of Margaret! That settled it! Face to face with such a proposition as that, doubt vanished. Each time when her image, her name, the merest thought of her, came before my mind, each event stood out stark as a living fact. My life upon her faith!

I was recalled from my reverie, which was fast becoming a dream of love, in a startling manner. A voice came from the bed; a deep, strong, masterful voice. The first note of it called up like a clarion my eyes and my ears. The sick man was awake and speaking!

"Who are you? What are you doing here?"

Whatever ideas any of us had ever formed of his waking, I am quite sure that none of us expected to see him start up all awake and full master of himself. I was so surprised that I answered almost mechanically:

"Ross is my name. I have been watching by you!" He looked surprised for an instant, and then I could see that his habit of judging for himself came into play.

"Watching by me! How do you mean? Why watching by me?" His eye had now lit on his heavily bandaged wrist. He went on in a different tone; less aggressive, more genial, as of one accepting facts:

"Are you a doctor?" I felt myself almost smiling as I answered; the relief from the long pressure of anxiety regarding his life was beginning to tell:

"No, sir!"

"Then why are you here? If you are not a doctor, what are you?" His tone was again more dictatorial. Thought is quick; the whole train of reasoning on which my answer must be based flooded through my brain before the words could leave my lips. Margaret! I must think of Margaret! This was her father, who as yet knew nothing of me; even of my very existence. He would be naturally curious, if not anxious, to know why I amongst men had been chosen as his daughter's friend on the occasion of his illness. Fathers are naturally a little jealous in such matters as a daughter's choice, and in the undeclared state of my love for Margaret I must do nothing which could ultimately embarrass her.

"I am a Barrister. It is not, however, in that capacity I am here; but simply as a friend of your daughter. It was probably her knowledge of my being a lawyer which first determined her to ask me to come when she thought you had been murdered. Afterwards she was good enough to consider me to be a friend, and to allow me to remain in accordance with your expressed wish that someone should remain to watch."

Mr. Trelawny was manifestly a man of quick thought, and of few words. He gazed at me keenly as I spoke, and his piercing eyes seemed to read my thought. To my relief he said no more on the subject just then, seeming to accept my words in simple faith. There was evidently in his own mind some cause for the acceptance deeper than my own knowledge. His eyes flashed, and there was an unconscious movement of the mouth—it could hardly be called a twitch—which betokened satisfaction. He was following out some train of reasoning in his own mind. Suddenly he said:

"She thought I had been murdered! Was that last night?"

"No! four days ago." He seemed surprised. Whilst he had been speaking the first time he had sat up in bed; now he made a movement as though he would jump out. With an effort, however, he restrained himself; leaning back on his pillows he said quietly:

"Tell me all about it! All you know! Every detail! Omit nothing! But stay; first lock the door! I want to know, before I see anyone, exactly how things stand."

Somehow his last words made my heart leap. "Anyone!" He evidently accepted me, then, as an exception. In my present state of feeling for his daughter, this was a comforting thought. I felt exultant as I went over to the door and softly turned the key. When I came back I found him sitting up again. He said:

"Go on!"

Accordingly, I told him every detail, even of the slightest which I could remember, of what had happened from the moment of my arrival at the house. Of course I said nothing of my feeling towards Margaret, and spoke only concerning those things already within his own knowledge. With regard to Corbeck, I simply said that he had brought back some lamps of which he had been in quest. Then I proceeded to tell him fully of their loss, and of their re-discovery in the house.

He listened with a self-control which, under the circumstances, was to me little less than marvellous. It was impassiveness, for at times his eyes would flash or blaze, and the strong fingers of his uninjured hand would grip the sheet, pulling it into far-extending wrinkles. This was most noticeable when I told him of the return of Corbeck, and the finding of the lamps in the boudoir. At times he spoke, but only a few words, and as if unconsciously in emotional comment. The mysterious parts, those which had most puzzled us, seemed to have no special interest for him; he seemed to know them already. The utmost concern he showed was when I told him of Daw's shooting. His muttered comment: "stupid ass!" together with a quick glance across the room at the injured cabinet, marked the measure of his disgust. As I told him of his daughter's harrowing anxiety for him, of her unending care and devotion, of the tender love which she had shown, he seemed much moved. There was a sort of veiled surprise in his unconscious whisper:

"Margaret! Margaret!"

When I had finished my narration, bringing matters up to the moment when Miss Trelawny had gone out for her walk—I thought of her as "Miss Trelawny', not as 'Margaret' now, in the presence of her father—he remained silent for quite a long time. It was probably two or three minutes; but it seemed interminable. All at once he turned and said to me briskly:

"Now tell me all about yourself!" This was something of a floorer; I felt myself grow red-hot. Mr. Trelawny's eyes were upon me; they were now calm and inquiring, but never ceasing in their soul-searching scrutiny. There was just a suspicion of a smile on the mouth which, though it added to my embarrassment, gave me a certain measure of relief. I was, however, face to face with difficulty; and the habit of my life stood me in good stead. I looked him straight in the eyes as I spoke:

"My name, as I told you, is Ross, Malcolm Ross. I am by profession a Barrister. I was made a Q. C. in the last year of the Queen's reign. I have been fairly successful in my work." To my relief he said:

"Yes, I know. I have always heard well of you! Where and when did you meet Margaret?"

"First at the Hay's in Belgrave Square, ten days ago. Then at a picnic up the river with Lady Strathconnell. We went from Windsor to Cookham. Mar—Miss Trelawny was in my boat. I scull a little, and I had my own boat at Windsor. We had a good deal of conversation—naturally."

"Naturally!" there was just a suspicion of something sardonic in the tone of acquiescence; but there was no other intimation of his feeling. I began to think that as I was in the presence of a strong man, I should show something of my own strength. My friends, and sometimes my opponents, say that I am a strong man. In my present circumstances, not to be absolutely truthful would be to be weak. So I stood up to the difficulty before me; always bearing in mind, however, that my words might affect Margaret's happiness through her love for her father. I went on:

"In conversation at a place and time and amid surroundings so pleasing, and in a solitude inviting to confidence, I got a glimpse of her inner life. Such a glimpse as a man of my years and experience may get from a young girl!" The father's face grew graver as I went on; but he said nothing. I was committed now to a definite line of speech, and went on with such mastery of my mind as I could exercise. The occasion might be fraught with serious consequences to me too.

"I could not but see that there was over her spirit a sense of loneliness which was habitual to her. I thought I understood it; I am myself an only child. I ventured to encourage her to speak to me freely; and was happy enough to succeed. A sort of confidence became established between us." There was something in the father's face which made me add hurriedly:

"Nothing was said by her, sir, as you can well imagine, which was not right and proper. She only told me in the impulsive way of one longing to give voice to thoughts long carefully concealed, of her yearning to be closer to the father whom she loved; more en rapport with him; more in his confidence; closer within the circle of his sympathies. Oh, believe me, sir, that it was all good! All that a father's heart could hope or wish for! It was all loyal! That she spoke it to me was perhaps because I was almost a stranger with whom there was no previous barrier to confidence."

Here I paused. It was hard to go on; and I feared lest I might, in my zeal, do Margaret a disservice. The relief of the strain came from her father.

"And you?"

"Sir, Miss Trelawny is very sweet and beautiful! She is young; and her mind is like crystal! Her sympathy is a joy! I am not an old man, and my affections were not engaged. They never had been till then. I hope I may say as much, even to a father!" My eyes involuntarily dropped. When I raised them again Mr. Trelawny was still gazing at me keenly. All the kindliness of his nature seemed to wreath itself in a smile as he held out his hand and said:

"Malcolm Ross, I have always heard of you as a fearless and honourable gentleman. I am glad my girl has such a friend! Go on!"

My heart leaped. The first step to the winning of Margaret's father was gained. I dare say I was somewhat more effusive in my words and my manner as I went on. I certainly felt that way.

"One thing we gain as we grow older: to use our age judiciously! I have had much experience. I have fought for it and worked for it all my life; and I felt that I was justified in using it. I ventured to ask Miss Trelawny to count on me as a friend; to let me serve her should occasion arise. She promised me that she would. I had little idea that my chance of serving her should come so soon or in such a way; but that very night you were stricken down. In her desolation and anxiety she sent for me!" I paused. He continued to look at me as I went on:

"When your letter of instructions was found, I offered my services. They were accepted, as you know."

"And these days, how did they pass for you?" The question startled me. There was in it something of Margaret's own voice and manner; something so greatly resembling her lighter moments that it brought out all the masculinity in me. I felt more sure of my ground now as I said:

"These days, sir, despite all their harrowing anxiety, despite all the pain they held for the girl whom I grew to love more and more with each passing hour, have been the happiest of my life!" He kept silence for a long time; so long that, as I waited for him to speak, with my heart beating, I began to wonder if my frankness had been too effusive. At last he said:

"I suppose it is hard to say so much vicariously. Her poor mother should have heard you; it would have made her heart glad!" Then a shadow swept across his face; and he went on more hurriedly.

"But are you quite sure of all this?"

"I know my own heart, sir; or, at least, I think I do!"

"No! no!" he answered, "I don't mean you. That is all right! But you spoke of my girl's affection for me ... and yet...! And yet she has been living here, in my house, a whole year... Still, she spoke to you of her loneliness—her desolation. I never—it grieves me to say it, but it is true—I never saw sign of such affection towards myself in all the year!..." His voice trembled away into sad, reminiscent introspection.

"Then, sir," I said, "I have been privileged to see more in a few days than you in her whole lifetime!" My words seemed to call him up from himself; and I thought that it was with pleasure as well as surprise that he said:

"I had no idea of it. I thought that she was indifferent to me. That what seemed like the neglect of her youth was revenging itself on me. That she was cold of heart.... It is a joy unspeakable to me that her mother's daughter loves me too!" Unconsciously he sank back upon his pillow, lost in memories of the past.

How he must have loved her mother! It was the love of her mother's child, rather than the love of his own daughter, that appealed to him. My heart went out to him in a great wave of sympathy and kindliness. I began to understand. To understand the passion of these two great, silent, reserved natures, that successfully concealed the burning hunger for the other's love! It did not surprise me when presently he murmured to himself:

"Margaret, my child! Tender, and thoughtful, and strong, and true, and brave! Like her dear mother! like her dear mother!"

And then to the very depths of my heart I rejoiced that I had spoken so frankly.

Presently Mr. Trelawny said:

"Four days! The sixteenth! Then this is the twentieth of July?" I nodded affirmation; he went on:

"So I have been lying in a trance for four days. It is not the first time. I was in a trance once under strange conditions for three days; and never even suspected it till I was told of the lapse of time. I shall tell you all about it some day, if you care to hear."

That made me thrill with pleasure. That he, Margaret's father, would so take me into his confidence made it possible.... The business-like, every-day alertness of his voice as he spoke next quite recalled me:

"I had better get up now. When Margaret comes in, tell her yourself that I am all right. It will avoid any shock! And will you tell Corbeck that I would like to see him as soon as I can. I want to see those lamps, and hear all about them!"

His attitude towards me filled me with delight. There was a possible father-in-law aspect that would have raised me from a death-bed. I was hurrying away to carry out his wishes; when, however, my hand was on the key of the door, his voice recalled me:

"Mr. Ross!"

I did not like to hear him say "Mr." After he knew of my friendship with his daughter he had called me Malcolm Ross; and this obvious return to formality not only pained, but filled me with apprehension. It must be something about Margaret. I thought of her as "Margaret" and not as "Miss Trelawny", now that there was danger of losing her. I know now what I felt then: that I was determined to fight for her rather than lose her. I came back, unconsciously holding myself erect. Mr. Trelawny, the keen observer of men, seemed to read my thought; his face, which was set in a new anxiety, relaxed as he said:

"Sit down a minute; it is better that we speak now than later. We are both men, and men of the world. All this about my daughter is very new to me, and very sudden; and I want to know exactly how and where I stand. Mind, I am making no objection; but as a father I have duties which are grave, and may prove to be painful. I—I"—he seemed slightly at a loss how to begin, and this gave me hope—"I suppose I am to take it, from what you have said to me of your feelings towards my girl, that it is in your mind to be a suitor for her hand, later on?" I answered at once:

"Absolutely! Firm and fixed; it was my intention the evening after I had been with her on the river, to seek you, of course after a proper and respectful interval, and to ask you if I might approach her on the subject. Events forced me into closer relationship more quickly than I had to hope would be possible; but that first purpose has remained fresh in my heart, and has grown in intensity, and multiplied itself with every hour which has passed since then." His face seemed to soften as he looked at me; the memory of his own youth was coming back to him instinctively. After a pause he said:

"I suppose I may take it, too, Malcolm Ross"—the return to the familiarity of address swept through me with a glorious thrill—"that as yet you have not made any protestation to my daughter?"

"Not in words, sir." The arriere pensee of my phrase struck me, not by its own humour, but through the grave, kindly smile on the father's face. There was a pleasant sarcasm in his comment:

"Not in words! That is dangerous! She might have doubted words, or even disbelieved them."

I felt myself blushing to the roots of my hair as I went on:

"The duty of delicacy in her defenceless position; my respect for her father—I did not know you then, sir, as yourself, but only as her father—restrained me. But even had not these barriers existed, I should not have dared in the presence of such grief and anxiety to have declared myself. Mr. Trelawny, I assure you on my word of honour that your daughter and I are as yet, on her part, but friends and nothing more!" Once again he held out his hands, and we clasped each other warmly. Then he said heartily:

"I am satisfied, Malcolm Ross. Of course, I take it that until I have seen her and have given you permission, you will not make any declaration to my daughter—in words," he added, with an indulgent smile. But his face became stern again as he went on:

"Time presses; and I have to think of some matters so urgent and so strange that I dare not lose an hour. Otherwise I should not have been prepared to enter, at so short a notice and to so new a friend, on the subject of my daughter's settlement in life, and of her future happiness." There was a dignity and a certain proudness in his manner which impressed me much.

"I shall respect your wishes, sir!" I said as I went back and opened the door. I heard him lock it behind me.

When I told Mr. Corbeck that Mr. Trelawny had quite recovered, he began to dance about like a wild man. But he suddenly stopped, and asked me to be careful not to draw any inferences, at all events at first, when in the future speaking of the finding of the lamps, or of the first visits to the tomb. This was in case Mr. Trelawny should speak to me on the subject; "as, of course, he will," he added, with a sidelong look at me which meant knowledge of the affairs of my heart. I agreed to this, feeling that it was quite right. I did not quite understand why; but I knew that Mr. Trelawny was a peculiar man. In no case could one make a mistake by being reticent. Reticence is a quality which a strong man always respects.

The manner in which the others of the house took the news of the recovery varied much. Mrs. Grant wept with emotion; then she hurried off to see if she could do anything personally, and to set the house in order for "Master", as she always called him. The Nurse's face fell: she was deprived of an interesting case. But the disappointment was only momentary; and she rejoiced that the trouble was over. She was ready to come to the patient the moment she should be wanted; but in the meantime she occupied herself in packing her portmanteau.

I took Sergeant Daw into the study, so that we should be alone when I told him the news. It surprised even his iron self-control when I told him the method of the waking. I was myself surprised in turn by his first words:

"And how did he explain the first attack? He was unconscious when the second was made."

Up to that moment the nature of the attack, which was the cause of my coming to the house, had never even crossed my mind, except when I had simply narrated the various occurrences in sequence to Mr. Trelawny. The Detective did not seem to think much of my answer:

"Do you know, it never occurred to me to ask him!" The professional instinct was strong in the man, and seemed to supersede everything else.

"That is why so few cases are ever followed out," he said, "unless our people are in them. Your amateur detective neer hunts down to the death. As for ordinary people, the moment things begin to mend, and the strain of suspense is off them, they drop the matter in hand. It is like sea-sickness," he added philosophically after a pause; "the moment you touch the shore you never give it a thought, but run off to the buffet to feed! Well, Mr. Ross, I'm glad the case is over; for over it is, so far as I am concerned. I suppose that Mr. Trelawny knows his own business; and that now he is well again, he will take it up himself. Perhaps, however, he will not do anything. As he seemed to expect something to happen, but did not ask for protection from the police in any way, I take it that he don't want them to interfere with an eye to punishment. We'll be told officially, I suppose, that it was an accident, or sleep-walking, or something of the kind, to satisfy the conscience of our Record Department; and that will be the end. As for me, I tell you frankly, sir, that it will be the saving of me. I verily believe I was beginning to get dotty over it all. There were too many mysteries, that aren't in my line, for me to be really satisfied as to either facts or the causes of them. Now I'll be able to wash my hands of it, and get back to clean, wholesome, criminal work. Of course, sir, I'll be glad to know if you ever do light on a cause of any kind. And I'll be grateful if you can ever tell me how the man was dragged out of bed when the cat bit him, and who used the knife the second time. For master Silvio could never have done it by himself. But there! I keep thinking of it still. I must look out and keep a check on myself, or I shall think of it when I have to keep my mind on other things!"

When Margaret returned from her walk, I met her in the hall. She was still pale and sad; somehow, I had expected to see her radiant after her walk. The moment she saw me her eyes brightened, and she looked at me keenly.

"You have some good news for me?" she said. "Is Father better?"

"He is! Why did you think so?"

"I saw it in your face. I must go to him at once." She was hurrying away when I stopped her.

"He said he would send for you the moment he was dressed."

"He said he would send for me!" she repeated in amazement. "Then he is awake again, and conscious? I had no idea he was so well as that! O Malcolm!"

She sat down on the nearest chair and began to cry. I felt overcome myself. The sight of her joy and emotion, the mention of my own name in such a way and at such a time, the rush of glorious possibilities all coming together, quite unmanned me. She saw my emotion, and seemed to understand. She put out her hand. I held it hard, and kissed it. Such moments as these, the opportunities of lovers, are gifts of the gods! Up to this instant, though I knew I loved her, and though I believed she returned my affection, I had had only hope. Now, however, the self-surrender manifest in her willingness to let me squeeze her hand, the ardour of her pressure in return, and the glorious flush of love in her beautiful, deep, dark eyes as she lifted them to mine, were all the eloquences which the most impatient or exacting lover could expect or demand.

No word was spoken; none was needed. Even had I not been pledged to verbal silence, words would have been poor and dull to express what we felt. Hand in hand, like two little children, we went up the staircase and waited on the landing, till the summons from Mr. Trelawny should come.

I whispered in her ear—it was nicer than speaking aloud and at a greater distance—how her father had awakened, and what he had said; and all that had passed between us, except when she herself had been the subject of conversation.

Presently a bell rang from the room. Margaret slipped from me, and looked back with warning finger on lip. She went over to her father's door and knocked softly.

"Come in!" said the strong voice.

"It is I, Father!" The voice was tremulous with love and hope.

There was a quick step inside the room; the door was hurriedly thrown open, and in an instant Margaret, who had sprung forward, was clasped in her father's arms. There was little speech; only a few broken phrases.

"Father! Dear, dear Father!"

"My child! Margaret! My dear, dear child!"

"O Father, Father! At last! At last!"

Here the father and daughter went into the room together, and the door closed.

Chapter XIV - The Birth-Mark

During my waiting for the summons to Mr. Trelawny's room, which I knew would come, the time was long and lonely. After the first few moments of emotional happiness at Margaret's joy, I somehow felt apart and alone; and for a little time the selfishness of a lover possessed me. But it was not for long. Margaret's happiness was all to me; and in the conscious sense of it I lost my baser self. Margaret's last words as the door closed on them gave the key to the whole situation, as it had been and as it was. These two proud, strong people, though father and daughter, had only come to know each other when the girl was grown up. Margaret's nature was of that kind which matures early.

The pride and strength of each, and the reticence which was their corollary, made a barrier at the beginning. Each had respected the other's reticence too much thereafter; and the misunderstanding grew to habit. And so these two loving hearts, each of which yearned for sympathy from the other, were kept apart. But now all was well, and in my heart of hearts I rejoiced that at last Margaret was happy. Whilst I was still musing on the subject, and dreaming dreams of a personal nature, the door was opened, and Mr. Trelawny beckoned to me.

"Come in, Mr. Ross!" he said cordially, but with a certain formality which I dreaded. I entered the room, and he closed the door again. He held out his hand, and I put mine in it. He did not let it go, but still held it as he drew me over toward his daughter. Margaret looked from me to him, and back again; and her eyes fell. When I was close to her, Mr. Trelawny let go my hand, and, looking his daughter straight in the face, said:

"If things are as I fancy, we shall not have any secrets between us. Malcolm Ross knows so much of my affairs already, that I take it he must either let matters stop where they are and go away in silence, or else he must know more. Margaret! are you willing to let Mr. Ross see your wrist?"

She threw one swift look of appeal in his eyes; but even as she did so she seemed to make up her mind. Without a word she raised her right hand, so that the bracelet of spreading wings which covered the wrist fell back, leaving the flesh bare. Then an icy chill shot through me.

On her wrist was a thin red jagged line, from which seemed to hang red stains like drops of blood!

She stood there, a veritable figure of patient pride.

Oh! but she looked proud! Through all her sweetness, all her dignity, all her high-souled negation of self which I had known, and which never seemed more marked than now—through all the fire that seemed to shine from the dark depths of her eyes into my very soul, pride shone conspicuously. The pride that has faith; the pride that is born of conscious purity; the pride of a veritable queen of Old Time, when to be royal was to be the first and greatest and bravest in all high things. As we stood thus for some seconds, the deep, grave voice of her father seemed to sound a challenge in my ears:

"What do you say now?"

My answer was not in words. I caught Margaret's right hand in mine as it fell, and, holding it tight, whilst with the other I pushed back the golden cincture, stooped and kissed the wrist. As I looked up at her, but never letting go her hand, there was a look of joy on her face such as I dream of when I think of heaven. Then I faced her father.

"You have my answer, sir!" His strong face looked gravely sweet. He only said one word as he laid his hand on our clasped ones, whilst he bent over and kissed his daughter:

"Good!"

We were interrupted by a knock at the door. In answer to an impatient "Come in!" from Mr. Trelawny, Mr. Corbeck entered. When he saw us grouped he would have drawn back; but in an instant Mr. Trelawny had sprung forth and dragged him forward. As he shook him by both hands, he seemed a transformed man. All the enthusiasm of his youth, of which Mr. Corbeck had told us, seemed to have come back to him in an instant.

"So you have got the lamps!" he almost shouted. "My reasoning was right after all. Come to the library, where we will be alone, and tell me all about it! And while he does it, Ross," said he, turning to me, "do you, like a good fellow, get the key from the safe deposit, so that I may have a look at the lamps!"

Then the three of them, the daughter lovingly holding her father's arm, went into the library, whilst I hurried off to Chancery Lane.

When I returned with the key, I found them still engaged in the narrative; but Doctor Winchester, who had arrived soon after I left, was with them. Mr. Trelawny, on hearing from Margaret of his great attention and kindness, and how he had, under much pressure to the contrary, steadfastly obeyed his written wishes, had asked him to remain and listen. "It will interest you, perhaps," he said, "to learn the end of the story!"

We all had an early dinner together. We sat after it a good while, and then Mr. Trelawny said:

"Now, I think we had all better separate and go quietly to bed early. We may have much to talk about tomorrow; and tonight I want to think."

Doctor Winchester went away, taking, with a courteous forethought, Mr. Corbeck with him, and leaving me behind. When the others had gone Mr. Trelawny said:

"I think it will be well if you, too, will go home for tonight. I want to be quite alone with my daughter; there are many things I wish to speak of to her, and to her alone. Perhaps, even tomorrow, I will be able to tell you also of them; but in the meantime there will be less distraction to us both if we are alone in the house." I quite understood and sympathised with his feelings; but the experiences of the last few days were strong on me, and with some hesitation I said:

"But may it not be dangerous? If you knew as we do—" To my surprise Margaret interrupted me:

"There will be no danger, Malcolm. I shall be with Father!" As she spoke she clung to him in a protective way. I said no more, but stood up to go at once. Mr. Trelawny said heartily:

"Come as early as you please, Ross. Come to breakfast. After it, you and I will want to have a word together." He went out of the room quietly, leaving us together. I clasped and kissed Margaret's hands, which she held out to me, and then drew her close to me, and our lips met for the first time.

I did not sleep much that night. Happiness on the one side of my bed and Anxiety on the other kept sleep away. But if I had anxious care, I had also happiness which had not equal in my life—or ever can have. The night went by so quickly that the dawn seemed to rush on me, not stealing as is its wont.

Before nine o'clock I was at Kensington. All anxiety seemed to float away like a cloud as I met Margaret, and saw that already the pallor of her face had given to the rich bloom which I knew. She told me that her father had slept well, and that he would be with us soon.

"I do believe," she whispered, "that my dear and thoughtful Father has kept back on purpose, so that I might meet you first, and alone!"

After breakfast Mr. Trelawny took us into the study, saying as he passed in:

"I have asked Margaret to come too." When we were seated, he said gravely:

"I told you last night that we might have something to say to each other. I dare say that you may have thought that it was about Margaret and yourself. Isn't that so?"

"I thought so."

"Well, my boy, that is all right. Margaret and I have been talking, and I know her wishes." He held out his hand. When I wrung it, and had kissed Margaret, who drew her chair close to mine, so that we could hold hands as we listened, he went on, but with a certain hesitation—it could hardly be called nervousness—which was new to me.

"You know a good deal of my hunt after this mummy and her belongings; and I dare say you have guessed a good deal of my theories. But these at any rate I shall explain later, concisely and categorically, if it be necessary. What I want to consult you about now is this: Margaret and I disagree on one point. I am about to make an experiment; the experiment which is to crown all that I have devoted twenty years of research, and danger, and labour to prepare for. Through it we may learn things that have been hidden from the eyes and the knowledge of men for centuries; for scores of centuries. I do not want my daughter to be present; for I cannot blind myself to the fact that there may be danger in it—great danger, and of an unknown kind. I have, however, already faced very great dangers, and of an unknown kind; and so has that brave scholar who has helped me in the work. As to myself, I am willing to run any risk. For science, and history, and philosophy may benefit; and we may turn one old page of a wisdom unknown in this prosaic age. But for my daughter to run such a risk I am loth. Her young bright life is too precious to throw lightly away; now especially when she is on the very threshold of new happiness. I do not wish to see her life given, as her dear mother's was—"

He broke down for a moment, and covered his eyes with his hands. In an instant Margaret was beside him, clasping him close, and kissing him, and comforting him with loving words. Then, standing erect, with one hand on his head, she said:

"Father! mother did not bid you stay beside her, even when you wanted to go on that journey of unknown danger to Egypt; though that country was then upset from end to end with war and the dangers that follow war. You have told me how she left you free to go as you wished; though that she thought of danger for you and feared it for you, is proved by this!" She held up her wrist with the scar that seemed to run blood. "Now, mother's daughter does as mother would have done herself!" Then she turned to me:

"Malcolm, you know I love you! But love is trust; and you must trust me in danger as well as in joy. You and I must stand beside Father in this unknown peril. Together we shall come through it; or together we shall fail; together we shall die. That is my wish; my first wish to my husband that is to be! Do you not think that, as a daughter, I am right? Tell my Father what you think!"

She looked like a Queen stooping to plead. My love for her grew and grew. I stood up beside her; and took her hand and said:

"Mr. Trelawny! in this Margaret and I are one!"

He took both our hands and held them hard. Presently he said with deep emotion:

"It is as her mother would have done!"

Mr. Corbeck and Doctor Winchester came exactly at the time appointed, and joined us in the library. Despite my great happiness I felt our meeting to be a very solemn function. For I could never forget the strange things that had been; and the idea of the strange things which might be, was with me like a cloud, pressing down on us all. From the gravity of my companions I gathered that each of them also was ruled by some such dominating thought.

Instinctively we gathered our chairs into a circle round Mr. Trelawny, who had taken the great armchair near the window. Margaret sat by him on his right, and I was next to her. Mr. Corbeck was on his left, with Doctor Winchester on the other side. After a few seconds of silence Mr. Trelawny said to Mr. Corbeck:

"You have told Doctor Winchester all up to the present, as we arranged?"

"Yes," he answered; so Mr. Trelawny said:

"And I have told Margaret, so we all know!" Then, turning to the Doctor, he asked:

"And am I to take it that you, knowing all as we know it who have followed the matter for years, wish to share in the experiment which we hope to make?" His answer was direct and uncompromising:

"Certainly! Why, when this matter was fresh to me, I offered to go on with it to the end. Now that it is of such strange interest, I would not miss it for anything which you could name. Be quite easy in your mind, Mr. Trelawny. I am a scientist and an investigator of phenomena. I have no one belonging to me or dependent on me. I am quite alone, and free to do what I like with my own—including my life!" Mr. Trelawny bowed gravely, and turning to Mr. Corbeck said:

"I have known your ideas for many years past, old friend; so I need ask you nothing. As to Margaret and Malcolm Ross, they have already told me their wishes in no uncertain way." He paused a few seconds, as though to put his thoughts or his words in order; then he began to explain his views and intentions. He spoke very carefully, seeming always to bear in mind that some of us who listened were ignorant of the very root and nature of some things touched upon, and explaining them to us as he went on:

"The experiment which is before us is to try whether or no there is any force, any reality, in the old Magic. There could not possibly be more favourable conditions for the test; and it is my own desire to do all that is possible to make the original design effective. That there is some such existing power I firmly believe. It might not be possible to create, or arrange, or organise such a power in our own time; but I take it that if in Old Time such a power existed, it may have some exceptional survival. After all, the Bible is not a myth; and we read there that the sun stood still at a man's command, and that an ass—not a human one—spoke. And if the Witch at Endor could call up to Saul the spirit of Samuel, why may not there have been others with equal powers; and why may not one among them survive? Indeed, we are told in the Book of Samuel that the Witch of Endor was only one of many, and her being consulted by Saul was a matter of chance. He only sought one among the many whom he had driven out of Israel; 'all those that had Familiar Spirits, and the Wizards.' This Egyptian Queen, Tera, who reigned nearly two thousand years before Saul, had a Familiar, and was a Wizard too. See how the priests of her time, and those after it tried to wipe out her name from the face of the earth, and put a curse over the very door of her tomb so that none might ever discover the lost name. Ay, and they succeeded so well that even Manetho, the historian of the Egyptian Kings, writing in the tenth century before Christ, with all the lore of the priesthood for forty centuries behind him, and with possibility of access to every existing record, could not even find her name. Did it strike any of you, in thinking of the late events, who or what her Familiar was?" There was an interruption, for Doctor Winchester struck one hand loudly on the other as he ejaculated:

"The cat! The mummy cat! I knew it!" Mr. Trelawny smiled over at him.

"You are right! There is every indication that the Familiar of the Wizard Queen was that cat which was mummied when she was, and was not only placed in her tomb, but was laid in the sarcophagus with her. That was what bit into my wrist, what cut me with sharp claws." He paused. Margaret's comment was a purely girlish one:

"Then my poor Silvio is acquitted! I am glad!" Her father stroked her hair and went on:

"This woman seems to have had an extraordinary foresight. Foresight far, far beyond her age and the philosophy of her time. She seems to have seen through the weakness of her own religion, and even prepared for emergence into a different world. All her aspirations were for the North, the point of the compass whence blew the cool invigorating breezes that make life a joy. From the first, her eyes seem to have been attracted to the seven stars of the Plough from the fact, as recorded in the hieroglyphics in her tomb, that at her birth a great aerolite fell, from whose heart was finally extracted that Jewel of Seven Stars which she regarded as the talisman of her life. It seems to have so far ruled her destiny that all her thought and care circled round it. The Magic Coffer, so wondrously wrought with seven sides, we learn from the same source, came from the aerolite. Seven was to her a magic number; and no wonder. With seven fingers on one hand, and seven toes on one foot. With a talisman of a rare ruby with seven stars in the same position as in that constellation which ruled her birth, each star of the seven having seven points—in itself a geological wonder—

it would have been odd if she had not been attracted by it. Again, she was born, we learn in the Stele of her tomb, in the seventh month of the year—the month beginning with the Inundation of the Nile. Of which month the presiding Goddess was Hathor, the Goddess of her own house, of the Antefs of the Theban line—the Goddess who in various forms symbolises beauty, and pleasure, and resurrection. Again, in this seventh month—which, by later Egyptian astronomy began on October 28th, and ran to the 27th of our November—on the seventh day the Pointer of the Plough just rises above the horizon of the sky at Thebes.

"In a marvellously strange way, therefore, are grouped into this woman's life these various things. The number seven; the Pole Star, with the constellation of seven stars; the God of the month, Hathor, who was her own particular God, the God of her family, the Antefs of the Theban Dynasty, whose Kings' symbol it was, and whose seven forms ruled love and the delights of life and resurrection. If ever there was ground for magic; for the power of symbolism carried into mystic use; for a belief in finites spirits in an age which knew not the Living God, it is here.

"Remember, too, that this woman was skilled in all the science of her time. Her wise and cautious father took care of that, knowing that by her own wisdom she must ultimately combat the intrigues of the Hierarchy. Bear in mind that in old Egypt the science of Astronomy began and was developed to an extraordinary height; and that Astrology followed Astronomy in its progress. And it is possible that in the later developments of science with regard to light rays, we may yet find that Astrology is on a scientific basis. Our next wave of scientific thought may deal with this. I shall have something special to call your minds to on this point presently. Bear in mind also that the Egyptians knew sciences, of which today, despite all our advantages, we are profoundly ignorant. Acoustics, for instance, an exact science with the builders of the temples of Karnak, of Luxor, of the Pyramids, is today a mystery to Bell, and Kelvin, and Edison, and Marconi. Again, these old miracle-workers probably understood some practical way of using other forces, and amongst them the forces of light that at present we do not dream of. But of this matter I shall speak later. That Magic Coffer of Queen Tera is probably a magic box in more ways than one. It may—possibly it does—contain forces that we wot not of. We cannot open it; it must be closed from within. How then was it closed? It is a coffer of solid stone, of amazing hardness, more like a jewel than an ordinary marble, with a lid equally solid; and yet all is so finely wrought that the finest tool made today cannot be inserted under the flange. How was it wrought to such perfection? How was the stone so chosen that those translucent patches match the relations of the seven stars of the constellation? How is it, or from what cause, that when the starlight shines on it, it glows from within—that when I fix the lamps in similar form the glow grows greater still; and yet the box is irresponsive to ordinary light however great? I tell you that that box hides some great mystery of science. We shall find that the light will open it in some way: either by striking on some substance, sensitive in a peculiar way to its effect, or in releasing some greater power. I only trust that in our ignorance we may not so bungle things as to do harm to its mechanism; and so deprive the knowledge of our time of a lesson handed down, as by a miracle, through nearly five thousand years.

"In another way, too, there may be hidden in that box secrets which, for good or ill, may enlighten the world. We know from their records, and inferentially also, that the Egyptians studied the properties of herbs and minerals for magic purposes—white magic as well as black. We know that some of the wizards of old could induce from sleep dreams of any given kind. That this purpose was mainly effected by hypnotism, which was another art or science of Old Nile, I have little doubt. But still, they must have had a mastery of drugs that is far beyond anything we know. With our own pharmacopoeia we can, to a certain extent, induce dreams. We may even differentiate between good and bad—dreams of pleasure, or disturbing and harrowing dreams. But these old practitioners seemed to have been able to command at will any form or colour of dreaming; could work round any given subject or thought in almost any was required. In that coffer, which you have seen, may rest a very armoury of dreams. Indeed, some of the forces that lie within it may have been already used in my household." Again there was an interruption from Doctor Winchester.

"But if in your case some of these imprisoned forces were used, what set them free at the opportune time, or how? Besides, you and Mr. Corbeck were once before put into a trance for three whole days, when you were in the Queen's tomb for the second time. And then, as I gathered from Mr. Corbeck's story, the coffer was not back in the tomb, though the mummy was. Surely in both these cases there must have been some active intelligence awake, and with some other power to wield." Mr. Trelawny's answer was equally to the point:

"There was some active intelligence awake. I am convinced of it. And it wielded a power which it never lacks. I believe that on both those occasions hypnotism was the power wielded."

"And wherein is that power contained? What view do you hold on the subject?" Doctor Winchester's voice vibrated with the intensity of his excitement as he leaned forward, breathing hard, and with eyes staring. Mr. Trelawny said solemnly:

"In the mummy of the Queen Tera! I was coming to that presently. Perhaps we had better wait till I clear the ground a little. What I hold is, that the preparation of that box was made for a special occasion; as indeed were all the preparations of the tomb and all belonging to it. Queen Tera did not trouble herself to guard against snakes and scorpions, in that rocky tomb cut in the sheer cliff face a hundred feet above the level of the valley, and fifty down from the summit. Her precautions were against the disturbances of human hands; against the jealousy and hatred of the priests, who, had they known of her real aims, would have tried to baffle them. From her point of view, she made all ready for the time of resurrection, whenever that might be. I gather from the symbolic pictures in the tomb that she so far differed from the belief of her time that she looked for a resurrection in the flesh. It was doubtless this that intensified the hatred of the priesthood, and gave them an acceptable cause for obliterating the very existence, present and future, of one who had outrage their theories and blasphemed their gods. All that she might require, either in the accomplishment of the resurrection or after it, were contained in that almost hermetically sealed suite of chambers in the rock. In the great sarcophagus, which as you know is of a size quite unusual even for kings, was the mummy of her Familiar, the cat, which from its great size I take to be a sort of tiger-cat. In the tomb, also in a strong receptacle, were the canopic jars usually containing those internal organs which are separately embalmed, but which in this case had no such contents. So that, I take it, there was in her case a departure in embalming; and that the organs were restored to the body, each in its proper place—if, indeed, they had ever been removed. If this surmise be true, we shall find that the brain of the Queen either was never extracted in the usual way, or, if so taken out, that it was duly replaced, instead of being enclosed within the mummy wrappings. Finally, in the sarcophagus there was the Magic Coffer on which her feet rested. Mark you also, the care taken in the preservance of her power to control the elements. According to her belief, the open hand outside the wrappings controlled the Air, and the strange Jewel Stone with the shining stars controlled Fire. The symbolism inscribed on the soles of her feet gave sway over Land and Water. About the Star Stone I shall tell you later; but whilst we are speaking of the sarcophagus, mark how she guarded her secret in case of grave-wrecking or intrusion. None could open her Magic Coffer without the lamps, for we know now that ordinary light will not be effective. The great lid of the sarcophagus was not sealed down as usual, because she wished to control the air. But she hid the lamps, which in structure belong to the Magic Coffer, in a place where none could find them, except by following the secret guidance which she had prepared for only the eyes of wisdom. And even here she had guarded against chance discovery, by preparing a bolt of death for the unwary discoverer. To do this she had applied the lesson of the tradition of the avenging guard of the treasures of the pyramid, built by her great predecessor of the Fourth Dynasty of the throne of Egypt.

"You have noted, I suppose, how there were, in the case of her tomb, certain deviations from the usual rules. For instance, the shaft of the Mummy Pit, which is usually filled up solid with stones and rubbish, was left open. Why was this? I take it that she had made arrangements for leaving the tomb when, after her resurrection, she should be a new woman, with a different personality, and less inured to the hardships that in her first existence she had suffered. So far as we can judge of her intent, all things needful for her exit into the world had been thought of, even to the iron chain, described by Van Huyn, close to the door in the rock, by which she might be able to lower herself to the ground. That she expected a long period to elapse was shown in the choice of material. An ordinary rope would be rendered weaker or unsafe in process of time, but she imagined, and rightly, that the iron would endure.

"What her intentions were when once she trod the open earth afresh we do not know, and we never shall, unless her own dead lips can soften and speak."

Chapter XV - The Purpose of Queen Tera

"Now, as to the Star Jewel! This she manifestly regarded as the greatest of her treasures. On it she had engraven words which none of her time dared to speak.

"In the old Egyptian belief it was held that there were words, which, if used properly—for the method of speaking them was as important as the words themselves—could command the Lords of the Upper and the Lower Worlds. The 'hekau', or word of power, was all-important in certain ritual. On the Jewel of Seven Stars, which, as you know, is carved into the image of a scarab, are graven in hieroglyphic two such hekau, one above, the other underneath. But you will understand better when you see it! Wait here! Do not stir!"

As he spoke, he rose and left the room. A great fear for him came over me; but I was in some strange way relieved when I looked at Margaret. Whenever there had been any possibility of danger to her father, she had shown great fear for him; now she was calm and placid. I said nothing, but waited.

In two or three minutes, Mr. Trelawny returned. He held in his hand a little golden box. This, as he resumed his seat, he placed before him on the table. We all leaned forward as he opened it.

On a lining of white satin lay a wondrous ruby of immense size, almost as big as the top joint of Margaret's little finger. It was carven—it could not possibly have been its natural shape, but jewels do not show the working of the tool—into the shape of a scarab, with its wings folded, and its legs and feelers pressed back to its sides. Shining through its wondrous "pigeon's blood" colour were seven different stars, each of seven points, in such position that they reproduced exactly the figure of the Plough. There could be no possible mistake as to this in the mind of anyone who had ever noted the constellation. On it were some hieroglyphic figures, cut with the most exquisite precision, as I could see when it came to my turn to use the magnifying-glass, which Mr. Trelawny took from his pocket and handed to us.

When we all had seen it fully, Mr. Trelawny turned it over so that it rested on its back in a cavity made to hold it in the upper half of the box. The reverse was no less wonderful than the upper, being carved to resemble the under side of the beetle. It, too, had some hieroglyphic figures cut on it. Mr. Trelawny resumed his lecture as we all sat with our heads close to this wonderful jewel:

"As you see, there are two words, one on the top, the other underneath. The symbols on the top represent a single word, composed of one syllable prolonged, with its determinatives. You know, all of you, I suppose, that the Egyptian language was phonetic, and that the hieroglyphic symbol represented the sound. The first symbol here, the hoe, means 'mer', and the two pointed ellipses the prolongation of the final r: mer-r-r. The sitting figure with the hand to its face is what we call the 'determinative' of 'thought'; and the roll of papyrus that of 'abstraction'. Thus we get the word 'mer', love, in its abstract, general, and fullest sense. This is the hekau which can command the Upper World."

Margaret's face was a glory as she said in a deep, low, ringing tone:

"Oh, but it is true. How the old wonder-workers guessed at almighty Truth!" Then a hot blush swept her face, and her eyes fell. Her father smiled at her lovingly as he resumed:

"The symbolisation of the word on the reverse is simpler, though the meaning is more abstruse. The first symbol means 'men', 'abiding', and the second, 'ab', 'the heart'. So that we get 'abiding of heart', or in our own language 'patience'. And this is the hekau to control the Lower World!"

He closed the box, and motioning us to remain as we were, he went back to his room to replace the Jewel in the safe. When he had returned and resumed his seat, he went on:

"That Jewel, with its mystic words, and which Queen Tera held under her hand in the sarcophagus, was to be an important factor—probably the most important—in the working out of the act of her resurrection. From the first I seemed by a sort of instinct to realise this. I kept the Jewel within my great safe, whence none could extract it; not even Queen Tera herself with her astral body."

"Her 'astral body'? What is that, Father? What does that mean?" There was a keenness in Margaret's voice as she asked the question which surprised me a little; but Trelawny smiled a sort of indulgent parental smile, which came through his grim solemnity like sunshine through a rifted cloud, as he spoke:

"The astral body, which is a part of Buddhist belief, long subsequent to the time I speak of, and which is an accepted fact of modern mysticism, had its rise in Ancient Egypt; at least, so far as we know. It is that the gifted individual can at will, quick as thought itself, transfer his body whithersoever he chooses, by the dissolution and re-incarnation of particles. In the ancient belief there were several parts of a human being. You may as well know them; so that you will understand matters relative to them or dependent on them as they occur.

"First there is the 'Ka', or 'Double', which, as Doctor Budge explains, may be defined as 'an abstract individuality of personality' which was imbued with all the characteristic attributes of the individual it represented, and possessed an absolutely independent existence. It was free to move from place to place on earth at will; and it could enter into heaven and hold converse with the gods. Then there was the 'Ba', or 'soul', which dwelt in the 'Ka', and had the power of becoming corporeal or incorporeal at will; 'it had both substance and form.... It had power to leave the tomb.... It could revisit the body in the tomb ... and could reincarnate it and hold converse with it.' Again there was the 'Khu', the 'spiritual intelligence', or spirit. It took the form of 'a shining, luminous, intangible shape of the body.'... Then, again, there was the 'Sekhem', or 'power' of a man, his strength or vital force personified. These were the 'Khaibit', or 'shadow', the 'Ren', or 'name', the 'Khat', or 'physical body', and 'Ab', the 'heart', in which life was seated, went to the full making up of a man.

"Thus you will see, that if this division of functions, spiritual and bodily, ethereal and corporeal, ideal and actual, be accepted as exact, there are all the possibilities and capabilities of corporeal transference, guided always by an unimprisonable will or intelligence." As he paused I murmured the lines from Shelley's "Prometheus Unbound":

"'The Magnus Zoroaster...
Met his own image walking in the garden.'"

Mr. Trelawny was not displeased. "Quite so!" he said, in his quiet way. "Shelley had a better conception of ancient beliefs than any of our poets." With a voice changed again he resumed his lecture, for so it was to some of us:

"There is another belief of the ancient Egyptian which you must bear in mind; that regarding the ushaptiu figures of Osiris, which were placed with the dead to its work in the Under World. The enlargement of this idea came to a belief that it was possible to transmit, by magical formulae, the soul and qualities of any living creature to a figure made in its image. This would give a terrible extension of power to one who held the gift of magic.

"It is from a union of these various beliefs, and their natural corollaries, that I have come to the conclusion that Queen Tera expected to be able to effect her own resurrection, when, and where, and how, she would. That she may have held before her a definite time for making her effort is not only possible but likely. I shall not stop now to explain it, but shall enter upon the subject later on. With a soul with the Gods, a spirit which could wander the earth at will, and a power of corporeal transference, or an astral body, there need be no bounds or limits to her ambition. The belief is forced upon us that for these forty or fifty centuries she lay dormant in her tomb—waiting. Waiting with that 'patience' which could rule the Gods of the Under World, for that 'love' which could command those of the Upper World. What she may have dreamt we know not; but her dream must have been broken when the Dutch explorer entered her sculptured cavern, and his follower violated the sacred privacy of her tomb by his rude outrage in the theft of her hand.

"That theft, with all that followed, proved to us one thing, however: that each part of her body, though separated from the rest, can be a central point or rallying place for the items or particles of her astral body. That hand in my room could ensure her instantaneous presence in the flesh, and its equally rapid dissolution.

"Now comes the crown of my argument. The purpose of the attack on me was to get the safe open, so that the sacred Jewel of Seven Stars could be extracted. That immense door of the safe could not keep out her astral body, which, or any part of it, could gather itself as well within as without the safe. And I doubt not that in the darkness of the night that mummied hand sought often the Talisman Jewel, and drew new inspiration from its touch. But despite all its power, the astral body could not remove the Jewel through the chinks of the safe. The Ruby is not astral; and it could only be moved in the ordinary way by the opening of the doors. To this end, the Queen used her astral body and the fierce force of her Familiar, to bring to the keyhole of the safe the master key which debarred her wish. For years I have suspected, nay, have believed as much; and I, too, guarded myself against powers of the Nether World. I, too, waited in patience till I should have gathered together all the factors required for the opening of the Magic Coffer and the resurrection of the mummied Queen!" He paused, and his daughter's voice came out sweet and clear, and full of intense feeling:

"Father, in the Egyptian belief, was the power of resurrection of a mummied body a general one, or was it limited? That is: could it achieve resurrection many times in the course of ages; or only once, and that one final?"

"There was but one resurrection," he answered. "There were some who believed that this was to be a definite resurrection of the body into the real world. But in the common belief, the Spirit found joy in the Elysian Fields, where there was plenty of food and no fear of famine. Where there was moisture and deep-rooted reeds, and all the joys that are to be expected by the people of an arid land and burning clime."

Then Margaret spoke with an earnestness which showed the conviction of her inmost soul:

"To me, then, it is given to understand what was the dream of this great and far-thinking and high-souled lady of old; the dream that held her soul in patient waiting for its realisation through the passing of all those tens of centuries. The dream of a love that might be; a love that she felt she might, even under new conditions, herself evoke. The love that is the dream of every woman's life; of the Old and of the New; Pagan or Christian; under whatever sun; in whatever rank or calling; however may have been the joy or pain of her life in other ways. Oh! I know it! I know it! I am a woman, and I know a woman's heart. What were the lack of food or the plenitude of it; what were feast or famine to this woman, born in a palace, with the shadow of the Crown of the Two Egypts on her brows! What were reedy morasses or the tinkle of running water to her whose barges could sweep the great Nile from the mountains to the sea. What were petty joys and absence of petty fears to her, the raising of whose hand could hurl armies, or draw to the water-stairs of her palaces the commerce of the world! At whose word rose temples filled with all the artistic beauty of the Times of Old which it was her aim and pleasure to restore! Under whose guidance the solid rock yawned into the sepulchre that she designed!

"Surely, surely, such a one had nobler dreams! I can feel them in my heart; I can see them with my sleeping eyes!"

As she spoke she seemed to be inspired; and her eyes had a far-away look as though they saw something beyond mortal sight. And then the deep eyes filled up with unshed tears of great emotion. The very soul of the woman seemed to speak in her voice; whilst we who listened sat entranced.

"I can see her in her loneliness and in the silence of her mighty pride, dreaming her own dream of things far different from those around her. Of some other land, far, far away under the canopy of the silent night, lit by the cool, beautiful light of the stars. A land under that Northern star, whence blew the sweet winds that cooled the feverish desert air. A land of wholesome greenery, far, far away. Where were no scheming and malignant priesthood; whose ideas were to lead to power through gloomy temples and more gloomy caverns of the dead, through an endless ritual of death! A land where love was not base, but a divine possession of the soul! Where there might be some one kindred spirit which could speak to hers through mortal lips like her own; whose being could merge with hers in a sweet communion of soul to soul, even as their breaths could mingle in the ambient air! I know the feeling, for I have shared it myself. I may speak of it now, since the blessing has come into my own life. I may speak of it since it enables me to interpret the feelings, the very longing soul, of that sweet and lovely Queen, so different from her surroundings, so high above her time! Whose nature, put into a word, could control the forces of the Under World; and the name of whose aspiration, though but graven on a star-lit jewel, could command all the powers in the Pantheon of the High Gods.

"And in the realisation of that dream she will surely be content to rest!"

We men sat silent, as the young girl gave her powerful interpretation of the design or purpose of the woman of old. Her every word and tone carried with it the conviction of her own belief. The loftiness of her thoughts seemed to uplift us all as we listened. Her noble words, flowing in musical cadence and vibrant with internal force, seemed to issue from some great instrument of elemental power. Even her tone was new to us all; so that we listened as to some new and strange being from a new and strange world. Her father's face was full of delight. I knew now its cause. I understood the happiness that had come into his life, on his return to the world that he knew, from that prolonged sojourn in the world of dreams. To find in his daughter, whose nature he had never till now known, such a wealth of affection, such a splendour of spiritual insight, such a scholarly imagination, such... The rest of his feeling was of hope!

The two other men were silent unconsciously. One man had had his dreaming; for the other, his dreams were to come.

For myself, I was like one in a trance. Who was this new, radiant being who had won to existence out of the mist and darkness of our fears? Love has divine possibilities for the lover's heart! The wings of the soul may expand at any time from the shoulders of the loved one, who then may sweep into angel form. I knew that in my Margaret's nature were divine possibilities of many kinds. When under the shade of the overhanging willow-tree on the river, I had gazed into the depths of her beautiful eyes, I had thenceforth a strict belief in the manifold beauties and excellences of her nature; but this soaring and understanding spirit was, indeed, a revelation. My pride, like her father's, was outside myself; my joy and rapture were complete and supreme!

When we had all got back to earth again in our various ways, Mr. Trelawny, holding his daughter's hand in his, went on with his discourse:

"Now, as to the time at which Queen Tera intended her resurrection to take place! We are in contact with some of the higher astronomical calculations in connection with true orientation. As you know, the stars shift their relative positions in the heavens; but though the real distances traversed are beyond all ordinary comprehension, the effects as we see them are small. Nevertheless, they are susceptible of measurement, not by years, indeed, but by centuries. It was by this means that Sir John Herschel arrived at the date of the building of the Great Pyramid—a date fixed by the time necessary to change the star of the true north from Draconis to the Pole Star, and since then verified by later discoveries. From the above there can be no doubt whatever that astronomy was an exact science with the Egyptians at least a thousand years before the time of Queen Tera. Now, the stars that go to make up a constellation change in process of time their relative positions, and the Plough is a notable example. The changes in the position of stars in even forty centuries is so small as to be hardly noticeable by an eye not trained to minute observances, but they can be measured and verified. Did you, or any of you, notice how exactly the stars in the Ruby correspond to the position of the stars in the Plough; or how the same holds with regard to the translucent places in the Magic Coffer?"

We all assented. He went on:

"You are quite correct. They correspond exactly. And yet when Queen Tera was laid in her tomb, neither the stars in the Jewel nor the translucent places in the Coffer corresponded to the position of the stars in the Constellation as they then were!"

We looked at each other as he paused: a new light was breaking upon us. With a ring of mastery in his voice he went on:

"Do you not see the meaning of this? Does it not throw a light on the intention of the Queen? She, who was guided by augury, and magic, and superstition, naturally chose a time for her resurrection which seemed to have been pointed out by the High Gods themselves, who had sent their message on a thunderbolt from other worlds. When such a time was fixed by supernal wisdom, would it not be the height of human wisdom to avail itself of it? Thus it is"—here his voice deepened and trembled with the intensity of his feeling—"that to us and our time is given the opportunity of this wondrous peep into the old world, such as has been the privilege of none other of our time; which may never be again.

"From first to last the cryptic writing and symbolism of that wondrous tomb of that wondrous woman is full of guiding light; and the key of the many mysteries lies in that most wondrous Jewel which she held in her dead hand over the dead heart, which she hoped and believed would beat again in a newer and nobler world!

"There are only loose ends now to consider. Margaret has given us the true inwardness of the feeling of the other Queen!" He looked at her fondly, and stroked her hand as he said it. "For my own part I sincerely hope she is right; for in such case it will be a joy, I am sure, to all of us to assist at such a realisation of hope. But we must not go too fast, or believe too much in our present state of knowledge. The voice that we hearken for comes out of times strangely other than our own; when human life counted for little, and when the morality of the time made little account of the removing of obstacles in the way to achievement of desire. We must keep our eyes fixed on the scientific side, and wait for the developments on the psychic side.

"Now, as to this stone box, which we call the Magic Coffer. As I have said, I am convinced that it opens only in obedience to some principle of light, or the exercise of some of its forces at present unknown to us. There is here much ground for conjecture and for experiment; for as yet the scientists have not thoroughly differentiated the kinds, and powers, and degrees of light. Without analysing various rays we may, I think, take it for granted that there are different qualities and powers of light; and this great field of scientific investigation is almost virgin soil. We know as yet so little of natural forces, that imagination need set no bounds to its flights in considering the possibilities of the future. Within but a few years we have made such discoveries as two centuries ago would have sent the discoverer's to the flames. The liquefaction of oxygen; the existence of radium, of helium, of polonium, of argon; the different powers of Roentgen and Cathode and Bequerel rays. And as we may finally prove that there are different kinds and qualities of light, so we may find that combustion may have its own powers of differentiation; that there are qualities in some flames non-existent in others. It may be that some of the essential conditions of substance are continuous, even in the destruction of their bases. Last night I was thinking of this, and reasoning that as there are certain qualities in some oils which are not in others, so there may be certain similar or corresponding qualities or powers in the combinations of each. I suppose we have all noticed some time or other that the light of colza oil is not quite the same as that of paraffin, or that the flames of coal gas and whale oil are different. They find it so in the light-houses! All at once it occurred to me that there might be some special virtue in the oil which had been found in the jars when Queen Tera's tomb was opened. These had not been used to preserve the intestines as usual, so they must have been placed there for some other purpose. I remembered that in Van Huyn's narrative he had commented on the way the jars were sealed. This was lightly, though effectually; they could be opened without force. The jars were themselves preserved in a sarcophagus which, though of immense strength and hermetically sealed, could be opened easily. Accordingly, I went at once to examine the jars. A little—a very little of the oil still remained, but it had grown thick in the two and a half centuries in which the jars had been open. Still, it was not rancid; and on examining it I found it was cedar oil, and that it still exhaled something of its original aroma. This gave me the idea that it was to be used to fill the lamps. Whoever had placed the oil in the jars, and the jars in the sarcophagus, knew that there might be shrinkage in process of time, even in vases of alabaster, and fully allowed for it; for each of the jars would have filled the lamps half a dozen times. With part of the oil remaining I made some experiments, therefore, which may give useful results. You know, Doctor, that cedar oil, which was much used in the preparation and ceremonials of the Egyptian dead, has a certain refractive power which we do not find in other oils. For instance, we use it on the lenses of our microscopes to give additional clearness of vision. Last night I put some in one of the lamps, and placed it near a translucent part of the Magic Coffer. The effect was very great; the glow of light within was fuller and more intense than I could have imagined, where an electric light similarly placed had little, if any, effect. I should have tried others of the seven lamps, but that my supply of oil ran out. This, however, is on the road to rectification. I have sent for more cedar oil, and expect to have before long an ample supply. Whatever may happen from other causes, our experiment shall not, at all events, fail from this. We shall see! We shall see!"

Doctor Winchester had evidently been following the logical process of the other's mind, for his comment was:

"I do hope that when the light is effective in opening the box, the mechanism will not be impaired or destroyed."

His doubt as to this gave anxious thought to some of us.

Chapter XVI - The Cavern

In the evening Mr. Trelawny took again the whole party into the study. When we were all attention he began to unfold his plans:

"I have come to the conclusion that for the proper carrying out of what we will call our Great Experiment we must have absolute and complete isolation. Isolation not merely for a day or two, but for as long as we may require. Here such a thing would be impossible; the needs and habits of a great city with its ingrained possibilities of interruption, would, or might, quite upset us. Telegrams, registered letters, or express messengers would alone be sufficient; but the great army of those who want to get something would make disaster certain. In addition, the occurrences of the last week have drawn police attention to this house. Even if special instructions to keep an eye on it have not been issued from Scotland Yard or the District Station, you may be sure that the individual policeman on his rounds will keep it well under observation. Besides, the servants who have discharged themselves will before long begin to talk. They must; for they have, for the sake of their own characters, to give some reason for the termination of a service which has I should say a position in the neighbourhood. The servants of the neighbours will begin to talk, and, perhaps the neighbours themselves. Then the active and intelligent Press will, with its usual zeal for the enlightenment of the public and its eye to increase of circulation, get hold of the matter. When the reporter is after us we shall not have much chance of privacy. Even if we were to bar ourselves in, we should not be free from interruption, possibly from intrusion. Either would ruin our plans, and so we must take measures to effect a retreat, carrying all our impedimenta with us. For this I am prepared. For a long time past I have foreseen such a possibility, and have made preparation for it. Of course, I had no foreknowledge of what has happened; but I knew something would, or might, happen. For more than two years past my house in Cornwall has been made ready to receive all the curios which are preserved here. When Corbeck went off on his search for the lamps I had the old house at Kyllion made ready; it is fitted with electric light all over, and all the appliances for manufacture of the light are complete. I had perhaps better tell you, for none of you, not even Margaret, knows anything of it, that the house is absolutely shut out from public access or even from view. It stands on a little rocky promontory behind a steep hill, and except from the sea cannot be seen. Of old it was fenced in by a high stone wall, for the house which it succeeded was built by an ancestor of mine in the days when a great house far away from a centre had to be prepared to defend itself. Here, then, is a place so well adapted to our needs that it might have been prepared on purpose. I shall explain it to you when we are all there. This will not be long, for already our movement is in train. I have sent word to Marvin to have all preparation for our transport ready. He is to have a special train, which is to run at night so as to avoid notice. Also a number of carts and stone-wagons, with sufficient men and appliances to take all our packing-cases to Paddington. We shall be away before the Argus-eyed Pressman is on the watch. We shall today begin our packing up; and I dare say that by tomorrow night we shall be ready. In the outhouses I have all the packing-cases which were used for bringing the things from Egypt, and I am satisfied that as they were sufficient for the journey across the desert and down the Nile to Alexandria and thence on to London, they will serve without fail between here and Kyllion. We four men, with Margaret to hand us such things as we may require, will be able to get the things packed safely; and the carrier's men will take them to the trucks.

"Today the servants go to Kyllion, and Mrs. Grant will make such arrangements as may be required. She will take a stock of necessaries with her, so that we will not attract local attention by our daily needs; and will keep us supplied with perishable food from London. Thanks to Margaret's wise and generous treatment of the servants who decided to remain, we have got a staff on which we can depend. They have been already cautioned to secrecy, so that we need not fear gossip from within. Indeed, as the servants will be in London after their preparations at Kyllion are complete, there will not be much subject for gossip, in detail at any rate.

"As, however, we should commence the immediate work of packing at once, we will leave over the after proceedings till later when we have leisure."

Accordingly we set about our work. Under Mr. Trelawny's guidance, and aided by the servants, we took from the outhouses great packing-cases. Some of these were of enormous strength, fortified by many thicknesses of wood, and by iron bands and rods with screw-ends and nuts. We placed them throughout the house, each close to the object which it was to contain. When this preliminary work had been effected, and there had been placed in each room and in the hall great masses of new hay, cotton-waste and paper, the servants were sent away. Then we set about packing.

No one, not accustomed to packing, could have the slightest idea of the amount of the amount of work involved in such a task as that in which in we were engaged. For my own part I had had a vague idea that there were a large number of Egyptian objects in Mr. Trelawny's house; but until I came to deal with them seriatim I had little idea of either their importance, the size of some of them, or of their endless number. Far into the night we worked. At times we used all the strength which we could muster on a single object; again we worked separately, but always under Mr. Trelawny's immediate direction. He himself, assisted by Margaret, kept an exact tall of each piece.

It was only when we sat down, utterly wearied, to a long-delayed supper that we began to realised that a large part of the work was done. Only a few of the packing-cases, however, were closed; for a vast amount of work still remained. We had finished some of the cases, each of which held only one of the great sarcophagi. The cases which held many objects could not be closed till all had been differentiated and packed.

I slept that night without movement or without dreams; and on our comparing notes in the morning, I found that each of the others had had the same experience.

Chapter XVI - The Cavern

By dinner-time next evening the whole work was complete, and all was ready for the carriers who were to come at midnight. A little before the appointed time we heard the rumble of carts; then we were shortly invaded by an army of workmen, who seemed by sheer force of numbers to move without effort, in an endless procession, all our prepared packages. A little over an hour sufficed them, and when the carts had rumbled away, we all got ready to follow them to Paddington. Silvio was of course to be taken as one of our party.

Before leaving we went in a body over the house, which looked desolate indeed. As the servants had all gone to Cornwall there had been no attempt at tidying-up; every room and passage in which we had worked, and all the stairways, were strewn with paper and waste, and marked with dirty feet.

The last thing which Mr. Trelawny did before coming away was to take from the great safe the Ruby with the Seven Stars. As he put it safely into his pocket-book, Margaret, who had all at once seemed to grow deadly tired and stood beside her father pale and rigid, suddenly became all aglow, as though the sight of the Jewel had inspired her. She smiled at her father approvingly as she said:

"You are right, Father. There will not be any more trouble tonight. She will not wreck your arrangements for any cause. I would stake my life upon it."

"She—or something—wrecked us in the desert when we had come from the tomb in the Valley of the Sorcerer!" was the grim comment of Corbeck, who was standing by. Margaret answered him like a flash:

"Ah! she was then near her tomb from which for thousands of years her body had not been moved. She must know that things are different now."

"How must she know?" asked Corbeck keenly.

"If she has that astral body that Father spoke of, surely she must know! How can she fail to, with an invisible presence and an intellect that can roam abroad even to the stars and the worlds beyond us!" She paused, and her father said solemnly:

"It is on that supposition that we are proceeding. We must have the courage of our convictions, and act on them—to the last!"

Margaret took his hand and held it in a dreamy kind of way as we filed out of the house. She was holding it still when he locked the hall door, and when we moved up the road to the gateway, whence we took a cab to Paddington.

When all the goods were loaded at the station, the whole of the workmen went on to the train; this took also some of the stone-wagons used for carrying the cases with the great sarcophagi. Ordinary carts and plenty of horses were to be found at Westerton, which was our station for Kyllion. Mr. Trelawny had ordered a sleeping-carriage for our party; as soon as the train had started we all turned into our cubicles.

That night I slept sound. There was over me a conviction of security which was absolute and supreme. Margaret's definite announcement: "There will not be any trouble tonight!" seemed to carry assurance with it. I did not question it; nor did anyone else. It was only afterwards that I began to think as to how she was so sure. The train was a slow one, stopping many times and for considerable intervals. As Mr. Trelawny did not wish to arrive at Westerton before dark, there was no need to hurry; and arrangements had been made to feed the workmen at certain places on the journey. We had our own hamper with us in the private car.

All that afternoon we talked over the Great Experiment, which seemed to have become a definite entity in our thoughts. Mr. Trelawny became more and more enthusiastic as the time wore on; hope was with him becoming certainty. Doctor Winchester seemed to become imbued with some of his spirit, though at times he would throw out some scientific fact which would either make an impasse to the other's line of argument, or would come as an arresting shock. Mr. Corbeck, on the other hand, seemed slightly antagonistic to the theory. It may have been that whilst the opinions of the others advanced, his own stood still; but the effect was an attitude which appeared negative, if not wholly one of negation.

As for Margaret, she seemed to be in some way overcome. Either it was some new phase of feeling with her, or else she was taking the issue more seriously than she had yet done. She was generally more or less distraite, as though sunk in a brown study; from this she would recover herself with a start. This was usually when there occurred some marked episode in the journey, such as stopping at a station, or when the thunderous rumble of crossing a viaduct woke the echoes of the hills or cliffs around us. On each such occasion she would plunge into the conversation, taking such a part in it as to show that, whatever had been her abstracted thought, her senses had taken in fully all that had gone on around her. Towards myself her manner was strange. Sometimes it was marked by a distance, half shy, half haughty, which was new to me. At other times there were moments of passion in look and gesture which almost made me dizzy with delight. Little, however, of a marked nature transpired during the journey. There was but one episode which had in it any element of alarm, but as we were all asleep at the time it did not disturb us. We only learned it from a communicative guard in the morning. Whilst running between Dawlish and Teignmouth the train was stopped by a warning given by someone who moved a torch to and fro right on the very track. The driver had found on pulling up that just ahead of the train a small landslip had taken place, some of the red earth from the high bank having fallen away. It did not however reach to the metals; and the driver had resumed his way, none too well pleased at the delay. To use his own words, the guard thought "there was too much bally caution on this 'ere line!"

We arrived at Westerton about nine o'clock in the evening. Carts and horses were in waiting, and the work of unloading the train began at once. Our own party did not wait to see the work done, as it was in the hands of competent people. We took the carriage which was in waiting, and through the darkness of the night sped on to Kyllion.

We were all impressed by the house as it appeared in the bright moonlight. A great grey stone mansion of the Jacobean period; vast and spacious, standing high over the sea on the very verge of a high cliff. When we had swept round the curve of the avenue cut through the rock, and come out on the high plateau on which the house stood, the crash and murmur of waves breaking against rock far below us came with an invigorating breath of moist sea air. We understood then in an instant how well we were shut out from the world on that rocky shelf above the sea.

Within the house we found all ready. Mrs. Grant and her staff had worked well, and all was bright and fresh and clean. We took a brief survey of the chief rooms and then separated to have a wash and to change our clothes after our long journey of more than four-and-twenty hours.

We had supper in the great dining-room on the south side, the walls of which actually hung over the sea. The murmur came up muffled, but it never ceased. As the little promontory stood well out into the sea, the northern side of the house was open;

and the due north was in no way shut out by the great mass of rock, which, reared high above us, shut out the rest of the world. Far off across the bay we could see the trembling lights of the castle, and here and there along the shore the faint light of a fisher's window. For the rest the sea was a dark blue plain with an occasional flicker of light as the gleam of starlight fell on the slope of a swelling wave.

When supper was over we all adjourned to the room which Mr. Trelawny had set aside as his study, his bedroom being close to it. As we entered, the first thing I noticed was a great safe, somewhat similar to that which stood in his room in London. When we were in the room Mr. Trelawny went over to the table, and, taking out his pocket-book, laid it on the table. As he did so he pressed down on it with the palm of his hand. A strange pallor came over his face. With fingers that trembled he opened the book, saying as he did so:

"Its bulk does not seem the same; I hope nothing has happened!"

All three of us men crowded round close. Margaret alone remained calm; she stood erect and silent, and still as a statue. She had a far-away look in her eyes, as though she did not either know or care what was going on around her.

With a despairing gesture Trelawny threw open the pouch of the pocket-book wherein he had placed the Jewel of Seven Stars. As he sank down on the chair which stood close to him, he said in a hoarse voice:

"My God! it is gone. Without it the Great Experiment can come to nothing!"

His words seemed to wake Margaret from her introspective mood. An agonised spasm swept her face; but almost on the instant she was calm. She almost smiled as she said:

"You may have left it in your room, Father. Perhaps it has fallen out of the pocket-book whilst you were changing." Without a word we all hurried into the next room through the open door between the study and the bedroom. And then a sudden calm fell on us like a cloud of fear.

There! on the table, lay the Jewel of Seven Stars, shining and sparkling with lurid light, as though each of the seven points of each the seven stars gleamed through blood!

Timidly we each looked behind us, and then at each other. Margaret was now like the rest of us. She had lost her statuesque calm. All the introspective rigidity had gone from her; and she clasped her hands together till the knuckles were white.

Without a word Mr. Trelawny raised the Jewel, and hurried with it into the next room. As quietly as he could he opened the door of the safe with the key fastened to his wrist and placed the Jewel within. When the heavy doors were closed and locked he seemed to breathe more freely.

Somehow this episode, though a disturbing one in many ways, seemed to bring us back to our old selves. Since we had left London we had all been overstrained; and this was a sort of relief. Another step in our strange enterprise had been effected.

The change back was more marked in Margaret than in any of us. Perhaps it was that she was a woman, whilst we were men; perhaps it was that she was younger than the rest; perhaps both reasons were effective, each in its own way. At any rate the change was there, and I was happier than I had been through the long journey. All her buoyancy, her tenderness, her deep feeling seemed to shine forth once more; now and again as her father's eyes rested on her, his face seemed to light up.

Whilst we waited for the carts to arrive, Mr. Trelawny took us through the house, pointing out and explaining where the objects which we had brought with us were to be placed. In one respect only did he withhold confidence. The positions of all those things which had connection with the Great Experiment were not indicated. The cases containing them were to be left in the outer hall, for the present.

By the time we had made the survey, the carts began to arrive; and the stir and bustle of the previous night were renewed. Mr. Trelawny stood in the hall beside the massive ironbound door, and gave directions as to the placing of each of the great packing-cases. Those containing many items were placed in the inner hall where they were to be unpacked.

In an incredibly short time the whole consignment was delivered; and the men departed with a douceur for each, given through their foreman, which made them effusive in their thanks. Then we all went to our own rooms. There was a strange confidence over us all. I do not think that any one of us had a doubt as the quiet passing of the remainder of the night.

The faith was justified, for on our re-assembling in the morning we found that all had slept well and peaceably.

During that day all the curios, except those required for the Great Experiment, were put into the places designed for them. Then it was arranged that all the servants should go back with Mrs. Grant to London on the next morning.

When they had all gone Mr. Trelawny, having seen the doors locked, took us into the study.

"Now," said he when we were seated, "I have a secret to impart; but, according to an old promise which does not leave me free, I must ask you each to give me a solemn promise not to reveal it. For three hundred years at least such a promise has been exacted from everyone to whom it was told, and more than once life and safety were secured through loyal observance of the promise. Even as it is, I am breaking the letter, if not the spirit of the tradition; for I should only tell it to the immediate members of my family."

We all gave the promise required. Then he went on:

"There is a secret place in this house, a cave, natural originally but finished by labour, underneath this house. I will not undertake to say that it has always been used according to the law. During the Bloody Assize more than a few Cornishmen found refuge in it; and later, and earlier, it formed, I have no doubt whatever, a useful place for storing contraband goods. 'Tre Pol and Pen', I suppose you know, have always been smugglers; and their relations and friends and neighbours have not held back from the enterprise. For all such reasons a safe hiding-place was always considered a valuable possession; and as the heads of our House have always insisted on preserving the secret, I am in honour bound to it. Later on, if all be well, I shall of course tell you, Margaret, and you too, Ross, under the conditions that I am bound to make."

He rose up, and we all followed him. Leaving us in the outer hall, he went away alone for a few minutes; and returning, beckoned us to follow him.

In the inside hall we found a whole section of an outstanding angle moved away, and from the cavity saw a great hole dimly dark, and the beginning of a rough staircase cut in the rock. As it was not pitch dark there was manifestly some means of lighting it naturally, so without pause we followed our host as he descended. After some forty or fifty steps cut in a winding passage, we came to a great cave whose further end tapered away into blackness. It was a huge place, dimly lit by a few irregular slits of eccentric shape. Manifestly these were faults in the rock which would readily allow the windows be disguised. Close to each of them was a hanging shutter which could be easily swung across by means of a dangling rope. The sound of the ceaseless beat of the waves came up muffled from far below. Mr. Trelawny at once began to speak:

"This is the spot which I have chosen, as the best I know, for the scene of our Great Experiment. In a hundred different ways it fulfils the conditions which I am led to believe are primary with regard to success. Here, we are, and shall be, as isolated as Queen Tera herself would have been in her rocky tomb in the Valley of the Sorcerer, and still in a rocky cavern. For good or ill we must here stand by our chances, and abide by results. If we are successful we shall be able to let in on the world of modern science such a flood of light from the Old World as will change every condition of thought and experiment and practice. If we fail, then even the knowledge of our attempt will die with us. For this, and all else which may come, I believe we are prepared!" He paused. No one spoke, but we all bowed our heads gravely in acquiescence. He resumed, but with a certain hesitancy:

"It is not yet too late! If any of you have a doubt or misgiving, for God's sake speak it now! Whoever it may be, can go hence without let or hindrance. The rest of us can go on our way alone!"

Again he paused, and looked keenly at us in turn. We looked at each other; but no one quailed. For my own part, if I had had any doubt as to going on, the look on Margaret's face would have reassured me. It was fearless; it was intense; it was full of a divine calm.

Mr. Trelawny took a long breath, and in a more cheerful, as well as in a more decided tone, went on:

"As we are all of one mind, the sooner we get the necessary matters in train the better. Let me tell you that this place, like all the rest of the house, can be lit with electricity. We could not join the wires to the mains lest our secret should become known, but I have a cable here which we can attach in the hall and complete the circuit!" As he was speaking, he began to ascend the steps. From close to the entrance he took the end of a cable; this he drew forward and attached to a switch in the wall. Then, turning on a tap, he flooded the whole vault and staircase below with light. I could now see from the volume of light streaming up into the hallway that the hole beside the staircase went direct into the cave. Above it was a pulley and a mass of strong tackle with multiplying blocks of the Smeaton order. Mr. Trelawny, seeing me looking at this, said, correctly interpreting my thoughts:

"Yes! it is new. I hung it there myself on purpose. I knew we should have to lower great weights; and as I did not wish to take too many into my confidence, I arranged a tackle which I could work alone if necessary."

We set to work at once; and before nightfall had lowered, unhooked, and placed in the positions designated for each by Trelawny, all the great sarcophagi and all the curios and other matters which we had taken with us.

It was a strange and weird proceeding, the placing of those wonderful monuments of a bygone age in that green cavern, which represented in its cutting and purpose and up-to-date mechanism and electric lights both the old world and the new. But as time went on I grew more and more to recognise the wisdom and correctness of Mr.

Trelawny's choice. I was much disturbed when Silvio, who had been brought into the cave in the arms of his mistress, and who was lying asleep on my coat which I had taken off, sprang up when the cat mummy had been unpacked, and flew at it with the same ferocity which he had previously exhibited. The incident showed Margaret in a new phase, and one which gave my heart a pang. She had been standing quite still at one side of the cave leaning on a sarcophagus, in one of those fits of abstraction which had of late come upon her; but on hearing the sound, and seeing Silvio's violent onslaught, she seemed to fall into a positive fury of passion. Her eyes blazed, and her mouth took a hard, cruel tension which was new to me. Instinctively she stepped towards Silvio as if to interfere in the attack. But I too had stepped forward; and as she caught my eye a strange spasm came upon her, and she stopped. Its intensity made me hold my breath; and I put up my hand to clear my eyes. When I had done this, she had on the instant recovered her calm, and there was a look of brief wonder on her face. With all her old grace and sweetness she swept over and lifted Silvio, just as she had done on former occasions, and held him in her arms, petting him and treating him as though he were a little child who had erred.

As I looked a strange fear came over me. The Margaret that I knew seemed to be changing; and in my inmost heart I prayed that the disturbing cause might soon come to an end. More than ever I longed at that moment that our terrible Experiment should come to a prosperous termination.

When all had been arranged in the room as Mr. Trelawny wished he turned to us, one after another, till he had concentrated the intelligence of us all upon him. Then he said:

"All is now ready in this place. We must only await the proper time to begin."

We were silent for a while. Doctor Winchester was the first to speak:

"What is the proper time? Have you any approximation, even if you are not satisfied as to the exact day?" He answered at once:

"After the most anxious thought I have fixed on July 31!"

"May I ask why that date?" He spoke his answer slowly:

"Queen Tera was ruled in great degree by mysticism, and there are so many evidences that she looked for resurrection that naturally she would choose a period ruled over by a God specialised to such a purpose. Now, the fourth month of the season of Inundation was ruled by Harmachis, this being the name for 'Ra', the Sun-God, at his rising in the morning, and therefore typifying the awakening or arising. This arising is manifestly to physical life, since it is of the mid-world of human daily life. Now as this month begins on our 25th July, the seventh day would be July 31st, for you may be sure that the mystic Queen would not have chosen any day but the seventh or some power of seven.

"I dare say that some of you have wondered why our preparations have been so deliberately undertaken. This is why! We must be ready in every possible way when the time comes; but there was no use in having to wait round for a needless number of days."

And so we waited only for the 31st of July, the next day but one, when the Great Experiment would be made.

Chapter XVII - Doubts and Fears

We learn of great things by little experiences. The history of ages is but an indefinite repetition of the history of hours. The record of a soul is but a multiple of the story of a moment. The Recording Angel writes in the Great Book in no rainbow tints; his pen is dipped in no colours but light and darkness. For the eye of infinite wisdom there is no need of shading. All things, all thoughts, all emotions, all experiences, all doubts and hopes and fears, all intentions, all wishes seen down to the lower strata of their concrete and multitudinous elements, are finally resolved into direct opposites.

Did any human being wish for the epitome of a life wherein were gathered and grouped all the experiences that a child of Adam could have, the history, fully and frankly written, of my own mind during the next forty-eight hours would afford him all that could be wanted. And the Recorder could have wrought as usual in sunlight and shadow, which may be taken to represent the final expressions of Heaven and Hell. For in the highest Heaven is Faith; and Doubt hangs over the yawning blackness of Hell.

There were of course times of sunshine in those two days; moments when, in the realisation of Margaret's sweetness and her love for me, all doubts were dissipated like morning mist before the sun. But the balance of the time—and an overwhelming balance it was—gloom hung over me like a pall. The hour, in whose coming I had acquiesced, was approaching so quickly and was already so near that the sense of finality was bearing upon me! The issue was perhaps life or death to any of us; but for this we were all prepared. Margaret and I were one as to the risk. The question of the moral aspect of the case, which involved the religious belief in which I had been reared, was not one to trouble me; for the issues, and the causes that lay behind them, were not within my power even to comprehend. The doubt of the success of the Great Experiment was such a doubt as exists in all enterprises which have great possibilities. To me, whose life was passed in a series of intellectual struggles, this form of doubt was a stimulus, rather than deterrent. What then was it that made for me a trouble, which became an anguish when my thoughts dwelt long on it?

I was beginning to doubt Margaret!

What it was that I doubted I knew not. It was not her love, or her honour, or her truth, or her kindness, or her zeal. What then was it?

It was herself!

Margaret was changing! At times during the past few days I had hardly known her as the same girl whom I had met at the picnic, and whose vigils I had shared in the sick-room of her father. Then, even in her moments of greatest sorrow or fright or anxiety, she was all life and thought and keenness. Now she was generally distraite, and at times in a sort of negative condition as though her mind—her very being—was not present. At such moments she would have full possession of observation and memory. She would know and remember all that was going on, and had gone on around her; but her coming back to her old self had to me something the sensation of a new person coming into the room. Up to the time of leaving London I had been content whenever she was present. I had over me that delicious sense of security which comes with the consciousness that love is mutual. But now doubt had taken its place. I never knew whether the personality present was my Margaret—the old Margaret whom I had loved at the first glance—or the other new Margaret, whom I hardly understood, and whose intellectual aloofness made an impalpable barrier between us. Sometimes she would become, as it were, awake all at once. At such times, though she would say to me sweet and pleasant things which she had often said before, she would seem most unlike herself. It was almost as if she was speaking parrot-like or at dictation of one who could read words or acts, but not thoughts. After one or two experiences of this kind, my own doubting began to make a barrier; for I could not speak with the ease and freedom which were usual to me. And so hour by hour we drifted apart. Were it not for the few odd moments when the old Margaret was back with me full of her charm I do not know what would have happened. As it was, each such moment gave me a fresh start and kept my love from changing.

I would have given the world for a confidant; but this was impossible. How could I speak a doubt of Margaret to anyone, even her father! How could I speak a doubt to Margaret, when Margaret herself was the theme! I could only endure—and hope. And of the two the endurance was the lesser pain.

I think that Margaret must have at times felt that there was some cloud between us, for towards the end of the first day she began to shun me a little; or perhaps it was that she had become more diffident that usual about me. Hitherto she had sought every opportunity of being with me, just as I had tried to be with her; so that now any avoidance, one of the other, made a new pain to us both.

On this day the household seemed very still. Each one of us was about his own work, or occupied with his own thoughts. We only met at meal times; and then, though we talked, all seemed more or less preoccupied. There was not in the house even the stir of the routine of service. The precaution of Mr. Trelawny in having three rooms prepared for each of us had rendered servants unnecessary. The dining-room was solidly prepared with cooked provisions for several days. Towards evening I went out by myself for a stroll. I had looked for Margaret to ask her to come with me; but when I found her, she was in one of her apathetic moods, and the charm of her presence seemed lost to me. Angry with myself, but unable to quell my own spirit of discontent, I went out alone over the rocky headland.

On the cliff, with the wide expanse of wonderful sea before me, and no sound but the dash of waves below and the harsh screams of the seagulls above, my thoughts ran free. Do what I would, they returned continuously to one subject, the solving of the doubt that was upon me. Here in the solitude, amid the wide circle of Nature's force and strife, my mind began to work truly. Unconsciously I found myself asking a question which I would not allow myself to answer. At last the persistence of a mind working truly prevailed; I found myself face to face with my doubt. The habit of my life began to assert itself, and I analysed the evidence before me.

It was so startling that I had to force myself into obedience to logical effort. My starting-place was this: Margaret was changed—in what way, and by what means? Was it her character, or her mind, or her nature? for her physical appearance remained the same. I began to group all that I had ever heard of her, beginning at her birth.

It was strange at the very first. She had been, according to Corbeck's statement, born of a dead mother during the time that her father and his friend were in a trance in the tomb at Aswan. That trance was presumably effected by a woman; a woman mummied, yet preserving as we had every reason to believe from after experience, an astral body subject to a free will and an active intelligence. With that astral body, space ceased to exist. The vast distance between London and Aswan became as naught; and whatever power of necromancy the Sorceress had might have been exercised over the dead mother, and possibly the dead child.

The dead child! Was it possible that the child was dead and was made alive again? Whence then came the animating spirit—the soul? Logic was pointing the way to me now with a vengeance!

If the Egyptian belief was true for Egyptians, then the "Ka" of the dead Queen and her "Khu" could animate what she might choose. In such case Margaret would not be an individual at all, but simply a phase of Queen Tera herself; an astral body obedient to her will!

Here I revolted against logic. Every fibre of my being resented such a conclusion. How could I believe that there was no Margaret at all; but just an animated image, used by the Double of a woman of forty centuries ago to its own ends...! Somehow, the outlook was brighter to me now, despite the new doubts.

At least I had Margaret!

Back swung the logical pendulum again. The child then was not dead. If so, had the Sorceress had anything to do with her birth at all? It was evident—so I took it again from Corbeck—that there was a strange likeness between Margaret and the pictures of Queen Tera. How could this be? It could not be any birth-mark reproducing what had been in the mother's mind; for Mrs. Trelawny had never seen the pictures. Nay, even her father had not seen them till he had found his way into the tomb only a few days before her birth. This phase I could not get rid of so easily as the last; the fibres of my being remained quiet. There remained to me the horror of doubt. And even then, so strange is the mind of man, Doubt itself took a concrete image; a vast and impenetrable gloom, through which flickered irregularly and spasmodically tiny points of evanescent light, which seemed to quicken the darkness into a positive existence.

The remaining possibility of relations between Margaret and the mummied Queen was, that in some occult way the Sorceress had power to change places with the other. This view of things could not be so lightly thrown aside. There were too many suspicious circumstances to warrant this, now that my attention was fixed on it and my intelligence recognised the possibility. Hereupon there began to come into my mind all the strange incomprehensible matters which had whirled through our lives in the last few days. At first they all crowded in upon me in a jumbled mass; but again the habit of mind of my working life prevailed, and they took order. I found it now easier to control myself; for there was something to grasp, some work to be done; though it was of a sorry kind, for it was or might be antagonistic to Margaret. But Margaret was herself at stake! I was thinking of her and fighting for her; and yet if I were to work in the dark, I might be even harmful to her. My first weapon in her defence was truth. I must know and understand; I might then be able to act. Certainly, I could not act beneficently without a just conception and recognition of the facts. Arranged in order these were as follows:

Firstly: the strange likeness of Queen Tera to Margaret who had been born in another country a thousand miles away, where her mother could not possibly have had even a passing knowledge of her appearance.

Secondly: the disappearance of Van Huyn's book when I had read up to the description of the Star Ruby.

Thirdly: the finding of the lamps in the boudoir. Tera with her astral body could have unlocked the door of Corbeck's room in the hotel, and have locked it again after her exit with the lamps. She could in the same way have opened the window, and put the lamps in the boudoir. It need not have been that Margaret in her own person should have had any hand in this; but—but it was at least strange.

Fourthly: here the suspicions of the Detective and the Doctor came back to me with renewed force, and with a larger understanding.

Fifthly: there were the occasions on which Margaret foretold with accuracy the coming occasions of quietude, as though she had some conviction or knowledge of the intentions of the astral-bodied Queen.

Sixthly: there was her suggestion of the finding of the Ruby which her father had lost. As I thought now afresh over this episode in the light of suspicion in which her own powers were involved, the only conclusion I could come to was—always supposing that the theory of the Queen's astral power was correct—that Queen Tera being anxious that all should go well in the movement from London to Kyllion had in her own way taken the Jewel from Mr. Trelawny's pocket-book, finding it of some use in her supernatural guardianship of the journey. Then in some mysterious way she had, through Margaret, made the suggestion of its loss and finding.

Seventhly, and lastly, was the strange dual existence which Margaret seemed of late to be leading; and which in some way seemed a consequence or corollary of all that had gone before.

The dual existence! This was indeed the conclusion which overcame all difficulties and reconciled opposites. If indeed Margaret were not in all ways a free agent, but could be compelled to speak or act as she might be instructed; or if her whole being could be changed for another without the possibility of any one noticing the doing of it, then all things were possible. All would depend on the spirit of the individuality by which she could be so compelled. If this individuality were just and kind and clean, all might be well. But if not! ... The thought was too awful for words. I ground my teeth with futile rage, as the ideas of horrible possibilities swept through me.

Up to this morning Margaret's lapses into her new self had been few and hardly noticeable, save when once or twice her attitude towards myself had been marked by a bearing strange to me. But today the contrary was the case; and the change presaged badly. It might be that that other individuality was of the lower, not of the better sort! Now that I thought of it I had reason to fear. In the history of the mummy, from the time of Van Huyn's breaking into the tomb, the record of deaths that we knew of, presumably effected by her will and agency, was a startling one. The Arab who had stolen the hand from the mummy; and the one who had taken it from his body. The Arab chief who had tried to steal the Jewel from Van Huyn, and whose throat bore the marks of seven fingers. The two men found dead on the first night of Trelawny's taking away the sarcophagus; and the three on the return to the tomb. The Arab who had opened the secret serdab. Nine dead men, one of them slain manifestly by the Queen's own hand! And beyond this again the several savage attacks on Mr. Trelawny in his own room, in which, aided by her Familiar, she had tried to open the safe and to extract the Talisman jewel. His device of fastening the key to his wrist by a steel bangle, though successful in the end, had wellnigh cost him his life.

If then the Queen, intent on her resurrection under her own conditions had, so to speak, waded to it through blood, what might she not do were her purpose thwarted? What terrible step might she not take to effect her wishes? Nay, what were her wishes; what was her ultimate purpose? As yet we had had only Margaret's statement of them, given in all the glorious enthusiasm of her lofty soul. In her record there was no expression of love to be sought or found. All we knew for certain was that she had set before her the object of resurrection, and that in it the North which she had manifestly loved was to have a special part. But that the resurrection was to be accomplished in the lonely tomb in the Valley of the Sorcerer was apparent. All preparations had been carefully made for accomplishment from within, and for her ultimate exit in her new and living form. The sarcophagus was unlidded. The oil jars, though hermetically sealed, were to be easily opened by hand; and in them provision was made for shrinkage through a vast period of time. Even flint and steel were provided for the production of flame. The Mummy Pit was left open in violation of usage; and beside the stone door on the cliff side was fixed an imperishable chain by which she might in safety descend to earth. But as to what her after intentions were we had no clue. If it was that she meant to begin life again as a humble individual, there was something so noble in the thought that it even warmed my heart to her and turned my wishes to her success.

The very idea seemed to endorse Margaret's magnificent tribute to her purpose, and helped to calm my troubled spirit.

Then and there, with this feeling strong upon me, I determined to warn Margaret and her father of dire possibilities; and to await, as well content as I could in my ignorance, the development of things over which I had no power.

I returned to the house in a different frame of mind to that in which I had left it; and was enchanted to find Margaret—the old Margaret—waiting for me.

After dinner, when I was alone for a time with the father and daughter, I opened the subject, though with considerable hesitation:

"Would it not be well to take every possible precaution, in case the Queen may not wish what we are doing, with regard to what may occur before the Experiment; and at or after her waking, if it comes off?" Margaret's answer came back quickly; so quickly that I was convinced she must have had it ready for some one:

"But she does approve! Surely it cannot be otherwise. Father is doing, with all his brains and all his energy and all his great courage, just exactly what the great Queen had arranged!"

"But," I answered, "that can hardly be. All that she arranged was in a tomb high up in a rock, in a desert solitude, shut away from the world by every conceivable means.

She seems to have depended on this isolation to insure against accident. Surely, here in another country and age, with quite different conditions, she may in her anxiety make mistakes and treat any of you—of us—as she did those others in times gone past. Nine men that we know of have been slain by her own hand or by her instigation. She can be remorseless if she will." It did not strike me till afterwards when I was thinking over this conversation, how thoroughly I had accepted the living and conscious condition of Queen Tera as a fact. Before I spoke, I had feared I might offend Mr. Trelawny; but to my pleasant surprise he smiled quite genially as he answered me:

"My dear fellow, in a way you are quite right. The Queen did undoubtedly intend isolation; and, all told, it would be best that her experiment should be made as she arranged it. But just think, that became impossible when once the Dutch explorer had broken into her tomb. That was not my doing. I am innocent of it, though it was the cause of my setting out to rediscover the sepulchre. Mind, I do not say for a moment that I would not have done just the same as Van Huyn. I went into the tomb from curiosity; and I took away what I did, being fired with the zeal of acquisitiveness which animates the collector. But, remember also, that at this time I did not know of the Queen's intention of resurrection; I had no idea of the completeness of her preparations. All that came long afterwards. But when it did come, I have done all that I could to carry out her wishes to the full. My only fear is that I may have misinterpreted some of her cryptic instructions, or have omitted or overlooked something. But of this I am certain; I have left undone nothing that I can imagine right to be done; and I have done nothing that I know of to clash with Queen Tera's arrangement. I want her Great Experiment to succeed. To this end I have not spared labour or time or money—or myself. I have endured hardship, and braved danger. All my brains; all my knowledge and learning, such as they are; all my endeavours such as they can be, have been, are, and shall be devoted to this end, till we either win or lose the great stake that we play for."

"The great stake?" I repeated; "the resurrection of the woman, and the woman's life? The proof that resurrection can be accomplished; by magical powers; by scientific knowledge; or by use of some force which at present the world does not know?"

Then Mr. Trelawny spoke out the hopes of his heart which up to now he had indicated rather than expressed. Once or twice I had heard Corbeck speak of the fiery energy of his youth; but, save for the noble words of Margaret when she had spoken of Queen Tera's hope—which coming from his daughter made possible a belief that her power was in some sense due to heredity—I had seen no marked sign of it. But now his words, sweeping before them like a torrent all antagonistic thought, gave me a new idea of the man.

"'A woman's life!' What is a woman's life in the scale with what we hope for! Why, we are risking already a woman's life; the dearest life to me in all the world, and that grows more dear with every hour that passes. We are risking as well the lives of four men; yours and my own, as well as those two others who have been won to our confidence. 'The proof that resurrection can be accomplished!' That is much. A marvellous thing in this age of science, and the scepticism that knowledge makes. But life and resurrection are themselves but items in what may be won by the accomplishment of this Great Experiment. Imagine what it will be for the world of thought—the true world of human progress—the veritable road to the Stars, the itur ad astra of the Ancients—if there can come back to us out of the unknown past one who can yield to us the lore stored in the great Library of Alexandria, and lost in its consuming flames. Not only history can be set right, and the teachings of science made veritable from their beginnings; but we can be placed on the road to the knowledge of lost arts, lost learning, lost sciences, so that our feet may tread on the indicated path to their ultimate and complete restoration. Why, this woman can tell us what the world was like before what is called 'the Flood'; can give us the origin of that vast astounding myth; can set the mind back to the consideration of things which to us now seem primeval, but which were old stories before the days of the Patriarchs. But this is not the end! No, not even the beginning! If the story of this woman be all that we think—which some of us most firmly believe; if her powers and the restoration of them prove to be what we expect, why, then we may yet achieve a knowledge beyond what our age has ever known—beyond what is believed today possible for the children of men. If indeed this resurrection can be accomplished, how can we doubt the old knowledge, the old magic, the old belief! And if this be so, we must take it that the 'Ka' of this great and learned Queen has won secrets of more than mortal worth from her surroundings amongst the stars. This woman in her life voluntarily went down living to the grave, and came back again, as we learn from the records in her tomb; she chose to die her mortal death whilst young, so that at her resurrection in another age, beyond a trance of countless magnitude, she might emerge from her tomb in all the fulness and splendour of her youth and power. Already we have evidence that though her body slept in patience through those many centuries, her intelligence never passed away, that her resolution never flagged, that her will remained supreme; and, most important of all, that her memory was unimpaired. Oh, what possibilities are there in the coming of such a being into our midst! One whose history began before the concrete teaching of our Bible; whose experiences were antecedent to the formulation of the Gods of Greece; who can link together the Old and the New, Earth and Heaven, and yield to the known worlds of thought and physical existence the mystery of the Unknown—of the Old World in its youth, and of Worlds beyond our ken!"

He paused, almost overcome. Margaret had taken his hand when he spoke of her being so dear to him, and held it hard. As he spoke she continued to hold it. But there came over her face that change which I had so often seen of late; that mysterious veiling of her own personality which gave me the subtle sense of separation from her. In his impassioned vehemence her father did not notice; but when he stopped she seemed all at once to be herself again. In her glorious eyes came the added brightness of unshed tears; and with a gesture of passionate love and admiration, she stooped and kissed her father's hand. Then, turning to me, she too spoke:

"Malcolm, you have spoken of the deaths that came from the poor Queen; or rather that justly came from meddling with her arrangements and thwarting her purpose. Do you not think that, in putting it as you have done, you have been unjust? Who would not have done just as she did? Remember she was fighting for her life! Ay, and for more than her life! For life, and love, and all the glorious possibilities of that dim future in the unknown world of the North which had such enchanting hopes for her! Do you not think that she, with all the learning of her time, and with all the great and resistless force of her mighty nature, had hopes of spreading in a wider way the lofty aspirations of her soul! That she hoped to bring to the conquering of unknown worlds, and using to the advantage of her people, all that she had won from sleep and death and time; all of which might and could have been frustrated by the ruthless hand of an assassin or a thief. Were it you, in such case would you not struggle by all means to achieve the object of your life and hope; whose possibilities grew and grew in the passing of those endless years? Can you think that that active brain was at rest during all those weary centuries, whilst her free soul was flitting from world to world amongst the boundless regions of the stars? Had these stars in their myriad and varied life no lessons for her; as they have had for us since we followed the glorious path which she and her people marked for us, when they sent their winged imaginations circling amongst the lamps of the night!"

Here she paused. She too was overcome, and the welling tears ran down her cheeks. I was myself more moved than I can say. This was indeed my Margaret; and in the consciousness of her presence my heart leapt. Out of my happiness came boldness, and I dared to say now what I had feared would be impossible: something which would call the attention of Mr. Trelawny to what I imagined was the dual existence of his daughter. As I took Margaret's hand in mine and kissed it, I said to her father:

"Why, sir! she couldn't speak more eloquently if the very spirit of Queen Tera was with her to animate her and suggest thoughts!"

Mr. Trelawny's answer simply overwhelmed me with surprise. It manifested to me that he too had gone through just such a process of thought as my own.

"And what if it was; if it is! I know well that the spirit of her mother is within her. If in addition there be the spirit of that great and wondrous Queen, then she would be no less dear to me, but doubly dear! Do not have fear for her, Malcolm Ross; at least have no more fear than you may have for the rest of us!" Margaret took up the theme, speaking so quickly that her words seemed a continuation of her father's, rather than an interruption of them.

"Have no special fear for me, Malcolm. Queen Tera knows, and will offer us no harm. I know it! I know it, as surely as I am lost in the depth of my own love for you!"

There was something in her voice so strange to me that I looked quickly into her eyes. They were bright as ever, but veiled to my seeing the inward thought behind them as are the eyes of a caged lion.

Then the two other men came in, and the subject changed.

Chapter XVIII - The Lesson of the "Ka"

That night we all went to bed early. The next night would be an anxious one, and Mr. Trelawny thought that we should all be fortified with what sleep we could get. The day, too, would be full of work. Everything in connection with the Great Experiment would have to be gone over, so that at the last we might not fail from any unthought-of flaw in our working. We made, of course, arrangements for summoning aid in case such should be needed; but I do not think that any of us had any real apprehension of danger. Certainly we had no fear of such danger from violence as we had had to guard against in London during Mr. Trelawny's long trance.

For my own part I felt a strange sense of relief in the matter. I had accepted Mr. Trelawny's reasoning that if the Queen were indeed such as we surmised—such as indeed we now took for granted—there would not be any opposition on her part; for we were carrying out her own wishes to the very last. So far I was at ease—far more at ease than earlier in the day I should have thought possible; but there were other sources of trouble which I could not blot out from my mind. Chief amongst them was Margaret's strange condition. If it was indeed that she had in her own person a dual existence, what might happen when the two existences became one? Again, and again, and again I turned this matter over in my mind, till I could have shrieked out in nervous anxiety. It was no consolation to me to remember that Margaret was herself satisfied, and her father acquiescent. Love is, after all, a selfish thing; and it throws a black shadow on anything between which and the light it stands. I seemed to hear the hands go round the dial of the clock; I saw darkness turn to gloom, and gloom to grey, and grey to light without pause or hindrance to the succession of my miserable feelings. At last, when it was decently possible without the fear of disturbing others, I got up. I crept along the passage to find if all was well with the others; for we had arranged that the door of each of our rooms should be left slightly open so that any sound of disturbance would be easily and distinctly heard.

One and all slept; I could hear the regular breathing of each, and my heart rejoiced that this miserable night of anxiety was safely passed. As I knelt in my own room in a burst of thankful prayer, I knew in the depths of my own heart the measure of my fear. I found my way out of the house, and went down to the water by the long stairway cut in the rock. A swim in the cool bright sea braced my nerves and made me my old self again.

As I came back to the top of the steps I could see the bright sunlight, rising from behind me, turning the rocks across the bay to glittering gold. And yet I felt somehow disturbed. It was all too bright; as it sometimes is before the coming of a storm. As I paused to watch it, I felt a soft hand on my shoulder; and, turning, found Margaret close to me; Margaret as bright and radiant as the morning glory of the sun! It was my own Margaret this time! My old Margaret, without alloy of any other; and I felt that, at least, this last and fatal day was well begun.

But alas! the joy did not last. When we got back to the house from a stroll around the cliffs, the same old routine of yesterday was resumed: gloom and anxiety, hope, high spirits, deep depression, and apathetic aloofness.

But it was to be a day of work; and we all braced ourselves to it with an energy which wrought its own salvation.

After breakfast we all adjourned to the cave, where Mr. Trelawny went over, point by point, the position of each item of our paraphernalia. He explained as he went on why each piece was so placed. He had with him the great rolls of paper with the measured plans and the signs and drawings which he had had made from his own and Corbeck's rough notes. As he had told us, these contained the whole of the hieroglyphics on walls and ceilings and floor of the tomb in the Valley of the Sorcerer. Even had not the measurements, made to scale, recorded the position of each piece of furniture, we could have eventually placed them by a study of the cryptic writings and symbols.

Mr. Trelawny explained to us certain other things, not laid down on the chart. Such as, for instance, that the hollowed part of the table was exactly fitted to the bottom of the Magic Coffer, which was therefore intended to be placed on it. The respective legs of this table were indicated by differently shaped uraei outlined on the floor, the head of each being extended in the direction of the similar uraeus twined round the leg. Also that the mummy, when laid on the raised portion in the bottom of the sarcophagus, seemingly made to fit the form, would lie head to the West and feet to the East, thus receiving the natural earth currents. "If this be intended," he said, "as I presume it is, I gather that the force to be used has something to do with magnetism or electricity, or both. It may be, of course, that some other force, such, for instance, as that emanating from radium, is to be employed. I have experimented with the latter, but only in such small quantity as I could obtain; but so far as I can ascertain the stone of the Coffer is absolutely impervious to its influence. There must be some such unsusceptible substances in nature. Radium does not seemingly manifest itself when distributed through pitchblende; and there are doubtless other such substances in which it can be imprisoned. Possibly these may belong to that class of "inert" elements discovered or isolated by Sir William Ramsay. It is therefore possible that in this Coffer, made from an aerolite and therefore perhaps containing some element unknown in our world, may be imprisoned some mighty power which is to be released on its opening."

This appeared to be an end of this branch of the subject; but as he still kept the fixed look of one who is engaged in a theme we all waited in silence. After a pause he went on:

"There is one thing which has up to now, I confess, puzzled me. It may not be of prime importance; but in a matter like this, where all is unknown, we must take it that everything is important. I cannot think that in a matter worked out with such extraordinary scrupulosity such a thing should be overlooked. As you may see by the ground-plan of the tomb the sarcophagus stands near the north wall, with the Magic

Coffer to the south of it. The space covered by the former is left quite bare of symbol or ornamentation of any kind. At the first glance this would seem to imply that the drawings had been made after the sarcophagus had been put into its place. But a more minute examination will show that the symbolisation on the floor is so arranged that a definite effect is produced. See, here the writings run in correct order as though they had jumped across the gap. It is only from certain effects that it becomes clear that there is a meaning of some kind. What that meaning may be is what we want to know. Look at the top and bottom of the vacant space, which lies West and East corresponding to the head and foot of the sarcophagus. In both are duplications of the same symbolisation, but so arranged that the parts of each one of them are integral portions of some other writing running crosswise. It is only when we get a coup d'oeil from either the head or the foot that you recognise that there are symbolisations. See! they are in triplicate at the corners and the centre of both top and bottom. In every case there is a sun cut in half by the line of the sarcophagus, as by the horizon. Close behind each of these and faced away from it, as though in some way dependent on it, is the vase which in hieroglyphic writing symbolises the heart—'Ab' the Egyptians called it. Beyond each of these again is the figure of a pair of widespread arms turned upwards from the elbow; this is the determinative of the 'Ka' or 'Double'. But its relative position is different at top and bottom. At the head of the sarcophagus the top of the 'Ka' is turned towards the mouth of the vase, but at the foot the extended arms point away from it.

"The symbolisation seems to mean that during the passing of the Sun from West to East—from sunset to sunrise, or through the Under World, otherwise night—the Heart, which is material even in the tomb and cannot leave it, simply revolves, so that it can always rest on 'Ra' the Sun-God, the origin of all good; but that the Double, which represents the active principle, goes whither it will, the same by night as by day. If this be correct it is a warning—a caution—a reminder that the consciousness of the mummy does not rest but is to be reckoned with.

"Or it may be intended to convey that after the particular night of the resurrection, the 'Ka' would leave the heart altogether, thus typifying that in her resurrection the Queen would be restored to a lower and purely physical existence. In such case what would become of her memory and the experiences of her wide-wandering soul? The chiefest value of her resurrection would be lost to the world! This, however, does not alarm me. It is only guess-work after all, and is contradictory to the intellectual belief of the Egyptian theology, that the 'Ka' is an essential portion of humanity." He paused and we all waited. The silence was broken by Doctor Winchester:

"But would not all this imply that the Queen feared intrusion of her tomb?" Mr. Trelawny smiled as he answered:

"My dear sir, she was prepared for it. The grave robber is no modern application of endeavour; he was probably known in the Queen's own dynasty. Not only was she prepared for intrusion, but, as shown in several ways, she expected it. The hiding of the lamps in the serdab, and the institution of the avenging 'treasurer' shows that there was defence, positive as well as negative. Indeed, from the many indications afforded in the clues laid out with the most consummated thought, we may almost gather that she entertained it as a possibility that others—like ourselves, for instance—might in all seriousness undertake the work which she had made ready for her own hands when the time should have come. This very matter that I have been speaking of is an instance. The clue is intended for seeing eyes!"

Again we were silent. It was Margaret who spoke:

"Father, may I have that chart? I should like to study it during the day!"

"Certainly, my dear!" answered Mr. Trelawny heartily, as he handed it to her. He resumed his instructions in a different tone, a more matter-of-fact one suitable to a practical theme which had no mystery about it:

"I think you had better all understand the working of the electric light in case any sudden contingency should arise. I dare say you have noticed that we have a complete supply in every part of the house, so that there need not be a dark corner anywhere. This I had specially arranged. It is worked by a set of turbines moved by the flowing and ebbing tide, after the manner of the turbines at Niagara. I hope by this means to nullify accident and to have without fail a full supply ready at any time. Come with me and I will explain the system of circuits, and point out to you the taps and the fuses." I could not but notice, as we went with him all over the house, how absolutely complete the system was, and how he had guarded himself against any disaster that human thought could foresee.

But out of the very completeness came a fear! In such an enterprise as ours the bounds of human thought were but narrow. Beyond it lay the vast of Divine wisdom, and Divine power!

When we came back to the cave, Mr. Trelawny took up another theme:

"We have now to settle definitely the exact hour at which the Great Experiment is to be made. So far as science and mechanism go, if the preparations are complete, all hours are the same. But as we have to deal with preparations made by a woman of extraordinarily subtle mind, and who had full belief in magic and had a cryptic meaning in everything, we should place ourselves in her position before deciding. It is now manifest that the sunset has an important place in the arrangements. As those suns, cut so mathematically by the edge of the sarcophagus, were arranged of full design, we must take our cue from this. Again, we find all along that the number seven has had an important bearing on every phase of the Queen's thought and reasoning and action. The logical result is that the seventh hour after sunset was the time fixed on. This is borne out by the fact that on each of the occasions when action was taken in my house, this was the time chosen. As the sun sets tonight in Cornwall at eight, our hour is to be three in the morning!" He spoke in a matter-of-fact way, though with great gravity; but there was nothing of mystery in his word or manner. Still, we were all impressed to a remarkable degree. I could see this in the other men by the pallor that came on some of their faces, and by the stillness and unquestioning silence with which the decision was received. The only one who remained in any way at ease was Margaret, who had lapsed into one of her moods of abstraction, but who seemed to wake up to a note of gladness. Her father, who was watching her intently, smiled; her mood was to him a direct confirmation of his theory.

For myself I was almost overcome. The definite fixing of the hour seemed like the voice of Doom. When I think of it now, I can realise how a condemned man feels at his sentence, or at the sounding of the last hour he is to hear.

There could be no going back now! We were in the hands of God!

The hands of God...! And yet...! What other forces were arrayed? ... What would become of us all, poor atoms of earthly dust whirled in the wind which cometh whence and goeth whither no man may know. It was not for myself... Margaret...!

I was recalled by Mr. Trelawny's firm voice:

"Now we shall see to the lamps and finish our preparations." Accordingly we set to work, and under his supervision made ready the Egyptian lamps, seeing that they were well filled with the cedar oil, and that the wicks were adjusted and in good order. We lighted and tested them one by one, and left them ready so that they would light at once and evenly. When this was done we had a general look round; and fixed all in readiness for our work at night.

All this had taken time, and we were I think all surprised when as we emerged from the cave we heard the great clock in the hall chime four.

We had a late lunch, a thing possible without trouble in the present state of our commissariat arrangements. After it, by Mr. Trelawny's advice, we separated; each to prepare in our own way for the strain of the coming night. Margaret looked pale and somewhat overwrought, so I advised her to lie down and try to sleep. She promised that she would. The abstraction which had been upon her fitfully all day lifted for the time; with all her old sweetness and loving delicacy she kissed me good-bye for the present! With the sense of happiness which this gave me I went out for a walk on the cliffs. I did not want to think; and I had an instinctive feeling that fresh air and God's sunlight, and the myriad beauties of the works of His hand would be the best preparation of fortitude for what was to come.

When I got back, all the party were assembling for a late tea. Coming fresh from the exhilaration of nature, it struck me as almost comic that we, who were nearing the end of so strange—almost monstrous—an undertaking, should be yet bound by the needs and habits of our lives.

All the men of the party were grave; the time of seclusion, even if it had given them rest, had also given opportunity for thought. Margaret was bright, almost buoyant; but I missed about her something of her usual spontaneity. Towards myself there was a shadowy air of reserve, which brought back something of my suspicion. When tea was over, she went out of the room; but returned in a minute with the roll of drawing which she had taken with her earlier in the day. Coming close to Mr. Trelawny, she said:

"Father, I have been carefully considering what you said today about the hidden meaning of those suns and hearts and 'Ka's', and I have been examining the drawings again."

"And with what result, my child?" asked Mr. Trelawny eagerly.

"There is another reading possible!"

"And that?" His voice was now tremulous with anxiety. Margaret spoke with a strange ring in her voice; a ring that cannot be, unless there is the consciousness of truth behind it:

"It means that at the sunset the 'Ka' is to enter the 'Ab'; and it is only at the sunrise that it will leave it!"

"Go on!" said her father hoarsely.

"It means that for this night the Queen's Double, which is otherwise free, will remain in her heart, which is mortal and cannot leave its prison-place in the mummy-shrouding. It means that when the sun has dropped into the sea, Queen Tera will cease to exist as a conscious power, till sunrise; unless the Great Experiment can recall her to waking life. It means that there will be nothing whatever for you or others to fear from her in such way as we have all cause to remember. Whatever change may come from the working of the Great Experiment, there can come none from the poor, helpless, dead woman who has waited all those centuries for this night; who has given up to the coming hour all the freedom of eternity, won in the old way, in hope of a new life in a new world such as she longed for...!" She stopped suddenly. As she had gone on speaking there had come with her words a strange pathetic, almost pleading, tone which touched me to the quick. As she stopped, I could see, before she turned away her head, that her eyes were full of tears.

For once the heart of her father did not respond to her feeling. He looked exultant, but with a grim masterfulness which reminded me of the set look of his stern face as he had lain in the trance. He did not offer any consolation to his daughter in her sympathetic pain. He only said:

"We may test the accuracy of your surmise, and of her feeling, when the time comes!" Having said so, he went up the stone stairway and into his own room. Margaret's face had a troubled look as she gazed after him.

Strangely enough her trouble did not as usual touch me to the quick.

When Mr. Trelawny had gone, silence reigned. I do not think that any of us wanted to talk. Presently Margaret went to her room, and I went out on the terrace over the sea. The fresh air and the beauty of all before helped to restore the good spirits which I had known earlier in the day. Presently I felt myself actually rejoicing in the belief that the danger which I had feared from the Queen's violence on the coming night was obviated. I believed in Margaret's belief so thoroughly that it did not occur to me to dispute her reasoning. In a lofty frame of mind, and with less anxiety than I had felt for days, I went to my room and lay down on the sofa.

I was awaked by Corbeck calling to me, hurriedly:

"Come down to the cave as quickly as you can. Mr. Trelawny wants to see us all there at once. Hurry!"

I jumped up and ran down to the cave. All were there except Margaret, who came immediately after me carrying Silvio in her arms. When the cat saw his old enemy he struggled to get down; but Margaret held him fast and soothed him. I looked at my watch. It was close to eight.

When Margaret was with us her father said directly, with a quiet insistence which was new to me:

"You believe, Margaret, that Queen Tera has voluntarily undertaken to give up her freedom for this night? To become a mummy and nothing more, till the Experiment has been completed? To be content that she shall be powerless under all and any circumstances until after all is over and the act of resurrection has been accomplished, or the effort has failed?" After a pause Margaret answered in a low voice:

"Yes!"

In the pause her whole being, appearance, expression, voice, manner had changed. Even Silvio noticed it, and with a violent effort wriggled away from her arms; she did not seem to notice the act. I expected that the cat, when he had achieved his freedom, would have attacked the mummy; but on this occasion he did not. He seemed too cowed to approach it. He shrunk away, and with a piteous "miaou" came over and rubbed himself against my ankles. I took him up in my arms, and he nestled there content. Mr. Trelawny spoke again:

"You are sure of what you say! You believe it with all your soul?" Margaret's face had lost the abstracted look; it now seemed illuminated with the devotion of one to whom is given to speak of great things. She answered in a voice which, though quiet, vibrated with conviction:

"I know it! My knowledge is beyond belief!" Mr. Trelawny spoke again:

"Then you are so sure, that were you Queen Tera herself, you would be willing to prove it in any way that I might suggest?"

"Yes, any way!" the answer rang out fearlessly. He spoke again, in a voice in which was no note of doubt:

"Even in the abandonment of your Familiar to death—to annihilation."

She paused, and I could see that she suffered—suffered horribly. There was in her eyes a hunted look, which no man can, unmoved, see in the eyes of his beloved. I was about to interrupt, when her father's eyes, glancing round with a fierce determination, met mine. I stood silent, almost spellbound; so also the other men. Something was going on before us which we did not understand!

With a few long strides Mr. Trelawny went to the west side of the cave and tore back the shutter which obscured the window. The cool air blew in, and the sunlight streamed over them both, for Margaret was now by his side. He pointed to where the sun was sinking into the sea in a halo of golden fire, and his face was as set as flint. In a voice whose absolute uncompromising hardness I shall hear in my ears at times till my dying day, he said:

"Choose! Speak! When the sun has dipped below the sea, it will be too late!" The glory of the dying sun seemed to light up Margaret's face, till it shone as if lit from within by a noble light, as she answered:

"Even that!"

Then stepping over to where the mummy cat stood on the little table, she placed her hand on it. She had now left the sunlight, and the shadows looked dark and deep over her. In a clear voice she said:

"Were I Tera, I would say 'Take all I have! This night is for the Gods alone!'"

As she spoke the sun dipped, and the cold shadow suddenly fell on us. We all stood still for a while. Silvio jumped from my arms and ran over to his mistress, rearing himself up against her dress as if asking to be lifted. He took no notice whatever of the mummy now.

Margaret was glorious with all her wonted sweetness as she said sadly:

"The sun is down, Father! Shall any of us see it again? The night of nights is come!"

Chapter XIX - The Great Experiment

If any evidence had been wanted of how absolutely one and all of us had come to believe in the spiritual existence of the Egyptian Queen, it would have been found in the change which in a few minutes had been effected in us by the statement of voluntary negation made, we all believed, through Margaret. Despite the coming of the fearful ordeal, the sense of which it was impossible to forget, we looked and acted as though a great relief had come to us. We had indeed lived in such a state of terrorism during the days when Mr. Trelawny was lying in a trance that the feeling had bitten deeply into us. No one knows till he has experienced it, what it is to be in constant dread of some unknown danger which may come at any time and in any form.

The change was manifested in different ways, according to each nature. Margaret was sad. Doctor Winchester was in high spirits, and keenly observant; the process of thought which had served as an antidote to fear, being now relieved from this duty, added to his intellectual enthusiasm. Mr. Corbeck seemed to be in a retrospective rather than a speculative mood. I was myself rather inclined to be gay; the relief from certain anxiety regarding Margaret was sufficient for me for the time.

As to Mr. Trelawny he seemed less changed than any. Perhaps this was only natural, as he had had in his mind the intention for so many years of doing that in which we were tonight engaged, that any event connected with it could only seem to him as an episode, a step to the end. His was that commanding nature which looks so to the end of an undertaking that all else is of secondary importance. Even now, though his terrible sternness relaxed under the relief from the strain, he never flagged nor faltered for a moment in his purpose. He asked us men to come with him; and going to the hall we presently managed to lower into the cave an oak table, fairly long and not too wide, which stood against the wall in the hall. This we placed under the strong cluster of electric lights in the middle of the cave. Margaret looked on for a while; then all at once her face blanched, and in an agitated voice she said:

"What are you going to do, Father?"

"To unroll the mummy of the cat! Queen Tera will not need her Familiar tonight. If she should want him, it might be dangerous to us; so we shall make him safe. You are not alarmed, dear?"

"Oh no!" she answered quickly. "But I was thinking of my Silvio, and how I should feel if he had been the mummy that was to be unswathed!"

Mr. Trelawny got knives and scissors ready, and placed the cat on the table. It was a grim beginning to our work; and it made my heart sink when I thought of what might happen in that lonely house in the mid-gloom of the night. The sense of loneliness and isolation from the world was increased by the moaning of the wind which had now risen ominously, and by the beating of waves on the rocks below. But we had too grave a task before us to be swayed by external manifestations: the unrolling of the mummy began.

There was an incredible number of bandages; and the tearing sound—they being stuck fast to each other by bitumen and gums and spices—and the little cloud of red pungent dust that arose, pressed on the senses of all of us. As the last wrappings came away, we saw the animal seated before us. He was all hunkered up; his hair and teeth and claws were complete. The eyes were closed, but the eyelids had not the fierce look which I expected. The whiskers had been pressed down on the side of the face by the bandaging; but when the pressure was taken away they stood out, just as they would have done in life. He was a magnificent creature, a tiger-cat of great size. But as we looked at him, our first glance of admiration changed to one of fear, and a shudder ran through each one of us; for here was a confirmation of the fears which we had endured.

His mouth and his claws were smeared with the dry, red stains of recent blood!

Doctor Winchester was the first to recover; blood in itself had small disturbing quality for him. He had taken out his magnifying-glass and was examining the stains on the cat's mouth. Mr. Trelawny breathed loudly, as though a strain had been taken from him.

"It is as I expected," he said. "This promises well for what is to follow."

By this time Doctor Winchester was looking at the red stained paws. "As I expected!" he said. "He has seven claws, too!" Opening his pocket-book, he took out the piece of blotting-paper marked by Silvio's claws, on which was also marked in pencil a diagram of the cuts made on Mr. Trelawny's wrist. He placed the paper under the mummy cat's paw. The marks fitted exactly.

When we had carefully examined the cat, finding, however, nothing strange about it but its wonderful preservation, Mr. Trelawny lifted it from the table. Margaret started forward, crying out:

"Take care, Father! Take care! He may injure you!"

"Not now, my dear!" he answered as he moved towards the stairway. Her face fell. "Where are you going?" she asked in a faint voice.

"To the kitchen," he answered. "Fire will take away all danger for the future; even an astral body cannot materialise from ashes!" He signed to us to follow him. Margaret turned away with a sob. I went to her; but she motioned me back and whispered:

"No, no! Go with the others. Father may want you. Oh! it seems like murder! The poor Queen's pet...!" The tears were dropping from under the fingers that covered her eyes.

In the kitchen was a fire of wood ready laid. To this Mr. Trelawny applied a match; in a few seconds the kindling had caught and the flames leaped. When the fire was solidly ablaze, he threw the body of the cat into it. For a few seconds it lay a dark mass amidst the flames, and the room was rank with the smell of burning hair. Then the dry body caught fire too. The inflammable substances used in embalming became new fuel, and the flames roared. A few minutes of fierce conflagration; and then we breathed freely. Queen Tera's Familiar was no more!

When we went back to the cave we found Margaret sitting in the dark. She had switched off the electric light, and only a faint glow of the evening light came through the narrow openings. Her father went quickly over to her and put his arms round her in a loving protective way. She laid her head on his shoulder for a minute and seemed comforted. Presently she called to me:

"Malcolm, turn up the light!" I carried out her orders, and could see that, though she had been crying, her eyes were now dry. Her father saw it too and looked glad. He said to us in a grave tone:

"Now we had better prepare for our great work. It will not do to leave anything to the last!" Margaret must have had a suspicion of what was coming, for it was with a sinking voice that she asked:

"What are you going to do now?" Mr. Trelawny too must have had a suspicion of her feelings, for he answered in a low tone:

"To unroll the mummy of Queen Tera!" She came close to him and said pleadingly in a whisper:

"Father, you are not going to unswathe her! All you men...! And in the glare of light!"

"But why not, my dear?"

"Just think, Father, a woman! All alone! In such a way! In such a place! Oh! it's cruel, cruel!" She was manifestly much overcome. Her cheeks were flaming red, and her eyes were full of indignant tears. Her father saw her distress; and, sympathising with it, began to comfort her. I was moving off; but he signed to me to stay. I took it that after the usual manner of men he wanted help on such an occasion, and man-like wished to throw on someone else the task of dealing with a woman in indignant distress. However, he began to appeal first to her reason:

"Not a woman, dear; a mummy! She has been dead nearly five thousand years!"

"What does that matter? Sex is not a matter of years! A woman is a woman, if she had been dead five thousand centuries! And you expect her to arise out of that long sleep! It could not be real death, if she is to rise out of it! You have led me to believe that she will come alive when the Coffer is opened!"

"I did, my dear; and I believe it! But if it isn't death that has been the matter with her all these years, it is something uncommonly like it. Then again, just think; it was men who embalmed her. They didn't have women's rights or lady doctors in ancient Egypt, my dear! And besides," he went on more freely, seeing that she was accepting his argument, if not yielding to it, "we men are accustomed to such things. Corbeck and I have unrolled a hundred mummies; and there were as many women as men amongst them. Doctor Winchester in his work has had to deal with women as well of men, till custom has made him think nothing of sex. Even Ross has in his work as a barrister..." He stopped suddenly.

"You were going to help too!" she said to me, with an indignant look.

I said nothing; I thought silence was best. Mr. Trelawny went on hurriedly; I could see that he was glad of interruption, for the part of his argument concerning a barrister's work was becoming decidedly weak:

"My child, you will be with us yourself. Would we do anything which would hurt or offend you? Come now! be reasonable! We are not at a pleasure party. We are all grave men, entering gravely on an experiment which may unfold the wisdom of old times, and enlarge human knowledge indefinitely; which may put the minds of men on new tracks of thought and research. An experiment," as he went on his voice deepened, "which may be fraught with death to any one of us—to us all! We know from what has been, that there are, or may be, vast and unknown dangers ahead of us, of which none in the house today may ever see the end. Take it, my child, that we are not acting lightly; but with all the gravity of deeply earnest men! Besides, my dear, whatever feelings you or any of us may have on the subject, it is necessary for the success of the experiment to unswathe her. I think that under any circumstances it would be necessary to remove the wrappings before she became again a live human being instead of a spiritualised corpse with an astral body. Were her original intention carried out, and did she come to new life within her mummy wrappings, it might be to exchange a coffin for a grave! She would die the death of the buried alive! But now, when she has voluntarily abandoned for the time her astral power, there can be no doubt on the subject."

Margaret's face cleared. "All right, Father!" she said as she kissed him. "But oh! it seems a horrible indignity to a Queen, and a woman."

I was moving away to the staircase when she called me:

"Where are you going?" I came back and took her hand and stroked it as I answered:

"I shall come back when the unrolling is over!" She looked at me long, and a faint suggestion of a smile came over her face as she said:

"Perhaps you had better stay, too! It may be useful to you in your work as a barrister!" She smiled out as she met my eyes: but in an instant she changed. Her face grew grave, and deadly white. In a far away voice she said:

"Father is right! It is a terrible occasion; we need all to be serious over it. But all the same—nay, for that very reason you had better stay, Malcolm! You may be glad, later on, that you were present tonight!"

My heart sank down, down, at her words; but I thought it better to say nothing. Fear was stalking openly enough amongst us already!

By this time Mr. Trelawny, assisted by Mr. Corbeck and Doctor Winchester, had raised the lid of the ironstone sarcophagus which contained the mummy of the Queen. It was a large one; but it was none too big. The mummy was both long and broad and high; and was of such weight that it was no easy task, even for the four of us, to lift it out. Under Mr. Trelawny's direction we laid it out on the table prepared for it.

Then, and then only, did the full horror of the whole thing burst upon me! There, in the full glare of the light, the whole material and sordid side of death seemed staringly real. The outer wrappings, torn and loosened by rude touch, and with the colour either darkened by dust or worn light by friction, seemed creased as by rough treatment; the jagged edges of the wrapping-cloths looked fringed; the painting was patchy, and the varnish chipped. The coverings were evidently many, for the bulk was great. But through all, showed that unhidable human figure, which seems to look more horrible when partially concealed than at any other time. What was before us was Death, and nothing else. All the romance and sentiment of fancy had disappeared. The two elder men, enthusiasts who had often done such work, were not disconcerted; and Doctor Winchester seemed to hold himself in a business-like attitude, as if before the operating-table. But I felt low-spirited, and miserable, and ashamed; and besides I was pained and alarmed by Margaret's ghastly pallor.

Then the work began. The unrolling of the mummy cat had prepared me somewhat for it; but this was so much larger, and so infinitely more elaborate, that it seemed a different thing. Moreover, in addition to the ever present sense of death and humanity, there was a feeling of something finer in all this. The cat had been embalmed with coarser materials; here, all, when once the outer coverings were removed, was more delicately done. It seemed as if only the finest gums and spices had been used in this embalming. But there were the same surroundings, the same attendant red dust and pungent presence of bitumen; there was the same sound of rending which marked the tearing away of the bandages. There were an enormous number of these, and their bulk when opened was great. As the men unrolled them, I grew more and more excited. I did not take a part in it myself; Margaret had looked at me gratefully as I drew back. We clasped hands, and held each other hard. As the unrolling went on, the wrappings became finer, and the smell less laden with bitumen, but more pungent. We all, I think, began to feel it as though it caught or touched us in some special way. This, however, did not interfere with the work; it went on uninterruptedly. Some of the inner wrappings bore symbols or pictures. These were done sometimes wholly in pale green colour, sometimes in many colours; but always with a prevalence of green. Now and again Mr. Trelawny or Mr. Corbeck would point out some special drawing before laying the bandage on the pile behind them, which kept growing to a monstrous height.

At last we knew that the wrappings were coming to an end. Already the proportions were reduced to those of a normal figure of the manifest height of the Queen, who was more than average height. And as the end drew nearer, so Margaret's pallor grew; and her heart beat more and more wildly, till her breast heaved in a way that frightened me.

Just as her father was taking away the last of the bandages, he happened to look up and caught the pained and anxious look of her pale face. He paused, and taking her concern to be as to the outrage on modesty, said in a comforting way:

"Do not be uneasy, dear! See! there is nothing to harm you. The Queen has on a robe.—Ay, and a royal robe, too!"

The wrapping was a wide piece the whole length of the body. It being removed, a profusely full robe of white linen had appeared, covering the body from the throat to the feet.

And such linen! We all bent over to look at it.

Margaret lost her concern, in her woman's interest in fine stuff. Then the rest of us looked with admiration; for surely such linen was never seen by the eyes of our age. It was as fine as the finest silk. But never was spun or woven silk which lay in such gracious folds, constrict though they were by the close wrappings of the mummy cloth, and fixed into hardness by the passing of thousands of years.

Round the neck it was delicately embroidered in pure gold with tiny sprays of sycamore; and round the feet, similarly worked, was an endless line of lotus plants of unequal height, and with all the graceful abandon of natural growth.

Across the body, but manifestly not surrounding it, was a girdle of jewels. A wondrous girdle, which shone and glowed with all the forms and phases and colours of the sky!

The buckle was a great yellow stone, round of outline, deep and curved, as if a yielding globe had been pressed down. It shone and glowed, as though a veritable sun lay within; the rays of its light seemed to strike out and illumine all round. Flanking it were two great moonstones of lesser size, whose glowing, beside the glory of the sun-stone, was like the silvery sheen of moonlight.

And then on either side, linked by golden clasps of exquisite shape, was a line of flaming jewels, of which the colours seemed to glow. Each of these stones seemed to hold a living star, which twinkled in every phase of changing light.

Margaret raised her hands in ecstasy. She bent over to examine more closely; but suddenly drew back and stood fully erect at her grand height. She seemed to speak with the conviction of absolute knowledge as she said:

"That is no cerement! It was not meant for the clothing of death! It is a marriage robe!"

Mr. Trelawny leaned over and touched the linen robe. He lifted a fold at the neck, and I knew from the quick intake of his breath that something had surprised him. He lifted yet a little more; and then he, too, stood back and pointed, saying:

"Margaret is right! That dress is not intended to be worn by the dead! See! her figure is not robed in it. It is but laid upon her." He lifted the zone of jewels and handed it to Margaret. Then with both hands he raised the ample robe, and laid it across the arms which she extended in a natural impulse. Things of such beauty were too precious to be handled with any but the greatest care.

We all stood awed at the beauty of the figure which, save for the face cloth, now lay completely nude before us. Mr. Trelawny bent over, and with hands that trembled slightly, raised this linen cloth which was of the same fineness as the robe. As he stood back and the whole glorious beauty of the Queen was revealed, I felt a rush of shame sweep over me. It was not right that we should be there, gazing with irreverent eyes on such unclad beauty: it was indecent; it was almost sacrilegious! And yet the white wonder of that beautiful form was something to dream of. It was not like death at all; it was like a statue carven in ivory by the hand of a Praxiteles. There was nothing of that horrible shrinkage which death seems to effect in a moment. There was none of the wrinkled toughness which seems to be a leading characteristic of most mummies. There was not the shrunken attenuation of a body dried in the sand, as I had seen before in museums. All the pores of the body seemed to have been preserved in some wonderful way. The flesh was full and round, as in a living person; and the skin was as smooth as satin. The colour seemed extraordinary. It was like ivory, new ivory; except where the right arm, with shattered, bloodstained wrist and missing hand had lain bare to exposure in the sarcophagus for so many tens of centuries.

With a womanly impulse; with a mouth that drooped with pity, with eyes that flashed with anger, and cheeks that flamed, Margaret threw over the body the beautiful robe which lay across her arm. Only the face was then to be seen. This was more startling even than the body, for it seemed not dead, but alive. The eyelids were closed; but the long, black, curling lashes lay over on the cheeks. The nostrils, set in grave pride, seemed to have the repose which, when it is seen in life, is greater than the repose of death. The full, red lips, though the mouth was not open, showed the tiniest white line of pearly teeth within. Her hair, glorious in quantity and glossy black as the raven's wing, was piled in great masses over the white forehead, on which a few curling tresses strayed like tendrils. I was amazed at the likeness to Margaret, though I had had my mind prepared for this by Mr. Corbeck's quotation of her father's statement. This woman—I could not think of her as a mummy or a corpse—was the image of Margaret as my eyes had first lit on her. The likeness was increased by the jewelled ornament which she wore in her hair, the "Disk and Plumes", such as Margaret, too, had worn. It, too, was a glorious jewel; one noble pearl of moonlight lustre, flanked by carven pieces of moonstone.

Mr. Trelawny was overcome as he looked. He quite broke down; and when Margaret flew to him and held him close in her arms and comforted him, I heard him murmur brokenly:

"It looks as if you were dead, my child!"

There was a long silence. I could hear without the roar of the wind, which was now risen to a tempest, and the furious dashing of the waves far below. Mr. Trelawny's voice broke the spell:

"Later on we must try and find out the process of embalming. It is not like any that I know. There does not seem to have been any opening cut for the withdrawing of the viscera and organs, which apparently remain intact within the body. Then, again, there is no moisture in the flesh; but its place is supplied with something else, as though wax or stearine had been conveyed into the veins by some subtle process. I wonder could it be possible that at that time they could have used paraffin. It might have been, by some process that we know not, pumped into the veins, where it hardened!"

Margaret, having thrown a white sheet over the Queen's body, asked us to bring it to her own room, where we laid it on her bed. Then she sent us away, saying:

"Leave her alone with me. There are still many hours to pass, and I do not like to leave her lying there, all stark in the glare of light. This may be the Bridal she prepared for—the Bridal of Death; and at least she shall wear her pretty robes."

When presently she brought me back to her room, the dead Queen was dressed in the robe of fine linen with the embroidery of gold; and all her beautiful jewels were in place. Candles were lit around her, and white flowers lay upon her breast.

Hand in hand we stood looking at her for a while. Then with a sigh, Margaret covered her with one of her own snowy sheets. She turned away; and after softly closing the door of the room, went back with me to the others who had now come into the dining room. Here we all began to talk over the things that had been, and that were to be.

Now and again I could feel that one or other of us was forcing conversation, as if we were not sure of ourselves. The long wait was beginning to tell on our nerves. It was apparent to me that Mr. Trelawny had suffered in that strange trance more than we suspected, or than he cared to show. True, his will and his determination were as strong as ever; but the purely physical side of him had been weakened somewhat. It was indeed only natural that it should be. No man can go through a period of four days of absolute negation of life without being weakened by it somehow.

As the hours crept by, the time passed more and more slowly. The other men seemed to get unconsciously a little drowsy. I wondered if in the case of Mr. Trelawny and Mr. Corbeck, who had already been under the hypnotic influence of the Queen, the same dormance was manifesting itself. Doctor Winchester had periods of distraction which grew longer and more frequent as the time wore on.

As to Margaret, the suspense told on her exceedingly, as might have been expected in the case of a woman. She grew paler and paler still; till at last about midnight, I began to be seriously alarmed about her. I got her to come into the library with me, and tried to make her lie down on a sofa for a little while. As Mr. Trelawny had decided that the experiment was to be made exactly at the seventh hour after sunset, it would be as nearly as possible three o'clock in the morning when the great trial should be made. Even allowing a whole hour for the final preparations, we had still two hours of waiting to go through, and I promised faithfully to watch her and to awake her at any time she might name. She would not hear of it, however. She thanked me sweetly and smiled at me as she did so; but she assured me that she was not sleepy, and that she was quite able to bear up. That it was only the suspense and excitement of waiting that made her pale. I agreed perforce; but I kept her talking of many things in the library for more than an hour; so that at last, when she insisted on going back to her father's room I felt that I had at least done something to help her pass the time.

We found the three men sitting patiently in silence. With manlike fortitude they were content to be still when they felt they had done all in their power. And so we waited.

The striking of two o'clock seemed to freshen us all up. Whatever shadows had been settling over us during the long hours preceding seemed to lift at once; and we went about our separate duties alert and with alacrity. We looked first to the windows to see that they were closed, and we got ready our respirators to put them on when the time should be close at hand. We had from the first arranged to use them for we did not know whether some noxious fume might not come from the magic coffer when it should be opened. Somehow, it never seemed to occur to any of us that there was any doubt as to its opening.

Then, under Margaret's guidance, we carried the mummied body of Queen Tera from her room into her father's, and laid it on a couch. We put the sheet lightly over it, so that if she should wake she could at once slip from under it. The severed hand was placed in its true position on her breast, and under it the Jewel of Seven Stars which Mr. Trelawny had taken from the great safe. It seemed to flash and blaze as he put it in its place.

It was a strange sight, and a strange experience. The group of grave silent men carried the white still figure, which looked like an ivory statue when through our moving the sheet fell back, away from the lighted candles and the white flowers. We placed it on the couch in that other room, where the blaze of the electric lights shone on the great sarcophagus fixed in the middle of the room ready for the final experiment, the great experiment consequent on the researches during a lifetime of these two travelled scholars. Again, the startling likeness between Margaret and the mummy, intensified by her own extraordinary pallor, heightened the strangeness of it all. When all was finally fixed three-quarters of an hour had gone, for we were deliberate in all our doings. Margaret beckoned me, and I went out with her to bring in Silvio. He came to her purring. She took him up and handed him to me; and then did a thing which moved me strangely and brought home to me keenly the desperate nature of the enterprise on which we were embarked. One by one, she blew out the candles carefully and placed them back in their usual places. When she had finished she said to me:

"They are done with now. Whatever comes—life or death—there will be no purpose in their using now." Then taking Silvio into her arms, and pressing him close to her bosom where he purred loudly, we went back to the room. I closed the door carefully behind me, feeling as I did so a strange thrill as of finality. There was to be no going back now. Then we put on our respirators, and took our places as had been arranged. I was to stand by the taps of the electric lights beside the door, ready to turn them off or on as Mr. Trelawny should direct. Doctor Winchester was to stand behind the couch so that he should not be between the mummy and the sarcophagus; he was to watch carefully what should take place with regard to the Queen. Margaret was to be beside him; she held Silvio ready to place him upon the couch or beside it when she might think right. Mr. Trelawny and Mr. Corbeck were to attend to the lighting of the lamps. When the hands of the clock were close to the hour, they stood ready with their linstocks.

The striking of the silver bell of the clock seemed to smite on our hearts like a knell of doom. One! Two! Three!

Before the third stroke the wicks of the lamps had caught, and I had turned out the electric light. In the dimness of the struggling lamps, and after the bright glow of the electric light, the room and all within it took weird shapes, and all seemed in an instant to change. We waited with our hearts beating. I know mine did, and I fancied I could hear the pulsation of the others.

The seconds seemed to pass with leaden wings. It were as though all the world were standing still. The figures of the others stood out dimly, Margaret's white dress alone showing clearly in the gloom. The thick respirators which we all wore added to the strange appearance. The thin light of the lamps showed Mr. Trelawny's square jaw and strong mouth and the brown shaven face of Mr. Corbeck. Their eyes seemed to glare in the light. Across the room Doctor Winchester's eyes twinkled like stars, and Margaret's blazed like black suns. Silvio's eyes were like emeralds.

Would the lamps never burn up!

It was only a few seconds in all till they did blaze up. A slow, steady light, growing more and more bright, and changing in colour from blue to crystal white. So they stayed for a couple of minutes without change in the coffer; till at last there began to appear all over it a delicate glow. This grew and grew, till it became like a blazing jewel, and then like a living thing whose essence of life was light. We waited and waited, our hearts seeming to stand still.

All at once there was a sound like a tiny muffled explosion and the cover lifted right up on a level plane a few inches; there was no mistaking anything now, for the whole room was full of a blaze of light. Then the cover, staying fast at one side rose slowly up on the other, as though yielding to some pressure of balance. The coffer still continued to glow; from it began to steal a faint greenish smoke. I could not smell it fully on account of the respirator; but, even through that, I was conscious of a strange pungent odour. Then this smoke began to grow thicker, and to roll out in volumes of ever increasing density till the whole room began to get obscure. I had a terrible desire to rush over to Margaret, whom I saw through the smoke still standing erect behind the couch. Then, as I looked, I saw Doctor Winchester sink down. He was not unconscious; for he waved his hand back and forward, as though to forbid any one to come to him. At this time the figures of Mr. Trelawny and Mr. Corbeck were becoming indistinct in the smoke which rolled round them in thick billowy clouds. Finally I lost sight of them altogether. The coffer still continued to glow; but the lamps began to grow dim. At first I thought that their light was being overpowered by the thick black smoke; but presently I saw that they were, one by one, burning out. They must have burned quickly to produce such fierce and vivid flames.

I waited and waited, expecting every instant to hear the command to turn up the light; but none came. I waited still, and looked with harrowing intensity at the rolling billows of smoke still pouring out of the glowing casket, whilst the lamps sank down and went out one by one.

Finally there was but one lamp alight, and that was dimly blue and flickering. The only effective light in the room was from the glowing casket. I kept my eyes fixed toward Margaret; it was for her now that all my anxiety was claimed. I could just see her white frock beyond the still white shrouded figure on the couch. Silvio was troubled; his piteous mewing was the only sound in the room. Deeper and denser grew the black mist and its pungency began to assail my nostrils as well as my eyes. Now the volume of smoke coming from the coffer seemed to lessen, and the smoke itself to be less dense. Across the room I saw something white move where the couch was. There were several movements. I could just catch the quick glint of white through the dense smoke in the fading light; for now the glow of the coffer began quickly to subside. I could still hear Silvio, but his mewing came from close under; a moment later I could feel him piteously crouching on my foot.

Then the last spark of light disappeared, and through the Egyptian darkness I could see the faint line of white around the window blinds. I felt that the time had come to speak; so I pulled off my respirator and called out:

"Shall I turn up the light?" There was no answer; so before the thick smoke choked me, I called again but more loudly:

"Mr. Trelawny, shall I turn up the light?" He did not answer; but from across the room I heard Margaret's voice, sounding as sweet and clear as a bell:

"Yes, Malcolm!" I turned the tap and the lamps flashed out. But they were only dim points of light in the midst of that murky ball of smoke. In that thick atmosphere there was little possibility of illumination. I ran across to Margaret, guided by her white dress, and caught hold of her and held her hand. She recognised my anxiety and said at once:

"I am all right."

"Thank God!" I said. "How are the others? Quick, let us open all the windows and get rid of this smoke!" To my surprise, she answered in a sleepy way:

"They will be all right. They won't get any harm." I did not stop to inquire how or on what ground she formed such an opinion, but threw up the lower sashes of all the windows, and pulled down the upper. Then I threw open the door.

A few seconds made a perceptible change as the thick, black smoke began to roll out of the windows. Then the lights began to grow into strength and I could see the room. All the men were overcome. Beside the couch Doctor Winchester lay on his back as though he had sunk down and rolled over; and on the farther side of the sarcophagus, where they had stood, lay Mr. Trelawny and Mr. Corbeck. It was a relief to me to see that, though they were unconscious, all three were breathing heavily as though in a stupor. Margaret still stood behind the couch. She seemed at first to be in a partially dazed condition; but every instant appeared to get more command of herself. She stepped forward and helped me to raise her father and drag him close to a window. Together we placed the others similarly, and she flew down to the dining-room and returned with a decanter of brandy. This we proceeded to administer to them all in turn. It was not many minutes after we had opened the windows when all three were struggling back to consciousness. During this time my entire thoughts and efforts had been concentrated on their restoration; but now that this strain was off, I looked round the room to see what had been the effect of the experiment. The thick smoke had nearly cleared away; but the room was still misty and was full of a strange pungent acrid odour.

The great sarcophagus was just as it had been. The coffer was open, and in it, scattered through certain divisions or partitions wrought in its own substance, was a scattering of black ashes. Over all, sarcophagus, coffer and, indeed, all in the room, was a sort of black film of greasy soot. I went over to the couch. The white sheet still lay over part of it; but it had been thrown back, as might be when one is stepping out of bed.

But there was no sign of Queen Tera! I took Margaret by the hand and led her over. She reluctantly left her father to whom she was administering, but she came docilely enough. I whispered to her as I held her hand:

"What has become of the Queen? Tell me! You were close at hand, and must have seen if anything happened!" She answered me very softly:

"There was nothing that I could see. Until the smoke grew too dense I kept my eyes on the couch, but there was no change. Then, when all grew so dark that I could not see, I thought I heard a movement close to me. It might have been Doctor Winchester who had sunk down overcome; but I could not be sure. I thought that it might be the Queen waking, so I put down poor Silvio. I did not see what became of him; but I felt as if he had deserted me when I heard him mewing over by the door. I hope he is not offended with me!" As if in answer, Silvio came running into the room and reared himself against her dress, pulling it as though clamouring to be taken up. She stooped down and took him up and began to pet and comfort him.

I went over and examined the couch and all around it most carefully. When Mr. Trelawny and Mr. Corbeck recovered sufficiently, which they did quickly, though Doctor Winchester took longer to come round, we went over it afresh. But all we could find was a sort of ridge of impalpable dust, which gave out a strange dead odour. On the couch lay the jewel of the disk and plumes which the Queen had worn in her hair, and the Star Jewel which had words to command the Gods.

Other than this we never got clue to what had happened. There was just one thing which confirmed our idea of the physical annihilation of the mummy. In the sarcophagus in the hall, where we had placed the mummy of the cat, was a small patch of similar dust.

In the autumn Margaret and I were married. On the occasion she wore the mummy robe and zone and the jewel which Queen Tera had worn in her hair. On her breast, set in a ring of gold make like a twisted lotus stalk, she wore the strange Jewel of Seven Stars which held words to command the God of all the worlds. At the marriage the sunlight streaming through the chancel windows fell on it, and it seemed to glow like a living thing.

The graven words may have been of efficacy; for Margaret holds to them, and there is no other life in all the world so happy as my own.

We often think of the great Queen, and we talk of her freely. Once, when I said with a sigh that I was sorry she could not have waked into a new life in a new world, my wife, putting both her hands in mine and looking into my eyes with that far-away eloquent dreamy look which sometimes comes into her own, said lovingly:

"Do not grieve for her! Who knows, but she may have found the joy she sought? Love and patience are all that make for happiness in this world; or in the world of the past or of the future; of the living or the dead. She dreamed her dream; and that is all that any of us can ask!"

THE END

THE MAN

FORE-GLIMPSE

'I would rather be an angel than God!'

The voice of the speaker sounded clearly through the hawthorn tree. The young man and the young girl who sat together on the low tombstone looked at each other. They had heard the voices of the two children talking, but had not noticed what they said; it was the sentiment, not the sound, which roused their attention.

The girl put her finger to her lips to impress silence, and the man nodded; they sat as still as mice whilst the two children went on talking.

* * * * *

The scene would have gladdened a painter's heart. An old churchyard. The church low and square-towered, with long mullioned windows, the yellow-grey stone roughened by age and tender-hued with lichens. Round it clustered many tomb-stones tilted in all directions. Behind the church a line of gnarled and twisted yews.

The churchyard was full of fine trees. On one side a magnificent cedar; on the other a great copper beech. Here and there among the tombs and headstones many beautiful blossoming trees rose from the long green grass. The laburnum glowed in the June afternoon sunlight; the lilac, the hawthorn and the clustering meadowsweet which fringed the edge of the lazy stream mingled their heavy sweetness in sleepy fragrance. The yellow-grey crumbling walls were green in places with wrinkled harts-tongues, and were topped with sweet-williams and spreading house-leek and stone-crop and wild-flowers whose delicious sweetness made for the drowsy repose of perfect summer.

But amid all that mass of glowing colour the two young figures seated on the grey old tomb stood out conspicuously. The man was in conventional hunting-dress: red coat, white stock, black hat, white breeches, and top-boots. The girl was one of the richest, most glowing, and yet withal daintiest figures the eye of man could linger on. She was in riding-habit of hunting scarlet cloth; her black hat was tipped forward by piled-up masses red-golden hair. Round her neck was a white lawn scarf in the fashion of a man's hunting-stock, close fitting, and sinking into a gold-buttoned waistcoat of snowy twill. As she sat with the long skirt across her left arm her tiny black top-boots appeared underneath. Her gauntleted gloves were of white buckskin; her riding-whip was plaited of white leather, topped with ivory and banded with gold.

Even in her fourteenth year Miss Stephen Norman gave promise of striking beauty; beauty of a rarely composite character. In her the various elements of her race seemed to have cropped out. The firm-set jaw, with chin broader and more square than is usual in a woman, and the wide fine forehead and aquiline nose marked the high descent from Saxon through Norman. The glorious mass of red hair, of the true flame colour, showed the blood of another ancient ancestor of Northern race, and suited well with the voluptuous curves of the full, crimson lips. The purple-black eyes, the raven eyebrows and eyelashes, and the fine curve of the nostrils spoke of the Eastern blood of the far-back wife of the Crusader. Already she was tall for her age, with something of that lankiness which marks the early development of a really fine figure. Long-legged, long-necked, as straight as a lance, with head poised on the proud neck like a lily on its stem.

Stephen Norman certainly gave promise of a splendid womanhood. Pride, self-reliance and dominance were marked in every feature; in her bearing and in her lightest movement.

Her companion, Harold An Wolf, was some five years her senior, and by means of those five years and certain qualities had long stood in the position of her mentor. He was more than six feet two in height, deep-chested, broad-shouldered, lean-flanked, long-armed and big-handed. He had that appearance strength, with well-poised neck and forward set of the head, which marks the successful athlete.

The two sat quiet, listening. Through the quiet hum of afternoon came the voices of the two children. Outside the lich-gate, under the shade of the spreading cedar, the horses stamped occasionally as the flies troubled them. The grooms were mounted; one held the delicate-limbed white Arab, the other the great black horse.

'I would rather be an angel than God!'

The little girl who made the remark was an ideal specimen of the village Sunday-school child. Blue-eyed, rosy-cheeked, thick-legged, with her straight brown hair tied into a hard bunch with a much-creased, cherry-coloured ribbon. A glance at the girl would have satisfied the most sceptical as to her goodness. Without being in any way smug she was radiant with self-satisfaction and well-doing. A child of the people; an early riser; a help to her mother; a good angel to her father; a little mother to her brothers and sisters; cleanly in mind and body; self-reliant, full of faith, cheerful.

The other little girl was prettier, but of a more stubborn type; more passionate, less organised, and infinitely more assertive. Black-haired, black-eyed, swarthy, large-mouthed, snub-nosed; the very type and essence of unrestrained, impulsive, emotional, sensual nature. A seeing eye would have noted inevitable danger for the early years of her womanhood. She seemed amazed by the self-abnegation implied by her companion's statement; after a pause she replied:

'I wouldn't! I'd rather be up at the top of everything and give orders to the angels if I chose. I can't think, Marjorie, why you'd rather take orders than give them.'

'That's just it, Susan. I don't want to give orders; I'd rather obey them. It must be very terrible to have to think of things so much, that you want everything done your own way. And besides, I shouldn't like to have to be just!'

'Why not?' the voice was truculent, though there was wistfulness in it also.

'Oh Susan. Just fancy having to punish; for of course justice needs punishing as well as praising. Now an angel has such a nice time, helping people and comforting them, and bringing sunshine into dark places. Putting down fresh dew every morning; making the flowers grow, and bringing babies and taking care of them till their mothers find them. Of course God is very good and very sweet and very merciful, but oh, He must be very terrible.'

'All the same I would rather be God and able to do things!'

Then the children moved off out of earshot. The two seated on the tombstone looked after them. The first to speak was the girl, who said:

'That's very sweet and good of Marjorie; but do you know, Harold, I like Susie's idea better.'

'Which idea was that, Stephen?'

'Why, didn't you notice what she said: "I'd like to be God and be able to do things"?'

'Yes,' he said after a moment's reflection. 'That's a fine idea in the abstract; but I doubt of its happiness in the long-run.'

'Doubt of its happiness? Come now? what could there be better, after all? Isn't it good enough to be God? What more do you want?'

The girl's tone was quizzical, but her great black eyes blazed with some thought of sincerity which lay behind the fun. The young man shook his head with a smile of kindly tolerance as he answered:

'It isn't that—surely you must know it. I'm ambitious enough, goodness knows; but there are bounds to satisfy even me. But I'm not sure that the good little thing isn't right. She seemed, somehow, to hit a bigger truth than she knew: "fancy having to be just."'

'I don't see much difficulty in that. Anyone can be just!'

'Pardon me,' he answered, 'there is perhaps nothing so difficult in the whole range of a man's work.' There was distinct defiance in the girl's eyes as she asked:

'A man's work! Why a man's work? Isn't it a woman's work also?'

'Well, I suppose it ought to be, theoretically; practically it isn't.'

'And why not, pray?' The mere suggestion of any disability of woman as such aroused immediate antagonism. Her companion suppressed a smile as he answered deliberately:

'Because, my dear Stephen, the Almighty has ordained that justice is not a virtue women can practise. Mind, I do not say women are unjust. Far from it, where there are no interests of those dear to them they can be of a sincerity of justice that can make a man's blood run cold. But justice in the abstract is not an ordinary virtue: it has to be considerate as well as stern, and above all interest of all kinds and of every one—' The girl interrupted hotly:

'I don't agree with you at all. You can't give an instance where women are unjust. I don't mean of course individual instances, but classes of cases where injustice is habitual.' The suppressed smile cropped out now unconsciously round the man's lips in a way which was intensely aggravating to the girl.

'I'll give you a few,' he said. 'Did you ever know a mother just to a boy who beat her own boy at school?' The girl replied quietly:

'Ill-treatment and bullying are subjects for punishment, not justice.'

'Oh, I don't mean that kind of beating. I mean getting the prizes their own boys contended for; getting above them in class; showing superior powers in running or cricket or swimming, or in any of the forms of effort in which boys vie with each other.' The girl reflected, then she spoke:

'Well, you may be right. I don't altogether admit it, but I accept it as not on my side. But this is only one case.'

'A pretty common one. Do you think that Sheriff of Galway, who in default of a hangman hanged his son with his own hands, would have done so if he had been a woman?' The girl answered at once:

'Frankly, no. I don't suppose the mother was ever born who would do such a thing. But that is not a common case, is it? Have you any other?' The young man paused before he spoke:

'There is another, but I don't think I can go into it fairly with you.'

'Why not?'

'Well, because after all you know, Stephen, you are only a girl and you can't be expected to know.' The girl laughed:

'Well, if it's anything about women surely a girl, even of my tender age, must know something more of it, or be able to guess at, than any young man can. However, say what you think and I'll tell you frankly if I agree—that is if a woman can be just, in such a matter.'

'Shortly the point is this: Can a woman be just to another woman, or to a man for the matter of that, where either her own affection or a fault of the other is concerned?'

'I don't see any reason to the contrary. Surely pride alone should ensure justice in the former case, and the consciousness of superiority in the other.' The young man shook his head:

'Pride and the consciousness of superiority! Are they not much the same thing. But whether or no, if either of them has to be relied on, I'm afraid the scales of Justice would want regulating, and her sword should be blunted in case its edge should be turned back on herself. I have an idea that although pride might be a guiding principle with you individually, it would be a failure with the average. However, as it would be in any case a rule subject to many exceptions I must let it go.'

Harold looked at his watch and rose. Stephen followed him; transferring her whip into the hand which held up the skirt, she took his arm with her right hand in the pretty way in which a young girl clings to her elders. Together they went out at the lichgate. The groom drew over with the horses. Stephen patted hers and gave her a lump of sugar. Then putting her foot into Harold's ready hand she sprang lightly into the saddle. Harold swung himself into his saddle with the dexterity of an accomplished rider.

As the two rode up the road, keeping on the shady side under the trees, Stephen said quietly, half to herself, as if the sentence had impressed itself on her mind:

'To be God and able to do things!'

Harold rode on in silence. The chill of some vague fear was upon him.

CHAPTER I—STEPHEN

Stephen Norman of Normanstand had remained a bachelor until close on middle age, when the fact took hold of him that there was no immediate heir to his great estate. Whereupon, with his wonted decision, he set about looking for a wife.

He had been a close friend of his next neighbour, Squire Rowly, ever since their college days. They had, of course, been often in each other's houses, and Rowly's young sister—almost a generation younger than himself, and the sole fruit of his father's second marriage—had been like a little sister to him too. She had, in the twenty years which had elapsed, grown to be a sweet and beautiful young woman. In all the past years, with the constant opportunity which friendship gave of close companionship, the feeling never altered. Squire Norman would have been surprised had he been asked to describe Margaret Rowly and found himself compelled to present the picture of a woman, not a child.

Now, however, when his thoughts went womanward and wifeward, he awoke to the fact that Margaret came within the category of those he sought. His usual decision ran its course. Semi-brotherly feeling gave place to a stronger and perhaps more selfish feeling. Before he even knew it, he was head over ears in love with his pretty neighbour.

Norman was a fine man, stalwart and handsome; his forty years sat so lightly on him that his age never seemed to come into question in a woman's mind. Margaret had always liked him and trusted him; he was the big brother who had no duty in the way of scolding to do. His presence had always been a gladness; and the sex of the girl, first unconsciously then consciously, answered to the man's overtures, and her consent was soon obtained.

When in the fulness of time it was known that an heir was expected, Squire Norman took for granted that the child would be a boy, and held the idea so tenaciously that his wife, who loved him deeply, gave up warning and remonstrance after she had once tried to caution him against too fond a hope. She saw how bitterly he would be disappointed in case it should prove to be a girl. He was, however, so fixed on the point that she determined to say no more. After all, it might be a boy; the chances were equal. The Squire would not listen to any one else at all; so as the time went on his idea was more firmly fixed than ever. His arrangements were made on the base that he would have a son. The name was of course decided. Stephen had been the name of all the Squires of Normanstand for ages—as far back as the records went; and Stephen the new heir of course would be.

Like all middle-aged men with young wives he was supremely anxious as the time drew near. In his anxiety for his wife his belief in the son became passive rather than active. Indeed, the idea of a son was so deeply fixed in his mind that it was not disturbed even by his anxiety for the young wife he idolised.

When instead of a son a daughter was born, the Doctor and the nurse, who knew his views on the subject, held back from the mother for a little the knowledge of the sex. Dame Norman was so weak that the Doctor feared lest anxiety as to how her husband would bear the disappointment, might militate against her. Therefore the Doctor sought the Squire in his study, and went resolutely at his task.

'Well, Squire, I congratulate you on the birth of your child!' Norman was of course struck with the use of the word 'child'; but the cause of his anxiety was manifested by his first question:

'How is she, Doctor? Is she safe?' The child was after all of secondary importance! The Doctor breathed more freely; the question had lightened his task. There was, therefore, more assurance in his voice as he answered:

'She is safely through the worst of her trouble, but I am greatly anxious yet. She is very weak. I fear anything that might upset her.'

The Squire's voice came quick and strong:

'There must be no upset! And now tell me about my son?' He spoke the last word half with pride, half bashfully.

'Your son is a daughter!' There was silence for so long that the Doctor began to be anxious. Squire Norman sat quite still; his right hand resting on the writing-table before him became clenched so hard that the knuckles looked white and the veins red. After a long slow breath he spoke:

'She, my daughter, is well?' The Doctor answered with cheerful alacrity:

'Splendid!—I never saw a finer child in my life. She will be a comfort and an honour to you!' The Squire spoke again:

'What does her mother think? I suppose she's very proud of her?'

'She does not know yet that it is a girl. I thought it better not to let her know till I had told you.'

'Why?'

'Because—because—Norman, old friend, you know why! Because you had set your heart on a son; and I know how it would grieve that sweet young wife and mother to feel your disappointment. I want your lips to be the first to tell her; so that on may assure her of your happiness in that a daughter has been born to you.'

The Squire put out his great hand and laid it on the other's shoulder. There was almost a break in his voice as he said:

'Thank you, my old friend, my true friend, for your thought. When may I see her?'

'By right, not yet. But, as knowing your views, she may fret herself till she knows, I think you had better come at once.'

All Norman's love and strength combined for his task. As he leant over and kissed his young wife there was real fervour in his voice as he said:

'Where is my dear daughter that you may place her in my arms?' For an instant there came a chill to the mother's heart that her hopes had been so far disappointed; but then came the reaction of her joy that her husband, her baby's father, was pleased. There was a heavenly dawn of red on her pale face as she drew her husband's head down and kissed him.

'Oh, my dear,' she said, 'I am so happy that you are pleased!' The nurse took the mother's hand gently and held it to the baby as she laid it in the father's arms.

He held the mother's hand as he kissed the baby's brow.

The Doctor touched him gently on the arm and beckoned him away. He went with careful footsteps, looking behind as he went.

After dinner he talked with the Doctor on various matters; but presently he asked:

'I suppose, Doctor, it is no sort of rule that the first child regulates the sex of a family?'

'No, of course not. Otherwise how should we see boys and girls mixed in one family, as is nearly always the case. But, my friend,' he went on, 'you must not build hopes so far away. I have to tell you that your wife is far from strong. Even now she is not so well as I could wish, and there yet may be change.' The Squire leaped impetuously to his feet as he spoke quickly:

'Then why are we waiting here? Can nothing be done? Let us have the best help, the best advice in the world.' The Doctor raised his hand.

'Nothing can be done as yet. I have only fear.'

'Then let us be ready in case your fears should be justified! Who are the best men in London to help in such a case?' The Doctor mentioned two names; and within a few minutes a mounted messenger was galloping to Norcester, the nearest telegraph centre. The messenger was to arrange for a special train if necessary. Shortly afterwards the Doctor went again to see his patient. After a long absence he came back, pale and agitated. Norman felt his heart sink when he saw him; a groan broke from him as the Doctor spoke:

'She is much worse! I am in great fear that she may pass away before the morning!' The Squire's strong voice was clouded, with a hoarse veil as he asked:

'May I see her?'

'Not yet; at present she is sleeping. She may wake strengthened; in which case you may see her. But if not—'

'If not?'—the voice was not like his own.

'Then I shall send for you at once!' The Doctor returned to his vigil. The Squire, left alone, sank on his knees, his face in his hands; his great shoulders shook with the intensity of his grief.

An hour or more passed before he heard hurried steps. He sprang to the door:

'Well?'

'You had better come now.'

'Is she better?'

'Alas! no. I fear her minutes are numbered. School yourself, my dear old friend! God will help you in this bitter hour. All you can do now is to make her last moments happy.'

'I know! I know!' he answered in a voice so calm that his companion wondered.

When they came into the room Margaret was dozing. When her eyes opened and she found her husband beside her bed there spread over her face a glad look; which, alas! soon changed to one of pain. She motioned to him to bend down. He knelt and put his head beside her on the pillow; his arms went tenderly round her as though by his iron devotion and strength he would shield her from all harm. Her voice came very low and in broken gasps; she was summoning all her strength that she might speak:

'My dear, dear husband, I am so sad at leaving you! You have made me so happy, and I love you so! Forgive me, dear, for the pain I know you will suffer when I am gone! And oh, Stephen, I know you will cherish our little one—yours and mine—when I am gone. She will have no mother; you will have to be father and mother too.'

'I will hold her in my very heart's core, my darling, as I hold you!' He could hardly speak from emotion. She went on:

'And oh, my dear, you will not grieve that she is not a son to carry on your name?' And then a sudden light came into her eyes; and there was exultation in her weak voice as she said:

'She is to be our only one; let her be indeed our son! Call her the name we both love!' For answer he rose and laid his hand very, very tenderly on the babe as he said:

'This dear one, my sweet wife, who will carry your soul in her breast, will be my son; the only son I shall ever have. All my life long I shall, please Almighty God, so love her—our little Stephen—as you and I love each other!'

She laid her hand on his so that it touched at once her husband and her child. Then she raised the other weak arm, and placed it round his neck, and their lips met. Her soul went out in this last kiss.

CHAPTER II—THE HEART OF A CHILD

For some weeks after his wife's death Squire Norman was overwhelmed with grief. He made a brave effort, however, to go through the routine of his life; and succeeded so far that he preserved an external appearance of bearing his loss with resignation. But within, all was desolation.

Little Stephen had winning ways which sent deep roots into her father's heart. The little bundle of nerves which the father took into his arms must have realised with all its senses that, in all that it saw and heard and touched, there was nothing but love and help and protection. Gradually the trust was followed by expectation. If by some chance the father was late in coming to the nursery the child would grow impatient and cast persistent, longing glances at the door. When he came all was joy.

Time went quickly by, and Norman was only recalled to its passing by the growth of his child. Seedtime and harvest, the many comings of nature's growth were such commonplaces to him, and had been for so many years, that they made on him no impressions of comparison. But his baby was one and one only. Any change in it was not only in itself a new experience, but brought into juxtaposition what is with what was. The changes that began to mark the divergence of sex were positive shocks to him, for they were unexpected. In the very dawn of babyhood dress had no special import; to his masculine eyes sex was lost in youth. But, little by little, came the tiny changes which convention has established. And with each change came to Squire Norman the growing realisation that his child was a woman. A tiny woman, it is true, and requiring more care and protection and devotion than a bigger one; but still a woman. The pretty little ways, the eager caresses, the graspings and holdings of the childish hands, the little roguish smiles and pantings and flirtings were all but repetitions in little of the dalliance of long ago. The father, after all, reads in the same book in which the lover found his knowledge.

At first there was through all his love for his child a certain resentment of her sex. His old hope of a son had been rooted too deeply to give way easily. But when the conviction came, and with it the habit of its acknowledgment, there came also a certain resignation, which is the halting-place for satisfaction. But he never, not then nor afterwards, quite lost the old belief that Stephen was indeed a son. Could there ever have been a doubt, the remembrance of his wife's eyes and of her faint voice, of her hope and her faith, as she placed her baby in his arms would have refused it a resting-place. This belief tinged all his after-life and moulded his policy with regard to his girl's upbringing. If she was to be indeed his son as well as his daughter, she must from the first be accustomed to boyish as well as to girlish ways. This, in that she was an only child, was not a difficult matter to accomplish. Had she had brothers and sisters, matters of her sex would soon have found their own level.

There was one person who objected strongly to any deviation from the conventional rule of a girl's education. This was Miss Laetitia Rowly, who took after a time, in so far as such a place could be taken, that of the child's mother. Laetitia Rowly was a young aunt of Squire Rowly of Norwood; the younger sister of his father and some sixteen years his own senior. When the old Squire's second wife had died, Laetitia, then a conceded spinster of thirty-six, had taken possession of the young Margaret. When Margaret had married Squire Norman, Miss Rowly was well satisfied; for she had known Stephen Norman all her life. Though she could have wished a younger bridegroom for her darling, she knew it would be hard to get a better man or one of more suitable station in life. Also she knew that Margaret loved him, and the woman who had never found the happiness of mutual love in her own life found a pleasure in the romance of true love, even when the wooer was middle-aged. She had been travelling in the Far East when the belated news of Margaret's death came to her. When she had arrived home she announced her intention of taking care of Margaret's child, just as she had taken care of Margaret. For several reasons this could not be done in the same way. She was not old enough to go and live at Normanstand without exciting comment; and the Squire absolutely refused to allow that his daughter should live anywhere except in his own house. Educational supervision, exercised at such distance and so intermittently, could neither be complete nor exact.

Though Stephen was a sweet child she was a wilful one, and very early in life manifested a dominant nature. This was a secret pleasure to her father, who, never losing sight of his old idea that she was both son and daughter, took pleasure as well as pride out of each manifestation of her imperial will. The keen instinct of childhood, which reasons in feminine fashion, and is therefore doubly effective in a woman-child, early grasped the possibilities of her own will. She learned the measure of her nurse's foot and then of her father's; and so, knowing where lay the bounds of possibility of the achievement of her wishes, she at once avoided trouble and learned how to make the most of the space within the limit of her tether.

It is not those who 'cry for the Moon' who go furthest or get most in this limited world of ours. Stephen's pretty ways and unfailing good temper were a perpetual joy to her father; and when he found that as a rule her desires were reasonable, his wish to yield to them became a habit.

Miss Rowly seldom saw any individual thing to disapprove of. She it was who selected the governesses and who interviewed them from time to time as to the child's progress. Not often was there any complaint, for the little thing had such a pretty way of showing affection, and such a manifest sense of justified trust in all whom she encountered, that it would have been hard to name a specific fault.

But though all went in tears of affectionate regret, and with eminently satisfactory emoluments and references, there came an irregularly timed succession of governesses.

Stephen's affection for her 'Auntie' was never affected by any of the changes. Others might come and go, but there no change came. The child's little hand would steal into one of the old lady's strong ones, or would clasp a finger and hold it tight.

And then the woman who had never had a child of her own would feel, afresh each time, as though the child's hand was gripping her heart.

With her father she was sweetest of all. And as he seemed to be pleased when she did anything like a little boy, the habit of being like one insensibly grew on her.

An only child has certain educational difficulties. The true learning is not that which we are taught, but that which we take in for ourselves from experience and observation, and children's experiences and observation, especially of things other than repressive, are mainly of children. The little ones teach each other. Brothers and sisters are more with each other than are ordinary playmates, and in the familiarity of their constant intercourse some of the great lessons, so useful in after-life, are learned. Little Stephen had no means of learning the wisdom of give-and-take. To her everything was given, given bountifully and gracefully. Graceful acceptance of good things came to her naturally, as it does to one who is born to be a great lady. The children of the farmers in the neighbourhood, with whom at times she played, were in such habitual awe of the great house, that they were seldom sufficiently at ease to play naturally. Children cannot be on equal terms on special occasions with a person to whom they have been taught to bow or courtesy as a public habit. The children of neighbouring landowners, who were few and far between, and of the professional people in Norcester, were at such times as Stephen met them, generally so much on their good behaviour, that the spontaneity of play, through which it is that sharp corners of individuality are knocked off or worn down, did not exist.

And so Stephen learned to read in the Book of Life; though only on one side of it. At the age of six she had, though surrounded with loving care and instructed by skilled teachers, learned only the accepting side of life. Giving of course there was in plenty, for the traditions of Normanstand were royally benevolent; many a blessing followed the little maid's footsteps as she accompanied some timely aid to the sick and needy sent from the Squire's house. Moreover, her Aunt tried to inculcate certain maxims founded on that noble one that it is more blessed to give than to receive. But of giving in its true sense: the giving that which we want for ourselves, the giving that is as a temple built on the rock of self-sacrifice, she knew nothing. Her sweet and spontaneous nature, which gave its love and sympathy so readily, was almost a bar to education: it blinded the eyes that would have otherwise seen any defect that wanted altering, any evil trait that needed repression, any lagging virtue that required encouragement—or the spur.

CHAPTER III—HAROLD

Squire Norman had a clerical friend whose rectory of Carstone lay some thirty miles from Normanstand. Thirty miles is not a great distance for railway travel; but it is a long drive. The days had not come, nor were they ever likely to come, for the making of a railway between the two places. For a good many years the two men had met in renewal of their old University days. Squire Norman and Dr. An Wolf had been chums at Trinity, Cambridge, and the boyish friendship had ripened and lasted. When Harold An Wolf had put in his novitiate in a teeming Midland manufacturing town, it was Norman's influence which obtained the rectorship for his friend. It was not often that they could meet, for An Wolf's work, which, though not very exacting, had to be done single-handed, kept him to his post. Besides, he was a good scholar and eked out a small income by preparing a few pupils for public school. An occasional mid-week visit to Normanstand in the slack time of school work on the Doctor's part, and now and again a drive by Norman over to the rectory, returning the next day, had been for a good many years the measure of their meeting. Then An Wolf's marriage and the birth of a son had kept him closer to home. Mrs. An Wolf had been killed in a railway accident a couple of years after her only child had been born; and at the time Norman had gone over to render any assistance in his power to the afflicted man, and to give him what was under the circumstances his best gift, sympathy. After an interval of a few years the Squire's courtship and marriage, at which his old friend had assisted, had confined his activities to a narrower circle. The last time they had met was when An Wolf had come over to Norcester to aid in the burial of his friend's wife. In the process of years, however, the shadow over Norman's life had begun to soften; when his baby had grown to be something of a companion, they met again. Norman, 'who had never since his wife's death been able to tear himself, even for a night, away from Normanstand and Stephen, wrote to his old friend asking him to come to him. An Wolf gladly promised, and for a week of growing expectation the Squire looked forward to their meeting. Each found the other somewhat changed, in all but their old affection.

An Wolf was delighted with the little Stephen. Her dainty beauty seemed to charm him; and the child, seeming to realise what pleasure she was giving, exercised all her little winning ways. The rector, who knew more of children than did his, friend, told her as she sat on his knee of a very interesting person: his own son. The child listened, interested at first, then enraptured. She asked all kinds of questions; and the father's eyes brightened as he gladly answered the pretty sympathetic child, already deep in his heart for her father's sake. He told her about the boy who was so big and strong, and who could run and leap and swim and play cricket and football better than any other boy with whom he played. When, warmed himself by the keen interest of the little girl, and seeing her beautiful black eyes beginning to glow, he too woke to the glory of the time; and all the treasured moments of the father's lonely heart gave out their store. And the other father, thrilled with delight because of his baby's joy with, underlying all, an added pleasure that the little Stephen's interest was in sports that were for boys, looked on approvingly, now and again asking questions himself in furtherance of the child's wishes.

All the afternoon they sat in the garden, close to the stream that came out of the rock, and An Wolf told father's tales of his only son. Of the great cricket match with Castra Puerorum when he had made a hundred not out. Of the school races when he had won so many prizes. Of the swimming match in the Islam River when, after he had won the race and had dressed himself, he went into the water in his clothes to help some children who had upset a boat. How when Widow Norton's only son could not be found, he dived into the deep hole of the intake of the milldam of the great Carstone mills where Wingate the farrier had been drowned. And how, after diving twice without success, he had insisted on going down the third time though people had tried to hold him back; and how he had brought up in his arms the child all white and so near death that they had to put him in the ashes of the baker's oven before he could be brought back to life.

When her nurse came to take her to bed, she slid down from her father's knee and coming over to Dr. An Wolf, gravely held out her hand and said: 'Good-bye!' Then she kissed him and said:

'Thank you so much, Mr. Harold's daddy. Won't you come soon again, and tell us more?' Then she jumped again upon her father's knee and hugged him round the neck and kissed him, and whispered in his ear:

'Daddy, please make Mr. Harold's daddy when he comes again, bring Harold with him!'

After all it is natural for women to put the essence of the letter in the postscript!

Two weeks afterwards Dr. An Wolf came again and brought Harold with him. The time had gone heavily with little Stephen when she knew that Harold was coming with his father. Stephen had been all afire to see the big boy whose feats had so much interested her, and for a whole week had flooded Mrs. Jarrold with questions which she was unable to answer. At last the time came and she went out to the hall door with her father to welcome the guests. At the top of the great granite steps, down which in time of bad weather the white awning ran, she stood holding her father's hand and waving a welcome.

'Good morning, Harold! Good morning, Mr. Harold's daddy!'

The meeting was a great pleasure to both the children, and resulted in an immediate friendship. The small girl at once conceived a great admiration for the big, strong boy nearly twice her age and more than twice her size. At her time of life the convenances are not, and love is a thing to be spoken out at once and in the open. Mrs. Jarrold, from the moment she set eyes on him, liked the big kindly-faced boy who treated her like a lady, and who stood awkwardly blushing and silent in the middle of the nursery listening to the tiny child's proffers of affection. For whatever kind of love it is that boys are capable of, Harold had fallen into it. 'Calf-love' is a thing habitually treated with contempt. It may be ridiculous; but all the same it is a serious reality—to the calf.

Harold's new-found affection was as deep as his nature. An only child who had in his memory nothing of a mother's love, his naturally affectionate nature had in his childish days found no means of expression. A man child can hardly pour out his full heart to a man, even a father or a comrade; and this child had not, in a way, the consolations of other children. His father's secondary occupation of teaching brought other boys to the house and necessitated a domestic routine which had to be exact. There was no place for little girls in a boys' school; and though many of Dr. An Wolf's friends who were mothers made much of the pretty, quiet boy, and took him to play with their children, he never seemed to get really intimate with them. The equality of companionship was wanting. Boys he knew, and with them he could hold his own and yet be on affectionate terms. But girls were strange to him, and in their presence he was shy. With this lack of understanding of the other sex, grew up a sort of awe of it. His opportunities of this kind of study were so few that the view never could become rectified.

And so it was that from his boyhood up to his twelfth year, Harold's knowledge of girlhood never increased nor did his awe diminish. When his father had told him all about his visit to Normanstand and of the invitation which had been extended to him there came first awe, then doubt, then expectation. Between Harold and his father there was love and trust and sympathy. The father's married love so soon cut short found expression towards his child; and between them there had never been even the shadow of a cloud. When his father told him how pretty the little Stephen was, how dainty, how sweet, he began to picture her in his mind's eye and to be bashfully excited over meeting her.

His first glimpse of Stephen was, he felt, one that he never could forget. She had made up her mind that she would let Harold see what she could do. Harold could fly kites and swim and play cricket; she could not do any of these, but she could ride. Harold should see her pony, and see her riding him all by herself. And there would be another pony for Harold, a big, big, big one—she had spoken about its size herself to Topham, the stud-groom. She had coaxed her daddy into promising that after lunch she should take Harold riding. To this end she had made ready early. She had insisted on putting on the red riding habit which Daddy had given her for her birthday, and now she stood on the top of the steps all glorious in hunting pink, with the habit held over her arms, with the tiny hunting-hoots all shiny underneath. She had no hat on, and her beautiful hair of golden red shone in its glory. But even it was almost outshone by the joyous flush on her cheeks as she stood waving the little hand that did not hold Daddy's. She was certainly a picture to dream of! Her father's eyes lost nothing of her dainty beauty. He was so proud of her that he almost forgot to wish that she had been a boy. The pleasure he felt in her appearance was increased by the fact that her dress was his own idea.

During luncheon Stephen was fairly silent; she usually chattered all through as freely as a bird sings. Stephen was silent because the occasion was important. Besides, Daddy wasn't all alone, and therefore had not to be cheered up. Also—this in postscript form—Harold was silent! In her present frame of mind Harold could do no wrong, and what Harold did was right. She was unconsciously learning already a lesson from his presence.

CHAPTER III—HAROLD

That evening when going to bed she came to say good-night to Daddy. After she had kissed him she also kissed 'old Mr. Harold,' as she now called him, and as a matter of course kissed Harold also. He coloured up at once. It was the first time a girl had ever kissed him.

The next day from early morning until bed-time was one long joy to Stephen, and there were few things of interest that Harold had not been shown; there were few of the little secrets which had not been shared with him as they went about hand in hand. Like all manly boys Harold was good to little children and patient with them. He was content to follow Stephen about and obey all her behests. He had fallen in love with her to the very bottom of his boyish heart.

When the guests were going, Stephen stood with her father on the steps to see them off. When the carriage had swept behind the farthest point in the long avenue, and when Harold's cap waving from the window could no longer be seen, Squire Norman turned to go in, but paused in obedience to the unconscious restraint of Stephen's hand. He waited patiently till with a long sigh she turned to him and they went in together.

That night before she went to bed Stephen came and sat on her father's knee, and after sundry pattings and kissings whispered in his ear:

'Daddy, wouldn't it be nice if Harold could come here altogether? Couldn't you ask him to? And old Mr. Harold could come too. Oh, I wish he was here!'

CHAPTER IV—HAROLD AT NORMANSTAND

Two years afterwards a great blow fell upon Harold. His father, who had been suffering from repeated attacks of influenza, was, when in the low condition following this, seized with pneumonia, to which in a few days he succumbed. Harold was heart-broken. The affection which had been between him and his father had been so consistent that he had never known a time when it was not.

When Squire Norman had returned to the house with him after the funeral, he sat in silence holding the boy's hand till he had wept his heart out. By this time the two were old friends, and the boy was not afraid or too shy to break down before him. There was sufficient of the love of the old generation to begin with trust in the new.

Presently, when the storm was past and Harold had become his own man again, Norman said:

'And now, Harold, I want you to listen to me. You know, my dear boy, that I am your father's oldest friend, and right sure I am that he would approve of what I say. You must come home with me to live. I know that in his last hours the great concern of your dear father's heart would have been for the future of his boy. And I know, too, that it was a comfort to him to feel that you and I are such friends, and that the son of my dearest old friend would be as a son to me. We have been friends, you and I, a long time, Harold; and we have learned to trust, and I hope to love, one another. And you and my little Stephen are such friends already that your coming into the house will be a joy to us all. Why, long ago, when first you came, she said to me the night you went away: "Daddy, wouldn't it be nice if Harold could come here altogether?"'

And so Harold An Wolf came back with the Squire to Normanstand, and from that day on became a member of his house, and as a son to him. Stephen's delight at his coming was of course largely qualified by her sympathy with his grief; but it would have been hard to give him more comfort than she did in her own pretty way. Putting her lips to his she kissed him, and holding his big hand in both of her little ones, she whispered softly:

'Poor Harold! You and I should love each other, for we have both lost our mother. And now you have lost your father. But you must let my dear daddy be yours too!'

At this time Harold was between fourteen and fifteen years old. He was well educated in so far as private teaching went. His father had devoted much care to him, so that he was well grounded in all the Academic branches of learning. He was also, for his years, an expert in most manly exercises. He could ride anything, shoot straight, fence, run, jump or swim with any boy more than his age and size.

In Normanstand his education was continued by the rector. The Squire used often to take him with him when he went to ride, or fish, or shoot; frankly telling him that as his daughter was, as yet, too young to be his companion in these matters, he would act as her locum tenens. His living in the house and his helping as he did in Stephen's studies made familiarity perpetual. He was just enough her senior to command her childish obedience; and there were certain qualities in his nature which were eminently calculated to win and keep the respect of women as well as of men. He was the very incarnation of sincerity, and had now and again, in certain ways, a sublime self-negation which, at times, seemed in startling contrast to a manifestly militant nature. When at school he had often been involved in fights which were nearly always on matters of principle, and by a sort of unconscious chivalry he was generally found fighting on the weaker side. Harold's father had been very proud of his ancestry, which was Gothic through the Dutch, as the manifestly corrupted prefix of the original name implied, and he had gathered from a constant study of the Sagas something of the philosophy which lay behind the ideas of the Vikings.

This new stage of Harold's life made for quicker development than any which had gone before. Hitherto he had not the same sense of responsibility. To obey is in itself a relief; and as it is an actual consolation to weak natures, so it is only a retarding of the strong. Now he had another individuality to think of. There was in his own nature a vein of anxiety of which the subconsciousness of his own strength threw up the outcrop.

Little Stephen with the instinct of her sex discovered before long this weakness. For it is a weakness when any quality can be assailed or used. The using of a man's weakness is not always coquetry; but it is something very like it. Many a time the little girl, who looked up to and admired the big boy who could compel her to anything when he was so minded, would, for her own ends, work on his sense of responsibility, taking an elfin delight in his discomfiture.

The result of Stephen's harmless little coquetries was that Harold had occasionally either to thwart some little plan of daring, or else cover up its results. In either case her confidence in him grew, so that before long he became an established fact in her life, a being in whose power and discretion and loyalty she had absolute, blind faith. And this feeling seemed to grow with her own growth. Indeed at one time it came to be more than an ordinary faith. It happened thus:

The old Church of St. Stephen, which was the parish church of Normanstand, had a peculiar interest for the Norman family. There, either within the existing walls or those which had preceded them when the church was rebuilt by that Sir Stephen who was standard-bearer to Henry VI., were buried all the direct members of the line. It was an unbroken record of the inheritors since the first Sir Stephen, who had his place in the Domesday Book. Without, in the churchyard close to the church, were buried all such of the collaterals as had died within hail of Norcester. Some there were of course who, having achieved distinction in various walks of life, were further honoured by a resting-place within the chancel. The whole interior was full of records of the family. Squire Norman was fond of coming to the place; and often from the very beginning had taken Stephen with him. One of her earliest recollections was kneeling down with her father, who held her hand in his, whilst with the other he wiped the tears from his eyes, before a tomb sculptured beautifully in snowy marble. She never forgot the words he had said to her:

'You will always remember, darling, that your dear mother rests in this sacred place. When I am gone, if you are ever in any trouble come here. Come alone and open out your heart. You need never fear to ask God for help at the grave of your mother!' The child had been impressed, as had been many and many another of her race. For seven hundred years each child of the house of Norman had been brought alone by either parent and had heard some such words. The custom had come to be almost a family ritual, and it never failed to leave its impress in greater or lesser degree.

Whenever Harold had in the early days paid a visit to Normanstand, the church had generally been an objective of their excursions. He was always delighted to go. His love for his own ancestry made him admire and respect that of others; so that Stephen's enthusiasm in the matter was but another cord to bind him to her.

In one of their excursions they found the door into the crypt open; and nothing would do Stephen but that they should enter it. To-day, however, they had no light; but they arranged that on the morrow they would bring candles with them and explore the place thoroughly. The afternoon of the next day saw them at the door of the crypt with a candle, which Harold proceeded to light. Stephen looked on admiringly, and said in a half-conscious way, the half-consciousness being shown in the implication:

'You are not afraid of the crypt?'

'Not a bit! In my father's church there was a crypt, and I was in it several times.' As he spoke the memory of the last time he had been there swept over him. He seemed to see again the many lights, held in hands that were never still, making a grim gloom where the black shadows were not; to hear again the stamp and hurried shuffle of the many feet, as the great oak coffin was borne by the struggling mass of men down the steep stairway and in through the narrow door . . . And then the hush when voices faded away; and the silence seemed a real thing, as for a while he stood alone close to the dead father who had been all in all to him. And once again he seemed to feel the recall to the living world of sorrow and of light, when his inert hand was taken in the strong loving one of Squire Norman.

He paused and drew back.

'Why don't you go on?' she asked, surprised.

He did not like to tell her then. Somehow, it seemed out of place. He had often spoken to her of his father, and she had always been a sympathetic listener; but here, at the entrance of the grim vault, he did not wish to pain her with his own thoughts of sorrow and all the terrible memories which the similarity of the place evoked. And even whilst he hesitated there came to him a thought so laden with pain and fear that he rejoiced at the pause which gave it to him in time. It was in that very crypt that Stephen's mother had been buried, and had they two gone in, as they had intended, the girl might have seen her mother's coffin as he had seen his father's, but under circumstances which made him shiver. He had been, as he said, often in the crypt at Carstone; and well he knew the sordidness of the chamber of death. His imagination was alive as well as his memory; he shuddered, not for himself, but for Stephen. How could he allow the girl to suffer in such a way as she might, as she infallibly would, if it were made apparent to her in such a brutal way? How pitiful, how meanly pitiful, is the aftermath of death. Well he remembered how many a night he woke in an agony, thinking of how his father lay in that cold, silent, dust-strewn vault, in the silence and the dark, with never a ray of light or hope or love! Gone, abandoned, forgotten by all, save perhaps one heart which bled . . . He would save little Stephen, if he could, from such a memory. He would not give any reason for refusing to go in.

He blew out the candle, and turned the key in the lock, took it out, and put it in his pocket.

'Come, Stephen!' he said, 'let us go somewhere else. We will not go into the crypt to-day!'

'Why not?' The lips that spoke were pouted mutinously and the face was flushed. The imperious little lady was not at all satisfied to give up the cherished project. For a whole day and night she had, whilst waking, thought of the coming adventure; the thrill of it was not now to be turned to cold disappointment without even an explanation. She did not think that Harold was afraid; that would be ridiculous. But she wondered; and mysteries always annoyed her. She did not like to be at fault, more especially when other people knew. All the pride in her revolted.

'Why not?' she repeated more imperiously still.

Harold said kindly:

'Because, Stephen, there is really a good reason. Don't ask me, for I can't tell you. You must take it from me that I am right. You know, dear, that I wouldn't willingly disappoint you; and I know that you had set your heart on this. But indeed, indeed I have a good reason.'

Stephen was really angry now. She was amenable to reason, though she did not consciously know what reason was; but to accept some one else's reason blindfold was repugnant to her nature, even at her then age. She was about to speak angrily, but looking up she saw that Harold's mouth was set with marble firmness. So, after her manner, she acquiesced in the inevitable and said:

'All right! Harold.'

But in the inner recesses of her firm-set mind was a distinct intention to visit the vault when more favourable circumstances would permit.

CHAPTER V—THE CRYPT

It was some weeks before Stephen got the chance she wanted. She knew it would be difficult to evade Harold's observation, for the big boy's acuteness as to facts had impressed itself on her. It was strange that out of her very trust in Harold came a form of distrust in others. In the little matter of evading him she inclined to any one in whom there was his opposite, in whose reliability she instinctively mistrusted. 'There is nothing bad or good but thinking makes it so!' To enter that crypt, which had seemed so small a matter at first, had now in process of thinking and wishing and scheming become a thing to be much desired. Harold saw, or rather felt, that something was in the girl's mind, and took for granted that it had something to do with the crypt. But he thought it better not to say anything lest he should keep awake a desire which he hoped would die naturally.

One day it was arranged that Harold should go over to Carstone to see the solicitor who had wound up his father's business. He was to stay the night and ride back next day. Stephen, on hearing of the arrangement, so contrived matters that Master Everard, the son of a banker who had recently purchased an estate in the neighbourhood, was asked to come to play with her on the day when Harold left. It was holiday time at Eton, and he was at home. Stephen did not mention to Harold the fact of his coming; it was only from a chance allusion of Mrs. Jarrold before he went that he inferred it. He did not think the matter of sufficient importance to wonder why Stephen, who generally told him everything, had not mentioned this.

During their play, Stephen, after pledging him to secrecy, told Leonard of her intention of visiting the crypt, and asked him to help her in it. This was an adventure, and as such commended itself to the schoolboy heart. He entered at once into the scheme con amore; and the two discussed ways and means. Leonard's only regret was that he was associated with a little girl in such a project. It was something of a blow to his personal vanity, which was a large item in his moral equipment, that such a project should have been initiated by the girl and not by himself. He was to get possession of the key and in the forenoon of the next day he was to be waiting in the churchyard, when Stephen would join him as soon as she could evade her nurse. She was now more than eleven, and had less need of being watched than in her earlier years. It was possible, with strategy, to get away undiscovered for an hour.

* * * * *

CHAPTER V—THE CRYPT

At Carstone Harold got though what he had to do that same afternoon and arranged to start early in the morning for Normanstand. After an early breakfast he set out on his thirty-mile journey at eight o'clock. Littlejohn, his horse, was in excellent form, notwithstanding his long journey of the day before, and with his nose pointed for home, put his best foot foremost. Harold felt in great spirits. The long ride the day before had braced him physically, though there were on his journey times of great sadness when the thought of his father came back to him and the sense of loss was renewed with each thought of his old home. But youth is naturally buoyant. His visit to the church, the first thing on his arrival at Carstone, and his kneeling before the stone made sacred to his father's memory, though it entailed a silent gush of tears, did him good, and even seemed to place his sorrow farther away. When he came again in the morning before leaving Carstone there were no tears. There was only a holy memory which seemed to sanctify loss; and his father seemed nearer to him than ever.

As he drew near Normanstand he looked forward eagerly to seeing Stephen, and the sight of the old church lying far below him as he came down the steep road over Alt Hill, which was the short-cut from Norcester, set his mind working. His visit to the tomb of his own father made him think of the day when he kept Stephen from entering the crypt.

The keenest thought is not always conscious. It was without definite intention that when he came to the bridle-path Harold turned his horse's head and rode down to the churchyard. As he pushed open the door of the church he half expected to see Stephen; and there was a vague possibility that Leonard Everard might be with her.

The church was cool and dim. Coming from the hot glare the August sunshine it seemed, at the first glance, dark. He looked around, and a sense of relief came over him. The place was empty.

But even as he stood, there came a sound which made his heart grow cold. A cry, muffled, far away and full of anguish; a sobbing cry, which suddenly ceased.

It was the voice of Stephen. He instinctively knew where it came from; the crypt. Only for the experience he had had of her desire to enter the place, he would never have suspected that it was so close to him. He ran towards the corner where commenced the steps leading downward. As he reached the spot a figure came rushing up the steps. A boy in Eton jacket and wide collar, careless, pale, and agitated. It was Leonard Everard. Harold seized him as he came.

'Where is Stephen?' he cried in a quick, low voice.

'In the vault below there. She dropped her light and then took mine, and she dropped it too. Let me go! Let me go!' He struggled to get away; but Harold held him tight.

'Where are the matches?'

'In my pocket. Let me go! Let me go!'

'Give me them—this instant!' He was examining the frightened boy's waistcoat pockets as he spoke. When he had got the matches he let the boy go, and ran down the steps and through the open door into the crypt, calling out as he came:

'Stephen! Stephen dear, where are you? It is I—Harold!' There was no response; his heart seemed to grow cold and his knees to weaken. The match spluttered and flashed, and in the momentary glare he saw across the vault, which was not a large place, a white mass on the ground. He had to go carefully, lest the match should be blown out by the wind of his passage; but on coming close he saw that it was Stephen lying senseless in front of a great coffin which rested on a built-out pile of masonry. Then the match went out. In the flare of the next one he lit he saw a piece of candle lying on top of the coffin. He seized and lit it. He was able to think coolly despite his agitation, and knew that light was the first necessity. The bruised wick was slow to catch; he had to light another match, his last one, before it flamed. The couple of seconds that the light went down till the grease melted and the flame leaped again seemed of considerable length. When the lit candle was placed steadily on top of the coffin, and a light, dim, though strong enough to see with, spread around, he stooped and lifted Stephen in his arms. She was quite senseless, and so limp that a great fear came upon him that she might be dead. He did not waste time, but carried her across the vault where the door to the church steps stood out sharp against the darkness, and bore her up into the church. Holding her in one arm, with the other hand he dragged some long cushions from one of the pews and spread them on the floor; on these he laid her. His heart was smitten with love and pity as he looked. She was so helpless; so pitifully helpless! Her arms and legs were doubled up as though broken, disjointed; the white frock was smeared with patches of thick dust. Instinctively he stooped and pulled the frock down and straightened out the arms and feet. He knelt beside her, and felt if her heart was still beating, a great fear over him, a sick apprehension. A gush of thankful prayer came from his heart. Thank God! she was alive; he could feel her heart beat, though faintly underneath his hand. He started to his feet and ran towards the door, seizing his hat, which lay on a seat. He wanted it to bring back some water. As he passed out of the door he saw Leonard a little distance off, but took no notice of him. He ran to the stream, filled his hat with water, and brought it back. When he came into the church he saw Stephen, already partially restored, sitting up on the cushions with Leonard supporting her.

He was rejoiced; but somehow disappointed. He would rather Leonard had not been there. He remembered—he could not forget—the white face of the boy who fled out of the crypt leaving Stephen in a faint within, and who had lingered outside the church door whilst he ran for water. Harold came forward quickly and raised Stephen, intending to bring her into the fresh air. He had a shrewd idea that the sight of the sky and God's greenery would be the best medicine for her after her fright. He lifted her in his strong arms as he used to do when she was a very little child and had got tired in their walks together; and carried her to the door. She lent herself unconsciously to the movement, holding fast with her arm round his neck as she used to do. In her clinging was the expression of her trust in him. The little sigh with which she laid her head on his shoulder was the tribute to his masculine power, and her belief in it. Every instant her senses were coming back to her more and more. The veil of oblivion was passing from her half-closed eyes, as the tide of full remembrance swept in upon her. Her inner nature was expressed in the sequence of her emotions. Her first feeling was one of her own fault. The sight of Harold and his proximity recalled to her vividly how he had refused to go into the crypt, and how she had intentionally deceived him, negatively, as to her intention of doing that of which he disapproved. Her second feeling was one of justice; and was perhaps partially evoked by the sight of Leonard, who followed close as Harold brought her to the door. She did not wish to speak of herself or Harold before him; but she did not hesitate to speak of him to Harold:

'You must not blame Leonard. It was all my fault. I made him come!' Her generosity appealed to Harold. He was angry with the boy for being there at all; but more for his desertion of the girl in her trouble.

'I'm not blaming him for being with you!' he said simply. Leonard spoke at once. He had been waiting to defend himself, for that was what first concerned that young gentleman; next to his pleasure, his safety most appealed to him.

'I went to get help. You had let the candle drop; and how could I see in the dark? You would insist on looking at the plate on the coffin!'

A low moan broke from Stephen, a long, low, trembling moan which went to Harold's heart. Her head drooped over again on his shoulder; and she clung close to him as the memory of her shock came back to her. Harold spoke to Leonard over his shoulder in a low, fierce whisper, which Stephen did not seem to hear:

'There! that will do. Go away! You have done enough already. Go! Go!' he added more sternly, as the boy seemed disposed to argue. Leonard ran a few steps, then walked to the lich-gate, where he waited.

Stephen clung close to Harold in a state of agitation which was almost hysterical. She buried her face in his shoulder, sobbing brokenly:

'Oh, Harold! It was too awful. I never thought, never for a moment, that my poor dear mother was buried in the crypt. And when I went to look at the name on the coffin that was nearest to where I was, I knocked away the dust, and then I saw her name: "Margaret Norman, aetat 22." I couldn't bear it. She was only a girl herself, only just twice my age—lying there in that terrible dark place with all the thick dust and the spiders' webs. Oh, Harold, Harold! How shall I ever bear to think of her lying there, and that I shall never see her dear face? Never! Never!'

He tried to soothe her by patting and holding her hands. For a good while the resolution of the girl faltered, and she was but as a little child. Then her habitual strength of mind asserted itself. She did not ask Harold how she came to be out in the church instead of in the crypt when she recovered her senses. She seemed to take it for granted that Leonard had carried her out; and when she said how brave it had been of him, Harold, with his customary generosity, allowed her to preserve the belief. When they had made their way to the gate Leonard came up to them; but before he could speak Stephen had begun to thank him. He allowed her to do so, though the sight of Harold's mouth set in scorn, and his commanding eyes firmly fixed on him, made him grow hot and cold alternately. He withdrew without speaking; and took his way home with a heart full of bitterness and revengeful feelings.

In the park Stephen tried to dust herself, and then Harold tried to assist her. But her white dress was incurably soiled, the fine dust of the vault seemed to have got ingrained in the muslin. When she got to the house she stole upstairs, so that no one might notice her till she had made herself tidy.

The next day but one she took Harold for a walk in the afternoon. When they were quite alone and out of earshot she said:

'I have been thinking all night about poor mother. Of course I know she cannot be moved from the crypt. She must remain there. But there needn't be all that dust. I want you to come there with me some time soon. I fear I am afraid to go alone. I want to bring some flowers and to tidy up the place. Won't you come with me this time? I know now, Harold, why you didn't let me go in before. But now it is different. This is not curiosity. It is Duty and Love. Won't you come with me, Harold?'

Harold leaped from the edge of the ha-ha where he had been sitting and held up his hand. She took it and leaped down lightly beside him.

'Come,' he said, 'let us go there now!' She took his arm when they got on the path again, and clinging to him in her pretty girlish way they went together to the piece of garden which she called her own; there they picked a great bunch of beautiful white flowers. Then they walked to the old church. The door was open and they passed in. Harold took from his pocket a tiny key. This surprised her, and heightened the agitation which she naturally suffered from revisiting the place. She said nothing whilst he opened the door to the crypt. Within, on a bracket, stood some candles in glass shades and boxes of matches. Harold lit three candles, and leaving one of them on the shelf, and placing his cap beside it, took the other two in his hands. Stephen, holding her flowers tightly to her breast with her right hand, took Harold's arm with the left, and with beating heart entered the crypt.

For several minutes Harold kept her engaged, telling her about the crypt in his father's church, and how he went down at his last visit to see the coffin of his dear father, and how he knelt before it. Stephen was much moved, and held tight to his arm, her heart beating. But in the time she was getting accustomed to the place. Her eyes, useless at first on coming out of the bright sunlight, and not able to distinguish anything, began to take in the shape of the place and to see the rows of great coffins that stood out along the far wall. She also saw with surprise that the newest coffin, on which for several reasons her eyes rested, was no longer dusty but was scrupulously clean. Following with her eyes as well as she could see into the further corners she saw that there the same reform had been effected. Even the walls and ceiling had been swept of the hanging cobwebs, and the floor was clean with the cleanliness of ablution. Still holding Harold's arm, she moved over towards her mother's coffin and knelt before it. Harold knelt with her; for a little while she remained still and silent, praying inwardly. Then she rose, and taking her great bunch of flowers placed them lovingly on the lid of the coffin above where she thought her mother's heart would be. Then she turned to Harold, her eyes flowing and her cheeks wet with tears, and laid her head against his breast. Her arms could not go round his neck till he had bent his head, for with his great height he simply towered above her. Presently she was quiet; the paroxysm of her grief had passed. She took Harold's hand in both hers, and together they went to the door. With his disengaged hand, for he would not have disturbed the other for worlds, Harold put out the lights and locked the door behind them.

In the church she held him away from her, and looked him fairly in the face. She said slowly:

'Harold, was it you who had the crypt cleaned?' He answered in a low voice:

'I knew you would want to go again!'

She took the great hand which she held between hers, and before he knew what she was doing and could prevent her, raised it to her lips and kissed it, saying lovingly:

'Oh, Harold! No brother in all the wide world could be kinder. And—and—' this with a sob, 'we both thank you; mother and I!'

CHAPTER VI—A VISIT TO OXFORD

The next important move in the household was Harold's going to Cambridge. His father had always intended this, and Squire Norman had borne his wishes in mind. Harold joined Trinity, the college which had been his father's, and took up his residence in due course.

Stephen was now nearly twelve. Her range of friendships, naturally limited by her circumstances in life, was enlarged to the full; and if she had not many close friends there were at least of them all that was numerically possible. She still kept up to certain degree the little gatherings which in her childhood were got together for her amusement, and in the various games then instituted she still took a part. She never lost sight of the fact that her father took a certain pleasure in her bodily vigour. And though with her growing years and the conscious acceptance of her womanhood, she lost sight of the old childish fancy of being a boy instead of a girl, she could not lose sight of the fact that strength and alertness are sources of feminine as well as of masculine power.

Amongst the young friends who came from time to time during his holidays was Leonard Everard, now a tall, handsome boy. He was one of those boys who develop young, and who seem never to have any of that gawky stage so noticeable in the youth of men made in a large pattern. He was always well-poised, trim-set, alert; fleet of foot, and springy all over. In games he was *facile princeps*, seeming to make his effort always in the right way and without exertion, as if by an instinct of physical masterdom. His universal success in such matters helped to give him an easy debonair manner which was in itself winning. So physically complete a youth has always a charm. In its very presence there is a sort of sympathetic expression, such as comes with the sunshine.

Stephen always in Leonard's presence showed something of the common attitude. His youth and beauty and sex all had their influence on her. The influence of sex, as it is understood with regard to a later period of life, did not in her case exist; Cupid's darts are barbed and winged for more adult victims. But in her case Leonard's masculine superiority, emphasised by the few years between their age, his sublime self-belief, and, above all, his absolute disregard for herself or her wishes or her feelings, put him on a level at which she had to look up to him. The first step in the ladder of pre-eminence had been achieved when she realised that he was not on her level; the second when she experienced rather than thought that he had more influence on her than she had on him. Here again was a little morsel of hero worship, which, though based on a misconception of fact, was still of influence. In that episode of the crypt she had always believed that it was Leonard who had carried her out and laid her on the church floor in light and safety. He had been strong enough and resolute enough to do this, whilst she had fainted! Harold's generous forbearance had really worked to a false end.

It was not strange, therefore, that she found occasional companionship with the handsome, wilful, domineering boy somewhat of luxury. She did not see him often enough to get tired of him; to find out the weakness of his character; to realise his deep-seated, remorseless selfishness. But after all he was only an episode in a young life which was full of interests. Term after term came and went; the holidays had their seasonable pleasures, occasionally shared in common. That was all.

Harold's attitude was the same as ever. He was of a constant nature; and now that manhood was within hail the love of his boyhood was ripening to a man's love. That was all. He was with regard to Stephen the same devoted, worshipping protector, without thought of self; without hope of reward. Whatever Stephen wished Harold did; and Stephen, knowing their old wishes and their old pleasures, was content with their renewal. Each holiday between the terms became mainly a repetition of the days of the old life. They lived in the past.

Amongst the things that did not change was Stephen's riding dress. The scarlet habit had never been a thing for everyday wear, but had from the first been kept for special occasions. Stephen herself knew that it was not a conventional costume; but she rather preferred it, if on that account alone. In a certain way she felt justified in using it; for a red habit was a sort of tradition in the family.

It was on one of these occasions that she had gone with Harold into the churchyard where they had heard the discussion regarding God and the Angels.

* * * * *

When Stephen was about sixteen she went for a short visit to Oxford. She stayed at Somerville with Mrs. Egerton, an old friend of her mother's, who was a professor at the college. She sent back her maid who had travelled with her, as she knew that the college girls did not have servants of their own. The visit was prolonged by mutual consent into a duration of some weeks. Stephen fell in love with the place and the life, and had serious thoughts of joining the college herself. Indeed she had made up her mind to ask her father to allow her, knowing well that he would consent to that or to any other wholesome wish of hers. But then came the thought that he would be all alone at home; and following that came another thought, and one of more poignant feeling. He was alone now! Already, for many days, she had left him, for the first time in her life! Stephen was quick to act; well she knew that at home there would be no fault found with her for a speedy return. Within a few hours she had brought her visit to an end, and was by herself, despite Mrs. Egerton's protest, in the train on the way back to Norcester.

In the train she began to review, for the first time, her visit to the university. All had been so strange and new and delightful to her that she had never stopped for retrospect. Life in the new and enchanting place had been in the moving present. The mind had been receptive only, gathering data for later thought. During her visit she had had no one to direct her thought, and so it had been all personal, with the freedom of individuality at large. Of course her mother's friend, skilled in the mind-workings of average girls, and able to pick her way through intellectual and moral quagmires, had taken good care to point out to her certain intellectual movements and certain moral lessons; just as she had in their various walks and drives pointed out matters of interest—architectural beauties and spots of historic import. And she had taken in, loyally accepted, and thoroughly assimilated all that she had been told. But there were other lessons which were for her young eyes; facts which the older eyes had ceased to notice, if they had ever noticed them at all. The self-content, the sex-content in the endless tide of young men that thronged the streets and quads and parks; the all-sufficing nature of sport or study, to whichever their inclinations tended. The small part which womankind seemed to have in their lives. Stephen had had, as we know, a peculiar training; whatever her instincts were, her habits were largely boy habits. Here she was amongst boys, a glorious tide of them; it made now and again her heart beat to look at them. And yet amongst them all she was only an outsider. She could not do anything better than any of them. Of course, each time she went out, she became conscious of admiring glances; she could not be woman without such consciousness. But it was as a girl that men looked at her, not as an equal. As well as personal experience and the lessons of eyes and ears and intelligence, there were other things to classify and adjust; things which were entirely from the outside of her own life. The fragments of common-room gossip, which it had been her fortune to hear accidentally now and again. The half confidences of scandals, borne on whispered breaths. The whole confidences of dormitory and study which she had been privileged to share. All were parts of the new and strange world, the great world which had swum into her ken.

As she sat now in the train, with some formulation of memory already accomplished in the two hours of solitude, her first comment, spoken half audibly, would have surprised her teachers as much as it would have surprised herself, if she had been conscious of it; for as yet her thinking was not self-conscious:

'Surely, I am not like that!'

It was of the women she had been thinking, not of the men. The glimpse which she had had of her own sex had been an awakening to her; and the awakening had not been to a pleasant world. All at once she seemed to realise that her sex had defects—littlenesses, meannesses, cowardices, falsenesses. That their occupations were apt to be trivial or narrow or selfish; that their desires were earthly, and their tastes coarse; that what she held to be goodness was apt to be realised only as fear. That innocence was but ignorance, or at least baffled curiosity. That . . .

A flood of shame swept over her, and instinctively she put her hands before her burning face. As usual, she was running all at once into extremes.

And above all these was borne upon her, and for the first time in her life, that she was herself a woman!

For a long time she sat quite still. The train thrilled and roared on its way. Crowded stations took and gave their quantum of living freight; but the young girl sat abstracted, unmoved, seemingly unconscious. All the dominance and energy of her nature were at work.

If, indeed, she was a woman, and had to abide by the exigencies of her own sex, she would at least not be ruled and limited by woman's weakness. She would plan and act and manage things for herself, in her own way.

Whatever her thoughts might be, she could at least control her acts. And those acts should be based not on woman's weakness, but on man's strength!

CHAPTER VII—THE NEED OF KNOWING

When Stephen announced her intention of going with her father to the Petty Sessions Court, there was consternation amongst the female population of Normanstand and Norwood. Such a thing had not been heard of in the experiences of any of them. Courts of Justice were places for men; and the lower courts dealt with a class of cases . . . It was quite impossible to imagine where any young lady could get such an idea . . .

Miss Laetitia Rowly recognised that she had a difficult task before her, for she was by now accustomed to Stephen's quiet method of having her own way.

She made a careful toilet before driving over to Normanstand. Her wearing her best bonnet was a circumstance not unattended with dread for some one. Behold her then, sailing into the great drawing-room at Normanstand with her mind so firmly fixed on the task before her as to be oblivious of minor considerations. She was so fond of Stephen, and admired so truly her many beauties and fine qualities, that she was secure and without flaw in her purpose. Stephen was in danger, and though she doubted if she would be able to effect any change, she was determined that at least she should not go into danger with her eyes unopened.

Stephen entered hastily and ran to her. She loved her great-aunt; really and truly loved her. And indeed it would have been strange if she had not, for from the earliest hour which she could recollect she had received from her nothing but the truest, fondest affection. Moreover she deeply respected the old lady, her truth, her resolution, her kindliness, her genuine common-sense ability. Stephen always felt safe with her aunt. In the presence of others she might now and again have a qualm or a doubt; but not with her. There was an abiding calm in her love, answering love realised and respected. Her long and intimate knowledge of Laetitia made her aware of her moods. She could read the signs of them. She knew well the meaning of the bonnet which actually seemed to quiver as though it had a sentience of its own. She knew well the cause of her aunt's perturbation; the pain which must be caused to her was perhaps the point of most resistance in herself—she having made up her mind to her new experience. All she could do would be to try to reconcile her by the assurance of good intention; by reason, and by sweetness of manner. When she had kissed her and sat beside her, holding her hand after her pretty way, she, seeing the elder woman somewhat at a loss, opened the subject herself:

'You look troubled, auntie! I hope it is nothing serious?'

'It is, my dear! Very serious! Everything is serious to me which touches you.'

'Me, Auntie!' Hypocrisy is a fine art.

'Yes! yes, Stephen. Oh! my dear child, what is this I hear about your going to Petty Sessions with your father?'

'Oh, that! Why, Auntie dear, you must not let that trouble you. It is all right. That is necessary!'

'Necessary!' the old lady's figure grew rigid and her voice was loud and high. 'Necessary for a young lady to go to a court house. To hear low people speaking of low crimes. To listen to cases of the most shocking kind; cases of low immorality; cases of a kind, of a nature of a—a—class that you are not supposed to know anything about. Really, Stephen! . . . ' She was drawing away her hand in indignation. But Stephen held it tight, as she said very sweetly:

'That is just it, Auntie. I am so ignorant that I feel I should know more of the lives of those very people!' Miss Laetitia interrupted:

'Ignorant! Of course you are ignorant. That is what you ought to be. Isn't it what we have all been devoting ourselves to effect ever since you were born? Read your third chapter of Genesis and remember what came of eating of the fruit of the Tree of Knowledge.'

'I think the Tree of Knowledge must have been an orange tree.' The old lady looked up, her interest aroused:

'Why?'

'Because ever since Eden other brides have worn its blossom!' Her tone was demure. Miss Rowly looked sharply at her, but her sharpness softened off into a smile.

'H'm!' she said, and was silent. Stephen seized the opportunity to put her own case:

'Auntie dear, you must forgive me! You really must, for my heart is set on this. I assure you I am not doing it merely to please myself. I have thought over the whole matter. Father has always wished me to be in a position—a position of knowledge and experience—to manage Normanstand if I should ever succeed him. From the earliest time I can remember he has always kept this before me, and though of course I did not at first understand what it meant, I have seemed in the last few years to know better. Accordingly I learned all sorts of things under his care, and sometimes even without his help. I have studied the estate map, and I have been over the estate books and read some of the leases and all such matters which they deal with in the estate office. This only told me the bones of the thing. I wanted to know more of our people; and so I made a point of going now and again to each house that we own. Of seeing the people and talking with them familiarly; as familiarly as they would let me, and indeed so far as was possible considering my position. For, Auntie dear, I soon began to learn—to learn in a way there was no mistaking—what my position is. And so I want to get to know more of their ordinary lives; the darker as well as the lighter side. I would like to do them good. I can see how my dear daddy has always been a sort of power to help them, and I would like to carry on his work; to carry it further if I may. But I must know.'

Her aunt had been listening with growing interest, and with growing respect too, for she realised the intense earnestness which lay behind the girl's words and her immediate purpose. Her voice and manner were both softened:

'But, my dear, surely it is not necessary to go into the Court to know these things. The results of each case become known.'

'That is just it, Auntie,' she answered quickly. 'The magistrates have to hear the two sides of the case before even they can make up their minds. I want to hear both sides, too! If people are guilty, I want to know the cause of their guilt. If they are innocent, I want to know what the circumstances can be which make innocence look like guilt. In my own daily life I may be in the way of just such judgments; and surely it is only right that judgment should be just!'

Again she paused; there rose before her mind that conversation in the churchyard when Harold had said that it was difficult for women to be just.

Miss Rowly reflected too. She was becoming convinced that in principle the girl was right. But the details were repugnant as ever to her; concentrating her mind on the point where she felt the ground firm under her, she made her objection:

'But, Stephen dear, there are so many cases that are sordid and painful!'

'The more need to know of sordid things; if sordidness plays so important a part in the tragedy of their lives!'

'But there are cases which are not within a woman's province. Cases that touch sin . . . '

'What kind of sin do you mean? Surely all wrong-doing is sin!' The old lady was embarrassed. Not by the fact, for she had been for too many years the mistress of a great household not to know something of the subject on which she spoke, but that she had to speak of such a matter to the young girl whom she so loved.

'The sin, my dear, of . . . of woman's wrong-doing . . . as woman . . . of motherhood, without marriage!' All Stephen's nature seemed to rise in revolt.

'Why, Auntie,' she spoke out at once, 'you yourself show the want of the very experience I look for!'

'How? what?' asked the old lady amazed and bristling. Stephen took her hand and held it affectionately as she spoke:

'You speak of a woman's wrong-doing, when surely it is a man's as well. There does not seem to be blame for him who is the more guilty. Only for poor women! . . . And, Auntie dear, it is such poor women that I should like to help . . . Not when it is too late, but before! But how can I help unless I know? Good girls cannot tell me, and good women won't! You yourself, Auntie, didn't want to speak on the subject; even to me!'

'But, my dear child, these are not things for unmarried women. I never speak of them myself except with matrons.' Stephen's answer flashed out like a sword; and cut like one:

'And yet you are unmarried! Oh, Auntie dear, I did not and I do not mean to be offensive, or to hurt you in any way. I know, dear, your goodness and your kindness to all. But you limit yourself to one side!' The elder lady interrupted:

'How do you mean? one side! which side?'

'The punishment side. I want to know the cause of that which brings the punishment. There surely is some cross road in a girl's life where the ways part. I want to stand there if I can, with warning in one hand and help in the other. Oh! Auntie, Auntie, can't you see that my heart is in this . . . These are our people; Daddy says they are to be my people; and I want to know their lives right through; to understand their wants, and their temptations, and their weakness. Bad and good, whatever it be, I must know it all; or I shall be working in the dark, and may injure or crush where I had looked to help and raise.'

As she spoke she looked glorified. The afternoon autumn sun shone full through the great window and lighted her up till she looked like a spirit. Lighted her white diaphanous dress till it seemed to take shape as an ethereal robe; lighted her red hair till it looked like a celestial crown; lighted her great dark eyes till their black beauty became swept in the tide of glory.

The heart of the old woman who loved her best heaved, and her bosom swelled with pride. Instinctively she spoke:

'Oh, you noble, beautiful creature! Of course you are right, and your way is God's way!' With tears that rained down her furrowed cheeks, she put her arms round the girl and kissed her fondly. Still holding her in her arms she gave her the gentle counsel which was the aftermath of her moment of inspiration.

'But Stephen dear, do be careful! Knowledge is a two-edged sword, and it is apt to side with pride. Remember what was the last temptation of the serpent to Eve: "Your eyes shall be opened, and ye shall be as gods, knowing good and evil."'

'I shall be very careful,' she said gravely; and then added as if by an afterthought, 'of course you understand that my motive is the acquisition of knowledge?'

'Yes?' the answer was given interrogatively.

'Don't you think, dear, that Eve's object was not so much the acquisition of knowledge as the gratification of curiosity.'

'That may be,' said the elder lady in a doubtful tone; 'but my dear, who is to enlighten us as to which is which? We are apt in such matters to deceive ourselves. The more we know, the better are we able to deceive others; and the better we are able to deceive others the better we are able to deceive ourselves. As I tell you, dear, knowledge is two-edged and needs extra carefulness in its use!'

'True!' said Stephen reflectively. Long after her aunt had gone she sat thinking.

* * * * *

Once again did Miss Rowly try to restrain Stephen from a project. This was when a little later she wished to go for a few days to the University Mission House in the East end of London. Ever since her visit to Oxford she had kept up a correspondence with her mother's old friend. It was this lady's habit to spend a part of vacation in the Mission; and Stephen had had much correspondence with her regarding the work. At last she wrote that if she might, she would like to come and see for herself. The answer was a cordial invitation, armed with which she asked her father to allow her to go. He at once assented. He had been watching keenly the development of her character, and had seen with pride and satisfaction that as time went on she seemed to acquire greater resolution, larger self-dependence. She was becoming more and more of his ideal. Without losing any of her womanhood, she was beginning to look at things more from a man's point of view than is usually done by, or possible to, women.

When she returned at the end of a week she was full of new gravity. After a while this so far changed that her old lighter moods began to have their place, but it seemed that she never lost, and that she never would lose, the effect of that week of bitter experience amongst the 'submerged tenth.'

The effect of the mental working was shown by a remark made by Harold when home on his next college vacation. He had been entering with her on a discussion of an episode on the estate:

'Stephen, you are learning to be just!'

At the moment she was chagrined by the remark, though she accepted it in silence; but later, when she had thought the matter over, she took from it infinite pleasure. This was indeed to share man's ideas and to think with the workings of man's mind. It encouraged her to further and larger ideas, and to a greater toleration than she had hitherto dreamed of.

Of all those who loved her, none seemed to understand so fully as Laetitia Rowly the change in her mental attitude, or rather the development of it. Now and again she tried to deflect or modify certain coming forces, so that the educational process in which she had always had a part would continue in the right direction. But she generally found that the girl had been over the ground so thoroughly that she was able to defend her position. Once, when she had ventured to remonstrate with her regarding her attitude of woman's equality with man, she felt as if Stephen's barque was indeed entering on dangerous seas. The occasion had arisen thus: Stephen had been what her aunt had stigmatised as 'laying down the law' with regard to the position a married woman, and Miss Rowly, seeing a good argumentative opening, remarked:

'But what if a woman does not get the opportunity of being married?' Stephen looked at her a moment before saying with conviction:

'It is a woman's fault if she does not get the opportunity!' The old lady smiled as she answered:

'Her fault? My dear, what if no man asks her?' This seemed to her own mind a poser.

'Still her own fault! Why doesn't she ask him?' Her aunt's lorgnon was dropped in horrified amazement.

Stephen went on impassively.

'Certainly! Why shouldn't she? Marriage is a union. As it is in the eye of the law a civil contract, either party to it should be at liberty to originate the matter. If a woman is not free to think of a man in all ways, how is she to judge of the suitability of their union? And if she is free in theory, why not free to undertake if necessary the initiative in a matter so momentous to herself?' The old lady actually groaned and wrung her hands; she was horrified at such sentiments. They were daring enough to think; but to put them in words! . . .

'Oh, my dear, my dear!' she moaned, 'be careful what you say. Some one might hear you who would not understand, as I do, that you are talking theory.' Stephen's habit of thought stood to her here. She saw that her aunt was distressed, and as she did not wish to pain her unduly, was willing to divert the immediate channel of her fear. She took the hand which lay in her lap and held it firmly whilst she smiled in the loving old eyes.

'Of course, Auntie dear, it is theory. But still it is a theory which I hold very strongly!' . . . Here a thought struck her and she said suddenly:

'Did you ever . . . How many proposals did you have, Auntie?' The old lady smiled; her thoughts were already diverted.

'Several, my dear! It is so long ago that I don't remember!'

'Oh yes, you do, Auntie! No woman ever forgets that, no matter what else she may or may not remember! Tell me, won't you?' The old lady blushed slightly as she answered:

'There is no need to specify, my dear. Let it be at this, that there were more than you could count on your right hand!'

'And why did you refuse them?' The tone was wheedling, and the elder woman loved to hear it. Wheedling is the courtship, by the young of the old.

'Because, my dear, I didn't love them.'

'But tell me, Auntie, was there never any one that you did love?'

'Ah! my dear, that is a different matter. That is the real tragedy of a woman's life.' In flooding reminiscent thought she forgot her remonstrating; her voice became full of natural pathos:

'To love; and be helpless! To wait, and wait, and wait; with your heart all aflame! To hope, and hope; till time seems to have passed away, and all the world to stand still on your hopeless misery! To know that a word might open up Heaven; and yet to have to remain mute! To keep back the glances that could enlighten; to modulate the tones that might betray! To see all you hoped for passing away . . . to another! . . . '

Stephen bent over and kissed her, then standing up said:

'I understand! Isn't it wrong, Auntie, that there should be such tragedies? Should not that glance be given? Why should that tone be checked? Why should one be mute when a single word might, would, avert the tragedy? Is it not possible, Auntie, that there is something wrong in our social system when such things can happen; and can happen so often?'

She looked remorseless as well as irresistible in the pride of her youthful strength as with eyes that blazed, not flashing as in passion but with a steady light that seemed to burn, she continued:

'Some day women must learn their own strength, as well as they have learned their own weakness. They are taught this latter from their cradles up; but no one ever seems to teach them wherein their power lies. They have to learn this for themselves; and the process and the result of the self-teaching are not good. In the University Settlement I learned much that made my heart ache; but out of it there seemed some lesson for good.' She paused; and her aunt, wishing to keep the subject towards higher things, asked:

'And that lesson, Stephen dear?' The blazing eyes turned to her so that she was stirred by them as the answer came:

'It is bad women who seem to know men best, and to be able to influence them most. They can make men come and go at will. They can turn and twist and mould them as they choose. And *they* never hesitate to speak their own wishes; to ask for what they want. There are no tragedies, of the negative kind, in *their* lives. Their tragedies have come and gone already; and their power remains. Why should good women leave power to such as they? Why should good women's lives be wrecked for a convention? Why in the blind following of some society fetish should life lose its charm, its possibilities? Why should love eat its heart out, in vain? The time will come when women will not be afraid to speak to men, as they should speak, as free and equal. Surely if a woman is to be the equal and lifelong companion of a man, the closest to him—nay, the only one really close to him: the mother of his children—she should be free at the very outset to show her inclination to him just as he would to her. Don't be frightened, Auntie dear; your eyes are paining me! . . . There! perhaps I said too much. But after all it is only theory. Take for your comfort, Auntie dear, that I am free an heart-whole. You need not fear for me; I can see what your dear eyes tell me. Yes! I am very young; perhaps too young to think such things. But I have thought of them. Thought them all over in every way and phase I can imagine.'

She stopped suddenly; bending over, she took the old lady in her arms and kissed her fondly several times, holding her tight. Then, as suddenly releasing her, she ran away before she could say a word.

CHAPTER VIII—THE T-CART

When Harold took his degree, Stephen's father took her to Cambridge. She enjoyed the trip very much; indeed, it seemed under conditions that were absolutely happy.

When they had returned to Normanstand, the Squire took an early opportunity of bringing Harold alone into his study. He spoke to him with what in a very young man would have seemed diffidence:

'I have been thinking, Harold, that the time has come when you should be altogether your own master. I am more than pleased, my boy, with the way you have gone through college; it is, I am sure, just as your dear father would have wished it, and as it would have pleased him best.' He paused, and Harold said in a low voice:

'I tried hard, sir, to do what I thought he would like; and what you would.' The Squire went on more cheerfully:

'I know that, my boy! I know that well. And I can tell you that it is not the least of the pleasures we have all had in your success, how you have justified yourself. You have won many honours in the schools, and you have kept the reputation as an athlete which your father was so proud of. Well, I suppose in the natural order of things you would go into a profession; and of course if you so desire you can do that. But if you can see your way to it I would rather that you stayed here. My house is your home as long as I live; but I don't wish you to feel in any way dependent. I want you to stay here if you will; but to do it just because you wish to. To this end I have made over to you the estate at Camp which was my father's gift to me when I came of age. It is not a very large one; but it will give you a nice position of your own, and a comfortable income. And with it goes my blessing, my dear boy. Take it as a gift from your father and myself!'

Harold was much moved, not only by the act itself but by the gracious way of doing it. There were tears in his eyes as he wrung the Squire's hand; his voice thrilled with feeling as he said:

'Your many goodnesses to my father's son, sir, will, I hope, be justified by his love and loyalty. If I don't say much it is because I do not feel quite master of myself. I shall try to show in time, as I cannot say it all at once, all that I feel.'

Harold continued to live at Normanstand. The house at Camp was in reality a charming cottage. A couple of servants were installed, and now and again he stayed there for a few days as he wished to get accustomed to the place. In a couple of months every one accepted the order of things; and life at Normanstand went on much as it had done before Harold had gone to college. There was a man in the house now instead of a boy: that was all. Stephen too was beginning to be a young woman, but the relative positions were the same as they had been. Her growth did not seem to make an ostensible difference to any one. The one who might have noticed it most, Mrs. Jarrold, had died during the last year of Harold's life at college.

When the day came for the quarterly meeting of the magistrates of the county of Norcester, Squire Rowly arranged as usual to drive Squire Norman. This had been their habit for good many years. The two men usually liked to talk over the meeting as they returned home together. It was a beautiful morning for a drive, and when Rowly came flying up the avenue in his T-cart with three magnificent bays, Stephen ran out on the top of the steps to see him draw up. Rowly was a fine whip, and his horses felt it. Squire Norman was ready, and, after a kiss from Stephen, climbed into the high cart. The men raised their hats and waved good-bye. A word from Rowly; with a bound the horses were off. Stephen stood looking at them delighted; all was so sunny, so bright, so happy. The world was so full of life and happiness to-day that it seemed as if it would never end; that nothing except good could befall.

Harold, later on that morning, was to go into Norcester also; so Stephen with a lonely day before her set herself to take up loose-ends of all sorts of little personal matters. They would all meet at dinner as Rowly was to stop the night at Normanstand.

Harold left the club in good time to ride home to dinner. As he passed the County Hotel he stopped to ask if Squire Norman had left; and was told that he had started only a short time before with Squire Rowly in his T-cart. He rode on fast, thinking that perhaps he might overtake them and ride on with them. But the bays knew their work, and did it. They kept their start; it was only at the top of the North hill, five miles out of Norcester, that he saw them in the distance, flying along the level road. He knew he would not now overtake them, and so rode on somewhat more leisurely.

The Norcester highroad, when it has passed the village of Brackling, turns away to the right behind the great clump of oaks. From this the road twists to the left again, making a double curve, and then runs to Norling Parva in a clear stretch of some miles before reaching the sharp turn down the hill which is marked 'Dangerous to Cyclists.' From the latter village branches the by-road over the hill which is the short cut to Normanstand.

When Harold turned the corner under the shadow of the oaks he saw a belated road-mender, surrounded by some gaping peasants, pointing excitedly in the distance. The man, who of course knew him, called to him to stop.

'What is it?' he asked, reining up.

'It be Squire Rowly's bays which have run away with him. Three on 'em, all in a row and comin' like the wind. Squire he had his reins all right, but they 'osses didn't seem to mind 'un. They was fair mad and bolted. The leader he had got frightened at the heap o' stones theer, an' the others took scare from him.'

Without a word Harold shook his reins and touched the horse with his whip. The animal seemed to understand and sprang forward, covering the ground at a terrific pace. Harold was not given to alarms, but here might be serious danger. Three spirited horses in a light cart made for pace, all bolting in fright, might end any moment in calamity. Never in his life did he ride faster than on the road to Norling Parva. Far ahead of him he could see at the turn, now and again, a figure running. Something had happened. His heart grew cold: he knew as well as though he had seen it, the high cart swaying on one wheel round the corner as the maddened horses tore on their way; the one jerk too much, and the momentary reaction in the crash! . . .

With beating heart and eyes aflame in his white face he dashed on.

It was all too true. By the side of the roadway on the inner curve lay the cart on its side with broken shafts. The horses were prancing and stamping about along the roadway not recovered from their fright. Each was held by several men.

And on the grass two figures were still lying where they had been thrown out. Rowly, who had of course been on the off-side, had been thrown furthest. His head had struck the milestone that stood back on the waste ground before the ditch. There was no need for any one to tell that his neck had been broken. The way his head lay on one side, and the twisted, inert limbs, all told their story plainly enough.

Squire Norman lay on his back stretched out. Some one had raised him to a sitting posture and then lowered him again, straightening his limbs. He did not therefore look so dreadful as Rowly, but there were signs of coming death in the stertorous breathing, the ooze of blood from nostrils and ears as well as mouth. Harold knelt down by him at once and examined him. Those who were round all knew him and stood back. He felt the ribs and limbs; so far as he could ascertain by touch no bone was broken.

Just then the local doctor, for whom some one had run, arrived in his gig. He, too, knelt beside the injured man, a quick glance having satisfied him that there was only one patient requiring his care. Harold stood up and waited. The doctor looked up, shaking his head. Harold could hardly suppress the groan which was rising in his throat. He asked:

'Is it immediate? Should his daughter be brought here?'

'How long would it take her to arrive?'

'Perhaps half an hour; she would not lose an instant.'

'Then you had better send for her.'

'I shall go at once!' answered Harold, turning to jump on his horse, which was held on the road.

'No, no!' said the doctor, 'send some one else. You had better stay here yourself. He may become conscious just before the end; and he may want to say something!' It seemed to Harold that a great bell was sounding in his ears.—'Before the end! Good God! Poor Stephen!' . . . But this was no time for sorrow, or for thinking of it. That would come later. All that was possible must be done; and to do it required a cool head. He called to one of the lads he knew could ride and said to him:

'Get on my horse and ride as fast as you can to Normanstand. Send at once to Miss Norman and tell her that she is wanted instantly. Tell her that there has been an accident; that her father is alive, but that she must come at once without a moment's delay. She had better ride my horse back as it will save time. She will understand from that the importance of time. Quick!'

The lad sprang to the saddle, and was off in a flash. Whilst Harold was speaking, the doctor had told the men, who, accustomed to hunting accidents, had taken a gate from its hinges and held it in readiness, to bring it closer. Then under his direction the Squire was placed on the gate. The nearest house was only about a hundred yards away; and thither they bore him. He was lifted on a bed, and then the doctor made fuller examination. When he stood up he looked very grave and said to Harold:

'I greatly fear she cannot arrive in time. That bleeding from the ears means rupture of the brain. It is relieving the pressure, however, and he may recover consciousness before he dies. You had better be close to him. There is at present nothing that can be done. If he becomes conscious at all it will be suddenly. He will relapse and probably die as quickly.'

All at once Norman opened his eyes, and seeing him said quietly, as he looked around:

'What place is this, Harold?'

'Martin's—James Martin's, sir. You were brought here after the accident.'

'Yes, I remember! Am I badly hurt? I can feel nothing!'

'I fear so, sir! I have sent for Stephen.'

'Sent for Stephen! Am I about to die?' His voice, though feeble, was grave and even.

'Alas! sir, I fear so!' He sank on his knees as he spoke and took him, his second father, in his arms.

'Is it close?'

'Yes.'

'Then listen to me! If I don't see Stephen, give her my love and blessing! Say that with my last breath I prayed God to keep her and make her happy! You will tell her this?'

'I will! I will!' He could hardly speak for the emotion which was choking him. Then the voice went on, but slower and weaker:

'And Harold, my dear boy, you will look after her, will you not? Guard her and cherish her, as if you were indeed my son and she your sister!'

'I will. So help me God!' There was a pause of a few seconds which seemed an interminable time. Then in a feebler voice Squire Norman spoke again:

'And Harold—bend down—I must whisper! If it should be that in time you and Stephen should find that there is another affection between you, remember that I sanction it—with my dying breath. But give her time! I trust that to you! She is young, and the world is all before her. Let her choose . . . and be loyal to her if it is another! It may be a hard task, but I trust you, Harold. God bless you, my other son!' He rose slightly and listened. Harold's heart leaped. The swift hoof-strokes of a galloping horse were heard . . . The father spoke joyously:

'There she is! That is my brave girl! God grant that she may be in time. I know what it will mean to her hereafter!'

The horse stopped suddenly.

A quick patter of feet along the passage and then Stephen half dressed with a peignoir thrown over her, swept into the room. With the soft agility of a leopard she threw herself on her knees beside her father and put her arms round him. The dying man motioned to Harold to raise him. When this had been done he laid his hand tenderly on his daughter's head, saying:

'Let now, O Lord, Thy servant depart in peace! God bless and keep you, my dear child! You have been all your life a joy and a delight to me! I shall tell your mother when I meet her all that you have been to me! Harold, be good to her! Good-bye—Stephen! . . . Margaret! . . . '

His head fell over, and Harold, laying him gently down, knelt beside Stephen. He put his arm round her; and she, turning to him, laid her hand on his breast and sobbed as though her heart would break.

* * * * *

The bodies of the two squires were brought to Normanstand. Rowly had long ago said that if he died unmarried he would like to lie beside his half-sister, and that it was fitting that, as Stephen would be the new Squire of Norwood, her dust should in time lie by his. When the terrible news of her nephew's and of Norman's death came to Norwood, Miss Laetitia hurried off to Normanstand as fast as the horses could bring her.

Her coming was an inexpressible comfort to Stephen. After the first overwhelming burst of grief she had settled into an acute despair. Of course she had been helped by the fact that Harold had been with her, and she was grateful for that too. But it did not live in her memory of gratitude in the same way. Of course Harold was with her in trouble! He had always been; would always be.

But the comfort which Aunt Laetitia could give was of a more positive kind.

From that hour Miss Rowly stayed at Normanstand. Stephen wanted her; and she wanted to be with Stephen.

After the funeral Harold, with an instinctive delicacy of feeling, had gone to live in his own house; but he came to Normanstand every day. Stephen had so long been accustomed to consulting him about everything that there was no perceptible change in their relations. Even necessary business to be done did not come as a new thing.

And so things went on outwardly at Normanstand very much as they had done before the coming of the tragedy. But for a long time Stephen had occasional bursts of grief which to witness was positive anguish to those who loved her.

Then her duty towards her neighbours became a sort of passion. She did not spare herself by day or by night. With swift intuition she grasped the needs of any ill case which came before her, and with swift movement she took the remedy in hand.

Her aunt saw and approved. Stephen, she felt, was in this way truly fulfilling her duty as a woman. The old lady began to secretly hope, and almost to believe, that she had laid aside those theories whose carrying into action she so dreaded.

But theories do not die so easily. It is from theory that practice takes its real strength, as well as its direction. And did the older woman whose life had been bound under more orderly restraint but know, Stephen was following out her theories, remorselessly and to the end.

CHAPTER IX—IN THE SPRING

The months since her father's death spread into the second year before Stephen began to realise the loneliness of her life. She had no companion now but her aunt; and though the old lady adored her, and she returned her love in full, the mere years between them made impossible the companionship that youth craves. Miss Rowly's life was in the past. Stephen's was in the future. And loneliness is a feeling which comes unbidden to a heart.

Stephen felt her loneliness all round. In old days Harold was always within hail, and companionship of equal age and understanding was available. But now his very reticence in her own interest, and by her father's wishes, made for her pain. Harold had put his strongest restraint on himself, and in his own way suffered a sort of silent martyrdom. He loved Stephen with every fibre of his being. Day by day he came toward her with eager step; day by day he left her with a pang that made his heart ache and seemed to turn the brightness of the day to gloom. Night by night he tossed for hours thinking, thinking, wondering if the time would ever come when her kisses would be his . . . But the tortures and terrors of the night had their effect on his days. It seemed as if the mere act of thinking, of longing, gave him ever renewed self-control, so that he was able in his bearing to carry out the task he had undertaken: to give Stephen time to choose a mate for herself. Herein lay his weakness—a weakness coming from his want of knowledge of the world of women. Had he ever had a love affair, be it never so mild a one, he would have known that love requires a positive expression. It is not sufficient to sigh, and wish, and hope, and long, all to oneself. Stephen felt instinctively that his guarded speech and manner were due to the coldness—or rather the trusting abated worship—of the brotherhood to which she had been always accustomed. At the time when new forces were manifesting and expanding themselves within her; when her growing instincts, cultivated by the senses and the passions of young nature, made her aware of other forces, new and old, expanding themselves outside her; at the time when the heart of a girl is eager for new impressions and new expansions, and the calls of sex are working within her all unconsciously, Harold, to whom her heart would probably have been the first to turn, made himself in his effort to best show his love, a *quantité negligeable*.

Thus Stephen, whilst feeling that the vague desires of budding womanhood were trembling within her, had neither thought nor knowledge of their character or their ultimate tendency. She would have been shocked, horrified, had that logical process, which she applied so freely to less personal matters, been used upon her own intimate nature. In her case logic would of course act within a certain range; and as logic is a conscious intellectual process, she became aware that her objective was man. Man—in the abstract. 'Man,' not 'a man.' Beyond that, she could not go. It is not too much to say that she did not ever, even in her most errant thought, apply her reasoning, or even dream of its following out either the duties, the responsibilities, or the consequences of having a husband. She had a vague longing for younger companionship, and of the kind naturally most interesting to her. There thought stopped.

One only of her male acquaintances did not at this time appear. Leonard Everard, who had some time ago finished his course at college, was living partly in London and partly on the Continent. His very absence made him of added interest to his old play-fellow. The image of his grace and comeliness, of his dominance and masculine force, early impressed on her mind, began to compare favourably with the actualities of her other friends; those of them at least who were within the circle of her personal interest. 'Absence makes the heart grow fonder.' In Stephen's mind had been but a very mustard-seed of fondness. But new lights were breaking for her; and all of them, in greater or lesser degree, shone in turn on the memory of the pretty self-willed dominant boy, who now grew larger and more masculine in stature under the instance of each successive light. Stephen knew the others fairly well through and through. The usual mixture of good and evil, of strength and weakness, of purpose and vacillation, was quite within the scope of her own feeling and of her observation. But this man was something of a problem to her; and, as such, had a prominence in her thoughts quite beyond his own worthiness.

In movement of some form is life; and even ideas grow when the pulses beat and thought quickens. Stephen had long had in her mind the idea of sexual equality. For a long time, in deference to her aunt's feelings, she had not spoken of it; for the old lady winced in general under any suggestion of a breach of convention. But though her outward expression being thus curbed had helped to suppress or minimise the opportunities of inward thought, the idea had never left her. Now, when sex was, consciously or unconsciously, a dominating factor in her thoughts, the dormant idea woke to new life. She had held that if men and women were equal the woman should have equal rights and opportunities as the man. It had been, she believed, an absurd conventional rule that such a thing as a proposal of marriage should be entirely the prerogative of man.

And then came to her, as it ever does to woman, opportunity. Opportunity, the cruelest, most remorseless, most unsparing, subtlest foe that womanhood has. Here was an opportunity for her to test her own theory; to prove to herself, and others, that she was right. They—'they' being the impersonal opponents of, or unbelievers in, her theory—would see that a woman could propose as well as a man; and that the result would be good.

It is a part of self-satisfaction, and perhaps not the least dangerous part of it, that it has an increasing or multiplying power of its own. The desire to do increases the power to do; and desire and power united find new ways for the exercise of strength. Up to now Stephen's inclination towards Leonard had been vague, nebulous; but now that theory showed a way to its utilisation it forthwith began to become, first definite, then concrete, then substantial. When once the idea had become a possibility, the mere passing of time did the rest.

Her aunt saw—and misunderstood. The lesson of her own youth had not been applied; not even of those long hours and days and weeks at which she hinted when she had spoken of the tragedy of life which by inference was her own tragedy: 'to love and to be helpless. To wait, and wait, and wait, with your heart all aflame!'

Stephen recognised her aunt's concern for her health in time to protect herself from the curiosity of her loving-kindness. Her youth and readiness and adaptability, and that power of play-acting which we all have within us and of which she had her share, stood to her. With but little effort, based on a seeming acquiescence in her aunt's views, she succeeded in convincing the old lady that her incipient feverish cold had already reached its crisis and was passing away. But she had gained certain knowledge in the playing of her little part. All this self-protective instinct was new; for good or ill she had advanced one more step in not only the knowledge but the power of duplicity which is so necessary in the conventional life of a woman.

Oh! did we but see! Could we but see! Here was a woman, dowered in her youth with all the goods and graces in the power of the gods to bestow, who fought against convention; and who yet found in convention the strongest as well as the readiest weapon of defence.

For nearly two weeks Stephen's resolution was held motionless, neither advancing nor receding; it was veritably the slack water of her resolution. She was afraid to go on. Not afraid in sense of fear as it is usually understood, but with the opposition of virginal instincts; those instincts which are natural, but whose uses as well as whose powers are unknown to us.

CHAPTER X—THE RESOLVE

The next few days saw Stephen abnormally restless. She had fairly well made up her mind to test her theory of equality of the sexes by asking Leonard Everard to marry her; but her difficulty was as to the doing it. She knew well that it would not do to depend on a chance meeting for an opportunity. After all, the matter was too serious to allow of the possibility of levity. There were times when she thought she would write to him and make her proffer of affection in this way; but on every occasion when such thought recurred it was forthwith instantly abandoned. During the last few days, however, she became more reconciled to even this method of procedure. The fever of growth was unabated. At last came an evening which she had all to herself. Miss Laetitia was going over to Norwood to look after matters there, and would remain the night. Stephen saw in her absence an opportunity for thought and action, and said that, having a headache, she would remain at home. Her aunt offered to postpone her visit. But she would not hear of it; and so she had the evening to herself.

After dinner in her boudoir she set herself to the composition of a letter to Leonard which would convey at least something of her feelings and wishes towards him. In the depths of her heart, which now and again beat furiously, she had a secret hope that when once the idea was broached Leonard would do the rest. And as she thought of that 'rest' a languorous dreaminess came upon her. She thought how he would come to her full of love, of yearning passion; how she would try to keep towards him, at first, an independent front which would preserve her secret anxiety until the time should come when she might yield herself to his arms and tell him all. For hours she wrote letter after letter, destroying them as quickly as she wrote, as she found that she had but swayed pendulum fashion between overtness and coldness. Some of the letters were so chilly in tone that she felt they would defeat their own object. Others were so frankly warm in the expression of—regard she called it, that with burning blushes she destroyed them at once at the candle before her.

At last she made up her mind. Just as she had done when a baby she realised that the opposing forces were too strong for her; she gave in gracefully. It would not do to deal directly in a letter with the matter in hand. She would write to Leonard merely asking him to see her. Then, when they were together without fear of interruption, she would tell him her views.

She got as far as 'Dear Mr. Leonard,' when she stood up, saying to herself:

'I shall not be in a hurry. I must sleep on it before I write!' She took up the novel she had been reading in the afternoon, and read on at it steadily till her bedtime.

That night she did not sleep. It was not that she was agitated. Indeed, she was more at ease than she had been for days; she had after much anxious thought made up her mind to a definite course of action. Therefore her sleeplessness was not painful. It was rather that she did not want to sleep, than that she could not. She lay still, thinking, thinking; dreaming such dreams as are the occasions of sanctified privacy to her age and sex.

In the morning she was no worse for her vigil. When at luncheon-time Aunt Laetitia had returned she went into all the little matters of which she had to report. It was after tea-time when she found herself alone, and with leisure to attend to what was, she felt, directly her own affair. During the night she had made up her mind exactly what to say to Leonard; and as her specific resolution bore the test of daylight she was satisfied. The opening words had in their inception caused her some concern; but after hours of thought she had come to the conclusion that to address, under the circumstance, the recipient of the letter as 'Dear Mr. Everard' would hardly do. The only possible justification of her unconventional act was that there existed already a friendship, an intimacy of years, since childhood; that there were already between them knowledge and understanding of each other; that what she was doing, and about to do, was but a further step in a series of events long ago undertaken.

She thought it better to send by post rather than messenger, as the latter did away with all privacy with regard to the act.

The letter was as follows:

> 'DEAR LEONARD,—Would it be convenient for you to meet me to-morrow, Tuesday, at half-past twelve o'clock on the top of Caester Hill? I want to speak about a matter that may have some interest to you, and it will be more private there than in the house. Also it will be cooler in the shade on the hilltop.—
>
> Yours sincerely, STEPHEN NORMAN.'

Having posted the letter she went about the usual routine of her life at Normanstand, and no occasion of suspicion or remark regarding her came to her aunt.

In her room that night when she had sent away her maid, she sat down to think, and all the misgivings of the day came back. One by one they were conquered by one protective argument:

'I am free to do as I like. I am my own mistress; and I am doing nothing that is wrong. Even if it is unconventional, what of that? God knows there are enough conventions in the world that are wrong, hopelessly, unalterably wrong. After all, who are the people who are most bound by convention? Those who call themselves "smart!" If Convention is the god of the smart set, then it is about time that honest people chose another!'

* * * * *

Leonard received the letter at breakfast-time. He did not give it any special attention, as he had other letters at the same time, some of which were, if less pleasant, of more immediate importance. He had of late been bombarded with dunning letters from tradesmen; for during his University life, and ever since, he had run into debt.

The moderate allowance his father made him he had treated as cash for incidental expenses, but everything else had been on credit. Indeed he was beginning to get seriously alarmed about the future, for his father, who had paid his debts once, and at a time when they were by comparison inconsiderable, had said that he would not under any circumstances pay others. He was not sorry, therefore, for an opportunity of getting away for a few hours from home; from himself—from anxieties, possibilities. The morning was a sweltering one, and he grumbled to himself as he set out on his journey through the woods.

* * * * *

Stephen rose fresh and in good spirits, despite her sleepless night. When youth and strength are to the fore, a night's sleep is not of much account, for the system once braced up is not allowed to slacken. It was a notable sign of her strong nature that she was not even impatient, but waited with calm fixity the hour at which she had asked Leonard Everard to meet her. It is true that as the time grew closer her nerve was less marked. And just before it she was a girl—and nothing more; with all girl's diffidence, a girl's self-distrust, a girl's abnegation, a girl's plasticity.

In the more purely personal aspect of her enterprise Stephen's effort was more conscious. It is hardly possible for a pretty woman to seek in her study of perfection the aid of her mirror and to be unconscious of her aims. There must certainly be at least one dominant purpose: the achievement of success. Stephen did not attempt to deny her own beauty; on the contrary she gave it the fullest scope. There was a certain triumph in her glance as she took her last look in her mirror; a gratification of her wish to show herself in the best way possible. It was a very charming picture which the mirror reflected.

It may be that there is a companionship in a mirror, especially to a woman; that the reflection of oneself is an emboldening presence, a personality which is better than the actuality of an unvalued stranger. Certainly, when Stephen closed the door and stood in the wainscoted passage, which was only dimly lit by the high window at either end, her courage seemed at once to ooze away.

Probably for the first time in her life, as she left the shade of the long passage and came out on the staircase flooded with the light of the noonday sun, Stephen felt that she was a girl—'girl' standing as some sort of synonym for weakness, pretended or actual. Fear, in whatever form or degree it may come, is a vital quality and must move. It cannot stand at a fixed point; if it be not sent backward it must progress. Stephen felt this, and, though her whole nature was repugnant to the task, forced herself to the effort of repression. It would, she felt, have been to her a delicious pleasure to have abandoned all effort; to have sunk in the lassitude of self-surrender.

The woman in her was working; her sex had found her out!

She turned and looked around her, as though conscious of being watched. Then, seeing that she was alone, she went her way with settled purpose; with flashing eyes and glowing cheeks—and a beating heart. A heart all woman's since it throbbed the most with apprehension when the enemy, Man, was the objective of her most resolute attack. She knew that she must keep moving; that she must not stop or pause; or her whole resolution must collapse. And so she hurried on, fearful lest a chance meeting with any one might imperil her purpose.

CHAPTER X—THE RESOLVE

On she went through the faint moss-green paths; through meadows rich with flowering grasses and the many reds of the summer wild-flowers. And so up through the path cut in the natural dipping of the rock that rose over Caester Hill and formed a strong base for the clump of great trees that made a landmark for many a mile around. During the first part of her journey between the house and the hilltop, she tried to hold her purpose at arm's length; it would be sufficient to face its terrors when the time had come. In the meantime the matter was of such overwhelming importance that nothing else could take its place; all she could do was to suspend the active part of the thinking faculties and leave the mind only receptive.

But when she had passed through the thin belt of stunted oak and beech which hedged in the last of the lush meadows, and caught sight of the clump of trees on the hilltop, she unconsciously braced herself as a young regiment loses its tremors when the sight of the enemy breaks upon it. No longer her eyes fell earthward; they were raised, and raised proudly. Stephen Norman was fixed in her intention. Like the woman of old, her feet were on the ploughshares and she would not hesitate.

As she drew near the appointed place her pace grew slower and slower; the woman in her was unconsciously manifesting itself. She would not be first in her tryst with a man. Unconsciousness, however, is not a working quality which can be relied upon for staying power; the approach to the trysting-place brought once more home to her the strange nature of her enterprise. She had made up her mind to it; there was no use in deceiving herself. What she had undertaken to do was much more unconventional than being first at a meeting. It was foolish and weak to delay. The last thought braced her up; and it was with a hurried gait, which alone would have betrayed her to an intelligent observer, that she entered the grove.

CHAPTER XI—THE MEETING

Had Stephen been better acquainted with men and women, she would have been more satisfied with herself for being the first at the tryst. The conventional idea, in the minds of most women and of all men, is that a woman should never be the first. But real women, those in whom the heart beats strong, and whose blood can leap, know better. These are the commanders of men. In them sex calls to sex, all unconsciously at first; and men answer to their call, as they to men's.

Two opposite feelings strove for dominance as Stephen found herself on the hilltop, alone. One a feeling natural enough to any one, and especially to a girl, of relief that a dreaded hour had been postponed; the other of chagrin that she was the first.

After a few moments, however, one of the two militant thoughts became dominant: the feeling of chagrin. With a pang she thought if she had been a man and summoned for such a purpose, how she would have hurried to the trysting-place; how the flying of her feet would have vied with the quick rapturous beating of her heart! With a little sigh and a blush, she remembered that Leonard did not know the purpose of the meeting; that he was a friend almost brought up with her since boy and girl times; that he had often been summoned in similar terms and for the most trivial of social purposes.

For nearly half an hour Stephen sat on the rustic seat under the shadow of the great oak, looking, half unconscious of its beauty and yet influenced by it, over the wide landscape stretched at her feet.

In spite of her disregard of conventions, she was no fool; the instinct of wisdom was strong within her, so strong that in many ways it ruled her conscious efforts. Had any one told her that her preparations for this interview were made deliberately with some of the astuteness that dominated the Devil when he took Jesus to the top of a high mountain and showed him all the kingdoms of the earth at His feet, she would have, and with truth, denied it with indignation. Nevertheless it was a fact that she had, in all unconsciousness, chosen for the meeting a spot which would evidence to a man, consciously or unconsciously, the desirability for his own sake of acquiescence in her views and wishes. For all this spreading landscape was her possession, which her husband would share. As far as the eye could reach was within the estate which she had inherited from her father and her uncle.

The half-hour passed in waiting had in one way its advantages to the girl: though she was still as high strung as ever, she acquired a larger measure of control over herself. The nervous tension, however, was so complete physically that all her faculties were acutely awake; very early she became conscious of a distant footstep.

To Stephen's straining ears the footsteps seemed wondrous slow, and more wondrous regular; she felt instinctively that she would have liked to have listened to a more hurried succession of less evenly-marked sounds. But notwithstanding these thoughts, and the qualms which came in their turn, the sound of the coming feet brought great joy. For, after all, they were coming; and coming just in time to prevent the sense of disappointment at their delay gaining firm foothold. It was only when the coming was assured that she felt how strong had been the undercurrent of her apprehension lest they should not come at all.

Very sweet and tender and beautiful Stephen looked at this moment. The strong lines of her face were softened by the dark fire in her eyes and the feeling which glowed in the deep blushes which mantled her cheeks. The proudness of her bearing was no less marked than ever, but in the willowy sway of her body there was a yielding of mere sorry pride. In all the many moods which the gods allow to good women there is none so dear or so alluring, consciously as well as instinctively, to true men as this self-surrender. As Leonard drew near, Stephen sank softly into a seat, doing so with a guilty feeling of acting a part. When he actually came into the grove he found her seemingly lost in a reverie as she gazed out over the wide expanse in front of her. He was hot after his walk, and with something very like petulance threw himself into a cane armchair, exclaiming as he did so with the easy insolence of old familiarity:

'What a girl you are, Stephen! dragging a fellow all the way up here. Couldn't you have fixed it down below somewhere if you wanted to see me?'

Strangely enough, as it seemed to her, Stephen did not dislike his tone of mastery. There was something in it which satisfied her. The unconscious recognition of his manhood, as opposed to her womanhood, soothed her in a peaceful way. It was easy to yield to a dominant man. She was never more womanly than when she answered him softly:

'It was rather unfair; but I thought you would not mind coming so far. It is so cool and delightful here; and we can talk without being disturbed.' Leonard was lying back in his chair fanning himself with his wide-brimmed straw hat, with outstretched legs wide apart and resting on the back of his heels. He replied with grudging condescension:

'Yes, it's cool enough after the hot tramp over the fields and through the wood. It's not so good as the house, though, in one way: a man can't get a drink here. I say, Stephen, it wouldn't be half bad if there were a shanty put up here like those at the Grands Mulets or on the Matterhorn. There could be a tap laid on where a fellow could quench his thirst on a day like this!'

Before Stephen's eyes floated a momentary vision of a romantic châlet with wide verandah and big windows looking over the landscape; a great wide stone hearth; quaint furniture made from the gnarled branches of trees; skins on the floor; and the walls adorned with antlers, great horns, and various trophies of the chase. And amongst them Leonard, in a picturesque suit, lolling back just as at present and smiling with a loving look in his eyes as she handed him a great blue-and-white Munich beer mug topped with cool foam. There was a soft mystery in her voice as she answered:

'Perhaps, Leonard, there will some day be such a place here!' He seemed to grumble as he replied:

'I wish it was here now. Some day seems a long way off!'

This seemed a good opening for Stephen; for the fear of the situation was again beginning to assail her, and she felt that if she did not enter on her task at once, its difficulty might overwhelm her. She felt angry with herself that there was a change in her voice as she said:

'Some day may mean—can mean everything. Things needn't be a longer way off than we choose ourselves, sometimes!'

'I say, that's a good one! Do you mean to say that because I am some day to own Brindehow I can do as I like with it at once, whilst the governor's all there, and a better life than I am any day? Unless you want me to shoot the old man by accident when we go out on the First.' He laughed a short, unmeaning masculine laugh which jarred somewhat on her. She did not, however, mean to be diverted from her main purpose, so she went on quickly:

'You know quite well, Leonard, that I don't mean anything of the kind. But there was something I wanted to say to you, and I wished that we should be alone. Can you not guess what it is?'

'No, I'll be hanged if I can!' was his response, lazily given.

Despite her resolution she turned her head; she could not meet his eyes. It cut her with a sharp pain to notice when she turned again that he was not looking at her. He continued fanning himself with his hat as he gazed out at the view. She felt that the critical moment of her life had come, that it was now or never as to her fulfilling her settled intention. So with a rush she went on her way:

'Leonard, you and I have been friends a long time. You know my views on some points, and that I think a woman should be as free to act as a man!' She paused; words and ideas did not seem to flow with the readiness she expected. Leonard's arrogant assurance completed the dragging her back to earth which her own self-consciousness began:

'Drive on, old girl! I know you're a crank from Crankville on some subjects. Let us have it for all you're worth. I'm on the grass and listening.'

Stephen paused. 'A crank from Crankville!'—this after her nights of sleepless anxiety; after the making of the resolution which had cost her so much, and which was now actually in process of realisation. Was it all worth so much? why not abandon it now? . . . Abandon it! Abandon a resolution! All the obstinacy of her nature—she classed it herself as firmness—rose in revolt. She shook her head angrily, pulled herself together, and went on:

'That may be! though it's not what I call myself, or what I am usually called, so far as I know. At any rate my convictions are honest, and I am sure you will respect them as such, even if you do not share them.' She did not see the ready response in his face which she expected, and so hurried on:

'It has always seemed to me that a—when a woman has to speak to a man she should do so as frankly as she would like him to speak to her, and as freely. Leonard, I—I,' as she halted, a sudden idea, winged with possibilities of rescuing procrastination came to her. She went on more easily:

'I know you are in trouble about money matters. Why not let me help you?' He sat up and looked at her and said genially:

'Well, Stephen, you are a good old sort! No mistake about it. Do you mean to say you would help me to pay my debts, when the governor has refused to do so any more?'

'It would be a great pleasure to me, Leonard, to do anything for your good or your pleasure.'

There was a long pause; they both sat looking down at the ground. The woman's heart beat loud; she feared that the man must hear it. She was consumed with anxiety, and with a desolating wish to be relieved from the strain of saying more. Surely, surely Leonard could not be so blind as not to see the state of things! . . . He would surely seize the occasion; throw aside his diffidence and relieve her! . . . His words made a momentary music in her ears as he spoke:

'And is this what you asked me to come here for?'

The words filled her with a great shame. She felt herself a dilemma. It had been no part of her purpose to allude his debts. Viewed in the light of what was to follow, it would seem to him that she was trying to foreclose his affection. That could not be allowed to pass; the error must be rectified. And yet! . . . And yet this very error must be cleared up before she could make her full wish apparent. She seemed to find herself compelled by inexorable circumstances into an unlooked-for bluntness. In any case she must face the situation. Her pluck did not fail her; it was with a very noble and graceful simplicity that she turned to her companion and said:

'Leonard, I did not quite mean that. It would be a pleasure to me to be of that or any other service to you, if I might be so happy! But I never meant to allude to your debts. Oh! Leonard, can't you understand! If you were my husband—or—or going to be, all such little troubles would fall away from you. But I would not for the world have you think . . . '

Her very voice failed her. She could not speak what was in her mind; she turned away, hiding in her hands her face which fairly seemed to burn. This, she thought, was the time for a true lover's opportunity! Oh, if she had been a man, and a woman had so appealed, how he would have sprung to her side and taken her in his arms, and in a wild rapture of declared affection have swept away all the pain of her shame!

But she remained alone. There was no springing to her side; no rapture of declared affection; no obliteration of her shame. She had to bear it all alone. There, in the open; under the eyes that she would fain have seen any other phase of her distress. Her heart beat loud and fast; she waited to gain her self-control.

Leonard Everard had his faults, plenty of them, and he was in truth composed of an amalgam of far baser metals than Stephen thought; but he had been born of gentle blood and reared amongst gentlefolk. He did not quite understand the cause or the amount of his companion's concern; but he could not but recognise her distress. He realised that it had followed hard upon her most generous intention towards himself. He could not, therefore, do less than try to comfort her, and he began his task in a conventional way, but with a blundering awkwardness which was all manlike. He took her hand and held it in his; this much at any rate he had learned in sitting on stairs or in conservatories after extra dances. He said as tenderly as he could, but with an impatient gesture unseen by her:

'Forgive me, Stephen! I suppose I have said or done something which I shouldn't. But I don't know what it is; upon my honour I don't. Anyhow, I am truly sorry for it. Cheer up, old girl! I'm not your husband, you know; so you needn't be distressed.'

Stephen took her courage *à deux mains*. If Leonard would not speak she must. It was manifestly impossible that the matter could be left in its present state.

'Leonard,' she said softly and solemnly, 'might not that some day be?'

Leonard, in addition to being an egotist and the very incarnation of selfishness, was a prig of the first water. He had been reared altogether in convention. Home life and Eton and Christchurch had taught him many things, wise as well as foolish; but had tended to fix his conviction that affairs of the heart should proceed on adamantine lines of conventional decorum. It never even occurred to him that a lady could so far step from the confines of convention as to take the initiative in a matter of affection. In his blind ignorance he blundered brutally. He struck better than he knew, as, meaning only to pass safely by an awkward conversational corner, he replied:

'No jolly fear of that! You're too much of a boss for me!' The words and the levity with which they were spoken struck the girl as with a whip. She turned for an instant as pale as ashes; then the red blood rushed from her heart, and face and neck were dyed crimson. It was not a blush, it was a suffusion. In his ignorance Leonard thought it was the former, and went on with what he considered his teasing.

'Oh yes! You know you always want to engineer a chap your own way and make him do just as you wish. The man who has the happiness of marrying you, Stephen, will have a hard row to hoe!' His 'chaff' with its utter want of refinement seemed to her, in her high-strung earnest condition, nothing short of brutal, and for a few seconds produced a feeling of repellence. But it is in the nature of things that opposition of any kind arouses the fighting instinct of a naturally dominant nature. She lost sight of her femininity in the pursuit of her purpose; and as this was to win the man to her way of thinking, she took the logical course of answering his argument. If Leonard Everard had purposely set himself to stimulate her efforts in this direction he could hardly have chosen a better way. It came somewhat as a surprise to Stephen, when she heard her own words:

'I would make a good wife, Leonard! A husband whom I loved and honoured would, I think, not be unhappy!' The sound of her own voice speaking these words, though the tone was low and tender and more self-suppressing by far than was her wont, seemed to peal like thunder in her own ears. Her last bolt seemed to have sped. The blood rushed to her head, and she had to hold on to the arms of the rustic chair or she would have fallen forward.

The time seemed long before Leonard spoke again; every second seemed an age. She seemed to have grown tired of waiting for the sound of his voice; it was with a kind of surprise that she heard him say:

'You limit yourself wisely, Stephen!'

'How do you mean?' she asked, making a great effort to speak.

'You would promise to love and honour; but there isn't anything about obeying.'

As he spoke Leonard stretched himself again luxuriously, and laughed with the intellectual arrogance of a man who is satisfied with a joke, however inferior, of his own manufacture. Stephen looked at him with a long look which began in anger—that anger which comes from an unwonted sense of impotence, and ends in tolerance, the intermediate step being admiration. It is the primeval curse that a woman's choice is to her husband; and it is an important part of the teaching of a British gentlewoman, knit in the very fibres of her being by the remorseless etiquette of a thousand years, that she be true to him. The man who has in his person the necessary powers or graces to evoke admiration in his wife, even for a passing moment, has a stronghold unconquerable as a rule by all the deadliest arts of mankind.

Leonard Everard was certainly good to look upon as he lolled at his ease on that summer morning. Tall, straight, supple; a typical British gentleman of the educated class, with all parts of the body properly developed and held in some kind of suitable poise.

As Stephen looked, the anxiety and chagrin which tormented her seemed to pass. She realised that here was a nature different from her own, and which should be dealt with in a way unsuitable to herself; and the conviction seemed to make the action which it necessitated more easy as well as more natural to her. Perhaps for the first time in her life Stephen understood that it may be necessary to apply to individuals a standard of criticism unsuitable to self-judgment. Her recognition might have been summed up in the thought which ran through her mind:

'One must be a little lenient with a man one loves!'

Stephen, when once she had allowed the spirit of toleration to work within her, felt immediately its calming influence. It was with brighter thoughts and better humour that she went on with her task. A task only, it seemed now; a means to an end which she desired.

'Leonard, tell me seriously, why do you think I gave you the trouble of coming out here?'

'Upon my soul, Stephen, I don't know.'

'You don't seem to care either, lolling like that when I am serious!' The words were acid, but the tone was soft and friendly, familiar and genuine, putting quite a meaning of its own on them. Leonard looked at her indolently:

'I like to loll.'

'But can't you even guess, or try to guess, what I ask you?'

'I can't guess. The day's too hot, and that shanty with the drinks is not built yet.'

'Or may never be!' Again he looked at her sleepily.

'Never be! Why not?'

'Because, Leonard, it may depend on you.'

'All right then. Drive on! Hurry up the architect and the jerry-builder!'

A quick blush leaped to Stephen's cheeks. The words were full of meaning, though the tone lacked something; but the news was too good. She could not accept it at once; she decided to herself to wait a short time. Ere many seconds had passed she rejoiced that she had done so as he went on:

'I hope you'll give me a say before that husband of yours comes along. He might be a blue-ribbonite; and it wouldn't do to start such a shanty for rot-gut!'

Again a cold wave swept over her. The absolute difference of feeling between the man and herself; his levity against her earnestness, his callous blindness to her purpose, even the commonness of his words chilled her. For a few seconds she wavered again in her intention; but once again his comeliness and her own obstinacy joined hands and took her back to her path. With chagrin she felt that her words almost stuck in her throat, as summoning up all her resolution she went on:

'It would be for you I would have it built, Leonard!' The man sat up quickly.

'For me?' he asked in a sort of wonderment.

'Yes, Leonard, for you and me!' She turned away; her blushes so overcame her that she could not look at him. When she faced round again he was standing up, his back towards her.

She stood up also. He was silent for a while; so long that the silence became intolerable, and she spoke:

'Leonard, I am waiting!' He turned round and said slowly, the absence of all emotion from his face chilling her till her face blanched:

'I don't think I would worry about it!'

Stephen Norman was plucky, and when she was face to face with any difficulty she was all herself. Leonard did not look pleasant; his face was hard and there was just a suspicion of anger. Strangely enough, this last made the next step easier to the girl; she said slowly:

'All right! I think I understand!'

He turned from her and stood looking out on the distant prospect. Then she felt that the blow which she had all along secretly feared had fallen on her. But her pride as well as her obstinacy now rebelled. She would not accept a silent answer. There must be no doubt left to torture her afterwards. She would take care that there was no mistake. Schooling herself to her task, and pressing one hand for a moment to her side as though to repress the beating of her heart, she came behind him and touched him tenderly on the arm.

'Leonard,' she said softly, 'are you sure there is no mistake? Do you not see that I am asking you,' she intended to say 'to be my husband,' but she could not utter the words, they seemed to stick in her mouth, so she finished the sentence: 'that I be your wife?'

The moment the words were spoken—the bare, hard, naked, shameless words—the revulsion came. As a lightning flash shows up the blackness of the night the appalling truth of what she had done was forced upon her. The blood rushed to her head till cheeks and shoulders and neck seemed to burn. Covering her face with her hands she sank back on the seat crying silently bitter tears that seemed to scald her eyes and her cheeks as they ran.

Leonard was angry. When it began to dawn upon him what was the purpose of Stephen's speech, he had been shocked. Young men are so easily shocked by breaches of convention made by women they respect! And his pride was hurt. Why should he have been placed in such a ridiculous position! He did not love Stephen in that way; and she should have known it. He liked her and all that sort of thing; but what right had she to assume that he loved her? All the weakness of his moral nature came out in his petulance. It was boyish that his eyes filled with tears. He knew it, and that made him more angry than ever. Stephen might well have been at a loss to understand his anger, as, with manifest intention to wound, he answered her:

'What a girl you are, Stephen. You are always doing something or other to put a chap in the wrong and make him ridiculous. I thought you were joking—not a good joke either! Upon my soul, I don't know what I've done that you should fix on me! I wish to goodness—'

If Stephen had suffered the red terror before, she suffered the white terror now. It was not injured pride, it was not humiliation, it was not fear; it was something vague and terrible that lay far deeper than any of these. Under ordinary circumstances she would have liked to have spoken out her mind and given back as good as she got; and even as the thoughts whirled through her brain they came in a torrent of vague vituperative eloquence. But now her tongue was tied. Instinctively she knew that she had put it out of her power to revenge, or even to defend herself. She was tied to the stake, and must suffer without effort and in silence.

Most humiliating of all was the thought that she must propitiate the man who had so wounded her. All love for him had in the instant passed from her; or rather she realised fully the blank, bare truth that she had never really loved him at all. Had she really loved him, even a blow at his hands would have been acceptable; but now . . .

She shook the feelings and thoughts from her as a bird does the water from its wings; and, with the courage and strength and adaptability of her nature, addressed herself to the hard task which faced her in the immediate present. With eloquent, womanly gesture she arrested the torrent of Leonard's indignation; and, as he paused in surprised obedience, she said:

'That will do, Leonard! It is not necessary to say any more; and I am sure you will see, later on, that at least there was no cause for your indignation! I have done an unconventional thing, I know; and I dare say I shall have to pay for it in humiliating bitterness of thought later on! But please remember we are all alone! This is a secret between us; no one else need ever know or suspect it!'

She rose as she concluded. The quiet dignity of her speech and bearing brought back Leonard in some way to his sense of duty as a gentleman. He began, in a sheepish way, to make an apology:

'I'm sure I beg your pardon, Stephen.' But again she held the warning hand:

'There is no need for pardon; the fault, if there were any, was mine alone. It was I, remember, who asked you to come here and who introduced and conducted this melancholy business. I have asked you several things, Leonard, and one more I will add—'tis only one: that you will forget!'

As she moved away, her dismissal of the subject was that of an empress to a serf. Leonard would have liked to answer her; to have given vent to his indignation that, even when he had refused her offer, she should have the power to treat him if he was the one refused, and to make him feel small and ridiculous in his own eyes. But somehow he felt constrained to silence; her simple dignity outclassed him.

There was another factor too, in his forming his conclusion of silence. He had never seen Stephen look so well, or so attractive. He had never respected her so much as when her playfulness had turned to majestic gravity. All the boy and girl strife of the years that had gone seemed to have passed away. The girl whom he had played with, and bullied, and treated as frankly as though she had been a boy, had in an instant become a woman—and such a woman as demanded respect and admiration even from such a man.

CHAPTER XII—ON THE ROAD HOME

When Leonard Everard parted from Stephen he did so with a feeling of dissatisfaction: firstly, with Stephen; secondly, with things in general; thirdly, with himself. The first was definite, concrete, and immediate; he could give himself chapter and verse for all the girl's misdoing. Everything she had said or done had touched some nerve painfully, or had offended his feelings; and to a man of his temperament his feelings are very sacred things, to himself.

'Why had she put him in such a ridiculous position? That was the worst of women. They were always wanting him to do something he didn't want to do, or crying . . . there was that girl at Oxford.'

Here he turned his head slowly, and looked round in a furtive way, which was getting almost a habit with him. 'A fellow should go away so that he wouldn't have to swear lies. Women were always wanting money; or worse: to be married! Confound women; they all seemed to want him to marry them! There was the Oxford girl, and then the Spaniard, and now Stephen!' This put his thoughts in a new channel. He wanted money himself. Why, Stephen had spoken of it herself; had offered to pay his debts. Gad! it was a good idea that every one round the countryside seemed to know his affairs. What a flat he had been not to accept her offer then and there before matters had gone further. Stephen had lots of money, more than any girl could want. But she didn't give him time to get the thing fixed . . . If he had only known beforehand what she wanted he could have come prepared . . . that was the way with women! Always thinking of themselves! And now? Of course she wouldn't stump up after his refusing her. What would his father say if he came to hear of it? And he must speak to him soon, for these chaps were threatening to County Court him if he didn't pay. Those harpies in Vere Street were quite nasty . . . ' He wondered if he could work Stephen for a loan.

He walked on through the woodland path, his pace slower than before. 'How pretty she had looked!' Here he touched his little moustache. 'Gad! Stephen was a fine girl anyhow! If it wasn't for all that red hair . . . I like 'em dark better! . . . And her being such an infernal boss!'. . . Then he said unconsciously aloud:

'If I was her husband I'd keep her to rights!'

Poor Stephen!

'So that's what the governor meant by telling me that fortune was to be had, and had easily, if a man wasn't a blind fool. The governor is a starchy old party. He wouldn't speak out straight and say, "Here's Stephen Norman, the richest girl you are ever likely to meet; why don't you make up to her and marry her?" But that would be encouraging his son to be a fortune-hunter! Rot! . . . And now, just because she didn't tell me what she wanted to speak about, or the governor didn't give me a hint so that I might be prepared, I have gone and thrown away the chance. After all it mightn't be so bad. Stephen is a fine girl! . . . But she mustn't ever look at me as she did when I spoke about her not obeying. I mean to be master in my own house anyhow!

'A man mustn't be tied down too tight, even if he is married. And if there's plenty of loose cash about it isn't hard to cover up your tracks . . . I think I'd better think this thing over calmly and be ready when Stephen comes at me again. That's the way with women. When a woman like Stephen fixes her cold grey on a man she does not mean to go asleep over it. I daresay my best plan will be to sit tight, and let her work herself up a bit. There's nothing like a little wholesome neglect for bringing a girl to her bearings!' . . .

For a while he walked on in satisfied self-complacency.

'Confound her! why couldn't she have let me know that she was fond of me in some decent way, without all that formal theatrical proposing? It's a deuced annoying thing in the long run the way the women get fond of me. Though it's nice enough in some ways while it lasts!' he added, as if in unwilling recognition of fact. As the path debouched on the highroad he said to himself half aloud:

'Well, she's a mighty fine girl, anyhow! And if she is red I've had about enough of the black! . . . That Spanish girl is beginning to kick too! I wish I had never come across . . . '

'Shut up, you fool!' he said to himself as he walked on.

When he got home he found a letter from his father. He took it to his room before breaking the seal. It was at least concise and to the point:

> 'The enclosed has been sent to me. You will have to deal with it yourself. You know my opinion and also my intention. The items which I have marked have been incurred since I spoke to you last about your debts. I shall not pay another farthing for you. So take your own course!
>
> 'JASPER EVERARD.'

The enclosed was a jeweller's bill, the length and the total of which lengthened his face and drew from him a low whistle. He held it in his hand for a long time, standing quite still and silent. Then drawing a deep breath he said aloud:

'That settles it! The halter is on me! It's no use squealing. If it's to be a red head on my pillow! . . . All right! I must only make the best of it. Anyhow I'll have a good time to-day, even if it must be the last!'

That day Harold was in Norcester on business. It was late when he went to the club to dine. Whilst waiting for dinner he met Leonard Everard, flushed and somewhat at uncertain in his speech. It was something of a shock to Harold to see him in such a state.

Leonard was, however, an old friend, and man is as a rule faithful to friends in this form of distress. So in his kindly feeling Harold offered to drive him home, for he knew that he could thus keep him out of further harm. Leonard thanked him in uncertain speech, and said he would be ready. In the meantime he would go and play billiards with the marker whilst Harold was having his dinner.

At ten o'clock Harold's dogcart was ready and he went to look for Leonard, who had not since come near him. He found him half asleep in the smoking-room, much drunker than he had been earlier in the evening.

The drive was fairly long, so Harold made up his mind for a prolonged term of uneasiness and anxiety. The cool night-air, whose effect was increased by the rapid motion, soon increased Leonard's somnolence and for a while he slept soundly, his companion watching carefully lest he should sway over and fall out of the trap. He even held him up as they swung round sharp corners.

After a time he woke up, and woke in a nasty temper. He began to find fault in an incoherent way with everything. Harold said little, just enough to prevent any cause for further grievance. Then Leonard changed and became affectionate. This mood was a greater bore than the other, but Harold managed to bear it with stolid indifference. Leonard was this by time making promises to do things for him, that as he was what he called a 'goo' fell',' he might count on his help and support in the future. As Harold knew him to be a wastrel, over head and ears in debt and with only the succession to a small estate, he did not take much heed to his maunderings. At last the drunken man said something which startled him so much that he instinctively drew himself together with such suddenness as to frighten the horse and almost make him rear up straight.

'Woa! Woa! Steady, boy. Gently!' he said, quieting him. Then turning to his companion said in a voice hollow with emotion and vibrant with suppressed passion:

'What was it you said?'

Leonard, half awake, and not half of that half master of himself, answered:

'I said I will make you agent of Normanstand when I marry Stephen.'

Harold grew cold. To hear of any one marrying Stephen was to him like plunging him in a glacier stream; but to hear her name so lightly spoken, and by such a man, was a bewildering shock which within a second set his blood on fire.

'What do you mean?' he thundered. 'You marry Ste . . . Miss Norman! You're not worthy to untie her shoe! You indeed! She wouldn't look on the same side of the street with a drunken brute like you! How dare you speak of her in such a way!'

'Brute!' said Leonard angrily, his vanity reaching inward to heart and brain through all the numbing obstacle of his drunken flesh. 'Who's brute? Brute yourself! Tell you goin' to marry Stephen, 'cos Stephen wants it. Stephen loves me. Loves me with all her red head! Wha're you doin'! Wha!!'

His words merged in a lessening gurgle, for Harold had now got him by the throat.

'Take care what you say about that lady! damn you!' he said, putting his face close the other's with eyes that blazed. 'Don't you dare to mention her name in such a way, or you will regret it longer than you can think. Loves you, you swine!'

The struggle and the fierce grip on his throat sobered Leonard somewhat. Momentarily sobbed him to that point when he could be coherent and vindictive, though not to the point where he could think ahead. Caution, wisdom, discretion, taste, were not for him at such a moment. Guarding his throat with both hands in an instinctive and spasmodic manner he answered the challenge:

'Who are you calling swine? I tell you she loves me. She ought to know. Didn't she tell me so this very day!' Harold drew back his arm to strike him in the face, his anger too great for words. But the other, seeing the motion and in the sobering recognition of danger, spoke hastily:

'Keep your hair on! You know so jolly much more than I do. I tell you that she told me this and a lot more this morning when she asked me to marry her.'

Harold's heart grew cold as ice. There is something in the sound of a voice speaking truthfully which a true man can recognise. Through all Leonard's half-drunken utterings came such a ring of truth; and Harold recognised it. He felt that his voice was weak and hollow as he spoke, thinking it necessary to give at first a sort of official denial to such a monstrous statement:

'Liar!'

'I'm no liar!' answered Leonard. He would like to have struck him in answer to such a word had he felt equal to it. 'She asked me to marry her to-day on the hill above the house, where I went to meet her by appointment. Here! I'll prove it to you. Read this!' Whilst he was speaking he had opened the greatcoat and was fumbling in the breast-pocket of his coat. He produced a letter which he handed to Harold, who took it with trembling hand. By this time the reins had fallen slack and the horse was walking quietly. There was moonlight, but not enough to read by. Harold bent over and lifted the driving-lamp next to him and turned it so that he could read the envelope. He could hardly keep either lamp or paper still, his hand trembled so when he saw that the direction was in Stephen's handwriting. He was handing it back when Leonard said again:

'Open it! Read it! You must do so; I tell you, you must! You called me a liar, and now must read the proof that I am not. If you don't I shall have to ask Stephen to make you!' Before Harold's mind flashed a rapid thought of what the girl might suffer in being asked to take part in such a quarrel. He could not himself even act to the best advantage unless he knew the truth . . . he took the letter from the envelope and held it before the lamp, the paper fluttering as though in a breeze from the trembling of his hand. Leonard looked on, the dull glare of his eyes brightening with malignant pleasure as he beheld the other's concern. He owed him a grudge, and by God he would pay it. Had he not been struck—throttled—called a liar! . . .

As he read the words Harold's face cleared. 'Why, you infernal young scoundrel!' he said angrily, 'that letter is nothing but a simple note from a young girl to an old friend—playmate asking him to come to see her about some trivial thing. And you construe it into a proposal of marriage. You hound!' He held the letter whilst he spoke, heedless of the outstretched hand of the other waiting to take it back. There was a dangerous glitter in Leonard's eyes. He knew his man and he knew the truth of what he had himself said, and he felt, with all the strength of his base soul, how best he could torture him. In the very strength of Harold's anger, in the poignancy of his concern, in the relief to his soul expressed in his eyes and his voice, his antagonist realised the jealousy of one who honours—and loves. Second by second Leonard grew more sober, and more and better able to carry his own idea into act.

'Give me my letter!' he began.

'Wait!' said Harold as he put the lamp back into its socket. 'That will do presently. Take back what you said just now!'

'What? Take back what?'

'That base lie; that Miss Norman asked you to marry her.'

Leonard felt that in a physical struggle for the possession of the letter he would be outmatched; but his passion grew colder and more malignant, and in a voice that cut like the hiss of a snake he spoke slowly and deliberately. He was all sober now; the drunkenness of brain and blood was lost, for the time, in the strength of his cold passion.

'It is true. By God it is true; every word of it! That letter, which you want to steal, is only a proof that I went to meet her on Caester Hill by her own appointment. When I got there, she was waiting for me. She began to talk about a châlet there, and at first I didn't know what she meant—'

There was such conviction, such a triumphant truth in his voice, that Harold was convinced.

'Stop!' he thundered; 'stop, don't tell me anything. I don't want to hear. I don't want to know.' He covered his face with his hands and groaned. It was not as though the speaker were a stranger, in which case he would have been by now well on in his death by strangulation; he had known Leonard all his life, and he was a friend of Stephen's. And he was speaking truth.

The baleful glitter of Leonard's eyes grew brighter still. He was as a serpent when he goes to strike. In this wise he struck.

'I shall not stop. I shall go on and tell you all I choose. You have called me liar—twice. You have also called me other names. Now you shall hear the truth, the whole truth, and nothing but the truth. And if you won't listen to me some one else will.' Harold groaned again; Leonard's eyes brightened still more, and the evil smile on his face grew broader as he began more and more to feel his power. He went on to speak with a cold deliberate malignancy, but instinctively so sticking to absolute truth that he could trust himself to hurt most. The other listened, cold at heart and physically; his veins and arteries seemed stagnant.

'I won't tell you anything of her pretty embarrassments; how her voice fell as she pleaded; how she blushed and stammered. Why, even I, who am used to women and their pretty ways and their passions and their flushings and their stormy upbraidings, didn't quite know for a while what she was driving at. So at last she spoke out pretty plainly, and told me what a fond wife she'd make me if I would only take her!' Harold said nothing; he only rocked a little as one in pain, and his hands fell. The other went on:

'That is what happened this morning on Caester Hill under the trees where I met Stephen Norman by her own appointment; honestly what happened. If you don't believe me now you can ask Stephen. My Stephen!' he added in a final burst of venom as in a gleam of moonlight through a rift in the shadowy wood he saw the ghastly pallor of Harold's face. Then he added abruptly as he held out his hand:

'Now give me my letter!'

In the last few seconds Harold had been thinking. And as he had been thinking for the good, the safety, of Stephen, his thoughts flew swift and true. This man's very tone, the openness of his malignity, the underlying scorn when he spoke of her whom others worshipped, showed him the danger—the terrible immediate danger in which she stood from such a man. With the instinct of a mind working as truly for the woman he loved as the needle does to the Pole he spoke quietly, throwing a sneer into the tone so as to exasperate his companion—it was brain against brain now, and for Stephen's sake:

'And of course you accepted. You naturally would!' The other fell into the trap. He could not help giving an extra dig to his opponent by proving him once more in the wrong.

'Oh no, I didn't! Stephen is a fine girl; but she wants taking down a bit. She's too high and mighty just at present, and wants to boss a chap too much. I mean to be master in my own house; and she's got to begin as she will have to go on. I'll let her wait a bit: and then I'll yield by degrees to her lovemaking. She's a fine girl, for all her red head; and she won't be so bad after all!'

Harold listened, chilled into still and silent amazement. To hear Stephen spoken of in such a way appalled him. She of all women! . . . Leonard never knew how near sudden death he was, as he lay back in his seat, his eyes getting dull again and his chin sinking. The drunkenness which had been arrested by his passion was reasserting itself. Harold saw his state in time and arrested his own movement to take him by the throat and dash him to the ground. Even as he looked at him in scornful hate, the cart gave a lurch and Leonard fell forward. Instinctively Harold swept an arm round him and held him up. As he did so the unconsciousness of arrested sleep came; Leonard's chin sank on his breast and he breathed stertorously.

As he drove on, Harold's thoughts circled in a tumult. Vague ideas of extreme measures which he ought to take flashed up and paled away. Intention revolved upon itself till its weak side was exposed, and, it was abandoned. He could not doubt the essential truth of Leonard's statement regarding the proposal of marriage. He did not understand this nor did he try to. His own love for the girl and the bitter awaking to its futility made him so hopeless that in his own desolation all the mystery of her doing and the cause of it was merged and lost.

His only aim and purpose now was her safety. One thing at least he could do: by fair means or foul stop Leonard's mouth, so that others need not know her shame! He groaned aloud as the thought came to him. Beyond this first step he could do nothing, think of nothing as yet. And he could not take this first step till Leonard had so far sobered that he could understand.

And so waiting for that time to come, he drove on through the silent night.

CHAPTER XIII—HAROLD'S RESOLVE

As they went on their way Harold noticed that Leonard's breathing became more regular, as in honest sleep. He therefore drove slowly so that the other might be sane again before they should arrive at the gate of his father's place; he had something of importance to say before they should part.

Seeing him sleeping so peacefully, Harold passed a strap round him to prevent him falling from his seat. Then he could let his thoughts run more freely. Her safety was his immediate concern; again and again he thought over what he should say to Leonard to ensure his silence.

Whilst he was pondering with set brows, he was startled by Leonard's voice at his side:

'Is that you, Harold? I must have been asleep!' Harold remained silent, amazed at the change. Leonard went on, quite awake and coherent:

'By George! I must have been pretty well cut. I don't remember a thing after coming down the stairs of the club and you and the hall-porter helping me up here. I say, old chap, you have strapped me up all safe and tight. It was good of you to take charge of me. I hope I haven't been a beastly nuisance!' Harold answered grimly:

'It wasn't exactly what I should have called it!' Then, after looking keenly at his companion, he said: 'Are you quite awake and sober now?'

'Quite.' The answer came defiantly; there was something in his questioner's tone which was militant and aggressive. Before speaking further Harold pulled up the horse. They were now crossing bare moorland, where anything within a mile could have easily been seen. They were quite alone, and would be undisturbed. Then he turned to his companion.

'You talked a good deal in your drunken sleep—if sleep it was. You appeared to be awake!' Leonard answered:

'I don't remember anything of it. What did I say?'

'I am going to tell you. You said something so strange and so wrong that you must answer for it. But first I must know its truth.'

'Must! You are pretty dictatorial,' said Leonard angrily. 'Must answer for it! What do you mean?'

'Were you on Caester Hill to-day?'

'What's that to you?' There was no mistaking the defiant, quarrelsome intent.

'Answer me! were you?' Harold's voice was strong and calm.

'What if I was? It is none of your affair. Did I say anything in what you have politely called my drunken sleep?'

'You did.'

'What did I say?'

'I shall tell you in time. But I must know the truth as I proceed. There is some one else concerned in this, and I must know as I go on. You can easily judge by what I say if I am right.'

'Then ask away and be damned to you!' Harold's calm voice seemed to quell the other's turbulence as he went on:

'Were you on Caester Hill this morning?'

'I was.'

'Did you meet Miss --- a lady there?'

'What . . . I did!'

'Was it by appointment?' Some sort of idea or half-recollection seemed to come to Leonard; he fumbled half consciously in his breast-pocket. Then he broke out angrily:

'You have taken my letter!'

'I know the answer to that question,' said Harold slowly. 'You showed me the letter yourself, and insisted on my reading it.' Leonard's heart began to quail. He seemed to have an instinctive dread of what was coming. Harold went on calmly and remorselessly:

'Did a proposal of marriage pass between you?'

'Yes!' The answer was defiantly given; Leonard began to feel that his back was against the wall.

'Who made it?' The answer was a sudden attempt at a blow, but Harold struck down his hand in time and held it. Leonard, though a fairly strong man, was powerless in that iron grasp.

'You must answer! It is necessary that I know the truth.'

'Why must you? What have you to do with it? You are not my keeper! Nor Stephen's; though I dare say you would like to be!' The insult cooled Harold's rising passion, even whilst it wrung his heart.

'I have to do with it because I choose. You may find the answer if you wish in your last insult! Now, clearly understand me, Leonard Everard. You know me of old; and you know that what I say I shall do. One way or another, your life or mine may hang on your answers to me—if necessary!' Leonard felt himself pulled up. He knew well the strength and purpose of the man. With a light laugh, which he felt to be, as it was, hollow, he answered:

'Well, schoolmaster, as you are asking questions, I suppose I may as well answer them. Go on! Next!' Harold went on in the same calm, cold voice:

'Who made the proposal of marriage?'

'She did.'

'Did . . . Was it made at once and directly, or after some preliminary suggestion?'

'After a bit. I didn't quite understand at first what she was driving at.' There was a long pause. With an effort Harold went on:

'Did you accept?' Leonard hesitated. With a really wicked scowl he eyed his big, powerfully-built companion, who still had his hand as in a vice. Then seeing no resource, he answered:

'I did not! That does not mean that I won't, though!' he added defiantly. To his surprise Harold suddenly released his hand. There was a grimness in his tone as he said:

'That will do! I know now that you have spoken the truth, sober as well as drunk. You need say no more. I know the rest. Most men—even brutes like you, if there are any—would have been ashamed even to think the things you said, said openly to me, you hound. You vile, traitorous, mean-souled hound!'

'What did I say?'

'I know what you said; and I shall not forget it.' He went on, his voice deepening into a stern judicial utterance, as though he were pronouncing a sentence of death:

'Leonard Everard, you have treated vilely a lady whom I love and honour more than I love my own soul. You have insulted her to her face and behind her back. You have made such disloyal reference to her and to her mad act in so trusting you, and have so shown your intention of causing, intentionally or unintentionally, woe to her, that I tell you here and now that you hold henceforth your life in your hand. If you ever mention to a living soul what you have told me twice to-night, even though you should be then her husband; if you should cause her harm though she should then be your wife; if you should cause her dishonour in public or in private, I shall kill you. So help me God!'

Not a word more did he say; but, taking up the reins, drove on in silence till they arrived at the gate of Brindehow, where he signed to him to alight.

He drove off in silence.

When he arrived at his own house he sent the servant to bed, and then went to his study, where he locked himself in. Then, and then only, did he permit his thoughts to have full range. For the first time since the blow had fallen he looked straight in the face the change in his own life. He had loved Stephen so long and so honestly that it seemed to him now as if that love had been the very foundation of his life. He could not remember a time when he had not loved her; away back to the time when he, a big boy, took her, a little girl, under his care, and devoted himself to her. He had grown into the belief that so strong and so consistent an affection, though he had never spoken it or even hinted at it or inferred it, had become a part of her life as well as of his own. And this was the end of that dreaming! Not only did she not care for him, but found herself with a heart so empty that she needs must propose marriage to another man! There was surely something, more than at present he knew of or could understand, behind such an act done by her. Why should she ask Everard to marry her? Why should she ask any man? Women didn't do such things! . . . Here he paused. 'Women didn't do such things.' All at once there came back to him fragments of discussions—in which Stephen had had a part, in which matters of convention had been dealt with. Out of these dim and shattered memories came a comfort to his heart, though his brain could not as yet grasp the reason of it. He knew that Stephen had held an unconventional idea as to the equality of the sexes. Was it possible that she was indeed testing one of her theories?

The idea stirred him so that he could not remain quiet. He stood up, and walked the room. Somehow he felt light beginning to dawn, though he could not tell its source, or guess at the final measure of its fulness. The fact of Stephen having done such a thing was hard to bear; but it was harder to think that she should have done such a thing without a motive; or worse: with love of Leonard as a motive! He shuddered as he paused. She could not love such a man. It was monstrous! And yet she had done this thing . . . 'Oh, if she had had any one to advise her, to restrain her! But she had no mother! No mother! Poor Stephen!'

The pity of it, not for himself but for the woman he loved, overcame him. Sitting down heavily before his desk, he put his face on his hands, and his great shoulders shook.

Long, long after the violence of his emotion had passed, he sat there motionless, thinking with all the power and sincerity he knew; thinking for Stephen's good.

When a strong man thinks unselfishly some good may come out of it. He may blunder; but the conclusion of his reasoning must be in the main right. So it was with Harold. He knew that he was ignorant of women, and of woman's nature, as distinguished from man's. The only woman he had ever known well was Stephen; and she in her youth and in her ignorance of the world and herself was hardly sufficient to supply to him data for his present needs. To a clean-minded man of his age a woman is something divine. It is only when in later life disappointment and experience have hammered bitter truth into his brain, that he begins to realise that woman is not angelic but human. When he knows more, and finds that she is like himself, human and limited but with qualities of purity and sincerity and endurance which put his own to shame, he realises how much better a helpmate she is for man than could be the vague, unreal creations of his dreams. And then he can thank God for His goodness that when He might have given us Angels He did give us women!

Of one thing, despite the seeming of facts, he was sure: Stephen did not love Leonard. Every fibre of his being revolted at the thought. She of so high a nature; he of so low. She so noble; he so mean. Bah! the belief was impossible.

Impossible! Herein was the manifestation of his ignorance; anything is possible where love is concerned! It was characteristic of the man that in his mind he had abandoned, for the present at all events, his own pain. He still loved Stephen with all the strength of his nature, but for him the selfish side ceased to exist. He was trying to serve Stephen; and every other thought had to give way. He had been satisfied that in a manner she loved him in some way and in some degree; and he had hoped that in the fulness of time the childish love would ripen, so that in the end would come a mutual affection which was of the very essence of Heaven. He believed still that she loved him in some way; but the future that was based on hope had now been wiped out with a sudden and unsparing hand. She had actually proposed marriage to another man. If the idea of a marriage with him had ever crossed her mind she could have had no doubt of her feeling toward another. . . . And yet? And yet he could not believe that she loved Leonard; not even if all trains of reasoning should end by leading to that point. One thing he had at present to accept, that whatever might be the measure of affection Stephen might have for him, it was not love as he understood it. He resolutely turned his back on the thought of his own side of the matter, and tried to find some justification of Stephen's act.

'Seek and ye shall find; knock and it shall be opened to ye' has perhaps a general as well as a special significance. It is by patient tireless seeking that many a precious thing has been found. It was after many a long cycle of thought that the seeking and the knocking had effectual result. Harold came to believe, vaguely at first but more definitely as the evidence nucleated, that Stephen's act was due to some mad girlish wish to test her own theory; to prove to herself the correctness of her own reasoning, the fixity of her own purpose. He did not go on analysing further; for as he walked the room with a portion of the weight taken from his heart he noticed that the sky was beginning to quicken. The day would soon be upon him, and there was work to be done. Instinctively he knew that there was trouble in store for Stephen, and he felt that in such an hour he should be near her. All her life she had been accustomed to him. In her sorrows to confide in him, to tell him her troubles so that they might dwindle and pass away; to enhance her pleasures by making him a sharer in them.

Harold was inspirited by the coming of the new day. There was work to be done, and the work must be based on thought. His thoughts must take a practical turn; what was he to do that would help Stephen? Here there dawned on him for the first time the understanding of a certain humiliation which she had suffered; she had been refused! She who had stepped so far out of the path of maidenly reserve in which she had always walked as to propose marriage to a man, had been refused! He did not, could not, know to the full the measure of such humiliation to a woman; but he could guess at any rate a part. And that guessing made him grind his teeth in impotent rage.

But out of that rage came an inspiration. If Stephen had been humiliated by the refusal of one man, might not this be minimised if she in turn might refuse another? Harold knew so well the sincerity of his own love and the depth of his own devotion that he was satisfied that he could not err in giving the girl the opportunity of refusing him. It would be some sort of balm to her wounded spirit to know that Leonard's views were not shared by all men. That there were others who would deem it a joy to serve as her slaves. When she had refused him she would perhaps feel easier in her mind. Of course if she did not refuse him . . . Ah! well, then would the gates of Heaven open . . . But that would never be. The past could not be blotted out! All he could do would be to serve her. He would go early. Such a man as Leonard Everard might make some new complication, and the present was quite bad enough.

It was a poor enough thing for him, he thought at length. She might trample on him; but it was for her sake. And to him what did it matter? The worst had come. All was over now!

CHAPTER XIV—THE BEECH GROVE

On the morning following the proposal Stephen strolled out into a beech grove, some little distance from the house, which from childhood had been a favourite haunt of hers. It was not in the immediate road to anywhere, and so there was no occasion for any of the household or the garden to go through it or near it. She did not put on a hat, but took only a sunshade, which she used in passing over the lawn. The grove was on the side of the house away from her own room and the breakfast-room. When she had reached its shade she felt that at last she was alone.

The grove was a privileged place. Long ago a great number of young beeches had been planted so thickly that as they grew they shot up straight and branchless in their struggle for the light. Not till they had reached a considerable altitude had they been thinned; and then the thinning had been so effected that, as the high branches began to shoot out in the freer space, they met in time and interlaced so closely that they made in many places a perfect screen of leafy shade. Here and there were rifts or openings through which the light passed; under such places the grass was fine and green, or the wild hyacinths in due season tinged the earth with blue. Through the grove some wide alleys had been left: great broad walks where the soft grass grew short and fine, and to whose edges came a drooping of branches and an upspringing of undergrowth of laurel and rhododendron. At the far ends of these walks were little pavilions of marble built in the classic style which ruled for garden use two hundred years ago. At the near ends some of them were close to the broad stretch of water from whose edges ran back the great sloping banks of emerald sward dotted here and there with great forest trees. The grove was protected by a ha-ha, so that it was never invaded from without, and the servants of the house, both the domestics and the gardeners and grooms, had been always forbidden to enter it. Thus by long usage it had become a place of quiet and solitude for the members of the family.

To this soothing spot had come Stephen in her pain. The long spell of self-restraint during that morning had almost driven her to frenzy, and she sought solitude as an anodyne to her tortured soul. The long anguish of a third sleepless night, following on a day of humiliation and terror, had destroyed for a time the natural resilience of a healthy nature. She had been for so long in the prison of her own purpose with Fear as warder; the fetters of conventional life had so galled her that here in the accustomed solitude of this place, in which from childhood she had been used to move and think freely, she felt as does a captive who has escaped from an irksome durance. As Stephen had all along been free of movement and speech, no such opportunities of freedom called to her. The pent-up passion in her, however, found its own relief. Her voice was silent, and she moved with slow steps, halting often between the green tree-trunks in the cool shade; but her thoughts ran free, and passion found a vent. No stranger seeing the tall, queenly girl moving slowly through the trees could have imagined the fierce passion which blazed within her, unless he had been close enough to see her eyes. The habit of physical restraint to which all her life she had been accustomed, and which was intensified by the experience of the past thirty-six hours, still ruled her, even here. Gradually the habit of security began to prevail, and the shackles to melt away. Here had she come in all her childish troubles. Here had she fought with herself, and conquered herself. Here the spirits of the place were with her and not against her. Here memory in its second degree, habit, gave her the full sense of spiritual freedom.

As she walked to and fro the raging of her spirit changed its objective: from restraint to its final causes; and chief amongst them the pride which had been so grievously hurt. How she loathed the day that had passed, and how more than all she hated herself for her part in it; her mad, foolish, idiotic, self-importance which gave her the idea of such an act and urged her to the bitter end of its carrying out; her mulish obstinacy in persisting when every fibre of her being had revolted at the doing, and when deep in her inmost soul was a deterring sense of its futility. How could she have stooped to have done such a thing: to ask a man . . . oh! the shame of it, the shame of it all! How could she have been so blind as to think that such a man was worthy! . . .

In the midst of her whirlwind of passion came a solitary gleam of relief: she knew with certainty that she did not love Leonard; that she had never loved him. The coldness of disdain to him, the fear of his future acts which was based on disbelief of the existence of that finer nature with which she had credited him, all proved to her convincingly that he could never really have been within the charmed circle of her inner life. Did she but know it, there was an even stronger evidence of her indifference to him in the ready manner in which her thoughts flew past him in their circling sweep. For a moment she saw him as the centre of a host of besetting fears; but her own sense of superior power nullified the force of the vision. She was able to cope with him and his doings, were there such need. And so her mind flew back to the personal side of her trouble: her blindness, her folly, her shame.

In truth she was doing good work for herself. Her mind was working truly and to a beneficent end. One by one she was overcoming the false issues of her passion and drifting to an end in which she would see herself face to face and would place so truly the blame for what had been as to make it a warning and ennobling lesson of her life. She moved more quickly, passing to and fro as does a panther in its cage when the desire of forest freedom is heavy upon it.

That which makes the irony of life will perhaps never be understood in its casual aspect by the finite mind of man. The 'why' and 'wherefore' and the 'how' of it is only to be understood by that All-wise intelligence which can scan the future as well as the present, and see the far far-reaching ramifications of those schemes of final development to which the manifestation of completed character tend.

To any mortal it would seem a pity that to Stephen in her solitude, when her passion was working itself out to an end which might be good, should come an interruption which would throw it back upon itself in such a way as to multiply its malignant force. But again it is a part of the Great Plan that instruments whose use man's finite mind could never predicate should be employed: the seeming good to evil, the seeming evil to good.

As she swept to and fro, her raging spirit compelling to violent movement, Stephen's eyes were arrested by the figure of a man coming through the aisles of the grove. At such a time any interruption of her passion was a cause for heightening anger; but the presence of a person was as a draught to a full-fed furnace. Most of all, in her present condition of mind, the presence of a man—for the thought of a man lay behind all her trouble, was as a tornado striking a burning forest. The blood of her tortured heart seemed to leap to her brain and to suffuse her eyes. She 'saw blood'!

It mattered not that the man whom she saw she knew and trusted. Indeed, this but added fuel to the flame. In the presence of a stranger some of her habitual self-restraint would doubtless have come back to her. But now the necessity for such was foregone; Harold was her alter ego, and in his presence was safety. He was, in this aspect, but a higher and more intelligent rendering of the trees around her. In another aspect he was an opportune victim, something to strike at. When the anger of a poison snake opens its gland, and the fang is charged with venom, it must strike at something. It does not pause or consider what it may be; it strikes, though it may be at stone or iron. So Stephen waited till her victim was within distance to strike. Her black eyes, fierce with passion and blood-rimmed as a cobra's, glittered as he passed among the tree-trunks towards her, eager with his errand of devotion.

Harold was a man of strong purpose. Had he not been, he would never have come on his present errand. Never, perhaps, had any suitor set forth on his quest with a heavier heart. All his life, since his very boyhood, had been centred round the girl whom to-day he had come to serve. All his thought had been for her: and to-day all he could expect was a gentle denial of all his hopes, so that his future life would be at best a blank.

But he would be serving Stephen! His pain might be to her good; ought to be, to a certain extent, to her mental ease. Her wounded pride would find some solace . . . As he came closer the feeling that he had to play a part, veritably to act one, came stronger and stronger upon him, and filled him with bitter doubt as to his power. Still he went on boldly. It had been a part of his plan to seem to come eagerly, as a lover should come; and so he came. When he got close to Stephen, all the witchery of her presence came upon him as of old. After all, he loved her with his whole soul; and the chance had come to tell her so. Even under the distressing conditions of his suit, the effort had its charm.

Stephen schooled herself to her usual attitude with him; and that, too, since the effort was based on truth came with a certain ease to her. At the present time, in her present frame of mind, nothing in the wide world could give her pleasure; the ease which came, if it did not change her purpose, increased her power. Their usual salutation, begun when she was a little baby, was 'Good morning, Stephen!' 'Good morning, Harold!' It had become so much a custom that now it came mechanically on her part. The tender reference to childhood's days, though it touched her companion to the quick, did not appeal to her since she had no special thought of it. Had such a thought come to her it might have softened her even to tears, for Harold had been always deep in her heart. As might have been expected from her character and condition of mind, she was the first to begin:

'I suppose you want to see me about something special, Harold, you have come so early.'

'Yes, Stephen. Very special!'

'Were you at the house?' she asked in a voice whose quietness might have conveyed a warning. She was so suspicious now that she suspected even Harold of—of what she did not know. He answered in all simplicity:

'No. I came straight here.'

'How did you know I should be here?' Her voice was now not only quiet but sweet. Without thinking, Harold blundered on. His intention was so single-minded, and his ignorance of woman so complete, that he did not recognise even elementary truths:

'I knew you always came here long ago when you were a child when you were in—' Here it suddenly flashed upon him that if he seemed to expect that she was in trouble as he had purposed saying, he would give away his knowledge of what had happened and so destroy the work to which he had set himself. So he finished the sentence in a lame and impotent manner, which, however, saved complete annihilation as it was verbally accurate: 'in short frocks.' Stephen needed to know little more. Her quick intelligence grasped the fact that there was some purpose afoot which she did not know or understand. She surmised, of course, that it was some way in connection with her mad act, and she grew cooler in her brain as well as colder in her heart as she prepared to learn more. Stephen had changed from girl to woman in the last twenty-four hours; and all the woman in her was now awake. After a moment's pause she said with a winning smile:

'Why, Harold, I've been in long frocks for years. Why should I come here on this special day on that account?' Even as she was speaking she felt that it would be well to abandon this ground of inquiry. It had clearly told her all it could. She would learn more by some other means. So she went on in a playful way, as a cat—not a kitten—does when it has got a mouse:

'That reason won't work, Harold. It's quite rusty in the joints. But never mind it! Tell me why you have come so early?' This seemed to Harold to be a heaven-sent opening; he rushed in at once:

'Because, Stephen, I wanted to ask you to be my wife! Oh! Stephen, don't you know that I love you? Ever since you were a little girl! When you were a little girl and I a big boy I loved you. I have loved you ever since with all my heart, and soul, and strength. Without you the world is a blank to me! For you and your happiness I would do anything—anything!'

This was no acting. When once the barrier of beginning had been broken, his soul seemed to pour itself out. The man was vibrant through all his nature; and the woman's very soul realised its truth. For an instant a flame of gladness swept through her; and for the time it lasted put all other thought aside.

But suspicion is a hard metal which does not easily yield to fire. It can come to white heat easily enough, but its melting-point is high indeed. When the flame had leaped it had spent its force; the reaction came quick. Stephen's heart seemed to turn to ice, all the heat and life rushing to her brain. Her thoughts flashed with convincing quickness; there was no time for doubting amid their rush. Her life was for good or ill at the crossing of the ways. She had trusted Harold thoroughly. The habit of her whole life from her babyhood up had been to so look to him as comrade and protector and sympathetic friend. She was so absolutely sure of his earnest devotion that this new experience of a riper feeling would have been a joy to her, if it should be that his act was all spontaneous and done in ignorance of her shame. 'Shame' was the generic word which now summarised to herself her thought of her conduct in proposing to Leonard. But of this she must be certain. She could not, dare not, go farther till this was settled. With the same craving for certainty with which she convinced herself that Leonard understood her overtures, and with the same dogged courage with which she pressed the matter on him, she now went on to satisfy her mind.

'What did you do yesterday?'

'I was at Norcester all day. I went early. By the way, here is the ribbon you wanted; I think it's exactly the same as the pattern.' As he spoke he took a tissue-piper parcel from his pocket and handed it to her.

'Thanks!' she said. 'Did you meet any friends there?'

'Not many.' He answered guardedly; he had a secret to keep.

'Where did you dine?'

'At the club!' He began to be uneasy at this questioning; but he did not see any way to avoid answering without creating some suspicion.

'Did you see any one you knew at the club?' Her voice as she spoke was a little harder, a little more strained. Harold noticed the change, rather by instinct than reason. He felt that there was danger in it, and paused. The pause seemed to suddenly create a new fury in the breast of Stephen. She felt that Harold was playing with her. Harold! If she could not trust him, where then was she to look for trust in the world? If he was not frank with her, what then meant his early coming; his seeking her in the grove; his proposal of marriage, which seemed so sudden and so inopportune? He must have seen Leonard, and by some means have become acquainted with her secret of shame . . . His motive?

Here her mind halted. She knew as well as if it had been trumpeted from the skies that Harold knew all. But she must be certain . . . Certain!

She was standing erect, her hands held down by her sides and clenched together till the knuckles were white; all her body strung high—like an over-pitched violin. Now she raised her right hand and flung it downward with a passionate jerk.

'Answer me!' she cried imperiously. 'Answer me! Why are you playing with me? Did you see Leonard Everard last night? Answer me, I say. Harold An Wolf, you do not lie! Answer me!'

As she spoke Harold grew cold. From the question he now knew that Stephen had guessed his secret. The fat was in the fire with a vengeance. He did not know what to do, and still remained silent. She did not give him time to think, but spoke again, this time more coldly. The white terror had replaced the red:

'Are you not going to answer me a simple question, Harold? To be silent now is to wrong me! I have a right to know!'

In his trouble, for he felt that say what he would he could only give her new pain, he said humbly:

'Don't ask me, Stephen! Won't you understand that I want to do what is best for you? Won't you trust me?' Her answer came harshly. A more experienced man than Harold, one who knew women better, would have seen how overwrought she was, and would have made pity the pivot of his future bearing and acts and words while the interview lasted; pity, and pity only. But to Harold the high ideal was ever the same. The Stephen whom he loved was no subject for pity, but for devotion only. He knew the nobility of her nature and must trust it to the end. When her silence and her blazing eyes denied his request, he answered her query in a low voice:

'I did!' Even whilst he spoke he was thankful for one thing, he had not been pledged in any way to confidence. Leonard had forced the knowledge on him; and though he would have preferred a million times over to be silent, he was still free to speak. Stephen's next question came more coldly still:

'Did he tell you of his meeting with me?'

'He did.'

'Did he tell you all?' It was torture to him to answer; but he was at the stake and must bear it.

'I think so! If it was true.'

'What did he tell you? Stay! I shall ask you the facts myself; the broad facts. We need not go into details . . . '

'Oh, Stephen!' She silenced his pleading with an imperious hand.

'If I can go into this matter, surely you can. If I can bear the shame of telling, you can at least bear that of listening. Remember that knowing—knowing what you know, or at least what you have heard—you could come here and propose marriage to me!' This she said with a cold, cutting sarcasm which sounded like the rasping of a roughly-sharpened knife through raw flesh. Harold groaned in spirit; he felt a weakness which began at his heart to steal through him. It took all his manhood to bear himself erect. He dreaded what was coming, as of old the once-tortured victim dreaded the coming torment of the rack.

CHAPTER XV—THE END OF THE MEETING

Stephen went on in her calm, cold voice:

'Did he tell you that I had asked him to marry me?' Despite herself, as she spoke the words a red tide dyed her face. It was not a flush; it was not a blush; it was a sort of flood which swept through her, leaving her in a few seconds whiter than before. Harold saw and understood. He could not speak; he lowered his head silently. Her eyes glittered more coldly. The madness that every human being may have once was upon her. Such a madness is destructive, and here was something more vulnerable than herself.

'Did he tell you how I pressed him?' There was no red tide this time, nor ever again whilst the interview lasted. To bow in affirmation was insufficient; with an effort he answered:

'I understood so.' She answered with an icy sarcasm:

'You understood so! Oh, I don't doubt he embellished the record with some of his own pleasantries. But you understood it; and that is sufficient.' After a pause she went on:

'Did he tell you that he had refused me?'

'Yes!' Harold knew now that he was under the torture, and that there was no refusing. She went on, with a light laugh, which wrung his heart even more than her pain had done . . . Stephen to laugh like that!

'And I have no doubt that he embellished that too, with some of his fine masculine witticisms. I understood myself that he was offended at my asking him. I understood it quite well; he told me so!' Then with feminine intuition she went on:

'I dare say that before he was done he said something kindly of the poor little thing that loved him; that loved him so much, and that she had to break down all the bounds of modesty and decorum that had made the women of her house honoured for a thousand years! And you listened to him whilst he spoke! Oh-h-h!' she quivered with her white-hot anger, as the fierce heat in the heart of a furnace quivers. But her voice was cold again as she went on:

'But who could help loving him? Girls always did. It was such a beastly nuisance! You "understood" all that, I dare say; though perhaps he did not put it in such plain words!' Then the scorn, which up to now had been imprisoned, turned on him; and he felt as though some hose of deathly chill was being played upon him.

'And yet you, knowing that only yesterday, he had refused me—refused my pressing request that he should marry me, come to me hot-foot in the early morning and ask me to be your wife. I thought such things did not take place; that men were more honourable, or more considerate, or more merciful! Or at least I used to think so; till yesterday. No! till to-day. Yesterday's doings were my own doings, and I had to bear the penalty of them myself. I had come here to fight out by myself the battle of my shame . . . '

Here Harold interrupted her. He could not bear to hear Stephen use such a word in connection with herself.

'No! You must not say "shame." There is no shame to you, Stephen. There can be none, and no one must say it in my presence!' In her secret heart of hearts she admired him for his words; she felt them at the moment sink into her memory, and knew that she would never forget the mastery of his face and bearing. But the blindness of rage was upon her, and it is of the essence of this white-hot anger that it preys not on what is basest in us, but on what is best. That Harold felt deeply was her opportunity to wound him more deeply than before.

'Even here in the solitude which I had chosen as the battleground of my shame you had need to come unasked, unthought of, when even a lesser mind than yours, for you are no fool, would have thought to leave me alone. My shame was my own, I tell you; and I was learning to take my punishment. My punishment! Poor creatures that we are, we think our punishment will be what we would like best: to suffer in silence, and not to have spread abroad our shame!' How she harped on that word, though she knew that every time she uttered it, it cut to the heart of the man who loved her. 'And yet you come right on top of my torture to torture me still more and illimitably. You come, you who alone had the power to intrude yourself on my grief and sorrow; power given you by my father's kindness. You come to me without warning, considerately telling me that you knew I would be here because I had always come here when I had been in trouble. No—I do you an injustice. "In trouble" was not what you said, but that I had come when I had been in short frocks. Short frocks! And you came to tell me that you loved me. You thought, I suppose, that as I had refused one man, I would jump at the next that came along. I wanted a man. God! God! what have I done that such an affront should come upon me? And come, too, from a hand that should have protected me if only in gratitude for my father's kindness!' She was eyeing him keenly, with eyes that in her unflinching anger took in everything with the accuracy of sun-painting. She wanted to wound; and she succeeded.

But Harold had nerves and muscles of steel; and when the call came to them they answered. Though the pain of death was upon him he did not flinch. He stood before her like a rock, in all his great manhood; but a rock on whose summit the waves had cast the wealth of their foam, for his face was as white as snow. She saw and understood; but in the madness upon her she went on trying new places and new ways to wound:

'You thought, I suppose, that this poor, neglected, despised, rejected woman, who wanted so much to marry that she couldn't wait for a man to ask her, would hand herself over to the first chance comer who threw his handkerchief to her; would hand over herself—and her fortune!'

'Oh, Stephen! How can you say such things, think such things?' The protest broke from him with a groan. His pain seemed to inflame her still further; to gratify her hate, and to stimulate her mad passion:

'Why did I ever see you at all? Why did my father treat you as a son; that when you had grown and got strong on his kindness you could thus insult his daughter in the darkest hour of her pain and her shame!' She almost choked with passion. There was now nothing in the whole world that she could trust. In the pause he spoke:

'Stephen, I never meant you harm. Oh, don't speak such wild words. They will come back to you with sorrow afterwards! I only meant to do you good. I wanted . . . ' Her anger broke out afresh:

'There; you speak it yourself! You only wanted to do me good. I was so bad that any kind of a husband . . . Oh, get out of my sight! I wish to God I had never seen you! I hope to God I may never see you again! Go! Go! Go!'

This was the end! To Harold's honest mind such words would have been impossible had not thoughts of truth lain behind them. That Stephen—his Stephen, whose image in his mind shut out every other woman in the world, past, present, and future—should say such things to any one, that she should think such things, was to him a deadly blow. But that she should say them to him! . . . Utterance, even the utterance which speaks in the inmost soul, failed him. He had in some way that he knew not hurt—wounded—killed Stephen; for the finer part was gone from the Stephen that he had known and worshipped so long. She wished him gone; she wished she had never seen him; she hoped to God never to see him again. Life for him was over and done! There could be no more happiness in the world; no more wish to work, to live! . . .

He bowed gravely; and without a word turned and walked away.

Stephen saw him go, his tall form moving amongst the tree trunks till finally it was lost in their massing. She was so filled with the tumult of her passion that she looked, unmoved. Even the sense of his going did not change her mood. She raged to and fro amongst the trees, her movements getting quicker and quicker as her excitement began to change from mental to physical; till the fury began to exhaust itself. All at once she stopped, as though arrested by a physical barrier; and with a moan sank down in a helpless heap on the cool moss.

* * * * *

Harold went from the grove as one seems to move in a dream. Little things and big were mixed up in his mind. He took note, as he went towards the town by the byroads, of everything around him in his usual way, for he had always been one of those who notice unconsciously, or rather unintentionally. Long afterwards he could shut his eyes and recall every step of the way from the spot where he had turned from Stephen to the railway station outside Norcester. And on many and many such a time when he opened them again the eyelids were wet. He wanted to get away quickly, silently, unobserved. With the instinct of habitual thought his mind turned London-ward. He met but few persons, and those only cottiers. He saluted them in his usual cheery way, but did not stop to speak with any. He was about to take a single ticket to London when it struck him that this might look odd, so he asked for a return. Then, his mind being once more directed towards concealment of purpose, he sent a telegram to his housekeeper telling her that he was called away to London on business. It was only when he was far on his journey that he gave thought to ways and means, and took stock of his possessions. Before he took out his purse and pocket-book he made up his mind that he would be content with what it was, no matter how little. He had left Normanstand and all belonging to it for ever, and was off to hide himself in whatever part of the world would afford him the best opportunity. Life was over! There was nothing to look forward to; nothing to look back at! The present was a living pain whose lightest element was despair. As, however, he got further and further away, his practical mind began to work; he thought over matters so as to arrange in his mind how best he could dispose of his affairs, so to cause as little comment as might be, and to save the possibility of worry or distress of any kind to Stephen.

Even then, in his agony of mind, his heart was with her; it was not the least among his troubles that he would have to be away from her when perhaps she would need him most. And yet whenever he would come to this point in his endless chain of thought, he would have to stop for a while, overcome with such pain that his power of thinking was paralysed. He would never, could never, be of service to her again. He had gone out of her life, as she had gone out of his life; though she never had, nor never could out of his thoughts. It was all over! All the years of sweetness, of hope, and trust, and satisfied and justified faith in each other, had been wiped out by that last terrible, cruel meeting. Oh! how could she have said such things to him! How could she have thought them! And there she was now in all the agony of her unrestrained passion. Well he knew, from his long experience of her nature, how she must have suffered to be in such a state of mind, to have so forgotten all the restraint of her teaching and her life! Poor, poor Stephen! Fatherless now as well as motherless; and friendless as well as fatherless! No one to calm her in the height of her wild abnormal passion! No one to comfort her when the fit had passed! No one to sympathise with her for all that she had suffered! No one to help her to build new and better hopes out of the wreck of her mad ideas! He would cheerfully have given his life for her. Only last night he was prepared to kill, which was worse than to die, for her sake. And now to be far away, unable to help, unable even to know how she fared. And behind her eternally the shadow of that worthless man who had spurned her love and flouted her to a chance comer in his drunken delirium. It was too bitter to bear. How could God lightly lay such a burden on his shoulders who had all his life tried to walk in sobriety and chastity and in all worthy and manly ways! It was unfair! It was unfair! If he could do anything for her? Anything! Anything! . . . And so the unending whirl of thoughts went on!

The smoke of London was dim on the horizon when he began to get back to practical matters. When the train drew up at Euston he stepped from it as one to whom death would be a joyous relief!

He went to a quiet hotel, and from there transacted by letter such business matters as were necessary to save pain and trouble to others. As for himself, he made up his mind that he would go to Alaska, which he took to be one of the best places in the as yet uncivilised world for a man to lose his identity. As a security at the start he changed his name; and as John Robinson, which was not a name to attract public attention, he shipped as a passenger on the *Scoriac* from London to New York.

The *Scoriac* was one of the great cargo boats which take a certain number of passengers. The few necessaries which he took with him were chosen with an eye to utility in that frozen land which he sought. For the rest, he knew nothing, nor did he care how or whither he went. His vague purpose was to cross the American Continent to San Francisco, and there to take passage for the high latitudes north of the Yukon River.

* * * * *

When Stephen began to regain consciousness her first sensation was one of numbness. She was cold in the back, and her feet did not seem to exist; but her head was hot and pulsating as though her brain were a living thing. Then her half-open eyes began to take in her surroundings. For another long spell she began to wonder why all around her was green. Then came the inevitable process of reason. Trees! It is a wood! How did I come here? why am I lying on the ground?

All at once wakened memory opened on her its flood-gates, and overwhelmed her with pain. With her hands pressed to her throbbing temples and her burning face close to the ground, she began to recall what she could of the immediate past. It all seemed like a terrible dream. By degrees her intelligence came back to its normal strength, and all at once, as does one suddenly wakened from sleep to the knowledge of danger, she sat up.

Somehow the sense of time elapsed made Stephen look at her watch. It was half-past twelve. As she had come into the grove immediately after breakfast, and as Harold had almost immediately joined her, and as the interview between them had been but short, she must have lain on the ground for more than three hours. She rose at once, trembling in every limb. A new fear began to assail her; that she had been missed at home, and that some one might have come to look for her. Up to now she had not been able to feel the full measure of pain regarding what had passed, but which would, she knew, come to her in the end. It was too vague as yet; she could not realise that it had really been. But the fear of discovery was immediate, and must be guarded against without delay. As well as she could, she tidied herself and began to walk slowly back to the house, hoping to gain her own room unnoticed. That her general intelligence was awake was shown by the fact that before she left the grove she remembered that she had forgotten her sunshade. She went back and searched till she had found it.

Gaining her room without meeting any one, she at once change her dress, fearing that some soil or wrinkle might betray her. Resolutely she put back from her mind all consideration of the past; there would be time for that later on. Her nerves were already much quieter than they had been. That long faint, or lapse into insensibility, had for the time taken the place of sleep. There would be a price to be paid for it later; but for the present it had served its purpose. Now and again she was disturbed by one thought; she could not quite remember what had occurred after Harold had left, and just before she became unconscious. She dared not dwell upon it, however. It would doubtless all come back to her when she had leisure to think the whole matter over as a connected narrative.

When the gong sounded for lunch she went down, with a calm exterior, to face the dreaded ordeal of another meal.

Luncheon passed off without a hitch. She and her aunt talked as usual over all the small affairs of the house and the neighbourhood, and the calm restraint was in itself soothing. Even then she could not help feeling how much convention is to a woman's life. Had it not been for these recurring trials of set hours and duties she could never have passed the last day and night without discovery of her condition of mind.

That one terrible, hysterical outburst was perhaps the safety valve. Had it been spread over the time occupied in conventional duties its force even then might have betrayed her; but without the necessity of nerving herself to conventional needs, she would have infallibly betrayed herself by her negative condition.

After lunch she went to her own boudoir where, when she had shut the inner door, no one was allowed to disturb her without some special need in the house or on the arrival of visitors. This 'sporting oak' was the sign of 'not at home' which she had learned in her glimpse of college life. Here in the solitude of safety, she began to go over the past, resolutely and systematically.

She had already been so often over the memory of the previous humiliating and unhappy day that she need not revert to it at present. Since then had she not quarrelled with Harold, whom she had all her life so trusted that her quarrel with him seemed to shake the very foundations of her existence? As yet she had not remembered perfectly all that had gone on under the shadow of the beech grove. She dared not face it all at once, even as yet. Time must elapse before she should dare to cry; to think of her loss of Harold was to risk breaking down altogether. Already she felt weak. The strain of the last forty-eight hours was too much for her physical strength. She began to feel, as she lay back in her cushioned chair, that a swoon is no worthy substitute for sleep. Indeed it had seemed to make the need for sleep even more imperative.

It was all too humiliating! She wanted to think over what had been; to recall it as far as possible so as to fix it in her mind, whilst it was still fresh. Later on, some action might have to be based on her recollection. And yet . . . How could she think when she was so tired . . . tired . . .

Nature came to the poor girl's relief at last, and she fell into a heavy sleep . . .

It was like coming out of the grave to be dragged back to waking life out of such a sleep, and so soon after it had begun. But the voice seemed to reach to her inner consciousness in some compelling way. For a second she could not understand; but as she rose from the cushions the maid's message repeated, brought her wide awake and alert in an instant:

'Mr. Everard, young Mr. Everard, to see you, miss!'

CHAPTER XVI—A PRIVATE CONVERSATION

The name braced Stephen at once. Here was danger, an enemy to be encountered; all the fighting blood of generations leaped to the occasion. The short spell of sleep had helped to restore her. There remained still quite enough of mental and nervous excitement to make her think quickly; the words were hardly out of the maid's mouth before her resolution was taken. It would never do to let Leonard Everard see she was diffident about meeting him; she would go down at once. But she would take the precaution of having her aunt present; at any rate, till she should have seen how the land lay. Her being just waked from sleep would be an excuse for asking her aunt to see the visitor till she came down. So she said to the maid:

'I have been asleep. I must have got tired walking in the wood in the heat. Ask Auntie to kindly see Mr. Everard in the blue drawing-room till I come down. I must tidy my hair; but I will be down in a few minutes.'

'Shall I send Marjorie to you, miss?'

'No! Don't mind; I can do what I want myself. Hurry down to Miss Rowly!'

How she regarded Leonard Everard now was shown in her instinctive classing him amongst her enemies.

When she entered the room she seemed all aglow. She wanted not only to overcome but to punish; and all the woman in her had risen to the effort. Never in her life had Stephen Norman looked more radiantly beautiful, more adorable, more desirable. Even Leonard Everard felt his pulses quicken as he saw that glowing mass of beauty standing out against the cold background of old French tapestry. All the physical side of him leaped in answer to the call of her beauty; and even his cold heart and his self-engrossed brain followed with slower gait. He had been sitting opposite Miss Rowly in one of the windows, twirling his hat in nervous suspense. He jumped up, and, as she came towards him, went forward rapidly to greet her. No one could mistake the admiration in his eyes. Ever since he had made up his mind to marry her she had assumed a new aspect in his thoughts. But now her presence swept away all false imaginings; from the moment that her loveliness dawned upon him something like love began to grow within his breast. Stephen saw the look and it strengthened her. He had so grievously wounded her pride the previous day that her victory on this was a compensation which set her more at her old poise.

Her greeting was all sweetness: she was charmed to see him. How was his father, and what was the news? Miss Rowly looked on with smiling visage. She too had seen the look of admiration in his eyes, and it pleased her. Old ladies, especially when they are maiden ladies, always like to see admiration in the eyes of young men when they are turned in the direction of any girl dear to them.

They talked for some time, keeping all the while, by Stephen's clever generalship, to the small-talk of the neighbourhood and the minor events of social importance. As the time wore on she could see that Leonard was growing impatient, and evidently wanted to see her alone. She ignored, however, all his little private signalling, and presently ordered tea to be brought. This took some little time; when it had been brought and served and drunk, Leonard was in a smothered fume of impatience. She was glad to see that as yet her aunt had noticed nothing, and she still hoped that she would be able to so prolong matters, that she would escape without a private interview. She did not know the cause of Leonard's impatience: that he must see her before the day passed. She too was an egoist, in her own way; in the flush of belief of his subjugation she did not think of attributing to him any other motive than his desire for herself. As she had made up her mind on the final issue she did not want to be troubled by a new 'scene.'

But, after all, Leonard was a man; and man's ways are more direct than woman's. Seeing that he could not achieve his object in any other way, he said out suddenly, thinking, and rightly, that she would not wish to force an issue in the presence of her aunt:

'By the way, Miss Norman,' he had always called her 'Miss Norman' in her aunt's presence: 'I want to have two minutes with you before I go. On a matter of business,' he added, noticing Miss Rowly's surprised look. The old lady was old-fashioned even for her age; in her time no young man would have asked to see a young lady alone on business. Except on one kind of business; and with regard to that kind of business gentlemen had to obtain first the confidence and permission of guardians. Leonard saw the difficulty and said quickly:

'It is on the matter you wrote to me about!'

Stephen was prepared for a nasty shock, but hardly for so nasty a one as this. There was an indelicacy about it which went far beyond the bounds of thoughtless conventionality. That such an appeal should be made to her, and in such a way, savoured of danger. Her woman's intuition gave her the guard, and at once she spoke, smilingly and gently as one recalling a matter in which the concern is not her own:

'Of course! It was selfish of me not to have thought of it, and to have kept you so long waiting. The fact is, Auntie, that Leonard—I like to call him Leonard, since we were children together, and he is so young; though perhaps it would be more decorous nowadays to say "Mr. Everard"—has consulted me about his debts. You know, Auntie dear, that young men will be young men in such matters; or perhaps you do not, since the only person who ever worried you has been myself. But I stayed at Oxford and I know something of young men's ways; and as I am necessarily more or less of a man of business, he values my help. Don't you, Leonard?' The challenge was so direct, and the position he was in so daringly put, that he had to acquiesce. Miss Rowly, who had looked on with a frown of displeasure, said coldly:

'I know you are your own mistress, my dear. But surely it would be better if Mr. Everard would consult with his solicitor or his father's agent, or some of his gentlemen friends, rather than with a young lady whose relations with him, after all, are only those of a neighbour on visiting terms. For my own part, I should have thought that Mr. Everard's best course would have been to consult his own father! But the things that gentlemen, as well as ladies do, have been sadly changed since my time!' Then, rising in formal dignity, she bowed gravely to the visitor before leaving the room.

But the position of being left alone in the room with Leonard did not at all suit Stephen's plans. Rising quickly she said to her aunt:

'Don't stir, Auntie. I dare say you are right in what you say; but I promised Mr. Everard to go into the matter. And as I have brought the awkwardness on myself, I suppose I must bear it. If Mr. Everard wants to see me alone, and I suppose he is diffident in speaking on such a matter before you—he didn't play with you, you know!—we can go out on the lawn. We shan't be long!' Before Leonard could recover his wits she had headed him out on the lawn.

Her strategy was again thoroughly good. The spot she chose, though beyond ear-shot, was quite in the open and commanded by all the windows in that side of the house. A person speaking there might say what he liked, but his actions must be discreet.

On the lawn Stephen tripped ahead; Leonard followed inwardly raging. By her clever use of the opening she had put him in a difficulty from which there was no immediate means of extrication. He could not quarrel overtly with Stephen; if he did so, how could he enter on the pressing matter of his debts? He dared not openly proclaim his object in wishing to marry her, for had he done so her aunt might have interfered, with what success he could not be sure. In any case it would cause delay, and delay was what he could not afford. He felt that in mentioning his debts at just such a movement he had given Stephen the chance she had so aptly taken. He had to be on his good behaviour, however; and with an apprehension that was new to him he followed her.

An old Roman marble seat was placed at an angle from the house so that the one of the two occupants within its curve must almost face the house, whilst the other gave to it at least a quarter-face. Stephen seated herself on the near side, leaving to Leonard the exposed position. As soon as he was seated, she began:

'Now, Leonard, tell me all about the debts?' She spoke in tones of gay friendliness, but behind the mask of her cheerfulness was the real face of fear. Down deep in her mind was a conviction that her letter was a pivotal point of future sorrow. It was in the meantime quite apparent to her that Leonard kept it as his last resource; so her instinct was to keep it to the front and thus minimise its power.

Leonard, though inwardly weakened by qualms of growing doubt, had the animal instinct that, as he was in opposition, his safety was in attacking where his opponent most feared. He felt that there was some subtle change in his companion; this was never the same Stephen Norman whom only yesterday he had met upon the hill! He plunged at once into his purpose.

'But it wasn't about my debts you asked me to meet you, Stephen.'

'You surprise me, Leonard! I thought I simply asked you to come to meet me. I know the first subject I mentioned when we began to talk, after your grumbling about coming in the heat, was your money matters.' Leonard winced, but went on:

'It was very good of you, Stephen; but really that is not what I came to speak of to-day. At first, at all events!' he added with a sublime naïvetté, as the subject of his debts and his imperative want of money rose before him. Stephen's eyes flashed; she saw more clearly than ever through his purpose. Such as admission at the very outset of the proffer of marriage, which she felt was coming, was little short of monstrous. Her companion did not see the look of mastery on her face; he was looking down at the moment. A true lover would have been looking up.

'I wanted to tell you, Stephen, that I have been thinking over what you said to me in your letter, and what you said in words; and I want to accept!' As he was speaking he was looking her straight in the face.

Stephen answered slowly with a puzzled smile which wrinkled up her forehead:

'Accept what I said in my letter! why, Leonard, what do you mean? That letter must have had a lot more in it than I thought. I seem to remember that it was simply a line asking you to meet me. Just let me look at it; I should like to be sure of what actually is!' As she spoke she held out her hand. Leonard was nonplussed; he did not know what to say. Stephen made up her mind to have the letter back. Leonard was chafing under the position forced upon him, and tried to divert his companion from her purpose. He knew well why she had chosen that exposed position for their interview. Now, as her outstretched hand embarrassed him, he made reprisal; he tried to take it in his in a tender manner.

She instantly drew back her hand and put it behind her in a decided manner. She was determined that whatever might happen she would not let any watcher at the windows, by chance or otherwise, see any sign of tenderness on her part. Leonard, thinking that his purpose had been effected, went on, breathing more freely:

'Your letter wasn't much. Except of course that it gave me the opportunity of listening to what you said; to all your sweet words. To your more than sweet proposal!'

'Yes! It must have been sweet to have any one, who was in a position to do so, offer to help you when you knew that you were overwhelmed with debts!' The words were brutal. Stephen felt so; but she had no alternative. Leonard had some of the hard side of human nature; but he had also some of the weak side. He went on blindly:

'I have been thinking ever since of what you said, and I want to tell you that I would like to do as you wish!' As he spoke, his words seemed even to him to be out of place. He felt it would be necessary to throw more fervour into the proceedings. The sudden outburst which followed actually amused Stephen, even in her state of fear:

'Oh, Stephen, don't you know that I love you! You are so beautiful! I love you! I love you! Won't you be my wife?'

This was getting too much to close quarters. Stephen said in a calm, business-like way:

'My dear Leonard, one thing at a time! I came out here, you know, to speak of your debts; and until that is done, I really won't go into any other matter. Of course if you'd rather not . . . ' Leonard really could not afford this; matters were too pressing with him. So he tried to affect a cheery manner; but in his heart was a black resolve that she should yet pay for this.

'All right! Stephen. Whatever you wish I will do; you are the queen of my heart, you know!'

'How much is the total amount?' said Stephen.

This was a change to the prosaic which made sentiment impossible. He gave over, for the time.

'Go on!' said Stephen, following up her advantage. 'Don't you even know how much you owe?'

'The fact is, I don't. Not exactly. I shall make up the amount as well as I can and let you know. But that's not what I came about to-day.' Stephen was going to make an angry gesture of dissent. She was not going to have that matter opened up. She waited, however, for Leonard was going on after his momentary pause. She breathed more freely after his first sentence. He was unable evidently to carry on a double train of thought.

'It was about that infernal money-lenders' letter that the Governor got!' Stephen got still less anxious. This open acknowledgment of his true purpose seemed to clear the air.

'What is the amount?' Leonard looked quickly at her; the relief of her mind made her tone seem joyful.

'A monkey! Five hundred pounds, you know. But then there's three hundred for interest that has to be paid also. It's an awful lot of money, isn't it?' The last phrase was added on seeing Stephen's surprised look.

'Yes!' she answered quietly. 'A great deal of money—to waste!' They were both silent for a while. Then she said:

'What does your father say to it?'

'He was in an awful wax. One of these beastly duns had written to him about another account and he was in a regular fury. When I told him I would pay it within a week, he said very little, which was suspicious; and then, just when I was going out, he sprung this on me. Mean of him! wasn't it? I need expect no help from him.' As he was speaking he took a mass of letters from his pocket and began to look among them for the money-lenders' letter.

'Why, what a correspondence you have there. Do you keep all your letters in your pockets?' said Stephen quietly.

'All I don't tear up or burn. It wouldn't do to let the Governor into my secrets. He might know too much!'

'And are all those letters from duns?'

'Mostly, but I only keep those letters I have to attend to and those I care for.'

'Show me the bundle!' she said. Then seeing him hesitate, added:

'You know if I am to help you to get clear you must take me into your confidence. I dare say I shall have to see a lot more letters than these before you are quite clear!' Her tone was too quiet. Knowing already the silent antagonism between them he began to suspect her; knowing also that her own letter was not amongst them, he used his wits and handed them over without a word. She, too, suspected him. After his tacit refusal to give her the letter, she almost took it for granted that it was not amongst them. She gave no evidence of her feeling, however, but opened and read the letters in due sequence; all save two, which, being in a female hand, she gave back without a word. There was a calmness and an utter absence of concern, much less of jealousy, about this which disconcerted him. Throughout her reading Stephen's face showed surprise now and again; but when she came to the last, which was that of the usurers, it showed alarm. Being a woman, a legal threat had certain fears of its own.

'There must be no delay about this!' she said.

'What am I to do?' he answered, a weight off his mind that the fiscal matter had been practically entered on.

'I shall see that you get the money!' she said quietly. 'It will be really a gift, but I prefer it to be as a loan for many reasons.' Leonard made no comment. He found so many reasons in his own mind that he thought it wise to forbear from asking any of hers. Then she took the practical matter in hand:

'You must wire to these people at once to say that you will pay the amount on the day after to-morrow. If you will come here to-morrow at four o'clock the money will be ready for you. You can go up to town by the evening train and pay off the debt first thing in the morning. When you bring the receipt I shall speak to you about the other debts; but you must make out a full list of them. We can't have any half-measure. I will not go into the matter till I have all the details before me!' Then she stood up to go.

As they walked across the lawn, she said:

'By the way, don't forget to bring that letter with you. I want to see what I really did say in it!' Her tone was quiet enough, and the wording was a request; but Leonard knew as well as if it had been spoken outright as a threat that if he did not have the letter with him when he came things were likely to be unpleasant.

The farther he got from Normanstand on his way home the more discontented Leonard grew. Whilst he had been in Stephen's presence she had so dominated him, not only by her personality but by her use of her knowledge of his own circumstances, that he had not dared to make protest or opposition; but now he began to feel how much less he was to receive than he had expected. He had come prepared to allow Stephen to fall into his arms, fortune and all. But now, although he had practical assurance that the weight of his debts would be taken from him, he was going away with his tail between his legs. He had not even been accepted as a suitor, he who had himself been wooed only a day before. His proposal of marriage had not been accepted, had not even been considered by the woman who had so lately broken ironclad convention to propose marriage to him. He had been treated merely as a scapegrace debtor who had come to ask favours from an old friend. He had even been treated like a bad boy; had been told that he had wasted money; had been ordered, in no doubtful way, to bring the full schedule of his debts. And all the time he dared not say anything lest the thing shouldn't come off at all. Stephen had such an infernally masterly way with her! It didn't matter whether she was proposing to him, or he was proposing to her, he was made to feel small all the same. He would have to put up with it till he had got rid of the debts!

And then as to the letter. Why was she so persistent about seeing it? Did she want to get it into her hands and then keep it, as Harold An Wolf had done? Was it possible that she suspected he would use it to coerce her; she would call it 'blackmail,' he supposed. This being the very thing he had intended to do, and had done, he grew very indignant at the very thought of being accused of it. It was, he felt, a very awkward thing that he had lost possession of the letter. He might need it if Stephen got nasty. Then Harold might give it to her, as he had threatened to do. He thought he would call round that evening by Harold's house, and see if he couldn't get back the letter. It belonged to him; Harold had no right to keep it. He would see him before he and Stephen got putting their heads together. So, on his way home, he turned his steps at once to Harold's house.

CHAPTER XVI—A PRIVATE CONVERSATION

He did not find him in. The maid who opened the door could give him no information; all she could say was that Mrs. Dingle the housekeeper had got a telegram from Master saying that he had been called suddenly away on business.

This was a new source of concern to Leonard. He suspected a motive of some sort; though what that motive could be he could not hazard the wildest guess. On his way home he called at the post-office and sent a telegram to Cavendish and Cecil, the name of the usurers' firm, in accordance with Stephen's direction. He signed it: 'Jasper Everard.'

CHAPTER XVII—A BUSINESS TRANSACTION

When Stephen had sent off her letter to the bank she went out for a stroll; she knew it would be no use trying to get rest before dinner. That ordeal, too, had to be gone through. She found herself unconsciously going in the direction of the grove; but when she became aware of it a great revulsion overcame her, and she shuddered.

Slowly she took her way across the hard stretch of finely-kept grass which lay on the side of the house away from the wood. The green sward lay like a sea, dotted with huge trees, singly, or in clumps as islands. In its far-stretching stateliness there was something soothing. She came back to the sound of the dressing-gong with a better strength to resist the trial before her. Well she knew her aunt would have something to say on the subject of her interference in Leonard Everard's affairs.

Her fears were justified, for when they had come into the drawing-room after dinner Miss Rowly began:

'Stephen dear, is it not unwise of you to interfere in Mr. Everard's affairs?'

'Why unwise, Auntie?'

'Well, my dear, the world is censorious. And when a young lady, of your position and your wealth, takes a part in a young man's affairs tongues are apt to wag. And also, dear, debts, young men's debts, are hardly the subjects for a girl's investigation. Remember, that we ladies live very different lives from men; from some men, I should say, for your dear father was the best of men, and I should think that in all his life there was nothing which he would have wished concealed. But, my dear, young men are less restrained in their ways than we are, than we have to be for our own safety and protection.' The poor lady was greatly perturbed at having to speak in such a way. Stephen saw her distress; coming over to her, she sat down and took her hand. Stephen had a very tender side to her nature, and she loved very truly the dear old lady who had taken her mother's place and had shown her all a mother's love. Now, in her loneliness and woe and fear, she clung to her in spirit. She would have liked to have clung to her physically; to have laid her head on her bosom, and have cried her heart out. The time for tears had not come. Hourly she felt more and more the weight that a shameful secret is to carry. She knew, however, that she could set her aunt's mind at rest on the present subject; so she said:

'I think you are right, Auntie dear. It would have been better if I had asked you first; but I saw that Leonard was in distress, and wormed the cause of it from him. When I heard that it was only debt I offered to help him. He is an old friend, you know, Auntie. We were children together; and as I have much more money than I can ever want or spend, I thought I might help him. I am afraid I have let myself in for a bigger thing than I intended; but as I have promised I must go on with it. I dare say, Auntie, that you are afraid that I may end by getting in love with him, and marrying him. Don't you, dear?' This was said with a hug and a kiss which gave the old lady delight. Her instinct told her what was coming. She nodded her head in acquiescence. Stephen went on gravely:

'Put any such fear out of your mind. I shall never marry him. I can never love him.' She was going to say 'could never love him,' when she remembered.

'Are you sure, my dear? The heart is not always under one's own control.'

'Quite sure, Auntie. I know Leonard Everard; and though I have always liked him, I do not respect him. Why, the very fact of his coming to me for money would make me reconsider any view I had formed, had nothing else ever done so. You may take it, Auntie dear, that in the way you mean Leonard is nothing to me; can never be anything to me!' Here a sudden inspiration took her. In its light a serious difficulty passed, and the doing of a thing which had a fear of its own became easy. With a conviction in her tone, which in itself aided her immediate purpose, she said:

'I shall prove it to you. That is, if you will not mind doing something which will save me an embarrassment.'

'You know I will do anything, my dearest, which an old woman can do for a young one!' Stephen squeezed the mittened hand which she held as she went on:

'As I said, I have promised to lend him some money. The first instalment is to be given him to-morrow; he is to call for it in the afternoon. Will you give it to him for me?'

'Gladly, my dear,' said the old lady, much relieved. Stephen continued:

'One other thing, Auntie, I want you to do for me: not to think of the amount, or to say a word to me about it. It is a large sum, and I dare say it will frighten you a little. But I have made up my mind to it. I am learning a great deal out of this, Auntie dear; and I am quite willing to pay for my knowledge. After all, money is the easiest and cheapest way of paying for knowledge! Don't you agree with me?'

Miss Rowly gulped down her disappointment. She felt that she ought not to say too much, now that Stephen had set aside her graver fears. She consoled herself with the thought that even a large amount of money would cause no inconvenience to so wealthy a woman as Stephen. Beyond this, as she would have the handing over of the money to Leonard, she would know the amount. If advisable, she could remonstrate. She could if necessary consult, in confidence, with Harold. Her relief from her greater fear, and her gladness at this new proof of her niece's confidence, were manifested in the extra affection with which she bade her good-night.

Stephen did not dare to breathe freely till she was quite alone; and as she lay quiet in her bed in the dark she thought before sleep came.

Her first feeling was one of thankfulness that immediate danger was swerving from her. Things were so shaping themselves that she need not have any fear concerning Leonard. For his own sake he would have to keep silent. If he intended to blackmail her she would have the protection of her aunt's knowledge of the loan, and of her participation in it. The only weapon that remained to him was her letter; and that she would get from him before furnishing the money for the payment of his other debts.

These things out of the way, her thoughts turned to the matter of the greater dread; that of which all along she had feared to think for a moment: Harold!

Harold! and her treatment of him!

The first reception of the idea was positive anguish. From the moment he had left her till now there had been no time when a consideration of the matter was possible. Time pressed, or circumstances had interfered, or her own personal condition had forbidden. Now, when she was alone, the whole awful truth burst on her like an avalanche. Stephen felt the issue of her thinking before the thinking itself was accomplished; and it was with a smothered groan that she, in the darkness, held up her arms with fingers linked in desperate concentration of appeal.

Oh, if she could only take back one hour of her life, well she knew what that hour would be! Even that shameful time with Leonard on the hill-top seemed innocuous beside the degrading remembrance of her conduct to the noble friend of her whole life.

Sadly she turned over in her bed, and with shut eyes put her burning face on the pillow, to hide, as it were, from herself her abject depth of shame.

Leonard lounged through the next morning with what patience he could. At four o'clock he was at the door of Normanstand in his dogcart. This time he had a groom with him and a suitcase packed for a night's use, as he was to go on to London after his interview with Stephen. He had lost sight altogether of the matter of Stephen's letter, or else he would have been more nervous.

He was taken into the blue drawing-room, where shortly Miss Rowly joined him. He had not expected this. His mental uneasiness manifested itself in his manner, and his fidgeting was not unobserved by the astute old lady. He was disconcerted; 'overwhelmed' would better have described his feelings when she said:

'Miss Norman is sorry she can't see you to-day as she is making a visit; but she has given me a message for you, or rather a commission to discharge. Perhaps you had better sit down at the table; there are writing materials there, and I shall want a receipt of some sort.'

'Stephen did not say anything about a receipt!' The other smiled sweetly as she said in a calm way:

'But unfortunately Miss Norman is not here; and so I have to do the best I can. I really must have some proof that I have fulfilled my trust. You see, Mr. Everard, though it is what lawyers call a "friendly" transaction, it is more or less a business act; and I must protect myself.'

Leonard saw that he must comply, for time pressed. He sat down at the table. Taking up a pen and drawing a sheet of paper towards him, he said with what command of his voice he could:

'What am I to write?' The old lady took from her basket a folded sheet of notepaper, and, putting on her reading-glasses, said as she smoothed it out:

'I think it would be well to say something like this—"I, Leonard Everard, of Brindehow, in the Parish of Normanstand, in the County of Norcester, hereby acknowledge the receipt from Miss Laetitia Rowly of nine hundred pounds sterling lent to me in accordance with my request, the same being to clear me of a pressing debt due by me.'

When he had finished writing the receipt Miss Rowly looked it over, and handing it back to him, said:

'Now sign; and date!' He did so with suppressed anger.

She folded the document carefully and put it in her pocket. Then taking from the little pouch which she wore at her belt a roll of notes, she counted out on the table nine notes of one hundred pounds each. As she put down the last she said:

'Miss Norman asked me to say that a hundred pounds is added to the sum you specified to her, as doubtless the usurers would, since you are actually behind the time promised for repayment, require something extra as a solatium or to avoid legal proceedings already undertaken. In fact that they would "put more salt on your tail." The expression, I regret to say, is not mine.'

Leonard folded up the notes, put them into his pocket-book, and walked away. He did not feel like adding verbal thanks to the document already signed. As he got near the door the thought struck him; turning back he said:

'May I ask if Stephen said anything about getting the document?'

'I beg your pardon,' she said icily, 'did you speak of any one?'

'Miss Norman, I meant!' Miss Rowly's answer to this came so smartly that it left an added sting. Her arrow was fledged with two feathers so that it must shoot true: her distrust of him and his own impotence.

'Oh no! Miss Norman knows nothing of this. She simply asked me to give you the money. This is my own doing entirely. You see, I must exercise my judgment on my dear niece's behalf. Of course it may not be necessary to show her the receipt; but if it should ever be advisable it is always there.'

He looked at her with anger, not unmixed with admiration, as, bowing rather lower than necessary, he went out of the door, saying sotto voce, between his teeth:

'When my turn comes out you go! Neck and crop! Quick! Normanstand isn't big enough to hold us both!'

CHAPTER XVIII—MORE BUSINESS

When Leonard tendered the eight hundred pounds in payment of his debt of five hundred, Mr. Cavendish at first refused to take it. But when Leonard calmly but firmly refused to pay a single penny beyond the obligations already incurred, including interest on the full sum for one day, he acquiesced. He knew the type of man fully; and knew also that in all probability it would not be long before he would come to the Firm again on a borrowing errand. When such time should come, he would put an extra clause into his Memorandum of Agreement which would allow the Firm full power to make whatever extra charge they might choose in case of the slightest default in making payment.

Leonard's visits to town had not of late been many, and such as he had had were not accompanied with a plethora of cash. He now felt that he had earned a holiday; and it was not till the third morning that he returned to Brindehow. His father made no comment on his absence; his only allusion to the subject was:

'Back all right! Any news in town?' There was, however, an unwonted suavity in his manner which made Leonard a little anxious. He busied himself for the balance of the morning in getting together all his unpaid accounts and making a schedule of them. The total at first amazed almost as much as it frightened him. He feared what Stephen would say. She had already commented unfavourably on the one amount she had seen. When she was face to face with this she might refuse to pay altogether. It would therefore be wise to propitiate her. What could he do in this direction? His thoughts naturally turned to the missing letter. If he could get possession of it, it would either serve as a sop or a threat. In the one case she would be so glad to have it back that she would not stick at a few pounds; in the other it would 'bring her to her senses' as he put in his own mind his intention of blackmail.

He was getting so tightened up in situation that as yet he could only do as he was told, and keep his temper as well as he could.

Altogether it was in a chastened mood that he made his appearance at Normanstand later in the afternoon. He was evidently expected, for he was shown into the study without a word. Here Miss Rowly and Stephen joined him. Both were very kind in manner. After the usual greetings and commonplaces Stephen said in a brisk, businesslike way:

'Have you the papers with you?' He took the bundle of accounts from his pocket and handed them to her. After his previous experience he would have suggested, had he dared, that he should see Stephen alone; but he feared the old lady. He therefore merely said:

'I am afraid you will find the amount very large. But I have put down everything!'

So he had; and more than everything. At the last an idea struck him that as he was getting so much he might as well have a little more. He therefore added several good-sized amounts which he called 'debts of honour.' This would, he thought, appeal to the feminine mind. Stephen did not look at the papers at once. She stood up, holding them, and said to Miss Rowly:

'Now, if you will talk to Mr. Everard I will go over these documents quietly by myself. When I have been through them and understand them all I shall come back; and we will see what can be done.' She moved gracefully out of the room, closing the door behind her. As is usual with women, she had more than one motive for her action in going away. In the first place, she wished to be alone whilst she went over the schedule of the debts. She feared she might get angry; and in the present state of her mind towards Leonard the expression of any feeling, even contempt, would not be wise. Her best protection from him would be a manifest kindly negation of any special interest. In the second place, she believed that he would have her letter with the other papers, and she did not wish her aunt to see it, lest she should recognise the writing. In her boudoir, with a beating heart, she untied the string and looked through the papers.

Her letter was not among them.

For a few seconds she stood stock still, thinking. Then, with a sigh, she sat down and began to read the list of debts, turning to the originals now and again for details. As she went on, her wonder and disgust grew; and even a sense of fear came into her thoughts. A man who could be so wildly reckless and so selfishly unscrupulous was to be feared. She knew his father was a comparatively poor man, who could not possibly meet such a burden. If he were thus to his father, what might he be to her if he got a chance.

The thought of what he might have been to her, had he taken the chance she had given him, never occurred to her. This possibility had already reached the historical stage in her mind.

She made a few pencil notes on the list; and went back to the study. Her mind was made up.

She was quite businesslike and calm, did not manifest the slightest disapproval, but seemed to simply accept everything as facts. She asked Leonard a few questions on subjects regarding which she had made notes, such as discounts. Then she held the paper out to him and without any preliminary remark said:

'Will you please put the names to these?'

'How do you mean?' he asked, flushing.

'The names of the persons to whom these sums marked "debt of honour" are due.' His reply came quickly, and was a little aggressive; he thought this might be a good time to make a bluff:

'I do not see that that is necessary. I can settle them when I have the money.' Slowly and without either pause or flurry Stephen replied, looking him straight in the eyes as she handed him the papers:

'Of course it is not necessary! Few things in the world really are! I only wanted to help you out of your troubles; but if you do not wish me to . . . !' Leonard interrupted in alarm:

'No! no! I only spoke of these items. You see, being "debts of honour" I ought not to give the names.' Looking with a keen glance at her set face he saw she was obdurate; and, recognising his defeat, said as calmly as he could, for he felt raging:

'All right! Give me the paper!' Bending over the table he wrote. When she took the paper, a look half surprised, half indignant, passed over her face. Her watchful aunt saw it, and bending over looked also at the paper. Then she too smiled bitterly.

Leonard had printed in the names! The feminine keenness of both women had made his intention manifest. He did not wish for the possibility of his handwriting being recognised. His punishment came quickly. With a dazzling smile Stephen said to him:

'But, Leonard, you have forgotten to put the addresses!'

'Is that necessary?'

'Of course it is! Why, you silly, how is the money to be paid if there are no addresses?'

Leonard felt like a rat in a trap; but he had no alternative. So irritated was he, and so anxious to hide his irritation that, forgetting his own caution, he wrote, not in printing characters but in his own handwriting, addresses evolved from his own imagination. Stephen's eyes twinkled as he handed her the paper: he had given himself away all round.

Leonard having done all that as yet had been required of him, felt that he might now ask a further favour, so he said:

'There is one of those bills which I have promised to pay by Monday.'

'Promised?' said Stephen with wide-opened eyes. She had no idea of sparing him, she remembered the printed names. 'Why, Leonard, I thought you said you were unable to pay any of those debts?'

Again he had put himself in a false position. He could not say that it was to his father he had made the promise; for he had already told Stephen that he had been afraid to tell him of his debts. In his desperation, for Miss Rowly's remorseless glasses were full on him, he said:

'I thought I was justified in making the promise after what you said about the pleasure it would be to help me. You remember, that day on the hilltop?'

If he had wished to disconcert her he was mistaken; she had already thought over and over again of every form of embarrassment her unhappy action might bring on her at his hands. She now said sweetly and calmly, so sweetly and so calmly that he, with knowledge of her secret, was alarmed:

'But that was not a promise to pay. If you will remember it was only an offer, which is a very different thing. You did not accept it then!' She was herself somewhat desperate, or she would not have sailed so close to the wind.

'Ah, but I accepted later!' he said quickly, feeling in his satisfaction in an epigrammatic answer a certain measure of victory. He felt his mistake when she went on calmly:

'Offers like that are not repeated. They are but phantoms, after all. They come at their own choice, when they do come; and they stay but the measure of a breath or two. You cannot summon them!' Leonard fell into the current of the metaphor and answered:

'I don't know that even that is impossible. There are spells which call, and recall, even phantoms!'

'Indeed!' Stephen was anxious to find his purpose.

Leonard felt that he was getting on, that he was again acquiring the upper hand; so he pushed on the metaphor, more and more satisfied with himself:

'And it is wonderful how simple some spells, and these the most powerful, can be. A remembered phrase, the recollection of a pleasant meeting, the smell of a forgotten flower, or the sight of a forgotten letter; any or all of these can, through memory, bring back the past. And it is often in the past that the secret of the future lies!'

Miss Rowly felt that something was going on before her which she could not understand. Anything of this man's saying which she could not fathom must be at least dangerous; so she determined to spoil his purpose, whatever it might be.

'Dear me! That is charmingly poetic! Past and future; memory and the smell of flowers; meetings and letters! It is quite philosophy. Do explain it all, Mr. Everard!' Leonard was not prepared to go on under the circumstances. His own mention of 'letter,' although he had deliberately used it with the intention of frightening Stephen, had frightened himself. It reminded him that he had not brought, had not got, the letter; and that as yet he was not certain of getting the money. Stephen also had noted the word, and determined not to pass the matter by. She said gaily:

'If a letter is a spell, I think you have a spell of mine, which is a spell of my own weaving. You were to show me the letter in which I asked you to come to see me. It was in that, I think you said, that I mentioned your debts; but I don't remember doing so. Show it to me!'

'I have not got it with me!' This was said with mulish sullenness.

'Why not?'

'I forgot.'

'That is a pity! It is always a pity to forget things in a business transaction; as this is. I think, Auntie, we must wait till we have all the documents, before we can complete this transaction!'

Leonard was seriously alarmed. If the matter of the loan were not gone on with at once the jeweller's bill could not be paid by Monday, and the result would be another scene with his father. He turned to Stephen and said as charmingly as he could, and he was all in earnest now:

'I'm awfully sorry! But these debts have been so worrying me that they put lots of things out of my head. That bill to be paid on Monday, when I haven't a feather to fly with, is enough to drive a fellow off his chump. The moment I lay my hands on the letter I shall keep it with me so that I can't forget it again. Won't you forgive me for this time?'

'Forgive!' she answered, with a laugh. 'Why it's not worth forgiveness! It is not worth a second thought! All right! Leonard, make your mind easy; the bill will be paid on Monday!' Miss Rowly said quietly:

'I have to be in London on Monday afternoon; I can pay it for you.' This was a shock to Leonard; he said impulsively:

'Oh, I say! Can't I . . . ' His words faded away as the old lady again raised her lorgnon and gazed at him calmly. She went on:

'You know, my dear, it won't be even out of my way, as I have to call at Mr. Malpas's office, and I can go there from the hotel in Regent Street.' This was all news to Stephen. She did not know that her aunt had intended going to London; and indeed she did not know of any business with Mr. Malpas, whose firm had been London solicitor to the Rowlys for several generations. She had no doubt, however, as to the old lady's intention. It was plain to her that she wanted to help. So she thanked her sweetly. Leonard could say nothing. He seemed to be left completely out of it. When Stephen rose, as a hint to him that it was time for him to go, he said humbly, as he left:

'Would it be possible that I should have the receipt before Monday evening? I want to show it to my father.'

'Certainly!' said the old lady, answering him. 'I shall be back by the two o'clock train; and if you happen to be at the railway station at Norcester when I arrive I can give it to you!'

He went away relieved, but vindictive; determined in his own mind that when he had received the money for the rest of the debts he would see Stephen, when the old lady was not present, and have it out with her.

CHAPTER XIX—A LETTER

On Monday evening after dinner Mr. Everard and his son sat for a while in silence. They had not met since morning; and in the presence of the servants conversation had been scrupulously polite. Now, though they were both waiting to talk, neither liked to begin. The older man was outwardly placid, when Leonard, a little flushed and a little nervous of voice, began:

'Have you had any more bills?' He had expected none, and thus hoped to begin by scoring against his father. It was something of a set-down when the latter, taking some papers from his breast-pocket, handed them to him, saying:

'Only these!' Leonard took them in silence and looked at them. All were requests for payment of debts due by his son.

In each case the full bill was enclosed. He was silent a while; but his father spoke:

'It would almost seem as if all these people had made up their minds that you were of no further use to them.' Then without pausing he said, but in a sharper voice:

'Have you paid the jewellers? This is Monday!' Without speaking Leonard took leisurely from his pocket folded paper. This he opened, and, after deliberately smoothing out the folds, handed it to his father. Doubtless something in his manner had already convinced the latter that the debt was paid. He took the paper in as leisurely a way as it had been given, adjusted his spectacles, and read it. Seeing that his son had scored this time, he covered his chagrin with an appearance of paternal satisfaction.

'Good!' For many reasons he was glad the debt was paid He was himself too poor a man to allow the constant drain his son's debts, and too careful of his position to be willing have such exposure as would come with a County Court action against his son. All the same, his exasperation continued. Neither was his quiver yet empty. He shot his next arrow:

'I am glad you paid off those usurers!' Leonard did not like the definite way he spoke. Still in silence, he took from his pocket a second paper, which he handed over unfolded. Mr. Everard read it, and returned it politely, with again one word:

'Good!' For a few minutes there was silence. The father spoke again:

'Those other debts, have you paid them?' With a calm deliberation so full of tacit rudeness that it made his father flush Leonard answered:

'Not yet, sir! But I shall think of them presently. I don't care to be bustled by them; and I don't mean to!' It was apparent that though he spoke verbally of his creditors, his meaning was with regard to others also.

'When will they be paid?' As his son hesitated, he went on:

'I am alluding to those who have written to me. I take it that as my estate is not entailed, and as you have no income except from me, the credit which has been extended to you has been rather on my account than your own. Therefore, as the matter touches my own name, I am entitled to know something of what is going on.' His manner as well as his words was so threatening that Leonard was a little afraid. He might imperil his inheritance. He answered quickly:

'Of course, sir, you shall know everything. After all, you know, my affairs are your affairs!'

'I know nothing of the sort. I may of course be annoyed by your affairs, even dishonoured, in a way, by them. But I accept no responsibility whatever. As you have made your bed, so must you lie on it!'

'It's all right, sir, I assure you. All my debts, both those you know of and some you don't, I shall settle very shortly.'

'How soon?' The question was sternly put.

'In a few days. I dare say a week at furthest will see everything straightened out.'

The elder man stood, saying gravely as he went to the door:

'You will do well to tell me when the last of them is paid. There is something which I shall then want to tell you!' Without waiting for reply he went to his study.

Leonard went to his room and made a systematic, though unavailing, search for Stephen's letter; thinking that by some chance he might have recovered it from Harold and had overlooked it.

The next few days he passed in considerable suspense. He did not dare go near Normanstand until he was summoned, as he knew he would be when he was required.

* * * * *

When Miss Rowly returned from her visit to London she told Stephen that she had paid the bill at the jeweller's, and had taken the precaution of getting a receipt, together with a duplicate for Mr. Everard. The original was by her own request made out as received from Miss Laetitia Rowly in settlement of the account of Leonard Everard, Esq.; the duplicate merely was 'recd. in settlement of the account of—,' etc. Stephen's brows bent hit thought as she said:

'Why did you have it done that way, Auntie dear?' The other answered quietly:

'I had a reason, my dear; good reason! Perhaps I shall tell you all about it some day; in the meantime I want you not to ask me anything about it. I have a reason for that too. Stephen, won't you trust me in this, blindfold?' There was something so sweet and loving in the way she made the request that Stephen was filled with emotion. She put her arms round her aunt's neck and hugged her tight. Then laying her head on her bosom she said with a sigh:

'Oh, my dear, you can't know how I trust you; or how much your trust is to me. You never can know!'

The next day the two women held a long consultation over the schedule of Leonard's debts. Neither said a word of disfavour, or even commented on the magnitude. The only remark touching on the subject was made by Miss Rowly:

'We must ask for proper discounts. Oh, the villainy of those tradesmen! I do believe they charge double in the hope of getting half. As to jewellers . . . !' Then she announced her intention of going up to town again on Thursday, at which visit she would arrange for the payment of the various debts. Stephen tried to remonstrate, but she was obdurate. She held Stephen's hand in hers and stroked it lovingly as she kept on repeating:

'Leave it all to me, dear! Leave it all to me! Everything shall be paid as you wish; but leave it to me!'

Stephen acquiesced. This gentle yielding was new in her; it touched the elder lady to the quick, even whilst it pained her. Well she knew that some trouble must have gone to the smoothing of that imperious nature.

Stephen's inner life in these last few days was so bitterly sad that she kept it apart from all the routine of social existence. Into it never came now, except as the exciting cause of all the evil, a thought of Leonard. The saddening memory was of Harold. And of him the sadness was increased and multiplied by a haunting fear. Since he had walked out of the grove she had not seen him nor heard from him. This was in itself strange; for in all her life, when she was at home and he too, never a day passed without her seeing him. She had heard her aunt say that word had come of his having made a sudden journey to London, from which he had not yet returned. She was afraid to make inquiries. Partly lest she might hear bad news—this was her secret fear; partly lest she might bring some attention to herself in connection with his going. Of some things in connection with her conduct to him she was afraid to think at all. Thought, she felt, would come in time, and with it new pains and new shames, of which as yet she dared not think.

One morning came an envelope directed in Harold's hand. The sight made her almost faint. She rejoiced that she had been first down, and had opened the postbag with her own key. She took the letter to her room and shut herself in before opening it. Within were a few lines of writing and her own letter to Leonard in its envelope. Her head beat so hard that she could scarcely see; but gradually the writing seemed to grow out of the mist:

'The enclosed should be in your hands. It is possible that it may comfort you to know that it is safe. Whatever may come, God love and guard you.'

For a moment joy, hot and strong, blazed through her. The last words were ringing through her brain. Then came the cold shock, and the gloom of fear. Harold would never have written thus unless he was going away! It was a farewell!

For a long time she stood, motionless, holding the letter in her hand. Then she said, half aloud:

'Comfort! Comfort! There is no more comfort in the world for me! Never, never again! Oh, Harold! Harold!'

She sank on her knees beside her bed, and buried her face in her cold hands, sobbing in all that saddest and bitterest phase of sorrow which can be to a woman's heart: the sorrow that is dry-eyed and without hope.

Presently the habit of caution which had governed her last days woke her to action. She bathed her eyes, smoothed her hair, locked the letter and its enclosure in the little jewel-safe let into the wall, and came down to breakfast.

The sense of loss was so strong on her that she forgot herself. Habit carried her on without will or voluntary effort, and, so faithfully worked to her good that even the loving eyes of her aunt—and the eyes of love are keen—had no suspicion that any new event had come into her life.

Not till she was alone in her room that night did Stephen dare to let her thoughts run freely. In the darkness her mind began to work truly, so truly that she began at the first step of logical process: to study facts. And to study them she must question till she found motive.

Why had Harold sent her the letter? His own words said that it should be in her hands. Then, again, he said it might comfort her to know the letter was safe. How could it comfort her? How did he get possession of the letter?

There she began to understand; her quick intuition and her old knowledge of Harold's character and her new knowledge of Leonard's, helped her to reconstruct causes. In his interview with her he had admitted that Leonard had told him much, all. He would no doubt have refused to believe him, and Leonard would have shown him, as proof, her letter asking him to meet her. He would have seen then, as she did now, how much the possession of that letter might mean to any one.

Good God! to 'any one.' Could it have been so to Harold himself . . . that he thought to use it as an engine, to force her to meet his wishes—as Leonard had already tried to do! The mistrust, founded on her fear, was not dead yet . . . No! no! no! Her whole being resented such a monstrous proposition! Besides, there was proof. Thank God! there was proof. A blackmailer would have stayed close to her, and would have kept the letter; Harold did neither. Her recognition of the truth was shown in her act, when, stretching out her arms in the darkness, she whispered pleadingly:

'Forgive me, Harold!'

And Harold, far away where the setting sun was lying red on the rim of the western sea, could not hear her. But perhaps God did.

As, then, Harold's motive was not of the basest, it must have been of the noblest. What would be a man's noblest motive under such circumstances? Surely self-sacrifice!

And yet there could be no doubt as to Harold's earnestness when he had told her that he loved her . . .

Here Stephen covered her face in one moment of rapture. But the gloom that followed was darker than the night. She did not pursue the thought. That would come later when she should understand.

And yet, so little do we poor mortals know the verities of things, so blind are we to things thrust before our eyes, that she understood more in that moment of ecstasy than in all the reasoning that preceded and followed it. But the reasoning went on:

If he really loved, and told her so, wherein was the self-sacrifice? She had reproached him with coming to her with his suit hotfoot upon his knowledge of her shameful proffer of herself to another man; of her refusal by him. Could he have been so blind as not to have seen, as she did, the shameful aspect of his impulsive act? Surely, if he had thought, he must have seen! . . . And he must have thought; there had been time for it. It was at dinner that he had seen Leonard; it was after breakfast when he had seen her . . . And if he had seen then . . .

In an instant it all burst upon her; the whole splendid truth. He had held back the expression of his long love for her, waiting for the time when her maturity might enable her to understand truly and judge wisely; waiting till her grief for the loss of her father had become a story of the past; waiting for God knows what a man's mind sees of obstacles when he loves. But he had spoken it out when it was to her benefit. What, then, had been his idea of her benefit? Was it that he wished to meet the desire that she had manifested to have some man to—to love? . . . The way she covered her face with her hands whilst she groaned aloud made her answer to her own query a perfect negative.

Was it, then, to save her from the evil of marrying Leonard in case he should repent of his harshness, and later on yield himself to her wooing? The fierce movement of her whole body, which almost threw the clothes from her bed, as the shameful recollection rolled over her, marked the measure of her self-disdain.

One other alternative there was; but it seemed so remote, so far-fetched, so noble, so unlike what a woman would do, that she could only regard it in a shamefaced way. She put the matter to herself questioningly, and with a meekness which had its roots deeper than she knew. And here out of the depths of her humility came a noble thought. A noble thought, which was a noble truth. Through the darkness of the night, through the inky gloom of her own soul came with that thought a ray of truth which, whilst it showed her her own shrivelled unworthiness, made the man whom she had dishonoured with insults worse than death stand out in noble relief. In that instant she guessed at, and realised, Harold's unselfish nobility of purpose, the supreme effort of his constant love. Knowing the humiliation she must have suffered at Leonard's hands, he had so placed himself that even her rejection of him might be some solace to her wounded spirit, her pride.

Here at last was truth! She knew it in the very marrow of her bones.

This time she did not move. She thought and thought of that noble gentleman who had used for her sake even that pent-up passion which, for her sake also, he had suppressed so long.

In that light, which restored in her eyes and justified so fully the man whom she had always trusted, her own shame and wrongdoing, and the perils which surrounded her, were for the time forgotten.

And its glory seemed to rest upon her whilst she slept.

CHAPTER XX—CONFIDENCES

Miss Rowly had received a bulky letter by the morning's post. She had not opened it, but had allowed it to rest beside her plate all breakfast-time. Then she had taken it away with her to her own sitting-room. Stephen did not appear to take any notice of it. She knew quite well that it was from some one in London whom her aunt had asked to pay Leonard's bills. She also knew that the old lady had some purpose in her reticence, so she waited. She was learning to be patient in these days. Miss Rowly did say anything about it that day, or the next, or the next. The third-morning, she received another letter which she had read in an enlightening manner. She began its perusal with set brow frowning, then she nodded her head and smiled. She put the letter back in its envelope and placed it in the little bag always carried. But she said nothing. Stephen wondered, but waited.

That night, when Stephen's maid had left her, there came a gentle tap at her door, and an instant after the door opened. The tap had been a warning, not a request; it had in a measure prepared Stephen, who was not surprised to see her Aunt in dressing-gown, though it was many a long day since she had visited her niece's room at night. She closed the door behind her, saying:

'There is something I want to talk to you about, dearest, and I thought it would be better to do so when there could not be any possible interruption. And besides,' here there was a little break in her voice, 'I could hardly summon up my courage in the daylight.' She stopped, and the stopping told its own story. In an instant Stephen's arm's were round her, all the protective instinct in her awake, at the distress of the woman she loved. The old lady took comfort from the warmth of the embrace, and held her tight whilst she went on:

'It is about these bills, my dear. Come and sit down and put a candle near me. I want you to read something.'

'Go on, Auntie dear,' she said gravely. The old lady, after a pause, spoke with a certain timidity:

'They are all paid; at least all that can be. Perhaps I had better read you the letter I have had from my solicitors:

'"Dear Madam,—In accordance with your instructions we have paid all the accounts mentioned in Schedule A (enclosed). We have placed for your convenience three columns: (1) the original amount of each account, (2) the amount of discount we were able to arrange, and (3) the amount paid. We regret that we have been unable to carry out your wishes with regard to the items enumerated in Schedule B (enclosed). We have, we assure you, done all in our power to find the gentlemen whose names and addresses are therein given. These were marked 'Debt of honour' in the list you handed to us. Not having been able to obtain any reply to our letters, we sent one of our clerks first to the addresses in London, and afterwards to Oxford. That clerk, who is well used to such inquiries, could not find trace of any of the gentlemen, or indeed of their existence. We have, therefore, come to the conclusion that, either there must be some error with regard to (a) names, (b) addresses, or (c) both; or that no such persons exist. As it would be very unlikely that such errors could occur in all the cases, we can only conclude that there have not been any such persons. If we may hazard an opinion: it is possible that, these debts being what young men call 'debts of honour,' the debtor, or possibly the creditors, may not have wished the names mentioned. In such case fictitious names and addresses may have been substituted for the real ones. If you should like any further inquiry instituted we would suggest that you ascertain the exact names and addresses from the debtor. Or should you prefer it we would see the gentleman on your behalf, on learning from you his name and address. We can keep, in the person of either one of the Firm or a Confidential Clerk as you might prefer, any appointment in such behalf you may care to make.

'"We have already sent to you the receipted account from each of the creditors as you directed, viz. 'Received from Miss Laetitia Rowly in full settlement to date of the account due by Mr. Leonard Everard the sum of,' etc. etc. And also, as you further directed, a duplicate receipt of the sum-total due in each case made out as 'Received in full settlement to date of account due by,' etc. etc. The duplicate receipt was pinned at the back of each account so as to be easily detachable.

'"With regard to finance we have carried out your orders, etc."' She hurried on the reading. "These sums, together with the amounts of nine hundred pounds sterling, and seven hundred pounds sterling lodged to the account of Miss Stephen Norman in the Norcester branch of the Bank as repayment of moneys advanced to you as by your written instructions, have exhausted the sum, etc."' She folded up the letter with the schedules, laying the bundle of accounts on the table. Stephen paused; she felt it necessary to collect herself before speaking.

'Auntie dear, will you let me see that letter? Oh, my dear, dear Auntie, don't think I mistrust you that I ask it. I do because I love you, and because I want to love you more if it is possible to do so.' Miss Rowly handed her the letter. She rose from the arm of the chair and stood beside the table as though to get better light from the candle than she could get from where she had sat.

She read slowly and carefully to the end; then folded up the letter and handed it to her aunt. She came back to her seat on the edge of the chair, and putting her arms round her companion's neck looked her straight in the eyes. The elder woman grew embarrassed under the scrutiny; she coloured up and smiled in a deprecatory way as she said:

'Don't look at me like that, darling; and don't shake your head so. It is all right! I told you I had my reasons, and you said you would trust me. I have only done what I thought best!'

'But, Auntie, you have paid away more than half your little fortune. I know all the figures. Father and uncle told me everything. Why did you do it? Why did you do it?' The old woman held out her arms as she said:

'Come here, dear one, and sit on my knee as you used to when you were a child, and I will whisper you.' Stephen sprang from her seat and almost threw herself into the loving arms. For a few seconds the two, clasped tight to each other's heart, rocked gently to and fro. The elder kissed the younger and was kissed impulsively in return. Then she stroked the beautiful bright hair with her wrinkled hand, and said admiringly:

'What lovely hair you have, my dear one!' Stephen held her closer and waited.

'Well, my dear, I did it because I love you!'

'I know that, Auntie; you have never done anything else my life!'

'That is true, dear one. But it is right that I should do this. Now you must listen to me, and not speak till I have done. Keep your thoughts on my words, so that you may follow my thoughts. You can do your own thinking about them afterwards. And your own talking too; I shall listen as long as you like!'

'Go on, I'll be good!'

'My dear, it is not right that you should appear to have paid the debts of a young man who is no relation to you and who will, I know well, never be any closer to you than he is now.' She hurried on, as though fearing an interruption, but Stephen felt that her clasp tightened. 'We never can tell what will happen as life goes on. And, as the world is full of scandal, one cannot be too careful not to give the scandalmongers anything to exercise their wicked spite upon. I don't trust that young man! he is a bad one all round, or I am very much mistaken. And, my dear, come close to me! I cannot but see that you and he have some secret which he is using to distress you!' She paused, and her clasp grew closer still as Stephen's head sank on her breast. 'I know you have done something or said something foolish of which he has a knowledge. And I know my dear one, that whatever it was, and no matter how foolish it may have been, it was not a wrong thing. God knows, we are all apt to do wrong things as well as foolish ones; the best of us. But such is not for you! Your race, your father and mother, your upbringing, yourself and the truth and purity which are yours would save you from anything which was in itself wrong. That I know, my dear, as well as I know myself! Ah! better, far better! for the gods did not think it well to dower me as they have dowered you. The God of all the gods has given you the ten talents to guard; and He knows, as I do, that you will be faithful to your trust.'

There was a solemn ring in her voce as the words were spoken which went through the young girl's heart. Love and confidence demanded in return that she should have at least the relief of certain acquiescence; there is a possible note of pain in the tensity of every string! Stephen lifted her head proudly and honestly, though her cheeks were scarlet, saying with a consciousness of integrity which spoke directly soul to soul:

'You are right, dear! I have done something very foolish; very, very foolish! But it was nothing which any one could call wrong. Do not ask me what it was. I need only tell you this: that it was an outrage on convention. It was so foolish, and based on such foolish misconception; it sprang from such over-weening, arrogant self-opinion that it deserves the bitter punishment which will come; which is coming; which is with me now! It was the cause of something whose blackness I can't yet realise; but of which I will tell you when I can speak of it. But it was not wrong in itself, or in the eyes of God or man!' The old woman said not a word. No word was needed, for had she not already expressed her belief? But Stephen felt her relief in the glad pressure of her finger-tips. In a voice less strained and tense Miss Rowly went on:

'What need have I for money, dear? Here I have all that any woman, especially at my age, can need. There is no room even for charity; you are so good to all your people that my help is hardly required. And, my dear one, I know—I know,' she emphasised the word as she stroked the beautiful hair, 'that when I am gone my own poor, the few that I have looked after all my life, will, not suffer when my darling thinks of me!' Stephen fairly climbed upon her as she said, looking in the brave old eyes:

'So help me God, my darling, they shall never want!'

Silence for a time; and then Miss Rowly's voice again:

'Though it would not do for the world to know that a young maiden lady had paid the debts of a vicious young man, it makes no matter if they be paid by an old woman, be the same maid, wife, or widow! And really, my dear, I do not see how any money I might have could be better spent than in keeping harm away from you.'

'There need not be any harm at all, Auntie.'

'Perhaps not, dear! I hope not with all my heart. But I fear that young man. Just fancy him threatening you, and in your own house; in my very presence! Oh! yes, my dear. He meant to threaten, anyhow! Though I could not exactly understand what he was driving at, I could see that he was driving at something. And after all that you were doing for him, and had done for him! I mean, of course, after all that I had done for him, and was doing for him. It is mean enough, surely, for a man to beg, and from a woman; but to threaten afterwards. Ach! But I think, my dear, it is checkmate to him this time. All along the line the only proof that is of there being any friendliness towards him from this house points to me. And moreover, my dear, I have a little plan in my head that will tend to show him up even better, in case he may ever try to annoy us. Look at me when next he is here. I mean to do a little play-acting which will astonish him, I can tell you, if it doesn't frighten him out of the house altogether. But we won't talk of that yet. You will understand when you see it!' Her eyes twinkled and her mouth shut with a loud snap as she spoke.

After a few minutes of repose, which was like a glimpse of heaven to Stephen's aching heart, she spoke again:

'There was something else that troubled you more than even this. You said you would tell me when you were able to speak of it . . . Why not speak now? Oh! my dear, our hearts are close together to-night; and in all your life, you will never have any one who will listen with greater sympathy than I will, or deal more tenderly with your fault, whatever it may have been. Tell me, dear! Dear!' she whispered after a pause, during which she realised the depth of the girl's emotion by her convulsive struggling to keep herself in check.

All at once the tortured girl seemed to yield herself, and slipped inertly from her grasp till kneeling down she laid her head in the motherly lap and sobbed. Miss Rowly kept stroking her hair in silence. Presently the girl looked up, and with a pang the aunt saw that her eyes were dry. In her pain she said:

'You sob like that, my child, and yet you are not crying; what is it, oh! my dear one? What is it that hurts you so that you cannot cry?'

And then the bitter sobbing broke out again, but still alas! without tears. Crouching low, and still enclosing her aunt's waist with her outstretched arms and hiding her head in her breast; she said:

'Oh! Auntie, I have sent Harold away!'

'What, my dear? What?' said the old lady astonished. 'Why, I thought there was no one in the world that you trusted so much as Harold!'

'It is true. There was—there is no one except you whom I trust so much. But I mistook something he said. I was in a blind fury at the time, and I said things that I thought my father's daughter never could have said. And she never thought them, even then! Oh, Auntie, I drove him away with all the horrible things I could say that would wound him. And all because he acted in a way that I see now was the most noble and knightly in which any man could act. He that my dear father had loved, and honoured, and trusted as another son. He that was a real son to him, and not a mock sop like me. I sent him away with such fierce and bitter pain that his poor face was ashen grey, and there was woe in his eyes that shall make woe in mine whenever I shall see them in my mind, waking or sleeping. He, the truest friend . . . the most faithful, the most tender, the most strong, the most unselfish! Oh! Auntie, Auntie, he just turned and bowed and went away. And he couldn't do anything else with the way I spoke to him; and now I shall never see him again!'

The young girl's eyes were still dry, but the old woman's were wet. For a few minutes she kept softly stroking the bowed heat till the sobbing grew less and less, and then died away; and the girl lay still, collapsed in the abandonment of dry-eyed grief.

Then she rose, and taking off her dressing-gown, said tenderly:

'Let me stay with you to-night, dear one? Go to sleep in my arms, as you did long ago when there was any grief that you could not bear.'

So Stephen lay in those loving arms till her own young breast ceased heaving, and she breathed softly. Till dawn she slept on the bosom of her who loved her so well.

CHAPTER XXI—THE DUTY OF COURTESY

Leonard was getting tired of waiting when he received his summons to Normanstand. But despite his impatience he was ill pleased with the summons, which came in the shape of a polite note from Miss Rowly asking him to come that afternoon at tea-time. He had expected to hear from Stephen.

'Damn that old woman! You'd think she was working the whole show!' However, he turned up at a little before five o'clock, spruce and dapper and well dressed and groomed as usual. He was shown, as before, into the blue drawing-room. Miss Rowly, who sat there, rose as he entered, and coming across the room, greeted him, as he thought, effusively. He actually winced when she called him 'my dear boy' before the butler.

She ordered tea to be served at once, and when it had been brought she said to the butler:

'Tell Mannerly to bring me a large thick envelope which is on the table in my room. It is marked L.E. on the outside.' Presently an elderly maid handed her the envelope and withdrew. When tea was over she opened the envelope, and taking from it a number of folios, looked over them carefully; holding them in her lap, she said quietly:

'You will find writing materials on the table. I am all ready now to hand you over the receipts.' His eyes glistened. This was good news at all events; the debts were paid. In a rapid flash of thought he came to the conclusion that if the debts were actually paid he need not be civil to the old lady. He felt that he could have been rude to her if he had actual possession of the receipts. As it was, however, he could not yet afford to have any unpleasantness. There was still to come that lowering interview with his father; and he could not look towards it satisfactorily until he had the assurance of the actual documents that he was safe. Miss Rowly was, in her own way, reading his mind in his face. Her lorgnon seemed to follow his every expression like a searchlight. He remembered his former interview with her, and how he had been bested in it; so he made up his mind to acquiesce in time. He went over to the table and sat down. Taking a pen he turned to Miss Rowly and said:

'What shall I write?' She answered calmly:

'Date it, and then say, "Received from Miss Laetitia Rowly the receipts for the following amounts from the various firms hereunder enumerated."' She then proceeded to read them, he writing and repeating as he wrote. Then she added:

'"The same being the total amount of my debts which she has kindly paid for me."' He paused here; she asked.

'Why don't you go on?'

'I thought it was Stephen—Miss Norman,' he corrected, catching sight of her lorgnon, 'who was paying them.'

'Good Lord, man,' she answered, 'what does it matter who has paid them, so long as they are paid?'

'But I didn't ask you to pay them,' he went on obstinately. There was a pause, and then the old lady, with a distinctly sarcastic smile, said:

'It seems to me, young man, that you are rather particular as to how things are done for you. If you had begun to be just a little bit as particular in making the debts as you are in the way of having them paid, there would be a little less trouble and expense all round. However, the debts have been paid, and we can't unpay them. But of course you can repay me the money if you like. It amounts in all to four thousand three hundred and seventeen pounds, twelve shillings and sixpence, and I have paid every penny of it out of my own pocket. If you can't pay it yourself, perhaps your father would like to do so.'

The last shot told; he went on writing: '"Kindly paid for me,"' she continued in the same even voice:

'"In remembrance of my mother, of whom she was an acquaintance." Now sign it!' He did so and handed it to her. She read it over carefully, folded it, and put it in her pocket. She then stood. He rose also; and as he moved to the door—he had not offered to shake hands with her—he said:

'I should like to see, Miss Norman.'

'I am afraid you will have to wait.'

'Why?'

'She is over at Heply Regis. She went there for Lady Heply's ball, and will remain for a few days. Good afternoon!' The tone in which the last two words were spoken seemed in his ears like the crow of the victor after a cock-fight.

As he was going out of the room a thought struck her. She felt he deserved some punishment for his personal rudeness to her. After all, she had paid half her fortune for him, though not on his account; and not only had he given no thanks, but had not even offered the usual courtesy of saying good-bye. She had intended to have been silent on the subject, and to have allowed him to discover it later. Now she said, as if it was an after-thought:

'By the way, I did not pay those items you put down as "debts of honour"; you remember you gave the actual names and addresses.'

'Why not?' the question came from him involuntarily. The persecuting lorgnon rose again:

'Because they were all bogus! Addresses, names, debts, honour! Good afternoon!'

He went out flaming; free from debt, money debts; all but one. And some other debts—not financial—whose magnitude was exemplified in the grinding of his teeth.

After breakfast next morning he said to his father:

'By the way, you said you wished to speak to me, sir.' There was something in the tone of his voice which called up antagonism.

'Then you have paid your debts?'

'All!'

'Good! Now there is something which it is necessary I should call your attention to. Do you remember the day on which I handed you that pleasing epistle from Messrs. Cavendish and Cecil?'

'Certainly, sir.'

'Didn't you send a telegram to them?'

'I did.'

'You wrote it yourself?'

'Certainly.'

'I had a courteous letter from the money-lenders, thanking me for my exertions in securing the settlement of their claim, and saying that in accordance with the request in my telegram they had held over proceedings until the day named. I did not quite remember having sent any telegram to them, or any letter either. So, being at a loss, I went to our excellent postmaster and requested that he would verify the sending of a telegram to London from me. He courteously looked up the file; which was ready for transference to the G.P.O., and showed me the form. It was in your handwriting.' He paused so long that Leonard presently said:

'Well!'

'It was signed Jasper Everard. Jasper Everard! my name; and yet it was sent by my son, who was christened, if I remember rightly, Leonard!' Then he went on, only in a cold acrid manner which made his son feel as though a February wind was blowing on his back:

'I think there need not have been much trouble in learning to avoid confusing our names. They are really dissimilar. Have you any explanation to offer of the—the error, let us call it?' A bright thought struck Leonard.

'Why, sir,' he said, 'I put it in your name as they had written to you. I thought it only courteous.' The elder man winced; he had not expected the excuse. We went on speaking in the same calm way, but his tone was more acrid than before:

'Good! of course! It was only courteous of you! Quite so! But I think it will be well in the future to let me look after my own courtesy; as regards my signature at any rate. You see, my dear boy, a signature is queer sort of thing, and judges and juries are apt to take a poor view of courtesy as over against the conventions regarding a man, writing his own name. What I want to tell you is this, that on seeing that signature I made a new will. You see, my estate is not entailed, and therefore I think it only right to see that in such a final matter justice is done all round. I therefore made a certain provision of which I am sure you will approve. Indeed, since I am assured of the payment of your debts, I feel justified in my action. I may say, inter alia, that I congratulate you on either the extent of your resources or the excellence of your friendships, or both. I confess that the amounts brought to my notice were rather large; more especially in proportion to the value of the estate which you are some day to inherit. For you are of course to inherit some day, my dear boy. You are my only son, and it would be hardly—hardly courteous of me not to leave it to you. But I have put a clause in my will to the effect that the trustee's are to pay all debts of your accruing which can be proved against you, before handing over to you either the estate itself or the remainder after its sale and the settlement of all claims. That's all. Now run away, my boy; I have some important work to do.'

* * * * *

The day after her return from Heply Regis, Stephen was walking in the wood when she thought she heard a slight rustling of leaves some way behind her. She looked round, expecting to see some one; but the leafy path was quite clear. Her suspicion was confirmed; some one was secretly following her. A short process of exclusions pointed to the personality of the some one. Tramps and poachers were unknown in Normanstand, and there was no one else whom she could think of who had any motive in following her in such a way; it must be Leonard Everard. She turned and walked rapidly in the opposite direction. As this would bring her to the house Leonard had to declare his presence at once or else lose the opportunity of a private interview which he sought. When she saw him she said at once and without any salutation:

'What are you doing there; why are you following me?'

'I wanted to see you alone. I could not get near you on account of that infernal old woman.' Stephen's face grew hard.

'On account of whom?' she asked with dangerous politeness.

'Miss Rowly; your aunt.'

'Don't you think, Mr. Everard,' she said icily, 'that it is at least an unpardonable rudeness to speak that way, and to me, of the woman I love best in all the world?'

'Sorry!' he said in the offhand way of younger days, 'I apologise. Fact is, I was angry that she wouldn't let me see you.'

'Not let you see me!' she said as if amazed. 'What do mean?'

'Why, I haven't been able to see you alone ever since I went to meet you on Caester Hill.'

'But why should you see me alone?' she asked as if still in amazement. 'Surely you can say anything you have to say before my aunt.' With an unwisdom for which an instant later he blamed himself he blurted out:

'Why, old girl, you yourself did not think her presence necessary when you asked me to meet you on the hill.'

'When was that?' She saw that he was angry and wanted to test him; to try how far he would venture. He was getting dangerous; she must know the measure of what she had to fear.

He fell into the trap at once. His debts being paid, fear was removed, and all the hectoring side of the man was aroused. His antagonist was a woman; and he had already had in his life so many unpleasant scenes with women that this was no new experience. This woman had, by her own indiscretion, put a whip into his hand; and, if necessary to secure his own way, by God! he meant to use it! These last days had made her a more desirable possession in his eyes. The vastness of her estate had taken hold on him, and his father's remorseless intention with regard to his will would either keep him with very limited funds, or leave him eventually a pauper if he forestalled his inheritance. The desire of her wealth had grown daily, and it was now the main force in bringing him here to-day. And to this was now added the personal desire which her presence evoked. Stephen, at all times beautiful, had never looked more lovely. In the days since she had met him on the hilltop, a time that to her seemed so long ago, she had grown to be a woman, and there is some subtle inconceivable charm in completed womanhood. The reaction from her terrible fear and depression had come, and her strong brilliant youth was manifesting itself. Her step was springy and her eyes were bright; and the glow of fine health, accentuated by the militant humour of the present moment, seemed to light up her beautiful skin. In herself she was desirable, very desirable; Leonard felt his pulses quicken and his blood leap as he looked at her. Even his prejudice against her red hair had changed to something like hungry admiration. Leonard felt for the first moment since he had known her that she was a woman; and that, with relation to her, he was a man.

And at the moment all the man in him asserted itself. It was with half love, as he saw it, and half self-assertion that he answered her question:

'The day you asked me to marry you! Oh! what a fool I was not to leap at such a chance! I should have taken you in my arms then and kissed you till I showed you how much I loved you. But that will all come yet; the kissing is still to come! Oh! Stephen, don't you see that I love you? Won't you tell me that you love me still? Darling!' He almost sprang at her, his arms extended to clasp her.

'Stop!' Her voice rang like a trumpet. She did not mean to submit to physical violence, and in the present state of her feeling, an embrace from him would be a desecration. He was now odious to her; she positively loathed him.

Before her uplifted hand and those flashing eyes, he stopped as one stricken into stone. In that instant she knew she was safe; and with a woman's quickness of apprehension and resolve, made up her mind what course to pursue. In a calm voice she said quietly:

'Mr. Everard, you have followed me in secret, and without my permission. I cannot talk here with you, alone. I absolutely refuse to do so; now or at any other time. If you have anything especial to say to me you will find me at home at noon to-morrow. Remember, I do not ask you to come. I simply yield to the pressure of your importunity. And remember also that I do not authorise you in any way to resume this conversation. In fact, I forbid it. If you come to my house you must control yourself to my wish!'

Then with a stately bow, whose imperious distance inflamed him more than ever, and without once looking back she took her way home, all agitated inwardly and with fast beating heart.

CHAPTER XXII—FIXING THE BOUNDS

Leonard came towards Normanstand next forenoon in considerable mental disturbance. In the first place he was seriously in love with Stephen, and love is in itself a disturbing influence.

Leonard's love was all of the flesh; and as such had power at present to disturb him, as it would later have power to torture him. Again, he was disturbed by the fear of losing Stephen, or rather of not being able to gain her. At first, ever since she had left him on the path from the hilltop till his interview the next day, he had looked on her possession as an 'option,' to the acceptance of which circumstances seemed to be compelling him. But ever since, that asset seemed to have been dwindling; and now he was almost beginning to despair. He was altogether cold at heart, and yet highly strung with apprehension, as he was shown into the blue drawing-room.

Stephen came in alone, closing the door behind her. She shook hands with him, and sat down by a writing-table near the window, pointing to him to sit on an ottoman a little distance away. The moment he sat down he realised that he was at a disadvantage; he was not close to her, and he could not get closer without manifesting his intention of so doing. He wanted to be closer, both for the purpose of his suit and for his own pleasure; the proximity of Stephen began to multiply his love for her. He thought that to-day she looked better than ever, of a warm radiant beauty which touched his senses with unattainable desire. She could not but notice the passion in his eyes, and instinctively her eyes wandered to a silver gong placed on the table well within reach. The more he glowed, the more icily calm she sat, till the silence between them began to grow oppressive. She waited, determined that he should be the first to speak. Recognising the helplessness of silence, he began huskily:

'I came here to-day in the hope that you would listen to me.' Her answer, given with a conventional smile, was not helpful:

'I am listening.'

'I cannot tell you how sorry I am that I did not accept your offer. If I had know when I was coming that day that you loved me . . . ' She interrupted him, calm of voice, and with uplifted hand:

'I never said so, did I? Surely I could not have said such a thing! I certainly don't remember it?' Leonard was puzzled.

'You certainly made me think so. You asked me to marry you, didn't you?' Her answer came calmly, though in a low voice:

'I did.'

'Then if you didn't love me, why did you ask me to marry you?' It was his nature to be more or less satisfied when he had put any one opposed to him proportionally in the wrong; and now his exultation at having put a poser manifested itself in his tone. This, however, braced up Stephen to cope with a difficult and painful situation. It was with a calm, seemingly genial frankness, that she answered, smilingly:

'Do you know, that is what has been puzzling me from that moment to this!' Her words appeared to almost stupefy Leonard. This view of the matter had not occurred to him, and now the puzzle of it made him angry.

'Do you mean to say,' he asked hotly, 'that you asked a man to marry you when you didn't even love him?'

'That is exactly what I do mean! Why I did it is, I assure you, as much a puzzle to me as it is to you. I have come to the conclusion that it must have been from my vanity. I suppose I wanted to dominate somebody; and you were the weakest within range!'

'Thank you!' He was genuinely angry by this time, and, but for a wholesome fear of the consequences, would have used strong language.

'I don't see that I was the weakest about.' Somehow this set her on her guard. She wanted to know more, so she asked:

'Who else?'

'Harold An Wolf! You had him on a string already!' The name came like a sword through her heart, but the bitter comment braced her to further caution. Her voice seemed to her to sound as though far away:

'Indeed! And may I ask you how you came to know that?' Her voice seemed so cold and sneering to him that he lost his temper still further.

'Simply because he told me so himself.' It pleased him to do an ill turn to Harold. He did not forget that savage clutch at his throat; and he never would. Stephen's senses were all alert. She saw an opportunity of learning something, and went on with the same cold voice:

'And I suppose it was that pleasing confidence which was the cause of your refusal of my offer of marriage; of which circumstance you have so thoughtfully and so courteously reminded me.' This, somehow, seemed of good import to Leonard. If he could show her that his intention to marry her was antecedent to Harold's confidence, she might still go back to her old affection for him. He could not believe that it did not still exist; his experience of other women showed him that their love outlived their anger, whether the same had been hot or cold.

'It had nothing in the world to do with it. He never said a word about it till he threatened to kill me—the great brute!' This was learning something indeed! She went on in the same voice:

'And may I ask you what was the cause of such sanguinary intention?'

'Because he knew that I was going to marry you!' As he spoke he felt that he had betrayed himself; he went on hastily, hoping that it might escape notice:

'Because he knew that I loved you. Oh! Stephen, don't you know it now! Can't you see that I love you; and that I want you for my wife!'

'But did he threaten to kill you out of mere jealousy? Do you still go in fear of your life? Will it be necessary to arrest him?' Leonard was chagrined at her ignoring of his love-suit, and in his self-engrossment answered sulkily:

'I'm not afraid of him! And, besides, I believe he has bolted. I called at his house yesterday, and his servant said they hadn't heard a word from him.' Stephen's heart sank lower and lower. This was what she had dreaded. She said in as steady a voice as she could muster:

'Bolted! Has he gone altogether?'

'Oh, he'll come back all right, in time. He's not going to give up the jolly good living he has here!'

'But why has he bolted? When he threatened to kill you did he give any reason?' There was too much talk about Harold. It made him angry; so he answered in an offhand way:

'Oh, I don't know. And, moreover, I don't care!'

'And now,' said Stephen, having ascertained what she wanted to know, 'what is it that you want to speak to me about?'

Her words fell on Leonard like a cold douche. Here had he been talking about his love for her, and yet she ignored the whole thing, and asked him what he wanted to talk about.

'What a queer girl you are. You don't seem to attend to what a fellow is saying. Here have I been telling you that I love you, and asking you to marry me; and yet you don't seem to have even heard me!' She answered at once, quite sweetly, and with a smile of superiority which maddened him:

'But that subject is barred!'

'How do you mean? Barred!'

'Yes. I told you yesterday!'

'But, Stephen,' he cried out quickly, all the alarm in him and all the earnestness of which he was capable uniting to his strengthening, 'can't you understand that I love you, with all my heart? You are so beautiful; so beautiful!' He felt now in reality what he was saying.

The torrent of his words left no opening for her objection; it swept all merely verbal obstacles before it. She listened, content in a measure. So long as he sat at the distance which she had arranged before his coming she did not fear any personal violence. Moreover, it was a satisfaction to her now to hear him, who had refused her, pleading in vain. The more sincere his eloquence, the larger her satisfaction; she had no pity for him now.

'I know I was a fool, Stephen! I had my chance that day on the hilltop; and if I had felt then as I feel now, as I have felt every moment since, I would not have been so cold. I would have taken you in my arms and held you close and kissed you, again, and again, and again. Oh, darling! I love you! I love you! I love you!' He held out his arms imploringly. 'Won't you love me? Won't—'

He stopped, paralysed with angry amazement. She was laughing.

He grew purple in the face; his hands were still outstretched. The few seconds seemed like hours.

'Forgive me!' she said in a polite tone, suddenly growing grave. 'But really you looked so funny, sitting there so quietly, and speaking in such a way, that I couldn't help it. You really must forgive me! But remember, I told you the subject was barred; and as, knowing that, you went on, you really have no one but yourself to blame!' Leonard was furious, but managed to say as he dropped his arms:

'But I love you!'

'That may be, now,' she went on icily. 'But it is too late. I do not love you; and I have never loved you! Of course, had you accepted my offer of marriage you should never have known that. No matter how great had been my shame and humiliation when I had come to a sense of what I had done, I should have honourably kept my part of the tacit compact entered into when I made that terrible mistake. I cannot tell you how rejoiced and thankful I am that you took my mistake in such a way. Of course, I do not give you any credit for it; you thought only of yourself, and did that which you liked best!'

'That is a nice sort of thing to tell a man!' he interrupted with cynical frankness.

'Oh, I do not want to hurt you unnecessarily; but I wish there to be no possible misconception in the matter. Now that I have discovered my error I am not likely to fall into it again; and that you may not have any error at all, I tell you now again, that I have not loved you, do not love you, and never will and never can love you.' Here an idea struck Leonard and he blurted out:

'But do you not think that something is due to me?'

'How do you mean?' Her brows were puckered with real wonder this time.

'For false hopes raised in my mind. If I did not love you before, the very act of proposing to me has made me love you; and now I love you so well that I cannot live without you!' In his genuine agitation he was starting up, when the sight of her hand laid upon the gong arrested him. She laughed as she said:

'I thought that the privilege of changing one's mind was a female prerogative! Besides, I have done already something to make reparation to you for the wrong of . . . of—I may put it fairly, as the suggestion is your own—of not having treated you as a woman!'

'Damn!'

'As you observe so gracefully, it is annoying to have one's own silly words come back at one, boomerang fashion. I made up my mind to do something for you; to pay off your debts.' This so exasperated him that he said out brutally:

'No thanks to you for that! As I had to put up with the patronage and the lecturings, and the eyeglass of that infernal old woman, I don't intend . . . '

Stephen stood up, her hand upon the gong:

'Mr. Everard, if you do not remember that you are in my drawing-room, and speaking of my dear and respected aunt, I shall not detain you longer!'

He sat down at once, saying surlily:

'I beg your pardon. I forgot. You make me so wild that—that . . . ' He chewed the ends of his moustache angrily. She resumed her seat, taking her hand from the gong. Without further pause she continued:

'Quite right! It has been Miss Rowly who paid your debts. At first I had promised myself the pleasure; but from something in your speech and manner she thought it better that such an act should not be done by a woman in my position to a man in yours. It might, if made public, have created quite a wrong impression in the minds of many of our friends.'

There was something like a snort from Leonard. She ignored it:

'So she paid the money herself out of her own fortune. And, indeed, I must say that you do not seem to have treated her with much gratitude.'

'What did I say or do that put you off doing the thing yourself?'

'I shall answer it frankly: It was because you manifested, several times, in a manner there was no mistaking, both by words and deeds, an intention of levying blackmail on me by using your knowledge of my ridiculous, unmaidenly act. No one can despise, or deplore, or condemn that act more than I do; so that rather than yield a single point to you, I am, if necessary, ready to face the odium which the public knowledge of it might produce. What I had intended to do for you in the way of compensation for false hopes raised to you by that act has now been done. That it was done by my aunt on my behalf, and not by me, matters to you no more than it did to your creditors, who, when they received the money, made no complaint of injury to their feelings on that account.

'Now, when you think the whole matter over in quietness, you will, knowing that I am ready at any time to face if necessary the unpleasant publicity, be able to estimate what damage you would do to yourself by any exposé. It seems to me that you would come out of it pretty badly all round. That, however, is not my affair; it entirely rests with yourself. I think I know how women would regard it. I dare say you best know how men would look at it; and at you!'

Leonard knew already how the only man who knew of it had taken it, and the knowledge did not reassure him!

'You jade! You infernal, devilish, cruel, smooth-tongued jade!' He stood as bespoke. She stood too, and stood watching him with her hand on the gong. After a pause of a couple of seconds she said gravely:

'One other thing I should wish to say, and I mean it. Understand me clearly, that I mean it! You must not come again into my grounds without my special permission. I shall not allow my liberty to be taken away, or restricted, by you. If there be need at any time to come to the house, come in ceremonious fashion, by the avenues which are used by others. You can always speak to me in public, or socially, in the most friendly manner; as I shall hope to be able to speak to you. But you must never transgress the ordinary rules of decorum. If you do, I shall have to take, for my own protection, another course. I know you now! I am willing to blot out the past; but it must be the whole past that is wiped out!'

She stood facing him; and as he looked at her clear-cut aquiline face, her steady eyes, her resolute mouth, her carriage, masterly in its self-possessed poise, he saw that there was no further hope for him. There was no love and no fear.

'You devil!' he hissed.

She struck the gong; her aunt entered the room.

'Oh, is that you, Auntie? Mr. Everard has finished his business with me!' Then to the servant, who had entered after Miss Rowly:

'Mr. Everard would like his carriage. By the way,' she added, turning to him in a friendly way as an afterthought, 'will you not stay, Mr. Everard, and take lunch with us? My aunt has been rather moping lately; I am sure your presence would cheer her up.'

'Yes, do stay, Mr. Everard!' added Miss Rowly placidly. 'It would make a pleasant hour for us all.'

Leonard, with a great effort, said with conventional politeness:

'Thanks, awfully! But I promised my father to be home for lunch!' and he withdrew to the door which the servant held open.

He went out filled with anger and despair, and, sad for him, with a fierce, overmastering desire—love he called it—for the clever, proud, imperious beauty who had so outmatched and crushed him.

That beautiful red head, which he had at first so despised, was henceforth to blaze in his dreams.

CHAPTER XXIII—THE MAN

On the *Scoriac* Harold An Wolf, now John Robinson, kept aloof from every one. He did not make any acquaintances, did not try to. Some of those at table with him, being ladies and gentlemen, now and again made a polite remark; to which he answered with equal politeness. Being what he was he could not willingly offend any one; and there was nothing in his manner to repel any kindly overture to acquaintance. But this was the full length his acquaintanceship went; so he gradually felt himself practically alone. This was just what he wished; he sat all day silent and alone, or else walked up and down the great deck that ran from stem to stern, still always alone. As there were no second-class or steerage passengers on the *Scoriac*, there were no deck restraints, and so there was ample room for individual solitude. The travellers, however, were a sociable lot, and a general feeling of friendliness was abroad. The first four days of the journey were ideally fine, and life was a joy. The great ship, with bilge keels, was as steady as a rock.

Among the other passengers was an American family consisting of Andrew Stonehouse, the great ironmaster and contractor, with his wife and little daughter.

Stonehouse was a remarkable man in his way, a typical product of the Anglo-Saxon under American conditions. He had started in young manhood with nothing but a good education, due in chief to his own industry and his having taken advantage to the full of such opportunities as life had afforded to him. By unremitting work he had at thirty achieved a great fortune, which had, however; been up to then entirely invested and involved in his businesses. With, however, the colossal plant at his disposal, and by aid of the fine character he had won for honesty and good work, he was able within the next ten years to pile up a fortune vast even in a nation where multi-millionaires are scattered freely. Then he had married, wisely and happily. But no child had come to crown the happiness of the pair who so loved each other till a good many years had come and gone. Then, when the hope of issue had almost passed away, a little daughter came. Naturally the child was idolised by her parents, and thereafter every step taken by either was with an eye to her good. When the rigour of winter and the heat of summer told on the child in a way which the more hardy parents had never felt, she was whirled away to some place with more promising conditions of health and happiness. When the doctors hinted that an ocean voyage and a winter in Italy would be good, those too were duly undertaken. And now, the child being in perfect health, the family was returning before the weather should get too hot to spend the summer at their châlet amongst the great pines on the slopes of Mount Ranier. Like the others on board, Mr. and Mrs. Stonehouse had proffered travellers' civilities to the sad, lonely young man. As to the others, he had shown thanks for their gracious courtesy; but friendship, as in other cases, did not advance. The Stonehouses were not in any way chagrined; their lives were too happy and too full for them to take needless offence. They respected the young man's manifest desire for privacy; and there, so far as they were concerned, the matter rested.

But this did not suit the child. Pearl was a sweet little thing, a real blue-eyed, golden-haired little fairy, full of loving-kindness. All the mother-instinct in her, and even at six a woman-child can be a mother—theoretically, went out towards the huge, lonely, sad, silent young man. She insisted on friendship with him; insisted shamelessly, with the natural inclination of innocence which rises high above shame. Even the half-hearted protests of the mother, who loved to see the child happy, did not deter her; after the second occasion of Pearl's seeking him, as she persisted, Harold could but remonstrate with the mother in turn; the ease of the gentle lady and the happiness of her child were more or less at stake. When Mrs. Stonehouse would say:

'There, darling! You must be careful not to annoy the gentleman,' Pearl would turn a rosy all-commanding face to her and answer:

'But, mother, I want him to play with me. You must play with me!' Then, as the mother would look at him, he would say quickly, and with genuine heartiness too:

'Oh please, madam, do let her play with me! Come, Pearl, shall you ride a cock-horse or go to market the way the gentleman rides?' Then the child would spring on his knee with a cry of delight, and their games began.

The presence of the child and her loving ways were unutterably sweet to Harold; but his pleasure was always followed by a pain that rent him as he thought of that other little one, now so far away, and of those times that seemed so long since gone.

But the child never relaxed in her efforts to please; and in the long hours of the sea voyage the friendship between her and the man grew, and grew. He was the biggest and strongest and therefore most lovely thing on board the ship, and that sufficed her. As for him, the child manifestly loved and trusted him, and that was all-in-all to his weary, desolate heart.

The fifth day out the weather began to change; the waves grew more and more mountainous as the day wore on and the ship advanced west. Not even the great bulk and weight of the ship, which ordinarily drove through the seas without pitch or roll, were proof against waves so gigantic. Then the wind grew fiercer and fiercer, coming in roaring squalls from the south-west. Most of those on board were alarmed, for the great waves were dreadful to see, and the sound of the wind was a trumpet-call to fear.

The sick stayed in their cabins; the rest found an interest if not a pleasure on deck. Among the latter were the Stonehouses, who were old travellers. Even Pearl had already had more sea-voyages than fall to most people in their lives. As for Harold, the storm seemed to come quite naturally to him and he paced the deck like a ship-master.

It was fortunate for the passengers that most of them had at this period of the voyage got their sea legs; otherwise walking on the slippery deck, that seemed to heave as the rolling of the vessel threw its slopes up or down, would have been impossible. Pearl was, like most children, pretty sure-footed; holding fast to Harold's hand she managed to move about ceaselessly. She absolutely refused to go with any one else. When her mother said that she had better sit still she answered:

'But, mother, I am quite safe with The Man!' 'The Man' was the name she had given Harold, and by which she always now spoke of him. They had had a good many turns together, and Harold had, with the captain's permission, taken her up on the bridge and showed her how to look out over the 'dodger' without the wind hurting her eyes. Then came the welcome beef-tea hour, and all who had come on deck were cheered and warmed with the hot soup. Pearl went below, and Harold, in the shelter of the charthouse, together with a good many others, looked out over the wild sea.

Harold, despite the wild turmoil of winds and seas around him, which usually lifted his spirits, was sad, feeling lonely and wretched; he was suffering from the recoil of his little friend's charming presence. Pearl came on deck again looking for him. He did not see her, and the child, seeing an opening for a new game, avoided both her father and mother, who also stood in the shelter of the charthouse, and ran round behind it on the weather side, calling a loud 'Boo!' to attract Harold's attention as she ran.

A few seconds later the *Scoriac* put her nose into a coming wave at just the angle which makes for the full exercise of the opposing forces. The great wave seemed to strike the ship on the port quarter like a giant hammer; and for an instant she stood still, trembling. Then the top of the wave seemed to leap up and deluge her. The wind took the flying water and threw it high in volumes of broken spray, which swept not only the deck but the rigging as high as the top of the funnels. The child saw the mass of water coming, and shrieking flew round the port side of the charthouse. But just as she turned down the open space between it and the funnel the vessel rolled to starboard. At the same moment came a puff of wind of greater violence than ever. The child, calling out, half in simulated half in real fear, flew down the slope. As she did so the gale took her, and in an instant whirled her, almost touching her mother, over the rail into the sea.

Mrs. Stonehouse shrieked and sprang forward as though to follow her child. She was held back by the strong arm of her husband. They both slipped on the sloping deck and fell together into the scuppers. There was a chorus of screams from all the women present. Harold, with an instinctive understanding of the dangers yet to be encountered, seized a red tam-o'-shanter from the head of a young girl who stood near.

Her exclamation of surprise was drowned in the fearful cry 'Man overboard!' and all rushed down to the rail and saw Harold, as he emerged from the water, pull the red cap over his head and then swim desperately towards the child, whose golden hair was spread on the rising wave.

The instant after Pearl's being swept overboard might be seen the splendid discipline of a well-ordered ship. Every man to his post, and every man with a knowledge of his duty. The First Officer called to the Quartermaster at the wheel in a voice which cut through the gale like a trumpet:

'Hard a port! Hard!'

The stern of the great ship swung away to port in time to clear the floating child from the whirling screw, which would have cut her to pieces in an instant. Then the Officer after tearing the engine-room signal to 'Starboard engine full speed astern,' ran for the lifebuoy hanging at the starboard end of the bridge. This he hurled far into the sea. As it fell the attached rope dragged with it the signal, which so soon as it reaches water bursts into smoke and flame—signal by day and night. This done, and it had all been done in a couple of seconds, he worked the electric switch of the syren, which screamed out quickly once, twice, thrice. This is the dread sound which means 'man overboard,' and draws to his post every man on the ship, waking or sleeping.

The Captain was now on the bridge and in command, and the First Officer, freed from his duty there, ran to the emergency boat, swung out on its davits on the port side.

All this time, though only numbered by seconds, the *Scoriac* was turning hard to starboard, making a great figure of eight; for it is quicker to turn one of these great sea monsters round than to stop her in mid career. The aim of her Captain in such cases is to bring her back to the weather side of the floating buoy before launching the boat.

On deck the anguish of the child's parents was pitiable. Close to the rail, with her husband's arms holding her tight to it, the distressed mother leaned out; but always moving so that she was at the nearest point of the ship to her child. As the ship passed on it became more difficult to see the heads. In the greater distance they seemed to be quite close together. All at once, just as a great wave which had hidden them in the farther trough passed on, the mother screamed out:

'She's sinking! she's sinking! Oh, God! Oh, God!' and she fell on her knees, her horrified eyes, set in a face of ashen grey, looking out between the rails.

But at the instant all eyes saw the man's figure rise in the water as he began to dive. There was a hush which seemed deadly; the onlookers feared to draw breath. And then the mother's heart leaped and her cry rang out again as two heads rose together in the waste of sea:

'He has her! He has her! He has her! Oh, thank God! Thank God!' and for a single instant she hid her face in her hands.

Then when the fierce 'hurrah' of all on board had been hushed in expectation, the comments broke forth. Most of the passengers had by this time got glasses of one kind or another.

'See! He's putting the cap on the child's head. He's a cool one that. Fancy him thinking of a red cap at such a time!'

'Ay! we could see that cap, when it might be we couldn't see anything else.'

'Look!' this from an old sailor standing by his boat, 'how he's raisin' in the water. He's keeping his body between her an' the spindrift till the squall has passed. That would choke them both in a wind like this if he didn't know how to guard against it. He's all right; he is! The little maid is safe wi' him.'

'Oh, bless you! Bless you for those words,' said the mother, turning towards him. 'At this moment the Second Officer, who had run down from the bridge, touched Mr. Stonehouse on the shoulder.

'The captain asked me to tell you, sir, that you and Mrs. Stonehouse had better come to him on the bridge. You'll see better from there.'

They both hurried up, and the mother again peered out with fixed eyes. The Captain tried to comfort her; laying his strong hand on her shoulder, he said:

'There, there! Take comfort, ma'am. She is in the hands of God! All that mortal man can do is being done. And she is safer with that gallant young giant than she could be with any other man on the ship. Look, how he is protecting her! Why he knows that all that can be done is being done. He is waiting for us to get to him, and is saving himself for it. Any other man who didn't know so much about swimming as he does would try to reach the lifebuoy; and would choke the two of them with the spindrift in the trying. Mind how he took the red cap to help us see them. He's a fine lad that; a gallant lad!'

CHAPTER XXIV—FROM THE DEEPS

Presently the Captain handed Mrs. Stonehouse a pair of binoculars. For an instant she looked through them, then handed them back and continued gazing out to where the two heads appeared—when they did appear on the crest of the waves like pin-heads. The Captain said half to himself and half to the father:

'Mother's eyes! Mother's eyes!' and the father understood.

As the ship swept back to the rescue, her funnels sending out huge volumes of smoke which the gale beat down on the sea to leeward, the excitement grew tenser and tenser. Men dared hardly breathe; women wept and clasped their hands convulsively as they prayed. In the emergency boat the men sat like statues, their oars upright, ready for instant use. The officer stood with the falls in his hand ready to lower away.

When opposite the lifebuoy, and about a furlong from Harold and Pearl, the Captain gave the signal 'Stop,' and then a second later: 'Full speed astern.'

'Ready, men! Steady!' As the coming wave slipping under the ship began to rise up her side, the officer freed the falls and the boat sank softly into the lifting sea.

Instantly the oars struck the water, and as the men bent to them a cheer rang out.

* * * * *

Harold and Pearl heard, and the man turning his head for a moment saw that the ship was close at hand, gradually drifting down to the weather side of them. He raised the child in his arms, saying:

'Now, Pearl, wave your hand to mother and say, hurrah!' The child, fired into fresh hope, waved her tiny hand and cried 'Hurrah! Hurrah!' The sound could not reach the mother's ears; but she saw, and her heart leaped. She too waved her hand, but she uttered no sound. The sweet high voice of the child crept over the water to the ears of the men in the boat, and seemed to fire their arms with renewed strength.

A few more strokes brought them close, Harold with a last effort raised the child in his arms as the boat drove down on them. The boatswain leaning over the bow grabbed the child, and with one sweep of his strong arm took her into the boat. The bow oarsman caught Harold by the wrist. The way of the boat took him for a moment under water; but the next man; pulling his oar across the boat, stooped over and caught him by the collar, and clung fast. A few seconds more and he was hauled abroad. A wild cheer from all on the *Scoriac* came, sweeping down on the wind.

When once the boat's head had been turned towards the ship, and the oars had bent again to their work, they came soon within shelter. When they had got close enough ropes were thrown out, caught and made fast; and then came down one of the bowlines which the seamen held ready along the rail of the lower deck. This was seized by the boatswain, who placed it round him under his armpits. Then, standing with the child in his arms he made ready to be pulled up. Pearl held out her arms to Harold, crying in fear:

'No, no, let The Man take me! I want to go with The Man!' He said quietly so as not to frighten her:

'No, no, dear! Go with him! He can do this better than I can!' So she clung quietly to the seaman, holding her face pressed close against his shoulder. As the men above pulled at the rope, keeping it as far as possible from the side of the vessel, the boatswain fended himself off with his feet. In a few seconds he was seized by eager hands and pulled over the rail, tenderly holding and guarding the child all the while. In an instant she was in the arms of her mother, who had thrown herself upon her knees and pressed her close to her loving heart. The child put her little arms around her neck and clung to her. Then looking up and seeing the grey pallor of her face, which even her great joy could not in a moment efface, she stroked it and said:

'Poor mother! Poor mother! And now I have made you all wet!' Then, feeling her father's hand on her head she turned and leaped into his arms, where he held her close.

Harold was the next to ascend. He came amid a regular tempest of cheers, the seamen joining with the passengers. The officers, led by the Captain waving his cap from the bridge, joined in the paean.

The boat was cast loose. An instant after the engine bells tinkled: 'Full speed ahead.'

Mrs. Stonehouse had no eyes but for her child, except for one other. When Harold leaped down from the rail she rushed at him, all those around instinctively making way for her. She flung her arms around him and kissed him, and then before he could stop her sank to her knees at his feet, and taking his hand kissed it. Harold was embarrassed beyond all thinking. He tried to take away his hand, but she clung tight to it.

'No, no!' she cried. 'You saved my child!'

Harold was a gentleman and a kindly one. He said no word till she had risen, still holding his hand, when he said quietly:

'There! there! Don't cry. I was only too happy to be of service. Any other man on board would have done the same. I was the nearest, and therefore had to be first. That was all!'

Mr. Stonehouse came to him and said as he grasped Harold's hand so hard that his fingers ached:

'I cannot thank you as I would. But you are a man and will understand. God be good to you as you have been good to my child; and to her mother and myself!' As he turned away Pearl, who had now been holding close to her mother's hand, sprang to him holding up her arms. He raised her up and kissed her. Then he placed her back in her mother's arms.

All at once she broke down as the recollection of danger swept back upon her. ‘Oh, Mother! Mother!’ she cried, with a long, low wail, which touched every one of her hearers to the heart’s core.

‘The hot blankets are all ready. Come, there is not a moment to be lost. I’ll be with you when I have seen the men attended to!’

So the mother, holding her in her arms and steadied by two seamen lest she should slip on the wet and slippery deck, took the child below.

Harold was taken by another set of men, who rubbed him down till he glowed, and poured hot brandy and water into him till he had to almost use force against the superabundance of their friendly ministrations.

For the remainder of that day a sort of solemn gladness ruled on the *Scoriac*. The Stonehouse family remained in their suite, content in glad thankfulness to be with Pearl, who lay well covered up on the sofa sleeping off the effects of the excitement and the immersion, and the result of the potation which the Doctor had forced upon her. Harold was simply shy, and objecting to the publicity which he felt to be his fate, remained in his cabin till the trumpet had blown the dinner call.

CHAPTER XXV—A LITTLE CHILD SHALL LEAD

After dinner Harold went back to his cabin; locking himself in, he lay down on the sofa. The gloom of his great sorrow was heavy on him; the reaction from the excitement of the morning had come.

He was recalled to himself by a gentle tapping. Unlocking and opening the door he saw Mr. Stonehouse, who said with trouble in his voice:

'I came to you on account of my little child.' There he stopped with a break in his voice. Harold, with intent to set his mind at ease and to stave off further expressions of gratitude, replied:

'Oh, pray don't say anything. I am only too glad that I was privileged to be of service. I only trust that the dear little girl is no worse for her—her adventure!'

'That is why I am here,' said the father quickly. 'My wife and I are loth to trouble you. But the poor little thing has worked herself into a paroxysm of fright and is calling for you. We have tried in vain to comfort or reassure her. She will not be satisfied without you. She keeps calling on "The Man" to come and help her. I am loth to put you to further strain after all you have gone through to-day; but if you would come—' Harold was already in the passage as he spoke:

'Of course I'm coming. If I can in any way help it is both a pleasure and a duty to be with her.' Turning to the father he added:

'She is indeed a very sweet and good child. I shall never forget how she bore herself whilst we waited for aid to come.'

'You must tell her mother and me all about it,' said the father; much moved.

When they came close to the Stonehouses' suite of rooms they heard Pearl's voice rising with a pitiful note of fear:

'Where is The Man? Oh! where is The Man? Why doesn't he come to me? He can save me! I want to be with The Man!' When the door opened and she saw him she gave shriek of delight, and springing from the arms of her mother fairly leaped into Harold's arms which were outstretched to receive her. She clung to him and kissed him again and again, rubbing her little hands all over his face as though to prove to herself that he was real and not a dream. Then with a sigh she laid her head on his breast, the reaction of sleep coming all at once to her. With a gesture of silence Harold sat down, holding the child in his arms. Her mother laid a thick shawl over and sat down close to Harold. Mr. Stonehouse stood quiet in the doorway with the child's nurse peering anxiously over his shoulder.

After a little while, when he thought she was asleep, Harold rose and began to place her gently in the bunk. But the moment he did so she waked with a scream. The fright in her eyes was terrible. She clung to him, moaning and crying out between her sobs:

'Don't leave me! Don't leave me! Don't leave me!' Harold was much moved and held the little thing tight in his strong arms, saying to her:

'No darling! I shan't leave you! Look in my eyes, dear, and I will promise you, and then you will be happy. Won't you?'

She looked quickly up in his face. Then she kissed him lovingly, and rested her head, but not sleepily this time, on his breast said:

'Yes! I'm not afraid now! I'm going to stay with The Man!' Presently Mrs. Stonehouse, who had been thinking of ways and means, and of the comfort of the strange man who had been so good to her child, said:

'You will sleep with mother to-night, darling. Mr. . . . The Man,' she said this with an appealing look of apology to Harold, 'The Man will stay by you till you are asleep . . . ' But she interrupted, not fretfully or argumentatively, but with a settled air of content:

'No! I'm going to sleep with The Man!'

'But, dear one,' the mother expostulated, 'The Man will want sleep too.'

'All right, mother. He can sleep too. I'll be very good and lie quite quiet; but oh! mother, I can't sleep unless his arms are round me. I'm afraid if they're not the sea will get me!' and she clung closer to Harold, tightening her arms round his neck.

'You will not mind?' asked Mrs. Stonehouse timidly to Harold; and, seeing acquiescence in his face, added in a burst of tearful gratitude:

'Oh! you are good to her to us all!'

'Hush!' Harold said quietly. Then he said to Pearl, in a cheerful matter-of-fact way which carried conviction to the child's mind:

'Now, darling, it is time for all good little girls to be asleep, especially when they have had an—an interesting day. You wait here till I put my pyjamas on, and then I'll come back for you. And mother and father shall come and see you nicely tucked in!'

'Don't be long!' the child anxiously called after him as he hurried away. Even trust can have its doubts.

In a few minutes Harold was back, in pyjamas and slipper and a dressing-gown. Pearl, already wrapped in a warm shawl by her mother, held out her arms to Harold, who lifted her.

The Stonehouses' suite of rooms was close to the top of the companion-way, and as Harold's stateroom was on the saloon deck, the little procession had, much to the man's concern, run the gauntlet of the thong of passengers whom the bad weather had kept indoors. When he came out of the day cabin carrying the child there was a rush of all the women to make much of the little girl. They were all very kind and no troublesome; their interest was natural enough, and Harold stopped whilst they petted the little thing.

The little procession followed. Mr. and Mrs. Stonehouse coming next, and last the nurse, who manifested a phase of the anxiety of a hen who sees her foster ducklings waddling toward a pond.

When Harold was in his bunk the little maid was brought in.

When they had all gone and the cabin was dark, save for the gleam from the nightlight which the careful mother had placed out of sight in the basin at the foot of the bunk, Harold lay a long time in a negative state, if such be possible, in so far as thought was concerned.

Presently he became conscious of a movement of the child his arms; a shuddering movement, and a sort of smothered groan. The little thing was living over again in sleep the perils and fears of the day. Instinctively she put up her hands and felt the a round her. Then with a sigh clasped her arms round his neck, and with a peaceful look laid her head upon his breast. Even through the gates of sleep her instinct had recognised and realised protection.

And then this trust of a little child brought back the man to his nobler self. Once again came back to him that love which he had had, and which he knew now that he had never lost, for the little child that he had seen grow into full womanhood; whose image must dwell in his heart of hearts for evermore.

The long night's sleep quite restored Pearl. She woke fairly early and without any recurrence of fear. At first she lay still, fearing she would wake The Man, but finding that he was awake—he had not slept a wink all night—she kissed him and then scrambled out of bed.

It was still early morning, but early hours rule on shipland. Harold rang for the steward, and when the man came he told him to tell Mr. Stonehouse that the child was awake. His delight when he found the child unfrightened looking out of the port was unbounded.

CHAPTER XXVI—A NOBLE OFFER

That day Harold passed in unutterable gloom. The reaction was strong on him; and all his woe, his bitter remembrance of the past and his desolation for the future, were with him unceasingly.

In the dusk of the evening he wandered out to his favourite spot, the cable-tank on top of the aft wheelhouse. Here he had been all alone, and his loneliness had the added advantage that from the isolated elevation he could see if anyone approached. He had been out there during the day, and the Captain, who had noticed his habit had had rigged up a canvas dodger on the rail on the weather side. When he sat down on the coiled hawsers in the tank he was both secluded and sheltered. In this peaceful corner his thoughts ran freely and in sympathy with the turmoil of wind and wave.

How unfair it all was! Why had he been singled out for such misery? What gleam of hope or comfort was left to his miserable life since he had heard the words of Stephen; those dreadful words which had shattered in an instant all the cherished hopes of his life. Too well he remembered the tone and look of scorn with which the horrible truths had been conveyed to him. In his inmost soul he accepted them as truths; Stephen's soul had framed them and Stephen's lips had sent them forth.

From his position behind the screen he did not see the approaching figure of Mr. Stonehouse, and was astonished when he saw his head rise above the edge of the tank as he climbed the straight Jacob's ladder behind the wheelhouse. The elder man paused as he saw him and said in an apologetic way:

'Will you forgive my intruding on your privacy? I wanted to speak to you alone; and as I saw you come here a while ago I thought it would be a good opportunity.' Harold was rising as he spoke.

'By all means. This place is common property. But all the same I am honoured in your seeking me.' The poor fellow wished to be genial; but despite his efforts there was a strange formality in the expression of his words. The elder man understood, and said as he hurried forward and sank beside him:

'Pray don't stir! Why, what a cosy corner this is. I don't believe at this moment there is such peace in the ship!'

Once again the bitterness of Harold's heart broke out in sudden words:

'I hope not! There is no soul on board to whom I could wish such evil!' The old man said as he laid his hand softly on the other's shoulder:

'God help you, my poor boy, if such pain is in your heart!' Mr. Stonehouse looked out at the sea, at last turning his face to him again he spoke:

'If you feel that I intrude on you I earnestly ask you to forgive me; but I think that the years between your age and mine as well as my feeling towards the great obligation which I owe you will plead for excuse. There is something I would like to say to you, sir; but I suppose I must not without your permission. May I have it?'

'If you wish, sir. I can at least hear it.'

The old man bowed and went on:

'I could not but notice that you have some great grief bearing upon you; and from one thing or another—I can tell you the data if you wish me to do so—I have come to the conclusion that you are leaving your native land because of it.' Here Harold, wakened to amazement by the readiness with which his secret had been divined, said quickly, rather as an exclamation than interrogation:

'How on earth did you know that!' His companion, taking it as a query, answered:

'Sir, at your age and with your strength life should be a joy; and yet you are sad: Companionship should be a pleasure; yet you prefer solitude. That you are brave and unselfish I know; I have reason, thank God! to know it. That you are kindly and tolerant is apparent from your bearing to my little child this morning; as well as your goodness of last night, the remembrance of which her mother and I will bear to our graves; and to me now. I have not lived all these years without having had trouble in my own heart; and although the happiness of late years has made it dim, my gratitude to you who are so sad brings it all back to me.' He bowed, and Harold, wishing to avoid speaking of his sorrow, said:

'You are quite right so far as I have a sorrow; and it is because of it I have turned my back on home. Let it rest at that!' His companion bowed gravely and went on.

'I take it that you are going to begin life afresh in the new country. In such case I have a proposition to make. I have a large business; a business so large that I am unable to manage it all myself. I was intending that when I arrived at home I would set about finding a partner. The man I want is not an ordinary man. He must have brains and strength and daring.' He paused. Harold felt what was coming, but realised, as he jumped at the conclusion, that it would not do for him to take for granted that he was the man sought. He waited; Mr. Stonehouse went on:

'As to brains, I am prepared to take the existence of such on my own judgment. I have been reading men, and in this aspect specially, all my life. The man I have thought of has brains. I am satisfied of that, without proof. I have proof of the other qualities.' He paused again; as Harold said nothing he continued in a manner ill at ease:

'My difficulty is to make the proposal to the man I want. It is so difficult to talk business to a man to whom you under great obligation; to whom you owe everything. He might take a friendly overture ill.' There was but one thing to be said and Harold said it. His heart warmed to the kindly old man and he wished to spare him pain; even if he could not accept him proposition:

'He couldn't take it ill; unless he was an awful bounder.'

'It was you I thought of!'

'I thought so much, sir;' said Harold after a pause, 'and I thank you earnestly and honestly. But it is impossible.'

'Oh, my dear sir!' said the other, chagrined as well as surprised. 'Think again! It is really worth your while to think of it, no matter what your ultimate decision may be!'

Harold shook his head. There was a long silence. The old man wished to give his companion time to think; and indeed he thought that Harold was weighing the proposition in his mind. As for Harold, he was thinking how best he could make his absolute refusal inoffensive. He must, he felt, give some reason; and his thoughts were bent on how much of the truth he could safely give without endangering his secret. Therefore he spoke at last in general terms:

'I can only ask you, sir, to bear with me and to believe that I am very truly and sincerely grateful to you for your trust. But the fact is, I cannot go anywhere amongst people. Of course you understand that I am speaking in confidence; to you alone and to none other?'

'Absolutely!' said Mr. Stonehouse gravely. Harold went on:

'I must be alone. I can only bear to see people on this ship because it is a necessary way to solitude.'

'You "cannot go anywhere amongst people"! Pardon me. I don't wish to be unduly inquisitive; but on my word I fail to understand!' Harold was in a great difficulty. Common courtesy alone forbade that he should leave the matter where it was; and in addition both the magnificently generous offer which had been made to him, and the way in which accident had thrown him to such close intimacy with Pearl's family, required that he should be at least fairly frank. At last in a sort of cold desperation he said:

'I cannot meet anyone . . . There is something that happened . . . Something I did . . . Nothing can make it right . . . All I can do is to lose myself in the wildest, grimmest, wilderness in the world; and fight my pain . . . my shame . . . !'

A long silence. Then the old man's voice came clear and sweet, something like music, in the shelter from the storm:

'But perhaps time may mend things. God is very good . . . !' Harold answered out of the bitterness of his heart. He felt that his words were laden with an anger which he did not feel, but he did not see his way to alter them:

'Nothing can mend this thing! It is at the farthest point of evil; and there is no going on or coming back. Nothing can wipe out what is done; what is past!'

Again silence, and again the strong, gentle voice:

'God can do much! Oh my dear young friend, you who have been such a friend to me and mine, think of this.'

'God Himself can do nothing here! It is done! And that is the end!' He turned his head; it was all he could do to keep from groaning. The old man's voice vibrated with earnest conviction as he spoke:

'You are young and strong and brave! Your heart is noble! You can think quickly in moments of peril; therefore your brain is sound and alert. Now, may I ask you a favour? it is not much. Only that you will listen, without interruption, to what, if I have your permission, I am going to say. Do not ask me anything; do not deny; do not interrupt! Only listen! May I ask this?'

'By all means! It is not much!' he almost felt like smiling as he spoke. Mr. Stonehouse, after a short pause, as if arranging his thoughts, spoke:

'Let me tell you what I am. I began life with nothing but a fair education such as all our American boys get. But from a good mother I got an idea that to be honest was the best of all things; from a strenuous father, who, however, could not do well for himself, I learned application to work and how best to use and exercise such powers as were in me. From the start things prospered with me. Men who knew me trusted me; some came with offers to share in my enterprise. Thus I had command of what capital I could use; I was able to undertake great works and to carry them through. Fortune kept growing and growing; for as I got wealthier I found newer and larger and more productive uses for my money. And in all my work I can say before God I never willingly wronged any man. I am proud to be able to say that my name stands good wherever it has been used. It may seem egotistical that I say such things of myself. It may seem bad taste; but I speak because I have a motive in so doing. I want you to understand at the outset that in my own country, wherever I am known and in my own work, my name is a strength.'

He paused a while. Harold sat still; he knew that such man would not, could not, speak in such a way without a strong motive; and to learn that motive he waited.

'When you were in the water making what headway you could in that awful sea—when my little child's life hung in the balance, and the anguish of my wife's heart nearly tore my heart in two, I said to myself, "If we had a son I should wish him to be like that." I meant it then, and I mean it now! Come to me as you are! Faults, and past, and all. Forget the past! Whatever it was we will together try to wipe it out. Much may be done in restoring where there has been any wrong-doing. Take my name as your own. It will protect you from the result of what ever has been, and give you an opportunity to find your place again. You are not bad in heart I know. Whatever you have done has not been from base motives. Few of us are spotless as to facts. You and I will show ourselves—for unless God wills to the opposite we shall confide in none other—that a strong, brave man may win back all that was lost. Let me call you by my name and hold you as the son of my heart; and it will be a joy and pleasure to my declining years.'

As he had spoken, Harold's thought's had at first followed in some wonderment. But gradually, as his noble purpose unfolded, based as it was on a misconception as to the misdoing of which he himself had spoken, he had been almost stricken dumb. At the first realisation of what was intended he could not have spoken had he tried; but at the end he had regained his thoughts and his voice. There was still wonderment in it, as realising from the long pause that the old man had completed his suggestion, he spoke:

'If I understand aright you are offering me your name! Offering to share your honour with me. With me, whom, if again I understand, you take as having committed some crime?'

'I inferred from what you said and from your sadness, your desire to shun your kind, that there was, if not a crime, some fault which needed expiation.'

'But your honour, sir; your honour!' There was a proud look in the old man's eyes as he said quietly:

'It was my desire, is my desire, to share with you what I have that is best; and that, I take it, is not the least valuable of my possessions, such as they are! And why not? You have given to me all that makes life sweet; without which it would be unbearable. That child who came to my wife and me when I was old and she had passed her youth is all in all to us both. Had your strength and courage been for barter in the moments when my child was quivering between life and death, I would have cheerfully purchased them with not half but all! Sir, I should have given my soul! I can say this now, for gratitude is above all barter; and surely it is allowed to a father to show gratitude for the life of his child!'

This great-hearted generosity touched Harold to the quick. He could hardly speak for a few minutes. Then instinctively grasping the old man's hand he said:

'You overwhelm me. Such noble trust and generosity as you have shown me demands a return of trust. But I must think! Will you remain here and let me return to you in a little while?'

He rose quickly and slipped down the iron ladder, passing into the darkness and the mist and the flying spray.

CHAPTER XXVII—AGE'S WISDOM

Harold went to and fro on the deserted deck. All at once the course he had to pursue opened out before him. He was aware that what the noble-minded old man offered him was fortune, great fortune in any part of the world. He would have to be refused, but the refusal should be gently done. He, believing that the other had done something very wrong, had still offered to share with him his name, his honour. Such confidence demanded full confidence in return; the unwritten laws which governed the men amongst whom he had been brought up required it.

And the shape that confidence should take? He must first disabuse his new friend's mind of criminal or unworthy cause for his going away. For the sake of his own name and that of his dead father that should be done. Then he would have to suggest the real cause . . . He would in this have to trust Mr. Stonehouse's honour for secrecy. But he was worthy of trust. He would, of course, give no name, no clue; but he would put things generally in a way that he could understand.

When his mind was so far made up he wanted to finish the matter, so he turned to the wheelhouse and climbed the ladder again. It was not till he sat in the shelter by his companion that he became aware that he had become wet with the spray. The old man wishing to help him in his embarrassment said:

'Well?' Harold began at once; the straightforward habit of his life stood to him now:

'Let me say first, sir, what will I know give you pleasure.' The old man extended his hand; he had been hoping for acceptance, and this seemed like it. Harold laid his hand on it for an instant only, and then raised it as if to say 'Wait':

'You have been so good to me, so nobly generous in your wishes that I feel I owe you a certain confidence. But as it concerns not myself alone I will ask that it be kept a secret between us two. Not to be told to any other; not even your wife!'

'I will hold your secret sacred. Even from my wife; the first secret I shall have ever kept from her.'

'First, then, let me say, and this is what I know will rejoice you, that I am not leaving home and country because of any crime I have committed; not from any offence against God or man, or law. Thank God! I am free from such. I have always tried to live uprightly . . . ' Here a burst of pain overcame him, and with a dry sob he added: 'And that is what makes the terrible unfairness of it all!'

The old man laid a kindly hand on his shoulder and kept it there for a few moments.

'My poor boy! My poor boy!' was all he said. Harold shook himself as if to dislodge the bitter thoughts. Mastering himself he went on:

'There was a lady with whom I was very much thrown in contact since we were children. Her father was my father's friend. My friend too, God knows; for almost with his dying breath he gave sanction to my marrying his daughter, if it should ever be that she should care for me in that way. But he wished me to wait, and, till she was old enough to choose, to leave her free. For she is several years younger than I am; and I am not very old yet—except in heart! All this, you understand, was said in private to me; none other knew it. None knew of it even till this moment when I tell you that such a thing has been.' He paused; the other said:

'Believe me that I value your confidence, beyond all words!' Harold felt already the good effects of being able to speak of his pent-up trouble. Already this freedom from the nightmare loneliness of his own thoughts seemed to be freeing his very soul.

'I honestly kept to his wishes. Before God, I did! No man who loved a woman, honoured her, worshipped her, could have been more scrupulously careful as to leaving her free. What it was to me to so hold myself no one knows; no one ever will know. For I loved her, do love her, with every nerve and fibre of my heart. All our lives we had been friends; and I believed we loved and trusted each other. But . . . but then there came a day when I found by chance that a great trouble threatened her. Not from anything wrong that she had done; but from something perhaps foolish, harmlessly foolish except that she did not know . . . ' He stopped suddenly, fearing he might have said overmuch of Stephen's side of the affair. 'When I came to her aid, however, meaning the best, and as single-minded as a man can be, she misunderstood my words, my meaning, my very coming; and she said things which cannot be unsaid. Things . . . matters were so fixed that I could not explain; and I had to listen. She said things that I did not believe she could have said to me, to anyone. Things that I did not think she could have thought . . . I dare say she was right in some ways. I suppose I bungled in my desire to be unselfish. What she said came to me in new lights upon what I had done . . . But anyhow her statements were such that I felt I could not, should not, remain. My very presence must have been a trouble to her hereafter. There was nothing for it but to come away. There was no place for me! No hope for me! There is none on this side of the grave! . . . For I love her still, more than ever. I honour and worship her still, and ever will, and ever must! . . . I am content to forego my own happiness; but I feel there is a danger to her from what has been. That there is and must be to her unhappiness even from the fact that it was I who was the object of her wrath; and this adds to my woe. Worst of all is . . . the thought and the memory that she should have done so; she who . . . she . . . '

He turned away overcome and hid his face in his hands. The old man sat still; he knew that at such a moment silence is the best form of sympathy. But his heart glowed; the wisdom of his years told him that he had heard as yet of no absolute bar to his friend's ultimate happiness.

'I am rejoiced, my dear boy, at what you tell me of your own conduct. It would have made no difference to me had it been otherwise. But it would have meant a harder and longer climb back to the place you should hold. But it really seems that nothing is so hopeless as you think. Believe me, my dear young friend who are now as a son to my heart, that there will be bright days for you yet . . . ' He paused a moment, but mastering himself went on in a quiet voice:

'I think you are wise to go away. In the solitudes and in danger things that are little in reality will find their true perspective; and things that are worthy will appear in their constant majesty.'

He stood, and laying once again his hand on the young man's shoulder said:

'I recognise that I—that we, for my wife and little girl would be at one with me in my wish, did they know of it, must not keep you from your purpose of fighting out your trouble alone. Every man, as the Scotch proverb says, must "dree his own weird." I shall not, I must not, ask you for any promise; but I trust that if ever you do come back you will make us all glad by seeing you. And remember that what I said of myself and of all I have—all—holds good so long as I shall live!'

Before Harold could reply he had slipped down the ladder and was gone.

During the rest of the voyage, with the exception of one occasion, he did not allude to the subject again by word or implication, and Harold was grateful to him for it.

On the night before Fire Island should be sighted Harold was in the bow of the great ship looking out with eyes in which gleamed no hope. To him came through the darkness Mr. Stonehouse. He heard the footsteps and knew them; so with the instinct of courtesy, knowing that his friend would not intrude on his solitude without purpose, he turned and met him. When the American stood beside him he said, studiously avoiding looking at his companion:

'This is the last night we shall be together, and, if I may, there is one thing I would like to say to you.'

'Say all you like, sir,' said Harold as heartily as he could, 'I am sure it is well meant; and for that at any rate I shall be grateful to you.'

'You will yet be grateful, I think!' he answered gravely. 'When it comes back to you in loneliness and solitude you will, I believe, think it worth being grateful for. I don't mean that you will be grateful to me, but for the thing itself. I speak out of the wisdom of many years. At your time of life the knowledge cannot come from observation. It may my poor boy, come through pain; and if what I think is correct you will even in due time be grateful to the pain which left such golden residuum.' He paused, and Harold grew interested. There was something in the old man's manner which presaged a truth; he, at least, believed it. So the young man listened at first with his ears; and as the other spoke, his heart listened too:

'Young men are apt to think somewhat wrongly of women they love and respect. We are apt to think that such women are of a different clay from ourselves. Nay! that they are not compact of clay at all, but of some faultless, flawless material which the Almighty keeps for such fine work. It is only in middle age that men—except scamps, who learn this bad side of knowledge young—realise that women are human beings like themselves. It may be, you know, that you may have misjudged this young lady! That you have not made sufficient allowance for her youth, her nature, even the circumstances under which she spoke. You have told me that she was in some deep grief or trouble. May it not have been that this in itself unnerved her, distorted her views, aroused her passion till all within and around was tinged with the jaundice of her concern, her humiliation—whatever it was that destroyed for the time that normal self which you had known so long. May it not have been that her bitterest memory even since may be of the speaking of these very words which sent you out into the wide world to hide yourself from men. I have thought, waking and sleeping, of your position ever since you honoured me with your confidence; and with every hour the conviction has strengthened in me that there is a way out of this situation which sends a man like you into solitude with a heart hopeless and full of pain; and which leaves her perhaps in greater pain, for she has not like you the complete sense of innocence. But at present there is no way out but through time and thought. Whatever may be her ideas or wishes she is powerless. She does not know your thoughts, no matter how she may guess at them. She does not know where you are or how to reach you, no matter how complete her penitence may be. And oh! my dear young friend, remember that you are a strong man, and she is a woman. Only a woman in her passion and her weakness after all. Think this all over, my poor boy! You will have time and opportunity where you are going. God help you to judge wisely!' After a pause of a few seconds he said abruptly: 'Good night!' and moved quickly away.

* * * * *

When the time for parting came Pearl was inconsolable. Not knowing any reason why The Man should not do as she wished she was persistent in her petitions to Harold that he should come with her, and to her father and mother that they should induce him to do so. Mrs. Stonehouse would have wished him to join them if only for a time. Her husband, unable to give any hint without betraying confidence, had to content himself with trying to appease his little daughter by vague hopes rather than promises that her friend would join them at some other time.

When the *Scoriac* was warped at the pier there was a tendency on the part of the passengers to give Harold a sort of public send-off; but becoming aware of it he hurried down the gangway without waiting. Having only hand luggage, for he was to get his equipment in New York, he had cleared and passed the ring of customs officers before the most expeditious of the other passengers had collected their baggage. He had said good-bye to the Stonehouses in their own cabin. Pearl had been so much affected at saying good-bye, and his heart had so warmed to her, that at last he had said impulsively:

'Don't cry, darling. If I am spared I shall come back to you within three years. Perhaps I will write before then; but there are not many post-offices where I am going to!'

Children are easily satisfied. Their trust makes a promise a real thing; and its acceptance is the beginning of satisfaction. But for weeks after the parting she had often fits of deep depression, and at such times her tears always flowed. She took note of the date, and there was never a day that she did not think of and sigh for The Man.

And The Man, away in the wilds of Alaska, was feeling, day by day and hour by hour, the chastening and purifying influences of the wilderness. Hot passions cooled before the breath of the snowfield and the glacier. The moaning of a tortured spirit was lost in the roar of the avalanche and the scream of the cyclone. Pale sorrow and cold despair were warmed and quickened by the fierce sunlight which came suddenly and stayed only long enough to vitalise all nature.

And as the first step to understanding, The Man forgot himself.

CHAPTER XXVIII—DE LANNOY

Two years!

Not much to look back upon, but a world to look forward to. To Stephen, dowered though she was with rare personal gifts and with wealth and position accorded to but few, the hours of waiting were longer than the years that were past. Yet the time had new and startling incidents for her. Towards Christmas in the second year the Boer war had reached its climax of evil. As the news of disaster after disaster was flashed through the cable she like others felt appalled at the sacrifices that were being exacted by the God of War.

One day she casually read in The Times that the Earl de Lannoy had died in his London mansion, and further learned that he had never recovered from the shock of hearing that his two sons and his nephew had been killed. The paragraph concluded: "By his death the title passes to a distant relative. The new Lord de Lannoy is at present in India with his regiment, the 35th or 'Grey' Hussars, of which he is Colonel." She gave the matter a more than passing thought, for it was sad to find a whole family thus wiped out at a blow.

Early in February she received a telegram from her London solicitor saying that he wished to see her on an important matter. Her answer was: "Come at once"; and at tea-time Mr. Copleston arrived. He was an old friend and she greeted him warmly. She was a little chilled when he answered with what seemed unusual deference:

'I thank your Ladyship for your kindness!' She raised her eyebrows but made no comment: she was learning to be silent under surprise. When she had handed the old gentleman his tea she said:

'My aunt has chosen to remain away, thinking that you might wish to see me privately. But I take it that there is nothing which she may not share. I have no secrets from her.'

He rubbed his hands genially as he replied:

'Not at all; not at all! I should like her to be present. It will, I am sure, be a delight to us all.'

Again raised eyebrows; again silence on the subject. When a servant answered her bell she told him to ask Miss Rowly if she would kindly join them.

Aunt Laetitia and the solicitor were old cronies, and their greeting was most friendly. When the old gentlewoman had seated herself and taken her cup of tea, Mr. Copleston said to Stephen, with a sort of pomposity:

'I have to announce your succession to the Earldom de Lannoy!'

Stephen sat quite still. She knew the news was true; Mr. Copleston was not one who would jest on a business subject, and too accurate a lawyer to make an error in a matter of fact. But the fact did not seem to touch her. It was not that she was indifferent to it; few women could hear such news without a thrill. Mr. Copleston seemed at a loss. Miss Rowly rose and quietly kissed her, and saying simply, 'God bless you, my dear!' went back to her seat.

Realising that Mr. Copleston expected some acknowledgment, Stephen held out her hand to him and said quietly:

'Thank you!'

After a long pause she added quietly:

'Now, won't you tell us about it? I am in absolute ignorance; and don't understand.'

'I had better not burden you, at first, with too many details, which can come later; but give you a rough survey of the situation.'

'Your title of Countess de Lannoy comes to you through your ancestor Isobel, third and youngest daughter of the sixth Earl; Messrs Collinbrae and Jackson, knowing that my firm acted for your family, communicated with us. Lest there should be any error we followed most carefully every descendant and every branch of the family, for we thought it best not to communicate with you till your right of inheritance was beyond dispute. We arrived independently at the same result as Messrs. Collinbrae and Jackson. There is absolutely no doubt whatever of your claim. You will petition the Crown, and on reference to the House of Lords the Committee for Privileges will admit your right. May I offer my congratulations, Lady de Lannoy on your acquisition? By the way, I may say that all the estates of the Earldom, which have been from the first kept in strict entail, go with the title de Lannoy.'

During the recital Stephen was conscious of a sort of bitter comment on the tendencies of good fortune.

'Too late! too late!' something seemed to whisper, 'what delight it would have been had Father inherited . . . If Harold had not gone . . . !' All the natural joy seemed to vanish, as bubbles break into empty air.

To Aunt Laetitia the new title was a source of pride and joy, far greater than would have been the case had it come to herself. She had for so many years longed for new honours for Stephen that she had almost come to regard them as a right whose coming should not be too long delayed. Miss Rowly had never been to Lannoy; and, indeed, she knew personally nothing of the county Angleshire in which it was situated. She was naturally anxious to see the new domain; but kept her feeling concealed during the months that elapsed until Stephen's right had been conceded by the Committee for Privileges. But after that her impatience became manifest to Stephen, who said one day in a teasing, caressing way, as was sometimes her wont:

'Why, Auntie, what a hurry you are in! Lannoy will keep, won't it?'

'Oh, my dear,' she replied, shaking her head, 'I can understand your own reticence, for you don't want to seem greedy and in a hurry about your new possessions. But when people come to my age there's no time to waste. I feel I would not have complete material for happiness in the World-to-come, if there were not a remembrance of my darling in her new home!'

Stephen was much touched; she said impulsively:

'We shall go to-morrow, Auntie. No! Let us go to-day. You shall not wait an hour that I can help!' She ran to the bell; but before her hand was on the cord the other said:

'Not yet! Stephen dear. It would flurry me to start all at once; to-morrow will be time enough. And that will give you time to send word so that they will be prepared for your coming.'

How often do we look for that to-morrow which never comes? How often do we find that its looked-for rosy tints are none other than the gloom-laden grey of the present?

Before the morrow's sun was high in the heavens Stephen was hurriedly summoned to her aunt's bedside. She lay calm and peaceful; but one side of her face was alive and the other seemingly dead. In the night a paralytic stroke had seized her. The doctors said she might in time recover a little, but she would never be her old active self again. She herself, with much painful effort, managed to convey to Stephen that she knew the end was near. Stephen, knowing the wish of her heart and thinking that it might do her good to gratify her wish, asked if she should arrange that she be brought to Lannoy. Feebly and slowly, word by word, she managed to convey her idea.

'Not now, dear one. I shall see it all in time!—Soon! And I shall understand and rejoice!' For a long time she lay still, holding with her right hand, which was not paralysed, the other's hand. Then she murmured:

'You will find happiness there!' She said no more; but seemed to sleep.

From that sleep she never woke, but faded slowly, softly away.

Stephen was broken-hearted. Now, indeed, she felt alone and desolate. All were gone. Father, uncle, aunt!—And Harold. The kingdoms of the Earth which lay at her feet were of no account. One hour of the dead or departed, any of them, back again were worth them all!

Normanstand was now too utterly lonely to be endurable; so Stephen determined to go, for a time at any rate, to Lannoy. She was becoming accustomed to be called 'my lady' and 'your ladyship,' and the new loneness made her feel better prepared to take her place amongst new surroundings.

In addition, there was another spur to her going. Leonard Everard, knowing of her absolute loneliness, and feeling that in it was a possibility of renewing his old status, was beginning to make himself apparent. He had learned by experience a certain wisdom, and did not put himself forward obtrusively. But whenever they met he looked at her so meekly and so lovingly that it brought remembrances which came with blushes. So, all at once, without giving time for the news to permeate through the neighbourhood, she took her way to Lannoy with a few servants.

Stephen's life had hitherto been spent inland. She had of course now and again been for short periods to various places; but the wonder of the sea as a constant companion had been practically unknown to her.

Now at her new home its full splendour burst upon her; and so impressed itself upon her that new life seemed to open.

Lannoy was on the north-eastern coast, the castle standing at the base of a wide promontory stretching far into the North Sea. From the coast the land sloped upward to a great rolling ridge. The outlook seaward was over a mighty expanse of green sward, dotted here and there with woods and isolated clumps of trees which grew fewer and smaller as the rigour of the northern sea was borne upon them by the easterly gales.

The coast was a wild and lonely one. No habitation other than an isolated fisher's cottage was to be seen between the little fishing-port at the northern curve away to the south, where beyond a waste of sandhills and strand another tiny fishing-village nestled under a high cliff, sheltering it from northerly wind. For centuries the lords of Lannoy had kept their magnificent prospect to themselves; and though they had treated their farmers and cottagers well, none had ever been allowed to settle in the great park to seaward of the castle.

From the terrace of the castle only than one building, other than the cottage on the headland, could be seen. Far off on the very crest of the ridge was the tower of an old windmill.

CHAPTER XXIX—THE SILVER LADY

When it was known that Lady de Lannoy had come to Lannoy there was a prompt rush of such callers as the county afforded. Stephen, however, did not wish to see anyone just at present. Partly to avoid the chance meeting with strangers, and partly because she enjoyed and benefited by the exercise, she was much away from home every day. Sometimes, attended only by a groom, she rode long distances north or south along the coast; or up over the ridge behind the castle and far inland along the shaded roads through the woods; or over bleak wind-swept stretches of moorland. Sometimes she would walk, all alone, far down to the sea-road, and would sit for hours on the shore or high up on some little rocky headland where she could enjoy the luxury of solitude.

Now and again in her journeyings she made friends, most of them humble ones. She was so great a lady in her station that she could be familiar without seeming to condescend. The fishermen of the little ports to north and south came to know her, and to look gladly for her coming. Their goodwives had for her always a willing curtsy and a ready smile. As for the children, they looked on her with admiration and love, tempered with awe. She was so gentle with them, so ready to share their pleasures and interests, that after a while they came to regard her as some strange embodiment of Fairydom and Dreamland. Many a little heart was made glad by the arrival of some item of delight from the Castle; and the hearts of the sick seemed never to hope, or their eyes to look, in vain.

One friend she made who became very dear and of great import. Often she had looked up at the old windmill on the crest of the ridge and wondered who inhabited it; for that some one lived in it, or close by, was shown at times by the drifting smoke. One day she made up her mind to go and see for herself. She had a fancy not to ask anyone about it. The place was a little item of mystery; and as such to be treasured and exploited, and in due course explored. The mill itself was picturesque, and the detail at closer acquaintance sustained the far-off impression. The roadway forked on the near side of the mill, reuniting again the further side, so that the place made a sort of island—mill, out-offices and garden. As the mill was on the very top of the ridge the garden which lay seawards was sheltered by the building from the west, and from the east by a thick hedge of thorn and privet, which quite hid it from the roadway. Stephen took the lower road. Finding no entrance save a locked wooden door she followed round to the western side, where the business side of the mill had been. It was all still now and silent, and that it had long fallen into disuse was shown by the grey faded look of everything. Grass, green and luxuriant, grew untrodden between the cobble-stones with which the yard was paved. There was a sort of old-world quietude about everything which greatly appealed to Stephen.

Stephen dismounted and walked round the yard admiring everything. She did not feel as if intruding; for the gateway was wide open.

A low door in the base of the mill tower opened, and a maid appeared, a demure pretty little thing of sixteen or seventeen years, dressed in a prim strait dress and an old-fashioned Puritan cap. Seeing a stranger, she made an ejaculation and drew back hastily. Stephen called out to her:

'Don't be afraid, little girl! Will you kindly tell me who lives here?' The answer came with some hesitation:

'Sister Ruth.'

'And who is Sister Ruth?' The question came instinctively and without premeditation. The maid, embarrassed, held hard to the half-open door and shifted from foot to foot uneasily.

'I don't know!' she said at last. 'Only Sister Ruth, I suppose!' It was manifest that the matter had never afforded her anything in the nature of a problem. There was an embarrassing silence. Stephen did not wish to seem, or even to be, prying; but her curiosity was aroused. What manner of woman was this who lived so manifestly alone, and who had but a Christian name! Stephen, however, had all her life been accustomed to dominance, and at Normanstand and Norwood had made many acquaintances amongst her poorer neighbours. She was just about to ask if she might see Sister Ruth, when behind the maid in the dark of the low passage-way appeared the tall, slim figure of a silver woman. Truly a silver woman! The first flash of Stephen's thought was correct. White-haired, white-faced, white-capped, white-kerchiefed; in a plain-cut dress of light-grey silk, without adornment of any kind. The whole ensemble was as a piece of old silver. The lines of her face were very dignified, very sweet, very beautiful. Stephen felt at once that she was in the presence of no common woman. She looked an admiration which all her Quaker garments could not forbid the other to feel. She was not the first to speak; in such a noble presence the dignity of Stephen's youth imperatively demanded silence, if not humility. So she waited. The Silver Lady, for so Stephen ever after held her in her mind, said quietly, but with manifest welcome:

'Didst thou wish to see me? Wilt thou come in?' Stephen answered frankly:

'I should like to come in; if you will not think me rude. The fact is, I was struck when riding by with the beautiful situation of the mill. I thought it was only an old mill till I saw the garden hedges; and I came round to ask if I might go in.' The Silver Lady came forward at a pace that by itself expressed warmth as she said heartily:

'Indeed thou mayest. Stay! it is tea-time. Let us put thy horse in one of the sheds; there is no man here at present to do it. Then thou shalt come with me and see my beautiful view!' She was about to take the horse herself, but Stephen forestalled her with a quick: 'No, no! pray let me. I am quite accustomed.' She led the horse to a shed, and having looped the rein over a hook, patted him and ran back. The Silver Lady gave her a hand, and they entered the dark passage together.

Stephen was thinking if she ought to begin by telling her name. But the Haroun al Raschid feeling for adventure incognito is an innate principle of the sons of men. It was seldom indeed that her life had afforded her such an opportunity.

The Silver Lady on her own part also wished for silence, as she looked for the effect on her companion when the glory of the view should break upon her. When they had climbed the winding stone stair, which led up some twenty feet, there was a low wide landing with the remains of the main shaft of the mill machinery running through it. From one side rose a stone stair curving with the outer wall of the mill tower and guarded by a heavy iron rail. A dozen steps there were, and then a landing a couple of yards square; then a deep doorway cut in the thickness of the wall, round which the winding stair continued.

The Silver Lady, who had led the way, threw open the door, and motioned to her guest to enter. Stephen stood for a few moments, surprised as well as delighted, for the room before her as not like anything which she had ever seen or thought of.

It was a section of almost the whole tower, and was of considerable size, for the machinery and even the inner shaft had been removed. East and south and west the wall had been partially cut away so that great wide windows nearly the full height of the room showed the magnificent panorama. In the depths of the ample windows were little cloistered nooks where one might with a feeling of super-solitude be away from and above the world.

The room was beautifully furnished and everywhere were flowers, with leaves and sprays and branches where possible.

Even from where she stood in the doorway Stephen had a bird's-eye view of the whole countryside; not only of the coast, with which she was already familiar, and on which her windows at the Castle looked, but to the south and west, which the hill rising steep behind the castle and to southward shut out.

The Silver Lady could not but notice her guest's genuine admiration.

'Thou likest my room and my view. There is no use asking thee, I see thou dost!' Stephen answered with a little gasp.

'I think it is the quaintest and most beautiful place I have ever seen!'

'I am so glad thou likest it. I have lived here for nearly forty years; and they have been years of unutterable peace and earthly happiness! And now, thou wilt have some tea!'

Stephen left the mill that afternoon with a warmth of heart that she had been a stranger to for many a day. The two women had accepted each other simply. 'I am called Ruth,' said the Silver Lady. 'And I am Stephen,' said the Countess de Lannoy in reply. And that was all; neither had any clue to the other's identity. Stephen felt that some story lay behind that calm, sweet personality; much sorrow goes to the making of fearless quietude. The Quaker lady moved so little out of her own environment that she did not even suspect the identity of her visitor. All that she knew of change was a notice from the solicitor to the estate that, as the headship had lapsed into another branch of the possessing family, she must be prepared, if necessary, to vacate her tenancy, which was one 'at will.'

It was not long before Stephen availed herself of the permission to come again. This time she made up her mind to tell who she was, lest the concealment of her identity might lead to awkwardness. At that meeting friendship became union.

The natures of the two women expanded to each other; and after a very few meetings there was established between them a rare confidence. Even the personal austerity of Quakerdom, or the state and estate of the peeress, could not come between. Their friendship seemed to be for the life of one. To the other it would be a memory.

The Silver Lady never left the chosen routine of her own life. Whatever was the reason of her giving up the world, she kept it to herself; and Stephen respected her reticence as much as she did her confidence.

It had become a habit, early in their friendship, for Stephen to ride or walk over to the windmill in the dusk of the evening when she felt especially lonely. On one such occasion she pushed open the outer door, which was never shut, and took her way up the stone stair. She knew she would find her friend seated in the window with hands folded on lap, looking out into the silent dusk with that absorbed understanding of things which is holier than reverence, and spiritually more active than conscious prayer.

She tapped the door lightly, and stepped into the room.

With a glad exclamation, which coming through her habitual sedateness showed how much she loved the young girl, Sister Ruth started to her feet. There was something of such truth in the note she had sounded, that the lonely girl's heart went out to her in abandoned fulness. She held out her arms; and, as she came close to the other, fell rather than sank at her feet. The elder woman recognised, and knew. She made no effort to restrain her; but sinking back into her own seat laid the girl's head in her lap, and held her hands close against her breast.

'Tell me,' she whispered. 'Won't you tell me, dear child, what troubles you? Tell me! dear. It may bring peace!'

'Oh, I am miserable, miserable, miserable!' moaned Stephen in a low voice whose despair made the other's heart grow cold. The Silver Lady knew that here golden silence was the best of help; holding close the other's hands, she waited. Stephen's breast began to heave; with an impulsive motion she drew away her hands and put them before her burning face, which she pressed lower still on the other's lap. Sister Ruth knew that the trouble, whatever it was, was about to find a voice. And then came in a low shuddering whisper a voice muffled in the folds of the dress:

'I killed a man!'

In all her life the Silver Lady had never been so startled or so shocked. She had grown so to love the bright, brilliant young girl that the whispered confession cut through the silence of the dusk as a shriek of murder goes through the silent gloom of night. Her hands flew wide from her breast, and the convulsive shudder which shook her all in an instant woke Stephen through all her own deep emotion to the instinct of protection of the other. The girl looked up, shaking her head, and said with a sadness which stilled all the other's fear:

'Ah! Don't be frightened! It is not murder that I tell you of. Perhaps if it were, the thought would be easier to bear! He would have been hurt less if it had been only his body that I slew. Well I know now that his life would have been freely given if I wished it; if it had been for my good. But it was the best of him that I killed; his soul. His noble, loving, trusting, unselfish soul. The bravest and truest soul that ever had place in a man's breast! . . . ' Her speaking ended with a sob; her body sank lower.

Sister Ruth's heart began to beat more freely. She understood now, and all the womanhood, all the wifehood, motherhood suppressed for a lifetime, awoke to the woman's need. Gently she stroked the beautiful head that lay so meekly on her lap; and as the girl sobbed with but little appearance of abatement, she said to her softly:

'Tell me, dear child. Tell me all about it! See! we are alone together. Thou and I; and God! In God's dusk; with only the silent land and sea before us! Won't thou trust me, dear one, and speak!'

And then, as the shadows fell, and far-off lights at sea began to twinkle over the waste of waters, Stephen found voice and told without reserve the secret of her shame and her remorse.

At last, when her broken voice had trailed away into gentle catchings of the breath, the older woman, knowing that the time come for comfort, took her in her strong arms, holding her face wet against her own, their tears mingling.

'Cry on, dear heart!' she said as she kissed her. 'Cry on! It will do thee good!' She was startled once again as the other seemed for an instant to grow rigid in her arms, and raising her hands cried out in a burst of almost hysterical passion:

'Cry! cry! Oh my God! my God!' Then becoming conscious of her wet face she seemed to become in an instant all limp, and sank on her knees again. There was so different a note in her voice that the other's heart leaped as she heard her say:

'God be thanked for these tears! Oh, thank God! Thank God!' Looking up she saw through the gloom the surprise in her companion's eyes and answered their query in words:

'Oh! you don't know! You can't know what it is to me! I have not cried since last I saw him pass from me in the wood!'

* * * * *

That time of confession seemed to have in some way cleared, purified and satisfied Stephen's soul. Life was now easier to bear. She was able to adapt herself, justifiably to the needs of her position; and all around her and dependent on her began to realise that amongst them was a controlling force, far-reaching sympathy, and a dominant resolution that made for good.

She began to shake off the gloom of her sorrows and to take her place in her new high station. Friends there were in many, and quondam lovers by the score. Lovers of all sorts. Fortune-hunters there were be sure, not a few. But no need was there for baseness when the lady herself was so desirable; so young, so fair, so lovable. That she was of great estate and 'richly left' made all things possible to any man who had sufficient acquisitiveness, or a good conceit of himself. In a wide circle of country were many true-lovers who would have done aught to win her praise.

And so in the East the passing of the two years of silence and gloom seemed to be the winning of something brighter to follow.

CHAPTER XXX—THE LESSON OF THE WILDERNESS

In the West the two years flew. Time seemed to go faster there, because life was more strenuous. Harold, being mainly alone, found endless work always before him. From daylight to dark labour never ceased; and for his own part he never wished that it should. In the wilderness, and especially under such conditions as held in Northern Alaska, labour is not merely mechanical. Every hour of the day is fraught with danger in some new form, and the head has to play its part in the strife against nature. In such a life there is not much time for thinking or brooding.

At first, when the work and his surroundings were strange to him, Harold did many useless things and ran many unnecessary risks. But his knowledge grew with experience. Privations he had in plenty; and all the fibre of his body and the strength of his resolution and endurance were now and again taxed to their utmost. But with a man of his nature and race the breaking strain is high; and endurance and resolution are qualities which develop with practice.

Gradually his mind came back to normal level; he had won seemingly through the pain that shadowed him. Without anguish he could now think, remember, look forward. Then it was that the kindly wisdom of the American came back to him, and came to stay. He began to examine himself as to his own part of the unhappy transaction; and stray moments of wonderment came as to whether the fault may not, at the very base, have his own. He began to realise that it is insufficient in this strenuous world to watch and wait; to suppress one's self; to put aside, in the wish to benefit others, all the hopes, ambitions, cravings which make for personal gain.

Thus it was that Harold's thoughts, ever circling round Stephen, came back with increasing insistence to his duty towards her. He often thought, and with a bitter feeling against himself that it came too late, of the dying trust of her father:

'Guard her and cherish her, as if you were indeed my son and she your sister . . . If it should be that you and Stephen should find that there is another affection between you remember I sanction it. But give her time! I trust that to you! She is young, and the world is all before her. Let her choose . . . And be loyal to her, if it is another! It may be a hard task; but I trust you, Harold!'

Here he would groan, as all the anguish of the past would rush back upon him; and keenest of all would be the fear, suspicion, thought which grew towards belief, that he may have betrayed that trust. . . .

At first the side of this memory personal to his own happiness was faintly emphasised; the important side was of the duty to Stephen. But as time went on the other thought became a sort of corollary; a timid, halting, blushing thought which followed sheepishly, borne down by trembling hope. No matter what adventure came to him, the thought of neglected duty returned ever afresh. Once, when he lay sick for weeks in an Indian wigwam, the idea so grew with each day of the monotony, that when he was able to crawl out by himself into the sunshine he had almost made up his mind to start back for home.

Luck is a strange thing. It seems in some mysterious way to be the divine machinery for adjusting averages. Whatever may be the measure of happiness or unhappiness, good or evil, allotted to anyone, luck is the cause or means of counterbalancing so that the main result reaches the standard set.

From the time of Harold's illness Dame Fortune seemed to change her attitude to him. The fierce frown, nay! the malignant scowl, to which he had become accustomed, changed to a smile. Hitherto everything seemed to have gone wrong with him; but now all at once all seemed to go right. He grew strong and hardy again. Indeed, he seemed by contrast to his late helplessness to be so strong and hard that it looked as if that very illness had done him good instead of harm. Game was plentiful, and he never seemed to want. Everywhere he went there were traces of gold, as though by some instinct he was tracking it to its home. He did not value gold for its own sake; but he did for the ardour of the search. Harold was essentially a man, and as a man an adventurer. To such a man of such a race adventure is the very salt of existence.

The adventurer's instinct took with it the adventurer's judgment; Harold was not content with small results. Amidst the vast primeval forces there were, he felt, vast results of their prehistoric working; and he determined to find some of them. In such a quest, purpose is much. It was hardly any wonder, then, that in time Harold found himself alone in the midst of one of the great treasure-places of the world. Only labour was needed to take from the earth riches beyond the dreams of avarice. But that labour was no easy problem; great and difficult distance had to be overcome; secrecy must be observed, for even a whisper of the existence of such a place would bring a horde of desperadoes. But all these difficulties were at least sources of interest, if not in themselves pleasures. The new Harold, seemingly freshly created by a year of danger and strenuous toil, of self-examining and humiliation, of the realisation of duty, and—though he knew it not as yet—of the dawning of hope, found delight in the thought of dangers and difficulties to be overcome. Having taken his bearings exactly so as to be safe in finding the place again, he took his specimens with him and set out to find the shortest and best route to the nearest port.

At length he came to the port and set quietly about finding men. This he did very carefully and very systematically. Finally, with the full complement, and with ample supply of stores, he started on his expedition to the new goldfields.

It is not purposed to set out here the extraordinary growth of Robinson City, for thus the mining camp soon became. Its history has long ago been told for all the world. In the early days, when everything had to be organised and protected, Harold worked like a giant, and with a system and energy which from the first established him as a master. But when the second year of his exile was coming to a close, and Robinson City was teeming with life and commerce, when banks and police and soldiers made life and property comparatively safe, he began to be restless again. This was not the life to which he had set himself. He had gone into the wilderness to be away from cities and from men; and here a city had sprung up around him and men claimed him as their chief. Moreover, with the restless feeling there began to come back to him the old thoughts and the old pain.

But he felt strong enough by this time to look forward in life as well as backward. With him now to think was to act; so much at least he had gained from his position of dominance in an upspringing city. He quietly consolidated such outlying interests as he had, placed the management of his great estate in the hands of a man he had learned to trust, and giving out that he was going to San Francisco to arrange some business, left Robinson City. He had already accumulated such a fortune that the world was before him in any way he might choose to take.

Knowing that at San Francisco, to which he had booked, he would have to run the gauntlet of certain of his friends and business connections, he made haste to leave the ship quietly at Portland, the first point she touched on her southern journey. Thence he got on the Canadian Pacific Line and took his way to Montreal.

What most arrested his attention, and in a very disconcerting way, were the glimpses of English life one sees reproduced so faithfully here and there in Canada. The whole of the past rushed back on him so overpoweringly that he was for the moment unnerved. The acute feeling of course soon became mitigated; but it was the beginning of a re-realisation of what had been, and which grew stronger with each mile as the train swept back eastward.

At first he tried to fight it; tried with all the resources of his strong nature. His mind was made up, he assured himself over and over again. The past was past, and what had been was no more to him than to any of the other passengers of the train. Destiny had long ago fulfilled itself. Stephen no doubt had by now found some one worthy of her and had married. In no dream, sleeping or waking, could he ever admit that she had married Leonard; that was the only gleam of comfort in what had grown to be remorse for his neglected duty.

And so it was that Harold An Wolf slowly drifted, though he knew it not, into something of the same intellectual position which had dominated him when he had started on his journeying and the sunset fell nightly on his despairing face. The life in the wilderness, and then in the dominance and masterdom of enterprise, had hardened and strengthened him into more self-reliant manhood, giving him greater forbearance and a more practical view of things.

When he took ship in the *Dominion*, a large cargo-boat with some passengers running to London, he had a vague purpose of visiting in secret Norcester, whence he could manage to find out how matters were at Normanstand. He would then, he felt, be in a better position to regulate his further movements. He knew that he had already a sufficient disguise in his great beard. He had nothing to fear from the tracing of him on his journey from Alaska or the interest of his fellow-passengers. He had all along been so fortunate as to be able to keep his identity concealed. The name John Robinson told nothing in itself, and the width of a whole great continent lay between him and the place of his fame. He was able to take his part freely amongst both the passengers and the officers. Even amongst the crew he soon came to be known; the men liked his geniality, and instinctively respected his enormous strength and his manifest force of character. Men who work and who know danger soon learn to recognise the forces which overcome both. And as sufficient time had not elapsed to impair his hardihood or lower his vast strength he was facile princeps. And so the crew acknowledged him; to them he was a born Captain whom to obey would be a natural duty.

After some days the weather changed. The great ship, which usually rested even-keeled on two waves, and whose bilge keels under normal conditions rendered rolling impossible, began to pitch and roll like a leviathan at play. The decks, swept by gigantic seas, were injured wherever was anything to injure. Bulwarks were torn away as though they had been compact of paper. More than once the double doors at the head of the companion stairs had been driven in. The bull's eye glasses of some of the ports were beaten from their brazen sockets. Nearly all the boats had been wrecked, broken or torn from their cranes as the great ship rolled heavily in the trough, or giant waves had struck her till she quivered like a frightened horse.

At that season she sailed on the far northern course. Driven still farther north by the gales, she came within a short way of south of Greenland. Then avoiding Moville, which should have been her place of call, she ran down the east of Britain, the wild weather still prevailing.

CHAPTER XXXI—THE LIFE-LINE

On the coast of Angleshire the weather in the early days of September had been stormy. With the south-west wind had come deluges of rain, not a common thing for the time of year on the east coast. Stephen, whose spirits always rose with high wind, was in a condition of prolonged excitement. She could not keep still; every day she rode long distances, and found a wonderful satisfaction in facing the strong winds. Like a true horsewoman she did not mind the wet, and had glorious gallops over the grassy ridge and down the slopes on the farther side, out on the open road or through the endless grass rides amid the pine woods.

On the Tuesday morning the storm was in full sweep, and Stephen was in wild spirits. Nothing would do her but to go out on the tower of the castle where she could walk about, and leaning on the crenellated parapet look over all the coast stretching far in front and sweeping away to the left and right. The prospect so enchanted her, and the fierce sweep of the wind so suited her exalted mood, that she remained there all the morning. The whole coast was a mass of leaping foam and flying spray, and far away to the horizon white-topped waves rolled endlessly. That day she did not even ride out, but contented herself with watching the sea and the storm from the tower. After lunch she went to her tower again; and again after tea. The storm was now furious. She made up her mind that after dinner she would ride down and see its happenings close at hand.

When she had finished dinner she went to her room to dress for her ride. The rush and roar of the storm were in her ears, and she was in wild tumultuous spirits. All her youth seemed to sweep back on her; or perhaps it was that the sickness of the last two years was swept away. Somewhere deep down in Stephen's heart, below her intention or even her consciousness, was a desire to be her old self if only for an hour. And to this end externals were of help. Without weighing the matter in her mind, and acting entirely on impulse, she told her maid to get the red habit she had not worn for years. When she was dressed she sent round to have out her white Arab; while it was getting ready she went once more to the tower to see the storm-effect in the darkening twilight. As she looked, her heart for an instant stood still. Half-way to the horizon a great ship, ablaze in the bows, was driving through the waves with all her speed. She was heading towards the little port, beyond which the shallows sent up a moving wall of white spray.

Stephen tore down the turret stair, and gave hurried directions to have beds prepared in a number of rooms, fires everywhere, and plenty of provisions. She also ordered that carriages should be sent at once to the fishing port with clothing and restoratives. There would, she felt, be need for such help before a time to be measured by minutes should have passed; and as some of her servants were as yet strange to her ways she did not leave anything to chance. One carriage was to go for the doctor who lived at Lannoy, the village over the hill, whence nothing could be seen of what was happening. She knew that others within sight or hailing would be already on their way. Work was afoot, and had she time, or thought of it, she would have chosen a more sedate garb. But in the excitement no thought of herself came to her.

In a few seconds she was in the saddle, tearing at full speed down the road that led to the port. The wind was blowing so strongly in her face that only in the lulls could she hear the hoof-strokes of the groom's horse galloping behind her.

At first the height of the road allowed her to see the ship and the port towards which she was making. But presently the road dipped, and the curving of the hill shut both from her sight; it was only when she came close that she could see either again.

Now the great ship was close at hand. The flames had gained terribly, and it was a race for life or death. There was no time do more than run her aground if life was to be saved at all. The captain, who in the gaps of the smoke could be seen upon the bridge, knew his work well. As he came near the shoal he ran a little north, and then turned sharply so as to throw the boat's head to the south of the shoal. Thus the wind would drive fire and smoke forward and leave the after part of the vessel free for a time.

The shock of her striking the sand was terrific, though the tinkle of the bell borne in on the gale showed that the engines had been slowed down. The funnels were shaken down, and the masts broke off, falling forward. A wild shriek from a hundred throats cleft the roaring of wind and wave. The mast fell, the foremast, with all its cumbering top-hamper on the bridge, which was in an instant blotted out of existence, together with the little band of gallant men who stood on it, true to their last duty. As the wind took the smoke south a man was seen to climb on the wreck of the mast aft and make fast the end of a great coil of rope which he carried. He was a huge man with a full dark beard. Two sailors working with furious haste helped him with the rope. The waves kept raising the ship a little, each time bumping her on the sand with a shock. The people on deck held frantically to the wreckage around them.

Then the bearded man, stripping to his waist and cutting off his trousers above the knee, fastened an end of the rope round his waist. The sailors stood ready one behind the other to pay it out. As a great wave rolled under the ship, he threw himself into the sea.

In the meantime the coastguard had fixed Board of Trade rocket-apparatus, and in a few seconds the prolonged roar of a rocket was heard. It flew straight towards the ship, rising at a high angle so as to fall beyond it. But the force of the wind took it up as it rose, and the gale increased so that it rose nearly vertically; and in this position the wind threw it south of its objective, and short of it. Another rocket was got ready at once, and blue lights were burned so that the course of the venturous swimmer might be noted. He swam strongly; but the great weight of the rope behind kept pulling him back, and the southern trend of the tide current and the force of the wind kept dragging him from the pier. Within the bar the waves were much less than without; but they were still so unruly that no boat in the harbour—which was not a lifeboat station—could venture out. Indeed, in the teeth of the storm it would have been a physical impossibility to have driven one seaward.

As the gathered crowd saw Stephen approach they made way for her. She had left her horse with the groom, and despite the drenching spray fought a way against the wind out on the pier. As in the glare of the blue light, which brought many things into harsh unnatural perspective, she caught sight of the set face of the swimmer rising and falling with the waves, her heart leaped. This was indeed a man! a brave man; and all the woman in her went out to him. For him, and to aid him and his work, she would have given everything, done anything; and in her heart, which beat in an ecstasy of anxiety, she prayed with that desperate conviction of hope which comes in such moments of exaltation.

But it soon became apparent that no landing could be effected. The force of the current and the wind were taking the man too far southward for him ever to win a way back. Then one of coastguards took the lead-topped cane which they use for throwing practice, and, after carefully coiling the line attached it so that it would run free, managed with a desperate effort to fling it far out. The swimmer, to whom it fell close, fought towards it frantically; and as the cord began to run through the water, managed to grasp it. A wild cheer rose from the shore and the ship. A stout line was fastened to the shore end of the cord, and the swimmer drew it out to him. He bent it on the rope which trailed behind him; then, seeing that he was himself a drag on it, with the knife which he drew from the sheath at the back of his waist, he cut himself free. One of the coastguards on the pier, helped by a host of willing hands, began drawing the end of the rope on shore. The swimmer still held the line thrown to him, and several men on the pier began to draw on it. Unhappily the thin cord broke under the strain, and within a few seconds the swimmer had drifted out of possible help. Seeing that only wild rocks lay south of the sea-wall, and that on them seas beat furiously, he turned and made out for sea. In the light beyond the glare he could see vaguely the shore bending away to the west in a deep curve of unbroken white leaping foam. There was no hope of landing there. To the south was the headland, perhaps two miles away as the crow flies. Here was the only chance for him. If he could round the headland, he might find shelter beyond; or somewhere along the farther shore some opening might present itself. Whilst the light from the blue fires still reached him he turned and made for the headland.

In the meantime on ship and on shore men worked desperately. Before long the end of the hawser was carried round on the high cliff, and pulled as taut as the force at hand could manage, and made fast. Soon endless ropes were bringing in passengers and crew as fast as place could be found for them. It became simply a race for time. If the fire, working against the wind, did not reach the hawser, and if the ship lasted the furious bumping on the sandbank, which threatened to shake her to pieces each moment, all on board might yet be saved.

Stephen's concern was now for the swimmer alone. Such a gallant soul should not perish without help, if help could be on this side of heaven. She asked the harbour-master, an old fisherman who knew every inch of the coast for miles, if anything could be done. He shook his head sadly as he answered:

'I fear no, my lady. The lifeboat from Granport is up north, no boat from here could get outside the harbour. There's never a spot in the bay where he could land, even in a less troubled sea than this. Wi' the wind ashore, there's no hope for ship or man here that cannot round the point. And a stranger is no like to do that.'

'Why not?' she asked breathlessly.

'Because, my lady, there's a wheen o' sunken rocks beyond the Head. No one that didn't know would ever think to keep out beyond them, for the cliff itself goes down sheer. He's a gallant soul yon; an' it's a sore pity he's goin' to his death. But it must be! God can save him if He wishes; but I fear none other!'

Even as he spoke rose to Stephen's mind a memory of an old churchyard with great trees and the scent of many flowers, and a child's voice that sounded harsh through the monotonous hum of bees:

'To be God, and able to do things!'

Oh; to be God, if but an hour; and able to do things! To do anything to help a brave man! A wild prayer surged up in the girl's heart:

'Oh! God, give me this man's life! Give it to me to atone for the other I destroyed! Let me but help him, and do with me as Thou wilt!'

The passion of her prayer seemed to help her, and her brain cleared. Surely something could be done! She would do what she could; but first she must understand the situation. She turned again to the old harbour-master:

'How long would it take him to reach the headland, if he can swim so far?' The answer came with a settled conviction bearing hope with it:

'The wind and tide are wi' him, an' he's a strong swimmer. Perhaps half an hour will take him there. He's all right in himself. He can swim it, sure. But alack! it's when he gets there his trouble will be, when none can warn him. Look how the waves are lashing the cliff; and mark the white water beyond! What voice can sound to him out in those deeps? How could he see if even one were there to warn?'

Here was a hope at any rate. Light and sound were the factors of safety. Some good might be effected if she could get a trumpet; and there were trumpets in the rocket-cart. Light could be had—must be had if all the fences round the headland had to be gathered for a bonfire! There was not a moment to be lost. She ran to the rocket-cart, and got a trumpet from the man in charge. Then she ran to where she had left her horse. She had plenty of escort, for by this time many gentlemen had arrived on horseback from outlying distances, and all offered their services. She thanked them and said:

'You may be useful here. When all these are ashore send on the rocket-cart, and come yourselves to the headland as quick as you can. Tell the coastguards that all those saved are to be taken to the castle. In the rocket-cart bring pitch and tar and oil, and anything that will flame. Stay!' she cried to the chief boatman. 'Give me some blue lights!' His answer chilled her:

'I'm sorry, my lady, but they are all used. There are the last of them burning now. We have burned them ever since that man began to swim ashore.'

'Then hurry on the rocket-cart!' she said as she sprang to the saddle, and swept out on the rough track that ran by the cliffs, following in bold curves the windings of the shore. The white Arab seemed to know that his speed was making for life. As he swept along, far outdistancing the groom, Stephen's heart went out in silent words which seemed to keep time to the gallop:

'Oh, to be God, and be able to do things! Give me this man's life, oh, God! Give me this man's life, to atone for that noble one which I destroyed!'

CHAPTER XXXI—THE LIFE-LINE

Faster and faster, over rough road, cattle track, and grassy sward; over rising and falling ground; now and again so close to the edge of the high cliff that the spume swept up the gulleys in the rocks like a snowstorm, the white Arab swept round the curve of the bay, and came out on the high headland where stood the fisher's house. On the very brink of the cliff all the fisher folk, men, women and children, stood looking at the far-off burning ship, from which the flames rose in leaping columns.

So intent were all on the cliff that they did not notice her coming; as the roar of the wind came from them to her, they could not hear her voice when she spoke from a distance. She had drawn quite close, having dismounted and hung her rein over the post of the garden paling, when one of the children saw her, and cried out:

'The lady! the lady! an' she's all in red!' The men were so intent on something that they did not seem to hear. They were peering out to the north, and were arguing in dumb show as though on something regarding which they did not agree. She drew closer, and touching the old fisherman on the shoulder, called out at his ear:

'What is it?' He answered without turning, keeping his eyes fixed:

'*I* say it's a man swimmin'. Joe and Garge here say as it's only a piece o' wood or sea-wrack. But I know I'm right. That's a man swimmin', or my old eyes have lost their power!' His words carried conviction; the seed of hope in her beating heart grew on the instant into certainty.

'It *is* a man. I saw him swim off towards here when he had taken the rope on shore. Do not turn round. Keep your eyes on him so that you may not lose sight of him in the darkness!' The old man chuckled.

'This darkness! Hee! hee! There be no differ to me between light and dark. But I'll watch him! It's you, my lady! I shan't turn round to do my reverence as you tell me to watch. But, poor soul, it'll not be for long to watch. The Skyres will have him, sure enow!'

'We can warn him!' she said, 'when he comes close enough. I have a trumpet here!' He shook his head sorrowfully:

'Ah! my lady, what trumpet could sound against that storm an' from this height?' Stephen's heart sank. But there was still hope. If the swimmer's ears could not be reached, his eyes might. Eagerly she looked back for the coming of the rocket-cart. Far off across the deep bay she could see its lamp sway as it passed over the rough ground; but alas! it would never arrive in time. With a note of despair in her voice she asked:

'How long before he reaches the rocks?' Still without turning the old man answered:

'At the rate he's going he will be in the sweep of the current through the rocks within three minutes. If he's to be saved he must turn seaward ere the stream grips him.'

'Would there be time to build a bonfire?'

'No, no! my lady. The wood couldn't catch in the time!'

For an instant a black film of despair seemed to fall on her. The surging of the blood in her head made her dizzy, and once again the prayer of the old memory rang in her brain:

'Oh to be God, and able to do things!'

On the instant an inspiration flashed through her. She, too could do things in a humble way. She could do something at any rate. If there was no time to build a fire, there was a fire already built.

The house would burn!

The two feet deep of old thatch held down with nets and battened with wreck timber would flare like a beacon. Forthwith she spoke:

'Good people, this noble man who has saved a whole shipload of others must not die without an effort. There must be light so that he can see our warning to pass beyond the rocks! The only light can be from the house. I buy it of you. It is mine; but I shall pay you for it and build you such another as you never thought of. But it must be fired at once. You have one minute to clear out all you want. In, quick and take all can. Quick! quick! for God's sake! It is for a brave man's life!'

The men and women without a word rushed into the house. They too knew the danger, and the only hope there was for a life. The assurance of the Countess took the sting from the present loss. Before the minute, which she timed watch in hand, was over, all came forth bearing armloads of their lares and penates. Then one of the younger men ran in again and out bearing a flaming stick from the fire. Stephen nodded, he held it to the northern edge of the thatch. The straw caught in a flash and the flame ran up the slope and along the edge of the roof like a quick match. The squeaking of many rats was heard and their brown bodies streamed over the roof. Before another minute had passed a great mass of flame towered into the sky and shed a red light far out over the waste of sea.

It lit up the wilderness of white water where the sea churned savagely amongst the sunken rocks; and it lit too the white face of a swimmer, now nearly spent, who rising and falling with each wave, drifted in the sea whose current bore him on towards the fatal rocks.

CHAPTER XXXII—'TO BE GOD AND ABLE TO DO THINGS'

When the swimmer saw the light he looked up; even at the distance they could see the lift of his face; but he did not seem to realise that there was any intention in the lighting, or that it was created for his benefit. He was manifestly spent with his tremendous exertions, and with his long heavy swim in the turbulent sea. Stephen's heart went out to him in a wave of infinite pity. She tried to use the trumpet. But simple as it is, a trumpet needs skill or at least practice in its use; she could only make an unintelligible sound, and not much even of that. One of the young men said:

'Let me try it, my lady!' She handed him the trumpet and he in turn used with a will. But it was of no avail; even his strong lungs and lusty manhood availed nothing in the teeth of that furious gale. The roof and the whole house was now well alight, and the flame roared and leapt. Stephen began to make gestures bidding the swimmer, in case he might see her and understand, move round the rocks. But he made no change in his direction, and was fast approaching a point in the tide-race whence to avoid the sunken rocks would be an impossibility. The old whaler, accustomed to use all his wits in times of difficulty, said suddenly:

'How can he understand when we're all between him and the light. We are only black shadows to him; all he can see are waving arms!' His sons caught his meaning and were already dashing towards the burning house. They came back with piles of blazing wood and threw them down on the very edge of the cliff; brought more and piled them up, flinging heaps of straw on the bonfire and pouring on oil and pitch till the flames rose high. Stephen saw what was necessary and stood out of the way, but close to the old whaler, where the light fell on both of their faces as they looked in the direction of the swimmer. Stephen's red dress itself stood out like a flame. The gale tearing up the front of the cliff had whirled away her hat; in the stress of the wind her hair was torn from its up-pinning and flew wide, itself like leaping flame.

Her gestures as she swept her right arm round, as though demonstrating the outward curve of a circle, or raising the hand above her head motioned with wide palm and spread fingers 'back! back!' seemed to have reached the swimmer's intelligence. He half rose in the water and looked about. As if seeing something that he realised, he sank back again and began swim frantically out to sea. A great throb of joy made Stephen almost faint. At last she had been able to do something to help this gallant man. In half a minute his efforts seemed to tell in his race for life. He drew sufficiently far from dangerous current for there to be a hope that he might be saved if he could last out the stress to come.

The fishermen kept watch in silent eagerness; and in their presence Stephen felt a comfort, though, like her, they could do nothing at present.

When the swimmer had passed sufficiently far out to be clear of the rocks, the fire began to lose its flame, though not its intensity. It would be fiery still for hours to come, and of great heat; but the flames ceased to leap, and in the moderated light Stephen only saw the white face for one more instant ere it faded out of her ken, when, turning, the man looked towards the light and made a gesture which she did not understand: for he put for an instant both hands before his face.

Just then there was a wild noise on the cliff. The rocket-cart drawn by sixteen splendid horses, some of them hunters, came tearing up the slope, and with it many men on horseback afoot. Many of the runners were the gentlemen who had given their horses for the good work.

As the coastguards jumped from the cart, and began to get out the rocket stand, the old whaler pointed out the direction where the swimmer's head could still be seen. Some of the sailors could see it too; though to Stephen and the laymen it was invisible. The chief boatman shook his head:

'No use throwing a line there! Even if he got it we could never drag him alive through these rocks. He would be pounded to death before twenty fathom!' Stephen's heart grew cold as she listened. Was this the end? Then with a bitter cry she wailed:

'Oh! can nothing be done? Can nothing be done? Can no boat come from the other side of the point? Must such a brave man be lost!' and her tears began to flow.

One of the young men who had just arrived, a neighbouring squire, a proved wastrel but a fine horseman, who had already regarded Stephen at the few occasions of their meeting with eyes of manifest admiration, spoke up:

'Don't cry, Lady de Lannoy. There's a chance for him yet. I'll see what I can do.'

'Bless you! oh! bless you!' she cried impulsively as she caught his hand. Then came the chill of doubt. 'But what can you do?' she added despairingly.

'Hector and I may be able to do something together.' Turning to one of the fishermen he asked:

'Is there any way down to the water in the shelter of the point?'

'Ay! ay! sir,' came the ready answer. 'There's the path as we get down by to our boats.'

'Come on, then!' he said. 'Some of you chaps show us a light on the way down. If Hector can manage the scramble there's a chance. You see,' he said, turning again to Stephen, 'Hector can swim like a fish. When he was a racer I trained him in the sea so that none of the touts could spy out his form. Many's the swim we've had together; and in rough water too, though in none so wild as this!'

'But it is a desperate chance for you!' said Stephen, woman-like drawing somewhat back from a danger she had herself evoked. The young man laughed lightly:

'What of that! I may do one good thing before I die. That fine fellow's life is worth a hundred of my wasted one! Here! some of you fellows help me with Hector. We must take him from the cart and get a girth on him instead of the saddle. We shall want something to hold on to without pulling his head down by using the bridle.'

He, followed by some others, ran to the rocket-cart where the horses stood panting, their steam rising in a white cloud in the glow of the burning house. In an incredibly short time the horse was ready with only the girth. The young squire took him by the mane and he followed eagerly; he had memories of his own. As they passed close to Stephen the squire said to one of his friends:

'Hold him a minute, Jack!' He ran over to Stephen and looked at her hard:

'Good-bye! Wish me luck; and give us light!' Tears were in her eyes and a flush on her cheek as she took his hand and clasped it hard:

'Oh, you brave man! God bless you!' He stooped suddenly and impulsively kissed the back of her hand lightly and was gone. For a fleeting moment she was angry. No man had kissed her hand before; but the thought of his liberty was swept away by another:

'Little enough when he may be going to his death!'

It was a sight to see that man and horse, surrounded by an eager crowd of helpers, scrambling down the rough zigzag, cut and worn in the very face of the cliff. They stumbled, and slipped; pebbles and broken rock fell away under their feet. Alone close to the bonfire stood Stephen, following every movement with racing blood and beating heart. The bonfire was glowing; a constant stream of men and women were dragging and hauling all sorts of material for its increase. The head of the swimmer could be seen, rising and falling amid the waves beyond the Skyres.

When about twenty feet from the water-level the path jutted out to one side left of the little beach whereon the sea now broke fiercely. This was a place where men watched, and whence at times they fished with rods; the broad rock overhung the water. The fire above, though it threw shadows, made light enough for everything. The squire held up his hand.

'Stop! We can take off this rock, if the water is deep enough. How much is it?'

'Ten fathoms sheer.'

'Good!' He motioned to them all to keep back. Then threw off all his clothes except shirt and trousers. For an instant he patted Hector and then sprang upon his back. Holding him by the mane he urged him forward with a cry. The noble animal did not hesitate an instant. He knew that grasp of the mane; that cry; that dig of the spurless heels. He sprang forward with wide dilated nostrils, and from the edge of the jutting rock jumped far out into the sea. Man and horse disappeared for a few seconds, but rose safely. The man slid from the horse's back; and, holding by the girth with one hand, swam beside him out to sea in the direction the swimmer must come on rounding the sunken rocks.

A wild cheer broke from all on the cliff above and those already scrambling back up the zigzag. Stephen kept encouraging the men to bring fuel to the bonfire:

'Bring everything you can find; the carts, the palings, the roofs, the corn, the dried fish; anything and everything that will burn. We must have light; plenty of light! Two brave men's lives are at stake now!'

The whole place was a scene of activity. Stephen stood on the edge of the cliff with the old whaler and the chief boatman and some of the women. The rest of the coastguards were by orders of their chief rigging up a whip which they thought might be necessary to hoist the men up from the water, if they could ever get close enough. One of the young men who had ridden with the rocket-cart kept tight hold of Hector's bridle; he knew it would be wanted if the horse ever had a chance of landing.

* * * * *

When Harold turned away from the dazzling blue lights on the pier, and saw the far white line of the cliffs beyond the bay, his heart sank within him. Even his great strength and hardihood, won by work and privation in the far North-West, had been already taxed in the many days of the battling with the gale when all on board who could lend a hand were taken into service. Again by the frantic struggle of the last hour or two, when the ship ran shoreward at the utmost of her speed in the last hope of beaching in time to save life. Finally in that grim struggle to draw the life-line shoreward. The cold and then the great heat, and on top of it the chill of the long swim, seemed to have struck at him. Alone on the dark sea, for soon the current and his own exertions were taking him away from the rocks, the light of the burning ship was ceasing to be effective. It was just enough to hinder his vision; looking from the patch of light which bathed the light and him he could just see far off the white water which marked the cliff fronts, and on the edge of his horizon the grim moving white wall where the waves broke on the headland.

On and on he toiled. His limbs were becoming more cramped with the cold and the terrible strain of swimming in such waves. But still the brave heart bore him up; and resolutely, sternly he forced himself afresh to the effort before him. He reasoned that where there was such a headland standing out so stark into the sea there ought to be some shelter in its lee. If he could pass it he might find calmer water and even a landing-place beyond.

Here at least was hope. He would try to round the point at any rate. Now he drew so close that the great rocks seemed to tower vast above him. He was not yet close enough to feel as though lapped in their shadow; but even the overcast sky seemed full of light above the line of the cliff. There was a strange roaring, rushing sound around him. He thought that it was not merely the waves dashing on the rocks, but that partly it came from his own ears; that his ebbing strength was feeling the frantic struggle which he was making. The end was coming, he thought; but still he kept valiantly on, set and silent, as is the way with brave men.

Suddenly from the top of the cliff a bright light flashed. He looked at it sideways as he fought his way on, and saw the light rise and fall and flicker as the flames leaped. High over him he saw fantastic figures which seemed to dance on the edge of the high cliff. They had evidently noticed him, and were making signals of some sort; but what the motions were he could not see or understand, for they were but dark silhouettes, edged with light, against the background of fire. The only thing he could think was that they meant to encourage him, and so he urged himself to further effort. It might be that help was at hand!

Several times as he turned his head sideways he saw the figures and the light, but not so clearly; it was as though the light was lessening in power. When again he looked he saw a new fire leap out on the edge of the cliff, and some figures to the right of it. They were signalling in some way. So, pausing in his swimming, he rose a little from the water and looked at them.

A thrill shot through him, and a paralysing thought that he must have gone mad. With his wet hand he cleared his eyes, though the touching them pained him terribly, and for an instant saw clearly:

There on the edge of the cliff, standing beside some men and waving her arms in a wild sweep as though motioning frantically 'Keep out! keep out!' was a woman. Instinctively he glanced to his left and saw a white waste of leaping water, through which sharp rocks rose like monstrous teeth. On the instant he saw the danger, and made out seaward, swimming frantically to clear the dangerous spot before the current would sweep him upon the rocks.

But the woman! As one remembers the last sight when the lightning has banished sight, so that vision seemed burned into his brain. A woman with a scarlet riding-habit and masses of long red hair blowing in the gale like leaping flame! Could there be two such persons in the world? No! no! It was a vision! A vision of the woman he loved, come to save him in the direst moment of great peril!

His heart beat with new hope; only the blackness of the stormy sea was before him as he strove frantically on.

Presently when he felt the current slacken, for he had been swimming across it and could feel its power, he turned and looked back. As he did so he murmured aloud:

'A dream! A vision! She came to warn me!' For as he looked all had disappeared. Cliff and coastline, dark rocks and leaping seas, blazing fire, and the warning vision of the woman he loved.

Again he looked where the waste of sea churning amongst the sunken rocks had been. He could hear the roaring of waters, the thunder of great waves beating on the iron-bound coast; but nothing could he see. He was alone on the wild sea; in the dark.

Then truly the swift shadow of despair fell upon him.

'Blind Blind!' he moaned, and for the moment, stricken with despair, sank into the trough of the waves. But the instinctive desire for life recalled him. Once more he fought his way up to the surface, and swam blindly, desperately on. Seeing nothing, he did not know which way he was going. He might have heard better had his eyes been able to help his ears; but in the sudden strange darkness all the senses were astray. In the agony of his mind he could not even feel the pain of his burnt face; the torture of his eyes had passed. But with the instinct of a strong man he kept on swimming blindly, desperately.

* * * * *

It seemed as if ages of untold agony had gone by, when he heard a voice seemingly beside him:

'Lay hold here! Catch the girth!' The voice came muffled by wind and wave. His strength was now nearly at its last.

The shock of his blindness and the agony of the moments that had passed had finished his exhaustion. But a little longer and he must have sunk into his rest. But the voice and the help it promised rallied him for a moment. He had hardly strength to speak, but he managed to gasp out:

'Where? where? Help me! I am blind!' A hand took his and guided it to a tightened girth. Instinctively his fingers closed round it, and he hung on grimly. His senses were going fast. He felt as if it was all a strange dream. A voice here in the sea! A girth! A horse; he could hear its hard breathing.

The voice came again.

'Steady! Hold on! My God! he's fainted! I must tie him on!' He heard a tearing sound, and something was wound round his wrists. Then his nerveless fingers relaxed their hold; and all passed into oblivion.

CHAPTER XXXIII—THE QUEEN'S ROOM

To Stephen all that now happened seemed like a dream. She saw Hector and his gallant young master forge across the smoother water of the current whose boisterous stream had been somewhat stilled in the churning amongst the rocks, and then go north in the direction of the swimmer who, strange to say, was drifting in again towards the sunken rocks. Then she saw the swimmer's head sink under the water; and her heart grew cold. Was this to be the end! Was such a brave man to be lost after such gallant effort as he had made, and just at the moment when help was at hand!

The few seconds seemed ages. Instinctively she shut her eyes and prayed again. 'Oh! God. Give me this man's life that I may atone!'

God seemed to have heard her prayer. Nay, more! He had mercifully allowed her to be the means of averting great danger. She would never, could never, forget the look on the man's face when he saw, by the flame that she had kindled, ahead of him the danger from the sunken rocks. She had exulted at the thought. And now . . .

She was recalled by a wild cheer beside her. Opening her eyes she saw that the man's head had risen again from the water. He was swimming furiously, this time seaward. But close at hand were the heads of the swimming horse and man . . . She saw the young squire seize the man . . .

And then the rush of her tears blinded her. When she could see again the horse had turned and was making back again to the shelter of the point. The squire had his arm stretched across the horse's back; he was holding up the sailor's head, which seemed to roll helplessly with every motion of the cumbering sea.

For a little she thought he was dead, but the voice of the old whaler reassured her:

'He was just in time! The poor chap was done!' And so with beating heart and eyes that did not flinch now she watched the slow progress to the shelter of the point. The coastguards and fishermen had made up their minds where the landing could be made, and were ready; on the rocky shelf, whence Hector had at jumped, they stood by with lines. When the squire had steered and encouraged the horse, whose snorting could be heard from the sheltered water, till he was just below the rocks, they lowered a noosed rope. This he fastened round the senseless man below his shoulders. One strong, careful pull, and he was safe on land; and soon was being borne up the steep zigzag on the shoulders of the willing crowd.

In the meantime other ropes were passed down to the squire. One he placed round his own waist; two others he fastened one on each side of the horse's girth. Then his friend lowered the bridle, and he managed to put it on the horse and attached a rope to it. The fishermen took the lines, and, paying out as they went so as to leave plenty of slack line, got on the rocks just above the little beach whereon, sheltered though it was, the seas broke heavily. There they waited, ready to pull the horse through the surf when he should have come close enough.

Stephen did not see the rescue of the horse; for just then a tall grave man spoke to her:

'Pardon me, Lady de Lannoy, but is the man to be brought up to the Castle? I am told you have given orders that all the rescued shall be taken there.' She answered unhesitatingly:

'Certainly! I gave orders before coming out that preparation was to be made for them.'

'I am Mr. Hilton. I have just come down to do lacum tenens for Dr. Winter at Lannoch Port. I rode over on hearing there was a wreck, and came here with the rocket-cart. I shall take charge of the man and bring him up. He will doubtless want some special care.'

'If you will be so good!' she answered, feeling a diffidence which was new to her. At that moment the crowd carrying the senseless man began to appear over the cliff, coming up the zig-zag. The Doctor hurried towards him; she followed at a little distance, fearing lest she should hamper him. Under his orders they laid the patient on the weather side of the bonfire so that the smoke would not reach him. The Doctor knelt by his side.

An instant after he looked up and said:

'He is alive; his heart is beating, though faintly. He had better be taken away at once. There is no means here of shelter.'

'Bring him in the rocket-cart; it is the only conveyance here,' cried Stephen. 'And bring Mr. Hepburn too. He also will need some care after his gallant service. I shall ride on and advise my household of your coming. And you good people come all to the Castle. You are to be my guests if you will so honour me. No! No! Really I should prefer to ride alone!'

She said this impulsively, seeing that several of the gentlemen were running for their horses to accompany her. 'I shall not wait to thank that valiant young gentleman. I shall see him at Lannoy.'

As she was speaking she had taken the bridle of her horse. One of the young men stooped and held his hand; she bowed, put her foot in it and sprang to the saddle. In an instant she was flying across country at full speed, in the dark. A wild mood was on her, reaction from the prolonged agony of apprehension. There was little which she would not have done just then.

The gale whistled round her and now and again she shouted with pure joy. It seemed as if God Himself had answered her prayer and given her the returning life!

By the time she had reached the Castle the wild ride had done its soothing work. She was calm again, comparatively; her wits and feelings were her own.

There was plenty to keep her occupied, mind and body. The train of persons saved from the wreck were arriving in all sorts of vehicles, and as clothes had to be found for them as well as food and shelter there was no end to the exertions necessary. She felt as though the world were not wide enough for the welcome she wished to extend. Its exercise was a sort of reward of her exertions; a thank-offering for the response to her prayer. She moved amongst her guests, forgetful of herself; of her strange attire; of the state of dishevelment and grime in which she was, the result of the storm, her long ride over rough ground with its share of marshes and pools, and the smoke from the bonfire and the blazing house. The strangers wondered at first, till they came to understand that she was the Lady Bountiful who had stretched her helpful hands to them. Those who could, made themselves useful with the new batches of arrivals. The whole Castle was lit from cellar to tower. The kitchens were making lordly provision, the servants were carrying piles of clothes of all sorts, and helping to fit those who came still wet from their passage through or over the heavy sea.

In the general disposition of chambers Stephen ordered to be set apart for the rescued swimmer the Royal Chamber where Queen Elizabeth had lain; and for Mr. Hepburn that which had been occupied by the Second George. She had a sort of idea that the stranger was God's guest who was coming to her house; and that nothing could be too good for him. As she waited for his coming, even though she swept to and fro in her ministrations to others, she felt as though she trod on air. Some great weight seemed to have been removed from her. Her soul was free again!

At last the rocket-cart arrived, and with it many horsemen and such men and women as could run across country with equal speed to the horses labouring by the longer road.

The rescued man was still senseless, but that alone did not seem to cause anxiety to the Doctor, who hurried him at once into the prepared room. When, assisted by some of the other men, he had undressed him, rubbed him down and put him to bed, and had seen some of the others who had been rescued from the wreck, he sought out Lady de Lannoy. He told her that his anxiety was for the man's sight; an announcement which blanched his hearer's cheeks. She had so made up her mind as to his perfect safety that the knowledge of any kind of ill came like a cruel shock. She questioned Mr. Hilton closely; so closely that he thought it well to tell her at once all that he surmised and feared:

'That fine young fellow who swam out with his horse to him, tells me that when he neared him he cried out that he was blind. I have made some inquiries from those on the ship, and they tell me that he was a passenger, named Robinson. Not only was he not blind then, but he was the strongest and most alert man on the ship. If it be blindness it must have come on during that long swim. It may be that before leaving the ship he received some special injury—indeed he has several cuts and burns and bruises—and that the irritation of the sea-water increased it. I can do nothing till he wakes. At present he is in such a state that nothing can be done for him. Later I shall if necessary give him a hypodermic to ensure sleep. In the morning when I come again I shall examine him fully.'

'But you are not going away to-night!' said Stephen in dismay. 'Can't you manage to stay here? Indeed you must! Look at all these people, some of whom may need special attention or perhaps treatment. We do not know yet if any may be injured.' He answered at once:

'Of course I shall stay if you wish it. But there are two other doctors here already. I must go over to my own place to get some necessary instruments for the examination of this special patient. But that I can do in the early morning.'

'Can I not send for what you want; the whole household are at your service. All that can be done for that gallant man must be done. You can send to London for special help if you wish. If that man is blind, or in danger of blindness, we must have the best oculist in the world for him.'

'All shall be done that is possible,' said he earnestly. 'But till I examine him in the morning we can do nothing. I am myself an oculist; that is my department in St. Stephen's Hospital. I have an idea of what is wrong, but I cannot diagnose exactly until I can use the ophthalmoscope.' His words gave Stephen confidence. Laying her hand on his arm unconsciously in the extremity of pity she said earnestly:

'Oh, do what you can for him. He must be a noble creature; and all that is possible must be done. I shall never rest happily if through any failing on my part he suffers as you fear.'

'I shall do all I can,' he said with equal earnestness, touched with her eager pity. 'And I shall not trust myself alone, if any other can be of service. Depend upon it, Lady de Lannoy, all shall be as you wish.'

There was little sleep in the Castle that night till late. Mr. Hilton slept on a sofa in the Queen's Room after he had administered a narcotic to his patient.

As soon as the eastern sky began to quicken, he rode, as he had arranged during the evening, to Dr. Winter's house at Lannoch Port where he was staying. After selecting such instruments and drugs as he required, he came back in the dogcart.

It was still early morning when he regained the Castle. He found Lady de Lannoy up and looking anxiously for him. Her concern was somewhat abated when he was able to tell her that his patient still slept.

It was a painful scene for Mr. Hilton when his patient woke. Fortunately some of the after-effects of the narcotic remained, for his despair at realising that he was blind was terrible. It was not that he was violent; to be so under his present circumstances would have been foreign to Harold's nature. But there was a despair which was infinitely more sad to witness than passion. He simply moaned to himself:

'Blind! Blind!' and again in every phase of horrified amazement, as though he could not realise the truth: 'Blind! Blind!' The Doctor laid his hand on his breast and said very gently:

'My poor fellow, it is a dreadful thing to face, to think of. But as yet I have not been able to come to any conclusion; unable even to examine you. I do not wish to encourage hopes that may be false, but there are cases when injury is not vital and perhaps only temporary. In such case your best chance, indeed your only chance, is to keep quiet. You must not even think if possible of anything that may excite you. I am now about to examine you with the ophthalmoscope. You are a man; none of us who saw your splendid feat last night can doubt your pluck. Now I want you to use some of it to help us both. You, for your recovery, if such is possible; me, to help me in my work. I have asked some of your late companions who tell me that on shipboard you were not only well and of good sight, but that you were remarkable even amongst strong men. Whatever it is you suffer from must have come on quickly. Tell me all you can remember of it.'

The Doctor listened attentively whilst Harold told all he could remember of his sufferings. When he spoke of the return of old rheumatic pains his hearer said involuntarily: 'Good!' Harold paused; but went on at once. The Doctor recognised that he had rightly appraised his remark, and by it judged that he was a well-educated man. Something in the method of speaking struck him, and he said, as nonchalantly as he could:

'By the way, which was your University?'

'Cambridge. Trinity.' He spoke without thinking, and the instant he had done so stopped. The sense of his blindness rushed back on him. He could not see; and his ears were not yet trained to take the place of his eyes. He must guard himself. Thenceforward he was so cautious in his replies that Mr. Hilton felt convinced there was some purpose in his reticence. He therefore stopped asking questions, and began to examine him. He was unable to come to much result; his opinion was shown in his report to Lady de Lannoy:

'I am unable to say anything definite as yet. The case is a most interesting one; as a case and quite apart from the splendid fellow who is the subject of it. I have hopes that within a few days I may be able to know more. I need not trouble you with surgical terms; but later on if the diagnosis supports the supposition at present in my mind I shall be able to speak more fully. In the meantime I shall, with your permission, wait here so that I may watch him myself.'

'Oh you are good. Thank you! Thank you!' said Stephen. She had so taken the man under her own care that she was grateful for any kindness shown to him.

'Not at all,' said Mr. Hilton. 'Any man who behaved as that fellow did has a claim on any of us who may help him. No time of mine could be better spent.'

When he went back to the patient's room he entered softly, for he thought he might be asleep. The room was, according to his instructions, quite dark, and as it was unfamiliar to him he felt his way cautiously. Harold, however, heard the small noise he made and said quietly:

'Who is there?'

'It is I; Hilton.'

'Are you alone?'

'Yes.'

'Look round the room and see. Then lock the door and come and talk to me if you will. You will pity a poor blind fellow, I know. The darkness has come down upon me so quickly that I am not accustomed to it!' There was a break in his voice which moved the other. He lit a candle, feeling that the doing so would impress his patient, and went round the room; not with catlike movement this time—he wanted the other to hear him. When he had turned the key in the lock, as sharply as he could, he came to the bedside and sat down. Harold spoke again after a short pause:

'Is that candle still lit?'

'Yes! Would you like it put out?'

'If you don't mind! Again I say pity me and pardon me. But I want to ask you something privately, between our two selves; and I will feel more of equality than if you were looking at me, whilst I cannot see you.' Mr Hilton blew out the candle.

'There! We are equal now.'

'Thank you!' A long pause; then he went on:

'When a man becomes suddenly blind is there usually, or even occasionally, any sort of odd sight? . . . Does he see anything like a dream, a vision?'

'Not that I know of. I have never heard of such a case. As a rule people struck blind by lightning, which is the most common cause, sometimes remember with extraordinary accuracy the last thing they have seen. Just as though it were photographed on the retina!'

'Thank you! Is such usually the recurrence of any old dream or anything they have much thought of?'

'Not that I know of. It would be unusual!' Harold waited a long time before he spoke again. When he did so it was in a different voice; a constrained voice. The Doctor, accustomed to take enlightenment from trivial details, noted it:

'Now tell me, Mr. Hilton, something about what has happened. Where am I?'

'In Lannoy Castle.'

'Where is it?'

'In Angleshire!'

'Who does it belong to?'

'Lady de Lannoy. The Countess de Lannoy; they tell me she is a Countess in her own right.'

'It is very good of her to have me here. Is she an old lady?'

'No! A young one. Young and very beautiful.' After a pause before his query:

'What's she like? Describe her to me!'

'She is young, a little over twenty. Tall and of a very fine figure. She has eyes like black diamonds, and hair like a flame!' For a long time Harold remained still. Then he said:

'Tell me all you know or have learned of this whole affair. How was I rescued, and by whom?' So the Doctor proceeded to give him every detail he knew of. When he was quite through, the other again lay still for a long time. The silence was broken by a gentle tap at the door. The Doctor lit a candle. He turned the key softly, so that no one would notice that the door was locked. Something was said in a low whisper. Then the door was gently closed, and the Doctor returning said:

'Lady Lannoy wants, if it will not disturb you, to ask how you are. Ordinarily I should not let anyone see you. But she is not only your hostess, but, as I have just told you, it was her ride to the headland, where she burned the house to give you light, which was the beginning of your rescue. Still if you think it better not . . . !'

'I hardly like anybody to see me like this!' said Harold, feebly seeking an excuse.

'My dear man,' said the other, 'you may be easy in your mind, she won't see much of you. You are all bandages and beard. She'll have to wait a while before she sees you.'

'Didn't she see me last night?'

'Not she! Whilst we were trying to restore you she was rushing back to the Castle to see that all was ready for you, and for the others from the wreck.' This vaguely soothed Harold.

If his surmise was correct, and if she had not seen him then, it was well that he was bandaged now. He felt that it would not do to refuse to let her see him; it might look suspicious. So after pausing a short while he said in a low voice:

'I suppose she had better come now. We must not keep her waiting!' When the Doctor brought her to his bedside Stephen felt in a measure awed. His bandaged face and head and his great beard, singed in patches, looked to her in the dim light rather awesome. In a very gentle voice she said kind things to the sick man, who acknowledged them in a feeble whisper. The Doctor, a keen observer, noticed the change in his voice, and determined to understand more. Stephen spoke of his bravery, and of how it was due to him that all on the ship were saved; and as she spoke her emotion moved her so much that her sweet voice shook and quivered. To the ears of the man who had now only sound to guide him, it was music of the sweetest he had ever heard. Fearing lest his voice should betray him, he whispered his own thanks feebly and in few words.

When Stephen went away the Doctor went with her; it was more than an hour before he returned. He found his patient in what he considered a state of suppressed excitement; for, though his thoughts were manifestly collected and his words were calm, he was restless and excited in other ways. He had evidently been thinking of his own condition; for shortly after the Doctor came in he said:

'Are we alone?'

'Quite!'

'I want you to arrange that there shall not be any nurse with me.'

'My dear sir! Don't handicap me, and yourself, with such a restriction. It is for your own good that you should have regular and constant attention.'

'But I don't wish it. Not for the present at all events. I am not accustomed to a nurse, and shall not feel comfortable. In a few days perhaps . . . ' The decided tone of his voice struck the other. Keeping his own thoughts and intentions in abeyance, even to himself, he answered heartily:

'All right! I shall not have any nurse, at present.'

'Thanks!' There was relief in the tone which seemed undue, and Mr. Hilton again took mental note. Presently he asked a question, but in such a tone that the Doctor pricked up his ears. There was a premeditated self-suppression, a gravity of restraint, which implied some falsity; some intention other than the words conveyed:

'It must have been a job to carry me up those stairs.' The Doctor was doubting everything, but as the safest attitude he stuck to literal truth so far as his words conveyed it:

'Yes. You are no light weight!' To himself he mused:

'How did he know there were stairs? He cannot know it; he was senseless! Therefore he must be guessing or inquiring!' Harold went on:

'I suppose the Castle is on high ground. Can you see far from the windows? I suppose we are up a good height?'

'From the windows you can see all round the promontory. But we are not high up; that is, the room is not high from the ground, though the Castle is from the sea.' Harold asked again, his voice vibrating in the note of gladness:

'Are we on the ground floor then?'

'Yes.'

'And I suppose the gardens are below us?'

'Yes.' The answer was given quickly, for a thought was floating through him: Why did this strong brave man, suddenly stricken blind, wish to know whether his windows were at a height? He was not surprised when his patient reaching out a hand rested it on his arm and said in an imploring tone:

'It should be moonlight; full moon two nights ago. Won't you pull up the blind and describe to me all you see? . . . Tell me fully . . . Remember, I am blind!'

This somehow fixed the Doctor's thought:

'Suicide! But I must convey the inutility of such effort by inference, not falsity.'

Accordingly he began to describe the scene, from the very base of the wall, where below the balcony the great border was glorious with a mass of foliage plants, away to the distant sea, now bathed in the flood of moonlight. Harold asked question after question; the Doctor replying accurately till he felt that the patient was building up a concrete idea of his surroundings near and far. Then he left him. He stood for a long time out in the passage thinking. He said to himself as he moved away:

'The poor fellow has some grim intention in his mind. I must not let him know that I suspect; but to-night I will watch without his knowing it!'

CHAPTER XXXIV—WAITING

Mr. Hilton telegraphed at once countermanding, for the present, the nurse for whom he had sent.

That night, when the household had all retired, he came quietly to his patient's room, and entering noiselessly, sat silent in a far corner. There was no artificial right; the patient had to be kept in darkness. There was, however, a bright moonlight; sufficient light stole in through the edges of the blinds to allow him, when his eyes grew accustomed, to see what might happen.

Harold lay quite still till the house was quiet. He had been thinking, ever since he had ascertained the identity of Stephen. In his weakness and the paralysing despair of his blindness all his former grief and apprehension had come bank upon him in a great wave; veritably the tide of circumstances seemed to run hard against him. He had had no idea of forcing himself upon Stephen; and yet here he was a guest in her house, without her knowledge or his own. She had saved his life by her energy and resource. Fortunately she did not as yet know him; the bandages, and his act in suppressing his voice, had so far protected him. But such could not last for long. He could not see to protect himself, and take precautions as need arose. And he knew well that Stephen's nature would not allow her to be satisfied without doing all that was possible to help one who had under her eyes made a great effort on behalf of others, and to whom there was the added bond that his life was due to her. In but a little time she must find out to whom she ministered.

What then would happen? Her kindness was such that when she realised the blindness of her old friend she might so pity him that out of the depths of her pity she would forgive. She would take back all the past; and now that she knew of his old love for her, would perhaps be willing to marry him. Back flooded the old memory of her independence and her theory of sexual equality. If out of any selfish or mistaken idea she did not hesitate to ask a man to marry her, would it be likely that when the nobler and more heroic side of her nature spoke she would hesitate to a similar act in pursuance of her self-sacrifice?

So it might be that she would either find herself once again flouted, or else married to a man she did not love.

Such a catastrophe should not happen, whatever the cost to him. He would, blind as he was, steal away in the night and take himself out of her life; this time for ever. Better the ingratitude of an unknown man, the saving of whose life was due to her, than the long dull routine of a spoiled life, which would otherwise be her unhappy lot.

When once this idea had taken root in his mind he had taken such steps as had been open to him without endangering the secrecy of his motive. Thanks to his subtle questioning of the Doctor, he now knew that his room was close to the ground, so that he would easily drop from the window and steal away with out immediate danger of any restraining accident. If he could once get away he would be all right. There was a large sum to his credit in each of two London banks. He would manage somehow to find his way to London; even if he had to walk and beg his way.

He felt that now in the silence of the night the time had come. Quietly he rose and felt his way to the door, now and again stumbling and knocking against unknown obstacles in the manner of the recently blind. After each such noise he paused and listened. He felt as if the very walls had ears. When he reached the door he turned the key softly. Then he breathed more freely. He felt that he was at last alone and free to move without suspicion.

Then began a great and arduous search; one that was infinitely difficult and exasperating; and full of pathos to the sympathetic man who watched him in silence. Mr. Hilton could not understand his movements as he felt his way about the room, opening drawers and armoires, now and again stooping down and feeling along the floor. He did not betray his presence, however, but moved noiselessly away as the other approached. It was a hideously real game of blindman's-buff, with perhaps a life as the forfeit.

Harold went all over the room, and at last sat down on the edge of his bed with a hollow suppressed groan that was full of pain. He had found his clothes, but realised that they were now but rags. He put on the clothes, and then for a long time sat quiet, rocking gently to and fro as one in pain, a figure of infinite woe. At last he roused himself. His mind was made up; the time for action had come. He groped his way towards the window looking south. The Doctor, who had taken off his shoes, followed him with catlike stealthiness.

He easily threw open the window, for it was already partly open for ventilation.

When Mr. Hilton saw him sit on the rail of the balcony and begin to raise his feet, getting ready to drop over, he rushed forward and seized him. Harold instinctively grappled with him; the habit of his Alaskan life amidst continual danger made in such a case action swift as thought. Mr. Hilton, with the single desire to prevent him from killing himself, threw himself backward and pulled Harold with him to the stone floor.

Harold, as he held him in a grip of iron, thundered out, forgetful in the excitement of the moment the hushed voice to which he had limited himself:

'What do you want? who are you?'

'H-s-s-sh! I am Mr. Hilton.' Harold relaxed the rigour of his grasp but still held him firmly:

'How did you come here? I locked my door!'

'I have been in the room a long time. I suspected something, and came to watch; to prevent your rash act.'

'Rash act! How?'

'Why, man, if you didn't kill, you would at least cripple yourself.'

'How can I cripple myself when the flower-bed is only a few feet below?'

'There are other dangers for a man who—a man in your sad state. And, besides, have I no duty to prevent a suicide!' Here a brilliant idea struck Harold. This man had evidently got some wrong impression; but it would serve to shield his real purpose. He would therefore encourage it. For the moment, of course, his purpose to escape unnoticed was foiled; but he would wait, and in due time seize another opportunity. In a harder and more determined tone than he had yet used he said:

'I don't see what right you have to interfere. I shall kill myself if I like.'

'Not whilst you are in my care!' This was spoken with a resolution equal to his own. Then Mr. Hilton went on, more softly and with infinite compassion: 'Moreover, I want to have a talk with you which may alter your views.' Harold interrupted, still playing the game of hiding his real purpose:

'I shall do as I wish; as I intend.'

'You are injuring yourself even now by standing in the draught of that open window. Your eyes will feel it before long . . . Are you mad . . . ?'

Harold felt a prick like a pin in his neck; and turned to seize his companion. He could not find him, and for a few moments stumbled through the dark, raging . . .

It seemed a long time before he remembered anything. He had a sense of time lapsed; of dreamland thoughts and visions. Then gradually recollection came back. He tried to move; but found it impossible. His arms and legs were extended wide and were tied; he could feel the cord hurting his wrists and ankles as he moved. To him it was awful to be thus blind and helpless; and anger began to surge up. He heard the voice of Mr. Hilton close by him speaking in a calm, grave, sympathetic tone:

'My poor fellow, I hated to take such a step; but it was really necessary for your own safety. You are a man, and a brave one. Won't you listen to me for a few minutes? When you have heard what I have to say I shall release you. In the meantime I apologise for the outrage, as I dare say you consider it!' Harold was reasonable; and he was now blind and helpless. Moreover, there was something in the Doctor's voice that carried a sense of power with it.

'Go on! I shall listen!' He compelled himself to quietude. The Doctor saw, and realised that he was master of himself. There were some snips of scissors, and he was free.

'See! all I want is calm for a short time, and you have it. May I go on?'

'Go on!' said Harold, not without respect. The Doctor after a pause spoke:

'My poor fellow, I want you to understand that I wish to help you, to do all in my power to restore to you that which you seem to have lost! I can sympathise with your desire to quit life altogether now that the best part of it, sight, seems gone. I do not pretend to judge the actions of my fellows; and if you determine to carry out your purpose I shall not be able to prevent you for ever. I shall not try to. But you certainly shall not do so till you know what I know! I had wished to wait till I could be a little more certain before I took you into confidence with regard to my guessing as to the future. But your desire to destroy yourself forces my hand. Now let me tell you that there is a possibility of the removal of the cause of your purpose.'

'What do you mean?' gasped Harold. He was afraid to think outright and to the full what the other's words seemed to imply.

'I mean,' said the other solemnly, 'that there is a possibility, more than a possibility, that you may recover your sight!' As he spoke there was a little break in his voice. He too was somewhat unnerved at the situation.

Harold lay still. The whole universe seemed to sway, and then whirl round him in chaotic mass. Through it at length he seemed to hear the calm voice:

'At first I could not be sure of my surmise, for when I used the ophthalmoscope your suffering was too recent to disclose the cause I looked for. Now I am fairly sure of it. What I have since heard from you has convinced me; your having suffered from rheumatic fever, and the recrudescence of the rheumatic pain after your terrible experience of the fire and that long chilling swim with so seemingly hopeless an end to it; the symptoms which I have since noticed, though they have not been as enlightening to me as they might be. Your disease, as I have diagnosed it, is an obscure one and not common. I have not before been able to study a case. All these things give me great hopes.'

'Thank God! Thank God!' the voice from the bed was now a whisper.

'Thank God! say I too. This that you suffer from is an acute form of inflammation of the optic nerve. It may of course end badly; in permanent loss of sight. But I hope—I believe, that in your case it will not be so. You are young, and you are immensely strong; not merely muscularly, but in constitution. I can see that you have been an athlete, and no mean one either. All this will stand to you. But it will take time. It will need all your own help; all the calm restraint of your body and your mind. I am doing all that science knows; you must do the rest!' He waited, giving time to the other to realise his ideas. Harold lay still for a long time before he spoke:

'Doctor.' The voice was so strangely different that the other was more hopeful at once. He had feared opposition, or conflict of some kind. He answered as cheerily as he could:

'Yes! I am listening.'

'You are a good fellow; and I am grateful to you, both for what you have done and what you have told me. I cannot say how grateful just yet; hope unmans me at present. But I think you deserve that I should tell you the truth!' The other nodded; he forgot that the speaker could not see.

'I was not intending to commit suicide. Such an idea didn't even enter my head. To me, suicide is the resource of a coward. I have been in too many tight places to ever fear that.'

'Then in the name of goodness why were you trying to get out of that window?'

'I wanted to escape; to get away!'

'In your shirt and trousers; and they are not over much! Without even slippers!' A faint smile curled round the lips of the injured man. Hope was beginning to help already.

'Even that way!'

'But man alive! you were going to your death. How could you expect to get away in such an outfit without being discovered? When you were missed the whole countryside would have been up, and even before the hue-and-cry the first person who saw you would have taken charge of you.'

'I know! I know! I had thought of it all. But I was willing to chance it. I had my own reasons!' He was silent a while. The Doctor was silent too. Each man was thinking in his own way. Presently the Doctor spoke:

'Look here, old chap! I don't want to pry into your secrets; but, won't you let me help you? I can hold my tongue. I want to help you. You have earned that wish from any man, and woman too, who saw the burning ship and what you did to save those on board. There is nothing I would not do for you. Nothing! I don't ask you to tell me all; only enough for me to understand and help. I can see that you have some overpowering wish to get away. Some reason that I cannot fathom, certainly without a clue. You may trust me, I assure you. If you could look into my face, my eyes, you would understand. But—There! take my hand. It may tell you something!'

Harold took the hand placed in his, and held it close. He pressed his other hand over it also, as though the effect of the two hands would bring him double knowledge. It was infinitely pathetic to see him trying to make his untrained fingers do the duty of his trained eyes. But, trained or not, his hands had their instinct. Laying down gently the hand he held he said, turning his bandaged eyes in the direction of his companion:

'I shall trust you! Are we alone; absolutely alone?'

'Absolutely!'

'Have I your solemn promise that anything I say shall never go beyond yourself?'

'I promise. I can swear, if it will make your mind more easy in the matter.'

'What do you hold most sacred in the world?' Harold had an odd thought; his question was its result.

'All told, I should think my profession! Perhaps it doesn't seem to you much to swear by; but it is all my world! But I have been brought up in honour, and you may trust my promise—as much as anything I could swear.'

'All right! My reason for wanting to get away was because I knew Lady de Lannoy!'

'What!' Then after a pause: 'I should have thought that was a reason for wanting to stay. She seems not only one of the most beautiful, but the sweetest woman I ever met.'

'She is all that! And a thousand times more!'

'Then why—Pardon me!'

'I cannot tell you all; but you must take it that my need to get away is imperative.' After pondering a while Mr. Hilton said suddenly:

'I must ask your pardon again. Are you sure there is no mistake. Lady de Lannoy is not married; has not been. She is Countess in her own right. It is quite a romance. She inherited from some old branch of more than three hundred years ago.' Again Harold smiled; he quite saw what the other meant.

He answered gravely

'I understand. But it does not alter my opinion; my purpose. It is needful—absolutely and imperatively needful that I get away without her recognising me, or knowing who I am.'

'She does not know you now. She has not seen you yet.'

'That is why I hoped to get away in time; before she should recognise me. If I stay quiet and do all you wish, will you help me?'

'I will! And what then?'

'When I am well, if it should be so, I shall steal away, this time clothed, and disappear out of her life without her knowing. She may think it ungrateful that one whom she has treated so well should behave so badly. But that can't be helped. It is the lesser evil of the two.'

'And I must abet you? All right! I will do it; though you must forgive me if you should ever hear that I have abused you and said bad things of you. It will have to be all in the day's work if I am not ultimately to give you away. I must take steps at once to keep her from seeing you. I shall have to invent some story; some new kind of dangerous disease, perhaps. I shall stay here and nurse you myself!' Harold spoke in joyful gratitude:

'Oh, you *are* good. But can you spare the time? How long will it all take?'

'Some weeks! Perhaps!' He paused as if thinking. 'Perhaps in a month's time I shall unbandage your eyes. You will then see; or . . . '

'I understand! I shall be patient!'

In the morning Mr. Hilton in reporting to Lady de Lannoy told her that he considered it would be necessary to keep his patient very quiet, both in mind and body. In the course of the conversation he said:

'Anything which might upset him must be studiously avoided. He is not an easy patient to deal with; he doesn't like people to go near him. I think, therefore, it will be well if even you do not see him. He seems to have an odd distrust of people, especially of women. It may be that he is fretful in his blindness, which is in itself so trying to a strong man. But besides, the treatment is not calculated to have a very buoyant effect. It is apt to make a man fretful to lie in the dark, and know that he has to do so for indefinite weeks. Pilocarpin, and salicylate of soda, and mercury do not tend towards cheerfulness. Nor do blisters on the forehead add to the content of life!'

'I quite understand,' said Stephen, 'and I will be careful not to go near him till he is well. Please God! it may bring him back his sight. Thank you a thousand times for your determination to stay with him.'

So it was that for more than two weeks Harold was kept all alone. No one attended him but the Doctor. He slept in the patient's room for the whole of the first week, and never had him out of sight for more than a few minutes at a time. He was then able to leave him alone for longer periods, and settled himself in the bedroom next to him. Every hour or two he would visit him. Occasionally he would be away for half a day, but never for more. Stephen rigidly observed the Doctor's advice herself, and gave strict orders that his instructions were to be obeyed.

Harold himself went through a period of mental suffering. It was agony to him to think of Stephen being so near at hand, and yet not to be able to see her, or even to hear her voice. All the pain of his loss of her affection seemed to crowd back on him, and with it the new need of escaping from her unknown. More than ever he felt it would not do that she should ever learn his identity. Her pity for him, and possibly her woman's regard for a man's effort in time of stress, might lead through the gates of her own self-sacrifice to his restoration to his old place in her affections. Nay! it could not be his old place; for at the close of those days she had learned of his love for her.

CHAPTER XXXV—A CRY

The third week had nearly elapsed, and as yet no one was allowed to see the patient.

For a time Stephen was inclined to be chagrined. It is not pleasant to have even the most generous and benevolent intentions thwarted; and she had set her mind on making much of this man whom fate and his own bravery had thrown athwart her life. But in these days Stephen was in some ways a changed woman. She had so much that she wished to forget and that she would have given worlds to recall, that she could not bear even to think of any militant or even questioning attitude. She even began to take herself to task more seriously than she had ever done with regard to social and conventional duties. When she found her house full of so many and so varied guests, it was borne in upon her that such a position as her own, with such consequent duties, called for the presence of some elder person of her own sex and of her own class.

No better proof of Stephen's intellectual process and its result could be adduced than her first act of recognition: she summoned an elderly lady to live with her and matronise her house. This lady, the widow of a distant relation, complied with all the charted requirements of respectability, and had what to Stephen's eyes was a positive gift: that of minding her own business and not interfering in any matter whatever. Lady de Lannoy, she felt, was her own master and quite able to take care of herself. Her own presence was all that convention required. So she limited herself to this duty, with admirable result to all, herself included. After a few days Stephen would almost forget that she was present.

Mr. Hilton kept bravely to his undertaking. He never gave even a hint of his hopes of the restoration of sight; and he was so assiduous in his attention that there arose no opportunity of accidental discovery of the secret. He knew that when the time did come he would find himself in a very unpleasant situation. Want of confidence, and even of intentional deceit, might be attributed to him; and he would not be able to deny nor explain. He was, however; determined to stick to his word. If he could but save his patient's sight he would be satisfied.

But to Stephen all the mystery seemed to grow out of its first shadowy importance into something real. There was coming to her a vague idea that she would do well not to manifest any concern, any anxiety, any curiosity. Instinct was at work; she was content to trust it, and wait.

One forenoon she received by messenger a letter which interested her much. So much that at first she was unwilling to show it to anyone, and took it to her own boudoir to read over again in privacy. She had a sort of feeling of expectancy with regard to it; such as sensitive natures feel before a thunderstorm. The letter was natural enough in itself. It was dated that morning from Varilands, a neighbouring estate which marched with Lannoy to the south.

> 'MY DEAR MADAM,—Will you pardon me a great liberty, and allow my little girl and me to come to see you to-day? I shall explain when we meet. When I say that we are Americans and have come seven thousand miles for the purpose, you will, I am sure, understand that it is no common interest which has brought us, and it will be the excuse for our eagerness. I should write you more fully, but as the matter is a confidential one I thought it would be better to speak. We shall be doubly grateful if you will have the kindness to see us alone. I write as a mother in making this appeal to your kindness; for my child—she is only a little over eight years old—has the matter so deeply in her heart that any disappointment or undue delay would I fear affect her health. We presume to take your kindness for granted and will call a little before twelve o'clock.
>
> 'I may perhaps say (in case you should feel any hesitation as to my *bona fides*) that my husband purchased some years ago this estate. We were to have come here to live in the early summer, but were kept in the West by some important business of his.
>
> 'Believe me, yours sincerely,
> 'ALICE STONEHOUSE.'

Stephen had, of course, no hesitation as to receiving the lady. Even had there been objection, the curiosity she had in common with her kind would have swept difficulties aside. She gave orders that when Mrs. Stonehouse arrived with her daughter they were to be shown at once into the Mandarin drawing-room. That they would probably stay for lunch. She would see them alone.

A little before twelve o'clock Mrs. Stonehouse and Pearl arrived, and were shown into the room where Lady de Lannoy awaited them. The high sun, streaming in from the side, shone on her beautiful hair, making it look like living gold. When the Americans came in they were for an instant entranced by her beauty. One glance at Mrs. Stonehouse's sweet sympathetic face was enough to establish her in Stephen's good graces forever. As for Pearl, she was like one who has unexpectedly seen a fairy or a goddess. She had been keeping guardedly behind her mother, but on the instant she came out fearlessly into the open.

Stephen advanced quickly and shook hands with Mrs. Stonehouse, saying heartily:

'I am so glad you have come. I am honoured in being trusted.'

'Thank you so much, Lady de Lannoy. I felt that you would not mind, especially when you know why we came. Indeed I had no choice. Pearl insisted on it; and when Pearl is urgent—we who love her have all to give way. This is Pearl!'

In an instant Stephen was on her knees by the beautiful child.

The red rosebud of a mouth was raised to her kiss, and the little arms went lovingly round her neck and clung to her. As the mother looked on delighted she thought she had never seen a more beautiful sight. The two faces so different, and yet with so much in common. The red hair and the flaxen, both tints of gold. The fine colour of each heightened to a bright flush in their eagerness. Stephen was so little used to children, and yet loved them so, that all the womanhood in her, which is possible motherhood, went out in an instant to the lovely eager child. She felt the keenest pleasure when the little thing, having rubbed her silk-gloved palms over her face, and then holding her away so that she could see her many beauties, whispered in her ear:

'How pretty you are!'

'You darling!' whispered Stephen in reply. 'We must love each other very much, you and I!'

When the two ladies had sat down, Stephen holding Pearl in her lap, Mrs. Stonehouse said:

'I suppose you have wondered, Lady de Lannoy, what has brought us here?'

'Indeed I was very much interested.'

'Then I had better tell you all from the beginning so that you may understand.' She proceeded to give the details of the meeting with Mr. Robinson on the *Scoriac*. Of how Pearl took to him and insisted on making him her special friend; of the terrible incident of her being swept overboard, and of the gallant rescue. Mrs. Stonehouse was much moved as she spoke. All that fearful time, of which the minutes had seemed years of agony, came back to her so vividly at times that she could hardly speak. Pearl listened too; all eagerness, but without fear. Stephen was greatly moved and held Pearl close to her all the time, as though protecting her. When the mother spoke of her feeling when she saw the brave man struggling up and down the giant waves, and now and again losing sight of him in the trough of the sea, she put out one hand and held the mother's with a grasp which vibrated in sympathy, whilst the great tears welled over in her eyes and ran down her cheeks. Pearl, watching her keenly, said nothing, but taking her tiny cambric handkerchief from her pocket silently wiped the tears away, and clung all the tighter. It was her turn to protect now!

Pearl's own time for tears came when her mother began to tell this new and sympathetic friend of how she became so much attached to her rescuer that when she knew he would not be coming to the West with them, but going off to the wildest region of the far North, her health became impaired; and that it was only when Mr. Robinson promised to come back to see her within three years that she was at all comforted. And how, ever since, she had held the man in her heart and thought of him every day; sleeping as well as waking, for he was a factor in her dreams!

Stephen was more than ever moved, for the child's constancy touched her as well as her grief. She strained the little thing in her strong young arms, as though the fervency of her grasp would bring belief and comfort; as it did. She in her turn dried the others' eyes. Then Mrs. Stonehouse went on with her story:

'We were at Banff, high up in the Rockies, when we read of the burning and wrecking of the *Dominion*. It is, as you know, a Montreal boat of the Allan Line; so that naturally there was a full telegraphic report in all the Canadian papers. When we read of the brave man who swam ashore with the line and who was unable to reach the port but swam out across the bay, Pearl took it for granted that it must have been "The Man," as she always called Mr. Robinson. When by the next paper we learned that the man's name *was* Robinson nothing would convince her that it was not *her* Mr. Robinson. My husband, I may tell you, had firmly come to the same conclusion. He had ever since the rescue of our child always looked for any news from Alaska, whither he knew Mr. Robinson had gone. He learned that up away in the very far North a new goldfield had been discovered by a man of the same name; and that a new town, Robinson City, began to grow up in the wilderness, where the condition of life from the cold was a new experience to even the most hardy gold miners. Then we began to think that the young hero who had so gallantly saved our darling was meeting some of his reward . . . !'

She paused, her voice breaking. Stephen was in a glow of holy feeling. Gladness, joy, gratitude, enthusiasm; she knew not which. It all seemed like a noble dream which was coming true. Mrs. Stonehouse went on:-

'From Californian papers of last month we learned that Robinson, of Robinson City, had sailed for San Francisco, but had disappeared when the ship touched at Portland; and then the whole chain of his identity seemed complete. Nothing would satisfy Pearl but that we should come at once to England and see "The Man," who was wounded and blind, and do what we could for him. Her father could not then come himself; he had important work on hand which he could not leave without some preparation. But he is following us and may be here at any time.

'And now, we want you to help us, Lady de Lannoy. We are not sure yet of the identity of Mr. Robinson, but we shall know the instant we see him, or hear his voice. We have learned that he is still here. Won't you let us? Do let us see him as soon as ever you can!' There was a pleading tone in her voice which alone would have moved Stephen, even had she not been wrought up already by the glowing fervour of her new friend.

But she paused. She did not know what to say; how to tell them that as yet she herself knew nothing. She, too, in the depths of her own heart knew—*knew*—that it was the same Robinson. And she also knew that both identities were one with another. The beating of her heart and the wild surging of her blood told her all. She was afraid to speak lest her voice should betray her.

She could not even think. She would have to be alone for that.

Mrs. Stonehouse, with the wisdom and power of age, waited, suspending judgment. But Pearl was in a fever of anxiety; she could imagine nothing which could keep her away from The Man. But she saw that there was some difficulty, some cause of delay. So she too added her pleading. Putting her mouth close to Lady de Lannoy's ear she whispered very faintly, very caressingly:

'What is your name? Your own name? Your very own name?'

'Stephen, my darling!'

'Oh, won't you let us see The Man, Stephen; dear Stephen! I love him so; and I do *so* want to see him. It is ages till I see him! Won't you let me? I shall be so good—Stephen!' And she strained her closer in her little arms and kissed her all over face, cheeks and forehead and eyes and mouth wooingly. Stephen returned the embrace and the kisses, but remained silent a little longer. Then she found voice:

'I hardly know what to say. Believe me, I should—I shall, do all I can; but the fact is that I am not in authority. The Doctor has taken him in charge and will not let anyone go near him: He will not even have a nurse, but watches and attends to him himself. He says it might be fatal if anything should occur to agitate him. Why, even I am not allowed to see him!'

'Haven't you seen him yet at all; ever, ever, Stephen?' asked Pearl, all her timidity gone. Stephen smiled—a wan smile it was, as she answered:

'I saw him in the water, but it was too far away to distinguish. And it was only by firelight.'

'Oh yes, I know,' said Pearl; 'Mother and Daddy told me how you had burned the house down to give him light. Didn't you want to see him more after that? I should!' Stephen drew the impulsive child closer as she answered:

'Indeed I did, dear. But I had to think of what was good for him. I went to his room the next day when he was awake, and the Doctor let me come in for only a moment.'

'Well! What did you see. Didn't you know him?' She forgot that the other did not know him from her point of view. But the question went through Stephen's heart like a sword. What would she not have given to have known him! What would she not give to know him now! . . . She spoke mechanically:

'The room was quite dark. It is necessary, the Doctor says, that he be kept in the dark. I saw only a big beard, partly burned away by the fire; and a great bandage which covered his eyes!' Pearl's hold relaxed, she slipped like an eel to the floor and ran over to her mother. Her new friend was all very well, but no one would do as well as mother when she was in trouble.

'Oh mother, mother! My Robinson had no beard!' Her mother stroked her face comfortingly as she answered:

'But, my dear, it is more than two years since you saw him. Two years and three months, for it was in June that we crossed.' How the date thrilled Stephen. It verified her assumption.

Mrs. Stonehouse did not notice, but went on:

'His beard would have grown. Men wear beards up in the cold place where he was.' Pearl kissed her; there was no need for words. Throwing herself again on Stephen's knees she went on with her questioning:

'But didn't you hear him?'

'I heard very little, darling. He was very weak. It was only the morning after the wreck, and he spoke in a whisper!' Then with an instinct of self-preservation she added: 'But how could I learn anything by hearing him when he was a stranger to me? I had never even heard of Mr. Robinson!'

As she was speaking she found her own ideas, the proofs of her own conviction growing. This was surely another link in the chain of proving that all three men were but one. But in such case Harold must know; must have tried to hide his identity!

She feared, with keen eyes upon her, to pursue the thought. But her blood began to grow cold and her brain to swim. With an effort she went on:

'Even since then I have not been allowed to go near him. Of course I must obey orders. I am waiting as patiently as I can. But we must ask the Doctor if he thinks his patient will see you—will let you see him—though he will not let me.' This she added with a touch of what she felt: regret rather than bitter ness. There was no room for bitterness in her full heart where Harold was concerned.

'Will you ask the Doctor now?' Pearl did not let grass grow under her feet. For answer Stephen rang the bell, and when a servant appeared asked:

'Is Mr. Hilton in the house?'

'I think not, your Ladyship. He said he was going over to Port Lannoch. Shall I inquire if he left word at what time he would be back?'

'If you please!' The man returned in a few minutes with the butler, who said:

'Mr. Hilton said, your Ladyship, that he expected to be back by one o'clock at latest.'

'Please ask him on his arrival if he will kindly come here at once. Do not let us be disturbed until then.' The butler bowed and withdrew.

'Now,' said Stephen, 'as we have to wait till our tyrant comes, won't you tell me all that went on after The Man had left you?' Pearl brightened up at once. Stephen would have given anything to get away even for a while. Beliefs and hopes and fears were surging up, till she felt choking. But the habit of her life, especially her life of the last two years, gave her self-control. And so she waited, trying with all her might to follow the child's prattle.

After a long wait Pearl exclaimed: 'Oh! I do wish that Doctor would come. I want to see The Man!' She was so restless, marching about the room, that Stephen said:

'Would you like to go out on the balcony, darling; of course if Mother will let you? It is quite safe, I assure you, Mrs. Stonehouse. It is wide and open and is just above the flower-borders, with a stone tail. You can see the road from it by which Mr. Hilton comes from Port Lannoch. He will be riding.' Pearl yielded at once to the diversion. It would at any rate be something to do, to watch. Stephen opened the French window and the child ran out on the balcony.

When Stephen came back to her seat Mrs. Stonehouse said quietly:

'I am glad she is away for a few minutes. She has been over wrought, and I am always afraid for her. She is so sensitive. And after all she is only a baby!'

'She is a darling!' said Stephen impulsively; and she meant it. Mrs. Stonehouse smiled gratefully as she went on:

'I suppose you noticed what a hold on her imagination that episode of Mollie Watford at the bank had. Mr. Stonehouse is, as perhaps you know, a very rich man. He has made his fortune himself, and most honourably; and we are all very proud of him, and of it. So Pearl does not think of the money for itself. But the feeling was everything; she really loves Mr. Robinson; as indeed she ought! He has done so much for us that it would be a pride and a privilege for us to show our gratitude. My husband, between ourselves, wanted to make him his partner. He tells me that, quite independent of our feeling towards him, he is just the man he wanted. And if indeed it was he who discovered the Alaskan goldfield and organised and ruled Robinson City, it is a proof that Mr. Stonehouse's judgment was sound. Now he is injured, and blind; and our little Pearl loves him. If indeed he be the man we believe he is, then we may be able to do something which all his millions cannot buy. He will come to us, and be as a son to us, and a brother to Pearl. We will be his eyes; and nothing but love and patience will guide his footsteps!' She paused, her mouth quivering; then she went on:

'If it is not our Mr. Robinson, then it will be our pleasure to do all that is necessary for his comfort. If he is a poor man he will never want . . . It will be a privilege to save so gallant a man from hardship . . . ' Here she came to a stop.

CHAPTER XXXV—A CRY

Stephen too was glad of the pause, for the emotion which the words and their remembrances evoked was choking her. Had not Harold been as her own father's son. As her own brother! . . . She turned away, fearing lest her face should betray her.

All at once Mrs. Stonehouse started to her feet, her face suddenly white with fear; for a cry had come to their ears. A cry which even Stephen knew as Pearl's. The mother ran to the window.

The balcony was empty. She came back into the room, and, ran to the door.

But on the instant a voice that both women knew was heard from without:

'Help there! Help, I say! The child has fainted. Is there no one there? And I am blind!'

CHAPTER XXXVI—LIGHT

Harold had been in a state of increasing restlessness. The month of waiting which Dr. Hilton had laid down for him seemed to wear away with extraordinary slowness; this was increased by the lack of companionship, and further by the cutting off of even the little episodes usual to daily life. His patience, great as it was naturally and trained as it had been by the years of self-repression, was beginning to give way. Often and often there came over him a wild desire to tear off the irksome bandages and try for himself whether the hopes held out to him were being even partially justified. He was restrained only by the fear of perpetual blindness, which came over him in a sort of cold wave at each reaction. Time, too, added to his fear of discovery; but he could not but think that his self-sought isolation must be a challenge to the curiosity of each and all who knew of it. And with all these disturbing causes came the main one, which never lessened but always grew: that whatever might happen Stephen would be further from him than ever. Look at the matter how he would; turn it round in whatsoever possible or impossible way, he could see no relief to this gloomy conclusion.

For it is in the nature of love that it creates or enlarges its own pain. If troubles or difficulties there be from natural causes, then it will exaggerate them into nightmare proportions. But if there be none, it will create them. Love is in fact the most serious thing that comes to man; where it exists all else seem as phantoms, or at best as actualities of lesser degree. During the better part of two years his troubles had but slept; and as nothing wakes the pangs of old love better than the sound of a voice, all the old acute pain of love and the agony that followed its denial were back with him. Surely he could never, never believe that Stephen did not mean what she had said to him that morning in the beech grove. All his new resolution not to hamper her with the burden of a blind and lonely-hearted man was back to the full.

In such mood had he been that morning. He was additionally disturbed because the Doctor had gone early to Port Lannoch; and as he was the only person with whom he could talk, he clung to him with something of the helpless feeling of a frightened child to its nurse.

The day being full of sunshine the window was open, and only the dark-green blind which crackled and rustled with every passing breeze made the darkness of the room. Harold was dressed and lay on a sofa placed back in the room, where the few rays of light thus entering could not reach him. His eyes and forehead were bandaged as ever. For some days the Doctor, who had his own reasons and his own purpose, had not taken them off; so the feeling of blind helplessness was doubly upon him. He knew he was blind; and he knew also that if he were not he could not in his present condition see.

All at once he started up awake. His hearing had in the weeks of darkness grown abnormally acute, and some trifling sound had recalled him to himself. It might have been inspiration, but he seemed to be conscious of some presence in the room.

As he rose from the sofa, with the violent motion of a strong man startled into unconscious activity, he sent a shock of fear to the eager child who had strayed into the room through the open window. Had he presented a normal appearance, she would not have been frightened. She would have recognised his identity despite the changes, and have sprung to him so impulsively that she would have been in his arms before she had time to think. But now all she saw was a great beard topped with a mass of linen and lint, which obscured all the rest of the face and seemed in the gloom like a gigantic and ominous turban.

In her fright she screamed out. He in turn, forgetful for the moment of his intention of silence, called aloud:

'Who is that?' Pearl, who had been instinctively backing towards the window by which she had entered, and whose thoughts in her fright had gone back to her mother—refuge in time of danger—cried out:

'Mother, Mother! It is him! It is The Man!' She would have run towards him in spite of his forbidding appearance; but the shock had been too much for her. The little knees trembled and gave way; the brain reeled; and with a moan she sank on the floor in a swoon.

Harold knew the voice the instant she spoke; there was no need for the enlightening words

'Pearl! Pearl!' he cried. 'Come to me, darling!' But as he spoke he heard her moan, and the soft thud of her little body on the thick carpet. He guessed the truth and groped his way towards where the sound had been, for he feared lest he might trample upon her in too great eagerness. Kneeling by her he touched her little feet, and then felt his way to her face. And as he did so, such is the double action of the mind, even in the midst of his care the remembrance swept across his mind of how he had once knelt in just such manner in an old church by another little senseless form. In his confusion of mind he lost the direction of the door, and coming to the window pushed forward the flapping blind and went out on the balcony. He knew from the freshness of the air and the distant sounds that he was in the open. This disturbed him, as he wished to find someone who could attend to the fainting child. But as he had lost the way back to the room now, he groped along the wall of the Castle with one hand, whilst he held Pearl securely in the other. As he went he called out for help.

When he came opposite the window of the Mandarin room Mrs. Stonehouse saw him; she ran to him and caught Pearl in her arms. She was so agitated, so lost in concern for the child that she never even thought to speak to the man whom she had come so far to seek. She wailed over the child:

'Pearl! Pearl! What is it, darling? It is Mother!' She laid the girl on the sofa, and taking the flowers out of a glass began to sprinkle water on the child's face. Harold knew her voice and waited in patience. Presently the child sighed; the mother, relieved, thought of other things at last and looked around her.

There was yet another trouble. There on the floor, where she had slipped down, lay Lady de Lannoy in a swoon. She called out instinctively, forgetting for the moment that the man was blind, but feeling all the old confidence which he had won in her heart:

'Oh! Mr. Robinson, help me! Lady de Lannoy has fainted too, and I do not know what to do!' As she spoke she looked up at him and remembered his blindness. But she had no time to alter her words; the instant she had spoken Harold, who had been leaning against the window-sash, and whose mind was calmer since with his acute hearing he too had heard Pearl sigh, seemed to leap into the room.

'Where is she? Where is she? Oh, God, now am I blind indeed!'

It gave her a pang to hear him and to see him turn helplessly with his arms and hands outstretched as though he would feel for her in the air.

Without pause, and under an instinctive and uncontrollable impulse, he tore the bandages from his eyes. The sun was streaming in. As he met it his eyes blinked and a cry burst from him; a wild cry whose joy and surprise pierced even through the shut portals of the swooning woman's brain. Not for worlds would she ever after have lost the memory of that sound:

'Light! light! Oh, God! Oh, God! I am not blind!'

But he looked round him still in terrified wonder:

'Where is she? Where is she? I cannot see her! Stephen! Stephen! where are you?' Mrs. Stonehouse, bewildered, pointed where Stephen's snow-white face and brilliant hair seemed in the streaming sunlight like ivory and gold:

'There! There!' He caught her arm mechanically, and putting his eyes to her wrist, tried to look along her pointed finger. In an instant he dropped her arm moaning.

'I cannot see her! What is it that is over me? This is worse than to be blind!' He covered his face with his hands and sobbed.

He felt light strong fingers on his forehead and hands; fingers whose touch he would have known had they been laid on him were he no longer quick. A voice whose music he had heard in his dreams for two long years said softly:

'I am here, Harold! I am here! Oh! do not sob like that; it breaks my heart to hear you!' He took his hands from his face and held hers in them, staring intently at her as though his passionate gaze would win through every obstacle.

That moment he never forgot. Never could forget! He saw the room all rich in yellow. He saw Pearl, pale but glad-eyed, lying on a sofa holding the hand of her mother, who stood beside her. He saw the great high window open, the lines of the covered stone balcony without, the stretch of green sward all vivid in the sunshine, and beyond it the blue quivering sea. He saw all but that for which his very soul longed; without to see which sight itself was valueless . . . But still he looked, and looked; and Stephen saw in his dark eyes, though he could not see her, that which made her own eyes fill and the warm red glow on her face again . . . Then she raised her eyes again, and the gladness of her beating heart seemed the answer to his own.

For as he looked he saw, as though emerging from a mist whose obscurity melted with each instant, what was to him the one face in all the world. He did not think then of its beauty—that would come later; and besides no beauty of one born of woman could outmatch the memorised beauty which had so long held his heart. But that he had so schooled himself in long months of gloomy despair, he would have taken her in his arms there and then; and, heedless of the presence of others, have poured out his full heart to her.

Mrs. Stonehouse saw and understood. So too Pearl, who though a child was a woman-child; softly they rose up to steal away. But Stephen saw them; her own instincts, too, told her that her hour had not come. What she hoped for must come alone! So she called to her guests:

'Don't go! Don't go, Mrs. Stonehouse. You know now that Harold and I are old friends, though neither of us knew it—till this moment. We were brought up as . . . almost as brother and sister. Pearl, isn't it lovely to see your friend . . . to see The Man again?'

She was so happy that she could only express herself, with dignity, through the happiness of others.

Pearl actually shrieked with joy as she rushed across the room and flung herself into Harold's arms as he stooped to her. He raised her; and she kissed him again and again, and put her little hands all over his face and stroked, very, very gently, his eyes, and said:

'Oh, I am so glad! And so glad your poor eyes are unbind again! May I call you Harold, too?'

'You darling!' was all he could say as he kissed her, and holding her in one arm went across and shook hands with Mrs. Stonehouse, who wrung his hand hard.

There was a little awkwardness in the group, for none of them knew what would be best to do next. In the midst of it there came a light knock at the door, and Mr. Hilton entered saying:

'They told me you wished to see me at once—Hulloa!' He rushed across the room and took Harold by the shoulders, turning his face to the light. He looked in his eyes long and earnestly, the others holding their breaths. Presently he said, without relaxing his gaze:

'Did you see mistily at first?'

'Yes.'

'Seeing at the periphery; but the centre being opaque?'

'Yes! How did you know? Why, I couldn't see'—see pointing to Stephen—'Lady de Lannoy; though her face was right in front of me!'

Dr. Hilton took his hands from his patient's shoulders and shook him warmly by both hands:-

'I am glad, old fellow! It was worth waiting for, wasn't it? But I say, it was a dangerous thing to take off those bandages before I permitted. However, it has done no harm! But it was lucky that I mistrusted your patience and put the time for the experiment a week later than I thought necessary . . . What is it?' He turned from one to the other questioningly; there was a look on Harold's face that he did not quite comprehend.

'H-s-h,' said the latter warningly, 'I'll tell you all about it . . . some time!'

The awkward pause was broken by Pearl, who came to the Doctor and said:

'I must kiss you, you know. It was you who saved The Man's eyes. Stephen has told me how you watched him!' The Doctor was somewhat taken aback; as yet he was ignorant of Pearl's existence. However, he raised the child in his arms and kissed her, saying:

'Thank you, my dear! I did all I could. But he helped much himself; except at the very last. Don't you ever go and take off bandages, if you should ever have the misfortune to have them on, without the doctor's permission!' Pearl nodded her head wisely and then wriggled out of his arms and came again to Harold, looking up at him protectingly and saying in an old-fashioned way:

'How are you feeling now? None the worse, I hope, *Harold*!'

The Man lifted her up and kissed her again. When he set her down she came over to Lady de Lannoy and held up her arms to be lifted:

'And I must kiss you again too, Stephen!' If Lady de Lannoy hadn't loved the sweet little thing already she would have loved her for that!

The door was opened, and the butler announced:

'Luncheon is served, your Ladyship.'

* * * * *

After a few days Harold went over to Varilands to stay for a while with the Stonehouses. Mr. Stonehouse had arrived, and both men were rejoiced to meet again. The elder never betrayed by word or sign that he recognised the identity of the other person of the drama of whom he had told him and who had come so accidentally into his life; and the younger was grateful to him for it. Harold went almost every day to Lannoy, and sometimes the Stonehouses went with him; at other times Stephen paid flying visits to Varilands. She did not make any effort to detain Harold; she would not for worlds have made a sign which might influence him. She was full now of that diffidence which every woman has who loves. She felt that she must wait; must wait even if the waiting lasted to her grave. She felt, as every woman does who really loves, that she had found her Master.

And Harold, to whom something of the same diffidence was an old story, got the idea that her reticence was a part of the same feeling whose violent expression had sent him out into the wilderness. And with the thought came the idea of his duty, implied in her father's dying trust: 'Give her time! . . . Let her choose!' For him the clock seemed to have stopped for two whole years, and he was back at the time when the guardianship of his boy life was beginning to yield to the larger and more selfish guardianship of manhood.

Stephen, noticing that he did not come near her as closely as she felt he might, and not realising his true reason—for when did love ever realise the true reason of the bashfulness of love?—felt a chillness which in turn reacted on her own manner.

And so these two ardent souls, who yearned for each other's love and the full expression of it, seemed as if they might end after all in drifting apart. Each thought that their secret was concealed. But both secrets were already known to Mrs. Stonehouse, who knew nothing; and to Mr. Stonehouse, who knew everything. Even Pearl had her own ideas, as was once shown in a confidence when they were alone in Stephen's bedroom after helping her to finish her dressing, just as Stephen herself had at a similar age helped her Uncle Gilbert. After some coy leading up to the subject of pretty dresses, the child putting her little mouth to the other's ear whispered:

'May I be your bridesmaid, Stephen?' The woman was taken aback; but she had to speak at once, for the child's eyes were on her:

'Of course you will, darling. But I—I may never be married.'

'You! You must! I know someone who will make you!' Stephen's heart beat hard and rapidly. The child's talk, though sweet and dear, was more than embarrassing. With, however, the desire to play with fire, which is a part of the nature of women, she answered:

'You have some queer ideas, little one, in that pretty knowledge-box of yours.'

'Oh! he never told me. But I know it all the same! And you know it too, Stephen!' This was getting too close to be without danger; so she tried to divert the thought from herself:

'My darling, you may guess about other people, though I don't say you ought; but you must not guess about me!'

'All right!' then she held up her arms to be lifted on the other's knee and said:

'I want to whisper to you!' Her voice and manner were so full of feeling that somehow the other was moved. She bent her head, and Pearl taking her neck in her little palms, said:

'I thought, oh! long ago, that I would marry him myself. But you knew him first . . . And he only saved me . . . But you saved him!' . . . And then she laid her head down on the throbbing bosom, and sobbed . . .

And Stephen sobbed too.

Before they left the room, Stephen said to her, very gravely, for the issue might be one of great concern:

'Of course, Pearl dear, our secrets are all between ourselves!' Pearl crossed her two forefingers and kissed them. But she said nothing; she had sworn! Stephen went on:

'And, darling, you will remember too that one must never speak or even think if they can help it about anyone's marrying anyone else till they say so themselves! What is it, dear, that you are smiling at?'

'I know, Stephen! I musn't take off the bandage till the Doctor says so!'

Stephen smiled and kissed her. Hand in hand, Pearl chattering merrily, they went down to the drawing-room.

CHAPTER XXXVII—GOLDEN SILENCE

Each day that passed seemed to add to the trouble in the heart of these young people; to widen the difficulty of expressing themselves. To Stephen, who had accepted the new condition of things and whose whole nature had bloomed again under the sunshine of hope, it was the less intolerable. She had set herself to wait, as had countless thousands of women before her; and as due proportion will, till the final cataclysm abolishes earthly unions. But Harold felt the growth, both positive and negative, as a new torture; and he began to feel that he would be unable to go through with it. In his heart was the constant struggle of hope; and in opposition to it the seeming realisation of every new fancy of evil. That bitter hour, when the whole of creation was for him turned upside down, was having its sad effect at last. Had it not been for that horrid remembrance he would have come to believe enough in himself to put his future to the test. He would have made an opportunity at which Stephen and himself would have with the fires of their mutual love burned away the encircling mist. There are times when a single minute of commonsense would turn sorrow into joy; and yet that minute, our own natures being the opposing forces, will be allowed to pass.

Those who loved these young people were much concerned about them. Mrs. Stonehouse took their trouble so much to heart that she spoke to her husband about it, seriously advising that one or other of them should make an effort to bring things in the right way for their happiness. The woman was sure of the woman's feeling. It is from men, not women, that women hide their love. By side-glances and unthinking moments women note and learn. The man knew already, from his own lips, of the man's passion. But his lips were sealed by his loyalty; and he said earnestly:

'My dear, we must not interfere. Not now, at any rate; we might cause them great trouble. I am as sure as you are that they really love each other. But they must win happiness by themselves and through themselves alone. Otherwise it would never be to them what it ought to be; what it might be; what it will be!'

So these friends were silent, and the little tragedy developed. Harold's patience began to give way under the constant strain of self-suppression. Stephen tried to hide her love and fear, under the mask of a gracious calm. This the other took for indifference.

At last there came an hour which was full of new, hopeless agony to Stephen. She heard Harold, in a fragment of conversation, speak to Mr. Stonehouse of the need of returning to Alaska. That sounded like a word of doom. In her inmost heart she knew that Harold loved her; and had she been free she would have herself spoken the words which would have drawn the full truth to them both. But how could she do so, having the remembrance of that other episode; when, without the reality of love, she had declared herself? . . . Oh! the shame of it . . . The folly! . . . And Harold knew it all! How could he ever believe that it was real this time! . . .

By the exercise of that self-restraint which long suffering had taught her, Stephen so managed to control herself that none of her guests realised what a blow she had received from a casual word. She bore herself gallantly till the last moment. After the old fashion of her youth, she had from the Castle steps seen their departure. Then she took her way to her own room, and locked herself in. She did not often, in these days, give way to tears; when she did cry it was as a luxury, and not from poignant cause. Her deep emotion was dry-eyed as of old. Now, she did not cry, she sat still, her hands clasped below her knees, with set white face gazing out on the far-off sea. For hours she sat there lonely; staring fixedly all the time, though her thoughts were whirling wildly. At first she had some vague purpose, which she hoped might eventually work out into a plan. But thought would not come. Everywhere there was the same beginning: a wild, burning desire to let Harold understand her feeling towards him; to blot out, with the conviction of trust and love, those bitter moments when in the madness of her overstrung passion she had heaped such insult upon him. Everywhere the same end: an impasse. He seemingly could not, would not, understand. She knew now that the man had diffidences, forbearances, self-judgments and self-denials which made for the suppression, in what he considered to be her interest, of his own desires. This was tragedy indeed! Again and again came back the remembrance of that bitter regret of her Aunt Laetitia, which no happiness and no pain of her own had ever been able to efface:

'To love; and be helpless! To wait, and wait, and wait; with heart all aflame! To hope, and hope; till time seemed to have passed away, and all the world to stand still on your hopeless misery! To know that a word might open up Heaven; and yet to have to remain mute! To keep back the glances that could enlighten, to modulate the tones that might betray! To see all you hoped for passing away . . . !'

At last she seemed to understand the true force of pride; which has in it a thousand forces of its own, positive, negative, restrainful. Oh! how blind she had been! How little she had learned from the miseries that the other woman whom she loved had suffered! How unsympathetic she had been; how self-engrossed; how callous to the sensibilities of others! And now to her, in her turn, had come the same suffering; the same galling of the iron fetters of pride, and of convention which is its original expression! Must it be that the very salt of youth must lose its savour, before the joys of youth could be won! What, after all, was youth if out of its own inherent power it must work its own destruction! If youth was so, why not then trust the wisdom of age? If youth could not act for its own redemption . . .

Here the rudiment of a thought struck her and changed the current of her reason. A thought so winged with hope that she dared not even try to complete it! . . . She thought, and thought till the long autumn shadows fell around her. But the misty purpose had become real.

After dinner she went up alone to the mill. It was late for a visit, for the Silver Lady kept early hours. But she found her friend as usual in her room, whose windows swept the course of the sun. Seeing that her visitor was in a state of mental disturbance such as she had once before exhibited, she blew out the candles and took the same seat in the eastern window she had occupied on the night which they both so well remembered.

Stephen understood both acts, and was grateful afresh. The darkness would be a help to her in what she had to say; and the resumption of the old seat and attitude did away with the awkwardness of new confidence. During the weeks that had passed Stephen had kept her friend informed of the rescue and progress of the injured man. Since the discovery of Harold's identity she had allowed her to infer her feeling towards him.

Shyly she had conveyed her hopes that all the bitter part of the past might be wiped out. To the woman who already knew of the love that had always been, but had only awakened to consciousness in the absence of its object, a hint was sufficient to build upon. She had noticed the gloom that had of late been creeping over the girl's happiness; and she had been much troubled about it. But she had thought it wiser to be silent; she well knew that should unhappily the time for comfort come, it must be precluded by new and more explicit confidence. So she too had been anxiously waiting the progress of events. Now; as she put her arms round the girl she said softly; not in the whisper which implies doubt of some kind, but in the soft voices which conveys sympathy and trust:

'Tell me, dear child!'

And then in broken words shyly spoken, and spoken in such a way that the silences were more eloquent than the words, the girl conveyed what was in her heart. The other listened, now and again stroking the beautiful hair. When all was said, there was a brief pause. The Silver Lady spoke no word; but the pressure of her delicate hand conveyed sympathy.

In but a half-conscious way, in words that came so shrinkingly through the darkness that they hardly reached the ear bent low to catch them, came Stephen's murmured thought:

'Oh, if he only knew! And I can't tell him; I can't! dare not! I must not. How could I dishonour him by bearing myself towards him as to that other . . . worthless . . . ! Oh! the happy, happy girls, who have mothers . . . !' All the muscles of her body seemed to shrink and collapse, till she was like an inert mass at the Silver Lady's feet.

But the other understood!

After a long, long pause; when Stephen's sobbing had died away; when each muscle of her body had become rigid on its return to normal calm; the Silver Lady began to talk of other matters, and conversation became normal. Stephen's courage seemed somehow to be restored, and she talked brightly.

Before they parted the Silver Lady made a request. She said in her natural voice:

'Couldst thou bring that gallant man who saved so many lives, and to whom the Lord was so good in the restoration of his sight, to see me? Thou knowest I have made a resolution not to go forth from this calm place whilst I may remain. But I should like to see him before he returns to that far North where he has done such wonders. He is evidently a man of kind heart; perhaps he will not mind coming to see a lonely woman who is no longer young. There is much I should like to ask him of that land of which nothing was known in my own youth. Perhaps he will not mind seeing me alone.' Stephen's heart beat furiously. She felt suffocating with new hope, for what could be but good from Harold's meeting with that sweet woman who had already brought so much comfort into her own life? She was abashed, and yet radiant; she seemed to tread on air as she stood beside her friend saying farewell. She did not wish to speak. So the two women kissed and parted.

It had been arranged that two days hence the Stonehouse party were to spend the day at Lannoy, coming before lunch and staying the night, as they wanted in the afternoon to return a visit at some distance to the north of Lannoy. Harold was to ride over with them.

When the Varilands party arrived, Stephen told them of Sister Ruth's wish to see Harold. Pearl at once proffered a request that she also should be taken at some other time to see the Silver Lady. Harold acquiesced heartily; and it was agreed that some time in the late afternoon he should pay the visit. Stephen would bring him.

Strangely enough, she felt no awkwardness, no trepidation, as they rode up the steep road to the Mill.

When the introduction had been effected, and half an hour had been consumed in conventional small talk, Stephen, obedience to a look from the Silver Lady, rose. She said in the most natural way she could:

'Now Sister Ruth, I will leave you two alone, if you do not mind. Harold can tell you all you want to know about Alaska; and perhaps, if you are very good, he will tell some of his adventures! Good afternoon, dear. I wish you were to be with us to-night; but I know your rule. I go for my ride. Sultan has had no exercise for five days; and he looked at me quite reproachfully when we met this morning. Au revoir, Harold. We shall meet at dinner!'

When she had gone Harold came back from the door, and stood in the window looking east. The Silver Lady came and stood beside him. She did not seem to notice his face, but in the mysterious way of women she watched him keenly. She wished to satisfy her own mind before she undertook her self-appointed task.

Her eyes were turned towards the headland towards which Stephen on her white Arab was galloping at breakneck speed. He was too good a horseman himself, and he knew her prowess on horseback too well to have any anxiety regarding such a rider at Stephen. It was not fear, then, that made his face so white, and his eyes to have such an illimitable sadness.

The Silver Lady made up her mind. All her instincts were to trust him. She recognised a noble nature, with which truth would be her surest force.

'Come,' she said, 'sit here, friend; where another friend has often sat with me. From this you can see all the coastline, and all that thou wilt!' Harold put a chair beside the one she pointed out; and when she was seated he sat also. She began at once with a desperate courage:

'I have wanted much to see thee. I have heard much of thee, before thy coming.' There was something in the tone of her voice which arrested his attention, and he looked keenly at her. Here, in the full light, her face looked sadly white and he noticed that her lips trembled. He said with all the kindliness of his nature, for from the first moment he had seen her he had taken to her, her purity and earnestness and sweetness appealing to some aspiration within him:

'You are pale! I fear you are not well! May I call your maid? Can I do anything for you?' She waved her hand gently:

'Nay! It is nothing. It is but the result of a sleepless night and much thought.'

'Oh! I wish I had known! I could have put off my visit; and I could have come any other time to suit you.' She smiled gently:

'I fear that would have availed but little. It was of thy coming that I was concerned.' Seeing his look of amazement, she went on quickly, her voice becoming more steady as she lost sight of herself in her task:

'Be patient a little with me. I am an old woman; and until recently it has been many and many years since the calm which I sought here has been ruffled. I had come to believe that for me earthly troubles were no more. But there has come into my life a new concern. I have heard so much of thee, and before thy coming.' The recurrence of the phrase struck him. He would have asked how such could be, but he deemed it better to wait. She went on:

'I have been wishful to ask thy advice. But why should not I tell thee outright that which troubles me? I am not used, at least for these many years, to dissemble. I can but trust thee in all; and lean on thy man's mercy to understand, and to aid me!'

'I shall do all in my power, believe me!' said Harold simply. 'Speak freely!' She pointed out of the window, where Stephen's white horse seemed on the mighty sweep of green sward like a little dot.

'It is of her that I would speak to thee!' Harold's heart began to beat hard; he felt that something was coming. The Silver Lady went on:

'Why thinkest thou that she rideth at such speed? It is her habit!' He waited. She continued:

'Doth it not seem to thee that such reckless movement is the result of much trouble; that she seeketh forgetfulness?' He knew that she was speaking truly; and somehow the conviction was borne upon him that she knew his secret heart, and was appealing to it. If it was about Stephen! If her disquiet was about her; then God bless her! He would be patient and grateful. The Quaker's voice seemed to come through his thought, as though she had continued speaking whilst he had paused:

'We have all our own secrets. I have had mine; and I doubt not that thou hast had, may still have, thine own. Stephen hath hers! May I speak to thee of her?'

'I shall be proud! Oh! madam, I thank you with all my heart for your sweet kindness to her. I cannot say what I feel; for she has always been very dear to me!' In the pause before she spoke again the beating of his own heart seemed to re-echo the quick sounds of Stephen's galloping horse. He was surprised at the method of her speech when it did come; for she forgot her Quaker idiom, and spoke in the phrasing of her youth:

'Do you love her still?'

'With all my soul! More than ever!'

'Then, God be thanked; for it is in your power to do much good. To rescue a poor, human, grieving soul from despair!' Her words conveyed joy greater than she knew. Harold did not himself know why the air seemed filled with sounds that seemed to answer every doubt of his life. He felt, understood, with that understanding which is quicker than thought. The Silver Lady went on now with a rush:

'See, I have trusted you indeed! I have given away another woman's secret; but I do it without fear. I can see that you also are troubled; and when I look back on my own life and remember the trouble that sent me out of the world; a lonely recluse here in this spot far from the stress of life, I rejoice that any act of mine can save such another tragedy as my own. I see that I need not go into detail. You know that I am speaking truth. It was before you came so heroically on this new scene that she told me her secret. At a time when nothing was known of you except that you had disappeared. When she laid bare her poor bleeding heart to me, she did it in such wise that for an instant I feared that it was a murder which she had committed. Indeed, she called it so! You understand that I know all your secret; all her part in it at least. And I know that you understand what loving duty lies before you. I see it in your eyes; your brave, true eyes! Go! and the Lord be with thee!' Her accustomed idiom had returned with prayer. She turned her head away, and, standing up, leaned against the window. Bending over, he took her hand and said simply:

'God bless you! I shall come back to thank you either to-night or to-morrow; and I hope that she will be with me.'

He went quickly out of the room. The woman stood for long looking out of the window, and following with tear-dimmed eyes the movement of his great black horse as he swept across country straight as the crow flies, towards the headland whither Stephen had gone.

* * * * *

Stephen passed over the wide expanse without thought; certainly without memory of it. Never in her after-life could she recall any thought that had passed through her mind from the time she left the open gate of the windmill yard till she pulled up her smoking, panting horse beside the ruin of the fisher's house.

Stephen was not unhappy! She was not happy in any conscious form. She was satisfied rather than dissatisfied. She was a woman! A woman who waited the coming of a man!

For a while she stood at the edge of the cliff, and looked at the turmoil of the tide churning on the rocks below. Her heart went out in a great burst of thankfulness that it was her hand which had been privileged to aid in rescuing so dear a life. Then she looked around her. Ostensibly it was to survey the ruined house; but in reality to search, even then under her lashes, the whole green expanse sloping up to the windmill for some moving figure. She saw that which made her throat swell and her ears to hear celestial music. But she would not allow herself to think, of that at all events. She was all woman now; all-patient, and all-submissive. She waited the man; and the man was coming!

For a few minutes she walked round the house as though looking at it critically for some after-purpose. After the wreck Stephen had suggested to Trinity House that there should be a lighthouse on the point; and offered to bear the expense of building it. She was awaiting the answer of the Brethren; and of course nothing would be done in clearing the ground for any purpose till the answer had come. She felt now that if that reply was negative, she would herself build there a pleasure-house of her own.

Then she went to the edge of the cliff, and went down the zigzag by which the man and horse had gone to their gallant task. At the edge of the flat rock she sat and thought.

And through all her thoughts passed the rider who even now was thundering over the green sward on his way to her. In her fancy at first, and later in her ears, she could hear the sound of his sweeping gallop.

It was thus that a man should come to a woman!

She had no doubts now. Her quietude was a hymn of grateful praise!

The sound stopped. With all her ears she listened, her heart now beginning to beat furiously. The sea before her, all lines and furrows with the passing tide, was dark under the shadow of the cliff; and the edge of the shadow was marked with the golden hue of sunset.

And then she saw suddenly a pillar of shadow beyond the line of the cliff. It rested but a moment, moved swiftly along the edge, and then was lost to her eyes.

But to another sense there was greater comfort: she heard the clatter of rolling pebbles and the scramble of eager feet. Harold was hastening down the zigzag.

Oh! the music of that sound! It woke all the finer instincts of the woman. All the dross and thought of self passed away. Nature, sweet and simple and true, reigned alone. Instinctively she rose and came towards him. In the simple nobility of her self-surrender and her purpose, which were at one with the grandeur of nature around her, to be negative was to be false.

Since he had spoken with the Silver Lady Harold had swept through the air; the rush of his foaming horse over the sward had been but a slow physical progress, which mocked the on-sweep of his mind. In is rapid ride he too had been finding himself. By the reading of his own soul he knew now that love needs a voice; that a man's love, to be welcomed to the full, should be dominant and self-believing.

When the two saw each other's eyes there was no need for words. Harold came close, opening wide his arms, Stephen flew to them.

In that divine moment, when their mouths met, both knew that their souls were one.

THE LADY OF THE SHROUD

TO

MY DEAR OLD FRIEND

THE COMTESSE DE GUERBEL

(GENEVIÈVE WARD)

FROM "THE JOURNAL OF OCCULTISM" - MID-JANUARY, 1907.

A strange story comes from the Adriatic. It appears that on the night of the 9th, as the Italia Steamship Company's vessel "Victorine" was passing a little before midnight the point known as "the Spear of Ivan," on the coast of the Blue Mountains, the attention of the Captain, then on the bridge, was called by the look-out man to a tiny floating light close inshore. It is the custom of some South-going ships to run close to the Spear of Ivan in fine weather, as the water is deep, and there is no settled current; also there are no outlying rocks. Indeed, some years ago the local steamers had become accustomed to hug the shore here so closely that an intimation was sent from Lloyd's that any mischance under the circumstances would not be included in ordinary sea risks. Captain Mirolani is one of those who insist on a wholesome distance from the promontory being kept; but on his attention having been called to the circumstance reported, he thought it well to investigate it, as it might be some case of personal distress. Accordingly, he had the engines slowed down, and edged cautiously in towards shore. He was joined on the bridge by two of his officers, Signori Falamano and Destilia, and by one passenger on board, Mr. Peter Caulfield, whose reports of Spiritual Phenomena in remote places are well known to the readers of "The Journal of Occultism." The following account of the strange occurrence written by him, and attested by the signatures of Captain Mirolani and the other gentleman named, has been sent to us.

" . . . It was eleven minutes before twelve midnight on Saturday, the 9th day of January, 1907, when I saw the strange sight off the headland known as the Spear of Ivan on the coast of the Land of the Blue Mountains. It was a fine night, and I stood right on the bows of the ship, where there was nothing to obstruct my view. We were some distance from the Spear of Ivan, passing from northern to southern point of the wide bay into which it projects. Captain Mirolani, the Master, is a very careful seaman, and gives on his journeys a wide berth to the bay which is tabooed by Lloyd's. But when he saw in the moonlight, though far off, a tiny white figure of a woman drifting on some strange current in a small boat, on the prow of which rested a faint light (to me it looked like a corpse-candle!), he thought it might be some person in distress, and began to cautiously edge towards it. Two of his officers were with him on the bridge—Signori Falamano and Destilia. All these three, as well as myself, saw It. The rest of the crew and passengers were below. As we got close the true inwardness of It became apparent to me; but the mariners did not seem to realize till the very last. This is, after all, not strange, for none of them had either knowledge or experience in Occult matters, whereas for over thirty years I have made a special study of this subject, and have gone to and fro over the earth investigating to the nth all records of Spiritual Phenomena. As I could see from their movements that the officers did not comprehend that which was so apparent to myself, I took care not to enlighten them, lest such should result in the changing of the vessel's course before I should be near enough to make accurate observation. All turned out as I wished—at least, nearly so—as shall be seen. Being in the bow, I had, of course, a better view than from the bridge. Presently I made out that the boat, which had all along seemed to be of a queer shape, was none other than a *Coffin*, and that the woman standing up in it was clothed in a shroud. Her back was towards us, and she had evidently not heard our approach. As we were creeping along slowly, the engines were almost noiseless, and there was hardly a ripple as our fore-foot cut the dark water. Suddenly there was a wild cry from the bridge—Italians are certainly very excitable; hoarse commands were given to the Quartermaster at the wheel; the engine-room bell clanged. On the instant, as it seemed, the ship's head began to swing round to starboard; full steam ahead was in action, and before one could understand, the Apparition was fading in the distance. The last thing I saw was the flash of a white face with dark, burning eyes as the figure sank down into the coffin—just as mist or smoke disappears under a breeze."

BOOK I: THE WILL OF ROGER MELTON

THE READING OF THE WILL OF ROGER MELTON AND ALL THAT FOLLOWED

Record made by Ernest Roger Halbard Melton, law-student of the Inner Temple, eldest son of Ernest Halbard Melton, eldest son of Ernest Melton, elder brother of the said Roger Melton and his next of kin.

I consider it at least useful—perhaps necessary—to have a complete and accurate record of all pertaining to the Will of my late grand-uncle Roger Melton.

To which end let me put down the various members of his family, and explain some of their occupations and idiosyncrasies. My father, Ernest Halbard Melton, was the only son of Ernest Melton, eldest son of Sir Geoffrey Halbard Melton of Humcroft, in the shire of Salop, a Justice of the Peace, and at one time Sheriff. My great-grandfather, Sir Geoffrey, had inherited a small estate from his father, Roger Melton. In his time, by the way, the name was spelled Milton; but my great-great-grandfather changed the spelling to the later form, as he was a practical man not given to sentiment, and feared lest he should in the public eye be confused with others belonging to the family of a Radical person called Milton, who wrote poetry and was some sort of official in the time of Cromwell, whilst we are Conservatives. The same practical spirit which originated the change in the spelling of the family name inclined him to go into business. So he became, whilst still young, a tanner and leather-dresser. He utilized for the purpose the ponds and streams, and also the oak-woods on his estate—Torraby in Suffolk. He made a fine business, and accumulated a considerable fortune, with a part of which he purchased the Shropshire estate, which he entailed, and to which I am therefore heir-apparent.

Sir Geoffrey had, in addition to my grandfather, three sons and a daughter, the latter being born twenty years after her youngest brother. These sons were: Geoffrey, who died without issue, having been killed in the Indian Mutiny at Meerut in 1857, at which he took up a sword, though a civilian, to fight for his life; Roger (to whom I shall refer presently); and John—the latter, like Geoffrey, dying unmarried. Out of Sir Geoffrey's family of five, therefore, only three have to be considered: My grandfather, who had three children, two of whom, a son and a daughter, died young, leaving only my father, Roger and Patience. Patience, who was born in 1858, married an Irishman of the name of Sellenger—which was the usual way of pronouncing the name of St. Leger, or, as they spelled it, Sent Leger—restored by later generations to the still older form. He was a reckless, dare-devil sort of fellow, then a Captain in the Lancers, a man not without the quality of bravery—he won the Victoria Cross at the Battle of Amoaful in the Ashantee Campaign. But I fear he lacked the seriousness and steadfast strenuous purpose which my father always says marks the character of our own family. He ran through nearly all of his patrimony—never a very large one; and had it not been for my grand-aunt's little fortune, his days, had he lived, must have ended in comparative poverty. Comparative, not actual; for the Meltons, who are persons of considerable pride, would not have tolerated a poverty-stricken branch of the family. We don't think much of that lot—any of us.

Fortunately, my great-aunt Patience had only one child, and the premature decease of Captain St. Leger (as I prefer to call the name) did not allow of the possibility of her having more. She did not marry again, though my grandmother tried several times to arrange an alliance for her. She was, I am told, always a stiff, uppish person, who would not yield herself to the wisdom of her superiors. Her own child was a son, who seemed to take his character rather from his father's family than from my own. He was a wastrel and a rolling stone, always in scrapes at school, and always wanting to do ridiculous things. My father, as Head of the House and his own senior by eighteen years, tried often to admonish him; but his perversity of spirit and his truculence were such that he had to desist. Indeed, I have heard my father say that he sometimes threatened his life. A desperate character he was, and almost devoid of reverence. No one, not even my father, had any influence—good influence, of course, I mean—over him, except his mother, who was of my family; and also a woman who lived with her—a sort of governess—aunt, he called her. The way of it was this: Captain St. Leger had a younger brother, who made an improvident marriage with a Scotch girl when they were both very young. They had nothing to live on except what the reckless Lancer gave them, for he had next to nothing himself, and she was "bare"—which is, I understand, the indelicate Scottish way of expressing lack of fortune. She was, however, I understand, of an old and somewhat good family, though broken in fortune—to use an expression which, however, could hardly be used precisely in regard to a family or a person who never had fortune to be broken in! It was so far well that the MacKelpies—that was the maiden name of Mrs. St. Leger—were reputable—so far as fighting was concerned. It would have been too humiliating to have allied to our family, even on the distaff side, a family both poor and of no account. Fighting alone does not make a family, I think. Soldiers are not everything, though they think they are. We have had in our family men who fought; but I never heard of any of them who fought because they *wanted* to. Mrs. St. Leger had a sister; fortunately there were only those two children in the family, or else they would all have had to be supported by the money of my family.

Mr. St. Leger, who was only a subaltern, was killed at Maiwand; and his wife was left a beggar. Fortunately, however, she died—her sister spread a story that it was from the shock and grief—before the child which she expected was born. This all happened when my cousin—or, rather, my father's cousin, my first-cousin-once-removed, to be accurate—was still a very small child. His mother then sent for Miss MacKelpie, her brother-in-law's sister-in-law, to come and live with her, which she did—beggars can't be choosers; and she helped to bring up young St. Leger.

I remember once my father giving me a sovereign for making a witty remark about her. I was quite a boy then, not more than thirteen; but our family were always clever from the very beginning of life, and father was telling me about the St. Leger family. My family hadn't, of course, seen anything of them since Captain St. Leger died—the circle to which we belong don't care for poor relations—and was explaining where Miss MacKelpie came in. She must have been a sort of nursery governess, for Mrs. St. Leger once told him that she helped her to educate the child.

"Then, father," I said, "if she helped to educate the child she ought to have been called Miss MacSkelpie!"

When my first-cousin-once-removed, Rupert, was twelve years old, his mother died, and he was in the dolefuls about it for more than a year. Miss MacKelpie kept on living with him all the same. Catch her quitting! That sort don't go into the poor-house when they can keep out! My father, being Head of the Family, was, of course, one of the trustees, and his uncle Roger, brother of the testator, another. The third was General MacKelpie, a poverty-stricken Scotch laird who had a lot of valueless land at Croom, in Ross-shire. I remember father gave me a new ten-pound note when I interrupted him whilst he was telling me of the incident of young St. Leger's improvidence by remarking that he was in error as to the land. From what I had heard of MacKelpie's estate, it was productive of one thing; when he asked me "What?" I answered "Mortgages!" Father, I knew, had bought, not long before, a lot of them at what a college friend of mine from Chicago used to call "cut-throat" price. When I remonstrated with my father for buying them at all, and so injuring the family estate which I was to inherit, he gave me an answer, the astuteness of which I have never forgotten.

"I did it so that I might keep my hand on the bold General, in case he should ever prove troublesome. And if the worst should ever come to the worst, Croom is a good country for grouse and stags!" My father can see as far as most men!

When my cousin—I shall call him cousin henceforth in this record, lest it might seem to any unkind person who might hereafter read it that I wished to taunt Rupert St. Leger with his somewhat obscure position, in reiterating his real distance in kinship with my family—when my cousin, Rupert St. Leger, wished to commit a certain idiotic act of financial folly, he approached my father on the subject, arriving at our estate, Humcroft, at an inconvenient time, without permission, not having had even the decent courtesy to say he was coming. I was then a little chap of six years old, but I could not help noticing his mean appearance. He was all dusty and dishevelled. When my father saw him—I came into the study with him—he said in a horrified voice:

"Good God!" He was further shocked when the boy brusquely acknowledged, in reply to my father's greeting, that he had travelled third class. Of course, none of my family ever go anything but first class; even the servants go second. My father was really angry when he said he had walked up from the station.

"A nice spectacle for my tenants and my tradesmen! To see my—my—a kinsman of my house, howsoever remote, trudging like a tramp on the road to my estate! Why, my avenue is two miles and a perch! No wonder you are filthy and insolent!" Rupert—really, I cannot call him cousin here—was exceedingly impertinent to my father.

"I walked, sir, because I had no money; but I assure you I did not mean to be insolent. I simply came here because I wished to ask your advice and assistance, not because you are an important person, and have a long avenue—as I know to my cost—but simply because you are one of my trustees."

"*Your* trustees, sirrah!" said my father, interrupting him. "Your trustees?"

"I beg your pardon, sir," he said, quite quietly. "I meant the trustees of my dear mother's will."

"And what, may I ask you," said father, "do you want in the way of advice from one of the trustees of your dear mother's will?" Rupert got very red, and was going to say something rude—I knew it from his look—but he stopped, and said in the same gentle way:

"I want your advice, sir, as to the best way of doing something which I wish to do, and, as I am under age, cannot do myself. It must be done through the trustees of my mother's will."

"And the assistance for which you wish?" said father, putting his hand in his pocket. I know what that action means when I am talking to him.

"The assistance I want," said Rupert, getting redder than ever, "is from my—the trustee also. To carry out what I want to do."

"And what may that be?" asked my father. "I would like, sir, to make over to my Aunt Janet—" My father interrupted him by asking—he had evidently remembered my jest:

"Miss MacSkelpie?" Rupert got still redder, and I turned away; I didn't quite wish that he should see me laughing. He went on quietly:

"*MacKelpie*, sir! Miss Janet MacKelpie, my aunt, who has always been so kind to me, and whom my mother loved—I want to have made over to her the money which my dear mother left to me." Father doubtless wished to have the matter take a less serious turn, for Rupert's eyes were all shiny with tears which had not fallen; so after a little pause he said, with indignation, which I knew was simulated:

"Have you forgotten your mother so soon, Rupert, that you wish to give away the very last gift which she bestowed on you?" Rupert was sitting, but he jumped up and stood opposite my father with his fist clenched. He was quite pale now, and his eyes looked so fierce that I thought he would do my father an injury. He spoke in a voice which did not seem like his own, it was so strong and deep.

"Sir!" he roared out. I suppose, if I was a writer, which, thank God, I am not—I have no need to follow a menial occupation—I would call it "thundered." "Thundered" is a longer word than "roared," and would, of course, help to gain the penny which a writer gets for a line. Father got pale too, and stood quite still. Rupert looked at him steadily for quite half a minute—it seemed longer at the time—and suddenly smiled and said, as he sat down again:

"Sorry. But, of course, you don't understand such things." Then he went on talking before father had time to say a word.

"Let us get back to business. As you do not seem to follow me, let me explain that it is *because* I do not forget that I wish to do this. I remember my dear mother's wish to make Aunt Janet happy, and would like to do as she did."

"*Aunt* Janet?" said father, very properly sneering at his ignorance. "She is not your aunt. Why, even her sister, who was married to your uncle, was only your aunt by courtesy." I could not help feeling that Rupert meant to be rude to my father, though his words were quite polite. If I had been as much bigger than him as he was than me, I should have flown at him; but he was a very big boy for his age. I am myself rather thin. Mother says thinness is an "appanage of birth."

"My Aunt Janet, sir, is an aunt by love. Courtesy is a small word to use in connection with such devotion as she has given to us. But I needn't trouble you with such things, sir. I take it that my relations on the side of my own house do not affect you. I am a Sent Leger!" Father looked quite taken aback. He sat quite still before he spoke.

"Well, Mr. St. Leger, I shall think over the matter for a while, and shall presently let you know my decision. In the meantime, would you like something to eat? I take it that as you must have started very early, you have not had any breakfast?" Rupert smiled quite genially:

"That is true, sir. I haven't broken bread since dinner last night, and I am ravenously hungry." Father rang the bell, and told the footman who answered it to send the housekeeper. When she came, father said to her:

"Mrs. Martindale, take this boy to your room and give him some breakfast." Rupert stood very still for some seconds. His face had got red again after his paleness. Then he bowed to my father, and followed Mrs. Martindale, who had moved to the door.

Nearly an hour afterwards my father sent a servant to tell him to come to the study. My mother was there, too, and I had gone back with her. The man came back and said:

"Mrs. Martindale, sir, wishes to know, with her respectful service, if she may have a word with you." Before father could reply mother told him to bring her. The housekeeper could not have been far off—that kind are generally near a keyhole—for she came at once. When she came in, she stood at the door curtseying and looking pale. Father said:

"Well?"

"I thought, sir and ma'am, that I had better come and tell you about Master Sent Leger. I would have come at once, but I feared to disturb you."

"Well?" Father had a stern way with servants. When I'm head of the family I'll tread them under my feet. That's the way to get real devotion from servants!

"If you please, sir, I took the young gentleman into my room and ordered a nice breakfast for him, for I could see he was half famished—a growing boy like him, and so tall! Presently it came along. It was a good breakfast, too! The very smell of it made even me hungry. There were eggs and frizzled ham, and grilled kidneys, and coffee, and buttered toast, and bloater-paste—"

"That will do as to the menu," said mother. "Go on!"

"When it was all ready, and the maid had gone, I put a chair to the table and said, 'Now, sir, your breakfast is ready!' He stood up and said, 'Thank you, madam; you are very kind!' and he bowed to me quite nicely, just as if I was a lady, ma'am!"

"Go on," said mother.

"Then, sir, he held out his hand and said, 'Good-bye, and thank you,' and he took up his cap.

"'But aren't you going to have any breakfast, sir?' I says.

"'No, thank you, madam,' he said; 'I couldn't eat here . . . in this house, I mean!' Well, ma'am, he looked so lonely that I felt my heart melting, and I ventured to ask him if there was any mortal thing I could do for him. 'Do tell me, dear,' I ventured to say. 'I am an old woman, and you, sir, are only a boy, though it's a fine man you will be—like your dear, splendid father, which I remember so well, and gentle like your poor dear mother.'

"'You're a dear!' he says; and with that I took up his hand and kissed it, for I remember his poor dear mother so well, that was dead only a year. Well, with that he turned his head away, and when I took him by the shoulders and turned him round—he is only a young boy, ma'am, for all he is so big—I saw that the tears were rolling down his cheeks. With that I laid his head on my breast—I've had children of my own, ma'am, as you know, though they're all gone. He came willing enough, and sobbed for a little bit. Then he straightened himself up, and I stood respectfully beside him.

"'Tell Mr. Melton,' he said, 'that I shall not trouble him about the trustee business.'

"'But won't you tell him yourself, sir, when you see him?' I says.

"'I shall not see him again,' he says; 'I am going back now!'

"Well, ma'am, I knew he'd had no breakfast, though he was hungry, and that he would walk as he come, so I ventured to say: 'If you won't take it a liberty, sir, may I do anything to make your going easier? Have you sufficient money, sir? If not, may I give, or lend, you some? I shall be very proud if you will allow me to.'

"'Yes,' he says quite hearty. 'If you will, you might lend me a shilling, as I have no money. I shall not forget it.' He said, as he took the coin: 'I shall return the amount, though I never can the kindness. I shall keep the coin.' He took the shilling, sir—he wouldn't take any more—and then he said good-bye. At the door he turned and walked back to me, and put his arms round me like a real boy does, and gave me a hug, and says he:

"'Thank you a thousand times, Mrs. Martindale, for your goodness to me, for your sympathy, and for the way you have spoken of my father and mother. You have seen me cry, Mrs. Martindale,' he said; 'I don't often cry: the last time was when I came back to the lonely house after my poor dear was laid to rest. But you nor any other shall ever see a tear of mine again.' And with that he straightened out his big back and held up his fine proud head, and walked out. I saw him from the window striding down the avenue. My! but he is a proud boy, sir—an honour to your family, sir, say I respectfully. And there, the proud child has gone away hungry, and he won't, I know, ever use that shilling to buy food!"

Father was not going to have that, you know, so he said to her:

"He does not belong to my family, I would have you to know. True, he is allied to us through the female side; but we do not count him or his in my family." He turned away and began to read a book. It was a decided snub to her.

But mother had a word to say before Mrs. Martindale was done with. Mother has a pride of her own, and doesn't brook insolence from inferiors; and the housekeeper's conduct seemed to be rather presuming. Mother, of course, isn't quite our class, though her folk are quite worthy and enormously rich. She is one of the Dalmallingtons, the salt people, one of whom got a peerage when the Conservatives went out. She said to the housekeeper:

"I think, Mrs. Martindale, that I shall not require your services after this day month! And as I don't keep servants in my employment when I dismiss them, here is your month's wages due on the 25th of this month, and another month in lieu of notice. Sign this receipt." She was writing a receipt as she spoke. The other signed it without a word, and handed it to her. She seemed quite flabbergasted. Mother got up and sailed—that is the way that mother moves when she is in a wax—out of the room.

Lest I should forget it, let me say here that the dismissed housekeeper was engaged the very next day by the Countess of Salop. I may say in explanation that the Earl of Salop, K.G., who is Lord-Lieutenant of the County, is jealous of father's position and his growing influence. Father is going to contest the next election on the Conservative side, and is sure to be made a Baronet before long.

Letter from Major-General Sir Colin Alexander MacKelpie, V.C., K.C.B., of Croom, Ross, N.B., to Rupert Sent Leger, Esq., 14, Newland Park, Dulwich, London, S.E.

July 4, 1892.

MY DEAR GODSON,

I am truly sorry I am unable to agree with your request that I should acquiesce in your desire to transfer to Miss Janet MacKelpie the property bequeathed to you by your mother, of which property I am a trustee. Let me say at once that, had it been possible to me to do so, I should have held it a privilege to further such a wish—not because the beneficiare whom you would create is a near kinswoman of my own. That, in truth, is my real difficulty. I have undertaken a trust made by an honourable lady on behalf of her only son—son of a man of stainless honour, and a dear friend of my own, and whose son has a rich heritage of honour from both parents, and who will, I am sure, like to look back on his whole life as worthy of his parents, and of those whom his parents trusted. You will see, I am sure, that whatsoever I might grant regarding anyone else, my hands are tied in this matter.

And now let me say, my dear boy, that your letter has given me the most intense pleasure. It is an unspeakable delight to me to find in the son of your father—a man whom I loved, and a boy whom I love—the same generosity of spirit which endeared your father to all his comrades, old as well as young. Come what may, I shall always be proud of you; and if the sword of an old soldier—it is all I have—can ever serve you in any way, it and its master's life are, and shall be, whilst life remains to him, yours.

It grieves me to think that Janet cannot, through my act, be given that ease and tranquillity of spirit which come from competence. But, my dear Rupert, you will be of full age in seven years more. Then, if you are in the same mind—and I am sure you will not change—you, being your own master, can do freely as you will. In the meantime, to secure, so far as I can, my dear Janet against any malign stroke of fortune, I have given orders to my factor to remit semi-annually to Janet one full half of such income as may be derived in any form from my estate of Croom. It is, I am sorry to say, heavily mortgaged; but of such as is—or may be, free from such charge as the mortgage entails—something at least will, I trust, remain to her. And, my dear boy, I can frankly say that it is to me a real pleasure that you and I can be linked in one more bond in this association of purpose. I have always held you in my heart as though you were my own son. Let me tell you now that you have acted as I should have liked a son of my own, had I been blessed with one, to have acted. God bless you, my dear.

Yours ever,
COLIN ALEX. MACKELPIE.

Letter from Roger Melton, of Openshaw Grange, to Rupert Sent Leger, Esq., 14, Newland Park, Dulwich, London, S.E.

July 1, 1892.

MY DEAR NEPHEW,

Your letter of the 30th ult. received. Have carefully considered matter stated, and have come to the conclusion that my duty as a trustee would not allow me to give full consent, as you wish. Let me explain. The testator, in making her will, intended that such fortune as she had at disposal should be used to supply to you her son such benefits as its annual product should procure. To this end, and to provide against wastefulness or foolishness on your part, or, indeed, against any generosity, howsoever worthy, which might impoverish you and so defeat her benevolent intentions regarding your education, comfort, and future good, she did not place the estate directly in your hands, leaving you to do as you might feel inclined about it. But, on the contrary, she entrusted the corpus of it in the hands of men whom she believed should be resolute enough and strong enough to carry out her intent, even against any cajolements or pressure which might be employed to the contrary. It being her intention, then, that such trustees as she appointed would use for your benefit the interest accruing annually from the capital at command, *and that only* (as specifically directed in the will), so that on your arriving at full age the capital entrusted to us should be handed over to you intact, I find a hard-and-fast duty in the matter of adhering exactly to the directions given. I have no doubt that my co-trustees regard the matter in exactly the same light. Under the circumstances, therefore, we, the trustees, have not only a single and united duty towards you as the object of the testator's wishes, but towards each other as regards the manner of the carrying out of that duty. I take it, therefore, that it would not be consonant with the spirit of the trust or of our own ideas in accepting it that any of us should take a course pleasant to himself which would or might involve a stern opposition on the part of other of the co-trustees. We have each of us to do the unpleasant part of this duty without fear or favour. You understand, of course, that the time which must elapse before you come into absolute possession of your estate is a limited one. As by the terms of the will we are to hand over our trust when you have reached the age of twenty-one, there are only seven years to expire. But till then, though I should gladly meet your wishes if I could, I must adhere to the duty which I have undertaken. At the expiration of that period you will be quite free to divest yourself of your estate without protest or comment of any man.

Having now expressed as clearly as I can the limitations by which I am bound with regard to the corpus of your estate, let me say that in any other way which is in my power or discretion I shall be most happy to see your wishes carried out so far as rests with me. Indeed, I shall undertake to use what influence I may possess with my co-trustees to induce them to take a similar view of your wishes. In my own thinking you are quite free to use your own property in your own way. But as, until you shall have attained your majority, you have only life-user in your mother's bequest, you are only at liberty to deal with the annual increment. On our part as trustees we have a first charge on that increment to be used for purposes of your maintenance, clothes, and education. As to what may remain over each half-year, you will be free to deal with it as you choose. On receiving from you a written authorization to your trustees, if you desire the whole sum or any part of it to be paid over to Miss Janet MacKelpie, I shall see that it is effected. Believe me, that our duty is to protect the corpus of the estate, and to this end we may not act on any instruction to imperil it. But there our warranty stops. We can deal during our trusteeship with the corpus only. Further, lest there should arise any error on your part, we can deal with any general instruction for only so long as it may remain unrevoked. You are, and must be, free to alter your instructions or authorizations at any time. Thus your latest document must be used for our guidance.

As to the general principle involved in your wish I make no comment. You are at liberty to deal with your own how you will. I quite understand that your impulse is a generous one, and I fully believe that it is in consonance with what had always been the wishes of my sister. Had she been happily alive and had to give judgment of your intent, I am convinced that she would have approved. Therefore, my dear nephew, should you so wish, I shall be happy for her sake as well as your own to pay over on your account (as a confidential matter between you and me), but from my own pocket, a sum equal to that which you wish transferred to Miss Janet MacKelpie. On hearing from you I shall know how to act in the matter. With all good wishes,

Believe me to be,
Your affectionate uncle,
ROGER MELTON.

TO RUPERT SENT LEGER, ESQ.

Letter from Rupert Sent Leger to Roger Melton,

July 5, 1892.

MY DEAR UNCLE,

Thank you heartily for your kind letter. I quite understand, and now see that I should not have asked you as a trustee, such a thing. I see your duty clearly, and agree with your view of it. I enclose a letter directed to my trustees, asking them to pay over annually till further direction to Miss Janet MacKelpie at this address whatever sum may remain over from the interest of my mother's bequest after deduction of such expenses as you may deem fit for my maintenance, clothing, and education, together with a sum of one pound sterling per month, which was the amount my dear mother always gave me for my personal use—"pocket-money," she called it.

With regard to your most kind and generous offer to give to my dear Aunt Janet the sum which I would have given myself, had such been in my power, I thank you most truly and sincerely, both for my dear aunt (to whom, of course, I shall not mention the matter unless you specially authorize me) and myself. But, indeed, I think it will be better not to offer it. Aunt Janet is very proud, and would not accept any benefit. With me, of course, it is different, for since I was a wee child she has been like another mother to me, and I love her very much. Since my mother died—and she, of course, was all-in-all to me—there has been no other. And in such a love as ours pride has no place. Thank you again, dear uncle, and God bless you.

Your loving nephew,
RUPERT SENT LEGER.

ERNEST ROGER HALBARD MELTON'S RECORD—*Continued.*

And now *re* the remaining one of Sir Geoffrey's children, Roger. He was the third child and third son, the only daughter, Patience, having been born twenty years after the last of the four sons. Concerning Roger, I shall put down all I have heard of him from my father and grandfather. From my grand-aunt I heard nothing, I was a very small kid when she died; but I remember seeing her, but only once. A very tall, handsome woman of a little over thirty, with very dark hair and light-coloured eyes. I think they were either grey or blue, but I can't remember which. She looked very proud and haughty, but I am bound to say that she was very nice to me. I remember feeling very jealous of Rupert because his mother looked so distinguished. Rupert was eight years older than me, and I was afraid he would beat me if I said anything he did not like. So I was silent except when I forgot to be, and Rupert said very unkindly, and I think very unfairly, that I was "A sulky little beast." I haven't forgot that, and I don't mean to. However, it doesn't matter much what he said or thought. There he is—if he is at all—where no one can find him, with no money or nothing, for what little he had he settled when he came of age, on the MacSkelpie. He wanted to give it to her when his mother died, but father, who was a trustee, refused; and Uncle Roger, as I call him, who is another, thought the trustees had no power to allow Rupert to throw away his matrimony, as I called it, making a joke to father when he called it patrimony. Old Sir Colin MacSkelpie, who is the third, said he couldn't take any part in such a permission, as the MacSkelpie was his niece. He is a rude old man, that. I remember when, not remembering his relationship, I spoke of the MacSkelpie, he caught me a clip on the ear that sent me across the room. His Scotch is very broad. I can hear him say, "Hae some attempt at even Soothern manners, and dinna misca' yer betters, ye young puddock, or I'll wring yer snoot!" Father was, I could see, very much offended, but he didn't say anything. He remembered, I think, that the General is a V.C. man, and was fond of fighting duels. But to show that the fault was not his, *he* wrung *my* ear—and the same ear too! I suppose he thought that was justice! But it's only right to say that he made up for it afterwards. When the General had gone he gave me a five-pound note.

I don't think Uncle Roger was very pleased with the way Rupert behaved about the legacy, for I don't think he ever saw him from that day to this. Perhaps, of course, it was because Rupert ran away shortly afterwards; but I shall tell about that when I come to him. After all, why should my uncle bother about him? He is not a Melton at all, and I am to be Head of the House—of course, when the Lord thinks right to take father to Himself! Uncle Roger has tons of money, and he never married, so if he wants to leave it in the right direction he needn't have any trouble. He made his money in what he calls "the Eastern Trade." This, so far as I can gather, takes in the Levant and all east of it. I know he has what they call in trade "houses" in all sorts of places—Turkey, and Greece, and all round them, Morocco, Egypt, and Southern Russia, and the Holy Land; then on to Persia, India, and all round it; the Chersonese, China, Japan, and the Pacific Islands. It is not to be expected that we landowners can know much about trade, but my uncle covers—or alas! I must say "covered"—a lot of ground, I can tell you. Uncle Roger was a very grim sort of man, and only that I was brought up to try and be kind to him I shouldn't ever have dared to speak to him. But when was a child father and mother—especially mother—forced me to go and see him and be affectionate to him. He wasn't ever even civil to me, that I can remember—grumpy old bear! But, then, he never saw Rupert at all, so that I take it Master R--- is out of the running altogether for testamentary honours. The last time I saw him myself he was distinctly rude. He treated me as a boy, though I was getting on for eighteen years of age. I came into his office without knocking; and without looking up from his desk, where he was writing, he said: "Get out! Why do you venture to disturb me when I'm busy? Get out, and be damned to you!" I waited where I was, ready to transfix him with my eye when he should look up, for I cannot forget that when my father dies I shall be Head of my House. But when he did there was no transfixing possible. He said quite coolly:

"Oh, it's you, is it? I thought it was one of my office boys. Sit down, if you want to see me, and wait till I am ready." So I sat down and waited. Father always said that I should try to conciliate and please my uncle. Father is a very shrewd man, and Uncle Roger is a very rich one.

But I don't think Uncle R--- is as shrewd as he thinks he is. He sometimes makes awful mistakes in business. For instance, some years ago he bought an enormous estate on the Adriatic, in the country they call the "Land of Blue Mountains." At least, he says he bought it. He told father so in confidence. But he didn't show any title-deeds, and I'm greatly afraid he was "had." A bad job for me that he was, for father believes he paid an enormous sum for it, and as I am his natural heir, it reduces his available estate to so much less.

And now about Rupert. As I have said, he ran away when he was about fourteen, and we did not hear about him for years. When we—or, rather, my father—did hear of him, it was no good that he heard. He had gone as a cabin-boy on a sailing ship round the Horn. Then he joined an exploring party through the centre of Patagonia, and then another up in Alaska, and a third to the Aleutian Islands. After that he went through Central America, and then to Western Africa, the Pacific Islands, India, and a lot of places. We all know the wisdom of the adage that "A rolling stone gathers no moss"; and certainly, if there be any value in moss, Cousin Rupert will die a poor man. Indeed, nothing will stand his idiotic, boastful wastefulness. Look at the way in which, when he came of age, he made over all his mother's little fortune to the MacSkelpie! I am sure that, though Uncle Roger made no comment to my father, who, as Head of our House, should, of course, have been informed, he was not pleased. My mother, who has a good fortune in her own right, and has had the sense to keep it in her own control—as I am to inherit it, and it is not in the entail, I am therefore quite impartial—I can approve of her spirited conduct in the matter. We never did think much of Rupert, anyhow; but now, since he is in the way to be a pauper, and therefore a dangerous nuisance, we look on him as quite an outsider. We know what he really is. For my own part, I loathe and despise him. Just now we are irritated with him, for we are all kept on tenterhooks regarding my dear Uncle Roger's Will. For Mr. Trent, the attorney who regulated my dear uncle's affairs and has possession of the Will, says it is necessary to know where every possible beneficiary is to be found before making the Will public, so we all have to wait. It is especially hard on me, who am the natural heir. It is very thoughtless indeed of Rupert to keep away like that. I wrote to old MacSkelpie about it, but he didn't seem to understand or to be at all anxious—he is not the heir! He said that probably Rupert Sent Leger—he, too, keeps to the old spelling—did not know of his uncle's death, or he would have taken steps to relieve our anxiety. Our anxiety, forsooth! We are not anxious; we only wish to *know*. And if we—and especially me—who have all the annoyance of thinking of the detestable and unfair death-duties, are anxious, we should be so. Well, anyhow, he'll get a properly bitter disappointment and set down when he does turn up and discovers that he is a pauper without hope!

* * * * *

To-day we (father and I) had letters from Mr. Trent, telling us that the whereabouts of "Mr. Rupert Sent Leger" had been discovered, and that a letter disclosing the fact of poor Uncle Roger's death had been sent to him. He was at Titicaca when last heard of. So goodness only knows when he may get the letter, which "asks him to come home at once, but only gives to him such information about the Will as has already been given to every member of the testator's family." And that is nil. I dare say we shall be kept waiting for months before we get hold of the estate which is ours. It is too bad!

Letter from Edward Bingham Trent to Ernest Roger Halbard Melton.

176, LINCOLN'S INN FIELDS,
December 28, 1906.

DEAR SIR,

I am glad to be able to inform you that I have just heard by letter from Mr. Rupert St. Leger that he intended leaving Rio de Janeiro by the S.S. *Amazon*, of the Royal Mail Company, on December 15. He further stated that he would cable just before leaving Rio de Janeiro, to say on what day the ship was expected to arrive in London. As all the others possibly interested in the Will of the late Roger Melton, and whose names are given to me in his instructions regarding the reading of the Will, have been advised, and have expressed their intention of being present at that event on being apprised of the time and place, I now beg to inform you that by cable message received the date scheduled for arrival at the Port of London was January 1 prox. I therefore beg to notify you, subject to postponement due to the non-arrival of the *Amazon*, the reading of the Will of the late Roger Melton, Esq., will take place in my office on Thursday, January 3 prox., at eleven o'clock a.m.

I have the honour to be, sir,
Yours faithfully,
EDWARD BINGHAM TRENT.
TO ERNEST ROGER HALBARD MELTON, ESQ.,
HUMCROFT,
SALOP.

Cable: Rupert Sent Leger to Edward Bingham Trent.

Amazon arrives London January 1. SENT LEGER.

Telegram (per Lloyd's): Rupert Sent Leger to Edward Bingham Trent.

THE LIZARD,
December 31.

Amazon arrives London to-morrow morning. All well.—LEGER.

Telegram: Edward Bingham Trent to Ernest Roger Halbard Mellon.

Rupert Sent Leger arrived. Reading Will takes place as arranged.—TRENT.

ERNEST ROGER HALBARD MELTON'S RECORD.

January 4, 1907.

The reading of Uncle Roger's Will is over. Father got a duplicate of Mr. Trent's letter to me, and of the cable and two telegrams pasted into this Record. We both waited patiently till the third—that is, we did not say anything. The only impatient member of our family was my mother. She *did* say things, and if old Trent had been here his ears would have been red. She said what ridiculous nonsense it was delaying the reading of the Will, and keeping the Heir waiting for the arrival of an obscure person who wasn't even a member of the family, inasmuch as he didn't bear the name. I don't think it's quite respectful to one who is some day to be Head of the House! I thought father was weakening in his patience when he said: "True, my dear—true!" and got up and left the room. Some time afterwards when I passed the library I heard him walking up and down.

Father and I went up to town on the afternoon of Wednesday, January 2. We stayed, of course, at Claridge's, where we always stay when we go to town. Mother wanted to come, too, but father thought it better not. She would not agree to stay at home till we both promised to send her separate telegrams after the reading.

At five minutes to eleven we entered Mr. Trent's office. Father would not go a moment earlier, as he said it was bad form to seem eager at any time, but most of all at the reading of a will. It was a rotten grind, for we had to be walking all over the neighbourhood for half an hour before it was time, not to be too early.

When we went into the room we found there General Sir Colin MacKelpie and a big man, very bronzed, whom I took to be Rupert St. Leger—not a very creditable connection to look at, I thought! He and old MacKelpie took care to be in time! Rather low, I thought it. Mr. St. Leger was reading a letter. He had evidently come in but lately, for though he seemed to be eager about it, he was only at the first page, and I could see that there were many sheets. He did not look up when we came in, or till he had finished the letter; and you may be sure that neither I nor my father (who, as Head of the House, should have had more respect from him) took the trouble to go to him. After all, he is a pauper and a wastrel, and he has not the honour of bearing our Name. The General, however, came forward and greeted us both cordially. He evidently had forgotten—or pretended to have—the discourteous way he once treated me, for he spoke to me quite in a friendly way—I thought more warmly than he did to father. I was pleased to be spoken to so nicely, for, after all, whatever his manners may be, he is a distinguished man—has won the V.C. and a Baronetcy. He got the latter not long ago, after the Frontier War in India. I was not, however, led away into cordiality myself. I had not forgotten his rudeness, and I thought that he might be sucking up to me. I knew that when I had my dear Uncle Roger's many millions I should be a rather important person; and, of course, he knew it too. So I got even with him for his former impudence. When he held out his hand I put one finger in it, and said, "How do?" He got very red and turned away. Father and he had ended by glaring at each other, so neither of us was sorry to be done with him. All the time Mr. St. Leger did not seem to see or hear anything, but went on reading his letter. I thought the old MacSkelpie was going to bring him into the matter between us, for as he turned away I heard him say something under his breath. It sounded like "Help!" but Mr. S--- did not hear. He certainly no notice of it.

As the MacS--- and Mr. S--- sat quite silent, neither looking at us, and as father was sitting on the other side of the room with his chin in his hand, and as I wanted to show that I was indifferent to the two S's, I took out this notebook, and went on with the Record, bringing it up to this moment.

THE RECORD—*Continued.*

When I had finished writing I looked over at Rupert.

When he saw us, he jumped up and went over to father and shook his hand quite warmly. Father took him very coolly. Rupert, however, did not seem to see it, but came towards me heartily. I happened to be doing something else at the moment, and at first I did not see his hand; but just as I was looking at it the clock struck eleven. Whilst it was striking Mr. Trent came into the room. Close behind him came his clerk, carrying a locked tin box. There were two other men also. He bowed to us all in turn, beginning with me. I was standing opposite the door; the others were scattered about. Father sat still, but Sir Colin and Mr. St. Leger rose. Mr. Trent not did shake hands with any of us—not even me. Nothing but his respectful bow. That is the etiquette for an attorney, I understand, on such formal occasions.

He sat down at the end of the big table in the centre of the room, and asked us to sit round. Father, of course, as Head of the Family, took the seat at his right hand. Sir Colin and St. Leger went to the other side, the former taking the seat next to the attorney. The General knows, of course, that a Baronet takes precedence at a ceremony. I may be a Baronet some day myself, and have to know these things.

The clerk took the key which his master handed to him, opened the tin box, and took from it a bundle of papers tied with red tape. This he placed before the attorney, and put the empty box behind him on the floor. Then he and the other man sat at the far end of the table; the latter took out a big notebook and several pencils, and put them before him. He was evidently a shorthand-writer. Mr. Trent removed the tape from the bundle of papers, which he placed a little distance in front of him. He took a sealed envelope from the top, broke the seal, opened the envelope, and from it took a parchment, in the folds of which were some sealed envelopes, which he laid in a heap in front of the other paper. Then he unfolded the parchment, and laid it before him with the outside page up. He fixed his glasses, and said:

"Gentlemen, the sealed envelope which you have seen me open is endorsed 'My Last Will and Testament—ROGER MELTON, *June*, 1906.' This document"—holding it up—"is as follows:

> "'I Roger Melton of Openshaw Grange in the County of Dorset; of number one hundred and twenty-three Berkeley Square London; and of the Castle of Vissarion in the Land of the Blue Mountains, being of sound mind do make this my Last Will and Testament on this day Monday the eleventh day of the month of June in the year of Our Lord one

thousand nine hundred and six at the office of my old friend and Attorney Edward Bingham Trent in number one hundred and seventy-six Lincoln's Inn Fields London hereby revoking all other wills that I may have formerly made and giving this as my sole and last Will making dispositions of my property as follows:

"'1. To my kinsman and nephew Ernest Halbard Melton Esquire, justice of the Peace, Humcroft the County of Salop, for his sole use and benefit the sum of twenty thousand pounds sterling free of all Duties Taxes and charges whatever to be paid out of my Five per centum Bonds of the City of Montreal, Canada.

"'2. To my respected friend and colleague as co-trustee to the Will of my late sister Patience late widow of the late Captain Rupert Sent Leger who predeceased her, Major-General Sir Colin Alexander MacKelpie, Baronet, holder of the Victoria Cross, Knight Commander of the Order of the Bath, of Croom in the county of Ross Scotland a sum of Twenty thousand pounds sterling free of all Taxes and charges whatsoever; to be paid out of my Five per centum Bonds of the City of Toronto, Canada.

"'3. To Miss Janet MacKelpie presently residing at Croom in the County of Ross Scotland the sum of Twenty thousand pounds sterling free of all Duties Taxes and Charges whatsoever, to be paid out of my Five per centum Bonds of the London County Council.

"'4. To the various persons charities and Trustees named in the schedule attached to this Will and marked A. the various sums mentioned therein, all free of Duties and Taxes and charges whatsoever.'"

Here Mr. Trent read out the list here following, and announced for our immediate understanding of the situation the total amount as two hundred and fifty thousand pounds. Many of the beneficiaries were old friends, comrades, dependents, and servants, some of them being left quite large sums of money and specific objects, such as curios and pictures.

"'5. To my kinsman and nephew Ernest Roger Halbard Melton presently living in the house of his father at Humcroft Salop the sum of Ten thousand pounds sterling.

"'6. To my old and valued friend Edward Bingham Trent of one hundred and seventy-six Lincoln's Inn Fields sum of Twenty thousand pounds sterling free from all Duties Taxes and Charges whatsoever to be paid out of my Five per centum Bonds of the city of Manchester England.

"'7. To my dear nephew Rupert Sent Leger only son of my dear sister Patience Melton by her marriage with Captain Rupert Sent Leger the sum of one thousand pounds sterling. I also bequeath to the said Rupert Sent Leger a further sum conditional upon his acceptance of the terms of a letter addressed to him marked B, and left in the custody of the above Edward Bingham Trent and which letter is an integral part of this my Will. In case of the non-acceptance of the conditions of such letter, I devise and bequeath the whole of the sums and properties reserved therein to the executors herein appointed Colin Alexander MacKelpie and Edward Bingham Trent in trust to distribute the same in accordance with the terms of the letter in the present custody of Edward Bingham Trent marked C, and now deposited sealed with my seal in the sealed envelope containing my last Will to be kept in the custody of the said Edward Bingham Trent and which said letter C is also an integral part of my Will. And in case any doubt should arise as to my ultimate intention as to the disposal of my property the above-mentioned Executors are to have full power to arrange and dispose all such matters as may seem best to them without further appeal. And if any beneficiary under this Will shall challenge the same or any part of it, or dispute the validity thereof, he shall forfeit to the general estate the bequest made herein to him, and any such bequest shall cease and be void to all intents and purposes whatsoever.

"'8. For proper compliance with laws and duties connected with testamentary proceedings and to keep my secret trusts secret I direct my Executors to pay all Death, Estate, Settlement, Legacy, Succession, or other duties charges impositions and assessments whatever on the residue of my estate beyond the bequests already named, at the scale charged in the case of most distant relatives or strangers in blood.

"'9. I hereby appoint as my Executors Major-General Sir Colin Alexander MacKelpie, Baronet, of Croom in the County of Ross, and Edward Bingham Trent Attorney at Law of one hundred and seventy-six Lincoln's Inn Fields London West Central with full power to exercise their discretion in any circumstance which may arise in the carrying out my wishes as expressed in this Will. As reward for their services in this capacity as Executors they are to receive each out of the general estate a sum of one hundred thousand pounds sterling free of all Duties and impositions whatsoever.

"12. The two Memoranda contained in the letters marked B and C are Integral Parts of this my Last Will are ultimately at the Probate of the Will to be taken as Clauses 10 and 11 of it. The envelopes are marked B and C on both envelope and contents and the contents of each is headed thus: B to be read as Clause 10 of my Will and the other C to be read as Clause 11 of my Will.

"13. Should either of the above-mentioned Executors die before the completion of the above year and a half from the date of the Reading of my Will or before the Conditions rehearsed in Letter C the remaining Executor shall have all and several the Rights and Duties entrusted by my Will to both. And if both Executors should die then the matter of interpretation and execution of all matters in connection with this my Last Will shall rest with the Lord Chancellor of England for the time being or with whomsoever he may appoint for the purpose.

"'This my Last Will is given by me on the first day of January in the year of Our Lord one thousand nine hundred and seven.

"'ROGER MELTON.

"We Andrew Rossiter and John Colson here in the presence of each other and of the Testator have seen the Testator Roger Melton sign and seal this document. In witness thereof we hereby set our names

"'ANDREW ROSSITER clerk of 9 Primrose Avenue London W.C.

"'JOHN COLSON caretaker of 176 Lincoln's Inn Fields and Verger of St. Tabitha's Church Clerkenwell London.'"

When Mr. Trent had finished the reading he put all the papers together, and tied them up in a bundle again with the red tape. Holding the bundle in his hand, he stood up, saying as he did so:

"That is all, gentlemen, unless any of you wish to ask me any questions; in which case I shall answer, of course, to the best of my power. I shall ask you, Sir Colin, to remain with me, as we have to deal with some matters, or to arrange a time when we may meet to do so. And you also, Mr. Sent Leger, as there is this letter to submit to you. It is necessary that you should open it in the presence of the executors, but there is no necessity that anyone else should be present."

The first to speak was my father. Of course, as a county gentleman of position and estate, who is sometimes asked to take the chair at Sessions—of course, when there is not anyone with a title present—he found himself under the duty of expressing himself first. Old MacKelpie has superior rank; but this was a family affair, in which my father is Head of the House, whilst old MacKelpie is only an outsider brought into it—and then only to the distaff side, by the wife of a younger brother of the man who married into our family. Father spoke with the same look on his face as when he asks important questions of witnesses at Quarter Sessions.

"I should like some points elucidated." The attorney bowed (he gets his 120 thou', any way, so he can afford to be oily—suave, I suppose he would call it); so father looked at a slip of paper in his hand and asked:

"How much is the amount of the whole estate?"

The attorney answered quickly, and I thought rather rudely. He was red in the face, and didn't bow this time; I suppose a man of his class hasn't more than a very limited stock of manners:

"That, sir, I am not at liberty to tell you. And I may say that I would not if I could."

"Is it a million?" said father again. He was angry this time, and even redder than the old attorney. The attorney said in answer, very quietly this time:

"Ah, that's cross-examining. Let me say, sir, that no one can know that until the accountants to be appointed for the purpose have examined the affairs of the testator up to date."

Mr. Rupert St. Leger, who was looking all this time angrier than even the attorney or my father—though at what he had to be angry about I can't imagine—struck his fist on the table and rose up as if to speak, but as he caught sight of both old MacKelpie and the attorney he sat down again. *Mem.*—Those three seem to agree too well. I must keep a sharp eye on them. I didn't think of this part any more at the time, for father asked another question which interested me much:

"May I ask why the other matters of the Will are not shown to us?" The attorney wiped his spectacles carefully with a big silk bandanna handkerchief before he answered:

"Simply because each of the two letters marked 'B' and 'C' is enclosed with instructions regarding their opening and the keeping secret of their contents. I shall call your attention to the fact that both envelopes are sealed, and that the testator and both witnesses have signed their names across the flap of each envelope. I shall read them. The letter marked 'B,' directed to 'Rupert Sent Leger,' is thus endorsed:

> "'This letter is to be given to Rupert Sent Leger by the Trustees and is to be opened by him in their presence. He is to take such copy or make such notes as he may wish and is then to hand the letter with envelope to the Executors who are at once to read it, each of them being entitled to make copy or notes if desirous of so doing. The letter is then to be replaced in its envelope and letter and envelope are to be placed in another envelope to be endorsed on outside as to its contents and to be signed across the flap by both the Executors and by the said Rupert Sent Leger.
>
> "'(Signed) ROGER MELTON 1/6/'06.

"The letter marked 'C,' directed to 'Edward Bingham Trent,' is thus endorsed:

> "'This letter directed to Edward Bingham Trent is to be kept by him unopened for a term of two years after the reading of my Last Will unless said period is earlier terminated by either the acceptance or refusal of Rupert Sent Leger to accept the conditions mentioned in my letter to him marked 'B' which he is to receive and read in the presence of my Executors at the same meeting as but subsequent to the Reading of the clauses (except those to be ultimately numbers ten and eleven) of my Last Will. This letter contains instructions as to what both the Executors and the said Rupert Sent Leger are to do when such acceptance or refusal of the said Rupert Sent Leger has been made known, or if he omit or refuse to make any such acceptance or refusal, at the end of two years next after my decease.
>
> "'(Signed) ROGER MELTON 1/6/'06.'"

When the attorney had finished reading the last letter he put it carefully in his pocket. Then he took the other letter in his hand, and stood up. "Mr. Rupert Sent Leger," he said, "please to open this letter, and in such a way that all present may see that the memorandum at top of the contents is given as—

> "'B. To be read as clause ten of my Will.'"

St. Leger rolled up his sleeves and cuffs just as if he was going to perform some sort of prestidigitation—it was very theatrical and ridiculous—then, his wrists being quite bare, he opened the envelope and took out the letter. We all saw it quite well. It was folded with the first page outward, and on the top was written a line just as the attorney said. In obedience to a request from the attorney, he laid both letter and envelope on the table in front of him. The clerk then rose up, and, after handing a piece of paper to the attorney, went back to his seat. Mr. Trent, having written something on the paper, asked us all who were present, even the clerk and the shorthand man, to look at the memorandum on the letter and what was written on the envelope, and to sign the paper, which ran:

"We the signatories of this paper hereby declare that we have seen the sealed letter marked B and enclosed in the Will of Roger Melton opened in the presence of us all including Mr. Edward Bingham Trent and Sir Colin Alexander MacKelpie and we declare that the paper therein contained was headed 'B. To be read as clause ten of my Will' and that there were no other contents in the envelope. In attestation of which we in the presence of each other append our signatures."

The attorney motioned to my father to begin. Father is a cautious man, and he asked for a magnifying-glass, which was shortly brought to him by a clerk for whom the clerk in the room called. Father examined the envelope all over very carefully, and also the memorandum at top of the paper. Then, without a word, he signed the paper. Father is a just man. Then we all signed. The attorney folded the paper and put it in an envelope. Before closing it he passed it round, and we all saw that it had not been tampered with. Father took it out and read it, and then put it back. Then the attorney asked us all to sign it across the flap, which we did. Then he put the sealing-wax on it and asked father to seal it with his own seal. He did so. Then he and MacKelpie sealed it also with their own seals, Then he put it in another envelope, which he sealed himself, and he and MacKelpie signed it across the flap.

Then father stood up, and so did I. So did the two men—the clerk and the shorthand writer. Father did not say a word till we got out into the street. We walked along, and presently we passed an open gate into the fields. He turned back, saying to me:

"Come in here. There is no one about, and we can be quiet. I want to speak to you." When we sat down on a seat with none other near it, father said:

"You are a student of the law. What does all that mean?" I thought it a good occasion for an epigram, so I said one word:

"Bilk!"

"H'm!" said father; "that is so far as you and I are concerned. You with a beggarly ten thousand, and I with twenty. But what is, or will be, the effect of those secret trusts?"

"Oh, that," I said, "will, I dare say, be all right. Uncle Roger evidently did not intend the older generation to benefit too much by his death. But he only gave Rupert St. Leger one thousand pounds, whilst he gave me ten. That looks as if he had more regard for the direct line. Of course—" Father interrupted me:

"But what was the meaning of a further sum?"

"I don't know, father. There was evidently some condition which he was to fulfil; but he evidently didn't expect that he would. Why, otherwise, did he leave a second trust to Mr. Trent?"

"True!" said father. Then he went on: "I wonder why he left those enormous sums to Trent and old MacKelpie. They seem out of all proportion as executors' fees, unless—"

"Unless what, father?"

"Unless the fortune he has left is an enormous one. That is why I asked."

"And that," I laughed, "is why he refused to answer."

"Why, Ernest, it must run into big figures."

"Right-ho, father. The death-duties will be annoying. What a beastly swindle the death-duties are! Why, I shall suffer even on your own little estate . . . "

"That will do!" he said curtly. Father is so ridiculously touchy. One would think he expects to live for ever. Presently he spoke again:

"I wonder what are the conditions of that trust. They are as important—almost—as the amount of the bequest—whatever it is. By the way, there seems to be no mention in the will of a residuary legatee. Ernest, my boy, we may have to fight over that."

"How do you make that out, father?" I asked. He had been very rude over the matter of the death-duties of his own estate, though it is entailed and I *must* inherit. So I determined to let him see that I know a good deal more than he does—of law, at any rate. "I fear that when we come to look into it closely that dog won't fight. In the first place, that may be all arranged in the letter to St. Leger, which is a part of the Will. And if that letter should be inoperative by his refusal of the conditions (whatever they may be), then the letter to the attorney begins to work. What it is we don't know, and perhaps even he doesn't—I looked at it as well as I could—and we law men are trained to observation. But even if the instructions mentioned as being in Letter C fail, then the corpus of the Will gives full power to Trent to act just as he darn pleases. He can give the whole thing to himself if he likes, and no one can say a word. In fact, he is himself the final court of appeal."

"H'm!" said father to himself. "It is a queer kind of will, I take it, that can override the Court of Chancery. We shall perhaps have to try it before we are done with this!" With that he rose, and we walked home together—without saying another word.

My mother was very inquisitive about the whole thing—women always are. Father and I between us told her all it was necessary for her to know. I think we were both afraid that, woman-like, she would make trouble for us by saying or doing something injudicious. Indeed, she manifested such hostility towards Rupert St. Leger that it is quite on the cards that she may try to injure him in some way. So when father said that he would have to go out shortly again, as he wished to consult his solicitor, I jumped up and said I would go with him, as I, too, should take advice as to how I stood in the matter.

The Contents of Letter marked "B" attached as an Integral Part to the Last Will of Roger Melton.

June 11, 1907.

"This letter an integral part of my Last Will regards the entire residue of my estate beyond the specific bequests made in the body of my Will. It is to appoint as Residuary Legatee of such Will—in case he may accept in due form the Conditions herein laid down—my dear Nephew Rupert Sent Leger only son of my sister Patience Melton now deceased by her marriage with Captain Rupert Sent Leger also now deceased. On his acceptance of the Conditions and the fulfilment of the first of them the Entire residue of my estate after payments of all specific Legacies and of all my debts and other obligations is to become his absolute property to be dealt with or disposed of as he may desire. The following are the conditions.

"1. He is to accept provisionally by letter addressed to my Executors a sum of nine hundred and ninety-nine thousand pounds sterling free of all Duties Taxes or other imposts. This he will hold for a period of six months from the date of the Reading of my Last Will and have user of the accruements thereto calculated at the rate of ten per centum per annum which amount he shall under no circumstances be required to replace. At the end of said six months he must express in writing directed to the Executors of my Will his acceptance or refusal of the other conditions herein to follow. But if he may so choose he shall be free to declare in writing to the Executors within one week from the time of the Reading of the Will his wish to accept or to withdraw altogether from the responsibility of this Trust. In case of withdrawal he is to retain absolutely and for his own use the above-mentioned sum of nine hundred and ninety-nine thousand pounds sterling free of all Duties Taxes and imposts whatsoever making with the specific bequest of one thousand pounds a clear sum of one million pounds sterling free of all imposts. And he will from the moment of the delivery of such written withdrawal cease to have any right or interest whatsoever in the further disposition of my estate under this instrument. Should such written withdrawal be received by my Executors they shall have possession of such residue of my estate as shall remain after the payment of the above sum of nine hundred and ninety-nine thousand pounds sterling and the payment of all Duties Taxes assessments or Imposts as may be entailed by law by its conveyance to the said Rupert Sent Leger and these my Executors shall hold the same for the further disposal of it according to the instructions given in the letter marked C and which is also an integral part of my Last Will and Testament.

"2. If at or before the expiration of the six months above-mentioned the said Rupert Sent Leger shall have accepted the further conditions herein stated, he is to have user of the entire income produced by such residue of my estate the said income being paid to him Quarterly on the usual Quarter Days by the aforesaid Executors to wit Major General Sir Colin Alexander MacKelpie Bart. and Edward Bingham Trent to be used by him in accordance with the terms and conditions hereinafter mentioned.

"3. The said Rupert Sent Leger is to reside for a period of at least six months to begin not later than three months from the reading of my Will in the Castle of Vissarion in the Land of the Blue Mountains. And if he fulfil the Conditions imposed on him and shall thereby become possessed of the residue of my estate he is to continue to reside there in part for a period of one year. He is not to change his British Nationality except by a formal consent of the Privy Council of Great Britain.

"At the end of a year and a half from the Reading of my Will he is to report in person to my Executors of the expenditure of amounts paid or due by him in the carrying out of the Trust and if they are satisfied that same are in general accord with the conditions named in above-mentioned letter marked C and which is an integral part of my Will they

are to record their approval on such Will which can then go for final Probate and Taxation. On the Completion of which the said Rupert Sent Leger shall become possessed absolutely and without further act or need of the entire residue of my estate. In witness whereof, etc.

"(Signed) ROGER MELTON."

This document is attested by the witnesses to the Will on the same date.

(*Personal and Confidential.*)

Memoranda made by Edward Bingham Trent in Connection with the Will of Roger Melton.

January 3, 1907.

The interests and issues of all concerned in the Will and estate of the late Roger Melton of Openshaw Grange are so vast that in case any litigation should take place regarding the same, I, as the solicitor, having the carriage of the testator's wishes, think it well to make certain memoranda of events, conversations, etc., not covered by documentary evidence. I make the first memorandum immediately after the event, whilst every detail of act and conversation is still fresh in my mind. I shall also try to make such comments thereon as may serve to refresh my memory hereafter, and which in case of my death may perhaps afford as opinions contemporaneously recorded some guiding light to other or others who may later on have to continue and complete the tasks entrusted to me.

I.

Concerning the Reading of the Will of Roger Melton.

When, beginning at 11 o'clock a.m. on this the forenoon of Thursday, the 3rd day of January, 1907, I opened the Will and read it in full, except the clauses contained in the letters marked "B" and "C"; there were present in addition to myself, the following:

1. Ernest Halbard Melton, J.P, nephew of the testator.
2. Ernest Roger Halbard Melton, son of the above.
3. Rupert Sent Leger, nephew of the testator.
4. Major-General Sir Colin Alexander MacKelpie, Bart., co-executor with myself of the Will.
5. Andrew Rossiter, my clerk, one of the witnesses of the testator's Will.
6. Alfred Nugent, stenographer (of Messrs. Castle's office, 21, Bream's Buildings, W.C.).

When the Will had been read, Mr. E. H. Melton asked the value of the estate left by the testator, which query I did not feel empowered or otherwise able to answer; and a further query, as to why those present were not shown the secret clauses of the

Will. I answered by reading the instructions endorsed on the envelopes of the two letters marked "B" and "C," which were sufficiently explanatory.

But, lest any question should hereafter arise as to the fact that the memoranda in letters marked "B" and "C," which were to be read as clauses 10 and 11 of the Will, I caused Rupert Sent Leger to open the envelope marked "B" in the presence of all in the room. These all signed a paper which I had already prepared, to the effect that they had seen the envelope opened, and that the memorandum marked "B. To be read as clause ten of my Will," was contained in the envelope, of which it was to be the sole contents. Mr. Ernest Halbard Melton, J.P., before signing, carefully examined with a magnifying-glass, for which he had asked, both the envelope and the heading of the memorandum enclosed in the letter. He was about to turn the folded paper which was lying on the table over, by which he might have been able to read the matter of the memorandum had he so desired. I at once advised him that the memorandum he was to sign dealt only with the heading of the page, and not with the matter. He looked very angry, but said nothing, and after a second scrutiny signed. I put the memorandum in an envelope, which we all signed across the flap. Before signing, Mr Ernest Halbard Melton took out the paper and verified it. I then asked him to close it, which he did, and when the sealing-wax was on it he sealed it with his own seal. Sir Colin A. MacKelpie and I also appended our own seals. I put the envelope in another, which I sealed with my own seal, and my co-executor and I signed it across the flap and added the date. I took charge of this. When the others present had taken their departure, my co-executor and I, together with Mr. Rupert Sent Leger, who had remained at my request, went into my private room.

Here Mr. Rupert Sent Leger read the memorandum marked "B," which is to be read as clause 10 of the Will. He is evidently a man of considerable nerve, for his face was quite impassive as he read the document, which conveyed to him (subject to the conditions laid down) a fortune which has no equal in amount in Europe, even, so far as I know, amongst the crowned heads. When he had read it over a second time he stood up and said:

"I wish I had known my uncle better. He must have had the heart of a king. I never heard of such generosity as he has shown me. Mr. Trent, I see, from the conditions of this memorandum, or codicil, or whatever it is, that I am to declare within a week as to whether I accept the conditions imposed on me. Now, I want you to tell me this: must I wait a week to declare?" In answer, I told him that the testator's intention was manifestly to see that he had full time to consider fully every point before making formal decision and declaration. But, in answer to the specific question, I could answer that he might make declaration when he would, provided it was *within*, or rather not after, the week named. I added:

"But I strongly advise you not to act hurriedly. So enormous a sum is involved that you may be sure that all possible efforts will be made by someone or other to dispossess you of your inheritance, and it will be well that everything shall be done, not only in perfect order, but with such manifest care and deliberation that there can be no question as to your intention."

"Thank you, sir," he answered; "I shall do as you shall kindly advise me in this as in other things. But I may tell you now—and you, too, my dear Sir Colin—that I not only accept my Uncle Roger's conditions in this, but that when the time comes in the other matters I shall accept every condition that he had in his mind—and that I may

know of—in everything." He looked exceedingly in earnest, and it gave me much pleasure to see and hear him. It was just what a young man should do who had seen so generously treated. As the time had now come, I gave him the bulky letter addressed to him, marked "D" which I had in my safe. As I fulfilled my obligation in the matter, I said:

"You need not read the letter here. You can take it away with you, and read it by yourself at leisure. It is your own property, without any obligation whatever attached to it. By the way, perhaps it would be well if you knew. I have a copy sealed up in an envelope, and endorsed, 'To be opened if occasion should arise,' but not otherwise. Will you see me to-morrow, or, better still, dine with me alone here to-night? I should like to have a talk with you, and you may wish to ask me some questions." He answered me cordially. I actually felt touched by the way he said good-bye before he went away. Sir Colin MacKelpie went with him, as Sent Leger was to drop him at the Reform.

Letter from Roger Melton to Rupert Sent Leger, endorsed "D. re Rupert Sent Leger. To be given to him by Edward Bingham Trent if and as soon as he has declared (formally or informally) his intention of accepting the conditions named in Letter B., forming Clause 10 in my Will. R. M., 1/1/'07.

"*Mem.*—Copy (sealed) left in custody of E. B. Trent, to be opened if necessary, as directed."

June 11, 1906.

My Dear Nephew,

When (if ever) you receive this you will know that (with the exception of some definite bequests) I have left to you, under certain conditions, the entire bulk of my fortune—a fortune so great that by its aid as a help, a man of courage and ability may carve out for himself a name and place in history. The specific conditions contained in Clause 10 of my Will have to be observed, for such I deem to be of service to your own fortune; but herein I give my advice, which you are at liberty to follow or not as you will, and my wishes, which I shall try to explain fully and clearly, so that you may be in possession of my views in case you should desire to carry them out, or, at least, to so endeavour that the results I hope for may be ultimately achieved. First let me explain—for your understanding and your guidance—that the power, or perhaps it had better be called the pressure, behind the accumulation of my fortune has been ambition. In obedience to its compulsion, I toiled early and late until I had so arranged matters that, subject to broad supervision, my ideas could be carried out by men whom I had selected and tested, and not found wanting. This was for years to the satisfaction, and ultimately to the accumulation by these men of fortune commensurate in some measure to their own worth and their importance to my designs. Thus I had accumulated, whilst still a young man, a considerable fortune. This

I have for over forty years used sparingly as regards my personal needs, daringly with regard to speculative investments. With the latter I took such very great care, studying the conditions surrounding them so thoroughly, that even now my schedule of bad debts or unsuccessful investments is almost a blank. Perhaps by such means things flourished with me, and wealth piled in so fast that at times I could hardly use it to advantage. This was all done as the forerunner of ambition, but I was over fifty years of age when the horizon of ambition itself opened up to me. I speak thus freely, my dear Rupert, as when you read it I shall have passed away, and not ambition nor the fear of misunderstanding, nor even of scorn can touch me. My ventures in commerce and finance covered not only the Far East, but every foot of the way to it, so that the Mediterranean and all its opening seas were familiar to me. In my journeyings up and down the Adriatic I was always struck by the great beauty and seeming richness—native richness—of the Land of the Blue Mountains. At last Chance took me into that delectable region. When the "Balkan Struggle" of '90 was on, one of the great Voivodes came to me in secret to arrange a large loan for national purposes. It was known in financial circles of both Europe and Asia that I took an active part in the *haute politique* of national treasuries, and the Voivode Vissarion came to me as to one able and willing to carry out his wishes. After confidential pour-parlers, he explained to me that his nation was in the throes of a great crisis. As you perhaps know, the gallant little Nation in the Land of the Blue Mountains has had a strange history. For more than a thousand years—ever since its settlement after the disaster of Rossoro—it had maintained its national independence under several forms of Government. At first it had a King whose successors became so despotic that they were dethroned. Then it was governed by its Voivodes, with the combining influence of a Vladika somewhat similar in power and function to the Prince-Bishops of Montenegro; afterwards by a Prince; or, as at present, by an irregular elective Council, influenced in a modified form by the Vladika, who was then supposed to exercise a purely spiritual function. Such a Council in a small, poor nation did not have sufficient funds for armaments, which were not immediately and imperatively necessary; and therefore the Voivode Vissarion, who had vast estates in his own possession, and who was the present representative a family which of old had been leaders in the land, found it a duty to do on his own account that which the State could not do. For security as to the loan which he wished to get, and which was indeed a vast one, he offered to sell me his whole estate if I would secure to him a right to re-purchase it within a given time (a time which I may say has some time ago expired). He made it a condition that the sale and agreement should remain a strict secret between us, as a widespread knowledge that his estate had changed hands would in all probability result in my death and his own at the hands of the mountaineers, who are beyond everything loyal, and were jealous to the last degree. An attack by Turkey was feared, and new armaments were required; and the patriotic Voivode

was sacrificing his own great fortune for the public good. What a sacrifice this was he well knew, for in all discussions regarding a possible change in the Constitution of the Blue Mountains it was always taken for granted that if the principles of the Constitution should change to a more personal rule, his own family should be regarded as the Most Noble. It had ever been on the side of freedom in olden time; before the establishment of the Council, or even during the rule of the Voivodes, the Vissarion had every now and again stood out against the King or challenged the Princedom. The very name stood for freedom, for nationality, against foreign oppression; and the bold mountaineers were devoted to it, as in other free countries men follow the flag.

Such loyalty was a power and a help in the land, for it knew danger in every form; and anything which aided the cohesion of its integers was a natural asset. On every side other powers, great and small, pressed the land, anxious to acquire its suzerainty by any means—fraud or force. Greece, Turkey, Austria, Russia, Italy, France, had all tried in vain. Russia, often hurled back, was waiting an opportunity to attack. Austria and Greece, although united by no common purpose or design, were ready to throw in their forces with whomsoever might seem most likely to be victor. Other Balkan States, too, were not lacking in desire to add the little territory of the Blue Mountains to their more ample possessions. Albania, Dalmatia, Herzegovina, Servia, Bulgaria, looked with lustful eyes on the land, which was in itself a vast natural fortress, having close under its shelter perhaps the finest harbour between Gibraltar and the Dardanelles.

But the fierce, hardy mountaineers were unconquerable. For centuries they had fought, with a fervour and fury that nothing could withstand or abate, attacks on their independence. Time after time, century after century, they had opposed with dauntless front invading armies sent against them. This unquenchable fire of freedom had had its effect. One and all, the great Powers knew that to conquer that little nation would be no mean task, but rather that of a tireless giant. Over and over again had they fought with units against hundreds, never ceasing until they had either wiped out their foes entirely or seen them retreat across the frontier in diminished numbers.

For many years past, however, the Land of the Blue Mountains had remained unassailable, for all the Powers and States had feared lest the others should unite against the one who should begin the attack.

At the time I speak of there was a feeling throughout the Blue Mountains—and, indeed, elsewhere—that Turkey was preparing for a war of offence. The objective of her attack was not known anywhere, but here there was evidence that the Turkish "Bureau of Spies" was in active exercise towards their sturdy little neighbour. To prepare for this, the Voivode Peter Vissarion approached me in order to obtain the necessary "sinews of war."

The situation was complicated by the fact that the Elective Council was at present largely held together by the old Greek Church, which was

the religion of the people, and which had had since the beginning its destinies linked in a large degree with theirs. Thus it was possible that if a war should break out, it might easily become—whatever might have been its cause or beginnings—a war of creeds. This in the Balkans must be largely one of races, the end of which no mind could diagnose or even guess at.

I had now for some time had knowledge of the country and its people, and had come to love them both. The nobility of Vissarion's self-sacrifice at once appealed to me, and I felt that I, too, should like to have a hand in the upholding of such a land and such a people. They both deserved freedom. When Vissarion handed me the completed deed of sale I was going to tear it up; but he somehow recognized my intention, and forestalled it. He held up his hand arrestingly as he said:

"I recognize your purpose, and, believe me, I honour you for it from the very depths of my soul. But, my friend, it must not be. Our mountaineers are proud beyond belief. Though they would allow me—who am one of themselves, and whose fathers have been in some way leaders and spokesmen amongst them for many centuries—to do all that is in my power to do—and what, each and all, they would be glad to do were the call to them—they would not accept aid from one outside themselves. My good friend, they would resent it, and might show to you, who wish us all so well, active hostility, which might end in danger, or even death. That was why, my friend, I asked to put a clause in our agreement, that I might have right to repurchase my estate, regarding which you would fain act so generously."

Thus it is, my dear nephew Rupert, only son of my dear sister, that I hereby charge you solemnly as you value me—as you value yourself—as you value honour, that, should it ever become known that that noble Voivode, Peter Vissarion, imperilled himself for his country's good, and if it be of danger or evil repute to him that even for such a purpose he sold his heritage, you shall at once and to the knowledge of the mountaineers—though not necessarily to others—reconvey to him or his heirs the freehold that he was willing to part with—and that he has *de facto* parted with by the effluxion of the time during which his right of repurchase existed. This is a secret trust and duty which is between thee and me alone in the first instance; a duty which I have undertaken on behalf of my heirs, and which must be carried out, at whatsoever cost may ensue. You must not take it that it is from any mistrust of you or belief that you will fail that I have taken another measure to insure that this my cherished idea is borne out. Indeed, it is that the law may, in case of need—for no man can know what may happen after his own hand be taken from the plough—be complied with, that I have in another letter written for the guidance of others, directed that in case of any failure to carry out this trust—death or other—the direction become a clause or codicil to my Will. But in the meantime I wish that this be kept a secret between us two. To show you the full extent of my confidence, let me here tell you that the letter alluded to above is marked "C," and directed

to my solicitor and co-executor, Edward Bingham Trent, which is finally to be regarded as clause eleven of my Will. To which end he has my instructions and also a copy of this letter, which is, in case of need, and that only, to be opened, and is to be a guide to my wishes as to the carrying out by you of the conditions on which you inherit.

And now, my dear nephew, let me change to another subject more dear to me—yourself. When you read this I shall have passed away, so that I need not be hampered now by that reserve which I feel has grown upon me through a long and self-contained life. Your mother was very dear to me. As you know, she was twenty years younger than her youngest brother, who was two years younger than me. So we were all young men when she was a baby, and, I need not say, a pet amongst us—almost like our own child to each of us, as well as our sister. You knew her sweetness and high quality, so I need say nothing of these; but I should like you to understand that she was very dear to me. When she and your father came to know and love each other I was far away, opening up a new branch of business in the interior of China, and it was not for several months that I got home news. When I first heard of him they had already been married. I was delighted to find that they were very happy. They needed nothing that I could give. When he died so suddenly I tried to comfort her, and all I had was at her disposal, did she want it. She was a proud woman—though not with me. She had come to understand that, though I seemed cold and hard (and perhaps was so generally), I was not so to her. But she would not have help of any kind. When I pressed her, she told me that she had enough for your keep and education and her own sustenance for the time she must still live; that your father and she had agreed that you should be brought up to a healthy and strenuous life rather than to one of luxury; and she thought that it would be better for the development of your character that you should learn to be self-reliant and to be content with what your dear father had left you. She had always been a wise and thoughtful girl, and now all her wisdom and thought were for you, your father's and her child. When she spoke of you and your future, she said many things which I thought memorable. One of them I remember to this day. It was apropos of my saying that there is a danger of its own kind in extreme poverty. A young man might know too much want. She answered me: "True! That is so! But there is a danger that overrides it;" and after a time went on:

"It is better not to know wants than not to know want!" I tell you, boy, that is a great truth, and I hope you will remember it for yourself as well as a part of the wisdom of your mother. And here let me say something else which is a sort of corollary of that wise utterance:

I dare say you thought me very hard and unsympathetic that time I would not, as one of your trustees, agree to your transferring your little fortune to Miss MacKelpie. I dare say you bear a grudge towards me about it up to this day. Well, if you have any of that remaining, put it aside when you know the truth. That request of yours was an unspeakable delight to me. It was like your mother coming back from the dead. That little letter of yours made me wish for the first time that I had a son—and that he should be like you. I fell into a sort of reverie, thinking if I were yet too old to marry, so that a son might be with me in my declining years—if such were to ever be for me. But I concluded that this might not be. There was no woman whom I knew or had ever met with that I could love as your mother loved your father and as he loved her. So I resigned myself to my fate. I must go my lonely road on to the end. And then came a ray of light into my darkness: there was you. Though you might not feel like a son to me—I could not expect it when the memory of that sweet relationship was more worthily filled. But I could feel like a father to you. Nothing could prevent that or interfere with it, for I would keep it as my secret in the very holy of holies of my heart, where had been for thirty years the image of a sweet little child—your mother. My boy, when in your future life you shall have happiness and honour and power, I hope you will sometimes give a thought to the lonely old man whose later years your very existence seemed to brighten.

The thought of your mother recalled me to my duty. I had undertaken for her a sacred task: to carry out her wishes regarding her son. I knew how she would have acted. It might—would—have been to her a struggle of inclination and duty; and duty would have won. And so I carried out my duty, though I tell you it was a harsh and bitter task to me at the time. But I may tell you that I have since been glad when I think of the result. I tried, as you may perhaps remember, to carry out your wishes in another way, but your letter put the difficulty of doing so so clearly before me that I had to give it up. And let me tell you that that letter endeared you to me more than ever.

I need not tell you that thenceforth I followed your life very closely. When you ran away to sea, I used in secret every part of the mechanism of commerce to find out what had become of you. Then, until you had reached your majority, I had a constant watch kept upon you—not to interfere with you in any way, but so that I might be able to find you should need arise. When in due course I heard of your first act on coming of age I was satisfied. I had to know of the carrying out of your original intention towards Janet Mac Kelpie, for the securities had to be transferred.

From that time on I watched—of course through other eyes—your chief doings. It would have been a pleasure to me to have been able to help in carrying out any hope or ambition of yours, but I realized that in the years intervening between your coming of age and the present moment you were fulfilling your ideas and ambitions in your own way, and, as I shall try to explain to you presently, my ambitions also. You were of so adventurous a nature that even my own widely-spread machinery of acquiring information—what I may call my private "intelligence department"—was inadequate. My machinery was fairly adequate for the East—in great part, at all events. But you went North and South, and West also, and, in addition, you essayed realms where commerce and purely real affairs have no foothold—worlds of thought, of spiritual import, of psychic phenomena—speaking generally, of mysteries. As now and again I was baffled in my inquiries, I had to enlarge my mechanism, and to this end started—not in my own name, of course—some new magazines devoted to certain branches of inquiry and adventure. Should you ever care to know more of these things, Mr. Trent, in whose name the stock is left, will be delighted to give you all details. Indeed, these stocks, like all else I have, shall be yours when the time comes, if you care to ask for them. By means of *The Journal of Adventure*, *The Magazine of Mystery*, *Occultism*, *Balloon and Aeroplane*, *The Submarine*, *Jungle and Pampas*, *The Ghost World*, *The Explorer*, *Forest and Island*, *Ocean and Creek*, I was often kept informed when I should otherwise have been ignorant of your whereabouts and designs. For instance, when you had disappeared into the Forest of the Incas, I got the first whisper of your strange adventures and discoveries in the buried cities of Eudori from a correspondent of *The Journal of Adventure* long before the details given in *The Times* of the rock-temple of the primeval savages, where only remained the little dragon serpents, whose giant ancestors were rudely sculptured on the sacrificial altar. I well remember how I thrilled at even that meagre account of your going in alone into that veritable hell. It was from *Occultism* that I learned how you had made a stay alone in the haunted catacombs of Elora, in the far recesses of the Himalayas, and of the fearful experiences which, when you came out shuddering and ghastly, overcame to almost epileptic fear those who had banded themselves together to go as far as the rock-cut approach to the hidden temple.

All such things I read with rejoicing. You were shaping yourself for a wider and loftier adventure, which would crown more worthily your matured manhood. When I read of you in a description of Mihask, in Madagascar, and the devil-worship there rarely held, I felt I had only to wait for your home-coming in order to broach the enterprise I had so long contemplated. This was what I read:

"He is a man to whom no adventure is too wild or too daring. His reckless bravery is a byword amongst many savage peoples and amongst many others not savages, whose fears are not of material things, but of the world of mysteries in and beyond the grave. He dares not only wild animals and savage men; but has tackled African magic and Indian mysticism. The Psychical Research Society has long exploited his deeds of valiance, and looked upon him as perhaps their most trusted agent or source of discovery. He is in the very prime of life, of almost giant stature and strength, trained to the use of all arms of all countries, inured to every kind of hardship, subtle-minded and resourceful, understanding human nature from its elemental form up. To say that he is fearless would be inadequate. In a word, he is a man whose strength and daring fit him for any enterprise of any kind. He would dare and do anything in the world or out of it, on the earth or under it, in the sea or—in the air, fearing nothing material or unseen, not man or ghost, nor God nor Devil."

If you ever care to think of it, I carried that cutting in my pocketbook from that hour I read it till now.

Remember, again, I say, that I never interfered in the slightest way in any of your adventures. I wanted you to "dree your own weird," as the Scotch say; and I wanted to know of it—that was all. Now, as I hold you fully equipped for greater enterprise, I want to set your feet on the road and to provide you with the most potent weapon—beyond personal qualities—for the winning of great honour—a gain, my dear nephew, which, I am right sure, does and will appeal to you as it has ever done to me. I have worked for it for more than fifty years; but now that the time has come when the torch is slipping from my old hands, I look to you, my dearest kinsman, to lift it and carry it on.

The little nation of the Blue Mountains has from the first appealed to me. It is poor and proud and brave. Its people are well worth winning, and I would advise you to throw in your lot with them. You may find them hard to win, for when peoples, like individuals, are poor and proud, these qualities are apt to react on each other to an endless degree. These men are untamable, and no one can ever succeed with them unless he is with them in all-in-all, and is a leader recognized. But if you can win them they are loyal to death. If you are ambitious—and I know you are—there may be a field for you in such a country. With your qualifications, fortified by the fortune which I am happy enough to be able to leave you, you may dare much and go far. Should I be alive when you return from your exploration in Northern South America, I may have the happiness of helping you to this or any other ambition, and I shall deem it a privilege to share it with you; but time is going on. I am in my seventy-second year . . . the years of man are three-score and ten—I suppose you understand; I do . . . Let me point out this: For ambitious projects the great nationalities are impossible to a stranger—and in our own we are limited by loyalty (and common-sense). It is only in a small nation that great ambitions can be achieved. If you share my own views and wishes, the Blue Mountains is your ground. I hoped at one time that I might yet become a Voivode—even a great one. But age has dulled my personal ambitions as it has cramped my powers. I no longer dream of such honour for myself, though I do look on it as a possibility for you if you care for it. Through my Will you will have a great position and a great estate, and though you may have to yield up the latter in accordance with my wish, as already expressed in this letter, the very doing so will give you an even greater hold than this possession in the hearts of the mountaineers, should they ever come to know it. Should it be that at the time you inherit from me the Voivode Vissarion should not be alive, it may serve or aid you to know that in such case you would be absolved from any conditions of mine, though I trust you would in that, as in all other matters, hold obligation enforced by your own honour as to my wishes. Therefore the matter stands thus: If Vissarion lives, you will relinquish the estates. Should such not be the case, you will act as you believe that I would wish you to. In either case the mountaineers should not know from you in any way of the secret contracts between Vissarion and myself. Enlightenment of the many should (if ever) come from others than yourself. And unless such take place, you would leave the estates without any *quid pro quo* whatever. This you need not mind, for the fortune you will inherit will leave you free and able to purchase other estates in the Blue Mountains or elsewhere that you may select in the world.

If others attack, attack them, and quicker and harder than they can, if such be a possibility. Should it ever be that you inherit the Castle of Vissarion on the Spear of Ivan, remember that I had it secretly fortified and armed against attack. There are not only massive grilles, but doors of chilled bronze where such be needed. My adherent Rooke, who has faithfully served me for nearly forty years, and has gone on my behalf on many perilous expeditions, will, I trust, serve you in the same way. Treat him well for my sake, if not for your own. I have left him provision for a life of ease; but he would rather take a part in dangerous enterprises. He is silent as the grave and as bold as a lion. He knows every detail of the fortification and of the secret means of defence. A word in your ear—he was once a pirate. He was then in his extreme youth, and long since changed his ways in this respect; but from this fact you can understand his nature. You will find him useful should occasion ever arise. Should you accept the conditions of my letter, you are to make the Blue Mountains—in part, at least—your home, living there a part of the year, if only for a week, as in England men of many estates share the time amongst them. To this you are not bound, and no one shall have power to compel you or interfere with you. I only express a hope. But one thing I do more than hope—I desire, if you will honour my wishes, that, come what may, you are to keep your British nationality, unless by special arrangement with and consent of the Privy Council. Such arrangement to be formally made by my friend, Edward Bingham Trent, or whomsoever he may appoint by deed or will to act in the matter, and made in such a way that no act save that alone of Parliament in all its estates, and endorsed by the King, may or can prevail against it.

My last word to you is, Be bold and honest, and fear not. Most things—even kingship—*somewhere* may now and again be won by the sword. A brave heart and a strong arm may go far. But whatever is so won cannot be held merely by the sword. Justice alone can hold in the long run. Where men trust they will follow, and the rank and file of people want to follow, not to lead. If it be your fortune to lead, be bold. Be wary, if you will; exercise any other faculties that may aid or guard. Shrink from nothing. Avoid nothing that is honourable in itself. Take responsibility when such presents itself. What others shrink from, accept. That is to be great in what world, little or big, you move. Fear nothing, no matter of what kind danger may be or whence it come. The only real way to meet danger is to despise it—except with your brains. Meet it in the gate, not the hall.

My kinsman, the name of my race and your own, worthily mingled in your own person, now rests with you!

Letter from Rupert Sent Leger, 32 Bodmin Street, Victoria, S.W., to Miss Janet MacKelpie, Croom, Ross-shire.

January 3, 1907.

MY DEAREST AUNT JANET,

You will, I know, be rejoiced to hear of the great good-fortune which has come to me through the Will of Uncle Roger. Perhaps Sir Colin will have written to you, as he is one of the executors, and there is a bequest to you, so I must not spoil his pleasure of telling you of that part himself. Unfortunately, I am not free to speak fully of my own legacy yet, but I want you to know that at worst I am to receive an amount many times more than I ever dreamt of possessing through any possible stroke of fortune. So soon as I can leave London—where, of course, I must remain until things are settled—I am coming up to Croom to see you, and I hope I shall by then be able to let you know so much that you will be able to guess at the extraordinary change that has come to my circumstances. It is all like an impossible dream: there is nothing like it in the "Arabian Nights." However, the details must wait, I am pledged to secrecy for the present. And you must be pledged too. You won't mind, dear, will you? What I want to do at present is merely to tell you of my own good-fortune, and that I shall be going presently to live for a while at Vissarion. Won't you come with me, Aunt Janet? We shall talk more of this when I come to Croom; but I want you to keep the subject in your mind.

Your loving
RUPERT.

From Rupert Sent Leger's Journal.

January 4, 1907.

Things have been humming about me so fast that I have had hardly time to think. But some of the things have been so important, and have so changed my entire outlook on life, that it may be well to keep some personal record of them. I may some day want to remember some detail—perhaps the sequence of events, or something like that—and it may be useful. It ought to be, if there is any justice in things, for it will be an awful swot to write it when I have so many things to think of now. Aunt Janet, I suppose, will like to keep it locked up for me, as she does with all my journals and papers. That is one good thing about Aunt Janet amongst many: she has no curiosity, or else she has some other quality which keeps her from prying as other women would. It would seem that she has not so much as opened the cover of one of my journals ever in her life, and that she would not without my permission. So this can in time go to her also.

I dined last night with Mr. Trent, by his special desire. The dinner was in his own rooms. Dinner sent in from the hotel. He would not have any waiters at all, but made them send in the dinner all at once, and we helped ourselves. As we were quite alone, we could talk freely, and we got over a lot of ground while we were dining. He began to tell me about Uncle Roger. I was glad of that, for, of course, I wanted to know all I could of him, and the fact was I had seen very little of him. Of course, when I was a small kid he was often in our house, for he was very fond of mother, and she of him. But I fancy that a small boy was rather a nuisance to him. And then I was at school, and he was away in the East. And then poor mother died while he was living in the Blue Mountains, and I never saw him again. When I wrote to him about Aunt Janet he answered me very kindly but he was so very just in the matter that I got afraid of him. And after that I ran away, and have been roaming ever since; so there was never a chance of our meeting. But that letter of his has opened my eyes. To think of him following me that way all over the world, waiting to hold out a helping hand if I should want it, I only wish I had known, or even suspected, the sort of man he was, and how he cared for me, and I would sometimes have come back to see him, if I had to come half round the world. Well, all I can do now is to carry out his wishes; that will be my expiation for my neglect. He knew what he wanted exactly, and I suppose I shall come in time to know it all and understand it, too.

I was thinking something like this when Mr. Trent began to talk, so that all he said fitted exactly into my own thought. The two men were evidently great friends—I should have gathered that, anyhow, from the Will—and the letters—so I was not surprised when Mr. Trent told me that they had been to school together, Uncle Roger being a senior when he was a junior; and had then and ever after shared each other's confidence. Mr. Trent, I gathered, had from the very first been in love with my mother, even when she was a little girl; but he was poor and shy, and did not like to speak. When he had made up his mind to do so, he found that she had by then met my father, and could not help seeing that they loved each other. So he was silent. He told me he had never said a word about it to anyone—not even to my Uncle Roger, though he knew from one thing and another, though he never spoke of it, that he would like it. I could not help seeing that the dear old man regarded me in a sort of parental way—I have heard of such romantic attachments being transferred to the later generation. I was not displeased with it; on the contrary, I liked him better for it. I love my mother so much—I always think of her in the present—that I cannot think of her as dead. There is a tie between anyone else who loved her and myself. I tried to let Mr. Trent see that I liked him, and it pleased him so much that I could see his liking for me growing greater. Before we parted he told me that he was going to give up business. He must have understood how disappointed I was—for how could I ever get along at all without him?—for he said, as he laid a hand quite affectionately, I thought—on my shoulder:

"I shall have one client, though, whose business I always hope to keep, and for whom I shall be always whilst I live glad to act—if he will have me." I did not care to speak as I took his hand. He squeezed mine, too, and said very earnestly:

"I served your uncle's interests to the very best of my ability for nearly fifty years. He had full confidence in me, and I was proud of his trust. I can honestly say, Rupert—you won't mind me using that familiarity, will you?—that, though the interests which I guarded were so vast that without abusing my trust I could often have used my knowledge to my personal advantage, I never once, in little matters or big, abused that trust—no, not even rubbed the bloom off it. And now that he has remembered me in his Will so generously that I need work no more, it will be a very genuine pleasure and pride to me to carry out as well as I can the wishes that I partly knew, and now realize more fully towards you, his nephew."

In the long chat which we had, and which lasted till midnight, he told me many very interesting things about Uncle Roger. When, in the course of conversation, he mentioned that the fortune Uncle Roger left must be well over a hundred millions, I was so surprised that I said out loud—I did not mean to ask a question:

"How on earth could a man beginning with nothing realize such a gigantic fortune?"

"By all honest ways," he answered, "and his clever human insight. He knew one half of the world, and so kept abreast of all public and national movements that he knew the critical moment to advance money required. He was always generous, and always on the side of freedom. There are nations at this moment only now entering on the consolidation of their liberty, who owe all to him, who knew when and how to help. No wonder that in some lands they will drink to his memory on great occasions as they used to drink his health."

"As you and I shall do now, sir!" I said, as I filled my glass and stood up. We drank it in bumpers. We did not say a word, either of us; but the old gentleman held out his hand, and I took it. And so, holding hands, we drank in silence. It made me feel quite choky; and I could see that he, too, was moved.

From E. B. Trent's Memoranda.

January 4, 1907.

I asked Mr. Rupert Sent Leger to dine with me at my office alone, as I wished to have a chat with him. To-morrow Sir Colin and I will have a formal meeting with him for the settlement of affairs, but I thought it best to have an informal talk with him alone first, as I wished to tell him certain matters which will make our meeting to-morrow more productive of utility, as he can now have more full understanding of the subjects which we have to discuss. Sir Colin is all that can be in manhood, and I could wish no better colleague in the executorship of this phenomenal Will; but he has not had the privilege of a lifelong friendship with the testator as I have had. And as Rupert Sent Leger had to learn intimate details regarding his uncle, I could best make my confidences alone. To-morrow we shall have plenty of formality. I was delighted with Rupert. He is just what I could have wished his mother's boy to be—or a son of my own to be, had I had the good-fortune to have been a father. But this is not for me. I remember long, long ago reading a passage in Lamb's Essays which hangs in my mind: "The children of Alice call Bartrum father." Some of my old friends would laugh to see *me* write this, but these memoranda are for my eyes alone, and no one shall see them till after my death, unless by my own permission. The boy takes some qualities after his father; he has a daring that is disturbing to an old dryasdust lawyer like me. But somehow I like him more than I ever liked anyone—any man—in my life—more even than his uncle, my old friend, Roger Melton; and Lord knows I had much cause to like him. I have more than ever now. It was quite delightful to see the way the young adventurer was touched by his uncle's thought of him. He is a truly gallant fellow, but venturesome exploits have not affected the goodness of heart. It is a pleasure to me to think that Roger and Colin came together apropos of the boy's thoughtful generosity towards Miss MacKelpie. The old soldier will be a good friend to him, or I am much mistaken. With an old lawyer like me, and an old soldier like him, and a real old gentlewoman like Miss MacKelpie, who loves the very ground he walks on, to look after him, together with all his own fine qualities and his marvellous experience of the world, and the gigantic wealth that will surely be his, that young man will go far.

Letter from Rupert Sent Leger to Miss Janet MacKelpie, Croom.

January 5, 1907.

MY DEAREST AUNT JANET,

It is all over—the first stage of it; and that is as far as I can get at present. I shall have to wait for a few days—or it may be weeks—in London for the doing of certain things now necessitated by my acceptance of Uncle Roger's bequest. But as soon as I can, dear, I shall come down to Croom and spend with you as many days as possible. I shall then tell you all I am at liberty to tell, and I shall thank you personally for your consent to come with me to Vissarion. Oh, how I wish my dear mother had lived to be with us! It would have made her happy, I know, to have come; and then we three who shared together the old dear, hard days would have shared in the same way the new splendour. I would try to show all my love and gratitude to you both . . . You must take the whole burden of it now, dear, for you and I are alone. No, not alone, as we used to be, for I have now two old friends who are already dear to me. One is so to you already. Sir Colin is simply splendid, and so, in his own way, is Mr. Trent. I am lucky, Aunt Janet, to have two such men to think of affairs for me. Am I not? I shall send you a wire as soon as ever I can see my way to get through my work; and I want you to think over all the things you ever wished for in your life, so that I may—if there is any mortal way of doing so—get them for you. You will not stand in the way of my having this great pleasure, will you, dear? Good-bye.

Your loving
RUPERT.

E. B. Trent's Memoranda.

January 6, 1907.

The formal meeting of Sir Colin and myself with Rupert Sent Leger went off quite satisfactorily. From what he had said yesterday, and again last night, I had almost come to expect an unreserved acceptance of everything stated or implied in Roger Melton's Will; but when we had sat round the table—this appeared, by the way, to be a formality for which we were all prepared, for we sat down as if by instinct—the very first words he said were:

"As I suppose I must go through this formality, I may as well say at once that I accept every possible condition which was in the mind of Uncle Roger; and to this end I am prepared to sign, seal, and deliver—or whatever is the ritual—whatever document you, sir"—turning to me—"may think necessary or advisable, and of which you both approve." He stood up and walked about the room for a few moments, Sir Colin and I sitting quite still, silent. He came back to his seat, and after a few seconds of nervousness—a rare thing with him, I fancy—said: "I hope you both understand—of course, I know you do; I only speak because this is an occasion for formality—that I am willing to accept, and at once! I do so, believe me, not to get possession of this vast fortune, but because of him who has given it. The man who was fond of me, and who trusted me, and yet had strength to keep his own feelings in check—who followed me in spirit to far lands and desperate adventures, and who, though he might be across the world from me, was ready to put out a hand to save or help me, was no common man; and his care of my mother's son meant no common love for my dear mother. And so she and I together accept his trust, come of it what may. I have been thinking it over all night, and all the time I could not get out of the idea that mother was somewhere near me. The only thought that could debar me from doing as I wished to do—and intend to do—would be that she would not approve. Now that I am satisfied she would approve, I accept. Whatever may result or happen, I shall go on following the course that he has set for me. So help me, God!" Sir Colin stood up, and I must say a more martial figure I never saw. He was in full uniform, for he was going on to the King's levee after our business. He drew his sword from the scabbard and laid it naked on the table before Rupert, and said:

"You are going, sir, into a strange and danger country—I have been reading about it since we met—and you will be largely alone amongst fierce mountaineers who resent the very presence of a stranger, and to whom you are, and must be, one. If you should ever be in any trouble and want a man to stand back to back with you, I hope you will give me the honour!" As he said this pointed to his sword. Rupert and I were also standing now—one cannot sit down in the presence of such an act as that. "You are, I am proud to say, allied with my family: and I only wish to God it was closer to myself." Rupert took him by the hand and bent his head before him as answered:

"The honour is mine, Sir Colin; and no greater can come to any man than that which you have just done me. The best way I can show how I value it will be to call on you if I am ever in such a tight place. By Jove, sir, this is history repeating itself. Aunt Janet used to tell me when I was a youngster how MacKelpie of Croom laid his sword before Prince Charlie. I hope I may tell her of this; it would make her so proud and happy. Don't imagine, sir, that I am thinking myself a Charles Edward. It is only that Aunt Janet is so good to me that I might well think I was."

Sir Colin bowed grandly:

"Rupert Sent Leger, my dear niece is a woman of great discretion and discernment. And, moreover, I am thinking she has in her some of the gift of Second Sight that has been a heritage of our blood. And I am one with my niece—in everything!" The whole thing was quite regal in manner; it seemed to take me back to the days of the Pretender.

It was not, however, a time for sentiment, but for action—we had met regarding the future, not the past; so I produced the short document I had already prepared. On the strength of his steadfast declaration that he would accept the terms of the Will and the secret letters, I had got ready a formal acceptance. When I had once again formally asked Mr. Sent Leger's wishes, and he had declared his wish to accept, I got in a couple of my clerks as witnesses.

Then, having again asked him in their presence if it was his wish to declare acceptance of the conditions, the document was signed and witnessed, Sir Colin and I both appending our signatures to the Attestation.

And so the first stage of Rupert Sent Leger's inheritance is completed. The next step will not have to be undertaken on my part until the expiration of six months from his entry on his estate at Vissarion. As he announces his intention of going within a fortnight, this will mean practically a little over six months from now.

BOOK II: VISSARION

VISSARION

Letter from Rupert Sent Leger, Castle of Vissarion, the Spear of Ivan, Land of the Blue Mountains, to Miss Janet MacKelpie, Croom Castle, Ross-shire, N.B.

January 23, 1907.

MY DEAREST AUNT JANET,

As you see, I am here at last. Having got my formal duty done, as you made me promise—my letters reporting arrival to Sir Colin and Mr. Trent are lying sealed in front of me ready to post (for nothing shall go before yours)—I am free to speak to you.

This is a most lovely place, and I hope you will like it. I am quite sure you will. We passed it in the steamer coming from Trieste to Durazzo. I knew the locality from the chart, and it was pointed out to me by one of the officers with whom I had become quite friendly, and who kindly showed me interesting places whenever we got within sight of shore. The Spear of Ivan, on which the Castle stands, is a headland running well out into the sea. It is quite a peculiar place—a sort of headland on a headland, jutting out into a deep, wide bay, so that, though it is a promontory, it is as far away from the traffic of coast life as anything you can conceive. The main promontory is the end of a range of mountains, and looms up vast, towering over everything, a mass of sapphire blue. I can well understand how the country came to be called the "Land of the Blue Mountains," for it is all mountains, and they are all blue! The coast-line is magnificent—what is called "iron-bound"—being all rocky; sometimes great frowning precipices; sometimes jutting spurs of rock; again little rocky islets, now and again clad with trees and verdure, at other places stark and bare. Elsewhere are little rocky bays and indentations—always rock, and often with long, interesting caves. Some of the shores of the bays are sandy, or else ridges of beautiful pebbles, where the waves make endless murmur.

But of all the places I have seen—in this land or any other—the most absolutely beautiful is Vissarion. It stands at the ultimate point of the promontory—I mean the little, or, rather, lesser promontory—that continues on the spur of the mountain range. For the lesser promontory or extension of the mountain is in reality vast; the lowest bit of cliff along the sea-front is not less than a couple of hundred feet high. That point of rock is really very peculiar. I think Dame Nature must, in the early days of her housekeeping—or, rather, house-*building*—have intended to give her little child, man, a rudimentary lesson in self-protection. It is just a natural bastion such as a titanic Vauban might have designed in primeval times. So far as the Castle is concerned, it is alone visible from the sea. Any enemy approaching could see only that frowning wall of black rock, of vast height and perpendicular steepness. Even the old fortifications which crown it are not built, but cut in the solid rock. A long nar-narrow creek of very deep water, walled in by high, steep cliffs, runs in behind the Castle, bending north and west, making safe and secret anchorage. Into the creek falls over a precipice a mountain-stream, which never fails in volume of water. On the western shore of that creek is the Castle, a huge pile of buildings of every style of architecture, from the Twelfth century to where such things seemed to stop in this dear old-world land—about the time of Queen Elizabeth. So it is pretty picturesque. I can tell you. When we got the first glimpse of the place from the steamer the officer, with whom I was on the bridge, pointed towards it and said:

"That is where we saw the dead woman floating in a coffin." That was rather interesting, so I asked him all about it. He took from his pocket-book a cutting from an Italian paper, which he handed to me. As I can read and speak Italian fairly well, it was all right; but as you, my dear Aunt Janet, are not skilled in languages, and as I doubt if there is any assistance of the kind to be had at Croom, I do not send it. But as I have heard that the item has been produced in the last number of *The Journal of Occultism*, you will be easily able to get it. As he handed me the cutting he said: "I am Destilia!" His story was so strange that I asked him a good many questions about it. He answered me quite frankly on every point, but always adhering stoutly to the main point—namely, that it was no phantom or mirage, no dream or imperfect vision in a fog. "We were four in all who saw it," he said—"three from the bridge and the Englishman, Caulfield—from the bows—whose account exactly agreed with what we saw. Captain Mirolani and Falamano and I were all awake and in good trim. We looked with our night-glasses, which are more than usually powerful. You know, we need good glasses for the east shore of the Adriatic and for among the islands to the south. There was a full moon and a brilliant light. Of course we were a little way off, for though the Spear of Ivan is in deep water, one has to be careful of currents, for it is in just such places that the dangerous currents run." The agent of Lloyd's told me only a few weeks ago that it was only after a prolonged investigation of the tidal and sea currents that the house decided to except from ordinary sea risks losses due to a too close course by the Spear of Ivan. When I tried to get a little more definite account of the coffin-boat and the dead lady that is given in *The*

Journal of Occultism he simply shrugged his shoulders. "Signor, it is all," he said. "That Englishman wrote everything after endless questioning."

So you see, my dear, that our new home is not without superstitious interests of its own. It is rather a nice idea, is it not, to have a dead woman cruising round our promontory in a coffin? I doubt if even at Croom you can beat that. "Makes the place kind of homey," as an American would say. When you come, Aunt Janet, you will not feel lonesome, at any rate, and it will save us the trouble of importing some of your Highland ghosts to make you feel at home in the new land. I don't know, but we might ask the stiff to come to tea with us. Of course, it would be a late tea. Somewhere between midnight and cock-crow would be about the etiquette of the thing, I fancy!

But I must tell you all the realities of the Castle and around it. So I will write again within a day or two, and try to let you know enough to prepare you for coming here. Till then adieu, my dear.

Your loving
RUPERT.

From Rupert Sent Leger, Vissarion, to Janet MacKelpie, Croom.

January 25, 1907.

I hope I did not frighten you, dear Aunt Janet, by the yarn of the lady in the coffin. But I know you are not afraid; you have told me too many weird stories for me to dread that. Besides, you have Second Sight—latent, at all events. However, there won't be any more ghosts, or about ghosts, in this letter. I want to tell you all about our new home. I am so glad you are coming out so soon; I am beginning to feel so lonesome—I walk about sometimes aimlessly, and find my thoughts drifting in such an odd way. If I didn't know better, I might begin to think I was in love! There is no one here to be in love with; so make your mind easy, Aunt Janet. Not that you would be unhappy, I know, dear, if I *did* fall in love. I suppose I must marry some day. It is a duty now, I know, when there is such an estate as Uncle Roger has left me. And I know this: I shall never marry any woman unless I love her. And I am right sure that if I do love her you will love her, too, Aunt Janet! Won't you, dear? It wouldn't be half a delight if you didn't. It won't if you don't. There, now!

But before I begin to describe Vissarion I shall throw a sop to you as a chatelaine; that may give you patience to read the rest. The Castle needs a lot of things to make it comfortable—as you would consider it. In fact, it is absolutely destitute of everything of a domestic nature. Uncle Roger had it vetted on the defence side, and so far it could stand a siege. But it couldn't cook a dinner or go through a spring-cleaning! As you know, I am not much up in domestic matters, and so I cannot give you details; but you may take it that it wants everything. I don't mean furniture, or silver, or even gold-plate, or works of art, for it is full of the most magnificent old things that you can imagine. I think Uncle Roger must have been a collector, and gathered a lot of good things in all sorts of places, stored them for years, and then sent them here. But as to glass, china, delft, all sorts of crockery, linen, household appliances and machinery, cooking utensils—except of the simplest—there are none. I don't think Uncle Roger could have lived here more than on a temporary picnic. So far as I only am concerned, I am all right; a gridiron and a saucepan are all *I* want—and I can use them myself. But, dear Aunt Janet, I don't want you to pig it. I would like you to have everything you can imagine, and all of the very best. Cost doesn't count now for us, thanks to Uncle Roger; and so I want you to order all. I know you, dear—being a woman—won't object to shopping. But it will have to be wholesale. This is an enormous place, and will swallow up all you can buy—like a quicksand. Do as you like about choosing, but get all the help you can. Don't be afraid of getting too much. You can't, or of being idle when you are here. I assure you that when you come there will be so much to do and so many things to think of that you will want to get away from it all. And, besides, Aunt Janet, I hope you won't be too long. Indeed, I don't wish to be selfish, but your boy is lonely, and wants you. And when you get here you will be an EMPRESS. I don't altogether like doing so, lest I should offend a millionairess like you; but it may facilitate matters, and the way's of commerce are strict, though devious. So I send you a cheque for £1,000 for the little things: and a letter to the bank to honour your own cheques for any amount I have got.

I think, by the way, I should, if I were you, take or send out a few servants—not too many at first, only just enough to attend on our two selves. You can arrange to send for any more you may want later. Engage them, and arrange for their being paid—when they are in our service we must treat them well—and then they can be at our call as you find that we want them. I think you should secure, say, fifty or a hundred—'tis an awfu' big place, Aunt Janet! And in the same way will you secure—and, of course, arrange for pay similarly—a hundred men, exclusive of any servants you think it well to have. I should like the General, if he can give the time, to choose or pass them. I want clansmen that I can depend on, if need be. We are going to live in a country which is at present strange to us, and it is well to look things in the face. I know Sir Colin will only have men who are a credit to Scotland and to Ross and to Croom—men who will impress the Blue Mountaineers. I know they will take them to their hearts—certainly if any of them are bachelors the girls will! Forgive me! But if we are to settle here, our followers will probably want to settle also. Moreover, the Blue Mountaineers may want followers also! And will want them to settle, too, and have successors!

Now for the description of the place. Well, I simply can't just now. It is all so wonderful and so beautiful. The Castle—I have written so much already about other things that I really must keep the Castle for another letter! Love to Sir Colin if he is at Croom. And oh, dear Aunt Janet, how I wish that my dear mother was coming out! It all seems so dark and empty without her. How she would have enjoyed it! How proud she would have been! And, my dear, if she could be with us again, how grateful she would have been to you for all you have done for her boy! As I am, believe me, most truly and sincerely and affectionately grateful.

Your loving
RUPERT.

Rupert Sent Leger, Vissarion, to Janet MacKelpie, Croom.

January 26, 1907.

MY DEAR AUNT JANET,

Please read this as if it was a part of the letter I wrote yesterday.

The Castle itself is so vast that I really can't describe it in detail. So I am waiting till you come; and then you and I will go over it together and learn all that we can about it. We shall take Rooke with us, and, as he is supposed to know every part of it, from the keep to the torture-chamber, we can spend a few days over it. Of course, I have been over most of it, since I came—that, is, I went at various times to see different portions—the battlements, the bastions, the old guard-room, the hall, the chapel, the walls, the roof. And I have been through some of the network of rock passages. Uncle Roger must have spent a mint of money on it, so far as I can see; and though I am not a soldier, I have been in so many places fortified in different ways that I am not entirely ignorant of the subject. He has restored it in such an up-to-date way that it is practically impregnable to anything under big guns or a siege-train. He has gone so far as to have certain outworks and the keep covered with armoured plating of what looks like harveyized steel. You will wonder when you see it. But as yet I really know only a few rooms, and am familiar with only one—my own room. The drawing-room—not the great hall, which is a vast place; the library—a magnificent one, but in sad disorder—we must get a librarian some day to put it in trim; and the drawing-room and boudoir and bedroom suite which I have selected for you, are all fine. But my own room is what suits me best, though I do not think you would care for it for yourself. If you do, you shall have it. It was Uncle Roger's own room when he stayed here; living in it for a few days served to give me more insight to his character—or rather to his mind—than I could have otherwise had. It is just the kind of place I like myself; so, naturally, I understand the other chap who liked it too. It is a fine big room, not quite within the Castle, but an outlying part of it. It is not detached, or anything of that sort, but is a sort of garden-room built on to it. There seems to have been always some sort of place where it is, for the passages and openings inside seem to accept or recognize it. It can be shut off if necessary—it would be in case of attack—by a great slab of steel, just like the door of a safe, which slides from inside the wall, and can be operated from either inside or outside—if you know how. That is from my room or from within the keep. The mechanism is a secret, and no one but Rooke and I know it. The room opens out through a great French window—the French window is modern, I take it, and was arranged by or for Uncle Roger; I think there must have been always a large opening there, for centuries at least—which opens on a wide terrace or balcony of white marble, extending right and left. From this a white marble stair lies straight in front of the window, and leads down to the garden. The balcony and staircase are quite ancient—of old Italian work, beautifully carved, and, of course, weather-worn through centuries. There is just that little tinging of green here and there which makes all outdoor marble so charming. It is hard to believe at times that it is a part of a fortified castle, it is so elegant and free and open. The first glance of it would make a burglar's heart glad. He would say to himself: "Here is the sort of crib I like when I'm on the job. You can just walk in and out as you choose." But, Aunt Janet, old Roger was cuter than any burglar. He had the place so guarded that the burglar would have been a baffled burglar. There are two steel shields which can slide out from the wall and lock into the other side right across the whole big window. One is a grille of steel bands that open out into diamond-shaped lozenges. Nothing bigger than a kitten could get through; and yet you can see the garden and the mountains and the whole view—much the same as you ladies can see through your veils. The other is a great sheet of steel, which slides out in a similar way in different grooves. It is not, of course, so heavy and strong as the safe-door which covers the little opening in the main wall, but Rooke tells me it is proof against the heaviest rifle-hall.

Having told you this, I must tell you, too, Aunt Janet, lest you should be made anxious by the *arrière-pensée* of all these warlike measures of defence, that I always sleep at night with one of these iron screens across the window. Of course, when I am awake I leave it open. As yet I have tried only, but not used, the grille; and I don't think I shall ever use anything else, for it is a perfect guard. If it should be tampered with from outside it would sound an alarm at the head of the bed, and the pressing of a button would roll out the solid steel screen in front of it. As a matter of fact, I have been so used to the open that I don't feel comfortable shut in. I only close windows against cold or rain. The weather here is delightful—as yet, at all events—but they tell me that the rainy season will be on us before very long.

I think you will like my den, aunty dear, though it will doubtless be a worry to you to see it so untidy. But that can't be helped. I must be untidy *somewhere*; and it is best in my own den!

Again I find my letter so long that I must cut it off now and go on again to-night. So this must go as it stands. I shall not cause you to wait to hear all I can tell you about our new home.

Your loving
RUPERT.

From Rupert Sent Leger, Vissarion, to Janet MacKelpie, Croom.

January 29, 1907.

MY DEAR AUNT JANET,

My den looks out, as I told you in my last letter, on the garden, or, to speak more accurately, on *one* of the gardens, for there are acres of them. This is the old one, which must be almost as old as the Castle itself, for it was within the defences in the old days of bows. The wall that surrounds the inner portion of it has long ago been levelled, but sufficient remains at either end where it joined the outer defences to show the long casemates for the bowmen to shoot through and the raised stone gallery where they stood. It is just the same kind of building as the stone-work of the sentry's walk on the roof and of the great old guardroom under it.

But whatever the garden may have been, and no matter how it was guarded, it is a most lovely place. There are whole sections of garden here of various styles—Greek, Italian, French, German, Dutch, British, Spanish, African, Moorish—all the older nationalities. I am going to have a new one laid out for you—a Japanese garden. I have sent to the great gardener of Japan, Minaro, to make the plans for it, and to come over with workmen to carry it out. He is to bring trees and shrubs and flowers and stone-work, and everything that can be required; and you shall superintend the finishing, if not the doing, of it yourself. We have such a fine head of water here, and the climate is, they tell me, usually so lovely that we can do anything in the gardening way. If it should ever turn out that the climate does not suit, we shall put a great high glass roof over it, and *make* a suitable climate.

This garden in front of my room is the old Italian garden. It must have been done with extraordinary taste and care, for there is not a bit of it which is not rarely beautiful. Sir Thomas Browne himself, for all his *Quincunx*, would have been delighted with it, and have found material for another "Garden of Cyrus." It is so big that there are endless "episodes" of garden beauty I think all Italy must have been ransacked in old times for garden stone-work of exceptional beauty; and these treasures have been put together by some master-hand. Even the formal borders of the walks are of old porous stone, which takes the weather-staining so beautifully, and are carved in endless variety. Now that the gardens have been so long neglected or left in abeyance, the green staining has become perfect. Though the stone-work is itself intact, it has all the picturesque effect of the wear and ruin wrought by many centuries. I am having it kept for you just as it is, except that I have had the weeds and undergrowth cleared away so that its beauties might be visible.

But it is not merely the architect work of the garden that is so beautiful, nor is the assembling there of the manifold wealth of floral beauty—there is the beauty that Nature creates by the hand of her servant, Time. You see, Aunt Janet, how the beautiful garden inspires a danger-hardened old tramp like me to high-grade sentiments of poetic fancy! Not only have limestone and sandstone, and even marble, grown green in time, but even the shrubs planted and then neglected have developed new kinds of beauty of their own. In some far-distant time some master-gardener of the Vissarions has tried to realize an idea—that of tiny plants that would grow just a little higher than the flowers, so that the effect of an uneven floral surface would be achieved without any hiding of anything in the garden seen from anywhere. This is only my reading of what has been from the effect of what is! In the long period of neglect the shrubs have outlived the flowers. Nature has been doing her own work all the time in enforcing the survival of the fittest. The shrubs have grown and grown, and have overtopped flower and weed, according to their inherent varieties of stature; to the effect that now you see irregularly scattered through the garden quite a number—for it is a big place—of vegetable products which from a landscape standpoint have something of the general effect of statues without the cramping feeling of detail. Whoever it was that laid out that part of the garden or made the choice of items, must have taken pains to get strange specimens, for all those taller shrubs are in special colours, mostly yellow or white—white cypress, white holly, yellow yew, grey-golden box, silver juniper, variegated maple, spiraea, and numbers of dwarf shrubs whose names I don't know. I only know that when the moon shines—and this, my dear Aunt Janet, is the very land of moonlight itself!—they all look ghastly pale. The effect is weird to the last degree, and I am sure that you will enjoy it. For myself, as you know, uncanny things hold no fear. I suppose it is that I have been up against so many different kinds of fears, or, rather, of things which for most people have terrors of their own, that I have come to have a contempt—not an active contempt, you know, but a tolerative contempt—for the whole family of them. And you, too, will enjoy yourself here famously, I know. You'll have to collect all the stories of such matters in our new world and make a new book of facts for the Psychical Research Society. It will be nice to see your own name on a title-page, won't it, Aunt Janet?

From Rupert Sent Leger, Vissarion, to Janet MacKelpie, Croom.

January 30, 1907.

MY DEAR AUNT JANET,

I stopped writing last night—do you know why? Because I wanted to write more! This sounds a paradox, but it is true. The fact is that, as I go on telling you of this delightful place, I keep finding out new beauties myself. Broadly speaking, it *is all* beautiful. In the long view or the little view—as the telescope or the microscope directs—it is all the same. Your eye can turn on nothing that does not entrance you. I was yesterday roaming about the upper part of time Castle, and came across some delightful nooks, which at once I became fond of, and already like them as if I had known them all my life. I felt at first a sense of greediness when I had appropriated to myself several rooms in different places—I who have never in my life had more than one room which I could call my own—and that only for a time! But when I slept on it the feeling changed, and its aspect is now not half bad. It is now under another classification—under a much more important label—*proprietorship*. If I were writing philosophy, I should here put in a cynical remark:

"Selfishness is an appanage of poverty. It might appear in the studbook as by 'Morals' out of 'Wants.'"

I have now three bedrooms arranged as my own particular dens. One of the other two was also a choice of Uncle Roger's. It is at the top of one of the towers to the extreme east, and from it I can catch the first ray of light over the mountains. I slept in it last night, and when I woke, as in my travelling I was accustomed to do, at dawn, I saw from my bed through an open window—a small window, for it is in a fortress tower—the whole great expanse to the east. Not far off, and springing from the summit of a great ruin, where long ago a seed had fallen, rose a great silver-birch, and the half-transparent, drooping branches and hanging clusters of leaf broke the outline of the grey hills beyond, for the hills were, for a wonder, grey instead of blue. There was a mackerel sky, with the clouds dropping on the mountain-tops till you could hardly say which was which. It was a mackerel sky of a very bold and extraordinary kind—not a dish of mackerel, but a world of mackerel! The mountains are certainly most lovely. In this clear air they usually seem close at hand. It was only this morning, with the faint glimpse of the dawn whilst the night clouds were still unpierced by the sunlight, that I seemed to realize their greatness. I have seen the same enlightening effect of aerial perspective a few times before—in Colorado, in Upper India, in Thibet, and in the uplands amongst the Andes.

There is certainly something in looking at things from above which tends to raise one's own self-esteem. From the height, inequalities simply disappear. This I have often felt on a big scale when ballooning, or, better still, from an aeroplane. Even here from the tower the outlook is somehow quite different from below. One realizes the place and all around it, not in detail, but as a whole. I shall certainly sleep up here occasionally, when you have come and we have settled down to our life as it is to be. I shall live in my own room downstairs, where I can have the intimacy of the garden. But I shall appreciate it all the more from now and again losing the sense of intimacy for a while, and surveying it without the sense of one's own self-importance.

I hope you have started on that matter of the servants. For myself, I don't care a button whether or not there are any servants at all; but I know well that you won't come till you have made your arrangements regarding them! Another thing, Aunt Janet. You must not be killed with work here, and it is all so vast . . . Why can't you get some sort of secretary who will write your letters and do all that sort of thing for you? I know you won't have a man secretary; but there are lots of women now who can write shorthand and typewrite. You could doubtless get one in the clan—someone with a desire to better herself. I know you would make her happy here. If she is not too young, all the better; she will have learned to hold her tongue and mind her own business, and not be too inquisitive. That would be a nuisance when we are finding our way about in a new country and trying to reconcile all sorts of opposites in a whole new country with new people, whom at first we shan't understand, and who certainly won't understand us; where every man carries a gun with as little thought of it as he has of buttons! Good-bye for a while.

Your loving
RUPERT.

From Rupert Sent Leger, Vissarion, to Janet MacKelpie, Croom.

February 3, 1907.

I am back in my own room again. Already it seems to me that to get here again is like coming home. I have been going about for the last few days amongst the mountaineers and trying to make their acquaintance. It is a tough job; and I can see that there will be nothing but to stick to it. They are in reality the most primitive people I ever met—the most fixed to their own ideas, which belong to centuries back. I can understand now what people were like in England—not in Queen Elizabeth's time, for that was civilized time, but in the time of Coeur-de-Lion, or even earlier—and all the time with the most absolute mastery of weapons of precision. Every man carries a rifle—and knows how to use it, too. I do believe they would rather go without their clothes than their guns if they had to choose between them. They also carry a handjar, which used to be their national weapon. It is a sort of heavy, straight cutlass, and they are so expert with it as well as so strong that it is as facile in the hands of a Blue Mountaineer as is a foil in the hands of a Persian *maître d'armes*. They are so proud and reserved that they make one feel quite small, and an "outsider" as well. I can see quite well that they rather resent my being here at all. It is not personal, for when alone with me they are genial, almost brotherly; but the moment a few of them get together they are like a sort of jury, with me as the criminal before them. It is an odd situation, and quite new to me. I am pretty well accustomed to all sorts of people, from cannibals to Mahatmas, but I'm blessed if I ever struck such a type as this—so proud, so haughty, so reserved, so distant, so absolutely fearless, so honourable, so hospitable. Uncle Roger's head was level when he chose them out as a people to live amongst. Do you know, Aunt Janet, I can't help feeling that they are very much like your own Highlanders—only more so. I'm sure of one thing: that in the end we shall get on capitally together. But it will be a slow job, and will need a lot of patience. I have a feeling in my bones that when they know me better they will be very loyal and very true; and I am not a hair's-breadth afraid of them or anything they shall or might do. That is, of course, if I live long enough for them to have time to know me. Anything may happen with such an indomitable, proud people to whom pride is more than victuals. After all, it only needs one man out of a crowd to have a wrong idea or to make a mistake as to one's motive—and there you are. But it will be all right that way, I am sure. I am come here to stay, as Uncle Roger wished. And stay I shall even if it has to be in a little bed of my own beyond the garden—seven feet odd long, and not too narrow—or else a stone-box of equal proportions in the vaults of St. Sava's Church across the Creek—the old burial-place of the Vissarions and other noble people for a good many centuries back . . .

I have been reading over this letter, dear Aunt Janet, and I am afraid the record is rather an alarming one. But don't you go building up superstitious horrors or fears on it. Honestly, I am only joking about death—a thing to which I have been rather prone for a good many years back. Not in very good taste, I suppose, but certainly very useful when the old man with the black wings goes flying about you day and night in strange places, sometimes visible and at others invisible. But you can always hear wings, especially in the dark, when you cannot see them. *You* know that, Aunt Janet, who come of a race of warriors, and who have special sight behind or through the black curtain.

Honestly, I am in no whit afraid of the Blue Mountaineers, nor have I a doubt of them. I love them already for their splendid qualities, and I am prepared to love them for themselves. I feel, too, that they will love me (and incidentally they are sure to love you). I have a sort of undercurrent of thought that there is something in their minds concerning me—something not painful, but disturbing; something that has a base in the past; something that has hope in it and possible pride, and not a little respect. As yet they can have had no opportunity of forming such impression from seeing me or from any thing I have done. Of course, it may be that, although they are fine, tall, stalwart men, I am still a head and shoulders over the tallest of them that I have yet seen. I catch their eyes looking up at me as though they were measuring me, even when they are keeping away from me, or, rather, keeping me from them at arm's length. I suppose I shall understand what it all means some day.

In the meantime there is nothing to do but to go on my own way—which is Uncle Roger's—and wait and be patient and just. I have learned the value of that, any way, in my life amongst strange peoples. Good-night.

Your loving
RUPERT.

From Rupert Sent Leger, Vissarion, to Janet MacKelpie, Croom.

February 24, 1907.

MY DEAR AUNT JANET,

I am more than rejoiced to hear that you are coming here so soon. This isolation is, I think, getting on my nerves. I thought for a while last night that I was getting on, but the reaction came all too soon. I was in my room in the east turret, the room on the *corbeille*, and saw here and there men passing silently and swiftly between the trees as though in secret. By-and-by I located their meeting-place, which was in a hollow in the midst of the wood just outside the "natural" garden, as the map or plan of the castle calls it. I stalked that place for all I was worth, and suddenly walked straight into the midst of them. There were perhaps two or three hundred gathered, about the very finest lot of men I ever saw in my life. It was in its way quite an experience, and one not likely to be repeated, for, as I told you, in this country every man carries a rifle, and knows how to use it. I do not think I have seen a single man (or married man either) without his rifle since I came here. I wonder if they take them with them to bed! Well, the instant after I stood amongst them every rifle in the place was aimed straight at me. Don't be alarmed, Aunt Janet; they did not fire at me. If they had I should not be writing to you now. I should be in that little bit of real estate or the stone box, and about as full of lead as I could hold. Ordinarily, I take it, they would have fired on the instant; that is the etiquette here. But this time they—all separately but all together—made a new rule. No one said a word or, so far as I could see, made a movement. Here came in my own experience. I had been more than once in a tight place of something of the same kind, so I simply behaved in the most natural way I could. I felt conscious—it was all in a flash, remember—that if I showed fear or cause for fear, or even acknowledged danger by so much as even holding up my hands, I should have drawn all the fire. They all remained stock-still, as though they had been turned into stone, for several seconds. Then a queer kind of look flashed round them like wind over corn—something like the surprise one shows unconsciously on waking in a strange place. A second after they each dropped the rifle to the hollow of his arm and stood ready for anything. It was all as regular and quick and simultaneous as a salute at St. James's Palace.

Happily I had no arms of any kind with me, so that there could be no complication. I am rather a quick hand myself when there is any shooting to be done. However, there was no trouble here, but the contrary;

the Blue Mountaineers—it sounds like a new sort of Bond Street band, doesn't it?—treated me in quite a different way than they did when I first met them. They were amazingly civil, almost deferential. But, all time same, they were more distant than ever, and all the time I was there I could get not a whit closer to them. They seemed in a sort of way to be afraid or in awe of me. No doubt that will soon pass away, and when we know one another better we shall become close friends. They are too fine fellows not to be worth a little waiting for. (That sentence, by the way, is a pretty bad sentence! In old days you would have slippered me for it!) Your journey is all arranged, and I hope you will be comfortable. Rooke will meet you at Liverpool Street and look after everything.

I shan't write again, but when we meet at Fiume I shall begin to tell you all the rest. Till then, good-bye. A good journey to you, and a happy meeting to us both.

RUPERT.

Letter from Janet MacKelpie, Vissarion, to Sir Colin MacKelpie, United Service Club, London.

February 28, 1907.

DEAREST UNCLE,

I had a very comfortable journey all across Europe. Rupert wrote to me some time ago to say that when I got to Vissarion I should be an Empress, and he certainly took care that on the way here I should be treated like one. Rooke, who seems a wonderful old man, was in the next compartment to that reserved for me. At Harwich he had everything arranged perfectly, and so right on to Fiume. Everywhere there were attentive officials waiting. I had a carriage all to myself, which I joined at Antwerp—a whole carriage with a suite of rooms, dining-room, drawing-room, bedroom, even bath-room. There was a cook with a kitchen of his own on board, a real chef like a French nobleman in disguise. There were also a waiter and a servant-maid. My own maid Maggie was quite awed at first. We were as far as Cologne before she summoned up courage to order them about. Whenever we stopped Rooke was on the platform with local officials, and kept the door of my carriage like a sentry on duty.

At Fiume, when the train slowed down, I saw Rupert waiting on the platform. He looked magnificent, towering over everybody there like a giant. He is in perfect health, and seemed glad to see me. He took me off at once on an automobile to a quay where an electric launch was waiting. This took us on board a beautiful big steam-yacht, which was waiting with full steam up and—how he got there I don't know—Rooke waiting at the gangway.

I had another suite all to myself. Rupert and I had dinner together—I think the finest dinner I ever sat down to. This was very nice of Rupert, for it was all for me. He himself only ate a piece of steak and drank a glass of water. I went to bed early, for, despite the luxury of the journey, I was very tired.

I awoke in the grey of the morning, and came on deck. We were close to the coast. Rupert was on the bridge with the Captain, and Rooke was acting as pilot. When Rupert saw me, he ran down the ladder and took me up on the bridge. He left me there while he ran down again and brought me up a lovely fur cloak which I had never seen. He put it on me and kissed me. He is the tenderest-hearted boy in the world, as well as the best and bravest! He made me take his arm whilst he pointed out Vissarion, towards which we were steering. It is the most lovely place I ever saw. I won't stop to describe it now, for it will be better that you see it for yourself and enjoy it all fresh as I did.

The Castle is an immense place. You had better ship off, as soon as all is ready here and you can arrange it, the servants whom I engaged; and I am not sure that we shall not want as many more. There has hardly been a mop or broom on the place for centuries, and I doubt if it ever had a thorough good cleaning all over since it was built. And, do you know, Uncle, that it might be well to double that little army of yours that you are arranging for Rupert? Indeed, the boy told me himself that he was going to write to you about it. I think old Lachlan and his wife, Sandy's Mary, had better be in charge of the maids when they come over. A lot of lassies like yon will be iller to keep together than a flock of sheep. So it will be wise to have authority over them, especially as none of them speaks a word of foreign tongues. Rooke—you saw him at the station at Liverpool Street—will, if he be available, go over to bring the whole body here. He has offered to do it if I should wish. And, by the way, I think it will be well, when the time comes for their departure, if not only the lassies, but Lachlan and Sandy's Mary, too, will call him *Mister* Rooke. He is a very important person indeed here. He is, in fact, a sort of Master of the Castle, and though he is very self-suppressing, is a man of rarely fine qualities. Also it will be well to keep authority. When your clansmen come over, he will have charge of them, too. Dear me! I find I have written such a long letter, I must stop and get to work. I shall write again.

Your very affectionate
JANET.

From the Same to the Same.

March 3, 1907.

DEAREST UNCLE,

All goes well here, and as there is no news, I only write because you are a dear, and I want to thank you for all the trouble you have taken for me—and for Rupert. I think we had better wait awhile before bringing out the servants. Rooke is away on some business for Rupert, and will not be back for some time; Rupert thinks it may be a couple of months. There is no one else that he could send to take charge of the party from home, and I don't like the idea of all those lassies coming out without an escort. Even Lachlan and Sandy's Mary are ignorant of foreign languages and foreign ways. But as soon as Rooke returns we can have them all out. I dare say you will have some of your clansmen ready by then, and I think the poor girls, who may feel a bit strange in a new country like this, where the ways are so different from ours, will feel easier when they know that there are some of their own mankind near them. Perhaps it might be well that those of them who are engaged to each other—I know there are some—should marry before they come out here. It will be more convenient in many ways, and will save lodgment, and, besides, these Blue Mountaineers are very handsome men. Good-night.

JANET.

Sir Colin MacKelpie, Croom, to Janet MacKelpie, Vissarion.

March 9, 1907.

MY DEAR JANET,

I have duly received both your letters, and am delighted to find you are so well pleased with your new home. It must certainly be a very lovely and unique place, and I am myself longing to see it. I came up here three days ago, and am, as usual, feeling all the better for a breath of my native air. Time goes on, my dear, and I am beginning to feel not so young as I was. Tell Rupert that the men are all fit, and longing to get out to him. They are certainly a fine lot of men. I don't think I ever saw a finer. I have had them drilled and trained as soldiers, and, in addition, have had them taught a lot of trades just as they selected themselves. So he shall have nigh him men who can turn their hands to anything—not, of course, that they all know every trade, but amongst them there is someone who can do whatever may be required. There are blacksmiths, carpenters, farriers, saddle-makers, gardeners, plumbers, cutlers, gunsmiths, so, as they all are farmers by origin and sportsmen by practice, they will make a rare household body of men. They are nearly all first-class shots, and I am having them practise with revolvers. They are being taught fencing and broadsword and ju-jitsu; I have organized them in military form, with their own sergeants and corporals. This morning I had an inspection, and I assure you, my dear, they could give points to the Household troop in matters of drill. I tell you I am proud of my clansmen!

I think you are quite wise about waiting to bring out the lassies, and wiser still about the marrying. I dare say there will be more marrying when they all get settled in a foreign country. I shall be glad of it, for as Rupert is going to settle there, it will be good for him to have round him a little colony of his own people. And it will be good for them, too, for I know he will be good to them—as you will, my dear. The hills are barren here, and life is hard, and each year there is more and more demand for crofts, and sooner or later our people must thin out. And mayhap our little settlement of MacKelpie clan away beyond the frontiers of the Empire may be some service to the nation and the King. But this is a dream! I see that here I am beginning to realise in myself one part of Isaiah's prophecy:

"Your young men shall see visions, and your old men shall dream dreams."

By the way, my dear, talking about dreams, I am sending you out some boxes of books which were in your rooms. They are nearly all on odd subjects that *we* understand—Second Sight, Ghosts, Dreams (that was what brought the matter to my mind just now), superstitions, Vampires, Wehr-Wolves, and all such uncanny folk and things. I looked over some of these books, and found your marks and underlining and comments, so I fancy you will miss them in your new home. You will, I am sure, feel more at ease with such old friends close to you. I have taken the names and sent the list to London, so that when you pay me a visit again you will be at home in all ways. If you come to me altogether, you will be more welcome still—if possible. But I am sure that Rupert, who I know loves you very much, will try to make you so happy that you will not want to leave him. So I will have to come out often to see you both, even at the cost of leaving Croom for so long. Strange, is it not? that now, when, through Roger Melton's more than kind remembrance of me, I am able to go where I will and do what I will, I want more and more to remain at home by my own ingle. I don't think that anyone but you or Rupert could get me away from it. I am working very hard at my little regiment, as I call it. They are simply fine, and will, I am sure, do us credit. The uniforms are all made, and well made, too. There is not a man of them that does not look like an officer. I tell you, Janet, that when we turn out the Vissarion Guard we shall feel proud of them. I dare say that a couple of months will do all that can be done here. I shall come out with them myself. Rupert writes me that he thinks it will be more comfortable to come out direct in a ship of our own. So when I go up to London in a few weeks' time I shall see about chartering a suitable vessel. It will certainly save a lot of trouble to us and anxiety to our people. Would it not be well when I am getting the ship, if I charter one big enough to take out all your lassies, too? It is not as if they were strangers. After all, my dear, soldiers are soldiers and lassies are lassies. But these are all kinsfolk, as well as clansmen and clanswomen, and I, their Chief, shall be there. Let me know your views and wishes in this respect. Mr. Trent, whom I saw before leaving London, asked me to "convey to you his most respectful remembrances"—these were his very words, and here they are. Trent is a nice fellow, and I like him. He has promised to pay me a visit here before the month is up, and I look forward to our both enjoying ourselves.

Good-bye, my dear, and the Lord watch over you and our dear boy.

Your affectionate Uncle,
COLIN ALEXANDER MACKELPIE.

BOOK III: THE COMING OF THE LADY

RUPERT SENT LEGER'S JOURNAL.

April 3, 1907.

I have waited till now—well into midday—before beginning to set down the details of the strange episode of last night. I have spoken with persons whom I know to be of normal type. I have breakfasted, as usual heartily, and have every reason to consider myself in perfect health and sanity. So that the record following may be regarded as not only true in substance, but exact as to details. I have investigated and reported on too many cases for the Psychical Research Society to be ignorant of the necessity for absolute accuracy in such matters of even the minutest detail.

Yesterday was Tuesday, the second day of April, 1907. I passed a day of interest, with its fair amount of work of varying kinds. Aunt Janet and I lunched together, had a stroll round the gardens after tea—especially examining the site for the new Japanese garden, which we shall call "Janet's Garden." We went in mackintoshes, for the rainy season is in its full, the only sign of its not being a repetition of the Deluge being that breaks in the continuance are beginning. They are short at present but will doubtless enlarge themselves as the season comes towards an end. We dined together at seven. After dinner I had a cigar, and then joined Aunt Janet for an hour in her drawing-room. I left her at half-past ten, when I went to my own room and wrote some letters. At ten minutes past eleven I wound my watch, so I know the time accurately. Having prepared for bed, I drew back the heavy curtain in front of my window, which opens on the marble steps into the Italian garden. I had put out my light before drawing back the curtain, for I wanted to have a look at the scene before turning in. Aunt Janet has always had an old-fashioned idea of the need (or propriety, I hardly know which) of keeping windows closed and curtains drawn. I am gradually getting her to leave my room alone in this respect, but at present the change is in its fitful stage, and of course I must not hurry matters or be too persistent, as it would hurt her feelings. This night was one of those under the old régime. It was a delight to look out, for the scene was perfect of its own kind. The long spell of rain—the ceaseless downpour which had for the time flooded everywhere—had passed, and water in abnormal places rather trickled than ran. We were now beginning to be in the sloppy rather than the deluged stage. There was plenty of light to see by, for the moon had begun to show out fitfully through the masses of flying clouds. The uncertain light made weird shadows with the shrubs and statues in the garden. The long straight walk which leads from the marble steps is strewn with fine sand white from the quartz strand in the nook to the south of the Castle. Tall shrubs of white holly, yew, juniper, cypress, and variegated maple and spiraea, which stood at intervals along the walk and its branches, appeared ghost-like in the fitful moonlight. The many vases and statues and urns, always like phantoms in a half-light, were more than ever weird. Last night the moonlight was unusually effective, and showed not only the gardens down to the defending wall, but the deep gloom of the great forest-trees beyond; and beyond that, again, to where the mountain chain began, the forest running up their silvered slopes flamelike in form, deviated here and there by great crags and the outcropping rocky sinews of the vast mountains.

Whilst I was looking at this lovely prospect, I thought I saw something white flit, like a modified white flash, at odd moments from one to another of the shrubs or statues—anything which would afford cover from observation. At first I was not sure whether I really saw anything or did not. This was in itself a little disturbing to me, for I have been so long trained to minute observation of facts surrounding me, on which often depend not only my own life, but the lives of others, that I have become accustomed to trust my eyes; and anything creating the faintest doubt in this respect is a cause of more or less anxiety to me. Now, however, that my attention was called to myself, I looked more keenly, and in a very short time was satisfied that something was moving—something clad in white. It was natural enough that my thoughts should tend towards something uncanny—the belief that this place is haunted, conveyed in a thousand ways of speech and inference. Aunt Janet's eerie beliefs, fortified by her books on occult subjects—and of late, in our isolation from the rest of the world, the subject of daily conversations—helped to this end. No wonder, then, that, fully awake and with senses all on edge, I waited for some further manifestation from this ghostly visitor—as in my mind I took it to be. It must surely be a ghost or spiritual manifestation of some kind which moved in this silent way. In order to see and hear better, I softly moved back the folding grille, opened the French window, and stepped out, bare-footed and pyjama-clad as I was, on the marble terrace. How cold the wet marble was! How heavy smelled the rain-laden garden! It was as though the night and the damp, and even the moonlight, were drawing the aroma from all the flowers that blossomed. The whole night seemed to exhale heavy, half-intoxicating odours! I stood at the head of the marble steps, and all immediately before me was ghostly in the extreme—the white marble terrace and steps, the white walks of quartz-sand glistening under the fitful moonlight; the shrubs of white or pale green or yellow,—all looking dim and ghostly in the glamorous light; the white statues and vases. And amongst them, still flitting noiselessly, that mysterious elusive figure which I could not say was based on fact or imagination. I held my breath, listening intently for every sound; but sound there was none, save those of the night and its denizens. Owls hooted in the forest; bats, taking advantage of the cessation of the rain, flitted about silently, like shadows in the air. But there was no more sign of moving ghost or phantom, or whatever I had seen might have been—if, indeed, there had been anything except imagination.

So, after waiting awhile, I returned to my room, closed the window, drew the grille across again, and dragged the heavy curtain before the opening; then, having extinguished my candles, went to bed in the dark. In a few minutes I must have been asleep.

"What was that?" I almost heard the words of my own thought as I sat up in bed wide awake. To memory rather than present hearing the disturbing sound had seemed like the faint tapping at the window. For some seconds I listened, mechanically but intently, with bated breath and that quick beating of the heart which in a timorous person speaks for fear, and for expectation in another. In the stillness the sound came again—this time a very, very faint but unmistakable tapping at the glass door.

I jumped up, drew back the curtain, and for a moment stood appalled.

There, outside on the balcony, in the now brilliant moonlight, stood a woman, wrapped in white grave-clothes saturated with water, which dripped on the marble floor, making a pool which trickled slowly down the wet steps. Attitude and dress and circumstance all conveyed the idea that, though she moved and spoke, she was not quick, but dead. She was young and very beautiful, but pale, like the grey pallor of death. Through the still white of her face, which made her look as cold as the wet marble she stood on, her dark eyes seemed to gleam with a strange but enticing lustre. Even in the unsearching moonlight, which is after all rather deceptive than illuminative, I could not but notice one rare quality of her eyes. Each had some quality of refraction which made it look as though it contained a star. At every movement she made, the stars exhibited new beauties, of more rare and radiant force. She looked at me imploringly as the heavy curtain rolled back, and in eloquent gestures implored me to admit her. Instinctively I obeyed; I rolled back the steel grille, and threw open the French window. I noticed that she shivered and trembled as the glass door fell open. Indeed, she seemed so overcome with cold as to seem almost unable to move. In the sense of her helplessness all idea of the strangeness of the situation entirely disappeared. It was not as if my first idea of death taken from her cerements was negatived. It was simply that I did not think of it at all; I was content to accept things as they were—she was a woman, and in some dreadful trouble; that was enough.

I am thus particular about my own emotions, as I may have to refer to them again in matters of comprehension or comparison. The whole thing is so vastly strange and abnormal that the least thing may afterwards give some guiding light or clue to something otherwise not understandable. I have always found that in recondite matters first impressions are of more real value than later conclusions. We humans place far too little reliance on instinct as against reason; and yet instinct is the great gift of Nature to all animals for their protection and the fulfilment of their functions generally.

When I stepped out on the balcony, not thinking of my costume, I found that the woman was benumbed and hardly able to move. Even when I asked her to enter, and supplemented my words with gestures in case she should not understand my language, she stood stock-still, only rocking slightly to and fro as though she had just strength enough left to balance herself on her feet. I was afraid, from the condition in which she was, that she might drop down dead at any moment. So I took her by the hand to lead her in. But she seemed too weak to even make the attempt. When I pulled her slightly forward, thinking to help her, she tottered, and would have fallen had I not caught her in my arms. Then, half lifting her, I moved her forwards. Her feet, relieved of her weight, now seemed able to make the necessary effort; and so, I almost carrying her, we moved into the room. She was at the very end of her strength; I had to lift her over the sill. In obedience to her motion, I closed the French window and bolted it. I supposed the warmth of the room—though cool, it was warmer than the damp air without—affected her quickly, for on the instant she seemed to begin to recover herself. In a few seconds, as though she had reacquired her strength, she herself pulled the heavy curtain across the window. This left us in darkness, through which I heard her say in English:

"Light. Get a light!"

I found matches, and at once lit a candle. As the wick flared, she moved over to the door of the room, and tried if the lock and bolt were fastened. Satisfied as to this, she moved towards me, her wet shroud leaving a trail of moisture on the green carpet. By this time the wax of the candle had melted sufficiently to let me see her clearly. She was shaking and quivering as though in an ague; she drew the wet shroud around her piteously. Instinctively I spoke:

"Can I do anything for you?"

She answered, still in English, and in a voice of thrilling, almost piercing sweetness, which seemed somehow to go straight to my heart, and affected me strangely: "Give me warmth."

I hurried to the fireplace. It was empty; there was no fire laid. I turned to her, and said:

"Wait just a few minutes here. I shall call someone, and get help—and fire."

Her voice seemed to ring with intensity as she answered without a pause:

"No, no! Rather would I be"—here she hesitated for an instant, but as she caught sight of her cerements went on hurriedly—"as I am. I trust you—not others; and you must not betray my trust." Almost instantly she fell into a frightful fit of shivering, drawing again her death-clothes close to her, so piteously that it wrung my heart. I suppose I am a practical man. At any rate, I am accustomed to action. I took from its place beside my bed a thick Jaeger dressing-gown of dark brown—it was, of course, of extra length—and held it out to her as I said:

"Put that on. It is the only warm thing here which would be suitable. Stay; you must remove that wet—wet"—I stumbled about for a word that would not be offensive—"that frock—dress—costume—whatever it is." I pointed to where, in the corner of the room, stood a chintz-covered folding-screen which fences in my cold sponge bath, which is laid ready for me overnight, as I am an early riser.

She bowed gravely, and taking the dressing-gown in a long, white, finely-shaped hand, bore it behind the screen. There was a slight rustle, and then a hollow "flop" as the wet garment fell on the floor; more rustling and rubbing, and a minute later she emerged wrapped from head to foot in the long Jaeger garment, which trailed on the floor behind her, though she was a tall woman. She was still shivering painfully, however. I took a flask of brandy and a glass from a cupboard, and offered her some; but with a motion of her hand she refused it, though she moaned grievously.

"Oh, I am so cold—so cold!" Her teeth were chattering. I was pained at her sad condition, and said despairingly, for I was at my wits' end to know what to do:

"Tell me anything that I can do to help you, and I will do it. I may not call help; there is no fire—nothing to make it with; you will not take some brandy. What on earth can I do to give you warmth?"

Her answer certainly surprised me when it came, though it was practical enough—so practical that I should not have dared to say it. She looked me straight in the face for a few seconds before speaking. Then, with an air of girlish innocence which disarmed suspicion and convinced me at once of her simple faith, she said in a voice that at once thrilled me and evoked all my pity:

"Let me rest for a while, and cover me up with rugs. That may give me warmth. I am dying of cold. And I have a deadly fear upon me—a deadly fear. Sit by me, and let me hold your hand. You are big and strong, and you look brave. It will reassure me. I am not myself a coward, but to-night fear has got me by the throat. I can hardly breathe. Do let me stay till I am warm. If you only knew what I have gone through, and have to go through still, I am sure you would pity me and help me."

To say that I was astonished would be a mild description of my feelings. I was not shocked. The life which I have led was not one which makes for prudery. To travel in strange places amongst strange peoples with strange views of their own is to have odd experiences and peculiar adventures now and again; a man without human passions is not the type necessary for an adventurous life, such as I myself have had. But even a man of passions and experiences can, when he respects a woman, be shocked—even prudish—where his own opinion of her is concerned. Such must bring to her guarding any generosity which he has, and any self-restraint also. Even should she place herself in a doubtful position, her honour calls to his honour. This is a call which may not be—*must* not be—unanswered. Even passion must pause for at least a while at sound of such a trumpet-call.

This woman I did respect—much respect. Her youth and beauty; her manifest ignorance of evil; her superb disdain of convention, which could only come through hereditary dignity; her terrible fear and suffering—for there must be more in her unhappy condition than meets the eye—would all demand respect, even if one did not hasten to yield it. Nevertheless, I thought it necessary to enter a protest against her embarrassing suggestion. I certainly did feel a fool when making it, also a cad. I can truly say it was made only for her good, and out of the best of me, such as I am. I felt impossibly awkward; and stuttered and stumbled before I spoke:

"But surely—the convenances! Your being here alone at night! Mrs. Grundy—convention—the—"

She interrupted me with an incomparable dignity—a dignity which had the effect of shutting me up like a clasp-knife and making me feel a decided inferior—and a poor show at that. There was such a gracious simplicity and honesty in it, too, such self-respecting knowledge of herself and her position, that I could be neither angry nor hurt. I could only feel ashamed of myself, and of my own littleness of mind and morals. She seemed in her icy coldness—now spiritual as well as bodily—like an incarnate figure of Pride as she answered:

"What are convenances or conventions to me! If you only knew where I have come from—the existence (if it can be called so) which I have had—the loneliness—the horror! And besides, it is for me to *make* conventions, not to yield my personal freedom of action to them. Even as I am—even here and in this garb—I am above convention. Convenances do not trouble me or hamper me. That, at least, I have won by what I have gone through, even if it had never come to me through any other way. Let me stay." She said the last words, in spite of all her pride, appealingly. But still, there was a note of high pride in all this—in all she said and did, in her attitude and movement, in the tones of her voice, in the loftiness of her carriage and the steadfast look of her open, starlit eyes. Altogether, there was something so rarely lofty in herself and all that clad her that, face to face with it and with her, my feeble attempt at moral precaution seemed puny, ridiculous, and out of place. Without a word in the doing, I took from an old chiffonier chest an armful of blankets, several of which I threw over her as she lay, for in the meantime, having replaced the coverlet, she had lain down at length on the bed. I took a chair, and sat down beside her. When she stretched out her hand from beneath the pile of wraps, I took it in mine, saying:

"Get warm and rest. Sleep if you can. You need not fear; I shall guard you with my life."

She looked at me gratefully, her starry eyes taking a new light more full of illumination than was afforded by the wax candle, which was shaded from her by my body . . . She was horribly cold, and her teeth chattered so violently that I feared lest she should have incurred some dangerous evil from her wetting and the cold that followed it. I felt, however, so awkward that I could find no words to express my fears; moreover, I hardly dared say anything at all regarding herself after the haughty way in which she had received my well-meant protest. Manifestly I was but to her as a sort of refuge and provider of heat, altogether impersonal, and not to be regarded in any degree as an individual. In these humiliating circumstances what could I do but sit quiet—and wait developments?

Little by little the fierce chattering of her teeth began to abate as the warmth of her surroundings stole through her. I also felt, even in this strangely awakening position, the influence of the quiet; and sleep began to steal over me. Several times I tried to fend it off, but, as I could not make any overt movement without alarming my strange and beautiful companion, I had to yield myself to drowsiness. I was still in such an overwhelming stupor of surprise that I could not even think freely. There was nothing for me but to control myself and wait. Before I could well fix my thoughts I was asleep.

I was recalled to consciousness by hearing, even through the pall of sleep that bound me, the crowing of a cock in some of the out-offices of the castle. At the same instant the figure, lying deathly still but for the gentle heaving of her bosom, began to struggle wildly. The sound had won through the gates of her sleep also. With a swift, gliding motion she slipped from the bed to the floor, saying in a fierce whisper as she pulled herself up to her full height:

"Let me out! I must go! I must go!"

By this time I was fully awake, and the whole position of things came to me in an instant which I shall never—can never—forget: the dim light of the candle, now nearly burned down to the socket, all the dimmer from the fact that the first grey gleam of morning was stealing in round the edges of the heavy curtain; the tall, slim figure in the brown dressing-gown whose over-length trailed on the floor, the black hair showing glossy in the light, and increasing by contrast the marble whiteness of the face, in which the black eyes sent through their stars fiery gleams. She appeared quite in a frenzy of haste; her eagerness was simply irresistible.

I was so stupefied with amazement, as well as with sleep, that I did not attempt to stop her, but began instinctively to help her by furthering her wishes. As she ran behind the screen, and, as far as sound could inform me,—began frantically to disrobe herself of the warm dressing-gown and to don again the ice-cold wet shroud, I pulled back the curtain from the window, and drew the bolt of the glass door. As I did so she was already behind me, shivering. As I threw open the door she glided out with a swift silent movement, but trembling in an agonized way. As she passed me, she murmured in a low voice, which was almost lost in the chattering of her teeth:

"Oh, thank you—thank you a thousand times! But I must go. I *must*! I *must*! I shall come again, and try to show my gratitude. Do not condemn me as ungrateful—till then." And she was gone.

I watched her pass the length of the white path, flitting from shrub to shrub or statue as she had come. In the cold grey light of the undeveloped dawn she seemed even more ghostly than she had done in the black shadow of the night.

When she disappeared from sight in the shadow of the wood, I stood on the terrace for a long time watching, in case I should be afforded another glimpse of her, for there was now no doubt in my mind that she had for me some strange attraction. I felt even then that the look in those glorious starry eyes would be with me always so long as I might live. There was some fascination which went deeper than my eyes or my flesh or my heart—down deep into the very depths of my soul. My mind was all in a whirl, so that I could hardly think coherently. It all was like a dream; the reality seemed far away. It was not possible to doubt that the phantom figure which had been so close to me during the dark hours of the night was actual flesh and blood. Yet she was so cold, so cold! Altogether I could not fix my mind to either proposition: that it was a living woman who had held my hand, or a dead body reanimated for the time or the occasion in some strange manner.

The difficulty was too great for me to make up my mind upon it, even had I wanted to. But, in any case, I did not want to. This would, no doubt, come in time. But till then I wished to dream on, as anyone does in a dream which can still be blissful though there be pauses of pain, or ghastliness, or doubt, or terror.

So I closed the window and drew the curtain again, feeling for the first time the cold in which I had stood on the wet marble floor of the terrace when my bare feet began to get warm on the soft carpet. To get rid of the chill feeling I got into the bed on which *she* had lain, and as the warmth restored me tried to think coherently. For a short while I was going over the facts of the night—or what seemed as facts to my remembrance. But as I continued to think, the possibilities of any result seemed to get less, and I found myself vainly trying to reconcile with the logic of life the grim episode of the night. The effort proved to be too much for such concentration as was left to me; moreover, interrupted sleep was clamant, and would not be denied. What I dreamt of—if I dreamt at all—I know not. I only know that I was ready for waking when the time came. It came with a violent knocking at my door. I sprang from bed, fully awake in a second, drew the bolt, and slipped back to bed. With a hurried "May I come in?" Aunt Janet entered. She seemed relieved when she saw me, and gave without my asking an explanation of her perturbation:

"Oh, laddie, I hae been so uneasy aboot ye all the nicht. I hae had dreams an' veesions an' a' sorts o' uncanny fancies. I fear that—" She was by now drawing back the curtain, and as her eyes took in the marks of wet all over the floor the current of her thoughts changed:

"Why, laddie, whativer hae ye been doin' wi' yer baith? Oh, the mess ye hae made! 'Tis sinful to gie sic trouble an' waste . . . " And so she went on. I was glad to hear the tirade, which was only what a good housewife, outraged in her sentiments of order, would have made. I listened in patience—with pleasure when I thought of what she would have thought (and said) had she known the real facts. I was well pleased to have got off so easily.

RUPERT'S JOURNAL—*Continued.*

April 10, 1907.

For some days after what I call "the episode" I was in a strange condition of mind. I did not take anyone—not even Aunt Janet—into confidence. Even she dear, and open-hearted and liberal-minded as she is, might not have understood well enough to be just and tolerant; and I did not care to hear any adverse comment on my strange visitor. Somehow I could not bear the thought of anyone finding fault with her or in her, though, strangely enough, I was eternally defending her to myself; for, despite my wishes, embarrassing thoughts *would* come again and again, and again in all sorts and variants of queries difficult to answer. I found myself defending her, sometimes as a woman hard pressed by spiritual fear and physical suffering, sometimes as not being amenable to laws that govern the Living. Indeed, I could not make up my mind whether I looked on her as a living human being or as one with some strange existence in another world, and having only a chance foothold in our own. In such doubt imagination began to work, and thoughts of evil, of danger, of doubt, even of fear, began to crowd on me with such persistence and in such varied forms that I found my instinct of reticence growing into a settled purpose. The value of this instinctive precaution was promptly shown by Aunt Janet's state of mind, with consequent revelation of it. She became full of gloomy prognostications and what I thought were morbid fears. For the first time in my life I discovered that Aunt Janet had nerves! I had long had a secret belief that she was gifted, to some degree at any rate, with Second Sight, which quality, or whatever it is, skilled in the powers if not the lore of superstition, manages to keep at stretch not only the mind of its immediate pathic, but of others relevant to it. Perhaps this natural quality had received a fresh impetus from the arrival of some cases of her books sent on by Sir Colin. She appeared to read and reread these works, which were chiefly on occult subjects, day and night, except when she was imparting to me choice excerpts of the most baleful and fearsome kind. Indeed, before a week was over I found myself to be an expert in the history of the cult, as well as in its manifestations, which latter I had been versed in for a good many years.

The result of all this was that it set me brooding. Such, at least, I gathered was the fact when Aunt Janet took me to task for it. She always speaks out according to her convictions, so that her thinking I brooded was to me a proof that I did; and after a personal examination I came—reluctantly—to the conclusion that she was right, so far, at any rate, as my outer conduct was concerned. The state of mind I was in, however, kept me from making any acknowledgment of it—the real cause of my keeping so much to myself and of being so *distrait*. And so I went on, torturing myself as before with introspective questioning; and she, with her mind set on my actions, and endeavouring to find a cause for them, continued and expounded her beliefs and fears.

Her nightly chats with me when we were alone after dinner—for I had come to avoid her questioning at other times—kept my imagination at high pressure. Despite myself, I could not but find new cause for concern in the perennial founts of her superstition. I had thought, years ago, that I had then sounded the depths of this branch of psychicism; but this new phase of thought, founded on the really deep hold which the existence of my beautiful visitor and her sad and dreadful circumstances had taken upon me, brought me a new concern in the matter of self-importance. I came to think that I must reconstruct my self-values, and begin a fresh understanding of ethical beliefs. Do what I would, my mind would keep turning on the uncanny subjects brought before it. I began to apply them one by one to my own late experience, and unconsciously to try to fit them in turn to the present case.

The effect of this brooding was that I was, despite my own will, struck by the similarity of circumstances bearing on my visitor, and the conditions apportioned by tradition and superstition to such strange survivals from earlier ages as these partial existences which are rather Undead than Living—still walking the earth, though claimed by the world of the Dead. Amongst them are the Vampire, or the Wehr-Wolf. To this class also might belong in a measure the Doppelgänger—one of whose dual existences commonly belongs to the actual world around it. So, too, the denizens of the world of Astralism. In any of these named worlds there is a material presence—which must be created, if only for a single or periodic purpose. It matters not whether a material presence already created can be receptive of a disembodied soul, or a soul unattached can have a body built up for it or around it; or, again, whether the body of a dead person can be made seeming quick through some diabolic influence manifested in the present, or an inheritance or result of some baleful use of malefic power in the past. The result is the same in each case, though the ways be widely different: a soul and a body which are not in unity but brought together for strange purposes through stranger means and by powers still more strange.

Through much thought and a process of exclusions the eerie form which seemed to be most in correspondence with my adventure, and most suitable to my fascinating visitor, appeared to be the Vampire. Doppelgänger, Astral creations, and all suchlike, did not comply with the conditions of my night experience. The Wehr-Wolf is but a variant of the Vampire, and so needed not to be classed or examined at all. Then it was that, thus focussed, the Lady of the Shroud (for so I came to hold her in my mind) began to assume a new force. Aunt Janet's library afforded me clues which I followed with avidity. In my secret heart I hated the quest, and did not wish to go on with it. But in this I was not my own master. Do what I would—brush away doubts never so often, new doubts and imaginings came in their stead. The circumstance almost repeated the parable of the Seven Devils who took the place of the exorcised one. Doubts I could stand. Imaginings I could stand. But doubts and imaginings together made a force so fell that I was driven to accept any reading of the mystery which might presumably afford a foothold for satisfying thought. And so I came to accept tentatively the Vampire theory—accept it, at least, so far as to examine it as judicially as was given me to do. As the days wore on, so the conviction grew. The more I read on the subject, the more directly the evidences pointed towards this view. The more I thought, the more obstinate became the conviction. I ransacked Aunt Janet's volumes again and again to find anything to the contrary; but in vain. Again, no matter how obstinate were my convictions at any given time, unsettlement came with fresh thinking over the argument, so that I was kept in a harassing state of uncertainty.

Briefly, the evidence in favour of accord between the facts of the case and the Vampire theory were:

Her coming was at night—the time the Vampire is according to the theory, free to move at will.

She wore her shroud—a necessity of coming fresh from grave or tomb; for there is nothing occult about clothing which is not subject to astral or other influences.

She had to be helped into my room—in strict accordance with what one sceptical critic of occultism has called "the Vampire etiquette."

She made violent haste in getting away at cock-crow.

She seemed preternaturally cold; her sleep was almost abnormal in intensity, and yet the sound of the cock-crowing came through it.

These things showed her to be subject to *some* laws, though not in exact accord within those which govern human beings. Under the stress of such circumstances as she must have gone through, her vitality seemed more than human—the quality of vitality which could outlive ordinary burial. Again, such purpose as she had shown in donning, under stress of some compelling direction, her ice-cold wet shroud, and, wrapt in it, going out again into the night, was hardly normal for a woman.

But if so, and if she was indeed a Vampire, might not whatever it may be that holds such beings in thrall be by some means or other exorcised? To find the means must be my next task. I am actually pining to see her again. Never before have I been stirred to my depths by anyone. Come it from Heaven or Hell, from the Earth or the Grave, it does not matter; I shall make it my task to win her back to life and peace. If she be indeed a Vampire, the task may be hard and long; if she be not so, and if it be merely that circumstances have so gathered round her as to produce that impression, the task may be simpler and the result more sweet. No, not more sweet; for what can be more sweet than to restore the lost or seemingly lost soul of the woman you love! There, the truth is out at last! I suppose that I have fallen in love with her. If so, it is too late for me to fight against it. I can only wait with what patience I can till I see her again. But to that end I can do nothing. I know absolutely nothing about her—not even her name. Patience!

RUPERT'S JOURNAL—*Continued.*

April 16, 1907.

The only relief I have had from the haunting anxiety regarding the Lady of the Shroud has been in the troubled state of my adopted country. There has evidently been something up which I have not been allowed to know. The mountaineers are troubled and restless; are wandering about, singly and in parties, and holding meetings in strange places. This is what I gather used to be in old days when intrigues were on foot with Turks, Greeks, Austrians, Italians, Russians. This concerns me vitally, for my mind has long been made up to share the fortunes of the Land of the Blue Mountains. For good or ill I mean to stay here: *J'y suis, j'y reste.* I share henceforth the lot of the Blue Mountaineers; and not Turkey, nor Greece, nor Austria, nor Italy, nor Russia—no, not France nor Germany either; not man nor God nor Devil shall drive me from my purpose. With these patriots I throw in my lot! My only difficulty seemed at first to be with the men themselves. They are so proud that at the beginning I feared they would not even accord me the honour of being one of them! However, things always move on somehow, no matter what difficulties there be at the beginning. Never mind! When one looks back at an accomplished fact the beginning is not to be seen—and if it were it would not matter. It is not of any account, anyhow.

I heard that there was going to be a great meeting near here yesterday afternoon, and I attended it. I think it was a success. If such is any proof, I felt elated as well as satisfied when I came away. Aunt Janet's Second Sight on the subject was comforting, though grim, and in a measure disconcerting. When I was saying good-night she asked me to bend down my head. As I did so, she laid her hands on it and passed them all over it. I heard her say to herself:

"Strange! There's nothing there; yet I could have sworn I saw it!" I asked her to explain, but she would not. For once she was a little obstinate, and refused point blank to even talk of the subject. She was not worried nor unhappy; so I had no cause for concern. I said nothing, but I shall wait and see. Most mysteries become plain or disappear altogether in time. But about the meeting—lest I forget!

When I joined the mountaineers who had assembled, I really think they were glad to see me; though some of them seemed adverse, and others did not seem over well satisfied. However, absolute unity is very seldom to be found. Indeed, it is almost impossible; and in a free community is not altogether to be desired. When it is apparent, the gathering lacks that sense of individual feeling which makes for the real consensus of opinion—which is the real unity of purpose. The meeting was at first, therefore, a little cold and distant. But presently it began to thaw, and after some fiery harangues I was asked to speak. Happily, I had begun to learn the Balkan language as soon as ever Uncle Roger's wishes had been made known to me, and as I have some facility of tongues and a great deal of experience, I soon began to know something of it. Indeed, when I had been here a few weeks, with opportunity of speaking daily with the people themselves, and learned to understand the intonations and vocal inflexions, I felt quite easy in speaking it. I understood every word which had up to then been spoken at the meeting, and when I spoke myself I felt that they understood. That is an experience which every speaker has in a certain way and up to a certain point. He knows by some kind of instinct if his hearers are with him; if they respond, they must certainly have understood. Last night this was marked. I felt it every instant I was talking and when I came to realize that the men were in strict accord with my general views, I took them into confidence with regard to my own personal purpose. It was the beginning of a mutual trust; so for peroration I told them that I had come to the conclusion that what they wanted most for their own protection and the security and consolidation of their nation was arms—arms of the very latest pattern. Here they interrupted me with wild cheers, which so strung me up that I went farther than I intended, and made a daring venture. "Ay," I repeated, "the security and consolidation of your country—of *our* country, for I have come to live amongst you. Here is my home whilst I live. I am with you heart and soul. I shall live with you, fight shoulder to shoulder with you, and, if need be, shall die with you!" Here the shouting was terrific, and the younger men raised their guns to fire a salute in Blue Mountain fashion. But on the instant the Vladika [1] held up his hands and motioned them to desist. In the immediate silence he spoke, sharply at first, but later ascending to a high pitch of single-minded, lofty eloquence. His words rang in my ears long after the meeting was over and other thoughts had come between them and the present.

"Silence!" he thundered. "Make no echoes in the forest or through the hills at this dire time of stress and threatened danger to our land. Bethink ye of this meeting, held here and in secret, in order that no whisper of it may be heard afar. Have ye all, brave men of the Blue Mountains, come hither through the forest like shadows that some of you, thoughtless, may enlighten your enemies as to our secret purpose? The thunder of your guns would doubtless sound well in the ears of those who wish us ill and try to work us wrong. Fellow-countrymen, know ye not that the Turk is awake once more for our harming? The Bureau of Spies has risen from the torpor which came on it when the purpose against our Teuta roused our mountains to such anger that the

---

[1] Vladika, a high functionary in the Land of the Blue Mountains. He is a sort of official descendant of the old Prince-Bishops who used at one time to govern the State. In process of time the system has changed, but the function—shorn of its personal dominance—remains. The nation is at present governed by the Council. The Church (which is, of course, the Eastern Church) is represented by the Archbishop, who controls the whole spiritual functions and organization. The connecting-link between them—they being quite independent organizations—is the Vladika, who is ex officio a member of the National Council. By custom he does not vote, but is looked on as an independent adviser who is in the confidence of both sides of national control.

frontiers blazed with passion, and were swept with fire and sword. Moreover, there is a traitor somewhere in the land, or else incautious carelessness has served the same base purpose. Something of our needs—our doing, whose secret we have tried to hide, has gone out. The myrmidons of the Turk are close on our borders, and it may be that some of them have passed our guards and are amidst us unknown. So it behoves us doubly to be discreet. Believe me that I share with you, my brothers, our love for the gallant Englishman who has come amongst us to share our sorrows and ambitions—and I trust it may be our joys. We are all united in the wish to do him honour—though not in the way by which danger might be carried on the wings of love. My brothers, our newest brother comes to us from the Great Nation which amongst the nations has been our only friend, and which has ere now helped us in our direst need—that mighty Britain whose hand has ever been raised in the cause of freedom. We of the Blue Mountains know her best as she stands with sword in hand face to face with our foes. And this, her son and now our brother, brings further to our need the hand of a giant and the heart of a lion. Later on, when danger does not ring us round, when silence is no longer our outer guard; we shall bid him welcome in true fashion of our land. But till then he will believe—for he is great-hearted—that our love and thanks and welcome are not to be measured by sound. When the time comes, then shall be sound in his honour—not of rifles alone, but bells and cannon and the mighty voice of a free people shouting as one. But now we must be wise and silent, for the Turk is once again at our gates. Alas! the cause of his former coming may not be, for she whose beauty and nobility and whose place in our nation and in our hearts tempted him to fraud and violence is not with us to share even our anxiety."

Here his voice broke, and there arose from all a deep wailing sound, which rose and rose till the woods around us seemed broken by a mighty and long-sustained sob. The orator saw that his purpose was accomplished, and with a short sentence finished his harangue: "But the need of our nation still remains!" Then, with an eloquent gesture to me to proceed, he merged in the crowd and disappeared.

How could I even attempt to follow such a speaker with any hope of success? I simply told them what I had already done in the way of help, saying:

"As you needed arms, I have got them. My agent sends me word through the code between us that he has procured for me—for us—fifty thousand of the newest-pattern rifles, the French Ingis-Malbron, which has surpassed all others, and sufficient ammunition to last for a year of war. The first section is in hand, and will soon be ready for consignment. There are other war materials, too, which, when they arrive, will enable every man and woman—even the children—of our land to take a part in its defence should such be needed. My brothers, I am with you in all things, for good or ill!"

It made me very proud to hear the mighty shout which arose. I had felt exalted before, but now this personal development almost unmanned me. I was glad of the long-sustained applause to recover my self-control.

I was quite satisfied that the meeting did not want to hear any other speaker, for they began to melt away without any formal notification having been given. I doubt if there will be another meeting soon again. The weather has begun to break, and we are in for another spell of rain. It is disagreeable, of course; but it has its own charm.

It was during a spell of wet weather that the Lady of the Shroud came to me. Perhaps the rain may bring her again. I hope so, with all my soul.

RUPERT'S JOURNAL—*Continued.*

April 23, 1907.

The rain has continued for four whole days and nights, and the low-lying ground is like a quagmire in places. In the sunlight the whole mountains glisten with running streams and falling water. I feel a strange kind of elation, but from no visible cause. Aunt Janet rather queered it by telling me, as she said good-night, to be very careful of myself, as she had seen in a dream last night a figure in a shroud. I fear she was not pleased that I did not take it with all the seriousness that she did. I would not wound her for the world if I could help it, but the idea of a shroud gets too near the bone to be safe, and I had to fend her off at all hazards. So when I doubted if the Fates regarded the visionary shroud as of necessity appertaining to me, she said, in a way that was, for her, almost sharp:

"Take care, laddie. 'Tis ill jesting wi' the powers o' time Unknown."

Perhaps it was that her talk put the subject in my mind. The woman needed no such aid; she was always there; but when I locked myself into my room that night, I half expected to find her in the room. I was not sleepy, so I took a book of Aunt Janet's and began to read. The title was "On the Powers and Qualities of Disembodied Spirits." "Your grammar," said I to the author, "is hardly attractive, but I may learn something which might apply to her. I shall read your book." Before settling down to it, however, I thought I would have a look at the garden. Since the night of the visit the garden seemed to have a new attractiveness for me: a night seldom passed without my having a last look at it before turning in. So I drew the great curtain and looked out.

The scene was beautiful, but almost entirely desolate. All was ghastly in the raw, hard gleams of moonlight coming fitfully through the masses of flying cloud. The wind was rising, and the air was damp and cold. I looked round the room instinctively, and noticed that the fire was laid ready for lighting, and that there were small-cut logs of wood piled beside the hearth. Ever since that night I have had a fire laid ready. I was tempted to light it, but as I never have a fire unless I sleep in the open, I hesitated to begin. I went back to the window, and, opening the catch, stepped out on the terrace. As I looked down the white walk and let my eyes range over the expanse of the garden, where everything glistened as the moonlight caught the wet, I half expected to see some white figure flitting amongst the shrubs and statues. The whole scene of the former visit came back to me so vividly that I could hardly believe that any time had passed since then. It was the same scene, and again late in the evening.

Life in Vissarion was primitive, and early hours prevailed—though not so late as on that night.

As I looked I thought I caught a glimpse of something white far away. It was only a ray of moonlight coming through the rugged edge of a cloud. But all the same it set me in a strange state of perturbation. Somehow I seemed to lose sight of my own identity. It was as though I was hypnotized by the situation or by memory, or perhaps by some occult force. Without thinking of what I was doing, or being conscious of any reason for it, I crossed the room and set light to the fire. Then I blew out the candle and came to the window again. I never thought it might be a foolish thing to do—to stand at a window with a light behind me in this country, where every man carries a gun with him always. I was in my evening clothes, too, with my breast well marked by a white shirt. I opened the window and stepped out on the terrace. There I stood for many minutes, thinking. All the time my eyes kept ranging over the garden. Once I thought I saw a white figure moving, but it was not followed up, so, becoming conscious that it was again beginning to rain, I stepped back into the room, shut the window, and drew the curtain. Then I realized the comforting appearance of the fire, and went over and stood before it.

Hark! Once more there was a gentle tapping at the window. I rushed over to it and drew the curtain.

There, out on the rain-beaten terrace, stood the white shrouded figure, more desolate-appearing than ever. Ghastly pale she looked, as before, but her eyes had an eager look which was new. I took it that she was attracted by the fire, which was by now well ablaze, and was throwing up jets of flame as the dry logs crackled. The leaping flames threw fitful light across the room, and every gleam threw the white-clad figure into prominence, showing the gleam of the black eyes, and fixing the stars that lay in them.

Without a word I threw open the window, and, taking the white hand extended to me, drew into the room the Lady of the Shroud.

As she entered and felt the warmth of the blazing fire, a glad look spread over her face. She made a movement as if to run to it. But she drew back an instant after, looking round with instinctive caution. She closed the window and bolted it, touched the lever which spread the grille across the opening, and pulled close the curtain behind it. Then she went swiftly to the door and tried if it was locked. Satisfied as to this, she came quickly over to the fire, and, kneeling before it, stretched out her numbed hands to the blaze. Almost on the instant her wet shroud began to steam. I stood wondering. The precautions of secrecy in the midst of her suffering—for that she did suffer was only too painfully manifest—must have presupposed some danger. Then and there my mind was made up that there should no harm assail her that I by any means could fend off. Still, the present must be attended to; pneumonia and other ills stalked behind such a chill as must infallibly come on her unless precautions were taken. I took again the dressing-gown which she had worn before and handed it to her, motioning as I did so towards the screen which had made a dressing-room for her on the former occasion. To my surprise she hesitated. I waited. She waited, too, and then laid down the dressing-gown on the edge of the stone fender. So I spoke:

"Won't you change as you did before? Your—your frock can then be dried. Do! It will be so much safer for you to be dry clad when you resume your own dress."

"How can I whilst you are here?"

Her words made me stare, so different were they from her acts of the other visit. I simply bowed—speech on such a subject would be at least inadequate—and walked over to the window. Passing behind the curtain, I opened the window. Before stepping out on to the terrace, I looked into the room and said:

"Take your own time. There is no hurry. I dare say you will find there all you may want. I shall remain on the terrace until you summon me." With that I went out on the terrace, drawing close the glass door behind me.

I stood looking out on the dreary scene for what seemed a very short time, my mind in a whirl. There came a rustle from within, and I saw a dark brown figure steal round the edge of the curtain. A white hand was raised, and beckoned me to come in. I entered, bolting the window behind me. She had passed across the room, and was again kneeling before the fire with her hands outstretched. The shroud was laid in partially opened folds on one side of the hearth, and was steaming heavily. I brought over some cushions and pillows, and made a little pile of them beside her.

"Sit there," I said, "and rest quietly in the heat." It may have been the effect of the glowing heat, but there was a rich colour in her face as she looked at me with shining eyes. Without a word, but with a courteous little bow, she sat down at once. I put a thick rug across her shoulders, and sat down myself on a stool a couple of feet away.

For fully five or six minutes we sat in silence. At last, turning her head towards me she said in a sweet, low voice:

"I had intended coming earlier on purpose to thank you for your very sweet and gracious courtesy to me, but circumstances were such that I could not leave my—my"—she hesitated before saying—"my abode. I am not free, as you and others are, to do what I will. My existence is sadly cold and stern, and full of horrors that appal. But I *do* thank you. For myself I am not sorry for the delay, for every hour shows me more clearly how good and understanding and sympathetic you have been to me. I only hope that some day you may realize how kind you have been, and how much I appreciate it."

"I am only too glad to be of any service," I said, feebly I felt, as I held out my hand. She did not seem to see it. Her eyes were now on the fire, and a warm blush dyed forehead and cheek and neck. The reproof was so gentle that no one could have been offended. It was evident that she was something coy and reticent, and would not allow me to come at present more close to her, even to the touching of her hand. But that her heart was not in the denial was also evident in the glance from her glorious dark starry eyes. These glances—veritable lightning flashes coming through her pronounced reserve—finished entirely any wavering there might be in my own purpose. I was aware now to the full that my heart was quite subjugated. I knew that I was in love—veritably so much in love as to feel that without this woman, be she what she might, by my side my future must be absolutely barren.

It was presently apparent that she did not mean to stay as long on this occasion as on the last. When the castle clock struck midnight she suddenly sprang to her feet with a bound, saying:

"I must go! There is midnight!" I rose at once, the intensity of her speech having instantly obliterated the sleep which, under the influence of rest and warmth, was creeping upon me. Once more she was in a frenzy of haste, so I hurried towards the window, but as I looked back saw her, despite her haste, still standing. I motioned towards the screen, and slipping behind the curtain, opened the window and went out on the terrace. As I was disappearing behind the curtain I saw her with the tail of my eye lifting the shroud, now dry, from the hearth.

She was out through the window in an incredibly short time, now clothed once more in that dreadful wrapping. As she sped past me barefooted on the wet, chilly marble which made her shudder, she whispered:

"Thank you again. You *are* good to me. You can understand."

Once again I stood on the terrace, saw her melt like a shadow down the steps, and disappear behind the nearest shrub. Thence she flitted away from point to point with exceeding haste. The moonlight had now disappeared behind heavy banks of cloud, so there was little light to see by. I could just distinguish a pale gleam here and there as she wended her secret way.

For a long time I stood there alone thinking, as I watched the course she had taken, and wondering where might be her ultimate destination. As she had spoken of her "abode," I knew there was some definitive objective of her flight.

It was no use wondering. I was so entirely ignorant of her surroundings that I had not even a starting-place for speculation. So I went in, leaving the window open. It seemed that this being so made one barrier the less between us. I gathered the cushions and rugs from before the fire, which was no longer leaping, but burning with a steady glow, and put them back in their places. Aunt Janet might come in the morning, as she had done before, and I did not wish to set her thinking. She is much too clever a person to have treading on the heels of a mystery—especially one in which my own affections are engaged. I wonder what she would have said had she seen me kiss the cushion on which my beautiful guest's head had rested?

When I was in bed, and in the dark save for the fading glow of the fire, my thoughts became fixed that whether she came from Earth or Heaven or Hell, my lovely visitor was already more to me than aught else in the world. This time she had, on going, said no word of returning. I had been so much taken up with her presence, and so upset by her abrupt departure, that I had omitted to ask her. And so I am driven, as before, to accept the chance of her returning—a chance which I fear I am or may be unable to control.

Surely enough Aunt Janet did come in the morning, early. I was still asleep when she knocked at my door. With that purely physical subconsciousness which comes with habit I must have realized the cause of the sound, for I woke fully conscious of the fact that Aunt Janet had knocked and was waiting to come in. I jumped from bed, and back again when I had unlocked the door. When Aunt Janet came in she noticed the cold of the room.

"Save us, laddie, but ye'll get your death o' cold in this room." Then, as she looked round and noticed the ashes of the extinct fire in the grate:

"Eh, but ye're no that daft after a'; ye've had the sense to light yer fire. Glad I am that we had the fire laid and a wheen o' dry logs ready to yer hand." She evidently felt the cold air coming from the window, for she went over and drew the curtain. When she saw the open window, she raised her hands in a sort of dismay, which to me, knowing how little base for concern could be within her knowledge, was comic. Hurriedly she shut the window, and then, coming close over to my bed, said:

"Yon has been a fearsome nicht again, laddie, for yer poor auld aunty."

"Dreaming again, Aunt Janet?" I asked—rather flippantly as it seemed to me. She shook her head:

"Not so, Rupert, unless it be that the Lord gies us in dreams what we in our spiritual darkness think are veesions." I roused up at this. When Aunt Janet calls me Rupert, as she always used to do in my dear mother's time, things are serious with her. As I was back in childhood now, recalled by her word, I thought the best thing I could do to cheer her would be to bring her back there too—if I could. So I patted the edge of the bed as I used to do when I was a wee kiddie and wanted her to comfort me, and said:

"Sit down, Aunt Janet, and tell me." She yielded at once, and the look of the happy old days grew over her face as though there had come a gleam of sunshine. She sat down, and I put out my hands as I used to do, and took her hand between them. There was a tear in her eye as she raised my hand and kissed it as in old times. But for the infinite pathos of it, it would have been comic:

Aunt Janet, old and grey-haired, but still retaining her girlish slimness of figure, petite, dainty as a Dresden figure, her face lined with the care of years, but softened and ennobled by the unselfishness of those years, holding up my big hand, which would outweigh her whole arm; sitting dainty as a pretty old fairy beside a recumbent giant—for my bulk never seems so great as when I am near this real little good fairy of my life—seven feet beside four feet seven.

So she began as of old, as though she were about to soothe a frightened child with a fairy tale:

"'Twas a veesion, I think, though a dream it may hae been. But whichever or whatever it was, it concerned my little boy, who has grown to be a big giant, so much that I woke all of a tremble. Laddie dear, I thought that I saw ye being married." This gave me an opening, though a small one, for comforting her, so I took it at once:

"Why, dear, there isn't anything to alarm you in that, is there? It was only the other day when you spoke to me about the need of my getting married, if it was only that you might have children of your boy playing around your knees as their father used to do when he was a helpless wee child himself."

"That is so, laddie," she answered gravely. "But your weddin' was none so merry as I fain would see. True, you seemed to lo'e her wi' all yer hairt. Yer eyes shone that bright that ye might ha' set her afire, for all her black locks and her winsome face. But, laddie, that was not all—no, not though her black een, that had the licht o' all the stars o' nicht in them, shone in yours as though a hairt o' love an' passion, too, dwelt in them. I saw ye join hands, an' heard a strange voice that talked stranger still, but I saw none ither. Your eyes an' her eyes, an' your hand an' hers, were all I saw. For all else was dim, and the darkness was close around ye twa. And when the benison was spoken—I knew that by the voices that sang, and by the gladness of her een, as well as by the pride and glory of yours—the licht began to glow a wee more, an' I could see yer bride. She was in a veil o' wondrous fine lace. And there were orange-flowers in her hair, though there were twigs, too, and there was a crown o' flowers on head wi' a golden band round it. And the heathen candles that stood on the table wi' the Book had some strange effect, for the reflex o' it hung in the air o'er her head like the shadow of a crown. There was a gold ring on her finger and a silver one on yours." Here she paused and trembled, so that, hoping to dispel her fears, I said, as like as I could to the way I used to when I was a child:

"Go on, Aunt Janet."

She did not seem to recognize consciously the likeness between past and present; but the effect was there, for she went on more like her old self, though there was a prophetic gravity in her voice, more marked than I had ever heard from her:

"All this I've told ye was well; but, oh, laddie, there was a dreadful lack o' livin' joy such as I should expect from the woman whom my boy had chosen for his wife—and at the marriage coupling, too! And no wonder, when all is said; for though the marriage veil o' love was fine, an' the garland o' flowers was fresh-gathered, underneath them a' was nane ither than a ghastly shroud. As I looked in my veesion—or maybe dream—I expectit to see the worms crawl round the flagstane at her feet. If 'twas not Death, laddie dear, that stood by ye, it was the shadow o' Death that made the darkness round ye, that neither the light o' candles nor the smoke o' heathen incense could pierce. Oh, laddie, laddie, wae is me that I hae seen sic a veesion—waking or sleeping, it matters not! I was sair distressed—so sair that I woke wi' a shriek on my lips and bathed in cold sweat. I would hae come doon to ye to see if you were hearty or no—or even to listen at your door for any sound o' yer being quick, but that I feared to alarm ye till morn should come. I've counted the hours and the minutes since midnight, when I saw the veesion, till I came hither just the now."

"Quite right, Aunt Janet," I said, "and I thank you for your kind thought for me in the matter, now and always." Then I went on, for I wanted to take precautions against the possibility of her discovery of my secret. I could not bear to think that she might run my precious secret to earth in any well-meant piece of bungling. That would be to me disaster unbearable. She might frighten away altogether my beautiful visitor, even whose name or origin I did not know, and I might never see her again:

"You must never do that, Aunt Janet. You and I are too good friends to have sense of distrust or annoyance come between us—which would surely happen if I had to keep thinking that you or anyone else might be watching me."

RUPERT'S JOURNAL—*Continued.*

April 27, 1907.

After a spell of loneliness which has seemed endless I have something to write. When the void in my heart was becoming the receptacle for many devils of suspicion and distrust I set myself a task which might, I thought, keep my thoughts in part, at any rate, occupied—to explore minutely the neighbourhood round the Castle. This might, I hoped, serve as an anodyne to my pain of loneliness, which grew more acute as the days, the hours, wore on, even if it should not ultimately afford me some clue to the whereabouts of the woman whom I had now grown to love so madly.

My exploration soon took a systematic form, as I intended that it should be exhaustive. I would take every day a separate line of advance from the Castle, beginning at the south and working round by the east to the north. The first day only took me to the edge of the creek, which I crossed in a boat, and landed at the base of the cliff opposite. I found the cliffs alone worth a visit. Here and there were openings to caves which I made up my mind to explore later. I managed to climb up the cliff at a spot less beetling than the rest, and continued my journey. It was, though very beautiful, not a specially interesting place. I explored that spoke of the wheel of which Vissarion was the hub, and got back just in time for dinner.

The next day I took a course slightly more to the eastward. I had no difficulty in keeping a straight path, for, once I had rowed across the creek, the old church of St. Sava rose before me in stately gloom. This was the spot where many generations of the noblest of the Land of the Blue Mountains had from time immemorial been laid to rest, amongst them the Vissarions. Again, I found the opposite cliffs pierced here and there with caves, some with wide openings,—others the openings of which were partly above and partly below water. I could, however, find no means of climbing the cliff at this part, and had to make a long detour, following up the line of the creek till further on I found a piece of beach from which ascent was possible. Here I ascended, and found that I was on a line between the Castle and the southern side of the mountains. I saw the church of St. Sava away to my right, and not far from the edge of the cliff. I made my way to it at once, for as yet I had never been near it. Hitherto my excursions had been limited to the Castle and its many gardens and surroundings. It was of a style with which I was not familiar—with four wings to the points of the compass. The great doorway, set in a magnificent frontage of carved stone of manifestly ancient date, faced west, so that, when one entered, he went east. To my surprise—for somehow I expected the contrary—I found the door open. Not wide open, but what is called ajar—manifestly not locked or barred, but not sufficiently open for one to look in. I entered, and after passing through a wide vestibule, more like a section of a corridor than an ostensible entrance, made my way through a spacious doorway into the body of the church. The church itself was almost circular, the openings of the four naves being spacious enough to give the appearance of the interior as a whole, being a huge cross. It was strangely dim, for the window openings were small and high-set, and were, moreover, filled with green or blue glass, each window having a colour to itself. The glass was very old, being of the thirteenth or fourteenth century. Such appointments as there were—for it had a general air of desolation—were of great beauty and richness,—especially so to be in a place—even a church—where the door lay open, and no one was to be seen. It was strangely silent even for an old church on a lonesome headland. There reigned a dismal solemnity which seemed to chill me, accustomed as I have been to strange and weird places. It seemed abandoned, though it had not that air of having been neglected which is so often to be noticed in old churches. There was none of the everlasting accumulation of dust which prevails in places of higher cultivation and larger and more strenuous work.

In the church itself or its appending chambers I could find no clue or suggestion which could guide me in any way in my search for the Lady of the Shroud. Monuments there were in profusion—statues, tablets, and all the customary memorials of the dead. The families and dates represented were simply bewildering. Often the name of Vissarion was given, and the inscription which it held I read through carefully, looking to find some enlightenment of any kind. But all in vain: there was nothing to see in the church itself. So I determined to visit the crypt. I had no lantern or candle with me, so had to go back to the Castle to secure one.

It was strange, coming in from the sunlight, here overwhelming to one so recently accustomed to northern skies, to note the slender gleam of the lantern which I carried, and which I had lit inside the door. At my first entry to the church my mind had been so much taken up with the strangeness of the place, together with the intensity of wish for some sort of clue, that I had really no opportunity of examining detail. But now detail became necessary, as I had to find the entrance to the crypt. My puny light could not dissipate the semi-Cimmerian gloom of the vast edifice; I had to throw the feeble gleam into one after another of the dark corners.

At last I found, behind the great screen, a narrow stone staircase which seemed to wind down into the rock. It was not in any way secret, but being in the narrow space behind the great screen, was not visible except when close to it. I knew I was now close to my objective, and began to descend. Accustomed though I have been to all sorts of mysteries and dangers, I felt awed and almost overwhelmed by a sense of loneliness and desolation as I descended the ancient winding steps. These were many in number, roughly hewn of old in the solid rock on which the church was built.

I met a fresh surprise in finding that the door of the crypt was open. After all, this was different from the church-door being open; for in many places it is a custom to allow all comers at all times to find rest and comfort in the sacred place. But I did expect that at least the final resting-place of the historic dead would be held safe against casual intrusion. Even I, on a quest which was very near my heart, paused with an almost overwhelming sense of decorum before passing through that open door. The crypt was a huge place, strangely lofty for a vault. From its formation, however, I soon came to the conclusion that it was originally a natural cavern altered to its present purpose by the hand of man. I could hear somewhere near the sound of running water, but I could not locate it. Now and again at irregular intervals there was a prolonged booming, which could only come from a wave breaking in a confined place. The recollection then came to me of the proximity of the church to the top of the beetling cliff, and of the half-sunk cavern entrances which pierced it.

With the gleam of my lamp to guide me, I went through and round the whole place. There were many massive tombs, mostly rough-hewn from great slabs or blocks of stone. Some of them were marble, and the cutting of all was ancient. So large and heavy were some of them that it was a wonder to me how they could ever have been brought to this place, to which the only entrance was seemingly the narrow, tortuous stairway by which I had come. At last I saw near one end of the crypt a great chain hanging. Turning the light upward, I found that it depended from a ring set over a wide opening, evidently made artificially. It must have been through this opening that the great sarcophagi had been lowered.

Directly underneath the hanging chain, which did not come closer to the ground than some eight or ten feet, was a huge tomb in the shape of a rectangular coffer or sarcophagus. It was open, save for a huge sheet of thick glass which rested above it on two thick balks of dark oak, cut to exceeding smoothness, which lay across it, one at either end. On the far side from where I stood each of these was joined to another oak plank, also cut smooth, which sloped gently to the rocky floor. Should it be necessary to open the tomb, the glass could be made to slide along the supports and descend by the sloping planks.

Naturally curious to know what might be within such a strange receptacle, I raised the lantern, depressing its lens so that the light might fall within.

Then I started back with a cry, the lantern slipping from my nerveless hand and falling with a ringing sound on the great sheet of thick glass.

Within, pillowed on soft cushions, and covered with a mantle woven of white natural fleece sprigged with tiny sprays of pine wrought in gold, lay the body of a woman—none other than my beautiful visitor. She was marble white, and her long black eyelashes lay on her white cheeks as though she slept.

Without a word or a sound, save the sounds made by my hurrying feet on the stone flooring, I fled up the steep steps, and through the dim expanse of the church, out into the bright sunlight. I found that I had mechanically raised the fallen lamp, and had taken it with me in my flight.

My feet naturally turned towards home. It was all instinctive. The new horror had—for the time, at any rate—drowned my mind in its mystery, deeper than the deepest depths of thought or imagination.

BOOK IV: UNDER THE FLAGSTAFF

RUPERT'S JOURNAL—*Continued.*

May 1, 1907.

For some days after the last adventure I was in truth in a half-dazed condition, unable to think sensibly, hardly coherently. Indeed, it was as much as I could do to preserve something of my habitual appearance and manner. However, my first test happily came soon, and when I was once through it I reacquired sufficient self-confidence to go through with my purpose. Gradually the original phase of stupefaction passed, and I was able to look the situation in the face. I knew the worst now, at any rate; and when the lowest point has been reached things must begin to mend. Still, I was wofully sensitive regarding anything which might affect my Lady of the Shroud, or even my opinion of her. I even began to dread Aunt Janet's Second-Sight visions or dreams. These had a fatal habit of coming so near to fact that they always made for a danger of discovery. I had to realize now that the Lady of the Shroud might indeed be a Vampire—one of that horrid race that survives death and carries on a life-in-death existence eternally and only for evil. Indeed, I began to *expect* that Aunt Janet would ere long have some prophetic insight to the matter. She had been so wonderfully correct in her prophetic surmises with regard to both the visits to my room that it was hardly possible that she could fail to take cognizance of this last development.

But my dread was not justified; at any rate, I had no reason to suspect that by any force or exercise of her occult gift she might cause me concern by the discovery of my secret. Only once did I feel that actual danger in that respect was close to me. That was when she came early one morning and rapped at my door. When I called out, "Who is that? What is it?" she said in an agitated way:

"Thank God, laddie, you are all right! Go to sleep again."

Later on, when we met at breakfast, she explained that she had had a nightmare in the grey of the morning. She thought she had seen me in the crypt of a great church close beside a stone coffin; and, knowing that such was an ominous subject to dream about, came as soon as she dared to see if I was all right. Her mind was evidently set on death and burial, for she went on:

"By the way, Rupert, I am told that the great church on time top of the cliff across the creek is St. Sava's, where the great people of the country used to be buried. I want you to take me there some day. We shall go over it, and look at the tombs and monuments together. I really think I should be afraid to go alone, but it will be all right if you are with me." This was getting really dangerous, so I turned it aside:

"Really, Aunt Janet, I'm afraid it won't do. If you go off to weird old churches, and fill yourself up with a fresh supply of horrors, I don't know what will happen. You'll be dreaming dreadful things about me every night and neither you nor I shall get any sleep." It went to my heart to oppose her in any wish; and also this kind of chaffy opposition might pain her. But I had no alternative; the matter was too serious to be allowed to proceed. Should Aunt Janet go to the church, she would surely want to visit the crypt. Should she do so, and there notice the glass-covered tomb—as she could not help doing—the Lord only knew what would happen. She had already Second-Sighted a woman being married to me, and before I myself knew that I had such a hope. What might she not reveal did she know where the woman came from? It may have been that her power of Second Sight had to rest on some basis of knowledge or belief, and that her vision was but some intuitive perception of my own subjective thought. But whatever it was it should be stopped—at all hazards.

This whole episode set me thinking introspectively, and led me gradually but imperatively to self-analysis—not of powers, but of motives. I found myself before long examining myself as to what were my real intentions. I thought at first that this intellectual process was an exercise of pure reason; but soon discarded this as inadequate—even impossible. Reason is a cold manifestation; this feeling which swayed and dominated me is none other than passion, which is quick, hot, and insistent.

As for myself, the self-analysis could lead to but one result—the expression to myself of the reality and definiteness of an already-formed though unconscious intention. I wished to do the woman good—to serve her in some way—to secure her some benefit by any means, no matter how difficult, which might be within my power. I knew that I loved her—loved her most truly and fervently; there was no need for self-analysis to tell me that. And, moreover, no self-analysis, or any other mental process that I knew of, could help my one doubt: whether she was an ordinary woman (or an extraordinary woman, for the matter of that) in some sore and terrible straits; or else one who lay under some dreadful condition, only partially alive, and not mistress of herself or her acts. Whichever her condition might be, there was in my own feeling a superfluity of affection for her. The self-analysis taught me one thing, at any rate—that I had for her, to start with, an infinite pity which had softened towards her my whole being, and had already mastered merely selfish desire. Out of it I began to find excuses for her every act. In the doing so I knew now, though perhaps I did not at the time the process was going on, that my view in its true inwardness was of her as a living woman—the woman I loved.

In the forming of our ideas there are different methods of work, as though the analogy with material life holds good. In the building of a house, for instance, there are many persons employed; men of different trades and occupations—architect, builder, masons, carpenters, plumbers, and a host of others—and all these with the officials of each guild or trade. So in the world of thought and feelings: knowledge and understanding come through various agents, each competent to its task.

How far pity reacted with love I knew not; I only knew that whatever her state might be, were she living or dead, I could find in my heart no blame for the Lady of the Shroud. It could not be that she was dead in the real conventional way; for, after all, the Dead do not walk the earth in corporal substance, even if there be spirits which take the corporal form. This woman was of actual form and weight. How could I doubt that, at all events—I, who had held her in my arms? Might it not be that she was not quite dead, and that it had been given to me to restore her to life again? Ah! that would be, indeed, a privilege well worth the giving my life to accomplish. That such a thing may be is possible. Surely the old myths were not absolute inventions; they must have had a basis somewhere in fact. May not the world-old story of Orpheus and Eurydice have been based on some deep-lying principle or power of human nature? There is not one of us but has wished at some time to bring back the dead. Ay, and who has not felt that in himself or herself was power in the deep love for our dead to make them quick again, did we but know the secret of how it was to be done?

For myself, I have seen such mysteries that I am open to conviction regarding things not yet explained. These have been, of course, amongst savages or those old-world people who have brought unchecked traditions and beliefs—ay, and powers too—down the ages from the dim days when the world was young; when forces were elemental, and Nature's handiwork was experimental rather than completed. Some of these wonders may have been older still than the accepted period of our own period of creation. May we not have to-day other wonders, different only in method, but not more susceptible of belief? Obi-ism and Fantee-ism have been exercised in my own presence, and their results proved by the evidence of my own eyes and other senses. So, too, have stranger rites, with the same object and the same success, in the far Pacific Islands. So, too, in India and China, in Thibet and in the Golden Chersonese. On all and each of these occasions there was, on my own part, enough belief to set in motion the powers of understanding; and there were no moral scruples to stand in the way of realization. Those whose lives are so spent that they achieve the reputation of not fearing man or God or devil are not deterred in their doing or thwarted from a set purpose by things which might deter others not so equipped for adventure. Whatever may be before them—pleasant or painful, bitter or sweet, arduous or facile, enjoyable or terrible, humorous or full of awe and horror—they must accept, taking them in the onward course as a good athlete takes hurdles in his stride. And there must be no hesitating, no looking back. If the explorer or the adventurer has scruples, he had better give up that special branch of effort and come himself to a more level walk in life. Neither must there be regrets. There is no need for such; savage life has this advantage: it begets a certain toleration not to be found in conventional existence.

RUPERT'S JOURNAL—*Continued.*

May 2, 1907.

I had heard long ago that Second Sight is a terrible gift, even to its possessor. I am now inclined not only to believe, but to understand it. Aunt Janet has made such a practice of it of late that I go in constant dread of discovery of my secret. She seems to parallel me all the time, whatever I may do. It is like a sort of dual existence to her; for she is her dear old self all the time, and yet some other person with a sort of intellectual kit of telescope and notebook, which are eternally used on me. I know they are *for* me, too—for what she considers my good. But all the same it makes an embarrassment. Happily Second Sight cannot speak as clearly as it sees, or, rather, as it understands. For the translation of the vague beliefs which it inculcates is both nebulous and uncertain—a sort of Delphic oracle which always says things which no one can make out at the time, but which can be afterwards read in any one of several ways. This is all right, for in my case it is a kind of safety; but, then, Aunt Janet is a very clever woman, and some time she herself may be able to understand. Then she may begin to put two and two together. When she does that, it will not be long before she knows more than I do of the facts of the whole affair. And her reading of them and of the Lady of the Shroud, round whom they circle, may not be the same as mine. Well, that will be all right too. Aunt Janet loves me—God knows I have good reason to know that all through these years—and whatever view she may take, her acts will be all I could wish. But I shall come in for a good lot of scolding, I am sure. By the way, I ought to think of that; if Aunt Janet scolds me, it is a pretty good proof that I ought to be scolded. I wonder if I dare tell her all. No! It is too strange. She is only a woman, after all: and if she knew I loved . . . I wish I knew her name, and thought—as I might myself do, only that I resist it—that she is not alive at all. Well, what she would either think or do beats me. I suppose she would want to slipper me as she used to do when I was a wee kiddie—in a different way, of course.

May 3, 1907.

I really could not go on seriously last night. The idea of Aunt Janet giving me a licking as in the dear old days made me laugh so much that nothing in the world seemed serious then. Oh, Aunt Janet is all right whatever comes. That I am sure of, so I needn't worry over it. A good thing too; there will be plenty to worry about without that. I shall not check her telling me of her visions, however; I may learn something from them.

For the last four-and-twenty hours I have, whilst awake, been looking over Aunt Janet's books, of which I brought a wheen down here. Gee whizz! No wonder the old dear is superstitious, when she is filled up to the back teeth with that sort of stuff! There may be some truth in some of those yarns; those who wrote them may believe in them, or some of them, at all events. But as to coherence or logic, or any sort of reasonable or instructive deduction, they might as well have been written by so many hens! These occult book-makers seem to gather only a lot of bare, bald facts, which they put down in the most uninteresting way possible. They go by quantity only. One story of the kind, well examined and with logical comments, would be more convincing to a third party than a whole hecatomb of them.

RUPERT'S JOURNAL—*Continued.*

May 4, 1907.

There is evidently something up in the country. The mountaineers are more uneasy than they have been as yet. There is constant going to and fro amongst them, mostly at night and in the grey of the morning. I spend many hours in my room in the eastern tower, from which I can watch the woods, and gather from signs the passing to and fro. But with all this activity no one has said to me a word on the subject. It is undoubtedly a disappointment to me. I had hoped that the mountaineers had come to trust me; that gathering at which they wanted to fire their guns for me gave me strong hopes. But now it is apparent that they do not trust me in full—as yet, at all events. Well, I must not complain. It is all only right and just. As yet I have done nothing to prove to them the love and devotion that I feel to the country. I know that such individuals as I have met trust me, and I believe like me. But the trust of a nation is different. That has to be won and tested; he who would win it must justify, and in a way that only troublous times can allow. No nation will—can—give full meed of honour to a stranger in times of peace. Why should it? I must not forget that I am here a stranger in the land, and that to the great mass of people even my name is unknown. Perhaps they will know me better when Rooke comes back with that store of arms and ammunition that he has bought, and the little warship he has got from South America. When they see that I hand over the whole lot to the nation without a string on them, they may begin to believe. In the meantime all I can do is to wait. It will all come right in time, I have no doubt. And if it doesn't come right, well, we can only die once!

Is that so? What about my Lady of the Shroud? I must not think of that or of her in this gallery. Love and war are separate, and may not mix—cannot mix, if it comes to that. I must be wise in the matter; and if I have got the hump in any degree whatever, must not show it.

But one thing is certain: something is up, and it must be the Turks. From what the Vladika said at that meeting they have some intention of an attack on the Blue Mountains. If that be so, we must be ready; and perhaps I can help there. The forces must be organized; we must have some method of communication. In this country, where are neither roads nor railways nor telegraphs, we must establish a signalling system of some sort. *That* I can begin at once. I can make a code, or adapt one that I have used elsewhere already. I shall rig up a semaphore on the top of the Castle which can be seen for an enormous distance around. I shall train a number of men to be facile in signalling. And then, should need come, I may be able to show the mountaineers that I am fit to live in their hearts . . .

And all this work may prove an anodyne to pain of another kind. It will help, at any rate, to keep my mind occupied whilst I am waiting for another visit from my Lady of the Shroud.

RUPERT'S JOURNAL—*Continued.*

May 18, 1907.

The two weeks that have passed have been busy, and may, as time goes on, prove eventful. I really think they have placed me in a different position with the Blue Mountaineers—certainly so far as those in this part of the country are concerned. They are no longer suspicious of me—which is much; though they have not yet received me into their confidence. I suppose this will come in time, but I must not try to hustle them. Already they are willing, so far as I can see, to use me to their own ends. They accepted the signalling idea very readily, and are quite willing to drill as much as I like. This can be (and I think is, in its way) a pleasure to them. They are born soldiers, every man of them; and practice together is only a realization of their own wishes and a further development of their powers. I think I can understand the trend of their thoughts, and what ideas of public policy lie behind them. In all that we have attempted together as yet they are themselves in absolute power. It rests with them to carry out any ideas I may suggest, so they do not fear any assumption of power or governance on my part. Thus, so long as they keep secret from me both their ideas of high policy and their immediate intentions, I am powerless to do them ill, and I *may* be of service should occasion arise. Well, all told, this is much. Already they accept me as an individual, not merely one of the mass. I am pretty sure that they are satisfied of my personal *bona fides*. It is policy and not mistrust that hedges me in. Well, policy is a matter of time. They are a splendid people, but if they knew a little more than they do they would understand that the wisest of all policies is trust—when it can be given. I must hold myself in check, and never be betrayed into a harsh thought towards them. Poor souls! with a thousand years behind them of Turkish aggression, strenuously attempted by both force and fraud, no wonder they are suspicious. Likewise every other nation with whom they have ever come in contact—except one, my own—has deceived or betrayed them. Anyhow, they are fine soldiers, and before long we shall have an army that cannot be ignored. If I can get so that they trust me, I shall ask Sir Colin to come out here. He would be a splendid head for their army. His great military knowledge and tactical skill would come in well. It makes me glow to think of what an army he would turn out of this splendid material, and one especially adapted for the style of fighting which would be necessary in this country.

If a mere amateur like myself, who has only had experience of organizing the wildest kind of savages, has been able to advance or compact their individual style of fighting into systematic effort, a great soldier like MacKelpie will bring them to perfection as a fighting machine. Our Highlanders, when they come out, will foregather with them, as mountaineers always do with each other. Then we shall have a force which can hold its own against any odds. I only hope that Rooke will be returning soon. I want to see those Ingis-Malbron rifles either safely stored in the Castle or, what is better, divided up amongst the mountaineers—a thing which will be done at the very earliest moment that I can accomplish it. I have a conviction that when these men have received their arms and ammunition from me they will understand me better, and not keep any secrets from me.

All this fortnight when I was not drilling or going about amongst the mountaineers, and teaching them the code which I have now got perfected, I was exploring the side of the mountain nearest to here. I could not bear to be still. It is torture to me to be idle in my present condition of mind regarding my Lady of the Shroud . . . Strange I do not mind mentioning the word to myself now. I used to at first; but that bitterness has all gone away.

RUPERT'S JOURNAL—Continued.

May 19, 1907.

I was so restless early this morning that before daylight I was out exploring on the mountain-side. By chance I came across a secret place just as the day was breaking. Indeed, it was by the change of light as the first sun-rays seemed to fall down the mountain-side that my attention was called to an opening shown by a light behind it. It was, indeed, a secret place—so secret that I thought at first I should keep it to myself. In such a place as this either to hide in or to be able to prevent anyone else hiding in might on occasion be an asset of safety.

When, however, I saw indications rather than traces that someone had already used it to camp in, I changed my mind, and thought that whenever I should get an opportunity I would tell the Vladika of it, as he is a man on whose discretion I can rely. If we ever have a war here or any sort of invasion, it is just such places that may be dangerous. Even in my own case it is much too near the Castle to be neglected.

The indications were meagre—only where a fire had been on a little shelf of rock; and it was not possible, through the results of burning vegetation or scorched grass, to tell how long before the fire had been alight. I could only guess. Perhaps the mountaineers might be able to tell or even to guess better than I could. But I am not so sure of this. I am a mountaineer myself, and with larger and more varied experience than any of them. For myself, though I could not be certain, I came to the conclusion that whoever had used the place had done so not many days before. It could not have been quite recently; but it may not have been very long ago. Whoever had used it had covered up his tracks well. Even the ashes had been carefully removed, and the place where they had lain was cleaned or swept in some way, so that there was no trace on the spot. I applied some of my West African experience, and looked on the rough bark of the trees to leeward, to where the agitated air, however directed, must have come, unless it was wanted to call attention to the place by the scattered wood-ashes, however fine. I found traces of it, but they were faint. There had not been rain for several days; so the dust must have been blown there since the rain had fallen, for it was still dry.

The place was a tiny gorge, with but one entrance, which was hidden behind a barren spur of rock—just a sort of long fissure, jagged and curving, in the rock, like a fault in the stratification. I could just struggle through it with considerable effort, holding my breath here and there, so as to reduce my depth of chest. Within it was tree-clad, and full of possibilities of concealment.

As I came away I marked well its direction and approaches, noting any guiding mark which might aid in finding it by day or night. I explored every foot of ground around it—in front, on each side, and above. But from nowhere could I see an indication of its existence. It was a veritable secret chamber wrought by the hand of Nature itself. I did not return home till I was familiar with every detail near and around it. This new knowledge added distinctly to my sense of security.

Later in the day I tried to find the Vladika or any mountaineer of importance, for I thought that such a hiding-place which had been used so recently might be dangerous, and especially at a time when, as I had learned at the meeting where they did *not* fire their guns that there may have been spies about or a traitor in the land.

Even before I came to my own room to-night I had fully made up my mind to go out early in the morning and find some proper person to whom to impart the information, so that a watch might be kept on the place. It is now getting on for midnight, and when I have had my usual last look at the garden I shall turn in. Aunt Janet was uneasy all day, and especially so this evening. I think it must have been my absence at the usual breakfast-hour which got on her nerves; and that unsatisfied mental or psychical irritation increased as the day wore on.

RUPERT'S JOURNAL—*Continued.*

May 20, 1907.

The clock on the mantelpiece in my room, which chimes on the notes of the clock at St. James's Palace, was striking midnight when I opened the glass door on the terrace. I had put out my lights before I drew the curtain, as I wished to see the full effect of the moonlight. Now that the rainy season is over, the moon is quite as beautiful as it was in the wet, and a great deal more comfortable. I was in evening dress, with a smoking-jacket in lieu of a coat, and I felt the air mild and mellow on the warm side, as I stood on the terrace.

But even in that bright moonlight the further corners of the great garden were full of mysterious shadows. I peered into them as well as I could—and my eyes are pretty good naturally, and are well trained. There was not the least movement. The air was as still as death, the foliage as still as though wrought in stone.

I looked for quite a long time in the hope of seeing something of my Lady. The quarters chimed several times, but I stood on unheeding. At last I thought I saw far off in the very corner of the old defending wall a flicker of white. It was but momentary, and could hardly have accounted in itself for the way my heart beat. I controlled myself, and stood as though I, too, were a graven image. I was rewarded by seeing presently another gleam of white. And then an unspeakable rapture stole over me as I realized that my Lady was coming as she had come before. I would have hurried out to meet her, but that I knew well that this would not be in accord with her wishes. So, thinking to please her, I drew back into the room. I was glad I had done so when, from the dark corner where I stood, I saw her steal up the marble steps and stand timidly looking in at the door. Then, after a long pause, came a whisper as faint and sweet as the music of a distant Æolian harp:

"Are you there? May I come in? Answer me! I am lonely and in fear!" For answer I emerged from my dim corner so swiftly that she was startled. I could hear from the quivering intake of her breath that she was striving—happily with success—to suppress a shriek.

"Come in," I said quietly. "I was waiting for you, for I felt that you would come. I only came in from the terrace when I saw you coming, lest you might fear that anyone might see us. That is not possible, but I thought you wished that I should be careful."

"I did—I do," she answered in a low, sweet voice, but very firmly. "But never avoid precaution. There is nothing that may not happen here. There may be eyes where we least expect—or suspect them." As she spoke the last words solemnly and in a low whisper, she was entering the room. I closed the glass door and bolted it, rolled back the steel grille, and pulled the heavy curtain. Then, when I had lit a candle, I went over and put a light to the fire. In a few seconds the dry wood had caught, and the flames were beginning to rise and crackle. She had not objected to my closing the window and drawing the curtain; neither did she make any comment on my lighting the fire. She simply acquiesced in it, as though it was now a matter of course. When I made the pile of cushions before it as on the occasion of her last visit, she sank down on them, and held out her white, trembling hands to the warmth.

She was different to-night from what she had been on either of the two former visits. From her present bearing I arrived at some gauge of her self-concern, her self-respect. Now that she was dry, and not overmastered by wet and cold, a sweet and gracious dignity seemed to shine from her, enwrapping her, as it were, with a luminous veil. It was not that she was by this made or shown as cold or distant, or in any way harsh or forbidding. On the contrary, protected by this dignity, she seemed much more sweet and genial than before. It was as though she felt that she could afford to stoop now that her loftiness was realized—that her position was recognized and secure. If her inherent dignity made an impenetrable nimbus round her, this was against others; she herself was not bound by it, or to be bound. So marked was this, so entirely and sweetly womanly did she appear, that I caught myself wondering in flashes of thought, which came as sharp periods of doubting judgment between spells of unconscious fascination, how I had ever come to think she was aught but perfect woman. As she rested, half sitting and half lying on the pile of cushions, she was all grace, and beauty, and charm, and sweetness—the veritable perfect woman of the dreams of a man, be he young or old. To have such a woman sit by his hearth and hold her holy of holies in his heart might well be a rapture to any man. Even an hour of such entrancing joy might be well won by a lifetime of pain, by the balance of a long life sacrificed, by the extinction of life itself. Quick behind the record of such thoughts came the answer to the doubt they challenged: if it should turn out that she was not living at all, but one of the doomed and pitiful Un-Dead, then so much more on account of her very sweetness and beauty would be the winning of her back to Life and Heaven—even were it that she might find happiness in the heart and in the arms of another man.

Once, when I leaned over the hearth to put fresh logs on the fire, my face was so close to hers that I felt her breath on my cheek. It thrilled me to feel even the suggestion of that ineffable contact. Her breath was sweet—sweet as the breath of a calf, sweet as the whiff of a summer breeze across beds of mignonette. How could anyone believe for a moment that such sweet breath could come from the lips of the dead—the dead *in esse* or *in posse*—that corruption could send forth fragrance so sweet and pure? It was with satisfied happiness that, as I looked at her from my stool, I saw the dancing of the flames from the beech-logs reflected in her glorious black eyes, and the stars that were hidden in them shine out with new colours and new lustre as they gleamed, rising and falling like hopes and fears. As the light leaped, so did smiles of quiet happiness flit over her beautiful face, the merriment of the joyous flames being reflected in ever-changing dimples.

At first I was a little disconcerted whenever my eyes took note of her shroud, and there came a momentary regret that the weather had not been again bad, so that there might have been compulsion for her putting on another garment—anything lacking the loathsomeness of that pitiful wrapping. Little by little, however, this feeling disappeared, and I found no matter for even dissatisfaction in her wrapping. Indeed, my thoughts found inward voice before the subject was dismissed from my mind:

"One becomes accustomed to anything—even a shroud!" But the thought was followed by a submerging wave of pity that she should have had such a dreadful experience.

By-and-by we seemed both to forget everything—I know I did—except that we were man and woman, and close together. The strangeness of the situation and the circumstances did not seem of moment—not worth even a passing thought. We still sat apart and said little, if anything. I cannot recall a single word that either of us spoke whilst we sat before the fire, but other language than speech came into play; the eyes told their own story, as eyes can do, and more eloquently than lips whilst exercising their function of speech. Question and answer followed each other in this satisfying language, and with an unspeakable rapture I began to realize that my affection was returned. Under these circumstances it was unrealizable that there should be any incongruity in the whole affair. I was not myself in the mood of questioning. I was diffident with that diffidence which comes alone from true love, as though it were a necessary emanation from that delightful and overwhelming and commanding passion. In her presence there seemed to surge up within me that which forbade speech. Speech under present conditions would have seemed to me unnecessary, imperfect, and even vulgarly overt. She, too, was silent. But now that I am alone, and memory is alone with me, I am convinced that she also had been happy. No, not that exactly. "Happiness" is not the word to describe either her feeling or my own. Happiness is more active, a more conscious enjoyment. We had been content. That expresses our condition perfectly; and now that I can analyze my own feeling, and understand what the word implies, I am satisfied of its accuracy. "Content" has both a positive and negative meaning or antecedent condition. It implies an absence of disturbing conditions as well as of wants; also it implies something positive which has been won or achieved, or which has accrued. In our state of mind—for though it may be presumption on my part, I am satisfied that our ideas were mutual—it meant that we had reached an understanding whence all that might come must be for good. God grant that it may be so!

As we sat silent, looking into each other's eyes, and whilst the stars in hers were now full of latent fire, perhaps from the reflection of the flames, she suddenly sprang to her feet, instinctively drawing the horrible shroud round her as she rose to her full height in a voice full of lingering emotion, as of one who is acting under spiritual compulsion rather than personal will, she said in a whisper:

"I must go at once. I feel the morning drawing nigh. I must be in my place when the light of day comes."

She was so earnest that I felt I must not oppose her wish; so I, too, sprang to my feet and ran towards the window. I pulled the curtain aside sufficiently far for me to press back the grille and reach the glass door, the latch of which I opened. I passed behind the curtain again, and held the edge of it back so that she could go through. For an instant she stopped as she broke the long silence:

"You are a true gentleman, and my friend. You understand all I wish. Out of the depth of my heart I thank you." She held out her beautiful high-bred hand. I took it in both mine as I fell on my knees, and raised it to my lips. Its touch made me quiver. She, too, trembled as she looked down at me with a glance which seemed to search my very soul. The stars in her eyes, now that the firelight was no longer on them, had gone back to their own mysterious silver. Then she drew her hand from mine very, very gently, as though it would fain linger; and she passed out behind the curtain with a gentle, sweet, dignified little bow which left me on my knees.

When I heard the glass door pulled-to gently behind her, I rose from my knees and hurried without the curtain, just in time to watch her pass down the steps. I wanted to see her as long as I could. The grey of morning was just beginning to war with the night gloom, and by the faint uncertain light I could see dimly the white figure flit between shrub and statue till finally it merged in the far darkness.

I stood for a long time on the terrace, sometimes looking into the darkness in front of me, in case I might be blessed with another glimpse of her; sometimes with my eyes closed, so that I might recall and hold in my mind her passage down the steps. For the first time since I had met her she had thrown back at me a glance as she stepped on the white path below the terrace. With the glamour over me of that look, which was all love and enticement, I could have dared all the powers that be.

When the grey dawn was becoming apparent through the lightening of the sky I returned to my room. In a dazed condition—half hypnotized by love—I went to bed, and in dreams continued to think, all happily, of my Lady of the Shroud.

RUPERT'S JOURNAL—*Continued.*

May 27, 1907.

A whole week has gone since I saw my Love! There it is; no doubt whatever is left in my mind about it now! Since I saw her my passion has grown and grown by leaps and bounds, as novelists put it. It has now become so vast as to overwhelm me, to wipe out all thought of doubt or difficulty. I suppose it must be what men suffered—suffering need not mean pain—under enchantments in old times. I am but as a straw whirled in the resistless eddies of a whirlpool. I feel that I *must* see her again, even if it be but in her tomb in the crypt. I must, I suppose, prepare myself for the venture, for many things have to be thought of. The visit must not be at night, for in such case I might miss her, did she come to me again here . . .

The morning came and went, but my wish and intention still remained; and so in the full tide of noon, with the sun in all its fiery force, I set out for the old church of St. Sava. I carried with me a lantern with powerful lens. I had wrapped it up secretly, for I had a feeling that I should not like anyone to know that I had such a thing with me.

On this occasion I had no misgivings. On the former visit I had for a moment been overwhelmed at the unexpected sight of the body of the woman I thought I loved—I knew it now—lying in her tomb. But now I knew all, and it was to see this woman, though in her tomb, that I came.

When I had lit my lantern, which I did as soon as I had pushed open the great door, which was once again unlocked, I turned my steps to the steps of the crypt, which lay behind the richly carven wood screen. This I could see, with the better light, was a noble piece of work of priceless beauty and worth. I tried to keep my heart in full courage with thoughts of my Lady, and of the sweetness and dignity of our last meeting; but, despite all, it sank down, down, and turned to water as I passed with uncertain feet down the narrow, tortuous steps. My concern, I am now convinced, was not for myself, but that she whom I adored should have to endure such a fearful place. As anodyne to my own pain I thought what it would be, and how I should feel, when I should have won for her a way out of that horror, at any rate. This thought reassured me somewhat, and restored my courage. It was in something of the same fashion which has hitherto carried me out of tight places as well as into them that at last I pushed open the low, narrow door at the foot of the rock-hewn staircase and entered the crypt.

Without delay I made my way to the glass-covered tomb set beneath the hanging chain. I could see by the flashing of the light around me that my hand which held the lantern trembled. With a great effort I steadied myself, and raising the lantern, turned its light down into the sarcophagus.

Once again the fallen lantern rang on the tingling glass, and I stood alone in the darkness, for an instant almost paralyzed with surprised disappointment.

The tomb was empty! Even the trappings of the dead had been removed.

I knew not what happened till I found myself groping my way up the winding stair. Here, in comparison with the solid darkness of the crypt, it seemed almost light. The dim expanse of the church sent a few straggling rays down the vaulted steps, and as I could see, be it never so dimly, I felt I was not in absolute darkness. With the light came a sense of power and fresh courage, and I groped my way back into the crypt again. There, by now and again lighting matches, I found my way to the tomb and recovered my lantern. Then I took my way slowly—for I wished to prove, if not my own courage, at least such vestiges of self-respect as the venture had left me—through the church, where I extinguished my lantern, and out through the great door into the open sunlight. I seemed to have heard, both in the darkness of the crypt and through the dimness of the church, mysterious sounds as of whispers and suppressed breathing; but the memory of these did not count for much when once I was free. I was only satisfied of my own consciousness and identity when I found myself on the broad rock terrace in front of the church, with the fierce sunlight beating on my upturned face, and, looking downward, saw far below me the rippled blue of the open sea.

RUPERT'S JOURNAL—*Continued.*

June 3, 1907.

Another week has elapsed—a week full of movement of many kinds and in many ways—but as yet I have had no tale or tidings of my Lady of the Shroud. I have not had an opportunity of going again in daylight to St. Sava's as I should have liked to have done. I felt that I must not go at night. The night is her time of freedom, and it must be kept for her—or else I may miss her, or perhaps never see her again.

The days have been full of national movement. The mountaineers have evidently been organizing themselves, for some reason which I cannot quite understand, and which they have hesitated to make known to me. I have taken care not to manifest any curiosity, whatever I may have felt. This would certainly arouse suspicion, and might ultimately cause disaster to my hopes of aiding the nation in their struggle to preserve their freedom.

These fierce mountaineers are strangely—almost unduly—suspicious, and the only way to win their confidence is to begin the trusting. A young American attaché of the Embassy at Vienna, who had made a journey through the Land of the Blue Mountains, once put it to me in this form:

"Keep your head shut, and they'll open theirs. If you don't, they'll open it for you—down to the chine!"

It was quite apparent to me that they were completing some fresh arrangements for signalling with a code of their own. This was natural enough, and in no way inconsistent with the measure of friendliness already shown to me. Where there are neither telegraphs, railways, nor roads, any effective form of communication must—can only be purely personal. And so, if they wish to keep any secret amongst themselves, they must preserve the secret of their code. I should have dearly liked to learn their new code and their manner of using it, but as I want to be a helpful friend to them—and as this implies not only trust, but the appearance of it—I had to school myself to patience.

This attitude so far won their confidence that before we parted at our last meeting, after most solemn vows of faith and secrecy, they took me into the secret. This was, however, only to the extent of teaching me the code and method; they still withheld from me rigidly the fact or political secret, or whatever it was that was the mainspring of their united action.

When I got home I wrote down, whilst it was fresh in my memory, all they told me. This script I studied until I had it so thoroughly by heart that I *could* not forget it. Then I burned the paper. However, there is now one gain at least: with my semaphore I can send through the Blue Mountains from side to side, with expedition, secrecy, and exactness, a message comprehensible to all.

RUPERT'S JOURNAL—*Continued.*

June 6, 1907.

Last night I had a new experience of my Lady of the Shroud—in so far as form was concerned, at any rate. I was in bed, and just falling asleep, when I heard a queer kind of scratching at the glass door of the terrace. I listened acutely, my heart beating hard. The sound seemed to come from low down, close to the floor. I jumped out of bed, ran to the window, and, pulling aside the heavy curtains, looked out.

The garden looked, as usual, ghostly in the moonlight, but there was not the faintest sign of movement anywhere, and no one was on or near the terrace. I looked eagerly down to where the sound had seemed to come from.

There, just inside the glass door, as though it had been pushed under the door, lay a paper closely folded in several laps. I picked it up and opened it. I was all in a tumult, for my heart told me whence it came. Inside was written in English, in a large, sprawling hand, such as might be from an English child of seven or eight:

"Meet me at the Flagstaff on the Rock!"

I knew the place, of course. On the farthermost point of the rock on which the Castle stands is set a high flagstaff, whereon in old time the banner of the Vissarion family flew. At some far-off time, when the Castle had been liable to attack, this point had been strongly fortified. Indeed, in the days when the bow was a martial weapon it must have been quite impregnable.

A covered gallery, with loopholes for arrows, had been cut in the solid rock, running right round the point, quite surrounding the flagstaff and the great boss of rock on whose centre it was reared. A narrow drawbridge of immense strength had connected—in peaceful times, and still remained—the outer point of rock with an entrance formed in the outer wall, and guarded with flanking towers and a portcullis. Its use was manifestly to guard against surprise. From this point only could be seen the line of the rocks all round the point. Thus, any secret attack by boats could be made impossible.

Having hurriedly dressed myself, and taking with me both hunting-knife and revolver, I went out on the terrace, taking the precaution, unusual to me, of drawing the grille behind me and locking it. Matters around the Castle are in far too disturbed a condition to allow the taking of any foolish chances, either in the way of being unarmed or of leaving the private entrance to the Castle open. I found my way through the rocky passage, and climbed by the Jacob's ladder fixed on the rock—a device of convenience in time of peace—to the foot of the flagstaff.

I was all on fire with expectation, and the time of going seemed exceeding long; so I was additionally disappointed by the contrast when I did not see my Lady there when I arrived. However, my heart beat freely again—perhaps more freely than ever—when I saw her crouching in the shadow of the Castle wall. From where she was she could not be seen from any point save that alone which I occupied; even from there it was only her white shroud that was conspicuous through the deep gloom of the shadow. The moonlight was so bright that the shadows were almost unnaturally black.

I rushed over towards her, and when close was about to say impulsively, "Why did you leave your tomb?" when it suddenly struck me that the question would be malapropos and embarrassing in many ways. So, better judgment prevailing, I said instead:

"It has been so long since I saw you! It has seemed an eternity to me!" Her answer came as quickly as even I could have wished; she spoke impulsively and without thought:

"It has been long to me too! Oh, so long! so long! I have asked you to come out here because I wanted to see you so much that I could not wait any longer. I have been heart-hungry for a sight of you!"

Her words, her eager attitude, the ineffable something which conveys the messages of the heart, the longing expression in her eyes as the full moonlight fell on her face, showing the stars as living gold—for in her eagerness she had stepped out towards me from the shadow—all set me on fire. Without a thought or a word—for it was Nature speaking in the language of Love, which is a silent tongue—I stepped towards her and took her in my arms. She yielded with that sweet unconsciousness which is the perfection of Love, as if it was in obedience to some command uttered before the beginning of the world. Probably without any conscious effort on either side—I know there was none on mine—our mouths met in the first kiss of love.

At the time nothing in the meeting struck me as out of the common. But later in the night, when I was alone and in darkness, whenever I thought of it all—its strangeness and its stranger rapture—I could not but be sensible of the bizarre conditions for a love meeting. The place lonely, the time night, the man young and strong, and full of life and hope and ambition; the woman, beautiful and ardent though she was, a woman seemingly dead, clothed in the shroud in which she had been wrapped when lying in her tomb in the crypt of the old church.

Whilst we were together, anyhow, there was little thought of the kind; no reasoning of any kind on my part. Love has its own laws and its own logic. Under the flagstaff, where the Vissarion banner was wont to flap in the breeze, she was in my arms; her sweet breath was on my face; her heart was beating against my own. What need was there for reason at all? *Inter arma silent leges*—the voice of reason is silent in the stress of passion. Dead she may be, or Un-dead—a Vampire with one foot in Hell and one on earth. But I love her; and come what may, here or hereafter, she is mine. As my mate, we shall fare along together, whatsoever the end may be, or wheresoever our path may lead. If she is indeed to be won from the nethermost Hell, then be mine the task!

But to go back to the record. When I had once started speaking to her in words of passion I could not stop. I did not want to—if I could; and she did not appear to wish it either. Can there be a woman—alive or dead—who would not want to hear the rapture of her lover expressed to her whilst she is enclosed in his arms?

There was no attempt at reticence on my part now; I took it for granted that she knew all that I surmised, and, as she made neither protest nor comment, that she accepted my belief as to her indeterminate existence. Sometimes her eyes would be closed, but even then the rapture of her face was almost beyond belief. Then, when the beautiful eyes would open and gaze on me, the stars that were in them would shine and scintillate as though they were formed of living fire. She said little, very little; but though the words were few, every syllable was fraught with love, and went straight to the very core of my heart.

By-and-by, when our transport had calmed to joy, I asked when I might next see her, and how and where I might find her when I should want to. She did not reply directly, but, holding me close in her arms, whispered in my ear with that breathless softness which is a lover's rapture of speech:

"I have come here under terrible difficulties, not only because I love you—and that would be enough—but because, as well as the joy of seeing you, I wanted to warn you."

"To warn me! Why?" I queried. Her reply came with a bashful hesitation, with something of a struggle in it, as of one who for some ulterior reason had to pick her words:

"There are difficulties and dangers ahead of you. You are beset with them; and they are all the greater because they are, of grim necessity, hidden from you. You cannot go anywhere, look in any direction, do anything, say anything, but it may be a signal for danger. My dear, it lurks everywhere—in the light as well as in the darkness; in the open as well as in the secret places; from friends as well as foes; when you are least prepared; when you may least expect it. Oh, I know it, and what it is to endure; for I share it for you—for your dear sake!"

"My darling!" was all I could say, as I drew her again closer to me and kissed her. After a bit she was calmer; seeing this, I came back to the subject that she had—in part, at all events—come to me to speak about:

"But if difficulty and danger hedge me in so everlastingly, and if I am to have no indication whatever of its kind or purpose, what can I do? God knows I would willingly guard myself—not on my own account, but for your dear sake. I have now a cause to live and be strong, and to keep all my faculties, since it may mean much to you. If you may not tell me details, may you not indicate to me some line of conduct, of action, that would be most in accord with your wishes—or, rather, with your idea of what would be best?"

She looked at me fixedly before speaking—a long, purposeful, loving look which no man born of woman could misunderstand. Then she spoke slowly, deliberately, emphatically:

"Be bold, and fear not. Be true to yourself, to me—it is the same thing. These are the best guards you can use. Your safety does not rest with me. Ah, I wish it did! I wish to God it did!" In my inner heart it thrilled me not merely to hear the expression of her wish, but to hear her use the name of God as she did. I understand now, in the calm of this place and with the sunlight before me, that my belief as to her being all woman—living woman—was not quite dead: but though at the moment my heart did not recognize the doubt, my brain did. And I made up my mind that we should not part this time until she knew that I had seen her, and where; but, despite my own thoughts, my outer ears listened greedily as she went on.

"As for me, you may not find *me*, but *I* shall find *you*, be sure! And now we must say 'Good-night,' my dear, my dear! Tell me once again that you love me, for it is a sweetness that one does not wish to forego—even one who wears such a garment as this—and rests where I must rest." As she spoke she held up part of her cerements for me to see. What could I do but take her once again in my arms and hold her close, close. God knows it was all in love; but it was passionate love which surged through my every vein as I strained her dear body to mine. But yet this embrace was not selfish; it was not all an expression of my own passion. It was based on pity—the pity which is twin-born with true love. Breathless from our kisses, when presently we released each other, she stood in a glorious rapture, like a white spirit in the moonlight, and as her lovely, starlit eyes seemed to devour me, she spoke in a languorous ecstasy:

"Oh, how you love me! how you love me! It is worth all I have gone through for this, even to wearing this terrible drapery." And again she pointed to her shroud.

Here was my chance to speak of what I knew, and I took it. "I know, I know. Moreover, I know that awful resting-place."

I was interrupted, cut short in the midst of my sentence, not by any word, but by the frightened look in her eyes and the fear-mastered way in which she shrank away from me. I suppose in reality she could not be paler than she looked when the colour-absorbing moonlight fell on her; but on the instant all semblance of living seemed to shrink and fall away, and she looked with eyes of dread as if in I some awful way held in thrall. But for the movement of the pitiful glance, she would have seemed of soulless marble, so deadly cold did she look.

The moments that dragged themselves out whilst I waited for her to speak seemed endless. At length her words came in an awed whisper, so faint that even in that stilly night I could hardly hear it:

"You know—you know my resting-place! How—when was that?" There was nothing to do now but to speak out the truth:

"I was in the crypt of St. Sava. It was all by accident. I was exploring all around the Castle, and I went there in my course. I found the winding stair in the rock behind the screen, and went down. Dear, I loved you well before that awful moment, but then, even as the lantern fell tingling on the glass, my love multiplied itself, with pity as a factor." She was silent for a few seconds. When she spoke, there was a new tone in her voice:

"But were you not shocked?"

"Of course I was," I answered on the spur of the moment, and I now think wisely. "Shocked is hardly the word. I was horrified beyond anything that words can convey that you—*you* should have to so endure! I did not like to return, for I feared lest my doing so might set some barrier between us. But in due time I did return on another day."

"Well?" Her voice was like sweet music.

"I had another shock that time, worse than before, for you were not there. Then indeed it was that I knew to myself how dear you were—how dear you are to me. Whilst I live, you—living or dead—shall always be in my heart." She breathed hard. The elation in her eyes made them outshine the moonlight, but she said no word. I went on:

"My dear, I had come into the crypt full of courage and hope, though I knew what dreadful sight should sear my eyes once again. But we little know what may be in store for us, no matter what we expect. I went out with a heart like water from that dreadful desolation."

"Oh, how you love me, dear!" Cheered by her words, and even more by her tone, I went on with renewed courage. There was no halting, no faltering in my intention now:

"You and I, my dear, were ordained for each other. I cannot help it that you had already suffered before I knew you. It may be that there may be for you still suffering that I may not prevent, endurance that I may not shorten; but what a man can do is yours. Not Hell itself will stop me, if it be possible that I may win through its torments with you in my arms!"

"Will nothing stop you, then?" Her question was breathed as softly as the strain of an Æolian harp.

"Nothing!" I said, and I heard my own teeth snap together. There was something speaking within me stronger than I had ever known myself to be. Again came a query, trembling, quavering, quivering, as though the issue was of more than life or death:

"Not this?" She held up a corner of the shroud, and as she saw my face and realized the answer before I spoke, went on: "With all it implies?"

"Not if it were wrought of the cerecloths of the damned!" There was a long pause. Her voice was more resolute when she spoke again. It rang. Moreover, there was in it a joyous note, as of one who feels new hope:

"But do you know what men say? Some of them, that I am dead and buried; others, that I am not only dead and buried, but that I am one of those unhappy beings that may not die the common death of man. Who live on a fearful life-in-death, whereby they are harmful to all. Those unhappy Un-dead whom men call Vampires—who live on the blood of the living, and bring eternal damnation as well as death with the poison of their dreadful kisses!

"I know what men say sometimes," I answered. "But I know also what my own heart says; and I rather choose to obey its calling than all the voices of the living or the dead. Come what may, I am pledged to you. If it be that your old life has to be rewon for you out of the very jaws of Death and Hell, I shall keep the faith I have pledged, and that here I pledge again!" As I finished speaking I sank on my knees at her feet, and, putting my arms round her, drew her close to me. Her tears rained down on my face as she stroked my hair with her soft, strong hand and whispered to me:

"This is indeed to be one. What more holy marriage can God give to any of His creatures?" We were both silent for a time.

I think I was the first to recover my senses. That I did so was manifest by my asking her: "When may we meet again?"—a thing I had never remembered doing at any of our former partings. She answered with a rising and falling of the voice that was just above a whisper, as soft and cooing as the voice of a pigeon:

"That will be soon—as soon as I can manage it, be sure. My dear, my dear!" The last four words of endearment she spoke in a low but prolonged and piercing tone which made me thrill with delight.

"Give me some token," I said, "that I may have always close to me to ease my aching heart till we meet again, and ever after, for love's sake!" Her mind seemed to leap to understanding, and with a purpose all her own. Stooping for an instant, she tore off with swift, strong fingers a fragment of her shroud. This, having kissed it, she handed to me, whispering:

"It is time that we part. You must leave me now. Take this, and keep it for ever. I shall be less unhappy in my terrible loneliness whilst it lasts if I know that this my gift, which for good or ill is a part of me as you know me, is close to you. It may be, my very dear, that some day you may be glad and even proud of this hour, as I am." She kissed me as I took it.

"For life or death, I care not which, so long as I am with you!" I said, as I moved off. Descending the Jacob's ladder, I made my way down the rock-hewn passage.

The last thing I saw was the beautiful face of my Lady of the Shroud as she leaned over the edge of the opening. Her eyes were like glowing stars as her looks followed me. That look shall never fade from my memory.

After a few agitating moments of thought I half mechanically took my way down to the garden. Opening the grille, I entered my lonely room, which looked all the more lonely for the memory of the rapturous moments under the Flagstaff. I went to bed as one in a dream. There I lay till sunrise—awake and thinking.

BOOK V: A RITUAL AT MIDNIGHT

RUPERT'S JOURNAL—*Continued.*

June 20, 1907.

The time has gone as quickly as work can effect since I saw my Lady. As I told the mountaineers, Rooke, whom I had sent on the service, had made a contract for fifty thousand Ingis-Malbron rifles, and as many tons of ammunition as the French experts calculated to be a full supply for a year of warfare. I heard from him by our secret telegraph code that the order had been completed, and that the goods were already on the way. The morning after the meeting at the Flagstaff I had word that at night the vessel—one chartered by Rooke for the purpose—would arrive at Vissarion during the night. We were all expectation. I had always now in the Castle a signalling party, the signals being renewed as fast as the men were sufficiently expert to proceed with their practice alone or in groups. We hoped that every fighting-man in the country would in time become an expert signaller. Beyond these, again, we have always a few priests. The Church of the country is a militant Church; its priests are soldiers, its Bishops commanders. But they all serve wherever the battle most needs them. Naturally they, as men of brains, are quicker at learning than the average mountaineers; with the result that they learnt the code and the signalling almost by instinct. We have now at least one such expert in each community of them, and shortly the priests alone will be able to signal, if need be, for the nation; thus releasing for active service the merely fighting-man. The men at present with me I took into confidence as to the vessel's arrival, and we were all ready for work when the man on the lookout at the Flagstaff sent word that a vessel without lights was creeping in towards shore. We all assembled on the rocky edge of the creek, and saw her steal up the creek and gain the shelter of the harbour. When this had been effected, we ran out the boom which protects the opening, and after that the great armoured sliding-gates which Uncle Roger had himself had made so as to protect the harbour in case of need.

We then came within and assisted in warping the steamer to the side of the dock.

Rooke looked fit, and was full of fire and vigour. His responsibility and the mere thought of warlike action seemed to have renewed his youth.

When we had arranged for the unloading of the cases of arms and ammunition, I took Rooke into the room which we call my "office," where he gave me an account of his doings. He had not only secured the rifles and the ammunition for them, but he had purchased from one of the small American Republics an armoured yacht which had been especially built for war service. He grew quite enthusiastic, even excited, as he told me of her:

"She is the last word in naval construction—a torpedo yacht. A small cruiser, with turbines up to date, oil-fuelled, and fully armed with the latest and most perfect weapons and explosives of all kinds. The fastest boat afloat to-day. Built by Thorneycroft, engined by Parsons, armoured by Armstrong, armed by Crupp. If she ever comes into action, it will be bad for her opponent, for she need not fear to tackle anything less than a *Dreadnought*."

He also told me that from the same Government, whose nation had just established an unlooked-for peace, he had also purchased a whole park of artillery of the very latest patterns, and that for range and accuracy the guns were held to be supreme. These would follow before long, and with them their proper ammunition, with a shipload of the same to follow shortly after.

When he had told me all the rest of his news, and handed me the accounts, we went out to the dock to see the debarkation of the war material. Knowing that it was arriving, I had sent word in the afternoon to the mountaineers to tell them to come and remove it. They had answered the call, and it really seemed to me that the whole of the land must that night have been in motion.

They came as individuals, grouping themselves as they came within the defences of the Castle; some had gathered at fixed points on the way. They went secretly and in silence, stealing through the forests like ghosts, each party when it grouped taking the place of that which had gone on one of the routes radiating round Vissarion. Their coming and going was more than ghostly. It was, indeed, the outward manifestation of an inward spirit—a whole nation dominated by one common purpose.

The men in the steamer were nearly all engineers, mostly British, well conducted, and to be depended upon. Rooke had picked them separately, and in the doing had used well his great experience of both men and adventurous life. These men were to form part of the armoured yacht's crew when she should come into the Mediterranean waters. They and the priests and fighting-men in the Castle worked well together, and with a zeal that was beyond praise. The heavy cases seemed almost of their own accord to leave the holds, so fast came the procession of them along the gangways from deck to dock-wall. It was a part of my design that the arms should be placed in centres ready for local distribution. In such a country as this, without railways or even roads, the distribution of war material in any quantity is a great labour, for it has to be done individually, or at least from centres.

But of this work the great number of mountaineers who were arriving made little account. As fast as the ship's company, with the assistance of the priests and fighting-men, placed the cases on the quay, the engineers opened them and laid the contents ready for portage. The mountaineers seemed to come in a continuous stream; each in turn shouldered his burden and passed out, the captain of his section giving him as he passed his instruction where to go and in what route. The method had been already prepared in my office ready for such a distribution when the arms should arrive, and descriptions and quantities had been noted by the captains. The whole affair was treated by all as a matter of the utmost secrecy. Hardly a word was spoken beyond the necessary directions, and these were given in whispers. All night long the stream of men went and came, and towards dawn the bulk of the imported material was lessened by half. On the following night the remainder was removed, after my own men had stored in the Castle the rifles and ammunition reserved for its defence if necessary. It was advisable to keep a reserve supply in case it should ever be required. The following night Rooke went away secretly in the chartered vessel. He had to bring back with him the purchased cannon and heavy ammunition, which had been in the meantime stored on one of the Greek islands. The second morning, having had secret word that the steamer was on the way, I had given the signal for the assembling of the mountaineers.

A little after dark the vessel, showing no light, stole into the creek. The barrier gates were once again closed, and when a sufficient number of men had arrived to handle the guns, we began to unload. The actual deportation was easy enough, for the dock had all necessary appliances quite up to date, including a pair of shears for gun-lifting which could be raised into position in a very short time.

The guns were well furnished with tackle of all sorts, and before many hours had passed a little procession of them disappeared into the woods in ghostly silence. A number of men surrounded each, and they moved as well as if properly supplied with horses.

In the meantime, and for a week after the arrival of the guns, the drilling went on without pause. The gun-drill was wonderful. In the arduous work necessary for it the great strength and stamina of the mountaineers showed out wonderfully. They did not seem to know fatigue any more than they knew fear.

For a week this went on, till a perfect discipline and management was obtained. They did not practise the shooting, for this would have made secrecy impossible. It was reported all along the Turkish frontier that the Sultan's troops were being massed, and though this was not on a war footing, the movement was more or less dangerous. The reports of our own spies, although vague as to the purpose and extent of the movement, were definite as to something being on foot. And Turkey does not do something without a purpose that bodes ill to someone. Certainly the sound of cannon, which is a far-reaching sound, would have given them warning of our preparations, and would so have sadly minimized their effectiveness.

When the cannon had all been disposed of—except, of course, those destined for defence of the Castle or to be stored there—Rooke went away with the ship and crew. The ship he was to return to the owners; the men would be shipped on the war-yacht, of whose crew they would form a part. The rest of them had been carefully selected by Rooke himself, and were kept in secrecy at Cattaro, ready for service the moment required. They were all good men, and quite capable of whatever work they might be set to. So Rooke told me, and he ought to know. The experience of his young days as a private made him an expert in such a job.

RUPERT'S JOURNAL—*Continued.*

June 24, 1907.

Last night I got from my Lady a similar message to the last, and delivered in a similar way. This time, however, our meeting was to be on the leads of the Keep.

I dressed myself very carefully before going on this adventure, lest by any chance of household concern, any of the servants should see me; for if this should happen, Aunt Janet would be sure to hear of it, which would give rise to endless surmises and questionings—a thing I was far from desiring.

I confess that in thinking the matter over during the time I was making my hurried preparations I was at a loss to understand how any human body, even though it be of the dead, could go or be conveyed to such a place without some sort of assistance, or, at least, collusion, on the part of some of the inmates. At the visit to the Flagstaff circumstances were different. This spot was actually outside the Castle, and in order to reach it I myself had to leave the Castle privately, and from the garden ascend to the ramparts. But here was no such possibility. The Keep was an *imperium in imperio*. It stood within the Castle, though separated from it, and it had its own defences against intrusion. The roof of it was, so far as I knew, as little approachable as the magazine.

The difficulty did not, however, trouble me beyond a mere passing thought. In the joy of the coming meeting and the longing rapture at the mere thought of it, all difficulties disappeared. Love makes its own faith, and I never doubted that my Lady would be waiting for me at the place designated. When I had passed through the little arched passages, and up the doubly-grated stairways contrived in the massiveness of the walls, I let myself out on the leads. It was well that as yet the times were sufficiently peaceful not to necessitate guards or sentries at all such points.

There, in a dim corner where the moonlight and the passing clouds threw deep shadows, I saw her, clothed as ever in her shroud. Why, I know not. I felt somehow that the situation was even more serious than ever. But I was steeled to whatever might come. My mind had been already made up. To carry out my resolve to win the woman I loved I was ready to face death. But now, after we had for a few brief moments held each other in our arms, I was willing to accept death—or more than death. Now, more than before, was she sweet and dear to me. Whatever qualms there might have been at the beginning of our love-making, or during the progress of it, did not now exist. We had exchanged vows and confidences, and acknowledged our loves. What, then, could there be of distrust, or even doubt, that the present might not set at naught? But even had there been such doubts or qualms, they must have disappeared in the ardour of our mutual embrace. I was by now mad for her, and was content to be so mad. When she had breath to speak after the strictness of our embrace, she said:

"I have come to warn you to be more than ever careful." It was, I confess, a pang to me, who thought only of love, to hear that anything else should have been the initiative power of her coming, even though it had been her concern for my own safety. I could not but notice the bitter note of chagrin in my voice as I answered:

"It was for love's sake that *I* came." She, too, evidently felt the undercurrent of pain, for she said quickly:

"Ah, dearest, I, too, came for love's sake. It is because I love you that I am so anxious about you. What would the world—ay, or heaven—be to me without you?"

There was such earnest truth in her tone that the sense and realization of my own harshness smote me. In the presence of such love as this even a lover's selfishness must become abashed. I could not express myself in words, so simply raised her slim hand in mine and kissed it. As it lay warm in my own I could not but notice, as well as its fineness, its strength and the firmness of its clasp. Its warmth and fervour struck into my heart—and my brain. Thereupon I poured out to her once more my love for her, she listening all afire. When passion had had its say, the calmer emotions had opportunity of expression. When I was satisfied afresh of her affection, I began to value her care for my safety, and so I went back to the subject. Her very insistence, based on personal affection, gave me more solid ground for fear. In the moment of love transports I had forgotten, or did not think, of what wonderful power or knowledge she must have to be able to move in such strange ways as she did. Why, at this very moment she was within my own gates. Locks and bars, even the very seal of death itself, seemed unable to make for her a prison-house. With such freedom of action and movement, going when she would into secret places, what might she not know that was known to others? How could anyone keep secret from such an one even an ill intent? Such thoughts, such surmises, had often flashed through my mind in moments of excitement rather than of reflection, but never long enough to become fixed into belief. But yet the consequences, the convictions, of them were with me, though unconsciously, though the thoughts themselves were perhaps forgotten or withered before development.

"And you?" I asked her earnestly. "What about danger to you?" She smiled, her little pearl-white teeth gleaming in the moonlight, as she spoke:

"There is no danger for me. I am safe. I am the safest person, perhaps the only safe person, in all this land." The full significance of her words did not seem to come to me all at once. Some base for understanding such an assertion seemed to be wanting. It was not that I did not trust or believe her, but that I thought she might be mistaken. I wanted to reassure myself, so in my distress I asked unthinkingly:

"How the safest? What is your protection?" For several moments that spun themselves out endlessly she looked me straight in the face, the stars in her eyes seeming to glow like fire; then, lowering her head, she took a fold of her shroud and held it up to me.

"This!"

The meaning was complete and understandable now. I could not speak at once for the wave of emotion which choked me. I dropped on my knees, and taking her in my arms, held her close to me. She saw that I was moved, and tenderly stroked my hair, and with delicate touch pressed down my head on her bosom, as a mother might have done to comfort a frightened child.

Presently we got back to the realities of life again. I murmured:

"Your safety, your life, your happiness are all-in-all to me. When will you let them be my care?" She trembled in my arms, nestling even closer to me. Her own arms seemed to quiver with delight as she said:

"Would you indeed like me to be always with you? To me it would be a happiness unspeakable; and to you, what would it be?"

I thought that she wished to hear me speak my love to her, and that, woman-like, she had led me to the utterance, and so I spoke again of the passion that now raged in me, she listening eagerly as we strained each other tight in our arms. At last there came a pause, a long, long pause, and our hearts beat consciously in unison as we stood together. Presently she said in a sweet, low, intense whisper, as soft as the sighing of summer wind:

"It shall be as you wish; but oh, my dear, you will have to first go through an ordeal which may try you terribly! Do not ask me anything! You must not ask, because I may not answer, and it would be pain to me to deny you anything. Marriage with such an one as I am has its own ritual, which may not be foregone. It may . . . " I broke passionately into her speaking:

"There is no ritual that I fear, so long as it be that it is for your good, and your lasting happiness. And if the end of it be that I may call you mine, there is no horror in life or death that I shall not gladly face. Dear, I ask you nothing. I am content to leave myself in your hands. You shall advise me when the time comes, and I shall be satisfied, content to obey. Content! It is but a poor word to express what I long for! I shall shirk nothing which may come to me from this or any other world, so long as it is to make you mine!" Once again her murmured happiness was music to my ears:

"Oh, how you love me! how you love me, dear, dear!" She took me in her arms, and for a few seconds we hung together. Suddenly she tore herself apart from me, and stood drawn up to the full height, with a dignity I cannot describe or express. Her voice had a new dominance, as with firm utterance and in staccato manner she said:

"Rupert Sent Leger, before we go a step further I must say something to you, ask you something, and I charge you, on your most sacred honour and belief, to answer me truly. Do you believe me to be one of those unhappy beings who may not die, but have to live in shameful existence between earth and the nether world, and whose hellish mission is to destroy, body and soul, those who love them till they fall to their level? You are a gentleman, and a brave one. I have found you fearless. Answer me in sternest truth, no matter what the issue may be!"

She stood there in the glamorous moonlight with a commanding dignity which seemed more than human. In that mystic light her white shroud seemed diaphanous, and she appeared like a spirit of power. What was I to say? How could I admit to such a being that I had actually had at moments, if not a belief, a passing doubt? It was a conviction with me that if I spoke wrongly I should lose her for ever. I was in a desperate strait. In such a case there is but one solid ground which one may rest on—the Truth.

I really felt I was between the devil and the deep sea. There was no avoiding the issue, and so, out of this all-embracing, all-compelling conviction of truth, I spoke.

For a fleeting moment I felt that my tone was truculent, and almost hesitated; but as I saw no anger or indignation on my Lady's face, but rather an eager approval, I was reassured. A woman, after all, is glad to see a man strong, for all belief in him must be based on that.

"I shall speak the truth. Remember that I have no wish to hurt your feelings, but as you conjure me by my honour, you must forgive me if I pain. It is true that I had at first—ay, and later, when I came to think matters over after you had gone, when reason came to the aid of impression—a passing belief that you are a Vampire. How can I fail to have, even now, though I love you with all my soul, though I have held you in my arms and kissed you on the mouth, a doubt, when all the evidences seem to point to one thing? Remember that I have only seen you at night, except that bitter moment when, in the broad noonday of the upper world, I saw you, clad as ever in a shroud, lying seemingly dead in a tomb in the crypt of St. Sava's Church . . . But let that pass. Such belief as I have is all in you. Be you woman or Vampire, it is all the same to me. It is *you* whom I love! Should it be that you are—you are not woman, which I cannot believe, then it will be my glory to break your fetters, to open your prison, and set you free. To that I consecrate my life." For a few seconds I stood silent, vibrating with the passion which had been awakened in me. She had by now lost the measure of her haughty isolation, and had softened into womanhood again. It was really like a realization of the old theme of Pygmalion's statue. It was with rather a pleading than a commanding voice that she said:

"And shall you always be true to me?"

"Always—so help me, God!" I answered, and I felt that there could be no lack of conviction in my voice.

Indeed, there was no cause for such lack. She also stood for a little while stone-still, and I was beginning to expand to the rapture which was in store for me when she should take me again in her arms.

But there was no such moment of softness. All at once she started as if she had suddenly wakened from a dream, and on the spur of the moment said:

"Now go, go!" I felt the conviction of necessity to obey, and turned at once. As I moved towards the door by which I had entered, I asked:

"When shall I see you again?"

"Soon!" came her answer. "I shall let you know soon—when and where. Oh, go, go!" She almost pushed me from her.

When I had passed through the low doorway and locked and barred it behind me, I felt a pang that I should have had to shut her out like that; but I feared lest there should arise some embarrassing suspicion if the door should be found open. Later came the comforting thought that, as she had got to the roof though the door had been shut, she would be able to get away by the same means. She had evidently knowledge of some secret way into the Castle. The alternative was that she must have some supernatural quality or faculty which gave her strange powers. I did not wish to pursue that train of thought, and so, after an effort, shut it out from my mind.

When I got back to my room I locked the door behind me, and went to sleep in the dark. I did not want light just then—could not bear it.

This morning I woke, a little later than usual, with a kind of apprehension which I could not at once understand. Presently, however, when my faculties became fully awake and in working order, I realized that I feared, half expected, that Aunt Janet would come to me in a worse state of alarm than ever apropos of some new Second-Sight experience of more than usual ferocity.

But, strange to say, I had no such visit. Later on in the morning, when, after breakfast, we walked together through the garden, I asked her how she had slept, and if she had dreamt. She answered me that she had slept without waking, and if she had had any dreams, they must have been pleasant ones, for she did not remember them. "And you know, Rupert," she added, "that if there be anything bad or fearsome or warning in dreams, I always remember them."

Later still, when I was by myself on the cliff beyond the creek, I could not help commenting on the absence of her power of Second Sight on the occasion. Surely, if ever there was a time when she might have had cause of apprehension, it might well have been when I asked the Lady whom she did not know to marry me—the Lady of whose identity I knew nothing, even whose name I did not know—whom I loved with all my heart and soul—my Lady of the Shroud.

I have lost faith in Second Sight.

RUPERT'S JOURNAL—*Continued.*

July 1, 1907.

Another week gone. I have waited patiently, and I am at last rewarded by another letter. I was preparing for bed a little while ago, when I heard the same mysterious sound at the door as on the last two occasions. I hurried to the glass door, and there found another close-folded letter. But I could see no sign of my Lady, or of any other living being. The letter, which was without direction, ran as follows:

"If you are still of the same mind, and feel no misgivings, meet me at the Church of St. Sava beyond the Creek to-morrow night at a quarter before midnight. If you come, come in secret, and, of course, alone. Do not come at all unless you are prepared for a terrible ordeal. But if you love me, and have neither doubts nor fears, come. Come!"

Needless to say, I did not sleep last night. I tried to, but without success. It was no morbid happiness that kept me awake, no doubting, no fear. I was simply overwhelmed with the idea of the coming rapture when I should call my Lady my very, very own. In this sea of happy expectation all lesser things were submerged. Even sleep, which is an imperative force with me, failed in its usual effectiveness, and I lay still, calm, content.

With the coming of the morning, however, restlessness began. I did not know what to do, how to restrain myself, where to look for an anodyne. Happily the latter came in the shape of Rooke, who turned up shortly after breakfast. He had a satisfactory tale to tell me of the armoured yacht, which had lain off Cattaro on the previous night, and to which he had brought his contingent of crew which had waited for her coming. He did not like to take the risk of going into any port with such a vessel, lest he might be detained or otherwise hampered by forms, and had gone out upon the open sea before daylight. There was on board the yacht a tiny torpedo-boat, for which provision was made both for hoisting on deck and housing there. This last would run into the creek at ten o'clock that evening, at which time it would be dark. The yacht would then run to near Otranto, to which she would send a boat to get any message I might send. This was to be in a code, which we arranged, and would convey instructions as to what night and approximate hour the yacht would come to the creek.

The day was well on before we had made certain arrangements for the future; and not till then did I feel again the pressure of my personal restlessness. Rooke, like a wise commander, took rest whilst he could. Well he knew that for a couple of days and nights at least there would be little, if any, sleep for him.

For myself, the habit of self-control stood to me, and I managed to get through the day somehow without exciting the attention of anyone else. The arrival of the torpedo-boat and the departure of Rooke made for me a welcome break in my uneasiness. An hour ago I said good-night to Aunt Janet, and shut myself up alone here. My watch is on the table before me, so that I may make sure of starting to the moment. I have allowed myself half an hour to reach St. Sava. My skiff is waiting, moored at the foot of the cliff on the hither side, where the zigzag comes close to the water. It is now ten minutes past eleven.

I shall add the odd five minutes to the time for my journey so as to make safe. I go unarmed and without a light.

I shall show no distrust of anyone or anything this night.

RUPERT'S JOURNAL—*Continued.*

July 2, 1907.

When I was outside the church, I looked at my watch in the bright moonlight, and found I had one minute to wait. So I stood in the shadow of the doorway and looked out at the scene before me. Not a sign of life was visible around me, either on land or sea. On the broad plateau on which the church stands there was no movement of any kind. The wind, which had been pleasant in the noontide, had fallen completely, and not a leaf was stirring. I could see across the creek and note the hard line where the battlements of the Castle cut the sky, and where the keep towered above the line of black rock, which in the shadow of the land made an ebon frame for the picture. When I had seen the same view on former occasions, the line where the rock rose from the sea was a fringe of white foam. But then, in the daylight, the sea was sapphire blue; now it was an expanse of dark blue—so dark as to seem almost black. It had not even the relief of waves or ripples—simply a dark, cold, lifeless expanse, with no gleam of light anywhere, of lighthouse or ship; neither was there any special sound to be heard that one could distinguish—nothing but the distant hum of the myriad voices of the dark mingling in one ceaseless inarticulate sound. It was well I had not time to dwell on it, or I might have reached some spiritually-disturbing melancholy.

Let me say here that ever since I had received my Lady's message concerning this visit to St. Sava's I had been all on fire—not, perhaps, at every moment consciously or actually so, but always, as it were, prepared to break out into flame. Did I want a simile, I might compare myself to a well-banked furnace, whose present function it is to contain heat rather than to create it; whose crust can at any moment be broken by a force external to itself, and burst into raging, all-compelling heat. No thought of fear really entered my mind. Every other emotion there was, coming and going as occasion excited or lulled, but not fear. Well I knew in the depths of my heart the purpose which that secret quest was to serve. I knew not only from my Lady's words, but from the teachings of my own senses and experiences, that some dreadful ordeal must take place before happiness of any kind could be won. And that ordeal, though method or detail was unknown to me, I was prepared to undertake. This was one of those occasions when a man must undertake, blindfold, ways that may lead to torture or death, or unknown terrors beyond. But, then, a man—if, indeed, he have the heart of a man—can always undertake; he can at least make the first step, though it may turn out that through the weakness of mortality he may be unable to fulfil his own intent, or justify his belief in his own powers. Such, I take it, was the intellectual attitude of the brave souls who of old faced the tortures of the Inquisition.

But though there was no immediate fear, there was a certain doubt. For doubt is one of those mental conditions whose calling we cannot control. The end of the doubting may not be a reality to us, or be accepted as a possibility. These things cannot forego the existence of the doubt. "For even if a man," says Victor Cousin, "doubt everything else, at least he cannot doubt that he doubts." The doubt had at times been on me that my Lady of the Shroud was a Vampire. Much that had happened seemed to point that way, and here, on the very threshold of the Unknown, when, through the door which I was pushing open, my eyes met only an expanse of absolute blackness, all doubts which had ever been seemed to surround me in a legion. I have heard that, when a man is drowning, there comes a time when his whole life passes in review during the space of time which cannot be computed as even a part of a second. So it was to me in the moment of my body passing into the church. In that moment came to my mind all that had been, which bore on the knowledge of my Lady; and the general tendency was to prove or convince that she was indeed a Vampire. Much that had happened, or become known to me, seemed to justify the resolving of doubt into belief. Even my own reading of the books in Aunt Janet's little library, and the dear lady's comments on them, mingled with her own uncanny beliefs, left little opening for doubt. My having to help my Lady over the threshold of my house on her first entry was in accord with Vampire tradition; so, too, her flying at cock-crow from the warmth in which she revelled on that strange first night of our meeting; so, too, her swift departure at midnight on the second. Into the same category came the facts of her constant wearing of her Shroud, even her pledging herself, and me also, on the fragment torn from it, which she had given to me as a souvenir; her lying still in the glass-covered tomb; her coming alone to the most secret places in a fortified Castle where every aperture was secured by unopened locks and bolts; her very movements, though all of grace, as she flitted noiselessly through the gloom of night.

All these things, and a thousand others of lesser import, seemed, for the moment, to have consolidated an initial belief. But then came the supreme recollections of how she had lain in my arms; of her kisses on my lips; of the beating of her heart against my own; of her sweet words of belief and faith breathed in my ear in intoxicating whispers; of . . . I paused. No! I could not accept belief as to her being other than a living woman of soul and sense, of flesh and blood, of all the sweet and passionate instincts of true and perfect womanhood.

And so, in spite of all—in spite of all beliefs, fixed or transitory, with a mind whirling amid contesting forces and compelling beliefs—I stepped into the church overwhelmed with that most receptive of atmospheres—doubt.

In one thing only was I fixed: here at least was no doubt or misgiving whatever. I intended to go through what I had undertaken. Moreover, I felt that I was strong enough to carry out my intention, whatever might be of the Unknown—however horrible, however terrible.

When I had entered the church and closed the heavy door behind me, the sense of darkness and loneliness in all their horror enfolded me round. The great church seemed a living mystery, and served as an almost terrible background to thoughts and remembrances of unutterable gloom. My adventurous life has had its own schooling to endurance and upholding one's courage in trying times; but it has its contra in fulness of memory.

I felt my way forward with both hands and feet. Every second seemed as if it had brought me at last to a darkness which was actually tangible. All at once, and with no heed of sequence or order, I was conscious of all around me, the knowledge or perception of which—or even speculation on the subject—had never entered my mind. They furnished the darkness with which I was encompassed with all the crowded phases of a dream. I knew that all around me were memorials of the dead—that in the Crypt deep-wrought in the rock below my feet lay the dead themselves. Some of them, perhaps—one of them I knew—had even passed the grim portals of time Unknown, and had, by some mysterious power or agency, come back again to material earth. There was no resting-place for thought when I knew that the very air which I breathed might be full of denizens of the spirit-world. In that impenetrable blackness was a world of imagining whose possibilities of horror were endless.

I almost fancied that I could see with mortal eyes down through that rocky floor to where, in the lonely Crypt, lay, in her tomb of massive stone and under that bewildering coverlet of glass, the woman whom I love. I could see her beautiful face, her long black lashes, her sweet mouth—which I had kissed—relaxed in the sleep of death. I could note the voluminous shroud—a piece of which as a precious souvenir lay even then so close to my heart—the snowy woollen coverlet wrought over in gold with sprigs of pine, the soft dent in the cushion on which her head must for so long have lain. I could see myself—within my eyes the memory of that first visit—coming once again with glad step to renew that dear sight—dear, though it scorched my eyes and harrowed my heart—and finding the greater sorrow, the greater desolation of the empty tomb!

There! I felt that I must think no more of that lest the thought should unnerve me when I should most want all my courage. That way madness lay! The darkness had already sufficient terrors of its own without bringing to it such grim remembrances and imaginings . . . And I had yet to go through some ordeal which, even to her who had passed and repassed the portals of death, was full of fear.

It was a merciful relief to me when, in groping my way forwards through the darkness, I struck against some portion of the furnishing of the church. Fortunately I was all strung up to tension, else I should never have been able to control instinctively, as I did, the shriek which was rising to my lips.

I would have given anything to have been able to light even a match. A single second of light would, I felt, have made me my own man again. But I knew that this would be against the implied condition of my being there at all, and might have had disastrous consequences to her whom I had come to save. It might even frustrate my scheme, and altogether destroy my opportunity. At that moment it was borne upon me more strongly than ever that this was not a mere fight for myself or my own selfish purposes—not merely an adventure or a struggle for only life and death against unknown difficulties and dangers. It was a fight on behalf of her I loved, not merely for her life, but perhaps even for her soul.

And yet this very thinking—understanding—created a new form of terror. For in that grim, shrouding darkness came memories of other moments of terrible stress.

Of wild, mystic rites held in the deep gloom of African forests, when, amid scenes of revolting horror, Obi and the devils of his kind seemed to reveal themselves to reckless worshippers, surfeited with horror, whose lives counted for naught; when even human sacrifice was an episode, and the reek of old deviltries and recent carnage tainted the air, till even I, who was, at the risk of my life, a privileged spectator who had come through dangers without end to behold the scene, rose and fled in horror.

Of scenes of mystery enacted in rock-cut temples beyond the Himalayas, whose fanatic priests, cold as death and as remorseless, in the reaction of their phrenzy of passion, foamed at the mouth and then sank into marble quiet, as with inner eyes they beheld the visions of the hellish powers which they had invoked.

Of wild, fantastic dances of the Devil-worshippers of Madagascar, where even the very semblance of humanity disappeared in the fantastic excesses of their orgies.

Of strange doings of gloom and mystery in the rock-perched monasteries of Thibet.

Of awful sacrifices, all to mystic ends, in the innermost recesses of Cathay.

Of weird movements with masses of poisonous snakes by the medicine-men of the Zuni and Mochi Indians in the far south-west of the Rockies, beyond the great plains.

Of secret gatherings in vast temples of old Mexico, and by dim altars of forgotten cities in the heart of great forests in South America.

Of rites of inconceivable horror in the fastnesses of Patagonia.

Of . . . Here I once more pulled myself up. Such thoughts were no kind of proper preparation for what I might have to endure. My work that night was to be based on love, on hope, on self-sacrifice for the woman who in all the world was the closest to my heart, whose future I was to share, whether that sharing might lead me to Hell or Heaven. The hand which undertook such a task must have no trembling.

Still, those horrible memories had, I am bound to say, a useful part in my preparation for the ordeal. They were of fact which I had seen, of which I had myself been in part a sharer, and which I had survived. With such experiences behind me, could there be aught before me more dreadful? . . .

Moreover, if the coming ordeal was of supernatural or superhuman order, could it transcend in living horror the vilest and most desperate acts of the basest men? . . .

With renewed courage I felt my way before me, till my sense of touch told me that I was at the screen behind which lay the stair to the Crypt.

There I waited, silent, still.

My own part was done, so far as I knew how to do it. Beyond this, what was to come was, so far as I knew, beyond my own control. I had done what I could; the rest must come from others. I had exactly obeyed my instructions, fulfilled my warranty to the utmost in my knowledge and power. There was, therefore, left for me in the present nothing but to wait.

It is a peculiarity of absolute darkness that it creates its own reaction. The eye, wearied of the blackness, begins to imagine forms of light. How far this is effected by imagination pure and simple I know not. It may be that nerves have their own senses that bring thought to the depository common to all the human functions, but, whatever may be the mechanism or the objective, the darkness seems to people itself with luminous entities.

So was it with me as I stood lonely in the dark, silent church. Here and there seemed to flash tiny points of light.

In the same way the silence began to be broken now and again by strange muffled sounds—the suggestion of sounds rather than actual vibrations. These were all at first of the minor importance of movement—rustlings, creakings, faint stirrings, fainter breathings. Presently, when I had somewhat recovered from the sort of hypnotic trance to which the darkness and stillness had during the time of waiting reduced me, I looked around in wonder.

The phantoms of light and sound seemed to have become real. There were most certainly actual little points of light in places—not enough to see details by, but quite sufficient to relieve the utter gloom. I thought—though it may have been a mingling of recollection and imagination—that I could distinguish the outlines of the church; certainly the great altar-screen was dimly visible. Instinctively I looked up—and thrilled. There, hung high above me, was, surely enough, a great Greek Cross, outlined by tiny points of light.

I lost myself in wonder, and stood still, in a purely receptive mood, unantagonistic to aught, willing for whatever might come, ready for all things, in rather a negative than a positive mood—a mood which has an aspect of spiritual meekness. This is the true spirit of the neophyte, and, though I did not think of it at the time, the proper attitude for what is called by the Church in whose temple I stood a "neo-nymph."

As the light grew a little in power, though never increasing enough for distinctness, I saw dimly before me a table on which rested a great open book, whereon were laid two rings—one of sliver, the other of gold—and two crowns wrought of flowers, bound at the joining of their stems with tissue—one of gold, the other of silver. I do not know much of the ritual of the old Greek Church, which is the religion of the Blue Mountains, but the things which I saw before me could be none other than enlightening symbols. Instinctively I knew that I had been brought hither, though in this grim way, to be married. The very idea of it thrilled me to the heart's core. I thought the best thing I could do would be to stay quite still, and not show surprise at anything that might happen; but be sure I was all eyes and ears.

I peered anxiously around me in every direction, but I could see no sign of her whom I had come to meet.

Incidentally, however, I noticed that in the lighting, such as it was, there was no flame, no "living" light. Whatever light there was came muffled, as though through some green translucent stone. The whole effect was terribly weird and disconcerting.

Presently I started, as, seemingly out of the darkness beside me, a man's hand stretched out and took mine. Turning, I found close to me a tall man with shining black eyes and long black hair and beard. He was clad in some kind of gorgeous robe of cloth of gold, rich with variety of adornment. His head was covered with a high, over-hanging hat draped closely with a black scarf, the ends of which formed a long, hanging veil on either side. These veils, falling over the magnificent robes of cloth of gold, had an extraordinarily solemn effect.

I yielded myself to the guiding hand, and shortly found myself, so far as I could see, at one side of the sanctuary.

In the floor close to my feet was a yawning chasm, into which, from so high over my head that in the uncertain light I could not distinguish its origin, hung a chain. At the sight a strange wave of memory swept over me. I could not but remember the chain which hung over the glass-covered tomb in the Crypt, and I had an instinctive feeling that the grim chasm in the floor of the sanctuary was but the other side of the opening in the roof of the crypt from which the chain over the sarcophagus depended.

There was a creaking sound—the groaning of a windlass and the clanking of a chain. There was heavy breathing close to me somewhere. I was so intent on what was going on that I did not see that one by one, seeming to grow out of the surrounding darkness, several black figures in monkish garb appeared with the silence of ghosts. Their faces were shrouded in black cowls, wherein were holes through which I could see dark gleaming eyes. My guide held me tightly by the hand. This gave me a feeling of security in the touch which helped to retain within my breast some semblance of calm.

The strain of the creaking windlass and the clanking chain continued for so long that the suspense became almost unendurable. At last there came into sight an iron ring, from which as a centre depended four lesser chains spreading wide. In a few seconds more I could see that these were fixed to the corners of the great stone tomb with the covering of glass, which was being dragged upward. As it arose it filled closely the whole aperture. When its bottom had reached the level of the floor it stopped, and remained rigid. There was no room for oscillation. It was at once surrounded by a number of black figures, who raised the glass covering and bore it away into the darkness. Then there stepped forward a very tall man, black-bearded, and with head-gear like my guide, but made in triple tiers, he also was gorgeously arrayed in flowing robes of cloth of gold richly embroidered. He raised his hand, and forthwith eight other black-clad figures stepped forward, and bending over the stone coffin, raised from it the rigid form of my Lady, still clad in her Shroud, and laid it gently on the floor of the sanctuary.

I felt it a grace that at that instant the dim lights seemed to grow less, and finally to disappear—all save the tiny points that marked the outline of the great Cross high overhead. These only gave light enough to accentuate the gloom. The hand that held mine now released it, and with a sigh I realized that I was alone. After a few moments more of the groaning of the winch and clanking of the chain there was a sharp sound of stone meeting stone; then there was silence. I listened acutely, but could not hear near me the slightest sound. Even the cautious, restrained breathing around me, of which up to then I had been conscious, had ceased. Not knowing, in the helplessness of my ignorance, what I should do, I remained as I was, still and silent, for a time that seemed endless. At last, overcome by some emotion which I could not at the moment understand, I slowly sank to my knees and bowed my head. Covering my face with my hands, I tried to recall the prayers of my youth. It was not, I am certain, that fear in any form had come upon me, or that I hesitated or faltered in my intention. That much I know now; I knew it even then. It was, I believe, that the prolonged impressive gloom and mystery had at last touched me to the quick. The bending of the knees was but symbolical of the bowing of the spirit to a higher Power. When I had realized that much, I felt more content than I had done since I had entered the church, and with the renewed consciousness of courage, took my hands from my face, and lifted again my bowed head.

Impulsively I sprang to my feet and stood erect—waiting. All seemed to have changed since I had dropped on my knees. The points of light about time church, which had been eclipsed, had come again, and were growing in power to a partial revealing of the dim expanse. Before me was the table with the open book, on which were laid the gold and silver rings and the two crowns of flowers. There were also two tall candles, with tiniest flames of blue—the only living light to be seen.

Out of the darkness stepped the same tall figure in the gorgeous robes and the triple hat. He led by the hand my Lady, still clad in her Shroud; but over it, descending from the crown of her head, was a veil of very old and magnificent lace of astonishing fineness. Even in that dim light I could note the exquisite beauty of the fabric. The veil was fastened with a bunch of tiny sprays of orange-blossom mingled with cypress and laurel—a strange combination. In her hand she carried a great bouquet of the same. Its sweet intoxicating odour floated up to my nostrils. It and the sentiment which its very presence evoked made me quiver.

Yielding to the guiding of the hand which held hers, she stood at my left side before the table. Her guide then took his place behind her. At either end of the table, to right and left of us, stood a long-bearded priest in splendid robes, and wearing the hat with depending veil of black. One of them, who seemed to be the more important of the two, and took the initiative, signed to us to put our right hands on the open book. My Lady, of course, understood the ritual, and knew the words which the priest was speaking, and of her own accord put out her hand. My guide at the same moment directed my hand to the same end. It thrilled me to touch my Lady's hand, even under such mysterious conditions.

After the priest had signed us each thrice on the forehead with the sign of the Cross, he gave to each of us a tiny lighted taper brought to him for the purpose. The lights were welcome, not so much for the solace of the added light, great as that was, but because it allowed us to see a little more of each other's faces. It was rapture to me to see the face of my Bride; and from the expression of her face I was assured that she felt as I did. It gave me an inexpressible pleasure when, as her eyes rested on me, there grew a faint blush over the grey pallor of her cheeks.

The priest then put in solemn voice to each of us in turn, beginning with me, the questions of consent which are common to all such rituals. I answered as well as I could, following the murmured words of my guide. My Lady answered out proudly in a voice which, though given softly, seemed to ring. It was a concern—even a grief—to me that I could not, in the priest's questioning, catch her name, of which, strangely enough,—I was ignorant. But, as I did not know the language, and as the phrases were not in accord literally with our own ritual, I could not make out which word was the name.

After some prayers and blessings, rhythmically spoken or sung by an invisible choir, the priest took the rings from the open book, and, after signing my forehead thrice with the gold one as he repeated the blessing in each case, placed it on my right hand; then he gave my Lady the silver one, with the same ritual thrice repeated. I suppose it was the blessing which is the effective point in making two into one.

After this, those who stood behind us exchanged our rings thrice, taking them from one finger and placing them on the other, so that at the end my wife wore the gold ring and I the silver one.

Then came a chant, during which the priest swung the censer himself, and my wife and I held our tapers. After that he blessed us, the responses coming from the voices of the unseen singers in the darkness.

After a long ritual of prayer and blessing, sung in triplicate, the priest took the crowns of flowers, and put one on the head of each, crowning me first, and with the crown tied with gold. Then he signed and blessed us each thrice. The guides, who stood behind us, exchanged our crowns thrice, as they had exchanged the rings; so that at the last, as I was glad to see, my wife wore the crown of gold, and I that of silver.

Then there came, if it is possible to describe such a thing, a hush over even that stillness, as though some form of added solemnity were to be gone through. I was not surprised, therefore, when the priest took in his hands the great golden chalice. Kneeling, my wife and I partook together thrice.

When we had risen from our knees and stood for a little while, the priest took my left hand in his right, and I, by direction of my guide, gave my right hand to my wife. And so in a line, the priest leading, we circled round the table in rhythmic measure. Those who supported us moved behind us, holding the crowns over our heads, and replacing them when we stopped.

After a hymn, sung through the darkness, the priest took off our crowns. This was evidently the conclusion of the ritual, for the priest placed us in each other's arms to embrace each other. Then he blessed us, who were now man and wife!

The lights went out at once, some as if extinguished, others slowly fading down to blackness.

Left in the dark, my wife and I sought each other's arms again, and stood together for a few moments heart to heart, tightly clasping each other, and kissed each other fervently.

Instinctively we turned to the door of the church, which was slightly open, so that we could see the moonlight stealing in through the aperture. With even steps, she holding me tightly by the left arm—which is the wife's arm, we passed through the old church and out into the free air.

Despite all that the gloom had brought me, it was sweet to be in the open air and together—this quite apart from our new relations to each other. The moon rode high, and the full light, coming after the dimness or darkness in the church, seemed as bright as day. I could now, for the first time, see my wife's face properly. The glamour of the moonlight may have served to enhance its ethereal beauty, but neither moonlight nor sunlight could do justice to that beauty in its living human splendour. As I gloried in her starry eyes I could think of nothing else; but when for a moment my eyes, roving round for the purpose of protection, caught sight of her whole figure, there was a pang to my heart. The brilliant moonlight showed every detail in terrible effect, and I could see that she wore only her Shroud. In the moment of darkness, after the last benediction, before she returned to my arms, she must have removed her bridal veil. This may, of course, have been in accordance with the established ritual of her church; but, all the same, my heart was sore. The glamour of calling her my very own was somewhat obscured by the bridal adornment being shorn. But it made no difference in her sweetness to me. Together we went along the path through the wood, she keeping equal step with me in wifely way.

When we had come through the trees near enough to see the roof of the Castle, now gilded with the moonlight, she stopped, and looking at me with eyes full of love, said:

"Here I must leave you!"

"What?" I was all aghast, and I felt that my chagrin was expressed in the tone of horrified surprise in my voice. She went on quickly:

"Alas! It is impossible that I should go farther—at present!"

"But what is to prevent you?" I queried. "You are now my wife. This is our wedding-night; and surely your place is with me!" The wail in her voice as she answered touched me to the quick:

"Oh, I know, I know! There is no dearer wish in my heart—there can be none—than to share my husband's home. Oh, my dear, my dear, if you only knew what it would be to me to be with you always! But indeed I may not—not yet! I am not free! If you but knew how much that which has happened to-night has cost me—or how much cost to others as well as to myself may be yet to come—you would understand. Rupert"—it was the first time she had ever addressed me by name, and naturally it thrilled me through and through—"Rupert, my husband, only that I trust you with all the faith which is in perfect love—mutual love, I dare not have done what I have done this night. But, dear, I know that you will bear me out; that your wife's honour is your honour, even as your honour is mine. My honour is given to this; and you can help me—the only help I can have at present—by trusting me. Be patient, my beloved, be patient! Oh, be patient for a little longer! It shall not be for long. So soon as ever my soul is freed I shall come to you, my husband; and we shall never part again. Be content for a while! Believe me that I love you with my very soul; and to keep away from your dear side is more bitter for me than even it can be for you! Think, my dear one, I am not as other women are, as some day you shall clearly understand. I am at the present, and shall be for a little longer, constrained by duties and obligations put upon me by others, and for others, and to which I am pledged by the most sacred promises—given not only by myself, but by others—and which I must not forgo. These forbid me to do as I wish. Oh, trust me, my beloved—my husband!"

She held out her hands appealingly. The moonlight, falling through the thinning forest, showed her white cerements. Then the recollection of all she must have suffered—the awful loneliness in that grim tomb in the Crypt, the despairing agony of one who is helpless against the unknown—swept over me in a wave of pity. What could I do but save her from further pain? And this could only be by showing her my faith and trust. If she was to go back to that dreadful charnel-house, she would at least take with her the remembrance that one who loved her and whom she loved—to whom she had been lately bound in the mystery of marriage—trusted her to the full. I loved her more than myself—more than my own soul; and I was moved by pity so great that all possible selfishness was merged in its depths. I bowed my head before her—my Lady and my Wife—as I said:

"So be it, my beloved. I trust you to the full, even as you trust me. And that has been proven this night, even to my own doubting heart. I shall wait; and as I know you wish it, I shall wait as patiently as I can. But till you come to me for good and all, let me see you or hear from you when you can. The time, dear wife, must go heavily with me as I think of you suffering and lonely. So be good to me, and let not too long a time elapse between my glimpses of hope. And, sweetheart, when you *do* come to me, it shall be for ever!" There was something in the intonation of the last sentence—I felt its sincerity myself—some implied yearning for a promise, that made her beautiful eyes swim. The glorious stars in them were blurred as she answered with a fervour which seemed to me as more than earthly:

"For ever! I swear it!"

With one long kiss, and a straining in each others arms, which left me tingling for long after we had lost sight of each other, we parted. I stood and watched her as her white figure, gliding through the deepening gloom, faded as the forest thickened. It surely was no optical delusion or a phantom of the mind that her shrouded arm was raised as though in blessing or farewell before the darkness swallowed her up.

BOOK VI: THE PURSUIT IN THE FOREST

RUPERT'S JOURNAL—*Continued.*

July 3, 1907.

There is no anodyne but work to pain of the heart; and my pain is all of the heart. I sometimes feel that it is rather hard that with so much to make me happy I cannot know happiness. How can I be happy when my wife, whom I fondly love, and who I know loves me, is suffering in horror and loneliness of a kind which is almost beyond human belief? However, what is my loss is my country's gain, for the Land of the Blue Mountains is my country now, despite the fact that I am still a loyal subject of good King Edward. Uncle Roger took care of that when he said I should have the consent of the Privy Council before I might be naturalized anywhere else.

When I got home yesterday morning I naturally could not sleep. The events of the night and the bitter disappointment that followed my exciting joy made such a thing impossible. When I drew the curtain over the window, the reflection of the sunrise was just beginning to tinge the high-sailing clouds in front of me. I laid down and tried to rest, but without avail. However, I schooled myself to lie still, and at last, if I did not sleep, was at least quiescent.

Disturbed by a gentle tap at the door, I sprang up at once and threw on a dressing gown. Outside, when I opened the door, was Aunt Janet. She was holding a lighted candle in her hand, for though it was getting light in the open, the passages were still dark. When she saw me she seemed to breathe more freely, and asked if she might come in.

Whilst she sat on the edge of my bed, in her old-time way, she said in a hushed voice:

"Oh, laddie, laddie, I trust yer burden is no too heavy to bear."

"My burden! What on earth do you mean, Aunt Janet?" I said in reply. I did not wish to commit myself by a definite answer, for it was evident that she had been dreaming or Second Sighting again. She replied with the grim seriousness usual to her when she touched on occult matters:

"I saw your hairt bleeding, laddie. I kent it was yours, though how I kent it I don't know. It lay on a stone floor in the dark, save for a dim blue light such as corpse-lights are. On it was placed a great book, and close around were scattered many strange things, amongst them two crowns o' flowers—the one bound wi' silver, the other wi' gold. There was also a golden cup, like a chalice, o'erturned. The red wine trickled from it an' mingled wi' yer hairt's bluid; for on the great book was some vast dim weight wrapped up in black, and on it stepped in turn many men all swathed in black. An' as the weight of each came on it the bluid gushed out afresh. And oh, yer puir hairt, my laddie, was quick and leaping, so that at every beat it raised the black-clad weight! An' yet that was not all, for hard by stood a tall imperial shape o' a woman, all arrayed in white, wi' a great veil o' finest lace worn o'er a shrood. An' she was whiter than the snow, an' fairer than the morn for beauty; though a dark woman she was, wi' hair like the raven, an' eyes black as the sea at nicht, an' there was stars in them. An' at each beat o' yer puir bleeding hairt she wrung her white hands, an' the manin' o' her sweet voice rent my hairt in twain. Oh, laddie, laddie! what does it mean?"

I managed to murmur: "I'm sure I don't know, Aunt Janet. I suppose it was all a dream!"

"A dream it was, my dear. A dream or a veesion, whilka matters nane, for a' such are warnin's sent frae God . . . " Suddenly she said in a different voice:

"Laddie, hae ye been fause to any lassie? I'm no blamin' ye. For ye men are different frae us women, an' yer regard on recht and wrang differs from oors. But oh, laddie, a woman's tears fa' heavy when her hairt is for sair wi' the yieldin' to fause words. 'Tis a heavy burden for ony man to carry wi' him as he goes, an' may well cause pain to ithers that he fain would spare." She stopped, and in dead silence waited for me to speak. I thought it would be best to set her poor loving heart at rest, and as I could not divulge my special secret, spoke in general terms:

"Aunt Janet, I am a man, and have led a man's life, such as it is. But I can tell you, who have always loved me and taught me to be true, that in all the world there is no woman who must weep for any falsity of mine. If close there be any who, sleeping or waking, in dreams or visions or in reality, weeps because of me, it is surely not for my doing, but because of something outside me. It may be that her heart is sore because I must suffer, as all men must in some degree; but she does not weep for or through any act of mine."

She sighed happily at my assurance, and looked up through her tears, for she was much moved; and after tenderly kissing my forehead and blessing me, stole away. She was more sweet and tender than I have words to say, and the only regret that I have in all that is gone is that I have not been able to bring my wife to her, and let her share in the love she has for me. But that, too, will come, please God!

In the morning I sent a message to Rooke at Otranto, instructing him by code to bring the yacht to Vissarion in the coming night.

All day I spent in going about amongst the mountaineers, drilling them and looking after their arms. I *could* not stay still. My only chance of peace was to work, my only chance of sleep to tire myself out. Unhappily, I am very strong, so even when I came home at dark I was quite fresh. However, I found a cable message from Rooke that the yacht would arrive at midnight.

There was no need to summon the mountaineers, as the men in the Castle would be sufficient to make preparations for the yacht's coming.

Later.

The yacht has come. At half-past eleven the lookout signalled that a steamer without lights was creeping in towards the Creek. I ran out to the Flagstaff, and saw her steal in like a ghost. She is painted a steely blue-grey, and it is almost impossible to see her at any distance. She certainly goes wonderfully. Although there was not enough throb from the engines to mar the absolute stillness, she came on at a fine speed, and within a few minutes was close to the boom. I had only time to run down to give orders to draw back the boom when she glided in and stopped dead at the harbour wall. Rooke steered her himself, and he says he never was on a boat that so well or so quickly answered her helm. She is certainly a beauty, and so far as I can see at night perfect in every detail. I promise myself a few pleasant hours over her in the daylight. The men seem a splendid lot.

But I do not feel sleepy; I despair of sleep to-night. But work demands that I be fit for whatever may come, and so I shall try to sleep—to rest, at any rate.

RUPERT'S JOURNAL.—*Continued.*

July 4, 1907.

I was up with the first ray of sunrise, so by the time I had my bath and was dressed there was ample light. I went down to the dock at once, and spent the morning looking over the vessel, which fully justifies Rooke's enthusiasm about her. She is built on lovely lines, and I can quite understand that she is enormously fast. Her armour I can only take on the specifications, but her armament is really wonderful. And there are not only all the very newest devices of aggressive warfare—indeed, she has the newest up-to-date torpedoes and torpedo-guns—but also the old-fashioned rocket-tubes, which in certain occasions are so useful. She has electric guns and the latest Massillon water-guns, and Reinhardt electro-pneumatic "deliverers" for pyroxiline shells. She is even equipped with war-balloons easy of expansion, and with compressible Kitson aeroplanes. I don't suppose that there is anything quite like her in the world.

The crew are worthy of her. I can't imagine where Rooke picked up such a splendid lot of men. They are nearly all man-of-warsmen; of various nationalities, but mostly British. All young men—the oldest of them hasn't got into the forties—and, so far as I can learn, all experts of one kind or another in some special subject of warfare. It will go hard with me, but I shall keep them together.

How I got through the rest of the day I know not. I tried hard not to create any domestic trouble by my manner, lest Aunt Janet should, after her lurid dream or vision of last night, attach some new importance to it. I think I succeeded, for she did not, so far as I could tell, take any special notice of me. We parted as usual at half-past ten, and I came here and made this entry in my journal. I am more restless than ever to-night, and no wonder. I would give anything to be able to pay a visit to St. Sava's, and see my wife again—if it were only sleeping in her tomb. But I dare not do even that, lest she should come to see me here, and I should miss her. So I have done what I can. The glass door to the Terrace is open, so that she can enter at once if she comes. The fire is lit, and the room is warm. There is food ready in case she should care for it. I have plenty of light in the room, so that through the aperture where I have not fully drawn the curtain there may be light to guide her.

Oh, how the time drags! The clock has struck midnight. One, two! Thank goodness, it will shortly be dawn, and the activity of the day may begin! Work may again prove, in a way, to be an anodyne. In the meantime I must write on, lest despair overwhelm me.

Once during the night I thought I heard a footstep outside. I rushed to the window and looked out, but there was nothing to see, no sound to hear. That was a little after one o'clock. I feared to go outside, lest that should alarm her; so I came back to my table. I could not write, but I sat as if writing for a while. But I could not stand it, so rose and walked about the room. As I walked I felt that my Lady—it gives me a pang every time I remember that I do not know even her name—was not quite so far away from me. It made my heart beat to think that it might mean that she was coming to me. Could not I as well as Aunt Janet have a little Second Sight! I went towards the window, and, standing behind the curtain, listened. Far away I thought I heard a cry, and ran out on the Terrace; but there was no sound to be heard, and no sign of any living thing anywhere; so I took it for granted that it was the cry of some night bird, and came back to my room, and wrote at my journal till I was calm. I think my nerves must be getting out of order, when every sound of the night seems to have a special meaning for me.

RUPERT'S JOURNAL—*Continued.*

July 7, 1907

When the grey of the morning came, I gave up hope of my wife appearing, and made up my mind that, so soon as I could get away without exciting Aunt Janet's attention, I would go to St. Sava's. I always eat a good breakfast, and did I forgo it altogether, it would be sure to excite her curiosity—a thing I do not wish at present. As there was still time to wait, I lay down on my bed as I was, and—such is the way of Fate—shortly fell asleep.

I was awakened by a terrific clattering at my door. When I opened it I found a little group of servants, very apologetic at awaking me without instructions. The chief of them explained that a young priest had come from the Vladika with a message so urgent that he insisted on seeing me immediately at all hazards. I came out at once, and found him in the hall of the Castle, standing before the great fire, which was always lit in the early morning. He had a letter in his hand, but before giving it to me he said:

"I am sent by the Vladika, who pressed on me that I was not to lose a single instant in seeing you; that time is of golden price—nay, beyond price. This letter, amongst other things, vouches for me. A terrible misfortune has occurred. The daughter of our leader has disappeared during last night—the same, he commanded me to remind you, that he spoke of at the meeting when he would not let the mountaineers fire their guns. No sign of her can be found, and it is believed that she has been carried off by the emissaries of the Sultan of Turkey, who once before brought our nations to the verge of war by demanding her as a wife. I was also to say that the Vladika Plamenac would have come himself, but that it was necessary that he should at once consult with the Archbishop, Stevan Palealogue, as to what step is best to take in this dire calamity. He has sent out a search-party under the Archimandrite of Spazac, Petrof Vlastimir, who is to come on here with any news he can get, as you have command of the signalling, and can best spread the news. He knows that you, Gospodar, are in your great heart one of our compatriots, and that you have already proved your friendship by many efforts to strengthen our hands for war. And as a great compatriot, he calls on you to aid us in our need." He then handed me the letter, and stood by respectfully whilst I broke the seal and read it. It was written in great haste, and signed by the Vladika.

"Come with us now in our nation's peril. Help us to rescue what we most adore, and henceforth we shall hold you in our hearts. You shall learn how the men of the Blue Mountains can love faith and valour. Come!"

This was a task indeed—a duty worthy of any man. It thrilled me to the core to know that the men of the Blue Mountains had called on me in their dire need. It woke all the fighting instinct of my Viking forbears, and I vowed in my heart that they should be satisfied with my work. I called to me the corps of signallers who were in the house, and led them to the Castle roof, taking with me the young messenger-priest.

"Come with me," I said to him, "and see how I answer the Vladika's command."

The National flag was run up—the established signal that the nation was in need. Instantly on every summit near and far was seen the flutter of an answering flag. Quickly followed the signal that commanded the call to arms.

One by one I gave the signallers orders in quick succession, for the plan of search unfolded itself to me as I went on. The arms of the semaphore whirled in a way that made the young priest stare. One by one, as they took their orders, the signallers seemed to catch fire. Instinctively they understood the plan, and worked like demi-gods. They knew that so widespread a movement had its best chance in rapidity and in unity of action.

From the forest which lay in sight of the Castle came a wild cheering, which seemed to interpret the former stillness of the hills. It was good to feel that those who saw the signals—types of many—were ready. I saw the look of expectation on the face of the messenger-priest, and rejoiced at the glow that came as I turned to him to speak. Of course, he wanted to know something of what was going on. I saw the flashing of my own eyes reflected in his as I spoke:

"Tell the Vladika that within a minute of his message being read the Land of the Blue Mountains was awake. The mountaineers are already marching, and before the sun is high there will be a line of guards within hail of each other round the whole frontier—from Angusa to Ilsin; from Ilsin to Bajana; from Bajana to Ispazar; from Ispazar to Volok; from Volok to Tatra; from Tatra to Domitan; from Domitan to Gravaja; and from Gravaja back to Angusa. The line is double. The old men keep guard on the line, and the young men advance. These will close in at the advancing line, so that nothing can escape them. They will cover mountain-top and forest depth, and will close in finally on the Castle here, which they can behold from afar. My own yacht is here, and will sweep the coast from end to end. It is the fastest boat afloat, and armed against a squadron. Here will all signals come. In an hour where we stand will be a signal bureau, where trained eyes will watch night and day till the lost one has been found and the outrage has been avenged. The robbers are even now within a ring of steel, and cannot escape."

The young priest, all on fire, sprang on the battlements and shouted to the crowd, which was massing round the Castle in the gardens far below. The forest was giving up its units till they seemed like the nucleus of an army. The men cheered lustily, till the sound swung high up to us like the roaring of a winter sea. With bared heads they were crying:

"God and the Blue Mountains! God and the Blue Mountains!"

I ran down to them as quickly as I could, and began to issue their instructions. Within a time to be computed by minutes the whole number, organized by sections, had started to scour the neighbouring mountains. At first they had only understood the call to arms for general safety. But when they learned that the daughter of a chief had been captured, they simply went mad. From something which the messenger first said, but which I could not catch or did not understand, the blow seemed to have for them some sort of personal significance which wrought them to a frenzy.

When the bulk of the men had disappeared, I took with me a few of my own men and several of the mountaineers whom I had asked to remain, and together we went to the hidden ravine which I knew. We found the place empty; but there were unmistakable signs that a party of men had been encamped there for several days. Some of our men, who were skilled in woodcraft and in signs generally, agreed that there must have been some twenty of them. As they could not find any trail either coming to or going from the place, they came to the conclusion that they must have come separately from different directions and gathered there, and that they must have departed in something of the same mysterious way.

However, this was, at any rate, some sort of a beginning, and the men separated, having agreed amongst themselves to make a wide cast round the place in the search for tracks. Whoever should find a trail was to follow with at least one comrade, and when there was any definite news, it was to be signalled to the Castle.

I myself returned at once, and set the signallers to work to spread amongst our own people such news as we had.

When presently such discoveries as had been made were signalled with flags to the Castle, it was found that the marauders had, in their flight, followed a strangely zigzag course. It was evident that, in trying to baffle pursuit, they had tried to avoid places which they thought might be dangerous to them. This may have been simply a method to disconcert pursuit. If so, it was, in a measure, excellent, for none of those immediately following could possibly tell in what direction they were heading. It was only when we worked the course on the great map in the signaller's room (which was the old guard room of the Castle) that we could get an inkling of the general direction of their flight. This gave added trouble to the pursuit; for the men who followed, being ignorant of their general intent, could not ever take chance to head them off, but had to be ready to follow in any or every direction. In this manner the pursuit was altogether a stern chase, and therefore bound to be a long one.

As at present we could not do anything till the intended route was more marked, I left the signalling corps to the task of receiving and giving information to the moving bands, so that, if occasion served, they might head off the marauders. I myself took Rooke, as captain of the yacht, and swept out of the creek. We ran up north to Dalairi, then down south to Olesso, and came back to Vissarion. We saw nothing suspicious except, far off to the extreme southward, one warship which flew no flag. Rooke, however, who seemed to know ships by instinct, said she was a Turk; so on our return we signalled along the whole shore to watch her. Rooke held The Lady—which was the name I had given the armoured yacht—in readiness to dart out in case anything suspicious was reported. He was not to stand on any ceremony, but if necessary to attack. We did not intend to lose a point in this desperate struggle which we had undertaken. We had placed in different likely spots a couple of our own men to look after the signalling.

When I got back I found that the route of the fugitives, who had now joined into one party, had been definitely ascertained. They had gone south, but manifestly taking alarm from the advancing line of guards, had headed up again to the north-east, where the country was broader and the mountains wilder and less inhabited.

Forthwith, leaving the signalling altogether in the hands of the fighting priests, I took a small chosen band of the mountaineers of our own district, and made, with all the speed we could, to cut across the track of the fugitives a little ahead of them. The Archimandrite (Abbot) of Spazac, who had just arrived, came with us. He is a splendid man—a real fighter as well as a holy cleric, as good with his handjar as with his Bible, and a runner to beat the band. The marauders were going at a fearful pace, considering that they were all afoot; so we had to go fast also! Amongst these mountains there is no other means of progressing. Our own men were so aflame with ardour that I could not but notice that they, more than any of the others whom I had seen, had some special cause for concern.

When I mentioned it to the Archimandrite, who moved by my side, he answered:

"All natural enough; they are not only fighting for their country, but for their own!" I did not quite understand his answer, and so began to ask him some questions, to the effect that I soon began to understand a good deal more than he did.

Letter from Archbishop Stevan Palealogue, Head of the Eastern Church of the Blue Mountains, to the Lady Janet MacKelpie, Vissarion.

Written July 9, 1907.

HONOURED LADY,

As you wish for an understanding regarding the late lamentable occurrence in which so much danger was incurred to this our Land of the Blue Mountains, and one dear to us, I send these words by request of the Gospodar Rupert, beloved of our mountaineers.

When the Voivode Peter Vissarion made his journey to the great nation to whom we looked in our hour of need, it was necessary that he should go in secret. The Turk was at our gates, and full of the malice of baffled greed. Already he had tried to arrange a marriage with the Voivodin, so that in time to come he, as her husband, might have established a claim to the inheritance of the land. Well he knew, as do all men, that the Blue Mountaineers owe allegiance to none that they themselves do not appoint to rulership. This has been the history in the past. But now and again an individual has arisen or come to the front adapted personally for such government as this land requires. And so the Lady Teuta, Voivodin of the Blue Mountains, was put for her proper guarding in the charge of myself as Head of the Eastern Church in the Land of the Blue Mountains, steps being taken in such wise that no capture of her could be effected by unscrupulous enemies of this our Land. This task and guardianship was gladly held as an honour by all concerned. For the Voivodin Teuta of Vissarion must be taken as representing in her own person the glory of the old Serb race, inasmuch as being the only child of the Voivode Vissarion, last male of his princely race—the race which ever, during the ten centuries of our history, unflinchingly gave life and all they held for the protection, safety, and well-being of the Land of the Blue Mountains. Never during those centuries had any one of the race been known to fail in patriotism, or to draw back from any loss or hardship enjoined by high duty or stress of need. Moreover, this was the race of that first Voivode Vissarion, of whom, in legend, it was prophesied that he—once known as "The Sword of Freedom," a giant amongst men—would some day, when the nation had need of him, come forth from his water-tomb in the lost Lake of Reo, and lead once more the men of the Blue Mountains to lasting victory. This noble race, then, had come to be known as the last hope of the Land. So that when the Voivode was away on his country's service, his daughter should be closely guarded. Soon after the Voivode had gone, it was reported that he might be long delayed in his diplomacies, and also in studying the system of Constitutional Monarchy, for which it had been hoped to exchange our imperfect political system. I may say *inter alia* that he was mentioned as to be the first king when the new constitution should have been arranged.

Then a great misfortune came on us; a terrible grief overshadowed the land. After a short illness, the Voivodin Teuta Vissarion died mysteriously of a mysterious ailment. The grief of the mountaineers was so great that it became necessary for the governing Council to warn them not to allow their sorrow to be seen. It was imperatively necessary that the fact of her death should be kept secret. For there were dangers and difficulties of several kinds. In the first place it was advisable that even her father should be kept in ignorance of his terrible loss. It was well known that he held her as the very core of his heart and that if he should hear of her death, he would be too much prostrated to be able to do the intricate and delicate work which he had undertaken. Nay, more: he would never remain afar off, under the sad circumstances, but would straightway return, so as to be in the land where she lay. Then suspicions would crop up, and the truth must shortly be known afield, with the inevitable result that the Land would become the very centre of a war of many nations.

In the second place, if the Turks were to know that the race of Vissarion was becoming extinct, this would encourage them to further aggression, which would become immediate should they find out that the Voivode was himself away. It was well known that they were already only suspending hostilities until a fitting opportunity should arise. Their desire for aggression had become acute after the refusal of the nation, and of the girl herself, that she should become a wife of the Sultan.

The dead girl had been buried in the Crypt of the church of St. Sava, and day after day and night after night, singly and in parties, the sorrowing mountaineers had come to pay devotion and reverence at her tomb. So many had wished to have a last glimpse of her face that the Vladika had, with my own consent as Archbishop, arranged for a glass cover to be put over the stone coffin wherein her body lay.

After a little time, however, there came a belief to all concerned in the guarding of the body—these, of course, being the priests of various degrees of dignity appointed to the task—that the Voivodin was not really dead, but only in a strangely-prolonged trance. Thereupon a new complication arose. Our mountaineers are, as perhaps you know, by nature deeply suspicious—a characteristic of all brave and self-sacrificing people who are jealous of their noble heritage. Having, as they believed, seen the girl dead, they might not be willing to accept the fact of her being alive. They might even imagine that there was on foot some deep, dark plot which was, or might be, a menace, now or hereafter, to their independence. In any case, there would be certain to be two parties on the subject, a dangerous and deplorable thing in the present condition of affairs.

As the trance, or catalepsy, whatever it was, continued for many days, there had been ample time for the leaders of the Council, the Vladika, the priesthood represented by the Archimandrite of Spazac, myself as Archbishop and guardian of the Voivodin in her father's absence, to consult as to a policy to be observed in case of the girl awaking. For in such case the difficulty of the situation would be multiplied indefinitely. In the secret chambers of St. Sava's we had many secret meetings, and were finally converging on agreement when the end of the trance came.

The girl awoke!

She was, of course, terribly frightened when she found herself in a tomb in the Crypt. It was truly fortunate that the great candles around her tomb had been kept lighted, for their light mitigated the horror of the place. Had she waked in darkness, her reason might have become unseated.

She was, however, a very noble girl; brave, with extraordinary will, and resolution, and self-command, and power of endurance. When she had been taken into one of the secret chambers of the church, where she was warmed and cared for, a hurried meeting was held by the Vladika, myself, and the chiefs of the National Council. Word had been at once sent to me of the joyful news of her recovery; and with the utmost haste I came, arriving in time to take a part in the Council.

At the meeting the Voivodin was herself present, and full confidence of the situation was made to her. She herself proposed that the belief in her death should be allowed to prevail until the return of her father, when all could be effectively made clear. To this end she undertook to submit to the terrific strain which such a proceeding would involve. At first we men could not believe that any woman could go through with such a task, and some of us did not hesitate to voice our doubts—our disbelief. But she stood to her guns, and actually down-faced us. At the last we, remembering things that had been done, though long ages ago, by others of her race, came to believe not merely in her self-belief and intention, but even in the feasibility of her plan. She took the most solemn oaths not to betray the secret under any possible stress.

The priesthood undertook through the Vladika and myself to further a ghostly belief amongst the mountaineers which would tend to prevent a too close or too persistent observation. The Vampire legend was spread as a protection against partial discovery by any mischance, and other weird beliefs were set afoot and fostered. Arrangements were made that only on certain days were the mountaineers to be admitted to the Crypt, she agreeing that for these occasions she was to take opiates or carry out any other aid to the preservation of the secret. She was willing, she impressed upon us, to make any personal sacrifice which might be deemed necessary for the carrying out her father's task for the good of the nation.

Of course, she had at first terrible frights lying alone in the horror of the Crypt. But after a time the terrors of the situation, if they did not cease, were mitigated. There are secret caverns off the Crypt, wherein in troublous times the priests and others of high place have found safe retreat. One of these was prepared for the Voivodin, and there she remained, except for such times as she was on show—and certain other times of which I shall tell you. Provision was made for the possibility of any accidental visit to the church. At such times, warned by an automatic signal from the opening door, she was to take her place in the tomb. The mechanism was so arranged that the means to replace the glass cover, and to take the opiate, were there ready to her hand. There was to be always a watch of priests at night in the church, to guard her from ghostly fears as well as from more physical dangers; and if she was actually in her tomb, it was to be visited at certain intervals. Even the draperies which covered her in the sarcophagus were rested on a bridge placed from side to side just above her, so as to hide the rising and falling of her bosom as she slept under the narcotic.

After a while the prolonged strain began to tell so much on her that it was decided that she should take now and again exercise out of doors. This was not difficult, for when the Vampire story which we had spread began to be widely known, her being seen would be accepted as a proof of its truth. Still, as there was a certain danger in her being seen at all, we thought it necessary to exact from her a solemn oath that so long as her sad task lasted she should under no circumstances ever wear any dress but her shroud—this being the only way to insure secrecy and to prevail against accident.

There is a secret way from the Crypt to a sea cavern, whose entrance is at high-tide under the water-line at the base of the cliff on which the church is built. A boat, shaped like a coffin, was provided for her; and in this she was accustomed to pass across the creek whenever she wished to make excursion. It was an excellent device, and most efficacious in disseminating the Vampire belief.

This state of things had now lasted from before the time when the Gospodar Rupert came to Vissarion up to the day of the arrival of the armoured yacht.

That night the priest on duty, on going his round of the Crypt just before dawn, found the tomb empty. He called the others, and they made full search. The boat was gone from the cavern, but on making search they found it on the farther side of the creek, close to the garden stairs. Beyond this they could discover nothing. She seemed to have disappeared without leaving a trace.

Straightway they went to the Vladika, and signalled to me by the fire-signal at the monastery at Astrag, where I then was. I took a band of mountaineers with me, and set out to scour the country. But before going I sent an urgent message to the Gospodar Rupert, asking him, who showed so much interest and love to our Land, to help us in our trouble. He, of course, knew nothing then of all have now told you. Nevertheless, he devoted himself whole-heartedly to our needs—as doubtless you know.

But the time had now come close when the Voivode Vissarion was about to return from his mission; and we of the council of his daughter's guardianship were beginning to arrange matters so that at his return the good news of her being still alive could be made public. With her father present to vouch for her, no question as to truth could arise.

But by some means the Turkish "Bureau of Spies" must have got knowledge of the fact already. To steal a dead body for the purpose of later establishing a fictitious claim would have been an enterprise even more desperate than that already undertaken. We inferred from many signs, made known to us in an investigation, that a daring party of the Sultan's emissaries had made a secret incursion with the object of kidnapping the Voivodin. They must have been bold of heart and strong of resource to enter the Land of the Blue Mountains on any errand, let alone such a desperate one as this. For centuries we have been teaching the Turk through bitter lessons that it is neither a safe task nor an easy one to make incursion here.

How they did it we know not—at present; but enter they did, and, after waiting in some secret hiding-place for a favourable opportunity, secured their prey. We know not even now whether they had found entrance to the Crypt and stole, as they thought, the dead body, or whether, by some dire mischance, they found her abroad—under her disguise as a ghost. At any rate, they had captured her, and through devious ways amongst the mountains were bearing her back to Turkey. It was manifest that when she was on Turkish soil the Sultan would force a marriage on her so as eventually to secure for himself or his successors as against all other nations a claim for the suzerainty or guardianship of the Blue Mountains.

Such was the state of affairs when the Gospodar Rupert threw himself into the pursuit with fiery zeal and the Berserk passion which he inherited from Viking ancestors, whence of old came "The Sword of Freedom" himself.

But at that very time was another possibility which the Gospodar was himself the first to realize. Failing the getting the Voivodin safe to

Turkish soil, the ravishers might kill her! This would be entirely in accord with the base traditions and history of the Moslems. So, too, it would accord with Turkish customs and the Sultan's present desires. It would, in its way, benefit the ultimate strategetic ends of Turkey. For were once the Vissarion race at an end, the subjection of the Land of the Blue Mountains might, in their view, be an easier task than it had yet been found to be.

Such, illustrious lady, were the conditions of affairs when the Gospodar Rupert first drew his handjar for the Blue Mountains and what it held most dear.

PALEALOGUE,
Archbishop of the Eastern Church, in the Land of the Blue Mountains.

RUPERT'S JOURNAL—*Continued.*

July 8, 1907.

I wonder if ever in the long, strange history of the world had there come to any other such glad tidings as came to me—and even then rather inferentially than directly—from the Archimandrite's answers to my questioning. Happily I was able to restrain myself, or I should have created some strange confusion which might have evoked distrust, and would certainly have hampered us in our pursuit. For a little I could hardly accept the truth which wove itself through my brain as the true inwardness of each fact came home to me and took its place in the whole fabric. But even the most welcome truth has to be accepted some time by even a doubting heart. My heart, whatever it may have been, was not then a doubting heart, but a very, very grateful one. It was only the splendid magnitude of the truth which forbade its immediate acceptance. I could have shouted for joy, and only stilled myself by keeping my thoughts fixed on the danger which my wife was in. My wife! My wife! Not a Vampire; not a poor harassed creature doomed to terrible woe, but a splendid woman, brave beyond belief, patriotic in a way which has but few peers even in the wide history of bravery! I began to understand the true meaning of the strange occurrences that have come into my life. Even the origin and purpose of that first strange visit to my room became clear. No wonder that the girl could move about the Castle in so mysterious a manner. She had lived there all her life, and was familiar with the secret ways of entrance and exit. I had always believed that the place must have been honeycombed with secret passages. No wonder that she could find a way to the battlements, mysterious to everybody else. No wonder that she could meet me at the Flagstaff when she so desired.

To say that I was in a tumult would be to but faintly express my condition. I was rapt into a heaven of delight which had no measure in all my adventurous life—the lifting of the veil which showed that my wife—mine—won in all sincerity in the very teeth of appalling difficulties and dangers—was no Vampire, no corpse, no ghost or phantom, but a real woman of flesh and blood, of affection, and love, and passion. Now at last would my love be crowned indeed when, having rescued her from the marauders, I should bear her to my own home, where she would live and reign in peace and comfort and honour, and in love and wifely happiness if I could achieve such a blessing for her—and for myself.

But here a dreadful thought flashed across me, which in an instant turned my joy to despair, my throbbing heart to ice:

"As she is a real woman, she is in greater danger than ever in the hands of Turkish ruffians. To them a woman is in any case no more than a sheep; and if they cannot bring her to the harem of the Sultan, they may deem it the next wisest step to kill her. In that way, too, they might find a better chance of escape. Once rid of her the party could separate, and there might be a chance of some of them finding escape as individuals that would not exist for a party. But even if they did not kill her, to escape with her would be to condemn her to the worst fate of all the harem of the Turk! Lifelong misery and despair—however long that life might be—must be the lot of a Christian woman doomed to such a lot. And to her, just happily wedded, and after she had served her country in such a noble way as she had done, that dreadful life of shameful slavery would be a misery beyond belief.

"She must be rescued—and quickly! The marauders must be caught soon, and suddenly, so that they may have neither time nor opportunity to harm her, as they would be certain to do if they have warning of immediate danger.

"On! on!"

And "on" it was all through that terrible night as well as we could through the forest.

It was a race between the mountaineers and myself as to who should be first. I understood now the feeling that animated them, and which singled them out even from amongst their fiery comrades, when the danger of the Voivodin became known. These men were no mean contestants even in such a race, and, strong as I am, it took my utmost effort to keep ahead of them. They were keen as leopards, and as swift. Their lives had been spent among the mountains, and their hearts and souls on were in the chase. I doubt not that if the death of any one of us could have through any means effected my wife's release, we should, if necessary, have fought amongst ourselves for the honour.

From the nature of the work before us our party had to keep to the top of the hills. We had not only to keep observation on the flying party whom we followed, and to prevent them making discovery of us, but we had to be always in a position to receive and answer signals made to us from the Castle, or sent to us from other eminences.

Letter from Petrof Vlastimir, Archimandrite of Spazac, to the Lady Janet MacKelpie, of Vissarion.

Written July 8, 1907.

GREAT LADY,

I am asked to write by the Vladika, and have permission of the Archbishop. I have the honour of transmitting to you the record of the pursuit of the Turkish spies who carried off the Voivodin Teuta, of the noble House of Vissarion. The pursuit was undertaken by the Gospodar Rupert, who asked that I would come with his party, since what he was so good as to call my "great knowledge of the country and its people" might serve much. It is true that I have had much knowledge of the Land of the Blue Mountains and its people, amongst which and whom my whole life has been passed. But in such a cause no reason was required. There was not a man in the Blue Mountains who would not have given his life for the Voivodin Teuta, and when they heard that she had not been dead, as they thought, but only in a trance, and that it was she whom the marauders had carried off, they were in a frenzy. So why should I—to whom has been given the great trust of the Monastery of Spazac—hesitate at such a time? For myself, I wanted to hurry on, and to come at once to the fight with my country's foes; and well I knew that the Gospodar Rupert, with a lion's heart meet for his giant body, would press on with a matchless speed. We of the Blue Mountains do not lag when our foes are in front of us; most of all do we of the Eastern Church press on when the Crescent wars against the Cross!

We took with us no gear or hamper of any kind; no coverings except what we stood in; no food—nothing but our handjars and our rifles, with a sufficiency of ammunition. Before starting, the Gospodar gave hurried orders by signal from the Castle to have food and ammunition sent to us (as we might signal) by the nearest hamlet.

It was high noon when we started, only ten strong—for our leader would take none but approved runners who could shoot straight and use the handjar as it should be used. So as we went light, we expected to go fast. By this time we knew from the reports signalled to Vissarion that the enemies were chosen men of no despicable prowess.

The Keeper of the Green Flag of Islam is well served, and as though the Turk is an infidel and a dog, he is sometimes brave and strong. Indeed, except when he passes the confines of the Blue Mountains, he has been known to do stirring deeds. But as none who have dared to wander in amongst our hills ever return to their own land, we may not know of how they speak at home of their battles here. Still, these men were evidently not to be despised; and our Gospodar, who is a wise man as well as a valiant, warned us to be prudent, and not to despise our foes over much. We did as he counselled, and in proof we only took ten men, as we had only twenty against us. But then there was at stake much beyond life, and we took no risks. So, as the great clock at Vissarion clanged of noon, the eight fastest runners of the Blue Mountains, together with the Gospodar Rupert and myself, swept out on our journey. It had been signalled to us that the course which the marauders had as yet taken in their flight was a zigzag one, running eccentrically at all sorts of angles in all sorts of directions. But our leader had marked out a course where we might intercept our foes across the main line of their flight; and till we had reached that region we paused not a second, but went as fast as we could all night long. Indeed, it was amongst us a race as was the Olympic race of old Greece, each one vying with his fellows, though not in jealous emulation, but in high spirit, to best serve his country and the Voivodin Teuta. Foremost amongst us went the Gospodar, bearing himself as a Paladin of old, his mighty form pausing for no obstacle. Perpetually did he urge us on. He would not stop or pause for a moment, but often as he and I ran together—for, lady, in my youth I was the fleetest of all in the race, and even that now can head a battalion when duty calls—he would ask me certain questions as to the Lady Teuta and of the strange manner of her reputed death, as it was gradually unfolded in my answers to his questioning. And as each new phase of knowledge came to him, he would rush on as one possessed of fiends: whereat our mountaineers, who seem to respect even fiends for their thoroughness, would strive to keep pace with him till they too seemed worked into diabolic possession. And I myself, left alone in the calmness of sacerdotal office, forgot even that. With surging ears and eyes that saw blood, I rushed along with best of them.

Then truly the spirit of a great captain showed itself in the Gospodar, for when others were charged with fury he began to force himself into calm, so that out of his present self-command and the memory of his exalted position came a worthy strategy and thought for every contingency that might arise. So that when some new direction was required for our guidance, there was no hesitation in its coming. We, nine men of varying kinds, all felt that we had a master; and so, being willing to limit ourselves to strict obedience, we were free to use such thoughts as well as such powers as we had to the best advantage of the doing.

We came across the trail of the flying marauders on the second morning after the abduction, a little before noon. It was easy enough to see, for by this time the miscreants were all together, and our people, who were woodlanders, were able to tell much of the party that passed. These were evidently in a terrified hurry, for they had taken no precautions such as are necessary baffle pursuit, and all of which take time. Our foresters said that two went ahead and two behind. In the centre went the mass, moving close together, as though surrounding their prisoner. We caught not even a single glimpse her—could not have, they encompassed her so closely. But our foresters saw other than the mass; the ground that had been passed was before them. They knew that the prisoner had gone unwillingly—nay, more: one of them said as he rose from his knees, where he had been examining of the ground:

"The misbegotten dogs have been urging her on with their yataghans! There are drops of blood, though there are no blood-marks on her feet."

Whereupon the Gospodar flamed with passion. His teeth ground together, and with a deep-breathed "On, on!" he sprang off again, handjar in hand, on the track.

Before long we saw the party in the distance. They this were far below us in a deep valley, although the track of their going passed away to the right hand. They were making for the base of the great cliff, which rose before us all. Their reason was twofold, as we soon knew. Far off down the valley which they were crossing we saw signs of persons coming in haste, who must be of the search party coming from the north. Though the trees hid them, we could not mistake the signs. I was myself forester enough to have no doubt. Again, it was evident that the young Voivodin could travel no longer at the dreadful pace at which they had been going. Those blood-marks told their own tale! They meant to make a last stand here in case they should be discovered.

Then it was that he, who amongst us all had been most fierce and most bent on rapid pursuit, became the most the calm. Raising his hand for silence—though, God knows, we were and had been silent enough during that long rush through the forest—he said, in a low, keen whisper which cut the silence like a knife:

"My friends, the time is come for action. God be thanked, who has now brought us face to face with our foes! But we must be careful here—not on our own account, for we wish nothing more than to rush on and conquer or die—but for the sake of her whom you love, and whom I, too, love. She is in danger from anything which may give warning to those fiends. If they know or even suspect for an instant that we are near, they will murder her . . . "

Here his voice broke for an instant with the extremity of his passion or the depth of his feeling—I hardly know which; I think both acted on him.

"We know from those blood-marks what they can do—even to her." His teeth ground together again, but he went on without stopping further:

"Let us arrange the battle. Though we are but little distance from them as the crow flies, the way is far to travel. There is, I can see, but one path down to the valley from this side. That they have gone by, and that they will sure to guard—to watch, at any rate. Let us divide, as to surround them. The cliff towards which they make runs far to the left without a break. That to the right we cannot see from this spot; but from the nature of the ground it is not unlikely that it turns round in this direction, making the hither end of the valley like a vast pocket or amphitheatre. As they have studied the ground in other places, they may have done so in this, and have come hither as to a known refuge. Let one man, a marksman, stay here."

As he spoke a man stepped to the front. He was, I knew, an excellent shot.

"Let two others go to the left and try to find a way down the cliff before us. When they have descended to the level of the valley—path or no path—let them advance cautiously and secretly, keeping their guns in readiness. But they must not fire till need. Remember, my brothers," said, turning to those who stepped out a pace or two to the left, "that the first shot gives the warning which will be the signal for the Voivodin's death. These men will not hesitate. You must judge yourselves of the time to shoot. The others of us will move to the right and try to find a path on that side. If the valley be indeed a pocket between the cliffs, we must find a way down that is not a path!"

As he spoke thus there was a blaze in his eyes that betokened no good to aught that might stand in his way. I ran by his side as we moved to the right.

It was as he surmised about the cliff. When we got a little on our way we saw how the rocky formation trended to our right, till, finally, with a wide curve, it came round to the other side.

It was a fearful valley that, with its narrow girth and its towering walls that seemed to topple over. On the farther side from us the great trees that clothed the slope of the mountain over it grew down to the very edge of the rock, so that their spreading branches hung far over the chasm. And, so far as we could understand, the same condition existed on our own side. Below us the valley was dark even in the daylight. We could best tell the movement of the flying marauders by the flashes of the white shroud of their captive in the midst of them.

From where we were grouped, amid the great tree-trunks on the very brow of the cliff, we could, when our eyes were accustomed to the shadow, see them quite well. In great haste, and half dragging, half carrying the Voivodin, they crossed the open space and took refuge in a little grassy alcove surrounded, save for its tortuous entrance, by undergrowth. From the valley level it was manifestly impossible to see them, though we from our altitude could see over the stunted undergrowth. When within the glade, they took their hands from her. She, shuddering instinctively, withdrew to a remote corner of the dell.

And then, oh, shame on their manhood!—Turks and heathens though they were—we could see that they had submitted her to the indignity of gagging her and binding her hands!

Our Voivodin Teuta bound! To one and all of us it was like lashing us across the face. I heard the Gospodar's teeth grind again. But once more he schooled himself to calmness ere he said:

"It is, perhaps, as well, great though the indignity be. They are seeking their own doom, which is coming quickly . . . Moreover, they are thwarting their own base plans. Now that she is bound they will trust to their binding, so that they will delay their murderous alternative to the very last moment. Such is our chance of rescuing her alive!"

For a few moments he stood as still as a stone, as though revolving something in his mind whilst he watched. I could see that some grim resolution was forming in his mind, for his eyes ranged to the top of the trees above cliff, and down again, very slowly this time, as though measuring and studying the detail of what was in front of him. Then he spoke:

"They are in hopes that the other pursuing party may not come across them. To know that, they are waiting. If those others do not come up the valley, they will proceed on their way. They will return up the path the way they came. There we can wait them, charge into the middle of them when she is opposite, and cut down those around her. Then the others will open fire, and we shall be rid of them!

Whilst he was speaking, two of the men of our party, who I knew to be good sharpshooters, and who had just before lain on their faces and had steadied their rifles to shoot, rose to their feet.

"Command us, Gospodar!" they said simply, as they stood to attention. "Shall we go to the head of the ravine road and there take hiding?" He thought for perhaps a minute, whilst we all stood as silent as images. I could hear our hearts beating. Then he said:

"No, not yet. There is time for that yet. They will not—cannot stir or make plans in any way till they know whether the other party is coming towards them or not. From our height here we can see what course the others are taking long before those villains do. Then we can make our plans and be ready in time."

We waited many minutes, but could see no further signs the other pursuing party. These had evidently adopted greater caution in their movements as they came closer to where they expected to find the enemy. The marauders began to grow anxious. Even at our distance we could gather as much from their attitude and movements.

Presently, when the suspense of their ignorance grew too much for them, they drew to the entrance of the glade, which was the farthest place to which, without exposing themselves to anyone who might come to the valley, they could withdraw from their captive. Here they consulted together. We could follow from their gestures what they were saying, for as they did not wish their prisoner to hear, their gesticulation was enlightening to us as to each other. Our people, like all mountaineers, have good eyes, and the Gospodar is himself an eagle in this as in other ways. Three men stood back from the rest. They stacked their rifles so that they could seize them easily. Then they drew their scimitars, and stood ready, as though on guard.

These were evidently the appointed murderers. Well they knew their work; for though they stood in a desert place with none within long distance except the pursuing party, of whose approach they would have good notice, they stood so close to their prisoner that no marksman in the world—now or that ever had been; not William Tell himself—could have harmed any of them without at least endangering her. Two of them turned the Voivodin round so that her face was towards the precipice—in which position she could not see what was going on—whilst he who was evidently leader of the gang explained, in gesture, that the others were going to spy upon the pursuing party. When they had located them he, or one of his men, would come out of the opening of the wood wherein they had had evidence of them, and hold up his hand.

That was to be the signal for the cutting of the victim's throat—such being the chosen method (villainous even for heathen murderers) of her death. There was not one of our men who did not grind his teeth when we witnessed the grim action, only too expressive, of the Turk as he drew his right hand, clenched as though he held a yataghan in it, across his throat.

At the opening of the glade all the spying party halted whilst the leader appointed to each his place of entry of the wood, the front of which extended in an almost straight across the valley from cliff to cliff.

The men, stooping low when in the open, and taking instant advantage of every little obstacle on the ground, seemed to fade like spectres with incredible swiftness across the level mead, and were swallowed up in the wood.

When they had disappeared the Gospodar Rupert revealed to us the details of the plan of action which he had revolving in his mind. He motioned us to follow him: we threaded a way between the tree-trunks, keeping all the while on the very edge of the cliff, so that the space below was all visible to us. When we had got round the curve sufficiently to see the whole of the wood on the valley level, without losing sight of the Voivodin and her appointed assassins, we halted under his direction. There was an added advantage of this point over the other, for we could see directly the rising of the hill-road, up which farther side ran the continuation of the mountain path which the marauders had followed. It was somewhere on that path that the other pursuing party had hoped to intercept the fugitives. The Gospodar spoke quickly, though in a voice of command which true soldiers love to hear:

"Brothers, the time has come when we can strike a blow for Teuta and the Land. Do you two, marksmen, take position here facing the wood." The two men here lay down and got their rifles ready. "Divide the frontage of the wood between you; arrange between yourselves the limits of your positions. The very instant one of the marauders appears, cover him; drop him before he emerges from the wood. Even then still watch and treat similarly whoever else may take his place. Do this if they come singly till not a man is left. Remember, brothers, that brave hearts alone will not suffice at this grim crisis. In this hour the best safety of the Voivodin is in the calm spirit and the steady eye!" Then he turned to the rest of us, and spoke to me:

"Archimandrite of Plazac, you who are interpreter to God of the prayers of so many souls, my own hour has come. If I do not return, convey my love to my Aunt Janet—Miss MacKelpie, at Vissarion. There is but one thing left to us if we wish to save the Voivodin. Do you, when the time comes, take these men and join the watcher at the top of the ravine road. When the shots are fired, do you out handjar, and rush the ravine and across the valley. Brothers, you may be in time to avenge the Voivodin, if you cannot save her. For me there must be a quicker way, and to it I go. As there is not, and will not be, time to traverse the path, I must take a quicker way. Nature finds me a path that man has made it necessary for me to travel. See that giant beech-tree that towers above the glade where the Voivodin is held? There is my path! When you from here have marked the return of the spies, give me a signal with your hat—do not use a handkerchief, as others might see its white, and take warning. Then rush that ravine. I shall take that as the signal for my descent by the leafy road. If I can do naught else, I can crush the murderers with my falling weight, even if I have to kill her too. At least we shall die together—and free. Lay us together in the tomb at St. Sava's. Farewell, if it be the last!"

He threw down the scabbard in which he carried his handjar, adjusted the naked weapon in his belt behind his back, and was gone!

We who were not watching the wood kept our eyes fixed on the great beech-tree, and with new interest noticed the long trailing branches which hung low, and swayed even in the gentle breeze. For a few minutes, which seemed amazingly long, we saw no sign of him. Then, high up on one of the great branches which stood clear of obscuring leaves, we saw something crawling flat against the bark. He was well out on the branch, hanging far over the precipice. He was looking over at us, and I waved my hand so that he should know we saw him. He was clad in green—his usual forest dress—so that there was not any likelihood of any other eyes noticing him. I took off my hat, and held it ready to signal with when the time should come. I glanced down at the glade and saw the Voivodin standing, still safe, with her guards so close to her as to touch. Then I, too, fixed my eyes on the wood.

Suddenly the man standing beside me seized my arm and pointed. I could just see through the trees, which were lower than elsewhere in the front of the wood, a Turk moving stealthily; so I waved my hat. At the same time a rifle underneath me cracked. A second or two later the spy pitched forward on his face and lay still. At the same instant my eyes sought the beech-tree, and I saw the close-lying figure raise itself and slide forward to a joint of the branch. Then the Gospodar, as he rose, hurled himself forward amid the mass of the trailing branches. He dropped like a stone, and my heart sank.

But an instant later he seemed in poise. He had clutched the thin, trailing branches as he fell; and as he sank a number of leaves which his motion had torn off floated out round him.

Again the rifle below me cracked, and then again, and again, and again. The marauders had taken warning, and were coming out in mass. But my own eyes were fixed on the tree. Almost as a thunderbolt falls fell the giant body of the Gospodar, his size lost in the immensity of his surroundings. He fell in a series of jerks, as he kept clutching the trailing beech-branches whilst they lasted, and then other lesser verdure growing out from the fissures in the rock after the lengthening branches had with all their elasticity reached their last point.

At length—for though this all took place in a very few seconds the gravity of the crisis prolonged them immeasurably—there came a large space of rock some three times his own length. He did not pause, but swung himself to one side, so that he should fall close to the Voivodin and her guards. These men did not seem to notice, for their attention was fixed on the wood whence they expected their messenger to signal. But they raised their yataghans in readiness. The shots had alarmed them; and they meant to do the murder now—messenger or no messenger

But though the men did not see the danger from above, the Voivodin did. She raised her eyes quickly at the first sound, and even from where we were, before we began to run towards the ravine path, I could see the triumphant look in her glorious eyes when she recognized the identity of the man who was seemingly coming straight down from Heaven itself to help her—as, indeed, she, and we too, can very well imagine that he did; for if ever heaven had a hand in a rescue on earth, it was now.

Even during the last drop from the rocky foliage the Gospodar kept his head. As he fell he pulled his handjar free, and almost as he was falling its sweep took off the head of one of the assassins. As he touched ground he stumbled for an instant, but it was towards his enemies. Twice with lightning rapidity the handjar swept the air, and at each sweep a head rolled on the sward.

The Voivodin held up her tied hands. Again the handjar flashed, this time downwards, and the lady was free. Without an instant's pause the Gospodar tore off the gag, and with his left arm round her and handjar in right hand, stood face toward his living foes. The Voivodin stooped suddenly, and then, raising the yataghan which had fallen from the hand of one of the dead marauders, stood armed beside him.

The rifles were now cracking fast, as the marauders—those that were left of them—came rushing out into the open. But well the marksmen knew their work. Well they bore in mind the Gospodar's command regarding calmness. They kept picking off the foremost men only, so that the onward rush never seemed to get more forward.

As we rushed down the ravine we could see clearly all before us. But now, just as we were beginning to fear lest some mischance might allow some of them to reach the glade, there was another cause of surprise—of rejoicing.

From the face of the wood seemed to burst all at once a body of men, all wearing the national cap, so we knew them as our own. They were all armed with the handjar only, and they came like tigers. They swept on the rushing Turks as though, for all their swiftness, they were standing still—literally wiping them out as a child wipes a lesson from its slate.

A few seconds later these were followed by a tall figure with long hair and beard of black mingled with grey. Instinctively we all, as did those in the valley, shouted with joy. For this was the Vladika Milosh Plamenac himself.

I confess that, knowing what I knew, I was for a short space of time anxious lest, in the terrific excitement in which we were all lapped, someone might say or do something which might make for trouble later on. The Gospodar's splendid achievement, which was worthy of any hero of old romance, had set us all on fire. He himself must have been wrought to a high pitch of excitement to dare such an act; and it is not at such a time that discretion must be expected from any man. Most of all did I fear danger from the womanhood of the Voivodin. Had I not assisted at her marriage, I might not have understood then what it must have been to her to be saved from such a doom at such a time by such a man, who was so much to her, and in such a way. It would have been only natural if at such a moment of gratitude and triumph she had proclaimed the secret which we of the Council of the Nation and her father's Commissioners had so religiously kept. But none of us knew then either the Voivodin or the Gospodar Rupert as we do now. It was well that they were as they are, for the jealousy and suspicion of our mountaineers might, even at such a moment, and even whilst they throbbed at such a deed, have so manifested themselves as to have left a legacy of distrust. The Vladika and I, who of all (save the two immediately concerned) alone knew, looked at each other apprehensively. But at that instant the Voivodin, with a swift glance at her husband, laid a finger on her lip; and he, with quick understanding, gave assurance by a similar sign. Then she sank before him on one knee, and, raising his hand to her lips, kissed it, and spoke:

"Gospodar Rupert, I owe you all that a woman may owe, except to God. You have given me life and honour! I cannot thank you adequately for what you have done; my father will try to do so when he returns. But I am right sure that the men of the Blue Mountains, who so value honour, and freedom, and liberty, and bravery, will hold you in their hearts for ever!"

This was so sweetly spoken, with lips that trembled and eyes that swam in tears, so truly womanly and so in accord with the custom of our nation regarding the reverence that women owe to men, that the hearts of our mountaineers were touched to the quick. Their noble simplicity found expression in tears. But if the gallant Gospodar could have for a moment thought that so to weep was unmanly, his error would have had instant correction. When the Voivodin had risen to her feet, which she did with queenly dignity, the men around closed in on the Gospodar like a wave of the sea, and in a second held him above their heads, tossing on their lifted hands as if on stormy breakers. It was as though the old Vikings of whom we have heard, and whose blood flows in Rupert's veins, were choosing a chief in old fashion. I was myself glad that the men were so taken up with the Gospodar that they did not see the glory of the moment in the Voivodin's starry eyes; for else they might have guessed the secret. I knew from the Vladika's look that he shared my own satisfaction, even as he had shared my anxiety.

As the Gospodar Rupert was tossed high on the lifted hands of the mountaineers, their shouts rose to such a sudden volume that around us, as far as I could see, the frightened birds rose from the forest, and their noisy alarm swelled the tumult.

The Gospodar, ever thoughtful for others, was the first to calm himself.

"Come, brothers," he said, "let us gain the hilltop, where we can signal to the Castle. It is right that the whole nation should share in the glad tidings that the Voivodin Teuta of Vissarion is free. But before we go, let us remove the arms and clothing of these carrion marauders. We may have use for them later on."

The mountaineers set him down, gently enough. And he, taking the Voivodin by the hand, and calling the Vladika and myself close to them, led the way up the ravine path which the marauders had descended, and thence through the forest to the top of the hill that dominated the valley. Here we could, from an opening amongst the trees, catch a glimpse far off of the battlements of Vissarion. Forthwith the Gospodar signalled;

and on the moment a reply of their awaiting was given. Then the Gospodar signalled the glad news. It was received with manifest rejoicing. We could not hear any sound so far away, but we could see the movement of lifted faces and waving hands, and knew that it was well. But an instant after came a calm so dread that we knew before the semaphore had begun to work that there was bad news in store for us. When the news did come, a bitter wailing arose amongst us; for the news that was signalled ran:

"The Voivode has been captured by the Turks on his return, and is held by them at Ilsin."

In an instant the temper of the mountaineers changed. It was as though by a flash summer had changed to winter, as though the yellow glory of the standing corn had been obliterated by the dreary waste of snow. Nay, more: it was as when one beholds the track of the whirlwind when the giants of the forest are levelled with the sward. For a few seconds there was silence; and then, with an angry roar, as when God speaks in the thunder, came the fierce determination of the men of the Blue Mountains:

"To Ilsin! To Ilsin!" and a stampede in the direction of the south began. For, Illustrious Lady, you, perhaps, who have been for so short a time at Vissarion, may not know that at the extreme southern point of the Land of the Blue Mountains lies the little port of Ilsin, which long ago we wrested from the Turk.

The stampede was checked by the command, "Halt!" spoken in a thunderous voice by the Gospodar. Instinctively all stopped. The Gospodar Rupert spoke again:

"Had we not better know a little more before we start on our journey? I shall get by semaphore what details are known. Do you all proceed in silence and as swiftly as possible. The Vladika and I will wait here till we have received the news and have sent some instructions, when we shall follow, and, if we can, overtake you. One thing: be absolutely silent on what has been. Be secret of every detail—even as to the rescue of the Voivodin—except what I send."

Without a word—thus showing immeasurable trust—the whole body—not a very large one, it is true—moved on, and the Gospodar began signalling. As I was myself expert in the code, I did not require any explanation, but followed question and answer on either side. The first words the Gospodar Rupert signalled were:

"Silence, absolute and profound, as to everything which has been." Then he asked for details of the capture of the Voivode. The answer ran:

"He was followed from Flushing, and his enemies advised by the spies all along the route. At Ragusa quite a number of strangers—travellers seemingly—went on board the packet. When he got out, the strangers debarked too, and evidently followed him, though, as yet, we have no details. He disappeared at Ilsin from the Hotel Reo, whither he had gone. All possible steps are being taken to trace his movements, and strictest silence and secrecy are observed."

His answer was:

"Good! Keep silent and secret. Am hurrying back. Signal request to Archbishop and all members of National Council to come to Gadaar with all speed. There the yacht will meet him. Tell Rooke take yacht all speed to Gadaar; there meet Archbishop and Council—give him list of names—and return full speed. Have ready plenty arms, six flying artillery. Two hundred men, provisions three days. Silence, silence. All depends on that. All to go on as usual at Castle, except to those in secret."

When the receipt of his message had been signalled, we three—for, of course, the Voivodin was with us; she had refused to leave the Gospodar—set out hot-foot after our comrades. But by the time we had descended the hill it was evident that the Voivodin could not keep up the terrific pace at which we were going. She struggled heroically, but the long journey she had already taken, and the hardship and anxiety she had suffered, had told on her. The Gospodar stopped, and said that it would be better that he should press on—it was, perhaps, her father's life—and said he would carry her.

"No, no!" she answered. "Go on! I shall follow with the Vladika. And then you can have things ready to get on soon after the Archbishop and Council arrive." They kissed each other after, on her part, a shy glance at me; and he went on the track of our comrades at a great pace. I could see him shortly after catch them up,—though they, too, were going fast. For a few minutes they ran together, he speaking—I could note it from the way they kept turning their heads towards him. Then he broke away from them hurriedly. He went like a stag breaking covert, and was soon out of sight. They halted a moment or two. Then some few ran on, and all the rest came back towards us. Quickly they improvised a litter with cords and branches, and insisted that the Voivodin should use it. In an incredibly short time we were under way again, and proceeding with great rapidity towards Vissarion. The men took it in turns to help with the litter; I had the honour of taking a hand in the work myself.

About a third of the way out from Vissarion a number of our people met us. They were fresh, and as they carried the litter, we who were relieved were free for speed. So we soon arrived at the Castle.

Here we found all humming like a hive of bees. The yacht, which Captain Rooke had kept fired ever since the pursuing party under the Gospodar had left Vissarion, was already away, and tearing up the coast at a fearful rate. The rifles and ammunition were stacked on the quay. The field-guns, too, were equipped, and the cases of ammunition ready to ship. The men, two hundred of them, were paraded in full kit, ready to start at a moment's notice. The provision for three days was all ready to put aboard, and barrels of fresh water to trundle aboard when the yacht should return. At one end of the quay, ready to lift on board, stood also the Gospodar's aeroplane, fully equipped, and ready, if need were, for immediate flight.

I was glad to see that the Voivodin seemed none the worse for her terrible experience. She still wore her shroud; but no one seemed to notice it as anything strange. The whisper had evidently gone round of what had been. But discretion ruled the day. She and the Gospodar met as two who had served and suffered in common; but I was glad to notice that both kept themselves under such control that none of those not already in the secret even suspected that there was any love between them, let alone marriage.

We all waited with what patience we could till word was signalled from the Castle tower that the yacht had appeared over the northern horizon, and was coming down fast, keeping inshore as she came.

When she arrived, we heard to our joy that all concerned had done their work well. The Archbishop was aboard, and of the National Council not one was missing. The Gospodar hurried them all into the great hall of the Castle, which had in the meantime been got ready. I, too, went with him, but the Voivodin remained without.

When all were seated, he rose and said:

"My Lord Archbishop, Vladika, and Lords of the Council all, I have dared to summon you in this way because time presses, and the life of one you all love—the Voivode Vissarion—is at stake. This audacious attempt of the Turk is the old aggression under a new form. It is a new and more daring step than ever to try to capture your chief and his daughter, the Voivodin, whom you love. Happily, the latter part of the scheme is frustrated. The Voivodin is safe and amongst us. But the Voivode is held prisoner—if, indeed, he be still alive. He must be somewhere near Ilsin—but where exactly we know not as yet. We have an expedition ready to start the moment we receive your sanction—your commands. We shall obey your wishes with our lives. But as the matter is instant, I would venture to ask one question, and one only: 'Shall we rescue the Voivode at any cost that may present itself?' I ask this, for the matter has now become an international one, and, if our enemies are as earnest as we are, the issue is war!"

Having so spoken, and with a dignity and force which is inexpressible, he withdrew; and the Council, having appointed a scribe—the monk Cristoferos, whom I had suggested—began its work.

The Archbishop spoke:

"Lords of the Council of the Blue Mountains, I venture to ask you that the answer to the Gospodar Rupert be an instant 'Yes!' together with thanks and honour to that gallant Englisher, who has made our cause his own, and who has so valiantly rescued our beloved Voivodin from the ruthless hands of our enemies." Forthwith the oldest member of the Council—Nicolos of Volok—rose, and, after throwing a searching look round the faces of all, and seeing grave nods of assent—for not a word was spoken—said to him who held the door: "Summon the Gospodar Rupert forthwith!" When Rupert entered, he spoke to him:

"Gospodar Rupert, the Council of the Blue Mountains has only one answer to give: Proceed! Rescue the Voivode Vissarion, whatever the cost may be! You hold henceforth in your hand the handjar of our nation, as already, for what you have done in your valiant rescue of our beloved Voivodin, your breast holds the heart of our people. Proceed at once! We give you, I fear, little time; but we know that such is your own wish. Later, we shall issue formal authorization, so that if war may ensue, our allies may understand that you have acted for the nation, and also such letters credential as may be required by you in this exceptional service. These shall follow you within an hour. For our enemies we take no account. See, we draw the handjar that we offer you." As one man all in the hall drew their handjars, which flashed as a blaze of lightning.

There did not seem to be an instant's delay. The Council broke up, and its members, mingling with the people without, took active part in the preparations. Not many minutes had elapsed when the yacht, manned and armed and stored as arranged, was rushing out of the creek. On the bridge, beside Captain Rooke, stood the Gospodar Rupert and the still-shrouded form of the Voivodin Teuta. I myself was on the lower deck with the soldiers, explaining to certain of them the special duties which they might be called on to fulfil. I held the list which the Gospodar Rupert had prepared whilst we were waiting for the yacht to arrive from Gadaar.

PETROF VLASTIMIR.

FROM RUPERT'S JOURNAL—*Continued.*

July 9, 1907.

We went at a terrific pace down the coast, keeping well inshore so as to avoid, if possible, being seen from the south. Just north of Ilsin a rocky headland juts out, and that was our cover. On the north of the peninsula is a small land-locked bay, with deep water. It is large enough to take the yacht, though a much larger vessel could not safely enter. We ran in, and anchored close to the shore, which has a rocky frontage—a natural shelf of rock, which is practically the same as a quay. Here we met the men who had come from Ilsin and the neighbourhood in answer to our signalling earlier in the day. They gave us the latest information regarding the kidnapping of the Voivode, and informed us that every man in that section of the country was simply aflame about it. They assured us that we could rely on them, not merely to fight to the death, but to keep silence absolutely. Whilst the seamen, under the direction of Rooke, took the aeroplane on shore and found a suitable place for it, where it was hidden from casual view, but from which it could be easily launched, the Vladika and I—and, of course, my wife—were hearing such details as were known of the disappearance of her father.

It seems that he travelled secretly in order to avoid just such a possibility as has happened. No one knew of his coming till he came to Fiume, whence he sent a guarded message to the Archbishop, which the latter alone would understand. But this Turkish agents were evidently on his track all the time, and doubtless the Bureau of Spies was kept well advised. He landed at Ilsin from a coasting steamer from Ragusa to the Levant.

For two days before his coming there had been quite an unusual number of arrivals at the little port, at which arrivals are rare. And it turned out that the little hotel—the only fairly good one in Ilsin—was almost filled up. Indeed, only one room was left, which the Voivode took for the night. The innkeeper did not know the Voivode in his disguise, but suspected who it was from the description. He dined quietly, and went to bed. His room was at the back, on the ground-floor, looking out on the bank of the little River Silva, which here runs into the harbour. No disturbance was heard in the night. Late in the morning, when the elderly stranger had not made his appearance, inquiry was made at his door. He did not answer, so presently the landlord forced the door, and found the room empty. His luggage was seemingly intact, only the clothes which he had worn were gone. A strange thing was that, though the bed had been slept in and his clothes were gone, his night-clothes were not to be found, from which it was argued by the local authorities, when they came to make inquiry, that he had gone or been taken from the room in his night-gear, and that his clothes had been taken with him. There was evidently some grim suspicion on the part of the authorities, for they had commanded absolute silence on all in the house. When they came to make inquiry as to the other guests, it was found that one and all had gone in the course of the morning, after paying their bills. None of them had any heavy luggage, and there was nothing remaining by which they might be traced or which would afford any clue to their identity. The authorities, having sent a confidential report to the seat of government, continued their inquiries, and even now all available hands were at work on the investigation. When I had signalled to Vissarion, before my arrival there, word had been sent through the priesthood to enlist in the investigation the services of all good men, so that every foot of ground in that section of the Blue Mountains was being investigated. The port-master was assured by his watchmen that no vessel, large or small, had heft the harbour during the night. The inference, therefore, was that the Voivode's captors had made inland with him—if, indeed, they were not already secreted in or near the town.

Whilst we were receiving the various reports, a hurried message came that it was now believed that the whole party were in the Silent Tower. This was a well-chosen place for such an enterprise. It was a massive tower of immense strength, built as a memorial—and also as a "keep"—after one of the massacres of the invading Turks.

It stood on the summit of a rocky knoll some ten miles inland from the Port of Ilsin. It was a place shunned as a rule, and the country all around it was so arid and desolate that there were no residents near it. As it was kept for state use, and might be serviceable in time of war, it was closed with massive iron doors, which were kept locked except upon certain occasions. The keys were at the seat of government at Plazac. If, therefore, it had been possible to the Turkish marauders to gain entrance and exit, it might be a difficult as well as a dangerous task to try to cut the Voivode out. His presence with them was a dangerous menace to any force attacking them, for they would hold his life as a threat.

I consulted with the Vladika at once as to what was best to be done. And we decided that, though we should put a cordon of guards around it at a safe distance to prevent them receiving warning, we should at present make no attack.

We made further inquiry as to whether there had been any vessel seen in the neighbourhood during the past few days, and were informed that once or twice a warship had been seen on the near side of the southern horizon. This was evidently the ship which Rooke had seen on his rush down the coast after the abduction of the Voivodin, and which he had identified as a Turkish vessel. The glimpses of her which had been had were all in full daylight—there was no proof that she had not stolen up during the night-time without lights. But the Vladika and I were satisfied that the Turkish vessel was watching—was in league with both parties of marauders—and was intended to take off any of the strangers, or their prey, who might reach Ilsin undetected. It was evidently with this view that the kidnappers of Teuta had, in the first instance, made with all speed for the south. It was only when disappointed there that they headed up north, seeking in desperation for some chance of crossing the border. That ring of steel had so far well served its purpose.

I sent for Rooke, and put the matter before him. He had thought it out for himself to the same end as we had. His deduction was:

"Let us keep the cordon, and watch for any signal from the Silent Tower. The Turks will tire before we shall. I undertake to watch the Turkish warship. During the night I shall run down south, without lights, and have a look at her, even if I have to wait till the grey of the dawn to do so. She may see us; but if she does I shall crawl away at such pace that she shall not get any idea of our speed. She will certainly come nearer before a day is over, for be sure the bureau of spies is kept advised, and they know that when the country is awake each day increases the hazard of them and their plans being discovered. From their caution I gather that they do not court discovery; and from that that they do not wish for an open declaration of war. If this be so, why should we not come out to them and force an issue if need be?"

When Teuta and I got a chance to be alone, we discussed the situation in every phase. The poor girl was in a dreadful state of anxiety regarding her father's safety. At first she was hardly able to speak, or even to think, coherently. Her utterance was choked, and her reasoning palsied with indignation. But presently the fighting blood of her race restored her faculties, and then her woman's quick wit was worth the reasoning of a camp full of men. Seeing that she was all on fire with the subject, I sat still and waited, taking care not to interrupt her. For quite a long time she sat still, whilst the coming night thickened. When she spoke, the whole plan of action, based on subtle thinking, had mapped itself out in her mind:

"We must act quickly. Every hour increases the risk to my father." Here her voice broke for an instant; but she recovered herself and went on:

"If you go to the ship, I must not go with you. It would not do for me to be seen. The Captain doubtless knows of both attempts: that to carry me off as well as that against my father. As yet he is in ignorance of what has happened. You and your party of brave, loyal men did their work so well that no news could go forth. So long, therefore, as the naval Captain is ignorant, he must delay till the last. But if he saw me he would know that *that* branch of the venture had miscarried. He would gather from our being here that we had news of my father's capture, and as he would know that the marauders would fail unless they were relieved by force, he would order the captive to be slain."

"Yes, dear, to-morrow you had, perhaps, better see the Captain, but to-night we must try to rescue my father. Here I think I see a way. You have your aeroplane. Please take me with you into the Silent Tower."

"Not for a world of chrysolite!" said I, horrified. She took my hand and held it tight whilst she went on:

"Dear, I know, I know! Be satisfied. But it is the only way. You can, I know, get there, and in the dark. But if you were to go in it, it would give warning to the enemies, and besides, my father would not understand. Remember, he does not know you; he has never seen you, and does not, I suppose, even know as yet of your existence. But he would know me at once, and in any dress. You can manage to lower me into the Tower by a rope from the aeroplane. The Turks as yet do not know of our pursuit, and doubtless rely, at all events in part, on the strength and security of the Tower. Therefore their guard will be less active than it would at first or later on. I shall post father in all details, and we shall be ready quickly. Now, dear, let us think out the scheme together. Let your man's wit and experience help my ignorance, and we shall save my father!"

How could I have resisted such pleading—even had it not seemed wise? But wise it was; and I, who knew what the aeroplane could do under my own guidance, saw at once the practicalities of the scheme. Of course there was a dreadful risk in case anything should go wrong. But we are at present living in a world of risks—and her father's life was at stake. So I took my dear wife in my arms, and told her that my mind was hers for this, as my soul and body already were. And I cheered her by saying that I thought it might be done.

I sent for Rooke, and told him of the new adventure, and he quite agreed with me in the wisdom of it. I then told him that he would have to go and interview the Captain of the Turkish warship in the morning, if I did not turn up. "I am going to see the Vladika," I said. "He will lead our own troops in the attack on the Silent Tower. But it will rest with you to deal with the warship. Ask the Captain to whom or what nation the ship belongs. He is sure to refuse to tell. In such case mention to him that if he flies no nation's flag, his vessel is a pirate ship, and that you, who are in command of the navy of the Blue Mountains, will deal with him as a pirate is dealt with—no quarter, no mercy. He will temporize, and perhaps try a bluff; but when things get serious with him he will land a force, or try to, and may even prepare to shell the town. He will threaten to, at any rate. In such case deal with him as you think best, or as near to it as you can." He answered:

"I shall carry out your wishes with my life. It is a righteous task. Not that anything of that sort would ever stand in my way. If he attacks our nation, either as a Turk or a pirate, I shall wipe him out. We shall see what our own little packet can do. Moreover, any of the marauders who have entered the Blue Mountains, from sea or otherwise, shall never get out by sea! I take it that we of my contingent shall cover the attacking party. It will be a sorry time for us all if that happens without our seeing you and the Voivodin; for in such case we shall understand the worst!" Iron as he was, the man trembled.

"That is so, Rooke," I said. "We are taking a desperate chance, we know. But the case is desperate! But we all have our duty to do, whatever happens. Ours and yours is stern; but when we have done it, the result will be that life will be easier for others—for those that are left."

Before he left, I asked him to send up to me three suits of the Masterman bullet-proof clothes of which we had a supply on the yacht.

"Two are for the Voivodin and myself," I said; "the third is for the Voivode to put on. The Voivodin will take it with her when she descends from the aeroplane into the Tower."

Whilst any daylight was left I went out to survey the ground. My wife wanted to come with me, but I would not let her. "No," said I; "you will have at the best a fearful tax on your strength and your nerves. You will want to be as fresh as is possible when you get on the aeroplane." Like a good wife, she obeyed, and lay down to rest in the little tent provided for her.

I took with me a local man who knew the ground, and who was trusted to be silent. We made a long detour when we had got as near the Silent Tower as we could without being noticed. I made notes from my compass as to directions, and took good notice of anything that could possibly serve as a landmark. By the time we got home I was pretty well satisfied that if all should go well I could easily sail over the Tower in the dark. Then I had a talk with my wife, and gave her full instructions:

"When we arrive over the Tower," I said, "I shall lower you with a long rope. You will have a parcel of food and spirit for your father in case he is fatigued or faint; and, of course, the bullet-proof suit, which he must put on at once. You will also have a short rope with a belt at either end—one for your father, the other for you. When I turn the aeroplane and come back again, you will have ready the ring which lies midway between the belts. This you will catch into the hook at the end of the lowered rope. When all is secure, and I have pulled you both up by the windlass so as to clear the top, I shall throw out ballast which we shall carry on purpose, and away we go! I am sorry it must be so uncomfortable for you both, but there is no other way. When we get well clear of the Tower, I shall take you both up on the platform. If necessary, I shall descend to do it—and then we shall steer for Ilsin."

"When all is safe, our men will attack the Tower. We must let them do it, for they expect it. A few men in the clothes and arms which we took from your captors will be pursued by some of ours. It is all arranged. They will ask the Turks to admit them, and if the latter have not learned of your father's escape, perhaps they will do so. Once in, our men will try to open the gate. The chances are against them, poor fellows! but they are all volunteers, and will die fighting. If they win out, great glory will be theirs."

"The moon does not rise to-night till just before midnight, so we have plenty of time. We shall start from here at ten. If all be well, I shall place you in the Tower with your father in less than a quarter-hour from that. A few minutes will suffice to clothe him in bullet-proof and get on his belt. I shall not be away from the Tower more than a very few minutes, and, please God, long before eleven we shall be safe. Then the Tower can be won in an attack by our mountaineers. Perhaps, when the guns are heard on the ship of war—for there is sure to be firing—the Captain may try to land a shore party. But Rooke will stand in the way, and if I know the man and *The Lady*, we shall not be troubled with many Turks to-night. By midnight you and your father can be on the way to Vissarion. I can interview the naval Captain in the morning."

My wife's marvellous courage and self-possession stood to her. At half an hour before the time fixed she was ready for our adventure. She had improved the scheme in one detail. She had put on her own belt and coiled the rope round her waist, so the only delay would be in bringing her father's belt. She would keep the bullet-proof dress intended to be his strapped in a packet on her back, so that if occasion should be favourable he would not want to put it on till he and she should have reached the platform of the aeroplane. In such case, I should not steer away from the Tower at all, but would pass slowly across it and take up the captive and his brave daughter before leaving. I had learned from local sources that the Tower was in several stories. Entrance was by the foot, where the great iron-clad door was; then came living-rooms and storage, and an open space at the top. This would probably be thought the best place for the prisoner, for it was deep-sunk within the massive walls, wherein was no loophole of any kind. This, if it should so happen, would be the disposition of things best for our plan. The guards would at this time be all inside the Tower—probably resting, most of them—so that it was possible that no one might notice the coming of the airship. I was afraid to think that all might turn out so well, for in such case our task would be a simple enough one, and would in all human probability be crowned with success.

At ten o'clock we started. Teuta did not show the smallest sign of fear or even uneasiness, though this was the first time she had even seen an aeroplane at work. She proved to be an admirable passenger for an airship. She stayed quite still, holding herself rigidly in the position arranged, by the cords which I had fixed for her.

When I had trued my course by the landmarks and with the compass lit by the Tiny my electric light in the dark box, I had time to look about me. All seemed quite dark wherever I looked—to land, or sea, or sky. But darkness is relative, and though each quarter and spot looked dark in turn, there was not such absolute darkness as a whole. I could tell the difference, for instance, between land and sea, no matter how far off we might be from either. Looking upward, the sky was dark; yet there was light enough to see, and even distinguish broad effects. I had no difficulty in distinguishing the Tower towards which we were moving, and that, after all, was the main thing. We drifted slowly, very slowly, as the air was still, and I only used the minimum pressure necessary for the engine. I think I now understood for the first time the extraordinary value of the engine with which my Kitson was equipped. It was noiseless, it was practically of no weight, and it allowed the machine to progress as easily as the old-fashioned balloon used to drift before a breeze. Teuta, who had naturally very fine sight, seemed to see even better than I did, for as we drew nearer to the Tower, and its round, open top began to articulate itself, she commenced to prepare for her part of the task. She it was who uncoiled the long drag-rope ready for her lowering. We were proceeding so gently that she as well as I had hopes that I might be able to actually balance the machine on the top of the curving wall—a thing manifestly impossible on a straight surface, though it might have been possible on an angle.

On we crept—on, and on! There was no sign of light about the Tower, and not the faintest sound to be heard till we were almost close to the line of the rising wall; then we heard a sound of something like mirth, but muffled by distance and thick walls. From it we took fresh heart, for it told us that our enemies were gathered in the lower chambers. If only the Voivode should be on the upper stage, all would be well.

Slowly, almost inch by inch, and with a suspense that was agonizing, we crossed some twenty or thirty feet above the top of the wall. I could see as we came near the jagged line of white patches where the heads of the massacred Turks placed there on spikes in old days seemed to give still their grim warning. Seeing that they made in themselves a difficulty of landing on the wall, I deflected the plane so that, as we crept over the wall, we might, if they became displaced, brush them to the outside of the wall. A few seconds more, and I was able to bring the machine to rest with the front of the platform jutting out beyond the Tower wall. Here I anchored her fore and aft with clamps which had been already prepared.

Whilst I was doing so Teuta had leaned over the inner edge of the platform, and whispered as softly as the sigh of a gentle breeze:

"Hist! hist!" The answer came in a similar sound from some twenty feet below us, and we knew that the prisoner was alone. Forthwith, having fixed the hook of the rope in the ring to which was attached her belt, I lowered my wife. Her father evidently knew her whisper, and was ready. The hollow Tower—a smooth cylinder within—sent up the voices from it faint as were the whispers:

"Father, it is I—Teuta!"

"My child, my brave daughter!"

"Quick, father; strap the belt round you. See that it is secure. We have to be lifted into the air if necessary. Hold together. It will be easier for Rupert to lift us to the airship."

"Rupert?"

"Yes; I shall explain later. Quick, quick! There is not a moment to lose. He is enormously strong, and can lift us together; but we must help him by being still, so he won't have to use the windlass, which might creak." As she spoke she jerked slightly at the rope, which was our preconcerted signal that I was to lift. I was afraid the windlass might creak, and her thoughtful hint decided me. I bent my back to the task, and in a few seconds they were on the platform on which they, at Teuta's suggestion, lay flat, one at each side of my seat, so as to keep the best balance possible.

I took off the clamps, lifted the bags of ballast to the top of the wall, so that there should be no sound of falling, and started the engine. The machine moved forward a few inches, so that it tilted towards the outside of the wall. I threw my weight on the front part of the platform, and we commenced our downward fall at a sharp angle. A second enlarged the angle, and without further ado we slid away into the darkness. Then, ascending as we went, when the engine began to work at its strength, we turned, and presently made straight for Ilsin.

The journey was short—not many minutes. It almost seemed as if no time whatever had elapsed till we saw below us the gleam of lights, and by them saw a great body of men gathered in military array. We slackened and descended. The crowd kept deathly silence, but when we were amongst them we needed no telling that it was not due to lack of heart or absence of joy. The pressure of their hands as they surrounded us, and the devotion with which they kissed the hands and feet of both the Voivode and his daughter, were evidence enough for me, even had I not had my own share of their grateful rejoicing.

In the midst of it all the low, stern voice of Rooke, who had burst a way to the front beside the Vladika, said:

"Now is the time to attack the Tower. Forward, brothers, but in silence. Let there not be a sound till you are near the gate; then play your little comedy of the escaping marauders. And 'twill be no comedy for them in the Tower. The yacht is all ready for the morning, Mr. Sent Leger, in case I do not come out of the scrimmage if the bluejackets arrive. In such case you will have to handle her yourself. God keep you, my Lady; and you, too, Voivode! Forward!"

In a ghostly silence the grim little army moved forwards. Rooke and the men with him disappeared into the darkness in the direction of the harbour of Ilsin.

FROM THE SCRIPT OF THE VOIVODE, PETER VISSARION,

July 7, 1907.

I had little idea, when I started on my homeward journey, that it would have such a strange termination. Even I, who ever since my boyhood have lived in a whirl of adventure, intrigue, or diplomacy—whichever it may be called—statecraft, and war, had reason to be surprised. I certainly thought that when I locked myself into my room in the hotel at Ilsin that I would have at last a spell, however short, of quiet. All the time of my prolonged negotiations with the various nationalities I had to be at tension; so, too, on my homeward journey, lest something at the last moment should happen adversely to my mission. But when I was safe on my own Land of the Blue Mountains, and laid my head on my pillow, where only friends could be around me, I thought I might forget care.

But to wake with a rude hand over my mouth, and to feel myself grasped tight by so many hands that I could not move a limb, was a dreadful shock. All after that was like a dreadful dream. I was rolled in a great rug so tightly that I could hardly breathe, let alone cry out. Lifted by many hands through the window, which I could hear was softly opened and shut for the purpose, and carried to a boat. Again lifted into some sort of litter, on which I was borne a long distance, but with considerable rapidity. Again lifted out and dragged through a doorway opened on purpose—I could hear the clang as it was shut behind me. Then the rug was removed, and I found myself, still in my night-gear, in the midst of a ring of men. There were two score of them, all Turks, all strong-looking, resolute men, armed to the teeth. My clothes, which had been taken from my room, were thrown down beside me, and I was told to dress. As the Turks were going from the room—shaped like a vault—where we then were, the last of them, who seemed to be some sort of officer, said:

"If you cry out or make any noise whatever whilst you are in this Tower, you shall die before your time!" Presently some food and water were brought me, and a couple of blankets. I wrapped myself up and slept till early in the morning. Breakfast was brought, and the same men filed in. In the presence of them all the same officer said:

"I have given instructions that if you make any noise or betray your presence to anyone outside this Tower, the nearest man is to restore you to immediate quiet with his yataghan. It you promise me that you will remain quiet whilst you are within the Tower, I can enlarge your liberties somewhat. Do you promise?" I promised as he wished; there was no need to make necessary any stricter measure of confinement.

Any chance of escape lay in having the utmost freedom allowed to me. Although I had been taken away with such secrecy, I knew that before long there would be pursuit. So I waited with what patience I could. I was allowed to go on the upper platform—a consideration due, I am convinced, to my captors' wish for their own comfort rather than for mine.

It was not very cheering, for during the daytime I had satisfied myself that it would be quite impossible for even a younger and more active man than I am to climb the walls. They were built for prison purposes, and a cat could not find entry for its claws between the stones. I resigned myself to my fate as well as I could. Wrapping my blanket round me, I lay down and looked up at the sky. I wished to see it whilst I could. I was just dropping to sleep—the unutterable silence of the place broken only now and again by some remark by my captors in the rooms below me—when there was a strange appearance just over me—an appearance so strange that I sat up, and gazed with distended eyes.

Across the top of the tower, some height above, drifted, slowly and silently, a great platform. Although the night was dark, it was so much darker where I was within the hollow of the Tower that I could actually see what was above me. I knew it was an aeroplane—one of which I had seen in Washington. A man was seated in the centre, steering; and beside him was a silent figure of a woman all wrapped in white. It made my heart beat to see her, for she was figured something like my Teuta, but broader, less shapely. She leaned over, and a whispered "Ssh!" crept down to me. I answered in similar way. Whereupon she rose, and the man lowered her down into the Tower. Then I saw that it was my dear daughter who had come in this wonderful way to save me. With infinite haste she helped me to fasten round my waist a belt attached to a rope, which was coiled round her; and then the man, who was a giant in strength as well as stature, raised us both to the platform of the aeroplane, which he set in motion without an instant's delay.

Within a few seconds, and without any discovery being made of my escape, we were speeding towards the sea. The lights of Ilsin were in front of us. Before reaching the town, however, we descended in the midst of a little army of my own people, who were gathered ready to advance upon the Silent Tower, there to effect, if necessary, my rescue by force. Small chance would there have been of my life in case of such a struggle. Happily, however, the devotion and courage of my dear daughter and of her gallant companion prevented such a necessity. It was strange to me to find such joyous reception amongst my friends expressed in such a whispered silence. There was no time for comment or understanding or the asking of questions—I was fain to take things as they stood, and wait for fuller explanation.

This came later, when my daughter and I were able to converse alone.

When the expedition went out against the Silent Tower, Teuta and I went to her tent, and with us came her gigantic companion, who seemed not wearied, but almost overcome with sleep. When we came into the tent, over which at a little distance a cordon of our mountaineers stood on guard, he said to me:

"May I ask you, sir, to pardon me for a time, and allow the Voivodin to explain matters to you? She will, I know, so far assist me, for there is so much work still to be done before we are free of the present peril. For myself, I am almost overcome with sleep. For three nights I have had no sleep, but all during that time much labour and more anxiety. I could hold on longer; but at daybreak I must go out to the Turkish warship that lies in the offing. She is a Turk, though she does not confess to it; and she it is who has brought hither the marauders who captured both your daughter and yourself. It is needful that I go, for I hold a personal authority from the National Council to take whatever step may be necessary for our protection. And when I go I should be clear-headed, for war may rest on that meeting. I shall be in the adjoining tent, and shall come at once if I am summoned, in case you wish for me before dawn." Here my daughter struck in:

"Father, ask him to remain here. We shall not disturb him, I am sure, in our talking. And, moreover, if you knew how much I owe to him—to his own bravery and his strength—you would understand how much safer I feel when he is close to me, though we are surrounded by an army of our brave mountaineers."

"But, my daughter," I said, for I was as yet all in ignorance, "there are confidences between father and daughter which none other may share. Some of what has been I know, but I want to know all, and it might be better that no stranger—however valiant he may be, or no matter in what measure we are bound to him—should be present." To my astonishment, she who had always been amenable to my lightest wish actually argued with me:

"Father, there are other confidences which have to be respected in like wise. Bear with me, dear, till I have told you all, and I am right sure that you will agree with me. I ask it, father."

That settled the matter, and as I could see that the gallant gentleman who had rescued me was swaying on his feet as he waited respectfully, I said to him:

"Rest with us, sir. We shall watch over your sleep."

Then I had to help him, for almost on the instant he sank down, and I had to guide him to the rugs spread on the ground. In a few seconds he was in a deep sleep. As I stood looking at him, till I had realized that he was really asleep, I could not help marvelling at the bounty of Nature that could uphold even such a man as this to the last moment of work to be done, and then allow so swift a collapse when all was over, and he could rest peacefully.

He was certainly a splendid fellow. I think I never saw so fine a man physically in my life. And if the lesson of his physiognomy be true, he is as sterling inwardly as his external is fair. "Now," said I to Teuta, "we are to all intents quite alone. Tell me all that has been, so that I may understand."

Whereupon my daughter, making me sit down, knelt beside me, and told me from end to end the most marvellous story I had ever heard or read of. Something of it I had already known from the Archbishop Paleologue's later letters, but of all else I was ignorant. Far away in the great West beyond the Atlantic, and again on the fringe of the Eastern seas, I had been thrilled to my heart's core by the heroic devotion and fortitude of my daughter in yielding herself for her country's sake to that fearful ordeal of the Crypt; of the grief of the nation at her reported death, news of which was so mercifully and wisely withheld from me as long as possible; of the supernatural rumours that took root so deep; but no word or hint had come to me of a man who had come across the orbit of her life, much less of all that has resulted from it. Neither had I known of her being carried off, or of the thrice gallant rescue of her by Rupert. Little wonder that I thought so highly of him even at the first moment I had a clear view of him when he sank down to sleep before me. Why, the man must be a marvel. Even our mountaineers could not match such endurance as his. In the course of her narrative my daughter told me of how, being wearied with her long waiting in the tomb, and waking to find herself alone when the floods were out, and even the Crypt submerged, she sought safety and warmth elsewhere; and how she came to the Castle in the night, and found the strange man alone. I said: "That was dangerous, daughter, if not wrong. The man, brave and devoted as he is, must answer me—your father." At that she was greatly upset, and before going on with her narrative, drew me close in her arms, and whispered to me:

"Be gentle to me, father, for I have had much to bear. And be good to him, for he holds my heart in his breast!" I reassured her with a gentle pressure—there was no need to speak. She then went on to tell me about her marriage, and how her husband, who had fallen into the belief that she was a Vampire, had determined to give even his soul for her; and how she had on the night of the marriage left him and gone back to the tomb to play to the end the grim comedy which she had undertaken to perform till my return; and how, on the second night after her marriage, as she was in the garden of the Castle—going, as she shyly told me, to see if all was well with her husband—she was seized secretly, muffled up, bound, and carried off. Here she made a pause and a digression. Evidently some fear lest her husband and myself should quarrel assailed her, for she said:

"Do understand, father, that Rupert's marriage to me was in all ways regular, and quite in accord with our customs. Before we were married I told the Archbishop of my wish. He, as your representative during your absence, consented himself, and brought the matter to the notice of the Vladika and the Archimandrites. All these concurred, having exacted from me—very properly, I think—a sacred promise to adhere to my self-appointed task. The marriage itself was orthodox in all ways—though so far unusual that it was held at night, and in darkness, save for the lights appointed by the ritual. As to that, the Archbishop himself, or the Archimandrite of Spazac, who assisted him, or the Vladika, who acted as Paranymph, will, all or any of them, give you full details. Your representative made all inquiries as to Rupert Sent Leger, who lived in Vissarion, though he did not know who I was, or from his point of view who I had been. But I must tell you of my rescue."

And so she went on to tell me of that unavailing journey south by her captors; of their bafflement by the cordon which Rupert had established at the first word of danger to "the daughter of our leader," though he little knew who the "leader" was, or who was his "daughter"; of how the brutal marauders tortured her to speed with their daggers; and how her wounds left blood-marks on the ground as she passed along; then of the halt in the valley, when the marauders came to know that their road north was menaced, if not already blocked; of the choosing of the murderers, and their keeping ward over her whilst their companions went to survey the situation; and of her gallant rescue by that noble fellow, her husband—my son I shall call him henceforth, and thank God that I may have that happiness and that honour!

Then my daughter went on to tell me of the race back to Vissarion, when Rupert went ahead of all—as a leader should do; of the summoning of the Archbishop and the National Council; and of their placing the nation's handjar in Rupert's hand; of the journey to Ilsin, and the flight of my daughter—and my son—on the aeroplane.

The rest I knew.

As she finished, the sleeping man stirred and woke—broad awake in a second—sure sign of a man accustomed to campaign and adventure. At a glance he recalled everything that had been, and sprang to his feet. He stood respectfully before me for a few seconds before speaking. Then he said, with an open, engaging smile:

"I see, sir, you know all. Am I forgiven—for Teuta's sake as well as my own?" By this time I was also on my feet. A man like that walks straight into my heart. My daughter, too, had risen, and stood by my side. I put out my hand and grasped his, which seemed to leap to meet me—as only the hand of a swordsman can do.

"I am glad you are my son!" I said. It was all I could say, and I meant it and all it implied. We shook hands warmly. Teuta was pleased; she kissed me, and then stood holding my arm with one hand, whilst she linked her other hand in the arm of her husband.

He summoned one of the sentries without, and told him to ask Captain Rooke to come to him. The latter had been ready for a call, and came at once. When through the open flap of the tent we saw him coming, Rupert—as I must call him now, because Teuta wishes it; and I like to do it myself—said:

"I must be off to board the Turkish vessel before it comes inshore. Good-bye, sir, in case we do not meet again." He said the last few words in so low a voice that I only could hear them. Then he kissed his wife, and told her he expected to be back in time for breakfast, and was gone. He met Rooke—I am hardly accustomed to call him Captain as yet, though, indeed, he well deserves it—at the edge of the cordon of sentries, and they went quickly together towards the port, where the yacht was lying with steam up.

BOOK VII: THE EMPIRE OF THE AIR

FROM THE REPORT OF CRISTOFEROS, WAR-SCRIBE TO THE NATIONAL COUNCIL.

July 7, 1907.

When the Gospodar Rupert and Captain Rooke came within hailing distance of the strange ship, the former hailed her, using one after another the languages of England, Germany, France, Russia, Turkey, Greece, Spain, Portugal, and another which I did not know; I think it must have been American. By this time the whole line of the bulwark was covered by a row of Turkish faces. When, in Turkish, the Gospodar asked for the Captain, the latter came to the gangway, which had been opened, and stood there. His uniform was that of the Turkish navy—of that I am prepared to swear—but he made signs of not understanding what had been said; whereupon the Gospodar spoke again, but in French this time. I append the exact conversation which took place, none other joining in it. I took down in shorthand the words of both as they were spoken:

THE GOSPODAR. "Are you the Captain of this ship?"

THE CAPTAIN. "I am."

GOSPODAR. "To what nationality do you belong?"

CAPTAIN. "It matters not. I am Captain of this ship."

GOSPODAR. "I alluded to your ship. What national flag is she under?"

CAPTAIN (*throwing his eye over the top-hamper*). "I do not see that any flag is flying."

GOSPODAR. "I take it that, as commander, you can allow me on board with my two companions?"

CAPTAIN. "I can, upon proper request being made!"

GOSPODAR (*taking off his cap*). "I ask your courtesy, Captain. I am the representative and accredited officer of the National Council of the Land of the Blue Mountains, in whose waters you now are; and on their account I ask for a formal interview on urgent matters."

The Turk, who was, I am bound to say, in manner most courteous as yet, gave some command to his officers, whereupon the companion-ladders and stage were lowered and the gangway manned, as is usual for the reception on a ship of war of an honoured guest.

CAPTAIN. "You are welcome, sir—you and your two companions—as you request."

The Gospodar bowed. Our companion-ladder was rigged on the instant, and a launch lowered. The Gospodar and Captain Rooke—taking me with them—entered, and rowed to the warship, where we were all honourably received. There were an immense number of men on board, soldiers as well as seamen. It looked more like a warlike expedition than a fighting-ship in time of peace. As we stepped on the deck, the seamen and marines, who were all armed as at drill, presented arms. The Gospodar went first towards the Captain, and Captain Rooke and I followed close behind him. The Gospodar spoke:

"I am Rupert Sent Leger, a subject of his Britannic Majesty, presently residing at Vissarion, in the Land of the Blue Mountains. I am at present empowered to act for the National Council in all matters. Here is my credential!" As he spoke he handed to the Captain a letter. It was written in five different languages—Balkan, Turkish, Greek, English, and French. The Captain read it carefully all through, forgetful for the moment that he had seemingly been unable to understand the Gospodar's question spoken in the Turkish tongue. Then he answered:

"I see the document is complete. May I ask on what subject you wish to see me?"

GOSPODAR. "You are here in a ship of war in Blue Mountain waters, yet you fly no flag of any nation. You have sent armed men ashore in your boats, thus committing an act of war. The National Council of the Land of the Blue Mountains requires to know what nation you serve, and why the obligations of international law are thus broken."

The Captain seemed to wait for further speech, but the Gospodar remained silent; whereupon the former spoke.

CAPTAIN. "I am responsible to my own—chiefs. I refuse to answer your question."

The Gospodar spoke at once in reply.

GOSPODAR. "Then, sir, you, as commander of a ship—and especially a ship of war—must know that in thus violating national and maritime laws you, and all on board this ship, are guilty of an act of piracy. This is not even piracy on the high seas. You are not merely within territorial waters, but you have invaded a national port. As you refuse to disclose the nationality of your ship, I accept, as you seem to do, your status as that of a pirate, and shall in due season act accordingly."

CAPTAIN (*with manifest hostility*). "I accept the responsibility of my own acts. Without admitting your contention, I tell you now that whatever action you take shall be at your own peril and that of your National Council. Moreover, I have reason to believe that my men who were sent ashore on special service have been beleaguered in a tower which can be seen from the ship. Before dawn this morning firing was heard from that direction, from which I gather that attack was made on them. They, being only a small party, may have been murdered. If such be so, I tell you that you and your miserable little nation, as you call it, shall pay such blood-money as you never thought of. I am responsible for this, and, by Allah! there shall be a great revenge. You have not in all your navy—if navy you have at all—power to cope with even one ship like this, which is but one of many. My guns shall be trained on Ilsin, to which end I have come inshore. You and your companions have free conduct back to port; such is due to the white flag which you fly. Fifteen minutes will bring you back whence you came. Go! And remember that whatever you may do amongst your mountain defiles, at sea you cannot even defend yourselves."

GOSPODAR (*slowly and in a ringing voice*). "The Land of the Blue Mountains has its own defences on sea and land. Its people know how to defend themselves."

CAPTAIN (*taking out his watch*). "It is now close on five bells. At the first stroke of six bells our guns shall open fire."

GOSPODAR (*calmly*). "It is my last duty to warn you, sir—and to warn all on this ship—that much may happen before even the first stroke of six bells. Be warned in time, and give over this piratical attack, the very threat of which may be the cause of much bloodshed."

CAPTAIN (*violently*). "Do you dare to threaten me, and, moreover, my ship's company? We are one, I tell you, in this ship; and the last man shall perish like the first ere this enterprise fail. Go!"

With a bow, the Gospodar turned and went down the ladder, we following him. In a couple of minutes the yacht was on her way to the port.

FROM RUPERT'S JOURNAL.

July 10, 1907.

When we turned shoreward after my stormy interview with the pirate Captain—I can call him nothing else at present, Rooke gave orders to a quartermaster on the bridge, and *The Lady* began to make to a little northward of Ilsin port. Rooke himself went aft to the wheel-house, taking several men with him.

When we were quite near the rocks—the water is so deep here that there is no danger—we slowed down, merely drifting along southwards towards the port. I was myself on the bridge, and could see all over the decks. I could also see preparations going on upon the warship. Ports were opened, and the great guns on the turrets were lowered for action. When we were starboard broadside on to the warship, I saw the port side of the steering-house open, and Rooke's men sliding out what looked like a huge grey crab, which by tackle from within the wheel-house was lowered softly into the sea. The position of the yacht hid the operation from sight of the warship. The doors were shut again, and the yacht's pace began to quicken. We ran into the port. I had a vague idea that Rooke had some desperate project on hand. Not for nothing had he kept the wheel-house locked on that mysterious crab.

All along the frontage was a great crowd of eager men. But they had considerately left the little mole at the southern entrance, whereon was a little tower, on whose round top a signal-gun was placed, free for my own use. When I was landed on this pier I went along to the end, and, climbing the narrow stair within, went out on the sloping roof. I stood up, for I was determined to show the Turks that I was not afraid for myself, as they would understand when the bombardment should begin. It was now but a very few minutes before the fatal hour—six bells. But all the same I was almost in a state of despair. It was terrible to think of all those poor souls in the town who had done nothing wrong, and who were to be wiped out in the coming bloodthirsty, wanton attack. I raised my glasses to see how preparations were going on upon the warship.

As I looked I had a momentary fear that my eyesight was giving way. At one moment I had the deck of the warship focussed with my glasses, and could see every detail as the gunners waited for the word to begin the bombardment with the great guns of the barbettes. The next I saw nothing but the empty sea. Then in another instant there was the ship as before, but the details were blurred. I steadied myself against the signal-gun, and looked again. Not more than two, or at the most three, seconds had elapsed. The ship was, for the moment, full in view. As I looked, she gave a queer kind of quick shiver, prow and stern, and then sideways. It was for all the world like a rat shaken in the mouth of a skilled terrier. Then she remained still, the one placid thing to be seen, for all around her the sea seemed to shiver in little independent eddies, as when water is broken without a current to guide it.

I continued to look, and when the deck was, or seemed, quite still—for the shivering water round the ship kept catching my eyes through the outer rays of the lenses—I noticed that nothing was stirring. The men who had been at the guns were all lying down; the men in the fighting-tops had leaned forward or backward, and their arms hung down helplessly. Everywhere was desolation—in so far as life was concerned. Even a little brown bear, which had been seated on the cannon which was being put into range position, had jumped or fallen on deck, and lay there stretched out—and still. It was evident that some terrible shock had been given to the mighty war-vessel. Without a doubt or a thought why I did so, I turned my eyes towards where *The Lady* lay, port broadside now to the inside, in the harbour mouth. I had the key now to the mystery of Rooke's proceedings with the great grey crab.

As I looked I saw just outside the harbour a thin line of cleaving water. This became more marked each instant, till a steel disc with glass eyes that shone in the light of the sun rose above the water. It was about the size of a beehive, and was shaped like one. It made a straight line for the aft of the yacht. At the same moment, in obedience to some command, given so quietly that I did not hear it, the men went below—all save some few, who began to open out doors in the port side of the wheel-house. The tackle was run out through an opened gangway on that side, and a man stood on the great hook at the lower end, balancing himself by hanging on the chain. In a few seconds he came up again. The chain tightened and the great grey crab rose over the edge of the deck, and was drawn into the wheel-house, the doors of which were closed, shutting in a few only of the men.

I waited, quite quiet. After a space of a few minutes, Captain Rooke in his uniform walked out of the wheel-house. He entered a small boat, which had been in the meantime lowered for the purpose, and was rowed to the steps on the mole. Ascending these, he came directly towards the signal-tower. When he had ascended and stood beside me, he saluted.

"Well?" I asked.

"All well, sir," he answered. "We shan't have any more trouble with that lot, I think. You warned that pirate—I wish he had been in truth a clean, honest, straightforward pirate, instead of the measly Turkish swab he was—that something might occur before the first stroke of six bells. Well, something has occurred, and for him and all his crew that six bells will never sound. So the Lord fights for the Cross against the Crescent! Bismillah. Amen!" He said this in a manifestly formal way, as though declaiming a ritual. The next instant he went on in the thoroughly practical conventional way which was usual to him:

"May I ask a favour, Mr. Sent Leger?"

"A thousand, my dear Rooke," I said. "You can't ask me anything which I shall not freely grant. And I speak within my brief from the National Council. You have saved Ilsin this day, and the Council will thank you for it in due time."

"Me, sir?" he said, with a look of surprise on his face which seemed quite genuine. "If you think that, I am well out of it. I was afraid, when I woke, that you might court-martial me!"

"Court-martial you! What for?" I asked, surprised in my turn.

"For going to sleep on duty, sir! And the fact is, I was worn out in the attack on the Silent Tower last night, and when you had your interview with the pirate—all good pirates forgive me for the blasphemy! Amen!—and I knew that everything was going smoothly, I went into the wheel-house and took forty winks." He said all this without moving so much as an eyelid, from which I gathered that he wished absolute silence to be observed on my part. Whilst I was revolving this in my mind he went on:

"Touching that request, sir. When I have left you and the Voivode—and the Voivodin, of course—at Vissarion, together with such others as you may choose to bring there with you, may I bring the yacht back here for a spell? I rather think that there is a good deal of cleaning up to be done, and the crew of *The Lady* with myself are the men to do it. We shall be back by nightfall at the creek."

"Do as you think best, Admiral Rooke," I said.

"Admiral?"

"Yes, Admiral. At present I can only say that tentatively, but by to-morrow I am sure the National Council will have confirmed it. I am afraid, old friend, that your squadron will be only your flagship for the present; but later we may do better."

"So long as I am Admiral, your honour, I shall have no other flagship than *The Lady*. I am not a young man, but, young or old, my pennon shall float over no other deck. Now, one other favour, Mr. Sent Leger? It is a corollary of the first, so I do not hesitate to ask. May I appoint Lieutenant Desmond, my present First Officer, to the command of the battleship? Of course, he will at first only command the prize crew; but in such case he will fairly expect the confirmation of his rank later. I had better, perhaps, tell you, sir, that he is a very capable seaman, learned in all the sciences that pertain to a battleship, and bred in the first navy in the world."

"By all means, Admiral. Your nomination shall, I think I may promise you, be confirmed."

Not another word we spoke. I returned with him in his boat to *The Lady*, which was brought to the dock wall, where we were received with tumultuous cheering.

I hurried off to my Wife and the Voivode. Rooke, calling Desmond to him, went on the bridge of *The Lady*, which turned, and went out at terrific speed to the battleship, which was already drifting up northward on the tide.

FROM THE REPORT OF CRISTOFEROS, SCRIBE OF THE NATIONAL COUNCIL OF THE LAND OF THE BLUE MOUNTAINS.

July 8, 1907.

The meeting of the National Council, July 6, was but a continuation of that held before the rescue of the Voivodin Vissarion, the members of the Council having been during the intervening night housed in the Castle of Vissarion. When, in the early morning, they met, all were jubilant; for late at night the fire-signal had flamed up from Ilsin with the glad news that the Voivode Peter Vissarion was safe, having been rescued with great daring on an aeroplane by his daughter and the Gospodar Rupert, as the people call him—Mister Rupert Sent Leger, as he is in his British name and degree.

Whilst the Council was sitting, word came that a great peril to the town of Ilsin had been averted. A war-vessel acknowledging to no nationality, and therefore to be deemed a pirate, had threatened to bombard the town; but just before the time fixed for the fulfilment of her threat, she was shaken to such an extent by some sub-aqueous means that, though she herself was seemingly uninjured, nothing was left alive on board. Thus the Lord preserves His own! The consideration of this, as well as the other incident, was postponed until the coming Voivode and the Gospodar Rupert, together with who were already on their way hither.

THE SAME (LATER IN THE SAME DAY).

The Council resumed its sitting at four o'clock. The Voivode Peter Vissarion and the Voivodin Teuta had arrived with the "Gospodar Rupert," as the mountaineers call him (Mr. Rupert Sent Leger) on the armoured yacht he calls *The Lady*. The National Council showed great pleasure when the Voivode entered the hall in which the Council met. He seemed much gratified by the reception given to him. Mr. Rupert Sent Leger, by the express desire of the Council, was asked to be present at the meeting. He took a seat at the bottom of the hall, and seemed to prefer to remain there, though asked by the President of the Council to sit at the top of the table with himself and the Voivode.

When the formalities of such Councils had been completed, the Voivode handed to the President a memorandum of his report on his secret mission to foreign Courts on behalf of the National Council. He then explained at length, for the benefit of the various members of the Council, the broad results of his mission. The result was, he said, absolutely satisfactory. Everywhere he had been received with distinguished courtesy, and given a sympathetic hearing. Several of the Powers consulted had made delay in giving final answers, but this, he explained, was necessarily due to new considerations arising from the international complications which were universally dealt with throughout the world as "the Balkan Crisis." In time, however (the Voivode went on), these matters became so far declared as to allow the waiting Powers to form definite judgment—which, of course, they did not declare to him—as to their own ultimate action. The final result—if at this initial stage such tentative setting forth of their own attitude in each case can be so named—was that he returned full of hope (founded, he might say, upon a justifiable personal belief) that the Great Powers throughout the world—North, South, East, and West—were in thorough sympathy with the Land of the Blue Mountains in its aspirations for the continuance of its freedom. "I also am honoured," he continued, "to bring to you, the Great Council of the nation, the assurance of protection against unworthy aggression on the part of neighbouring nations of present greater strength."

Whilst he was speaking, the Gospodar Rupert was writing a few words on a strip of paper, which he sent up to the President. When the Voivode had finished speaking, there was a prolonged silence. The President rose, and in a hush said that the Council would like to hear Mr. Rupert Sent Leger, who had a communication to make regarding certain recent events.

THE SAME (LATER IN THE SAME DAY).

Mr. Rupert Sent Leger rose, and reported how, since he had been entrusted by the Council with the rescue of the Voivode Peter of Vissarion, he had, by aid of the Voivodin, effected the escape of the Voivode from the Silent Tower; also that, following this happy event, the mountaineers, who had made a great cordon round the Tower so soon as it was known that the Voivode had been imprisoned within it, had stormed it in the night. As a determined resistance was offered by the marauders, who had used it as a place of refuge, none of these escaped. He then went on to tell how he sought interview with the Captain of the strange warship, which, without flying any flag, invaded our waters. He asked the President to call on me to read the report of that meeting. This, in obedience to his direction, I did. The acquiescent murmuring of the Council showed how thoroughly they endorsed Mr. Sent Leger's words and acts.

When I resumed my seat, Mr. Sent Leger described how, just before the time fixed by the "pirate Captain"—so he designated him, as did every speaker thereafter—the warship met with some under-sea accident, which had a destructive effect on all on board her. Then he added certain words, which I give verbatim, as I am sure that others will some time wish to remember them in their exactness:

"By the way, President and Lords of the Council, I trust I may ask you to confirm Captain Rooke, of the armoured yacht *The Lady*, to be Admiral of the Squadron of the Land of the Blue Mountains, and also Captain (tentatively) Desmond, late First-Lieutenant of *The Lady*, to the command of the second warship of our fleet—the as yet unnamed vessel, whose former Captain threatened to bombard Ilsin. My Lords, Admiral Rooke has done great service to the Land of the Blue Mountains, and deserves well at your hands. You will have in him, I am sure, a great official. One who will till his last breath give you good and loyal service."

He had sat down, the President put to the Council resolutions, which were passed by acclamation. Admiral Rooke was given command of the navy, and Captain Desmond confirmed in his appointment to the captaincy of the new ship, which was, by a further resolution, named *The Gospodar Rupert*.

In thanking the Council for acceding to his request, and for the great honour done him in the naming of the ship, Mr. Sent Leger said:

"May I ask that the armoured yacht *The Lady* be accepted by you, the National Council, on behalf of the nation, as a gift on behalf of the cause of freedom from the Voivodin Teuta?"

In response to the mighty cheer of the Council with which the splendid gift was accepted the Gospodar Rupert—Mr. Sent Leger—bowed, and went quietly out of the room.

As no agenda of the meeting had been prepared, there was for a time, not silence, but much individual conversation. In the midst of it the Voivode rose up, whereupon there was a strict silence. All listened with an intensity of eagerness whilst he spoke.

"President and Lords of the Council, Archbishop, and Vladika, I should but ill show my respect did I hesitate to tell you at this the first opportunity I have had of certain matters personal primarily to myself, but which, in the progress of recent events, have come to impinge on the affairs of the nation. Until I have done so, I shall not feel that I have done a duty, long due to you or your predecessors in office, and which I hope you will allow me to say that I have only kept back for purposes of statecraft. May I ask that you will come back with me in memory to the year 1890, when our struggle against Ottoman aggression, later on so successfully brought to a close, was begun. We were then in a desperate condition. Our finances had run so low that we could not purchase even the bread which we required. Nay, more, we could not procure through the National Exchequer what we wanted more than bread—arms of modern effectiveness; for men may endure hunger and yet fight well, as the glorious past of our country has proved again and again and again. But when our foes are better armed than we are, the penalty is dreadful to a nation small as our own is in number, no matter how brave their hearts. In this strait I myself had to secretly raise a sufficient sum of money to procure the weapons we needed. To this end I sought the assistance of a great merchant-prince, to whom our nation as well as myself was known. He met me in the same generous spirit which he had shown to other struggling nationalities throughout a long and honourable career. When I pledged to him as security my own estates, he wished to tear up the bond, and only under pressure would he meet my wishes in this respect. Lords of the Council, it was his money, thus generously advanced, which procured for us the arms with which we hewed out our freedom.

"Not long ago that noble merchant—and here I trust you will pardon me that I am so moved as to perhaps appear to suffer in want of respect to this great Council—this noble merchant passed to his account—leaving to a near kinsman of his own the royal fortune which he had amassed. Only a few hours ago that worthy kinsman of the benefactor of our nation made it known to me that in his last will he had bequeathed to me, by secret trust, the whole of those estates which long ago I had forfeited by effluxion of time, inasmuch as I had been unable to fulfil the terms of my voluntary bond. It grieves me to think that I have had to keep you so long in ignorance of the good thought and wishes and acts of this great man.

"But it was by his wise counsel, fortified by my own judgment, that I was silent; for, indeed, I feared, as he did, lest in our troublous times some doubting spirit without our boundaries, or even within it, might mistrust the honesty of my purposes for public good, because I was no longer one whose whole fortune was invested within our confines. This prince-merchant, the great English Roger Melton—let his name be for ever graven on the hearts of our people!—kept silent during his own life, and enjoined on others to come after him to keep secret from the men of the Blue Mountains that secret loan made to me on their behalf, lest in their eyes I, who had striven to be their friend and helper, should suffer wrong repute. But, happily, he has left me free to clear myself in your eyes. Moreover, by arranging to have—under certain contingencies, which have come to pass—the estates which were originally my own retransferred to me, I have no longer the honour of having given what I could to the national cause. All such now belongs to him; for it was his money—and his only—which purchased our national armament.

"His worthy kinsman you already know, for he has not only been amongst you for many months, but has already done you good service in his own person. He it was who, as a mighty warrior, answered the summons of the Vladika when misfortune came upon my house in the capture by enemies of my dear daughter, the Voivodin Teuta, whom you hold in your hearts; who, with a chosen band of our brothers, pursued the marauders, and himself, by a deed of daring and prowess, of which poets shall hereafter sing, saved her, when hope itself seemed to be dead, from their ruthless hands, and brought her back to us; who administered condign punishment to the miscreants who had dared to so wrong her. He it was who later took me, your servant, out of the prison wherein another band of Turkish miscreants held me captive; rescued me, with the help of my dear daughter, whom he had already freed, whilst I had on my person the documents of international secrecy of which I have already advised you—rescued me whilst I had been as yet unsubjected to the indignity of search.

"Beyond this you know now that of which I was in partial ignorance: how he had, through the skill and devotion of your new Admiral, wrought destruction on a hecatomb of our malignant foes. You who have received for the nation the splendid gift of the little warship, which already represents a new era in naval armament, can understand the great-souled generosity of the man who has restored the vast possessions of my House. On our way hither from Ilsin, Rupert Sent Leger made known to me the terms of the trust of his noble uncle, Roger Melton, and—believe me that he did so generously, with a joy that transcended my own—restored to the last male of the Vissarion race the whole inheritance of a noble line.

"And now, my Lords of the Council, I come to another matter, in which I find myself in something of a difficulty, for I am aware that in certain ways you actually know more of it than even I myself do. It is regarding the marriage of my daughter to Rupert Sent Leger. It is known to me that the matter has been brought before you by the Archbishop, who, as guardian of my daughter during my absence on the service of the nation, wished to obtain your sanction, as till my return he held her safety in trust. This was so, not from any merit of mine, but because she, in her own person, had undertaken for the service of our nation a task of almost incredible difficulty. My Lords, were she child of another father, I should extol to the skies her bravery, her self-devotion, her loyalty to the land she loves. Why, then, should I hesitate to speak of her deeds in fitting terms, since it is my duty, my glory, to hold them in higher honour than can any in this land? I shall not shame her—or even myself—by being silent when such a duty urges me to speak, as Voivode, as trusted envoy of our nation, as father. Ages hence loyal men and women of our Land of the Blue Mountains will sing her deeds in song and tell them in story. Her name, Teuta, already sacred in these regions, where it was held by a great Queen, and honoured by all men, will hereafter be held as a symbol and type of woman's devotion. Oh, my Lords, we pass along the path of life, the best of us but a little time marching in the sunlight between gloom and gloom, and it is during that march that we must be judged for the future. This brave woman has won knightly spurs as well as any Paladin of old. So is it meet that ere she might mate with one worthy of her you, who hold in your hands the safety and honour of the State, should give your approval. To you was it given to sit in judgment on the worth of this gallant Englisher, now my son. You judged him then, before you had seen his valour, his strength, and skill exercised on behalf of a national cause. You judged wisely, oh, my brothers, and out of a grateful heart I thank you one and all for it. Well has he justified your trust by his later acts. When, in obedience to the summons of the Vladika, he put the nation in a blaze and ranged our boundaries with a ring of steel, he did so unknowing that what was dearest to him in the world was at stake. He saved my daughter's honour and happiness, and won her safety by an act of valour that outvies any told in history. He took my daughter with him to bring me out from the Silent Tower on the wings of the air, when earth had for me no possibility of freedom—I, that had even then in my possession the documents involving other nations which the Soldan would fain have purchased with the half of his empire.

"Henceforth to me, Lords of the Council, this brave man must ever be as a son of my heart, and I trust that in his name grandsons of my own may keep in bright honour the name which in glorious days of old my fathers made illustrious. Did I know how adequately to thank you for your interest in my child, I would yield up to you my very soul in thanks."

The speech of the Voivode was received with the honour of the Blue Mountains—the drawing and raising of handjars.

FROM RUPERT'S JOURNAL.

July 14, 1907.

For nearly a week we waited for some message from Constantinople, fully expecting either a declaration of war, or else some inquiry so couched as to make war an inevitable result. The National Council remained on at Vissarion as the guests of the Voivode, to whom, in accordance with my uncle's will, I had prepared to re-transfer all his estates. He was, by the way, unwilling at first to accept, and it was only when I showed him Uncle Roger's letter, and made him read the Deed of Transfer prepared in anticipation by Mr. Trent, that he allowed me to persuade him. Finally he said:

"As you, my good friends, have so arranged, I must accept, be it only in honour to the wishes of the dead. But remember, I only do so but for the present, reserving to myself the freedom to withdraw later if I so desire."

But Constantinople was silent. The whole nefarious scheme was one of the "put-up jobs" which are part of the dirty work of a certain order of statecraft—to be accepted if successful; to be denied in case of failure.

The matter stood thus: Turkey had thrown the dice—and lost. Her men were dead; her ship was forfeit. It was only some ten days after the warship was left derelict with every living thing—that is, everything that had been living—with its neck broken, as Rooke informed me, when he brought the ship down the creek, and housed it in the dock behind the armoured gates—that we saw an item in *The Roma* copied from *The Constantinople Journal* of July 9:

> "LOSS OF AN OTTOMAN IRONCLAD WITH ALL HANDS.
>
> "News has been received at Constantinople of the total loss, with all hands, of one of the newest and finest warships in the Turkish fleet—*The Mahmoud*, Captain Ali Ali—which foundered in a storm on the night of July 5, some distance off Cabrera, in the Balearic Isles. There were no survivors, and no wreckage was discovered by the ships which went in relief—the *Pera* and the *Mustapha*—or reported from anywhere along the shores of the islands, of which exhaustive search was made. *The Mahmoud* was double-manned, as she carried a full extra crew sent on an educational cruise on the most perfectly scientifically equipped warship on service in the Mediterranean waters."

When the Voivode and I talked over the matter, he said:

"After all, Turkey is a shrewd Power. She certainly seems to know when she is beaten, and does not intend to make a bad thing seem worse in the eyes of the world."

Well, 'tis a bad wind that blows good to nobody. As *The Mahmoud* was lost off the Balearics, it cannot have been her that put the marauders on shore and trained her big guns on Ilsin. We take it, therefore, that the latter must have been a pirate, and as we have taken her derelict in our waters, she is now ours in all ways. Anyhow, she is ours, and is the first ship of her class in the navy of the Blue Mountains. I am inclined to think that even if she was—or is still—a Turkish ship, Admiral Rooke would not be inclined to let her go. As for Captain Desmond, I think he would go straight out of his mind if such a thing was to be even suggested to him.

It will be a pity if we have any more trouble, for life here is very happy with us all now. The Voivode is, I think, like a man in a dream. Teuta is ideally happy, and the real affection which sprang up between them when she and Aunt Janet met is a joy to think of. I had posted Teuta about her, so that when they should meet my wife might not, by any inadvertence, receive or cause any pain. But the moment Teuta saw her she ran straight over to her and lifted her in her strong young arms, and, raising her up as one would lift a child, kissed her. Then, when she had put her sitting in the chair from which she had arisen when we entered the room, she knelt down before her, and put her face down in her lap. Aunt Janet's face was a study; I myself could hardly say whether at the first moment surprise or joy predominated. But there could be no doubt about it the instant after. She seemed to beam with happiness. When Teuta knelt to her, she could only say:

"My dear, my dear, I am glad! Rupert's wife, you and I must love each other very much." Seeing that they were laughing and crying in each other's arms, I thought it best to come away and leave them alone. And I didn't feel a bit lonely either when I was out of sight of them. I knew that where those two dear women were there was a place for my own heart.

When I came back, Teuta was sitting on Aunt Janet's knee. It seemed rather stupendous for the old lady, for Teuta is such a splendid creature that even when she sits on my own knee and I catch a glimpse of us in some mirror, I cannot but notice what a nobly-built girl she is.

My wife was jumping up as soon as I was seen, but Aunt Janet held her tight to her, and said:

"Don't stir, dear. It is such happiness to me to have you there. Rupert has always been my 'little boy,' and, in spite of all his being such a giant, he is so still. And so you, that he loves, must be my little girl—in spite of all your beauty and your strength—and sit on my knee, till you can place there a little one that shall be dear to us all, and that shall let me feel my youth again. When first I saw you I was surprised, for, somehow, though I had never seen you nor even heard of you, I seemed to know your face. Sit where you are, dear. It is only Rupert—and we both love him."

Teuta looked at me, flushing rosily; but she sat quiet, and drew the old lady's white head on her young breast.

JANET MACKELPIE'S NOTES.

July 8, 1907.

I used to think that whenever Rupert should get married or start on the way to it by getting engaged—I would meet his future wife with something of the same affection that I have always had for himself. But I know now that what was really in my mind was *jealousy*, and that I was really fighting against my own instincts, and pretending to myself that I was not jealous. Had I ever had the faintest idea that she would be anything the least like Teuta, that sort of feeling should never have had even a foothold. No wonder my dear boy is in love with her, for, truth to tell, I am in love with her myself. I don't think I ever met a creature—a woman creature, of course, I mean—with so many splendid qualities. I almost fear to say it, lest it should seem to myself wrong; but I think she is as good as a woman as Rupert is as a man. And what more than that can I say? I thought I loved her and trusted her, and knew her all I could, until this morning.

I was in my own room, as it is still called. For, though Rupert tells me in confidence that under his uncle's will the whole estate of Vissarion, Castle and all, really belongs to the Voivode, and though the Voivode has been persuaded to accept the position, he (the Voivode) will not allow anything to be changed. He will not even hear a word of my going, or changing my room, or anything. And Rupert backs him up in it, and Teuta too. So what am I to do but let the dears have their way?

Well, this morning, when Rupert was with the Voivode at a meeting of the National Council in the Great Hall, Teuta came to me, and (after closing the door and bolting it, which surprised me a little) came and knelt down beside me, and put her face in my lap. I stroked her beautiful black hair, and said:

"What is it, Teuta darling? Is there any trouble? And why did you bolt the door? Has anything happened to Rupert?" When she looked up I saw that her beautiful black eyes, with the stars in them, were overflowing with tears not yet shed. But she smiled through them, and the tears did not fall. When I saw her smile my heart was eased, and I said without thinking: "Thank God, darling, Rupert is all right."

"I thank God, too, dear Aunt Janet!" she said softly; and I took her in my arms and laid her head on my breast.

"Go on, dear," I said; "tell me what it is that troubles you?" This time I saw the tears drop, as she lowered her head and hid her face from me.

"I'm afraid I have deceived you, Aunt Janet, and that you will not—cannot—forgive me."

"Lord save you, child!" I said, "there's nothing that you could do that I could not and would not forgive. Not that you would ever do anything base, for that is the only thing that is hard to forgive. Tell me now what troubles you."

She looked up in my eyes fearlessly, this time with only the signs of tears that had been, and said proudly:

"Nothing base, Aunt Janet. My father's daughter would not willingly be base. I do not think she could. Moreover, had I ever done anything base I should not be here, for—for—I should never have been Rupert's wife!"

"Then what is it? Tell your old Aunt Janet, dearie." She answered me with another question:

"Aunt Janet, do you know who I am, and how I first met Rupert?"

"You are the Voivodin Teuta Vissarion—the daughter of the Voivode—Or, rather, you were; you are now Mrs. Rupert Sent Leger. For he is still an Englishman, and a good subject of our noble King."

"Yes, Aunt Janet," she said, "I am that, and proud to be it—prouder than I would be were I my namesake, who was Queen in the old days. But how and where did I see Rupert first?" I did not know, and frankly told her so. So she answered her question herself:

"I saw him first in his own room at night." I knew in my heart that in whatever she did had been nothing wrong, so I sat silent waiting for her to go on:

"I was in danger, and in deadly fear. I was afraid I might die—not that I fear death—and I wanted help and warmth. I was not dressed as I am now!"

On the instant it came to me how I knew her face, even the first time I had seen it. I wished to help her out of the embarrassing part of her confidence, so I said:

"Dearie, I think I know. Tell me, child, will you put on the frock . . . the dress . . . costume you wore that night, and let me see you in it? It is not mere idle curiosity, my child, but something far, far above such idle folly."

"Wait for me a minute, Aunt Janet," she said, as she rose up; "I shall not be long." Then she left the room.

In a very few minutes she was back. Her appearance might have frightened some people, for she was clad only in a shroud. Her feet were bare, and she walked across the room with the gait of an empress, and stood before me with her eyes modestly cast down. But when presently she looked up and caught my eyes, a smile rippled over her face. She threw herself once more before me on her knees, and embraced me as she said:

"I was afraid I might frighten you, dear." I knew I could truthfully reassure her as to that, so I proceeded to do so:

"Do not worry yourself, my dear. I am not by nature timid. I come of a fighting stock which has sent out heroes, and I belong to a family wherein is the gift of Second Sight. Why should we fear? We know! Moreover, I saw you in that dress before. Teuta, I saw you and Rupert married!" This time she herself it was that seemed disconcerted.

"Saw us married! How on earth did you manage to be there?"

"I was not there. My Seeing was long before! Tell me, dear, what day, or rather what night, was it that you first saw Rupert?" She answered sadly:

"I do not know. Alas! I lost count of the days as I lay in the tomb in that dreary Crypt."

"Was your—your clothing wet that night?" I asked.

"Yes. I had to leave the Crypt, for a great flood was out, and the church was flooded. I had to seek help—warmth—for I feared I might die. Oh, I was not, as I have told you, afraid of death. But I had undertaken a terrible task to which I had pledged myself. It was for my father's sake, and the sake of the Land, and I felt that it was a part of my duty to live. And so I lived on, when death would have been relief. It was to tell you all about this that I came to your room to-day. But how did you see me—us—married?"

"Ah, my child!" I answered, "that was before the marriage took place. The morn after the night that you came in the wet, when, having been troubled in uncanny dreaming, I came to see if Rupert was a'richt, I lost remembrance o' my dreaming, for the floor was all wet, and that took off my attention. But later, the morn after Rupert used his fire in his room for the first time, I told him what I had dreamt; for, lassie, my dear, I saw ye as bride at that weddin' in fine lace o'er yer shrood, and orange-flowers and ithers in yer black hair; an' I saw the stars in yer bonny een—the een I love. But oh, my dear, when I saw the shrood, and kent what it might mean, I ex-peckit to see the worms crawl round yer feet. But do ye ask yer man to tell ye what I tell't him that morn. 'Twill interest ye to know how the hairt o' men can learn by dreams. Has he ever tellt ye aught o' this?"

"No, dear," she said simply. "I think that perhaps he was afraid that one or other of us, if not both, might be upset by it if he did. You see, he did not tell you anything at all of our meeting, though I am sure that he will be glad when he knows that we both know all about it, and have told each other everything."

That was very sweet of her, and very thoughtful in all ways, so I said that which I thought would please her best—that is, the truth:

"Ah, lassie, that is what a wife should be—what a wife should do. Rupert is blessed and happy to have his heart in your keeping."

I knew from the added warmth of her kiss what I had said had pleased her.

Letter from Ernest Roger Halbard Melton, Humcroft, Salop, to Rupert Sent Leger, Vissarion, Land of the Blue Mountains.

July 29, 1907.

MY DEAR COUSIN RUPERT,

We have heard such glowing accounts of Vissarion that I am coming out to see you. As you are yourself now a landowner, you will understand that my coming is not altogether a pleasure. Indeed, it is a duty first. When my father dies I shall be head of the family—the family of which Uncle Roger, to whom we were related, was a member. It is therefore meet and fitting that I should know something of our family branches and of their Seats. I am not giving you time for much warning, so am coming on immediately—in fact, I shall arrive almost as soon as this letter. But I want to catch you in the middle of your tricks. I hear that the Blue Mountaineer girls are peaches, so don't send them *all* away when you hear I'm coming!

Do send a yacht up to Fiume to meet me. I hear you have all sorts of craft at Vissarion. The MacSkelpie, I hear, said you received her as a Queen; so I hope you will do the decent by one of your own flesh and blood, and the future Head of the House at that. I shan't bring much of a retinue with me. *I* wasn't made a billionaire by old Roger, so can only take my modest "man Friday"—whose name is Jenkinson, and a Cockney at that. So don't have too much gold lace and diamond-hilted scimitars about, like a good chap, or else he'll want the very worst—his wyges ryzed. That old image Rooke that came over for Miss McS., and whom by chance I saw at the attorney man's, might pilot me down from Fiume. The old gentleman-by-Act-of-Parliament Mr. Bingham Trent (I suppose he has hyphened it by this time) told me that Miss McS. said he "did her proud" when she went over under his charge. I shall be at Fiume on the evening of Wednesday, and shall stay at the Europa, which is, I am told, the least indecent hotel in the place. So you know where to find me, or any of your attendant demons can know, in case I am to suffer "substituted service."

Your affectionate Cousin,
ERNEST ROGER HALBARD MELTON.

Letter from Admiral Rooke to the Gospodar Rupert.

August 1, 1907.

SIR,

In obedience to your explicit direction that I should meet Mr. Ernest R. H. Melton at Fiume, and report to you exactly what occurred, "without keeping anything back,"—as you will remember you said, I beg to report.

I brought the steam-yacht *Trent* to Fiume, arriving there on the morning of Thursday. At 11.30 p.m. I went to meet the train from St. Peter, due 11.40. It was something late, arriving just as the clock was beginning to strike midnight. Mr. Melton was on board, and with him his valet Jenkinson. I am bound to say that he did not seem very pleased with his journey, and expressed much disappointment at not seeing Your Honour awaiting him. I explained, as you directed, that you had to attend with the Voivode Vissarion and the Vladika the National Council, which met at Plazac, or that otherwise you would have done yourself the pleasure of coming to meet him. I had, of course, reserved rooms (the Prince of Wales's suite), for him at the Re d'Ungheria, and had waiting the carriage which the proprietor had provided for the Prince of Wales when he stayed there. Mr. Melton took his valet with him (on the box-seat), and I followed in a *Stadtwagen* with the luggage. When I arrived, I found the *maître d'hôtel* in a stupor of concern. The English nobleman, he said, had found fault with everything, and used to him language to which he was not accustomed. I quieted him, telling him that the stranger was probably unused to foreign ways, and assuring him that

Your Honour had every faith in him. He announced himself satisfied and happy at the assurance. But I noticed that he promptly put everything in the hands of the headwaiter, telling him to satisfy the milor at any cost, and then went away to some urgent business in Vienna. Clever man!

I took Mr. Melton's orders for our journey in the morning, and asked if there was anything for which he wished. He simply said to me:

"Everything is rotten. Go to hell, and shut the door after you!" His man, who seems a very decent little fellow, though he is as vain as a peacock, and speaks with a Cockney accent which is simply terrible, came down the passage after me, and explained "on his own," as he expressed it, that his master, "Mr. Ernest," was upset by the long journey, and that I was not to mind. I did not wish to make him uncomfortable, so I explained that I minded nothing except what Your Honour wished; that the steam-yacht would be ready at 7 a.m.; and that I should be waiting in the hotel from that time on till Mr. Melton cared to start, to bring him aboard.

In the morning I waited till the man Jenkinson came and told me that Mr. Ernest would start at ten. I asked if he would breakfast on board; he answered that he would take his *café-complet* at the hotel, but breakfast on board.

We left at ten, and took the electric pinnace out to the *Trent*, which lay, with steam up, in the roads. Breakfast was served on board, by his orders, and presently he came up on the bridge, where I was in command. He brought his man Jenkinson with him. Seeing me there, and not (I suppose) understanding that I was in command, he unceremoniously ordered me to go on the deck. Indeed, he named a place much lower. I made a sign of silence to the quartermaster at the wheel, who had released the spokes, and was going, I feared, to make some impertinent remark. Jenkinson joined me presently, and said, as some sort of explanation of his master's discourtesy (of which he was manifestly ashamed), if not as an amende:

"The governor is in a hell of a wax this morning."

When we got in sight of Meleda, Mr. Melton sent for me and asked me where we were to land. I told him that, unless he wished to the contrary, we were to run to Vissarion; but that my instructions were to land at whatever port he wished. Whereupon he told me that he wished to stay the night at some place where he might be able to see some "life." He was pleased to add something, which I presume he thought jocular, about my being able to "coach" him in such matters, as doubtless even "an old has-been like you" had still some sort of an eye for a pretty girl. I told him as respectfully as I could that I had no knowledge whatever on such subjects, which were possibly of some interest to younger men, but of none to me. He said no more; so after waiting for further orders, but without receiving any, I said:

"I suppose, sir, we shall run to Vissarion?"

"Run to the devil, if you like!" was his reply, as he turned away. When we arrived in the creek at Vissarion, he seemed much milder—less aggressive in his manner; but when he heard that you were detained at Plazac, he got rather "fresh"—I use the American term—again. I greatly feared there would be a serious misfortune before we got into the Castle, for on the dock was Julia, the wife of Michael, the Master of the Wine, who is, as you know, very beautiful. Mr. Melton seemed much taken with her; and she, being flattered by the attention of a strange gentleman and Your Honour's kinsman, put aside the stand-offishness of most of the Blue Mountain women. Whereupon Mr. Melton, forgetting himself, took her in his arms and kissed her. Instantly there was a hubbub. The mountaineers present drew their handjars, and almost on the instant sudden death appeared to be amongst us. Happily the men waited as Michael, who had just arrived on the quay-wall as the outrage took place, ran forward, wheeling his handjar round his head, and manifestly intending to decapitate Mr. Melton. On the instant—I am sorry to say it, for it created a terribly bad effect—Mr. Melton dropped on his knees in a state of panic. There was just this good use in it—that there was a pause of a few seconds. During that time the little Cockney valet, who has the heart of a man in him, literally burst his way forward, and stood in front of his master in boxing attitude, calling out:

"'Ere, come on, the 'ole lot of ye! 'E ain't done no 'arm. He honly kissed the gal, as any man would. If ye want to cut off somebody's 'ed, cut off mine. I ain't afride!" There was such genuine pluck in this, and it formed so fine a contrast to the other's craven attitude (forgive me, Your Honour; but you want the truth!), that I was glad he was an Englishman, too. The mountaineers recognized his spirit, and saluted with their handjars, even Michael amongst the number. Half turning his head, the little man said in a fierce whisper:

"Buck up, guv'nor! Get up, or they'll slice ye! 'Ere's Mr. Rooke; 'e'll see ye through it."

By this time the men were amenable to reason, and when I reminded them that Mr. Melton was Your Honour's cousin, they put aside their handjars and went about their work. I asked Mr. Melton to follow, and led the way to the Castle.

When we got close to the great entrance within the walled courtyard, we found a large number of the servants gathered, and with them many of the mountaineers, who have kept an organized guard all round the Castle ever since the abducting of the Voivodin. As both Your Honour and the Voivode were away at Plazac, the guard had for the time been doubled. When the steward came and stood in the doorway, the servants stood off somewhat, and the mountaineers drew back to the farther sides and angles of the courtyard. The Voivodin had, of course, been informed of the guest's (your cousin) coming, and came to meet him in the old custom of the Blue Mountains. As Your Honour only came to the Blue Mountains recently, and as no occasion has been since then of illustrating the custom since the Voivode was away, and the Voivodin then believed to be dead, perhaps I, who have lived here so long, may explain:

When to an old Blue Mountain house a guest comes whom it is wished to do honour, the Lady, as in the vernacular the mistress of the house is called, comes herself to meet the guest at the door—or, rather, *outside* the door—so that she can herself conduct him within. It is a pretty ceremony, and it is said that of old in kingly days the monarch always set much store by it. The custom is that, when she approaches the honoured guest (he need not be royal), she bends—or more properly kneels—before him and kisses his hand. It has been explained by historians that the symbolism is that the woman, showing obedience to her husband, as the married woman of the Blue Mountains always does, emphasizes that obedience to her husband's guest. The custom is always observed in its largest formality when a young wife receives for the first time a guest, and especially one whom her husband wishes to honour. The Voivodin was, of course, aware that Mr. Melton was your kinsman, and naturally wished to make the ceremony of honour as marked as possible, so as to show overtly her sense of her husband's worth.

When we came into the courtyard, I held back, of course, for the honour is entirely individual, and is never extended to any other, no matter how worthy he may be. Naturally Mr. Melton did not know the etiquette of the situation, and so for that is not to be blamed. He took his valet with him when, seeing someone coming to the door, he went forward. I thought he was going to rush to his welcomer. Such, though not in the ritual, would have been natural in a young kinsman wishing to do honour to the bride of his host, and would to anyone have been both understandable and forgivable. It did not occur to me at the time, but I have since thought that perhaps he had not then heard of Your Honour's marriage, which I trust you will, in justice to the young gentleman, bear in mind when considering the matter. Unhappily, however, he did not show any such eagerness. On the contrary, he seemed to make a point of showing indifference. It seemed to me myself that he, seeing somebody wishing to make much of him, took what he considered a safe opportunity of restoring to himself his own good opinion, which must have been considerably lowered in the episode of the Wine Master's wife.

The Voivodin, thinking, doubtless, Your Honour, to add a fresh lustre to her welcome, had donned the costume which all her nation has now come to love and to accept as a dress of ceremonial honour. She wore her shroud. It moved the hearts of all of us who looked on to see it, and we appreciated its being worn for such a cause. But Mr. Melton did not seem to care. As he had been approaching she had begun to kneel, and was already on her knees whilst he was several yards away. There he stopped and turned to speak to his valet, put a glass in his eye, and looked all round him and up and down—indeed, everywhere except at the Great Lady, who was on her knees before him, waiting to bid him welcome. I could see in the eyes of such of the mountaineers as were within my range of vision a growing animosity; so, hoping to keep down any such expression, which I knew would cause harm to Your Honour and the Voivodin, I looked all round them straight in their faces with a fixed frown, which, indeed, they seemed to understand, for they regained, and for the time maintained, their usual dignified calm. The Voivodin, may I say, bore the trial wonderfully. No human being could see that she was in any degree pained or even surprised. Mr. Melton stood looking round him so long that I had full time to regain my own attitude of calm. At last he seemed to come back to the knowledge that someone was waiting for him, and sauntered leisurely forward. There was so much insolence—mind you, not insolence that was intended to appear as such—in his movement that the mountaineers began to steal forward. When he was close up to the Voivodin, and she put out her hand to take his, he put forward *one finger*! I could hear the intake of the breath of the men, now close around, for I had moved forward, too. I thought it would be as well to be close to your guest, lest something should happen to him. The Voivodin still kept her splendid self-control. Raising the finger put forward by the guest with the same deference as though it had been the hand of a King, she bent her head down and kissed it. Her duty of courtesy now done, she was preparing to rise, when he put his hand into his pocket, and, pulling out a sovereign, offered it to her. His valet moved his hand forward, as if to pull back his arm, but it was too late. I am sure, Your Honour, that no affront was intended. He doubtless thought that he was doing a kindness of the sort usual in England when one "tips" a housekeeper. But all the same, to one in her position, it was an affront, an insult, open and unmistakable. So it was received by the mountaineers, whose handjars flashed out as one. For a second it was so received even by the Voivodin, who, with face flushing scarlet, and the stars in her eves flaming red, sprang to her feet. But in that second she had regained herself, and to all appearances her righteous anger passed away. Stooping, she took the hand of her guest and raised it—you know how strong she is—and, holding it in hers, led him into the doorway, saying:

"You are welcome, kinsman of my husband, to the house of my father, which is presently my husband's also. Both are grieved that, duty having called them away for the time, they are unable to be here to help me to greet you."

I tell you, Your Honour, that it was a lesson in self-respect which anyone who saw it can never forget. As to me, it makes my flesh quiver, old as I am, with delight, and my heart leap.

May I, as a faithful servant who has had many years of experience, suggest that Your Honour should seem—for the present, at any rate—not to know any of these things which I have reported, as you wished me to do. Be sure that the Voivodin will tell you her gracious self aught that she would wish you to know. And such reticence on your part must make for her happiness, even if it did not for your own.

So that you may know all, as you desired, and that you may have time to school yourself to whatever attitude you think best to adopt, I send this off to you at once by fleet messenger. Were the aeroplane here, I should take it myself. I leave here shortly to await the arrival of Sir Colin at Otranto.

Your Honour's faithful servant,
ROOKE.

JANET MACKELPIE'S NOTES.

August 9, 1907.

To me it seems very providential that Rupert was not at home when that dreadful young man Ernest Melton arrived, though it is possible that if Rupert had been present he would not have dared to conduct himself so badly. Of course, I heard all about it from the maids; Teuta never opened her lips to me on the subject. It was bad enough and stupid enough for him to try to kiss a decent young woman like Julia, who is really as good as gold and as modest as one of our own Highland lassies; but to think of him insulting Teuta! The little beast! One would think that a champion idiot out of an Equatorial asylum would know better! If Michael, the Wine Master, wanted to kill him, I wonder what my Rupert and hers would have done? I am truly thankful that he was not present. And I am thankful, too, that I was not present either, for I should have made an exhibition of myself, and Rupert would not have liked that. He—the little beast! might have seen from the very dress that the dear girl wore that there was something exceptional about her. But on one account I should have liked to see her. They tell me that she was, in her true dignity, like a Queen, and that her humility in receiving her husband's kinsman was a lesson to every woman in the Land. I must be careful not to let Rupert know that I have heard of the incident. Later on, when it is all blown over and the young man has been got safely away, I shall tell him of it. Mr. Rooke—Lord High Admiral Rooke, I should say—must be a really wonderful man to have so held himself in check; for, from what I have heard of him, he must in his younger days have been worse than Old Morgan of Panama. Mr. Ernest Roger Halbard Melton, of Humcroft, Salop, little knows how near he was to being "cleft to the chine" also.

Fortunately, I had heard of his meeting with Teuta before he came to see me, for I did not get back from my walk till after he had arrived. Teuta's noble example was before me, and I determined that I, too, would show good manners under any circumstances. But I didn't know how mean he is. Think of his saying to me that Rupert's position here must be a great source of pride to me, who had been his nursery governess. He said "nursemaid" first, but then stumbled in his words, seeming to remember something. I did not turn a hair, I am glad to say. It is a mercy Uncle Colin was not here, for I honestly believe that, if he had been, he would have done the "cleaving to the chine" himself. It has been a narrow escape for Master Ernest, for only this morning Rupert had a message, sent on from Gibraltar, saying that he was arriving with his clansmen, and that they would not be far behind his letter. He would call at Otranto in case someone should come across to pilot him to Vissarion. Uncle told me all about that young cad having offered him one finger in Mr. Trent's office, though, of course, he didn't let the cad see that he noticed it. I have no doubt that, when he does arrive, that young man, if he is here still, will find that he will have to behave himself, if it be only on Sir Colin's account alone.

THE SAME (LATER).

I had hardly finished writing when the lookout on the tower announced that the *Teuta*, as Rupert calls his aeroplane, was sighted crossing the mountains from Plazac. I hurried up to see him arrive, for I had not as yet seen him on his "aero." Mr. Ernest Melton came up, too. Teuta was, of course, before any of us. She seems to know by instinct when Rupert is coming.

It was certainly a wonderful sight to see the little aeroplane, with outspread wings like a bird in flight, come sailing high over the mountains. There was a head-wind, and they were beating against it; otherwise we should not have had time to get to the tower before the arrival.

When once the "aero" had begun to drop on the near side of the mountains, however, and had got a measure of shelter from them, her pace was extraordinary. We could not tell, of course, what sort of pace she came at from looking at herself. But we gathered some idea from the rate at which the mountains and hills seemed to slide away from under her. When she got over the foot-hills, which are about ten miles away, she came on at a swift glide that seemed to throw the distance behind her. When quite close, she rose up a little till she was something higher than the Tower, to which she came as straight as an arrow from the bow, and glided to her moorings, stopping dead as Rupert pulled a lever, which seemed to turn a barrier to the wind. The Voivode sat beside Rupert, but I must say that he seemed to hold on to the bar in front of him even more firmly than Rupert held to his steering-gear.

When they had alighted, Rupert greeted his cousin with the utmost kindness, and bade him welcome to Vissarion.

"I see," he said, "you have met Teuta. Now you may congratulate me, if you wish."

Mr. Melton made a long rodomontade about her beauty, but presently, stumbling about in his speech, said something regarding it being unlucky to appear in grave-clothes. Rupert laughed, and clapped him on the shoulder as he answered:

"That pattern of frock is likely to become a national dress for loyal women of the Blue Mountains. When you know something of what that dress means to us all at present you will understand. In the meantime, take it that there is not a soul in the nation that does not love it and honour her for wearing it." To which the cad replied:

"Oh, indeed! I thought it was some preparation for a fancy-dress ball." Rupert's comment on this ill-natured speech was (for him) quite grumpily given:

"I should not advise you to think such things whilst you are in this part of the world, Ernest. They bury men here for much less."

The cad seemed struck with something—either what Rupert had said or his manner of saying it—for he was silent for several seconds before he spoke.

"I'm very tired with that long journey, Rupert. Would you and Mrs. Sent Leger mind if I go to my own room and turn in? My man can ask for a cup of tea and a sandwich for me."

RUPERT'S JOURNAL.

August 10, 1907.

When Ernest said he wished to retire it was about the wisest thing he could have said or done, and it suited Teuta and me down to the ground. I could see that the dear girl was agitated about something, so thought it would be best for her to be quiet, and not worried with being civil to the Bounder. Though he is my cousin, I can't think of him as anything else. The Voivode and I had certain matters to attend to arising out of the meeting of the Council, and when we were through the night was closing in. When I saw Teuta in our own rooms she said at once:

"Do you mind, dear, if I stay with Aunt Janet to-night? She is very upset and nervous, and when I offered to come to her she clung to me and cried with relief."

So when I had had some supper, which I took with the Voivode, I came down to my old quarters in the Garden Room, and turned in early.

I was awakened a little before dawn by the coming of the fighting monk Theophrastos, a notable runner, who had an urgent message for me. This was the letter to me given to him by Rooke. He had been cautioned to give it into no other hand, but to find me wherever I might be, and convey it personally. When he had arrived at Plazac I had left on the aeroplane, so he had turned back to Vissarion.

When I read Rooke's report of Ernest Melton's abominable conduct I was more angry with him than I can say. Indeed, I did not think before that that I could be angry with him, for I have always despised him. But this was too much. However, I realized the wisdom of Rooke's advice, and went away by myself to get over my anger and reacquire my self-mastery. The aeroplane *Teuta* was still housed on the tower, so I went up alone and took it out.

When I had had a spin of about a hundred miles I felt better. The bracing of the wind and the quick, exhilarating motion restored me to myself, and I felt able to cope with Master Ernest, or whatever else chagrinable might come along, without giving myself away. As Teuta had thought it better to keep silence as to Ernest's affront, I felt I must not acknowledge it; but, all the same, I determined to get rid of him before the day was much older.

When I had had my breakfast I sent word to him by a servant that I was coming to his rooms, and followed not long behind the messenger.

He was in a suit of silk pyjamas, such as not even Solomon in all his glory was arrayed in. I closed the door behind me before I began to speak. He listened, at first amazed, then disconcerted, then angry, and then cowering down like a whipped hound. I felt that it was a case for speaking out. A bumptious ass like him, who deliberately insulted everyone he came across—for if all or any of his efforts in that way were due to mere elemental ignorance he was not fit to live, but should be silenced on sight as a modern Caliban—deserved neither pity nor mercy. To extend to him fine feeling, tolerance, and such-like gentlenesses would be to deprive the world of them without benefit to any. So well as I can remember, what I said was something like this:

"Ernest, as you say, you've got to go, and to go quick, you understand. I dare say you look on this as a land of barbarians, and think that any of your high-toned refinements are thrown away on people here. Well, perhaps it is so. Undoubtedly, the structure of the country is rough; the mountains may only represent the glacial epoch; but so far as I can gather from some of your exploits—for I have only learned a small part as yet—you represent a period a good deal farther back. You seem to have given our folk here an exhibition of the playfulness of the hooligan of the Saurian stage of development; but the Blue Mountains, rough as they are, have come up out of the primeval slime, and even now the people aim at better manners. They may be rough, primitive, barbarian, elemental, if you will, but they are not low down enough to tolerate either your ethics or your taste. My dear cousin, your life is not safe here! I am told that yesterday, only for the restraint exercised by certain offended mountaineers on other grounds than your own worth, you would have been abbreviated by the head. Another day of your fascinating presence would do away with this restraint, and then we should have a scandal. I am a new-comer here myself—too new a comer to be able to afford a scandal of that kind—and so I shall not delay your going. Believe me, my dear cousin, Ernest Roger Halbard Melton, of Humcroft, Salop, that I am inconsolable about your resolution of immediate departure, but I cannot shut my eyes to its wisdom. At present the matter is altogether amongst ourselves, and when you have gone—if it be immediately—silence will be observed on all hands for the sake of the house wherein you are a guest; but if there be time for scandal to spread, you will be made, whether you be alive or dead, a European laughing-stock. Accordingly, I have anticipated your wishes, and have ordered a fast steam yacht to take you to Ancona, or to whatever other port you may desire. The yacht will be under the command of Captain Desmond, of one of our battleships—a most determined officer, who will carry out any directions which may be given to him. This will insure your safety so far as Italian territory. Some of his officials will arrange a special carriage for you up to Flushing, and a cabin on the steamer to Queenboro'. A man of mine will travel on the train and steamer with you, and will see that whatever you may wish in the way of food or comfort will be provided. Of course, you understand, my dear cousin, that you are my guest until you arrive in London. I have not asked Rooke to accompany you, as when he went to meet you, it was a mistake. Indeed, there might have been a danger to you which I never contemplated—a quite unnecessary danger, I assure you. But happily Admiral Rooke, though a man of strong passions, has wonderful self-control."

"Admiral Rooke?" he queried. "Admiral?"

"Admiral, certainly," I replied, "but not an ordinary Admiral—one of many. He is *the* Admiral—the Lord High Admiral of the Land of the Blue Mountains, with sole control of its expanding navy. When such a man is treated as a valet, there may be . . . But why go into this? It is all over. I only mention it lest anything of a similar kind should occur with Captain Desmond, who is a younger man, and therefore with probably less self-repression."

I saw that he had learned his lesson, and so said no more on the subject.

There was another reason for his going which I did not speak of. Sir Colin MacKelpie was coming with his clansmen, and I knew he did not like Ernest Melton. I well remembered that episode of his offering one finger to the old gentleman in Mr. Trent's office, and, moreover, I had my suspicions that Aunt Janet's being upset was probably in some measure due to some rudeness of his that she did not wish to speak about. He is really an impossible young man, and is far better out of this country than in it. If he remained here, there would be some sort of a tragedy for certain.

I must say that it was with a feeling of considerable relief that I saw the yacht steam out of the creek, with Captain Desmond on the bridge and my cousin beside him.

Quite other were my feelings when, an hour after, *The Lady* came flying into the creek with the Lord High Admiral on the bridge, and beside him, more splendid and soldier-like than ever, Sir Colin MacKelpie. Mr. Bingham Trent was also on the bridge.

The General was full of enthusiasm regarding his regiment, for in all, those he brought with him and those finishing their training at home, the force is near the number of a full regiment. When we were alone he explained to me that all was arranged regarding the non-commissioned officers, but that he had held over the question of officers until we should have had a suitable opportunity of talking the matter over together. He explained to me his reasons, which were certainly simple and cogent. Officers, according to him, are a different class, and accustomed to a different standard altogether of life and living, of duties and pleasures. They are harder to deal with and more difficult to obtain. "There was no use," he said, "in getting a lot of failures, with old-crusted ways of their own importance. We must have young men for our purpose—that is, men not old, but with some experience—men, of course, who know how to behave themselves, or else, from what little I have seen of the Blue Mountaineers, they wouldn't last long here if they went on as some of them do elsewhere. I shall start things here as you wish me to, for I am here, my dear boy, to stay with you and Janet, and we shall, if it be given to us by the Almighty, help to build up together a new 'nation'—an ally of Britain, who will stand at least as an outpost of our own nation, and a guardian of our eastern road. When things are organized here on the military side, and are going strong, I shall, if you can spare me, run back to London for a few weeks. Whilst I am there I shall pick up a lot of the sort of officers we want. I know that there are loads of them to be had. I shall go slowly, however, and carefully, too, and every man I bring back will be recommended to me by some old soldier whom I know, and who knows the man he recommends, and has seen him work. We shall have, I dare say, an army for its size second to none in the world, and the day may come when your old country will be proud of your new one. Now I'm off to see that all is ready for my people—your people now."

I had had arrangements made for the comfort of the clansmen and the women, but I knew that the good old soldier would see for himself that his men were to be comfortable. It was not for nothing that he was—is—looked on as perhaps the General most beloved by his men in the whole British Army.

When he had gone, and I was alone, Mr. Trent, who had evidently been waiting for the opportunity, came to me. When we had spoken of my marriage and of Teuta, who seems to have made an immense impression on him, he said suddenly:

"I suppose we are quite alone, and that we shall not be interrupted?" I summoned the man outside—there is always a sentry on guard outside my door or near me, wherever I may be—and gave orders that I was not to be disturbed until I gave fresh orders. "If," I said, "there be anything pressing or important, let the Voivodin or Miss MacKelpie know. If either of them brings anyone to me, it will be all right."

When we were quite alone Mr. Trent took a slip of paper and some documents from the bag which was beside him. He then read out items from the slip, placing as he did so the documents so checked over before him.

1. New Will made on marriage, to be signed presently.

2. Copy of the Re-conveyance of Vissarion estates to Peter Vissarion, as directed by Will of Roger Melton.

3. Report of Correspondence with Privy Council, and proceedings following.

Taking up the last named, he untied the red tape, and, holding the bundle in his hand, went on:

"As you may, later on, wish to examine the details of the Proceedings, I have copied out the various letters, the originals of which are put safely away in my strong-room where, of course, they are always available in case you may want them. For your present information I shall give you a rough synopsis of the Proceedings, referring where advisable to this paper.

"On receipt of your letter of instructions regarding the Consent of the Privy Council to your changing your nationality in accordance with the terms of Roger Melton's Will, I put myself in communication with the Clerk of the Privy Council, informing him of your wish to be naturalized in due time to the Land of the Blue Mountains. After some letters between us, I got a summons to attend a meeting of the Council.

"I attended, as required, taking with me all necessary documents, and such as I conceived might be advisable to produce, if wanted.

"The Lord President informed me that the present meeting of the Council was specially summoned in obedience to the suggestion of the King, who had been consulted as to his personal wishes on the subject—should he have any. The President then proceeded to inform me officially that all Proceedings of the Privy Council were altogether confidential, and were not to be made public under any circumstances. He was gracious enough to add:

"'The circumstances of this case, however, are unique; and as you act for another, we have thought it advisable to enlarge your permission in the matter, so as to allow you to communicate freely with your principal. As that gentleman is settling himself in a part of the world which has been in the past, and may be again, united to this nation by some common interest, His Majesty wishes Mr. Sent Leger to feel assured of the good-will of Great Britain to the Land of the Blue Mountains, and even of his own personal satisfaction that a gentleman of so distinguished a lineage and such approved personal character is about to be—within his own scope—a connecting-link between the nations. To which end he has graciously announced that, should the Privy Council acquiesce in the request of Denaturalization, he will himself sign the Patent therefor.

"'The Privy Council has therefore held private session, at which the matter has been discussed in its many bearings; and it is content that the change can do no harm, but may be of some service to the two nations. We have, therefore, agreed to grant the prayer of the Applicant; and the officials of the Council have the matter of the form of Grant in hand. So you, sir, may rest satisfied that as soon as the formalities—which will, of course, require the formal signing of certain documents by the Applicant—can be complied with, the Grant and Patent will obtain.'"

Having made this statement in formal style, my old friend went on in more familiar way:

"And so, my dear Rupert, all is in hand; and before very long you will have the freedom required under the Will, and will be at liberty to take whatever steps may be necessary to be naturalized in your new country.

"I may tell you, by the way, that several members of the Council made very complimentary remarks regarding you. I am forbidden to give names, but I may tell you facts. One old Field-Marshal, whose name is familiar to the whole world, said that he had served in many places with your father, who was a very valiant soldier, and that he was glad that Great Britain was to have in the future the benefit of your father's son in a friendly land now beyond the outposts of our Empire, but which had been one with her in the past, and might be again.

"So much for the Privy Council. We can do no more at present until you sign and have attested the documents which I have brought with me.

"We can now formally complete the settlement of the Vissarion estates, which must be done whilst you are a British citizen. So, too, with the Will, the more formal and complete document, which is to take the place of that short one which you forwarded to me the day after your marriage. It may be, perhaps, necessary or advisable that, later on, when you are naturalized here, you shall make a new Will in strictest accordance with local law."

TEUTA SENT LEGER'S DIARY.

August 19, 1907.

We had a journey to-day that was simply glorious. We had been waiting to take it for more than a week. Rupert not only wanted the weather suitable, but he had to wait till the new aeroplane came home. It is more than twice as big as our biggest up to now. None of the others could take all the party which Rupert wanted to go. When he heard that the aero was coming from Whitby, where it was sent from Leeds, he directed by cable that it should be unshipped at Otranto, whence he took it here all by himself. I wanted to come with him, but he thought it better not. He says that Brindisi is too busy a place to keep anything quiet—if not secret—and he wants to be very dark indeed about this, as it is worked by the new radium engine. Ever since they found radium in our own hills he has been obsessed by the idea of an aerial navy for our protection. And after to-day's experiences I think he is right. As he wanted to survey the whole country at a glimpse, so that the general scheme of defence might be put in hand, we had to have an aero big enough to take the party as well as fast enough to do it rapidly, and all at once. We had, in addition to Rupert, my father, and myself, Sir Colin and Lord High Admiral Rooke (I do like to give that splendid old fellow his full title!). The military and naval experts had with them scientific apparatus of various kinds, also cameras and range-finders, so that they could mark their maps as they required. Rupert, of course, drove, and I acted as his assistant. Father, who has not yet become accustomed to aerial travel, took a seat in the centre (which Rupert had thoughtfully prepared for him), where there is very little motion. I must say I was amazed to see the way that splendid old soldier Sir Colin bore himself. He had never been on an aeroplane before, but, all the same, he was as calm as if he was on a rock. Height or motion did not trouble him. Indeed, he seemed to *enjoy* himself all the time. The Admiral is himself almost an expert, but in any case I am sure he would have been unconcerned, just as he was in the *Crab* as Rupert has told me.

We left just after daylight, and ran down south. When we got to the east of Ilsin, we kept slightly within the border-line, and went north or east as it ran, making occasional loops inland over the mountains and back again. When we got up to our farthest point north, we began to go much slower. Sir Colin explained that for the rest all would be comparatively plain-sailing in the way of defence; but that as any foreign Power other than the Turk must attack from seaward, he would like to examine the seaboard very carefully in conjunction with the Admiral, whose advice as to sea defence would be invaluable.

Rupert was fine. No one could help admiring him as he sat working his lever and making the great machine obey every touch. He was wrapped up in his work. I don't believe that whilst he was working he ever thought of even me. He *is* splendid!

We got back just as the sun was dropping down over the Calabrian Mountains. It is quite wonderful how the horizon changes when you are sailing away up high on an aeroplane. Rupert is going to teach me how to manage one all by myself, and when I am fit he will give me one, which he is to have specially built for me.

I think I, too, have done some good work—at least, I have got some good ideas—from our journey to-day. Mine are not of war, but of peace, and I think I see a way by which we shall be able to develop our country in a wonderful way. I shall talk the idea over with Rupert to-night, when we are alone. In the meantime Sir Colin and Admiral Rooke will think their plans over individually, and to-morrow morning together. Then the next day they, too, are to go over their idea with Rupert and my father, and something may be decided then.

RUPERT'S JOURNAL—*Continued.*

August 21, 1907.

Our meeting on the subject of National Defence, held this afternoon, went off well. We were five in all, for with permission of the Voivode and the two fighting-men, naval and military, I brought Teuta with me. She sat beside me quite quietly, and never made a remark of any kind till the Defence business had been gone through. Both Sir Colin and Admiral Rooke were in perfect agreement as to the immediate steps to be taken for defence. In the first instance, the seaboard was to be properly fortified in the necessary places, and the navy largely strengthened. When we had got thus far I asked Rooke to tell of the navy increase already in hand. Whereupon he explained that, as we had found the small battleship *The Lady* of an excellent type for coast defence, acting only in home waters, and of a size to take cover where necessary at many places on our own shores, we had ordered nine others of the same pattern. Of these the first four were already in hand, and were proceeding with the greatest expedition. The General then supplemented this by saying that big guns could be used from points judiciously chosen on the seaboard, which was in all so short a length that no very great quantity of armament would be required.

"We can have," he said, "the biggest guns of the most perfect kind yet accomplished, and use them from land batteries of the most up-to-date pattern. The one serious proposition we have to deal with is the defence of the harbour—as yet quite undeveloped—which is known as the 'Blue Mouth.' Since our aerial journey I have been to it by sea with Admiral Rooke in *The Lady*, and then on land with the Vladika, who was born on its shores, and who knows every inch of it.

"It is worth fortifying—and fortifying well, for as a port it is peerless in Mediterranean seas. The navies of the world might ride in it, land-locked, and even hidden from view seawards. The mountains which enclose it are in themselves absolute protection. In addition, these can only be assailed from our own territory. Of course, Voivode, you understand when I say 'our' I mean the Land of the Blue Mountains, for whose safety and well-being I am alone concerned. Any ship anchoring in the roads of the Blue Mouth would have only one need—sufficient length of cable for its magnificent depth.

"When proper guns are properly placed on the steep cliffs to north and south of the entrance, and when the rock islet between has been armoured and armed as will be necessary, the Mouth will be impregnable. But we should not depend on the aiming of the entrance alone. At certain salient points—which I have marked upon this map—armour-plated sunken forts within earthworks should be established. There should be covering forts on the hillsides, and, of course, the final summits protected. Thus we could resist attack on any side or all sides—from sea or land. That port will yet mean the wealth as well as the strength of this nation, so it will be well to have it properly protected. This should be done soon, and the utmost secrecy observed in the doing of it, lest the so doing should become a matter of international concern."

Here Rooke smote the table hard.

"By God, that is true! It has been the dream of my own life for this many a year."

In the silence which followed the sweet, gentle voice of Teuta came clear as a bell:

"May I say a word? I am emboldened to, as Sir Colin has spoken so splendidly, and as the Lord High Admiral has not hesitated to mention his dreaming. I, too, have had a dream—a day-dream—which came in a flash, but no less a dream, for all that. It was when we hung on the aeroplane over the Blue Mouth. It seemed to me in an instant that I saw that beautiful spot as it will some time be—typical, as Sir Colin said, of the wealth as well as the strength of this nation; a mart for the world whence will come for barter some of the great wealth of the Blue Mountains. That wealth is as yet undeveloped. But the day is at hand when we may begin to use it, and through that very port. Our mountains and their valleys are clad with trees of splendid growth, virgin forests of priceless worth; hard woods of all kinds, which have no superior throughout the world. In the rocks, though hidden as yet, is vast mineral wealth of many kinds. I have been looking through the reports of the geological exports of the Commission of Investigation which my husband organized soon after he came to live here, and, according to them, our whole mountain ranges simply teem with vast quantities of minerals, almost more precious for industry than gold and silver are for commerce—though, indeed, gold is not altogether lacking as a mineral. When once our work on the harbour is done, and the place has been made secure against any attempt at foreign aggression, we must try to find a way to bring this wealth of woods and ores down to the sea.

"And then, perhaps, may begin the great prosperity of our Land, of which we have all dreamt."

She stopped, all vibrating, almost choked with emotion. We were all moved. For myself, I was thrilled to the core. Her enthusiasm was all-sweeping, and under its influence I found my own imagination expanding. Out of its experiences I spoke:

"And there is a way. I can see it. Whilst our dear Voivodin was speaking, the way seemed to clear. I saw at the back of the Blue Mouth, where it goes deepest into the heart of the cliffs, the opening of a great tunnel, which ran upward over a steep slope till it debouched on the first plateau beyond the range of the encompassing cliffs. Thither came by various rails of steep gradient, by timber-shoots and cable-rails, by aerial cables and precipitating tubes, wealth from over ground and under it; for as our Land is all mountains, and as these tower up to the clouds, transport to the sea shall be easy and of little cost when once the machinery is established. As everything of much weight goes downward, the cars of the main tunnel of the port shall return upward without cost. We can have from the mountains a head of water under good control, which will allow of endless hydraulic power, so that the whole port and the mechanism of the town to which it will grow can be worked by it.

"This work can be put in hand at once. So soon as the place shall be perfectly surveyed and the engineering plans got ready, we can start on the main tunnel, working from the sea-level up, so that the cost of the transport of material will be almost nil. This work can go on whilst the forts are building; no time need be lost.

"Moreover, may I add a word on National Defence? We are, though old in honour, a young nation as to our place amongst Great Powers. And so we must show the courage and energy of a young nation. The Empire of the Air is not yet won. Why should not we make a bid for it? As our mountains are lofty, so shall we have initial power of attack or defence. We can have, in chosen spots amongst the clouds, depots of war aeroplanes, with which we can descend and smite our enemies quickly on land or sea. We shall hope to live for Peace; but woe to those who drive us to War!"

There is no doubt that the Vissarions are a warlike race. As I spoke, Teuta took one of my hands and held it hard. The old Voivode, his eyes blazing, rose and stood beside me and took the other. The two old fighting-men of the land and the sea stood up and saluted.

This was the beginning of what ultimately became "The National Committee of Defence and Development."

I had other, and perhaps greater, plans for the future in my mind; but the time had not come for their utterance.

To me it seems not only advisable, but necessary, that the utmost discretion be observed by all our little group, at all events for the present. There seems to be some new uneasiness in the Blue Mountains. There are constant meetings of members of the Council, but no formal meeting of the Council, as such, since the last one at which I was present. There is constant coming and going amongst the mountaineers, always in groups, small or large. Teuta and I, who have been about very much on the aeroplane, have both noticed it. But somehow we—that is, the Voivode and myself—are left out of everything; but we have not said as yet a word on the subject to any of the others. The Voivode notices, but he says nothing; so I am silent, and Teuta does whatever I ask. Sir Colin does not notice anything except the work he is engaged on—the planning the defences of the Blue Mouth. His old scientific training as an engineer, and his enormous experience of wars and sieges—for he was for nearly fifty years sent as military representative to all the great wars—seem to have become directed on that point. He is certainly planning it all out in a wonderful way. He consults Rooke almost hourly on the maritime side of the question. The Lord High Admiral has been a watcher all his life, and very few important points have ever escaped him, so that he can add greatly to the wisdom of the defensive construction. He notices, I think, that something is going on outside ourselves; but he keeps a resolute silence.

What the movement going on is I cannot guess. It is not like the uneasiness that went before the abduction of Teuta and the Voivode, but it is even more pronounced. That was an uneasiness founded on some suspicion. This is a positive thing, and has definite meaning—of some sort. We shall, I suppose, know all about it in good time. In the meantime we go on with our work. Happily the whole Blue Mouth and the mountains round it are on my own property, the portion acquired long ago by Uncle Roger, exclusive of the Vissarion estate. I asked the Voivode to allow me to transfer it to him, but he sternly refused and forbade me, quite peremptorily, to ever open the subject to him again. "You have done enough already," he said. "Were I to allow you to go further, I should feel mean. And I do not think you would like your wife's father to suffer that feeling after a long life, which he has tried to live in honour."

I bowed, and said no more. So there the matter rests, and I have to take my own course. I have had a survey made, and on the head of it the Tunnel to the harbour is begun.

BOOK VIII: THE FLASHING OF THE HANDJAR

PRIVATE MEMORANDUM OF THE MEETING OF VARIOUS MEMBERS OF THE NATIONAL COUNCIL, HELD AT THE STATE HOUSE OF THE BLUE MOUNTAINS AT PLAZAC ON MONDAY, AUGUST 26, 1907.

(*Written by Cristoferos, Scribe of the Council, by instruction of those present.*)

When the private meeting of various Members of the National Council had assembled in the Council Hall of the State House at Plazac, it was as a preliminary decided unanimously that now or hereafter no names of those present were to be mentioned, and that officials appointed for the purposes of this meeting should be designated by office only, the names of all being withheld.

The proceedings assumed the shape of a general conversation, quite informal, and therefore not to be recorded. The nett outcome was the unanimous expression of an opinion that the time, long contemplated by very many persons throughout the nation, had now come when the Constitution and machinery of the State should be changed; that the present form of ruling by an Irregular Council was not sufficient, and that a method more in accord with the spirit of the times should be adopted. To this end Constitutional Monarchy, such as that holding in Great Britain, seemed best adapted. Finally, it was decided that each Member of the Council should make a personal canvass of his district, talk over the matter with his electors, and bring back to another meeting—or, rather, as it was amended, to this meeting postponed for a week, until September 2nd—the opinions and wishes received. Before separating, the individual to be appointed King, in case the new idea should prove grateful to the nation, was discussed. The consensus of opinion was entirely to the effect that the Voivode Peter Vissarion should, if he would accept the high office, be appointed. It was urged that, as his daughter, the Voivodin Teuta, was now married to the Englishman, Rupert Sent Leger—called generally by the mountaineers "the Gospodar Rupert"—a successor to follow the Voivode when God should call him would be at hand—a successor worthy in every way to succeed to so illustrious a post. It was urged by several speakers, with general acquiescence, that already Mr. Sent Leger's services to the State were such that he would be in himself a worthy person to begin the new Dynasty; but that, as he was now allied to the Voivode Peter Vissarion, it was becoming that the elder, born of the nation, should receive the first honour.

THE SAME—*Continued.*

The adjourned meeting of certain members of the National Council was resumed in the Hall of the State House at Plazac on Monday, September 2nd, 1907. By motion the same chairman was appointed, and the rule regarding the record renewed.

Reports were made by the various members of the Council in turn, according to the State Roll. Every district was represented. The reports were unanimously in favour of the New Constitution, and it was reported by each and all of the Councillors that the utmost enthusiasm marked in every case the suggestion of the Voivode Peter Vissarion as the first King to be crowned under the new Constitution, and that remainder should be settled on the Gospodar Rupert (the mountaineers would only receive his lawful name as an alternative; one and all said that he would be "Rupert" to them and to the nation—for ever).

The above matter having been satisfactorily settled, it was decided that a formal meeting of the National Council should be held at the State House, Plazac, in one week from to-day, and that the Voivode Peter Vissarion should be asked to be in the State House in readiness to attend. It was also decided that instruction should be given to the High Court of National Law to prepare and have ready, in skeleton form, a rescript of the New Constitution to be adopted, the same to be founded on the Constitution and Procedure of Great Britain, so far as the same may be applicable to the traditional ideas of free Government in the Land of the Blue Mountains.

By unanimous vote this private and irregular meeting of "Various National Councillors" was then dissolved.

RECORD OF THE FIRST MEETING OF THE NATIONAL COUNCIL OF THE LAND OF THE BLUE MOUNTAINS, HELD AT PLAZAC ON MONDAY, SEPTEMBER 9TH, 1907, TO CONSIDER THE ADOPTION OF A NEW CONSTITUTION, AND TO GIVE PERMANENT EFFECT TO THE SAME IF, AND WHEN, DECIDED UPON.

(*Kept by the Monk Cristoferos, Scribe to the National Council.*)

The adjourned meeting duly took place as arranged. There was a full attendance of Members of the Council, together with the Vladika, the Archbishop, the Archimandrites of Spazac, of Ispazar, of Domitan, and Astrag; the Chancellor; the Lord of the Exchequer; the President of the High Court of National Law; the President of the Council of Justice; and such other high officials as it is customary to summon to meetings of the National Council on occasions of great importance. The names of all present will be found in the full report, wherein are given the ipsissima verba of the various utterances made during the consideration of the questions discussed, the same having been taken down in shorthand by the humble scribe of this précis, which has been made for the convenience of Members of the Council and others.

The Voivode Peter Vissarion, obedient to the request of the Council, was in attendance at the State House, waiting in the "Chamber of the High Officers" until such time as he should be asked to come before the Council.

The President put before the National Council the matter of the new Constitution, outlining the headings of it as drawn up by the High Court of National Law, and the Constitution having been formally accepted *nem. con.* by the National Council on behalf of the people, he proposed that the Crown should be offered to the Voivode Peter Vissarion, with remainder to the "Gospodar Rupert" (legally, Rupert Sent Leger), husband of his only child, the Voivodin Teuta. This also was received with enthusiasm, and passed *nem. con.*

Thereupon the President of Council, the Archbishop, and the Vladika, acting together as a deputation, went to pray the attention of the Voivode Peter Vassarion.

When the Voivode entered, the whole Council and officials stood up, and for a few seconds waited in respectful silence with heads bowed down. Then, as if by a common impulse—for no word was spoken nor any signal given—they all drew their handjars, and stood to attention—with points raised and edges of the handjars to the front.

The Voivode stood very still. He seemed much moved, but controlled himself admirably. The only time when be seemed to lose his self-control was when, once again with a strange simultaneity, all present raised their handjars on high, and shouted: "Hail, Peter, King!" Then lowering their points till these almost touched the ground, they once again stood with bowed heads.

When he had quite mastered himself, the Voivode Peter Vissarion spoke:

"How can I, my brothers, sufficiently thank you, and, through you, the people of the Blue Mountains, for the honour done to me this day? In very truth it is not possible, and therefore I pray you to consider it as done, measuring my gratitude in the greatness of your own hearts. Such honour as you offer to me is not contemplated by any man in whose mind a wholesome sanity rules, nor is it even the dream of fervent imagination. So great is it, that I pray you, men with hearts and minds like my own, to extend to me, as a further measure of your generosity, a little time to think it over. I shall not want long, for even already, with the blaze of honour fresh upon me, I see the cool shadow of Duty, though his substance is yet hardly visible. Give me but an hour of solitude—an hour at most—if it do not prolong this your session unduly. It may be that a lesser time will serve, but in any case I promise you that, when I can see a just and fitting issue to my thought, I shall at once return."

The President of the Council looked around him, and, seeing everywhere the bowing heads of acquiescence, spoke with a reverent gravity:

"We shall wait in patience whatsoever time you will, and may the God who rules all worthy hearts guide you to His Will!"

And so in silence the Voivode passed out of the hall.

From my seat near a window I could watch him go, as with measured steps he passed up the hill which rises behind the State House, and disappeared into the shadow of the forest. Then my work claimed me, for I wished to record the proceedings so far whilst all was fresh in my mind. In silence, as of the dead, the Council waited, no man challenging opinion of his neighbour even by a glance.

Almost a full hour had elapsed when the Voivode came again to the Council, moving with slow and stately gravity, as has always been his wont since age began to hamper the movement which in youth had been so notable. The Members of the Council all stood up uncovered, and so remained while he made announcement of his conclusion. He spoke slowly; and as his answer was to be a valued record of this Land and its Race, I wrote down every word as uttered, leaving here and there space for description or comment, which spaces I have since then filled in.

"Lords of the National Council, Archbishop, Vladika, Lords of the Council of Justice and of National Law, Archimandrites, and my brothers all, I have, since I left you, held in the solitude of the forest counsel with myself—and with God; and He, in His gracious wisdom, has led my thinking to that conclusion which was from the first moment of knowledge of your intent presaged in my heart. Brothers, you know—or else a long life has been spent in vain—that my heart and mind are all for the nation—my experience, my life, my handjar. And when all is for her, why should I shrink to exercise on her behalf my riper judgment though the same should have to combat my own ambition? For ten centuries my race has not failed in its duty. Ages ago the men of that time trusted in the hands of my ancestors the Kingship, even as now you, their children, trust me. But to me it would be base to betray that trust, even by the smallest tittle. That would I do were I to take the honour of the crown which you have tendered to me, so long as there is another more worthy to wear it. Were there none other, I should place myself in your hands, and yield myself over to blind obedience of your desires. But such an one there is; dear to you already by his own deeds, now doubly dear to me, since he is my son by my daughter's love. He is young, whereas I am old. He is strong and brave and true; but my days of the usefulness of strength and bravery are over. For myself, I have long contemplated as the crown of my later years a quiet life in one of our monasteries, where I can still watch the whirl of the world around us on your behalf, and be a counsellor of younger men of more active minds. Brothers, we are entering on stirring times. I can see the signs of their coming all around us. North and South—the Old Order and the New, are about to clash, and we lie between the opposing forces. True it is that the Turk, after warring for a thousand years, is fading into insignificance. But from the North where conquests spring, have crept towards our Balkans the men of a mightier composite Power. Their march has been steady; and as they came, they fortified every step of the way. Now they are hard upon us, and are already beginning to swallow up the regions that we have helped to win from the dominion of Mahound. The Austrian is at our very gates. Beaten back by the Irredentists of Italy, she has so enmeshed herself with the Great Powers of Europe that she seems for the moment to be impregnable to a foe of our stature. There is but one hope for us—the uniting of the Balkan forces to turn a masterly front to North and West as well as to South and East. Is that a task for old hands to undertake? No; the hands must be young and supple; and the brain subtle, as well as the heart be strong, of whomsoever would dare such an accomplishment. Should I accept the crown, it would only postpone the doing of that which must ultimately be done. What avail would it be if, when the darkness closes over me, my daughter should be Queen Consort to the first King of a new dynasty? You know this man, and from your record I learn that you are already willing to have him as King to follow me. Why not begin with him? He comes of a great nation, wherein the principle of freedom is a vital principle that quickens all things. That nation has more than once shown to us its friendliness; and doubtless the very fact that an Englishman would become our King, and could carry into our Government the spirit and customs which have made his own country great, would do much to restore the old friendship, and even to create a new one, which would in times of trouble bring British fleets to our waters, and British bayonets to support our own handjars. It is within my own knowledge, though as yet unannounced to you, that Rupert Sent Leger has already obtained a patent, signed by the King of England himself, allowing him to be denaturalized in England, so that he can at once apply for naturalization here. I know also that he has brought hither a vast fortune, by aid of which he is beginning to strengthen our hands for war, in case that sad eventuality should arise. Witness his late ordering to be built nine other warships of the class that has already done such effective service in overthrowing the Turk—or the pirate, whichever he may have been. He has undertaken the defence of the Blue Mouth at his own cost in a way which will make it stronger than Gibraltar, and secure us against whatever use to which the Austrian may apply the vast forces already gathered in the Bocche di Cattaro. He is already founding aerial stations on our highest peaks for use of the war aeroplanes which are being built for him. It is such a man as this who makes a nation great; and right sure I am that in his hands this splendid land and our noble, freedom-loving people will flourish and become a power in the world. Then, brothers, let me, as one to whom this nation and its history and its future are dear, ask you to give to the husband of my daughter the honour which you would confer on me. For her I can speak as well as for myself. She shall suffer nothing in dignity either. Were I indeed King, she, as my daughter, would be a Princess of the world. As it will be, she shall be companion and Queen of a great King, and her race, which is mine, shall flourish in all the lustre of the new Dynasty.

"Therefore on all accounts, my brothers, for the sake of our dear Land of the Blue Mountains, make the Gospodar Rupert, who has so proved himself, your King. And make me happy in my retirement to the cloister."

When the Voivode ceased to speak, all still remained silent and standing. But there was no mistaking their acquiescence in his most generous prayer. The President of the Council well interpreted the general wish when he said:

"Lords of the National Council, Archbishop, Vladika, Lords of the Councils of Justice and National Law, Archimandrites, and all who are present, is it agreed that we prepare at leisure a fitting reply to the Voivode Peter of the historic House of Vissarion, stating our agreement with his wish?"

To which there was a unanimous answer:

"It is." He went on:

"Further. Shall we ask the Gospodar Rupert of the House of Sent Leger, allied through his marriage to the Voivodin Teuta, daughter and only child of the Voivode Peter of Vissarion, to come hither to-morrow? And that, when he is amongst us, we confer on him the Crown and Kingship of the Land of the Blue Mountains?"

Again came the answer: "It is."

But this time it rang out like the sound of a gigantic trumpet, and the handjars flashed.

Whereupon the session was adjourned for the space of a day.

THE SAME—*Continued.*

September 10, 1907.

When the National Council met to-day the Voivode Peter Vissarion sat with them, but well back, so that at first his presence was hardly noticeable. After the necessary preliminaries had been gone through, they requested the presence of the Gospodar Rupert—Mr. Rupert Sent Leger—who was reported as waiting in the "Chamber of the High Officers." He at once accompanied back to the Hall the deputation sent to conduct him. As he made his appearance in the doorway the Councillors stood up. There was a burst of enthusiasm, and the handjars flashed. For an instant he stood silent, with lifted hand, as though indicating that he wished to speak. So soon as this was recognized, silence fell on the assembly, and he spoke:

"I pray you, may the Voivodin Teuta of Vissarion, who has accompanied me hither, appear with me to hear your wishes?" There was an immediate and enthusiastic acquiescence, and, after bowing his thanks, he retired to conduct her.

Her appearance was received with an ovation similar to that given to Gospodar Rupert, to which she bowed with dignified sweetness. She, with her husband, was conducted to the top of the Hall by the President, who came down to escort them. In the meantime another chair had been placed beside that prepared for the Gospodar, and these two sat.

The President then made the formal statement conveying to the "Gospodar Rupert" the wishes of the Council, on behalf of the nation, to offer to him the Crown and Kingship of the Land of the Blue Mountains. The message was couched in almost the same words as had been used the previous day in making the offer to the Voivode Peter Vissarion, only differing to meet the special circumstances. The Gospodar Rupert listened in grave silence. The whole thing was manifestly quite new to him, but he preserved a self-control wonderful under the circumstances. When, having been made aware of the previous offer to the Voivode and the declared wish of the latter, he rose to speak, there was stillness in the Hall. He commenced with a few broken words of thanks; then he grew suddenly and strangely calm as he went on:

"But before I can even attempt to make a fitting reply, I should know if it is contemplated to join with me in this great honour my dear wife the Voivodin Teuta of Vissarion, who has so splendidly proved her worthiness to hold any place in the government of the Land. I fain would . . . "

He was interrupted by the Voivodin, who, standing up beside him and holding his left arm, said:

"Do not, President, and Lords all, think me wanting in that respect of a wife for husband which in the Blue Mountains we hold so dear, if I venture to interrupt my lord. I am here, not merely as a wife, but as Voivodin of Vissarion, and by the memory of all the noble women of that noble line I feel constrained to a great duty. We women of Vissarion, in all the history of centuries, have never put ourselves forward in rivalry of our lords. Well I know that my own dear lord will forgive me as wife if I err; but I speak to you, the Council of the nation, from another ground and with another tongue. My lord does not, I fear, know as you do, and as I do too, that of old, in the history of this Land, when Kingship was existent, that it was ruled by that law of masculine supremacy which, centuries after, became known as the *Lex Salica.* Lords of the Council of the Blue Mountains, I am a wife of the Blue Mountains—as a wife young as yet, but with the blood of forty generations of loyal women in my veins. And it would ill become me, whom my husband honours—wife to the man whom you would honour—to take a part in changing the ancient custom which has been held in honour for all the thousand years, which is the glory of Blue Mountain womanhood. What an example such would be in an age when self-seeking women of other nations seek to forget their womanhood in the struggle to vie in equality with men! Men of the Blue Mountains, I speak for our women when I say that we hold of greatest price the glory of our men. To be their companions is our happiness; to be their wives is the completion of our lives; to be mothers of their children is our share of the glory that is theirs.

"Therefore, I pray you, men of the Blue Mountains, let me but be as any other wife in our land, equal to them in domestic happiness, which is our woman's sphere; and if that priceless honour may be vouchsafed to me, and I be worthy and able to bear it, an exemplar of woman's rectitude." With a low, modest, graceful bow, she sat down.

There was no doubt as to the reception of her renunciation of Queenly dignity. There was more honour to her in the quick, fierce shout which arose, and the unanimous upward swing of the handjars, than in the wearing of any crown which could adorn the head of woman.

The spontaneous action of the Gospodar Rupert was another source of joy to all—a fitting corollary to what had gone before. He rose to his feet, and, taking his wife in his arms, kissed her before all. Then they sat down, with their chairs close, bashfully holding hands like a pair of lovers.

Then Rupert arose—he is Rupert now; no lesser name is on the lips of his people henceforth. With an intense earnestness which seemed to glow in his face, he said simply:

"What can I say except that I am in all ways, now and for ever, obedient to your wishes?" Then, raising his handjar and holding it before him, he kissed the hilt, saying:

"Hereby I swear to be honest and just—to be, God helping me, such a King as you would wish—in so far as the strength is given me. Amen."

This ended the business of the Session, and the Council showed unmeasured delight. Again and again the handjars flashed, as the cheers rose "three times three" in British fashion.

When Rupert—I am told I must not write him down as "King Rupert" until after the formal crowning, which is ordained for Wednesday, October 16th,—and Teuta had withdrawn, the Voivode Peter Vissarion, the President and Council conferred in committee with the Presidents of the High Courts of National Law and of Justice as to the formalities to be observed in the crowning of the King, and of the formal notification to be given to foreign Powers. These proceedings kept them far into the night.

FROM "The London Messenger."

CORONATION FESTIVITIES OF THE BLUE MOUNTAINS.
(*From our Special Correspondent.*)

PLAZAC,
October 14, 1907.

As I sat down to a poorly-equipped luncheon-table on board the Austro-Orient liner *Franz Joseph*, I mourned in my heart (and I may say incidentally in other portions of my internal economy) the comfort and gastronomic luxury of the King and Emperor Hotel at Trieste. A brief comparison between the menus of to-day's lunch and yesterday's will afford to the reader a striking object-lesson:

Trieste.	*Steamer.*
Eggs à la cocotte.	Scrambled eggs on toast.
Stewed chicken, with paprika.	Cold chicken.
Devilled slices of Westphalian ham (boiled in wine).	Cold ham.
Tunny fish, pickled.	Bismarck herrings.
Rice, burst in cream.	Stewed apples.
Guava jelly.	Swiss cheese.

Consequence: Yesterday I was well and happy, and looked forward to a good night's sleep, which came off. To-day I am dull and heavy, also restless, and I am convinced that at sleeping-time my liver will have it all its own way.

The journey to Ragusa, and thence to Plazac, is writ large with a pigment of misery on at least one human heart. Let a silence fall upon it! In such wise only can Justice and Mercy join hands.

Plazac is a miserable place. There is not a decent hotel in it. It was perhaps on this account that the new King, Rupert, had erected for the alleged convenience of his guests of the Press a series of large temporary hotels, such as were in evidence at the St. Louis Exposition. Here each guest was given a room to himself, somewhat after the nature of the cribs in a Rowton house. From my first night in it I am able to speak from experience of the sufferings of a prisoner of the third class. I am, however, bound to say that the dining and reception rooms were, though uncomfortably plain, adequate for temporary use. Happily we shall not have to endure many more meals here, as to-morrow we all dine with the King in the State House; and as the cuisine is under the control of that *cordon bleu*, Gaston de Faux Pas, who so long controlled the gastronomic (we might almost say Gastonomic) destinies of the Rois des Diamants in the Place Vendôme, we may, I think, look forward to not going to bed hungry. Indeed, the anticipations formed from a survey of our meagre sleeping accommodation were not realized at dinnertime to-night. To our intense astonishment, an excellent dinner was served, though, to be sure, the cold dishes predominated (a thing I always find bad for one's liver). Just as we were finishing, the King (nominated) came amongst us in quite an informal way, and, having bidden us a hearty welcome, asked that we should drink a glass of wine together. This we did in an excellent (if rather sweet) glass of Cliquot '93. King Rupert (nominated) then asked us to resume our seats. He walked between the tables, now and again recognizing some journalistic friend whom he had met early in life in his days of adventure. The men spoken to seemed vastly pleased—with themselves probably. Pretty bad form of them, I call it! For myself, I was glad I had not previously met him in the same casual way, as it saved me from what I should have felt a humiliation—the being patronized in that public way by a prospective King who had not (in a Court sense) been born. The writer, who is by profession a barrister-at-law, is satisfied at being himself a county gentleman and heir to an historic estate in the ancient county of Salop, which can boast a larger population than the Land of the Blue Mountains.

EDITORIAL NOTE.—We must ask our readers to pardon the report in yesterday's paper sent from Plazac. The writer was not on our regular staff, but asked to be allowed to write the report, as he was a kinsman of King Rupert of the Blue Mountains, and would therefore be in a position to obtain special information and facilities of description "from inside," as he puts it. On reading the paper, we cabled his recall; we cabled also, in case he did not obey, to have his ejectment effected forthwith.

We have also cabled Mr. Mordred Booth, the well-known correspondent, who was, to our knowledge, in Plazac for his own purposes, to send us full (and proper) details. We take it our readers will prefer a graphic account of the ceremony to a farrago of cheap menus, comments on his own liver, and a belittling of an Englishman of such noble character and achievements that a rising nation has chosen him for their King, and one whom our own nation loves to honour. We shall not, of course, mention our abortive correspondent's name, unless compelled thereto by any future utterance of his.

FROM "The London Messenger."

THE CORONATION OF KING RUPERT OF THE BLUE MOUNTAINS.
(*By our Special Correspondent, Mordred Booth.*)

PLAZAC,
October 17, 1907.

Plazac does not boast of a cathedral or any church of sufficient dimensions for a coronation ceremony on an adequate scale. It was therefore decided by the National Council, with the consent of the King, that it should be held at the old church of St. Sava at Vissarion—the former home of the Queen. Accordingly, arrangements had been made to bring thither on the warships on the morning of the coronation the whole of the nation's guests. In St. Sava's the religious ceremony would take place, after which there would be a banquet in the Castle of Vissarion. The guests would then return on the warships to Plazac, where would be held what is called here the "National Coronation."

In the Land of the Blue Mountains it was customary in the old days, when there were Kings, to have two ceremonies—one carried out by the official head of the national Church, the Greek Church; the other by the people in a ritual adopted by themselves, on much the same basis as the Germanic Folk-Moot. The Blue Mountains is a nation of strangely loyal tendencies. What was a thousand years ago is to be to-day—so far, of course, as is possible under the altered condition of things.

The church of St. Sava is very old and very beautiful, built in the manner of old Greek churches, full of monuments of bygone worthies of the Blue Mountains. But, of course, neither it nor the ceremony held in it to-day can compare in splendour with certain other ceremonials—for instance, the coronation of the penultimate Czar in Moscow, of Alfonso XII. in Madrid, of Carlos I. in Lisbon.

The church was arranged much after the fashion of Westminster Abbey for the coronation of King Edward VII., though, of course, not so many persons present, nor so much individual splendour. Indeed, the number of those present, outside those officially concerned and the Press of the world, was very few.

The most striking figure present—next to King Rupert, who is seven feet high and a magnificent man—was the Queen Consort, Teuta. She sat in front of a small gallery erected for the purpose just opposite the throne. She is a strikingly beautiful woman, tall and finely-formed, with jet-black hair and eyes like black diamonds, but with the unique quality that there are stars in them which seem to take varied colour according to each strong emotion. But it was not even her beauty or the stars in her eyes which drew the first glance of all. These details showed on scrutiny, but from afar off the attractive point was her dress. Surely never before did woman, be she Queen or peasant, wear such a costume on a festive occasion.

She was dressed in a white *Shroud*, and in that only. I had heard something of the story which goes behind that strange costume, and shall later on send it to you.[1]

When the procession entered the church through the great western door, the national song of the Blue Mountains, “Guide our feet through darkness, O Jehovah,” was sung by an unseen choir, in which the organ, supplemented by martial instruments, joined. The Archbishop was robed in readiness before the altar, and close around him stood the Archimandrites of the four great monasteries. The Vladika stood in front of the Members of the National Council. A little to one side of this body was a group of high officials, Presidents of the Councils of National Law and Justice, the Chancellor, etc.—all in splendid robes of great antiquity—the High Marshall of the Forces and the Lord high Admiral.

When all was ready for the ceremonial act of coronation, the Archbishop raised his hand, whereupon the music ceased. Turning around, so that he faced the Queen, who thereon stood up, the King drew his handjar and saluted her in Blue Mountain fashion—the point raised as high possible, and then dropped down till it almost touches the ground. Every man in the church, ecclesiastics and all, wear the handjar, and, following the King by the interval of a second, their weapons flashed out. There was something symbolic, as well as touching, in this truly royal salute, led by the King. His handjar is a mighty blade, and held high in the hands of a man of his stature, it overtowered everything in the church. It was an inspiriting sight. No one who saw will ever forget that noble flashing of blades in the thousand-year-old salute . . .

The coronation was short, simple, and impressive. Rupert knelt whilst the Archbishop, after a short, fervent prayer, placed on his head the bronze crown of the first King of the Blue Mountains, Peter. This was handed to him by the Vladika, to whom it was brought from the National Treasury by a procession of the high officers. A blessing of the new King and his Queen Teuta concluded the ceremony. Rupert’s first act on rising from his knees was to draw his handjar and salute his people.

After the ceremony in St. Sava, the procession was reformed, and took its way to the Castle of Vissarion, which is some distance off across a picturesque creek, bounded on either side by noble cliffs of vast height. The King led the way, the Queen walking with him and holding his hand . . . The Castle of Vissarion is of great antiquity, and picturesque beyond belief. I am sending later on, as a special article, a description of it . . .

The “Coronation Feast,” as it was called on the menu, was held in the Great Hall, which is of noble proportions. I enclose copy of the menu, as our readers may wish to know something of the details of such a feast in this part of the world.

One feature of the banquet was specially noticeable. As the National Officials were guests of the King and Queen, they were waited on and served by the King and

---

[1] Editorial Note—We shall, in our issue of Saturday week, give a full record of the romantic story of Queen Teuta and her Shroud, written by Mr. Mordred Booth, and illustrated by our special artist, Mr. Neillison Browne, who is Mr. Booth’s artistic collaborateur in the account of King Rupert’s Coronation.

Queen in person. The rest of the guests, including us of the Press, were served by the King's household, not the servants—none of that cult were visible—but by the ladies and gentlemen of the Court.

There was only one toast, and that was given by the King, all standing: "The Land of the Blue Mountains, and may we all do our duty to the Land we love!" Before drinking, his mighty handjar flashed out again, and in an instant every table at which the Blue Mountaineers sat was ringed with flashing steel. I may add parenthetically that the handjar is essentially the national weapon. I do not know if the Blue Mountaineers take it to bed with them, but they certainly wear it everywhere else. Its drawing seems to emphasize everything in national life . . .

We embarked again on the warships—one a huge, steel-plated Dreadnought, up to date in every particular, the other an armoured yacht most complete in every way, and of unique speed. The King and Queen, the Lords of the Council, together with the various high ecclesiastics and great officials, went on the yacht, which the Lord High Admiral, a man of remarkably masterful physiognomy, himself steered. The rest of those present at the Coronation came on the warship. The latter went fast, but the yacht showed her heels all the way. However, the King's party waited in the dock in the Blue Mouth. From this a new cable-line took us all to the State House at Plazac. Here the procession was reformed, and wound its way to a bare hill in the immediate vicinity. The King and Queen—the King still wearing the ancient bronze crown with which the Archbishop had invested him at St. Sava's—the Archbishop, the Vladika, and the four Archimandrites stood together at the top of the hill, the King and Queen being, of course, in the front. A courteous young gentleman, to whom I had been accredited at the beginning of the day—all guests were so attended—explained to me that, as this was the national as opposed to the religious ceremony, the Vladika, who is the official representative of the laity, took command here. The ecclesiastics were put prominently forward, simply out of courtesy, in obedience to the wish of the people, by whom they were all greatly beloved.

Then commenced another unique ceremony, which, indeed, might well find a place in our Western countries. As far as ever we could see were masses of men roughly grouped, not in any uniform, but all in national costume, and armed only with the handjar. In the front of each of these groups or bodies stood the National Councillor for that district, distinguishable by his official robe and chain. There were in all seventeen of these bodies. These were unequal in numbers, some of them predominating enormously over others, as, indeed, might be expected in so mountainous a country. In all there were present, I was told, over a hundred thousand men. So far as I can judge from long experience of looking at great bodies of men, the estimate was a just one. I was a little surprised to see so many, for the population of the Blue Mountains is never accredited in books of geography as a large one. When I made inquiry as to how the frontier guard was being for the time maintained, I was told:

"By the women mainly. But, all the same, we have also a male guard which covers the whole frontier except that to seaward. Each man has with him six women, so that the whole line is unbroken. Moreover, sir, you must bear in mind that in the Blue Mountains our women are trained to arms as well as our men—ay, and they could give a good account of themselves, too, against any foe that should assail us. Our history shows what women can do in defence. I tell you, the Turkish population would be bigger to-day but for the women who on our frontier fought of old for defence of their homes!"

"No wonder this nation has kept her freedom for a thousand years!" I said.

At a signal given by the President of the National Council one of the Divisions moved forwards. It was not an ordinary movement, but an intense rush made with all the *elan* and vigour of hardy and highly-trained men. They came on, not merely at the double, but as if delivering an attack. Handjar in hand, they rushed forward. I can only compare their rush to an artillery charge or to an attack of massed cavalry battalions. It was my fortune to see the former at Magenta and the latter at Sadowa, so that I know what such illustration means. I may also say that I saw the relief column which Roberts organized rush through a town on its way to relieve Mafeking; and no one who had the delight of seeing that inspiring progress of a flying army on their way to relieve their comrades needs to be told what a rush of armed men can be. With speed which was simply desperate they ran up the hill, and, circling to the left, made a ring round the topmost plateau, where stood the King. When the ring was complete, the stream went on lapping round and round till the whole tally was exhausted. In the meantime another Division had followed, its leader joining close behind the end of the first. Then came another and another. An unbroken line circled and circled round the hill in seeming endless array, till the whole slopes were massed with moving men, dark in colour, and with countless glittering points everywhere. When the whole of the Divisions had thus surrounded the King, there was a moment's hush—a silence so still that it almost seemed as if Nature stood still also. We who looked on were almost afraid to breathe.

Then suddenly, without, so far as I could see, any fugleman or word of command, the handjars of all that mighty array of men flashed upward as one, and like thunder pealed the National cry:

"The Blue Mountains and Duty!"

After the cry there was a strange subsidence which made the onlooker rub his eyes. It seemed as though the whole mass of fighting men had partially sunk into the ground. Then the splendid truth burst upon us—the whole nation was kneeling at the feet of their chosen King, who stood upright.

Another moment of silence, as King Rupert, taking off his crown, held it up in his left hand, and, holding his great handjar high in his right, cried in a voice so strong that it came ringing over that serried mass like a trumpet:

"To Freedom of our Nation, and to Freedom within it, I dedicate these and myself. I swear!"

So saying, he, too, sank on his knees, whilst we all instinctively uncovered.

The silence which followed lasted several seconds; then, without a sign, as though one and all acted instinctively, the whole body stood up. Thereupon was executed a movement which, with all my experience of soldiers and war, I never saw equalled—not with the Russian Royal Guard saluting the Czar at his Coronation, not with an impi of Cetewayo's Zulus whirling through the opening of a kraal.

For a second or two the whole mass seemed to writhe or shudder, and then, lo! the whole District Divisions were massed again in completeness, its Councillors next the King, and the Divisions radiating outwards down the hill like wedges.

This completed the ceremony, and everything broke up into units. Later, I was told by my official friend that the King's last movement—the oath as he sank to his knees—was an innovation of his own. All I can say is, if, in the future, and for all time, it is not taken for a precedent, and made an important part of the Patriotic Coronation ceremony, the Blue Mountaineers will prove themselves to be a much more stupid people than they seem at present to be.

The conclusion of the Coronation festivities was a time of unalloyed joy. It was the banquet given to the King and Queen by the nation; the guests of the nation were included in the royal party. It was a unique ceremony. Fancy a picnic-party of a hundred thousand persons, nearly all men. There must have been made beforehand vast and elaborate preparations, ramifying through the whole nation. Each section had brought provisions sufficient for their own consumption in addition to several special dishes for the guest-tables; but the contribution of each section was not consumed by its own members.

It was evidently a part of the scheme that all should derive from a common stock, so that the feeling of brotherhood and common property should be preserved in this monumental fashion.

The guest-tables were the only tables to be seen. The bulk of the feasters sat on the ground. The tables were brought forward by the men themselves—no such thing as domestic service was known on this day—from a wood close at hand, where they and the chairs had been placed in readiness. The linen and crockery used had been sent for the purpose from the households of every town and village. The flowers were plucked in the mountains early that morning by the children, and the gold and silver plate used for adornment were supplied from the churches. Each dish at the guest-tables was served by the men of each section in turn.

Over the whole array seemed to be spread an atmosphere of joyousness, of peace, of brotherhood. It would be impossible to adequately describe that amazing scene, a whole nation of splendid men surrounding their new King and Queen, loving to honour and serve them. Scattered about through that vast crowd were groups of musicians, chosen from amongst themselves. The space covered by this titanic picnic was so vast that there were few spots from which you could hear music proceeding from different quarters.

After dinner we all sat and smoked; the music became rather vocal than instrumental—indeed, presently we did not hear the sound of any instrument at all. Only knowing a few words of Balkan, I could not follow the meanings of the songs, but I gathered that they were all legendary or historical. To those who could understand, as I was informed by my tutelary young friend, who stayed beside me the whole of this memorable day, we were listening to the history of the Land of the Blue Mountains in ballad form. Somewhere or other throughout that vast concourse each notable record of ten centuries was being told to eager ears.

It was now late in the day. Slowly the sun had been dropping down over the Calabrian Mountains, and the glamorous twilight was stealing over the immediate scene. No one seemed to notice the coming of the dark, which stole down on us with an unspeakable mystery. For long we sat still, the clatter of many tongues becoming stilled into the witchery of the scene. Lower the sun sank, till only the ruddiness of the afterglow lit the expanse with rosy light; then this failed in turn, and the night shut down quickly.

At last, when we could just discern the faces close to us, a simultaneous movement began. Lights began to flash out in places all over the hillside. At first these seemed as tiny as glow-worms seen in a summer wood, but by degrees they grew till the space was set with little circles of light. These in turn grew and grew in both number and strength. Flames began to leap out from piles of wood, torches were lighted and held high. Then the music began again, softly at first, but then louder as the musicians began to gather to the centre, where sat the King and Queen. The music was wild and semi-barbaric, but full of sweet melody. It somehow seemed to bring before us a distant past; one and all, according to the strength of our imagination and the volume of our knowledge, saw episodes and phases of bygone history come before us. There was a wonderful rhythmic, almost choric, force in the time kept, which made it almost impossible to sit still. It was an invitation to the dance such as I had never before heard in any nation or at any time. Then the lights began to gather round. Once more the mountaineers took something of the same formation as at the crowning. Where the royal party sat was a level mead, with crisp, short grass, and round it what one might well call the Ring of the Nation was formed.

The music grew louder. Each mountaineer who had not a lit torch already lighted one, and the whole rising hillside was a glory of light. The Queen rose, and the King an instant after. As they rose men stepped forward and carried away their chairs, or rather thrones. The Queen gave the King her hand—this is, it seems, the privilege of the wife as distinguished from any other woman. Their feet took the time of the music, and they moved into the centre of the ring.

That dance was another thing to remember, won from the haunting memories of that strange day. At first the King and Queen danced all alone. They began with stately movement, but as the music quickened their feet kept time, and the swing of their bodies with movements kept growing more and more ecstatic at every beat till, in true Balkan fashion, the dance became a very agony of passionate movement.

At this point the music slowed down again, and the mountaineers began to join in the dance. At first slowly, one by one, they joined in, the Vladika and the higher priests leading; then everywhere the whole vast crowd began to dance, till the earth around us seemed to shake. The lights quivered, flickered, blazed out again, and rose and fell as that hundred thousand men, each holding a torch, rose and fell with the rhythm of the dance. Quicker, quicker grew the music, faster grew the rushing and pounding of the feet, till the whole nation seemed now in an ecstasy.

I stood near the Vladika, and in the midst of this final wildness I saw him draw from his belt a short, thin flute; then he put it to his lips and blew a single note—a fierce, sharp note, which pierced the volume of sound more surely than would the thunder of a cannon-shot. On the instant everywhere each man put his torch under his foot.

There was complete and immediate darkness, for the fires, which had by now fallen low, had evidently been trodden out in the measure of the dance. The music still kept in its rhythmic beat, but slower than it had yet been. Little by little this beat was pointed and emphasized by the clapping of hands—at first only a few, but spreading till everyone present was beating hands to the slow music in the darkness. This lasted a little while, during which, looking round, I noticed a faint light beginning to steal up behind the hills. The moon was rising.

Again there came a note from the Vladika's flute—a single note, sweet and subtle, which I can only compare with a note from a nightingale, vastly increased in powers. It, too, won through the thunder of the hand-claps, and on the second the sound ceased. The sudden stillness, together with the darkness, was so impressive that we could almost hear our hearts beating. And then came through the darkness the most beautiful and impressive sound heard yet. That mighty concourse, without fugleman of any sort, began, in low, fervent voice, to sing the National Anthem. At first it was of so low tone as to convey the idea of a mighty assembly of violinists playing with the mutes on. But it gradually rose till the air above us seemed to throb and quiver. Each syllable—each word—spoken in unison by the vast throng was as clearly enunciated as though spoken by a single voice:

"Guide our feet through darkness, O Jehovah."

This anthem, sung out of full hearts, remains on our minds as the last perfection of a perfect day. For myself, I am not ashamed to own that it made me weep like a child. Indeed, I cannot write of it now as I would; it unmans me so!

* * * * *

In the early morning, whilst the mountains were still rather grey than blue, the cable-line took us to the Blue Mouth, where we embarked in the King's yacht, *The Lady*, which took us across the Adriatic at a pace which I had hitherto considered impossible. The King and Queen came to the landing to see us off. They stood together at the right-hand side of the red-carpeted gangway, and shook hands with each guest as he went on board. The instant the last passenger had stepped on deck the gangway was withdrawn. The Lord High Admiral, who stood on the bridge, raised his hand, and we swept towards the mouth of the gulf. Of course, all hats were off, and we cheered frantically. I can truly say that if King Rupert and Queen Teuta should ever wish to found in the Blue Mountains a colony of diplomatists and journalists, those who were their guests on this great occasion will volunteer to a man. I think old Hempetch, who is the doyen of English-speaking journalists, voiced our sentiments when he said:

"May God bless them and theirs with every grace and happiness, and send prosperity to the Land and the rule!" I think the King and Queen heard us cheer, they turned to look at our flying ship again.

BOOK IX: BALKA

RUPERT'S JOURNAL—Continued (Longe Intervallo).

February 10, 1908.

It is so long since I even thought of this journal that I hardly know where to begin. I always heard that a married man is a pretty busy man; but since I became one, though it is a new life to me, and of a happiness undreamt of, I *know* what that life is. But I had no idea that this King business was anything like what it is. Why, it never leaves me a moment at all to myself—or, what is worse, to Teuta. If people who condemn Kings had only a single month of my life in that capacity, they would form an opinion different from that which they hold. It might be useful to have a Professor of Kingship in the Anarchists' College—whenever it is founded!

Everything has gone on well with us, I am glad to say. Teuta is in splendid health, though she has—but only very lately—practically given up going on her own aeroplane. It was, I know, a great sacrifice to make, just as she had become an expert at it. They say here that she is one of the best drivers in the Blue Mountains—and that is in the world, for we have made that form of movement our own. Ever since we found the pitch-blende pockets in the Great Tunnel, and discovered the simple process of extracting the radium from it, we have gone on by leaps and bounds. When first Teuta told me she would "aero" no more for a while, I thought she was wise, and backed her up in it: for driving an aeroplane is trying work and hard on the nerves. I only learned then the reason for her caution—the usual one of a young wife. That was three months ago, and only this morning she told me she would not go sailing in the air, even with me, till she could do so "without risk"—she did not mean risk to herself. Aunt Janet knew what she meant, and counselled her strongly to stick to her resolution. So for the next few months I am to do my air-sailing alone.

The public works which we began immediately after the Coronation are going strong. We began at the very beginning on an elaborate system. The first thing was to adequately fortify the Blue Mouth. Whilst the fortifications were being constructed we kept all the warships in the gulf. But when the point of safety was reached, we made the ships do sentry-go along the coast, whilst we trained men for service at sea. It is our plan to take by degrees all the young men and teach them this wise, so that at the end the whole population shall be trained for sea as well as for land. And as we are teaching them the airship service, too, they will be at home in all the elements—except fire, of course, though if that should become a necessity, we shall tackle it too!

We started the Great Tunnel at the farthest inland point of the Blue Mouth, and ran it due east at an angle of 45 degrees, so that, when complete, it would go right through the first line of hills, coming out on the plateau Plazac. The plateau is not very wide—half a mile at most—and the second tunnel begins on the eastern side of it. This new tunnel is at a smaller angle, as it has to pierce the second hill—a mountain this time. When it comes out on the east side of that, it will tap the real productive belt. Here it is that our hardwood-trees are finest, and where the greatest mineral deposits are found. This plateau is of enormous length, and runs north arid south round the great bulk of the central mountain, so that in time, when we put up a circular railway, we can bring, at a merely nominal cost, all sorts of material up or down. It is on this level that we have built the great factories for war material. We are tunnelling into the mountains, where are the great deposits of coal. We run the trucks in and out on the level, and can get perfect ventilation with little cost or labour. Already we are mining all the coal which we consume within our own confines, and we can, if we wish, within a year export largely. The great slopes of these tunnels give us the necessary aid of specific gravity, and as we carry an endless water-supply in great tubes that way also, we can do whatever we wish by hydraulic power. As one by one the European and Asiatic nations began to reduce their war preparations, we took over their disbanded workmen though our agents, so that already we have a productive staff of skilled workmen larger than anywhere else in the world. I think myself that we were fortunate in being able to get ahead so fast with our preparations for war manufacture, for if some of the "Great Powers," as they call themselves, knew the measure of our present production, they would immediately try to take active measures against us. In such case we should have to fight them, which would delay us. But if we can have another year untroubled, we shall, so far as war material is concerned, be able to defy any nation in the world. And if the time may only come peacefully till we have our buildings and machinery complete, we can prepare war-stores and implements for the whole Balkan nations. And then—But that is a dream. We shall know in good time.

In the meantime all goes well. The cannon foundries are built and active. We are already beginning to turn out finished work. Of course, our first guns are not very large, but they are good. The big guns, and especially siege-guns, will come later. And when the great extensions are complete, and the boring and wire-winding machines are in working order, we can go merrily on. I suppose that by that time the whole of the upper plateau will be like a manufacturing town—at any rate, we have plenty of raw material to hand. The haematite mines seem to be inexhaustible, and as the raising of the ore is cheap and easy by means of our extraordinary water-power, and as coal comes down to the plateau by its own gravity on the cable-line, we have natural advantages which exist hardly anywhere else in the world—certainly not all together, as here. That bird's eye view of the Blue Mouth which we had from the aeroplane when Teuta saw that vision of the future has not been in vain. The aeroplane works are having a splendid output. The aeroplane is a large and visible product; there is no mistaking when it is there! We have already a large and respectable aerial fleet. The factories for explosives are, of course, far away in bare valleys, where accidental effects are minimized. So, too, are the radium works, wherein unknown dangers may lurk. The turbines in the tunnel give us all the power we want at present, and, later on, when the new tunnel, which we call the "water tunnel," which is already begun, is complete, the available power will be immense. All these works are bringing up our shipping, and we are in great hopes for the future.

So much for our material prosperity. But with it comes a larger life and greater hopes. The stress of organizing and founding these great works is practically over. As they are not only self-supporting, but largely productive, all anxiety in the way of national expenditure is minimized. And, more than all, I am able to give my unhampered attention to those matters of even more than national importance on which the ultimate development, if not the immediate strength, of our country must depend.

I am well into the subject of a great Balkan Federation. This, it turns out, has for long been the dream of Teuta's life, as also that of the present Archimandrite of Plazac, her father, who, since I last touched this journal, having taken on himself a Holy Life, was, by will of the Church, the Monks, and the People, appointed to that great office on the retirement of Petrof Vlastimir.

Such a Federation had long been in the air. For myself, I had seen its inevitableness from the first. The modern aggressions of the Dual Nation, interpreted by her past history with regard to Italy, pointed towards the necessity of such a protective measure. And now, when Servia and Bulgaria were used as blinds to cover her real movements to incorporate with herself as established the provinces, once Turkish, which had been entrusted to her temporary protection by the Treaty of Berlin; when it would seem that Montenegro was to be deprived for all time of the hope of regaining the Bocche di Cattaro, which she had a century ago won, and held at the point of the sword, until a Great Power had, under a wrong conviction, handed it over to her neighbouring Goliath; when the Sandjack of Novi-Bazar was threatened with the fate which seemed to have already overtaken Bosnia and Herzegovina; when gallant little Montenegro was already shut out from the sea by the octopus-like grip of Dalmatia crouching along her western shore; when Turkey was dwindling down to almost ineptitude; when Greece was almost a byword, and when Albania as a nation—though still nominally subject—was of such unimpaired virility that there were great possibilities of her future, it was imperative that something must happen if the Balkan race was not to be devoured piecemeal by her northern neighbours. To the end of ultimate protection I found most of them willing to make defensive alliance.

And as the true defence consists in judicious attack, I have no doubt that an alliance so based must ultimately become one for all purposes. Albania was the most difficult to win to the scheme, as her own complications with her suzerain, combined with the pride and suspiciousness of her people, made approach a matter of extreme caution. It was only possible when I could induce her rulers to see that, no matter how great her pride and valour, the magnitude of northern advance, if unchecked, must ultimately overwhelm her.

I own that this map-making was nervous work, for I could not shut my eyes to the fact that German lust of enlargement lay behind Austria's advance. At and before that time expansion was the dominant idea of the three Great Powers of Central Europe. Russia went eastward, hoping to gather to herself the rich north-eastern provinces of China, till ultimately she should dominate the whole of Northern Europe and Asia from the Gulf of Finland to the Yellow Sea. Germany wished to link the North Sea to the Mediterranean by her own territory, and thus stand as a flawless barrier across Europe from north to south.

When Nature should have terminated the headship of the Empire-Kingdom, she, as natural heir, would creep southward through the German-speaking provinces. Thus Austria, of course kept in ignorance of her neighbour's ultimate aims, had to extend towards the south. She had been barred in her western movement by the rise of the Irredentist party in Italy, and consequently had to withdraw behind the frontiers of Carinthia, Carniola, and Istria.

My own dream of the new map was to make "Balka"—the Balkan Federation—take in ultimately all south of a line drawn from the Isle of Serpents to Aquileia. There would—must—be difficulties in the carrying out of such a scheme. Of course, it involved Austria giving up Dalmatia, Istria, and Sclavonia, as well as a part of Croatia and the Hungarian Banat. On the contrary, she might look for centuries of peace in the south. But it would make for peace so strongly that each of the States impinging on it would find it worth while to make a considerable sacrifice to have it effected. To its own integers it would offer a lasting settlement of interests which at present conflicted, and a share in a new world-power. Each of these integers would be absolutely self-governing and independent, being only united for purposes of mutual good. I did not despair that even Turkey and Greece, recognizing that benefit and safety would ensue without the destruction or even minimizing of individuality, would, sooner or later, come into the Federation. The matter is already so far advanced that within a month the various rulers of the States involved are to have a secret and informal meeting. Doubtless some larger plan and further action will be then evolved. It will be an anxious time for all in this zone—and outside it—till this matter is all settled. In any case, the manufacture of war material will go on until it is settled, one way or another.

RUPERT'S JOURNAL—*Continued.*

March 6, 1908.

I breathe more freely. The meeting has taken place here at Vissarion. Nominal cause of meeting: a hunting-party in the Blue Mountains. Not any formal affair. Not a Chancellor or Secretary of State or Diplomatist of any sort present. All headquarters. It was, after all, a real hunting-party. Good sportsmen, plenty of game, lots of beaters, everything organized properly, and an effective tally of results. I think we all enjoyed ourselves in the matter of sport; and as the political result was absolute unanimity of purpose and intention, there could be no possible cause of complaint.

So it is all decided. Everything is pacific. There is not a suggestion even of war, revolt, or conflicting purpose of any kind. We all go on exactly as we are doing for another year, pursuing our own individual objects, just as at present. But we are all to see that in our own households order prevails. All that is supposed to be effective is to be kept in good working order, and whatever is, at present, not adequate to possibilities is to be made so. This is all simply protective and defensive. We understand each other. But if any hulking stranger should undertake to interfere in our domestic concerns, we shall all unite on the instant to keep things as we wish them to remain. We shall be ready. Alfred's maxim of Peace shall be once more exemplified. In the meantime the factories shall work overtime in our own mountains, and the output shall be for the general good of our special community—the bill to be settled afterwards amicably. There can hardly be any difference of opinion about that, as the others will be the consumers of our surplus products. We are the producers, who produce for ourselves first, and then for the limited market of those within the Ring. As we undertake to guard our own frontiers—sea and land—and are able to do so, the goods are to be warehoused in the Blue Mountains until required—if at all—for participation in the markets of the world, and especially in the European market. If all goes well and the markets are inactive, the goods shall be duly delivered to the purchasers as arranged.

So much for the purely mercantile aspect.

THE VOIVODIN JANET MACKELPIE'S NOTES.

May 21, 1908.

As Rupert began to neglect his Journal when he was made a King, so, too, I find in myself a tendency to leave writing to other people. But one thing I shall not be content to leave to others—little Rupert. The baby of Rupert and Teuta is much too precious a thing to be spoken of except with love, quite independent of the fact that he will be, in natural course, a King! So I have promised Teuta that whatever shall be put into this record of the first King of the Sent Leger Dynasty relating to His Royal Highness the Crown Prince shall only appear in either her hand or my own. And she has deputed the matter to me.

Our dear little Prince arrived punctually and in perfect condition. The angels that carried him evidently took the greatest care of him, and before they left him they gave him dower of all their best. He is a dear! Like both his father and his mother, and that says everything. My own private opinion is that he is a born King! He does not know what fear is, and he thinks more of everyone else than he does of his dear little self. And if those things do not show a truly royal nature, I do not know what does . . .

Teuta has read this. She held up a warning finger, and said:

"Aunt Janet dear, that is all true. He is a dear, and a King, and an angel! But we mustn't have too much about him just yet. This book is to be about Rupert. So our little man can only be what we shall call a corollary." And so it is.

I should mention here that the book is Teuta's idea. Before little Rupert came she controlled herself wonderfully, doing only what was thought best for her under the circumstances. As I could see that it would be a help for her to have some quiet occupation which would interest her without tiring her, I looked up (with his permission, of course) all Rupert's old letters and diaries, and journals and reports—all that I had kept for him during his absences on his adventures. At first I was a little afraid they might harm her, for at times she got so excited over some things that I had to caution her. Here again came in her wonderful self-control. I think the most soothing argument I used with her was to point out that the dear boy had come through all the dangers safely, and was actually with us, stronger and nobler than ever.

After we had read over together the whole matter several times—for it was practically new to me too, and I got nearly as excited as she was, though I have known him so much longer—we came to the conclusion that this particular volume would have to be of selected matter. There is enough of Rupert's work to make a lot of volumes and we have an ambitious literary project of some day publishing an *edition de luxe* of his whole collected works. It will be a rare showing amongst the works of Kings. But this is to be all about himself, so that in the future it may serve as a sort of backbone of his personal history.

By-and-by we came to a part when we had to ask him questions; and he was so interested in Teuta's work—he is really bound up body and soul in his beautiful wife, and no wonder—that we had to take him into full confidence. He promised he would help us all he could by giving us the use of his later journals, and such letters and papers as he had kept privately. He said he would make one condition—I use his own words: "As you two dear women are to be my editors, you must promise to put in everything exactly as I wrote it. It will not do to have any fake about this. I do not wish anything foolish or egotistical toned down out of affection for me. It was all written in sincerity, and if I had faults, they must not be hidden. If it is to be history, it must be true history, even if it gives you and me or any of us away."

So we promised.

He also said that, as Sir Edward Bingham Trent, Bart.—as he is now—was sure to have some matter which we should like, he would write and ask him to send such to us. He also said that Mr. Ernest Roger Halbard Melton, of Humcroft, Salop (he always gives this name and address in full, which is his way of showing contempt), would be sure to have some relevant matter, and that he would have him written to on the subject. This he did. The Chancellor wrote him in his most grandiloquent style. Mr. E. R. H. Melton, of H., S., replied by return post. His letter is a document which speaks for itself:

HUMCROFT, SALOP,
May 30, 1908.

MY DEAR COUSIN KING RUPERT,

I am honoured by the request made on your behalf by the Lord High Chancellor of your kingdom that I should make a literary contribution to the volume which my cousin, Queen Teuta, is, with the help of your former governess, Miss MacKelpie, compiling. I am willing to do so, as you naturally wish to have in that work some contemporary record made by the Head of the House of Melton, with which you are connected, though only on the distaff side. It is a natural ambition enough, even on the part of a barbarian—or perhaps semi-barbarian—King, and far be it from me, as Head of the House, to deny you such a coveted privilege. Perhaps you may not know that I am now Head of the House; my father died three days ago. I offered my mother the use of the Dower House—to the incumbency of which, indeed, she is entitled by her marriage settlement. But she preferred to go to live at her seat, Carfax, in Kent. She went this morning after the funeral. In letting you have the use of my manuscript I make only one stipulation, but that I expect to be rigidly adhered to. It is that all that I have written be put in the book *in extenso*. I do not wish any record of mine to be garbled to suit other ends than those ostensible, or whatever may be to the honour of myself or my House to be burked. I dare say you have noticed, my dear Rupert, that the compilers of family histories often, through jealousy, alter matter that they are allowed to use so as to suit their own purpose or minister to their own vanity. I think it right to tell you that I have had a certified copy made by Petter and Galpin, the law stationers, so that I shall be able to verify whether my stipulation has been honourably observed. I am having the book, which is naturally valuable, carefully packed, and shall have it forwarded to Sir Edward Bingham Trent, Baronet (which he now is—Heaven save the mark!), the Attorney. Please see that he returns it to me, and in proper order. He is not to publish for himself anything in it about him. A man of that class is apt to advertise the fact of anyone of distinction taking any notice of him. I would bring out the MS. to you myself, and stay for a while with you for some sport, only your lot—subjects I suppose you call them!—are such bounders that a gentleman's life is hardly safe amongst them. I never met anyone who had so poor an appreciation of a joke as they have. By the way, how is Teuta? She is one of them. I heard all about the hatching business. I hope the kid is all right. This is only a word in your ear, so don't get cocky, old son. I am open to a godfathership. Think of that, Hedda! Of course, if the other godfather and the godmother are up to the mark; I don't want to have to boost up the whole lot! Savvy? Kiss Teuta and the kid for me. I must have the boy over here for a bit later on—when he is presentable, and has learned not to be a nuisance. It will be good for him to see something of a real first-class English country house like Humcroft. To a person only accustomed to rough ways and meagre living its luxury will make a memory which will serve in time as an example to be aimed at. I shall write again soon. Don't hesitate to ask any favour which I may be able to confer on you. So long!

Your affectionate cousin,
ERNEST ROGER HALBARD MELTON.

Extract from Letter from E. Bingham Trent to Queen Teuta of the Blue Mountains.

. . . So I thought the best way to serve that appalling cad would be to take him at his word, and put in his literary contribution in full. I have had made and attested a copy of his "Record," as he calls it, so as to save you trouble. But I send the book itself, because I am afraid that unless you see his words in his own writing, you will not believe that he or anyone else ever penned seriously a document so incriminating. I am sure he must have forgotten what he had written, for even such a dull dog as he is could never have made public such a thing knowingly. . . Such a nature has its revenges on itself. In this case the officers of revenge are his *ipsissima verba*.

RUPERT'S JOURNAL—*Continued.*

February 1, 1909.

All is now well in train. When the Czar of Russia, on being asked by the Sclavs (as was meet) to be the referee in the "Balkan Settlement," declined on the ground that he was himself by inference an interested party, it was unanimously agreed by the Balkan rulers that the Western King should be asked to arbitrate, as all concerned had perfect confidence in his wisdom, as well as his justice. To their wish he graciously assented. The matter has now been for more than six months in his hands, and he has taken endless trouble to obtain full information. He has now informed us through his Chancellor that his decision is almost ready, and will be communicated as soon as possible.

We have another hunting-party at Vissarion next week. Teuta is looking forward to it with extraordinary interest. She hopes then to present to our brothers of the Balkans our little son, and she is eager to know if they endorse her mother-approval of him.

RUPERT'S JOURNAL—*Continued.*

April 15, 1909.

The arbitrator's decision has been communicated to us through the Chancellor of the Western King, who brought it to us himself as a special act of friendliness. It met with the enthusiastic approval of all. The Premier remained with us during the progress of the hunting-party, which was one of the most joyous occasions ever known. We are all of good heart, for the future of the Balkan races is now assured. The strife—internal and external—of a thousand years has ceased, and we look with hope for a long and happy time. The Chancellor brought messages of grace and courtliness and friendliness to all. And when I, as spokesman of the party, asked him if we might convey a request of His Majesty that he would honour us by attending the ceremony of making known formally the Balkan Settlement, he answered that the King had authorized him to say that he would, if such were wished by us, gladly come; and that if he should come, he would attend with a fleet as an escort. The Chancellor also told me from himself that it might be possible to have other nationalities represented on such a great occasion by Ambassadors and even fleets, though the monarchs themselves might not be able to attend. He hinted that it might be well if I put the matter in train. (He evidently took it for granted that, though I was only one of several, the matter rested with me—possibly he chose me as the one to whom to make the confidence, as I was born a stranger.) As we talked it over, he grew more enthusiastic, and finally said that, as the King was taking the lead, doubtless all the nations of the earth friendly to him would like to take a part in the ceremony. So it is likely to turn out practically an international ceremony of a unique kind. Teuta will love it, and we shall all do what we can.

JANET MACKELPIE'S NOTES.

June 1, 1909.

Our dear Teuta is full of the forthcoming celebration of the Balkan Federation, which is to take place this day month, although I must say, for myself, that the ceremony is attaining to such dimensions that I am beginning to have a sort of vague fear of some kind. It almost seems uncanny. Rupert is working unceasingly—has been for some time. For weeks past he seems to have been out day and night on his aeroplane, going through and round over the country arranging matters, and seeing for himself that what has been arranged is being done. Uncle Colin is always about, too, and so is Admiral Rooke. But now Teuta is beginning to go with Rupert. That girl is simply fearless—just like Rupert. And they both seem anxious that little Rupert shall be the same. Indeed, he is the same. A few mornings ago Rupert and Teuta were about to start just after dawn from the top of the Castle. Little Rupert was there—he is always awake early and as bright as a bee. I was holding him in my arms, and when his mother leant over to kiss him good-bye, he held out his arms to her in a way that said as plainly as if he had spoken, "Take me with you."

She looked appealingly at Rupert, who nodded, and said: "All right. Take him, darling. He will have to learn some day, and the sooner the better." The baby, looking eagerly from one to the other with the same questioning in his eyes as there is sometimes in the eyes of a kitten or a puppy—but, of course, with an eager soul behind it—saw that he was going, and almost leaped into his mother's arms. I think she had expected him to come, for she took a little leather dress from Margareta, his nurse, and, flushing with pride, began to wrap him in it. When Teuta, holding him in her arms, stepped on the aeroplane, and took her place in the centre behind Rupert, the young men of the Crown Prince's Guard raised a cheer, amid which Rupert pulled the levers, and they glided off into the dawn.

The Crown Prince's Guard was established by the mountaineers themselves the day of his birth. Ten of the biggest and most powerful and cleverest young men of the nation were chosen, and were sworn in with a very impressive ceremony to guard the young Prince. They were to so arrange and order themselves and matters generally that two at least of them should always have him, or the place in which he was, within their sight. They all vowed that the last of their lives should go before harm came to him. Of course, Teuta understood, and so did Rupert. And these young men are the persons most privileged in the whole Castle. They are dear boys, every one of them, and we are all fond of them and respect them. They simply idolize the baby.

Ever since that morning little Rupert has, unless it is at a time appointed for his sleeping, gone in his mother's arms. I think in any other place there would be some State remonstrance at the whole royal family being at once and together in a dangerous position, but in the Blue Mountains danger and fear are not thought of—indeed, they can hardly be in their terminology. And I really think the child enjoys it even more than his parents. He is just like a little bird that has found the use of his wings. Bless him!

I find that even I have to study Court ritual a little. So many nationalities are to be represented at the ceremony of the "Balkan Settlement," and so many Kings and Princes and notabilities of all kinds are coming, that we must all take care not to make any mistakes. The Press alone would drive anyone silly. Rupert and Teuta come and sit with me sometimes in the evening when we are all too tired to work, and they rest themselves by talking matters over. Rupert says that there will be over five hundred reporters, and that the applications for permission are coming in so fast that there may be a thousand when the day comes. Last night he stopped in the middle of speaking of it, and said:

"I have an inspiration! Fancy a thousand journalists,—each wanting to get ahead of the rest, and all willing to invoke the Powers of Evil for exclusive information! The only man to look after this department is Rooke. He knows how to deal with men, and as we have already a large staff to look after the journalistic guests, he can be at the head, and appoint his own deputies to act for him. Somewhere and sometime the keeping the peace will be a matter of nerve and resolution, and Rooke is the man for the job."

We were all concerned about one thing, naturally important in the eyes of a woman: What robes was Teuta to wear? In the old days, when there were Kings and Queens, they doubtless wore something gorgeous or impressive; but whatever it was that they wore has gone to dust centuries ago, and there were no illustrated papers in those primitive days. Teuta was talking to me eagerly, with her dear beautiful brows all wrinkled, when Rupert who was reading a bulky document of some kind, looked up and said:

"Of course, darling, you will wear your Shroud?"

"Capital!" she said, clapping her hands like a joyous child. "The very thing, and our people will like it."

I own that for a moment I was dismayed. It was a horrible test of a woman's love and devotion. At a time when she was entertaining Kings and notabilities in her own house—and be sure they would all be decked in their finery—to have to appear in such a garment! A plain thing with nothing even pretty, let alone gorgeous, about it! I expressed my views to Rupert, for I feared that Teuta might be disappointed, though she might not care to say so; but before he could say a word Teuta answered:

"Oh, thank you so much, dear! I should love that above everything, but I did not like to suggest it, lest you should think me arrogant or presuming; for, indeed, Rupert, I am very proud of it, and of the way our people look on it."

"Why not?" said Rupert, in his direct way. "It is a thing for us all to be proud of; the nation has already adopted it as a national emblem—our emblem of courage and devotion and patriotism, which will always, I hope, be treasured beyond price by the men and women of our Dynasty, the Nation, that is—of the Nation that is to be."

Later on in the evening we had a strange endorsement of the national will. A "People's Deputation" of mountaineers, without any official notice or introduction, arrived at the Castle late in the evening in the manner established by Rupert's "Proclamation of Freedom," wherein all citizens were entitled to send a deputation to the King, at will and in private, on any subject of State importance. This deputation was composed of seventeen men, one selected from each political section, so that the body as a whole represented the entire nation. They were of all sorts of social rank and all degrees of fortune, but they were mainly "of the people." They spoke hesitatingly—possibly because Teuta, or even because I, was present—but with a manifest earnestness. They made but one request—that the Queen should, on the great occasion of the Balkan Federation, wear as robes of State the Shroud that they loved to see her in. The spokesman, addressing the Queen, said in tones of rugged eloquence:

"This is a matter, Your Majesty, that the women naturally have a say in, so we have, of course, consulted them. They have discussed the matter by themselves, and then with us, and they are agreed without a flaw that it will be good for the Nation and for Womankind that you do this thing. You have shown to them, and to the world at large, what women should do, what they can do, and they want to make, in memory of your great act, the Shroud a garment of pride and honour for women who have deserved well of their country. In the future it can be a garment to be worn only by privileged women who have earned the right. But they hope, and we hope with them, that on this occasion of our Nation taking the lead before the eyes of the world, all our women may wear it on that day as a means of showing overtly their willingness to do their duty, even to the death. And so"—here he turned to the King—"Rupert, we trust that Her Majesty Queen Teuta will understand that in doing as the women of the Blue Mountains wish, she will bind afresh to the Queen the loyal devotion which she won from them as Voivodin. Henceforth and for all time the Shroud shall be a dress of honour in our Land."

Teuta looked all ablaze with love and pride and devotion. Stars in her eyes shone like white fire as she assured them of the granting of their request. She finished her little speech:

"I feared that if I carried out my own wish, it might look arrogant, but Rupert has expressed the same wish, and now I feel that I am free to wear that dress which brought me to you and to Rupert"—here she beamed on him, and took his hand—"fortified as I am by your wishes and the command of my lord the King."

Rupert took her in his arms and kissed her fondly before them all, saying:

"Tell your wives, my brothers, and the rest of the Blue Mountain women, that that is the answer of the husband who loves and honours his wife. All the world shall see at the ceremony of the Federation of Balka that we men love and honour the women who are loyal and can die for duty. And, men of the Blue Mountains, some day before long we shall organize that great idea, and make it a permanent thing—that the Order of the Shroud is the highest guerdon that a noble-hearted woman can wear."

Teuta disappeared for a few moments, and came back with the Crown Prince in her arms. Everyone present asked to be allowed to kiss him, which they did kneeling.

THE FEDERATION BALKA.

By the Correspondents of "Free America."

The Editors of *Free America* have thought it well to put in consecutive order the reports and descriptions of their Special Correspondents, of whom there were present no less than eight. Not a word they wrote is omitted, but the various parts of their reports are placed in different order, so that, whilst nothing which any of them recorded is left out, the reader may be able to follow the proceedings from the various points of view of the writers who had the most favourable opportunity of moment. In so large an assemblage of journalists—there were present over a thousand—they could not all be present in one place; so our men, in consultation amongst themselves, arranged to scatter, so as to cover the whole proceeding from the various "coigns of vantage," using their skill and experience in selecting these points. One was situated on the summit of the steel-clad tower in the entrance to the Blue Mouth; another on the "Press-boat," which was moored alongside King Rupert's armoured yacht, *The Lady*, whereon were gathered the various Kings and rulers of the Balkan States, all of whom were in the Federation; another was in a swift torpedo-boat, with a roving commission to cruise round the harbour as desired; another took his place on the top of the great mountain which overlooks Plazac, and so had a bird's-eye view of the whole scene of operations; two others were on the forts to right and left of the Blue Mouth; another was posted at the entrance to the Great Tunnel which runs from the water level right up through the mountains to the plateau, where the mines and factories are situate; another had the privilege of a place on an aeroplane, which went everywhere and saw everything. This aeroplane was driven by an old Special Correspondent of *Free America*, who had been a chum of our Special in the Japanese and Russian War, and who has taken service on the Blue Mountain *Official Gazette*.

PLAZAC,
June 30, 1909.

Two days before the time appointed for the ceremony the guests of the Land of the Blue Mountains began to arrive. The earlier comers were mostly the journalists who had come from almost over the whole inhabited world. King Rupert, who does things well, had made a camp for their exclusive use. There was a separate tent for each—of course, a small one, as there were over a thousand journalists—but there were big tents for general use scattered about—refectories, reading and writing rooms, a library, idle rooms for rest, etc. In the rooms for reading and writing, which were the work-rooms for general use, were newspapers, the latest attainable from all over the world, Blue-Books, guides, directories, and all such aids to work as forethought could arrange. There was for this special service a body of some hundreds of capable servants in special dress and bearing identification numbers—in fact, King Rupert "did us fine," to use a slang phrase of pregnant meaning.

There were other camps for special service, all of them well arranged, and with plenty of facility for transport. Each of the Federating Monarchs had a camp of his own, in which he had erected a magnificent pavilion. For the Western King, who had acted as Arbitrator in the matter of the Federation, a veritable palace had been built by King Rupert—a sort of Aladdin's palace it must have been, for only a few weeks ago the place it occupied was, I was told, only primeval wilderness. King Rupert and his Queen, Teuta, had a pavilion like the rest of the Federators of Balka, but infinitely more modest, both in size and adornments.

Everywhere were guards of the Blue Mountains, armed only with the "handjar," which is the national weapon. They wore the national dress, but so arranged in colour and accoutrement that the general air of uniformity took the place of a rigid uniform. There must have been at least seventy or eighty thousand of them.

The first day was one of investigation of details by the visitors. During the second day the retinues of the great Federators came. Some of these retinues were vast. For instance, the Soldan (though only just become a Federator) sent of one kind or another more than a thousand men. A brave show they made, for they are fine men, and drilled to perfection. As they swaggered along, singly or in mass, with their gay jackets and baggy trousers, their helmets surmounted by the golden crescent, they looked a foe not to be despised. Landreck Martin, the Nestor of journalists, said to me, as we stood together looking at them:

"To-day we witness a new departure in Blue Mountain history. This is the first occasion for a thousand years that so large a Turkish body has entered the Blue Mountains with a reasonable prospect of ever getting out again."

July 1, 1909.

To-day, the day appointed for the ceremony, was auspiciously fine, even for the Blue Mountains, where at this time of year the weather is nearly always fine. They are early folk in the Blue Mountains, but to-day things began to hum before daybreak. There were bugle-calls all over the place—everything here is arranged by calls of musical instruments—trumpets, or bugles, or drums (if, indeed, the drum can be called a musical instrument)—or by lights, if it be after dark. We journalists were all ready; coffee and bread-and-butter had been thoughtfully served early in our sleeping-tents, and an elaborate breakfast was going on all the time in the refectory pavilions. We had a preliminary look round, and then there was a sort of general pause for breakfast. We took advantage of it, and attacked the sumptuous—indeed, memorable—meal which was served for us.

The ceremony was to commence at noon, but at ten o'clock the whole place was astir—not merely beginning to move, but actually moving; everybody taking their places for the great ceremony. As noon drew near, the excitement was intense and prolonged. One by one the various signatories to the Federation began to assemble. They all came by sea; such of them as had sea-boards of their own having their fleets around them. Such as had no fleets of their own were attended by at least one of the Blue Mountain ironclads. And I am bound to say that I never in my life saw more dangerous craft than these little warships of King Rupert of the Blue Mountains. As they entered the Blue Mouth each ship took her appointed station, those which carried the signatories being close together in an isolated group in a little bay almost surrounded by high cliffs in the farthest recesses of the mighty harbour. King Rupert's armoured yacht all the time lay close inshore, hard by the mouth of the Great Tunnel which runs straight into the mountain from a wide plateau, partly natural rock, partly built up with mighty blocks of stone. Here it is, I am told, that the inland products are brought down to the modern town of Plazac. Just as the clocks were chiming the half-hour before noon this yacht glided out into the expanse of the "Mouth." Behind her came twelve great barges, royally decked, and draped each in the colour of the signatory nation. On each of these the ruler entered with his guard, and was carried to Rupert's yacht, he going on the bridge, whilst his suite remained on the lower deck. In the meantime whole fleets had been appearing on the southern horizon; the nations were sending their maritime quota to the christening of "Balka"! In such wonderful order as can only be seen with squadrons of fighting ships, the mighty throng swept into the Blue Mouth, and took up their stations in groups. The only armament of a Great Power now missing was that of the Western King. But there was time. Indeed, as the crowd everywhere began to look at their watches a long line of ships began to spread up northward from the Italian coast. They came at great speed—nearly twenty knots. It was a really wonderful sight—fifty of the finest ships in the world; the very latest expression of naval giants, each seemingly typical of its class—Dreadnoughts, cruisers, destroyers. They came in a wedge, with the King's yacht flying the Royal Standard the apex. Every ship of the squadron bore a red ensign long enough to float from the masthead to the water. From the armoured tower in the waterway one could see the myriad of faces—white stars on both land and sea—for the great harbour was now alive with ships and each and all of them alive with men.

Suddenly, without any direct cause, the white masses became eclipsed—everyone had turned round, and was looking the other way. I looked across the bay and up the mountain behind—a mighty mountain, whose slopes run up to the very sky, ridge after ridge seeming like itself a mountain. Far away on the very top the standard of the Blue Mountains was run up on a mighty Flagstaff which seemed like a shaft of light. It was two hundred feet high, and painted white, and as at the distance the steel stays were invisible, it towered up in lonely grandeur. At its foot was a dark mass grouped behind a white space, which I could not make out till I used my field-glasses.

Then I knew it was King Rupert and the Queen in the midst of a group of mountaineers. They were on the aero station behind the platform of the aero, which seemed to shine—shine, not glitter—as though it were overlaid with plates of gold.

Again the faces looked west. The Western Squadron was drawing near to the entrance of the Blue Mouth. On the bridge of the yacht stood the Western King in uniform of an Admiral, and by him his Queen in a dress of royal purple, splendid with gold. Another glance at the mountain-top showed that it had seemed to become alive. A whole park of artillery seemed to have suddenly sprung to life, round each its crew ready for action. Amongst the group at the foot of the Flagstaff we could distinguish King Rupert; his vast height and bulk stood out from and above all round him. Close to him was a patch of white, which we understood to be Queen Teuta, whom the Blue Mountaineers simply adore.

By this time the armoured yacht, bearing all the signatories to "Balka" (excepting King Rupert), had moved out towards the entrance, and lay still and silent, waiting the coming of the Royal Arbitrator, whose whole squadron simultaneously slowed down, and hardly drifted in the seething water of their backing engines.

When the flag which was in the yacht's prow was almost opposite the armoured fort, the Western King held up a roll of vellum handed to him by one of his officers. We onlookers held our breath, for in an instant was such a scene as we can never hope to see again.

At the raising of the Western King's hand, a gun was fired away on the top of the mountain where rose the mighty Flagstaff with the standard of the Blue Mountains. Then came the thunder of salute from the guns, bright flashes and reports, which echoed down the hillsides in never-ending sequence. At the first gun, by some trick of signalling, the flag of the Federated "Balka" floated out from the top of the Flagstaff, which had been mysteriously raised, and flew above that of the Blue Mountains.

At the same moment the figures of Rupert and Teuta sank; they were taking their places on the aeroplane. An instant after, like a great golden bird, it seemed to shoot out into the air, and then, dipping its head, dropped downward at an obtuse angle. We could see the King and Queen from time waist upwards—the King in Blue Mountain dress of green; the Queen, wrapped in her white Shroud, holding her baby on her breast. When far out from the mountain-top and over the Blue Mouth, the wings and tail of the great bird-like machine went up, and the aero dropped like a stone, till it was only some few hundred feet over the water. Then the wings and tail went down, but with diminishing speed. Below the expanse of the plane the King and Queen were now seen seated together on the tiny steering platform, which seemed to have been lowered; she sat behind her husband, after the manner of matrons of the Blue Mountains. That coming of that aeroplane was the most striking episode of all this wonderful day.

After floating for a few seconds, the engines began to work, whilst the planes moved back to their normal with beautiful simultaneity. There was a golden aero finding its safety in gliding movement. At the same time the steering platform was rising, so that once more the occupants were not far below, but above the plane. They were now only about a hundred feet above the water, moving from the far end of the Blue Mouth towards the entrance in the open space between the two lines of the fighting ships of the various nationalities, all of which had by now their yards manned—a manoeuvre which had begun at the firing of the first gun on the mountain-top. As the aero passed along, all the seamen began to cheer—a cheering which they kept up till the King and Queen had come so close to the Western King's vessel that the two Kings and Queens could greet each other. The wind was now beginning to blow westward from the mountain-top, and it took the sounds towards the armoured fort, so that at moments we could distinguish the cheers of the various nationalities, amongst which, more keen than the others, came the soft "Ban Zai!" of the Japanese.

King Rupert, holding his steering levers, sat like a man of marble. Behind him his beautiful wife, clad in her Shroud, and holding in her arms the young Crown Prince, seemed like a veritable statue.

The aero, guided by Rupert's unerring hand, lit softly on the after-deck of the Western King's yacht; and King Rupert, stepping on deck, lifted from her seat Queen Teuta with her baby in her arms. It was only when the Blue Mountain King stood amongst other men that one could realize his enormous stature. He stood literally head and shoulders over every other man present.

Whilst the aeroplane was giving up its burden, the Western King and his Queen were descending from the bridge. The host and hostess, hand in hand—after their usual fashion, as it seems—hurried forward to greet their guests. The meeting was touching in its simplicity. The two monarchs shook hands, and their consorts, representatives of the foremost types of national beauty of the North and South, instinctively drew close and kissed each other. Then the hostess Queen, moving towards the Western King, kneeled before him with the gracious obeisance of a Blue Mountain hostess, and kissed his hand.

Her words of greeting were:

"You are welcome, sire, to the Blue Mountains. We are grateful to you for all you have done for Balka, and to you and Her Majesty for giving us the honour of your presence."

The King seemed moved. Accustomed as he was to the ritual of great occasions, the warmth and sincerity, together with the gracious humility of this old Eastern custom, touched him, monarch though he was of a great land and many races in the Far East. Impulsively he broke through Court ritual, and did a thing which, I have since been told, won for him for ever a holy place in the warm hearts of the Blue Mountaineers. Sinking on his knee before the beautiful shroud-clad Queen, he raised her hand and kissed it. The act was seen by all in and around the Blue Mouth, and a mighty cheering rose, which seemed to rise and swell as it ran far and wide up the hillsides, till it faded away on the far-off mountain-top, where rose majestically the mighty Flagstaff bearing the standard of the Balkan Federation.

For myself, I can never forget that wonderful scene of a nation's enthusiasm, and the core of it is engraven on my memory. That spotless deck, typical of all that is perfect in naval use; the King and Queen of the greatest nation of the earth [1] received by the newest King and Queen—a King and Queen who won empire for themselves, so that the former subject of another King received him as a brother-monarch on a history-making occasion, when a new world-power was, under his tutelage, springing into existence. The fair Northern Queen in the arms of the dark Southern Queen with the starry eyes. The simple splendour of Northern dress arrayed against that of almost peasant plainness of the giant King of the South. But all were eclipsed—even the thousand years of royal lineage of the Western King, Rupert's natural dower of stature, and the other Queen's bearing of royal dignity and sweetness—by the elemental simplicity of Teuta's Shroud. Not one of all that mighty throng but knew something of her wonderful story; and not one but felt glad and proud that such a noble woman had won an empire through her own bravery, even in the jaws of the grave.

The armoured yacht, with the remainder of the signatories to the Balkan Federation, drew close, and the rulers stepped on board to greet the Western King, the Arbitrator, Rupert leaving his task as personal host and joining them. He took his part modestly in the rear of the group, and made a fresh obeisance in his new capacity.

Presently another warship, *The Balka*, drew close. It contained the ambassadors of Foreign Powers, and the Chancellors and high officials of the Balkan nations. It was

---

[1] Greatest Kingdom—Editor Free America.

followed by a fleet of warships, each one representing a Balkan Power. The great Western fleet lay at their moorings, but with the exception of manning their yards, took no immediate part in the proceedings.

On the deck of the new-comer the Balkan monarchs took their places, the officials of each State grading themselves behind their monarch. The Ambassadors formed a foremost group by themselves.

Last came the Western King, quite alone (save for the two Queens), bearing in his hand the vellum scroll, the record of his arbitration. This he proceeded to read, a polyglot copy of it having been already supplied to every Monarch, Ambassador, and official present. It was a long statement, but the occasion was so stupendous—so intense—that the time flew by quickly. The cheering had ceased the moment the Arbitrator opened the scroll, and a veritable silence of the grave abounded.

When the reading was concluded Rupert raised his hand, and on the instant came a terrific salvo of cannon-shots from not only the ships in the port, but seemingly all up and over the hillsides away to the very summit.

When the cheering which followed the salute had somewhat toned down, those on board talked together, and presentations were made. Then the barges took the whole company to the armour-clad fort in the entrance-way to the Blue Mouth. Here, in front, had been arranged for the occasion, platforms for the starting of aeroplanes. Behind them were the various thrones of state for the Western King and Queen, and the various rulers of "Balka"—as the new and completed Balkan Federation had become—*de jure* as well as *de facto*. Behind were seats for the rest of the company. All was a blaze of crimson and gold. We of the Press were all expectant, for some ceremony had manifestly been arranged, but of all details of it we had been kept in ignorance. So far as I could tell from the faces, those present were at best but partially informed. They were certainly ignorant of all details, and even of the entire programme of the day. There is a certain kind of expectation which is not concerned in the mere execution of fore-ordered things.

The aero on which the King and Queen had come down from the mountain now arrived on the platform in the charge of a tall young mountaineer, who stepped from the steering-platform at once. King Rupert, having handed his Queen (who still carried her baby) into her seat, took his place, and pulled a lever. The aero went forward, and seemed to fall head foremost off the fort. It was but a dip, however, such as a skilful diver takes from a height into shallow water, for the plane made an upward curve, and in a few seconds was skimming upwards towards the Flagstaff. Despite the wind, it arrived there in an incredibly short time. Immediately after his flight another aero, a big one this time, glided to the platform. To this immediately stepped a body of ten tall, fine-looking young men. The driver pulled his levers, and the plane glided out on the track of the King. The Western King, who was noticing, said to the Lord High Admiral, who had been himself in command of the ship of war, and now stood close behind him:

"Who are those men, Admiral?"

"The Guard of the Crown Prince, Your Majesty. They are appointed by the Nation."

"Tell me, Admiral, have they any special duties?"

"Yes, Your Majesty," came the answer: "to die, if need be, for the young Prince!"

"Quite right! That is fine service. But how if any of them should die?"

"Your Majesty, if one of them should die, there are ten thousand eager to take his place."

"Fine, fine! It is good to have even one man eager to give his life for duty. But ten thousand! That is what makes a nation!"

When King Rupert reached the platform by the Flagstaff, the Royal Standard of the Blue Mountains was hauled up under it. Rupert stood up and raised his hand. In a second a cannon beside him was fired; then, quick as thought, others were fired in sequence, as though by one prolonged lightning-flash. The roar was incessant, but getting less in detonating sound as the distance and the hills subdued it. But in the general silence which prevailed round us we could hear the sound as though passing in a distant circle, till finally the line which had gone northward came back by the south, stopping at the last gun to south'ard of the Flagstaff.

"What was that wonderful circle?" asked the King of the Lord High Admiral.

"That, Your Majesty, is the line of the frontier of the Blue Mountains. Rupert has ten thousand cannon in line."

"And who fires them? I thought all the army must be here."

"The women, Your Majesty. They are on frontier duty to-day, so that the men can come here."

Just at that moment one of the Crown Prince's Guards brought to the side of the King's aero something like a rubber ball on the end of a string. The Queen held it out to the baby in her arms, who grabbed at it. The guard drew back. Pressing that ball must have given some signal, for on the instant a cannon, elevated to perpendicular, was fired. A shell went straight up an enormous distance. The shell burst, and sent out both a light so bright that it could be seen in the daylight, and a red smoke, which might have been seen from the heights of the Calabrian Mountains over in Italy.

As the shell burst, the King's aero seemed once more to spring from the platform out into mid-air, dipped as before, and glided out over the Blue Mouth with a rapidity which, to look at, took one's breath away.

As it came, followed by the aero of the Crown Prince's Guard and a group of other aeros, the whole mountain-sides seemed to become alive. From everywhere, right away up to the farthest visible mountain-tops, darted aeroplanes, till a host of them were rushing with dreadful speed in the wake of the King. The King turned to Queen Teuta, and evidently said something, for she beckoned to the Captain of the Crown Prince's Guard, who was steering the plane. He swerved away to the right, and instead of following above the open track between the lines of warships, went high over the outer line. One of those on board began to drop something, which, fluttering down, landed on every occasion on the bridge of the ship high over which they then were.

The Western King said again to the Gospodar Rooke (the Lord High Admiral):

"It must need some skill to drop a letter with such accuracy."

With imperturbable face the Admiral replied:

"It is easier to drop bombs, Your Majesty."

The flight of aeroplanes was a memorable sight. It helped to make history. Henceforth no nation with an eye for either defence or attack can hope for success without the mastery of the air.

In the meantime—and after that time, too—God help the nation that attacks "Balka" or any part of it, so long as Rupert and Teuta live in the hearts of that people, and bind them into an irresistible unity.

THE LAIR OF THE WHITE WORM

**To my friend Bertha Nicoll
with affectionate esteem.**

CHAPTER I—ADAM SALTON ARRIVES

Adam Salton sauntered into the Empire Club, Sydney, and found awaiting him a letter from his grand-uncle. He had first heard from the old gentleman less than a year before, when Richard Salton had claimed kinship, stating that he had been unable to write earlier, as he had found it very difficult to trace his grand-nephew's address. Adam was delighted and replied cordially; he had often heard his father speak of the older branch of the family with whom his people had long lost touch. Some interesting correspondence had ensued. Adam eagerly opened the letter which had only just arrived, and conveyed a cordial invitation to stop with his grand-uncle at Lesser Hill, for as long a time as he could spare.

"Indeed," Richard Salton went on, "I am in hopes that you will make your permanent home here. You see, my dear boy, you and I are all that remain of our race, and it is but fitting that you should succeed me when the time comes. In this year of grace, 1860, I am close on eighty years of age, and though we have been a long-lived race, the span of life cannot be prolonged beyond reasonable bounds. I am prepared to like you, and to make your home with me as happy as you could wish. So do come at once on receipt of this, and find the welcome I am waiting to give you. I send, in case such may make matters easy for you, a banker's draft for £200. Come soon, so that we may both of us enjoy many happy days together. If you are able to give me the pleasure of seeing you, send me as soon as you can a letter telling me when to expect you. Then when you arrive at Plymouth or Southampton or whatever port you are bound for, wait on board, and I will meet you at the earliest hour possible."

* * * * *

Old Mr. Salton was delighted when Adam's reply arrived and sent a groom hot-foot to his crony, Sir Nathaniel de Salis, to inform him that his grand-nephew was due at Southampton on the twelfth of June.

Mr. Salton gave instructions to have ready a carriage early on the important day, to start for Stafford, where he would catch the 11.40 a.m. train. He would stay that night with his grand-nephew, either on the ship, which would be a new experience for him, or, if his guest should prefer it, at a hotel. In either case they would start in the early morning for home. He had given instructions to his bailiff to send the postillion carriage on to Southampton, to be ready for their journey home, and to arrange for relays of his own horses to be sent on at once. He intended that his grand-nephew, who had been all his life in Australia, should see something of rural England on the drive. He had plenty of young horses of his own breeding and breaking, and could depend on a journey memorable to the young man. The luggage would be sent on by rail to Stafford, where one of his carts would meet it. Mr. Salton, during the journey to Southampton, often wondered if his grand-nephew was as much excited as he was at the idea of meeting so near a relation for the first time; and it was with an effort that he controlled himself. The endless railway lines and switches round the Southampton Docks fired his anxiety afresh.

As the train drew up on the dockside, he was getting his hand traps together, when the carriage door was wrenched open and a young man jumped in.

"How are you, uncle? I recognised you from the photo you sent me! I wanted to meet you as soon as I could, but everything is so strange to me that I didn't quite know what to do. However, here I am. I am glad to see you, sir. I have been dreaming of this happiness for thousands of miles; now I find that the reality beats all the dreaming!" As he spoke the old man and the young one were heartily wringing each other's hands.

The meeting so auspiciously begun proceeded well. Adam, seeing that the old man was interested in the novelty of the ship, suggested that he should stay the night on board, and that he would himself be ready to start at any hour and go anywhere that the other suggested. This affectionate willingness to fall in with his own plans quite won the old man's heart. He warmly accepted the invitation, and at once they became not only on terms of affectionate relationship, but almost like old friends. The heart of the old man, which had been empty for so long, found a new delight. The young man found, on landing in the old country, a welcome and a surrounding in full harmony with all his dreams throughout his wanderings and solitude, and the promise of a fresh and adventurous life. It was not long before the old man accepted him to full relationship by calling him by his Christian name. After a long talk on affairs of interest, they retired to the cabin, which the elder was to share. Richard Salton put his hands affectionately on the boy's shoulders—though Adam was in his twenty-seventh year, he was a boy, and always would be, to his grand-uncle.

"I am so glad to find you as you are, my dear boy—just such a young man as I had always hoped for as a son, in the days when I still had such hopes. However, that is all past. But thank God there is a new life to begin for both of us. To you must be the larger part—but there is still time for some of it to be shared in common. I have waited till we should have seen each other to enter upon the subject; for I thought it better not to tie up your young life to my old one till we should have sufficient personal knowledge to justify such a venture. Now I can, so far as I am concerned, enter into it freely, since from the moment my eyes rested on you I saw my son—as he shall be, God willing—if he chooses such a course himself."

"Indeed I do, sir—with all my heart!"

"Thank you, Adam, for that." The old, man's eyes filled and his voice trembled. Then, after a long silence between them, he went on: "When I heard you were coming I made my will. It was well that your interests should be protected from that moment on. Here is the deed—keep it, Adam. All I have shall belong to you; and if love and good wishes, or the memory of them, can make life sweeter, yours shall be a happy one. Now, my dear boy, let us turn in. We start early in the morning and have a long drive before us. I hope you don't mind driving? I was going to have the old travelling carriage in which my grandfather, your great-grand-uncle, went to Court when

William IV. was king. It is all right—they built well in those days—and it has been kept in perfect order. But I think I have done better: I have sent the carriage in which I travel myself. The horses are of my own breeding, and relays of them shall take us all the way. I hope you like horses? They have long been one of my greatest interests in life."

"I love them, sir, and I am happy to say I have many of my own. My father gave me a horse farm for myself when I was eighteen. I devoted myself to it, and it has gone on. Before I came away, my steward gave me a memorandum that we have in my own place more than a thousand, nearly all good."

"I am glad, my boy. Another link between us."

"Just fancy what a delight it will be, sir, to see so much of England—and with you!"

"Thank you again, my boy. I will tell you all about your future home and its surroundings as we go. We shall travel in old-fashioned state, I tell you. My grandfather always drove four-in-hand; and so shall we."

"Oh, thanks, sir, thanks. May I take the ribbons sometimes?"

"Whenever you choose, Adam. The team is your own. Every horse we use to-day is to be your own."

"You are too generous, uncle!"

"Not at all. Only an old man's selfish pleasure. It is not every day that an heir to the old home comes back. And—oh, by the way . . . No, we had better turn in now—I shall tell you the rest in the morning."

CHAPTER II—THE CASWALLS OF CASTRA REGIS

Mr. Salton had all his life been an early riser, and necessarily an early waker. But early as he woke on the next morning—and although there was an excuse for not prolonging sleep in the constant whirr and rattle of the "donkey" engine winches of the great ship—he met the eyes of Adam fixed on him from his berth. His grand-nephew had given him the sofa, occupying the lower berth himself. The old man, despite his great strength and normal activity, was somewhat tired by his long journey of the day before, and the prolonged and exciting interview which followed it. So he was glad to lie still and rest his body, whilst his mind was actively exercised in taking in all he could of his strange surroundings. Adam, too, after the pastoral habit to which he had been bred, woke with the dawn, and was ready to enter on the experiences of the new day whenever it might suit his elder companion. It was little wonder, then, that, so soon as each realised the other's readiness, they simultaneously jumped up and began to dress. The steward had by previous instructions early breakfast prepared, and it was not long before they went down the gangway on shore in search of the carriage.

They found Mr. Salton's bailiff looking out for them on the dock, and he brought them at once to where the carriage was waiting in the street. Richard Salton pointed out with pride to his young companion the suitability of the vehicle for every need of travel. To it were harnessed four useful horses, with a postillion to each pair.

"See," said the old man proudly, "how it has all the luxuries of useful travel—silence and isolation as well as speed. There is nothing to obstruct the view of those travelling and no one to overhear what they may say. I have used that trap for a quarter of a century, and I never saw one more suitable for travel. You shall test it shortly. We are going to drive through the heart of England; and as we go I'll tell you what I was speaking of last night. Our route is to be by Salisbury, Bath, Bristol, Cheltenham, Worcester, Stafford; and so home."

Adam remained silent a few minutes, during which he seemed all eyes, for he perpetually ranged the whole circle of the horizon.

"Has our journey to-day, sir," he asked, "any special relation to what you said last night that you wanted to tell me?"

"Not directly; but indirectly, everything."

"Won't you tell me now—I see we cannot be overheard—and if anything strikes you as we go along, just run it in. I shall understand."

So old Salton spoke:

CHAPTER II—THE CASWALLS OF CASTRA REGIS

"To begin at the beginning, Adam. That lecture of yours on 'The Romans in Britain,' a report of which you posted to me, set me thinking—in addition to telling me your tastes. I wrote to you at once and asked you to come home, for it struck me that if you were fond of historical research—as seemed a fact—this was exactly the place for you, in addition to its being the home of your own forbears. If you could learn so much of the British Romans so far away in New South Wales, where there cannot be even a tradition of them, what might you not make of the same amount of study on the very spot. Where we are going is in the real heart of the old kingdom of Mercia, where there are traces of all the various nationalities which made up the conglomerate which became Britain."

"I rather gathered that you had some more definite—more personal reason for my hurrying. After all, history can keep—except in the making!"

"Quite right, my boy. I had a reason such as you very wisely guessed. I was anxious for you to be here when a rather important phase of our local history occurred."

"What is that, if I may ask, sir?"

"Certainly. The principal landowner of our part of the county is on his way home, and there will be a great home-coming, which you may care to see. The fact is, for more than a century the various owners in the succession here, with the exception of a short time, have lived abroad."

"How is that, sir, if I may ask?"

"The great house and estate in our part of the world is Castra Regis, the family seat of the Caswall family. The last owner who lived here was Edgar Caswall, grandfather of the man who is coming here—and he was the only one who stayed even a short time. This man's grandfather, also named Edgar—they keep the tradition of the family Christian name—quarrelled with his family and went to live abroad, not keeping up any intercourse, good or bad, with his relatives, although this particular Edgar, as I told you, did visit his family estate, yet his son was born and lived and died abroad, while his grandson, the latest inheritor, was also born and lived abroad till he was over thirty—his present age. This was the second line of absentees. The great estate of Castra Regis has had no knowledge of its owner for five generations—covering more than a hundred and twenty years. It has been well administered, however, and no tenant or other connected with it has had anything of which to complain. All the same, there has been much natural anxiety to see the new owner, and we are all excited about the event of his coming. Even I am, though I own my own estate, which, though adjacent, is quite apart from Castra Regis.—Here we are now in new ground for you. That is the spire of Salisbury Cathedral, and when we leave that we shall be getting close to the old Roman county, and you will naturally want your eyes. So we shall shortly have to keep our minds on old Mercia. However, you need not be disappointed. My old friend, Sir Nathaniel de Salis, who, like myself, is a freeholder near Castra Regis—his estate, Doom Tower, is over the border of Derbyshire, on the Peak—is coming to stay with me for the festivities to welcome Edgar Caswall. He is just the sort of man you will like. He is devoted to history, and is President of the Mercian Archaeological Society. He knows more of our own part of the country, with its history and its people, than anyone else. I expect he will have arrived before us, and we three can have a long chat after dinner. He is also our local geologist and natural historian. So you and he will have many interests in common. Amongst other things he has a special knowledge of the Peak and its caverns, and knows all the old legends of prehistoric times."

They spent the night at Cheltenham, and on the following morning resumed their journey to Stafford. Adam's eyes were in constant employment, and it was not till Salton declared that they had now entered on the last stage of their journey, that he referred to Sir Nathaniel's coming.

As the dusk was closing down, they drove on to Lesser Hill, Mr. Salton's house. It was now too dark to see any details of their surroundings. Adam could just see that it was on the top of a hill, not quite so high as that which was covered by the Castle, on whose tower flew the flag, and which was all ablaze with moving lights, manifestly used in the preparations for the festivities on the morrow. So Adam deferred his curiosity till daylight. His grand-uncle was met at the door by a fine old man, who greeted him warmly.

"I came over early as you wished. I suppose this is your grand-nephew—I am glad to meet you, Mr. Adam Salton. I am Nathaniel de Salis, and your uncle is one of my oldest friends."

Adam, from the moment of their eyes meeting, felt as if they were already friends. The meeting was a new note of welcome to those that had already sounded in his ears.

The cordiality with which Sir Nathaniel and Adam met, made the imparting of information easy. Sir Nathaniel was a clever man of the world, who had travelled much, and within a certain area studied deeply. He was a brilliant conversationalist, as was to be expected from a successful diplomatist, even under unstimulating conditions. But he had been touched and to a certain extent fired by the younger man's evident admiration and willingness to learn from him. Accordingly the conversation, which began on the most friendly basis, soon warmed to an interest above proof, as the old man spoke of it next day to Richard Salton. He knew already that his old friend wanted his grand-nephew to learn all he could of the subject in hand, and so had during his journey from the Peak put his thoughts in sequence for narration and explanation. Accordingly, Adam had only to listen and he must learn much that he wanted to know. When dinner was over and the servants had withdrawn, leaving the three men at their wine, Sir Nathaniel began.

"I gather from your uncle—by the way, I suppose we had better speak of you as uncle and nephew, instead of going into exact relationship? In fact, your uncle is so old and dear a friend, that, with your permission, I shall drop formality with you altogether and speak of you and to you as Adam, as though you were his son."

"I should like," answered the young man, "nothing better!"

The answer warmed the hearts of both the old men, but, with the usual avoidance of Englishmen of emotional subjects personal to themselves, they instinctively returned to the previous question. Sir Nathaniel took the lead.

"I understand, Adam, that your uncle has posted you regarding the relationships of the Caswall family?"

"Partly, sir; but I understood that I was to hear minuter details from you—if you would be so good."

"I shall be delighted to tell you anything so far as my knowledge goes. Well, the first Caswall in our immediate record is an Edgar, head of the family and owner of the estate, who came into his kingdom just about the time that George III. did. He had one son of about twenty-four. There was a violent quarrel between the two. No one of this generation has any idea of the cause; but, considering the family characteristics, we may take it for granted that though it was deep and violent, it was on the surface trivial.

"The result of the quarrel was that the son left the house without a reconciliation or without even telling his father where he was going. He never came back again. A few years after, he died, without having in the meantime exchanged a word or a letter with his father. He married abroad and left one son, who seems to have been brought up in ignorance of all belonging to him. The gulf between them appears to have been unbridgable; for in time this son married and in turn had a son, but neither joy nor sorrow brought the sundered together. Under such conditions no *rapprochement* was to be looked for, and an utter indifference, founded at best on ignorance, took the place of family affection—even on community of interests. It was only due to the watchfulness of the lawyers that the birth of this new heir was ever made known. He actually spent a few months in the ancestral home.

"After this the family interest merely rested on heirship of the estate. As no other children have been born to any of the newer generations in the intervening years, all hopes of heritage are now centred in the grandson of this man.

"Now, it will be well for you to bear in mind the prevailing characteristics of this race. These were well preserved and unchanging; one and all they are the same: cold, selfish, dominant, reckless of consequences in pursuit of their own will. It was not that they did not keep faith, though that was a matter which gave them little concern, but that they took care to think beforehand of what they should do in order to gain their own ends. If they should make a mistake, someone else should bear the burthen of it. This was so perpetually recurrent that it seemed to be a part of a fixed policy. It was no wonder that, whatever changes took place, they were always ensured in their own possessions. They were absolutely cold and hard by nature. Not one of them—so far as we have any knowledge—was ever known to be touched by the softer sentiments, to swerve from his purpose, or hold his hand in obedience to the dictates of his heart. The pictures and effigies of them all show their adherence to the early Roman type. Their eyes were full; their hair, of raven blackness, grew thick and close and curly. Their figures were massive and typical of strength.

"The thick black hair, growing low down on the neck, told of vast physical strength and endurance. But the most remarkable characteristic is the eyes. Black, piercing, almost unendurable, they seem to contain in themselves a remarkable will power which there is no gainsaying. It is a power that is partly racial and partly individual: a power impregnated with some mysterious quality, partly hypnotic, partly mesmeric, which seems to take away from eyes that meet them all power of resistance—nay, all power of wishing to resist. With eyes like those, set in that all-commanding face, one would need to be strong indeed to think of resisting the inflexible will that lay behind.

"You may think, Adam, that all this is imagination on my part, especially as I have never seen any of them. So it is, but imagination based on deep study. I have made use of all I know or can surmise logically regarding this strange race. With such strange compelling qualities, is it any wonder that there is abroad an idea that in the race there is some demoniac possession, which tends to a more definite belief that certain individuals have in the past sold themselves to the Devil?

"But I think we had better go to bed now. We have a lot to get through to-morrow, and I want you to have your brain clear, and all your susceptibilities fresh. Moreover, I want you to come with me for an early walk, during which we may notice, whilst the matter is fresh in our minds, the peculiar disposition of this place—not merely your grand-uncle's estate, but the lie of the country around it. There are many things on which we may seek—and perhaps find—enlightenment. The more we know at the start, the more things which may come into our view will develop themselves."

CHAPTER III—DIANA'S GROVE

Curiosity took Adam Salton out of bed in the early morning, but when he had dressed and gone downstairs; he found that, early as he was, Sir Nathaniel was ahead of him. The old gentleman was quite prepared for a long walk, and they started at once.

Sir Nathaniel, without speaking, led the way to the east, down the hill. When they had descended and risen again, they found themselves on the eastern brink of a steep hill. It was of lesser height than that on which the Castle was situated; but it was so placed that it commanded the various hills that crowned the ridge. All along the ridge the rock cropped out, bare and bleak, but broken in rough natural castellation. The form of the ridge was a segment of a circle, with the higher points inland to the west. In the centre rose the Castle, on the highest point of all. Between the various rocky excrescences were groups of trees of various sizes and heights, amongst some of which were what, in the early morning light, looked like ruins. These—whatever they were—were of massive grey stone, probably limestone rudely cut—if indeed they were not shaped naturally. The fall of the ground was steep all along the ridge, so steep that here and there both trees and rocks and buildings seemed to overhang the plain far below, through which ran many streams.

Sir Nathaniel stopped and looked around, as though to lose nothing of the effect. The sun had climbed the eastern sky and was making all details clear. He pointed with a sweeping gesture, as though calling Adam's attention to the extent of the view. Having done so, he covered the ground more slowly, as though inviting attention to detail. Adam was a willing and attentive pupil, and followed his motions exactly, missing—or trying to miss—nothing.

"I have brought you here, Adam, because it seems to me that this is the spot on which to begin our investigations. You have now in front of you almost the whole of the ancient kingdom of Mercia. In fact, we see the whole of it except that furthest part, which is covered by the Welsh Marches and those parts which are hidden from where we stand by the high ground of the immediate west. We can see—theoretically—the whole of the eastern bound of the kingdom, which ran south from the Humber to the Wash. I want you to bear in mind the trend of the ground, for some time, sooner or later, we shall do well to have it in our mind's eye when we are considering the ancient traditions and superstitions, and are trying to find the *rationale* of them. Each legend, each superstition which we receive, will help in the understanding and possible elucidation of the others. And as all such have a local basis, we can come closer to the truth—or the probability—by knowing the local conditions as we go along. It will help us to bring to our aid such geological truth as we may have between us. For instance, the building materials used in various ages can afford their own lessons to understanding eyes. The very heights and shapes and materials of these hills—nay, even of the wide plain that lies between us and the sea—have in themselves the materials of enlightening books."

"For instance, sir?" said Adam, venturing a question.

"Well, look at those hills which surround the main one where the site for the Castle was wisely chosen—on the highest ground. Take the others. There is something ostensible in each of them, and in all probability something unseen and unproved, but to be imagined, also."

"For instance?" continued Adam.

"Let us take them *seriatim*. That to the east, where the trees are, lower down—that was once the location of a Roman temple, possibly founded on a pre-existing Druidical one. Its name implies the former, and the grove of ancient oaks suggests the latter."

"Please explain."

"The old name translated means 'Diana's Grove.' Then the next one higher than it, but just beyond it, is called '*Mercy*'—in all probability a corruption or familiarisation of the word *Mercia*, with a Roman pun included. We learn from early manuscripts that the place was called *Vilula Misericordiae*. It was originally a nunnery, founded by Queen Bertha, but done away with by King Penda, the reactionary to Paganism after St. Augustine. Then comes your uncle's place—Lesser Hill. Though it is so close to the Castle, it is not connected with it. It is a freehold, and, so far as we know, of equal age. It has always belonged to your family."

"Then there only remains the Castle!"

"That is all; but its history contains the histories of all the others—in fact, the whole history of early England." Sir Nathaniel, seeing the expectant look on Adam's face, went on:

"The history of the Castle has no beginning so far as we know. The furthest records or surmises or inferences simply accept it as existing. Some of these—guesses, let us call them—seem to show that there was some sort of structure there when the Romans came, therefore it must have been a place of importance in Druid times—if indeed that was the beginning. Naturally the Romans accepted it, as they did everything of the kind that was, or might be, useful. The change is shown or inferred in the name Castra. It was the highest protected ground, and so naturally became the most important of their camps. A study of the map will show you that it must have been a most important centre. It both protected the advances already made to the north, and helped to dominate the sea coast. It sheltered the western marches, beyond which lay savage Wales—and danger. It provided a means of getting to the Severn, round which lay the great Roman roads then coming into existence, and made possible the great waterway to the heart of England—through the Severn and its tributaries. It brought the east and the west together by the swiftest and easiest ways known to those times. And, finally, it provided means of descent on London and all the expanse of country watered by the Thames.

"With such a centre, already known and organised, we can easily see that each fresh wave of invasion—the Angles, the Saxons, the Danes, and the Normans—found it a desirable possession and so ensured its upholding. In the earlier centuries it was merely a vantage ground. But when the victorious Romans brought with them the heavy solid fortifications impregnable to the weapons of the time, its commanding position alone ensured its adequate building and equipment. Then it was that the fortified camp of the Caesars developed into the castle of the king. As we are as yet ignorant of the names of the first kings of Mercia, no historian has been able to guess which of them made it his ultimate defence; and I suppose we shall never know now. In process of time, as the arts of war developed, it increased in size and strength, and although recorded details are lacking, the history is written not merely in the stone of its building, but is inferred in the changes of structure. Then the sweeping changes which followed the Norman Conquest wiped out all lesser records than its own. To-day we must accept it as one of the earliest castles of the Conquest, probably not later than the time of Henry I. Roman and Norman were both wise in their retention of places of approved strength or utility. So it was that these surrounding heights, already established and to a certain extent proved, were retained. Indeed, such characteristics as already pertained to them were preserved, and to-day afford to us lessons regarding things which have themselves long since passed away.

"So much for the fortified heights; but the hollows too have their own story. But how the time passes! We must hurry home, or your uncle will wonder what has become of us."

He started with long steps towards Lesser Hill, and Adam was soon furtively running in order to keep up with him.

CHAPTER IV—THE LADY ARABELLA MARCH

"Now, there is no hurry, but so soon as you are both ready we shall start," Mr. Salton said when breakfast had begun. "I want to take you first to see a remarkable relic of Mercia, and then we'll go to Liverpool through what is called 'The Great Vale of Cheshire.' You may be disappointed, but take care not to prepare your mind"—this to Adam—"for anything stupendous or heroic. You would not think the place a vale at all, unless you were told so beforehand, and had confidence in the veracity of the teller. We should get to the Landing Stage in time to meet the *West African*, and catch Mr. Caswall as he comes ashore. We want to do him honour—and, besides, it will be more pleasant to have the introductions over before we go to his *fête* at the Castle."

The carriage was ready, the same as had been used the previous day, but there were different horses—magnificent animals, and keen for work. Breakfast was soon over, and they shortly took their places. The postillions had their orders, and were quickly on their way at an exhilarating pace.

Presently, in obedience to Mr. Salton's signal, the carriage drew up opposite a great heap of stones by the wayside.

"Here, Adam," he said, "is something that you of all men should not pass by unnoticed. That heap of stones brings us at once to the dawn of the Anglian kingdom. It was begun more than a thousand years ago—in the latter part of the seventh century—in memory of a murder. Wulfere, King of Mercia, nephew of Penda, here murdered his two sons for embracing Christianity. As was the custom of the time, each passer-by added a stone to the memorial heap. Penda represented heathen reaction after St. Augustine's mission. Sir Nathaniel can tell you as much as you want about this, and put you, if you wish, on the track of such accurate knowledge as there is."

Whilst they were looking at the heap of stones, they noticed that another carriage had drawn up beside them, and the passenger—there was only one—was regarding them curiously. The carriage was an old heavy travelling one, with arms blazoned on it gorgeously. The men took off their hats, as the occupant, a lady, addressed them.

"How do you do, Sir Nathaniel? How do you do, Mr. Salton? I hope you have not met with any accident. Look at me!"

As she spoke she pointed to where one of the heavy springs was broken across, the broken metal showing bright. Adam spoke up at once:

"Oh, that can soon be put right."

"Soon? There is no one near who can mend a break like that."

"I can."

"You!" She looked incredulously at the dapper young gentleman who spoke. "You—why, it's a workman's job."

"All right, I am a workman—though that is not the only sort of work I do. I am an Australian, and, as we have to move about fast, we are all trained to farriery and such mechanics as come into travel—I am quite at your service."

"I hardly know how to thank you for your kindness, of which I gladly avail myself. I don't know what else I can do, as I wish to meet Mr. Caswall of Castra Regis, who arrives home from Africa to-day. It is a notable home-coming; all the countryside want to do him honour." She looked at the old men and quickly made up her mind as to the identity of the stranger. "You must be Mr. Adam Salton of Lesser Hill. I am Lady Arabella March of Diana's Grove." As she spoke she turned slightly to Mr. Salton, who took the hint and made a formal introduction.

So soon as this was done, Adam took some tools from his uncle's carriage, and at once began work on the broken spring. He was an expert workman, and the breach was soon made good. Adam was gathering the tools which he had been using—which, after the manner of all workmen, had been scattered about—when he noticed that several black snakes had crawled out from the heap of stones and were gathering round him. This naturally occupied his mind, and he was not thinking of anything else when he noticed Lady Arabella, who had opened the door of the carriage, slip from it with a quick gliding motion. She was already among the snakes when he called out to warn her. But there seemed to be no need of warning. The snakes had turned and were wriggling back to the mound as quickly as they could. He laughed to himself behind his teeth as he whispered, "No need to fear there. They seem much more afraid of her than she of them." All the same he began to beat on the ground with a stick which was lying close to him, with the instinct of one used to such vermin. In an instant he was alone beside the mound with Lady Arabella, who appeared quite unconcerned at the incident. Then he took a long look at her, and her dress alone was sufficient to attract attention. She was clad in some kind of soft white stuff, which clung close to her form, showing to the full every movement of her sinuous figure. She wore a close-fitting cap of some fine fur of dazzling white. Coiled round her white throat was a large necklace of emeralds, whose profusion of colour dazzled when the sun shone on them. Her voice was peculiar, very low and sweet, and so soft that the dominant note was of sibilation. Her hands, too, were peculiar—long, flexible, white, with a strange movement as of waving gently to and fro.

She appeared quite at ease, and, after thanking Adam, said that if any of his uncle's party were going to Liverpool she would be most happy to join forces.

"Whilst you are staying here, Mr. Salton, you must look on the grounds of Diana's Grove as your own, so that you may come and go just as you do in Lesser Hill. There are some fine views, and not a few natural curiosities which are sure to interest you, if you are a student of natural history—specially of an earlier kind, when the world was younger."

The heartiness with which she spoke, and the warmth of her words—not of her manner, which was cold and distant—made him suspicious. In the meantime both his uncle and Sir Nathaniel had thanked her for the invitation—of which, however, they said they were unable to avail themselves. Adam had a suspicion that, though she answered regretfully, she was in reality relieved. When he had got into the carriage with the two old men, and they had driven off, he was not surprised when Sir Nathaniel spoke.

"I could not but feel that she was glad to be rid of us. She can play her game better alone!"

"What is her game?" asked Adam unthinkingly.

"All the county knows it, my boy. Caswall is a very rich man. Her husband was rich when she married him—or seemed to be. When he committed suicide, it was found that he had nothing left, and the estate was mortgaged up to the hilt. Her only hope is in a rich marriage. I suppose I need not draw any conclusion; you can do that as well as I can."

Adam remained silent nearly all the time they were travelling through the alleged Vale of Cheshire. He thought much during that journey and came to several conclusions, though his lips were unmoved. One of these conclusions was that he would be very careful about paying any attention to Lady Arabella. He was himself a rich man, how rich not even his uncle had the least idea, and would have been surprised had he known.

The remainder of the journey was uneventful, and upon arrival at Liverpool they went aboard the *West African*, which had just come to the landing-stage. There his uncle introduced himself to Mr. Caswall, and followed this up by introducing Sir Nathaniel and then Adam. The new-comer received them graciously, and said what a pleasure it was to be coming home after so long an absence of his family from their old seat. Adam was pleased at the warmth of the reception; but he could not avoid a feeling of repugnance at the man's face. He was trying hard to overcome this when a diversion was caused by the arrival of Lady Arabella. The diversion was welcome to all; the two Saltons and Sir Nathaniel were shocked at Caswall's face—so hard, so ruthless, so selfish, so dominant. "God help any," was the common thought, "who is under the domination of such a man!"

Presently his African servant approached him, and at once their thoughts changed to a larger toleration. Caswall looked indeed a savage—but a cultured savage. In him were traces of the softening civilisation of ages—of some of the higher instincts and education of man, no matter how rudimentary these might be. But the face of Oolanga, as his master called him, was unreformed, unsoftened savage, and inherent in it were all the hideous possibilities of a lost, devil-ridden child of the forest and the swamp—the lowest of all created things that could be regarded as in some form ostensibly human. Lady Arabella and Oolanga arrived almost simultaneously, and Adam was surprised to notice what effect their appearance had on each other. The woman seemed as if she would not—could not—condescend to exhibit any concern or interest in such a creature. On the other hand, the negro's bearing was such as in itself to justify her pride. He treated her not merely as a slave treats his master, but as a worshipper would treat a deity. He knelt before her with his hands out-stretched and his forehead in the dust. So long as she remained he did not move; it was only when she went over to Caswall that he relaxed his attitude of devotion and stood by respectfully.

Adam spoke to his own man, Davenport, who was standing by, having arrived with the bailiff of Lesser Hill, who had followed Mr. Salton in a pony trap. As he spoke, he pointed to an attentive ship's steward, and presently the two men were conversing.

"I think we ought to be moving," Mr. Salton said to Adam. "I have some things to do in Liverpool, and I am sure that both Mr. Caswall and Lady Arabella would like to get under weigh for Castra Regis."

"I too, sir, would like to do something," replied Adam. "I want to find out where Ross, the animal merchant, lives—I want to take a small animal home with me, if you don't mind. He is only a little thing, and will be no trouble."

"Of course not, my boy. What kind of animal is it that you want?"

"A mongoose."

"A mongoose! What on earth do you want it for?"

"To kill snakes."

"Good!" The old man remembered the mound of stones. No explanation was needed.

When Ross heard what was wanted, he asked:

"Do you want something special, or will an ordinary mongoose do?"

"Well, of course I want a good one. But I see no need for anything special. It is for ordinary use."

"I can let you have a choice of ordinary ones. I only asked, because I have in stock a very special one which I got lately from Nepaul. He has a record of his own. He killed a king cobra that had been seen in the Rajah's garden. But I don't suppose we have any snakes of the kind in this cold climate—I daresay an ordinary one will do."

When Adam got back to the carriage, carefully carrying the box with the mongoose, Sir Nathaniel said: "Hullo! what have you got there?"

"A mongoose."

"What for?"

"To kill snakes!"

Sir Nathaniel laughed.

"I heard Lady Arabella's invitation to you to come to Diana's Grove."

"Well, what on earth has that got to do with it?"

"Nothing directly that I know of. But we shall see." Adam waited, and the old man went on: "Have you by any chance heard the other name which was given long ago to that place."

"No, sir."

"It was called—Look here, this subject wants a lot of talking over. Suppose we wait till we are alone and have lots of time before us."

"All right, sir." Adam was filled with curiosity, but he thought it better not to hurry matters. All would come in good time. Then the three men returned home, leaving Mr. Caswall to spend the night in Liverpool.

The following day the Lesser Hill party set out for Castra Regis, and for the time Adam thought no more of Diana's Grove or of what mysteries it had contained—or might still contain.

The guests were crowding in, and special places were marked for important people. Adam, seeing so many persons of varied degree, looked round for Lady Arabella, but could not locate her. It was only when he saw the old-fashioned travelling carriage approach and heard the sound of cheering which went with it, that he realised that Edgar Caswall had arrived. Then, on looking more closely, he saw that Lady Arabella, dressed as he had seen her last, was seated beside him. When the carriage drew up at the great flight of steps, the host jumped down and gave her his hand.

It was evident to all that she was the chief guest at the festivities. It was not long before the seats on the daïs were filled, while the tenants and guests of lesser importance had occupied all the coigns of vantage not reserved. The order of the day had been carefully arranged by a committee. There were some speeches, happily neither many nor long; and then festivities were suspended till the time for feasting arrived. In the interval Caswall walked among his guests, speaking to all in a friendly manner and expressing a general welcome. The other guests came down from the daïs and followed his example, so there was unceremonious meeting and greeting between gentle and simple.

Adam Salton naturally followed with his eyes all that went on within their scope, taking note of all who seemed to afford any interest. He was young and a man and a stranger from a far distance; so on all these accounts he naturally took stock rather of the women than of the men, and of these, those who were young and attractive. There were lots of pretty girls among the crowd, and Adam, who was a handsome young man and well set up, got his full share of admiring glances. These did not concern him much, and he remained unmoved until there came along a group of three, by their dress and bearing, of the farmer class. One was a sturdy old man; the other two were good-looking girls, one of a little over twenty, the other not quite so old. So soon as Adam's eyes met those of the younger girl, who stood nearest to him, some sort of electricity flashed—that divine spark which begins by recognition, and ends in obedience. Men call it "Love."

Both his companions noticed how much Adam was taken by the pretty girl, and spoke of her to him in a way which made his heart warm to them.

"Did you notice that party that passed? The old man is Michael Watford, one of the tenants of Mr. Caswall. He occupies Mercy Farm, which Sir Nathaniel pointed out to you to-day. The girls are his grand-daughters, the elder, Lilla, being the only child of his elder son, who died when she was less than a year old. His wife died on the same day. She is a good girl—as good as she is pretty. The other is her first cousin, the daughter of Watford's second son. He went for a soldier when he was just over twenty, and was drafted abroad. He was not a good correspondent, though he was a good enough son. A few letters came, and then his father heard from the colonel of his regiment that he had been killed by dacoits in Burmah. He heard from the same source that his boy had been married to a Burmese, and that there was a daughter only a year old. Watford had the child brought home, and she grew up beside Lilla. The only thing that they heard of her birth was that her name was Mimi. The two children adored each other, and do to this day. Strange how different they are! Lilla all fair, like the old Saxon stock from which she is sprung; Mimi showing a trace of her mother's race. Lilla is as gentle as a dove, but Mimi's black eyes can glow whenever she is upset. The only thing that upsets her is when anything happens to injure or threaten or annoy Lilla. Then her eyes glow as do the eyes of a bird when her young are menaced."

CHAPTER V—THE WHITE WORM

Mr. Salton introduced Adam to Mr. Watford and his grand-daughters, and they all moved on together. Of course neighbours in the position of the Watfords knew all about Adam Salton, his relationship, circumstances, and prospects. So it would have been strange indeed if both girls did not dream of possibilities of the future. In agricultural England, eligible men of any class are rare. This particular man was specially eligible, for he did not belong to a class in which barriers of caste were strong. So when it began to be noticed that he walked beside Mimi Watford and seemed to desire her society, all their friends endeavoured to give the promising affair a helping hand. When the gongs sounded for the banquet, he went with her into the tent where her grandfather had seats. Mr. Salton and Sir Nathaniel noticed that the young man did not come to claim his appointed place at the daïs table; but they understood and made no remark, or indeed did not seem to notice his absence.

Lady Arabella sat as before at Edgar Caswall's right hand. She was certainly a striking and unusual woman, and to all it seemed fitting from her rank and personal qualities that she should be the chosen partner of the heir on his first appearance. Of course nothing was said openly by those of her own class who were present; but words were not necessary when so much could be expressed by nods and smiles. It seemed to be an accepted thing that at last there was to be a mistress of Castra Regis, and that she was present amongst them. There were not lacking some who, whilst admitting all her charm and beauty, placed her in the second rank, Lilla Watford being marked as first. There was sufficient divergence of type, as well as of individual beauty, to allow of fair comment; Lady Arabella represented the aristocratic type, and Lilla that of the commonalty.

When the dusk began to thicken, Mr. Salton and Sir Nathaniel walked home—the trap had been sent away early in the day—leaving Adam to follow in his own time. He came in earlier than was expected, and seemed upset about something. Neither of the elders made any comment. They all lit cigarettes, and, as dinner-time was close at hand, went to their rooms to get ready.

Adam had evidently been thinking in the interval. He joined the others in the drawing-room, looking ruffled and impatient—a condition of things seen for the first time. The others, with the patience—or the experience—of age, trusted to time to unfold and explain things. They had not long to wait. After sitting down and standing up several times, Adam suddenly burst out.

"That fellow seems to think he owns the earth. Can't he let people alone! He seems to think that he has only to throw his handkerchief to any woman, and be her master."

This outburst was in itself enlightening. Only thwarted affection in some guise could produce this feeling in an amiable young man. Sir Nathaniel, as an old diplomatist, had a way of understanding, as if by foreknowledge, the true inwardness of things, and asked suddenly, but in a matter-of-fact, indifferent voice:

"Was he after Lilla?"

"Yes, and the fellow didn't lose any time either. Almost as soon as they met, he began to butter her up, and tell her how beautiful she was. Why, before he left her side, he had asked himself to tea to-morrow at Mercy Farm. Stupid ass! He might see that the girl isn't his sort! I never saw anything like it. It was just like a hawk and a pigeon."

As he spoke, Sir Nathaniel turned and looked at Mr. Salton—a keen look which implied a full understanding.

"Tell us all about it, Adam. There are still a few minutes before dinner, and we shall all have better appetites when we have come to some conclusion on this matter."

"There is nothing to tell, sir; that is the worst of it. I am bound to say that there was not a word said that a human being could object to. He was very civil, and all that was proper—just what a landlord might be to a tenant's daughter . . . Yet—yet—well, I don't know how it was, but it made my blood boil."

"How did the hawk and the pigeon come in?" Sir Nathaniel's voice was soft and soothing, nothing of contradiction or overdone curiosity in it—a tone eminently suited to win confidence.

"I can hardly explain. I can only say that he looked like a hawk and she like a dove—and, now that I think of it, that is what they each did look like; and do look like in their normal condition."

"That is so!" came the soft voice of Sir Nathaniel.

Adam went on:

"Perhaps that early Roman look of his set me off. But I wanted to protect her; she seemed in danger."

"She seems in danger, in a way, from all you young men. I couldn't help noticing the way that even you looked—as if you wished to absorb her!"

"I hope both you young men will keep your heads cool," put in Mr. Salton. "You know, Adam, it won't do to have any quarrel between you, especially so soon after his home-coming and your arrival here. We must think of the feelings and happiness of our neighbours; mustn't we?"

"I hope so, sir. I assure you that, whatever may happen, or even threaten, I shall obey your wishes in this as in all things."

"Hush!" whispered Sir Nathaniel, who heard the servants in the passage bringing dinner.

After dinner, over the walnuts and the wine, Sir Nathaniel returned to the subject of the local legends.

"It will perhaps be a less dangerous topic for us to discuss than more recent ones."

"All right, sir," said Adam heartily. "I think you may depend on me now with regard to any topic. I can even discuss Mr. Caswall. Indeed, I may meet him tomorrow. He is going, as I said, to call at Mercy Farm at three o'clock—but I have an appointment at two."

"I notice," said Mr. Salton, "that you do not lose any time."

The two old men once more looked at each other steadily. Then, lest the mood of his listener should change with delay, Sir Nathaniel began at once:

"I don't propose to tell you all the legends of Mercia, or even to make a selection of them. It will be better, I think, for our purpose if we consider a few facts—recorded or unrecorded—about this neighbourhood. I think we might begin with Diana's Grove. It has roots in the different epochs of our history, and each has its special crop of legend. The Druid and the Roman are too far off for matters of detail; but it seems to me the Saxon and the Angles are near enough to yield material for legendary lore. We find that this particular place had another name besides Diana's Grove. This was manifestly of Roman origin, or of Grecian accepted as Roman. The other is more pregnant of adventure and romance than the Roman name. In Mercian tongue it was 'The Lair of the White Worm.' This needs a word of explanation at the beginning.

"In the dawn of the language, the word 'worm' had a somewhat different meaning from that in use to-day. It was an adaptation of the Anglo-Saxon 'wyrm,' meaning a dragon or snake; or from the Gothic 'waurms,' a serpent; or the Icelandic 'ormur,' or the German 'wurm.' We gather that it conveyed originally an idea of size and power, not as now in the diminutive of both these meanings. Here legendary history helps us. We have the well-known legend of the 'Worm Well' of Lambton Castle, and that of the 'Laidly Worm of Spindleston Heugh' near Bamborough. In both these legends the 'worm' was a monster of vast size and power—a veritable dragon or serpent, such as legend attributes to vast fens or quags where there was illimitable room for expansion. A glance at a geological map will show that whatever truth there may have been of the actuality of such monsters in the early geologic periods, at least there was plenty of possibility. In England there were originally vast plains where the plentiful supply of water could gather. The streams were deep and slow, and there were holes of abysmal depth, where any kind and size of antediluvian monster could find a habitat. In places, which now we can see from our windows, were mud-holes a hundred or more feet deep. Who can tell us when the age of the monsters which flourished in slime came to an end? There must have been places and conditions which made for greater longevity, greater size, greater strength than was usual. Such over-lappings may have come down even to our earlier centuries. Nay, are there not now creatures of a vastness of bulk regarded by the generality of men as impossible? Even in our own day there are seen the traces of animals, if not the animals themselves, of stupendous size—veritable survivals from earlier ages, preserved by some special qualities in their habitats. I remember meeting a distinguished man in India, who had the reputation of being a great shikaree, who told me that the greatest temptation he had ever had in his life was to shoot a giant snake which he had come across in the Terai of Upper India. He was on a tiger-shooting expedition, and as his elephant was crossing a nullah, it squealed. He looked down from his howdah and saw that the elephant had stepped across the body of a snake which was dragging itself through the jungle. 'So far as I could see,' he said, 'it must have been eighty or one hundred feet in length. Fully forty or fifty feet was on each side of the track, and though the weight which it dragged had thinned it, it was as thick round as a man's body. I suppose you know that when you are after tiger, it is a point of honour not to shoot at anything else, as life may depend on it. I could easily have spined this monster, but I felt that I must not—so, with regret, I had to let it go.'

"Just imagine such a monster anywhere in this country, and at once we could get a sort of idea of the 'worms,' which possibly did frequent the great morasses which spread round the mouths of many of the great European rivers."

"I haven't the least doubt, sir, that there may have been such monsters as you have spoken of still existing at a much later period than is generally accepted," replied Adam. "Also, if there were such things, that this was the very place for them. I have tried to think over the matter since you pointed out the configuration of the ground. But it seems to me that there is a hiatus somewhere. Are there not mechanical difficulties?"

"In what way?"

"Well, our antique monster must have been mighty heavy, and the distances he had to travel were long and the ways difficult. From where we are now sitting down to the level of the mud-holes is a distance of several hundred feet—I am leaving out of consideration altogether any lateral distance. Is it possible that there was a way by which a monster could travel up and down, and yet no chance recorder have ever seen him? Of course we have the legends; but is not some more exact evidence necessary in a scientific investigation?"

"My dear Adam, all you say is perfectly right, and, were we starting on such an investigation, we could not do better than follow your reasoning. But, my dear boy, you must remember that all this took place thousands of years ago. You must remember, too, that all records of the kind that would help us are lacking. Also, that the places to be considered were desert, so far as human habitation or population are considered. In the vast desolation of such a place as complied with the necessary conditions, there must have been such profusion of natural growth as would bar the progress of men formed as we are. The lair of such a monster would not have been disturbed for hundreds—or thousands—of years. Moreover, these creatures must have occupied places quite inaccessible to man. A snake who could make himself comfortable in a quagmire, a hundred feet deep, would be protected on the outskirts by such stupendous morasses as now no longer exist, or which, if they exist anywhere at all, can be on very few places on the earth's surface. Far be it from me to say that in more elemental times such things could not have been. The condition belongs to the geologic age—the great birth and growth of the world, when natural forces ran riot, when the struggle for existence was so savage that no vitality which was not founded in a gigantic form could have even a possibility of survival. That such a time existed, we have evidences in geology, but there only; we can never expect proofs such as this age demands. We can only imagine or surmise such things—or such conditions and such forces as overcame them."

CHAPTER VI—HAWK AND PIGEON

At breakfast-time next morning Sir Nathaniel and Mr. Salton were seated when Adam came hurriedly into the room.

"Any news?" asked his uncle mechanically.

"Four."

"Four what?" asked Sir Nathaniel.

"Snakes," said Adam, helping himself to a grilled kidney.

"Four snakes. I don't understand."

"Mongoose," said Adam, and then added explanatorily: "I was out with the mongoose just after three."

"Four snakes in one morning! Why, I didn't know there were so many on the Brow"—the local name for the western cliff. "I hope that wasn't the consequence of our talk of last night?"

"It was, sir. But not directly."

"But, God bless my soul, you didn't expect to get a snake like the Lambton worm, did you? Why, a mongoose, to tackle a monster like that—if there were one—would have to be bigger than a haystack."

"These were ordinary snakes, about as big as a walking-stick."

"Well, it's pleasant to be rid of them, big or little. That is a good mongoose, I am sure; he'll clear out all such vermin round here," said Mr. Salton.

Adam went quietly on with his breakfast. Killing a few snakes in a morning was no new experience to him. He left the room the moment breakfast was finished and went to the study that his uncle had arranged for him. Both Sir Nathaniel and Mr. Salton took it that he wanted to be by himself, so as to avoid any questioning or talk of the visit that he was to make that afternoon. They saw nothing further of him till about half-an-hour before dinner-time. Then he came quietly into the smoking-room, where Mr. Salton and Sir Nathaniel were sitting together, ready dressed.

"I suppose there is no use waiting. We had better get it over at once," remarked Adam.

His uncle, thinking to make things easier for him, said: "Get what over?"

There was a sign of shyness about him at this. He stammered a little at first, but his voice became more even as he went on.

"My visit to Mercy Farm."

Mr. Salton waited eagerly. The old diplomatist simply smiled.

"I suppose you both know that I was much interested yesterday in the Watfords?" There was no denial or fending off the question. Both the old men smiled acquiescence. Adam went on: "I meant you to see it—both of you. You, uncle, because you are my uncle and the nearest of my own kin, and, moreover, you couldn't have been more kind to me or made me more welcome if you had been my own father." Mr. Salton said nothing. He simply held out his hand, and the other took it and held it for a few seconds. "And you, sir, because you have shown me something of the same affection which in my wildest dreams of home I had no right to expect." He stopped for an instant, much moved.

Sir Nathaniel answered softly, laying his hand on the youth's shoulder.

"You are right, my boy; quite right. That is the proper way to look at it. And I may tell you that we old men, who have no children of our own, feel our hearts growing warm when we hear words like those."

Then Adam hurried on, speaking with a rush, as if he wanted to come to the crucial point.

"Mr. Watford had not come in, but Lilla and Mimi were at home, and they made me feel very welcome. They have all a great regard for my uncle. I am glad of that any way, for I like them all—much. We were having tea, when Mr. Caswall came to the door, attended by the negro. Lilla opened the door herself. The window of the living-room at the farm is a large one, and from within you cannot help seeing anyone coming. Mr. Caswall said he had ventured to call, as he wished to make the acquaintance of all his tenants, in a less formal way, and more individually, than had been possible to him on the previous day. The girls made him welcome—they are very sweet girls those, sir; someone will be very happy some day there—with either of them."

"And that man may be you, Adam," said Mr. Salton heartily.

A sad look came over the young man's eyes, and the fire his uncle had seen there died out. Likewise the timbre left his voice, making it sound lonely.

"Such might crown my life. But that happiness, I fear, is not for me—or not without pain and loss and woe."

"Well, it's early days yet!" cried Sir Nathaniel heartily.

The young man turned on him his eyes, which had now grown excessively sad.

"Yesterday—a few hours ago—that remark would have given me new hope—new courage; but since then I have learned too much."

The old man, skilled in the human heart, did not attempt to argue in such a matter.

"Too early to give in, my boy."

"I am not of a giving-in kind," replied the young man earnestly. "But, after all, it is wise to realise a truth. And when a man, though he is young, feels as I do—as I have felt ever since yesterday, when I first saw Mimi's eyes—his heart jumps. He does not need to learn things. He knows."

There was silence in the room, during which the twilight stole on imperceptibly. It was Adam who again broke the silence.

"Do you know, uncle, if we have any second sight in our family?"

"No, not that I ever heard about. Why?"

"Because," he answered slowly, "I have a conviction which seems to answer all the conditions of second sight."

"And then?" asked the old man, much perturbed.

"And then the usual inevitable. What in the Hebrides and other places, where the Sight is a cult—a belief—is called 'the doom'—the court from which there is no appeal. I have often heard of second sight—we have many western Scots in Australia; but I have realised more of its true inwardness in an instant of this afternoon than I did in the whole of my life previously—a granite wall stretching up to the very heavens, so high and so dark that the eye of God Himself cannot see beyond. Well, if the Doom must come, it must. That is all."

The voice of Sir Nathaniel broke in, smooth and sweet and grave.

"Can there not be a fight for it? There can for most things."

"For most things, yes, but for the Doom, no. What a man can do I shall do. There will be—must be—a fight. When and where and how I know not, but a fight there will be. But, after all, what is a man in such a case?"

"Adam, there are three of us." Salton looked at his old friend as he spoke, and that old friend's eyes blazed.

"Ay, three of us," he said, and his voice rang.

There was again a pause, and Sir Nathaniel endeavoured to get back to less emotional and more neutral ground.

"Tell us of the rest of the meeting. Remember we are all pledged to this. It is a fight *à l'outrance*, and we can afford to throw away or forgo no chance."

"We shall throw away or lose nothing that we can help. We fight to win, and the stake is a life—perhaps more than one—we shall see." Then he went on in a conversational tone, such as he had used when he spoke of the coming to the farm of Edgar Caswall: "When Mr. Caswall came in, the negro went a short distance away and there remained. It gave me the idea that he expected to be called, and intended to remain in sight, or within hail. Then Mimi got another cup and made fresh tea, and we all went on together."

"Was there anything uncommon—were you all quite friendly?" asked Sir Nathaniel quietly.

"Quite friendly. There was nothing that I could notice out of the common—except," he went on, with a slight hardening of the voice, "except that he kept his eyes fixed on Lilla, in a way which was quite intolerable to any man who might hold her dear."

"Now, in what way did he look?" asked Sir Nathaniel.

"There was nothing in itself offensive; but no one could help noticing it."

"You did. Miss Watford herself, who was the victim, and Mr. Caswall, who was the offender, are out of range as witnesses. Was there anyone else who noticed?"

"Mimi did. Her face flamed with anger as she saw the look."

"What kind of look was it? Over-ardent or too admiring, or what? Was it the look of a lover, or one who fain would be? You understand?"

"Yes, sir, I quite understand. Anything of that sort I should of course notice. It would be part of my preparation for keeping my self-control—to which I am pledged."

"If it were not amatory, was it threatening? Where was the offence?"

Adam smiled kindly at the old man.

"It was not amatory. Even if it was, such was to be expected. I should be the last man in the world to object, since I am myself an offender in that respect. Moreover, not only have I been taught to fight fair, but by nature I believe I am just. I would be as tolerant of and as liberal to a rival as I should expect him to be to me. No, the look I mean was nothing of that kind. And so long as it did not lack proper respect, I should not of my own part condescend to notice it. Did you ever study the eyes of a hound?"

"At rest?"

"No, when he is following his instincts! Or, better still," Adam went on, "the eyes of a bird of prey when he is following his instincts. Not when he is swooping, but merely when he is watching his quarry?"

"No," said Sir Nathaniel, "I don't know that I ever did. Why, may I ask?"

"That was the look. Certainly not amatory or anything of that kind—yet it was, it struck me, more dangerous, if not so deadly as an actual threatening."

Again there was a silence, which Sir Nathaniel broke as he stood up:

"I think it would be well if we all thought over this by ourselves. Then we can renew the subject."

CHAPTER VII—OOLANGA

Mr. Salton had an appointment for six o'clock at Liverpool. When he had driven off, Sir Nathaniel took Adam by the arm.

"May I come with you for a while to your study? I want to speak to you privately without your uncle knowing about it, or even what the subject is. You don't mind, do you? It is not idle curiosity. No, no. It is on the subject to which we are all committed."

"Is it necessary to keep my uncle in the dark about it? He might be offended."

"It is not necessary; but it is advisable. It is for his sake that I asked. My friend is an old man, and it might concern him unduly—even alarm him. I promise you there shall be nothing that could cause him anxiety in our silence, or at which he could take umbrage."

"Go on, sir!" said Adam simply.

"You see, your uncle is now an old man. I know it, for we were boys together. He has led an uneventful and somewhat self-contained life, so that any such condition of things as has now arisen is apt to perplex him from its very strangeness. In fact, any new matter is trying to old people. It has its own disturbances and its own anxieties, and neither of these things are good for lives that should be restful. Your uncle is a strong man, with a very happy and placid nature. Given health and ordinary conditions of life, there is no reason why he should not live to be a hundred. You and I, therefore, who both love him, though in different ways, should make it our business to protect him from all disturbing influences. I am sure you will agree with me that any labour to this end would be well spent. All right, my boy! I see your answer in your eyes; so we need say no more of that. And now," here his voice changed, "tell me all that took place at that interview. There are strange things in front of us—how strange we cannot at present even guess. Doubtless some of the difficult things to understand which lie behind the veil will in time be shown to us to see and to understand. In the meantime, all we can do is to work patiently, fearlessly, and unselfishly, to an end that we think is right. You had got so far as where Lilla opened the door to Mr. Caswall and the negro. You also observed that Mimi was disturbed in her mind at the way Mr. Caswall looked at her cousin."

"Certainly—though 'disturbed' is a poor way of expressing her objection."

"Can you remember well enough to describe Caswall's eyes, and how Lilla looked, and what Mimi said and did? Also Oolanga, Caswall's West African servant."

"I'll do what I can, sir. All the time Mr. Caswall was staring, he kept his eyes fixed and motionless—but not as if he was in a trance. His forehead was wrinkled up, as it is when one is trying to see through or into something. At the best of times his face has not a gentle expression; but when it was screwed up like that it was almost diabolical. It frightened poor Lilla so that she trembled, and after a bit got so pale that I thought she had fainted. However, she held up and tried to stare back, but in a feeble kind of way. Then Mimi came close and held her hand. That braced her up, and—still, never ceasing her return stare—she got colour again and seemed more like herself."

"Did he stare too?"

"More than ever. The weaker Lilla seemed, the stronger he became, just as if he were feeding on her strength. All at once she turned round, threw up her hands, and fell down in a faint. I could not see what else happened just then, for Mimi had thrown herself on her knees beside her and hid her from me. Then there was something like a black shadow between us, and there was the nigger, looking more like a malignant devil than ever. I am not usually a patient man, and the sight of that ugly devil is enough to make one's blood boil. When he saw my face, he seemed to realise danger—immediate danger—and slunk out of the room as noiselessly as if he had been blown out. I learned one thing, however—he is an enemy, if ever a man had one."

"That still leaves us three to two!" put in Sir Nathaniel.

"Then Caswall slunk out, much as the nigger had done. When he had gone, Lilla recovered at once."

"Now," said Sir Nathaniel, anxious to restore peace, "have you found out anything yet regarding the negro? I am anxious to be posted regarding him. I fear there will be, or may be, grave trouble with him."

"Yes, sir, I've heard a good deal about him—of course it is not official; but hearsay must guide us at first. You know my man Davenport—private secretary, confidential man of business, and general factotum. He is devoted to me, and has my full confidence. I asked him to stay on board the *West African* and have a good look round, and find out what he could about Mr. Caswall. Naturally, he was struck with the aboriginal savage. He found one of the ship's stewards, who had been on the regular voyages to South Africa. He knew Oolanga and had made a study of him. He is a man who gets on well with niggers, and they open their hearts to him. It seems that this Oolanga is quite a great person in the nigger world of the African West Coast. He has the two things which men of his own colour respect: he can make them afraid, and he is lavish with money. I don't know whose money—but that does not matter. They are always ready to trumpet his greatness. Evil greatness it is—but neither does that matter. Briefly, this is his history. He was originally a witch-finder—about as low an occupation as exists amongst aboriginal savages. Then he got up in the world and became an Obi-man, which gives an opportunity to wealth *via* blackmail. Finally, he reached the highest honour in hellish service. He became a user of Voodoo, which seems to be a service of the utmost baseness and cruelty. I was told some of his deeds of cruelty, which are simply sickening. They made me long for an opportunity of helping to drive him back to hell. You might think to look at him that you could measure in some way the extent of his vileness; but it would be a vain hope. Monsters such as he is belong to an earlier and more rudimentary stage of barbarism.

He is in his way a clever fellow—for a nigger; but is none the less dangerous or the less hateful for that. The men in the ship told me that he was a collector: some of them had seen his collections. Such collections! All that was potent for evil in bird or beast, or even in fish. Beaks that could break and rend and tear—all the birds represented were of a predatory kind. Even the fishes are those which are born to destroy, to wound, to torture. The collection, I assure you, was an object lesson in human malignity. This being has enough evil in his face to frighten even a strong man. It is little wonder that the sight of it put that poor girl into a dead faint!"

Nothing more could be done at the moment, so they separated.

Adam was up in the early morning and took a smart walk round the Brow. As he was passing Diana's Grove, he looked in on the short avenue of trees, and noticed the snakes killed on the previous morning by the mongoose. They all lay in a row, straight and rigid, as if they had been placed by hands. Their skins seemed damp and sticky, and they were covered all over with ants and other insects. They looked loathsome, so after a glance, he passed on.

A little later, when his steps took him, naturally enough, past the entrance to Mercy Farm, he was passed by the negro, moving quickly under the trees wherever there was shadow. Laid across one extended arm, looking like dirty towels across a rail, he had the horrid-looking snakes. He did not seem to see Adam. No one was to be seen at Mercy except a few workmen in the farmyard, so, after waiting on the chance of seeing Mimi, Adam began to go slowly home.

Once more he was passed on the way. This time it was by Lady Arabella, walking hurriedly and so furiously angry that she did not recognise him, even to the extent of acknowledging his bow.

When Adam got back to Lesser Hill, he went to the coach-house where the box with the mongoose was kept, and took it with him, intending to finish at the Mound of Stone what he had begun the previous morning with regard to the extermination. He found that the snakes were even more easily attacked than on the previous day; no less than six were killed in the first half-hour. As no more appeared, he took it for granted that the morning's work was over, and went towards home. The mongoose had by this time become accustomed to him, and was willing to let himself be handled freely. Adam lifted him up and put him on his shoulder and walked on. Presently he saw a lady advancing towards him, and recognised Lady Arabella.

Hitherto the mongoose had been quiet, like a playful affectionate kitten; but when the two got close, Adam was horrified to see the mongoose, in a state of the wildest fury, with every hair standing on end, jump from his shoulder and run towards Lady Arabella. It looked so furious and so intent on attack that he called a warning.

"Look out—look out! The animal is furious and means to attack."

Lady Arabella looked more than ever disdainful and was passing on; the mongoose jumped at her in a furious attack. Adam rushed forward with his stick, the only weapon he had. But just as he got within striking distance, the lady drew out a revolver and shot the animal, breaking his backbone. Not satisfied with this, she poured shot after shot into him till the magazine was exhausted. There was no coolness or hauteur about her now; she seemed more furious even than the animal, her face transformed with hate, and as determined to kill as he had appeared to be. Adam, not knowing exactly what to do, lifted his hat in apology and hurried on to Lesser Hill.

CHAPTER VIII—SURVIVALS

At breakfast Sir Nathaniel noticed that Adam was put out about something, but he said nothing. The lesson of silence is better remembered in age than in youth. When they were both in the study, where Sir Nathaniel followed him, Adam at once began to tell his companion of what had happened. Sir Nathaniel looked graver and graver as the narration proceeded, and when Adam had stopped he remained silent for several minutes, before speaking.

"This is very grave. I have not formed any opinion yet; but it seems to me at first impression that this is worse than anything I had expected."

"Why, sir?" said Adam. "Is the killing of a mongoose—no matter by whom—so serious a thing as all that?"

His companion smoked on quietly for quite another few minutes before he spoke.

"When I have properly thought it over I may moderate my opinion, but in the meantime it seems to me that there is something dreadful behind all this—something that may affect all our lives—that may mean the issue of life or death to any of us."

Adam sat up quickly.

"Do tell me, sir, what is in your mind—if, of course, you have no objection, or do not think it better to withhold it."

"I have no objection, Adam—in fact, if I had, I should have to overcome it. I fear there can be no more reserved thoughts between us."

"Indeed, sir, that sounds serious, worse than serious!"

"Adam, I greatly fear that the time has come for us—for you and me, at all events—to speak out plainly to one another. Does not there seem something very mysterious about this?"

"I have thought so, sir, all along. The only difficulty one has is what one is to think and where to begin."

"Let us begin with what you have told me. First take the conduct of the mongoose. He was quiet, even friendly and affectionate with you. He only attacked the snakes, which is, after all, his business in life."

"That is so!"

"Then we must try to find some reason why he attacked Lady Arabella."

"May it not be that a mongoose may have merely the instinct to attack, that nature does not allow or provide him with the fine reasoning powers to discriminate who he is to attack?"

"Of course that may be so. But, on the other hand, should we not satisfy ourselves why he does wish to attack anything? If for centuries, this particular animal is known to attack only one kind of other animal, are we not justified in assuming that when one of them attacks a hitherto unclassed animal, he recognises in that animal some quality which it has in common with the hereditary enemy?"

"That is a good argument, sir," Adam went on, "but a dangerous one. If we followed it out, it would lead us to believe that Lady Arabella is a snake."

"We must be sure, before going to such an end, that there is no point as yet unconsidered which would account for the unknown thing which puzzles us."

"In what way?"

"Well, suppose the instinct works on some physical basis—for instance, smell. If there were anything in recent juxtaposition to the attacked which would carry the scent, surely that would supply the missing cause."

"Of course!" Adam spoke with conviction.

"Now, from what you tell me, the negro had just come from the direction of Diana's Grove, carrying the dead snakes which the mongoose had killed the previous morning. Might not the scent have been carried that way?"

"Of course it might, and probably was. I never thought of that. Is there any possible way of guessing approximately how long a scent will remain? You see, this is a natural scent, and may derive from a place where it has been effective for thousands of years. Then, does a scent of any kind carry with it any form or quality of another kind, either good or evil? I ask you because one ancient name of the house lived in by the lady who was attacked by the mongoose was 'The Lair of the White Worm.' If any of these things be so, our difficulties have multiplied indefinitely. They may even change in kind. We may get into moral entanglements; before we know it, we may be in the midst of a struggle between good and evil."

Sir Nathaniel smiled gravely.

"With regard to the first question—so far as I know, there are no fixed periods for which a scent may be active—I think we may take it that that period does not run into thousands of years. As to whether any moral change accompanies a physical one, I can only say that I have met no proof of the fact. At the same time, we must remember that 'good' and 'evil' are terms so wide as to take in the whole scheme of creation, and all that is implied by them and by their mutual action and reaction. Generally, I would say that in the scheme of a First Cause anything is possible. So long as the inherent forces or tendencies of any one thing are veiled from us we must expect mystery."

"There is one other question on which I should like to ask your opinion. Suppose that there are any permanent forces appertaining to the past, what we may call 'survivals,' do these belong to good as well as to evil? For instance, if the scent of the primaeval monster can so remain in proportion to the original strength, can the same be true of things of good import?"

Sir Nathaniel thought for a while before he answered.

"We must be careful not to confuse the physical and the moral. I can see that already you have switched on the moral entirely, so perhaps we had better follow it up first. On the side of the moral, we have certain justification for belief in the utterances of revealed religion. For instance, 'the effectual fervent prayer of a righteous man availeth much' is altogether for good. We have nothing of a similar kind on the side of evil. But if we accept this dictum we need have no more fear of 'mysteries': these become thenceforth merely obstacles."

Adam suddenly changed to another phase of the subject.

"And now, sir, may I turn for a few minutes to purely practical things, or rather to matters of historical fact?"

Sir Nathaniel bowed acquiescence.

"We have already spoken of the history, so far as it is known, of some of the places round us—'Castra Regis,' 'Diana's Grove,' and 'The Lair of the White Worm.' I would like to ask if there is anything not necessarily of evil import about any of the places?"

"Which?" asked Sir Nathaniel shrewdly.

"Well, for instance, this house and Mercy Farm?"

"Here we turn," said Sir Nathaniel, "to the other side, the light side of things. Let us take Mercy Farm first. When Augustine was sent by Pope Gregory to Christianise England, in the time of the Romans, he was received and protected by Ethelbert, King of Kent, whose wife, daughter of Charibert, King of Paris, was a Christian, and did much for Augustine. She founded a nunnery in memory of Columba, which was named *Sedes misericordioe*, the House of Mercy, and, as the region was Mercian, the two names became involved. As Columba is the Latin for dove, the dove became a sort of signification of the nunnery. She seized on the idea and made the newly-founded nunnery a house of doves. Someone sent her a freshly-discovered dove, a sort of carrier, but which had in the white feathers of its head and neck the form of a religious cowl. The nunnery flourished for more than a century, when, in the time of Penda, who was the reactionary of heathendom, it fell into decay. In the meantime the doves, protected by religious feeling, had increased mightily, and were known in all Catholic communities. When King Offa ruled in Mercia, about a hundred and fifty years later, he restored Christianity, and under its protection the nunnery of St. Columba was restored and its doves flourished again. In process of time this religious house again fell into desuetude; but before it disappeared it had achieved a great name for good works, and in especial for the piety of its members. If deeds and prayers and hopes and earnest thinking leave anywhere any moral effect, Mercy Farm and all around it have almost the right to be considered holy ground."

"Thank you, sir," said Adam earnestly, and was silent. Sir Nathaniel understood.

After lunch that day, Adam casually asked Sir Nathaniel to come for a walk with him. The keen-witted old diplomatist guessed that there must be some motive behind the suggestion, and he at once agreed.

As soon as they were free from observation, Adam began.

"I am afraid, sir, that there is more going on in this neighbourhood than most people imagine. I was out this morning, and on the edge of the small wood, I came upon the body of a child by the roadside. At first, I thought she was dead, and while examining her, I noticed on her neck some marks that looked like those of teeth."

"Some wild dog, perhaps?" put in Sir Nathaniel.

"Possibly, sir, though I think not—but listen to the rest of my news. I glanced around, and to my surprise, I noticed something white moving among the trees. I placed the child down carefully, and followed, but I could not find any further traces. So I returned to the child and resumed my examination, and, to my delight, I discovered that she was still alive. I chafed her hands and gradually she revived, but to my disappointment she remembered nothing—except that something had crept up quietly from behind, and had gripped her round the throat. Then, apparently, she fainted."

"Gripped her round the throat! Then it cannot have been a dog."

"No, sir, that is my difficulty, and explains why I brought you out here, where we cannot possibly be overheard. You have noticed, of course, the peculiar sinuous way in which Lady Arabella moves—well, I feel certain that the white thing that I saw in the wood was the mistress of Diana's Grove!"

"Good God, boy, be careful what you say."

"Yes, sir, I fully realise the gravity of my accusation, but I feel convinced that the marks on the child's throat were human—and made by a woman."

Adam's companion remained silent for some time, deep in thought.

"Adam, my boy," he said at last, "this matter appears to me to be far more serious even than you think. It forces me to break confidence with my old friend, your uncle—but, in order to spare him, I must do so. For some time now, things have been happening in this district that have been worrying him dreadfully—several people have disappeared, without leaving the slightest trace; a dead child was found by the roadside, with no visible or ascertainable cause of death—sheep and other animals have been found in the fields, bleeding from open wounds. There have been other matters—many of them apparently trivial in themselves. Some sinister influence has been at work, and I admit that I have suspected Lady Arabella—that is why I questioned you so closely about the mongoose and its strange attack upon Lady Arabella. You will think it strange that I should suspect the mistress of Diana's Grove, a beautiful woman of aristocratic birth. Let me explain—the family seat is near my own place, Doom Tower, and at one time I knew the family well. When still a young girl, Lady Arabella wandered into a small wood near her home, and did not return. She was found unconscious and in a high fever—the doctor said that she had received a poisonous bite, and the girl being at a delicate and critical age, the result was serious—so much so that she was not expected to recover. A great London physician came down but could do nothing—indeed, he said that the girl would not survive the night. All hope had been abandoned, when, to everyone's surprise, Lady Arabella made a sudden and startling recovery. Within a couple of days she was going about as usual! But to the horror of her people, she developed a terrible craving for cruelty, maiming and injuring birds and small animals—even killing them. This was put down to a nervous disturbance due to her age, and it was hoped that her marriage to Captain March would put this right. However, it was not a happy marriage, and eventually her husband was found shot through the head. I have always suspected suicide, though no pistol was found near the body. He may have discovered something—God knows what!—so possibly Lady Arabella may herself have killed him. Putting together many small matters that have come to my knowledge, I have come to the conclusion that the foul White Worm obtained control of her body, just as her soul was leaving its earthly tenement—that would explain the sudden revival of energy, the strange and inexplicable craving for maiming and killing, as well as many other matters with which I need not trouble you now, Adam. As I said just now, God alone knows what poor Captain March discovered—it must have been something too ghastly for human endurance, if my theory is correct that the once beautiful human body of Lady Arabella is under the control of this ghastly White Worm."

Adam nodded.

"But what can we do, sir—it seems a most difficult problem."

"We can do nothing, my boy—that is the important part of it. It would be impossible to take action—all we can do is to keep careful watch, especially as regards Lady Arabella, and be ready to act, promptly and decisively, if the opportunity occurs."

Adam agreed, and the two men returned to Lesser Hill.

CHAPTER IX—SMELLING DEATH

Adam Salton, though he talked little, did not let the grass grow under his feet in any matter which he had undertaken, or in which he was interested. He had agreed with Sir Nathaniel that they should not do anything with regard to the mystery of Lady Arabella's fear of the mongoose, but he steadily pursued his course in being *prepared* to act whenever the opportunity might come. He was in his own mind perpetually casting about for information or clues which might lead to possible lines of action. Baffled by the killing of the mongoose, he looked around for another line to follow. He was fascinated by the idea of there being a mysterious link between the woman and the animal, but he was already preparing a second string to his bow. His new idea was to use the faculties of Oolanga, so far as he could, in the service of discovery. His first move was to send Davenport to Liverpool to try to find the steward of the *West African*, who had told him about Oolanga, and if possible secure any further information, and then try to induce (by bribery or other means) the nigger to come to the Brow. So soon as he himself could have speech of the Voodoo-man he would be able to learn from him something useful. Davenport was successful in his missions, for he had to get another mongoose, and he was able to tell Adam that he had seen the steward, who told him much that he wanted to know, and had also arranged for Oolanga to come to Lesser Hill the following day. At this point Adam saw his way sufficiently clear to admit Davenport to some extent into his confidence. He had come to the conclusion that it would be better—certainly at first—not himself to appear in the matter, with which Davenport was fully competent to deal. It would be time for himself to take a personal part when matters had advanced a little further.

If what the nigger said was in any wise true, the man had a rare gift which might be useful in the quest they were after. He could, as it were, "smell death." If any one was dead, if any one had died, or if a place had been used in connection with death, he seemed to know the broad fact by intuition. Adam made up his mind that to test this faculty with regard to several places would be his first task. Naturally he was anxious, and the time passed slowly. The only comfort was the arrival the next morning of a strong packing case, locked, from Ross, the key being in the custody of Davenport. In the case were two smaller boxes, both locked. One of them contained a mongoose to replace that killed by Lady Arabella; the other was the special mongoose which had already killed the king-cobra in Nepaul. When both the animals had been safely put under lock and key, he felt that he might breathe more freely. No one was allowed to know the secret of their existence in the house, except himself and

Davenport. He arranged that Davenport should take Oolanga round the neighbourhood for a walk, stopping at each of the places which he designated. Having gone all along the Brow, he was to return the same way and induce him to touch on the same subjects in talking with Adam, who was to meet them as if by chance at the farthest part—that beyond Mercy Farm.

The incidents of the day proved much as Adam expected. At Mercy Farm, at Diana's Grove, at Castra Regis, and a few other spots, the negro stopped and, opening his wide nostrils as if to sniff boldly, said that he smelled death. It was not always in the same form. At Mercy Farm he said there were many small deaths. At Diana's Grove his bearing was different. There was a distinct sense of enjoyment about him, especially when he spoke of many great deaths. Here, too, he sniffed in a strange way, like a bloodhound at check, and looked puzzled. He said no word in either praise or disparagement, but in the centre of the Grove, where, hidden amongst ancient oak stumps, was a block of granite slightly hollowed on the top, he bent low and placed his forehead on the ground. This was the only place where he showed distinct reverence. At the Castle, though he spoke of much death, he showed no sign of respect.

There was evidently something about Diana's Grove which both interested and baffled him. Before leaving, he moved all over the place unsatisfied, and in one spot, close to the edge of the Brow, where there was a deep hollow, he appeared to be afraid. After returning several times to this place, he suddenly turned and ran in a panic of fear to the higher ground, crossing as he did so the outcropping rock. Then he seemed to breathe more freely, and recovered some of his jaunty impudence.

All this seemed to satisfy Adam's expectations. He went back to Lesser Hill with a serene and settled calm upon him. Sir Nathaniel followed him into his study.

"By the way, I forgot to ask you details about one thing. When that extraordinary staring episode of Mr. Caswall went on, how did Lilla take it—how did she bear herself?"

"She looked frightened, and trembled just as I have seen a pigeon with a hawk, or a bird with a serpent."

"Thanks. It is just as I expected. There have been circumstances in the Caswall family which lead one to believe that they have had from the earliest times some extraordinary mesmeric or hypnotic faculty. Indeed, a skilled eye could read so much in their physiognomy. That shot of yours, whether by instinct or intention, of the hawk and the pigeon was peculiarly apposite. I think we may settle on that as a fixed trait to be accepted throughout our investigation."

When dusk had fallen, Adam took the new mongoose—not the one from Nepaul—and, carrying the box slung over his shoulder, strolled towards Diana's Grove. Close to the gateway he met Lady Arabella, clad as usual in tightly fitting white, which showed off her slim figure.

To his intense astonishment the mongoose allowed her to pet him, take him up in her arms and fondle him. As she was going in his direction, they walked on together.

Round the roadway between the entrances of Diana's Grove and Lesser Hill were many trees, with not much foliage except at the top. In the dusk this place was shadowy, and the view was hampered by the clustering trunks. In the uncertain, tremulous light which fell through the tree-tops, it was hard to distinguish anything clearly, and at last, somehow, he lost sight of her altogether, and turned back on his track to find her. Presently he came across her close to her own gate. She was leaning over the paling of split oak branches which formed the paling of the avenue. He could not see the mongoose, so he asked her where it had gone.

"He slipt out of my arms while I was petting him," she answered, "and disappeared under the hedges."

They found him at a place where the avenue widened so as to let carriages pass each other. The little creature seemed quite changed. He had been ebulliently active; now he was dull and spiritless—seemed to be dazed. He allowed himself to be lifted by either of the pair; but when he was alone with Lady Arabella he kept looking round him in a strange way, as though trying to escape. When they had come out on the roadway Adam held the mongoose tight to him, and, lifting his hat to his companion, moved quickly towards Lesser Hill; he and Lady Arabella lost sight of each other in the thickening gloom.

When Adam got home, he put the mongoose in his box, and locked the door of the room. The other mongoose—the one from Nepaul—was safely locked in his own box, but he lay quiet and did not stir. When he got to his study Sir Nathaniel came in, shutting the door behind him.

"I have come," he said, "while we have an opportunity of being alone, to tell you something of the Caswall family which I think will interest you. There is, or used to be, a belief in this part of the world that the Caswall family had some strange power of making the wills of other persons subservient to their own. There are many allusions to the subject in memoirs and other unimportant works, but I only know of one where the subject is spoken of definitely. It is *Mercia and its Worthies*, written by Ezra Toms more than a hundred years ago. The author goes into the question of the close association of the then Edgar Caswall with Mesmer in Paris. He speaks of Caswall being a pupil and the fellow worker of Mesmer, and states that though, when the latter left France, he took away with him a vast quantity of philosophical and electric instruments, he was never known to use them again. He once made it known to a friend that he had given them to his old pupil. The term he used was odd, for it was 'bequeathed,' but no such bequest of Mesmer was ever made known. At any rate the instruments were missing, and never turned up."

A servant came into the room to tell Adam that there was some strange noise coming from the locked room into which he had gone when he came in. He hurried off to the place at once, Sir Nathaniel going with him. Having locked the door behind them, Adam opened the packing-case where the boxes of the two mongooses were locked up. There was no sound from one of them, but from the other a queer restless struggling. Having opened both boxes, he found that the noise was from the Nepaul animal, which, however, became quiet at once. In the other box the new mongoose lay dead, with every appearance of having been strangled!

CHAPTER X—THE KITE

On the following day, a little after four o'clock, Adam set out for Mercy.

He was home just as the clocks were striking six. He was pale and upset, but otherwise looked strong and alert. The old man summed up his appearance and manner thus: "Braced up for battle."

"Now!" said Sir Nathaniel, and settled down to listen, looking at Adam steadily and listening attentively that he might miss nothing—even the inflection of a word.

"I found Lilla and Mimi at home. Watford had been detained by business on the farm. Miss Watford received me as kindly as before; Mimi, too, seemed glad to see me. Mr. Caswall came so soon after I arrived, that he, or someone on his behalf, must have been watching for me. He was followed closely by the negro, who was puffing hard as if he had been running—so it was probably he who watched. Mr. Caswall was very cool and collected, but there was a more than usually iron look about his face that I did not like. However, we got on very well. He talked pleasantly on all sorts of questions. The nigger waited a while and then disappeared as on the other occasion. Mr. Caswall's eyes were as usual fixed on Lilla. True, they seemed to be very deep and earnest, but there was no offence in them. Had it not been for the drawing down of the brows and the stern set of the jaws, I should not at first have noticed anything. But the stare, when presently it began, increased in intensity. I could see that Lilla began to suffer from nervousness, as on the first occasion; but she carried herself bravely. However, the more nervous she grew, the harder Mr. Caswall stared. It was evident to me that he had come prepared for some sort of mesmeric or hypnotic battle. After a while he began to throw glances round him and then raised his hand, without letting either Lilla or Mimi see the action. It was evidently intended to give some sign to the negro, for he came, in his usual stealthy way, quietly in by the hall door, which was open. Then Mr. Caswall's efforts at staring became intensified, and poor Lilla's nervousness grew greater. Mimi, seeing that her cousin was distressed, came close to her, as if to comfort or strengthen her with the consciousness of her presence. This evidently made a difficulty for Mr. Caswall, for his efforts, without appearing to get feebler, seemed less effective. This continued for a little while, to the gain of both Lilla and Mimi. Then there was a diversion. Without word or apology the door opened, and Lady Arabella March entered the room. I had seen her coming through the great window. Without a word she crossed the room and stood beside Mr. Caswall. It really was very like a fight of a peculiar kind; and the longer it was sustained the more earnest—the fiercer—it grew. That combination of forces—the over-lord, the white woman, and the black man—would have cost some—probably all of them—their lives in the Southern States of America. To us it was simply horrible. But all that you can understand. This time, to go on in sporting phrase, it was understood by all to be a 'fight to a finish,' and the mixed group did not slacken a moment or relax their efforts. On Lilla the strain began to tell disastrously. She grew pale—a patchy pallor, which meant that her nerves were out of order. She trembled like an aspen, and though she struggled bravely, I noticed that her legs would hardly support her. A dozen times she seemed about to collapse in a faint, but each time, on catching sight of Mimi's eyes, she made a fresh struggle and pulled through.

"By now Mr. Caswall's face had lost its appearance of passivity. His eyes glowed with a fiery light. He was still the old Roman in inflexibility of purpose; but grafted on to the Roman was a new Berserker fury. His companions in the baleful work seemed to have taken on something of his feeling. Lady Arabella looked like a soulless, pitiless being, not human, unless it revived old legends of transformed human beings who had lost their humanity in some transformation or in the sweep of natural savagery. As for the negro—well, I can only say that it was solely due to the self-restraint which you impressed on me that I did not wipe him out as he stood—without warning, without fair play—without a single one of the graces of life and death. Lilla was silent in the helpless concentration of deadly fear; Mimi was all resolve and self-forgetfulness, so intent on the soul-struggle in which she was engaged that there was no possibility of any other thought. As for myself, the bonds of will which held me inactive seemed like bands of steel which numbed all my faculties, except sight and hearing. We seemed fixed in an *impasse*. Something must happen, though the power of guessing was inactive. As in a dream, I saw Mimi's hand move restlessly, as if groping for something. Mechanically it touched that of Lilla, and in that instant she was transformed. It was as if youth and strength entered afresh into something already dead to sensibility and intention. As if by inspiration, she grasped the other's band with a force which blenched the knuckles. Her face suddenly flamed, as if some divine light shone through it. Her form expanded till it stood out majestically. Lifting her right hand, she stepped forward towards Caswall, and with a bold sweep of her arm seemed to drive some strange force towards him. Again and again was the gesture repeated, the man falling back from her at each movement. Towards the door he retreated, she following. There was a sound as of the cooing sob of doves, which seemed to multiply and intensify with each second. The sound from the unseen source rose and rose as he retreated, till finally it swelled out in a triumphant peal, as she with a fierce sweep of her arm, seemed to hurl something at her foe, and he, moving his hands blindly before his face, appeared to be swept through the doorway and out into the open sunlight.

"All at once my own faculties were fully restored; I could see and hear everything, and be fully conscious of what was going on. Even the figures of the baleful group were there, though dimly seen as through a veil—a shadowy veil. I saw Lilla sink down in a swoon, and Mimi throw up her arms in a gesture of triumph. As I saw her through the great window, the sunshine flooded the landscape, which, however, was momentarily becoming eclipsed by an onrush of a myriad birds."

By the next morning, daylight showed the actual danger which threatened. From every part of the eastern counties reports were received concerning the enormous immigration of birds. Experts were sending—on their own account, on behalf of learned societies, and through local and imperial governing bodies—reports dealing with the matter, and suggesting remedies.

The reports closer to home were even more disturbing. All day long it would seem that the birds were coming thicker from all quarters. Doubtless many were going as well as coming, but the mass seemed never to get less. Each bird seemed to sound some note of fear or anger or seeking, and the whirring of wings never ceased nor lessened. The air was full of a muttered throb. No window or barrier could shut out the sound, till the ears of any listener became dulled by the ceaseless murmur. So monotonous it was, so cheerless, so disheartening, so melancholy, that all longed, but in vain, for any variety, no matter how terrible it might be.

The second morning the reports from all the districts round were more alarming than ever. Farmers began to dread the coming of winter as they saw the dwindling of the timely fruitfulness of the earth. And as yet it was only a warning of evil, not the evil accomplished; the ground began to look bare whenever some passing sound temporarily frightened the birds.

Edgar Caswall tortured his brain for a long time unavailingly, to think of some means of getting rid of what he, as well as his neighbours, had come to regard as a plague of birds. At last he recalled a circumstance which promised a solution of the difficulty. The experience was of some years ago in China, far up-country, towards the head-waters of the Yang-tze-kiang, where the smaller tributaries spread out in a sort of natural irrigation scheme to supply the wilderness of paddy-fields. It was at the time of the ripening rice, and the myriads of birds which came to feed on the coming crop was a serious menace, not only to the district, but to the country at large. The farmers, who were more or less afflicted with the same trouble every season, knew how to deal with it. They made a vast kite, which they caused to be flown over the centre spot of the incursion. The kite was shaped like a great hawk; and the moment it rose into the air the birds began to cower and seek protection—and then to disappear. So long as that kite was flying overhead the birds lay low and the crop was saved. Accordingly Caswall ordered his men to construct an immense kite, adhering as well as they could to the lines of a hawk. Then he and his men, with a sufficiency of cord, began to fly it high overhead. The experience of China was repeated. The moment the kite rose, the birds hid or sought shelter. The following morning, the kite was still flying high, no bird was to be seen as far as the eye could reach from Castra Regis. But there followed in turn what proved even a worse evil. All the birds were cowed; their sounds stopped. Neither song nor chirp was heard—silence seemed to have taken the place of the normal voices of bird life. But that was not all. The silence spread to all animals.

The fear and restraint which brooded amongst the denizens of the air began to affect all life. Not only did the birds cease song or chirp, but the lowing of the cattle ceased in the fields and the varied sounds of life died away. In place of these things was only a soundless gloom, more dreadful, more disheartening, more soul-killing than any concourse of sounds, no matter how full of fear and dread. Pious individuals put up constant prayers for relief from the intolerable solitude. After a little there were signs of universal depression which those who ran might read. One and all, the faces of men and women seemed bereft of vitality, of interest, of thought, and, most of all, of hope. Men seemed to have lost the power of expression of their thoughts.

The soundless air seemed to have the same effect as the universal darkness when men gnawed their tongues with pain.

From this infliction of silence there was no relief. Everything was affected; gloom was the predominant note. Joy appeared to have passed away as a factor of life, and this creative impulse had nothing to take its place. That giant spot in high air was a plague of evil influence. It seemed like a new misanthropic belief which had fallen on human beings, carrying with it the negation of all hope.

After a few days, men began to grow desperate; their very words as well as their senses seemed to be in chains. Edgar Caswall again tortured his brain to find any antidote or palliative of this greater evil than before. He would gladly have destroyed the kite, or caused its flying to cease; but the instant it was pulled down, the birds rose up in even greater numbers; all those who depended in any way on agriculture sent pitiful protests to Castra Regis.

It was strange indeed what influence that weird kite seemed to exercise. Even human beings were affected by it, as if both it and they were realities. As for the people at Mercy Farm, it was like a taste of actual death. Lilla felt it most. If she had been indeed a real dove, with a real kite hanging over her in the air, she could not have been more frightened or more affected by the terror this created.

Of course, some of those already drawn into the vortex noticed the effect on individuals. Those who were interested took care to compare their information. Strangely enough, as it seemed to the others, the person who took the ghastly silence least to heart was the negro. By nature he was not sensitive to, or afflicted by, nerves. This alone would not have produced the seeming indifference, so they set their minds to discover the real cause. Adam came quickly to the conclusion that there was for him some compensation that the others did not share; and he soon believed that that compensation was in one form or another the enjoyment of the sufferings of others. Thus the black had a never-failing source of amusement.

Lady Arabella's cold nature rendered her immune to anything in the way of pain or trouble concerning others. Edgar Caswall was far too haughty a person, and too stern of nature, to concern himself about poor or helpless people, much less the lower order of mere animals. Mr. Watford, Mr. Salton, and Sir Nathaniel were all concerned in the issue, partly from kindness of heart—for none of them could see suffering, even of wild birds, unmoved—and partly on account of their property, which had to be protected, or ruin would stare them in the face before long.

Lilla suffered acutely. As time went on, her face became pinched, and her eyes dull with watching and crying. Mimi suffered too on account of her cousin's suffering. But as she could do nothing, she resolutely made up her mind to self-restraint and patience. Adam's frequent visits comforted her.

CHAPTER XI—MESMER'S CHEST

After a couple of weeks had passed, the kite seemed to give Edgar Caswall a new zest for life. He was never tired of looking at its movements. He had a comfortable armchair put out on the tower, wherein he sat sometimes all day long, watching as though the kite was a new toy and he a child lately come into possession of it. He did not seem to have lost interest in Lilla, for he still paid an occasional visit at Mercy Farm.

Indeed, his feeling towards her, whatever it had been at first, had now so far changed that it had become a distinct affection of a purely animal kind. Indeed, it seemed as though the man's nature had become corrupted, and that all the baser and more selfish and more reckless qualities had become more conspicuous. There was not so much sternness apparent in his nature, because there was less self-restraint. Determination had become indifference.

The visible change in Edgar was that he grew morbid, sad, silent; the neighbours thought he was going mad. He became absorbed in the kite, and watched it not only by day, but often all night long. It became an obsession to him.

Caswall took a personal interest in the keeping of the great kite flying. He had a vast coil of cord efficient for the purpose, which worked on a roller fixed on the parapet of the tower. There was a winch for the pulling in of the slack; the outgoing line being controlled by a racket. There was invariably one man at least, day and night, on the tower to attend to it. At such an elevation there was always a strong wind, and at times the kite rose to an enormous height, as well as travelling for great distances laterally. In fact, the kite became, in a short time, one of the curiosities of Castra Regis and all around it. Edgar began to attribute to it, in his own mind, almost human qualities. It became to him a separate entity, with a mind and a soul of its own. Being idle-handed all day, he began to apply to what he considered the service of the kite some of his spare time, and found a new pleasure—a new object in life—in the old schoolboy game of sending up "runners" to the kite. The way this is done is to get round pieces of paper so cut that there is a hole in the centre, through which the string of the kite passes. The natural action of the wind-pressure takes the paper along the string, and so up to the kite itself, no matter how high or how far it may have gone.

In the early days of this amusement Edgar Caswall spent hours. Hundreds of such messengers flew along the string, until soon he bethought him of writing messages on these papers so that he could make known his ideas to the kite. It may be that his brain gave way under the opportunities given by his illusion of the entity of the toy and its power of separate thought. From sending messages he came to making direct speech to the kite—without, however, ceasing to send the runners. Doubtless, the height of the tower, seated as it was on the hill-top, the rushing of the ceaseless wind, the hypnotic effect of the lofty altitude of the speck in the sky at which he gazed, and the rushing of the paper messengers up the string till sight of them was lost in distance, all helped to further affect his brain, undoubtedly giving way under the strain of beliefs and circumstances which were at once stimulating to the imagination, occupative of his mind, and absorbing.

The next step of intellectual decline was to bring to bear on the main idea of the conscious identity of the kite all sorts of subjects which had imaginative force or tendency of their own. He had, in Castra Regis, a large collection of curious and interesting things formed in the past by his forebears, of similar tastes to his own. There were all sorts of strange anthropological specimens, both old and new, which had been collected through various travels in strange places: ancient Egyptian relics from tombs and mummies; curios from Australia, New Zealand, and the South Seas; idols and images—from Tartar ikons to ancient Egyptian, Persian, and Indian objects of worship; objects of death and torture of American Indians; and, above all, a vast collection of lethal weapons of every kind and from every place—Chinese "high pinders," double knives, Afghan double-edged scimitars made to cut a body in two, heavy knives from all the Eastern countries, ghost daggers from Thibet, the terrible kukri of the Ghourka and other hill tribes of India, assassins' weapons from Italy and Spain, even the knife which was formerly carried by the slave-drivers of the Mississippi region. Death and pain of every kind were fully represented in that gruesome collection.

That it had a fascination for Oolanga goes without saying. He was never tired of visiting the museum in the tower, and spent endless hours in inspecting the exhibits, till he was thoroughly familiar with every detail of all of them. He asked permission to clean and polish and sharpen them—a favour which was readily granted. In addition to the above objects, there were many things of a kind to awaken human fear. Stuffed serpents of the most objectionable and horrid kind; giant insects from the tropics, fearsome in every detail; fishes and crustaceans covered with weird spikes; dried octopuses of great size. Other things, too, there were, not less deadly though seemingly innocuous—dried fungi, traps intended for birds, beasts, fishes, reptiles, and insects; machines which could produce pain of any kind and degree, and the only mercy of which was the power of producing speedy death.

Caswall, who had never before seen any of these things, except those which he had collected himself, found a constant amusement and interest in them. He studied them, their uses, their mechanism—where there was such—and their places of origin, until he had an ample and real knowledge of all concerning them. Many were secret and intricate, but he never rested till he found out all the secrets. When once he had become interested in strange objects, and the way to use them, he began to explore various likely places for similar finds. He began to inquire of his household where strange lumber was kept. Several of the men spoke of old Simon Chester as one who knew everything in and about the house. Accordingly, he sent for the old man, who came at once. He was very old, nearly ninety years of age, and very infirm. He had been born in the Castle, and had served its succession of masters—present or absent—ever since. When Edgar began to question him on the subject regarding which he had sent for him, old Simon exhibited much perturbation. In fact, he became so frightened that his master, fully believing that he was concealing something, ordered him to tell at once what remained unseen, and where it was hidden away. Face to face with discovery of his secret, the old man, in a pitiable state of concern, spoke out even more fully than Mr. Caswall had expected.

"Indeed, indeed, sir, everything is here in the tower that has ever been put away in my time except—except—" here he began to shake and tremble it—"except the chest which Mr. Edgar—he who was Mr. Edgar when I first took service—brought back from France, after he had been with Dr. Mesmer. The trunk has been kept in my room for safety; but I shall send it down here now."

"What is in it?" asked Edgar sharply.

"That I do not know. Moreover, it is a peculiar trunk, without any visible means of opening."

"Is there no lock?"

"I suppose so, sir; but I do not know. There is no keyhole."

"Send it here; and then come to me yourself."

The trunk, a heavy one with steel bands round it, but no lock or keyhole, was carried in by two men. Shortly afterwards old Simon attended his master. When he came into the room, Mr. Caswall himself went and closed the door; then he asked:

"How do you open it?"

"I do not know, sir."

"Do you mean to say that you never opened it?"

"Most certainly I say so, your honour. How could I? It was entrusted to me with the other things by my master. To open it would have been a breach of trust."

Caswall sneered.

"Quite remarkable! Leave it with me. Close the door behind you. Stay—did no one ever tell you about it—say anything regarding it—make any remark?"

Old Simon turned pale, and put his trembling hands together.

"Oh, sir, I entreat you not to touch it. That trunk probably contains secrets which Dr. Mesmer told my master. Told them to his ruin!"

"How do you mean? What ruin?"

"Sir, he it was who, men said, sold his soul to the Evil One; I had thought that that time and the evil of it had all passed away."

"That will do. Go away; but remain in your own room, or within call. I may want you."

The old man bowed deeply and went out trembling, but without speaking a word.

CHAPTER XII—THE CHEST OPENED

Left alone in the turret-room, Edgar Caswall carefully locked the door and hung a handkerchief over the keyhole. Next, he inspected the windows, and saw that they were not overlooked from any angle of the main building. Then he carefully examined the trunk, going over it with a magnifying glass. He found it intact: the steel bands were flawless; the whole trunk was compact. After sitting opposite to it for some time, and the shades of evening beginning to melt into darkness, he gave up the task and went to his bedroom, after locking the door of the turret-room behind him and taking away the key.

He woke in the morning at daylight, and resumed his patient but unavailing study of the metal trunk. This he continued during the whole day with the same result—humiliating disappointment, which overwrought his nerves and made his head ache. The result of the long strain was seen later in the afternoon, when he sat locked within the turret-room before the still baffling trunk, distrait, listless and yet agitated, sunk in a settled gloom. As the dusk was falling he told the steward to send him two men, strong ones. These he ordered to take the trunk to his bedroom. In that room he then sat on into the night, without pausing even to take any food. His mind was in a whirl, a fever of excitement. The result was that when, late in the night, he locked himself in his room his brain was full of odd fancies; he was on the high road to mental disturbance. He lay down on his bed in the dark, still brooding over the mystery of the closed trunk.

Gradually he yielded to the influences of silence and darkness. After lying there quietly for some time, his mind became active again. But this time there were round him no disturbing influences; his brain was active and able to work freely and to deal with memory. A thousand forgotten—or only half-known—incidents, fragments of conversations or theories long ago guessed at and long forgotten, crowded on his mind. He seemed to hear again around him the legions of whirring wings to which he had been so lately accustomed. Even to himself he knew that that was an effort of imagination founded on imperfect memory. But he was content that imagination should work, for out of it might come some solution of the mystery which surrounded him. And in this frame of mind, sleep made another and more successful essay. This time he enjoyed peaceful slumber, restful alike to his wearied body and his overwrought brain.

In his sleep he arose, and, as if in obedience to some influence beyond and greater than himself, lifted the great trunk and set it on a strong table at one side of the room, from which he had previously removed a quantity of books. To do this, he had to use an amount of strength which was, he knew, far beyond him in his normal state. As it was, it seemed easy enough; everything yielded before his touch. Then he became conscious that somehow—how, he never could remember—the chest was open. He unlocked his door, and, taking the chest on his shoulder, carried it up to the turret-room, the door of which also he unlocked. Even at the time he was amazed at his own strength, and wondered whence it had come. His mind, lost in conjecture, was too far off to realise more immediate things. He knew that the chest was enormously heavy. He seemed, in a sort of vision which lit up the absolute blackness around, to see the two sturdy servant men staggering under its great weight. He locked himself again in the turret-room, and laid the opened chest on a table, and in the darkness began to unpack it, laying out the contents, which were mainly of metal and glass—great pieces in strange forms—on another table. He was conscious of being still asleep, and of acting rather in obedience to some unseen and unknown command than in accordance with any reasonable plan, to be followed by results which he understood. This phase completed, he proceeded to arrange in order the component parts of some large instruments, formed mostly of glass. His fingers seemed to have acquired a new and exquisite subtlety and even a volition of their own. Then weariness of brain came upon him; his head sank down on his breast, and little by little everything became wrapped in gloom.

He awoke in the early morning in his bedroom, and looked around him, now clear-headed, in amazement. In its usual place on the strong table stood the great steel-hooped chest without lock or key. But it was now locked. He arose quietly and stole to the turret-room. There everything was as it had been on the previous evening. He looked out of the window where high in air flew, as usual, the giant kite. He unlocked the wicket gate of the turret stair and went out on the roof. Close to him was the great coil of cord on its reel. It was humming in the morning breeze, and when he touched the string it sent a quick thrill through hand and arm. There was no sign anywhere that there had been any disturbance or displacement of anything during the night.

Utterly bewildered, he sat down in his room to think. Now for the first time he *felt* that he was asleep and dreaming. Presently he fell asleep again, and slept for a long time. He awoke hungry and made a hearty meal. Then towards evening, having locked himself in, he fell asleep again. When he woke he was in darkness, and was quite at sea as to his whereabouts. He began feeling about the dark room, and was recalled to the consequences of his position by the breaking of a large piece of glass. Having obtained a light, he discovered this to be a glass wheel, part of an elaborate piece of mechanism which he must in his sleep have taken from the chest, which was now opened. He had once again opened it whilst asleep, but he had no recollection of the circumstances.

Caswall came to the conclusion that there had been some sort of dual action of his mind, which might lead to some catastrophe or some discovery of his secret plans; so he resolved to forgo for a while the pleasure of making discoveries regarding the chest. To this end, he applied himself to quite another matter—an investigation of the other treasures and rare objects in his collections. He went amongst them in simple, idle curiosity, his main object being to discover some strange item which he might use for experiment with the kite. He had already resolved to try some runners other than those made of paper. He had a vague idea that with such a force as the great kite straining at its leash, this might be used to lift to the altitude of the kite itself heavier articles. His first experiment with articles of little but increasing weight was eminently successful. So he added by degrees more and more weight, until he found out that the lifting power of the kite was considerable. He then determined to take a step further, and send to the kite some of the articles which lay in the steel-hooped chest. The last time he had opened it in sleep, it had not been shut again, and he had inserted a wedge so that he could open it at will. He made examination of the contents, but came to the conclusion that the glass objects were unsuitable. They were too light for testing weight, and they were so frail as to be dangerous to send to such a height.

So he looked around for something more solid with which to experiment. His eye caught sight of an object which at once attracted him. This was a small copy of one of the ancient Egyptian gods—that of Bes, who represented the destructive power of nature. It was so bizarre and mysterious as to commend itself to his mad humour. In lifting it from the cabinet, he was struck by its great weight in proportion to its size. He made accurate examination of it by the aid of some instruments, and came to the conclusion that it was carved from a lump of lodestone. He remembered that he had read somewhere of an ancient Egyptian god cut from a similar substance, and, thinking it over, he came to the conclusion that he must have read it in Sir Thomas Brown's *Popular Errors*, a book of the seventeenth century. He got the book from the library, and looked out the passage:

"A great example we have from the observation of our learned friend Mr. Graves, in an AEgyptian idol cut out of Loadstone and found among the Mummies; which still retains its attraction, though probably taken out of the mine about two thousand years ago."

The strangeness of the figure, and its being so close akin to his own nature, attracted him. He made from thin wood a large circular runner, and in front of it placed the weighty god, sending it up to the flying kite along the throbbing cord.

CHAPTER XIII—OOLANGA'S HALLUCINATIONS

During the last few days Lady Arabella had been getting exceedingly impatient. Her debts, always pressing, were growing to an embarrassing amount. The only hope she had of comfort in life was a good marriage; but the good marriage on which she had fixed her eye did not seem to move quickly enough—indeed, it did not seem to move at all—in the right direction. Edgar Caswall was not an ardent wooer. From the very first he seemed *difficile*, but he had been keeping to his own room ever since his struggle with Mimi Watford. On that occasion Lady Arabella had shown him in an unmistakable way what her feelings were; indeed, she had made it known to him, in a more overt way than pride should allow, that she wished to help and support him. The moment when she had gone across the room to stand beside him in his mesmeric struggle, had been the very limit of her voluntary action. It was quite bitter enough, she felt, that he did not come to her, but now that she had made that advance, she felt that any withdrawal on his part would, to a woman of her class, be nothing less than a flaming insult. Had she not classed herself with his nigger servant, an unreformed savage? Had she not shown her preference for him at the festival of his home-coming? Had she not . . . Lady Arabella was cold-blooded, and she was prepared to go through all that might be necessary of indifference, and even insult, to become chatelaine of Castra Regis. In the meantime, she would show no hurry—she must wait. She might, in an unostentatious way, come to him again. She knew him now, and could make a keen guess at his desires with regard to Lilla Watford. With that secret in her possession, she could bring pressure to bear on Caswall which would make it no easy matter for him to evade her. The great difficulty was how to get near him. He was shut up within his Castle, and guarded by a defence of convention which she could not pass without danger of ill repute to herself. Over this question she thought and thought for days and nights. At last she decided that the only way would be to go to him openly at Castra Regis. Her rank and position would make such a thing possible, if carefully done. She could explain matters afterwards if necessary. Then when they were alone, she would use her arts and her experience to make him commit himself. After all, he was only a man, with a man's dislike of difficult or awkward situations. She felt quite sufficient confidence in her own womanhood to carry her through any difficulty which might arise.

From Diana's Grove she heard each day the luncheon-gong from Castra Regis sound, and knew the hour when the servants would be in the back of the house. She would enter the house at that hour, and, pretending that she could not make anyone hear her, would seek him in his own rooms. The tower was, she knew, away from all the usual sounds of the house, and moreover she knew that the servants had strict orders not to interrupt him when he was in the turret chamber. She had found out, partly by the aid of an opera-glass and partly by judicious questioning, that several times lately a heavy chest had been carried to and from his room, and that it rested in the room each night. She was, therefore, confident that he had some important work on hand which would keep him busy for long spells.

Meanwhile, another member of the household at Castra Regis had schemes which he thought were working to fruition. A man in the position of a servant has plenty of opportunity of watching his betters and forming opinions regarding them. Oolanga was in his way a clever, unscrupulous rogue, and he felt that with things moving round him in this great household there should be opportunities of self-advancement. Being unscrupulous and stealthy—and a savage—he looked to dishonest means. He saw plainly enough that Lady Arabella was making a dead set at his master, and he was watchful of the slightest sign of anything which might enhance this knowledge. Like the other men in the house, he knew of the carrying to and fro of the great chest, and had got it into his head that the care exercised in its porterage indicated that it was full of treasure. He was for ever lurking around the turret-rooms on the chance of making some useful discovery. But he was as cautious as he was stealthy, and took care that no one else watched him.

It was thus that the negro became aware of Lady Arabella's venture into the house, as she thought, unseen. He took more care than ever, since he was watching another, that the positions were not reversed. More than ever he kept his eyes and ears open and his mouth shut. Seeing Lady Arabella gliding up the stairs towards his master's room, he took it for granted that she was there for no good, and doubled his watching intentness and caution.

Oolanga was disappointed, but he dared not exhibit any feeling lest it should betray that he was hiding. Therefore he slunk downstairs again noiselessly, and waited for a more favourable opportunity of furthering his plans. It must be borne in mind that he thought that the heavy trunk was full of valuables, and that he believed that Lady Arabella had come to try to steal it. His purpose of using for his own advantage the combination of these two ideas was seen later in the day. Oolanga secretly followed her home. He was an expert at this game, and succeeded admirably on this occasion. He watched her enter the private gate of Diana's Grove, and then, taking a roundabout course and keeping out of her sight, he at last overtook her in a thick part of the Grove where no one could see the meeting.

Lady Arabella was much surprised. She had not seen the negro for several days, and had almost forgotten his existence. Oolanga would have been startled had he known and been capable of understanding the real value placed on him, his beauty, his worthiness, by other persons, and compared it with the value in these matters in which he held himself. Doubtless Oolanga had his dreams like other men. In such cases he saw himself as a young sun-god, as beautiful as the eye of dusky or even white womanhood had ever dwelt upon. He would have been filled with all noble and captivating qualities—or those regarded as such in West Africa. Women would have loved him, and would have told him so in the overt and fervid manner usual in affairs of the heart in the shadowy depths of the forest of the Gold Coast.

Oolanga came close behind Lady Arabella, and in a hushed voice, suitable to the importance of his task, and in deference to the respect he had for her and the place, began to unfold the story of his love. Lady Arabella was not usually a humorous person, but no man or woman of the white race could have checked the laughter which rose spontaneously to her lips. The circumstances were too grotesque, the contrast too violent, for subdued mirth. The man a debased specimen of one of the most primitive races of the earth, and of an ugliness which was simply devilish; the woman of high degree, beautiful, accomplished. She thought that her first moment's consideration of the outrage—it was nothing less in her eyes—had given her the full material for thought. But every instant after threw new and varied lights on the affront. Her indignation was too great for passion; only irony or satire would meet the situation. Her cold, cruel nature helped, and she did not shrink to subject this ignorant savage to the merciless fire-lash of her scorn.

Oolanga was dimly conscious that he was being flouted; but his anger was no less keen because of the measure of his ignorance. So he gave way to it, as does a tortured beast. He ground his great teeth together, raved, stamped, and swore in barbarous tongues and with barbarous imagery. Even Lady Arabella felt that it was well she was within reach of help, or he might have offered her brutal violence—even have killed her.

"Am I to understand," she said with cold disdain, so much more effective to wound than hot passion, "that you are offering me your love? Your—love?"

For reply he nodded his head. The scorn of her voice, in a sort of baleful hiss, sounded—and felt—like the lash of a whip.

"And you dared! you—a savage—a slave—the basest thing in the world of vermin! Take care! I don't value your worthless life more than I do that of a rat or a spider. Don't let me ever see your hideous face here again, or I shall rid the earth of you."

As she was speaking, she had taken out her revolver and was pointing it at him. In the immediate presence of death his impudence forsook him, and he made a weak effort to justify himself. His speech was short, consisting of single words. To Lady Arabella it sounded mere gibberish, but it was in his own dialect, and meant love, marriage, wife. From the intonation of the words, she guessed, with her woman's quick intuition, at their meaning; but she quite failed to follow, when, becoming more pressing, he continued to urge his suit in a mixture of the grossest animal passion and ridiculous threats. He warned her that he knew she had tried to steal his master's treasure, and that he had caught her in the act. But if she would be his, he would share the treasure with her, and they could live in luxury in the African forests. But if she refused, he would tell his master, who would flog and torture her and then give her to the police, who would kill her.

CHAPTER XIV—BATTLE RENEWED

The consequences of that meeting in the dusk of Diana's Grove were acute and far-reaching, and not only to the two engaged in it. From Oolanga, this might have been expected by anyone who knew the character of the tropical African savage. To such, there are two passions that are inexhaustible and insatiable—vanity and that which they are pleased to call love. Oolanga left the Grove with an absorbing hatred in his heart. His lust and greed were afire, while his vanity had been wounded to the core. Lady Arabella's icy nature was not so deeply stirred, though she was in a seething passion. More than ever she was set upon bringing Edgar Caswall to her feet. The obstacles she had encountered, the insults she had endured, were only as fuel to the purpose of revenge which consumed her.

As she sought her own rooms in Diana's Grove, she went over the whole subject again and again, always finding in the face of Lilla Watford a key to a problem which puzzled her—the problem of a way to turn Caswall's powers—his very existence—to aid her purpose.

When in her boudoir, she wrote a note, taking so much trouble over it that she destroyed, and rewrote, till her dainty waste-basket was half-full of torn sheets of notepaper. When quite satisfied, she copied out the last sheet afresh, and then carefully burned all the spoiled fragments. She put the copied note in an emblazoned envelope, and directed it to Edgar Caswall at Castra Regis. This she sent off by one of her grooms. The letter ran:

> "DEAR MR. CASWALL,
>
> "I want to have a chat with you on a subject in which I believe you are interested. Will you kindly call for me one day after lunch—say at three or four o'clock, and we can walk a little way together. Only as far as Mercy Farm, where I want to see Lilla and Mimi Watford. We can take a cup of tea at the Farm. Do not bring your African servant with you, as I am afraid his face frightens the girls. After all, he is not pretty, is he? I have an idea you will be pleased with your visit this time.
>
> "Yours sincerely,
>
> "ARABELLA MARCH."

At half-past three next day, Edgar Caswall called at Diana's Grove. Lady Arabella met him on the roadway outside the gate. She wished to take the servants into her confidence as little as possible. She turned when she saw him coming, and walked beside him towards Mercy Farm, keeping step with him as they walked. When they got near Mercy, she turned and looked around her, expecting to see Oolanga or some sign of him. He was, however, not visible. He had received from his master peremptory orders to keep out of sight—an order for which the African scored a new offence up against her. They found Lilla and Mimi at home and seemingly glad to see them, though both the girls were surprised at the visit coming so soon after the other.

The proceedings were a repetition of the battle of souls of the former visit. On this occasion, however, Edgar Caswall had only the presence of Lady Arabella to support him—Oolanga being absent; but Mimi lacked the support of Adam Salton, which had been of such effective service before. This time the struggle for supremacy of will was longer and more determined. Caswall felt that if he could not achieve supremacy he had better give up the idea, so all his pride was enlisted against Mimi. When they had been waiting for the door to be opened, Lady Arabella, believing in a sudden attack, had said to him in a low voice, which somehow carried conviction:

"This time you should win. Mimi is, after all, only a woman. Show her no mercy. That is weakness. Fight her, beat her, trample on her—kill her if need be. She stands in your way, and I hate her. Never take your eyes off her. Never mind Lilla—she is afraid of you. You are already her master. Mimi will try to make you look at her cousin. There lies defeat. Let nothing take your attention from Mimi, and you will win. If she is overcoming you, take my hand and hold it hard whilst you are looking into her eyes. If she is too strong for you, I shall interfere. I'll make a diversion, and under cover of it you must retire unbeaten, even if not victorious. Hush! they are coming."

The two girls came to the door together. Strange sounds were coming up over the Brow from the west. It was the rustling and crackling of the dry reeds and rushes from the low lands. The season had been an unusually dry one. Also the strong east wind was helping forward enormous flocks of birds, most of them pigeons with white cowls. Not only were their wings whirring, but their cooing was plainly audible. From such a multitude of birds the mass of sound, individually small, assumed the volume of a storm. Surprised at the influx of birds, to which they had been strangers so long, they all looked towards Castra Regis, from whose high tower the great kite had been flying as usual. But even as they looked, the cord broke, and the great kite fell headlong in a series of sweeping dives. Its own weight, and the aerial force opposed to it, which caused it to rise, combined with the strong easterly breeze, had been too much for the great length of cord holding it.

Somehow, the mishap to the kite gave new hope to Mimi. It was as though the side issues had been shorn away, so that the main struggle was thenceforth on simpler lines. She had a feeling in her heart, as though some religious chord had been newly touched. It may, of course, have been that with the renewal of the bird voices a fresh courage, a fresh belief in the good issue of the struggle came too. In the misery of silence, from which they had all suffered for so long, any new train of thought was almost bound to be a boon. As the inrush of birds continued, their wings beating against the crackling rushes, Lady Arabella grew pale, and almost fainted.

"What is that?" she asked suddenly.

To Mimi, born and bred in Siam, the sound was strangely like an exaggeration of the sound produced by a snake-charmer.

CHAPTER XIV—BATTLE RENEWED

Edgar Caswall was the first to recover from the interruption of the falling kite. After a few minutes he seemed to have quite recovered his *sang froid*, and was able to use his brains to the end which he had in view. Mimi too quickly recovered herself, but from a different cause. With her it was a deep religious conviction that the struggle round her was of the powers of Good and Evil, and that Good was triumphing. The very appearance of the snowy birds, with the cowls of Saint Columba, heightened the impression. With this conviction strong upon her, she continued the strange battle with fresh vigour. She seemed to tower over Caswall, and he to give back before her oncoming. Once again her vigorous passes drove him to the door. He was just going out backward when Lady Arabella, who had been gazing at him with fixed eyes, caught his hand and tried to stop his movement. She was, however, unable to do any good, and so, holding hands, they passed out together. As they did so, the strange music which had so alarmed Lady Arabella suddenly stopped. Instinctively they all looked towards the tower of Castra Regis, and saw that the workmen had refixed the kite, which had risen again and was beginning to float out to its former station.

As they were looking, the door opened and Michael Watford came into the room. By that time all had recovered their self-possession, and there was nothing out of the common to attract his attention. As he came in, seeing inquiring looks all around him, he said:

"The new influx of birds is only the annual migration of pigeons from Africa. I am told that it will soon be over."

The second victory of Mimi Watford made Edgar Caswall more moody than ever. He felt thrown back on himself, and this, added to his absorbing interest in the hope of a victory of his mesmeric powers, became a deep and settled purpose of revenge. The chief object of his animosity was, of course, Mimi, whose will had overcome his, but it was obscured in greater or lesser degree by all who had opposed him. Lilla was next to Mimi in his hate—Lilla, the harmless, tender-hearted, sweet-natured girl, whose heart was so full of love for all things that in it was no room for the passions of ordinary life—whose nature resembled those doves of St. Columba, whose colour she wore, whose appearance she reflected. Adam Salton came next—after a gap; for against him Caswall had no direct animosity. He regarded him as an interference, a difficulty to be got rid of or destroyed. The young Australian had been so discreet that the most he had against him was his knowledge of what had been. Caswall did not understand him, and to such a nature as his, ignorance was a cause of alarm, of dread.

Caswall resumed his habit of watching the great kite straining at its cord, varying his vigils in this way by a further examination of the mysterious treasures of his house, especially Mesmer's chest. He sat much on the roof of the tower, brooding over his thwarted passion. The vast extent of his possessions, visible to him at that altitude, might, one would have thought, have restored some of his complacency. But the very extent of his ownership, thus perpetually brought before him, created a fresh sense of grievance. How was it, he thought, that with so much at command that others wished for, he could not achieve the dearest wishes of his heart?

In this state of intellectual and moral depravity, he found a solace in the renewal of his experiments with the mechanical powers of the kite. For a couple of weeks he did not see Lady Arabella, who was always on the watch for a chance of meeting him; neither did he see the Watford girls, who studiously kept out of his way. Adam Salton simply marked time, keeping ready to deal with anything that might affect his friends. He called at the farm and heard from Mimi of the last battle of wills, but it had only one consequence. He got from Ross several more mongooses, including a second king-cobra-killer, which he generally carried with him in its box whenever he walked out.

Mr. Caswall's experiments with the kite went on successfully. Each day he tried the lifting of greater weight, and it seemed almost as if the machine had a sentience of its own, which was increasing with the obstacles placed before it. All this time the kite hung in the sky at an enormous height. The wind was steadily from the north, so the trend of the kite was to the south. All day long, runners of increasing magnitude were sent up. These were only of paper or thin cardboard, or leather, or other flexible materials. The great height at which the kite hung made a great concave curve in the string, so that as the runners went up they made a flapping sound. If one laid a finger on the string, the sound answered to the flapping of the runner in a sort of hollow intermittent murmur. Edgar Caswall, who was now wholly obsessed by the kite and all belonging to it, found a distinct resemblance between that intermittent rumble and the snake-charming music produced by the pigeons flying through the dry reeds.

One day he made a discovery in Mesmer's chest which he thought he would utilise with regard to the runners. This was a great length of wire, "fine as human hair," coiled round a finely made wheel, which ran to a wondrous distance freely, and as lightly. He tried this on runners, and found it work admirably. Whether the runner was alone, or carried something much more weighty than itself, it worked equally well. Also it was strong enough and light enough to draw back the runner without undue strain. He tried this a good many times successfully, but it was now growing dusk and he found some difficulty in keeping the runner in sight. So he looked for something heavy enough to keep it still. He placed the Egyptian image of Bes on the fine wire, which crossed the wooden ledge which protected it. Then, the darkness growing, he went indoors and forgot all about it.

He had a strange feeling of uneasiness that night—not sleeplessness, for he seemed conscious of being asleep. At daylight he rose, and as usual looked out for the kite. He did not see it in its usual position in the sky, so looked round the points of the compass. He was more than astonished when presently he saw the missing kite struggling as usual against the controlling cord. But it had gone to the further side of the tower, and now hung and strained *against the wind* to the north. He thought it so strange that he determined to investigate the phenomenon, and to say nothing about it in the meantime.

In his many travels, Edgar Caswall had been accustomed to use the sextant, and was now an expert in the matter. By the aid of this and other instruments, he was able to fix the position of the kite and the point over which it hung. He was startled to find that exactly under it—so far as he could ascertain—was Diana's Grove. He had an inclination to take Lady Arabella into his confidence in the matter, but he thought better of it and wisely refrained. For some reason which he did not try to explain to himself, he was glad of his silence, when, on the following morning, he found, on looking out, that the point over which the kite then hovered was Mercy Farm. When he had verified this with his instruments, he sat before the window of the tower, looking out and thinking. The new locality was more to his liking than the other; but the why of it puzzled him, all the same. He spent the rest of the day in the turret-room, which he did not leave all day. It seemed to him that he was now drawn by forces which he could not control—of which, indeed, he had no knowledge—in directions which he did not understand, and which were without his own volition. In sheer helpless inability to think the problem out satisfactorily, he called up a servant and told him to tell Oolanga that he wanted to see him at once in the turret-room. The answer came back that the African had not been seen since the previous evening.

Caswall was now so irritable that even this small thing upset him. As he was distrait and wanted to talk to somebody, he sent for Simon Chester, who came at once, breathless with hurrying and upset by the unexpected summons. Caswall bade him sit down, and when the old man was in a less uneasy frame of mind, he again asked him if he had ever seen what was in Mesmer's chest or heard it spoken about.

Chester admitted that he had once, in the time of "the then Mr. Edgar," seen the chest open, which, knowing something of its history and guessing more, so upset him that he had fainted. When he recovered, the chest was closed. From that time the then Mr. Edgar had never spoken about it again.

When Caswall asked him to describe what he had seen when the chest was open, he got very agitated, and, despite all his efforts to remain calm, he suddenly went off into a faint. Caswall summoned servants, who applied the usual remedies. Still the old man did not recover. After the lapse of a considerable time, the doctor who had been summoned made his appearance. A glance was sufficient for him to make up his mind. Still, he knelt down by the old man, and made a careful examination. Then he rose to his feet, and in a hushed voice said:

"I grieve to say, sir, that he has passed away."

CHAPTER XV—ON THE TRACK

Those who had seen Edgar Caswall familiarly since his arrival, and had already estimated his cold-blooded nature at something of its true value, were surprised that he took so to heart the death of old Chester. The fact was that not one of them had guessed correctly at his character. They thought, naturally enough, that the concern which he felt was that of a master for a faithful old servant of his family. They little thought that it was merely the selfish expression of his disappointment, that he had thus lost the only remaining clue to an interesting piece of family history—one which was now and would be for ever wrapped in mystery. Caswall knew enough about the life of his ancestor in Paris to wish to know more fully and more thoroughly all that had been. The period covered by that ancestor's life in Paris was one inviting every form of curiosity.

Lady Arabella, who had her own game to play, saw in the *métier* of sympathetic friend, a series of meetings with the man she wanted to secure. She made the first use of the opportunity the day after old Chester's death; indeed, as soon as the news had filtered in through the back door of Diana's Grove. At that meeting, she played her part so well that even Caswall's cold nature was impressed.

Oolanga was the only one who did not credit her with at least some sense of fine feeling in the matter. In emotional, as in other matters, Oolanga was distinctly a utilitarian, and as he could not understand anyone feeling grief except for his own suffering, pain, or for the loss of money, he could not understand anyone simulating such an emotion except for show intended to deceive. He thought that she had come to Castra Regis again for the opportunity of stealing something, and was determined that on this occasion the chance of pressing his advantage over her should not pass. He felt, therefore, that the occasion was one for extra carefulness in the watching of all that went on. Ever since he had come to the conclusion that Lady Arabella was trying to steal the treasure-chest, he suspected nearly everyone of the same design, and made it a point to watch all suspicious persons and places. As Adam was engaged on his own researches regarding Lady Arabella, it was only natural that there should be some crossing of each other's tracks. This is what did actually happen.

Adam had gone for an early morning survey of the place in which he was interested, taking with him the mongoose in its box. He arrived at the gate of Diana's Grove just as Lady Arabella was preparing to set out for Castra Regis on what she considered her mission of comfort. Seeing Adam from her window going through the shadows of the trees round the gate, she thought that he must be engaged on some purpose similar to her own. So, quickly making her toilet, she quietly left the house, and, taking advantage of every shadow and substance which could hide her, followed him on his walk.

Oolanga, the experienced tracker, followed her, but succeeded in hiding his movements better than she did. He saw that Adam had on his shoulder a mysterious box, which he took to contain something valuable. Seeing that Lady Arabella was secretly following Adam, he was confirmed in this idea. His mind—such as it was—was fixed on her trying to steal, and he credited her at once with making use of this new opportunity.

In his walk, Adam went into the grounds of Castra Regis, and Oolanga saw her follow him with great secrecy. He feared to go closer, as now on both sides of him were enemies who might make discovery. When he realised that Lady Arabella was bound for the Castle, he devoted himself to following her with singleness of purpose. He therefore missed seeing that Adam branched off the track and returned to the high road.

That night Edgar Caswall had slept badly. The tragic occurrence of the day was on his mind, and he kept waking and thinking of it. After an early breakfast, he sat at the open window watching the kite and thinking of many things. From his room he could see all round the neighbourhood, but the two places that interested him most were Mercy Farm and Diana's Grove. At first the movements about those spots were of a humble kind—those that belong to domestic service or agricultural needs—the opening of doors and windows, the sweeping and brushing, and generally the restoration of habitual order.

From his high window—whose height made it a screen from the observation of others—he saw the chain of watchers move into his own grounds, and then presently break up—Adam Salton going one way, and Lady Arabella, followed by the nigger, another. Then Oolanga disappeared amongst the trees; but Caswall could see that he was still watching. Lady Arabella, after looking around her, slipped in by the open door, and he could, of course, see her no longer.

Presently, however, he heard a light tap at his door, then the door opened slowly, and he could see the flash of Lady Arabella's white dress through the opening.

CHAPTER XVI—A VISIT OF SYMPATHY

Caswall was genuinely surprised when he saw Lady Arabella, though he need not have been, after what had already occurred in the same way. The look of surprise on his face was so much greater than Lady Arabella had expected—though she thought she was prepared to meet anything that might occur—that she stood still, in sheer amazement. Cold-blooded as she was and ready for all social emergencies, she was nonplussed how to go on. She was plucky, however, and began to speak at once, although she had not the slightest idea what she was going to say.

"I came to offer you my very warm sympathy with the grief you have so lately experienced."

"My grief? I'm afraid I must be very dull; but I really do not understand."

Already she felt at a disadvantage, and hesitated.

"I mean about the old man who died so suddenly—your old . . . retainer."

Caswall's face relaxed something of its puzzled concentration.

"Oh, he was only a servant; and he had over-stayed his three-score and ten years by something like twenty years. He must have been ninety!"

"Still, as an old servant . . . "

Caswall's words were not so cold as their inflection.

"I never interfere with servants. He was kept on here merely because he had been so long on the premises. I suppose the steward thought it might make him unpopular if the old fellow had been dismissed."

How on earth was she to proceed on such a task as hers if this was the utmost geniality she could expect? So she at once tried another tack—this time a personal one.

"I am sorry I disturbed you. I am really not unconventional—though certainly no slave to convention. Still there are limits . . . it is bad enough to intrude in this way, and I do not know what you can say or think of the time selected, for the intrusion."

After all, Edgar Caswall was a gentleman by custom and habit, so he rose to the occasion.

"I can only say, Lady Arabella, that you are always welcome at any time you may deign to honour my house with your presence."

She smiled at him sweetly.

"Thank you *so* much. You *do* put one at ease. My breach of convention makes me glad rather than sorry. I feel that I can open my heart to you about anything."

Forthwith she proceeded to tell him about Oolanga and his strange suspicions of her honesty. Caswall laughed and made her explain all the details. His final comment was enlightening.

"Let me give you a word of advice: If you have the slightest fault to find with that infernal nigger, shoot him at sight. A swelled-headed nigger, with a bee in his bonnet, is one of the worst difficulties in the world to deal with. So better make a clean job of it, and wipe him out at once!"

"But what about the law, Mr. Caswall?"

"Oh, the law doesn't concern itself much about dead niggers. A few more or less do not matter. To my mind it's rather a relief!"

"I'm afraid of you," was her only comment, made with a sweet smile and in a soft voice.

"All right," he said, "let us leave it at that. Anyhow, we shall be rid of one of them!"

"I don't love niggers any more than you do," she replied, "and I suppose one mustn't be too particular where that sort of cleaning up is concerned." Then she changed in voice and manner, and asked genially: "And now tell me, am I forgiven?"

"You are, dear lady—if there is anything to forgive."

As he spoke, seeing that she had moved to go, he came to the door with her, and in the most natural way accompanied her downstairs. He passed through the hall with her and down the avenue. As he went back to the house, she smiled to herself.

"Well, that is all right. I don't think the morning has been altogether thrown away."

And she walked slowly back to Diana's Grove.

Adam Salton followed the line of the Brow, and refreshed his memory as to the various localities. He got home to Lesser Hill just as Sir Nathaniel was beginning lunch. Mr. Salton had gone to Walsall to keep an early appointment; so he was all alone. When the meal was over—seeing in Adam's face that he had something to speak about—he followed into the study and shut the door.

When the two men had lighted their pipes, Sir Nathaniel began.

"I have remembered an interesting fact about Diana's Grove—there is, I have long understood, some strange mystery about that house. It may be of some interest, or it may be trivial, in such a tangled skein as we are trying to unravel."

"Please tell me all you know' or suspect. To begin, then, of what sort is the mystery—physical, mental, moral, historical, scientific, occult? Any kind of hint will help me."

"Quite right. I shall try to tell you what I think; but I have not put my thoughts on the subject in sequence, so you must forgive me if due order is not observed in my narration. I suppose you have seen the house at Diana's Grove?"

"The outside of it; but I have that in my mind's eye, and I can fit into my memory whatever you may mention."

"The house is very old—probably the first house of some sort that stood there was in the time of the Romans. This was probably renewed—perhaps several times at later periods. The house stands, or, rather, used to stand here when Mercia was a kingdom—I do not suppose that the basement can be later than the Norman Conquest. Some years ago, when I was President of the Mercian Archaeological Society, I went all over it very carefully. This was when it was purchased by Captain March.

The house had then been done up, so as to be suitable for the bride. The basement is very strong,—almost as strong and as heavy as if it had been intended as a fortress. There are a whole series of rooms deep underground. One of them in particular struck me. The room itself is of considerable size, but the masonry is more than massive. In the middle of the room is a sunk well, built up to floor level and evidently going deep underground. There is no windlass nor any trace of there ever having been any—no rope—nothing. Now, we know that the Romans had wells of immense depth, from which the water was lifted by the 'old rag rope'; that at Woodhull used to be nearly a thousand feet. Here, then, we have simply an enormously deep well-hole. The door of the room was massive, and was fastened with a lock nearly a foot square. It was evidently intended for some kind of protection to someone or something; but no one in those days had ever heard of anyone having been allowed even to see the room. All this is *à propos* of a suggestion on my part that the well-hole was a way by which the White Worm (whatever it was) went and came. At that time I would have had a search made—even excavation if necessary—at my own expense, but all suggestions were met with a prompt and explicit negative. So, of course, I took no further step in the matter. Then it died out of recollection—even of mine."

"Do you remember, sir," asked Adam, "what was the appearance of the room where the well-hole was? Was there furniture—in fact, any sort of thing in the room?"

"The only thing I remember was a sort of green light—very clouded, very dim—which came up from the well. Not a fixed light, but intermittent and irregular—quite unlike anything I had ever seen."

"Do you remember how you got into the well-room? Was there a separate door from outside, or was there any interior room or passage which opened into it?"

"I think there must have been some room with a way into it. I remember going up some steep steps; they must have been worn smooth by long use or something of the kind, for I could hardly keep my feet as I went up. Once I stumbled and nearly fell into the well-hole."

"Was there anything strange about the place—any queer smell, for instance?"

"Queer smell—yes! Like bilge or a rank swamp. It was distinctly nauseating; when I came out I felt as if I had just been going to be sick. I shall try back on my visit and see if I can recall any more of what I saw or felt."

"Then perhaps, sir, later in the day you will tell me anything you may chance to recollect."

"I shall be delighted, Adam. If your uncle has not returned by then, I'll join you in the study after dinner, and we can resume this interesting chat."

CHAPTER XVII—THE MYSTERY OF "THE GROVE"

That afternoon Adam decided to do a little exploring. As he passed through the wood outside the gate of Diana's Grove, he thought he saw the African's face for an instant. So he went deeper into the undergrowth, and followed along parallel to the avenue to the house. He was glad that there was no workman or servant about, for he did not care that any of Lady Arabella's people should find him wandering about her grounds. Taking advantage of the denseness of the trees, he came close to the house and skirted round it. He was repaid for his trouble, for on the far side of the house, close to where the rocky frontage of the cliff fell away, he saw Oolanga crouched behind the irregular trunk of a great oak. The man was so intent on watching someone, or something, that he did not guard against being himself watched. This suited Adam, for he could thus make scrutiny at will.

The thick wood, though the trees were mostly of small girth, threw a heavy shadow, so that the steep declension, in front of which grew the tree behind which the African lurked, was almost in darkness. Adam drew as close as he could, and was amazed to see a patch of light on the ground before him; when he realised what it was, he was determined, more than ever to follow on his quest. The nigger had a dark lantern in his hand, and was throwing the light down the steep incline. The glare showed a series of stone steps, which ended in a low-lying heavy iron door fixed against the side of the house. All the strange things he had heard from Sir Nathaniel, and all those, little and big, which he had himself noticed, crowded into his mind in a chaotic way. Instinctively he took refuge behind a thick oak stem, and set himself down, to watch what might occur.

After a short time it became apparent that the African was trying to find out what was behind the heavy door. There was no way of looking in, for the door fitted tight into the massive stone slabs. The only opportunity for the entrance of light was through a small hole between the great stones above the door. This hole was too high up to look through from the ground level. Oolanga, having tried standing tiptoe on the highest point near, and holding the lantern as high as he could, threw the light round the edges of the door to see if he could find anywhere a hole or a flaw in the metal through which he could obtain a glimpse. Foiled in this, he brought from the shrubbery a plank, which he leant against the top of the door and then climbed up with great dexterity. This did not bring him near enough to the window-hole to look in, or even to throw the light of the lantern through it, so he climbed down and carried the plank back to the place from which he had got it. Then he concealed himself near the iron door and waited, manifestly with the intent of remaining there till someone came near. Presently Lady Arabella, moving noiselessly through the shade, approached the door. When he saw her close enough to touch it, Oolanga stepped forward from his concealment, and spoke in a whisper, which through the gloom sounded like a hiss.

"I want to see you, missy—soon and secret."

"What do you want?"

"You know well, missy; I told you already."

She turned on him with blazing eyes, the green tint in them glowing like emeralds.

"Come, none of that. If there is anything sensible which you wish to say to me, you can see me here, just where we are, at seven o'clock."

He made no reply in words, but, putting the backs of his hands together, bent lower and lower till his forehead touched the earth. Then he rose and went slowly away.

Adam Salton, from his hiding-place, saw and wondered. In a few minutes he moved from his place and went home to Lesser Hill, fully determined that seven o'clock would find him in some hidden place behind Diana's Grove.

At a little before seven Adam stole softly out of the house and took the back-way to the rear of Diana's Grove. The place seemed silent and deserted, so he took the opportunity of concealing himself near the spot whence he had seen Oolanga trying to investigate whatever was concealed behind the iron door. He waited, perfectly still, and at last saw a gleam of white passing soundlessly through the undergrowth. He was not surprised when he recognised the colour of Lady Arabella's dress. She came close and waited, with her face to the iron door. From some place of concealment near at hand Oolanga appeared, and came close to her. Adam noticed, with surprised amusement, that over his shoulder was the box with the mongoose. Of course the African did not know that he was seen by anyone, least of all by the man whose property he had with him.

Silent-footed as he was, Lady Arabella heard him coming, and turned to meet him. It was somewhat hard to see in the gloom, for, as usual, he was all in black, only his collar and cuffs showing white. Lady Arabella opened the conversation which ensued between the two.

"What do you want? To rob me, or murder me?"

"No, to lub you!"

This frightened her a little, and she tried to change the tone.

"Is that a coffin you have with you? If so, you are wasting your time. It would not hold me."

When a nigger suspects he is being laughed at, all the ferocity of his nature comes to the front; and this man was of the lowest kind.

"Dis ain't no coffin for nobody. Dis box is for you. Somefin you lub. Me give him to you!"

Still anxious to keep off the subject of affection, on which she believed him to have become crazed, she made another effort to keep his mind elsewhere.

"Is this why you want to see me?" He nodded. "Then come round to the other door. But be quiet. I have no desire to be seen so close to my own house in conversation with a—a—a nigger like you!"

She had chosen the word deliberately. She wished to meet his passion with another kind. Such would, at all events, help to keep him quiet. In the deep gloom she could not see the anger which suffused his face. Rolling eyeballs and grinding teeth are, however, sufficient signs of anger to be decipherable in the dark. She moved round the corner of the house to her right. Oolanga was following her, when she stopped him by raising her hand.

"No, not that door," she said; "that is not for niggers. The other door will do well enough for you!"

Lady Arabella took in her hand a small key which hung at the end of her watch-chain, and moved to a small door, low down, round the corner, and a little downhill from the edge of the Brow. Oolanga, in obedience to her gesture, went back to the iron door. Adam looked carefully at the mongoose box as the African went by, and was glad to see that it was intact. Unconsciously, as he looked, he fingered the key that was in his waistcoat pocket. When Oolanga was out of sight, Adam hurried after Lady Arabella.

CHAPTER XVIII—EXIT OOLANGA

The woman turned sharply as Adam touched her shoulder.

"One moment whilst we are alone. You had better not trust that nigger!" he whispered.

Her answer was crisp and concise:

"I don't."

"Forewarned is forearmed. Tell me if you will—it is for your own protection. Why do you mistrust him?"

"My friend, you have no idea of that man's impudence. Would you believe that he wants me to marry him?"

"No!" said Adam incredulously, amused in spite of himself.

"Yes, and wanted to bribe me to do it by sharing a chest of treasure—at least, he thought it was—stolen from Mr. Caswall. Why do you distrust him, Mr. Salton?"

"Did you notice that box he had slung on his shoulder? That belongs to me. I left it in the gun-room when I went to lunch. He must have crept in and stolen it. Doubtless he thinks that it, too, is full of treasure."

"He does!"

"How on earth do you know?" asked Adam.

"A little while ago he offered to give it to me—another bribe to accept him. Faugh! I am ashamed to tell you such a thing. The beast!"

Whilst they had been speaking, she had opened the door, a narrow iron one, well hung, for it opened easily and closed tightly without any creaking or sound of any kind. Within all was dark; but she entered as freely and with as little misgiving or restraint as if it had been broad daylight. For Adam, there was just sufficient green light from somewhere for him to see that there was a broad flight of heavy stone steps leading upward; but Lady Arabella, after shutting the door behind her, when it closed tightly without a clang, tripped up the steps lightly and swiftly. For an instant all was dark, but there came again the faint green light which enabled him to see the outlines of things. Another iron door, narrow like the first and fairly high, led into another large room, the walls of which were of massive stones, so closely joined together as to exhibit only one smooth surface. This presented the appearance of having at one time been polished. On the far side, also smooth like the walls, was the reverse of a wide, but not high, iron door. Here there was a little more light, for the high-up aperture over the door opened to the air.

CHAPTER XVIII—EXIT OOLANGA

Lady Arabella took from her girdle another small key, which she inserted in a keyhole in the centre of a massive lock. The great bolt seemed wonderfully hung, for the moment the small key was turned, the bolts of the great lock moved noiselessly and the iron doors swung open. On the stone steps outside stood Oolanga, with the mongoose box slung over his shoulder. Lady Arabella stood a little on one side, and the African, accepting the movement as an invitation, entered in an obsequious way. The moment, however, that he was inside, he gave a quick look around him.

"Much death here—big death. Many deaths. Good, good!"

He sniffed round as if he was enjoying the scent. The matter and manner of his speech were so revolting that instinctively Adam's hand wandered to his revolver, and, with his finger on the trigger, he rested satisfied that he was ready for any emergency.

There was certainly opportunity for the nigger's enjoyment, for the open well-hole was almost under his nose, sending up such a stench as almost made Adam sick, though Lady Arabella seemed not to mind it at all. It was like nothing that Adam had ever met with. He compared it with all the noxious experiences he had ever had—the drainage of war hospitals, of slaughter-houses, the refuse of dissecting rooms. None of these was like it, though it had something of them all, with, added, the sourness of chemical waste and the poisonous effluvium of the bilge of a water-logged ship whereon a multitude of rats had been drowned.

Then, quite unexpectedly, the negro noticed the presence of a third person—Adam Salton! He pulled out a pistol and shot at him, happily missing. Adam was himself usually a quick shot, but this time his mind had been on something else and he was not ready. However, he was quick to carry out an intention, and he was not a coward. In another moment both men were in grips. Beside them was the dark well-hole, with that horrid effluvium stealing up from its mysterious depths.

Adam and Oolanga both had pistols; Lady Arabella, who had not one, was probably the most ready of them all in the theory of shooting, but that being impossible, she made her effort in another way. Gliding forward, she tried to seize the African; but he eluded her grasp, just missing, in doing so, falling into the mysterious hole. As he swayed back to firm foothold, he turned his own gun on her and shot. Instinctively Adam leaped at his assailant; clutching at each other, they tottered on the very brink.

Lady Arabella's anger, now fully awake, was all for Oolanga. She moved towards him with her hands extended, and had just seized him when the catch of the locked box—due to some movement from within—flew open, and the king-cobra-killer flew at her with a venomous fury impossible to describe. As it seized her throat, she caught hold of it, and, with a fury superior to its own, tore it in two just as if it had been a sheet of paper. The strength used for such an act must have been terrific. In an instant, it seemed to spout blood and entrails, and was hurled into the well-hole. In another instant she had seized Oolanga, and with a swift rush had drawn him, her white arms encircling him, down with her into the gaping aperture.

Adam saw a medley of green and red lights blaze in a whirling circle, and as it sank down into the well, a pair of blazing green eyes became fixed, sank lower and lower with frightful rapidity, and disappeared, throwing upward the green light which grew more and more vivid every moment. As the light sank into the noisome depths, there came a shriek which chilled Adam's blood—a prolonged agony of pain and terror which seemed to have no end.

Adam Salton felt that he would never be able to free his mind from the memory of those dreadful moments. The gloom which surrounded that horrible charnel pit, which seemed to go down to the very bowels of the earth, conveyed from far down the sights and sounds of the nethermost hell. The ghastly fate of the African as he sank down to his terrible doom, his black face growing grey with terror, his white eyeballs, now like veined bloodstone, rolling in the helpless extremity of fear. The mysterious green light was in itself a milieu of horror. And through it all the awful cry came up from that fathomless pit, whose entrance was flooded with spots of fresh blood. Even the death of the fearless little snake-killer—so fierce, so frightful, as if stained with a ferocity which told of no living force above earth, but only of the devils of the pit—was only an incident. Adam was in a state of intellectual tumult, which had no parallel in his experience. He tried to rush away from the horrible place; even the baleful green light, thrown up through the gloomy well-shaft, was dying away as its source sank deeper into the primeval ooze. The darkness was closing in on him in overwhelming density—darkness in such a place and with such a memory of it!

He made a wild rush forward—slipt on the steps in some sticky, acrid-smelling mass that felt and smelt like blood, and, falling forward, felt his way into the inner room, where the well-shaft was not.

Then he rubbed his eyes in sheer amazement. Up the stone steps from the narrow door by which he had entered, glided the white-clad figure of Lady Arabella, the only colour to be seen on her being blood-marks on her face and hands and throat. Otherwise, she was calm and unruffled, as when earlier she stood aside for him to pass in through the narrow iron door.

CHAPTER XIX—AN ENEMY IN THE DARK

Adam Salton went for a walk before returning to Lesser Hill; he felt that it might be well, not only to steady his nerves, shaken by the horrible scene, but to get his thoughts into some sort of order, so as to be ready to enter on the matter with Sir Nathaniel. He was a little embarrassed as to telling his uncle, for affairs had so vastly progressed beyond his original view that he felt a little doubtful as to what would be the old gentleman's attitude when he should hear of the strange events for the first time. Mr. Salton would certainly not be satisfied at being treated as an outsider with regard to such things, most of which had points of contact with the inmates of his own house. It was with an immense sense of relief that Adam heard that his uncle had telegraphed to the housekeeper that he was detained by business at Walsall, where he would remain for the night; and that he would be back in the morning in time for lunch.

When Adam got home after his walk, he found Sir Nathaniel just going to bed. He did not say anything to him then of what had happened, but contented himself with arranging that they would walk together in the early morning, as he had much to say that would require serious attention.

Strangely enough he slept well, and awoke at dawn with his mind clear and his nerves in their usual unshaken condition. The maid brought up, with his early morning cup of tea, a note which had been found in the letter-box. It was from Lady Arabella, and was evidently intended to put him on his guard as to what he should say about the previous evening.

He read it over carefully several times, before he was satisfied that he had taken in its full import.

> "DEAR MR. SALTON,
>
> "I cannot go to bed until I have written to you, so you must forgive me if I disturb you, and at an unseemly time. Indeed, you must also forgive me if, in trying to do what is right, I err in saying too much or too little. The fact is that I am quite upset and unnerved by all that has happened in this terrible night. I find it difficult even to write; my hands shake so that they are not under control, and I am trembling all over with memory of the horrors we saw enacted before our eyes. I am grieved beyond measure that I should be, however remotely, a cause of this horror coming on you. Forgive me if you can, and do not think too hardly of me. This I ask with confidence, for since we shared together the dan-

ger—the very pangs—of death, I feel that we should be to one another something more than mere friends, that I may lean on you and trust you, assured that your sympathy and pity are for me. You really must let me thank you for the friendliness, the help, the confidence, the real aid at a time of deadly danger and deadly fear which you showed me. That awful man—I shall see him for ever in my dreams. His black, malignant face will shut out all memory of sunshine and happiness. I shall eternally see his evil eyes as he threw himself into that well-hole in a vain effort to escape from the consequences of his own misdoing. The more I think of it, the more apparent it seems to me that he had premeditated the whole thing—of course, except his own horrible death.

"Perhaps you have noticed a fur collar I occasionally wear. It is one of my most valued treasures—an ermine collar studded with emeralds. I had often seen the nigger's eyes gleam covetously when he looked at it. Unhappily, I wore it yesterday. That may have been the cause that lured the poor man to his doom. On the very brink of the abyss he tore the collar from my neck—that was the last I saw of him. When he sank into the hole, I was rushing to the iron door, which I pulled behind me. When I heard that soul-sickening yell, which marked his disappearance in the chasm, I was more glad than I can say that my eyes were spared the pain and horror which my ears had to endure.

"When I tore myself out of the negro's grasp as he sank into the well-hole; I realised what freedom meant. Freedom! Freedom! Not only from that noisome prison-house, which has now such a memory, but from the more noisome embrace of that hideous monster. Whilst I live, I shall always thank you for my freedom. A woman must sometimes express her gratitude; otherwise it becomes too great to bear. I am not a sentimental girl, who merely likes to thank a man; I am a woman who knows all, of bad as well as good, that life can give. I have known what it is to love and to lose. But you must not let me bring any unhappiness into your life. I must live on—as I have lived—alone, and, in addition, bear with other woes the memory of this latest insult and horror. In the meantime, I must get away as quickly as possible from Diana's Grove. In the morning I shall go up to town, where I shall remain for a week—I cannot stay longer, as business affairs demand my presence here. I think, however, that a week in the rush of busy London, surrounded with multitudes of commonplace people, will help to soften—I cannot expect total obliteration—the terrible images of the bygone night. When I can sleep easily—which will be, I hope, after a day or two—I shall be fit to return home and take up again the burden which will, I suppose, always be with me.

"I shall be most happy to see you on my return—or earlier, if my good fortune sends you on any errand to London. I shall stay at the Mayfair Hotel. In that busy spot we may forget some of the dangers and horrors we have shared together. Adieu, and thank you, again and again, for all your kindness and consideration to me.

"ARABELLA MARSH."

Adam was surprised by this effusive epistle, but he determined to say nothing of it to Sir Nathaniel until he should have thought it well over. When Adam met Sir Nathaniel at breakfast, he was glad that he had taken time to turn things over in his mind. The result had been that not only was he familiar with the facts in all their bearings, but he had already so far differentiated them that he was able to arrange them in his own mind according to their values. Breakfast had been a silent function, so it did not interfere in any way with the process of thought.

So soon as the door was closed, Sir Nathaniel began:

"I see, Adam, that something has occurred, and that you have much to tell me."

"That is so, sir. I suppose I had better begin by telling you all I know—all that has happened since I left you yesterday?"

Accordingly Adam gave him details of all that had happened during the previous evening. He confined himself rigidly to the narration of circumstances, taking care not to colour events by any comment of his own, or any opinion of the meaning of things which he did not fully understand. At first, Sir Nathaniel seemed disposed to ask questions, but shortly gave this up when he recognised that the narration was concise and self-explanatory. Thenceforth, he contented himself with quick looks and glances, easily interpreted, or by some acquiescent motions of his hands, when such could be convenient, to emphasise his idea of the correctness of any inference. Until Adam ceased speaking, having evidently come to an end of what he had to say with regard to this section of his story, the elder man made no comment whatever. Even when Adam took from his pocket Lady Arabella's letter, with the manifest intention of reading it, he did not make any comment. Finally, when Adam folded up the letter and put it, in its envelope, back in his pocket, as an intimation that he had now quite finished, the old diplomatist carefully made a few notes in his pocket-book.

"Your narrative, my dear Adam, is altogether admirable. I think I may now take it that we are both well versed in the actual facts, and that our conference had better take the shape of a mutual exchange of ideas. Let us both ask questions as they may arise; and I do not doubt that we shall arrive at some enlightening conclusions."

"Will you kindly begin, sir? I do not doubt that, with your longer experience, you will be able to dissipate some of the fog which envelops certain of the things which we have to consider."

"I hope so, my dear boy. For a beginning, then, let me say that Lady Arabella's letter makes clear some things which she intended—and also some things which she did not intend. But, before I begin to draw deductions, let me ask you a few questions. Adam, are you heart-whole, quite heart-whole, in the matter of Lady Arabella?"

His companion answered at once, each looking the other straight in the eyes during question and answer.

"Lady Arabella, sir, is a charming woman, and I should have deemed it a privilege to meet her—to talk to her—even—since I am in the confessional—to flirt a little with her. But if you mean to ask if my affections are in any way engaged, I can emphatically answer 'No!'—as indeed you will understand when presently I give you the reason. Apart from that, there are the unpleasant details we discussed the other day."

"Could you—would you mind giving me the reason now? It will help us to understand what is before us, in the way of difficulty."

"Certainly, sir. My reason, on which I can fully depend, is that I love another woman!"

"That clinches it. May I offer my good wishes, and, I hope, my congratulations?"

"I am proud of your good wishes, sir, and I thank you for them. But it is too soon for congratulations—the lady does not even know my hopes yet. Indeed, I hardly knew them myself, as definite, till this moment."

"I take it then, Adam, that at the right time I may be allowed to know who the lady is?"

Adam laughed a low, sweet laugh, such as ripples from a happy heart.

"There need not be an hour's, a minute's delay. I shall be glad to share my secret with you, sir. The lady, sir, whom I am so happy as to love, and in whom my dreams of life-long happiness are centred, is Mimi Watford!"

"Then, my dear Adam, I need not wait to offer congratulations. She is indeed a very charming young lady. I do not think I ever saw a girl who united in such perfection the qualities of strength of character and sweetness of disposition. With all my heart, I congratulate you. Then I may take it that my question as to your heart-wholeness is answered in the affirmative?"

"Yes; and now, sir, may I ask in turn why the question?"

"Certainly! I asked because it seems to me that we are coming to a point where my questions might be painful to you."

"It is not merely that I love Mimi, but I have reason to look on Lady Arabella as her enemy," Adam continued.

"Her enemy?"

"Yes. A rank and unscrupulous enemy who is bent on her destruction."

Sir Nathaniel went to the door, looked outside it and returned, locking it carefully behind him.

CHAPTER XX—METABOLISM

"Am I looking grave?" asked Sir Nathaniel inconsequently when he re-entered the room.

"You certainly are, sir."

"We little thought when first we met that we should be drawn into such a vortex. Already we are mixed up in robbery, and probably murder, but—a thousand times worse than all the crimes in the calendar—in an affair of ghastly mystery which has no bottom and no end—with forces of the most unnerving kind, which had their origin in an age when the world was different from the world which we know. We are going back to the origin of superstition—to an age when dragons tore each other in their slime. We must fear nothing—no conclusion, however improbable, almost impossible it may be. Life and death is hanging on our judgment, not only for ourselves, but for others whom we love. Remember, I count on you as I hope you count on me."

"I do, with all confidence."

"Then," said Sir Nathaniel, "let us think justly and boldly and fear nothing, however terrifying it may seem. I suppose I am to take as exact in every detail your account of all the strange things which happened whilst you were in Diana's Grove?"

"So far as I know, yes. Of course I may be mistaken in recollection of some detail or another, but I am certain that in the main what I have said is correct."

"You feel sure that you saw Lady Arabella seize the negro round the neck, and drag him down with her into the hole?"

"Absolutely certain, sir, otherwise I should have gone to her assistance."

"We have, then, an account of what happened from an eye-witness whom we trust—that is yourself. We have also another account, written by Lady Arabella under her own hand. These two accounts do not agree. Therefore we must take it that one of the two is lying."

"Apparently, sir."

"And that Lady Arabella is the liar!"

"Apparently—as I am not."

"We must, therefore, try to find a reason for her lying. She has nothing to fear from Oolanga, who is dead. Therefore the only reason which could actuate her would be to convince someone else that she was blameless. This 'someone' could not be you, for you had the evidence of your own eyes. There was no one else present; therefore it must have been an absent person."

"That seems beyond dispute, sir."

"There is only one other person whose good opinion she could wish to keep—Edgar Caswall. He is the only one who fills the bill. Her lies point to other things besides the death of the African. She evidently wanted it to be accepted that his falling into the well was his own act. I cannot suppose that she expected to convince you, the eye-witness; but if she wished later on to spread the story, it was wise of her to try to get your acceptance of it."

"That is so!"

"Then there were other matters of untruth. That, for instance, of the ermine collar embroidered with emeralds. If an understandable reason be required for this, it would be to draw attention away from the green lights which were seen in the room, and especially in the well-hole. Any unprejudiced person would accept the green lights to be the eyes of a great snake, such as tradition pointed to living in the well-hole. In fine, therefore, Lady Arabella wanted the general belief to be that there was no snake of the kind in Diana's Grove. For my own part, I don't believe in a partial liar—this art does not deal in veneer; a liar is a liar right through. Self-interest may prompt falsity of the tongue; but if one prove to be a liar, nothing that he says can ever be believed. This leads us to the conclusion that because she said or inferred that there was no snake, we should look for one—and expect to find it, too.

"Now let me digress. I live, and have for many years lived, in Derbyshire, a county more celebrated for its caves than any other county in England. I have been through them all, and am familiar with every turn of them; as also with other great caves in Kentucky, in France, in Germany, and a host of other places—in many of these are tremendously deep caves of narrow aperture, which are valued by intrepid explorers, who descend narrow gullets of abysmal depth—and sometimes never return. In many of the caverns in the Peak I am convinced that some of the smaller passages were used in primeval times as the lairs of some of the great serpents of legend and tradition. It may have been that such caverns were formed in the usual geologic way—bubbles or flaws in the earth's crust—which were later used by the monsters of the period of the young world. It may have been, of course, that some of them were worn originally by water; but in time they all found a use when suitable for living monsters.

"This brings us to another point, more difficult to accept and understand than any other requiring belief in a base not usually accepted, or indeed entered on—whether such abnormal growths could have ever changed in their nature. Some day the study of metabolism may progress so far as to enable us to accept structural changes proceeding from an intellectual or moral base. We may lean towards a belief that great animal strength may be a sound base for changes of all sorts. If this be so, what could be a more fitting subject than primeval monsters whose strength was such as to allow a survival of thousands of years? We do not know yet if brain can increase and develop independently of other parts of the living structure.

"After all, the mediaeval belief in the Philosopher's Stone which could transmute metals, has its counterpart in the accepted theory of metabolism which changes living tissue. In an age of investigation like our own, when we are returning to science as the base of wonders—almost of miracles—we should be slow to refuse to accept facts, however impossible they may seem to be.

"Let us suppose a monster of the early days of the world—a dragon of the prime—of vast age running into thousands of years, to whom had been conveyed in some way—it matters not—a brain just sufficient for the beginning of growth. Suppose the monster to be of incalculable size and of a strength quite abnormal—a veritable incarnation of animal strength. Suppose this animal is allowed to remain in one place, thus being removed from accidents of interrupted development; might not, would not this creature, in process of time—ages, if necessary—have that rudimentary intelligence developed? There is no impossibility in this; it is only the natural process of evolution. In the beginning, the instincts of animals are confined to alimentation, self-protection, and the multiplication of their species. As time goes on and the needs of life become more complex, power follows need. We have been long accustomed to consider growth as applied almost exclusively to size in its various aspects. But Nature, who has no doctrinaire ideas, may equally apply it to concentration. A developing thing may expand in any given way or form. Now, it is a scientific law that increase implies gain and loss of various kinds; what a thing gains in one direction it may lose in another. May it not be that Mother Nature may deliberately encourage decrease as well as increase—that it may be an axiom that what is gained in concentration is lost in size? Take, for instance, monsters that tradition has accepted and localised, such as the Worm of Lambton or that of Spindleston Heugh. If such a creature were, by its own process of metabolism, to change much of its bulk for intellectual growth, we should at once arrive at a new class of creature—more dangerous, perhaps, than the world has ever had any experience of—a force which can think, which has no soul and no morals, and therefore no acceptance of responsibility. A snake would be a good illustration of this, for it is cold-blooded, and therefore removed from the temptations which often weaken or restrict warm-blooded creatures. If, for instance, the Worm of Lambton—if such ever existed—were guided to its own ends by an organised intelligence capable of expansion, what form of creature could we imagine which would equal it in potentialities of evil? Why, such a being would devastate a whole country. Now, all these things require much thought, and we want to apply the knowledge usefully, and we should therefore be exact. Would it not be well to resume the subject later in the day?"

"I quite agree, sir. I am in a whirl already; and want to attend carefully to what you say; so that I may try to digest it."

Both men seemed fresher and better for the "easy," and when they met in the afternoon each of them had something to contribute to the general stock of information. Adam, who was by nature of a more militant disposition than his elderly friend, was glad to see that the conference at once assumed a practical trend. Sir Nathaniel recognised this, and, like an old diplomatist, turned it to present use.

"Tell me now, Adam, what is the outcome, in your own mind, of our conversation?"

"That the whole difficulty already assumes practical shape; but with added dangers, that at first I did not imagine."

"What is the practical shape, and what are the added dangers? I am not disputing, but only trying to clear my own ideas by the consideration of yours—"

So Adam went on:

"In the past, in the early days of the world, there were monsters who were so vast that they could exist for thousands of years. Some of them must have overlapped the

Christian era. They may have progressed intellectually in process of time. If they had in any way so progressed, or even got the most rudimentary form of brain, they would be the most dangerous things that ever were in the world. Tradition says that one of these monsters lived in the Marsh of the East, and came up to a cave in Diana's Grove, which was also called the Lair of the White Worm. Such creatures may have grown down as well as up. They *may* have grown into, or something like, human beings. Lady Arabella March is of snake nature. She has committed crimes to our knowledge. She retains something of the vast strength of her primal being—can see in the dark—has the eyes of a snake. She used the nigger, and then dragged him through the snake's hole down to the swamp; she is intent on evil, and hates some one we love. Result . . . "

"Yes, the result?"

"First, that Mimi Watford should be taken away at once—then—"

"Yes?"

"The monster must be destroyed."

"Bravo! That is a true and fearless conclusion. At whatever cost, it must be carried out."

"At once?"

"Soon, at all events. That creature's very existence is a danger. Her presence in this neighbourhood makes the danger immediate."

As he spoke, Sir Nathaniel's mouth hardened and his eyebrows came down till they met. There was no doubting his concurrence in the resolution, or his readiness to help in carrying it out. But he was an elderly man with much experience and knowledge of law and diplomacy. It seemed to him to be a stern duty to prevent anything irrevocable taking place till it had been thought out and all was ready. There were all sorts of legal cruxes to be thought out, not only regarding the taking of life, even of a monstrosity in human form, but also of property. Lady Arabella, be she woman or snake or devil, owned the ground she moved in, according to British law, and the law is jealous and swift to avenge wrongs done within its ken. All such difficulties should be—must be—avoided for Mr. Salton's sake, for Adam's own sake, and, most of all, for Mimi Watford's sake.

Before he spoke again, Sir Nathaniel had made up his mind that he must try to postpone decisive action until the circumstances on which they depended—which, after all, were only problematical—should have been tested satisfactorily, one way or another. When he did speak, Adam at first thought that his friend was wavering in his intention, or "funking" the responsibility. However, his respect for Sir Nathaniel was so great that he would not act, or even come to a conclusion on a vital point, without his sanction.

He came close and whispered in his ear:

"We will prepare our plans to combat and destroy this horrible menace, after we have cleared up some of the more baffling points. Meanwhile, we must wait for the night—I hear my uncle's footsteps echoing down the hall."

Sir Nathaniel nodded his approval.

CHAPTER XXI—GREEN LIGHT

When old Mr. Salton had retired for the night, Adam and Sir Nathaniel returned to the study. Things went with great regularity at Lesser Hill, so they knew that there would be no interruption to their talk.

When their cigars were lighted, Sir Nathaniel began.

"I hope, Adam, that you do not think me either slack or changeable of purpose. I mean to go through this business to the bitter end—whatever it may be. Be satisfied that my first care is, and shall be, the protection of Mimi Watford. To that I am pledged; my dear boy, we who are interested are all in the same danger. That semi-human monster out of the pit hates and means to destroy us all—you and me certainly, and probably your uncle. I wanted especially to talk with you to-night, for I cannot help thinking that the time is fast coming—if it has not come already—when we must take your uncle into our confidence. It was one thing when fancied evils threatened, but now he is probably marked for death, and it is only right that he should know all."

"I am with you, sir. Things have changed since we agreed to keep him out of the trouble. Now we dare not; consideration for his feelings might cost his life. It is a duty—and no light or pleasant one, either. I have not a shadow of doubt that he will want to be one with us in this. But remember, we are his guests; his name, his honour, have to be thought of as well as his safety."

"All shall be as you wish, Adam. And now as to what we are to do? We cannot murder Lady Arabella off-hand. Therefore we shall have to put things in order for the killing, and in such a way that we cannot be taxed with a crime."

"It seems to me, sir, that we are in an exceedingly tight place. Our first difficulty is to know where to begin. I never thought this fighting an antediluvian monster would be such a complicated job. This one is a woman, with all a woman's wit, combined with the heartlessness of a *cocotte*. She has the strength and impregnability of a diplodocus. We may be sure that in the fight that is before us there will be no semblance of fair-play. Also that our unscrupulous opponent will not betray herself!"

"That is so—but being feminine, she will probably over-reach herself. Now, Adam, it strikes me that, as we have to protect ourselves and others against feminine nature, our strong game will be to play our masculine against her feminine. Perhaps we had better sleep on it. She is a thing of the night; and the night may give us some ideas."

So they both turned in.

Adam knocked at Sir Nathaniel's door in the grey of the morning, and, on being bidden, came into the room. He had several letters in his hand. Sir Nathaniel sat up in bed.

"Well!"

"I should like to read you a few letters, but, of course, I shall not send them unless you approve. In fact"—with a smile and a blush—"there are several things which I want to do; but I hold my hand and my tongue till I have your approval."

"Go on!" said the other kindly. "Tell me all, and count at any rate on my sympathy, and on my approval and help if I can see my way."

Accordingly Adam proceeded:

"When I told you the conclusions at which I had arrived, I put in the foreground that Mimi Watford should, for the sake of her own safety, be removed—and that the monster which had wrought all the harm should be destroyed."

"Yes, that is so."

"To carry this into practice, sir, one preliminary is required—unless harm of another kind is to be faced. Mimi should have some protector whom all the world would recognise. The only form recognised by convention is marriage!"

Sir Nathaniel smiled in a fatherly way.

"To marry, a husband is required. And that husband should be you."

"Yes, yes."

"And the marriage should be immediate and secret—or, at least, not spoken of outside ourselves. Would the young lady be agreeable to that proceeding?"

"I do not know, sir!"

"Then how are we to proceed?"

"I suppose that we—or one of us—must ask her."

"Is this a sudden idea, Adam, a sudden resolution?"

"A sudden resolution, sir, but not a sudden idea. If she agrees, all is well and good. The sequence is obvious."

"And it is to be kept a secret amongst ourselves?"

"I want no secret, sir, except for Mimi's good. For myself, I should like to shout it from the house-tops! But we must be discreet; untimely knowledge to our enemy might work incalculable harm."

"And how would you suggest, Adam, that we could combine the momentous question with secrecy?"

Adam grew red and moved uneasily.

"Someone must ask her—as soon as possible!"

"And that someone?"

"I thought that you, sir, would be so good!"

"God bless my soul! This is a new kind of duty to take on—at my time of life. Adam, I hope you know that you can count on me to help in any way I can!"

"I have already counted on you, sir, when I ventured to make such a suggestion. I can only ask," he added, "that you will be more than ever kind to me—to us—and look on the painful duty as a voluntary act of grace, prompted by kindness and affection."

"Painful duty!"

"Yes," said Adam boldly. "Painful to you, though to me it would be all joyful."

"It is a strange job for an early morning! Well, we all live and learn. I suppose the sooner I go the better. You had better write a line for me to take with me. For, you see, this is to be a somewhat unusual transaction, and it may be embarrassing to the lady, even to myself. So we ought to have some sort of warrant, something to show that we have been mindful of her feelings. It will not do to take acquiescence for granted—although we act for her good."

"Sir Nathaniel, you are a true friend; I am sure that both Mimi and I shall be grateful to you for all our lives—however long they may be!"

So the two talked it over and agreed as to points to be borne in mind by the ambassador. It was striking ten when Sir Nathaniel left the house, Adam seeing him quietly off.

As the young man followed him with wistful eyes—almost jealous of the privilege which his kind deed was about to bring him—he felt that his own heart was in his friend's breast.

The memory of that morning was like a dream to all those concerned in it. Sir Nathaniel had a confused recollection of detail and sequence, though the main facts stood out in his memory boldly and clearly. Adam Salton's recollection was of an illimitable wait, filled with anxiety, hope, and chagrin, all dominated by a sense of the slow passage of time and accompanied by vague fears. Mimi could not for a long time think at all, or recollect anything, except that Adam loved her and was saving her from a terrible danger. When she had time to think, later on, she wondered when she had any ignorance of the fact that Adam loved her, and that she loved him with all her heart. Everything, every recollection however small, every feeling, seemed to fit into those elemental facts as though they had all been moulded together. The main and crowning recollection was her saying goodbye to Sir Nathaniel, and entrusting to him loving messages, straight from her heart, to Adam Salton, and of his bearing when—with an impulse which she could not check—she put her lips to his and kissed him. Later, when she was alone and had time to think, it was a passing grief to her that she would have to be silent, for a time, to Lilla on the happy events of that strange mission.

She had, of course, agreed to keep all secret until Adam should give her leave to speak.

The advice and assistance of Sir Nathaniel was a great help to Adam in carrying out his idea of marrying Mimi Watford without publicity. He went with him to London, and, with his influence, the young man obtained the license of the Archbishop of Canterbury for a private marriage. Sir Nathaniel then persuaded old Mr. Salton to allow his nephew to spend a few weeks with him at Doom Tower, and it was here that Mimi became Adam's wife. But that was only the first step in their plans; before going further, however, Adam took his bride off to the Isle of Man. He wished to place a stretch of sea between Mimi and the White Worm, while things matured. On their return, Sir Nathaniel met them and drove them at once to Doom, taking care to avoid any one that he knew on the journey.

Sir Nathaniel had taken care to have the doors and windows shut and locked—all but the door used for their entry. The shutters were up and the blinds down. Moreover, heavy curtains were drawn across the windows. When Adam commented on this, Sir Nathaniel said in a whisper:

"Wait till we are alone, and I'll tell you why this is done; in the meantime not a word or a sign. You will approve when we have had a talk together."

They said no more on the subject till after dinner, when they were ensconced in Sir Nathaniel's study, which was on the top storey. Doom Tower was a lofty structure, situated on an eminence high up in the Peak. The top commanded a wide prospect, ranging from the hills above the Ribble to the near side of the Brow, which marked the northern bound of ancient Mercia. It was of the early Norman period, less than a century younger than Castra Regis. The windows of the study were barred and locked, and heavy dark curtains closed them in. When this was done not a gleam of light from the tower could be seen from outside.

When they were alone, Sir Nathaniel explained that he had taken his old friend, Mr. Salton, into full confidence, and that in future all would work together.

"It is important for you to be extremely careful. In spite of the fact that our marriage was kept secret, as also your temporary absence, both are known."

"How? To whom?"

"How, I know not; but I am beginning to have an idea."

"To her?" asked Adam, in momentary consternation.

Sir Nathaniel shivered perceptibly.

"The White Worm—yes!"

Adam noticed that from now on, his friend never spoke of Lady Arabella otherwise, except when he wished to divert the suspicion of others.

Sir Nathaniel switched off the electric light, and when the room was pitch dark, he came to Adam, took him by the hand, and led him to a seat set in the southern window. Then he softly drew back a piece of the curtain and motioned his companion to look out.

Adam did so, and immediately shrank back as though his eyes had opened on pressing danger. His companion set his mind at rest by saying in a low voice:

"It is all right; you may speak, but speak low. There is no danger here—at present!"

Adam leaned forward, taking care, however, not to press his face against the glass. What he saw would not under ordinary circumstances have caused concern to anybody. With his special knowledge, it was appalling—though the night was now so dark that in reality there was little to be seen.

On the western side of the tower stood a grove of old trees, of forest dimensions. They were not grouped closely, but stood a little apart from each other, producing the effect of a row widely planted. Over the tops of them was seen a green light, something like the danger signal at a railway-crossing. It seemed at first quite still; but presently, when Adam's eye became accustomed to it, he could see that it moved as if trembling. This at once recalled to Adam's mind the light quivering above the well-hole in the darkness of that inner room at Diana's Grove, Oolanga's awful shriek, and the hideous black face, now grown grey with terror, disappearing into the impenetrable gloom of the mysterious orifice. Instinctively he laid his hand on his revolver, and stood up ready to protect his wife. Then, seeing that nothing happened, and that the light and all outside the tower remained the same, he softly pulled the curtain over the window.

Sir Nathaniel switched on the light again, and in its comforting glow they began to talk freely.

CHAPTER XXII—AT CLOSE QUARTERS

"She has diabolical cunning," said Sir Nathaniel. "Ever since you left, she has ranged along the Brow and wherever you were accustomed to frequent. I have not heard whence the knowledge of your movements came to her, nor have I been able to learn any data whereon to found an opinion. She seems to have heard both of your marriage and your absence; but I gather, by inference, that she does not actually know where you and Mimi are, or of your return. So soon as the dusk fails, she goes out on her rounds, and before dawn covers the whole ground round the Brow, and away up into the heart of the Peak. The White Worm, in her own proper shape, certainly has great facilities for the business on which she is now engaged. She can look into windows of any ordinary kind. Happily, this house is beyond her reach, if she wishes—as she manifestly does—to remain unrecognised. But, even at this height, it is wise to show no lights, lest she might learn something of our presence or absence."

"Would it not be well, sir, if one of us could see this monster in her real shape at close quarters? I am willing to run the risk—for I take it there would be no slight risk in the doing. I don't suppose anyone of our time has seen her close and lived to tell the tale."

Sir Nathaniel held up an expostulatory hand.

"Good God, lad, what are you suggesting? Think of your wife, and all that is at stake."

"It is of Mimi that I think—for her sake that I am willing to risk whatever is to be risked."

Adam's young bride was proud of her man, but she blanched at the thought of the ghastly White Worm. Adam saw this and at once reassured her.

"So long as her ladyship does not know whereabout I am, I shall have as much safety as remains to us; bear in mind, my darling, that we cannot be too careful."

Sir Nathaniel realised that Adam was right; the White Worm had no supernatural powers and could not harm them until she discovered their hiding place. It was agreed, therefore, that the two men should go together.

When the two men slipped out by the back door of the house, they walked cautiously along the avenue which trended towards the west. Everything was pitch dark—so dark that at times they had to feel their way by the palings and tree-trunks. They could still see, seemingly far in front of them and high up, the baleful light which at the height and distance seemed like a faint line. As they were now on the level of the ground, the light seemed infinitely higher than it had from the top of the tower. At the sight Adam's heart fell; the danger of the desperate enterprise which he had undertaken burst upon him. But this feeling was shortly followed by another which restored him to himself—a fierce loathing, and a desire to kill, such as he had never experienced before.

They went on for some distance on a level road, fairly wide, from which the green light was visible. Here Sir Nathaniel spoke softly, placing his lips to Adam's ear for safety.

"We know nothing whatever of this creature's power of hearing or smelling, though I presume that both are of no great strength. As to seeing, we may presume the opposite, but in any case we must try to keep in the shade behind the tree-trunks. The slightest error would be fatal to us."

Adam only nodded, in case there should be any chance of the monster seeing the movement.

After a time that seemed interminable, they emerged from the circling wood. It was like coming out into sunlight by comparison with the misty blackness which had been around them. There was light enough to see by, though not sufficient to distinguish things at a distance. Adam's eyes sought the green light in the sky. It was still in about the same place, but its surroundings were more visible. It was now at the summit of what seemed to be a long white pole, near the top of which were two pendant white masses, like rudimentary arms or fins. The green light, strangely enough, did not seem lessened by the surrounding starlight, but had a clearer effect and a deeper green. Whilst they were carefully regarding this—Adam with the aid of an opera-glass—their nostrils were assailed by a horrid stench, something like that which rose from the well-hole in Diana's Grove.

By degrees, as their eyes got the right focus, they saw an immense towering mass that seemed snowy white. It was tall and thin. The lower part was hidden by the trees which lay between, but they could follow the tall white shaft and the duplicate green lights which topped it. As they looked there was a movement—the shaft seemed to bend, and the line of green light descended amongst the trees. They could see the green light twinkle as it passed between the obstructing branches.

Seeing where the head of the monster was, the two men ventured a little further forward, and saw that the hidden mass at the base of the shaft was composed of vast coils of the great serpent's body, forming a base from which the upright mass rose. As they looked, this lower mass moved, the glistening folds catching the moonlight, and they could see that the monster's progress was along the ground. It was coming towards them at a swift pace, so they turned and ran, taking care to make as little noise as possible, either by their footfalls or by disturbing the undergrowth close to them. They did not stop or pause till they saw before them the high dark tower of Doom.

CHAPTER XXIII—IN THE ENEMY'S HOUSE

Sir Nathaniel was in the library next morning, after breakfast, when Adam came to him carrying a letter.

"Her ladyship doesn't lose any time. She has begun work already!"

Sir Nathaniel, who was writing at a table near the window, looked up.

"What is it?" said he.

Adam held out the letter he was carrying. It was in a blazoned envelope.

"Ha!" said Sir Nathaniel, "from the White Worm! I expected something of the kind."

"But," said Adam, "how could she have known we were here? She didn't know last night."

"I don't think we need trouble about that, Adam. There is so much we do not understand. This is only another mystery. Suffice it that she does know—perhaps it is all the better and safer for us."

"How is that?" asked Adam with a puzzled look.

"General process of reasoning, my boy; and the experience of some years in the diplomatic world. This creature is a monster without heart or consideration for anything or anyone. She is not nearly so dangerous in the open as when she has the dark to protect her. Besides, we know, by our own experience of her movements, that for some reason she shuns publicity. In spite of her vast bulk and abnormal strength, she is afraid to attack openly. After all, she is only a snake and with a snake's nature, which is to keep low and squirm, and proceed by stealth and cunning. She will never attack when she can run away, although she knows well that running away would probably be fatal to her. What is the letter about?"

Sir Nathaniel's voice was calm and self-possessed. When he was engaged in any struggle of wits he was all diplomatist.

"She asks Mimi and me to tea this afternoon at Diana's Grove, and hopes that you also will favour her."

Sir Nathaniel smiled.

"Please ask Mrs. Salton to accept for us all."

"She means some deadly mischief. Surely—surely it would be wiser not."

"It is an old trick that we learn early in diplomacy, Adam—to fight on ground of your own choice. It is true that she suggested the place on this occasion; but by accepting it we make it ours. Moreover, she will not be able to understand our reason for doing so, and her own bad conscience—if she has any, bad or good—and her own fears and doubts will play our game for us. No, my dear boy, let us accept, by all means."

Adam said nothing, but silently held out his hand, which his companion shook: no words were necessary.

When it was getting near tea-time, Mimi asked Sir Nathaniel how they were going.

"We must make a point of going in state. We want all possible publicity." Mimi looked at him inquiringly. "Certainly, my dear, in the present circumstances publicity is a part of safety. Do not be surprised if, whilst we are at Diana's Grove, occasional messages come for you—for all or any of us."

"I see!" said Mrs. Salton. "You are taking no chances."

"None, my dear. All I have learned at foreign courts, and amongst civilised and uncivilised people, is going to be utilised within the next couple of hours."

Sir Nathaniel's voice was full of seriousness, and it brought to Mimi in a convincing way the awful gravity of the occasion

In due course, they set out in a carriage drawn by a fine pair of horses, who soon devoured the few miles of their journey. Before they came to the gate, Sir Nathaniel turned to Mimi.

"I have arranged with Adam certain signals which may be necessary if certain eventualities occur. These need be nothing to do with you directly. But bear in mind that if I ask you or Adam to do anything, do not lose a second in the doing of it. We must try to pass off such moments with an appearance of unconcern. In all probability, nothing requiring such care will occur. The White Worm will not try force, though she has so much of it to spare. Whatever she may attempt to-day, of harm to any of us, will be in the way of secret plot. Some other time she may try force, but—if I am able to judge such a thing—not to-day. The messengers who may ask for any of us will not be witnesses only, they may help to stave off danger." Seeing query in her face, he went on: "Of what kind the danger may be, I know not, and cannot guess. It will doubtless be some ordinary circumstance; but none the less dangerous on that account. Here we are at the gate. Now, be careful in all matters, however small. To keep your head is half the battle."

There were a number of men in livery in the hall when they arrived. The doors of the drawing-room were thrown open, and Lady Arabella came forth and offered them cordial welcome. This having been got over, Lady Arabella led them into another room where tea was served.

Adam was acutely watchful and suspicious of everything, and saw on the far side of this room a panelled iron door of the same colour and configuration as the outer door of the room where was the well-hole wherein Oolanga had disappeared. Something in the sight alarmed him, and he quietly stood near the door. He made no movement, even of his eyes, but he could see that Sir Nathaniel was watching him intently, and, he fancied, with approval.

They all sat near the table spread for tea, Adam still near the door. Lady Arabella fanned herself, complaining of heat, and told one of the footmen to throw all the outer doors open.

Tea was in progress when Mimi suddenly started up with a look of fright on her face; at the same moment, the men became cognisant of a thick smoke which began to spread through the room—a smoke which made those who experienced it gasp and choke. The footmen began to edge uneasily towards the inner door. Denser and denser grew the smoke, and more acrid its smell. Mimi, towards whom the draught from the open door wafted the smoke, rose up choking, and ran to the inner door, which she threw open to its fullest extent, disclosing on the outside a curtain of thin silk, fixed to the doorposts. The draught from the open door swayed the thin silk towards her, and in her fright, she tore down the curtain, which enveloped her from head to foot. Then she ran through the still open door, heedless of the fact that she could not see where she was going. Adam, followed by Sir Nathaniel, rushed forward and joined her—Adam catching his wife by the arm and holding her tight. It was well that he did so, for just before her lay the black orifice of the well-hole, which, of course, she could not see with the silk curtain round her head. The floor was extremely slippery; something like thick oil had been spilled where she had to pass; and close to the edge of the hole her feet shot from under her, and she stumbled forward towards the well-hole.

When Adam saw Mimi slip, he flung himself backward, still holding her. His weight told, and he dragged her up from the hole and they fell together on the floor outside the zone of slipperiness. In a moment he had raised her up, and together they rushed out through the open door into the sunlight, Sir Nathaniel close behind them. They were all pale except the old diplomatist, who looked both calm and cool. It sustained and cheered Adam and his wife to see him thus master of himself. Both managed to follow his example, to the wonderment of the footmen, who saw the three who had just escaped a terrible danger walking together gaily, as, under the guiding pressure of Sir Nathaniel's hand, they turned to re-enter the house.

Lady Arabella, whose face had blanched to a deadly white, now resumed her ministrations at the tea-board as though nothing unusual had happened. The slop-basin was full of half-burned brown paper, over which tea had been poured.

Sir Nathaniel had been narrowly observing his hostess, and took the first opportunity afforded him of whispering to Adam:

"The real attack is to come—she is too quiet. When I give my hand to your wife to lead her out, come with us—and caution her to hurry. Don't lose a second, even if you have to make a scene. Hs-s-s-h!"

Then they resumed their places close to the table, and the servants, in obedience to Lady Arabella's order, brought in fresh tea.

Thence on, that tea-party seemed to Adam, whose faculties were at their utmost intensity, like a terrible dream. As for poor Mimi, she was so overwrought both with present and future fear, and with horror at the danger she had escaped, that her faculties were numb. However, she was braced up for a trial, and she felt assured that whatever might come she would be able to go through with it. Sir Nathaniel seemed just as usual—suave, dignified, and thoughtful—perfect master of himself.

To her husband, it was evident that Mimi was ill at ease. The way she kept turning her head to look around her, the quick coming and going of the colour of her face, her hurried breathing, alternating with periods of suspicious calm, were evidences of mental perturbation. To her, the attitude of Lady Arabella seemed compounded of social sweetness and personal consideration. It would be hard to imagine more thoughtful and tender kindness towards an honoured guest.

When tea was over and the servants had come to clear away the cups, Lady Arabella, putting her arm round Mimi's waist, strolled with her into an adjoining room, where she collected a number of photographs which were scattered about, and, sitting down beside her guest, began to show them to her. While she was doing this, the servants closed all the doors of the suite of rooms, as well as that which opened from the room outside—that of the well-hole into the avenue. Suddenly, without any seeming cause, the light in the room began to grow dim. Sir Nathaniel, who was sitting close to Mimi, rose to his feet, and, crying, "Quick!" caught hold of her hand and began to drag her from the room. Adam caught her other hand, and between them they drew her through the outer door which the servants were beginning to close. It was difficult at first to find the way, the darkness was so great; but to their relief when Adam whistled shrilly, the carriage and horses, which had been waiting in the angle of the avenue, dashed up. Her husband and Sir Nathaniel lifted—almost threw—Mimi into the carriage. The postillion plied whip and spur, and the vehicle, rocking with its speed, swept through the gate and tore up the road. Behind them was a hubbub—servants rushing about, orders being shouted out, doors shutting, and somewhere, seemingly far back in the house, a strange noise. Every nerve of the horses was strained as they dashed recklessly along the road. The two men held Mimi between them, the arms of both of them round her as though protectingly. As they went, there was a sudden rise in the ground; but the horses, breathing heavily, dashed up it at racing speed, not slackening their pace when the hill fell away again, leaving them to hurry along the downgrade.

It would be foolish to say that neither Adam nor Mimi had any fear in returning to Doom Tower. Mimi felt it more keenly than her husband, whose nerves were harder, and who was more inured to danger. Still she bore up bravely, and as usual the effort was helpful to her. When once she was in the study in the top of the turret, she almost forgot the terrors which lay outside in the dark. She did not attempt to peep out of the window; but Adam did—and saw nothing. The moonlight showed all the surrounding country, but nowhere was to be observed that tremulous line of green light.

The peaceful night had a good effect on them all; danger, being unseen, seemed far off. At times it was hard to realise that it had ever been. With courage restored, Adam rose early and walked along the Brow, seeing no change in the signs of life in Castra Regis. What he did see, to his wonder and concern, on his returning homeward, was Lady Arabella, in her tight-fitting white dress and ermine collar, but without her emeralds; she was emerging from the gate of Diana's Grove and walking towards the Castle. Pondering on this and trying to find some meaning in it, occupied his thoughts till he joined Mimi and Sir Nathaniel at breakfast. They began the meal in silence. What had been had been, and was known to them all. Moreover, it was not a pleasant topic.

A fillip was given to the conversation when Adam told of his seeing Lady Arabella, on her way to Castra Regis. They each had something to say of her, and of what her wishes or intentions were towards Edgar Caswall. Mimi spoke bitterly of her in every aspect. She had not forgotten—and never would—never could—the occasion when, to harm Lilla, the woman had consorted even with the nigger. As a social matter, she was disgusted with her for following up the rich landowner—"throwing herself at his head so shamelessly," was how she expressed it. She was interested to know that the great kite still flew from Caswall's tower. But beyond such matters she did not try to go. The only comment she made was of strongly expressed surprise at her ladyship's "cheek" in ignoring her own criminal acts, and her impudence in taking it for granted that others had overlooked them also.

CHAPTER XXIV—A STARTLING PROPOSITION

The more Mimi thought over the late events, the more puzzled she was. What did it all mean—what could it mean, except that there was an error of fact somewhere. Could it be possible that some of them—all of them had been mistaken, that there had been no White Worm at all? On either side of her was a belief impossible of reception. Not to believe in what seemed apparent was to destroy the very foundations of belief . . . yet in old days there had been monsters on the earth, and certainly some people had believed in just such mysterious changes of identity. It was all very strange. Just fancy how any stranger—say a doctor—would regard her, if she were to tell him that she had been to a tea-party with an antediluvian monster, and that they had been waited on by up-to-date men-servants.

Adam had returned, exhilarated by his walk, and more settled in his mind than he had been for some time. Like Mimi, he had gone through the phase of doubt and inability to believe in the reality of things, though it had not affected him to the same extent. The idea, however, that his wife was suffering ill-effects from her terrible ordeal, braced him up. He remained with her for a time, then he sought Sir Nathaniel in order to talk over the matter with him. He knew that the calm common sense and self-reliance of the old man, as well as his experience, would be helpful to them all.

Sir Nathaniel had come to the conclusion that, for some reason which he did not understand, Lady Arabella had changed her plans, and, for the present at all events, was pacific. He was inclined to attribute her changed demeanour to the fact that her influence over Edgar Caswall was so far increased, as to justify a more fixed belief in his submission to her charms.

As a matter of fact, she had seen Caswall that morning when she visited Castra Regis, and they had had a long talk together, during which the possibility of their union had been discussed. Caswall, without being enthusiastic on the subject, had been courteous and attentive; as she had walked back to Diana's Grove, she almost congratulated herself on her new settlement in life. That the idea was becoming fixed in her mind, was shown by a letter which she wrote later in the day to Adam Salton, and sent to him by hand. It ran as follows:

> "DEAR MR. SALTON,
>
> "I wonder if you would kindly advise, and, if possible, help me in a matter of business. I have been for some time trying to make up my

mind to sell Diana's Grove, I have put off and put off the doing of it till now. The place is my own property, and no one has to be consulted with regard to what I may wish to do about it. It was bought by my late husband, Captain Adolphus Ranger March, who had another residence, The Crest, Appleby. He acquired all rights of all kinds, including mining and sporting. When he died, he left his whole property to me. I shall feel leaving this place, which has become endeared to me by many sacred memories and affections—the recollection of many happy days of my young married life, and the more than happy memories of the man I loved and who loved me so much. I should be willing to sell the place for any fair price—so long, of course, as the purchaser was one I liked and of whom I approved. May I say that you yourself would be the ideal person. But I dare not hope for so much. It strikes me, however, that among your Australian friends may be someone who wishes to make a settlement in the Old Country, and would care to fix the spot in one of the most historic regions in England, full of romance and legend, and with a never-ending vista of historical interest—an estate which, though small, is in perfect condition and with illimitable possibilities of development, and many doubtful—or unsettled—rights which have existed before the time of the Romans or even Celts, who were the original possessors. In addition, the house has been kept up to the *dernier cri.* Immediate possession can be arranged. My lawyers can provide you, or whoever you may suggest, with all business and historical details. A word from you of acceptance or refusal is all that is necessary, and we can leave details to be thrashed out by our agents. Forgive me, won't you, for troubling you in the matter, and believe me, yours very sincerely.

"ARABELLA MARCH."

Adam read this over several times, and then, his mind being made up, he went to Mimi and asked if she had any objection. She answered—after a shudder—that she was, in this, as in all things, willing to do whatever he might wish.

"Dearest, I am willing that you should judge what is best for us. Be quite free to act as you see your duty, and as your inclination calls. We are in the hands of God, and He has hitherto guided us, and will do so to His own end."

From his wife's room Adam Salton went straight to the study in the tower, where he knew Sir Nathaniel would be at that hour. The old man was alone, so, when he had entered in obedience to the "Come in," which answered his query, he closed the door and sat down beside him.

"Do you think, sir, that it would be well for me to buy Diana's Grove?"

"God bless my soul!" said the old man, startled, "why on earth would you want to do that?"

"Well, I have vowed to destroy that White Worm, and my being able to do whatever I may choose with the Lair would facilitate matters and avoid complications."

Sir Nathaniel hesitated longer than usual before speaking. He was thinking deeply.

"Yes, Adam, there is much common sense in your suggestion, though it startled me at first. I think that, for all reasons, you would do well to buy the property and to have the conveyance settled at once. If you want more money than is immediately convenient, let me know, so that I may be your banker."

"Thank you, sir, most heartily; but I have more money at immediate call than I shall want. I am glad you approve."

"The property is historic, and as time goes on it will increase in value. Moreover, I may tell you something, which indeed is only a surmise, but which, if I am right, will add great value to the place." Adam listened. "Has it ever struck you why the old name, 'The Lair of the White Worm,' was given? We know that there was a snake which in early days was called a worm; but why white?"

"I really don't know, sir; I never thought of it. I simply took it for granted."

"So did I at first—long ago. But later I puzzled my brain for a reason."

"And what was the reason, sir?"

"Simply and solely because the snake or worm *was* white. We are near the county of Stafford, where the great industry of china-burning was originated and grew. Stafford owes much of its wealth to the large deposits of the rare china clay found in it from time to time. These deposits become in time pretty well exhausted; but for centuries Stafford adventurers looked for the special clay, as Ohio and Pennsylvania farmers and explorers looked for oil. Anyone owning real estate on which china clay can be discovered strikes a sort of gold mine."

"Yes, and then—" The young man looked puzzled.

"The original 'Worm' so-called, from which the name of the place came, had to find a direct way down to the marshes and the mud-holes. Now, the clay is easily penetrable, and the original hole probably pierced a bed of china clay. When once the way was made it would become a sort of highway for the Worm. But as much movement was necessary to ascend such a great height, some of the clay would become attached to its rough skin by attrition. The downway must have been easy work, but the ascent was different, and when the monster came to view in the upper world, it would be fresh from contact with the white clay. Hence the name, which has no cryptic significance, but only fact. Now, if that surmise be true—and I do not see why not—there must be a deposit of valuable clay—possibly of immense depth."

Adam's comment pleased the old gentleman.

"I have it in my bones, sir, that you have struck—or rather reasoned out—a great truth."

Sir Nathaniel went on cheerfully. "When the world of commerce wakes up to the value of your find, it will be as well that your title to ownership has been perfectly secured. If anyone ever deserved such a gain, it is you."

With his friend's aid, Adam secured the property without loss of time. Then he went to see his uncle, and told him about it. Mr. Salton was delighted to find his young relative already constructively the owner of so fine an estate—one which gave him an important status in the county. He made many anxious enquiries about Mimi, and the doings of the White Worm, but Adam reassured him.

The next morning, when Adam went to his host in the smoking-room, Sir Nathaniel asked him how he purposed to proceed with regard to keeping his vow.

"It is a difficult matter which you have undertaken. To destroy such a monster is something like one of the labours of Hercules, in that not only its size and weight and power of using them in little-known ways are against you, but the occult side is alone an unsurpassable difficulty. The Worm is already master of all the elements except fire—and I do not see how fire can be used for the attack. It has only to sink into the earth in its usual way, and you could not overtake it if you had the resources of the biggest coal-mine in existence. But I daresay you have mapped out some plan in your mind," he added courteously.

"I have, sir. But, of course, it may not stand the test of practice."

"May I know the idea?"

"Well, sir, this was my argument: At the time of the Chartist trouble, an idea spread amongst financial circles that an attack was going to be made on the Bank of England. Accordingly, the directors of that institution consulted many persons who were supposed to know what steps should be taken, and it was finally decided that the best protection against fire—which is what was feared—was not water but sand. To carry the scheme into practice great store of fine sea-sand—the kind that blows about and is used to fill hour-glasses—was provided throughout the building, especially at the points liable to attack, from which it could be brought into use.

"I propose to provide at Diana's Grove, as soon as it comes into my possession, an enormous amount of such sand, and shall take an early occasion of pouring it into the well-hole, which it will in time choke. Thus Lady Arabella, in her guise of the White Worm, will find herself cut off from her refuge. The hole is a narrow one, and is some hundreds of feet deep. The weight of the sand this can contain would not in itself be sufficient to obstruct; but the friction of such a body working up against it would be tremendous."

"One moment. What use would the sand be for destruction?"

"None, directly; but it would hold the struggling body in place till the rest of my scheme came into practice."

"And what is the rest?"

"As the sand is being poured into the well-hole, quantities of dynamite can also be thrown in!"

"Good. But how would the dynamite explode—for, of course, that is what you intend. Would not some sort of wire or fuse he required for each parcel of dynamite?"

Adam smiled.

"Not in these days, sir. That was proved in New York. A thousand pounds of dynamite, in sealed canisters, was placed about some workings. At the last a charge of gunpowder was fired, and the concussion exploded the dynamite. It was most successful. Those who were non-experts in high explosives expected that every pane of glass in New York would be shattered. But, in reality, the explosive did no harm outside the area intended, although sixteen acres of rock had been mined and only the supporting walls and pillars had been left intact. The whole of the rocks were shattered."

Sir Nathaniel nodded approval.

"That seems a good plan—a very excellent one. But if it has to tear down so many feet of precipice, it may wreck the whole neighbourhood."

"And free it for ever from a monster," added Adam, as he left the room to find his wife.

CHAPTER XXV—THE LAST BATTLE

Lady Arabella had instructed her solicitors to hurry on with the conveyance of Diana's Grove, so no time was lost in letting Adam Salton have formal possession of the estate. After his interview with Sir Nathaniel, he had taken steps to begin putting his plan into action. In order to accumulate the necessary amount of fine sea-sand, he ordered the steward to prepare for an elaborate system of top-dressing all the grounds. A great heap of the sand, brought from bays on the Welsh coast, began to grow at the back of the Grove. No one seemed to suspect that it was there for any purpose other than what had been given out.

Lady Arabella, who alone could have guessed, was now so absorbed in her matrimonial pursuit of Edgar Caswall, that she had neither time nor inclination for thought extraneous to this. She had not yet moved from the house, though she had formally handed over the estate.

Adam put up a rough corrugated-iron shed behind the Grove, in which he stored his explosives. All being ready for his great attempt whenever the time should come, he was now content to wait, and, in order to pass the time, interested himself in other things—even in Caswall's great kite, which still flew from the high tower of Castra Regis.

The mound of fine sand grew to proportions so vast as to puzzle the bailiffs and farmers round the Brow. The hour of the intended cataclysm was approaching apace. Adam wished—but in vain—for an opportunity, which would appear to be natural, of visiting Caswall in the turret of Castra Regis. At last, one morning, he met Lady Arabella moving towards the Castle, so he took his courage *à deux mains* and asked to be allowed to accompany her. She was glad, for her own purposes, to comply with his wishes. So together they entered, and found their way to the turret-room. Caswall was much surprised to see Adam come to his house, but lent himself to the task of seeming to be pleased. He played the host so well as to deceive even Adam. They all went out on the turret roof, where he explained to his guests the mechanism for raising and lowering the kite, taking also the opportunity of testing the movements of the multitudes of birds, how they answered almost instantaneously to the lowering or raising of the kite.

As Lady Arabella walked home with Adam from Castra Regis, she asked him if she might make a request. Permission having been accorded, she explained that before she finally left Diana's Grove, where she had lived so long, she had a desire to know the depth of the well-hole. Adam was really happy to meet her wishes, not from any sentiment, but because he wished to give some valid and ostensible reason for examining the passage of the Worm, which would obviate any suspicion resulting from his being on the premises. He brought from London a Kelvin sounding apparatus, with a sufficient length of piano-wire for testing any probable depth. The wire passed easily over the running wheel, and when this was once fixed over the hole, he was satisfied to wait till the most advantageous time for his final experiment.

* * * * *

In the meantime, affairs had been going quietly at Mercy Farm. Lilla, of course, felt lonely in the absence of her cousin, but the even tenor of life went on for her as for others. After the first shock of parting was over, things went back to their accustomed routine. In one respect, however, there was a marked difference. So long as home conditions had remained unchanged, Lilla was content to put ambition far from her, and to settle down to the life which had been hers as long as she could remember. But Mimi's marriage set her thinking; naturally, she came to the conclusion that she too might have a mate. There was not for her much choice—there was little movement in the matrimonial direction at the farmhouse. She did not approve of the personality of Edgar Caswall, and his struggle with Mimi had frightened her; but he was unmistakably an excellent *parti*, much better than she could have any right to expect. This weighs much with a woman, and more particularly one of her class. So, on the whole, she was content to let things take their course, and to abide by the issue.

As time went on, she had reason to believe that things did not point to happiness. She could not shut her eyes to certain disturbing facts, amongst which were the existence of Lady Arabella and her growing intimacy with Edgar Caswall; as well as his own cold and haughty nature, so little in accord with the ardour which is the foundation of a young maid's dreams of happiness. How things would, of necessity, alter if she were to marry, she was afraid to think. All told, the prospect was not happy for her, and she had a secret longing that something might occur to upset the order of things as at present arranged.

When Lilla received a note from Edgar Caswall asking if he might come to tea on the following afternoon, her heart sank within her. If it was only for her father's sake, she must not refuse him or show any disinclination which he might construe into incivility. She missed Mimi more than she could say or even dared to think. Hitherto, she had always looked to her cousin for sympathy, for understanding, for loyal support. Now she and all these things, and a thousand others—gentle, assuring, supporting—were gone. And instead there was a horrible aching void.

For the whole afternoon and evening, and for the following forenoon, poor Lilla's loneliness grew to be a positive agony. For the first time she began to realise the sense of her loss, as though all the previous suffering had been merely a preparation. Everything she looked at, everything she remembered or thought of, became laden with poignant memory. Then on the top of all was a new sense of dread. The reaction from the sense of security, which had surrounded her all her life, to a never-quieted apprehension, was at times almost more than she could bear. It so filled her with fear that she had a haunting feeling that she would as soon die as live. However, whatever might be her own feelings, duty had to be done, and as she had been brought up to consider duty first, she braced herself to go through, to the very best of her ability, what was before her.

Still, the severe and prolonged struggle for self-control told upon Lilla. She looked, as she felt, ill and weak. She was really in a nerveless and prostrate condition, with black circles round her eyes, pale even to her lips, and with an instinctive trembling which she was quite unable to repress. It was for her a sad mischance that Mimi was away, for her love would have seen through all obscuring causes, and have brought to light the girl's unhappy condition of health. Lilla was utterly unable to do anything to escape from the ordeal before her; but her cousin, with the experience of her former struggles with Mr. Caswall and of the condition in which these left her, would have taken steps—even peremptory ones, if necessary—to prevent a repetition.

Edgar arrived punctually to the time appointed by herself. When Lilla, through the great window, saw him approaching the house, her condition of nervous upset was pitiable. She braced herself up, however, and managed to get through the interview in its preliminary stages without any perceptible change in her normal appearance and bearing. It had been to her an added terror that the black shadow of Oolanga, whom she dreaded, would follow hard on his master. A load was lifted from her mind when he did not make his usual stealthy approach. She had also feared, though in lesser degree, lest Lady Arabella should be present to make trouble for her as before.

With a woman's natural forethought in a difficult position, she had provided the furnishing of the tea-table as a subtle indication of the social difference between her and her guest. She had chosen the implements of service, as well as all the provender set forth, of the humblest kind. Instead of arranging the silver teapot and china cups, she had set out an earthen teapot, such as was in common use in the farm kitchen. The same idea was carried out in the cups and saucers of thick homely delft, and in the cream-jug of similar kind. The bread was of simple whole-meal, home-baked. The butter was good, since she had made it herself, while the preserves and honey came from her own garden. Her face beamed with satisfaction when the guest eyed the appointments with a supercilious glance. It was a shock to the poor girl herself, for she enjoyed offering to a guest the little hospitalities possible to her; but that had to be sacrificed with other pleasures.

Caswall's face was more set and iron-clad than ever—his piercing eyes seemed from the very beginning to look her through and through. Her heart quailed when she thought of what would follow—of what would be the end, when this was only the beginning. As some protection, though it could be only of a sentimental kind, she brought from her own room the photographs of Mimi, of her grandfather, and of Adam Salton, whom by now she had grown to look on with reliance, as a brother whom she could trust. She kept the pictures near her heart, to which her hand naturally strayed when her feelings of constraint, distrust, or fear became so poignant as to interfere with the calm which she felt was necessary to help her through her ordeal.

At first Edgar Caswall was courteous and polite, even thoughtful; but after a little while, when he found her resistance to his domination grow, he abandoned all forms of self-control and appeared in the same dominance as he had previously shown. She was prepared, however, for this, both by her former experience and the natural fighting instinct within her. By this means, as the minutes went on, both developed the power and preserved the equality in which they had begun.

Without warning, the psychic battle between the two individualities began afresh. This time both the positive and negative causes were all in favour of the man. The woman was alone and in bad spirits, unsupported; nothing at all was in her favour except the memory of the two victorious contests; whereas the man, though unaided, as before, by either Lady Arabella or Oolanga, was in full strength, well rested, and in flourishing circumstances. It was not, therefore, to be wondered at that his native dominance of character had full opportunity of asserting itself. He began his preliminary stare with a conscious sense of power, and, as it appeared to have immediate effect on the girl, he felt an ever-growing conviction of ultimate victory.

After a little Lilla's resolution began to flag. She felt that thc contest was unequal—that she was unable to put forth her best efforts. As she was an unselfish person, she could not fight so well in her own battle as in that of someone whom she loved and to whom she was devoted. Edgar saw the relaxing of the muscles of face and brow, and the almost collapse of the heavy eyelids which seemed tumbling downward in sleep. Lilla made gallant efforts to brace her dwindling powers, but for a time unsuccessfully. At length there came an interruption, which seemed like a powerful stimulant. Through the wide window she saw Lady Arabella enter the plain gateway of the farm, and advance towards the hall door. She was clad as usual in tight-fitting white, which accentuated her thin, sinuous figure.

The sight did for Lilla what no voluntary effort could have done. Her eyes flashed, and in an instant she felt as though a new life had suddenly developed within her. Lady Arabella's entry, in her usual unconcerned, haughty, supercilious way, heightened the effect, so that when the two stood close to each other battle was joined. Mr. Caswall, too, took new courage from her coming, and all his masterfulness and power came back to him. His looks, intensified, had more obvious effect than had been noticeable that day. Lilla seemed at last overcome by his dominance. Her face became red and pale—violently red and ghastly pale—by rapid turns. Her strength seemed gone. Her knees collapsed, and she was actually sinking on the floor, when to her surprise and joy Mimi came into the room, running hurriedly and breathing heavily.

Lilla rushed to her, and the two clasped hands. With that, a new sense of power, greater than Lilla had ever seen in her, seemed to quicken her cousin. Her hand swept the air in front of Edgar Caswall, seeming to drive him backward more and more by each movement, till at last he seemed to be actually hurled through the door which Mimi's entrance had left open, and fell at full length on the gravel path without.

Then came the final and complete collapse of Lilla, who, without a sound, sank down on the floor.

CHAPTER XXVI—FACE TO FACE

Mimi was greatly distressed when she saw her cousin lying prone. She had a few times in her life seen Lilla on the verge of fainting, but never senseless; and now she was frightened. She threw herself on her knees beside Lilla, and tried, by rubbing her hands and other measures commonly known, to restore her. But all her efforts were unavailing. Lilla still lay white and senseless. In fact, each moment she looked worse; her breast, that had been heaving with the stress, became still, and the pallor of her face grew like marble.

At these succeeding changes Mimi's fright grew, till it altogether mastered her. She succeeded in controlling herself only to the extent that she did not scream.

Lady Arabella had followed Caswall, when he had recovered sufficiently to get up and walk—though stumblingly—in the direction of Castra Regis. When Mimi was quite alone with Lilla and the need for effort had ceased, she felt weak and trembled. In her own mind, she attributed it to a sudden change in the weather—it was momentarily becoming apparent that a storm was coming on.

She raised Lilla's head and laid it on her warm young breast, but all in vain. The cold of the white features thrilled through her, and she utterly collapsed when it was borne in on her that Lilla had passed away.

The dusk gradually deepened and the shades of evening closed in, but Mimi did not seem to notice or to care. She sat on the floor with her arms round the body of the girl whom she loved. Darker and blacker grew the sky as the coming storm and the closing night joined forces. Still she sat on—alone—tearless—unable to think. Mimi did not know how long she sat there. Though it seemed to her that ages had passed, it could not have been more than half-an-hour. She suddenly came to herself, and was surprised to find that her grandfather had not returned. For a while she lay quiet, thinking of the immediate past. Lilla's hand was still in hers, and to her surprise it was still warm. Somehow this helped her consciousness, and without any special act of will she stood up. She lit a lamp and looked at her cousin. There was no doubt that Lilla was dead; but when the lamp-light fell on her eyes, they seemed to look at Mimi with intent—with meaning. In this state of dark isolation a new resolution came to her, and grew and grew until it became a fixed definite purpose. She would face Caswall and call him to account for his murder of Lilla—that was what she called it to herself. She would also take steps—she knew not what or how—to avenge the part taken by Lady Arabella.

In this frame of mind she lit all the lamps in the room, got water and linen from her room, and set about the decent ordering of Lilla's body. This took some time; but when it was finished, she put on her hat and cloak, put out the lights, and set out quietly for Castra Regis.

As Mimi drew near the Castle, she saw no lights except those in and around the tower room. The lights showed her that Mr. Caswall was there, so she entered by the hall door, which as usual was open, and felt her way in the darkness up the staircase to the lobby of the room. The door was ajar, and the light from within showed brilliantly through the opening. She saw Edgar Caswall walking restlessly to and fro in the room, with his hands clasped behind his back. She opened the door without knocking, and walked right into the room. As she entered, he ceased walking, and stared at her in surprise. She made no remark, no comment, but continued the fixed look which he had seen on her entrance.

For a time silence reigned, and the two stood looking fixedly at each other. Mimi was the first to speak.

"You murderer! Lilla is dead!"

"Dead! Good God! When did she die?"

"She died this afternoon, just after you left her."

"Are you sure?"

"Yes—and so are you—or you ought to be. You killed her!"

"I killed her! Be careful what you say!"

"As God sees us, it is true; and you know it. You came to Mercy Farm on purpose to break her—if you could. And the accomplice of your guilt, Lady Arabella March, came for the same purpose."

"Be careful, woman," he said hotly. "Do not use such names in that way, or you shall suffer for it."

"I am suffering for it—have suffered for it—shall suffer for it. Not for speaking the truth as I have done, but because you two, with devilish malignity, did my darling to death. It is you and your accomplice who have to dread punishment, not I."

"Take care!" he said again.

"Oh, I am not afraid of you or your accomplice," she answered spiritedly. "I am content to stand by every word I have said, every act I have done. Moreover, I believe in God's justice. I fear not the grinding of His mills; if necessary I shall set the wheels in motion myself. But you don't care for God, or believe in Him. Your god is your great kite, which cows the birds of a whole district. But be sure that His hand, when it rises, always falls at the appointed time. It may be that your name is being called even at this very moment at the Great Assize. Repent while there is still time. Happy you, if you may be allowed to enter those mighty halls in the company of the pure-souled angel whose voice has only to whisper one word of justice, and you disappear for ever into everlasting torment."

The sudden death of Lilla caused consternation among Mimi's friends and well-wishers. Such a tragedy was totally unexpected, as Adam and Sir Nathaniel had been expecting the White Worm's vengeance to fall upon themselves.

Adam, leaving his wife free to follow her own desires with regard to Lilla and her grandfather, busied himself with filling the well-hole with the fine sand prepared for the purpose, taking care to have lowered at stated intervals quantities of the store of dynamite, so as to be ready for the final explosion. He had under his immediate supervision a corps of workmen, and was assisted by Sir Nathaniel, who had come over for the purpose, and all were now staying at Lesser Hill.

Mr. Salton, too, showed much interest in the job, and was constantly coming in and out, nothing escaping his observation.

Since her marriage to Adam and their coming to stay at Doom Tower, Mimi had been fettered by fear of the horrible monster at Diana's Grove. But now she dreaded it no longer. She accepted the fact of its assuming at will the form of Lady Arabella. She had still to tax and upbraid her for her part in the unhappiness which had been wrought on Lilla, and for her share in causing her death.

One evening, when Mimi entered her own room, she went to the window and threw an eager look round the whole circle of sight. A single glance satisfied her that the White Worm in *propriâ personâ* was not visible. So she sat down in the window-seat and enjoyed the pleasure of a full view, from which she had been so long cut off. The maid who waited on her had told her that Mr. Salton had not yet returned home, so she felt free to enjoy the luxury of peace and quiet.

As she looked out of the window, she saw something thin and white move along the avenue. She thought she recognised the figure of Lady Arabella, and instinctively drew back behind the curtain. When she had ascertained, by peeping out several times, that the lady had not seen her, she watched more carefully, all her instinctive hatred flooding back at the sight of her. Lady Arabella was moving swiftly and stealthily, looking back and around her at intervals, as if she feared to be followed. This gave Mimi an idea that she was up to no good, so she determined to seize the occasion for watching her in more detail.

Hastily putting on a dark cloak and hat, she ran downstairs and out into the avenue. Lady Arabella had moved, but the sheen of her white dress was still to be seen among the young oaks around the gateway. Keeping in shadow, Mimi followed, taking care not to come so close as to awake the other's suspicion, and watched her quarry pass along the road in the direction of Castra Regis.

She followed on steadily through the gloom of the trees, depending on the glint of the white dress to keep her right. The wood began to thicken, and presently, when the road widened and the trees grew farther back, she lost sight of any indication of her whereabouts. Under the present conditions it was impossible for her to do any more, so, after waiting for a while, still hidden in the shadow to see if she could catch another glimpse of the white frock, she determined to go on slowly towards Castra Regis, and trust to the chapter of accidents to pick up the trail again. She went on slowly, taking advantage of every obstacle and shadow to keep herself concealed.

At last she entered on the grounds of the Castle, at a spot from which the windows of the turret were dimly visible, without having seen again any sign of Lady Arabella.

Meanwhile, during most of the time that Mimi Salton had been moving warily along in the gloom, she was in reality being followed by Lady Arabella, who had caught sight of her leaving the house and had never again lost touch with her. It was a case of the hunter being hunted. For a time Mimi's many turnings, with the natural obstacles that were perpetually intervening, caused Lady Arabella some trouble; but when she was close to Castra Regis, there was no more possibility of concealment, and the strange double following went swiftly on.

When she saw Mimi close to the hall door of Castra Regis and ascending the steps, she followed. When Mimi entered the dark hall and felt her way up the staircase, still, as she believed, following Lady Arabella, the latter kept on her way. When they reached the lobby of the turret-rooms, Mimi believed that the object of her search was ahead of her.

Edgar Caswall sat in the gloom of the great room, occasionally stirred to curiosity when the drifting clouds allowed a little light to fall from the storm-swept sky. But nothing really interested him now. Since he had heard of Lilla's death, the gloom of his remorse, emphasised by Mimi's upbraiding, had made more hopeless his cruel, selfish, saturnine nature. He heard no sound, for his normal faculties seemed benumbed.

Mimi, when she came to the door, which stood ajar, gave a light tap. So light was it that it did not reach Caswall's ears. Then, taking her courage in both hands, she boldly pushed the door and entered. As she did so, her heart sank, for now she was face to face with a difficulty which had not, in her state of mental perturbation, occurred to her.

CHAPTER XXVII—ON THE TURRET ROOF

The storm which was coming was already making itself manifest, not only in the wide scope of nature, but in the hearts and natures of human beings. Electrical disturbance in the sky and the air is reproduced in animals of all kinds, and particularly in the highest type of them all—the most receptive—the most electrical. So it was with Edgar Caswall, despite his selfish nature and coldness of blood. So it was with Mimi Salton, despite her unselfish, unchanging devotion for those she loved. So it was even with Lady Arabella, who, under the instincts of a primeval serpent, carried the ever-varying wishes and customs of womanhood, which is always old—and always new.

Edgar, after he had turned his eyes on Mimi, resumed his apathetic position and sullen silence. Mimi quietly took a seat a little way apart, whence she could look on the progress of the coming storm and study its appearance throughout the whole visible circle of the neighbourhood. She was in brighter and better spirits than she had been for many days past. Lady Arabella tried to efface herself behind the now open door.

Without, the clouds grew thicker and blacker as the storm-centre came closer. As yet the forces, from whose linking the lightning springs, were held apart, and the silence of nature proclaimed the calm before the storm. Caswall felt the effect of the gathering electric force. A sort of wild exultation grew upon him, such as he had sometimes felt just before the breaking of a tropical storm. As he became conscious of this, he raised his head and caught sight of Mimi. He was in the grip of an emotion greater than himself; in the mood in which he was he felt the need upon him of doing some desperate deed. He was now absolutely reckless, and as Mimi was associated with him in the memory which drove him on, he wished that she too should be engaged in this enterprise. He had no knowledge of the proximity of Lady Arabella, and thought that he was far removed from all he knew and whose interests he shared—alone with the wild elements, which were being lashed to fury, and with the woman who had struggled with him and vanquished him, and on whom he would shower the full measure of his hate.

The fact was that Edgar Caswall was, if not mad, close to the border-line. Madness in its first stage—monomania—is a lack of proportion. So long as this is general, it is not always noticeable, for the uninspired onlooker is without the necessary means of comparison. But in monomania the errant faculty protrudes itself in a way that may not be denied. It puts aside, obscures, or takes the place of something else—just as the head of a pin placed before the centre of the iris will block out the whole scope of vision. The most usual form of monomania has commonly the same beginning as that from which Edgar Caswall suffered—an over-large idea of self-importance. Alienists, who study the matter exactly, probably know more of human vanity and its effects than do ordinary men. Caswall's mental disturbance was not hard to identify. Every asylum is full of such cases—men and women, who, naturally selfish and egotistical, so appraise to themselves their own importance that every other circumstance in life becomes subservient to it. The disease supplies in itself the material for self-magnification. When the decadence attacks a nature naturally proud and selfish and vain, and lacking both the aptitude and habit of self-restraint, the development of the disease is more swift, and ranges to farther limits. It is such persons who become inbued with the idea that they have the attributes of the Almighty—even that they themselves are the Almighty.

Mimi had a suspicion—or rather, perhaps, an intuition—of the true state of things when she heard him speak, and at the same time noticed the abnormal flush on his face, and his rolling eyes. There was a certain want of fixedness of purpose which she had certainly not noticed before—a quick, spasmodic utterance which belongs rather to the insane than to those of intellectual equilibrium. She was a little frightened, not only by his thoughts, but by his staccato way of expressing them.

Caswall moved to the door leading to the turret stair by which the roof was reached, and spoke in a peremptory way, whose tone alone made her feel defiant.

"Come! I want you."

She instinctively drew back—she was not accustomed to such words, more especially to such a tone. Her answer was indicative of a new contest.

"Why should I go? What for?"

He did not at once reply—another indication of his overwhelming egotism. She repeated her questions; habit reasserted itself, and he spoke without thinking the words which were in his heart.

"I want you, if you will be so good, to come with me to the turret roof. I am much interested in certain experiments with the kite, which would be, if not a pleasure, at least a novel experience to you. You would see something not easily seen otherwise."

"I will come," she answered simply; Edgar moved in the direction of the stair, she following close behind him.

She did not like to be left alone at such a height, in such a place, in the darkness, with a storm about to break. Of himself she had no fear; all that had been seemed to have passed away with her two victories over him in the struggle of wills. Moreover, the more recent apprehension—that of his madness—had also ceased. In the conversation of the last few minutes he seemed so rational, so clear, so unaggressive, that she no longer saw reason for doubt. So satisfied was she that even when he put out a hand to guide her to the steep, narrow stairway, she took it without thought in the most conventional way.

Lady Arabella, crouching in the lobby behind the door, heard every word that had been said, and formed her own opinion of it. It seemed evident to her that there had been some rapprochement between the two who had so lately been hostile to each other, and that made her furiously angry. Mimi was interfering with her plans! She had made certain of her capture of Edgar Caswall, and she could not tolerate even the lightest and most contemptuous fancy on his part which might divert him from the main issue. When she became aware that he wished Mimi to come with him to the roof and that she had acquiesced, her rage got beyond bounds. She became oblivious to any danger there might be in a visit to such an exposed place at such a time, and to all lesser considerations, and made up her mind to forestall them. She stealthily and noiselessly crept through the wicket, and, ascending the stair, stepped out on the roof. It was bitterly cold, for the fierce gusts of the storm which swept round the turret drove in through every unimpeded way, whistling at the sharp corners and singing round the trembling flagstaff. The kite-string and the wire which controlled the runners made a concourse of weird sounds which somehow, perhaps from the violence which surrounded them, acting on their length, resolved themselves into some kind of harmony—a fitting accompaniment to the tragedy which seemed about to begin.

Mimi's heart beat heavily. Just before leaving the turret-chamber she had a shock which she could not shake off. The lights of the room had momentarily revealed to her, as they passed out, Edgar's face, concentrated as it was whenever he intended to use his mesmeric power. Now the black eyebrows made a thick line across his face, under which his eyes shone and glittered ominously. Mimi recognised the danger, and assumed the defiant attitude that had twice already served her so well. She had a fear that the circumstances and the place were against her, and she wanted to be forearmed.

The sky was now somewhat lighter than it had been. Either there was lightning afar off, whose reflections were carried by the rolling clouds, or else the gathered force, though not yet breaking into lightning, had an incipient power of light. It seemed to affect both the man and the woman. Edgar seemed altogether under its influence. His spirits were boisterous, his mind exalted. He was now at his worst; madder than he had been earlier in the night.

Mimi, trying to keep as far from him as possible, moved across the stone floor of the turret roof, and found a niche which concealed her. It was not far from Lady Arabella's place of hiding.

Edgar, left thus alone on the centre of the turret roof, found himself altogether his own master in a way which tended to increase his madness. He knew that Mimi was close at hand, though he had lost sight of her. He spoke loudly, and the sound of his own voice, though it was carried from him on the sweeping wind as fast as the words were spoken, seemed to exalt him still more. Even the raging of the elements round him appeared to add to his exaltation. To him it seemed that these manifestations were obedient to his own will. He had reached the sublime of his madness; he was now in his own mind actually the Almighty, and whatever might happen would be the direct carrying out of his own commands. As he could not see Mimi, nor fix whereabout she was, he shouted loudly:

"Come to me! You shall see now what you are despising, what you are warring against. All that you see is mine—the darkness as well as the light. I tell you that I am greater than any other who is, or was, or shall be. When the Master of Evil took Christ up on a high place and showed Him all the kingdoms of the earth, he was doing what he thought no other could do. He was wrong—he forgot *Me*. I shall send you light, up to the very ramparts of heaven. A light so great that it shall dissipate those black clouds that are rushing up and piling around us. Look! Look! At the very touch of my hand that light springs into being and mounts up—and up—and up!"

He made his way whilst he was speaking to the corner of the turret whence flew the giant kite, and from which the runners ascended. Mimi looked on, appalled and afraid to speak lest she should precipitate some calamity. Within the niche Lady Arabella cowered in a paroxysm of fear.

Edgar took up a small wooden box, through a hole in which the wire of the runner ran. This evidently set some machinery in motion, for a sound as of whirring came. From one side of the box floated what looked like a piece of stiff ribbon, which snapped and crackled as the wind took it. For a few seconds Mimi saw it as it rushed along the sagging line to the kite. When close to it, there was a loud crack, and a sudden light appeared to issue from every chink in the box. Then a quick flame flashed along the snapping ribbon, which glowed with an intense light—a light so great that the whole of the countryside around stood out against the background of black driving clouds. For a few seconds the light remained, then suddenly disappeared in the blackness around. It was simply a magnesium light, which had been fired by the mechanism within the box and carried up to the kite. Edgar was in a state of tumultuous excitement, shouting and yelling at the top of his voice and dancing about like a lunatic.

This was more than Lady Arabella's curious dual nature could stand—the ghoulish element in her rose triumphant, and she abandoned all idea of marriage with Edgar Caswall, gloating fiendishly over the thought of revenge.

She must lure him to the White Worm's hole—but how? She glanced around and quickly made up her mind. The man's whole thoughts were absorbed by his wonderful kite, which he was showing off, in order to fascinate her imaginary rival, Mimi.

On the instant she glided through the darkness to the wheel whereon the string of the kite was wound. With deft fingers she unshipped this, took it with her, reeling out the wire as she went, thus keeping, in a way, in touch with the kite. Then she glided swiftly to the wicket, through which she passed, locking the gate behind her as she went.

Down the turret stair she ran quickly, letting the wire run from the wheel which she carried carefully, and, passing out of the hall door, hurried down the avenue with all her speed. She soon reached her own gate, ran down the avenue, and with her key opened the iron door leading to the well-hole.

She felt well satisfied with herself. All her plans were maturing, or had already matured. The Master of Castra Regis was within her grasp. The woman whose interference she had feared, Lilla Watford, was dead. Truly, all was well, and she felt that she might pause a while and rest. She tore off her clothes, with feverish fingers, and in full enjoyment of her natural freedom, stretched her slim figure in animal delight. Then she lay down on the sofa—to await her victim! Edgar Caswall's life blood would more than satisfy her for some time to come.

CHAPTER XXVIII—THE BREAKING OF THE STORM

When Lady Arabella had crept away in her usual noiseless fashion, the two others remained for a while in their places on the turret roof: Caswall because he had nothing to say, Mimi because she had much to say and wished to put her thoughts in order. For quite a while—which seemed interminable—silence reigned between them. At last Mimi made a beginning—she had made up her mind how to act.

"Mr. Caswall," she said loudly, so as to make sure of being heard through the blustering of the wind and the perpetual cracking of the electricity.

Caswall said something in reply, but his words were carried away on the storm. However, one of her objects was effected: she knew now exactly whereabout on the roof he was. So she moved close to the spot before she spoke again, raising her voice almost to a shout.

"The wicket is shut. Please to open it. I can't get out."

As she spoke, she was quietly fingering a revolver which Adam had given to her in case of emergency and which now lay in her breast. She felt that she was caged like a rat in a trap, but did not mean to be taken at a disadvantage, whatever happened. Caswall also felt trapped, and all the brute in him rose to the emergency. In a voice which was raucous and brutal—much like that which is heard when a wife is being beaten by her husband in a slum—he hissed out, his syllables cutting through the roaring of the storm:

"You came of your own accord—without permission, or even asking it. Now you can stay or go as you choose. But you must manage it for yourself; I'll have nothing to do with it."

Her answer was spoken with dangerous suavity

"I am going. Blame yourself if you do not like the time and manner of it. I daresay Adam—my husband—will have a word to say to you about it!"

"Let him say, and be damned to him, and to you too! I'll show you a light. You shan't be able to say that you could not see what you were doing."

As he spoke, he was lighting another piece of the magnesium ribbon, which made a blinding glare in which everything was plainly discernible, down to the smallest detail. This exactly suited Mimi. She took accurate note of the wicket and its fastening before the glare had died away. She took her revolver out and fired into the lock, which was shivered on the instant, the pieces flying round in all directions, but happily without causing hurt to anyone. Then she pushed the wicket open and ran down the narrow stair, and so to the hall door. Opening this also, she ran down the avenue, never lessening her speed till she stood outside the door of Lesser Hill. The door was opened at once on her ringing.

"Is Mr. Adam Salton in?" she asked.

"He has just come in, a few minutes ago. He has gone up to the study," replied a servant.

She ran upstairs at once and joined him. He seemed relieved when he saw her, but scrutinised her face keenly. He saw that she had been in some concern, so led her over to the sofa in the window and sat down beside her.

"Now, dear, tell me all about it!" he said.

She rushed breathlessly through all the details of her adventure on the turret roof. Adam listened attentively, helping her all he could, and not embarrassing her by any questioning. His thoughtful silence was a great help to her, for it allowed her to collect and organise her thoughts.

"I must go and see Caswall to-morrow, to hear what he has to say on the subject."

"But, dear, for my sake, don't have any quarrel with Mr. Caswall. I have had too much trial and pain lately to wish it increased by any anxiety regarding you."

"You shall not, dear—if I can help it—please God," he said solemnly, and he kissed her.

Then, in order to keep her interested so that she might forget the fears and anxieties that had disturbed her, he began to talk over the details of her adventure, making shrewd comments which attracted and held her attention. Presently, *inter alia*, he said:

"That's a dangerous game Caswall is up to. It seems to me that that young man—though he doesn't appear to know it—is riding for a fall!"

"How, dear? I don't understand."

"Kite flying on a night like this from a place like the tower of Castra Regis is, to say the least of it, dangerous. It is not merely courting death or other accident from lightning, but it is bringing the lightning into where he lives. Every cloud that is blowing up here—and they all make for the highest point—is bound to develop into a flash of lightning. That kite is up in the air and is bound to attract the lightning. Its cord makes a road for it on which to travel to earth. When it does come, it will strike the top of the tower with a weight a hundred times greater than a whole park of artillery, and will knock Castra Regis into pieces. Where it will go after that, no one can tell. If there should be any metal by which it can travel, such will not only point the road, but be the road itself."

"Would it be dangerous to be out in the open air when such a thing is taking place?" she asked.

"No, little woman. It would be the safest possible place—so long as one was not in the line of the electric current."

"Then, do let us go outside. I don't want to run into any foolish danger—or, far more, to ask you to do so. But surely if the open is safest, that is the place for us."

Without another word, she put on again the cloak she had thrown off, and a small, tight-fitting cap. Adam too put on his cap, and, after seeing that his revolver was all right, gave her his hand, and they left the house together.

"I think the best thing we can do will be to go round all the places which are mixed up in this affair."

"All right, dear, I am ready. But, if you don't mind, we might go first to Mercy. I am anxious about grandfather, and we might see that—as yet, at all events—nothing has happened there."

So they went on the high-hung road along the top of the Brow. The wind here was of great force, and made a strange booming noise as it swept high overhead; though not the sound of cracking and tearing as it passed through the woods of high slender trees which grew on either side of the road. Mimi could hardly keep her feet. She was not afraid; but the force to which she was opposed gave her a good excuse to hold on to her husband extra tight.

At Mercy there was no one up—at least, all the lights were out. But to Mimi, accustomed to the nightly routine of the house, there were manifest signs that all was well, except in the little room on the first floor, where the blinds were down. Mimi could not bear to look at that, to think of it. Adam understood her pain, for he had been keenly interested in poor Lilla. He bent over and kissed her, and then took her hand and held it hard. Thus they passed on together, returning to the high road towards Castra Regis.

At the gate of Castra Regis they were extra careful. When drawing near, Adam stumbled upon the wire that Lady Arabella had left trailing on the ground.

Adam drew his breath at this, and spoke in a low, earnest whisper:

"I don't want to frighten you, Mimi dear, but wherever that wire is there is danger."

"Danger! How?"

"That is the track where the lightning will go; at any moment, even now whilst we are speaking and searching, a fearful force may be loosed upon us. Run on, dear; you know the way to where the avenue joins the highroad. If you see any sign of the wire, keep away from it, for God's sake. I shall join you at the gateway."

"Are you going to follow that wire alone?"

"Yes, dear. One is sufficient for that work. I shall not lose a moment till I am with you."

"Adam, when I came with you into the open, my main wish was that we should be together if anything serious happened. You wouldn't deny me that right, would you, dear?"

"No, dear, not that or any right. Thank God that my wife has such a wish. Come; we will go together. We are in the hands of God. If He wishes, we shall be together at the end, whenever or wherever that may be."

They picked up the trail of the wire on the steps and followed it down the avenue, taking care not to touch it with their feet. It was easy enough to follow, for the wire, if not bright, was self-coloured, and showed clearly. They followed it out of the gateway and into the avenue of Diana's Grove.

Here a new gravity clouded Adam's face, though Mimi saw no cause for fresh concern. This was easily enough explained. Adam knew of the explosive works in progress regarding the well-hole, but the matter had been kept from his wife. As they stood near the house, Adam asked Mimi to return to the road, ostensibly to watch the course of the wire, telling her that there might be a branch wire leading somewhere else. She was to search the undergrowth, and if she found it, was to warn him by the Australian native "Coo-ee!"

CHAPTER XXVIII—THE BREAKING OF THE STORM

Whilst they were standing together, there came a blinding flash of lightning, which lit up for several seconds the whole area of earth and sky. It was only the first note of the celestial prelude, for it was followed in quick succession by numerous flashes, whilst the crash and roll of thunder seemed continuous.

Adam, appalled, drew his wife to him and held her close. As far as he could estimate by the interval between lightning and thunder-clap, the heart of the storm was still some distance off, so he felt no present concern for their safety. Still, it was apparent that the course of the storm was moving swiftly in their direction. The lightning flashes came faster and faster and closer together; the thunder-roll was almost continuous, not stopping for a moment—a new crash beginning before the old one had ceased. Adam kept looking up in the direction where the kite strained and struggled at its detaining cord, but, of course, the dull evening light prevented any distinct scrutiny.

At length there came a flash so appallingly bright that in its glare Nature seemed to be standing still. So long did it last, that there was time to distinguish its configuration. It seemed like a mighty tree inverted, pendent from the sky. The whole country around within the angle of vision was lit up till it seemed to glow. Then a broad ribbon of fire seemed to drop on to the tower of Castra Regis just as the thunder crashed. By the glare, Adam could see the tower shake and tremble, and finally fall to pieces like a house of cards. The passing of the lightning left the sky again dark, but a blue flame fell downward from the tower, and, with inconceivable rapidity, running along the ground in the direction of Diana's Grove, reached the dark silent house, which in the instant burst into flame at a hundred different points.

At the same moment there rose from the house a rending, crashing sound of woodwork, broken or thrown about, mixed with a quick scream so appalling that Adam, stout of heart as he undoubtedly was, felt his blood turn into ice. Instinctively, despite the danger and their consciousness of it, husband and wife took hands and listened, trembling. Something was going on close to them, mysterious, terrible, deadly! The shrieks continued, though less sharp in sound, as though muffled. In the midst of them was a terrific explosion, seemingly from deep in the earth.

The flames from Castra Regis and from Diana's Grove made all around almost as light as day, and now that the lightning had ceased to flash, their eyes, unblinded, were able to judge both perspective and detail. The heat of the burning house caused the iron doors to warp and collapse. Seemingly of their own accord, they fell open, and exposed the interior. The Saltons could now look through to the room beyond, where the well-hole yawned, a deep narrow circular chasm. From this the agonised shrieks were rising, growing ever more terrible with each second that passed.

But it was not only the heart-rending sound that almost paralysed poor Mimi with terror. What she saw was sufficient to fill her with evil dreams for the remainder of her life. The whole place looked as if a sea of blood had been beating against it. Each of the explosions from below had thrown out from the well-hole, as if it had been the mouth of a cannon, a mass of fine sand mixed with blood, and a horrible repulsive slime in which were great red masses of rent and torn flesh and fat. As the explosions kept on, more and more of this repulsive mass was shot up, the great bulk of it falling back again. Many of the awful fragments were of something which had lately been alive. They quivered and trembled and writhed as though they were still in torment, a supposition to which the unending scream gave a horrible credence. At moments some mountainous mass of flesh surged up through the narrow orifice, as though forced by a measureless power through an opening infinitely smaller than itself. Some of these fragments were partially covered with white skin as of a human being, and others—the largest and most numerous—with scaled skin as of a gigantic lizard or serpent. Once, in a sort of lull or pause, the seething contents of the hole rose, after the manner of a bubbling spring, and Adam saw part of the thin form of Lady Arabella, forced up to the top amid a mass of blood and slime, and what looked as if it had been the entrails of a monster torn into shreds. Several times some masses of enormous bulk were forced up through the well-hole with inconceivable violence, and, suddenly expanding as they came into larger space, disclosed sections of the White Worm which Adam and Sir Nathaniel had seen looking over the trees with its enormous eyes of emerald-green flickering like great lamps in a gale.

At last the explosive power, which was not yet exhausted, evidently reached the main store of dynamite which had been lowered into the worm hole. The result was appalling. The ground for far around quivered and opened in long deep chasms, whose edges shook and fell in, throwing up clouds of sand which fell back and hissed amongst the rising water. The heavily built house shook to its foundations. Great stones were thrown up as from a volcano, some of them, great masses of hard stone, squared and grooved with implements wrought by human hands, breaking up and splitting in mid air as though riven by some infernal power. Trees near the house—and therefore presumably in some way above the hole, which sent up clouds of dust and steam and fine sand mingled, and which carried an appalling stench which sickened the spectators—were torn up by the roots and hurled into the air. By now, flames were bursting violently from all over the ruins, so dangerously that Adam caught up his wife in his arms, and ran with her from the proximity of the flames.

Then almost as quickly as it had begun, the whole cataclysm ceased, though a deep-down rumbling continued intermittently for some time. Then silence brooded over all—silence so complete that it seemed in itself a sentient thing—silence which seemed like incarnate darkness, and conveyed the same idea to all who came within its radius. To the young people who had suffered the long horror of that awful night, it brought relief—relief from the presence or the fear of all that was horrible—relief which seemed perfected when the red rays of sunrise shot up over the far eastern sea, bringing a promise of a new order of things with the coming day.

* * * * *

His bed saw little of Adam Salton for the remainder of that night. He and Mimi walked hand in hand in the brightening dawn round by the Brow to Castra Regis and on to Lesser Hill. They did so deliberately, in an attempt to think as little as possible of the terrible experiences of the night. The morning was bright and cheerful, as a morning sometimes is after a devastating storm. The clouds, of which there were plenty in evidence, brought no lingering idea of gloom. All nature was bright and joyous, being in striking contrast to the scenes of wreck and devastation, the effects of obliterating fire and lasting ruin.

The only evidence of the once stately pile of Castra Regis and its inhabitants was a shapeless huddle of shattered architecture, dimly seen as the keen breeze swept aside the cloud of acrid smoke which marked the site of the once lordly castle. As for Diana's Grove, they looked in vain for a sign which had a suggestion of permanence.

The oak trees of the Grove were still to be seen—some of them—emerging from a haze of smoke, the great trunks solid and erect as ever, but the larger branches broken and twisted and rent, with bark stripped and chipped, and the smaller branches broken and dishevelled looking from the constant stress and threshing of the storm.

Of the house as such, there was, even at the short distance from which they looked, no trace. Adam resolutely turned his back on the devastation and hurried on. Mimi was not only upset and shocked in many ways, but she was physically "dog tired," and falling asleep on her feet. Adam took her to her room and made her undress and get into bed, taking care that the room was well lighted both by sunshine and lamps. The only obstruction was from a silk curtain, drawn across the window to keep out the glare. He sat beside her, holding her hand, well knowing that the comfort of his presence was the best restorative for her. He stayed with her till sleep had overmastered her wearied body. Then he went softly away. He found his uncle and Sir Nathaniel in the study, having an early cup of tea, amplified to the dimensions of a possible breakfast. Adam explained that he had not told his wife that he was going over the horrible places again, lest it should frighten her, for the rest and sleep in ignorance would help her and make a gap of peacefulness between the horrors.

Sir Nathaniel agreed.

"We know, my boy," he said, "that the unfortunate Lady Arabella is dead, and that the foul carcase of the Worm has been torn to pieces—pray God that its evil soul will never more escape from the nethermost hell."

They visited Diana's Grove first, not only because it was nearer, but also because it was the place where most description was required, and Adam felt that he could tell his story best on the spot. The absolute destruction of the place and everything in it seen in the broad daylight was almost inconceivable. To Sir Nathaniel, it was as a story of horror full and complete. But to Adam it was, as it were, only on the fringes. He knew what was still to be seen when his friends had got over the knowledge of externals. As yet, they had only seen the outside of the house—or rather, where the outside of the house once had been. The great horror lay within. However, age—and the experience of age—counts.

A strange, almost elemental, change in the aspect had taken place in the time which had elapsed since the dawn. It would almost seem as if Nature herself had tried to obliterate the evil signs of what had occurred. True, the utter ruin of the house was made even more manifest in the searching daylight; but the more appalling destruction which lay beneath was not visible. The rent, torn, and dislocated stonework looked worse than before; the upheaved foundations, the piled-up fragments of masonry, the fissures in the torn earth—all were at the worst. The Worm's hole was still evident, a round fissure seemingly leading down into the very bowels of the earth. But all the horrid mass of blood and slime, of torn, evil-smelling flesh and the sickening remnants of violent death, were gone. Either some of the later explosions had thrown up from the deep quantities of water which, though foul and corrupt itself, had still some cleansing power left, or else the writhing mass which stirred from far below had helped to drag down and obliterate the items of horror. A grey dust, partly of fine sand, partly of the waste of the falling ruin, covered everything, and, though ghastly itself, helped to mask something still worse.

After a few minutes of watching, it became apparent to the three men that the turmoil far below had not yet ceased. At short irregular intervals the hell-broth in the hole seemed as if boiling up. It rose and fell again and turned over, showing in fresh form much of the nauseous detail which had been visible earlier. The worst parts were the great masses of the flesh of the monstrous Worm, in all its red and sickening aspect. Such fragments had been bad enough before, but now they were infinitely worse. Corruption comes with startling rapidity to beings whose destruction has been due wholly or in part to lightning—the whole mass seemed to have become all at once corrupt! The whole surface of the fragments, once alive, was covered with insects, worms, and vermin of all kinds. The sight was horrible enough, but, with the awful smell added, was simply unbearable. The Worm's hole appeared to breathe forth death in its most repulsive forms. The friends, with one impulse, moved to the top of the Brow, where a fresh breeze from the sea was blowing up.

At the top of the Brow, beneath them as they looked down, they saw a shining mass of white, which looked strangely out of place amongst such wreckage as they had been viewing. It appeared so strange that Adam suggested trying to find a way down, so that they might see it more closely.

"We need not go down; I know what it is," Sir Nathaniel said. "The explosions of last night have blown off the outside of the cliffs—that which we see is the vast bed of china clay through which the Worm originally found its way down to its lair. I can catch the glint of the water of the deep quags far down below. Well, her ladyship didn't deserve such a funeral—or such a monument."

* * * * *

The horrors of the last few hours had played such havoc with Mimi's nerves, that a change of scene was imperative—if a permanent breakdown was to be avoided.

"I think," said old Mr. Salton, "it is quite time you young people departed for that honeymoon of yours!" There was a twinkle in his eye as he spoke.

Mimi's soft shy glance at her stalwart husband, was sufficient answer.

DRACULA'S GUEST

To MY SON

Preface

A few months before the lamented death of my husband—I might say even as the shadow of death was over him—he planned three series of short stories for publication, and the present volume is one of them. To his original list of stories in this book, I have added an hitherto unpublished episode from *Dracula*. It was originally excised owing to the length of the book, and may prove of interest to the many readers of what is considered my husband's most remarkable work. The other stories have already been published in English and American periodicals. Had my husband lived longer, he might have seen fit to revise this work, which is mainly from the earlier years of his strenuous life. But, as fate has entrusted to me the issuing of it, I consider it fitting and proper to let it go forth practically as it was left by him.

FLORENCE BRAM STOKER

Dracula's Guest

When we started for our drive the sun was shining brightly on Munich, and the air was full of the joyousness of early summer. Just as we were about to depart, Herr Delbrück (the maître d'hôtel of the Quatre Saisons, where I was staying) came down, bareheaded, to the carriage and, after wishing me a pleasant drive, said to the coachman, still holding his hand on the handle of the carriage door:

'Remember you are back by nightfall. The sky looks bright but there is a shiver in the north wind that says there may be a sudden storm. But I am sure you will not be late.' Here he smiled, and added, 'for you know what night it is.'

Johann answered with an emphatic, 'Ja, mein Herr,' and, touching his hat, drove off quickly. When we had cleared the town, I said, after signalling to him to stop:

'Tell me, Johann, what is tonight?'

He crossed himself, as he answered laconically: 'Walpurgis nacht.' Then he took out his watch, a great, old-fashioned German silver thing as big as a turnip, and looked at it, with his eyebrows gathered together and a little impatient shrug of his shoulders. I realised that this was his way of respectfully protesting against the unnecessary delay, and sank back in the carriage, merely motioning him to proceed. He started off rapidly, as if to make up for lost time. Every now and then the horses seemed to throw up their heads and sniffed the air suspiciously. On such occasions I often looked round in alarm. The road was pretty bleak, for we were traversing a sort of high, wind-swept plateau. As we drove, I saw a road that looked but little used, and which seemed to dip through a little, winding valley. It looked so inviting that, even at the risk of offending him, I called Johann to stop—and when he had pulled up, I told him I would like to drive down that road. He made all sorts of excuses, and frequently crossed himself as he spoke. This somewhat piqued my curiosity, so I asked him various questions. He answered fencingly, and repeatedly looked at his watch in protest. Finally I said:

'Well, Johann, I want to go down this road. I shall not ask you to come unless you like; but tell me why you do not like to go, that is all I ask.' For answer he seemed to throw himself off the box, so quickly did he reach the ground. Then he stretched out his hands appealingly to me, and implored me not to go. There was just enough of English mixed with the German for me to understand the drift of his talk. He seemed always just about to tell me something—the very idea of which evidently frightened him; but each time he pulled himself up, saying, as he crossed himself: 'Walpurgis-Nacht!'

I tried to argue with him, but it was difficult to argue with a man when I did not know his language. The advantage certainly rested with him, for although he began to speak in English, of a very crude and broken kind, he always got excited and broke into his native tongue—and every time he did so, he looked at his watch. Then the horses became restless and sniffed the air. At this he grew very pale, and, looking around in a frightened way, he suddenly jumped forward, took them by the bridles and led them on some twenty feet. I followed, and asked why he had done this. For answer he crossed himself, pointed to the spot we had left and drew his carriage in the direction of the other road, indicating a cross, and said, first in German, then in English: 'Buried him—him what killed themselves.'

I remembered the old custom of burying suicides at cross-roads: 'Ah! I see, a suicide. How interesting!' But for the life of me I could not make out why the horses were frightened.

Whilst we were talking, we heard a sort of sound between a yelp and a bark. It was far away; but the horses got very restless, and it took Johann all his time to quiet them. He was pale, and said, 'It sounds like a wolf—but yet there are no wolves here now.'

'No?' I said, questioning him; 'isn't it long since the wolves were so near the city?'

'Long, long,' he answered, 'in the spring and summer; but with the snow the wolves have been here not so long.'

Whilst he was petting the horses and trying to quiet them, dark clouds drifted rapidly across the sky. The sunshine passed away, and a breath of cold wind seemed to drift past us. It was only a breath, however, and more in the nature of a warning than a fact, for the sun came out brightly again. Johann looked under his lifted hand at the horizon and said:

'The storm of snow, he comes before long time.' Then he looked at his watch again, and, straightway holding his reins firmly—for the horses were still pawing the ground restlessly and shaking their heads—he climbed to his box as though the time had come for proceeding on our journey.

I felt a little obstinate and did not at once get into the carriage.

'Tell me,' I said, 'about this place where the road leads,' and I pointed down.

Again he crossed himself and mumbled a prayer, before he answered, 'It is unholy.'

'What is unholy?' I enquired.

'The village.'

'Then there is a village?'

'No, no. No one lives there hundreds of years.' My curiosity was piqued, 'But you said there was a village.'

'There was.'

'Where is it now?'

Whereupon he burst out into a long story in German and English, so mixed up that I could not quite understand exactly what he said, but roughly I gathered that long ago, hundreds of years, men had died there and been buried in their graves; and sounds were heard under the clay, and when the graves were opened, men and women were found rosy with life, and their mouths red with blood. And so, in haste to save their lives (aye, and their souls!—and here he crossed himself) those who were left fled away to other places, where the living lived, and the dead were dead and not—

not something. He was evidently afraid to speak the last words. As he proceeded with his narration, he grew more and more excited. It seemed as if his imagination had got hold of him, and he ended in a perfect paroxysm of fear—white-faced, perspiring, trembling and looking round him, as if expecting that some dreadful presence would manifest itself there in the bright sunshine on the open plain. Finally, in an agony of desperation, he cried:

'Walpurgis nacht!' and pointed to the carriage for me to get in. All my English blood rose at this, and, standing back, I said:

'You are afraid, Johann—you are afraid. Go home; I shall return alone; the walk will do me good.' The carriage door was open. I took from the seat my oak walking-stick—which I always carry on my holiday excursions—and closed the door, pointing back to Munich, and said, 'Go home, Johann—Walpurgis-nacht doesn't concern Englishmen.'

The horses were now more restive than ever, and Johann was trying to hold them in, while excitedly imploring me not to do anything so foolish. I pitied the poor fellow, he was deeply in earnest; but all the same I could not help laughing. His English was quite gone now. In his anxiety he had forgotten that his only means of making me understand was to talk my language, so he jabbered away in his native German. It began to be a little tedious. After giving the direction, 'Home!' I turned to go down the cross-road into the valley.

With a despairing gesture, Johann turned his horses towards Munich. I leaned on my stick and looked after him. He went slowly along the road for a while: then there came over the crest of the hill a man tall and thin. I could see so much in the distance. When he drew near the horses, they began to jump and kick about, then to scream with terror. Johann could not hold them in; they bolted down the road, running away madly. I watched them out of sight, then looked for the stranger, but I found that he, too, was gone.

With a light heart I turned down the side road through the deepening valley to which Johann had objected. There was not the slightest reason, that I could see, for his objection; and I daresay I tramped for a couple of hours without thinking of time or distance, and certainly without seeing a person or a house. So far as the place was concerned, it was desolation, itself. But I did not notice this particularly till, on turning a bend in the road, I came upon a scattered fringe of wood; then I recognised that I had been impressed unconsciously by the desolation of the region through which I had passed.

I sat down to rest myself, and began to look around. It struck me that it was considerably colder than it had been at the commencement of my walk—a sort of sighing sound seemed to be around me, with, now and then, high overhead, a sort of muffled roar. Looking upwards I noticed that great thick clouds were drifting rapidly across the sky from North to South at a great height. There were signs of coming storm in some lofty stratum of the air. I was a little chilly, and, thinking that it was the sitting still after the exercise of walking, I resumed my journey.

The ground I passed over was now much more picturesque. There were no striking objects that the eye might single out; but in all there was a charm of beauty. I took little heed of time and it was only when the deepening twilight forced itself upon me that I began to think of how I should find my way home. The brightness of the day had gone. The air was cold, and the drifting of clouds high overhead was more marked. They were accompanied by a sort of far-away rushing sound, through which seemed to come at intervals that mysterious cry which the driver had said came from a wolf. For a while I hesitated. I had said I would see the deserted village, so on I went, and presently came on a wide stretch of open country, shut in by hills all around. Their sides were covered with trees which spread down to the plain, dotting, in clumps, the gentler slopes and hollows which showed here and there. I followed with my eye the winding of the road, and saw that it curved close to one of the densest of these clumps and was lost behind it.

As I looked there came a cold shiver in the air, and the snow began to fall. I thought of the miles and miles of bleak country I had passed, and then hurried on to seek the shelter of the wood in front. Darker and darker grew the sky, and faster and heavier fell the snow, till the earth before and around me was a glistening white carpet the further edge of which was lost in misty vagueness. The road was here but crude, and when on the level its boundaries were not so marked, as when it passed through the cuttings; and in a little while I found that I must have strayed from it, for I missed underfoot the hard surface, and my feet sank deeper in the grass and moss. Then the wind grew stronger and blew with ever increasing force, till I was fain to run before it. The air became icy-cold, and in spite of my exercise I began to suffer. The snow was now falling so thickly and whirling around me in such rapid eddies that I could hardly keep my eyes open. Every now and then the heavens were torn asunder by vivid lightning, and in the flashes I could see ahead of me a great mass of trees, chiefly yew and cypress all heavily coated with snow.

I was soon amongst the shelter of the trees, and there, in comparative silence, I could hear the rush of the wind high overhead. Presently the blackness of the storm had become merged in the darkness of the night By-and-by the storm seemed to be passing away: it now only came in fierce puffs or blasts. At such moments the weird sound of the wolf appeared to be echoed by many similar sounds around me.

Now and again, through the black mass of drifting cloud, came a straggling ray of moonlight, which lit up the expanse, and showed me that I was at the edge of a dense mass of cypress and yew trees. As the snow had ceased to fall, I walked out from the shelter and began to investigate more closely. It appeared to me that, amongst so many old foundations as I had passed, there might be still standing a house in which, though in ruins, I could find some sort of shelter for a while. As I skirted the edge of the copse, I found that a low wall encircled it, and following this I presently found an opening. Here the cypresses formed an alley leading up to a square mass of some kind of building. Just as I caught sight of this, however, the drifting clouds obscured the moon, and I passed up the path in darkness. The wind must have grown colder, for I felt myself shiver as I walked; but there was hope of shelter, and I groped my way blindly on.

I stopped, for there was a sudden stillness. The storm had passed; and, perhaps in sympathy with nature's silence, my heart seemed to cease to beat. But this was only momentarily; for suddenly the moonlight broke through the clouds, showing me that I was in a graveyard, and that the square object before me was a great massive tomb of marble, as white as the snow that lay on and all around it. With the moonlight there came a fierce sigh of the storm, which appeared to resume its course with a long, low howl, as of many dogs or wolves. I was awed and shocked, and felt the cold perceptibly grow upon me till it seemed to grip me by the heart. Then while the flood of moonlight still fell on the marble tomb, the storm gave further evidence of renewing, as though it was returning on its track. Impelled by some sort of fascination, I approached the sepulchre to see what it was, and why such a thing stood alone in such a place. I walked around it, and read, over the Doric door, in German:

COUNTESS DOLINGEN OF GRATZ
IN STYRIA
SOUGHT AND FOUND DEATH
1801

On the top of the tomb, seemingly driven through the solid marble—for the structure was composed of a few vast blocks of stone—was a great iron spike or stake. On going to the back I saw, graven in great Russian letters:

'The dead travel fast.'

There was something so weird and uncanny about the whole thing that it gave me a turn and made me feel quite faint. I began to wish, for the first time, that I had taken Johann's advice. Here a thought struck me, which came under almost mysterious circumstances and with a terrible shock. This was Walpurgis Night!

Walpurgis Night, when, according to the belief of millions of people, the devil was abroad—when the graves were opened and the dead came forth and walked. When all evil things of earth and air and water held revel. This very place the driver had specially shunned. This was the depopulated village of centuries ago. This was where the suicide lay; and this was the place where I was alone—unmanned, shivering with cold in a shroud of snow with a wild storm gathering again upon me! It took all my philosophy, all the religion I had been taught, all my courage, not to collapse in a paroxysm of fright.

And now a perfect tornado burst upon me. The ground shook as though thousands of horses thundered across it; and this time the storm bore on its icy wings, not snow, but great hailstones which drove with such violence that they might have come from the thongs of Balearic slingers—hailstones that beat down leaf and branch and made the shelter of the cypresses of no more avail than though their stems were standing-corn. At the first I had rushed to the nearest tree; but I was soon fain to leave it and seek the only spot that seemed to afford refuge, the deep Doric doorway of the marble tomb. There, crouching against the massive bronze door, I gained a certain amount of protection from the beating of the hailstones, for now they only drove against me as they ricocheted from the ground and the side of the marble.

As I leaned against the door, it moved slightly and opened inwards. The shelter of even a tomb was welcome in that pitiless tempest, and I was about to enter it when there came a flash of forked-lightning that lit up the whole expanse of the heavens. In the instant, as I am a living man, I saw, as my eyes were turned into the darkness of the tomb, a beautiful woman, with rounded cheeks and red lips, seemingly sleeping on a bier. As the thunder broke overhead, I was grasped as by the hand of a giant and hurled out into the storm. The whole thing was so sudden that, before I could realise the shock, moral as well as physical, I found the hailstones beating me down. At the same time I had a strange, dominating feeling that I was not alone. I looked towards the tomb. Just then there came another blinding flash, which seemed to strike the iron stake that surmounted the tomb and to pour through to the earth, blasting and crumbling the marble, as in a burst of flame. The dead woman rose for a moment of agony, while she was lapped in the flame, and her bitter scream of pain was drowned in the thundercrash. The last thing I heard was this mingling of dreadful sound, as again I was seized in the giant-grasp and dragged away, while the hailstones beat on me, and the air around seemed reverberant with the howling of wolves. The last sight that I remembered was a vague, white, moving mass, as if all the graves around me had sent out the phantoms of their sheeted-dead, and that they were closing in on me through the white cloudiness of the driving hail.

Gradually there came a sort of vague beginning of consciousness; then a sense of weariness that was dreadful. For a time I remembered nothing; but slowly my senses returned. My feet seemed positively racked with pain, yet I could not move them. They seemed to be numbed. There was an icy feeling at the back of my neck and all down my spine, and my ears, like my feet, were dead, yet in torment; but there was in my breast a sense of warmth which was, by comparison, delicious. It was as a nightmare—a physical nightmare, if one may use such an expression; for some heavy weight on my chest made it difficult for me to breathe.

This period of semi-lethargy seemed to remain a long time, and as it faded away I must have slept or swooned. Then came a sort of loathing, like the first stage of seasickness, and a wild desire to be free from something—I knew not what. A vast stillness enveloped me, as though all the world were asleep or dead—only broken by the low panting as of some animal close to me. I felt a warm rasping at my throat, then came a consciousness of the awful truth, which chilled me to the heart and sent the blood surging up through my brain. Some great animal was lying on me and now licking my throat. I feared to stir, for some instinct of prudence bade me lie still; but the brute seemed to realise that there was now some change in me, for it raised its head. Through my eyelashes I saw above me the two great flaming eyes of a gigantic wolf. Its sharp white teeth gleamed in the gaping red mouth, and I could feel its hot breath fierce and acrid upon me.

For another spell of time I remembered no more. Then I became conscious of a low growl, followed by a yelp, renewed again and again. Then, seemingly very far away, I heard a 'Holloa! holloa!' as of many voices calling in unison. Cautiously I raised my head and looked in the direction whence the sound came; but the cemetery blocked my view. The wolf still continued to yelp in a strange way, and a red glare began to move round the grove of cypresses, as though following the sound. As the voices drew closer, the wolf yelped faster and louder. I feared to make either sound or motion. Nearer came the red glow, over the white pall which stretched into the darkness around me. Then all at once from beyond the trees there came at a trot a troop of horsemen bearing torches. The wolf rose from my breast and made for the cemetery. I saw one of the horsemen (soldiers by their caps and their long military cloaks) raise his carbine and take aim. A companion knocked up his arm, and I heard the ball whizz over my head. He had evidently taken my body for that of the wolf. Another sighted the animal as it slunk away, and a shot followed. Then, at a gallop, the troop rode forward—some towards me, others following the wolf as it disappeared amongst the snow-clad cypresses.

As they drew nearer I tried to move, but was powerless, although I could see and hear all that went on around me. Two or three of the soldiers jumped from their horses and knelt beside me. One of them raised my head, and placed his hand over my heart.

'Good news, comrades!' he cried. 'His heart still beats!'

Then some brandy was poured down my throat; it put vigour into me, and I was able to open my eyes fully and look around. Lights and shadows were moving among the trees, and I heard men call to one another. They drew together, uttering frightened exclamations; and the lights flashed as the others came pouring out of the cemetery pell-mell, like men possessed. When the further ones came close to us, those who were around me asked them eagerly:

'Well, have you found him?'

The reply rang out hurriedly:

'No! no! Come away quick—quick! This is no place to stay, and on this of all nights!'

'What was it?' was the question, asked in all manner of keys. The answer came variously and all indefinitely as though the men were moved by some common impulse to speak, yet were restrained by some common fear from giving their thoughts.

'It—it—indeed!' gibbered one, whose wits had plainly given out for the moment.

'A wolf—and yet not a wolf!' another put in shudderingly.

'No use trying for him without the sacred bullet,' a third remarked in a more ordinary manner.

'Serve us right for coming out on this night! Truly we have earned our thousand marks!' were the ejaculations of a fourth.

'There was blood on the broken marble,' another said after a pause—'the lightning never brought that there. And for him—is he safe? Look at his throat! See, comrades, the wolf has been lying on him and keeping his blood warm.'

The officer looked at my throat and replied:

'He is all right; the skin is not pierced. What does it all mean? We should never have found him but for the yelping of the wolf.'

'What became of it?' asked the man who was holding up my head, and who seemed the least panic-stricken of the party, for his hands were steady and without tremor. On his sleeve was the chevron of a petty officer.

'It went to its home,' answered the man, whose long face was pallid, and who actually shook with terror as he glanced around him fearfully. 'There are graves enough there in which it may lie. Come, comrades—come quickly! Let us leave this cursed spot.'

The officer raised me to a sitting posture, as he uttered a word of command; then several men placed me upon a horse. He sprang to the saddle behind me, took me in his arms, gave the word to advance; and, turning our faces away from the cypresses, we rode away in swift, military order.

As yet my tongue refused its office, and I was perforce silent. I must have fallen asleep; for the next thing I remembered was finding myself standing up, supported by a soldier on each side of me. It was almost broad daylight, and to the north a red streak of sunlight was reflected, like a path of blood, over the waste of snow. The officer was telling the men to say nothing of what they had seen, except that they found an English stranger, guarded by a large dog.

'Dog! that was no dog,' cut in the man who had exhibited such fear. 'I think I know a wolf when I see one.'

The young officer answered calmly: 'I said a dog.'

'Dog!' reiterated the other ironically. It was evident that his courage was rising with the sun; and, pointing to me, he said, 'Look at his throat. Is that the work of a dog, master?'

Instinctively I raised my hand to my throat, and as I touched it I cried out in pain. The men crowded round to look, some stooping down from their saddles; and again there came the calm voice of the young officer:

'A dog, as I said. If aught else were said we should only be laughed at.'

I was then mounted behind a trooper, and we rode on into the suburbs of Munich. Here we came across a stray carriage, into which I was lifted, and it was driven off to the Quatre Saisons—the young officer accompanying me, whilst a trooper followed with his horse, and the others rode off to their barracks.

When we arrived, Herr Delbrück rushed so quickly down the steps to meet me, that it was apparent he had been watching within. Taking me by both hands he solicitously led me in. The officer saluted me and was turning to withdraw, when I recognised his purpose, and insisted that he should come to my rooms. Over a glass of wine I warmly thanked him and his brave comrades for saving me. He replied simply that he was more than glad, and that Herr Delbrück had at the first taken steps to make all the searching party pleased; at which ambiguous utterance the maître d'hôtel smiled, while the officer pleaded duty and withdrew.

'But Herr Delbrück,' I enquired, 'how and why was it that the soldiers searched for me?'

He shrugged his shoulders, as if in depreciation of his own deed, as he replied:

'I was so fortunate as to obtain leave from the commander of the regiment in which I served, to ask for volunteers.'

'But how did you know I was lost?' I asked.

'The driver came hither with the remains of his carriage, which had been upset when the horses ran away.'

'But surely you would not send a search-party of soldiers merely on this account?'

'Oh, no!' he answered; 'but even before the coachman arrived, I had this telegram from the Boyar whose guest you are,' and he took from his pocket a telegram which he handed to me, and I read:

Bistritz.

> Be careful of my guest—his safety is most precious to me. Should aught happen to him, or if he be missed, spare nothing to find him and ensure his safety. He is English and therefore adventurous. There are often dangers from snow and wolves and night. Lose not a moment if you suspect harm to him. I answer your zeal with my fortune.—*Dracula.*

As I held the telegram in my hand, the room seemed to whirl around me; and, if the attentive maître d'hôtel had not caught me, I think I should have fallen. There was something so strange in all this, something so weird and impossible to imagine, that there grew on me a sense of my being in some way the sport of opposite forces—the mere vague idea of which seemed in a way to paralyse me. I was certainly under some form of mysterious protection. From a distant country had come, in the very nick of time, a message that took me out of the danger of the snow-sleep and the jaws of the wolf.

The Judge's House

When the time for his examination drew near Malcolm Malcolmson made up his mind to go somewhere to read by himself. He feared the attractions of the seaside, and also he feared completely rural isolation, for of old he knew it charms, and so he determined to find some unpretentious little town where there would be nothing to distract him. He refrained from asking suggestions from any of his friends, for he argued that each would recommend some place of which he had knowledge, and where he had already acquaintances. As Malcolmson wished to avoid friends he had no wish to encumber himself with the attention of friends' friends, and so he determined to look out for a place for himself. He packed a portmanteau with some clothes and all the books he required, and then took ticket for the first name on the local time-table which he did not know.

When at the end of three hours' journey he alighted at Benchurch, he felt satisfied that he had so far obliterated his tracks as to be sure of having a peaceful opportunity of pursuing his studies. He went straight to the one inn which the sleepy little place contained, and put up for the night. Benchurch was a market town, and once in three weeks was crowded to excess, but for the remainder of the twenty-one days it was as attractive as a desert, Malcolmson looked around the day after his arrival to try to find quarters more isolated than even so quiet an inn as 'The Good Traveller' afforded. There was only one place which took his fancy, and it certainly satisfied his wildest ideas regarding quiet; in fact, quiet was not the proper word to apply to it—desolation was the only term conveying any suitable idea of its isolation. It was an old rambling, heavy-built house of the Jacobean style, with heavy gables and windows, unusually small, and set higher than was customary in such houses, and was surrounded with a high brick wall massively built. Indeed, on examination, it looked more like a fortified house than an ordinary dwelling. But all these things pleased Malcolmson. 'Here,' he thought, 'is the very spot I have been looking for, and if I can get opportunity of using it I shall be happy.' His joy was increased when he realised beyond doubt that it was not at present inhabited.

From the post-office he got the name of the agent, who was rarely surprised at the application to rent a part of the old house. Mr. Carnford, the local lawyer and agent, was a genial old gentleman, and frankly confessed his delight at anyone being willing to live in the house.

'To tell you the truth,' said he, 'I should be only too happy, on behalf of the owners, to let anyone have the house rent free for a term of years if only to accustom the people here to see it inhabited. It has been so long empty that some kind of absurd prejudice has grown up about it, and this can be best put down by its occupation—if only,' he added with a sly glance at Malcolmson, 'by a scholar like yourself, who wants its quiet for a time.'

Malcolmson thought it needless to ask the agent about the 'absurd prejudice'; he knew he would get more information, if he should require it, on that subject from other quarters. He paid his three months' rent, got a receipt, and the name of an old woman who would probably undertake to 'do' for him, and came away with the keys in his pocket. He then went to the landlady of the inn, who was a cheerful and most kindly person, and asked her advice as to such stores and provisions as he would be likely to require. She threw up her hands in amazement when he told her where he was going to settle himself.

'Not in the Judge's House!' she said, and grew pale as she spoke. He explained the locality of the house, saying that he did not know its name. When he had finished she answered:

'Aye, sure enough—sure enough the very place! It is the Judge's House sure enough.' He asked her to tell him about the place, why so called, and what there was against it. She told him that it was so called locally because it had been many years before—how long she could not say, as she was herself from another part of the country, but she thought it must have been a hundred years or more—the abode of a judge who was held in great terror on account of his harsh sentences and his hostility to prisoners at Assizes. As to what there was against the house itself she could not tell. She had often asked, but no one could inform her; but there was a general feeling that there was *something*, and for her own part she would not take all the money in Drinkwater's Bank and stay in the house an hour by herself. Then she apologised to Malcolmson for her disturbing talk.

'It is too bad of me, sir, and you—and a young gentlemen, too—if you will pardon me saying it, going to live there all alone. If you were my boy—and you'll excuse me for saying it—you wouldn't sleep there a night, not if I had to go there myself and pull the big alarm bell that's on the roof!' The good creature was so manifestly in earnest, and was so kindly in her intentions, that Malcolmson, although amused, was touched. He told her kindly how much he appreciated her interest in him, and added:

'But, my dear Mrs. Witham, indeed you need not be concerned about me! A man who is reading for the Mathematical Tripos has too much to think of to be disturbed by any of these mysterious "somethings", and his work is of too exact and prosaic a kind to allow of his having any corner in his mind for mysteries of any kind. Harmonical Progression, Permutations and Combinations, and Elliptic Functions have sufficient mysteries for me!' Mrs. Witham kindly undertook to see after his commissions, and he went himself to look for the old woman who had been recommended to him. When he returned to the Judge's House with her, after an interval of a couple of hours, he found Mrs. Witham herself waiting with several men and boys carrying parcels, and an upholsterer's man with a bed in a car, for she said, though tables and chairs might be all very well, a bed that hadn't been aired for mayhap fifty years was not proper for young bones to lie on. She was evidently curious to see the inside of the house; and though manifestly so afraid of the 'somethings' that at the slightest sound she clutched on to Malcolmson, whom she never left for a moment, went over the whole place.

After his examination of the house, Malcolmson decided to take up his abode in the great dining-room, which was big enough to serve for all his requirements; and Mrs. Witham, with the aid of the charwoman, Mrs. Dempster, proceeded to arrange matters. When the hampers were brought in and unpacked, Malcolmson saw that with much kind forethought she had sent from her own kitchen sufficient provisions to last for a few days. Before going she expressed all sorts of kind wishes; and at the door turned and said:

'And perhaps, sir, as the room is big and draughty it might be well to have one of those big screens put round your bed at night—though, truth to tell, I would die myself if I were to be so shut in with all kinds of—of "things", that put their heads round the sides, or over the top, and look on me!' The image which she had called up was too much for her nerves, and she fled incontinently.

Mrs. Dempster sniffed in a superior manner as the landlady disappeared, and remarked that for her own part she wasn't afraid of all the bogies in the kingdom.

'I'll tell you what it is, sir,' she said; 'bogies is all kinds and sorts of things—except bogies! Rats and mice, and beetles; and creaky doors, and loose slates, and broken panes, and stiff drawer handles, that stay out when you pull them and then fall down in the middle of the night. Look at the wainscot of the room! It is old—hundreds of years old! Do you think there's no rats and beetles there! And do you imagine, sir, that you won't see none of them? Rats is bogies, I tell you, and bogies is rats; and don't you get to think anything else!'

'Mrs. Dempster,' said Malcolmson gravely, making her a polite bow, 'you know more than a Senior Wrangler! And let me say, that, as a mark of esteem for your indubitable soundness of head and heart, I shall, when I go, give you possession of this house, and let you stay here by yourself for the last two months of my tenancy, for four weeks will serve my purpose.'

'Thank you kindly, sir!' she answered, 'but I couldn't sleep away from home a night. I am in Greenhow's Charity, and if I slept a night away from my rooms I should lose all I have got to live on. The rules is very strict; and there's too many watching for a vacancy for me to run any risks in the matter. Only for that, sir, I'd gladly come here and attend on you altogether during your stay.'

'My good woman,' said Malcolmson hastily, 'I have come here on purpose to obtain solitude; and believe me that I am grateful to the late Greenhow for having so organised his admirable charity—whatever it is—that I am perforce denied the opportunity of suffering from such a form of temptation! Saint Anthony himself could not be more rigid on the point!'

The old woman laughed harshly. 'Ah, you young gentlemen,' she said, 'you don't fear for naught; and belike you'll get all the solitude you want here.' She set to work with her cleaning; and by nightfall, when Malcolmson returned from his walk—he always had one of his books to study as he walked—he found the room swept and tidied, a fire burning in the old hearth, the lamp lit, and the table spread for supper with Mrs. Witham's excellent fare. 'This is comfort, indeed,' he said, as he rubbed his hands.

When he had finished his supper, and lifted the tray to the other end of the great oak dining-table, he got out his books again, put fresh wood on the fire, trimmed his lamp, and set himself down to a spell of real hard work. He went on without pause till about eleven o'clock, when he knocked off for a bit to fix his fire and lamp, and to make himself a cup of tea. He had always been a tea-drinker, and during his college life had sat late at work and had taken tea late. The rest was a great luxury to him, and he enjoyed it with a sense of delicious, voluptuous ease. The renewed fire leaped and sparkled, and threw quaint shadows through the great old room; and as he sipped his hot tea he revelled in the sense of isolation from his kind. Then it was that he began to notice for the first time what a noise the rats were making.

'Surely,' he thought, 'they cannot have been at it all the time I was reading. Had they been, I must have noticed it!' Presently, when the noise increased, he satisfied himself that it was really new. It was evident that at first the rats had been frightened at the presence of a stranger, and the light of fire and lamp; but that as the time went on they had grown bolder and were now disporting themselves as was their wont.

How busy they were! and hark to the strange noises! Up and down behind the old wainscot, over the ceiling and under the floor they raced, and gnawed, and scratched! Malcolmson smiled to himself as he recalled to mind the saying of Mrs. Dempster, 'Bogies is rats, and rats is bogies!' The tea began to have its effect of intellectual and nervous stimulus, he saw with joy another long spell of work to be done before the night was past, and in the sense of security which it gave him, he allowed himself the luxury of a good look round the room. He took his lamp in one hand, and went all around, wondering that so quaint and beautiful an old house had been so long neglected. The carving of the oak on the panels of the wainscot was fine, and on and round the doors and windows it was beautiful and of rare merit. There were some old pictures on the walls, but they were coated so thick with dust and dirt that he could not distinguish any detail of them, though he held his lamp as high as he could over his head. Here and there as he went round he saw some crack or hole blocked for a moment by the face of a rat with its bright eyes glittering in the light, but in an instant it was gone, and a squeak and a scamper followed. The thing that most struck him, however, was the rope of the great alarm bell on the roof, which hung down in a corner of the room on the right-hand side of the fireplace. He pulled up close to the hearth a great high-backed carved oak chair, and sat down to his last cup of tea. When this was done he made up the fire, and went back to his work, sitting at the corner of the table, having the fire to his left. For a little while the rats disturbed him somewhat with their perpetual scampering, but he got accustomed to the noise as one does to the ticking of a clock or to the roar of moving water; and he became so immersed in his work that everything in the world, except the problem which he was trying to solve, passed away from him.

He suddenly looked up, his problem was still unsolved, and there was in the air that sense of the hour before the dawn, which is so dread to doubtful life. The noise of the rats had ceased. Indeed it seemed to him that it must have ceased but lately and that it was the sudden cessation which had disturbed him. The fire had fallen low, but still it threw out a deep red glow. As he looked he started in spite of his *sang froid*.

There on the great high-backed carved oak chair by the right side of the fireplace sat an enormous rat, steadily glaring at him with baleful eyes. He made a motion to it as though to hunt it away, but it did not stir. Then he made the motion of throwing something. Still it did not stir, but showed its great white teeth angrily, and its cruel eyes shone in the lamplight with an added vindictiveness.

Malcolmson felt amazed, and seizing the poker from the hearth ran at it to kill it. Before, however, he could strike it, the rat, with a squeak that sounded like the concentration of hate, jumped upon the floor, and, running up the rope of the alarm bell, disappeared in the darkness beyond the range of the green-shaded lamp. Instantly, strange to say, the noisy scampering of the rats in the wainscot began again.

By this time Malcolmson's mind was quite off the problem; and as a shrill cock-crow outside told him of the approach of morning, he went to bed and to sleep.

He slept so sound that he was not even waked by Mrs. Dempster coming in to make up his room. It was only when she had tidied up the place and got his breakfast ready and tapped on the screen which closed in his bed that he woke. He was a little tired still after his night's hard work, but a strong cup of tea soon freshened him up and, taking his book, he went out for his morning walk, bringing with him a few sandwiches lest he should not care to return till dinner time. He found a quiet walk between high elms some way outside the town, and here he spent the greater part of the day studying his Laplace. On his return he looked in to see Mrs. Witham and to thank her for her kindness. When she saw him coming through the diamond-paned bay window of her sanctum she came out to meet him and asked him in. She looked at him searchingly and shook her head as she said:

'You must not overdo it, sir. You are paler this morning than you should be. Too late hours and too hard work on the brain isn't good for any man! But tell me, sir, how did you pass the night? Well, I hope? But my heart! sir, I was glad when Mrs. Dempster told me this morning that you were all right and sleeping sound when she went in.'

'Oh, I was all right,' he answered smiling, 'the "somethings" didn't worry me, as yet. Only the rats; and they had a circus, I tell you, all over the place. There was one wicked looking old devil that sat up on my own chair by the fire, and wouldn't go till I took the poker to him, and then he ran up the rope of the alarm bell and got to somewhere up the wall or the ceiling—I couldn't see where, it was so dark.'

'Mercy on us,' said Mrs. Witham, 'an old devil, and sitting on a chair by the fireside! Take care, sir! take care! There's many a true word spoken in jest.'

'How do you mean? Pon my word I don't understand.'

'An old devil! The old devil, perhaps. There! sir, you needn't laugh,' for Malcolmson had broken into a hearty peal. 'You young folks thinks it easy to laugh at things that makes older ones shudder. Never mind, sir! never mind! Please God, you'll laugh all the time. It's what I wish you myself!' and the good lady beamed all over in sympathy with his enjoyment, her fears gone for a moment.

'Oh, forgive me!' said Malcolmson presently. 'Don't think me rude; but the idea was too much for me—that the old devil himself was on the chair last night!' And at the thought he laughed again. Then he went home to dinner.

This evening the scampering of the rats began earlier; indeed it had been going on before his arrival, and only ceased whilst his presence by its freshness disturbed them. After dinner he sat by the fire for a while and had a smoke; and then, having cleared his table, began to work as before. Tonight the rats disturbed him more than they had done on the previous night. How they scampered up and down and under and over! How they squeaked, and scratched, and gnawed! How they, getting bolder by degrees, came to the mouths of their holes and to the chinks and cracks and crannies in the wainscoting till their eyes shone like tiny lamps as the firelight rose and fell. But to him, now doubtless accustomed to them, their eyes were not wicked; only their playfulness touched him. Sometimes the boldest of them made sallies out on the floor or along the mouldings of the wainscot. Now and again as they disturbed him Malcolmson made a sound to frighten them, smiting the table with his hand or giving a fierce 'Hsh, hsh,' so that they fled straightway to their holes.

And so the early part of the night wore on; and despite the noise Malcolmson got more and more immersed in his work.

All at once he stopped, as on the previous night, being overcome by a sudden sense of silence. There was not the faintest sound of gnaw, or scratch, or squeak. The silence was as of the grave. He remembered the odd occurrence of the previous night, and instinctively he looked at the chair standing close by the fireside. And then a very odd sensation thrilled through him.

There, on the great old high-backed carved oak chair beside the fireplace sat the same enormous rat, steadily glaring at him with baleful eyes.

Instinctively he took the nearest thing to his hand, a book of logarithms, and flung it at it. The book was badly aimed and the rat did not stir, so again the poker performance of the previous night was repeated; and again the rat, being closely pursued, fled up the rope of the alarm bell. Strangely too, the departure of this rat was instantly followed by the renewal of the noise made by the general rat community. On this occasion, as on the previous one, Malcolmson could not see at what part of the room the rat disappeared, for the green shade of his lamp left the upper part of the room in darkness, and the fire had burned low.

On looking at his watch he found it was close on midnight; and, not sorry for the *divertissement*, he made up his fire and made himself his nightly pot of tea. He had got through a good spell of work, and thought himself entitled to a cigarette; and so he sat on the great oak chair before the fire and enjoyed it. Whilst smoking he began to think that he would like to know where the rat disappeared to, for he had certain ideas for the morrow not entirely disconnected with a rat-trap. Accordingly he lit another lamp and placed it so that it would shine well into the right-hand corner of the wall by the fireplace. Then he got all the books he had with him, and placed them handy to throw at the vermin. Finally he lifted the rope of the alarm bell and placed the end of it on the table, fixing the extreme end under the lamp. As he handled it he could not help noticing how pliable it was, especially for so strong a rope, and one not in use. 'You could hang a man with it,' he thought to himself. When his preparations were made he looked around, and said complacently:

'There now, my friend, I think we shall learn something of you this time!' He began his work again, and though as before somewhat disturbed at first by the noise of the rats, soon lost himself in his propositions and problems.

Again he was called to his immediate surroundings suddenly. This time it might not have been the sudden silence only which took his attention; there was a slight movement of the rope, and the lamp moved. Without stirring, he looked to see if his pile of books was within range, and then cast his eye along the rope. As he looked he saw the great rat drop from the rope on the oak arm-chair and sit there glaring at him. He raised a book in his right hand, and taking careful aim, flung it at the rat. The latter, with a quick movement, sprang aside and dodged the missile. He then took another book, and a third, and flung them one after another at the rat, but each time unsuccessfully. At last, as he stood with a book poised in his hand to throw, the rat squeaked and seemed afraid. This made Malcolmson more than ever eager to strike, and the book flew and struck the rat a resounding blow. It gave a terrified squeak, and turning on his pursuer a look of terrible malevolence, ran up the chair-back and made a great jump to the rope of the alarm bell and ran up it like lightning. The lamp rocked under the sudden strain, but it was a heavy one and did not topple over. Malcolmson kept his eyes on the rat, and saw it by the light of the second lamp leap to a moulding of the wainscot and disappear through a hole in one of the great pictures which hung on the wall, obscured and invisible through its coating of dirt and dust.

'I shall look up my friend's habitation in the morning,' said the student, as he went over to collect his books. 'The third picture from the fireplace; I shall not forget.' He picked up the books one by one, commenting on them as he lifted them. '*Conic Sections* he does not mind, nor *Cycloidal Oscillations*, nor the *Principia*, nor *Quaternions*, nor *Thermodynamics*. Now for the book that fetched him!' Malcolmson took it up and looked at it. As he did so he started, and a sudden pallor overspread his face. He looked round uneasily and shivered slightly, as he murmured to himself:

'The Bible my mother gave me! What an odd coincidence.' He sat down to work again, and the rats in the wainscot renewed their gambols. They did not disturb him, however; somehow their presence gave him a sense of companionship. But he could not attend to his work, and after striving to master the subject on which he was engaged gave it up in despair, and went to bed as the first streak of dawn stole in through the eastern window.

He slept heavily but uneasily, and dreamed much; and when Mrs. Dempster woke him late in the morning he seemed ill at ease, and for a few minutes did not seem to realise exactly where he was. His first request rather surprised the servant.

'Mrs. Dempster, when I am out to-day I wish you would get the steps and dust or wash those pictures—specially that one the third from the fireplace—I want to see what they are.'

Late in the afternoon Malcolmson worked at his books in the shaded walk, and the cheerfulness of the previous day came back to him as the day wore on, and he found that his reading was progressing well. He had worked out to a satisfactory conclusion all the problems which had as yet baffled him, and it was in a state of jubilation that he paid a visit to Mrs. Witham at 'The Good Traveller'. He found a stranger in the cosy sitting-room with the landlady, who was introduced to him as Dr. Thornhill. She was not quite at ease, and this, combined with the doctor's plunging at once into a series of questions, made Malcolmson come to the conclusion that his presence was not an accident, so without preliminary he said:

'Dr. Thornhill, I shall with pleasure answer you any question you may choose to ask me if you will answer me one question first.'

The doctor seemed surprised, but he smiled and answered at once, 'Done! What is it?'

'Did Mrs. Witham ask you to come here and see me and advise me?'

Dr. Thornhill for a moment was taken aback, and Mrs. Witham got fiery red and turned away; but the doctor was a frank and ready man, and he answered at once and openly.

'She did: but she didn't intend you to know it. I suppose it was my clumsy haste that made you suspect. She told me that she did not like the idea of your being in that house all by yourself, and that she thought you took too much strong tea. In fact, she wants me to advise you if possible to give up the tea and the very late hours. I was a keen student in my time, so I suppose I may take the liberty of a college man, and without offence, advise you not quite as a stranger.'

Malcolmson with a bright smile held out his hand. 'Shake! as they say in America,' he said. 'I must thank you for your kindness and Mrs. Witham too, and your kindness deserves a return on my part. I promise to take no more strong tea—no tea at all till you let me—and I shall go to bed tonight at one o'clock at latest. Will that do?'

'Capital,' said the doctor. 'Now tell us all that you noticed in the old house,' and so Malcolmson then and there told in minute detail all that had happened in the last two nights. He was interrupted every now and then by some exclamation from Mrs. Witham, till finally when he told of the episode of the Bible the landlady's pent-up emotions found vent in a shriek; and it was not till a stiff glass of brandy and water had been administered that she grew composed again. Dr. Thornhill listened with a face of growing gravity, and when the narrative was complete and Mrs. Witham had been restored he asked:

'The rat always went up the rope of the alarm bell?'

'Always.'

'I suppose you know,' said the Doctor after a pause, 'what the rope is?'

'No!'

'It is,' said the Doctor slowly, 'the very rope which the hangman used for all the victims of the Judge's judicial rancour!' Here he was interrupted by another scream from Mrs. Witham, and steps had to be taken for her recovery. Malcolmson having looked at his watch, and found that it was close to his dinner hour, had gone home before her complete recovery.

When Mrs. Witham was herself again she almost assailed the Doctor with angry questions as to what he meant by putting such horrible ideas into the poor young man's mind. 'He has quite enough there already to upset him,' she added. Dr. Thornhill replied:

'My dear madam, I had a distinct purpose in it! I wanted to draw his attention to the bell rope, and to fix it there. It may be that he is in a highly overwrought state, and has been studying too much, although I am bound to say that he seems as sound and healthy a young man, mentally and bodily, as ever I saw—but then the rats—and that suggestion of the devil.' The doctor shook his head and went on. 'I would have offered to go and stay the first night with him but that I felt sure it would have been a cause of offence. He may get in the night some strange fright or hallucination; and if he does I want him to pull that rope. All alone as he is it will give us warning, and we may reach him in time to be of service. I shall be sitting up pretty late tonight and shall keep my ears open. Do not be alarmed if Benchurch gets a surprise before morning.'

'Oh, Doctor, what do you mean? What do you mean?'

'I mean this; that possibly—nay, more probably—we shall hear the great alarm bell from the Judge's House tonight,' and the Doctor made about as effective an exit as could be thought of.

When Malcolmson arrived home he found that it was a little after his usual time, and Mrs. Dempster had gone away—the rules of Greenhow's Charity were not to be neglected. He was glad to see that the place was bright and tidy with a cheerful fire and a well-trimmed lamp. The evening was colder than might have been expected in April, and a heavy wind was blowing with such rapidly-increasing strength that there was every promise of a storm during the night. For a few minutes after his entrance the noise of the rats ceased; but so soon as they became accustomed to his presence they began again. He was glad to hear them, for he felt once more the feeling of companionship in their noise, and his mind ran back to the strange fact that they only ceased to manifest themselves when that other—the great rat with the baleful eyes—came upon the scene. The reading-lamp only was lit and its green shade kept the ceiling and the upper part of the room in darkness, so that the cheerful light from the hearth spreading over the floor and shining on the white cloth laid over the end of the table was warm and cheery. Malcolmson sat down to his dinner with a good appetite and a buoyant spirit. After his dinner and a cigarette he sat steadily down to work, determined not to let anything disturb him, for he remembered his promise to the doctor, and made up his mind to make the best of the time at his disposal.

For an hour or so he worked all right, and then his thoughts began to wander from his books. The actual circumstances around him, the calls on his physical attention, and his nervous susceptibility were not to be denied. By this time the wind had become a gale, and the gale a storm. The old house, solid though it was, seemed to shake to its foundations, and the storm roared and raged through its many chimneys and its queer old gables, producing strange, unearthly sounds in the empty rooms and corridors. Even the great alarm bell on the roof must have felt the force of the wind, for the rope rose and fell slightly, as though the bell were moved a little from time to time and the limber rope fell on the oak floor with a hard and hollow sound.

As Malcolmson listened to it he bethought himself of the doctor's words, 'It is the rope which the hangman used for the victims of the Judge's judicial rancour,' and he went over to the corner of the fireplace and took it in his hand to look at it. There seemed a sort of deadly interest in it, and as he stood there he lost himself for a moment in speculation as to who these victims were, and the grim wish of the Judge to have such a ghastly relic ever under his eyes. As he stood there the swaying of the bell on the roof still lifted the rope now and again; but presently there came a new sensation—a sort of tremor in the rope, as though something was moving along it.

Looking up instinctively Malcolmson saw the great rat coming slowly down towards him, glaring at him steadily. He dropped the rope and started back with a muttered curse, and the rat turning ran up the rope again and disappeared, and at the same instant Malcolmson became conscious that the noise of the rats, which had ceased for a while, began again.

All this set him thinking, and it occurred to him that he had not investigated the lair of the rat or looked at the pictures, as he had intended. He lit the other lamp without the shade, and, holding it up went and stood opposite the third picture from the fireplace on the right-hand side where he had seen the rat disappear on the previous night.

At the first glance he started back so suddenly that he almost dropped the lamp, and a deadly pallor overspread his face. His knees shook, and heavy drops of sweat came on his forehead, and he trembled like an aspen. But he was young and plucky, and pulled himself together, and after the pause of a few seconds stepped forward again, raised the lamp, and examined the picture which had been dusted and washed, and now stood out clearly.

It was of a judge dressed in his robes of scarlet and ermine. His face was strong and merciless, evil, crafty, and vindictive, with a sensual mouth, hooked nose of ruddy colour, and shaped like the beak of a bird of prey. The rest of the face was of a cadaverous colour. The eyes were of peculiar brilliance and with a terribly malignant expression. As he looked at them, Malcolmson grew cold, for he saw there the very counterpart of the eyes of the great rat. The lamp almost fell from his hand, he saw the rat with its baleful eyes peering out through the hole in the corner of the picture, and noted the sudden cessation of the noise of the other rats. However, he pulled himself together, and went on with his examination of the picture.

The Judge was seated in a great high-backed carved oak chair, on the right-hand side of a great stone fireplace where, in the corner, a rope hung down from the ceiling, its end lying coiled on the floor. With a feeling of something like horror, Malcolmson recognised the scene of the room as it stood, and gazed around him in an awestruck manner as though he expected to find some strange presence behind him. Then he looked over to the corner of the fireplace—and with a loud cry he let the lamp fall from his hand.

There, in the Judge's arm-chair, with the rope hanging behind, sat the rat with the Judge's baleful eyes, now intensified and with a fiendish leer. Save for the howling of the storm without there was silence.

The fallen lamp recalled Malcolmson to himself. Fortunately it was of metal, and so the oil was not spilt. However, the practical need of attending to it settled at once his nervous apprehensions. When he had turned it out, he wiped his brow and thought for a moment.

'This will not do,' he said to himself. 'If I go on like this I shall become a crazy fool. This must stop! I promised the doctor I would not take tea. Faith, he was pretty right! My nerves must have been getting into a queer state. Funny I did not notice it. I never felt better in my life. However, it is all right now, and I shall not be such a fool again.'

Then he mixed himself a good stiff glass of brandy and water and resolutely sat down to his work.

It was nearly an hour when he looked up from his book, disturbed by the sudden stillness. Without, the wind howled and roared louder than ever, and the rain drove in sheets against the windows, beating like hail on the glass; but within there was no sound whatever save the echo of the wind as it roared in the great chimney, and now and then a hiss as a few raindrops found their way down the chimney in a lull of the storm. The fire had fallen low and had ceased to flame, though it threw out a red glow. Malcolmson listened attentively, and presently heard a thin, squeaking noise, very faint. It came from the corner of the room where the rope hung down, and he thought it was the creaking of the rope on the floor as the swaying of the bell raised and lowered it. Looking up, however, he saw in the dim light the great rat clinging to the rope and gnawing it. The rope was already nearly gnawed through—he could see the lighter colour where the strands were laid bare. As he looked the job was completed, and the severed end of the rope fell clattering on the oaken floor, whilst for an instant the great rat remained like a knob or tassel at the end of the rope, which now began to sway to and fro. Malcolmson felt for a moment another pang of terror as he thought that now the possibility of calling the outer world to his assistance was cut off, but an intense anger took its place, and seizing the book he was reading he hurled it at the rat. The blow was well aimed, but before the missile could reach him the rat dropped off and struck the floor with a soft thud. Malcolmson instantly rushed over towards him, but it darted away and disappeared in the darkness of the shadows of the room. Malcolmson felt that his work was over for the night, and determined then and there to vary the monotony of the proceedings by a hunt for the rat, and took off the green shade of the lamp so as to insure a wider spreading light. As he did so the gloom of the upper part of the room was relieved, and in the new flood of light, great by comparison with the previous darkness, the pictures on the wall stood out boldly. From where he stood, Malcolmson saw right opposite to him the third picture on the wall from the right of the fireplace. He rubbed his eyes in surprise, and then a great fear began to come upon him.

In the centre of the picture was a great irregular patch of brown canvas, as fresh as when it was stretched on the frame. The background was as before, with chair and chimney-corner and rope, but the figure of the Judge had disappeared.

Malcolmson, almost in a chill of horror, turned slowly round, and then he began to shake and tremble like a man in a palsy. His strength seemed to have left him, and he was incapable of action or movement, hardly even of thought. He could only see and hear.

There, on the great high-backed carved oak chair sat the Judge in his robes of scarlet and ermine, with his baleful eyes glaring vindictively, and a smile of triumph on the resolute, cruel mouth, as he lifted with his hands a *black cap*. Malcolmson felt as if the blood was running from his heart, as one does in moments of prolonged suspense. There was a singing in his ears. Without, he could hear the roar and howl of the tempest, and through it, swept on the storm, came the striking of midnight by the great chimes in the market place. He stood for a space of time that seemed to him endless still as a statue, and with wide-open, horror-struck eyes, breathless. As the clock struck, so the smile of triumph on the Judge's face intensified, and at the last stroke of midnight he placed the black cap on his head.

Slowly and deliberately the Judge rose from his chair and picked up the piece of the rope of the alarm bell which lay on the floor, drew it through his hands as if he enjoyed its touch, and then deliberately began to knot one end of it, fashioning it into a noose. This he tightened and tested with his foot, pulling hard at it till he was satisfied and then making a running noose of it, which he held in his hand. Then he began to move along the table on the opposite side to Malcolmson keeping his eyes on him until he had passed him, when with a quick movement he stood in front of the door. Malcolmson then began to feel that he was trapped, and tried to think of what he should do. There was some fascination in the Judge's eyes, which he never took off him, and he had, perforce, to look. He saw the Judge approach—still keeping between him and the door—and raise the noose and throw it towards him as if to entangle him. With a great effort he made a quick movement to one side, and saw the rope fall beside him, and heard it strike the oaken floor. Again the Judge raised the noose and tried to ensnare him, ever keeping his baleful eyes fixed on him, and each time by a mighty effort the student just managed to evade it. So this went on for many times, the Judge seeming never discouraged nor discomposed at failure, but playing as a cat does with a mouse. At last in despair, which had reached its climax, Malcolmson cast a quick glance round him. The lamp seemed to have blazed up, and there was a fairly good light in the room. At the many rat-holes and in the chinks and crannies of the wainscot he saw the rats' eyes; and this aspect, that was purely physical, gave him a gleam of comfort. He looked around and saw that the rope of the great alarm bell was laden with rats. Every inch of it was covered with them, and more and more were pouring through the small circular hole in the ceiling whence it emerged, so that with their weight the bell was beginning to sway.

Hark! it had swayed till the clapper had touched the bell. The sound was but a tiny one, but the bell was only beginning to sway, and it would increase.

At the sound the Judge, who had been keeping his eyes fixed on Malcolmson, looked up, and a scowl of diabolical anger overspread his face. His eyes fairly glowed like hot coals, and he stamped his foot with a sound that seemed to make the house shake. A dreadful peal of thunder broke overhead as he raised the rope again, whilst the rats kept running up and down the rope as though working against time. This time, instead of throwing it, he drew close to his victim, and held open the noose as he approached. As he came closer there seemed something paralysing in his very presence, and Malcolmson stood rigid as a corpse. He felt the Judge's icy fingers touch his throat as he adjusted the rope. The noose tightened—tightened. Then the Judge, taking the rigid form of the student in his arms, carried him over and placed him standing in the oak chair, and stepping up beside him, put his hand up and caught the end of the swaying rope of the alarm bell. As he raised his hand the rats fled squeaking, and disappeared through the hole in the ceiling. Taking the end of the noose which was round Malcolmson's neck he tied it to the hanging-bell rope, and then descending pulled away the chair.

When the alarm bell of the Judge's House began to sound a crowd soon assembled. Lights and torches of various kinds appeared, and soon a silent crowd was hurrying to the spot. They knocked loudly at the door, but there was no reply. Then they burst in the door, and poured into the great dining-room, the doctor at the head.

There at the end of the rope of the great alarm bell hung the body of the student, and on the face of the Judge in the picture was a malignant smile.

The Squaw

Nurnberg at the time was not so much exploited as it has been since then. Irving had not been playing *Faust*, and the very name of the old town was hardly known to the great bulk of the travelling public. My wife and I being in the second week of our honeymoon, naturally wanted someone else to join our party, so that when the cheery stranger, Elias P. Hutcheson, hailing from Isthmian City, Bleeding Gulch, Maple Tree County, Neb. turned up at the station at Frankfort, and casually remarked that he was going on to see the most all-fired old Methuselah of a town in Yurrup, and that he guessed that so much travelling alone was enough to send an intelligent, active citizen into the melancholy ward of a daft house, we took the pretty broad hint and suggested that we should join forces. We found, on comparing notes afterwards, that we had each intended to speak with some diffidence or hesitation so as not to appear too eager, such not being a good compliment to the success of our married life; but the effect was entirely marred by our both beginning to speak at the same instant—stopping simultaneously and then going on together again. Anyhow, no matter how, it was done; and Elias P. Hutcheson became one of our party. Straightway Amelia and I found the pleasant benefit; instead of quarrelling, as we had been doing, we found that the restraining influence of a third party was such that we now took every opportunity of spooning in odd corners. Amelia declares that ever since she has, as the result of that experience, advised all her friends to take a friend on the honeymoon. Well, we 'did' Nurnberg together, and much enjoyed the racy remarks of our Transatlantic friend, who, from his quaint speech and his wonderful stock of adventures, might have stepped out of a novel. We kept for the last object of interest in the city to be visited the Burg, and on the day appointed for the visit strolled round the outer wall of the city by the eastern side.

The Burg is seated on a rock dominating the town and an immensely deep fosse guards it on the northern side. Nurnberg has been happy in that it was never sacked; had it been it would certainly not be so spick and span perfect as it is at present. The ditch has not been used for centuries, and now its base is spread with tea-gardens and orchards, of which some of the trees are of quite respectable growth. As we wandered round the wall, dawdling in the hot July sunshine, we often paused to admire the views spread before us, and in especial the great plain covered with towns and villages and bounded with a blue line of hills, like a landscape of Claude Lorraine. From this we always turned with new delight to the city itself, with its myriad of quaint old gables and acre-wide red roofs dotted with dormer windows, tier upon tier. A little to our right rose the towers of the Burg, and nearer still, standing grim, the Torture Tower, which was, and is, perhaps, the most interesting place in the city. For centuries the tradition of the Iron Virgin of Nurnberg has been handed down as an instance of the horrors of cruelty of which man is capable; we had long looked forward to seeing it; and here at last was its home.

In one of our pauses we leaned over the wall of the moat and looked down. The garden seemed quite fifty or sixty feet below us, and the sun pouring into it with an intense, moveless heat like that of an oven. Beyond rose the grey, grim wall seemingly of endless height, and losing itself right and left in the angles of bastion and counterscarp. Trees and bushes crowned the wall, and above again towered the lofty houses on whose massive beauty Time has only set the hand of approval. The sun was hot and we were lazy; time was our own, and we lingered, leaning on the wall. Just below us was a pretty sight—a great black cat lying stretched in the sun, whilst round her gambolled prettily a tiny black kitten. The mother would wave her tail for the kitten to play with, or would raise her feet and push away the little one as an encouragement to further play. They were just at the foot of the wall, and Elias P. Hutcheson, in order to help the play, stooped and took from the walk a moderate sized pebble.

'See!' he said, 'I will drop it near the kitten, and they will both wonder where it came from.'

'Oh, be careful,' said my wife; 'you might hit the dear little thing!'

'Not me, ma'am,' said Elias P. 'Why, I'm as tender as a Maine cherry-tree. Lor, bless ye. I wouldn't hurt the poor pooty little critter more'n I'd scalp a baby. An' you may bet your variegated socks on that! See, I'll drop it fur away on the outside so's not to go near her!' Thus saying, he leaned over and held his arm out at full length and dropped the stone. It may be that there is some attractive force which draws lesser matters to greater; or more probably that the wall was not plump but sloped to its base—we not noticing the inclination from above; but the stone fell with a sickening thud that came up to us through the hot air, right on the kitten's head, and shattered out its little brains then and there. The black cat cast a swift upward glance, and we saw her eyes like green fire fixed an instant on Elias P. Hutcheson; and then her attention was given to the kitten, which lay still with just a quiver of her tiny limbs, whilst a thin red stream trickled from a gaping wound. With a muffled cry, such as a human being might give, she bent over the kitten licking its wounds and moaning. Suddenly she seemed to realise that it was dead, and again threw her eyes up at us. I shall never forget the sight, for she looked the perfect incarnation of hate. Her green eyes blazed with lurid fire, and the white, sharp teeth seemed to almost shine through the blood which dabbled her mouth and whiskers. She gnashed her teeth, and her claws stood out stark and at full length on every paw. Then she made a wild rush up the wall as if to reach us, but when the momentum ended fell back, and further added to her horrible appearance for she fell on the kitten, and rose with her black fur smeared with its brains and blood. Amelia turned quite faint, and I had to lift her back from the wall. There was a seat close by in shade of a spreading plane-tree, and here I placed her whilst she composed herself. Then I went back to Hutcheson, who stood without moving, looking down on the angry cat below.

As I joined him, he said:

'Wall, I guess that air the savagest beast I ever see—'cept once when an Apache squaw had an edge on a half-breed what they nicknamed "Splinters" 'cos of the way he fixed up her papoose which he stole on a raid just to show that he appreciated the way they had given his mother the fire torture. She got that kinder look so set on her face that it jest seemed to grow there. She followed Splinters mor'n three year till at last the braves got him and handed him over to her. They did say that no man, white or Injun, had ever been so long a-dying under the tortures of the Apaches. The only time I ever see her smile was when I wiped her out. I kem on the camp just in time to see Splinters pass in his checks, and he wasn't sorry to go either. He was a hard citizen, and though I never could shake with him after that papoose business—for it was bitter bad, and he should have been a white man, for he looked like one—I see he had got paid out in full. Durn me, but I took a piece of his hide from one of his skinnin' posts an' had it made into a pocket-book. It's here now!' and he slapped the breast pocket of his coat.

Whilst he was speaking the cat was continuing her frantic efforts to get up the wall. She would take a run back and then charge up, sometimes reaching an incredible height. She did not seem to mind the heavy fall which she get each time but started with renewed vigour; and at every tumble her appearance became more horrible. Hutcheson was a kind-hearted man—my wife and I had both noticed little acts of kindness to animals as well as to persons—and he seemed concerned at the state of fury to which the cat had wrought herself.

'Wall, now!' he said, 'I du declare that that poor critter seems quite desperate. There! there! poor thing, it was all an accident—though that won't bring back your little one to you. Say! I wouldn't have had such a thing happen for a thousand! Just shows what a clumsy fool of a man can do when he tries to play! Seems I'm too darned slipperhanded to even play with a cat. Say Colonel!' it was a pleasant way he had to bestow titles freely—'I hope your wife don't hold no grudge against me on account of this unpleasantness? Why, I wouldn't have had it occur on no account.'

He came over to Amelia and apologised profusely, and she with her usual kindness of heart hastened to assure him that she quite understood that it was an accident. Then we all went again to the wall and looked over.

The cat missing Hutcheson's face had drawn back across the moat, and was sitting on her haunches as though ready to spring. Indeed, the very instant she saw him she did spring, and with a blind unreasoning fury, which would have been grotesque, only that it was so frightfully real. She did not try to run up the wall, but simply launched herself at him as though hate and fury could lend her wings to pass straight through the great distance between them. Amelia, womanlike, got quite concerned, and said to Elias P. in a warning voice:

'Oh! you must be very careful. That animal would try to kill you if she were here; her eyes look like positive murder.'

He laughed out jovially. 'Excuse me, ma'am,' he said, 'but I can't help laughin'. Fancy a man that has fought grizzlies an' Injuns bein' careful of bein' murdered by a cat!'

When the cat heard him laugh, her whole demeanour seemed to change. She no longer tried to jump or run up the wall, but went quietly over, and sitting again beside the dead kitten began to lick and fondle it as though it were alive.

'See!' said I, 'the effect of a really strong man. Even that animal in the midst of her fury recognises the voice of a master, and bows to him!'

'Like a squaw!' was the only comment of Elias P. Hutcheson, as we moved on our way round the city fosse. Every now and then we looked over the wall and each time saw the cat following us. At first she had kept going back to the dead kitten, and then as the distance grew greater took it in her mouth and so followed. After a while, however, she abandoned this, for we saw her following all alone; she had evidently hidden the body somewhere. Amelia's alarm grew at the cat's persistence, and more than once she repeated her warning; but the American always laughed with amusement, till finally, seeing that she was beginning to be worried, he said:

'I say, ma'am, you needn't be skeered over that cat. I go heeled, I du!' Here he slapped his pistol pocket at the back of his lumbar region. 'Why sooner'n have you worried, I'll shoot the critter, right here, an' risk the police interferin' with a citizen of the United States for carryin' arms contrairy to reg'lations!' As he spoke he looked over the wall, but the cat on seeing him, retreated, with a growl, into a bed of tall flowers, and was hidden. He went on: 'Blest if that ar critter ain't got more sense of what's good for her than most Christians. I guess we've seen the last of her! You bet, she'll go back now to that busted kitten and have a private funeral of it, all to herself!'

Amelia did not like to say more, lest he might, in mistaken kindness to her, fulfil his threat of shooting the cat: and so we went on and crossed the little wooden bridge leading to the gateway whence ran the steep paved roadway between the Burg and the pentagonal Torture Tower. As we crossed the bridge we saw the cat again down below us. When she saw us her fury seemed to return, and she made frantic efforts to get up the steep wall. Hutcheson laughed as he looked down at her, and said:

'Goodbye, old girl. Sorry I injured your feelin's, but you'll get over it in time! So long!' And then we passed through the long, dim archway and came to the gate of the Burg.

When we came out again after our survey of this most beautiful old place which not even the well-intentioned efforts of the Gothic restorers of forty years ago have been able to spoil—though their restoration was then glaring white—we seemed to have quite forgotten the unpleasant episode of the morning. The old lime tree with its great trunk gnarled with the passing of nearly nine centuries, the deep well cut through the heart of the rock by those captives of old, and the lovely view from the city wall whence we heard, spread over almost a full quarter of an hour, the multitudinous chimes of the city, had all helped to wipe out from our minds the incident of the slain kitten.

We were the only visitors who had entered the Torture Tower that morning—so at least said the old custodian—and as we had the place all to ourselves were able to make a minute and more satisfactory survey than would have otherwise been possible. The custodian, looking to us as the sole source of his gains for the day, was willing to meet our wishes in any way. The Torture Tower is truly a grim place, even now when many thousands of visitors have sent a stream of life, and the joy that follows life, into the place; but at the time I mention it wore its grimmest and most gruesome aspect. The dust of ages seemed to have settled on it, and the darkness and the horror of its memories seem to have become sentient in a way that would have satisfied the Pantheistic souls of Philo or Spinoza. The lower chamber where we entered was seemingly, in its normal state, filled with incarnate darkness; even the hot sunlight streaming in through the door seemed to be lost in the vast thickness of the walls, and only showed the masonry rough as when the builder's scaffolding had come down, but coated with dust and marked here and there with patches of dark stain which, if walls could speak, could have given their own dread memories of fear and pain. We were glad to pass up the dusty wooden staircase, the custodian leaving the outer door open to light us somewhat on our way; for to our eyes the one long-wick'd, evil-smelling candle stuck in a sconce on the wall gave an inadequate light. When we came up through the open trap in the corner of the chamber overhead, Amelia held on to me so tightly that I could actually feel her heart beat. I must say for my own part that I was not surprised at her fear, for this room was even more gruesome than that below. Here there was certainly more light, but only just sufficient to realise the horrible surroundings of the place. The builders of the tower had evidently intended that only they who should gain the top should have any of the joys of light and prospect. There, as we had noticed from below, were ranges of windows, albeit of mediaeval smallness, but elsewhere in the tower were only a very few narrow slits such as were habitual in places of mediaeval defence. A few of these only lit the chamber, and these so high up in the wall that from no part could the sky be seen through the thickness of the walls. In racks, and leaning in disorder against the walls, were a number of headsmen's swords, great double-handed weapons with broad blade and keen edge. Hard by were several blocks whereon the necks of the victims had lain, with here and there deep notches where the steel had bitten through the guard of flesh and shored into the wood. Round the chamber, placed in all sorts of irregular ways, were many implements of torture which made one's heart ache to see—chairs full of spikes which gave instant and excruciating pain; chairs and couches with dull knobs whose torture was seemingly less, but which, though slower, were equally efficacious; racks, belts, boots, gloves, collars, all made for compressing at will; steel baskets in which the head could be slowly crushed into a pulp if necessary; watchmen's hooks with long handle and knife that cut at resistance—this a speciality of the old Nurnberg police system; and many, many other devices for man's injury to man. Amelia grew quite pale with the horror of the things, but fortunately did not faint, for being a little overcome she sat down on a torture chair, but jumped up again with a shriek, all tendency to faint gone. We both pretended that it was the injury done to her dress by the dust of the chair, and the rusty spikes which had upset her, and Mr. Hutcheson acquiesced in accepting the explanation with a kind-hearted laugh.

But the central object in the whole of this chamber of horrors was the engine known as the Iron Virgin, which stood near the centre of the room. It was a rudely-shaped figure of a woman, something of the bell order, or, to make a closer comparison, of the figure of Mrs. Noah in the children's Ark, but without that slimness of waist and perfect *rondeur* of hip which marks the aesthetic type of the Noah family. One would hardly have recognised it as intended for a human figure at all had not the founder shaped on the forehead a rude semblance of a woman's face. This machine was coated with rust without, and covered with dust; a rope was fastened to a ring in the front of the figure, about where the waist should have been, and was drawn through a pulley, fastened on the wooden pillar which sustained the flooring above. The custodian pulling this rope showed that a section of the front was hinged like a door at one side; we then saw that the engine was of considerable thickness, leaving just room enough inside for a man to be placed. The door was of equal thickness and of great weight, for it took the custodian all his strength, aided though he was by the contrivance of the pulley, to open it. This weight was partly due to the fact that the door was of manifest purpose hung so as to throw its weight downwards, so that it might shut of its own accord when the strain was released. The inside was honeycombed with rust—nay more, the rust alone that comes through time would hardly have eaten so deep into the iron walls; the rust of the cruel stains was deep indeed! It was only, however, when we came to look at the inside of the door that the diabolical intention was manifest to the full. Here were several long spikes, square and massive, broad at the base and sharp at the points, placed in such a position that when the door should close the upper ones would pierce the eyes of the victim, and the lower ones his heart and vitals. The sight was too much for poor Amelia, and this time she fainted dead off, and I had to carry her down the stairs, and place her on a bench outside till she recovered. That she felt it to the quick was afterwards shown by the fact that my eldest son bears to this day a rude birthmark on his breast, which has, by family consent, been accepted as representing the Nurnberg Virgin.

When we got back to the chamber we found Hutcheson still opposite the Iron Virgin; he had been evidently philosophising, and now gave us the benefit of his thought in the shape of a sort of exordium.

'Wall, I guess I've been learnin' somethin' here while madam has been gettin' over her faint. 'Pears to me that we're a long way behind the times on our side of the big drink. We uster think out on the plains that the Injun could give us points in tryin' to make a man uncomfortable; but I guess your old mediaeval law-and-order party could raise him every time. Splinters was pretty good in his bluff on the squaw, but this here young miss held a straight flush all high on him. The points of them spikes air sharp enough still, though even the edges air eaten out by what uster be on them. It'd be a good thing for our Indian section to get some specimens of this here play-toy to send round to the Reservations jest to knock the stuffin' out of the bucks, and the squaws too, by showing them as how old civilisation lays over them at their best. Guess but I'll get in that box a minute jest to see how it feels!'

'Oh no! no!' said Amelia. 'It is too terrible!'

'Guess, ma'am, nothin's too terrible to the explorin' mind. I've been in some queer places in my time. Spent a night inside a dead horse while a prairie fire swept over me in Montana Territory—an' another time slept inside a dead buffler when the Comanches was on the war path an' I didn't keer to leave my kyard on them. I've been two days in a caved-in tunnel in the Billy Broncho gold mine in New Mexico, an' was one of the four shut up for three parts of a day in the caisson what slid over on her side when we was settin' the foundations of the Buffalo Bridge. I've not funked an odd experience yet, an' I don't propose to begin now!'

We saw that he was set on the experiment, so I said: 'Well, hurry up, old man, and get through it quick!'

'All right, General,' said he, 'but I calculate we ain't quite ready yet. The gentlemen, my predecessors, what stood in that thar canister, didn't volunteer for the office—not much! And I guess there was some ornamental tyin' up before the big stroke was made. I want to go into this thing fair and square, so I must get fixed up proper first. I dare say this old galoot can rise some string and tie me up accordin' to sample?'

This was said interrogatively to the old custodian, but the latter, who understood the drift of his speech, though perhaps not appreciating to the full the niceties of dialect and imagery, shook his head. His protest was, however, only formal and made to be overcome. The American thrust a gold piece into his hand, saying: 'Take it, pard! it's your pot; and don't be skeer'd. This ain't no necktie party that you're asked to assist in!' He produced some thin frayed rope and proceeded to bind our companion with sufficient strictness for the purpose. When the upper part of his body was bound, Hutcheson said:

'Hold on a moment, Judge. Guess I'm too heavy for you to tote into the canister. You jest let me walk in, and then you can wash up regardin' my legs!'

Whilst speaking he had backed himself into the opening which was just enough to hold him. It was a close fit and no mistake. Amelia looked on with fear in her eyes, but she evidently did not like to say anything. Then the custodian completed his task by tying the American's feet together so that he was now absolutely helpless and fixed in his voluntary prison. He seemed to really enjoy it, and the incipient smile which was habitual to his face blossomed into actuality as he said:

'Guess this here Eve was made out of the rib of a dwarf! There ain't much room for a full-grown citizen of the United States to hustle. We uster make our coffins more roomier in Idaho territory. Now, Judge, you jest begin to let this door down, slow, on to me. I want to feel the same pleasure as the other jays had when those spikes began to move toward their eyes!'

'Oh no! no! no!' broke in Amelia hysterically. 'It is too terrible! I can't bear to see it!—I can't! I can't!' But the American was obdurate. 'Say, Colonel,' said he, 'why not take Madame for a little promenade? I wouldn't hurt her feelin's for the world; but now that I am here, havin' kem eight thousand miles, wouldn't it be too hard to give up the very experience I've been pinin' an' pantin' fur? A man can't get to feel like canned goods every time! Me and the Judge here'll fix up this thing in no time, an' then you'll come back, an' we'll all laugh together!'

Once more the resolution that is born of curiosity triumphed, and Amelia stayed holding tight to my arm and shivering whilst the custodian began to slacken slowly inch by inch the rope that held back the iron door. Hutcheson's face was positively radiant as his eyes followed the first movement of the spikes.

'Wall!' he said, 'I guess I've not had enjoyment like this since I left Noo York. Bar a scrap with a French sailor at Wapping—an' that warn't much of a picnic neither—I've not had a show fur real pleasure in this dod-rotted Continent, where there ain't no b'ars nor no Injuns, an' wheer nary man goes heeled. Slow there, Judge! Don't you rush this business! I want a show for my money this game—I du!'

The custodian must have had in him some of the blood of his predecessors in that ghastly tower, for he worked the engine with a deliberate and excruciating slowness which after five minutes, in which the outer edge of the door had not moved half as many inches, began to overcome Amelia. I saw her lips whiten, and felt her hold upon my arm relax. I looked around an instant for a place whereon to lay her, and when I looked at her again found that her eye had become fixed on the side of the Virgin. Following its direction I saw the black cat crouching out of sight. Her green eyes shone like danger lamps in the gloom of the place, and their colour was heightened by the blood which still smeared her coat and reddened her mouth. I cried out:

'The cat! look out for the cat!' for even then she sprang out before the engine. At this moment she looked like a triumphant demon. Her eyes blazed with ferocity, her hair bristled out till she seemed twice her normal size, and her tail lashed about as does a tiger's when the quarry is before it. Elias P. Hutcheson when he saw her was amused, and his eyes positively sparkled with fun as he said:

'Darned if the squaw hain't got on all her war paint! Jest give her a shove off if she comes any of her tricks on me, for I'm so fixed everlastingly by the boss, that durn my skin if I can keep my eyes from her if she wants them! Easy there, Judge! don't you slack that ar rope or I'm euchered!'

At this moment Amelia completed her faint, and I had to clutch hold of her round the waist or she would have fallen to the floor. Whilst attending to her I saw the black cat crouching for a spring, and jumped up to turn the creature out.

But at that instant, with a sort of hellish scream, she hurled herself, not as we expected at Hutcheson, but straight at the face of the custodian. Her claws seemed to be tearing wildly as one sees in the Chinese drawings of the dragon rampant, and as I looked I saw one of them light on the poor man's eye, and actually tear through it and down his cheek, leaving a wide band of red where the blood seemed to spurt from every vein.

With a yell of sheer terror which came quicker than even his sense of pain, the man leaped back, dropping as he did so the rope which held back the iron door. I jumped for it, but was too late, for the cord ran like lightning through the pulley-block, and the heavy mass fell forward from its own weight.

As the door closed I caught a glimpse of our poor companion's face. He seemed frozen with terror. His eyes stared with a horrible anguish as if dazed, and no sound came from his lips.

And then the spikes did their work. Happily the end was quick, for when I wrenched open the door they had pierced so deep that they had locked in the bones of the skull through which they had crushed, and actually tore him—it—out of his iron prison till, bound as he was, he fell at full length with a sickly thud upon the floor, the face turning upward as he fell.

I rushed to my wife, lifted her up and carried her out, for I feared for her very reason if she should wake from her faint to such a scene. I laid her on the bench outside and ran back. Leaning against the wooden column was the custodian moaning in pain whilst he held his reddening handkerchief to his eyes. And sitting on the head of the poor American was the cat, purring loudly as she licked the blood which trickled through the gashed socket of his eyes.

I think no one will call me cruel because I seized one of the old executioner's swords and shore her in two as she sat.

The Secret of the Growing Gold

When Margaret Delandre went to live at Brent's Rock the whole neighbourhood awoke to the pleasure of an entirely new scandal. Scandals in connection with either the Delandre family or the Brents of Brent's Rock, were not few; and if the secret history of the county had been written in full both names would have been found well represented. It is true that the status of each was so different that they might have belonged to different continents—or to different worlds for the matter of that—for hitherto their orbits had never crossed. The Brents were accorded by the whole section of the country a unique social dominance, and had ever held themselves as high above the yeoman class to which Margaret Delandre belonged, as a blue-blooded Spanish hidalgo out-tops his peasant tenantry.

The Delandres had an ancient record and were proud of it in their way as the Brents were of theirs. But the family had never risen above yeomanry; and although they had been once well-to-do in the good old times of foreign wars and protection, their fortunes had withered under the scorching of the free trade sun and the 'piping times of peace.' They had, as the elder members used to assert, 'stuck to the land', with the result that they had taken root in it, body and soul. In fact, they, having chosen the life of vegetables, had flourished as vegetation does—blossomed and thrived in the good season and suffered in the bad. Their holding, Dander's Croft, seemed to have been worked out, and to be typical of the family which had inhabited it. The latter had declined generation after generation, sending out now and again some abortive shoot of unsatisfied energy in the shape of a soldier or sailor, who had worked his way to the minor grades of the services and had there stopped, cut short either from unheeding gallantry in action or from that destroying cause to men without breeding or youthful care—the recognition of a position above them which they feel unfitted to fill. So, little by little, the family dropped lower and lower, the men brooding and dissatisfied, and drinking themselves into the grave, the women drudging at home, or marrying beneath them—or worse. In process of time all disappeared, leaving only two in the Croft, Wykham Delandre and his sister Margaret. The man and woman seemed to have inherited in masculine and feminine form respectively the evil tendency of their race, sharing in common the principles, though manifesting them in different ways, of sullen passion, voluptuousness and recklessness.

The history of the Brents had been something similar, but showing the causes of decadence in their aristocratic and not their plebeian forms. They, too, had sent their shoots to the wars; but their positions had been different and they had often attained honour—for without flaw they were gallant, and brave deeds were done by them before the selfish dissipation which marked them had sapped their vigour.

The present head of the family—if family it could now be called when one remained of the direct line—was Geoffrey Brent. He was almost a type of worn out race, manifesting in some ways its most brilliant qualities, and in others its utter degradation. He might be fairly compared with some of those antique Italian nobles whom the painters have preserved to us with their courage, their unscrupulousness, their refinement of lust and cruelty—the voluptuary actual with the fiend potential. He was certainly handsome, with that dark, aquiline, commanding beauty which women so generally recognise as dominant. With men he was distant and cold; but such a bearing never deters womankind. The inscrutable laws of sex have so arranged that even a timid woman is not afraid of a fierce and haughty man. And so it was that there was hardly a woman of any kind or degree, who lived within view of Brent's Rock, who did not cherish some form of secret admiration for the handsome wastrel. The category was a wide one, for Brent's Rock rose up steeply from the midst of a level region and for a circuit of a hundred miles it lay on the horizon, with its high old towers and steep roofs cutting the level edge of wood and hamlet, and far-scattered mansions.

So long as Geoffrey Brent confined his dissipations to London and Paris and Vienna—anywhere out of sight and sound of his home—opinion was silent. It is easy to listen to far off echoes unmoved, and we can treat them with disbelief, or scorn, or disdain, or whatever attitude of coldness may suit our purpose. But when the scandal came close home it was another matter; and the feelings of independence and integrity which is in people of every community which is not utterly spoiled, asserted itself and demanded that condemnation should be expressed. Still there was a certain reticence in all, and no more notice was taken of the existing facts than was absolutely necessary. Margaret Delandre bore herself so fearlessly and so openly—she accepted her position as the justified companion of Geoffrey Brent so naturally that people came to believe that she was secretly married to him, and therefore thought it wiser to hold their tongues lest time should justify her and also make her an active enemy.

The one person who, by his interference, could have settled all doubts was debarred by circumstances from interfering in the matter. Wykham Delandre had quarrelled with his sister—or perhaps it was that she had quarrelled with him—and they were on terms not merely of armed neutrality but of bitter hatred. The quarrel had been antecedent to Margaret going to Brent's Rock. She and Wykham had almost come to blows. There had certainly been threats on one side and on the other; and in the end Wykham, overcome with passion, had ordered his sister to leave his house. She had risen straightway, and, without waiting to pack up even her own personal belongings, had walked out of the house. On the threshold she had paused for a moment to hurl a bitter threat at Wykham that he would rue in shame and despair to the last hour of his life his act of that day. Some weeks had since passed; and it was understood in the neighbourhood that Margaret had gone to London, when she suddenly appeared driving out with Geoffrey Brent, and the entire neighbourhood knew before nightfall that she had taken up her abode at the Rock. It was no subject of surprise that Brent had come back unexpectedly, for such was his usual custom. Even his own servants never knew when to expect him, for there was a private door, of which he alone had the key, by which he sometimes entered without anyone in the house being aware of his coming. This was his usual method of appearing after a long absence.

Wykham Delandre was furious at the news. He vowed vengeance—and to keep his mind level with his passion drank deeper than ever. He tried several times to see his sister, but she contemptuously refused to meet him. He tried to have an interview with Brent and was refused by him also. Then he tried to stop him in the road, but without avail, for Geoffrey was not a man to be stopped against his will. Several actual encounters took place between the two men, and many more were threatened and avoided. At last Wykham Delandre settled down to a morose, vengeful acceptance of the situation.

Neither Margaret nor Geoffrey was of a pacific temperament, and it was not long before there began to be quarrels between them. One thing would lead to another, and wine flowed freely at Brent's Rock. Now and again the quarrels would assume a bitter aspect, and threats would be exchanged in uncompromising language that fairly awed the listening servants. But such quarrels generally ended where domestic altercations do, in reconciliation, and in a mutual respect for the fighting qualities proportionate to their manifestation. Fighting for its own sake is found by a certain class of persons, all the world over, to be a matter of absorbing interest, and there is no reason to believe that domestic conditions minimise its potency. Geoffrey and Margaret made occasional absences from Brent's Rock, and on each of these occasions Wykham Delandre also absented himself; but as he generally heard of the absence too late to be of any service, he returned home each time in a more bitter and discontented frame of mind than before.

At last there came a time when the absence from Brent's Rock became longer than before. Only a few days earlier there had been a quarrel, exceeding in bitterness anything which had gone before; but this, too, had been made up, and a trip on the Continent had been mentioned before the servants. After a few days Wykham Delandre also went away, and it was some weeks before he returned. It was noticed that he was full of some new importance—satisfaction, exaltation—they hardly knew how to call it. He went straightway to Brent's Rock, and demanded to see Geoffrey Brent, and on being told that he had not yet returned, said, with a grim decision which the servants noted:

'I shall come again. My news is solid—it can wait!' and turned away. Week after week went by, and month after month; and then there came a rumour, certified later on, that an accident had occurred in the Zermatt valley. Whilst crossing a dangerous pass the carriage containing an English lady and the driver had fallen over a precipice, the gentleman of the party, Mr. Geoffrey Brent, having been fortunately saved as he had been walking up the hill to ease the horses. He gave information, and search was made. The broken rail, the excoriated roadway, the marks where the horses had struggled on the decline before finally pitching over into the torrent—all told the sad tale. It was a wet season, and there had been much snow in the winter, so that the river was swollen beyond its usual volume, and the eddies of the stream were packed with ice. All search was made, and finally the wreck of the carriage and the body of one horse were found in an eddy of the river. Later on the body of the driver was found on the sandy, torrent-swept waste near Täsch; but the body of the lady, like that of the other horse, had quite disappeared, and was—what was left of it by that time—whirling amongst the eddies of the Rhone on its way down to the Lake of Geneva.

Wykham Delandre made all the enquiries possible, but could not find any trace of the missing woman. He found, however, in the books of the various hotels the name of 'Mr. and Mrs. Geoffrey Brent'. And he had a stone erected at Zermatt to his sister's memory, under her married name, and a tablet put up in the church at Bretten, the parish in which both Brent's Rock and Dander's Croft were situated.

There was a lapse of nearly a year, after the excitement of the matter had worn away, and the whole neighbourhood had gone on its accustomed way. Brent was still absent, and Delandre more drunken, more morose, and more revengeful than before.

Then there was a new excitement. Brent's Rock was being made ready for a new mistress. It was officially announced by Geoffrey himself in a letter to the Vicar, that he had been married some months before to an Italian lady, and that they were then on their way home. Then a small army of workmen invaded the house; and hammer and plane sounded, and a general air of size and paint pervaded the atmosphere. One wing of the old house, the south, was entirely re-done; and then the great body of the workmen departed, leaving only materials for the doing of the old hall when Geoffrey Brent should have returned, for he had directed that the decoration was only to be done under his own eyes. He had brought with him accurate drawings of a hall in the house of his bride's father, for he wished to reproduce for her the place to which she had been accustomed. As the moulding had all to be re-done, some scaffolding poles and boards were brought in and laid on one side of the great hall, and also a great wooden tank or box for mixing the lime, which was laid in bags beside it.

When the new mistress of Brent's Rock arrived the bells of the church rang out, and there was a general jubilation. She was a beautiful creature, full of the poetry and fire and passion of the South; and the few English words which she had learned were spoken in such a sweet and pretty broken way that she won the hearts of the people almost as much by the music of her voice as by the melting beauty of her dark eyes.

Geoffrey Brent seemed more happy than he had ever before appeared; but there was a dark, anxious look on his face that was new to those who knew him of old, and he started at times as though at some noise that was unheard by others.

And so months passed and the whisper grew that at last Brent's Rock was to have an heir. Geoffrey was very tender to his wife, and the new bond between them seemed to soften him. He took more interest in his tenants and their needs than he had ever done; and works of charity on his part as well as on his sweet young wife's were not lacking. He seemed to have set all his hopes on the child that was coming, and as he looked deeper into the future the dark shadow that had come over his face seemed to die gradually away.

All the time Wykham Delandre nursed his revenge. Deep in his heart had grown up a purpose of vengeance which only waited an opportunity to crystallise and take a definite shape. His vague idea was somehow centred in the wife of Brent, for he knew that he could strike him best through those he loved, and the coming time seemed to hold in its womb the opportunity for which he longed. One night he sat alone in the living-room of his house. It had once been a handsome room in its way, but time and neglect had done their work and it was now little better than a ruin, without dignity or picturesqueness of any kind. He had been drinking heavily for some time and was more than half stupefied. He thought he heard a noise as of someone at the door and looked up. Then he called half savagely to come in; but there was no response. With a muttered blasphemy he renewed his potations. Presently he forgot all around him, sank into a daze, but suddenly awoke to see standing before him someone or something like a battered, ghostly edition of his sister. For a few moments there came upon him a sort of fear. The woman before him, with distorted features and burning eyes seemed hardly human, and the only thing that seemed a reality of his sister, as she had been, was her wealth of golden hair, and this was now streaked with grey. She eyed her brother with a long, cold stare; and he, too, as he looked and began to realise the actuality of her presence, found the hatred of her which he had had, once again surging up in his heart. All the brooding passion of the past year seemed to find a voice at once as he asked her:

'Why are you here? You're dead and buried.'

'I am here, Wykham Delandre, for no love of you, but because I hate another even more than I do you!' A great passion blazed in her eyes.

'Him?' he asked, in so fierce a whisper that even the woman was for an instant startled till she regained her calm.

'Yes, him!' she answered. 'But make no mistake, my revenge is my own; and I merely use you to help me to it.' Wykham asked suddenly:

'Did he marry you?'

The woman's distorted face broadened out in a ghastly attempt at a smile. It was a hideous mockery, for the broken features and seamed scars took strange shapes and strange colours, and queer lines of white showed out as the straining muscles pressed on the old cicatrices.

'So you would like to know! It would please your pride to feel that your sister was truly married! Well, you shall not know. That was my revenge on you, and I do not mean to change it by a hair's breadth. I have come here tonight simply to let you know that I am alive, so that if any violence be done me where I am going there may be a witness.'

'Where are you going?' demanded her brother.

'That is my affair! and I have not the least intention of letting you know!' Wykham stood up, but the drink was on him and he reeled and fell. As he lay on the floor he announced his intention of following his sister; and with an outburst of splenetic humour told her that he would follow her through the darkness by the light of her hair, and of her beauty. At this she turned on him, and said that there were others beside him that would rue her hair and her beauty too. 'As he will,' she hissed; 'for the hair remains though the beauty be gone. When he withdrew the lynch-pin and sent us over the precipice into the torrent, he had little thought of my beauty. Perhaps his beauty would be scarred like mine were he whirled, as I was, among the rocks of the Visp, and frozen on the ice pack in the drift of the river. But let him beware! His time is coming!' and with a fierce gesture she flung open the door and passed out into the night.

Later on that night, Mrs. Brent, who was but half-asleep, became suddenly awake and spoke to her husband:

'Geoffrey, was not that the click of a lock somewhere below our window?'

But Geoffrey—though she thought that he, too, had started at the noise—seemed sound asleep, and breathed heavily. Again Mrs. Brent dozed; but this time awoke to the fact that her husband had arisen and was partially dressed. He was deadly pale, and when the light of the lamp which he had in his hand fell on his face, she was frightened at the look in his eyes.

'What is it, Geoffrey? What dost thou?' she asked.

'Hush! little one,' he answered, in a strange, hoarse voice. 'Go to sleep. I am restless, and wish to finish some work I left undone.'

'Bring it here, my husband,' she said; 'I am lonely and I fear when thou art away.'

For reply he merely kissed her and went out, closing the door behind him. She lay awake for awhile, and then nature asserted itself, and she slept.

Suddenly she started broad awake with the memory in her ears of a smothered cry from somewhere not far off. She jumped up and ran to the door and listened, but there was no sound. She grew alarmed for her husband, and called out: 'Geoffrey! Geoffrey!'

After a few moments the door of the great hall opened, and Geoffrey appeared at it, but without his lamp.

'Hush!' he said, in a sort of whisper, and his voice was harsh and stern. 'Hush! Get to bed! I am working, and must not be disturbed. Go to sleep, and do not wake the house!'

With a chill in her heart—for the harshness of her husband's voice was new to her—she crept back to bed and lay there trembling, too frightened to cry, and listened to every sound. There was a long pause of silence, and then the sound of some iron implement striking muffled blows! Then there came a clang of a heavy stone falling, followed by a muffled curse. Then a dragging sound, and then more noise of stone on stone. She lay all the while in an agony of fear, and her heart beat dreadfully. She heard a curious sort of scraping sound; and then there was silence. Presently the door opened gently, and Geoffrey appeared. His wife pretended to be asleep; but through her eyelashes she saw him wash from his hands something white that looked like lime.

In the morning he made no allusion to the previous night, and she was afraid to ask any question.

From that day there seemed some shadow over Geoffrey Brent. He neither ate nor slept as he had been accustomed, and his former habit of turning suddenly as though someone were speaking from behind him revived. The old hall seemed to have some kind of fascination for him. He used to go there many times in the day, but grew impatient if anyone, even his wife, entered it. When the builder's foreman came to inquire about continuing his work Geoffrey was out driving; the man went into the hall, and when Geoffrey returned the servant told him of his arrival and where he was. With a frightful oath he pushed the servant aside and hurried up to the old hall. The workman met him almost at the door; and as Geoffrey burst into the room he ran against him. The man apologised:

'Beg pardon, sir, but I was just going out to make some enquiries. I directed twelve sacks of lime to be sent here, but I see there are only ten.'

'Damn the ten sacks and the twelve too!' was the ungracious and incomprehensible rejoinder.

The workman looked surprised, and tried to turn the conversation.

'I see, sir, there is a little matter which our people must have done; but the governor will of course see it set right at his own cost.'

'What do you mean?'

'That 'ere 'arth-stone, sir: Some idiot must have put a scaffold pole on it and cracked it right down the middle, and it's thick enough you'd think to stand hanythink.' Geoffrey was silent for quite a minute, and then said in a constrained voice and with much gentler manner:

'Tell your people that I am not going on with the work in the hall at present. I want to leave it as it is for a while longer.'

'All right sir. I'll send up a few of our chaps to take away these poles and lime bags and tidy the place up a bit.'

'No! No!' said Geoffrey, 'leave them where they are. I shall send and tell you when you are to get on with the work.' So the foreman went away, and his comment to his master was:

'I'd send in the bill, sir, for the work already done. 'Pears to me that money's a little shaky in that quarter.'

Once or twice Delandre tried to stop Brent on the road, and, at last, finding that he could not attain his object rode after the carriage, calling out:

'What has become of my sister, your wife?' Geoffrey lashed his horses into a gallop, and the other, seeing from his white face and from his wife's collapse almost into a faint that his object was attained, rode away with a scowl and a laugh.

That night when Geoffrey went into the hall he passed over to the great fireplace, and all at once started back with a smothered cry. Then with an effort he pulled himself together and went away, returning with a light. He bent down over the broken hearth-stone to see if the moonlight falling through the storied window had in any way deceived him. Then with a groan of anguish he sank to his knees.

There, sure enough, through the crack in the broken stone were protruding a multitude of threads of golden hair just tinged with grey!

He was disturbed by a noise at the door, and looking round, saw his wife standing in the doorway. In the desperation of the moment he took action to prevent discovery, and lighting a match at the lamp, stooped down and burned away the hair that rose through the broken stone. Then rising nonchalantly as he could, he pretended surprise at seeing his wife beside him.

For the next week he lived in an agony; for, whether by accident or design, he could not find himself alone in the hall for any length of time. At each visit the hair had grown afresh through the crack, and he had to watch it carefully lest his terrible secret should be discovered. He tried to find a receptacle for the body of the murdered woman outside the house, but someone always interrupted him; and once, when he was coming out of the private doorway, he was met by his wife, who began to question him about it, and manifested surprise that she should not have before noticed the key which he now reluctantly showed her. Geoffrey dearly and passionately loved his wife, so that any possibility of her discovering his dread secrets, or even of doubting him, filled him with anguish; and after a couple of days had passed, he could not help coming to the conclusion that, at least, she suspected something.

That very evening she came into the hall after her drive and found him there sitting moodily by the deserted fireplace. She spoke to him directly.

'Geoffrey, I have been spoken to by that fellow Delandre, and he says horrible things. He tells to me that a week ago his sister returned to his house, the wreck and ruin of her former self, with only her golden hair as of old, and announced some fell intention. He asked me where she is—and oh, Geoffrey, she is dead, she is dead! So how can she have returned? Oh! I am in dread, and I know not where to turn!'

For answer, Geoffrey burst into a torrent of blasphemy which made her shudder. He cursed Delandre and his sister and all their kind, and in especial he hurled curse after curse on her golden hair.

'Oh, hush! hush!' she said, and was then silent, for she feared her husband when she saw the evil effect of his humour. Geoffrey in the torrent of his anger stood up and moved away from the hearth; but suddenly stopped as he saw a new look of terror in his wife's eyes. He followed their glance, and then he too, shuddered—for there on the broken hearth-stone lay a golden streak as the point of the hair rose though the crack.

'Look, look!' she shrieked. 'Is it some ghost of the dead! Come away—come away!' and seizing her husband by the wrist with the frenzy of madness, she pulled him from the room.

That night she was in a raging fever. The doctor of the district attended her at once, and special aid was telegraphed for to London. Geoffrey was in despair, and in his anguish at the danger of his young wife almost forgot his own crime and its consequences. In the evening the doctor had to leave to attend to others; but he left Geoffrey in charge of his wife. His last words were:

'Remember, you must humour her till I come in the morning, or till some other doctor has her case in hand. What you have to dread is another attack of emotion. See that she is kept warm. Nothing more can be done.'

Late in the evening, when the rest of the household had retired, Geoffrey's wife got up from her bed and called to her husband.

'Come!' she said. 'Come to the old hall! I know where the gold comes from! I want to see it grow!'

Geoffrey would fain have stopped her, but he feared for her life or reason on the one hand, and lest in a paroxysm she should shriek out her terrible suspicion, and seeing that it was useless to try to prevent her, wrapped a warm rug around her and went with her to the old hall. When they entered, she turned and shut the door and locked it.

'We want no strangers amongst us three tonight!' she whispered with a wan smile.

'We three! nay we are but two,' said Geoffrey with a shudder; he feared to say more.

'Sit here,' said his wife as she put out the light. 'Sit here by the hearth and watch the gold growing. The silver moonlight is jealous! See, it steals along the floor towards the gold—our gold!' Geoffrey looked with growing horror, and saw that during the hours that had passed the golden hair had protruded further through the broken hearth-stone. He tried to hide it by placing his feet over the broken place; and his wife, drawing her chair beside him, leant over and laid her head on his shoulder.

'Now do not stir, dear,' she said; 'let us sit still and watch. We shall find the secret of the growing gold!' He passed his arm round her and sat silent; and as the moonlight stole along the floor she sank to sleep.

He feared to wake her; and so sat silent and miserable as the hours stole away.

Before his horror-struck eyes the golden-hair from the broken stone grew and grew; and as it increased, so his heart got colder and colder, till at last he had not power to stir, and sat with eyes full of terror watching his doom.

In the morning when the London doctor came, neither Geoffrey nor his wife could be found. Search was made in all the rooms, but without avail. As a last resource the great door of the old hall was broken open, and those who entered saw a grim and sorry sight.

There by the deserted hearth Geoffrey Brent and his young wife sat cold and white and dead. Her face was peaceful, and her eyes were closed in sleep; but his face was a sight that made all who saw it shudder, for there was on it a look of unutterable horror. The eyes were open and stared glassily at his feet, which were twined with tresses of golden hair, streaked with grey, which came through the broken hearth-stone.

The Gipsy Prophecy

'I really think,' said the Doctor, 'that, at any rate, one of us should go and try whether or not the thing is an imposture.'

'Good!' said Considine. 'After dinner we will take our cigars and stroll over to the camp.'

Accordingly, when the dinner was over, and the *La Tour* finished, Joshua Considine and his friend, Dr Burleigh, went over to the east side of the moor, where the gipsy encampment lay. As they were leaving, Mary Considine, who had walked as far as the end of the garden where it opened into the laneway, called after her husband:

'Mind, Joshua, you are to give them a fair chance, but don't give them any clue to a fortune—and don't you get flirting with any of the gipsy maidens—and take care to keep Gerald out of harm.'

For answer Considine held up his hand, as if taking a stage oath, and whistled the air of the old song, 'The Gipsy Countess.' Gerald joined in the strain, and then, breaking into merry laughter, the two men passed along the laneway to the common, turning now and then to wave their hands to Mary, who leaned over the gate, in the twilight, looking after them.

It was a lovely evening in the summer; the very air was full of rest and quiet happiness, as though an outward type of the peacefulness and joy which made a heaven of the home of the young married folk. Considine's life had not been an eventful one. The only disturbing element which he had ever known was in his wooing of Mary Winston, and the long-continued objection of her ambitious parents, who expected a brilliant match for their only daughter. When Mr. and Mrs. Winston had discovered the attachment of the young barrister, they had tried to keep the young people apart by sending their daughter away for a long round of visits, having made her promise not to correspond with her lover during her absence. Love, however, had stood the test. Neither absence nor neglect seemed to cool the passion of the young man, and jealousy seemed a thing unknown to his sanguine nature; so, after a long period of waiting, the parents had given in, and the young folk were married.

They had been living in the cottage a few months, and were just beginning to feel at home. Gerald Burleigh, Joshua's old college chum, and himself a sometime victim of Mary's beauty, had arrived a week before, to stay with them for as long a time as he could tear himself away from his work in London.

When her husband had quite disappeared Mary went into the house, and, sitting down at the piano, gave an hour to Mendelssohn.

It was but a short walk across the common, and before the cigars required renewing the two men had reached the gipsy camp. The place was as picturesque as gipsy camps—when in villages and when business is good—usually are. There were some few persons round the fire, investing their money in prophecy, and a large number of others, poorer or more parsimonious, who stayed just outside the bounds but near enough to see all that went on.

As the two gentlemen approached, the villagers, who knew Joshua, madc way a little, and a pretty, keen-eyed gipsy girl tripped up and asked to tell their fortunes. Joshua held out his hand, but the girl, without seeming to see it, stared at his face in a very odd manner. Gerald nudged him:

'You must cross her hand with silver,' he said. 'It is one of the most important parts of the mystery.' Joshua took from his pocket a half-crown and held it out to her, but, without looking at it, she answered:

'You have to cross the gipsy's hand with gold.'

Gerald laughed. 'You are at a premium as a subject,' he said. Joshua was of the kind of man—the universal kind—who can tolerate being stared at by a pretty girl; so, with some little deliberation, he answered:

'All right; here you are, my pretty girl; but you must give me a real good fortune for it,' and he handed her a half sovereign, which she took, saying:

'It is not for me to give good fortune or bad, but only to read what the Stars have said.' She took his right hand and turned it palm upward; but the instant her eyes met it she dropped it as though it had been red hot, and, with a startled look, glided swiftly away. Lifting the curtain of the large tent, which occupied the centre of the camp, she disappeared within.

'Sold again!' said the cynical Gerald. Joshua stood a little amazed, and not altogether satisfied. They both watched the large tent. In a few moments there emerged from the opening not the young girl, but a stately looking woman of middle age and commanding presence.

The instant she appeared the whole camp seemed to stand still. The clamour of tongues, the laughter and noise of the work were, for a second or two, arrested, and every man or woman who sat, or crouched, or lay, stood up and faced the imperial looking gipsy.

'The Queen, of course,' murmured Gerald. 'We are in luck tonight.' The gipsy Queen threw a searching glance around the camp, and then, without hesitating an instant, came straight over and stood before Joshua.

'Hold out your hand,' she said in a commanding tone.

Again Gerald spoke, *sotto voce*: 'I have not been spoken to in that way since I was at school.'

'Your hand must be crossed with gold.'

'A hundred per cent. at this game,' whispered Gerald, as Joshua laid another half sovereign on his upturned palm.

The gipsy looked at the hand with knitted brows; then suddenly looking up into his face, said:

'Have you a strong will—have you a true heart that can be brave for one you love?'

'I hope so; but I am afraid I have not vanity enough to say "yes".'

'Then I will answer for you; for I read resolution in your face—resolution desperate and determined if need be. You have a wife you love?'

'Yes,' emphatically.

'Then leave her at once—never see her face again. Go from her now, while love is fresh and your heart is free from wicked intent. Go quick—go far, and never see her face again!'

Joshua drew away his hand quickly, and said, 'Thank you!' stiffly but sarcastically, as he began to move away.

'I say!' said Gerald, 'you're not going like that, old man; no use in being indignant with the Stars or their prophet—and, moreover, your sovereign—what of it? At least, hear the matter out.'

'Silence, ribald!' commanded the Queen, 'you know not what you do. Let him go—and go ignorant, if he will not be warned.'

Joshua immediately turned back. 'At all events, we will see this thing out,' he said. 'Now, madam, you have given me advice, but I paid for a fortune.'

'Be warned!' said the gipsy. 'The Stars have been silent for long; let the mystery still wrap them round.'

'My dear madam, I do not get within touch of a mystery every day, and I prefer for my money knowledge rather than ignorance. I can get the latter commodity for nothing when I want any of it.'

Gerald echoed the sentiment. 'As for me I have a large and unsaleable stock on hand.'

The gipsy Queen eyed the two men sternly, and then said: 'As you wish. You have chosen for yourself, and have met warning with scorn, and appeal with levity. On your own heads be the doom!'

'Amen!' said Gerald.

With an imperious gesture the Queen took Joshua's hand again, and began to tell his fortune.

'I see here the flowing of blood; it will flow before long; it is running in my sight. It flows through the broken circle of a severed ring.'

'Go on!' said Joshua, smiling. Gerald was silent.

'Must I speak plainer?'

'Certainly; we commonplace mortals want something definite. The Stars are a long way off, and their words get somewhat dulled in the message.'

The gipsy shuddered, and then spoke impressively. 'This is the hand of a murderer—the murderer of his wife!' She dropped the hand and turned away.

Joshua laughed. 'Do you know,' said he, 'I think if I were you I should prophesy some jurisprudence into my system. For instance, you say "this hand is the hand of a murderer." Well, whatever it may be in the future—or potentially—it is at present not one. You ought to give your prophecy in such terms as "the hand which will be a murderer's", or, rather, "the hand of one who will be the murderer of his wife". The Stars are really not good on technical questions.'

The gipsy made no reply of any kind, but, with drooping head and despondent mien, walked slowly to her tent, and, lifting the curtain, disappeared.

Without speaking the two men turned homewards, and walked across the moor. Presently, after some little hesitation, Gerald spoke.

'Of course, old man, this is all a joke; a ghastly one, but still a joke. But would it not be well to keep it to ourselves?'

'How do you mean?'

'Well, not tell your wife. It might alarm her.'

'Alarm her! My dear Gerald, what are you thinking of? Why, she would not be alarmed or afraid of me if all the gipsies that ever didn't come from Bohemia agreed that I was to murder her, or even to have a hard thought of her, whilst so long as she was saying "Jack Robinson."'

Gerald remonstrated. 'Old fellow, women are superstitious—far more than we men are; and, also they are blessed—or cursed—with a nervous system to which we are strangers. I see too much of it in my work not to realise it. Take my advice and do not let her know, or you will frighten her.'

Joshua's lips unconsciously hardened as he answered: 'My dear fellow, I would not have a secret from my wife. Why, it would be the beginning of a new order of things between us. We have no secrets from each other. If we ever have, then you may begin to look out for something odd between us.'

'Still,' said Gerald, 'at the risk of unwelcome interference, I say again be warned in time.'

'The gipsy's very words,' said Joshua. 'You and she seem quite of one accord. Tell me, old man, is this a put-up thing? You told me of the gipsy camp—did you arrange it all with Her Majesty?' This was said with an air of bantering earnestness. Gerald assured him that he only heard of the camp that morning; but he made fun of every answer of his friend, and, in the process of this raillery, the time passed, and they entered the cottage.

Mary was sitting at the piano but not playing. The dim twilight had waked some very tender feelings in her breast, and her eyes were full of gentle tears. When the men came in she stole over to her husband's side and kissed him. Joshua struck a tragic attitude.

'Mary,' he said in a deep voice, 'before you approach me, listen to the words of Fate. The Stars have spoken and the doom is sealed.'

'What is it, dear? Tell me the fortune, but do not frighten me.'

'Not at all, my dear; but there is a truth which it is well that you should know. Nay, it is necessary so that all your arrangements can be made beforehand, and everything be decently done and in order.'

'Go on, dear; I am listening.'

'Mary Considine, your effigy may yet be seen at Madame Tussaud's. The jurisimprudent Stars have announced their fell tidings that this hand is red with blood—your blood. Mary! Mary! my God!' He sprang forward, but too late to catch her as she fell fainting on the floor.

'I told you,' said Gerald. 'You don't know them as well as I do.'

After a little while Mary recovered from her swoon, but only to fall into strong hysterics, in which she laughed and wept and raved and cried, 'Keep him from me—from me, Joshua, my husband,' and many other words of entreaty and of fear.

Joshua Considine was in a state of mind bordering on agony, and when at last Mary became calm he knelt by her and kissed her feet and hands and hair and called her all the sweet names and said all the tender things his lips could frame. All that night he sat by her bedside and held her hand. Far through the night and up to the early morning she kept waking from sleep and crying out as if in fear, till she was comforted by the consciousness that her husband was watching beside her.

Breakfast was late the next morning, but during it Joshua received a telegram which required him to drive over to Withering, nearly twenty miles. He was loth to go; but Mary would not hear of his remaining, and so before noon he drove off in his dog-cart alone.

When he was gone Mary retired to her room. She did not appear at lunch, but when afternoon tea was served on the lawn under the great weeping willow, she came to join her guest. She was looking quite recovered from her illness of the evening before. After some casual remarks, she said to Gerald: 'Of course it was very silly about last night, but I could not help feeling frightened. Indeed I would feel so still if I let myself think of it. But, after all these people may only imagine things, and I have got a test that can hardly fail to show that the prediction is false—if indeed it be false,' she added sadly.

'What is your plan?' asked Gerald.

'I shall go myself to the gipsy camp, and have my fortune told by the Queen.'

'Capital. May I go with you?'

'Oh, no! That would spoil it. She might know you and guess at me, and suit her utterance accordingly. I shall go alone this afternoon.'

When the afternoon was gone Mary Considine took her way to the gipsy encampment. Gerald went with her as far as the near edge of the common, and returned alone.

Half-an-hour had hardly elapsed when Mary entered the drawing-room, where he lay on a sofa reading. She was ghastly pale and was in a state of extreme excitement. Hardly had she passed over the threshold when she collapsed and sank moaning on the carpet. Gerald rushed to aid her, but by a great effort she controlled herself and motioned him to be silent. He waited, and his ready attention to her wish seemed to be her best help, for, in a few minutes, she had somewhat recovered, and was able to tell him what had passed.

'When I got to the camp,' she said, 'there did not seem to be a soul about, I went into the centre and stood there. Suddenly a tall woman stood beside me. "Something told me I was wanted!" she said. I held out my hand and laid a piece of silver on it. She took from her neck a small golden trinket and laid it there also; and then, seizing the two, threw them into the stream that ran by. Then she took my hand in hers and spoke: "Naught but blood in this guilty place," and turned away. I caught hold of her and asked her to tell me more. After some hesitation, she said: "Alas! alas! I see you lying at your husband's feet, and his hands are red with blood".'

Gerald did not feel at all at ease, and tried to laugh it off. 'Surely,' he said, 'this woman has a craze about murder.'

'Do not laugh,' said Mary, 'I cannot bear it,' and then, as if with a sudden impulse, she left the room.

Not long after Joshua returned, bright and cheery, and as hungry as a hunter after his long drive. His presence cheered his wife, who seemed much brighter, but she did not mention the episode of the visit to the gipsy camp, so Gerald did not mention it either. As if by tacit consent the subject was not alluded to during the evening. But there was a strange, settled look on Mary's face, which Gerald could not but observe.

In the morning Joshua came down to breakfast later than usual. Mary had been up and about the house from an early hour; but as the time drew on she seemed to get a little nervous and now and again threw around an anxious look.

Gerald could not help noticing that none of those at breakfast could get on satisfactorily with their food. It was not altogether that the chops were tough, but that the knives were all so blunt. Being a guest, he, of course, made no sign; but presently saw Joshua draw his thumb across the edge of his knife in an unconscious sort of way. At the action Mary turned pale and almost fainted.

After breakfast they all went out on the lawn. Mary was making up a bouquet, and said to her husband, 'Get me a few of the tea-roses, dear.'

Joshua pulled down a cluster from the front of the house. The stem bent, but was too tough to break. He put his hand in his pocket to get his knife; but in vain. 'Lend me your knife, Gerald,' he said. But Gerald had not got one, so he went into the breakfast room and took one from the table. He came out feeling its edge and grumbling. 'What on earth has happened to all the knives—the edges seem all ground off?' Mary turned away hurriedly and entered the house.

Joshua tried to sever the stalk with the blunt knife as country cooks sever the necks of fowl—as schoolboys cut twine. With a little effort he finished the task. The cluster of roses grew thick, so he determined to gather a great bunch.

He could not find a single sharp knife in the sideboard where the cutlery was kept, so he called Mary, and when she came, told her the state of things. She looked so agitated and so miserable that he could not help knowing the truth, and, as if astounded and hurt, asked her:

'Do you mean to say that *you* have done it?'

She broke in, 'Oh, Joshua, I was so afraid.'

He paused, and a set, white look came over his face. 'Mary!' said he, 'is this all the trust you have in me? I would not have believed it.'

'Oh, Joshua! Joshua!' she cried entreatingly, 'forgive me,' and wept bitterly.

Joshua thought a moment and then said: 'I see how it is. We shall better end this or we shall all go mad.'

He ran into the drawing-room.

'Where are you going?' almost screamed Mary.

Gerald saw what he meant—that he would not be tied to blunt instruments by the force of a superstition, and was not surprised when he saw him come out through the French window, bearing in his hand a large Ghourka knife, which usually lay on the centre table, and which his brother had sent him from Northern India. It was one of those great hunting-knives which worked such havoc, at close quarters with the enemies of the loyal Ghourkas during the mutiny, of great weight but so evenly balanced in the hand as to seem light, and with an edge like a razor. With one of these knives a Ghourka can cut a sheep in two.

When Mary saw him come out of the room with the weapon in his hand she screamed in an agony of fright, and the hysterics of last night were promptly renewed.

Joshua ran toward her, and, seeing her falling, threw down the knife and tried to catch her.

However, he was just a second too late, and the two men cried out in horror simultaneously as they saw her fall upon the naked blade.

When Gerald rushed over he found that in falling her left hand had struck the blade, which lay partly upwards on the grass. Some of the small veins were cut through, and the blood gushed freely from the wound. As he was tying it up he pointed out to Joshua that the wedding ring was severed by the steel.

They carried her fainting to the house. When, after a while, she came out, with her arm in a sling, she was peaceful in her mind and happy. She said to her husband:

'The gipsy was wonderfully near the truth; too near for the real thing ever to occur now, dear.'

Joshua bent over and kissed the wounded hand.

The Coming of Abel Behenna

The little Cornish port of Pencastle was bright in the early April, when the sun had seemingly come to stay after a long and bitter winter. Boldly and blackly the rock stood out against a background of shaded blue, where the sky fading into mist met the far horizon. The sea was of true Cornish hue—sapphire, save where it became deep emerald green in the fathomless depths under the cliffs, where the seal caves opened their grim jaws. On the slopes the grass was parched and brown. The spikes of furze bushes were ashy grey, but the golden yellow of their flowers streamed along the hillside, dipping out in lines as the rock cropped up, and lessening into patches and dots till finally it died away all together where the sea winds swept round the jutting cliffs and cut short the vegetation as though with an ever-working aerial shears. The whole hillside, with its body of brown and flashes of yellow, was just like a colossal yellow-hammer.

The little harbour opened from the sea between towering cliffs, and behind a lonely rock, pierced with many caves and blow-holes through which the sea in storm time sent its thunderous voice, together with a fountain of drifting spume. Hence, it wound westwards in a serpentine course, guarded at its entrance by two little curving piers to left and right. These were roughly built of dark slates placed endways and held together with great beams bound with iron bands. Thence, it flowed up the rocky bed of the stream whose winter torrents had of old cut out its way amongst the hills. This stream was deep at first, with here and there, where it widened, patches of broken rock exposed at low water, full of holes where crabs and lobsters were to be found at the ebb of the tide. From amongst the rocks rose sturdy posts, used for warping in the little coasting vessels which frequented the port. Higher up, the stream still flowed deeply, for the tide ran far inland, but always calmly for all the force of the wildest storm was broken below. Some quarter mile inland the stream was deep at high water, but at low tide there were at each side patches of the same broken rock as lower down, through the chinks of which the sweet water of the natural stream trickled and murmured after the tide had ebbed away. Here, too, rose mooring posts for the fishermen's boats. At either side of the river was a row of cottages down almost on the level of high tide. They were pretty cottages, strongly and snugly built, with trim narrow gardens in front, full of old-fashioned plants, flowering currants, coloured primroses, wallflower, and stonecrop. Over the fronts of many of them climbed clematis and wisteria. The window sides and door posts of all were as white as snow, and the little pathway to each was paved with light coloured stones. At some of the doors were tiny porches, whilst at others were rustic seats cut from tree trunks or from old barrels; in nearly every case the window ledges were filled with boxes or pots of flowers or foliage plants.

Two men lived in cottages exactly opposite each other across the stream. Two men, both young, both good-looking, both prosperous, and who had been companions and rivals from their boyhood. Abel Behenna was dark with the gypsy darkness which the Phœnician mining wanderers left in their track; Eric Sanson—which the local antiquarian said was a corruption of Sagamanson—was fair, with the ruddy hue which marked the path of the wild Norseman. These two seemed to have singled out each other from the very beginning to work and strive together, to fight for each other and to stand back to back in all endeavours. They had now put the coping-stone on their Temple of Unity by falling in love with the same girl. Sarah Trefusis was certainly the prettiest girl in Pencastle, and there was many a young man who would gladly have tried his fortune with her, but that there were two to contend against, and each of these the strongest and most resolute man in the port—except the other. The average young man thought that this was very hard, and on account of it bore no good will to either of the three principals: whilst the average young woman who had, lest worse should befall, to put up with the grumbling of her sweetheart, and the sense of being only second best which it implied, did not either, be sure, regard Sarah with friendly eye. Thus it came, in the course of a year or so, for rustic courtship is a slow process, that the two men and woman found themselves thrown much together. They were all satisfied, so it did not matter, and Sarah, who was vain and something frivolous, took care to have her revenge on both men and women in a quiet way. When a young woman in her 'walking out' can only boast one not-quite-satisfied young man, it is no particular pleasure to her to see her escort cast sheep's eyes at a better-looking girl supported by two devoted swains.

At length there came a time which Sarah dreaded, and which she had tried to keep distant—the time when she had to make her choice between the two men. She liked them both, and, indeed, either of them might have satisfied the ideas of even a more exacting girl. But her mind was so constituted that she thought more of what she might lose, than of what she might gain; and whenever she thought she had made up her mind she became instantly assailed with doubts as to the wisdom of her choice. Always the man whom she had presumably lost became endowed afresh with a newer and more bountiful crop of advantages than had ever arisen from the possibility of his acceptance. She promised each man that on her birthday she would give him his answer, and that day, the 11th of April, had now arrived. The promises had been given singly and confidentially, but each was given to a man who was not likely to forget. Early in the morning she found both men hovering round her door. Neither had taken the other into his confidence, and each was simply seeking an early opportunity of getting his answer, and advancing his suit if necessary. Damon, as a rule, does not take Pythias with him when making a proposal; and in the heart of each man his own affairs had a claim far above any requirements of friendship. So, throughout the day, they kept seeing each other out. The position was doubtless somewhat embarrassing to Sarah, and though the satisfaction of her vanity that she should be thus adored was very pleasing, yet there were moments when she was annoyed with both men for being so persistent. Her only consolation at such moments was that she saw, through the elaborate smiles of the other girls when in passing they noticed her door thus doubly guarded, the jealousy which filled their hearts. Sarah's mother was a person of commonplace and sordid ideas, and, seeing all along the state of affairs, her one intention, persistently expressed to her daughter in the plainest words, was to so arrange matters that Sarah should get all that was possible out of both men. With this purpose she had cunningly kept herself as far as possible in the background in the matter of her daughter's wooings, and watched in silence. At first Sarah had been indignant with her for her sordid views; but, as usual, her weak nature gave way before persistence, and she had now got to the stage of acceptance. She was not surprised when her mother whispered to her in the little yard behind the house:—

'Go up the hillside for a while; I want to talk to these two. They're both red-hot for ye, and now's the time to get things fixed!' Sarah began a feeble remonstrance, but her mother cut her short.

'I tell ye, girl, that my mind is made up! Both these men want ye, and only one can have ye, but before ye choose it'll be so arranged that ye'll have all that both have got! Don't argy, child! Go up the hillside, and when ye come back I'll have it fixed—I see a way quite easy!' So Sarah went up the hillside through the narrow paths between the golden furze, and Mrs. Trefusis joined the two men in the living-room of the little house.

She opened the attack with the desperate courage which is in all mothers when they think for their children, howsoever mean the thoughts may be.

'Ye two men, ye're both in love with my Sarah!'

Their bashful silence gave consent to the barefaced proposition. She went on.

'Neither of ye has much!' Again they tacitly acquiesced in the soft impeachment.

'I don't know that either of ye could keep a wife!' Though neither said a word their looks and bearing expressed distinct dissent. Mrs. Trefusis went on:

'But if ye'd put what ye both have together ye'd make a comfortable home for one of ye—and Sarah!' She eyed the men keenly, with her cunning eyes half shut, as she spoke; then satisfied from her scrutiny that the idea was accepted she went on quickly, as if to prevent argument:

'The girl likes ye both, and mayhap it's hard for her to choose. Why don't ye toss up for her? First put your money together—ye've each got a bit put by, I know. Let the lucky man take the lot and trade with it a bit, and then come home and marry her. Neither of ye's afraid, I suppose! And neither of ye'll say that he won't do that much for the girl that ye both say ye love!'

Abel broke the silence:

'It don't seem the square thing to toss for the girl! She wouldn't like it herself, and it doesn't seem—seem respectful like to her—' Eric interrupted. He was conscious that his chance was not so good as Abel's in case Sarah should wish to choose between them:

'Are ye afraid of the hazard?'

'Not me!' said Abel, boldly. Mrs. Trefusis, seeing that her idea was beginning to work, followed up the advantage.

'It is settled that ye put yer money together to make a home for her, whether ye toss for her or leave it for her to choose?'

'Yes,' said Eric quickly, and Abel agreed with equal sturdiness. Mrs. Trefusis' little cunning eyes twinkled. She heard Sarah's step in the yard, and said:

'Well! here she comes, and I leave it to her.' And she went out.

During her brief walk on the hillside Sarah had been trying to make up her mind. She was feeling almost angry with both men for being the cause of her difficulty, and as she came into the room said shortly:

'I want to have a word with you both—come to the Flagstaff Rock, where we can be alone.' She took her hat and went out of the house up the winding path to the steep rock crowned with a high flagstaff, where once the wreckers' fire basket used to burn. This was the rock which formed the northern jaw of the little harbour. There was only room on the path for two abreast, and it marked the state of things pretty well when, by a sort of implied arrangement, Sarah went first, and the two men followed, walking abreast and keeping step. By this time, each man's heart was boiling with jealousy. When they came to the top of the rock, Sarah stood against the flagstaff, and the two young men stood opposite her. She had chosen her position with knowledge and intention, for there was no room for anyone to stand beside her. They were all silent for a while; then Sarah began to laugh and said:—

'I promised the both of you to give you an answer to-day. I've been thinking and thinking and thinking, till I began to get angry with you both for plaguing me so; and even now I don't seem any nearer than ever I was to making up my mind.' Eric said suddenly:

'Let us toss for it, lass!' Sarah showed no indignation whatever at the proposition; her mother's eternal suggestion had schooled her to the acceptance of something of the kind, and her weak nature made it easy to her to grasp at any way out of the difficulty. She stood with downcast eyes idly picking at the sleeve of her dress, seeming to have tacitly acquiesced in the proposal. Both men instinctively realising this pulled each a coin from his pocket, spun it in the air, and dropped his other hand over the palm on which it lay. For a few seconds they remained thus, all silent; then Abel, who was the more thoughtful of the men, spoke:

'Sarah! is this good?' As he spoke he removed the upper hand from the coin and placed the latter back in his pocket. Sarah was nettled.

'Good or bad, it's good enough for me! Take it or leave it as you like,' she said, to which he replied quickly:

'Nay lass! Aught that concerns you is good enow for me. I did but think of you lest you might have pain or disappointment hereafter. If you love Eric better nor me, in God's name say so, and I think I'm man enow to stand aside. Likewise, if I'm the one, don't make us both miserable for life!' Face to face with a difficulty, Sarah's weak nature proclaimed itself; she put her hands before her face and began to cry, saying—

'It was my mother. She keeps telling me!' The silence which followed was broken by Eric, who said hotly to Abel:

'Let the lass alone, can't you? If she wants to choose this way, let her. It's good enough for me—and for you, too! She's said it now, and must abide by it!' Hereupon Sarah turned upon him in sudden fury, and cried:

'Hold your tongue! what is it to you, at any rate?' and she resumed her crying. Eric was so flabbergasted that he had not a word to say, but stood looking particularly foolish, with his mouth open and his hands held out with the coin still between them. All were silent till Sarah, taking her hands from her face laughed hysterically and said:

'As you two can't make up your minds, I'm going home!' and she turned to go.

'Stop,' said Abel, in an authoritative voice. 'Eric, you hold the coin, and I'll cry. Now, before we settle it, let us clearly understand: the man who wins takes all the money that we both have got, brings it to Bristol and ships on a voyage and trades with it. Then he comes back and marries Sarah, and they two keep all, whatever there may be, as the result of the trading. Is this what we understand?'

'Yes,' said Eric.

'I'll marry him on my next birthday,' said Sarah. Having said it the intolerably mercenary spirit of her action seemed to strike her, and impulsively she turned away with a bright blush. Fire seemed to sparkle in the eyes of both men. Said Eric: 'A year so be! The man that wins is to have one year.'

'Toss!' cried Abel, and the coin spun in the air. Eric caught it, and again held it between his outstretched hands.

'Heads!' cried Abel, a pallor sweeping over his face as he spoke. As he leaned forward to look Sarah leaned forward too, and their heads almost touched. He could feel her hair blowing on his cheek, and it thrilled through him like fire. Eric lifted his upper hand; the coin lay with its head up. Abel stepped forward and took Sarah in his arms. With a curse Eric hurled the coin far into the sea. Then he leaned against the flagstaff and scowled at the others with his hands thrust deep into his pockets. Abel whispered wild words of passion and delight into Sarah's ears, and as she listened she began to believe that fortune had rightly interpreted the wishes of her secret heart, and that she loved Abel best.

Presently Abel looked up and caught sight of Eric's face as the last ray of sunset struck it. The red light intensified the natural ruddiness of his complexion, and he looked as though he were steeped in blood. Abel did not mind his scowl, for now that his own heart was at rest he could feel unalloyed pity for his friend. He stepped over meaning to comfort him, and held out his hand, saying:

'It was my chance, old lad. Don't grudge it me. I'll try to make Sarah a happy woman, and you shall be a brother to us both!'

'Brother be damned!' was all the answer Eric made, as he turned away. When he had gone a few steps down the rocky path he turned and came back. Standing before Abel and Sarah, who had their arms round each other, he said:

'You have a year. Make the most of it! And be sure you're in time to claim your wife! Be back to have your banns up in time to be married on the 11th April. If you're not, I tell you I shall have my banns up, and you may get back too late.'

'What do you mean, Eric? You are mad!'

'No more mad than you are, Abel Behenna. You go, that's your chance! I stay, that's mine! I don't mean to let the grass grow under my feet. Sarah cared no more for you than for me five minutes ago, and she may come back to that five minutes after you're gone! You won by a point only—the game may change.'

'The game won't change!' said Abel shortly. 'Sarah, you'll be true to me? You won't marry till I return?'

'For a year!' added Eric, quickly, 'that's the bargain.'

'I promise for the year,' said Sarah. A dark look came over Abel's face, and he was about to speak, but he mastered himself and smiled.

'I mustn't be too hard or get angry tonight! Come, Eric! we played and fought together. I won fairly. I played fairly all the game of our wooing! You know that as well as I do; and now when I am going away, I shall look to my old and true comrade to help me when I am gone!'

'I'll help you none,' said Eric, 'so help me God!'

'It was God helped me,' said Abel simply.

'Then let Him go on helping you,' said Eric angrily. 'The Devil is good enough for me!' and without another word he rushed down the steep path and disappeared behind the rocks.

When he had gone Abel hoped for some tender passage with Sarah, but the first remark she made chilled him.

'How lonely it all seems without Eric!' and this note sounded till he had left her at home—and after.

Early on the next morning Abel heard a noise at his door, and on going out saw Eric walking rapidly away: a small canvas bag full of gold and silver lay on the threshold; on a small slip of paper pinned to it was written:

'Take the money and go. I stay. God for you! The Devil for me! Remember the 11th of April.—ERIC SANSON.' That afternoon Abel went off to Bristol, and a week later sailed on the *Star of the Sea* bound for Pahang. His money—including that which had been Eric's—was on board in the shape of a venture of cheap toys. He had been advised by a shrewd old mariner of Bristol whom he knew, and who knew the ways of the Chersonese, who predicted that every penny invested would be returned with a shilling to boot.

As the year wore on Sarah became more and more disturbed in her mind. Eric was always at hand to make love to her in his own persistent, masterful manner, and to this she did not object. Only one letter came from Abel, to say that his venture had proved successful, and that he had sent some two hundred pounds to the bank at Bristol, and was trading with fifty pounds still remaining in goods for China, whither the *Star of the Sea* was bound and whence she would return to Bristol. He suggested that Eric's share of the venture should be returned to him with his share of the profits. This proposition was treated with anger by Eric, and as simply childish by Sarah's mother.

More than six months had since then elapsed, but no other letter had come, and Eric's hopes which had been dashed down by the letter from Pahang, began to rise again. He perpetually assailed Sarah with an 'if!' If Abel did not return, would she then marry him? If the 11th April went by without Abel being in the port, would she give him over? If Abel had taken his fortune, and married another girl on the head of it, would she marry him, Eric, as soon as the truth were known? And so on in an endless variety of possibilities. The power of the strong will and the determined purpose over the woman's weaker nature became in time manifest. Sarah began to lose her faith in Abel and to regard Eric as a possible husband; and a possible husband is in a woman's eye different to all other men. A new affection for him began to arise in her breast, and the daily familiarities of permitted courtship furthered the growing affection. Sarah began to regard Abel as rather a rock in the road of her life, and had it not been for her mother's constantly reminding her of the good fortune already laid by in the Bristol Bank she would have tried to have shut her eyes altogether to the fact of Abel's existence.

The 11th April was Saturday, so that in order to have the marriage on that day it would be necessary that the banns should be called on Sunday, 22nd March. From the beginning of that month Eric kept perpetually on the subject of Abel's absence, and his outspoken opinion that the latter was either dead or married began to become a reality to the woman's mind. As the first half of the month wore on Eric became more jubilant, and after church on the 15th he took Sarah for a walk to the Flagstaff Rock. There he asserted himself strongly:

'I told Abel, and you too, that if he was not here to put up his banns in time for the eleventh, I would put up mine for the twelfth. Now the time has come when I mean to do it. He hasn't kept his word'—here Sarah struck in out of her weakness and indecision:

'He hasn't broken it yet!' Eric ground his teeth with anger.

'If you mean to stick up for him,' he said, as he smote his hands savagely on the flagstaff, which sent forth a shivering murmur, 'well and good. I'll keep my part of the bargain. On Sunday I shall give notice of the banns, and you can deny them in the church if you will. If Abel is in Pencastle on the eleventh, he can have them cancelled, and his own put up; but till then, I take my course, and woe to anyone who stands in my way!' With that he flung himself down the rocky pathway, and Sarah could not but admire his Viking strength and spirit, as, crossing the hill, he strode away along the cliffs towards Bude.

During the week no news was heard of Abel, and on Saturday Eric gave notice of the banns of marriage between himself and Sarah Trefusis. The clergyman would have remonstrated with him, for although nothing formal had been told to the neighbours, it had been understood since Abel's departure that on his return he was to marry Sarah; but Eric would not discuss the question.

'It is a painful subject, sir,' he said with a firmness which the parson, who was a very young man, could not but be swayed by. 'Surely there is nothing against Sarah or me. Why should there be any bones made about the matter?' The parson said no more, and on the next day he read out the banns for the first time amidst an audible buzz from the congregation. Sarah was present, contrary to custom, and though she blushed furiously enjoyed her triumph over the other girls whose banns had not yet come. Before the week was over she began to make her wedding dress. Eric used to come and look at her at work and the sight thrilled through him. He used to say all sorts of pretty things to her at such times, and there were to both delicious moments of lovemaking.

The banns were read a second time on the 29th, and Eric's hope grew more and more fixed though there were to him moments of acute despair when he realised that the cup of happiness might be dashed from his lips at any moment, right up to the last. At such times he was full of passion—desperate and remorseless—and he ground his teeth and clenched his hands in a wild way as though some taint of the old Berserker fury of his ancestors still lingered in his blood. On the Thursday of that week he looked in on Sarah and found her, amid a flood of sunshine, putting finishing touches to her white wedding gown. His own heart was full of gaiety, and the sight of the woman who was so soon to be his own so occupied, filled him with a joy unspeakable, and he felt faint with languorous ecstasy. Bending over he kissed Sarah on the mouth, and then whispered in her rosy ear—

'Your wedding dress, Sarah! And for me!' As he drew back to admire her she looked up saucily, and said to him—

'Perhaps not for you. There is more than a week yet for Abel!' and then cried out in dismay, for with a wild gesture and a fierce oath Eric dashed out of the house, banging the door behind him. The incident disturbed Sarah more than she could have thought possible, for it awoke all her fears and doubts and indecision afresh. She cried a little, and put by her dress, and to soothe herself went out to sit for a while on the summit of the Flagstaff Rock. When she arrived she found there a little group anxiously discussing the weather. The sea was calm and the sun bright, but across the sea were strange lines of darkness and light, and close in to shore the rocks were fringed with foam, which spread out in great white curves and circles as the currents drifted. The wind had backed, and came in sharp, cold puffs. The blow-hole, which ran under the Flagstaff Rock, from the rocky bay without to the harbour within, was booming at intervals, and the seagulls were screaming ceaselessly as they wheeled about the entrance of the port.

'It looks bad,' she heard an old fisherman say to the coastguard. 'I seen it just like this once before, when the East Indiaman *Coromandel* went to pieces in Dizzard Bay!' Sarah did not wait to hear more. She was of a timid nature where danger was concerned, and could not bear to hear of wrecks and disasters. She went home and resumed the completion of her dress, secretly determined to appease Eric when she should meet him with a sweet apology—and to take the earliest opportunity of being even with him after her marriage. The old fisherman's weather prophecy was justified. That night at dusk a wild storm came on. The sea rose and lashed the western coasts from Skye to Scilly and left a tale of disaster everywhere. The sailors and fishermen of Pencastle all turned out on the rocks and cliffs and watched eagerly. Presently, by a flash of lightning, a 'ketch' was seen drifting under only a jib about half-a-mile outside the port. All eyes and all glasses were concentrated on her, waiting for the next flash, and when it came a chorus went up that it was the *Lovely Alice*, trading between Bristol and Penzance, and touching at all the little ports between. 'God help them!' said the harbour-master, 'for nothing in this world can save them when they are between Bude and Tintagel and the wind on shore!' The coastguards exerted themselves, and, aided by brave hearts and willing hands, they brought the rocket apparatus up on the summit of the Flagstaff Rock. Then they burned blue lights so that those on board might see the harbour opening in case they could make any effort to reach it. They worked gallantly enough on board; but no skill or strength of man could avail. Before many minutes were over the *Lovely Alice* rushed to her doom on the great island rock that guarded the mouth of the port. The screams of those on board were faintly borne on the tempest as they flung themselves into the sea in a last chance for life. The blue lights were kept burning, and eager eyes peered into the depths of the waters in case any face could be seen; and ropes were held ready to fling out in aid. But never a face was seen, and the willing arms rested idle. Eric was there amongst his fellows. His old Icelandic origin was never more apparent than in that wild hour. He took a rope, and shouted in the ear of the harbour-master:

'I shall go down on the rock over the seal cave. The tide is running up, and someone may drift in there!'

'Keep back, man!' came the answer. 'Are you mad? One slip on that rock and you are lost: and no man could keep his feet in the dark on such a place in such a tempest!'

'Not a bit,' came the reply. 'You remember how Abel Behenna saved me there on a night like this when my boat went on the Gull Rock. He dragged me up from the deep water in the seal cave, and now someone may drift in there again as I did,' and he was gone into the darkness. The projecting rock hid the light on the Flagstaff Rock, but he knew his way too well to miss it. His boldness and sureness of foot standing to him, he shortly stood on the great round-topped rock cut away beneath by the action of the waves over the entrance of the seal cave, where the water was fathomless. There he stood in comparative safety, for the concave shape of the rock beat back the waves with their own force, and though the water below him seemed to boil like a seething cauldron, just beyond the spot there was a space of almost calm. The rock, too, seemed here to shut off the sound of the gale, and he listened as well as watched. As he stood there ready, with his coil of rope poised to throw, he thought he heard below him, just beyond the whirl of the water, a faint, despairing cry. He echoed it with a shout that rang into the night Then he waited for the flash of lightning, and as it passed flung his rope out into the darkness where he had seen a face rising through the swirl of the foam. The rope was caught, for he felt a pull on it, and he shouted again in his mighty voice:

'Tie it round your waist, and I shall pull you up.' Then when he felt that it was fast he moved along the rock to the far side of the sea cave, where the deep water was something stiller, and where he could get foothold secure enough to drag the rescued man on the overhanging rock. He began to pull, and shortly he knew from the rope taken in that the man he was now rescuing must soon be close to the top of the rock. He steadied himself for a moment, and drew a long breath, that he might at the next effort complete the rescue. He had just bent his back to the work when a flash of lightning revealed to each other the two men—the rescuer and the rescued.

Eric Sanson and Abel Behenna were face to face—and none knew of the meeting save themselves; and God.

On the instant a wave of passion swept through Eric's heart. All his hopes were shattered, and with the hatred of Cain his eyes looked out. He saw in the instant of recognition the joy in Abel's face that his was the hand to succour him, and this intensified his hate. Whilst the passion was on him he started back, and the rope ran out between his hands. His moment of hate was followed by an impulse of his better manhood, but it was too late.

Before he could recover himself, Abel encumbered with the rope that should have aided him, was plunged with a despairing cry back into the darkness of the devouring sea.

Then, feeling all the madness and the doom of Cain upon him, Eric rushed back over the rocks, heedless of the danger and eager only for one thing—to be amongst other people whose living noises would shut out that last cry which seemed to ring still in his ears. When he regained the Flagstaff Rock the men surrounded him, and through the fury of the storm he heard the harbour-master say:—

'We feared you were lost when we heard a cry! How white you are! Where is your rope? Was there anyone drifted in?'

'No one,' he shouted in answer, for he felt that he could never explain that he had let his old comrade slip back into the sea, and at the very place and under the very circumstances in which that comrade had saved his own life. He hoped by one bold lie to set the matter at rest for ever. There was no one to bear witness—and if he should have to carry that still white face in his eyes and that despairing cry in his ears for evermore—at least none should know of it. 'No one,' he cried, more loudly still. 'I slipped on the rock, and the rope fell into the sea!' So saying he left them, and, rushing down the steep path, gained his own cottage and locked himself within.

The remainder of that night he passed lying on his bed—dressed and motionless—staring upwards, and seeming to see through the darkness a pale face gleaming wet in the lightning, with its glad recognition turning to ghastly despair, and to hear a cry which never ceased to echo in his soul.

In the morning the storm was over and all was smiling again, except that the sea was still boisterous with its unspent fury. Great pieces of wreck drifted into the port, and the sea around the island rock was strewn with others. Two bodies also drifted into the harbour—one the master of the wrecked ketch, the other a strange seaman whom no one knew.

Sarah saw nothing of Eric till the evening, and then he only looked in for a minute. He did not come into the house, but simply put his head in through the open window.

'Well, Sarah,' he called out in a loud voice, though to her it did not ring truly, 'is the wedding dress done? Sunday week, mind! Sunday week!'

Sarah was glad to have the reconciliation so easy; but, womanlike, when she saw the storm was over and her own fears groundless, she at once repeated the cause of offence.

'Sunday so be it,' she said without looking up, 'if Abel isn't there on Saturday!' Then she looked up saucily, though her heart was full of fear of another outburst on the part of her impetuous lover. But the window was empty; Eric had taken himself off, and with a pout she resumed her work. She saw Eric no more till Sunday afternoon, after the banns had been called the third time, when he came up to her before all the people with an air of proprietorship which half-pleased and half-annoyed her.

'Not yet, mister!' she said, pushing him away, as the other girls giggled. 'Wait till Sunday next, if you please—the day after Saturday!' she added, looking at him saucily. The girls giggled again, and the young men guffawed. They thought it was the snub that touched him so that he became as white as a sheet as he turned away. But Sarah, who knew more than they did, laughed, for she saw triumph through the spasm of pain that overspread his face.

The week passed uneventfully; however, as Saturday drew nigh Sarah had occasional moments of anxiety, and as to Eric he went about at night-time like a man possessed. He restrained himself when others were by, but now and again he went down amongst the rocks and caves and shouted aloud. This seemed to relieve him somewhat, and he was better able to restrain himself for some time after. All Saturday he stayed in his own house and never left it. As he was to be married on the morrow, the neighbours thought it was shyness on his part, and did not trouble or notice him. Only once was he disturbed, and that was when the chief boatman came to him and sat down, and after a pause said:

'Eric, I was over in Bristol yesterday. I was in the ropemaker's getting a coil to replace the one you lost the night of the storm, and there I saw Michael Heavens of this place, who is a salesman there. He told me that Abel Behenna had come home the week ere last on the *Star of the Sea* from Canton, and that he had lodged a sight of money in the Bristol Bank in the name of Sarah Behenna. He told Michael so himself—and that he had taken passage on the *Lovely Alice* to Pencastle. 'Bear up, man,' for Eric had with a groan dropped his head on his knees, with his face between his hands. 'He was your old comrade, I know, but you couldn't help him. He must have gone down with the rest that awful night. I thought I'd better tell you, lest it might come some other way, and you might keep Sarah Trefusis from being frightened.

They were good friends once, and women take these things to heart. It would not do to let her be pained with such a thing on her wedding day!' Then he rose and went away, leaving Eric still sitting disconsolately with his head on his knees.

'Poor fellow!' murmured the chief boatman to himself; 'he takes it to heart. Well, well! right enough! They were true comrades once, and Abel saved him!'

The afternoon of that day, when the children had left school, they strayed as usual on half-holidays along' the quay and the paths by the cliffs. Presently some of them came running in a state of great excitement to the harbour, where a few men were unloading a coal ketch, and a great many were superintending the operation. One of the children called out:

'There is a porpoise in the harbour mouth! We saw it come through the blow-hole! It had a long tail, and was deep under the water!'

'It was no porpoise,' said another; 'it was a seal; but it had a long tail! It came out of the seal cave!' The other children bore various testimony, but on two points they were unanimous—it, whatever 'it' was, had come through the blow-hole deep under the water, and had a long, thin tail—a tail so long that they could not see the end of it. There was much unmerciful chaffing of the children by the men on this point, but as it was evident that they had seen something, quite a number of persons, young and old, male and female, went along the high paths on either side of the harbour mouth to catch a glimpse of this new addition to the fauna of the sea, a long-tailed porpoise or seal. The tide was now coming in. There was a slight breeze, and the surface of the water was rippled so that it was only at moments that anyone could see clearly into the deep water. After a spell of watching a woman called out that she saw something moving up the channel, just below where she was standing. There was a stampede to the spot, but by the time the crowd had gathered the breeze had freshened, and it was impossible to see with any distinctness below the surface of the water. On being questioned the woman described what she had seen, but in such an incoherent way that the whole thing was put down as an effect of imagination; had it not been for the children's report she would not have been credited at all. Her semi-hysterical statement that what she saw was 'like a pig with the entrails out' was only thought anything of by an old coastguard, who shook his head but did not make any remark. For the remainder of the daylight this man was seen always on the bank, looking into the water, but always with disappointment manifest on his face.

Eric arose early on the next morning—he had not slept all night, and it was a relief to him to move about in the light. He shaved himself with a hand that did not tremble, and dressed himself in his wedding clothes. There was a haggard look on his face, and he seemed as though he had grown years older in the last few days. Still there was a wild, uneasy light of triumph in his eyes, and he kept murmuring to himself over and over again:

'This is my wedding-day! Abel cannot claim her now—living or dead!—living or dead! Living or dead!' He sat in his arm-chair, waiting with an uncanny quietness for the church hour to arrive. When the bell began to ring he arose and passed out of his house, closing the door behind him. He looked at the river and saw the tide had just turned. In the church he sat with Sarah and her mother, holding Sarah's hand tightly in his all the time, as though he feared to lose her. When the service was over they stood up together, and were married in the presence of the entire congregation; for no one left the church. Both made the responses clearly—Eric's being even on the defiant side. When the wedding was over Sarah took her husband's arm, and they walked away together, the boys and younger girls being cuffed by their elders into a decorous behaviour, for they would fain have followed close behind their heels.

The way from the church led down to the back of Eric's cottage, a narrow passage being between it and that of his next neighbour. When the bridal couple had passed through this the remainder of the congregation, who had followed them at a little distance, were startled by a long, shrill scream from the bride. They rushed through the passage and found her on the bank with wild eyes, pointing to the river bed opposite Eric Sanson's door.

The falling tide had deposited there the body of Abel Behenna stark upon the broken rocks. The rope trailing from its waist had been twisted by the current round the mooring post, and had held it back whilst the tide had ebbed away from it. The right elbow had fallen in a chink in the rock, leaving the hand outstretched toward Sarah, with the open palm upward as though it were extended to receive hers, the pale drooping fingers open to the clasp.

All that happened afterwards was never quite known to Sarah Sanson. Whenever she would try to recollect there would become a buzzing in her ears and a dimness in her eyes, and all would pass away. The only thing that she could remember of it all—and this she never forgot—was Eric's breathing heavily, with his face whiter than that of the dead man, as he muttered under his breath:

'Devil's help! Devil's faith! Devil's price!'

The Burial of the Rats

Leaving Paris by the Orleans road, cross the Enceinte, and, turning to the right, you find yourself in a somewhat wild and not at all savoury district. Right and left, before and behind, on every side rise great heaps of dust and waste accumulated by the process of time.

Paris has its night as well as its day life, and the sojourner who enters his hotel in the Rue de Rivoli or the Rue St. Honore late at night or leaves it early in the morning, can guess, in coming near Montrouge—if he has not done so already—the purpose of those great waggons that look like boilers on wheels which he finds halting everywhere as he passes.

Every city has its peculiar institutions created out of its own needs; and one of the most notable institutions of Paris is its rag-picking population. In the early morning—and Parisian life commences at an early hour—may be seen in most streets standing on the pathway opposite every court and alley and between every few houses, as still in some American cities, even in parts of New York, large wooden boxes into which the domestics or tenement-holders empty the accumulated dust of the past day. Round these boxes gather and pass on, when the work is done, to fresh fields of labour and pastures new, squalid hungry-looking men and women, the implements of whose craft consist of a coarse bag or basket slung over the shoulder and a little rake with which they turn over and probe and examine in the minutest manner the dustbins. They pick up and deposit in their baskets, by aid of their rakes, whatever they may find, with the same facility as a Chinaman uses his chopsticks.

Paris is a city of centralisation—and centralisation and classification are closely allied. In the early times, when centralisation is becoming a fact, its forerunner is classification. All things which are similar or analogous become grouped together, and from the grouping of groups rises one whole or central point. We see radiating many long arms with innumerable tentaculae, and in the centre rises a gigantic head with a comprehensive brain and keen eyes to look on every side and ears sensitive to hear—and a voracious mouth to swallow.

Other cities resemble all the birds and beasts and fishes whose appetites and digestions are normal. Paris alone is the analogical apotheosis of the octopus. Product of centralisation carried to an *ad absurdum*, it fairly represents the devil fish; and in no respects is the resemblance more curious than in the similarity of the digestive apparatus.

DRACULA'S GUEST

Those intelligent tourists who, having surrendered their individuality into the hands of Messrs. Cook or Gaze, 'do' Paris in three days, are often puzzled to know how it is that the dinner which in London would cost about six shillings, can be had for three francs in a café in the Palais Royal. They need have no more wonder if they will but consider the classification which is a theoretic speciality of Parisian life, and adopt all round the fact from which the chiffonier has his genesis.

The Paris of 1850 was not like the Paris of to-day, and those who see the Paris of Napoleon and Baron Hausseman can hardly realise the existence of the state of things forty-five years ago.

Amongst other things, however, which have not changed are those districts where the waste is gathered. Dust is dust all the world over, in every age, and the family likeness of dust-heaps is perfect. The traveller, therefore, who visits the environs of Montrouge can go back in fancy without difficulty to the year 1850.

In this year I was making a prolonged stay in Paris. I was very much in love with a young lady who, though she returned my passion, so far yielded to the wishes of her parents that she had promised not to see me or to correspond with me for a year. I, too, had been compelled to accede to these conditions under a vague hope of parental approval. During the term of probation I had promised to remain out of the country and not to write to my dear one until the expiration of the year.

Naturally the time went heavily with me. There was not one of my own family or circle who could tell me of Alice, and none of her own folk had, I am sorry to say, sufficient generosity to send me even an occasional word of comfort regarding her health and well-being. I spent six months wandering about Europe, but as I could find no satisfactory distraction in travel, I determined to come to Paris, where, at least, I would be within easy hail of London in case any good fortune should call me thither before the appointed time. That 'hope deferred maketh the heart sick' was never better exemplified than in my case, for in addition to the perpetual longing to see the face I loved there was always with me a harrowing anxiety lest some accident should prevent me showing Alice in due time that I had, throughout the long period of probation, been faithful to her trust and my own love. Thus, every adventure which I undertook had a fierce pleasure of its own, for it was fraught with possible consequences greater than it would have ordinarily borne.

Like all travellers I exhausted the places of most interest in the first month of my stay, and was driven in the second month to look for amusement whithersoever I might. Having made sundry journeys to the better-known suburbs, I began to see that there was a *terra incognita*, in so far as the guide book was concerned, in the social wilderness lying between these attractive points. Accordingly I began to systematise my researches, and each day took up the thread of my exploration at the place where I had on the previous day dropped it.

In the process of time my wanderings led me near Montrouge, and I saw that hereabouts lay the Ultima Thule of social exploration—a country as little known as that round the source of the White Nile. And so I determined to investigate philosophically the chiffonier—his habitat, his life, and his means of life.

The job was an unsavoury one, difficult of accomplishment, and with little hope of adequate reward. However, despite reason, obstinacy prevailed, and I entered into my new investigation with a keener energy than I could have summoned to aid me in any investigation leading to any end, valuable or worthy.

One day, late in a fine afternoon, toward the end of September, I entered the holy of holies of the city of dust. The place was evidently the recognised abode of a number of chiffoniers, for some sort of arrangement was manifested in the formation of the dust heaps near the road. I passed amongst these heaps, which stood like orderly sentries, determined to penetrate further and trace dust to its ultimate location.

As I passed along I saw behind the dust heaps a few forms that flitted to and fro, evidently watching with interest the advent of any stranger to such a place. The district was like a small Switzerland, and as I went forward my tortuous course shut out the path behind me.

Presently I got into what seemed a small city or community of chiffoniers. There were a number of shanties or huts, such as may be met with in the remote parts of the Bog of Allan—rude places with wattled walls, plastered with mud and roofs of rude thatch made from stable refuse—such places as one would not like to enter for any consideration, and which even in water-colour could only look picturesque if judiciously treated. In the midst of these huts was one of the strangest adaptations—I cannot say habitations—I had ever seen. An immense old wardrobe, the colossal remnant of some boudoir of Charles VII, or Henry II, had been converted into a dwelling-house. The double doors lay open, so that the entire ménage was open to public view. In the open half of the wardrobe was a common sitting-room of some four feet by six, in which sat, smoking their pipes round a charcoal brazier, no fewer than six old soldiers of the First Republic, with their uniforms torn and worn threadbare. Evidently they were of the *mauvais sujet* class; their bleary eyes and limp jaws told plainly of a common love of absinthe; and their eyes had that haggard, worn look of slumbering ferocity which follows hard in the wake of drink. The other side stood as of old, with its shelves intact, save that they were cut to half their depth, and in each shelf of which there were six, was a bed made with rags and straw. The half-dozen of worthies who inhabited this structure looked at me curiously as I passed; and when I looked back after going a little way I saw their heads together in a whispered conference. I did not like the look of this at all, for the place was very lonely, and the men looked very, very villainous. However, I did not see any cause for fear, and went on my way, penetrating further and further into the Sahara. The way was tortuous to a degree, and from going round in a series of semi-circles, as one goes in skating with the Dutch roll, I got rather confused with regard to the points of the compass.

When I had penetrated a little way I saw, as I turned the corner of a half-made heap, sitting on a heap of straw an old soldier with threadbare coat.

'Hallo!' said I to myself; 'the First Republic is well represented here in its soldiery.'

As I passed him the old man never even looked up at me, but gazed on the ground with stolid persistency. Again I remarked to myself: 'See what a life of rude warfare can do! This old man's curiosity is a thing of the past.'

When I had gone a few steps, however, I looked back suddenly, and saw that curiosity was not dead, for the veteran had raised his head and was regarding me with a very queer expression. He seemed to me to look very like one of the six worthies in the press. When he saw me looking he dropped his head; and without thinking further of him I went on my way, satisfied that there was a strange likeness between these old warriors.

Presently I met another old soldier in a similar manner. He, too, did not notice me whilst I was passing.

By this time it was getting late in the afternoon, and I began to think of retracing my steps. Accordingly I turned to go back, but could see a number of tracks leading between different mounds and could not ascertain which of them I should take. In my perplexity I wanted to see someone of whom to ask the way, but could see no one. I determined to go on a few mounds further and so try to see someone—not a veteran.

I gained my object, for after going a couple of hundred yards I saw before me a single shanty such as I had seen before—with, however, the difference that this was not one for living in, but merely a roof with three walls open in front. From the evidences which the neighbourhood exhibited I took it to be a place for sorting. Within it was an old woman wrinkled and bent with age; I approached her to ask the way.

She rose as I came close and I asked her my way. She immediately commenced a conversation; and it occurred to me that here in the very centre of the Kingdom of Dust was the place to gather details of the history of Parisian rag-picking—particularly as I could do so from the lips of one who looked like the oldest inhabitant.

I began my inquiries, and the old woman gave me most interesting answers—she had been one of the ceteuces who sat daily before the guillotine and had taken an active part among the women who signalised themselves by their violence in the revolution. While we were talking she said suddenly: 'But m'sieur must be tired standing,' and dusted a rickety old stool for me to sit down. I hardly liked to do so for many reasons; but the poor old woman was so civil that I did not like to run the risk of hurting her by refusing, and moreover the conversation of one who had been at the taking of the Bastille was so interesting that I sat down and so our conversation went on.

While we were talking an old man—older and more bent and wrinkled even than the woman—appeared from behind the shanty. 'Here is Pierre,' said she. 'M'sieur can hear stories now if he wishes, for Pierre was in everything, from the Bastille to Waterloo.' The old man took another stool at my request and we plunged into a sea of revolutionary reminiscences. This old man, albeit clothed like a scarecrow, was like any one of the six veterans.

I was now sitting in the centre of the low hut with the woman on my left hand and the man on my right, each of them being somewhat in front of me. The place was full of all sorts of curious objects of lumber, and of many things that I wished far away. In one corner was a heap of rags which seemed to move from the number of vermin it contained, and in the other a heap of bones whose odour was something shocking. Every now and then, glancing at the heaps, I could see the gleaming eyes of some of the rats which infested the place. These loathsome objects were bad enough, but what looked even more dreadful was an old butcher's axe with an iron handle stained with clots of blood leaning up against the wall on the right hand side. Still, these things did not give me much concern. The talk of the two old people was so fascinating that I stayed on and on, till the evening came and the dust heaps threw dark shadows over the vales between them.

After a time I began to grow uneasy. I could not tell how or why, but somehow I did not feel satisfied. Uneasiness is an instinct and means warning. The psychic faculties are often the sentries of the intellect, and when they sound alarm the reason begins to act, although perhaps not consciously.

This was so with me. I began to bethink me where I was and by what surrounded, and to wonder how I should fare in case I should be attacked; and then the thought suddenly burst upon me, although without any overt cause, that I was in danger. Prudence whispered: 'Be still and make no sign,' and so I was still and made no sign, for I knew that four cunning eyes were on me. 'Four eyes—if not more.' My God, what a horrible thought! The whole shanty might be surrounded on three sides with villains! I might be in the midst of a band of such desperadoes as only half a century of periodic revolution can produce.

With a sense of danger my intellect and observation quickened, and I grew more watchful than was my wont. I noticed that the old woman's eyes were constantly wandering towards my hands. I looked at them too, and saw the cause—my rings. On my left little finger I had a large signet and on the right a good diamond.

I thought that if there was any danger my first care was to avert suspicion. Accordingly I began to work the conversation round to rag-picking—to the drains—of the things found there; and so by easy stages to jewels. Then, seizing a favourable opportunity, I asked the old woman if she knew anything of such things. She answered that she did, a little. I held out my right hand, and, showing her the diamond, asked her what she thought of that. She answered that her eyes were bad, and stooped over my hand. I said as nonchalantly as I could: 'Pardon me! You will see better thus!' and taking it off handed it to her. An unholy light came into her withered old face, as she touched it. She stole one glance at me swift and keen as a flash of lightning.

She bent over the ring for a moment, her face quite concealed as though examining it. The old man looked straight out of the front of the shanty before him, at the same time fumbling in his pockets and producing a screw of tobacco in a paper and a pipe, which he proceeded to fill. I took advantage of the pause and the momentary rest from the searching eyes on my face to look carefully round the place, now dim and shadowy in the gloaming. There still lay all the heaps of varied reeking foulness; there the terrible blood-stained axe leaning against the wall in the right hand corner, and everywhere, despite the gloom, the baleful glitter of the eyes of the rats. I could see them even through some of the chinks of the boards at the back low down close to the ground. But stay! these latter eyes seemed more than usually large and bright and baleful!

For an instant my heart stood still, and I felt in that whirling condition of mind in which one feels a sort of spiritual drunkenness, and as though the body is only maintained erect in that there is no time for it to fall before recovery. Then, in another second, I was calm—coldly calm, with all my energies in full vigour, with a self-control which I felt to be perfect and with all my feeling and instincts alert.

Now I knew the full extent of my danger: I was watched and surrounded by desperate people! I could not even guess at how many of them were lying there on the ground behind the shanty, waiting for the moment to strike. I knew that I was big and strong, and they knew it, too. They knew also, as I did, that I was an Englishman and would make a fight for it; and so we waited. I had, I felt, gained an advantage in the last few seconds, for I knew my danger and understood the situation. Now, I thought, is the test of my courage—the enduring test: the fighting test may come later!

The old woman raised her head and said to me in a satisfied kind of way:

'A very fine ring, indeed—a beautiful ring! Oh, me! I once had such rings, plenty of them, and bracelets and earrings! Oh! for in those fine days I led the town a dance! But they've forgotten me now! They've forgotten me! They? Why they never heard of me! Perhaps their grandfathers remember me, some of them!' and she laughed a harsh, croaking laugh. And then I am bound to say that she astonished me, for she handed me back the ring with a certain suggestion of old-fashioned grace which was not without its pathos.

The old man eyed her with a sort of sudden ferocity, half rising from his stool, and said to me suddenly and hoarsely:

'Let me see!'

I was about to hand the ring when the old woman said:

'No! no, do not give it to Pierre! Pierre is eccentric. He loses things; and such a pretty ring!'

'Cat!' said the old man, savagely. Suddenly the old woman said, rather more loudly than was necessary:

'Wait! I shall tell you something about a ring.' There was something in the sound of her voice that jarred upon me. Perhaps it was my hyper-sensitiveness, wrought up as I was to such a pitch of nervous excitement, but I seemed to think that she was not addressing me. As I stole a glance round the place I saw the eyes of the rats in the bone heaps, but missed the eyes along the back. But even as I looked I saw them again appear. The old woman's 'Wait!' had given me a respite from attack, and the men had sunk back to their reclining posture.

'I once lost a ring—a beautiful diamond hoop that had belonged to a queen, and which was given to me by a farmer of the taxes, who afterwards cut his throat because I sent him away. I thought it must have been stolen, and taxed my people; but I could get no trace. The police came and suggested that it had found its way to the drain. We descended—I in my fine clothes, for I would not trust them with my beautiful ring! I know more of the drains since then, and of rats, too! but I shall never forget the horror of that place—alive with blazing eyes, a wall of them just outside the light of our torches. Well, we got beneath my house. We searched the outlet of the drain, and there in the filth found my ring, and we came out.

'But we found something else also before we came! As we were coming toward the opening a lot of sewer rats—human ones this time—came towards us. They told the police that one of their number had gone into the drain, but had not returned. He had gone in only shortly before we had, and, if lost, could hardly be far off. They asked help to seek him, so we turned back. They tried to prevent me going, but I insisted. It was a new excitement, and had I not recovered my ring? Not far did we go till we came on something. There was but little water, and the bottom of the drain was raised with brick, rubbish, and much matter of the kind. He had made a fight for it, even when his torch had gone out. But they were too many for him! They had not been long about it! The bones were still warm; but they were picked clean. They had even eaten their own dead ones and there were bones of rats as well as of the man. They took it cool enough those other—the human ones—and joked of their comrade when they found him dead, though they would have helped him living. Bah! what matters it—life or death?'

'And had you no fear?' I asked her.

'Fear!' she said with a laugh. 'Me have fear? Ask Pierre! But I was younger then, and, as I came through that horrible drain with its wall of greedy eyes, always moving with the circle of the light from the torches, I did not feel easy. I kept on before the men, though! It is a way I have! I never let the men get it before me. All I want is a chance and a means! And they ate him up—took every trace away except the bones;

and no one knew it, nor no sound of him was ever heard!' Here she broke into a chuckling fit of the ghastliest merriment which it was ever my lot to hear and see. A great poetess describes her heroine singing: 'Oh! to see or hear her singing! Scarce I know which is the divinest.'

And I can apply the same idea to the old crone—in all save the divinity, for I scarce could tell which was the most hellish—the harsh, malicious, satisfied, cruel laugh, or the leering grin, and the horrible square opening of the mouth like a tragic mask, and the yellow gleam of the few discoloured teeth in the shapeless gums. In that laugh and with that grin and the chuckling satisfaction I knew as well as if it had been spoken to me in words of thunder that my murder was settled, and the murderers only bided the proper time for its accomplishment. I could read between the lines of her gruesome story the commands to her accomplices. 'Wait,' she seemed to say, 'bide your time. I shall strike the first blow. Find the weapon for me, and I shall make the opportunity! He shall not escape! Keep him quiet, and then no one will be wiser. There will be no outcry, and the rats will do their work!'

It was growing darker and darker; the night was coming. I stole a glance round the shanty, still all the same! The bloody axe in the corner, the heaps of filth, and the eyes on the bone heaps and in the crannies of the floor.

Pierre had been still ostensibly filling his pipe; he now struck a light and began to puff away at it. The old woman said:

'Dear heart, how dark it is! Pierre, like a good lad, light the lamp!'

Pierre got up and with the lighted match in his hand touched the wick of a lamp which hung at one side of the entrance to the shanty, and which had a reflector that threw the light all over the place. It was evidently that which was used for their sorting at night.

'Not that, stupid! Not that! the lantern!' she called out to him.

He immediately blew it out, saying: 'All right, mother I'll find it,' and he hustled about the left corner of the room—the old woman saying through the darkness:

The lantern! the lantern! Oh! That is the light that is most useful to us poor folks. The lantern was the friend of the revolution! It is the friend of the chiffonier! It helps us when all else fails.'

Hardly had she said the word when there was a kind of creaking of the whole place, and something was steadily dragged over the roof.

Again I seemed to read between the lines of her words. I knew the lesson of the lantern.

'One of you get on the roof with a noose and strangle him as he passes out if we fail within.'

As I looked out of the opening I saw the loop of a rope outlined black against the lurid sky. I was now, indeed, beset!

Pierre was not long in finding the lantern. I kept my eyes fixed through the darkness on the old woman. Pierre struck his light, and by its flash I saw the old woman raise from the ground beside her where it had mysteriously appeared, and then hide in the folds of her gown, a long sharp knife or dagger. It seemed to be like a butcher's sharpening iron fined to a keen point.

The lantern was lit.

'Bring it here, Pierre,' she said. 'Place it in the doorway where we can see it. See how nice it is! It shuts out the darkness from us; it is just right!'

Just right for her and her purposes! It threw all its light on my face, leaving in gloom the faces of both Pierre and the woman, who sat outside of me on each side.

I felt that the time of action was approaching, but I knew now that the first signal and movement would come from the woman, and so watched her.

I was all unarmed, but I had made up my mind what to do. At the first movement I would seize the butcher's axe in the right-hand corner and fight my way out. At least, I would die hard. I stole a glance round to fix its exact locality so that I could not fail to seize it at the first effort, for then, if ever, time and accuracy would be precious.

Good God! It was gone! All the horror of the situation burst upon me; but the bitterest thought of all was that if the issue of the terrible position should be against me Alice would infallibly suffer. Either she would believe me false—and any lover, or any one who has ever been one, can imagine the bitterness of the thought—or else she would go on loving long after I had been lost to her and to the world, so that her life would be broken and embittered, shattered with disappointment and despair. The very magnitude of the pain braced me up and nerved me to bear the dread scrutiny of the plotters.

I think I did not betray myself. The old woman was watching me as a cat does a mouse; she had her right hand hidden in the folds of her gown, clutching, I knew, that long, cruel-looking dagger. Had she seen any disappointment in my face she would, I felt, have known that the moment had come, and would have sprung on me like a tigress, certain of taking me unprepared.

I looked out into the night, and there I saw new cause for danger. Before and around the hut were at a little distance some shadowy forms; they were quite still, but I knew that they were all alert and on guard. Small chance for me now in that direction.

Again I stole a glance round the place. In moments of great excitement and of great danger, which is excitement, the mind works very quickly, and the keenness of the faculties which depend on the mind grows in proportion. I now felt this. In an instant I took in the whole situation. I saw that the axe had been taken through a small hole made in one of the rotten boards. How rotten they must be to allow of such a thing being done without a particle of noise.

The hut was a regular murder-trap, and was guarded all around. A garroter lay on the roof ready to entangle me with his noose if I should escape the dagger of the old hag. In front the way was guarded by I know not how many watchers. And at the back was a row of desperate men—I had seen their eyes still through the crack in the boards of the floor, when last I looked—as they lay prone waiting for the signal to start erect. If it was to be ever, now for it!

As nonchalantly as I could I turned slightly on my stool so as to get my right leg well under me. Then with a sudden jump, turning my head, and guarding it with my hands, and with the fighting instinct of the knights of old, I breathed my lady's name, and hurled myself against the back wall of the hut.

Watchful as they were, the suddenness of my movement surprised both Pierre and the old woman. As I crashed through the rotten timbers I saw the old woman rise with a leap like a tiger and heard her low gasp of baffled rage. My feet lit on something that moved, and as I jumped away I knew that I had stepped on the back of one of the row of men lying on their faces outside the hut. I was torn with nails and splinters, but otherwise unhurt. Breathless I rushed up the mound in front of me, hearing as I went the dull crash of the shanty as it collapsed into a mass.

It was a nightmare climb. The mound, though but low, was awfully steep, and with each step I took the mass of dust and cinders tore down with me and gave way under my feet. The dust rose and choked me; it was sickening, fœtid, awful; but my climb was, I felt, for life or death, and I struggled on. The seconds seemed hours; but the few moments I had in starting, combined with my youth and strength, gave me a great advantage, and, though several forms struggled after me in deadly silence which was more dreadful than any sound, I easily reached the top. Since then I have climbed the cone of Vesuvius, and as I struggled up that dreary steep amid the sulphurous fumes the memory of that awful night at Montrouge came back to me so vividly that I almost grew faint.

The mound was one of the tallest in the region of dust, and as I struggled to the top, panting for breath and with my heart beating like a sledge-hammer, I saw away to my left the dull red gleam of the sky, and nearer still the flashing of lights. Thank God! I knew where I was now and where lay the road to Paris!

For two or three seconds I paused and looked back. My pursuers were still well behind me, but struggling up resolutely, and in deadly silence. Beyond, the shanty was a wreck—a mass of timber and moving forms. I could see it well, for flames were already bursting out; the rags and straw had evidently caught fire from the lantern. Still silence there! Not a sound! These old wretches could die game, anyhow.

I had no time for more than a passing glance, for as I cast an eye round the mound preparatory to making my descent I saw several dark forms rushing round on either side to cut me off on my way. It was now a race for life. They were trying to head me on my way to Paris, and with the instinct of the moment I dashed down to the right-hand side. I was just in time, for, though I came as it seemed to me down the steep in a few steps, the wary old men who were watching me turned back, and one, as I rushed by into the opening between the two mounds in front, almost struck me a blow with that terrible butcher's axe. There could surely not be two such weapons about!

Then began a really horrible chase. I easily ran ahead of the old men, and even when some younger ones and a few women joined in the hunt I easily distanced them. But I did not know the way, and I could not even guide myself by the light in the sky, for I was running away from it. I had heard that, unless of conscious purpose, hunted men turn always to the left, and so I found it now; and so, I suppose, knew also my pursuers, who were more animals than men, and with cunning or instinct had found out such secrets for themselves: for on finishing a quick spurt, after which I intended to take a moment's breathing space, I suddenly saw ahead of me two or three forms swiftly passing behind a mound to the right.

I was in the spider's web now indeed! But with the thought of this new danger came the resource of the hunted, and so I darted down the next turning to the right. I continued in this direction for some hundred yards, and then, making a turn to the left again, felt certain that I had, at any rate, avoided the danger of being surrounded.

But not of pursuit, for on came the rabble after me, steady, dogged, relentless, and still in grim silence.

In the greater darkness the mounds seemed now to be somewhat smaller than before, although—for the night was closing—they looked bigger in proportion. I was now well ahead of my pursuers, so I made a dart up the mound in front.

Oh joy of joys! I was close to the edge of this inferno of dustheaps. Away behind me the red light of Paris was in the sky, and towering up behind rose the heights of Montmarte—a dim light, with here and there brilliant points like stars.

Restored to vigour in a moment, I ran over the few remaining mounds of decreasing size, and found myself on the level land beyond. Even then, however, the prospect was not inviting. All before me was dark and dismal, and I had evidently come on one of those dank, low-lying waste places which are found here and there in the neighbourhood of great cities. Places of waste and desolation, where the space is required for the ultimate agglomeration of all that is noxious, and the ground is so poor as to create no desire of occupancy even in the lowest squatter. With eyes accustomed to the gloom of the evening, and away now from the shadows of those dreadful dustheaps, I could see much more easily than I could a little while ago. It might have been, of course, that the glare in the sky of the lights of Paris, though the city was some miles away, was reflected here. Howsoever it was, I saw well enough to take bearings for certainly some little distance around me.

In front was a bleak, flat waste that seemed almost dead level, with here and there the dark shimmering of stagnant pools. Seemingly far off on the right, amid a small cluster of scattered lights, rose a dark mass of Fort Montrouge, and away to the left in the dim distance, pointed with stray gleams from cottage windows, the lights in the sky showed the locality of Bicêtre. A moment's thought decided me to take to the right and try to reach Montrouge. There at least would be some sort of safety, and I might possibly long before come on some of the cross roads which I knew. Somewhere, not far off, must lie the strategic road made to connect the outlying chain of forts circling the city.

Then I looked back. Coming over the mounds, and outlined black against the glare of the Parisian horizon, I saw several moving figures, and still a way to the right several more deploying out between me and my destination. They evidently meant to cut me off in this direction, and so my choice became constricted; it lay now between going straight ahead or turning to the left. Stooping to the ground, so as to get the advantage of the horizon as a line of sight, I looked carefully in this direction, but could detect no sign of my enemies. I argued that as they had not guarded or were not trying to guard that point, there was evidently danger to me there already. So I made up my mind to go straight on before me.

It was not an inviting prospect, and as I went on the reality grew worse. The ground became soft and oozy, and now and again gave way beneath me in a sickening kind of way. I seemed somehow to be going down, for I saw round me places seemingly more elevated than where I was, and this in a place which from a little way back seemed dead level. I looked around, but could see none of my pursuers. This was strange, for all along these birds of the night had followed me through the darkness as well as though it was broad daylight. How I blamed myself for coming out in my light-coloured tourist suit of tweed. The silence, and my not being able to see my enemies, whilst I felt that they were watching me, grew appalling, and in the hope of some one not of this ghastly crew hearing me I raised my voice and shouted several times. There was not the slightest response; not even an echo rewarded my efforts. For a while I stood stock still and kept my eyes in one direction. On one of the rising places around me I saw something dark move along, then another, and another. This was to my left, and seemingly moving to head me off.

I thought that again I might with my skill as a runner elude my enemies at this game, and so with all my speed darted forward.

Splash!

My feet had given way in a mass of slimy rubbish, and I had fallen headlong into a reeking, stagnant pool. The water and the mud in which my arms sank up to the elbows was filthy and nauseous beyond description, and in the suddenness of my fall I had actually swallowed some of the filthy stuff, which nearly choked me, and made me gasp for breath. Never shall I forget the moments during which I stood trying to recover myself almost fainting from the fœtid odour of the filthy pool, whose white mist rose ghostlike around. Worst of all, with the acute despair of the hunted animal when he sees the pursuing pack closing on him, I saw before my eyes whilst I stood helpless the dark forms of my pursuers moving swiftly to surround me.

It is curious how our minds work on odd matters even when the energies of thought are seemingly concentrated on some terrible and pressing need. I was in momentary peril of my life: my safety depended on my action, and my choice of alternatives coming now with almost every step I took, and yet I could not but think of the strange dogged persistency of these old men. Their silent resolution, their steadfast, grim, persistency even in such a cause commanded, as well as fear, even a measure of respect. What must they have been in the vigour of their youth. I could understand now that whirlwind rush on the bridge of Arcola, that scornful exclamation of the Old Guard at Waterloo! Unconscious cerebration has its own pleasures, even at such moments; but fortunately it does not in any way clash with the thought from which action springs.

I realised at a glance that so far I was defeated in my object, my enemies as yet had won. They had succeeded in surrounding me on three sides, and were bent on driving me off to the left-hand, where there was already some danger for me, for they had left no guard. I accepted the alternative—it was a case of Hobson's choice and run. I had to keep the lower ground, for my pursuers were on the higher places. However, though the ooze and broken ground impeded me my youth and training made me able to hold my ground, and by keeping a diagonal line I not only kept them from gaining on me but even began to distance them. This gave me new heart and strength, and by this time habitual training was beginning to tell and my second wind had come. Before me the ground rose slightly. I rushed up the slope and found before me a waste of watery slime, with a low dyke or bank looking black and grim beyond. I felt that if I could but reach that dyke in safety I could there, with solid ground under my feet and some kind of path to guide me, find with comparative ease a way out of my troubles. After a glance right and left and seeing no one near, I kept my eyes for a few minutes to their rightful work of aiding my feet whilst I crossed the swamp. It was rough, hard work, but there was little danger, merely toil; and a short time took me to the dyke. I rushed up the slope exulting; but here again I met a new shock. On either side of me rose a number of crouching figures. From right and left they rushed at me. Each body held a rope.

The cordon was nearly complete. I could pass on neither side, and the end was near.

There was only one chance, and I took it. I hurled myself across the dyke, and escaping out of the very clutches of my foes threw myself into the stream.

At any other time I should have thought that water foul and filthy, but now it was as welcome as the most crystal stream to the parched traveller. It was a highway of safety!

My pursuers rushed after me. Had only one of them held the rope it would have been all up with me, for he could have entangled me before I had time to swim a stroke; but the many hands holding it embarrassed and delayed them, and when the rope struck the water I heard the splash well behind me. A few minutes' hard swimming took me across the stream. Refreshed with the immersion and encouraged by the escape, I climbed the dyke in comparative gaiety of spirits.

From the top I looked back. Through the darkness I saw my assailants scattering up and down along the dyke. The pursuit was evidently not ended, and again I had to choose my course. Beyond the dyke where I stood was a wild, swampy space very similar to that which I had crossed. I determined to shun such a place, and thought for a moment whether I would take up or down the dyke. I thought I heard a sound—the muffled sound of oars, so I listened, and then shouted.

No response; but the sound ceased. My enemies had evidently got a boat of some kind. As they were on the up side of me I took the down path and began to run. As I passed to the left of where I had entered the water I heard several splashes, soft and stealthy, like the sound a rat makes as he plunges into the stream, but vastly greater; and as I looked I saw the dark sheen of the water broken by the ripples of several advancing heads. Some of my enemies were swimming the stream also.

And now behind me, up the stream, the silence was broken by the quick rattle and creak of oars; my enemies were in hot pursuit. I put my best leg foremost and ran on. After a break of a couple of minutes I looked back, and by a gleam of light through the ragged clouds I saw several dark forms climbing the bank behind me. The wind had now begun to rise, and the water beside me was ruffled and beginning to break in tiny waves on the bank. I had to keep my eyes pretty well on the ground before me, lest I should stumble, for I knew that to stumble was death. After a few minutes I looked back behind me. On the dyke were only a few dark figures, but crossing the waste, swampy ground were many more. What new danger this portended I did not know—could only guess. Then as I ran it seemed to me that my track kept ever sloping away to the right. I looked up ahead and saw that the river was much wider than before, and that the dyke on which I stood fell quite away, and beyond it was another stream on whose near bank I saw some of the dark forms now across the marsh. I was on an island of some kind.

My situation was now indeed terrible, for my enemies had hemmed me in on every side. Behind came the quickening roll of the oars, as though my pursuers knew that the end was close. Around me on every side was desolation; there was not a roof or light, as far as I could see. Far off to the right rose some dark mass, but what it was I knew not. For a moment I paused to think what I should do, not for more, for my pursuers were drawing closer. Then my mind was made up. I slipped down the bank and took to the water. I struck out straight ahead so as to gain the current by clearing the backwater of the island, for such I presume it was, when I had passed into the stream. I waited till a cloud came driving across the moon and leaving all in darkness. Then I took off my hat and laid it softly on the water floating with the stream, and a second after dived to the right and struck out under water with all my might. I was, I suppose, half a minute under water, and when I rose came up as softly as I could, and turning, looked back. There went my light brown hat floating merrily away. Close behind it came a rickety old boat, driven furiously by a pair of oars. The moon was still partly obscured by the drifting clouds, but in the partial light I could see a man in the bows holding aloft ready to strike what appeared to me to be that same dreadful pole-axe which I had before escaped. As I looked the boat drew closer, closer, and the man struck savagely. The hat disappeared. The man fell forward, almost out of the boat. His comrades dragged him in but without the axe, and then as I turned with all my energies bent on reaching the further bank, I heard the fierce whirr of the muttered 'Sacre!' which marked the anger of my baffled pursuers.

That was the first sound I had heard from human lips during all this dreadful chase, and full as it was of menace and danger to me it was a welcome sound for it broke that awful silence which shrouded and appalled me. It was as though an overt sign that my opponents were men and not ghosts, and that with them I had, at least; the chance of a man, though but one against many.

But now that the spell of silence was broken the sounds came thick and fast. From boat to shore and back from shore to boat came quick question and answer, all in the fiercest whispers. I looked back—a fatal thing to do—for in the instant someone caught sight of my face, which showed white on the dark water, and shouted. Hands pointed to me, and in a moment or two the boat was under weigh, and following hard after me. I had but a little way to go, but quicker and quicker came the boat after me. A few more strokes and I would be on the shore, but I felt the oncoming of the boat, and expected each second to feel the crash of an oar or other weapon on my head. Had I not seen that dreadful axe disappear in the water I do not think that I could have won the shore. I heard the muttered curses of those not rowing and the laboured breath of the rowers. With one supreme effort for life or liberty I touched the bank and sprang up it. There was not a single second to spare, for hard behind me the boat grounded and several dark forms sprang after me. I gained the top of the dyke, and keeping to the left ran on again. The boat put off and followed down the stream. Seeing this I feared danger in this direction, and quickly turning, ran down the dyke on the other side, and after passing a short stretch of marshy ground gained a wild, open flat country and sped on.

Still behind me came on my relentless pursuers. Far away, below me, I saw the same dark mass as before, but now grown closer and greater. My heart gave a great thrill of delight, for I knew that it must be the fortress of Bicêtre, and with new courage I ran on. I had heard that between each and all of the protecting forts of Paris there are strategic ways, deep sunk roads where soldiers marching should be sheltered from an enemy. I knew that if I could gain this road I would be safe, but in the darkness I could not see any sign of it, so, in blind hope of striking it, I ran on.

Presently I came to the edge of a deep cut, and found that down below me ran a road guarded on each side by a ditch of water fenced on either side by a straight, high wall.

Getting fainter and dizzier, I ran on; the ground got more broken—more and more still, till I staggered and fell, and rose again, and ran on in the blind anguish of the hunted. Again the thought of Alice nerved me. I would not be lost and wreck her life: I would fight and struggle for life to the bitter end. With a great effort I caught the top of the wall. As, scrambling like a catamount, I drew myself up, I actually felt a hand touch the sole of my foot. I was now on a sort of causeway, and before me I saw a dim light. Blind and dizzy, I ran on, staggered, and fell, rising, covered with dust and blood.

'Halt la!'

The words sounded like a voice from heaven. A blaze of light seemed to enwrap me, and I shouted with joy.

'Qui va la?' The rattle of musketry, the flash of steel before my eyes. Instinctively I stopped, though close behind me came a rush of my pursuers.

Another word or two, and out from a gateway poured, as it seemed to me, a tide of red and blue, as the guard turned out. All around seemed blazing with light, and the flash of steel, the clink and rattle of arms, and the loud, harsh voices of command. As I fell forward, utterly exhausted, a soldier caught me. I looked back in dreadful expectation, and saw the mass of dark forms disappearing into the night. Then I must have fainted. When I recovered my senses I was in the guard room. They gave me brandy, and after a while I was able to tell them something of what had passed. Then a commissary of police appeared, apparently out of the empty air, as is the way of the Parisian police officer. He listened attentively, and then had a moment's consultation with the officer in command. Apparently they were agreed, for they asked me if I were ready now to come with them.

'Where to?' I asked, rising to go.

'Back to the dust heaps. We shall, perhaps, catch them yet!'

'I shall try!' said I.

He eyed me for a moment keenly, and said suddenly:

'Would you like to wait a while or till tomorrow, young Englishman?' This touched me to the quick, as, perhaps, he intended, and I jumped to my feet.

'Come now!' I said; 'now! now! An Englishman is always ready for his duty!'

The commissary was a good fellow, as well as a shrewd one; he slapped my shoulder kindly. 'Brave garçon!' he said. 'Forgive me, but I knew what would do you most good. The guard is ready. Come!'

And so, passing right through the guard room, and through a long vaulted passage, we were out into the night. A few of the men in front had powerful lanterns. Through courtyards and down a sloping way we passed out through a low archway to a sunken road, the same that I had seen in my flight. The order was given to get at the double, and with a quick, springing stride, half run, half walk, the soldiers went swiftly along. I felt my strength renewed again—such is the difference between hunter and hunted. A very short distance took us to a low-lying pontoon bridge across the stream, and evidently very little higher up than I had struck it. Some effort had evidently been made to damage it, for the ropes had all been cut, and one of the chains had been broken. I heard the officer say to the commissary:

'We are just in time! A few more minutes, and they would have destroyed the bridge. Forward, quicker still!' and on we went. Again we reached a pontoon on the winding stream; as we came up we heard the hollow boom of the metal drums as the efforts to destroy the bridge was again renewed. A word of command was given, and several men raised their rifles.

'Fire!' A volley rang out. There was a muffled cry, and the dark forms dispersed. But the evil was done, and we saw the far end of the pontoon swing into the stream. This was a serious delay, and it was nearly an hour before we had renewed ropes and restored the bridge sufficiently to allow us to cross.

We renewed the chase. Quicker, quicker we went towards the dust heaps.

After a time we came to a place that I knew. There were the remains of a fire—a few smouldering wood ashes still cast a red glow, but the bulk of the ashes were cold. I knew the site of the hut and the hill behind it up which I had rushed, and in the flickering glow the eyes of the rats still shone with a sort of phosphorescence. The commissary spoke a word to the officer, and he cried:

'Halt!'

The soldiers were ordered to spread around and watch, and then we commenced to examine the ruins. The commissary himself began to lift away the charred boards and rubbish. These the soldiers took and piled together. Presently he started back, then bent down and rising beckoned me.

'See!' he said.

It was a gruesome sight. There lay a skeleton face downwards, a woman by the lines—an old woman by the coarse fibre of the bone. Between the ribs rose a long spike-like dagger made from a butcher's sharpening knife, its keen point buried in the spine.

'You will observe,' said the commissary to the officer and to me as he took out his note book, 'that the woman must have fallen on her dagger. The rats are many here—see their eyes glistening among that heap of bones—and you will also notice'—I shuddered as he placed his hand on the skeleton—'that but little time was lost by them, for the bones are scarcely cold!'

There was no other sign of any one near, living or dead; and so deploying again into line the soldiers passed on. Presently we came to the hut made of the old ward-robe. We approached. In five of the six compartments was an old man sleeping—sleeping so soundly that even the glare of the lanterns did not wake them. Old and grim and grizzled they looked, with their gaunt, wrinkled, bronzed faces and their white moustaches.

The officer called out harshly and loudly a word of command, and in an instant each one of them was on his feet before us and standing at 'attention!'

'What do you here?'

'We sleep,' was the answer.

'Where are the other chiffoniers?' asked the commissary.

'Gone to work.'

'And you?'

'We are on guard!'

'Peste!' laughed the officer grimly, as he looked at the old men one after the other in the face and added with cool deliberate cruelty: 'Asleep on duty! Is this the manner of the Old Guard? No wonder, then, a Waterloo!'

By the gleam of the lantern I saw the grim old faces grow deadly pale, and almost shuddered at the look in the eyes of the old men as the laugh of the soldiers echoed the grim pleasantry of the officer.

I felt in that moment that I was in some measure avenged.

For a moment they looked as if they would throw themselves on the taunter, but years of their life had schooled them and they remained still.

'You are but five,' said the commissary; 'where is the sixth?' The answer came with a grim chuckle.

'He is there!' and the speaker pointed to the bottom of the wardrobe. 'He died last night. You won't find much of him. The burial of the rats is quick!'

The commissary stooped and looked in. Then he turned to the officer and said calmly:

'We may as well go back. No trace here now; nothing to prove that man was the one wounded by your soldiers' bullets! Probably they murdered him to cover up the trace. See!' again he stooped and placed his hands on the skeleton. 'The rats work quickly and they are many. These bones are warm!'

I shuddered, and so did many more of those around me.

'Form!' said the officer, and so in marching order, with the lanterns swinging in front and the manacled veterans in the midst, with steady tramp we took ourselves out of the dustheaps and turned backward to the fortress of Bicêtre.

My year of probation has long since ended, and Alice is my wife. But when I look back upon that trying twelvemonth one of the most vivid incidents that memory recalls is that associated with my visit to the City of Dust.

A Dream of Red Hands

The first opinion given to me regarding Jacob Settle was a simple descriptive statement, 'He's a down-in-the-mouth chap': but I found that it embodied the thoughts and ideas of all his fellow-workmen. There was in the phrase a certain easy tolerance, an absence of positive feeling of any kind, rather than any complete opinion, which marked pretty accurately the man's place in public esteem. Still, there was some dissimilarity between this and his appearance which unconsciously set me thinking, and by degrees, as I saw more of the place and the workmen, I came to have a special interest in him. He was, I found, for ever doing kindnesses, not involving money expenses beyond his humble means, but in the manifold ways of forethought and forbearance and self-repression which are of the truer charities of life. Women and children trusted him implicitly, though, strangely enough, he rather shunned them, except when anyone was sick, and then he made his appearance to help if he could, timidly and awkwardly. He led a very solitary life, keeping house by himself in a tiny cottage, or rather hut, of one room, far on the edge of the moorland. His existence seemed so sad and solitary that I wished to cheer it up, and for the purpose took the occasion when we had both been sitting up with a child, injured by me through accident, to offer to lend him books. He gladly accepted, and as we parted in the grey of the dawn I felt that something of mutual confidence had been established between us.

The books were always most carefully and punctually returned, and in time Jacob Settle and I became quite friends. Once or twice as I crossed the moorland on Sundays I looked in on him; but on such occasions he was shy and ill at ease so that I felt diffident about calling to see him. He would never under any circumstances come into my own lodgings.

One Sunday afternoon, I was coming back from a long walk beyond the moor, and as I passed Settle's cottage stopped at the door to say 'How do you do?' to him. As the door was shut, I thought that he was out, and merely knocked for form's sake, or through habit, not expecting to get any answer. To my surprise, I heard a feeble voice from within, though what was said I could not hear. I entered at once, and found Jacob lying half-dressed upon his bed. He was as pale as death, and the sweat was simply rolling off his face. His hands were unconsciously gripping the bedclothes as a drowning man holds on to whatever he may grasp. As I came in he half arose, with a wild, hunted look in his eyes, which were wide open and staring, as though something of horror had come before him; but when he recognised me he sank back on the couch with a smothered sob of relief and closed his eyes. I stood by him for a while, quite a minute or two, while he gasped. Then he opened his eyes and looked at me, but with such a despairing, woeful expression that, as I am a living man, I would have rather seen that frozen look of horror. I sat down beside him and asked after his health. For a while he would not answer me except to say that he was not ill; but then, after scrutinising me closely, he half arose on his elbow and said:

'I thank you kindly, sir, but I'm simply telling you the truth. I am not ill, as men call it, though God knows whether there be not worse sicknesses than doctors know of. I'll tell you, as you are so kind, but I trust that you won't even mention such a thing to a living soul, for it might work me more and greater woe. I am suffering from a bad dream.'

'A bad dream!' I said, hoping to cheer him; 'but dreams pass away with the light—even with waking.' There I stopped, for before he spoke I saw the answer in his desolate look round the little place.

'No! no! that's all well for people that live in comfort and with those they love around them. It is a thousand times worse for those who live alone and have to do so. What cheer is there for me, waking here in the silence of the night, with the wide moor around me full of voices and full of faces that make my waking a worse dream than my sleep? Ah, young sir, you have no past that can send its legions to people the darkness and the empty space, and I pray the good God that you may never have!' As he spoke, there was such an almost irresistible gravity of conviction in his manner that I abandoned my remonstrance about his solitary life. I felt that I was in the presence of some secret influence which I could not fathom. To my relief, for I knew not what to say, he went on:

'Two nights past have I dreamed it. It was hard enough the first night, but I came through it. Last night the expectation was in itself almost worse than the dream—until the dream came, and then it swept away every remembrance of lesser pain. I stayed awake till just before the dawn, and then it came again, and ever since I have been in such an agony as I am sure the dying feel, and with it all the dread of tonight.' Before he had got to the end of the sentence my mind was made up, and I felt that I could speak to him more cheerfully.

'Try and get to sleep early tonight—in fact, before the evening has passed away. The sleep will refresh you, and I promise you there will not be any bad dreams after tonight.' He shook his head hopelessly, so I sat a little longer and then left him.

When I got home I made my arrangements for the night, for I had made up my mind to share Jacob Settle's lonely vigil in his cottage on the moor. I judged that if he got to sleep before sunset he would wake well before midnight, and so, just as the bells of the city were striking eleven, I stood opposite his door armed with a bag, in which were my supper, an extra large flask, a couple of candles, and a book. The moonlight was bright, and flooded the whole moor, till it was almost as light as day; but ever and anon black clouds drove across the sky, and made a darkness which by comparison seemed almost tangible. I opened the door softly, and entered without waking Jacob, who lay asleep with his white face upward. He was still, and again bathed in sweat. I tried to imagine what visions were passing before those closed eyes which could bring with them the misery and woe which were stamped on the face, but fancy failed me, and I waited for the awakening. It came suddenly, and in a fashion which touched me to the quick, for the hollow groan that broke from the man's white lips as he half arose and sank back was manifestly the realisation or completion of some train of thought which had gone before.

'If this be dreaming,' said I to myself, 'then it must be based on some very terrible reality. What can have been that unhappy fact that he spoke of?'

While I thus spoke, he realised that I was with him. It struck me as strange that he had no period of that doubt as to whether dream or reality surrounded him which commonly marks an expected environment of waking men. With a positive cry of joy, he seized my hand and held it in his two wet, trembling hands, as a frightened child clings on to someone whom it loves. I tried to soothe him:

'There, there! it is all right. I have come to stay with you tonight, and together we will try to fight this evil dream.' He let go my hand suddenly, and sank back on his bed and covered his eyes with his hands.

'Fight it?—the evil dream! Ah! no, sir, no! No mortal power can fight that dream, for it comes from God—and is burned in here;' and he beat upon his forehead. Then he went on:

'It is the same dream, ever the same, and yet it grows in its power to torture me every time it comes.'

'What is the dream?' I asked, thinking that the speaking of it might give him some relief, but he shrank away from me, and after a long pause said:

'No, I had better not tell it. It may not come again.'

There was manifestly something to conceal from me—something that lay behind the dream, so I answered:

'All right. I hope you have seen the last of it. But if it should come again, you will tell me, will you not? I ask, not out of curiosity, but because I think it may relieve you to speak.' He answered with what I thought was almost an undue amount of solemnity:

'If it comes again, I shall tell you all.'

Then I tried to get his mind away from the subject to more mundane things, so I produced supper, and made him share it with me, including the contents of the flask. After a little he braced up, and when I lit my cigar, having given him another, we smoked a full hour, and talked of many things. Little by little the comfort of his body stole over his mind, and I could see sleep laying her gentle hands on his eyelids. He felt it, too, and told me that now he felt all right, and I might safely leave him; but I told him that, right or wrong, I was going to see in the daylight. So I lit my other candle, and began to read as he fell asleep.

By degrees I got interested in my book, so interested that presently I was startled by its dropping out of my hands. I looked and saw that Jacob was still asleep, and I was rejoiced to see that there was on his face a look of unwonted happiness, while his lips seemed to move with unspoken words. Then I turned to my work again, and again woke, but this time to feel chilled to my very marrow by hearing the voice from the bed beside me:

'Not with those red hands! Never! never!' On looking at him, I found that he was still asleep. He woke, however, in an instant, and did not seem surprised to see me; there was again that strange apathy as to his surroundings. Then I said:

'Settle, tell me your dream. You may speak freely, for I shall hold your confidence sacred. While we both live I shall never mention what you may choose to tell me.'

He replied:

'I said I would; but I had better tell you first what goes before the dream, that you may understand. I was a schoolmaster when I was a very young man; it was only a parish school in a little village in the West Country. No need to mention any names. Better not. I was engaged to be married to a young girl whom I loved and almost reverenced. It was the old story. While we were waiting for the time when we could afford to set up house together, another man came along. He was nearly as young as I was, and handsome, and a gentleman, with all a gentleman's attractive ways for a woman of our class. He would go fishing, and she would meet him while I was at my work in school. I reasoned with her and implored her to give him up. I offered to get married at once and go away and begin the world in a strange country; but she would not listen to anything I could say, and I could see that she was infatuated with him. Then I took it on myself to meet the man and ask him to deal well with the girl, for I thought he might mean honestly by her, so that there might be no talk or chance of talk on the part of others. I went where I should meet him with none by, and we met!' Here Jacob Settle had to pause, for something seemed to rise in his throat, and he almost gasped for breath. Then he went on:

'Sir, as God is above us, there was no selfish thought in my heart that day, I loved my pretty Mabel too well to be content with a part of her love, and I had thought of my own unhappiness too often not to have come to realise that, whatever might come to her, my hope was gone. He was insolent to me—you, sir, who are a gentleman, cannot know, perhaps, how galling can be the insolence of one who is above you in station—but I bore with that. I implored him to deal well with the girl, for what might be only a pastime of an idle hour with him might be the breaking of her heart. For I never had a thought of her truth, or that the worst of harm could come to her—it was only the unhappiness to her heart I feared. But when I asked him when he intended to marry her his laughter galled me so that I lost my temper and told him that I would not stand by and see her life made unhappy. Then he grew angry too, and in his anger said such cruel things of her that then and there I swore he should not live to do her harm. God knows how it came about, for in such moments of passion it is hard to remember the steps from a word to a blow, but I found myself standing over his dead body, with my hands crimson with the blood that welled from his torn throat. We were alone and he was a stranger, with none of his kin to seek for him and murder does not always out—not all at once. His bones may be whitening still, for all I know, in the pool of the river where I left him. No one suspected his absence, or why it was, except my poor Mabel, and she dared not speak. But it was all in vain, for when I came back again after an absence of months—for I could not live in the place—I learned that her shame had come and that she had died in it. Hitherto I had been borne up by the thought that my ill deed had saved her future, but now, when I learned that I had been too late, and that my poor love was smirched with that man's sin, I fled away with the sense of my useless guilt upon me more heavily than I could bear. Ah! sir, you that have not done such a sin don't know what it is to carry it with you. You may think that custom makes it easy to you, but it is not so. It grows and grows with every hour, till it becomes intolerable, and with it growing, too, the feeling that you must for ever stand outside Heaven. You don't know what that means, and I pray God that you never may. Ordinary men, to whom all things are possible, don't often, if ever, think of Heaven. It is a name, and nothing more, and they are content to wait and let things be, but to those who are doomed to be shut out for ever you cannot think what it means, you cannot guess or measure the terrible endless longing to see the gates opened, and to be able to join the white figures within.

'And this brings me to my dream. It seemed that the portal was before me, with great gates of massive steel with bars of the thickness of a mast, rising to the very clouds, and so close that between them was just a glimpse of a crystal grotto, on whose shining walls were figured many white-clad forms with faces radiant with joy. When I stood before the gate my heart and my soul were so full of rapture and longing that I forgot. And there stood at the gate two mighty angels with sweeping wings, and, oh! so stern of countenance. They held each in one hand a flaming sword, and in the other the latchet, which moved to and fro at their lightest touch. Nearer were figures all draped in black, with heads covered so that only the eyes were seen, and they handed to each who came white garments such as the angels wear. A low murmur came that told that all should put on their own robes, and without soil, or the angels would not pass them in, but would smite them down with the flaming swords. I was eager to don my own garment, and hurriedly threw it over me and stepped swiftly to the gate; but it moved not, and the angels, loosing the latchet, pointed to my dress, I looked down, and was aghast, for the whole robe was smeared with blood. My hands were red; they glittered with the blood that dripped from them as on that day by the river bank. And then the angels raised their flaming swords to smite me down, and the horror was complete—I awoke. Again, and again, and again, that awful dream comes to me. I never learn from the experience, I never remember, but at the beginning the hope is ever there to make the end more appalling; and I know that the dream does not come out of the common darkness where the dreams abide, but that it is sent from God as a punishment! Never, never shall I be able to pass the gate, for the soil on the angel garments must ever come from these bloody hands!'

I listened as in a spell as Jacob Settle spoke. There was something so far away in the tone of his voice—something so dreamy and mystic in the eyes that looked as if through me at some spirit beyond—something so lofty in his very diction and in such marked contrast to his workworn clothes and his poor surroundings that I wondered if the whole thing were not a dream.

We were both silent for a long time. I kept looking at the man before me in growing wonderment. Now that his confession had been made, his soul, which had been crushed to the very earth, seemed to leap back again to uprightness with some resilient force. I suppose I ought to have been horrified with his story, but, strange to say, I was not. It certainly is not pleasant to be made the recipient of the confidence of a murderer, but this poor fellow seemed to have had, not only so much provocation, but so much self-denying purpose in his deed of blood that I did not feel called upon to pass judgment upon him. My purpose was to comfort, so I spoke out with what calmness I could, for my heart was beating fast and heavily:

'You need not despair, Jacob Settle. God is very good, and His mercy is great. Live on and work on in the hope that some day you may feel that you have atoned for the past.' Here I paused, for I could see that deep, natural sleep this time, was creeping upon him. 'Go to sleep,' I said; 'I shall watch with you here and we shall have no more evil dreams tonight.'

He made an effort to pull himself together, and answered:

'I don't know how to thank you for your goodness to me this night, but I think you had best leave me now. I'll try and sleep this out; I feel a weight off my mind since I have told you all. If there's anything of the man left in me, I must try and fight out life alone.'

'I'll go tonight, as you wish it,' I said; 'but take my advice, and do not live in such a solitary way. Go among men and women; live among them. Share their joys and sorrows, and it will help you to forget. This solitude will make you melancholy mad.'

'I will!' he answered, half unconsciously, for sleep was overmastering him.

I turned to go, and he looked after me. When I had touched the latch I dropped it, and, coming back to the bed, held out my hand. He grasped it with both his as he rose to a sitting posture, and I said my goodnight, trying to cheer him:

'Heart, man, heart! There is work in the world for you to do, Jacob Settle. You can wear those white robes yet and pass through that gate of steel!'

Then I left him.

A week after I found his cottage deserted, and on asking at the works was told that he had 'gone north', no one exactly knew whither.

Two years afterwards, I was staying for a few days with my friend Dr. Munro in Glasgow. He was a busy man, and could not spare much time for going about with me, so I spent my days in excursions to the Trossachs and Loch Katrine and down the Clyde. On the second last evening of my stay I came back somewhat later than I had arranged, but found that my host was late too. The maid told me that he had been sent for to the hospital—a case of accident at the gas-works, and the dinner was postponed an hour; so telling her I would stroll down to find her master and walk back with him, I went out. At the hospital I found him washing his hands preparatory to starting for home. Casually, I asked him what his case was.

'Oh, the usual thing! A rotten rope and men's lives of no account. Two men were working in a gasometer, when the rope that held their scaffolding broke. It must have occurred just before the dinner hour, for no one noticed their absence till the men had returned. There was about seven feet of water in the gasometer, so they had a hard fight for it, poor fellows. However, one of them was alive, just alive, but we have had a hard job to pull him through. It seems that he owes his life to his mate, for I have never heard of greater heroism. They swam together while their strength lasted, but at the end they were so done up that even the lights above, and the men slung with ropes, coming down to help them, could not keep them up. But one of them stood on the bottom and held up his comrade over his head, and those few breaths made all the difference between life and death. They were a shocking sight when they were taken out, for that water is like a purple dye with the gas and the tar. The man upstairs looked as if he had been washed in blood. Ugh!'

'And the other?'

'Oh, he's worse still. But he must have been a very noble fellow. That struggle under the water must have been fearful; one can see that by the way the blood has been drawn from the extremities. It makes the idea of the *Stigmata* possible to look at him. Resolution like this could, you would think, do anything in the world. Ay! it might almost unbar the gates of Heaven. Look here, old man, it is not a very pleasant sight, especially just before dinner, but you are a writer, and this is an odd case. Here is something you would not like to miss, for in all human probability you will never see anything like it again.' While he was speaking he had brought me into the mortuary of the hospital.

On the bier lay a body covered with a white sheet, which was wrapped close round it.

'Looks like a chrysalis, don't it? I say, Jack, if there be anything in the old myth that a soul is typified by a butterfly, well, then the one that this chrysalis sent forth was a very noble specimen and took all the sunlight on its wings. See here!' He uncovered the face. Horrible, indeed, it looked, as though stained with blood. But I knew him at once, Jacob Settle! My friend pulled the winding sheet further down.

The hands were crossed on the purple breast as they had been reverently placed by some tender-hearted person. As I saw them my heart throbbed with a great exultation, for the memory of his harrowing dream rushed across my mind. There was no stain now on those poor, brave hands, for they were blanched white as snow.

And somehow as I looked I felt that the evil dream was all over. That noble soul had won a way through the gate at last. The white robe had now no stain from the hands that had put it on.

Crooken Sands

Mr Arthur Fernlee Markam, who took what was known as the Red House above the Mains of Crooken, was a London merchant, and being essentially a cockney, thought it necessary when he went for the summer holidays to Scotland to provide an entire rig-out as a Highland chieftain, as manifested in chromolithographs and on the music-hall stage. He had once seen in the Empire the Great Prince—'The Bounder King'—bring down the house by appearing as 'The MacSlogan of that Ilk,' and singing the celebrated Scotch song, 'There's naething like haggis to mak a mon dry!' and he had ever since preserved in his mind a faithful image of the picturesque and warlike appearance which he presented. Indeed, if the true inwardness of Mr. Markam's mind on the subject of his selection of Aberdeenshire as a summer resort were known, it would be found that in the foreground of the holiday locality which his fancy painted stalked the many hued figure of the MacSlogan of that Ilk. However, be this as it may, a very kind fortune—certainly so far as external beauty was concerned—led him to the choice of Crooken Bay. It is a lovely spot, between Aberdeen and Peterhead, just under the rock-bound headland whence the long, dangerous reefs known as The Spurs run out into the North Sea. Between this and the 'Mains of Crooken'—a village sheltered by the northern cliffs—lies the deep bay, backed with a multitude of bent-grown dunes where the rabbits are to be found in thousands. Thus at either end of the bay is a rocky promontory, and when the dawn or the sunset falls on the rocks of red syenite the effect is very lovely. The bay itself is floored with level sand and the tide runs far out, leaving a smooth waste of hard sand on which are dotted here and there the stake nets and bag nets of the salmon fishers. At one end of the bay there is a little group or cluster of rocks whose heads are raised something above high water, except when in rough weather the waves come over them green. At low tide they are exposed down to sand level; and here is perhaps the only little bit of dangerous sand on this part of the eastern coast. Between the rocks, which are apart about some fifty feet, is a small quicksand, which, like the Goodwins, is dangerous only with the incoming tide. It extends outwards till it is lost in the sea, and inwards till it fades away in the hard sand of the upper beach. On the slope of the hill which rises beyond the dunes, midway between the Spurs and the Port of Crooken, is the Red House. It rises from the midst of a clump of fir-trees which protect it on three sides, leaving the whole sea front open. A trim old-fashioned garden stretches down to the roadway, on crossing which a grassy path, which can be used for light vehicles, threads a way to the shore, winding amongst the sand hills.

When the Markam family arrived at the Red House after their thirty-six hours of pitching on the Aberdeen steamer *Ban Righ* from Blackwall, with the subsequent train to Yellon and drive of a dozen miles, they all agreed that they had never seen a more delightful spot. The general satisfaction was more marked as at that very time none of the family were, for several reasons, inclined to find favourable anything or any place over the Scottish border. Though the family was a large one, the prosperity of the business allowed them all sorts of personal luxuries, amongst which was a wide latitude in the way of dress. The frequency of the Markam girls' new frocks was a source of envy to their bosom friends and of joy to themselves.

Arthur Fernlee Markam had not taken his family into his confidence regarding his new costume. He was not quite certain that he should be free from ridicule, or at least from sarcasm, and as he was sensitive on the subject, he thought it better to be actually in the suitable environment before he allowed the full splendour to burst upon them. He had taken some pains, to insure the completeness of the Highland costume. For the purpose he had paid many visits to 'The Scotch All-Wool Tartan Clothing Mart' which had been lately established in Copthall-court by the Messrs. MacCallum More and Roderick MacDhu. He had anxious consultations with the head of the firm—MacCallum as he called himself, resenting any such additions as 'Mr.' or 'Esquire.' The known stock of buckles, buttons, straps, brooches and ornaments of all kinds were examined in critical detail; and at last an eagle's feather of sufficiently magnificent proportions was discovered, and the equipment was complete. It was only when he saw the finished costume, with the vivid hues of the tartan seemingly modified into comparative sobriety by the multitude of silver fittings, the cairngorm brooches, the philibeg, dirk and sporran that he was fully and absolutely satisfied with his choice. At first he had thought of the Royal Stuart dress tartan, but abandoned it on the MacCallum pointing out that if he should happen to be in the neighbourhood of Balmoral it might lead to complications. The MacCallum, who, by the way, spoke with a remarkable cockney accent, suggested other plaids in turn; but now that the other question of accuracy had been raised, Mr. Markam foresaw difficulties if he should by chance find himself in the locality of the clan whose colours he had usurped. The MacCallum at last undertook to have, at Markam's expense, a special pattern woven which would not be exactly the same as any existing tartan, though partaking of the characteristics of many. It was based on the Royal Stuart, but contained suggestions as to simplicity of pattern from the Macalister and Ogilvie clans, and as to neutrality of colour from the clans of Buchanan, Macbeth, Chief of Macintosh and Macleod. When the specimen had been shown to Markam he had feared somewhat lest it should strike the eye of his domestic circle as gaudy; but as Roderick MacDhu fell into perfect ecstasies over its beauty he did not make any objection to the completion of the piece. He thought, and wisely, that if a genuine Scotchman like MacDhu liked it, it must be right—especially as the junior partner was a man very much of his own build and appearance. When the MacCallum was receiving his cheque—which, by the way, was a pretty stiff one—he remarked:

'I've taken the liberty of having some more of the stuff woven in case you or any of your friends should want it.' Markam was gratified, and told him that he should be only too happy if the beautiful stuff which they had originated between them should become a favourite, as he had no doubt it would in time. He might make and sell as much as he would.

Markam tried the dress on in his office one evening after the clerks had all gone home. He was pleased, though a little frightened, at the result. The MacCallum had done his work thoroughly, and there was nothing omitted that could add to the martial dignity of the wearer.

'I shall not, of course, take the claymore and the pistols with me on ordinary occasions,' said Markam to himself as he began to undress. He determined that he would wear the dress for the first time on landing in Scotland, and accordingly on the morning when the *Ban Righ* was hanging off the Girdle Ness lighthouse, waiting for the tide to enter the port of Aberdeen, he emerged from his cabin in all the gaudy splendour of his new costume. The first comment he heard was from one of his own sons, who did not recognise him at first.

'Here's a guy! Great Scott! It's the governor!' And the boy fled forthwith and tried to bury his laughter under a cushion in the saloon. Markam was a good sailor and had not suffered from the pitching of the boat, so that his naturally rubicund face was even more rosy by the conscious blush which suffused his cheeks when he had found himself at once the cynosure of all eyes. He could have wished that he had not been so bold for he knew from the cold that there was a big bare spot under one side of his jauntily worn Glengarry cap. However, he faced the group of strangers boldly. He was not, outwardly, upset even when some of the comments reached his ears.

'He's off his bloomin' chump,' said a cockney in a suit of exaggerated plaid.

'There's flies on him,' said a tall thin Yankee, pale with sea-sickness, who was on his way to take up his residence for a time as close as he could get to the gates of Balmoral.

'Happy thought! Let us fill our mulls; now's the chance!' said a young Oxford man on his way home to Inverness. But presently Mr. Markam heard the voice of his eldest daughter.

'Where is he? Where is he?' and she came tearing along the deck with her hat blowing behind her. Her face showed signs of agitation, for her mother had just been telling her of her father's condition; but when she saw him she instantly burst into laughter so violent that it ended in a fit of hysterics. Something of the same kind happened to each of the other children. When they had all had their turn Mr. Markam went to his cabin and sent his wife's maid to tell each member of the family that he wanted to see them at once. They all made their appearance, suppressing their feelings as well as they could. He said to them very quietly:

'My dears, don't I provide you all with ample allowances?'

'Yes, father!' they all answered gravely, 'no one could be more generous!'

'Don't I let you dress as you please?'

'Yes, father!'—this a little sheepishly.

'Then, my dears, don't you think it would be nicer and kinder of you not to try and make me feel uncomfortable, even if I do assume a dress which is ridiculous in your eyes, though quite common enough in the country where we are about to sojourn?' There was no answer except that which appeared in their hanging heads. He was a good father and they all knew it. He was quite satisfied and went on:

'There, now, run away and enjoy yourselves! We shan't have another word about it.' Then he went on deck again and stood bravely the fire of ridicule which he recognised around him, though nothing more was said within his hearing.

The astonishment and the amusement which his get-up occasioned on the *Ban Righ* was, however, nothing to that which it created in Aberdeen. The boys and loafers, and women with babies, who waited at the landing shed, followed *en masse* as the Markam party took their way to the railway station; even the porters with their old-fashioned knots and their new-fashioned barrows, who await the traveller at the foot of the gang-plank, followed in wondering delight. Fortunately the Peterhead train was just about to start, so that the martyrdom was not unnecessarily prolonged. In the carriage the glorious Highland costume was unseen, and as there were but few persons at the station at Yellon, all went well there. When, however, the carriage drew near the Mains of Crooken and the fisher folk had run to their doors to see who it was that was passing, the excitement exceeded all bounds. The children with one impulse waved their bonnets and ran shouting behind the carriage; the men forsook their nets and their baiting and followed; the women clutched their babies, and followed also. The horses were tired after their long journey to Yellon and back, and the hill was steep, so that there was ample time for the crowd to gather and even to pass on ahead.

Mrs. Markam and the elder girls would have liked to make some protest or to do something to relieve their feelings of chagrin at the ridicule which they saw on all faces, but there was a look of fixed determination on the face of the seeming Highlander which awed them a little, and they were silent. It might have been that the eagle's feather, even when arising above the bald head, the cairngorm brooch even on the fat shoulder, and the claymore, dirk and pistols, even when belted round the extensive paunch and protruding from the stocking on the sturdy calf, fulfilled their existence as symbols of martial and terrifying import! When the party arrived at the gate of the Red House there awaited them a crowd of Crooken inhabitants, hatless and respectfully silent; the remainder of the population was painfully toiling up the hill. The silence was broken by only one sound, that of a man with a deep voice.

'Man! but he's forgotten the pipes!'

The servants had arrived some days before, and all things were in readiness. In the glow consequent on a good lunch after a hard journey all the disagreeables of travel and all the chagrin consequent on the adoption of the obnoxious costume were forgotten.

That afternoon Markam, still clad in full array, walked through the Mains of Crooken. He was all alone, for, strange to say, his wife and both daughters had sick headaches, and were, as he was told, lying down to rest after the fatigue of the journey. His eldest son, who claimed to be a young man, had gone out by himself to explore the surroundings of the place, and one of the boys could not be found. The other boy, on being told that his father had sent for him to come for a walk, had managed—by accident, of course—to fall into the water butt, and had to be dried and rigged out afresh. His clothes not having been as yet unpacked this was of course impossible without delay.

Mr. Markam was not quite satisfied with his walk. He could not meet any of his neighbours. It was not that there were not enough people about, for every house and cottage seemed to be full; but the people when in the open were either in their doorways some distance behind him, or on the roadway a long distance in front. As he passed he could see the tops of heads and the whites of eyes in the windows or round the corners of doors. The only interview which he had was anything but a pleasant one. This was with an odd sort of old man who was hardly ever heard to speak except to join in the 'Amens' in the meeting-house. His sole occupation seemed to be to wait at the window of the post-office from eight o'clock in the morning till the arrival of the mail at one, when he carried the letter-bag to a neighbouring baronial castle. The remainder of his day was spent on a seat in a draughty part of the port, where the offal of the fish, the refuse of the bait, and the house rubbish was thrown, and where the ducks were accustomed to hold high revel.

When Saft Tammie beheld him coming he raised his eyes, which were generally fixed on the nothing which lay on the roadway opposite his seat, and, seeming dazzled as if by a burst of sunshine, rubbed them and shaded them with his hand. Then he started up and raised his hand aloft in a denunciatory manner as he spoke:—

'"Vanity of vanities, saith the preacher. All is vanity." Mon, be warned in time! "Behold the lilies of the field, they toil not, neither do they spin, yet Solomon in all his glory was not arrayed like one of these." Mon! Mon! Thy vanity is as the quicksand which swallows up all which comes within its spell. Beware vanity! Beware the quicksand, which yawneth for thee, and which will swallow thee up! See thyself! Learn thine own vanity! Meet thyself face to face, and then in that moment thou shalt learn the fatal force of thy vanity. Learn it, know it, and repent ere the quicksand swallow thee!' Then without another word he went back to his seat and sat there immovable and expressionless as before.

Markam could not but feel a little upset by this tirade. Only that it was spoken by a seeming madman, he would have put it down to some eccentric exhibition of Scottish humour or impudence; but the gravity of the message—for it seemed nothing else—made such a reading impossible. He was, however, determined not to give in to ridicule, and although he had not yet seen anything in Scotland to remind him even of a kilt, he determined to wear his Highland dress. When he returned home, in less than half-an-hour, he found that every member of the family was, despite the headaches, out taking a walk. He took the opportunity afforded by their absence of locking himself in his dressing-room, took off the Highland dress, and, putting on a suit of flannels, lit a cigar and had a snooze. He was awakened by the noise of the family coming in, and at once donning his dress made his appearance in the drawing-room for tea.

He did not go out again that afternoon; but after dinner he put on his dress again—he had, of course dressed for dinner as usual—and went by himself for a walk on the sea-shore. He had by this time come to the conclusion that he would get by degrees accustomed to the Highland dress before making it his ordinary wear. The moon was up and he easily followed the path through the sand-hills, and shortly struck the shore. The tide was out and the beach firm as a rock, so he strolled southwards to nearly the end of the bay. Here he was attracted by two isolated rocks some little way out from the edge of the dunes, so he strolled towards them. When he reached the nearest one he climbed it, and, sitting there elevated some fifteen or twenty feet over the waste of sand, enjoyed the lovely, peaceful prospect. The moon was rising behind the headland of Pennyfold, and its light was just touching the top of the furthermost rock of the Spurs some three-quarters of a mile out; the rest of the rocks were in dark shadow. As the moon rose over the headland, the rocks of the Spurs and then the beach by degrees became flooded with light.

For a good while Mr. Markam sat and looked at the rising moon and the growing area of light which followed its rise. Then he turned and faced eastwards and sat with his chin in his hand looking seawards, and revelling in the peace and beauty and freedom of the scene. The roar of London—the darkness and the strife and weariness of London life—seemed to have passed quite away, and he lived at the moment a freer and higher life. He looked at the glistening water as it stole its way over the flat waste of sand, coming closer and closer insensibly—the tide had turned. Presently he heard a distant shouting along the beach very far off.

'The fishermen calling to each other,' he said to himself and looked around. As he did so he got a horrible shock, for though just then a cloud sailed across the moon he saw, in spite of the sudden darkness around him, his own image. For an instant, on the top of the opposite rock he could see the bald back of the head and the Glengarry cap with the immense eagle's feather. As he staggered back his foot slipped, and he began to slide down towards the sand between the two rocks. He took no concern as to failing, for the sand was really only a few feet below him, and his mind was occupied with the figure or simulacrum of himself, which had already disappeared. As the easiest way of reaching *terra firma* he prepared to jump the remainder of the distance. All this had taken but a second, but the brain works quickly, and even as he gathered himself for the spring he saw the sand below him lying so marbly level shake and shiver in an odd way. A sudden fear overcame him; his knees failed, and instead of jumping he slid miserably down the rock, scratching his bare legs as he went. His feet touched the sand—went through it like water—and he was down below his knees before he realised that he was in a quicksand. Wildly he grasped at the rock to keep himself from sinking further, and fortunately there was a jutting spur or edge which he was able to grasp instinctively. To this he clung in grim desperation. He tried to shout, but his breath would not come, till after a great effort his voice rang out. Again he shouted, and it seemed as if the sound of his own voice gave him new courage, for he was able to hold on to the rock for a longer time than he thought possible—though he held on only in blind desperation. He was, however, beginning to find his grasp weakening, when, joy of joys! his shout was answered by a rough voice from just above him.

'God be thankit, I'm nae too late!' and a fisherman with great thigh-boots came hurriedly climbing over the rock. In an instant he recognised the gravity of the danger, and with a cheering 'Haud fast, mon! I'm comin'!' scrambled down till he found a firm foothold. Then with one strong hand holding the rock above, he leaned down, and catching Markam's wrist, called out to him, 'Haud to me, mon! Haud to me wi' ither hond!'

Then he lent his great strength, and with a steady, sturdy pull, dragged him out of the hungry quicksand and placed him safe upon the rock. Hardly giving him time to draw breath, he pulled and pushed him—never letting him go for an instant—over the rock into the firm sand beyond it, and finally deposited him, still shaking from the magnitude of his danger, high upon the beach. Then he began to speak:

'Mon! but I was just in time. If I had no laucht at yon foolish lads and begun to rin at the first you'd a bin sinkin' doon to the bowels o' the airth be the noo! Wully Beagrie thocht you was a ghaist, and Tom MacPhail swore ye was only like a goblin on a puddick-steel! "Na!" said I. "Yon's but the daft Englishman—the loony that had escapit frae the waxwarks." I was thinkin' that bein' strange and silly—if not a whole-made feel—ye'd no ken the ways o' the quicksan'! I shouted till warn ye, and then ran to drag ye aff, if need be. But God be thankit, be ye fule or only half-daft wi' yer vanity, that I was no that late!' and he reverently lifted his cap as he spoke.

Mr. Markam was deeply touched and thankful for his escape from a horrible death; but the sting of the charge of vanity thus made once more against him came through his humility. He was about to reply angrily, when suddenly a great awe fell upon him as he remembered the warning words of the half-crazy letter-carrier: 'Meet thyself face to face, and repent ere the quicksand shall swallow thee!'

Here, too, he remembered the image of himself that he had seen and the sudden danger from the deadly quicksand that had followed. He was silent a full minute, and then said:

'My good fellow, I owe you my life!'

The answer came with reverence from the hardy fisherman, 'Na! Na! Ye owe that to God; but, as for me, I'm only too glad till be the humble instrument o' His mercy.'

'But you will let me thank you,' said Mr. Markam, taking both the great hands of his deliverer in his and holding them tight. 'My heart is too full as yet, and my nerves are too much shaken to let me say much; but, believe me, I am very, very grateful!' It was quite evident that the poor old fellow was deeply touched, for the tears were running down his cheeks.

The fisherman said, with a rough but true courtesy:

'Ay, sir! thank me and ye will—if it'll do yer poor heart good. An' I'm thinking that if it were me I'd be thankful too. But, sir, as for me I need no thanks. I am glad, so I am!'

That Arthur Fernlee Markam was really thankful and grateful was shown practically later on. Within a week's time there sailed into Port Crooken the finest fishing smack that had ever been seen in the harbour of Peterhead. She was fully found with sails and gear of all kinds, and with nets of the best. Her master and men went away by the coach, after having left with the salmon-fisher's wife the papers which made her over to him.

As Mr. Markam and the salmon-fisher walked together along the shore the former asked his companion not to mention the fact that he had been in such imminent danger, for that it would only distress his dear wife and children. He said that he would warn them all of the quicksand, and for that purpose he, then and there, asked questions about it till he felt that his information on the subject was complete. Before they parted he asked his companion if he had happened to see a second figure, dressed like himself on the other rock as he had approached to succour him.

'Na! Na!' came the answer, 'there is nae sic another fule in these parts. Nor has there been since the time o' Jamie Fleeman—him that was fule to the Laird o' Udny. Why, mon! sic a heathenish dress as ye have on till ye has nae been seen in these pairts within the memory o' mon. An' I'm thinkin' that sic a dress never was for sittin' on the cauld rock, as ye done beyont. Mon! but do ye no fear the rheumatism or the lumbagy wi' floppin' doon on to the cauld stanes wi' yer bare flesh? I was thinking that it was daft ye waur when I see ye the mornin' doon be the port, but it's fule or eediot ye maun be for the like o' thot!' Mr. Markam did not care to argue the point, and as they were now close to his own home he asked the salmon-fisher to have a glass of whisky—which he did—and they parted for the night. He took good care to warn all his family of the quicksand, telling them that he had himself been in some danger from it.

All that night he never slept. He heard the hours strike one after the other; but try how he would he could not get to sleep. Over and over again he went through the horrible episode of the quicksand, from the time that Saft Tammie had broken his habitual silence to preach to him of the sin of vanity and to warn him. The question kept ever arising in his mind: 'Am I then so vain as to be in the ranks of the foolish?' and the answer ever came in the words of the crazy prophet: '"Vanity of vanities! All is vanity." Meet thyself face to face, and repent ere the quicksand shall swallow thee!' Somehow a feeling of doom began to shape itself in his mind that he would yet perish in that same quicksand, for there he had already met himself face to face.

In the grey of the morning he dozed off, but it was evident that he continued the subject in his dreams, for he was fully awakened by his wife, who said:

'Do sleep quietly! That blessed Highland suit has got on your brain. Don't talk in your sleep, if you can help it!' He was somehow conscious of a glad feeling, as if some terrible weight had been lifted from him, but he did not know any cause of it. He asked his wife what he had said in his sleep, and she answered:

'You said it often enough, goodness knows, for one to remember it—"Not face to face! I saw the eagle plume over the bald head! There is hope yet! Not face to face!" Go to sleep! Do!' And then he did go to sleep, for he seemed to realise that the prophecy of the crazy man had not yet been fulfilled. He had not met himself face to face—as yet at all events.

He was awakened early by a maid who came to tell him that there was a fisherman at the door who wanted to see him. He dressed himself as quickly as he could—for he was not yet expert with the Highland dress—and hurried down, not wishing to keep the salmon-fisher waiting. He was surprised and not altogether pleased to find that his visitor was none other than Saft Tammie, who at once opened fire on him:

'I maun gang awa' t' the post; but I thocht that I would waste an hour on ye, and ca' roond just to see if ye waur still that fou wi' vanity as on the nicht gane by. An I see that ye've no learned the lesson. Well! the time is comin', sure eneucht! However I have all the time i' the marnins to my ain sel', so I'll aye look roond jist till see how ye gang yer ain gait to the quicksan', and then to the de'il! I'm aff till ma wark the noo!' And he went straightway, leaving Mr. Markam considerably vexed, for the maids within earshot were vainly trying to conceal their giggles. He had fairly made up his mind to wear on that day ordinary clothes, but the visit of Saft Tammie reversed his decision. He would show them all that he was not a coward, and he would go on as he had begun—come what might. When he came to breakfast in full martial panoply the children, one and all, held down their heads and the backs of their necks became very red indeed. As, however, none of them laughed—except Titus, the youngest boy, who was seized with a fit of hysterical choking and was promptly banished from the room—he could not reprove them, but began to break his egg with a sternly determined air. It was unfortunate that as his wife was handing him a cup of tea one of the buttons of his sleeve caught in the lace of her morning wrapper, with the result that the hot tea was spilt over his bare knees. Not unnaturally, he made use of a swear word, whereupon his wife, somewhat nettled, spoke out:

'Well, Arthur, if you will make such an idiot of yourself with that ridiculous costume what else can you expect? You are not accustomed to it—and you never will be!' In answer he began an indignant speech with: 'Madam!' but he got no further, for now that the subject was broached, Mrs. Markam intended to have her say out. It was not a pleasant say, and, truth to tell, it was not said in a pleasant manner. A wife's manner seldom is pleasant when she undertakes to tell what she considers 'truths' to her husband. The result was that Arthur Fernlee Markam undertook, then and there, that during his stay in Scotland he would wear no other costume than the one she abused. Woman-like his wife had the last word—given in this case with tears:

'Very well, Arthur! Of course you will do as you choose. Make me as ridiculous as you can, and spoil the poor girls' chances in life. Young men don't seem to care, as a general rule, for an idiot father-in-law! But I must warn you that your vanity will some day get a rude shock—if indeed you are not before then in an asylum or dead!'

It was manifest after a few days that Mr. Markam would have to take the major part of his outdoor exercise by himself. The girls now and again took a walk with him, chiefly in the early morning or late at night, or on a wet day when there would be no one about; they professed to be willing to go out at all times, but somehow something always seemed to occur to prevent it. The boys could never be found at all on such occasions, and as to Mrs. Markam she sternly refused to go out with him on any consideration so long as he should continue to make a fool of himself. On the Sunday he dressed himself in his habitual broadcloth, for he rightly felt that church was not a place for angry feelings; but on Monday morning he resumed his Highland garb. By this time he would have given a good deal if he had never thought of the dress, but his British obstinacy was strong, and he would not give in. Saft Tammie called at his house every morning, and, not being able to see him nor to have any message taken to him, used to call back in the afternoon when the letter-bag had been delivered and watched for his going out. On such occasions he never failed to warn him against his vanity in the same words which he had used at the first. Before many days were over Mr. Markam had come to look upon him as little short of a scourge.

By the time the week was out the enforced partial solitude, the constant chagrin, and the never-ending brooding which was thus engendered, began to make Mr. Markam quite ill. He was too proud to take any of his family into his confidence since they had in his view treated him very badly. Then he did not sleep well at night, and when he did sleep he had constantly bad dreams. Merely to assure himself that his pluck was not failing him he made it a practice to visit the quicksand at least once every day, he hardly ever failed to go there the last thing at night. It was perhaps this habit that wrought the quicksand with its terrible experience so perpetually into his dreams. More and more vivid these became, till on waking at times he could hardly realise that he had not been actually in the flesh to visit the fatal spot. He sometimes thought that he might have been walking in his sleep.

One night his dream was so vivid that when he awoke he could not believe that it had only been a dream. He shut his eyes again and again, but each time the vision, if it was a vision, or the reality, if it was a reality, would rise before him. The moon was shining full and yellow over the quicksand as he approached it; he could see the expanse of light shaken and disturbed and full of black shadows as the liquid sand quivered and trembled and wrinkled and eddied as was its wont between its pauses of marble calm. As he drew close to it another figure came towards it from the opposite side with equal footsteps. He saw that it was his own figure, his very self, and in silent terror, compelled by what force he knew not, he advanced—charmed as the bird is by the snake, mesmerised or hypnotised—to meet this other self. As he felt the yielding sand closing over him he awoke in the agony of death, trembling with fear, and, strange to say, with the silly man's prophecy seeming to sound in his ears: '"Vanity of vanities! All is vanity!" See thyself and repent ere the quicksand swallow thee!'

So convinced was he that this was no dream that he arose, early as it was, and dressing himself without disturbing his wife took his way to the shore. His heart fell when he came across a series of footsteps on the sands, which he at once recognised as his own. There was the same wide heel, the same square toe; he had no doubt now that he had actually been there, and half horrified, and half in a state of dreamy stupor, he followed the footsteps, and found them lost in the edge of the yielding quicksand. This gave him a terrible shock, for there were no return steps marked on the sand, and he felt that there was some dread mystery which he could not penetrate, and the penetration of which would, he feared, undo him.

In this state of affairs he took two wrong courses. Firstly he kept his trouble to himself, and, as none of his family had any clue to it, every innocent word or expression which they used supplied fuel to the consuming fire of his imagination. Secondly he began to read books professing to bear upon the mysteries of dreaming and of mental phenomena generally, with the result that every wild imagination of every crank or half-crazy philosopher became a living germ of unrest in the fertilising soil of his disordered brain. Thus negatively and positively all things began to work to a common end. Not the least of his disturbing causes was Saft Tammie, who had now become at certain times of the day a fixture at his gate. After a while, being interested in the previous state of this individual, he made inquiries regarding his past with the following result.

Saft Tammie was popularly believed to be the son of a laird in one of the counties round the Firth of Forth. He had been partially educated for the ministry, but for some cause which no one ever knew threw up his prospects suddenly, and, going to Peterhead in its days of whaling prosperity, had there taken service on a whaler. Here off and on he had remained for some years, getting gradually more and more silent in his habits, till finally his shipmates protested against so taciturn a mate, and he had found service amongst the fishing smacks of the northern fleet. He had worked for many years at the fishing with always the reputation of being 'a wee bit daft,' till at length he had gradually settled down at Crooken, where the laird, doubtless knowing something of his family history, had given him a job which practically made him a pensioner. The minister who gave the information finished thus:—

'It is a very strange thing, but the man seems to have some odd kind of gift. Whether it be that "second sight" which we Scotch people are so prone to believe in, or some other occult form of knowledge, I know not, but nothing of a disastrous tendency ever occurs in this place but the men with whom he lives are able to quote after the event some saying of his which certainly appears to have foretold it. He gets uneasy or excited—wakes up, in fact—when death is in the air!'

This did not in any way tend to lessen Mr. Markam's concern, but on the contrary seemed to impress the prophecy more deeply on his mind. Of all the books which he had read on his new subject of study none interested him so much as a German one *Die Döppleganger*, by Dr. Heinrich von Aschenberg, formerly of Bonn. Here he learned for the first time of cases where men had led a double existence—each nature being quite apart from the other—the body being always a reality with one spirit, and a simulacrum with the other. Needless to say that Mr. Markam realised this theory as exactly suiting his own case. The glimpse which he had of his own back the night of his escape from the quicksand—his own footmarks disappearing into the quicksand with no return steps visible—the prophecy of Saft Tammie about his meeting himself and perishing in the quicksand—all lent aid to the conviction that he was in his own person an instance of the döppleganger. Being then conscious of a double life he took steps to prove its existence to his own satisfaction. To this end on one night before going to bed he wrote his name in chalk on the soles of his shoes. That night he dreamed of the quicksand, and of his visiting it—dreamed so vividly that on walking in the grey of the dawn he could not believe that he had not been there. Arising, without disturbing his wife, he sought his shoes.

The chalk signatures were undisturbed! He dressed himself and stole out softly. This time the tide was in, so he crossed the dunes and struck the shore on the further side of the quicksand. There, oh, horror of horrors! he saw his own footprints dying into the abyss!

He went home a desperately sad man. It seemed incredible that he, an elderly commercial man, who had passed a long and uneventful life in the pursuit of business in the midst of roaring, practical London, should thus find himself enmeshed in mystery and horror, and that he should discover that he had two existences. He could not speak of his trouble even to his own wife, for well he knew that she would at once require the fullest particulars of that other life—the one which she did not know; and that she would at the start not only imagine but charge him with all manner of infidelities on the head of it. And so his brooding grew deeper and deeper still. One evening—the tide then going out and the moon being at the full—he was sitting waiting for dinner when the maid announced that Saft Tammie was making a disturbance outside because he would not be let in to see him. He was very indignant, but did not like the maid to think that he had any fear on the subject, and so told her to bring him in. Tammie entered, walking more briskly than ever with his head up and a look of vigorous decision in the eyes that were so generally cast down. As soon as he entered he said:

'I have come to see ye once again—once again; and there ye sit, still just like a cockatoo on a pairch. Weel, mon, I forgie ye! Mind ye that, I forgie ye!' And without a word more he turned and walked out of the house, leaving the master in speechless indignation.

After dinner he determined to pay another visit to the quicksand—he would not allow even to himself that he was afraid to go. And so, about nine o'clock, in full array, he marched to the beach, and passing over the sands sat on the skirt of the nearer rock. The full moon was behind him and its light lit up the bay so that its fringe of foam, the dark outline of the headland, and the stakes of the salmon-nets were all emphasised. In the brilliant yellow glow the lights in the windows of Port Crooken and in those of the distant castle of the laird trembled like stars through the sky. For a long time he sat and drank in the beauty of the scene, and his soul seemed to feel a peace that it had not known for many days. All the pettiness and annoyance and silly fears of the past weeks seemed blotted out, and a new holy calm took the vacant place. In this sweet and solemn mood he reviewed his late action calmly, and felt ashamed of himself for his vanity and for the obstinacy which had followed it. And then and there he made up his mind that the present would be the last time he would wear the costume which had estranged him from those whom he loved, and which had caused him so many hours and days of chagrin, vexation, and pain.

But almost as soon as he arrived at this conclusion another voice seemed to speak within him and mockingly to ask him if he should ever get the chance to wear the suit again—that it was too late—he had chosen his course and must now abide the issue.

'It is not too late,' came the quick answer of his better self; and full of the thought, he rose up to go home and divest himself of the now hateful costume right away. He paused for one look at the beautiful scene. The light lay pale and mellow, softening every outline of rock and tree and house-top, and deepening the shadows into velvety-black, and lighting, as with a pale flame, the incoming tide, that now crept fringe-like across the flat waste of sand. Then he left the rock and stepped out for the shore.

But as he did so a frightful spasm of horror shook him, and for an instant the blood rushing to his head shut out all the light of the full moon. Once more he saw that fatal image of himself moving beyond the quicksand from the opposite rock to the shore. The shock was all the greater for the contrast with the spell of peace which he had just enjoyed; and, almost paralysed in every sense, he stood and watched the fatal vision and the wrinkly, crawling quicksand that seemed to writhe and yearn for something that lay between. There could be no mistake this time, for though the moon behind threw the face into shadow he could see there the same shaven cheeks as his own, and the small stubby moustache of a few weeks' growth. The light shone on the brilliant tartan, and on the eagle's plume. Even the bald space at one side of the Glengarry cap glistened, as did the cairngorm brooch on the shoulder and the tops of the silver buttons. As he looked he felt his feet slightly sinking, for he was still near the edge of the belt of quicksand, and he stepped back. As he did so the other figure stepped forward, so that the space between them was preserved.

So the two stood facing each other, as though in some weird fascination; and in the rushing of the blood through his brain Markam seemed to hear the words of the prophecy: 'See thyself face to face, and repent ere the quicksand swallow thee.' He did stand face to face with himself, he had repented—and now he was sinking in the quicksand! The warning and prophecy were coming true.

Above him the seagulls screamed, circling round the fringe of the incoming tide, and the sound being entirely mortal recalled him to himself. On the instant he stepped back a few quick steps, for as yet only his feet were merged in the soft sand. As he did so the other figure stepped forward, and coming within the deadly grip of the quicksand began to sink. It seemed to Markam that he was looking at himself going down to his doom, and on the instant the anguish of his soul found vent in a terrible cry. There was at the same instant a terrible cry from the other figure, and as Markam threw up his hands the figure did the same. With horror-struck eyes he saw him sink deeper into the quicksand; and then, impelled by what power he knew not, he advanced again towards the sand to meet his fate. But as his more forward foot began to sink he heard again the cries of the seagulls which seemed to restore his benumbed faculties. With a mighty effort he drew his foot out of the sand which seemed to clutch it, leaving his shoe behind, and then in sheer terror he turned and ran from the place, never stopping till his breath and strength failed him, and he sank half swooning on the grassy path through the sandhills.

Arthur Markam made up his mind not to tell his family of his terrible adventure—until at least such time as he should be complete master of himself. Now that the fatal double—his other self—had been engulfed in the quicksand he felt something like his old peace of mind.

That night he slept soundly and did not dream at all; and in the morning was quite his old self. It really seemed as though his newer and worser self had disappeared for ever; and strangely enough Saft Tammie was absent from his post that morning and never appeared there again, but sat in his old place watching nothing, as of old, with lack-lustre eye. In accordance with his resolution he did not wear his Highland suit again, but one evening tied it up in a bundle, claymore, dirk and philibeg and all, and bringing it secretly with him threw it into the quicksand. With a feeling of intense pleasure he saw it sucked below the sand, which closed above it into marble smoothness. Then he went home and announced cheerily to his family assembled for evening prayers:

'Well! my dears, you will be glad to hear that I have abandoned my idea of wearing the Highland dress. I see now what a vain old fool I was and how ridiculous I made myself! You shall never see it again!'

'Where is it, father?' asked one of the girls, wishing to say something so that such a self-sacrificing announcement as her father's should not be passed in absolute silence. His answer was so sweetly given that the girl rose from her seat and came and kissed him. It was:

'In the quicksand, my dear! and I hope that my worser self is buried there along with it—for ever.'

The remainder of the summer was passed at Crooken with delight by all the family, and on his return to town Mr. Markam had almost forgotten the whole of the incident of the quicksand, and all touching on it, when one day he got a letter from the MacCallum More which caused him much thought, though he said nothing of it to his family, and left it, for certain reasons, unanswered. It ran as follows:—

'The MacCallum More and Roderick MacDhu.
'The Scotch All-Wool Tartan Clothing Mart.
Copthall Court, E.C.,
30th September, 1892.

'Dear Sir,—I trust you will pardon the liberty which I take in writing to you, but I am desirous of making an inquiry, and I am informed that you have been sojourning during the summer in Aberdeenshire (Scotland, N.B.). My partner, Mr. Roderick MacDhu—as he appears for business reasons on our bill-heads and in our advertisements, his real name being Emmanuel Moses Marks of London—went early last month to Scotland (N.B.) for a tour, but as I have only once heard from him, shortly after his departure, I am anxious lest any misfortune may have befallen him. As I have been unable to obtain any news of him on making all inquiries in my power, I venture to appeal to you. His letter was written in deep dejection of spirit, and mentioned that he feared a judgment had come upon him for wishing to appear as a Scotchman on Scottish soil, as he had one moonlight night shortly after his arrival seen his 'wraith'. He evidently alluded to the fact that before his departure he had procured for himself a Highland costume similar to that which we had the honour to supply to you, with which, as perhaps you will remember, he was much struck. He may, however, never have worn it, as he was, to my own knowledge, diffident about putting it on, and even went so far as to tell me that he would at first only venture to wear it late at night or very early in the morning, and then only in remote places, until such time as he should get accustomed to it. Unfortunately he did not advise me of his route so that I am in complete ignorance of his whereabouts; and I venture to ask if you may have seen or heard of a Highland costume similar to your own having been seen anywhere in the neighbourhood in which I am told you have recently purchased the estate which you temporarily occupied. I shall not expect an answer to this letter unless you can give me some information regarding my friend and partner, so pray do not trouble to reply unless there be cause. I am encouraged to think that he may have been in your neighbourhood as, though his letter is not dated, the envelope is marked with the postmark of "Yellon" which I find is in Aberdeenshire, and not far from the Mains of Crooken.

'I have the honour to be, dear sir,

'Yours very respectfully,

'JOSHUA SHEENY COHEN BENJAMIN

'(The MacCallum More.)'

THE DUALITISTS

1. Bis Dat Qui Non Cito Dat

There was joy in the house of Bubb.

For ten long years had Ephraim and Sophonisba Bubb mourned in vain the loneliness of their life. Unavailingly had they gazed into the emporia of baby-linen, and fixed their searching glances on the basket-makers' warehouses where the cradles hung in tempting rows. In vain had they prayed, and sighed, and groaned, and wished, and waited, and wept, but never had even a ray of hope been held out by the family physician.

But now at last the wished-for moment had arrived. Month after month had flown by on leaden wings, and the destined days had slowly measured their course. The months had become weeks; the weeks had dwindled down to days; the days had been attenuated to hours; the hours had lapsed into minutes, the minutes had slowly died away, and but seconds remained.

Ephraim Bubb sat cowering on the stairs, and tried with high-strung ears to catch the strain of blissful music from the lips of his first- born. There was silence in the house--silence as of the deadly calm before the cyclone. Ah! Ephraim Bubb, little thinkest thou that another moment may for ever destroy the peaceful, happy course of thy life, and open to thy too-craving eyes the portals of that wondrous land where childhood reigns supreme, and where the tyrant infant with the wave of his tiny hand and the imperious treble of his tiny voice sentences his parent o the deadly vault beneath the castle moat. As the thought strikes thee thou becomest pale. How thou tremblest as thou findest thyself upon the brink of the abyss! Wouldst that thou could recall the past!

But hark! the die is cast for good or ill. The long years of praying and hoping have found an end at last. From the chamber within comes a sharp cry, which shortly after is repeated. Ah!

Ephraim, that cry is the feeble effort of childish lips as yet unused to the rough, worldly form of speech to frame the word 'father'. In the glow of thy transport all doubts are forgotten; and when the doctor cometh forth as the harbinger of joy he findeth thee radiant with new-found delight.

'My dear sir, allow me to congratulate you--to offer twofold felicitations. Mr Bubb, sir, you are the father of twins!'

2. Halcyon Days

The twins were the finest children that ever were seen--so at least said the cognoscenti, and the parents were not slow to believe. The nurse's opinion was in itself a proof.

It was not, ma'am, that they was fine for twins, but they was fine for singles, and she had ought to know, for she had nussed a many in her time, both twins and singles. All they wanted was to have their dear little legs cut off and little wings on their dear little shoulders, for to be put one on each side of a white marble tombstone, cut beautiful, sacred to the relic of Ephraim Bubb, that they might, sir, if so be that missus was to survive the father of two such lovely twins--although she would make bold to say, and no offence intended, that a handsome gentleman, though a trifle or two older than his good lady, though for the matter of that she heerd that gentlemen was never too old at all, and for her own part she liked them the better for it: not like bits of boys that didn't know their own minds--that a gentleman what was the father of two such 'eavenly twins (God bless them!) couldn't be called anything but a boy; though for the matter of that she never knowed in her experience--which it was much--of a boy as had such twins, or any twins at all so much for the matter of that. The twins were the idols of their parents, and at the same time their pleasure and their pain. Did Zerubbabel cough, Ephraim would start from his balmy slumbers with an agonized cry of consternation, for visions of innumerable twins black in the face from croup haunted his nightly pillow. Did Zacariah rail at ethereal expansion, Sophonisba with pallid hue and dishevelled locks would fly to the cradle of her offspring. Did pins torture or strings afflict, or flannel or flies tickle, or light dazzle, or darkness affright, or hunger or thirst assail the synchronous productions, the household of Bubb would be roused from quiet slumbers or the current of its manifold workings changed.

The twin's grew apace; were weaned; teethed; and at length arrived at the stage of three years!

They grew in beauty side by side, They filled one home, etc.

3. Rumours of Wars

Harry Merford and Tommy Santon lived in the same range of villas as Ephraim Bubb. Harry's parents had taken up their abode in no. 25, no. 27 was happy in the perpetual sunshine of Tommy's smiles, and between these two residences Ephraim Bubb reared his blossoms, the number of his mansion being 26. Harry and Tommy had been accustomed from the earliest times to meet each other daily. Their primal method of communication had been by the housetops, till their respective sires had been obliged to pay compensation to Bubb for damages to his roof and dormer windows; and from that time they had been forbidden by the home authorities to meet, whilst their mutual neighbour had taken the precaution of having his garden walls pebble-dashed and topped with broken glass to prevent their incursions. Harry and Tommy, however, being gifted with daring souls, lofty, ambitious, impetuous natures, and strong seats to their trousers, defied the rugged walls of Bubb and continued to meet in secret.

Compared with these two youths, Castor and Pollux, Damon and Pythias, Eloisa and Abelard are but tame examples of duality or constancy and friendship. All the poets from Hyginus to Schiller might sing of noble deeds and desperate dangers held as naught for friendship's sake, but they would have been mute had they but known of the mutual affection of Harry and Tommy. Day by day, and often night by night, would these two brave the perils of nurse, and father, and mother, of whip and imprisonment, and hunger and thirst, and solitude and darkness to meet together. What they discussed in secret none other knew. What deeds of darkness were perpetrated in their symposia none could tell. Alone they met, alone they remained, and alone they departed to their several abodes. There was in the garden of Bubb a summer-house overgrown with trailing plants, and surrounded by young poplars which the fond father had planted on his children's natal day, and whose rapid growth he had proudly watched. These trees quite obscured the summer-house, and here Harry and Tommy, knowing after a careful observation that none ever entered the place, held their conclaves. Time after time they met in full security and followed their customary pursuit of pleasure. Let us raise the mysterious veil and see what was the great Unknown at whose shrine they bent the knee. Harry and Tommy had each been given as a Christmas box a new knife; and for a long time---nearly a year--these knives, similar in size and pattern, were their chief delights. With them they cut and hacked in their respective homes all things which would not be likely to be noticed; for the young gentlemen were wary and had no wish that their moments of pleasure should be atoned for by moments of pain. The insides of drawers, and desks, and boxes, the underparts of tables and chairs, the backs of pictures frames, even the floors, where corners of the carpets could surreptitiously be turned up, all bore marks of their craftsmanship; and to compare notes on these artistic triumphs was a source of joy. At length, however, a critical time came, some new field of action should be opened up, for the old appetites were sated, and the old joys had begun to pall. It was absolutely necessary that the existing schemes of destruction should be enlarged; and yet this could hardly be done without a terrible risk of discovery, for the limits of safety had long since been reached and passed. But, be the risk great or small, some new ground should be broken--some new joy found, for the old earth was barren, and the craving for pleasure was growing fiercer with each successive day.

The crisis had come: who could tell the issue?

4. The Tucket Sounds

They met in the arbour, determined to discuss this grave question. The heart of each was big with revolution, the head of each was full of scheme and strategy, and the pocket of each was full of sweet-stuff, the sweeter for being stolen. After having dispatched the sweets, the conspirators proceeded to explain their respective views with regard to the enlargement of their artistic operations. Tommy unfolded with much pride a scheme which he had in contemplation of cutting a series of holes in the sounding board of the piano, so as to destroy its musical properties. Harry was in no wise behindhand in his ideas of reform. He had conceived the project of cutting the canvas at the back of his great-grandfather's portrait, which his father held in high regard among his lares and penates, so that in time when the picture should be moved the skin of paint would be broken, the head fall bodily out from the frame.

At this point of the council a brilliant thought occurred to Tommy. 'Why should not the enjoyment be doubled, and the musical instruments and family pictures of both establishments be sacrificed on the altar of pleasure?' This was agreed to nem. con.; and then the meeting adjourned for dinner. When they next met it was evident that there was a screw loose somewhere--that there was 'something rotten in the state of Denmark'. After a little fencing on both sides, it came out that all the schemes of domestic reform had been foiled by maternal vigilance, and that so sharp had been the reprimand consequent on a partial discovery of the schemes that they would have to be abandoned--till such time, at least, as increased physical strength would allow the reformers to laugh to scorn parental threats and injunctions.

Sadly the two forlorn youths took out their knives and regarded them; sadly, sadly they thought, as erst did Othello, of all the fair chances of honour and triumph and glory gone for ever. They compared knives with almost the fondness of doting parents. There they were--so equal in size and strength and beauty--dimmed by no corrosive rust, tarnished by no stain, and with unbroken edges of the keenness of Saladin's sword.

So like were the knives that but for the initials scratched in the handles neither boy could have been sure which was his own. After a little while they began mutually to brag of the superior excellence of their respective weapons. Tommy insisted that his was the sharper, Harry asserted that his was the stronger of the two. Hotter and hotter grew the war of words. The tempers of Harry and Tommy got inflamed, and their boyish bosoms glowed with manly thoughts of daring and hate. But there was abroad in that hour a spirit of a bygone age--one that penetrated even to that dim arbour in the grove of Bubb. The world-old scheme of ordeal was whispered by the spirit in the ear of each, and suddenly the tumult was allayed. With one impulse the boys suggested that they should test the quality of their knives by the ordeal of the Hack.

No sooner said than done. Harry held out his knife edge uppermost; and Tommy, grasping his firmly by the handle, brought down the edge of the blade crosswise on Harry's. The process was then reversed, and Harry became in turn the aggressor. Then they paused and eagerly looked for the result. It was not hard to see; in each knife were two great dents of equal depth; and so it was necessary to renew the contest, and seek a further proof.

What needs it to relate seriatim the details of that direful strife? The sun had long since gone down, and the moon with fair, smiling face had long risen over the roof of Bubb, when, wearied and jaded, Harry and Tommy sought their respective homes. Alas! the splendour of the knives was gone for ever. Ichabod!--Ichabod! the glory had departed and naught remained but two useless wrecks, with keen edges destroyed, and now like unto nothing save the serried hills of Spain.

But though they mourned for their fondly cherished weapons, the hearts of the boys were glad; for the bygone day had opened to their gaze a prospect of pleasure as boundless as the limits of the world.

5. The First Crusade

From that day a new era dawned in the lives of Harry and Tommy. So long as the resources of the parental establishments could hold out so long would their new amusement continue. Subtly they obtained surreptitious possession of articles of family cutlery not in general use, and brought them one by one to their rendezvous. These came fair and spotless from the sanctity of the butler's pantry. Alas! they returned not as they came.

But in course of time the stock of available cutlery became exhausted, and again the inventive faculties of the youths were called into requisition. They reasoned thus: 'The knife game, it is true, is played out, but the excitement of the hack is not to be dispensed with. Let us carry, then, this great idea into new worlds; let us still live in the sunshine of pleasure; let us continue to hack, but with objects other than knives.'

It was done. Not knives now engaged the attention of the ambitious youths. Spoons and forks were daily flattened and beaten out of shape; pepper castor met pepper castor in combat, and both were borne dying from the field; candlesticks met in fray to part no more on this side of the grave; even epergnes were used as weapons in the crusade of hack.

At last all the resources of the butler's pantry became exhausted, and then began a system of miscellaneous destruction that proved in a little time ruinous to the furniture of the respective homes of Harry and Tommy. Mrs Santon and Mrs Merford began to notice that the wear and tear in their households became excessive. Day after day some new domestic calamity seemed to have occurred. Today a valuable edition of some book whose luxurious binding made it an object for public display would appear to have suffered some dire misfortune, for the edges were frayed and broken and the back loose if not altogether displaced; tomorrow the same awful fate would seem to have followed some miniature frame; the day following the legs of some chair or spider- table would show signs of extraordinary hardship. Even in the nursery the sounds of lamentation were heard. It was a thing of daily occurrence for the little girls to state that when going to bed at night they had laid their dear dollies in their beds with tender care, but that when again seeking them in the period of recess they had found them with all their beauty gone, with legs and arms amputated and faces beaten from all semblance of human form.

Then articles of crockery began to be missed. The thief could in no case be discovered, and the wages of the servants, from constant stoppages, began to be nominal rather than real. Mrs Merford and Mrs Santon mourned their losses, but Harry and

Tommy gloated day after day over their spoils, which lay in an ever-increasing heap in the hidden grove of Bubb. To such an extent had the fondness of the hack now grown that with both youths it was an infatuation--a madness--a frenzy.

At length one awful day arrived. The butlers of the houses of Merford and Santon, harassed by constant losses and complaints, and finding that their breakage account was in excess of their wages, determined to seek some sphere of occupation where, if they did not meet with a suitable reward or recognition of their services, they would, at least, not lose whatever fortune and reputation they had already acquired. Accordingly, before rendering up their keys and the goods entrusted to their charge, they proceeded to take a preliminary stock of their own accounts, to make sure of their accredited accuracy. Dire indeed was their distress when they knew to the full the havoc which had been wrought; terrible their anguish of the present, bitter their thoughts of the future. Their hearts, bowed down with weight of woe, failed them quite; reeled the strong brains that had erst overcome foes of deadlier spirit than grief; and fell their stalwart forms prone on the floors of their respective sancta sanctorum.

Late in the day when their services were required they were sought for in bower and hail, and at length discovered where they lay.

But alas for justice! They were accused of being drunk and for having, whilst in that degraded condition, deliberately injured all the property on which they could lay hands. Were not the evidences of their guilt patent to all in the hecatombs of the destroyed? Then they were charged with all the evils wrought in the houses, and on their indignant denial Harry and Tommy, each in his own home, according to their concerted scheme of action, stepped forward and relieved their minds of the deadly weight that had for long in secret borne them down. The story of each ran that time after time he had seen the butler, when he thought that nobody was looking, knocking knives together in the pantry, chairs and books and pictures in the drawing- room and study, dolls in the nursery, and plates in the kitchen. Then, indeed, was the master of each household stern and uncompromising in his demands for justice. Each butler was committed to the charge of myrmidons of the law under the double charge of drunkenness and wilful destruction of property.

Softly and sweetly slept Harry and Tommy in their little beds that night. Angels seemed to whisper to them, for they smiled as though lost in pleasant dreams. The rewards given by proud and grateful parents lay in their pockets, and in their hearts the happy consciousness of having done their duty.

Truly sweet should be the slumbers of the just...

6. 'Let The Dead Past Bury Its Dead'

It might be supposed that now the operations of Harry and Tommy would be obliged to be abandoned. Not so, however. The minds of these youths were of no common order, nor were their souls of such weak nature as to yield at the first summons of necessity. Like Nelson, they knew not fear; like Napoleon, they held 'impossible' to be the adjective of fools; and they revelled in the glorious truth that in the lexicon of youth is no such word as 'fail'. Therefore on the day following the éclaircissement of the butlers' misdeeds, they met in the arbour to plan a new campaign. In the hour when all seemed blackest to them, and when the narrowing walls of possibility hedged them in on every side, thus ran the deliberations of these dauntless youths:

'We have played out the meaner things that are inanimate and inert; why not then trench on the domains of life? The dead have lapsed into the regions of the forgotten past--let the living look to themselves.'

That night they met when all households had retired to balmy sleep, and naught but the amorous wailings of nocturnal cats told of the existence of life and sentience. Each bore into the arbour in his arms a pet rabbit and a piece of sticking-plaster. Then, in the peaceful, quiet moonlight, commenced a work of mystery, blood, and gloom. The proceedings began by the fixing of a piece of sticking-plaster over the mouth of each rabbit to prevent it making a noise, if so inclined. Then Tommy held up his rabbit by its scutty tail, and it hung wriggling, a white mass in the moonlight. Slowly Harry raised his rabbit holding it in the same manner, and when level with his head brought it down on Tommy's client.

But the chances had been miscalculated. The boys held firmly to the tails, but the chief portions of the rabbits fell to earth. Ere the doomed beasts could escape, however, the operators had pounced upon them, and this time holding them by the hind legs renewed the trial.

Deep into the night the game was kept up, and the eastern sky began to show signs of approaching day as each boy bore triumphantly the dead corpse of his favourite bunny and placed it within its sometime hutch.

Next night the same game was renewed with a new rabbit on each side, and for more than a week--so long as the hutches supplied the wherewithal--the battle was sustained. True that there were sad hearts and red eyes in the juveniles of Santon and Merford as one by one the beloved pets were found dead, but Harry and Tommy, with the hearts of heroes steeled to suffering and deaf to the pitiful cries of childhood, still fought the good fight on to the bitter end.

When the supply of rabbits was exhausted, other munition was not wanting, and for some days the war was continued with white mice, dormice, hedgehogs, guinea pigs, pigeons, lambs, canaries, parakeets, linnets, squirrels, parrots, marmots, poodles, ravens, tortoises, terriers, and cats. Of these, as might be expected, the most difficult to manipulate were the terriers and the cats, and of these two classes the proportion of the difficulties in the way of terrier-hacking was, when compared with those of cat-hacking, about that which the simple lac of the British pharmacopoeia bears to water in the compound which dairymen palm off upon a too-confiding public as milk. More than once when engaged in the rapturous delights of cat-hacking had Harry and Tommy wished that the silent tomb could open its ponderous and massy jaws and engulf them, for the feline victims were not patient in their death agonies, and often broke the bonds in which the security of the artists rested, and turned fiercely on their executioners.

At last, however, all the animals available were sacrificed; but the passion for hacking still remained. How was it all to end?

7. A Cloud With Golden Lining

Tommy and Harry sat in the arbour dejected and disconsolate. They wept like two Alexanders because there were no more worlds to conquer. At last the conviction had been forced upon them that the resources available for hacking were exhausted. That very morning they had had a desperate battle, and their attire showed the ravages of direful war. Their hats were battered into shapeless masses, their shoes were soleless and heel-less and had the uppers broken, the ends of their braces, their sleeves, and their trousers were frayed, and had they indulged in the manly luxury of coat-tails these too would have gone.

Truly, hacking had become an absorbing passion with them. Long and fiercely had they been swept onwards on the wings of the demon of strife, and powerless at the best of times had been the promptings of good; but now, heated with combat, maddened by the equal success of arms, and with the lust for victory still unsated, they longed more fiercely than ever for some new pleasure: like tigers that have tasted blood they thirsted for a larger and more potent libation.

As they sat, with their souls in a tumult of desire and despair, some evil genius guided into the garden the twin blossoms of the tree of Bubb. Hand in hand Zacariah and Zerubbabel advanced from the back door; they had escaped from their nurses, and with the exploring instinct of humanity, advanced boldly into the great world--the terra incognita, the ultima Thule of the paternal domain.

In the course of time they approached the hedge of poplars, from behind which the anxious eyes of Harry and Tommy looked for their approach, for the boys knew that where the twins were the nurses were accustomed to be gathered together, and they feared discovery if their retreat should be cut off.

It was a touching sight, these lovely babes, alike in form, feature, size, expression, and dress; in fact, so like each other that one 'might not have told either from which'. When the startling similarity was recognized by Harry and Tommy, each suddenly turned, and, grasping the other by the shoulder, spoke in a keen whisper: 'Hack! They are exactly equal! This is the very apotheosis of our art!'

With excited faces and trembling hands they laid their plans to lure the unsuspecting babes within the precincts of their charnel house, and they were so successful in their efforts that in a little time the twins had toddled behind the hedge and were lost to the sight of the parental mansion.

Harry and Tommy were not famed for gentleness within the immediate precincts of their respective homes, but it would have delighted the heart of any philanthropist to see the kindly manner in which they arranged for the pleasures of the helpless babes. With smiling faces and playful words and gentle wiles they led them within the arbour, and then, under pretence of giving them some of those sudden jumps in which infants rejoice, they raised them from the ground. Tommy held Zacariah across his arm with his baby moon-face smiling up at the cobwebs on the arbour roof, and Harry, with a mighty effort, raised the cherubic Zerubbabel aloft.

Each nerved himself for a great endeavour, Harry to give, Tommy to endure a shock, and then the form of Zerubbabel was seen whirling through the air round Harry's glowing and determined face. There was a sickening crash and the arm of Tommy yielded visibly.

The pasty face of Zerubbabel had fallen fair on that of Zacariah, for Tommy and Harry were by this time artists of too great experience to miss so simple a mark. The putty-like noses collapsed, the putty-like cheeks became for a moment flattened, and when in an instant more they parted, the faces of both were dabbled in gore. Immediately the firmament was rent with a series of such yells as might have awakened the dead. Forthwith from the house of Bubb came the echoes in parental cries and footsteps. As the sounds of scurrying feet rang through the mansion, Harry cried to Tommy: 'They will be on us soon. Let us cut to the roof of the stable and draw up the ladder.'

Tommy answered by a nod, and the two boys, regardless of consequences, and bearing each a twin, ascended to the roof of the stable by means of a ladder which usually stood against the wall, and which they pulled up after them.

As Ephraim Bubb issued from his house in pursuit of his lost darlings, the sight which met his gaze froze his very soul. There, on the coping of the stable roof, stood Harry and Tommy renewing their game. They seemed like two young demons forging some diabolical implement, for each in turn the twins were lifted high in air and let fall with stunning force on the supine form of its fellow. How Ephraim felt none but a tender and imaginative father can conceive. It would be enough to wring the heart of even a callous parent to see his children, the darlings of his old age--his own beloved twins--being sacrificed to the brutal pleasure of unregenerate youths, without being made unconsciously and helplessly guilty of the crime of fratricide.

Loudly did Ephraim and also Sophonisba, who, with dishevelled locks, had now appeared upon the scene, bewail their unhappy lot and shriek in vain for aid; but by rare ill-chance no eyes save their own saw the work of butchery or heard the shrieks of anguish and despair. Wildly did Ephraim, mounting on the shoulders of his spouse, strive, but in vain, to scale the stable wall.

Baffled in every effort, he rushed into the house and appeared in a moment bearing in his hands a double-barrelled gun, into which he poured the contents of a shot pouch as he ran. He came anigh the stable and hailed the murderous youths: 'Drop them twins and come down here or I'll shoot you like a brace of dogs.'

'Never!' exclaimed the heroic two with one impulse, and continued their awful pastime with a zest tenfold as they knew that the agonized eyes of parents wept at the cause of their joy.

'Then die!' shrieked Ephraim, as he fired both barrels, right--left, at the hackers.

But, alas! love for his darlings shook the hand that never shook before. As the smoke cleared off and Ephraim recovered from the kick of his gun, he heard a loud twofold laugh of triumph and saw Harry and Tommy, all unhurt, waving in the air the trunks of the twins-the fond father had blown the heads completely off his own offspring.

Tommy and Harry shrieked aloud in glee, and after playing catch with the bodies for some time, seen only by the agonized eyes of the infanticide and his wife, flung them high in the air.

Ephraim leaped forward to catch what had once been Zacariah, and Sophonisba grabbed wildly for the loved remains of her Zerubbabel.

But the weight of the bodies and the height from which they fell were not reckoned by either parent, and from being ignorant of a simple dynamical formula each tried to effect an object which calm, common sense, united with scientific knowledge, would have told them was impossible. The masses fell, and Ephraim and Sophonisba were stricken dead by the falling twins, who were thus posthumously guilty of the crime of parricide.

An intelligent coroner's jury found the parents guilty of the crimes of infanticide and suicide, on the evidence of Harry and Tommy, who swore, reluctantly, that the inhuman monsters, maddened by drink, had killed their offspring by shooting them into the air out of a cannon---since stolen--whence like curses they had fallen on their own heads; and that then they had slain themselves suis manibus with their own hands. Accordingly Ephraim and Sophonisba were denied the solace of Christian burial, and were committed to the earth with 'maimed rites', and had stakes driven through their middles to pin them down in their unhallowed graves till the crack of doom.

Harry and Tommy were each rewarded with national honours and were knighted, even at their tender years.

Fortune seemed to smile upon them all the long after-years, and they lived to a ripe old age, hale of body, and respected and beloved of all.

Often in the golden summer eves, when all nature seemed at rest, when the oldest cask was opened and the largest lamp was lit, when the chestnuts glowed in the embers and the kid turned on the spit, when their great-grandchildren pretended to mend fictional armour and to trim an imaginary helmet's plume, when the shuttles of the good wives of their grandchildren went flashing each through its proper loom, with shouting and with laughter they were accustomed to tell the tale of THE DUALITISTS; OR, THE DEATH DOOM OF THE DOUBLE BORN.

THE END

The Power of Darkness and other Chilling Tales
Edith Nesbit
Benediction Classics, 2012
68 pages
ISBN: 978-1-78139-190-7

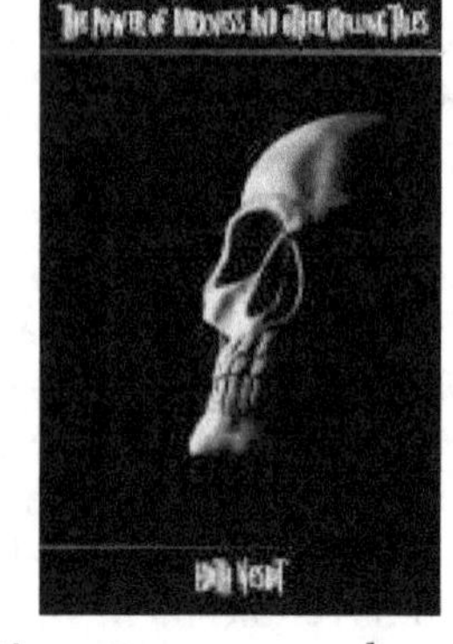

Available from www.amazon.com,
www.amazon.co.uk

Edith Nesbit is best known as the author of The Railway Children, but she was also a great writer of terror and ghost stories. Do not read this book at bedtime or you may be haunted in the night! Nesbit spins chilling tales, where we meet the undead, love transcends the grave, vampires stalk us and ghosts have their vengeance. These spooky stories, tinged with horror, are vibrant and bold, spanning the years to come and scare us today. In this collection are: Power of Darkness; Man-Size in Marble; John Charrington's Wedding; In the Dark; The Mystery of the Semi-Detached; The Ebony Frame.

Collected Twilight Stories - 18 Twilight tales
Marjorie Bowen
Oxford City Press, 2011
266 pages
ISBN: 978-1-84902-453-2

Available from www.amazon.com,
www.amazon.co.uk

Collected Twilight Stories' is a compilation of eighteen of Marjorie Bowen's supernatural horror stories. This collection comprises the following eighteen short stories: Scoured Silk; The Breakdown; One Remained Behind - A Romance A La Mode Gothique; The House By The Poppy Field; Half-Past Two; Elsie's Lonely Afternoon; The Extraordinary Adventure Of Mr John Proudie; Ann Mellor's Lover; Florence Flannery; Kecksies; The Avenging Of Ann Leete; The Bishop Of Hell; The Crown Derby Plate; The Fair Hair Of Ambrosine; The Housekeeper; Raw Material; The Hidden Ape; The Sign-Painter And The Crystal Fishes

The Weird Menace Collection
Robert Ervin Howard
Benediction Classics, 2011
182 pages
ISBN: 978-1-84902-450-1
Available from www.amazon.com, www.amazon.co.uk
Robert Ervin Howard (1906 - 1936) was an American writer of fantasy, horror, historical adventure, boxing, western, and detective fiction. He is most famous for creating the character Conan the Barbarian. His is a master of the weird and the gloomy, extremely well read and his stories have been reprinted endlessly since his premature death. 'The Weird Menace Collection' showcases his horror stories and comprises the four 'Weird Menace' books: Black Talons Moon of Zambebwei Skull-Face Black Wind Blowing

Collected Ghost Stories - 22 stories
M. R. James
Benediction Classics, 2011
284 pages
ISBN: 978-1-84902-454-9
Available from www.amazon.com, www.amazon.co.uk
Collected Ghost Stories by M R James is a collection of twenty-two ghost stories, plus a fascinating essay on the writing of ghost stories. The collection is comprised of the following twenty-two stories: The Uncommon Prayer-Book; A Neighbour's Landmark; Rats; The Experiment; The Malice Of Inanimate Objects; A Vignette; Canon Alberic's Scrap-Book; The Stalls Of Barchester Cathedral; An Episode Of Cathedral History; The Story Of A Disappearance And An Appearance; The Haunted Dolls' House; Lost Hearts; Mr. Humphreys And His Inheritance; Martin's Close; The Diary Of Mr. Poynter; The Rose-Garden; Casting The Runes; A School Story; The Tractate Middoth; Two Doctors; A View From A Hill; The Residence At Whitminster; Appendix: M. R. James On Ghost Stories Note: This is not to be confused with the Book "The Collected Ghost Stories of M R James" which was published in 1931.

Also from Benediction Books ...

Wandering Between Two Worlds: Essays on Faith and Art
Anita Mathias
Benediction Books, 2007
152 pages
ISBN: 0955373700

Available from www.amazon.com, www.amazon.co.uk

In these wide-ranging lyrical essays, Anita Mathias writes, in lush, lovely prose, of her naughty Catholic childhood in Jamshedpur, India; her large, eccentric family in Mangalore, a sea-coast town converted by the Portuguese in the sixteenth century; her rebellion and atheism as a teenager in her Himalayan boarding school, run by German missionary nuns, St. Mary's Convent, Nainital; and her abrupt religious conversion after which she entered Mother Teresa's convent in Calcutta as a novice. Later rich, elegant essays explore the dualities of her life as a writer, mother, and Christian in the United States-- Domesticity and Art, Writing and Prayer, and the experience of being "an alien and stranger" as an immigrant in America, sensing the need for roots.

About the Author

Anita Mathias is the author of *Wandering Between Two Worlds: Essays on Faith and Art*. She has a B.A. and M.A. in English from Somerville College, Oxford University, and an M.A. in Creative Writing from the Ohio State University, USA. Anita won a National Endowment of the Arts fellowship in Creative Non-fiction in 1997. She lives in Oxford, England with her husband, Roy, and her daughters, Zoe and Irene.

Anita's website:
http://www.anitamathias.com, and
Anita's blog Dreaming Beneath the Spires:
http://dreamingbeneaththespires.blogspot.com

The Church That Had Too Much
Anita Mathias
Benediction Books, 2010
52 pages
ISBN: 9781849026567

Available from www.amazon.com, www.amazon.co.uk

The Church That Had Too Much was very well-intentioned. She wanted to love God, she wanted to love people, but she was both hampered by her muchness and the abundance of her possessions, and beset by ambition, power struggles and snobbery. Read about the surprising way The Church That Had Too Much began to resolve her problems in this deceptively simple and enchanting fable.

About the Author

Anita Mathias is the author of *Wandering Between Two Worlds: Essays on Faith and Art*. She has a B.A. and M.A. in English from Somerville College, Oxford University, and an M.A. in Creative Writing from the Ohio State University, USA. Anita won a National Endowment of the Arts fellowship in Creative Non-fiction in 1997. She lives in Oxford, England with her husband, Roy, and her daughters, Zoe and Irene.

Anita's website:
 http://www.anitamathias.com, and
Anita's blog Dreaming Beneath the Spires:
 http://dreamingbeneaththespires.blogspot.com

www.ingramcontent.com/pod-product-compliance
Lightning Source LLC
Chambersburg PA
CBHW081129300726
48982CB00005B/904

* 9 7 8 1 7 8 1 3 9 3 7 8 9 *